The Lightstone

Voyager

The Lightstone

Book One of the Ea Cycle

DAVID ZINDELL

HarperCollins*Publishers*

ACKNOWLEDGMENTS

I would like to thank the people closest to this book, who made it possible: My daughters, who journeyed with me on many long and magical walks through Ea and helped generate this story with their pointed-questions, blazing imagination, dreams and delight. My agent, Donald Maass, for his great enthusiasm, brilliant suggestions and help in fine-tuning the story. And Jane Johnson and Joy Chamberlain, whose inspired editing, unstinting support and sheer hard work in the face of great pressure brought this book to life.

Voyager
An Imprint of HarperCollins*Publishers*
77–85 Fulham Palace Road,
Hammersmith, London W6 8JB

www.voyager-books.com

Published by *Voyager* 2001

1 3 5 7 9 8 6 4 2

A catalogue record for this book
is available from the British Library

Hardback ISBN 0 00 224765 9
Trade Paperback ISBN 0 00 224755 0

Typeset in Giovanni by Palimpsest Book Production Limited,
Polmont, Stirlingshire

Printed and bound in Great Britain by
Clays Limited, St Ives plc

For Justine and Jillian

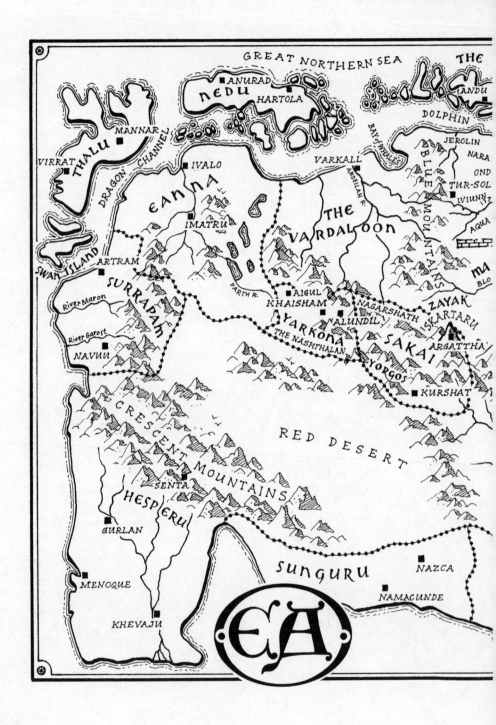

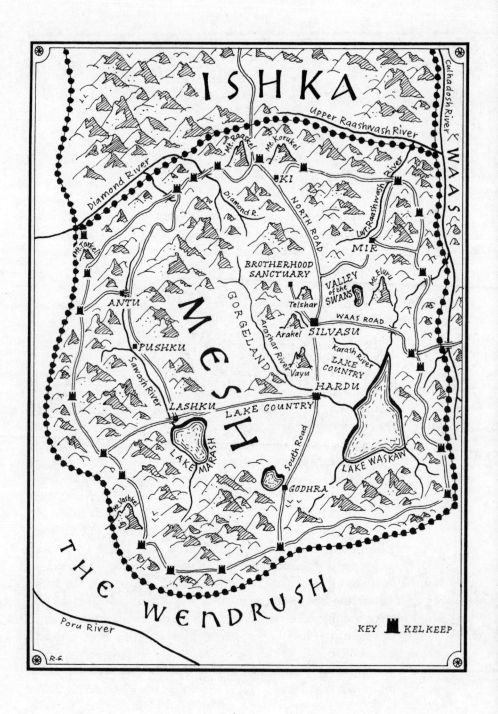

1

On clear winter nights, I have stood on mountains just to be closer to the stars. Some say that these shimmering lights are the souls of warriors who have died in battle; some say that at the beginning of time, Arwe himself cast an infinite number of diamonds into the sky to shine forever and defeat the darkness of night. But I believe the stars are other suns like our own. They speak along the blood in fiery whisperings of ancient dreams and promises unfulfilled. From there long ago our people came to earth bearing the cup called the Lightstone; to there we would someday return as angels holding light in our hands.

My grandfather believed this, too. It was he who taught me the stories of the Great Bear, the Dragon, the Seven Sisters and the other constellations. It was he who named me after the bright Morning Star, Valashu. He always said that we were born to shine. A Valari warrior, he once told me, should polish first his soul and then his sword. For only then can he see his fate and accept it. Or fight against it if he is one of the few men marked out to make their own fate. Such a man is a glory and gift to the earth. Such a man was my grandfather. But the Ishkans killed him all the same.

Elkasar Elahad would have found it a strange fate indeed that on the same day King Kiritan's messengers came from Alonia to announce a great quest for the Lightstone, a whole company of knights and nobles from Ishka rode into my father's castle to negotiate for peace or call for war. It was the first of Ashte in the 2,812th year in that span of centuries that the historians had named the Age of the Dragon. In the warmth of one of the loveliest springs that anyone could remember, with the snows melting from the mountains and wildflowers everywhere abloom, the forests surrounding Silvassu teemed with boar and deer and other animals that might be killed for food. My father's steward, upon counting the castle's guests that day, grumbled that the kitchens would require much food if any feast were to be made. And so my brothers and I, along with other knights, were called to go out and hunt for it. After all, even the murderers of a king must eat.

Just after noon I rode down from the hills upon which our ancient city is built with my eldest brother, Lord Asaru. My friend, Maram, and one of my brother's squires rode with us as well. We were a small hunting party, perhaps the smallest of the many to fill the woods that day. I was glad for such company, for I cared nothing for the sport of hounds yelping and men on snorting horses running down a fear-maddened pig. As for Asaru, he was like our father, King Shamesh: stern, serious and focused on his objective with an astonishing clarity of purpose. His soul had not only been polished but sharpened until it cut like the finest Godhran steel. He had said that we would take a deer, and for that we needed small numbers and stealth. Maram, who would have preferred the pageantry of hunting with the other knights, followed him anyway. In truth, he followed me. As he liked to say, he would never desert his best friend. As he didn't like to say, he was a coward who had once seen what the razor-like tusks of a boar could do to a man's groin. It was much safer to hunt a deer.

It was a warm day, and the air smelled of freshly turned earth and lila blossoms. Every quarter of a mile or so, a stout farmhouse stood out among fields demarcated by lines of low stone walls. There was new barley in the ground, and the golden sun in the sky. As we passed farther into the Valley of the Swans, the farmland gave out onto miles of unbroken forest. At the edge of a field, where the ancient oaks rose up like a wall of green, we drew up and dismounted. Asaru handed the reins of his horse to his young squire, Joshu Kadar, who had the square face and stolid temperament of his father, Lord Kadar. Joshu didn't like being left to tend the horses, and watched impatiently as Asaru drew out his great yew bow and strung it. For a moment I was tempted to give him my bow and let him hunt the deer while I waited in the sun. I hated hunting almost as much as I did war.

And then Asaru, tall and imperious in his flowing black cloak, handed me my bow and pointed at the forest. He said, 'Why *these* woods, Val?'

'Why not?' I countered. Asaru, knowing how I felt about slaughtering innocent animals, had given me my choice of where to hunt that day. Although he had remained silent during our ride down from the castle, he must have known where I was leading him. 'You know why,' I said more gently, looking at him.

And he looked at me, fearless as all Valari would hope to be. His eyes were those of the Valari kings: deep and mysterious, as black as space and as bright as stars. He had the bold face bones and long hawk's nose

2

of our ancient line. His skin, burnt brown in the hot spring sun, was like weathered ivory, and he had a great shock of glossy black hair, long and thick and blowing wild in the wind. Although he was very much a man of blood and steel and other elements of the earth, there was something otherworldly about him, too. My father said that we looked enough alike to be twins. But of the seven sons of Shavashar Elahad, he was the firstborn and I was the last. And that made all the difference in the world.

He drew closer and stood silently regarding me. Where I insisted on wearing a leather hunting jacket and a homespun shirt and trousers of a deep forest green, he was resplendent in a cloak and a black tunic embroidered with the silver swan and the seven silver stars of the royal house of Mesh. He would never think to be seen in any other garments. He was the tallest of my brothers, taller than I by half an inch. He seemed to look down at me, and his bright black eyes fell like blazing suns on the scar cut into my forehead above my left eye. It was a unique scar, shaped like a lightning bolt. I think it reminded him of things that he would rather not know.

'Why do you have to be so wild?' he said in a quickly exhaled breath.

I stood beneath his gaze listening to the thunder of my heart, but said nothing.

'Here, now!' a loud voice boomed out. 'What's this? What are you talking about?'

Maram, upon seeing the silent communication flowing between us, came up clutching his bow and making nervous rumbling noises in his throat. Though not as tall as Asaru, he was a big man with a big belly that pushed out ahead of him as if to knock any obstacles or lesser men from his path.

'What should I know about these woods?' he asked me.

'They're full of deer,' I said, smiling at him.

'And other animals,' Asaru added provocatively.

'What animals?' Maram asked. He licked his thick, sensuous lips. He rubbed his thick, brown beard where it curled across his blubbery cheeks.

'The last time we entered these woods,' Asaru said, 'we could hardly move without stepping on a rabbit. And there were squirrels every-where.'

'Good, good,' Maram said, 'I like squirrels.'

'So do the foxes,' Asaru said. 'So do the wolves.'

Maram coughed to clear his throat, and then swallowed a couple of times. 'In my country, I've only ever seen red foxes – they're not at all

3

like these huge gray ones of yours that might as well *be* wolves. And as for our wolves, ah, well, we hunted out most of them long ago.'

Maram was not of Mesh, not even of the Nine Kingdoms of the Valari. Everything about him was an affront to a Valari's sensibilities. His large brown eyes reminded one of the sugared coffee that the Delians drink, and were given to tears of rage or sentimentality as the situation might demand. He wore jeweled rings on each of the fingers of his hamlike hands; he wore the bright scarlet tunic and trousers of the Delian royalty. He liked red, of course, because it was an outward manifestation of the colors of his fiery heart. And even more he liked standing out and being seen, especially in a wood full of hungry men with bows and arrows. My brothers believed that he had been sent to the Brotherhood school in the mountains above Silvassu as a punishment for his cowardly ways. But the truth was he had been banished from court due to an indiscretion with his father's favorite concubine.

'Do not,' Asaru warned him, 'hunt wolves in Mesh. It's bad luck.'

'Ah, well,' Maram said, twanging his bowstring, 'I won't hunt them if they won't hunt *me*.'

'Wolves don't hunt men,' Asaru assured him. 'It's the bears that you have to watch for.'

'Bears?'

'This time of year, especially the mothers with their cubs.'

'I saw one of your bears last year,' Maram said. 'I hope I never see another.'

I rubbed my forehead as I caught the heat of Maram's fear. Of course, Mesh is famed for the ferociousness of its huge, brown bears, which had driven the much gentler black bears into gentler lands such as Delu ages ago.

'If the Brothers don't expel you and you stay with us long enough,' Asaru said, 'you'll see plenty of bears.'

'But I thought the bears kept mostly to the mountains.'

'Well, where do you think you *are*?' Asaru said, sweeping his hand out toward the snow-capped peaks all around us.

In truth, we stood in the Valley of the Swans, largest and loveliest of Mesh's valleys. Here the Kurash flowed through gentle terrain into Lake Waskaw. Here there were other lakes, too, where the swans came each spring to hatch their young and swim through clear blue waters.

But across the valley twenty miles due east, Mount Eluru stood like a vast pyramid of granite and ice. Beyond it were still greater peaks of the Culhadosh Range, which separates the kingdoms of Waas and Mesh. In the distance to the south forty-five miles as a raven flies, was the hazy wall of the Itarsu in whose narrow passes my ancestors had

4

more than once slaughtered invading Sarni armies from the great gray plains beyond. Behind us above the hills from where we had ridden that day, just to the west of the bear-infested woods that we proposed to enter, were three of the greatest and most beautiful peaks of the Central Range: Telshar, Arakel and Vayu. These were the mountains of my soul; here, I thought, was the heart of the Morning Mountains and possibly of all Ea. As a boy I had played in their forests and sung songs to their silent, stony faces. They rose up like gods just beyond the houses and battlements of Silvassu: the shining Vayu a few miles to the south, Arakel west just across the swift Kurash river, and Telshar the Great on whose lower slopes my grandfather's grandfathers had built the Elahad castle. Once I had climbed this luminous mountain. From the summit, looking north, I had seen Raaskel and Korukel glittering beyond the Diamond River, and beyond these guardian peaks, the cold white mountains of Ishka. But, of course, all my life I have tried not to look in that direction.

Now Maram followed the line of Asaru's outstretched hand. He looked into the dark, waiting forest and muttered, 'Ah, where am I, indeed? Lost, lost, truly lost.'

At that moment, as if in answer to some silent supplication of Maram's, there came the slow clip-clop of a horse's hooves. I turned to see a white-haired man leading a draft horse across the field straight toward us. He wore a patch over his right eye and walked with a severe limp as if his knee had been smashed with a mace or a flail. I knew that I had seen this old farmer before, but I couldn't quite remember where.

'Hello, lads,' he said as he drew up to us. 'It's a fine day for hunting, isn't it?'

Maram took in the farmer's work-stained woolens, which smelled of horse manure and pigs. He wrinkled up his fat nose disdainfully. But Asaru, who had a keener eye, immediately saw the ring glittering on the farmer's gnarled finger, and so did I. It was a plain silver ring set with four brilliant diamonds: the ring of a warrior and a lord at that.

'Lord Harsha,' Asaru said, finally recognizing him, 'it's been a long time.'

'Yes, it has,' Lord Harsha said. He looked at Asaru's squire, and then at Maram and me. 'Who are your friends?'

'Excuse me,' Asaru said. 'May I present Joshu Kadar of Lashku?'

Lord Harsha nodded his head at my brother's squire and told him, 'Your father is a fine man. We fought against Waas together.'

Young Joshu bowed deeply as befit his rank, and then stood silently basking in Lord Harsha's compliment.

5

'And this,' Asaru continued, 'is Prince Maram Marshayk of Delu. He's a student of the Brothers.'

Lord Harsha peered out at him with his single eye and said, 'Isn't it true that the Brothers don't hunt animals?'

'Ah, that *is* true,' Maram said, gripping his bow, 'we hunt knowledge. You see, I've come along only to protect my friend in case we run into any bears.'

Now Lord Harsha turned his attention toward me, and looked back and forth between me and my brother. The light of his eye bore into my forehead like the rays of the sun.

'You must be Valashu Elahad,' he said.

Just then Maram's face reddened in anger on my behalf. I knew that he didn't approve of the Valari system of honors and rank. It must have galled him that an old man of no noble blood, a mere farmer, could outrank a prince.

I looked down at the ring I wore around my finger. In it was set neither the four diamonds of a lord nor the three of a master – nor even the two sparkling stones of a full knight. A single diamond stood out against the silver: the ring of a simple warrior. In truth, I was lucky to have won it. If not for some skills with the sword and bow that my father had taught me, I never would have. What kind of warrior hates war? How is it that a Valari knight – or rather, a man who only dreamed of being a knight – should prefer playing the flute and writing poetry to trials of arms with his brothers and countrymen?

Lord Harsha smiled grimly at me and said, 'It's been a long time since you've come to these woods, hasn't it?'

'Yes, sir, it has,' I said.

'Well, you should have paid your respects before trampling over my fields. Young people have no manners these days.'

'My apologies, sir, but we were in a hurry. You see, we got a late start.'

I didn't explain that our hunting expedition had been delayed for an hour while I searched the castle for Maram – only to find him in bed with one of my father's chambermaids.

'Yes, very late,' Lord Harsha said, looking up at the sun. 'The Ishkans have already been here before you.'

'Which Ishkans?' I asked in alarm. I noticed that Asaru was now staring off into the woods intently.

'They didn't stop to present themselves either,' Lord Harsha said. 'But there were five of them – I heard them bragging they were going to take a bear.'

At this news, Maram gripped his bow even more tightly. Beads of sweat formed up among the brown curls of hair across his forehead. He said, 'Well, then – I suppose we should leave these woods to them.'

But Asaru only smiled as if Maram had suggested abandoning all of Mesh to the enemy. He said, 'The Ishkans like to hunt bears. Well, it's a big wood, and they've had more than an hour to become lost in it.'

'Please see to it that you don't become lost as well,' Lord Harsha said.

'My brother,' Asaru said, looking at me strangely, 'is more at home in the woods than in his own castle. We won't get lost.'

'Good. Then good luck hunting.' Lord Harsha nodded his head at me in a curt bow. 'Are you after a bear this time, too?'

'No, a deer,' I said. 'As we were the last time we came here.'

'But you found a bear all the same.'

'It might be more accurate to say the bear found us.'

Now Maram's knuckles grew white around his bow, and he looked at me with wide-open eyes. 'What do you *mean* a bear found you?'

Because I didn't want to tell him the story, I stood there looking off into the woods in silence. And so Lord Harsha answered for me.

'It was ten years ago,' he said. 'Lord Asaru had just received his knight's ring, and Val must have been what – eleven? Ten?'

'Ten,' I told him.

'That's right,' Lord Harsha said, nodding his head. 'And so the lads went into the woods alone after their deer. And then the bear –'

'Was it a large bear?' Maram interrupted.

Lord Harsha's single eye narrowed as he admonished Maram to silence as he might a child. And then he continued the story: 'And so the bear attacked them. It broke Lord Asaru's arm and some ribs. And mauled Valashu, as you can see.'

Here he paused to point his old finger at the scar on my forehead.

'But you told me that you were born with that scar!' Maram said, turning to me.

'Yes,' I said. 'That's right.'

Truly, I had been. My mother's labor in bringing me into the world was so hard and long that everyone had said I wanted to remain inside her in darkness. And so, finally, the midwife had had to use tongs to pull me out. The tongs had cut me, and the wound had healed raggedly, in the shape of a lightning bolt.

'The bear,' Asaru explained, 'opened up the scar again and cut it deeper.'

'He was lucky the bear didn't break his skull,' Lord Harsha said to Maram. 'And both of them were lucky that my son, may he abide in peace, was walking through the woods that day. He found these lads half-dead in the moss and killed the bear with his spear before it could kill them.'

Andaru Harsha – I knew the name of my rescuer very well. At the Battle of Red Mountain, I had taken a wound in my thigh protecting him from the Waashians' spears. And later, at the same battle, I had frozen up and been unable to kill one of our enemy who stood shieldless and helpless before me. Because of my hesitation, many still whispered that I was a coward. But Asaru never called me that.

'Then your son saved their lives,' Maram said to Lord Harsha.

'He always said it was the best thing he ever did.'

Maram came up to me and grabbed my arm. 'And you think to repay the courage of this man's son by going *back* into these woods?'

'Yes, that's right,' I said.

'Ah,' he said, looking at me with his soft brown eyes. 'I see.'

And he did see, which was why I loved him. Without being told, he understood that I had come back to these woods today not to seek vengeance by shooting arrows in some strange bear, but only because there are other monsters that must be faced.

'Well, then,' Lord Harsha said. 'Enough of bear stories. Would you like a bite to eat before your hunt?'

Due to Maram's peccadilloes, we had missed lunch and we were all of us hungry. Of course, that wouldn't have dismayed Asaru, but rejecting Lord Harsha's hospitality would. And so Asaru, speaking for all of us as if he were already king, bowed his head and said, 'We'd be honored.'

While Lord Harsha opened his horse's saddlebags, our horses stamped the earth impatiently and bent their heads to munch the sweet green grass growing between the field's stone wall and the forest. I glanced off across the field to study Lord Asaru's house. I liked its square lines and size and the cedar-shingled roof, which was almost as steeply gabled as the chalets you see higher in the mountains. It was built of oak and stone: austere, clean, quietly beautiful – very Valari. I remembered Andaru Harsha bringing me to this house, where I had lain in delirium for half a day while his father tended my wound.

'Here, now,' Lord Harsha said as he laid a cloth on the wall. 'Sit with me, and let's talk about the war.'

While we took our places along the wall, he set out two loaves of black, barley bread, a tub of goat cheese and some freshly pulled green onions. We cut the bread for sandwiches and ate them. I liked the tang of the onions against the saltiness of the cheese; I liked it even more when Lord Harsha drew out four silver goblets and filled them with brown beer that he poured from a small, wooden cask.

'This was brewed last fall,' Lord Harsha said. In turn, he handed goblets to Asaru, me and Joshu. Then he picked up his own goblet. 'It was a good harvest, and a better brew. Shall we make a toast?'

I saw Maram licking his lips as if he'd been stricken dumb with grief, and I said, 'Lord Harsha, you've forgotten Maram.'

'Indeed,' he said, smiling. 'But you said he's with the Brothers – hasn't he taken vows?'

'Ah, well, yes, I have,' Maram admitted. 'I've forsworn wine, women and war.'

'Well, then?'

'I never vowed not to drink beer.'

'You quibble, Prince Maram.'

'Yes, I do, don't I? But only when vital matters are at stake.'

'Such as the drinking of beer?'

'Such as the drinking of *Meshian* beer, which is known to be the finest in all of Ea.'

This compliment proved too much for Lord Harsha, who laughed and magically produced another goblet from the saddlebags. He picked up the cask and poured forth a stream of beer.

'Let's drink to the king,' he said, raising his goblet. 'May he abide in the One and find the wisdom to decide on peace or war.'

We all clinked goblets and drank the frothy beer. It tasted of barley and hops and roasted nuts of the talaru tree that grows only in the forests near Mount Arakel. Maram, of course, was the first to finish his beer. He gulped it down like a hound does milk. Then he held out his goblet for Lord Harsha to fill it again and said, 'Now *I* would like to propose a toast. To the lords and knights of Mesh who have fought faithfully for their king.'

'Excellent,' Lord Harsha said, once more filling Maram's goblet. 'Let's drink to that indeed.'

Again Maram drained his cup. He licked the froth from his mustache. He held the empty cup out yet again and said, 'And now, ah, to the courage and prowess of the warriors – how do you say it? To flawlessness and fearlessness.'

But Lord Harsha stoppered the cask with a cork, and said, 'No, that's enough if you're going hunting today – we can't have you young princes shooting arrows at each other, can we?'

'But Lord Harsha,' Maram protested, 'I was only going to suggest that the courage of your Meshian warriors is an inspiration to those of us who can only hope to –'

'You're quite the diplomat,' Lord Harsha said, laughing as he cut Maram off. 'Perhaps *you* should reason with the Ishkans. Perhaps you could talk them out of this war as easily as you talked me out of my beer.'

'I don't understand why there has to be a war at all,' Maram said.

'Well, there's bad blood between us,' Lord Harsha said simply.

'But it's the *same* blood, isn't it? You're all Valari, aren't you?'

'Yes, the same blood,' Lord Harsha said, slowly sipping from his goblet. Then he looked at me sadly. 'But the Ishkans shed it in ways shameful to any Valari. The way they killed Valashu's grandfather.'

'But he died in battle, didn't he? Ah, the Battle of the Diamond River?'

Now Lord Harsha swallowed the last of his beer as if someone had forced him to drink blood. He tapped his eye-patch and said, 'Yes, it was at the Diamond. Twelve years ago now. That's where the Ishkans took this eye. That's where the Ishkans sacrificed five companies just to close with King Elkamesh and kill him.'

'But that's war, isn't it?' Maram asked.

'No, that's dueling. The Ishkans hated King Elkamesh because when he was a young man such as yourself, he killed Lord Dorje in a duel. And so they used the battle as a duel to take their revenge.'

'Lord Dorje,' I explained, looking at Maram, 'was King Hadaru's oldest brother.'

'I see,' Maram said. 'And this duel took place, ah, fifty years ago? You Valari wait a long time to take your revenge.'

I looked north toward the dark clouds moving in from Ishka's mountains, and I lost myself in memories of wrongs and hurts that went back more than a hundred times fifty years.

'Please do not say "we Valari,"' Lord Harsha told Maram. He rubbed his broken knee and said, 'Sar Lensu of Waas caught me here with his mace, and *that's* war. There's no vengeance to be taken. They understand that in Waas. They would never have tried to kill King Elkamesh as the Ishkans did.'

While Lord Harsha rose abruptly and shook out the cloth of its crumbs for the sparrows to eat, I clenched my teeth together. And then I said, 'There was more to it than vengeance.'

At this, Asaru shot me a quick look as if warning me not to divulge family secrets in front of strangers. But I spoke not only for Maram's benefit, but for Asaru's and Lord Harsha's and my own.

'My grandfather,' I said, 'had a dream. He would have united all the Valari against Morjin.'

At the mention of this name, dreadful and ancient, Lord Harsha froze motionless while Joshu Kadar turned to stare at me. I felt fear fluttering in Maram's belly like a blackbird's wings. In the sky, the dark, distant clouds seemed to grow even darker.

And then Asaru's voice grew as cold as steel as it always did when he was angry at me. 'The Ishkans,' he said, 'don't want the Valari united under our banner. No one does, Val.'

I looked up to see a few crows circling the field in search of carrion or other easy feasts. I said nothing.

'You have to understand,' Asaru continued, 'there's no need.'

'No need?' I half-shouted. 'Morjin's armies swallow up half the continent, and you say there's no need?'

I looked west beyond the white diamond peak of Telshar as I tried to imagine the earthshaking events occurring far away. What little news of Morjin's acquisitions that had arrived in our isolated country was very bad. From his fastness of Sakai in the White Mountains, this warlock and would-be Lord of Ea had sent armies to conquer Hesperu and lands with strange names such as Uskudar and Karabuk. The enslaved peoples of Acadu, of course, had long since marched beneath the banner of the Red Dragon, while in Surrapam and Yarkona, and even in Eanna, Morjin's spies and assassins worked to undermine those realms from within. His terror had found its most recent success in Galda. The fall of this mighty kingdom, so near the Morning Mountains and Mesh, had shocked almost all of the free peoples from Delu to Thalu. But not the Meshians. Nor the Ishkans, the Kaashans, nor any of the other Valari.

'Morjin will never conquer us,' Asaru said proudly. 'Never.'

'He'll never conquer us if we stand against him,' I said.

'No army has ever successfully invaded the Nine Kingdoms.'

'Not *successfully*,' I agreed. 'But why should we invite an invasion at all?'

'If anyone invades Mesh,' Asaru said, 'we'll cut them to pieces. The way the Kaashans cut Morjin's priests to pieces.'

He was referring to the grisly events that had occurred half a year before in Kaash, that most mountainous and rugged of all Valari kingdoms. When King Talanu discovered that two of his most trusted lords had entered Morjin's secret order of assassin-priests, he had ordered them beheaded and quartered. The pieces of their bodies he had then sent to each of the Nine Kingdoms as a warning against traitors and others who would serve Morjin.

I shuddered as I remembered the day that King Talanu's messenger had arrived with his grisly trophy in Silvassu. Something sharp stabbed into my chest as I thought of worse things. In Galda, thousands of men and women had been put to the sword. Some few survivors of the

11

massacres there had found their way across the steppes to Mesh, only to be turned away at the passes. Their sufferings were grievous but not unique. The rattle of the chains of all those enslaved by Morjin would have shaken the mountains, if any had ears to hear it. On the Wendrush, it was said, the Sarni tribes were on the move again and roasting their captured enemies alive. From Karabuk had come stories of a terrible new plague and even a rumor that a city had been burned with a firestone. It seemed that all of Ea was going up in flames while here we sat by a small green field drinking beer and talking of yet another war with the Ishkans.

'There's more to the world than Mesh,' I said. I listened to the twittering of the birds in the forest. 'What of Eanna and Yarkona? What of Alonia? The Elyssu? And Delu?'

At the mention of his homeland, Maram stood up and grabbed his bow. Despite his renunciation of war, he shook it bravely and said, 'Ah, my friend is right. We defeated Morjin once. And we can defeat him again.'

For a moment I held my breath against the beery vapors wafting out of Maram's mouth. Defeating Morjin, of course, wasn't what I had suggested. But uniting against him so that we wouldn't have to fight at all was.

'We should send an army of Valari against him,' Maram bellowed.

I tried not to smile as I noted that in demanding that 'we' fight together against our enemy, Maram meant us: the Meshians and the other Valari.

I looked at him and asked, 'And to where would you send this army that you've so bravely assembled in your mind?'

'Why, to Sakai, of course. We should root out Morjin before he gains too much strength and then destroy him.'

At this Asaru's face paled, as did Lord Harsha's and, I imagined, my own. Once, long ago, a Valari army had crossed the Wendrush to join with the Alonians in an assault on Sakai. And at the Battle of Tarshid, Morjin had used firestones and treachery to defeat us utterly. It was said that he had crucified the thousand Valari survivors for twenty miles along the road leading to Sakai; his priests had pierced our warriors' veins with knives and had drunk their blood. All the histories cited this as the beginning of the War of the Stones.

Of course, no one knew if the Morjin who now ruled in Sakai was the same man who had tortured my ancestors: Morjin, Lord of Lies, the Great Red Dragon, who had stolen the Lightstone and kept it locked away in his underground city of Argattha. Many said that the present Morjin was only a sorcerer or usurper who had taken on the most

12

terrible name in history. But my grandfather had believed that these two Morjins were one and the same. And so did I.

Asaru stood staring at Maram, and said, 'So then, you want to defeat Morjin – do you hope to recover the Lightstone as well?'

'Ah, well,' Maram said, his face falling red, 'the Lightstone – now that's a different matter. It's been lost for three thousand years. Surely it's been destroyed.'

'Surely it has,' Lord Harsha agreed. 'The Lightstone, the firestones, most of the other gelstei – they were all destroyed in the War of the Stones.'

'Of course it was destroyed,' Asaru said as if that ended the matter.

I wondered if it was possible to destroy the gold gelstei, greatest of all the stones of power, from which the Lightstone was wrought. I was silent as I watched the clouds move down the valley and cover up the sun. I couldn't help noticing that despite the darkness of these monstrous gray shapes, some small amount of light fought its way through.

'You don't agree, do you?' Asaru said to me.

'No,' I said. 'The Lightstone exists, somewhere.'

'But three thousand years, Val.'

'I *know* it exists – it can't have been destroyed.'

'If not destroyed, then lost forever.'

'King Kiritan doesn't think so. Otherwise he wouldn't call a quest for knights to find it.'

Lord Harsha let loose a deep grumbling sound as he packed the uneaten food into his horse's saddlebags. He turned to me, and his remaining eyed bore into me like a spear. 'Who knows why foreign kings do what they do? But what would *you* do, Valashu Elahad, if you suddenly found the Lightstone in your hands?'

I looked north and east toward Anjo, Taron, Athar, Lagash and the other kingdoms of the Valari, and I said simply, 'End war.'

Lord Harsha shook his head as if he hadn't heard me correctly. He said, 'End the wars?'

'No, *war*,' I said. 'War itself.'

Now both Lord Harsha and Asaru – and Joshu Kadar as well – looked at me in amazement as if I had suggested ending the world itself.

'Ha!' Lord Harsha called out. 'No one but a scryer can see the future, but let's make this prediction anyway: when next the Ishkans and Meshians line up for battle, you'll be there at the front of our army.'

I smelled moisture in the air and bloodlust in Lord Harsha's fiery old heart, but I said nothing.

And then Asaru moved close to me and caught me with his brilliant eyes. He said quietly, 'You're too much like Grandfather: you've always loved this gold cup that doesn't exist.'

Did the world itself exist, I wondered? Did the light I saw shining in my brother's eyes?

'If it came to it,' he asked me, 'would you fight for this Lightstone or would you fight for your people?'

Behind the sadness of his noble face lingered the unspoken question: *Would you fight for me?*

Just then, as the clouds built even higher overhead and the air grew heavy and still, I felt something warm and bright welling up inside him. How could I *not* fight for him? I remembered the outing seven years ago when I had broken through the thin spring ice of Lake Waskaw after insisting that we take this dangerous shortcut toward home. Hadn't he, heedless of his own life, jumped into the black, churning waters to pull me out? How could I ever simply abandon this noble being and let him perish from the earth? Could I imagine the world without tall, straight oak trees or clear mountain streams? Could I imagine the world without the sun?

I looked at my brother, and felt this sun inside me. There were stars there, too. It was strange, I thought, that although he was firstborn and I was last, that although he wore four diamonds in his ring and I only one, it was he who always looked away from me, as he did now.

'Asaru,' I said, 'listen to me.'

The Valari see a man as a diamond to be slowly cut, polished and perfected. Cut it right and you have a perfect jewel; cut it wrong, hit a flaw, and it shatters. Outwardly, Asaru was the hardest and strongest of men. But deep inside him ran a vein of innocence as pure and soft as gold. I always had to be gentle with him lest my words – or even a flicker in my eyes – find this flaw. I had to guard his heart with infinitely more care than I would my own.

'It may be,' I told him, 'that in fighting for the Lightstone, we'd be fighting for our people. For all people. *We* would be, Asaru.'

'Perhaps,' he said, looking at me again.

Someday, I thought, he would be king and therefore the loneliest of men. And so he needed one other man whom he could trust absolutely.

'At least,' I said, 'please consider that our grandfather might not have been a fool. All right?'

He slowly nodded his head and grasped my shoulder. 'All right.'

'Good,' I said, smiling at him. I picked up my bow and nodded toward the woods. 'Then why don't we go get your deer?'

After that we helped Lord Harsha put away the remains of our lunch.

We slipped on our quivers full of hunting arrows. I said goodbye to Altaru, my fierce, black stallion, who reluctantly allowed Joshu Kadar to tend him in my absence. I thanked Lord Harsha for his hospitality, then turned and led the way into the woods.

2

As soon as we entered this stand of ancient trees, it grew cooler and darker. The forest that filled the Valley of Swans was mostly of elm, maple and oak with a scattering of the occasional alder or birch. Their great canopies opened out a hundred feet above the forest floor, nearly blocking out the rays of the cloud-shrouded sun. The light was softened by the millions of fluttering leaves, and deepened to a primeval green. I could almost smell this marvelous color as I could the ferns and flowers, the animal droppings and the loamy earth. Through the still air came the tap-tap-tap of a woodpecker and the buzzing of bees; I heard a pair of bluebirds calling to each other and the whispering of my own breath.

We walked deeper into the woods across the valley almost due east toward the unseen Mount Eluru. I was as sure of this direction as I was of the beating of my heart. Once a sea captain from the Elyssu, on a visit to our castle, had shown me a little piece of iron called a lodestone that pointed always toward the north. In my wandering of Mesh's forests and mountains, I had always found my way as if I had millions of tiny lodestones in my blood pointing always toward home. And now I moved steadily through the great trees toward something vast and deep that called to me from the forest farther within. What was calling me, however, I didn't quite know.

I felt something else there that seemed as out of place as a snow tiger in a jungle or the setting of the sun in the east. The air, dark and heavy, almost screamed with a sense of wrongness that chilled me to the bone. I felt eyes watching me: those of the squirrels and the cawing crows and perhaps others as well. For some reason, I suddenly thought of the lines from *The Death of Elahad* – Elahad the Great, my distant ancestor, the fabled first king of the Valari who had brought the Lightstone to Ea long, long ago. I shuddered as I thought of how Elahad's brother, Aryu, had killed Elahad in a dark wood very like this one, and then, ages before

16

Morjin had ever conceived of such a crime, claimed the Lightstone for his own :

> *The stealing of the gold,*
> *The evil knife, the cold –*
> *The cold that freezes breath,*
> *The nothingness of death.*

My breath steamed out into the coolness of the silent trees as I caught a faint, distant scent that disturbed me. The sense of wrongness pervading the woods grew stronger. Perhaps, I thought, I was only dwelling on the wrongness of Elahad's murder. I couldn't help it. Wasn't *all* killing of men by men wrong, I asked myself?

And what of killing, *itself*? Men hunted animals, and that was the way the world was. I thought of this as the scar above my eye began to tingle with a burning coldness. I remembered that once, not far from here, I had tried to kill a bear; I remembered that sometimes bears went wrong in their hearts and hunted men just for the sport of it.

I gripped my bow tightly as I listened for a bear or other large animal crashing through the bushes and bracken all about us. I listened to Maram stepping close behind me and to Asaru following him. Maram, curiously, despite his size, could move quietly when he wanted to. And he could shoot straight enough, as the Delian royalty are taught. We Valari, of course, are taught three fundamental things: to wield a sword, to tell the truth, and to abide in the One. But we are also taught to shoot our long yew bows with deadly accuracy, and some of us, as my grandfather had taught me, to move across even broken terrain almost silently. I believe that if we *had* chanced upon a bear feasting upon wild newberries or honey, we might have stepped up close to him unheard and touched him before being discovered.

That is, we might have done this if not for Maram's continual comments and complaints. Once, when I had bent low to examine the round, brown pellets left behind by a deer, he leaned up against a tree and grumbled, 'How much farther do we have to go? Are you sure we're not lost? Are you sure there are any deer in these wretched woods?'

Asaru's voice hissed out in a whisper, 'Shhh – if there *are* any deer about, you'll scare them away.'

'All right,' Maram muttered as we moved off again. He belched, and a bloom of beer vapor obliterated the perfume of the wildflowers. 'But don't go so fast. And watch out for snakes. Any poison ivy.'

I smiled as I tugged gently on the sleeve of his red tunic to get him going again. But I didn't watch for snakes, for the only deadly ones were

17

the water dragons which hunted mostly along the streams. And the only poison ivy that was to be found in Mesh grew in the mountains beyond the Lower Raaswash near Ishka.

We walked for most of an hour while the clouds built into great black thunderheads high in the sky and seemed to press down through the trees with an almost palpable pressure. Still I felt something calling me, and I moved still deeper into the woods. I saw an old elm shagged with moss, a clear sign that we were approaching a place I remembered very well. And then, as Maram drew in a quick breath, I turned to see him pointing at the exposed, gnarly root of a great oak tree.

'Look,' he murmured. 'What's wrong with that squirrel?'

A squirrel, I saw, was lying flat on the root with its arms and legs splayed out. Its dark eye stared out at us but appeared not to see us. Its sides shook with quick, shallow breathing.

I closed my eyes for a moment, and I could feel the pain where something sharp had punctured the squirrel beneath the fur of its hind leg. It was the sharp, hot pain of infection, which burned up the leg and consumed the squirrel with its fire.

'Val?'

Something dark and vast had its claws sunk into the squirrel's fluttering heart, and I could feel this terrible pulling just as surely as I could Maram's fear of death. This was my gift; this was my glory; this was my curse. What others feel, I feel as well. All my life I had suffered from this unwanted empathy. And I had told only one other person about its terrors and joys.

Asaru moved closer to Maram and pointed at the squirrel as he whispered, 'Val has always been able to talk to animals.'

It was not Asaru. Although he certainly knew of my love of animals and sometimes looked at me fearfully when I opened my heart to him, he sensed only that I was strange in ways that he could never quite understand. But my grandfather had known, for he had shared my gift; indeed, it was he who gave it to me. I thought that like the color of my eyes, it must have been passed along in my family's blood – but skipping generations and touching brother and sister capriciously. I thought as well that my grandfather regarded it as truly a gift and not an affliction. But he had died before he could teach me how to bear it.

For a few moments I stared at the squirrel, touching eyes. I suddenly remembered other lines from *The Death of Elahad*; I remembered that Master Juwain, at the Brotherhood's school, had never approved of this ancient song, because, as he said, it was full of dread and despair:

And down into the dark,
No eyes, no lips, no spark.
The dying of the light,
The neverness of night.

Maram asked softly, 'Should we finish him?'

'No,' I said, holding up my hand. 'It will be dead soon enough. Let it be.'

Let it be, I told myself, and so I tried. I closed myself to this dying animal then. To keep out the waves of pain nauseating me, by habit and instinct, I surrounded my heart with walls as high and thick as those of my father's castle. After a while, even as I watched the light go out of the squirrel's eye, I felt nothing.

Almost nothing. When I closed my eyes, I remembered for the thousandth time how much I had always hated living inside of castles. As much as fortresses keeping enemies out, they are prisons of cold stone keeping people within.

'Let's go,' I said abruptly.

Where does the light go when the light goes out, I wondered?

Asaru, it seemed, had also tried to distance himself from this little death. He moved off slowly through the woods, and we followed him. Soon, near a patchwork of ferns growing close to the ground, we came upon a splintered elm that had once been struck by lightning. Although the wood of this fallen tree was now brown and crumbling with rot, once it had been white and hard and freshly scorched.

Once, in this very place, I had come upon the bear that Lord Harsha had spoken of. It had been a huge, brown bear, a great-grandfather of the forest. Upon beholding this great being, I had frozen up and been unable to shoot him. Instead, I had lain down my bow and walked up to touch him. I had known the bear wouldn't hurt me: he had told me this in the rumbling of his well-filled belly and the playfulness of his eyes. But Asaru hadn't known this. Upon seeing me apparently abandoning all sense, he had panicked, shooting the bear in the chest with an arrow. The astonished bear had then fallen on him with his mighty paws, breaking his arm and smashing his ribs. And I had fallen on the bear. In truth, I had jumped on his back, pulling at his thick, musky fur and stabbing him with my knife in a desperate attempt to keep him from killing Asaru. And then the bear had turned on me as I had turned on him; he had hammered my forehead with his sharp claws. And then I had known only blackness until I awoke to see Andaru Harsha pulling his great hunting spear out of the bear's back.

Later that night, Asaru had told our father how I had saved his life.

19

It was a story that became widely known – and widely disbelieved. To this day, everyone assumed that Asaru had embellished my role in the bear's killing to save me from the shame of laying down my weapons in the face of the enemy.

'Look, Val,' Asaru whispered, pointing through the trees.

I turned to follow the line of his outstretched finger. Standing some thirty yards away, munching the leaves of a tender fern, was the deer that we had come for. He was a young buck, his new antlers fuzzy with velvet. Miraculously, he hadn't yet seen us. He kept eating quietly even as we slipped arrows from our quivers and nocked them to our bowstrings.

Asaru, kneeling ten paces to my left, drew his bow along with me, as did Maram who stood slightly behind me and to my right. I felt their excitement heating up their quickly indrawn breaths. I felt my own excitement, too. My mouth watered in anticipation of the coming night's feast. In truth, I loved the taste of meat as well as any man, even though very often I couldn't do what I had to do to get it.

'Abide in peace,' I whispered.

At that moment, as I pulled back the arrow toward my ear, the buck looked up at me. And I looked at him. His deep, liquid eyes were as full of life as the squirrel's had been of death. It was hard to kill so great an animal as a deer, much less that infinitely more complex being called man.

Valashu.

There was something about the buck's sudden awareness of the nearness of death that opened me to the nearness of my own. The light of his eyes was like flame from a firestone melting the granite walls that I hid behind; his booming heart was a battering ram beating open the gates of my heart. More strongly than ever I heard the thunder of that deep and soundless voice that had called me to the woods that day. I heard as well another voice calling my name; it was a voice from the past and future, and it roared with malevolence and murder.

Valashu Elahad.

The buck looked past me suddenly, and his eyes flickered as he tried to tell me something. The wrongness I had sensed in the woods was now very close; I felt it eating into the flesh between my shoulder blades like a mass of twisting, red worms. Instinctively, I moved to escape this terrible sensation.

And then came the moment of death. Arrows flew. They sang from our bows, and burned through the air. Maram's arrow hit the deer in the side even as I felt a sudden burning pain in my own side; my arrow missed altogether and buried itself in a tree. But Asaru's arrow drove straight behind the buck's shoulder into his heart. Although the buck gathered in all his strength for a last, desperate leap into life, I knew that he would be as good as dead before he struck the ground.

20

And down into the dark . . .

The fourth arrow, I saw, had nearly killed me. As the sky finally opened and thunderbolts lit up the forest, I looked down in astonishment to see a feathered shaft three feet long sticking out of the side of my torn jacket – its thick leather and the book of poetry in its pocket had entangled the arrow. I was reeling from the buck's death and something worse, but I still had the good sense to wonder who had shot it.

'Val, get down!'

And so did Asaru. Even as he shouted at me to protect myself, he whirled about to scan the forest. And there, more than a hundred yards farther into the forest, a dark, cloaked figure was running through the trees away from us. Asaru, ever the battle lord, tried to follow him, leaping across the bracken even as he drew another arrow from his quiver and nocked it. He got off a good shot, but my would-be murderer found cover behind a tree. And then he started running again with Asaru quickly closing the distance behind him.

'Val, behind you!' Maram called out.

I turned just in time to see another cloaked figure step out from behind a tree some eighty yards behind me. He was drawing back a black arrow aimed at my chest.

I tried to heed the urgency of the moment, but I found that I couldn't move. The burning in my side from the first assassin's arrow spread through my body like fire. But strangely, my hands, legs and feet – even my lips and eyes – felt cold.

The cold that freezes breath . . .

Maram, seeing my helplessness, cursed as he suddenly leaped from behind the tree where he had taken shelter. He cursed again as his fat arms and legs drove him puffing and crashing through the forest. He shot an arrow at the second assassin, but it missed. I heard the arrow skittering off through the leaves of a young oak tree. And then the assassin loosed his arrow, not at Maram, of course, but at me.

Again, just as the arrow was released, I felt in my chest the twisting of the man's hate. It was *my* hate, I think, that gave me the strength to turn to the side and pull my shoulders backward. The arrow hissed like a wooden snake only inches from my chin. I felt it slice through the air even as I heard my assassin howl with frustration and rage. And then Maram fell upon him like a fury, and I knew I had to find the strength to move very fast or my fat friend would soon be dead.

I felt Maram's fear quivering inside my own heart; there, I felt something deeper compelling me to move. It warmed my frozen limbs, and filled my hands with a terrible strength. Suddenly, I found the skill at arms that my father had taught me. With a speed that astonished me, I plucked out the arrow caught in my jacket and fit it to my bowstring.

But now Maram and the assassin whirled about each other as Maram slashed at the air with his dagger and the assassin tried to brain him with an evil-looking mace. I couldn't shoot lest I hit Maram, so I cast down my bow and started running through the trees toward them. Twigs broke beneath me; even through my boots, rocks bruised my feet. I kept my eyes fixed on the assassin even as he drew back his mace and swung it at Maram's head.

'No!' I cried out.

It was a miracle, I believe, that Maram got his arm up just in time to deflect the full force of the blow. But the mace's heavy iron head glanced off the side of his skull, knocking him to the ground. The assassin would surely have finished him then if I hadn't charged him with my dagger drawn and flashing with every lightning bolt that lit the forest.

Valashu Elahad.

The assassin stood back from Maram's stunned and bleeding form and watched me approach. He was a huge man, thicker even than Maram, though none of his bulk appeared to be fat. His hair was a dirty, tangled, coppery mass, and the skin of his face, pale and pocked with scars, glistened with grease. He was breathing hard with his bristly lips pulled back to reveal huge lower canines that looked more like a boar's tusks than they did teeth. He regarded me hatefully with small bloodshot eyes full of intelligence and cruelty.

And then, with frightening speed, he charged at me. I hadn't wanted to close with a man wielding a mace, but before I could check myself, we crashed into each other. I barely managed to catch his arm as his huge hand closed around *my* arm and twisted savagely to force me to drop my knife. We struggled this way, hands clutching each other's arms, as we thrashed about the forest floor trying to free our weapons.

Valashu.

I pulled and shifted and raged against this monster of a man trying to kill me. His vast bulk, like a mountain of spasming muscles, surrounded me and almost crushed me under. He grunted like a wild boar, and I smelled his stinking sweat. I felt his fingernails like fire tearing my forearm open. Suddenly I crashed against a tree. My face scraped along its rough bark, shredding off the skin. In my mouth, I tasted the iron-red tang of blood. And all the while, he kept trying to smash the mace against my head.

'Valashu,' I heard my father whisper, 'you must get away or he'll kill you.'

Somehow then, I managed to turn the point of my knife into his arm. A dark bloom of blood instantly soaked through his dirty woolens. It was a only small wound, but it weakened him enough that I was able to break free. With the force of sudden hate, he pulled back from me

22

at almost the same moment and shook his mace at me as he cried out, 'Damn you Elahads!'

He clenched the fist of his wounded arm and grimaced at the hurt of it. It hurt me, too. The nerves in *my* arm felt outraged, stunned. There was no way, I knew, that I could fight another human being and not leave myself open to the violence and pain I inflicted on him.

But I wasn't wounded in my body, and so I was able take up a good stance and keep a distance between us. I tried to clear my mind and let my will to life run through me like a cleansing river. My father had taught me to fight this way. It was he, the stern king, who had insisted that I train with every possible combination of weapons, even one so unlikely as a mace against a knife. Words and whispers of encouragement began sounding inside me; bits of strategy came to me unbidden. I found myself falling into motions drilled into my limbs by hours of exhausting practice beneath my father's grim, black eyes. It was vital, I remembered, that I keep outside of the killing arc of the mace, longer than my knife by nearly two feet. Its massive head was of iron cast into the shape of a coiled dragon and rusted red. One good blow from it would crush my skull and send me for ever into the land of night.

'Damn you all!'

The assassin swore as he swung the mace at my head and pressed me back. Big drops of rain splatted against my forehead, nearly blinding me; I was afraid that I would stumble over a tree root or branch and fall helpless beneath this onslaught. The best strategy, I knew, called for me to feint and maneuver and wait for the mace's momentum to throw my opponent off balance and create an opening. But the assassin was a powerful man, able to check his blow and aim a new one at me almost before the head of the mace swept past me. He came straight at me in full fury, spitting and swearing and swinging his terrible mace.

He might have killed me there in the pouring rain. He had the superior weapon and the skill. But I had skill, too, and something else.

I have said that my talent for feeling what others feel can be a curse. But it is also truly a gift, like a great, shimmering double-edged sword. Even now, as I felt the pounding red pain of his wounded arm, I sensed precisely how he would move almost before his muscles tensed and the mace burned past me.

It wasn't really like reading his mind. He wanted to frighten me with a feint toward my knife hand, and I felt the fear of it as an icy tingling in my fingers before he even moved; a desire to smash out my eyes formed up inside him, and I felt this sickening emotion as a blinding red pain in my own eyes. He whirled about me now, faster and faster, trying to crush me with his mace. And with each of his movements, I moved too,

23

anticipating him by a breath. It was as if we were locked together hand to hand and eye to eye, dancing a dance of death together in the quickness of iron and steel that flashed like the storm's brilliant lightning.

And then the assassin aimed a tremendous blow at my face, and the force of it carried the mace whooshing through the air. Just then his foot slipped against a sodden tree root, and I had the opening that I had been waiting for. But I couldn't take it; I froze up with fear as I had at the Battle of Red Mountain. Instantly, the assassin recovered his balance, and swung the mace back toward my chest. It was a weak blow, but it caught me on the muscle there with a sickening crunch that nearly staved in my ribs. It took all my strength to jump away from him and not let myself fall to the ground screaming in pain.

'Val, help me!' Maram screamed from the glistening bracken deeper in the trees.

I found a moment to watch as he struggled to rise grunting and groaning to his feet. And then I realized that the scream had never left his lips but was only forming up like thunder inside him. As it was inside of me.

'Val, Val.'

The assassin's lust to kill was like a black, ravenous, twisted thing. He fairly ached to bash open my brains. I suddenly knew that if I let him do this, he would gleefully finish off Maram. And then lie in wait for Asaru's return.

'No, no,' I cried out, 'never!'

The assassin came at me again. Hail began to fall, and little pieces of ice pinged off the mace's iron head. I slipped and skidded over an exposed, muddy expanse of the forest floor; the assassin quickly took advantage of my clumsiness, aiming a vicious blow at me that nearly took off my face. Despite the rain's bitter cold, I could feel him sweating as he growled and gasped and damned me to a death without end.

I knew that I had to find my courage and close with him, now, before I slipped again. But how could I ever kill him? He might be a swine of a man, a terrible man, evil – but he was still a man. Perhaps he had a woman somewhere who loved him; perhaps he had a child. But certainly he himself was a child of the One, and therefore a spark of the infinite glowed inside him. Who was I to put it out? Who was I to look into his tormented eyes and steal the light?

There is something called the joy of battle. Women don't like to know about this; most men would rather forget it. Combat with another man this way in the dark woods was truly dirty, ugly, awful – but there was a terrible beauty about it, too. For fighting for life brings one closer to life. I remembered, then, my father telling me that I had been born to fight. All of us were. As the assassin raged at me with his dragon-headed mace, a great surge of life welled up inside me. My hands and heart and every part of me knew that it was good to feel my blood rushing like a river in flood, that it was a miracle simply to be able to draw in one more breath.

'Asaru,' I whispered.

Some deep part of me must have realized that this wild joy was really just a love of life. And love of the finest creations of life, such as my brother, Asaru, and even Maram. I felt this beautiful force flowing into me like sunlight; I opened myself to it utterly. In moments, it filled my whole being with a terrible strength.

Maram cried out in pain from the bloody wound on his head. The assassin glanced at him as his pulse leaped in anticipation of an easy kill. Something broke inside me then. *My* heart swelled with a sudden fury that I feared almost more that any other thing. I found that secret place where love and hate, life and death, were as one. This time, when the mace swept past me, I rushed the assassin. I stepped in close enough to feel the heat steaming off his massive body. I got my arm up to block the return arc of his mace as he snorted in anger and spat into my face. I smelled his fear, with my nostrils as well as with a finer sense. And then I plunged my dagger into the soft spot above his big, hard belly; I angled it upward so that it pierced his heart.

'Maram!' I screamed out. 'Asaru!'

The pain of the assassin's death was like nothing I had ever felt before. It was like lightning striking through my eyes into my spine, like a mace as big as a tree crushing in my chest. As the assassin gasped and spasmed and crumpled to the sodden earth, I fell on top of him. I coughed and gasped for breath; I screamed and raged and wept, all at once. A river of blood spurted out of the wound where I had put my knife. But an entire ocean flowed out of me.

'Val – are you hurt?' I heard Maram's voice boom like thunder as from far away. I felt him hovering over me as he placed his hand on my shoulder and shook me gently. 'Come on now, get up – you killed him.'

But the assassin wasn't quite dead. Even in the violence of the pouring rain, I felt his last breath burn against my face. I watched the light die from his eyes. And only then came the darkness.

'Come on, Val. Here, let me help you.'

But I couldn't move. I was only dimly aware of Maram grunting and puffing as he rolled me off the assassin's body. Maram's frightened face suddenly seemed to thin and grow as insubstantial as smoke. The colors faded from the forest; the blood seeping from his wounded head wasn't red at all but a dark gray. Everything grew darker then. A terrible cold, centered in my heart, began spreading through my body. It was worse than being caught in a blizzard in one of the mountain passes, worse even than plunging through Lake Waskaw's broken ice into freezing waters. It was a cosmic cold: vast, empty, indifferent; it was the cold that brings on the neverness of night and the nothingness of death. And I was utterly open to it.

It was as I lay in this half-alive state that Asaru finally returned. He must have sprinted when he saw me – and the dead assassin – stretched out on the forest floor, for he was panting to catch his breath when he reached my side. He knelt over me, and I felt his warm, hard hand pressing gently against my throat as he tested my pulse. To Maram he said, 'The other one . . . escaped. They had horses waiting. What happened here?'

Maram quickly explained how I had frozen up after the first assassin's arrow had stuck in my jacket; his voice swelled with pride as he told of how he had charged the second assassin.

'Ah, Lord Asaru,' he said, 'you should have seen me! A Valari warrior couldn't have done any better. I don't think it's too much of an exaggeration to say that I saved Val's life.'

'Thank you,' Asaru said dryly. 'It seems that Val also saved yours.'

He looked down at me and smiled grimly. He said, 'Val, what's wrong – why can't you move?'

'It's cold,' I whispered, looking into the blackness of his eyes. 'So cold.'

With much grumbling from Maram, they lifted me and carried me over beneath a great elm tree. Maram lay down his cloak and helped Asaru prop me up against the tree's trunk. Then Asaru ran back through the woods to retrieve our bows that we had cast down. He brought back as well the arrow that the first assassin had shot at me.

'This is bad,' he said, looking at the black arrow. In the flashes of lightning, he scanned the woods to the north, east, south and west. 'There may be more of them,' he told us.

'No,' I whispered. To be open to death is to be open to life. The hateful presence that I had sensed in the woods that day was now gone. Already, the rain was washing the air clean. 'There are no more.'

Asaru peered at the arrow and said, 'They almost killed me. I felt this pass through my hair.'

I looked at Asaru's long black hair blowing about his shoulders, but I could only gasp silently in pain.

'Let's get your shirt off,' he said. It was one of his rules, I knew, that wounds must be tended as soon as possible.

26

In a moment they had carefully removed my jacket and shirt. It must have been cold, with the wind whipping raindrops against my suddenly exposed flesh. But all I could feel was a deeper cold that sucked me down into death.

Asaru touched the livid bruise that the assassin's mace had left on my chest. His fingers gently probed my ribs. 'You're lucky – it seems that nothing is broken.'

'What about *that*?' Maram asked, pointing at my side where the arrow had touched me.

'Why, it's only a scratch,' Asaru said. He soaked a cloth with some of the brandy that he carried in a wineskin, and then swabbed it over my skin.

I looked down at my throbbing side. To call the wound left by the arrow a scratch was to exaggerate its seriousness. Truly, no more than the faintest featherstroke of a single red line marked the place where the arrow had nicked the skin. But I could still feel the poison working in my veins.

'It's cold,' I whispered. 'Everywhere, cold.'

Now Asaru examined the arrow, which was fletched with raven feathers and tipped with a razor-sharp steel head like any common hunting arrow. But the steel, I saw, was enameled with some dark, blue substance. Asaru's eyes flashed with anger as he showed it to Maram.

He said, 'They tried to kill me with a poison arrow.'

I blinked my eyes at the cold crushing my skull. But I said nothing against my brother's prideful assumption that the arrow had been meant for him and not me.

'Do you think it was the Ishkans?' Maram asked.

Asaru pointed at the assassin's body and said, 'That's no Ishkan.'

'Perhaps they hired him.'

'They must have,' Asaru said.

'Oh, no,' I murmured. 'No, no, no.'

Not even the Ishkans, I thought, would ever kill a man with poison. Or would they?

Asaru quickly, but with great care, wrapped my torn and tainted jacket and shirt around the arrow's head to protect it from the falling rain. Then he took off his cloak and put it on me.

'Is that better?' he asked me.

'Yes,' I said, lying to him despite what I had been taught. 'Much better.'

Although he smiled down at me to encourage me, his face was grave. I didn't need my gift of empathy to feel his love and concern for me.

27

'This is hard to understand,' he said. 'You can't have taken enough poison to paralyze you this way.'

No, I thought, I couldn't have. It wasn't the poison that pinned me to the earth like a thousand arrows of ice. I wanted to explain to him that somehow the poison must have dissolved my shields and left me open to the assassin. But how could I tell my simple, courageous brother what it was like to feel another die? How I could make him understand the terror of a cold as vast and black as the emptiness between the stars?

I turned my head to watch the rain beating down on the assassin's bloody chest. Who could ever escape the great emptiness? Truly, I thought, the same fate awaited us all.

Asaru placed his warm hand on top of mine and said, 'If it's poison, Master Juwain will know a cure. We'll take you to him as soon as the rain stops.'

My grandfather had once warned me to beware of elms in thunder, but we took shelter beneath that great tree all the same. Its dense foliage protected us from the worst of the rain as we waited out the storm. As Asaru tended Maram's wounded head, I heard him reassuring Maram that it rains hard in the Morning Mountains, but not long.

As always, he spoke truly. After a while the downpour weakened to a sprinkle and then stopped. The clouds began to break up, and shafts of light drove down through gaps in the forest canopy and touched the rain-sparkled ferns with a deeper radiance. There was something in this golden light that I had never seen before. It seemed to struggle to take form even as I struggled to apprehend it. I somehow knew that I had to open myself to this wondrous thing as I had my brother's love or the inevitability of my death.

The stealing of the gold . . .

And then there, floating in the air five feet in front of me, appeared a plain golden cup that would have fit easily into the palm of my hand. Call it a vision; call it a waking dream; call it a derangement of my aching eyes. But I saw it as clearly as I might have a bird or a butterfly.

I was only dimly aware of Asaru kneeling by my side as he touched my throbbing head. Almost all that I could see was this marvelous cup shimmering before me. With my eyes, I drank in its golden light. And almost immediately, a warmth like that of my mother's honey tea began pouring into me.

'Do you see it?' I asked Asaru.

'See what?'

The Lightstone, I thought. *The healing stone.*

For this, I thought, Aryu had risen up and killed his brother with a knife even as I had killed the assassin. For this simple cup, men had fought and murdered and made war for more than ten thousand years.

'What is it, Val?' Asaru asked, gently shaking my shoulder.

But I couldn't tell him what I saw. After a while, as I leaned back against the solidity and strength of the great elm, the coldness left my body. I prayed then that someday the Lightstone would heal me completely so that the terror of my gift would leave me as well and I would suffer the pain of the world no more.

Although I was still very weak, I managed to press my hands down into the damp earth. And then to Asaru's and Maram's astonishment – and my own – I stood up.

Somehow I staggered over to where the assassin lay atop the glistening bracken. While my whole body shook and I gasped with the effort of it, I pulled my knife out of his chest and cleaned it. Then I closed the assassin's cold blue eyes. In my own eyes, I felt a sudden moist pain. My throat hurt as if I had swallowed a lump of cold iron. Somewhere deeper inside, my belly and being heaved with a sickness that wouldn't go away. There, I knew, the cold would always wait to freeze my breath and steal my soul. I vowed then that no matter the cause or need, I would never, never kill anyone again.

In the air above me – above the assassin's still form – the Lightstone poured out a golden radiance that filled the forest. It was the light of love, the light of life, the light of truth. In its shimmering presence, I couldn't lie to myself: I knew with a bitter certainty that it was my fate to kill many, many men.

And then, suddenly, the cup was gone.

'What are you staring at?' Asaru asked.

'It's nothing,' I told him. 'Nothing at all.'

Now a fire burned through me like the poison still in my veins. I struggled to remain standing. Asaru came over to my side. His strong arm wrapped itself around my back to help me.

'Can you walk now?' he asked.

I nodded and Asaru smiled in relief. After I had steadied myself, Asaru called Maram over to check his wounded head. He poked his finger into Maram's big gut and told him, 'Your head is as hard as your belly is soft. You'll be all right.'

'Ah, yes, indeed, I suppose I will – as soon as you bring back the horses.'

For a moment, Asaru looked up through the fluttering leaves at the sun. He looked down at the dead assassin. And then he turned to Maram and told him, 'No, it's getting late, and it wouldn't do to leave either of you alone here. Despite what Val says, there may be others about. We'll walk out together.'

'All right then, *Lord* Asaru,' Maram said.

Asaru bent down toward the assassin. And then, with a shocking strength, he hoisted the body onto his shoulder and straightened up. He pointed deeper into the woods. 'You'll carry back the deer,' he told Maram.

'Carry back the deer!' Maram protested. Asaru might as well have appointed him to bear the whole world on his shoulders. 'It must be two miles back to the horses!'

Asaru, straining under the great mass of the assassin's body, looked down at Maram with a sternness that reminded me of my father. He said, 'You wanted to be a warrior – why don't you act like one?'

Despite Maram's protests, beneath all his fear and fat, he was as strong as a bull. As there was no gainsaying my brother when he had decided on an action, Maram grudgingly went to fetch the deer.

'You look sick,' Asaru said as he freed a hand to touch my forehead. 'But at least the cold is gone.'

No, no, I thought, *it will never be gone.*

'Does it still hurt?' he asked me.

'Yes,' I said, wincing at the pain in my side. 'It hurts.'

Why, I wondered, had someone tainted an arrow with poison? Why would anyone try to kill me?

I drew in a deep breath as I steeled myself for the walk back through the forest. When I closed my eyes, I could still see the Lightstone shining like a sun.

With Asaru in the lead, we started walking west toward the place where we had left the horses. Maram puffed and grumbled beneath the deer flopped across his shoulders. At least, I thought, we had taken a deer, even as Asaru had said we would. And so we would have something to contribute to that night's feast with the Ishkans.

3

It was late afternoon by the time we broke free from the forest and rejoined Joshu Kadar at the edge of Lord Harsha's fields. The young squire blinked his eyes in amazement at the load slung across my brother's back; he had the good sense, however, not to beleaguer us with questions just then. He kept a grim silence and went to fetch Lord Harsha as my brother bade him.

The horses, however, practiced no such restraint. Joshu had them tied to a couple of saplings beyond the wall surrounding Lord Harsha's field; at the smell of fresh blood they began whinnying and stomping the ground as they pulled at the trees with almost enough force to uproot them. Maram tried to calm them but couldn't. They were already skittish from the bolts of lightning that had shaken the earth only an hour before.

I walked over to Altaru and laid my hand on him. His wet fur was pungent with the scent of anger and fear. As I stroked his trembling neck, I pressed my head against his head and then breathed into his huge nostrils. Gradually, he grew quieter. After a while, he looked at me with his soft brown eyes and then gently nudged my side where the arrow had burned me with its poison.

The gentleness of this great animal always touched me even as much as it astonished me. For Altaru stood eighteen hands high and weighed some two thousand pounds of quivering muscle and unyielding bone. He was the fiercest of stallions. He was one of the last of the black war horses who run wild on the plains of Anjo. For a thousand years, the kings of Anjo had bred his line for beauty no less than battle. But after the Sarni wars, when Anjo had broken apart into a dozen contending dukedoms, Altaru's sires had escaped into the fields surrounding the shattered castles, and Anjo's great horsebreeding tradition had been lost. From time to time, some brave Anjori would manage to capture one of these magnificent horses only to find him unbreakable. So it had been with Altaru: Duke Gorador had presented him as a gift to my father as if to say, 'You Meshians think you are the greatest knights of all the Valari; well, we'll see if you can ride *this* horse into battle.'

This my father had tried to do. But nothing in his power had persuaded Altaru to accept a bit in his mouth or a saddle on his back.

Five times he had bucked the proud king to the ground before my father gave up and pronounced Altaru incorrigibly wild.

As I knew he truly was. For Altaru had never seen a mare whom he didn't tremble to cover or another stallion he wouldn't fight. And he had never known a man whose hand he didn't want to bite or whose face he didn't want to crush with a kick from one of his mighty hooves. Except me. When my father, in a rare display of frustration, had finally ordered Altaru gelded, I had rushed into his stall and thrown myself against his side to keep the handlers away from him. Everyone supposed that I had fallen mad and would soon be stomped into pulp. But Altaru had astonished my father and brothers – and myself – by lowering his head to lick my sweating face. He had allowed me to mount him and race him bareback through the forest below Silvassu. And ever since that wild ride through the trees, for five years, we had been the best of friends.

'It's all right,' I reassured him as I stroked his great shoulder, 'everything will be all right.'

But Altaru, who spoke a language deeper than words, knew that I was lying to him. Again he nuzzled my side and shuddered as if it was *he* who had been poisoned. The fire in his dark eyes told me that he was ready to kill the man who had wounded me, if only we could find him.

A short time later, Joshu Kadar returned with Lord Harsha. The old man drove a stout, oak wagon, rough-cut and strong like Lord Harsha himself. A few hours had worked a transformation on him. Gone were the muddy workboots and homespun woolens that he wore tending his fields. Now he sported a fine new tunic, and I couldn't help noticing the sword fastened to his sleek, black belt. After he had stopped the wagon on the other side of the stone wall, he stepped down and smoothed back his freshly washed hair. He gazed for a long moment at the dead deer and the assassin's body spread out on the earth. Then he said, 'The king has asked me to contribute the beverage for tonight's feast. Now it seems we'll be carrying more than beer in my wagon.'

While Asaru stepped over to him and began telling of what had happened in the woods, Maram peeled back the wagon's covering tarp to reveal a dozen barrels of beer. His eyes went wide with the greed of thirst, and he eyed the contents of the wagon as if he had discovered a cave full of treasure.

32

With his fat knuckles, he rapped the barrels one by one. 'Oh, my beauties – have I ever seen such a beautiful, beautiful sight?'

I was sure that he would have begged Lord Harsha for a bowl of beer right there if not for the grim look on Lord Harsha's face as he stared at the dead assassin. Maram stared at him, too. Then, to everyone's surprise, Maram called for Joshu to help him lift the assassin's body into the wagon. The sweating and puffing Maram moved quickly as with new strength, and then loaded in the deer by himself. Only his anticipation of later helping to drain these barrels, I thought, could have caused him to take such initiative.

'Thank you for sparing an old man's joints,' Lord Harsha told him, patting his broken knee. 'Now if you will all accompany me, we'll collect my daughter and be on our way. She'll be joining us for the feast.'

So saying, Lord Harsha drove the groaning wagon across his fields while we followed him on horseback to his house. There, a rather plump, pretty woman with raven-dark hair stood in the doorway and watched us draw up. She was dressed in a silk gown and a flowing gray cloak gathered in above her ample breasts with a silver brooch. This was to be her first appearance at my father's castle, I gathered, and so she naturally wanted to be seen wearing her finest.

Lord Harsha stepped painfully down from his wagon and said, 'Lord Asaru, may I present my daughter, Behira?'

In turn, he presented this shy young woman to me, Joshu Kadar and Maram. To my dismay, Maram's face flushed a deep red at the first sight of her. I could almost feel his desire for her leaping like fire along his veins. Gone from him completely, it seemed, was any thought of beer.

'Oh, Lord, what a beauty!' he blurted out. 'Lord Harsha – you certainly have a talent for making beautiful things.'

It might have been thought that Lord Harsha would relish such a compliment. Instead, his single eye glared at Maram like a heated iron. Most likely, I thought, he wished to present Behira at my father's court to some of the greatest knights of Mesh; he would take advantage of the night's gathering to make the best match for her that he could – and that certainly wouldn't be a marriage to some cowardly outland prince who had forsworn wine, women and war.

'My daughter,' Lord Harsha coldly informed Maram, 'is *not* a thing. But thank you all the same.'

He limped over to his barn then, and returned a short time later leading a huge, gray mare. Despite the pain of his knee, he insisted on riding to my father's castle with all the dignity that he could command. And so he gritted his teeth as he pulled himself up into the saddle; he sat straight and tall like the battle lord he still was, and led the way down the road followed closely by Asaru, Joshu and myself. Behira seemed happy at being left to drive the wagon, while Maram was *very* happy lagging behind the rest of us so that he could talk to her.

'Well, Behira,' I overheard him say above the clopping of the horses' hooves, 'it's a lovely day for such a lovely woman to attend her first feast. Ah, how old *are* you? Sixteen? Seventeen?'

Behira, holding the reins of the wagon's horses in her strong, rough hands, looked over at me as if she wished that it was *I* who was lavishing my attention on her. But women terrified me even more than did war. Their passions were like deep, underground rivers flowing with unstoppable force. If I opened myself to a woman's love for only a moment, I thought, I would surely be swept away.

'I'm afraid we have no such women as you in Delu,' Maram went on. 'If we did, I never would have left home.'

I looked away from Behira to concentrate on a stand of oak trees by the side of the road. I sensed that, despite herself, she was quite taken by Maram's flattery. And probably Maram impressed her as well. After Alonia, Delu was the greatest kingdom of Ea, and Maram was Delu's eldest prince.

'Well, you should have let a *woman* tend your wound,' I heard Behira say to him. I could almost feel her touching the makeshift bandage that my brother had tied around Maram's head. 'Perhaps when we get to the castle I could look at it.'

'Would you? Would you?'

'Of course,' she told him. 'The outlander struck you with a mace, didn't he?'

'Ah, yes, a mace,' Maram said. And then his great, booming voice softened with the seductiveness of recounting his feats. 'I hope you're not alarmed by what happened in the woods today. It was quite a little battle, but of course we prevailed. I had the honor of being in a position to help Val at the critical moment.'

According to Maram, not only had he scared off the first assassin and weakened the second, but he had willingly taken a wound to his head in order to save my life. When he caught me smiling at the embellishments of his story – I didn't want to think of his braggadocio as mere lies – he shot me a quick, wounded look as if to say, 'Love is difficult, my friend, and wooing a woman calls for any weapon.'

Perhaps it did, I thought, but I didn't want to watch him bring down this particular quarry. Even as he began speaking of his father's bejeweled palaces and vast estates in far-off Delu, I nudged Altaru forward so that I might take part in other conversations.

'Val,' Asaru said to me as I pulled alongside him, 'Lord Harsha has agreed that no one should know about all this until we've had a chance to speak with the king.'

I was silent as I looked off at the rolling fields of Lord Harsha's neighbors. Then I said, 'And Master Juwain?'

'Yes. Speak with him while he attends your wound, but no one else.' Asaru said. 'All right?'

'All right,' I said.

We gave voice then to questions for which we had no answers: Who *were* these strange men who had shot poisoned arrows at us? Assassins sent by the Ishkans or some vengeful duke or king? How had they crossed the heavily guarded passes into Mesh? How had they picked up our trail and then stalked us so silently through the forest?

And why, I wondered above all else, *did they want to kill me*?

With this thought came the certainty that it had been my death they had sought and not Asaru's. Again I felt the wrongness that I had sensed earlier in the woods. It seemed not to emanate from any one direction but rather pervaded the sweet-smelling air itself. All about us were the familiar colors of my father's kingdom: the white granite farm houses; the greenness of fields rich with oats, rye and barley; the purple mountains of Mesh that soared into the deep blue sky. And yet all that I looked upon – even the bright red firebirds fluttering about in the trees – seemed darkened as with some indelible taint.

It touched me as well. I felt it as a poison burning in my blood and a coldness that sucked at my soul. As we rode across this beautiful country, more than once I wanted to call a halt so that I could slip down from my saddle and sleep – either that or sink down into the dark, rain-churned earth and cry out at the terror that had awakened inside me.

And this I might easily have done but for Altaru. Somehow he sensed the hurt of my wounded side and the deeper pain of the death that I had inflicted upon the assassin; somehow he moved with a slow, rhythmic grace that seemed to flow into me and ease my distress rather than aggravate it. The surging of his long muscles and great heart lent me a badly needed strength. The familiar, fermy smell steaming off his body reassured me of the basic goodness of life. I had no need to guide him or even to touch his reins, for he knew well enough where we were going: home, to where the setting sun hung above the mountains like a golden cup overflowing with light.

So it was that we finally came upon my father's castle. This great heap of stone stood atop a hill which was one of several 'steps' forming the lower slope of Telshar. The right branch of the Kurash River cut around the base of this hill, separating the castle from the buildings and streets of Silvassu itself. At least in the spring, the river was a natural moat of raging, icy, brown waters; the defensive advantages of such a site must have been obvious to my ancestors who had entered the Valley of Swans so long ago.

As I looked out at the castle's soaring white towers, I couldn't help remembering the story of the first Shavashar, who was the great-grandson of Elahad himself. It had been he who had led the Valari into the Morning Mountains at the beginning of the Lost Ages. This was in the time after the Hundred Year March when the small Valari tribe had wandered across all of Ea on a futile quest to recover the golden cup that Aryu had stolen. Shavashar had set the stones of the first Elahad castle and had begun the warrior tradition of the Valari, for it was told that the first Valari to come to Ea – like all the Star People – were warriors of the spirit only. It was Shavashar who forged my people into warriors of the sword. It was he who had foretold that the Valari would one day have to fight 'whole armies and all the demons of hell' to regain the Lightstone.

And so we had. Thousands of years later, in the year 2,292 of the Age of the Sword – every child older than five knew this date – the Valari had united under Aramesh's banner and defeated Morjin at the Battle of Sarburn. Aramesh had wrested the Lightstone from Morjin's very hands and brought this priceless cup back to the security of my family's castle. For a long time it had resided there, acting as a beacon that drew pilgrims from across all of Ea. These were the great years of Mesh, during which time Silvassu had grown out into the valley to become a great city.

I heard Asaru's voice calling me as from far away.

'Why have you stopped?'

In truth, I hadn't noticed that I had stopped. Or rather, Altaru, sensing my mood, had pulled up at the edge of the road while I gazed off into the past. Before us farther up the road, along the gentle slope leading up to the castle, fields of barley glistened in the slanting light where once great buildings had stood. I remembered my grandfather telling me of the second great tragedy of my people: that in the time of Godavanni the Glorious, Morjin had again stolen the Lightstone, and its radiance had left the Morning Mountains forever. And so, over the centuries, Silvassu had diminished to little more than a backwoods city in a forgotten kingdom. The stones of its streets and houses had been torn up to build the shield wall that surrounded the castle, for the golden age of Ea had ended and the Age of the Dragon had begun.

'Look,' I said to Asaru as I pointed at this great wall. Atop the mural towers protecting it, green pennants fluttered in the wind. This was a signal that the castle had received guests and a feast was to be held.

36

'It's late,' Asaru said. 'We should have been home an hour ago. Shall we go?'

Maram pulled up by my side then as the wagon creaked to a halt behind me. Lord Harsha, still sitting erect in his saddle, rubbed his head above his eye-patch as his mare pawed the muddy road.

And I continued staring at this great edifice of stone that dominated the Valley of the Swans. The shield wall, a hundred feet high, ran along the perimeter of the entire hill almost flush with its steep slopes. Indeed, it seemed to arise out of the hill itself as if the very earth had flung up its hardest parts toward the sky. Higher even than this mighty wall stood the main body of the castle with its many towers: the Swan Tower, the Aramesh Tower with its ancient, crenelated stonework, the Tower of the Stars. The keep was a massive cube of carefully cut rocks as was the adjoining great hall. And all of it – the watchtowers and turrets, the gatehouses and garden walls – had been made of white granite. In the falling sun, the whole of the castle shimmered with a terrible beauty, as even I had to admit. But I knew too well the horrors that waited inside: the catapults and sheaves of arrows tied together like so many stalks of wheat; the pots of sand to be heated red-hot and poured through the overhanging parapets on any enemy who dared to assault the walls. Truly, the castle had been built to keep whole armies out, if not demons from hell. And not, it seemed, the Ishkans. My father had invited them to break bread with us in the castle's very heart. There, in the great hall, I would find them waiting for me, and perhaps my would-be assassin as well.

'Yes,' I finally said to Asaru, 'let's go.'

I touched my ankles to Altaru's side, and the huge horse practically leapt forward as if to battle. We started up the north road that cut through an apple orchard before curving around the edge of Silvassu's least populated district; its slope was the most gentle of the three roads leading into the castle and therefore the easiest for the horses pulling the heavy wagon to negotiate. A short while later we passed through the two great towers guarding the Aramesh Gate and entered the castle.

In the north courtyard that day there was a riot of activity. Various wagons laden with foodstuffs had pulled up to the storehouses where the cooks' apprentices rushed to unload them. From the wheelwright's workshop came the sound of hammered steel, while the candlers were busy dipping the last of the night's tapers. Squires such as Joshu ran about completing errands assigned by their lords. We had to ride carefully through the courtyard lest our horses trample them, as well as the children playing with wooden swords or spinning tops along the flagstones. When we reached the stables, we dismounted and gave the tending of the horses over to Joshu. He took Altaru's reins in his hands as if his life depended on the care with which he handled the great, snorting stallion – as it very well did. There, in front of the stalls smelling of freshly spread straw and even fresher dung, we said our goodbyes. Asaru and Lord Harsha would accompany Behira to the kitchens to unload the wagon before attending their business with the steward and king. And Maram and I would seek out Master Juwain.

'But what about your head?' Behira said to Maram. 'It needs a proper dressing.'

'Ah,' Maram said as his voice swelled with anticipation, 'perhaps we could meet later in the infirmary.'

At this, Lord Harsha stepped between the wagon and Maram, and stood staring down at him. 'No, that won't be necessary,' he said to him. 'Isn't your Master Juwain a healer? Well, let *him* heal you, then.'

Asaru moved closer to me and laid his hand on my shoulder. 'Please give Master Juwain my regards,' he said.

And then, as his eyes flashed like a dark sky crackling with lightning, he added, 'Tonight there will be a feast to be remembered.'

Maram and I crossed the courtyard then, and walked through the middle ward which was full of chickens squawking and running for their lives. After passing through the gateway to the west ward, we found the arched doorway to the Adami Tower open. I went inside and fairly raced up the worn steps that wound up through the narrow staircase; Maram, however, puffed along behind me at a slower pace. I couldn't help reflecting on the fact that the stairs spiraled clockwise as they rose to the tower's upper floors. This allowed a defender to retreat upwards while wielding his sword with his right hand, whereas an attacker would have to lean around the corner in the wrong direction to wield his. I couldn't help noticing as well the castle's ever-present smell: rusting iron and sweating stone and the sharpness of burning tallow that over the centuries had coated the walls and ceilings with layers of black smoke.

Master Juwain was in the guest chamber on the highest floor. It was the grandest such room in the castle – indeed, in all of Mesh – and many would argue that it should have been reserved for the Ishkan prince or even King Kiritan's emissaries. But by tradition, whenever a master of the Brotherhoods was visiting, he took up residence there.

'Come in,' Master Juwain's voice croaked out after I had knocked at the door to his chamber.

I opened this great, iron-shod slab of oak and stepped into a large room. It was well-lit, with the shutters of its eight arched windows thrown open. In most other rooms of the castle, this would have let in gusts of cold air along with sunlight. But the windows here were some of the few to be fitted with glass panes. Even so, the room was rather cool, and Master Juwain had a few logs burning in the fireplace along the far wall. This, I thought, was an extravagance. As were the chamber's other appointments: the tiled floor, covered with Galdan carpets; the richly-colored tapestries; the shelves of books set into the wall near the great, canopied bed. As far as I knew, there was only one other true bed in the castle, and there my father and mother slept. The whole of the chamber bespoke a comfort at odds with the Brotherhoods' ideal of restraint and austerity, but the great Elemesh had proclaimed that these teachers of our people should be treated like kings, and so they were.

'Valashu Elahad – is that you?' Master Juwain called out as I entered the room. He was as short and stocky as I remembered, and one of the ugliest men I had ever seen.

'Sir,' I said, bowing. 'It's good to see you again.'

He was standing by one of the windows and looking up from a large book that he had been reading; he returned my bow politely and then stepped over to me. 'It's good to see *you*,' he said. 'It's been almost two years.'

To look upon Master Juwain was to be reminded at first of vegetables – and not the most attractive ones at that. His head, large and lumpy like a potato, was shaved smooth, the better to appreciate the puffy ears that stood out like cauliflowers. His nose was a big, brown squash, and of his mouth and lips, it is better not to speak. He clasped me on the shoulder with a hand as tough as old tree roots. Although he was first and foremost a scholar – perhaps the finest in all of Ea – he liked nothing better than working in his garden and keeping close to the earth. Although he might advise kings and teach their sons, I thought he would always be a farmer at heart.

'To what honor,' he asked, 'shall I attribute this visit after being ignored for so long?'

His gaze took in the rain-stained cloak that Asaru had lent me as he looked at me deeply. The saving feature of his face, I thought, were his eyes: they were large and luminous, all silver-gray like the moonlit sea. There was a keen intelligence there and great kindness, too. I have said that he was an ugly man, and ugly he truly was. But he was also one of those rare men transformed by a love of truth into a being of great beauty.

'My apologies, sir,' I told him. 'But it was never my intention to ignore you.'

Just then Maram came wheezing and panting into the room. He

39

bowed to Master Juwain and then said, 'Please excuse us, sir, but we needed to see you. Something has happened.'

While Master Juwain paced back and forth rubbing his bald head, Maram explained how we had fought for our lives in the woods that afternoon. He conveniently left out the part of the story in which he had shot the deer, but otherwise his account was reasonably accurate. By the time I had spoken as well, the room was growing dark.

'I see,' Master Juwain said. His head bowed down in deep thought as he dug his foot into the priceless carpet. Then he moved over to the window and gazed out at Telshar's white diamond peak. 'It's growing late, and I want to get a good look at this arrow you've brought me. And your wounds as well. Would you please light the candles, Brother Maram?'

While I tightly gripped the black arrow, still wrapped in my torn shirt, Maram went over to the fireplace where he stuck a long match into the flames to ignite it. Then he went about the room lighting the many candles in their stands. As the soft light of the tapers filled the room, I reflected on the fact that some two thousand candles would be burned throughout the castle before the night was through.

'Here, now,' Master Juwain said as his hand closed on Maram's arm. He pulled him over to the writing table, which was covered with maps, open books and many papers. There he sat him down in the carved, oak chair. 'We'll look at your head first.'

He went over to the basin by one of the windows and carefully washed his hands. Then, from beneath the bed, he retrieved two large wooden boxes which he set on the writing table. In the first box, as I saw when he opened it, were many small compartments filled with unguents, bottled medicines and twists of foul-smelling herbs. The second box contained various knives, probes, clamps, scissors and saws – all made of gleaming Godhran steel. I tried not to look into this box as Master Juwain lifted out a roll of clean white cloth and set it on the table.

It didn't take him very long to clean Maram's wound and wrap his head with a fresh dressing. But for me, standing by the window and looking out at the night's first stars as I tried not to listen to Maram's groans and gasps, it seemed like an hour. And then it was my turn.

After pulling back Asaru's cloak, I took Maram's place on the chair. Master Juwain's hard, gnarly fingers gently probed my bruised chest and then touched my side along the thin red line left by the arrow.

'It's hot,' Master Juwain said. 'A wound such as this shouldn't be so hot so soon.'

And with that, he dabbed an unguent on my side. The greenish cream was cool but stank of mold and other substances that I couldn't identify.

'All right,' Master Juwain said, 'now let's see the arrow.'

As Maram crowded closer and looked on, I unwrapped the arrow and handed it to Master Juwain. He seemed loath to touch it, as if it were a snake that might at any moment come alive and sink its venomous fangs into him. With great care he held it closer to the stand of candles burning by the table; he gazed at the coated head for a long time as his gray eyes darkened like the sea in a storm.

'What is it?' Maram blurted out. 'Is it truly poison?'

'You know it is,' Master Juwain told him.

'Well, which one?'

Master Juwain sighed and said, 'That we shall soon see.'

He instructed us to stand off toward the open window, and we did as he bade us. Then, from the second box, he produced a scalpel and a tiny spoon whose bowl was the size of a child's fingernail. With a meticulousness that I had always found daunting, he used the scalpel to scrape off a bit of the bluish substance that covered the head of the arrow. He caught these evil-looking flakes with a sheet of white paper, then funneled them into the spoon.

'Hold your breath, now,' he told us.

I drew in a draft of clean mountain air and watched as Master Juwain covered his nose and mouth with a thick cloth. Then he held the spoon over one of the candles. A moment later, the blue flakes caught fire. But strangely, I saw, they burned with an angry, red flame.

Still holding the cloth over his face, Master Juwain set down the spoon and joined us by the window. I could almost feel him silently counting the seconds to every beat of my heart. By this time, my lungs were burning for air. At last Master Juwain uncovered his mouth and told us, 'Go ahead and breathe – I think it should be all right now.'

Maram, whose face was red as an apple, gasped at the air streaming in the window, and so did I. Even so, I caught the faintness of a stench that was bitter beyond belief.

'Well?' Maram said, turning to Master Juwain, 'do you know what it is?'

'Yes, I know,' Master Juwain said. There was a great sadness in his voice. 'It's as I feared – the poison is kirax.'

'Kirax,' Maram repeated as if he didn't like the taste of the word on his tongue. 'I don't know about kirax.'

'Well, you should,' Master Juwain said. 'If you weren't so busy with the chambermaids, then you would.'

I thought Master Juwain was being unfair to him. Maram was studying

41

to become a Master of Poetry, and so couldn't be expected to know of every esoteric herb or poison.

'What is kirax, sir?' I asked him.

He turned to me and grasped my shoulder. There was a reassuring strength in his hand and tenderness as well. And then he said, 'It's a poison used only by Morjin and the Red Priests of the Kallimun. And their assassins.'

He went on to say that kirax was a derivative of the kirque plant, as was the more common drug called kiriol. Kiriol, of course, was known to open certain sensitives to others' minds – though at great cost to themselves. Kirax was much more dangerous: even a small amount opened its victim to a flood of sensations that overwhelmed and burned out the nerves. Death came quickly and agonizingly as if one's entire body had been plunged into a vat of boiling oil.

'You must have absorbed a minuscule amount of it,' Master Juwain told me. 'Not enough to kill but quite sufficient to torment you.'

Truly, I thought, enough to torment me even as my gift tormented me. I looked off at the candles' flickering flames, and it occurred to me that the kirax was a dark, blue, hidden knife cutting at my heart and further opening it to sufferings and secrets that I would rather not know.

'Do you have the antidote?' I asked him.

Master Juwain sighed as he looked at his box of medicines. 'I'm afraid there is no antidote,' he said. He told Maram and me that the hell of kirax was that once injected, it never left the body.

'Ah,' Maram said upon hearing this news, 'that's hard, Val – that's too bad.'

Yes, I thought, trying to close myself from the waves of pity and fear that poured from Maram, it was very bad indeed.

Master Juwain moved back over to the table and gingerly picked up the arrow. 'This came from Argattha,' he said.

At the mention of Morjin's stronghold in the White Mountains, a shudder ran through me. It was said that Argattha was carved out of the rock of a mountain, an entire city built underground where slaves were whipped to work and dreadful rites occurred far from the eyes of civilized men.

'I would guess,' Master Juwain told me, 'that the man you killed was sent from there. He might even be a full priest of the Kallimun.'

I closed my eyes as I recalled the assassin's fiercely intelligent eyes.

'I'd like to see the body,' Master Juwain said.

Maram wiped the sweat from his fat neck as he pointed at the arrow and said, 'But we don't *know* that the assassins are Kallimun priests,

42

do we? Isn't it also possible that one of the Ishkans has gone over to Morjin?'

Master Juwain suddenly stiffened with anger as he admonished Maram: 'Please do not call him by that name.' Then he turned to me. 'It worries me even more that the Lord of Lies has made traitor one of your own countrymen.'

'No,' I said, filling up with a rare anger of my own. 'No Meshian would ever betray us so.'

'Perhaps not willfully,' Master Juwain said. 'But you don't know the deceit of the Lord of Lies. You don't know his power.'

He told us then that all men, even warriors and kings, knew moments of darkness and despair. At such times, when the clouds of doubt shrouded the soul and the stars did not shine, they became more vulnerable to evil, most especially to the Master of Minds himself. Then Morjin might come for them, in their hatred or in their darkest dreams; he would send illusions to confuse them; he would seize the sinews of their will and control them at a distance as with a puppeteer pulling on strings. These soulless men were terrible and very deadly, though fortunately very rare. Master Juwain called them ghuls; he admitted to his fear that a ghul might be waiting in the great hall to take meat with us that very night.

To steady my racing heart, I stepped over to the window to get a breath of fresh air. As a child, I had heard rumors of ghuls, as of werewolves or the dreaded Gray Men who come at night to suck out your soul. But I had never really believed them.

'But why,' I asked Master Juwain, 'would the Lord of Lies send an assassin – or anyone else – to kill me with poison?'

He looked at me strangely, and asked, 'Are you sure the first assassin was shooting at you and not Asaru?'

'Yes.'

'But how *could* you be sure? Didn't Asaru say that he felt the arrow pass through his hair?'

Master Juwain's clear, gray eyes fell upon me with the weight of twin moons. How could I tell him about my gift of sensing what lay inside another's heart? How could I tell him that I had felt the assassin's intention to murder me as surely as I did the cold wind pouring through the window?

'There was the angle of the shot,' I tried to explain. 'There was something in the assassin's eyes.'

'You could see his eyes from a hundred yards away?'

'Yes,' I said. And then, 'No, that is, it wasn't really like seeing. But there was something about the way he looked at me. The concentration.'

Master Juwain was silent as he stared at me from beneath his bushy gray eyebrows. Then he said, 'I think there's something about *you*, Valashu Elahad. There was something about your grandfather, too.'

In silence I reached out to close the cold pane of glass against the night.

'I believe,' Master Juwain continued, 'that this *something* might have something to do with why the Lord of Lies is hunting you. If we understood it better, it might provide us with the crucial clue.'

I looked at Master Juwain then and I wanted him to help me understand how I could feel the fire of another's passions or the unbearable pressure of their longing for the peace of the One. But some things can never be understood. How could one feel the cold light of the stars on a perfect winter night? How could one feel the wind?

'The Lord of Lies *couldn't* know of me,' I said at last. 'He'd have no reason to hunt the seventh son of a faraway mountain king.'

'No reason? Wasn't it your ancestor, Aramesh, who took the Lightstone from him at the Battle of Sarburn?'

'Aramesh,' I said, 'is the ancestor of many Valari. The Lord of Lies can't hunt us all.'

'No? Can he not?' Master Juwain's eyebrows suddenly pulled down in anger. 'I'm afraid he would hunt any and all who oppose him.'

For a moment I stood there rubbing the scar on my forehead. Oppose Morjin? I wanted the Valari to stop fighting among ourselves and unite under one banner so that we wouldn't *have* to oppose him. Shouldn't that, I wondered, be enough?

'But I don't oppose him,' I said.

'No, you're too gentle of soul for that,' Master Juwain told me. There was doubt in his voice, and irony as well. 'But you needn't take up arms to be in opposition to the Red Dragon. You oppose him merely in your intelligence and love of freedom. And by seeking all that is beautiful, good and true.'

I looked down at the carpet and bit my lip against the tightness in my throat. It was the Brothers who sought those things, not I.

As if Master Juwain could read my thoughts, he caught my eyes and said, 'You have a gift, Val. What kind of gift, I'm not yet sure. But you could have been a Meditation Master or Music Master. Or possibly even a Master Healer.'

'Do you really think so, sir?' I asked, looking at him.

'You know I do,' he said in a voice heavy with accusation. 'But in the end, you quit.'

Because I couldn't bear the hurt in his eyes, I turned to stare at the fire, which seemed scarcely less angry and inflamed. Of all my brothers,

I had been the only one to attend the Brotherhood school past the age of sixteen. I had wanted to study music, poetry, languages and meditation. With great reluctance my father had agreed to this, so long as I didn't neglect the art of the sword. And so for two happy years, I had wandered the cloisters and gardens of the Brotherhood's great sanctuary ten miles up the valley from Silvassu; there I had memorized poems and played my flute and sneaked off into the ash grove to practice fencing with Maram. Though it had never occurred to my father that I might actually want to take vows and join the Brotherhood, for a long time I had nursed just such an ambition.

'It wasn't my choice,' I finally said.

'Not your choice?' Master Juwain huffed out. 'Everything we do, we choose. And you chose to quit.'

'But the Waashians were killing my friends!' I protested. 'Raising spears against my brothers! The king called me to war, and I had to go.'

'And what have all your wars ever changed?'

'Please do not call them *my* wars, sir. Nothing would make me happier than to see war ended forever.'

'No?' he said, pointing at the dagger that I wore on my belt. 'Is that why you bear arms wherever you go? Is that why you answered your father's call to battle?'

'But, sir,' I said, smiling as I thought of the words from one of his favorite books, 'isn't all life a battle?'

'Yes,' he said, 'a battle of the heart and soul.'

'Navsa Adami,' I said, 'believed in fighting with other weapons.'

At the mention of the name of the man who had founded the first Brotherhood, Master Juwain grimaced as if he had been forced to drink vinegar. Perhaps I shouldn't have touched upon the old wound between the Brotherhoods and the Valari. But I had read the history of the Brotherhoods in books collected in their own libraries. In Tria, the Eternal City, in the 2,177th year of the Age of the Mother, which ever after would be called the Dark Year, Navsa Adami had been among those who suffered the first invasion of the Aryans. The sack of Tria had been terrible and swift, for in that most peaceful of ages, the Alonians possessed hoes and spades for digging in their gardens but no true weapons. Navsa Adami had been bound in chains and forced to watch the violation and murder of his own wife on the steps of the Temple of Life. The Aryan warlord had then razed the great Temple and destroyed the Garden of the Earth as the slaughter began. And Navsa Adami, along with fifty priests, had escaped and fled into the Morning Mountains, vowing revenge.

45

This exile became known as the First Breaking of the Order. For the Order had been founded to use the green gelstei crystals to awaken the lands of Ea to a greater life whereas Navsa Adami now wished to bring about the Aryans' death. And so, in the mountains of Mesh, he founded the Great White Brotherhood to fight the Aryans by any means the Brothers could find. With him he brought a green gelstei meant to be used for healing and furthering the life forces; Navsa Adami, however, had planned to use it to breed a race of warriors to fight the Aryans and overthrow their reign of terror. But he found in Mesh men who were already warriors; it became his hope to unite the Valari and train us in the mystic arts so that we would one day defeat the Aryans and bring peace to Ea. And this, at the Battle of Sarburn, we had nearly done. As a consequence of this the Brotherhoods, early in the Age of Law, had forever renounced violence and war. They had pleaded with the Valari to do the same. The Valari knights, though, fearing the return of the Dragon, had kept their swords sharpened and close to their hands. And so the bond between the Brotherhoods and the Valari was broken.

I had thought to score a point by invoking the name of Navsa Adami. But Master Juwain let his anger melt away so that only a terrible sadness remained. Then he said softly, 'If Navsa Adami were alive today, he would be the first to warn you that once the killing begins, it never ends.'

I turned away as his sadness touched my eyes with a deep, hot pain. I suddenly recalled the overpowering wrongness that I had sensed earlier in the woods; now a bit of this wrongness, in the form of kirax and perhaps something worse, would burn forever inside me.

I wanted to look at Master Juwain and tell him that there had to be a way to end the killing. Instead, I looked into myself and said, 'There's always a time to fight.'

Master Juwain stepped closer to me and laid his hand on mine. Then he told me, 'Evil can't be vanquished with a sword, Val. Darkness can't be defeated in battle but only by shining a bright enough light.'

He looked at me with a new radiance pouring out of him and said, 'This is truly a dark time. But it's always darkest just before the dawn.'

He let go of me suddenly and walked over to his desk. There his hand closed on a large book bound in green leather. I immediately recognized it as the *Saganom Elu*, many passages of which I had memorized during my years at the Brotherhood's school.

'I think it's time for a little reading lesson,' he announced, moving back toward Maram and me. His fingers quickly flipped through the yellow, well-worn pages, and then he suddenly dropped the book into

Maram's hands. 'Brother Maram, would you please read from the *Trian Prophecies*. Chapter seven, beginning with verse twenty-six.'

Maram, who was as surprised as I was at this sudden call to scholarship, stood there sweating and blinking his eyes. 'You want me to read *now*, sir. Ah, shouldn't we be getting ready for the feast?'

'Indulge me if you will, please.'

'But you know I've no talent for ancient Ardik,' Maram grumbled. 'Now, if you would ask me to read Lorranda, which is the language of love and poetry, why then I would be delighted to –'

'Please just read us the lines,' Master Juwain interrupted, 'or we *will* miss the feast.'

Maram stood there glowering at him like a child asked to muck out a stable. He asked, 'Do I have to, sir?'

'Yes, you do,' Master Juwain told him. 'I'm afraid that Val never had the *time* to learn Ardik as well as you.'

Truly, I had left the Brotherhood's school before mastering this noblest of languages. And so I waited intently as Maram took a deep breath and ground his finger into the page of the book that Master Juwain had set before him. And then his huge voice rolled out into the room: '*Songan erathe ad valte kalanath li galdanaan* . . . ah, let me see . . . *Jin Ieldra, song Ieldra* –'

'Very good,' Master Juwain broke in, 'but why don't you translate as you read?'

'But, sir,' he said, pointing at a book on the writing table, 'you already have the translated version there. Why don't I just read from that?'

Master Juwain tapped the book that Maram was holding and said, 'Because I asked you to read from this.'

'Very well, sir,' Maram said, rolling his eyes. And then he swallowed a mouthful of air and continued, 'When the earth and stars enter the Golden Band . . . ah, I think this is right . . . the darkest age will end and a new age –'

'That's very good,' Master Juwain interrupted again. 'Your translation is very accurate but . . .'

'Yes, sir?'

'I'm afraid you've lost the flavor of the original. The poetry, as it were. Why don't you put the words to verse?'

Now sweat began pouring down Maram's beard and neck. He said, '*Now*, sir? Here?'

'You're studying to be a Master Poet, aren't you? Well, poets make poems.'

'Yes, yes, I know, but without time to make the music and to find the rhymes, you can't really expect me to –'

'Do your best, Brother Maram,' Master Juwain said with a broad smile. 'I have faith in you.'

Strangely, this immensely difficult prospect seemed suddenly to please Maram. He stared at the book for quite a long while as if burning its glyphs into his mind. Then he closed his eyes for an even longer time. And suddenly, as if reciting a sonnet to a lover, he looked toward the windows and said:

> When earth alights the Golden Band,
> The darkest age will pass away;
> When angel fire illumes the land,
> The stars will show the brightest day.
>
> The deathless day, the Age of Light;
> Ieldra's blaze befalls the earth;
> The end of war, the end of night
> Awaits the last Maitreya's birth.
>
> The Cup of Heaven in his hand,
> The One's clear light in heart and eye,
> He brings the healing of the land,
> And opens colors in the sky.
>
> And there, the stars, the ageless lights
> For which we ache and dream and burn,
> Upon the deep and dazzling heights –
> Our ancient home we shall return.

'There,' he said, wiping the sweat from his face as he finished. With a trembling hand, he gave the book back to Master Juwain.

'Very good,' Master Juwain told him. 'We'll make a Brother of you yet.'

He motioned us over to the window. He pointed up at the stars, and in a voice quavering with excitement, he said, 'This is the time. The earth entered the Golden Band twenty years ago, and I believe that somewhere on Ea, the Maitreya, the Shining One, has been born.'

I looked out at the Owl constellation and other clusters of stars that shimmered in the dark sky beyond Telshar's jagged peak. It was said that the earth and all the stars turned about the heavens like a great, diamond-studded wheel. At the center of this cosmic wheel – at the center of all things – dwelt the Ieldra, luminous beings who shone the light of their souls on all of creation. These great, golden beacons streamed out from the cosmic center like rivers of light, and the Brothers called them the Golden Bands. Every few thousand years, the earth would enter one of them and bask in its radiance. At such times the trumpets of doom would sound and mountains would ring; souls would be quickened and Maitreyas would be born as the old ages ended and the new ones began. Although it was impossible to behold this numinous light with one's eyes, the scryers and certain gifted children could apprehend it as a deep, golden glow that touched all things.

'This is the time,' Master Juwain said again as he turned toward me. 'The time for the ending of war. And perhaps the time that the Lightstone will be found as well. I'm sure that King Kiritan's messengers have come bearing the news of just such a prophecy.'

I gazed out at the stars and there, too, I felt a rushing of a wind that carried the call of strange and beautiful voices. The Ieldra, I knew, communicate the Law of the One not just in golden rays of light but in the deepest whisperings of the soul.

'If the Lightstone *is* found,' I said, wondering aloud, 'who would ever have the wisdom to use it?'

Master Juwain looked up at the stars, too, and I sensed in him the fierce pride that had taken him from the fields of a farm on the Elyssu to a mastership in the greatest of Brotherhoods. I expected him to tell me that only the Brothers had attained the purity of mind necessary to plumb the secrets of the Lightstone. Instead, he turned to me and said, 'The Maitreya would have such wisdom. It is for him that the Galadin sent the Lightstone to earth.'

Outside the window, high above the castle and the mountains, the stars of the Seven Sisters and other constellations gleamed brightly. Somewhere among them, I thought, the immortal Elijin gazed upon this cosmic glory and dreamed of becoming Galadin, just as the Star People aspired to advancement to the Elijik order. There, too, dwelled Arwe, Ashtoreth and Valoreth, and others of the Galadin. These great, angelic beings had so perfected themselves and mastered the physical realm that they could never be killed. They walked on other worlds even as men did the fields and forests of Mesh; in truth, they walked freely *between* worlds, though never yet on earth. Scryers had seen visions of them, and I had sensed their great beauty in my longings and dreams. It was Valoreth himself, my grandfather once told me, who had sent Elahad to Ea bearing the Lightstone in his hands.

For a while, as the night deepened and the stars turned through the sky, we stood there talking about the powers of this mysterious golden cup. I said nothing of my seeing it appear before me in the woods earlier that day. Although its splendor now seemed only that of a dream, the warmth that had revived me like a golden elixir was too real to doubt. Could the Lightstone itself, I wondered, truly heal me of the wound that cut through my heart? Or would it take a Maitreya, wielding the Lightstone as I might a sword, to accomplish this miracle?

I believe that I might have found the courage to ask Master Juwain these questions if we hadn't been interrupted. Just as I was wondering if those of the orders of the Galadin and Elijin had once suffered from the curse of empathy even as I did, footsteps sounded in the hallway and there came a loud knocking at the door.

'Just a moment,' Master Juwain called out.

He stepped briskly across the room and opened the door. And there, in the dimly-lit archway, stood Joshu Kadar breathing heavily from his long climb up the stairs.

'It's time,' the young squire gasped out. 'Lord Asaru has asked me to tell you that it's time for the feast to begin.'

'Thank you,' Master Juwain told him. Then he moved back to the desk where he had left the arrow. He carefully wrapped it in my shirt again and asked, 'Are you ready, Val?'

It seemed that the answers that I sought to the great riddles of life would have to wait. And so, with Joshu in the lead, I followed Maram and Master Juwain out into the cold, dark hallway.

4

We entered the great hall to the blare of trumpets announcing the feast. Along the room's north wall, hung with a great, black banner emblazoned with the swan and stars of the royal house of Mesh, three heralds stood blowing their brass horns. The sound that reverberated through the huge room and out into the castle was the same that I had twice heard calling the Valari to battle. Indeed, the knights of Mesh – and those of Ishka – crowded through the doorways five abreast and moved toward their various tables as if marching to war.

I found Asaru and my brothers standing by their chairs at my family's table along the north wall; there, too, my mother and grandmother waited for me to take my place, as did my father. I'm sure that he didn't like it that I was among the last to arrive. He stood tall and grave in a black tunic that was much like the one that I had hastily fetched from my rooms – only clean and embroidered with a freshly polished silver swan and seven bright, silver stars. As he watched me climb the steps to the dais upon which our table stood, his bright, black eyes blazed like stars; there was reproof in his fierce gaze, but also concern and much else as well. Although Shavashar Elahad was the hardest man I knew, the well of his emotions ran as deep as the sea.

When all the guests had finally found their places, my father pulled out his chair and sat down, and everyone did the same. He took the position of honor at the center of the table, with my mother at his immediate right and my grandmother on his left. And on *her* left, in order, sat Karshur, Jonathay and Mandru, the fiercest of all my brothers. Where the other Valari knights in the room were content to wear their swords buckled to their waists, Mandru always carried his scabbarded in his three-fingered left hand, ready to draw at a moment's notice should he need to defend his honor – or his kingdom's. He sat looking down the table in silent communication with Asaru, who must have told him what had occurred earlier in the woods. Asaru sat to the right of my mother,

51

Elianora wi Solaru, who was tall and regal in her brightly embroidered gown – and said to be the most beautiful woman in the Nine Kingdoms. Her dark, perceptive eyes moved from Asaru to Yarashan, who sat on Asaru's right, and then down the line of the table from the silent and secretive Ravar to me. As the youngest and least distinguished member of my family, I sat at the far right near the end of the table. There I had hoped to lose myself in the clamor and vastness of the room. But there was no eluding my mother's strength, goodness and grace. She was the most alive being I had ever known, and the most loyal, too, and she looked at me as if to say that she would gladly lay down her life to protect me should the unknown assassin try to kill me again.

'Do you see him here?' Ravar whispered to me. The fox-faced Ravar was older than I by three years and shorter by almost a head. I had to bend low to hear what he was saying.

I looked out at the sea of faces in the room as I tried to identify that of the assassin who had escaped us. At the table nearest the dais, on the right, sat the Brothers who were visiting the castle that night. Master Juwain was there, of course, accompanied by Master Kelem, the Music Master, and Master Tadeo and some twenty other Brothers besides Maram. I knew all of them by name, and I was sure that none of them could have drawn a bow against me.

Unfortunately, I couldn't say the same for King Kiritan's emissaries, who had taken the next two tables. All of them – the knights and squires, the minstrels and grooms – were strangers to me. Count Dario, the king's cousin, I recognized only by description and his emblem: he wore the gold caduceus of House Narmada on his blue tunic, and his carefully trimmed hair and goatee seemed like red flames shooting from his head.

At the left of the room, next to the Ishkan tables where I tried not to look, were the first of the Meshian tables. There I saw Lord Harsha beaming proudly at Behira, and Lord Tomavar and Lord Tanu talking with their wives. Lansar Raasharu, my father's seneschal, sat there, too, along with Mesh's other greatest lords. If any of these old warriors were traitors, I thought, then I couldn't be sure that the sun would rise in the east the next morning.

As well I had faith in my countrymen in the second tier of tables where the master knights and their ladies waited for my father's attendants to pour the wine. And so with the many lesser knights sitting at the tables beyond, out to the farthest corners of the hall. There, almost too far away to see clearly, I studied the faces of friends such as Sunjay Navaru and other common warriors at whose sides I had fought. There, I thought, near the great granite pillars holding

52

up the arched roof, I would have sat too but for the happenstance of birth.

I whispered back to Ravar. 'None of them looks like the one who shot at me.'

'But what of the Ishkans?' he asked with a gleam in his eyes. 'You haven't even looked at them, have you, Val?'

Of course, I hadn't. And of course Ravar had noticed that I hadn't. He had quick, black eyes and an even quicker wit. Mandru and the stolid Karshur often accused him of living in his mind, a battlefield upon which no Valari should dwell for too long. Like me he had no natural liking for war: he preferred fencing with words and ideas. Unlike me, however, he was very good at real war because he saw it as a way of perfecting both his mind and his will. Although there were some who thought him unworthy to wear the three diamonds of a master knight, I had seen him lead a company of men at the Battle of Red Mountain and cast his lance through Sar Manashu's eye at a distance of twenty yards.

As Ravar began to study the Ishkans, perhaps looking for weaknesses with the same concentration that he had turned on Waas's army, I did the same. And immediately my eyes fell upon an arrogant man with a great scar running down the side of his face. Although he had a great beak of a nose like an eagle, his father and mother had bestowed upon him scarcely any chin. His eyes, I thought, were like pools of stagnant black water, and seemed to suck me down into the coldness of his heart even as they challenged me. Because I didn't like the slimy feeling that crept into my belly just then, I gazed instead at his bright red tunic, which bore the great white bear of the Ishkan royalty. I recognized him as Prince Salmelu, King Hadaru's oldest son. Five years before, at the great tournament in Taron, in a game of chess, I had humiliated him in a crushing defeat that had taken only twenty-three moves. It wasn't enough that he had won the gold medal in the fencing competition and had acquitted himself honorably in the horsemanship and archery competitions; it seemed he had to be preeminent at everything, for he took insult easily, especially from those who had bested him. It was said that he had fought fifteen men in duels – and left all fifteen dead in pools of blood. One of his brothers, Lord Issur, shared the table with him, along with Lord Mestivan and Lord Nadhru and other prominent Ishkans whom Ravar pointed out to me.

'Do any of them look like your assassin?' Ravar asked me.

'No,' I said. 'It's hard to tell – the man's face was hooded.'

And then, even as I closed my eyes and opened myself to the hum of hundreds of voices, I felt the same taint of wrongness that I had in the woods. The red, twisting worms of someone's hate began eating their way up my spine. From what man in the hall this dreadful sensation emanated, however, I couldn't tell.

At last, the wine having been poured, my father lifted up his goblet and stood to make the opening toast. All eyes in the hall turned his way; all voices trailed off and then died into silence as he began to speak.

'Masters of the Brotherhood,' he began, 'princes and lords, ladies and knights, we would like to welcome you to this gathering tonight. It's a strange chance that brings King Kiritan's emissaries to Mesh at the same time that King Hadaru sends his eldest son to honor us. But let us hope that it's a good chance and a sign of good times to come.'

My father, I thought, had a fine, strong voice that rang from the stones of the hall. He fairly shone with strength, both in the inner steel of his soul and in his large, long hands that could still grip a sword with great ferocity. At fifty-four he was just entering the fullest flower of manhood, for the Valari age more slowly than do other peoples – no one knows why. His long black hair, shot with strands of snowy white, flowed out from beneath a silver crown whose points were set with brilliant white diamonds. Five other diamonds, arrayed into the shape of a star, shimmered from a great, silver ring. It was the ring of a king, and someday Asaru would wear it if no one killed him first.

'And so,' my father continued, 'in the hope of finding the way toward the peace that all desire, we invite you to take salt and bread with us – and perhaps a little meat and ale as well.'

My father smiled as he said this, to leaven the stiffness of his formal speech. Then he motioned for the grooms to bring out what he had called a 'little meat.' In truth, there were many platters laden with steaming hams and roasted beef, along with elk, venison and other game. There were fowls almost too numerous to count: nicely browned ducks, geese, pheasants and quail – though of course no swans. It seemed that hunters such as Asaru and I had slaughtered whole herds and flocks that day. The grooms served baskets heaped with black barley bread and the softer white breads, aged cheeses, butter, jams, apple pies, honeycomb and pitchers of frothing black beer. There was so much food that the long wooden tables fairly groaned beneath its weight.

Although I was very hungry, my belly seemed a knot of acid and pain, and I could hardly eat. And so I picked at my food as I looked out into the hall. Along the walls were tapestries depicting famous battles that my people had fought and many portraits of my ancestors. The light of hundreds of candles illuminated the faces of Aramesh, Duramesh, and the great Elemesh who had utterly crushed the Sarni at the Battle of the Song River. In their ancient countenances I saw traits that my brothers shared to this day: Yarashan's pride, Karshur's strength, Jonathay's almost unearthly calm and beauty. There was much to admire in these kings, who were a reminder of the debt that we owed to those who give us life.

My brothers seemed all too aware of this debt of blood. Between bites of wild turkey or bread, washed down with drafts of beer, they spoke of their willingness to make war with the Ishkans should it become necessary to fight. They spoke of the causes for this war, too: the killing of the Ishkan crown prince in a duel with my grandfather two generations earlier, and my grandfather's own death at the Battle of the Diamond River. Yarashan, who fancied himself a student of history (although he had studied only lineages and battles), brought up the War of the Two Stars early in the Age of Law in which Mesh and Ishka had taken opposing sides. The Ishkans had fought my ancestors over the possession of the Lightstone; we had badly defeated them at the Raaswash, where their king, Elsu Maruth, had been killed. It was the greatest of ironies, I thought, that this healing vessel had been the source of woe for so long.

'The Ishkans will never forget that battle,' I heard Asaru say to Ravar. 'But in the end, it will all come down to the mountain.'

Everyone, of course, knew of which mountain he spoke: Mount Korukel, one of the great guardian peaks that stood upon the border between Mesh and Ishka just beyond the feeder streams of the Upper Raaswash River. The Ishkans were pressing their old demand that the border of our two kingdoms should exactly bisect Mount Korukel, while we of the swan and stars claimed the whole mountain as Meshian soil.

'But Korukel is ours,' Yarashan said as he used a napkin to neatly wipe the beer from his lips. In his outward form, he was almost as beautiful a man as Jonathay and even prouder than Asaru.

What was half a mile of rock against men's lives, I wondered? Well, if many of those rocks were diamonds, it was a great deal indeed. For the lives of men – the Valari warriors of each of the Nine Kingdoms – had been connected to the fabulous mineral wealth of the Morning Mountains for thousands of years. From their silver we made our emblems and the gleaming rings with which we pledged our lives; from its iron we made our steel. And from the diamonds we found deep underground and sometimes sparkling in the shallows of clear mountain streams, we made our marvelous suits of armor. In the Age of Swords, before the Brotherhoods had broken with the Valari, it had been the Brothers who had learned to work these hardest and most beautiful of stones; they had discovered the secret of affixing them to corslets of black leather and then taught us this art. While it was not true that this diamond-encrusted armor afforded the Valari invulnerability in battle – an arrow or a well-aimed spear thrust could find a chink between the carefully set diamonds – many were the swords that had broken upon it. The mere sight of a Valari army marching into battle and glittering in their ranks as if raimented with millions of stars had struck terror into our enemies for most of three long ages. They called us the Diamond Warriors, and said that we could never be defeated by force of arms alone, but only through treachery or the fire of the red gelstei.

And recently a great new vein of diamonds had been discovered running through the heart of Mount Korukel. Naturally, the Ishkans wanted to mine it for themselves.

When the last pie had been eaten and nearly everyone's belly groaned from much more than a little meat, it came time for the rounds of toasting. It would have been more sensible, of course, to hold this drinking fest *after* discussing the rather serious business that the Alonians and Ishkans had come for. But we Valari honored our traditions, and the end of a meal was the time for paying one's respects to guests and hosts alike.

The first to stand that day was Count Dario. He was a compact man who moved with quick, deft gestures of his arms and hands. He took up a goblet of black beer and presented it toward my father, saying, 'To King Shamesh, whose hospitality is overmatched only by his wisdom.'

A clamor of approval rang through the hall, but Prince Salmelu, like the swordsman he was, took advantage of the opening that Count Dario had unwittingly presented him. Like an uncaged bear, he stood, stretched and planted his feet wide apart on the floor. He fingered the many colored battle ribbons tied to his long hair with his right hand before resting it on the hilt of his sword. Then with his left hand, he raised his goblet and said, 'To King Shamesh. May he find the wisdom to do what we all wish for in walking the road toward peace.'

As I touched my lips to my beer, he flashed me a quick, hard look as if testing me with a feint of his sword.

I knew that I should have thought of an immediate rejoinder to his thinly veiled demand. But the maliciousness in his eyes held me to my chair. Instead, it was my usually unimaginative brother, Karshur, who stood and raised his goblet.

'To King Shamesh,' he said in a voice that sounded like boulders rolling down a mountain. He himself was built like an inverted mountain: as if successive slabs of granite had been piled higher and deeper from his thick legs to his massive shoulders and chest. 'May he find the *strength* to do what he has to do no matter what others may wish.'

As soon as he had returned to his chair, Jonathay stood up beside him.

He had all of our mother's beauty and much of her grace as well. He was a fatalistic but cheerful man who liked to play at life, most especially at war – though with skillful and deadly effect. He laughed good-naturedly as if enjoying this duel of words. 'To Queen Elianora, may she always find the patience to endure men's talk of war.'

All at once, from the tables throughout the hall, the many women there raised their goblets as if by a single hand and called out, 'Yes, yes, to Queen Elianora!'

As a nervous laughter spread from table to table, my mother stood and smoothed out the folds of her black gown. Then she smiled kindly. Although she directed her words out into the hall, it seemed that she was speaking right at Salmelu.

'To all our guests this evening,' she said, 'thank you for making such long journeys to honor our home. May the food we've all shared nourish our bodies, and may the good company we bring open our hearts so that we act out of the true courage of compassion rather than fear.'

So saying, she turned to Salmelu and beamed a smile at him. In her bright eyes there was only an open desire for fellowship. But her natural grace seemed to infuriate Salmelu rather than soothe him. He sat deathly still in his chair gripping the hilt of his sword as his face flushed with blood. Although Salmelu had stood sword to naked sword with fifteen men in the ring of honor, he couldn't seem to bear the gentleness of my mother's gaze.

Because it would have been unseemly for him to stand again while others waited to make their toasts, he cast a quick, ferocious look at Lord Nadhru as if to order him to speak in his place. And so Lord Nadhru, a rather angry young man who might have been Salmelu's twin in his insolent nature if not appearance, sprang up from his chair.

'To Queen Elianora,' he said, looking over the rim of his goblet. 'We thank her for reminding us that we must always act with courage, which we promise to do. And we thank her for welcoming us into her house, even as she was once welcomed herself.'

This, I thought, was the Ishkans' way of reminding *her* that she was as much of an outsider in the castle as they were, and therefore that she had no real right to speak for Mesh. But of course this was just pure spite on their part. For Elianora wi Solaru, sister of King Talanu of Kaash, had chosen freely to wed my father and not their greedy, old king.

And so it went, toast after toast, both Ishkans and Meshians casting words back and forth as if they were velvet-covered spears. All this time my father sat as still and grave in his chair as any of our ancestors in the portraits lining the walls. Although he kept most of the fire from his eyes, I could feel a whole stew of emotions boiling up inside him: pride, anger, loyalty, outrage, love. One who didn't know him better might have thought that at any moment he might lose his patience and silence his attackers with a burst of kingly thunder. But my father practiced self-restraint as others did wielding their swords. No man, I thought, asked more of himself than he. In many ways he embodied the Valari ideal of flowingness, flawlessness and fearlessness. As I, too, struggled to keep my silence, he suddenly looked at me as if say, 'Never let the enemy know what you're thinking.'

I believe that my father might have allowed this part of the feast to continue half the night so that he might better have a chance to study the Ishkans – and his own countrymen and sons. But the toasting came to a sudden and unexpected end, from a most unexpected source.

'My lords and ladies!' a strong voice suddenly bellowed out from below our table, 'I would like to propose a toast.'

I turned just in time to see Maram push back his chair and stand away from the Brothers' table. How Maram had acquired a goblet full of beer in plain sight of his masters was a mystery. And clearly it was not his first glass either, for he used his fat, beer-stained fingers to wipe the dried froth from his mustache as he wobbled on his feet. And then he raised his goblet, spilling even more beer on his stained tunic.

'To Lord Harsha,' he said, nodding toward his table. 'May we all thank him for providing this wonderful drink tonight.'

That was a toast everyone could gladly drink to; all at once hundreds of goblets, both of glass and silver steel, clinked together, and a grateful laughter pealed out into the room. I looked across the hall as Lord Harsha shifted about in his chair. Although he was plainly embarrassed to have been singled out for his generosity, he smiled at Maram all the same. If Maram had left well enough alone and sat back down, he might even have gained Lord Harsha's favor. But Maram, it seemed, could never leave anything alone.

'And now I would like to drink to love and beautiful women,' he said. He turned to Behira, fairly drinking in the sight of her as if the sensibilities of the hundreds of people looking on didn't matter. 'Ah, the love *of* beautiful women – it's what makes the world turn and the stars shine, is it not?'

Master Juwain looked up at Maram but Maram ignored his icy stare.

'It's to the most beautiful woman in the world that I would now like to dedicate this poem, whose words came into my mind like flowers opening the first moment I saw her.'

He raised his goblet toward Behira. Forgetting that he was supposed to wait until *after* the toast before drinking, he took a huge gulp of beer. And all the while, Behira sat next to her father flushing with embarrassment. But it was clear that Maram's attentions delighted her, for she smiled back at him, glowing with an almost tangible heat.

'Brother Maram,' Lord Harsha suddenly called out in his gravelly old voice, 'this isn't the place for your poetry.'

But Maram ignored him, too, and began his poem:

> Star of my soul, how you shimmer
> Beyond the deep blue sky,
> Whirling and whirling – you and I whisperlessly
> Spinning sparks of joy into the night.

I stared at the rings glittering from Maram's fingers and the passion pouring from his eyes. The words of his poem outraged me. For it wasn't really his poem at all; he had stolen the verse of the great but forgotten Amun Amaduk and was passing it off as his own.

Lord Harsha pushed back his chair and called out even more strongly, 'Brother Maram!'

Maram would have done well to heed the warning in Lord Harsha's voice. But by this time he was drunk on his own words (or rather Amun's), and with childlike abandon began the second stanza of the poem:

> From long ago we came across the universe:
> Lost rays of light, we fell among strange new flowers
> And searched in fields and forests
> Until we found each other and remembered.

Now Lord Harsha, gritting his teeth against the pain of his broken knee, suddenly rose to his feet. With surprising speed, he began advancing down the row of tables straight at Maram. And still Maram continued reciting his poem:

> Soul of my soul, for how few moments
> Were we together on this wandering earth
> In the magic of our love
> Dancing in the eyelight, breathing as one?

Suddenly, with a sound of fury in his throat, Lord Harsha drew his sword. Its polished steel pointed straight at Maram, who finally closed his mouth as it occurred to him that he had gone too far. And Lord

Harsha, I was afraid, had gone too far to stop, too. Almost without thinking, I leaped up from my chair, crossed the dais, and jumped down to the lower level of the guests' tables. My boots hit the cold stone with a loud slap. Then I stepped in front of Maram just as Lord Harsha closed the distance between them and pointed the tip of his sword at my heart.

'Lord Harsha,' I said, 'will you please excuse my friend? He's obviously had too much of your fine beer.'

Lord Harsha's sword lowered perhaps half an inch. I felt his hot breath steaming out of his nostrils. I was afraid that at any moment he might try to get at Maram by pushing his sword through me. Then he growled out, 'Well, then he should remember his vows, shouldn't he? Particularly his vow to renounce women!'

Behind me, I heard Maram clear his throat as if to argue with Lord Harsha. And then my father, the king, finally spoke.

'Lord Harsha, would you please put down your sword? As a favor to me.'

If Maram had been Valari then there *would* have been a death that night, for he would have had to answer Lord Harsha's challenge with steel. But Maram was only a Delian and a Brother at that. Because no one could reasonably expect a Brother to fight a duel with a Valari lord, there was yet hope.

Lord Harsha took a deep breath and then another. I felt the heat of his blood begin to cool. Then he nodded his head in a quick bow to my father and said, 'Sire, as a favor to you, it would be my pleasure.'

Almost as suddenly as he had drawn his sword, he slipped it back into his sheath. When the king asked you to put down your sword – or take it up – there was no choice but to honor his request.

'Thank you,' my father called out to him, 'for your restraint.'

'Thank you,' I whispered to him, 'for sparing my friend.'

Then I turned to look at Maram as I laid my hand on his shoulder and pushed him back down into his chair. From the nearby table of Valari masters and their ladies, I swept up two goblets of beer and gave one to Lord Harsha.

'To brotherhood among men,' I said, raising my goblet. I looked from my family's table to that of Master Juwain, and then back across the room to the table of the Ishkans. 'In the end, all men are brothers.'

I listened with great hope as echoes of approval rang out to the clinking of many glasses. And then Maram, my stubborn, irrepressible friend, looked up at my father and said, 'Ah, King Shamesh – I suppose this isn't the best time to finish my poem?'

My father ignored him. 'The time for making toasts is at an end. Lord

Harsha, would you please take your seat so that we might move on to more important matters?'

Again Lord Harsha bowed, and he walked slowly back through the rows of tables to his chair. He sat down next to his greatly relieved daughter, whom he looked at sternly but with an obvious love. And then a silence fell over the room as all eyes turned toward my father.

'We have before us tonight the emissaries of two kings,' he said, nodding his head at Salmelu and then Count Dario. 'And two requests will be made of us here tonight; we should listen well to both and neither let our hearts shout down the wisdom of our heads nor our heads mock what our hearts know to be true. Why don't we have Prince Salmelu speak first, for it may be that in deciding upon his request, the answer to Count Dario's will become obvious.'

Without smiling, he then nodded at Salmelu, who eagerly sprang to his feet.

'King Shamesh,' he said in voice that snapped out like a whip, 'the request of King Hadaru is simple: that the border of our kingdoms be clearly established according to the agreement of our ancestors. Either that, or the king asks that we set a time and place for battle.'

So, I thought, the ultimatum that we had all been awaiting had finally been set before us. I felt the hands of three hundred Meshian warriors almost aching to grip the hilts of their swords.

'The border of our kingdoms *is* established thusly,' my father told Salmelu. 'The first Shavashar gave your people all the lands from Mount Korukel to the Aru River.'

This was true. Long, long ago in the Lost Ages before the millennia of recorded history, it was said that the first Shavashar Elahad had claimed most of the lands of the Morning Mountains for his kingdom. But his seventh son, Ishkavar, wanting lands of his own to rule, had despaired of ever coming into this great possession. And so he had rebelled against his own father. Because Shavashar refused to spill the blood of his favorite son, he had given him all the lands from Korukel to the Aru, and from the Culhadosh River to the grassy plains of the Wendrush. Such was the origin of the kingdom that came to be called Ishka.

'From Mount *Korukel*,' Salmelu snapped at my father. 'Which you now claim for your own!'

My father stared down at him with a face as cold as stone. Then he said, 'If a man gives his son all his fields from his house to a river, he has given him only his fields – not the house or the river.'

'But mountains,' Salmelu said, repeating the old argument, 'aren't houses. There's no clearly marked boundary where one begins and ends.'

'This is true,' my father said. 'But surely you can't think a mountain's boundary should be a line running through the center of its highest peak?'

'Given the spirit of the agreement, it's only way *to* think.'

'There are many ways of thinking,' my father said, 'and we're here tonight to determine what is most fair.'

'You speak of fairness?' Salmelu half-shouted. 'You who keep the richest lands of the Morning Mountains for yourselves? You who kept the Lightstone locked in your castle for an entire age when all the Valari should have shared in its possession?'

Some of what he said was true. After the Battle of Sarburn, when the combined might of the Valari had overthrown Morjin and he had been imprisoned in a great fortress on the Isle of Damoom, Aramesh had brought the Lightstone back to Silvassu. And it *had* resided in my family's castle for most of the Age of Law. But it had never been locked away. I turned to look at the white granite pedestal against the banner-covered wall behind my father's chair. There, on this dusty, old stand, now dark and empty, the Lightstone had sat in plain view for nearly three thousand years.

'All the Valari *did* share of its radiance,' my father told Salmelu. 'Although it was deemed unwise to move it about among the kingdoms, our castle was always open to any and all who came to see it. Especially to the Ishkans.'

'Yes, and we had to enter your castle as beggars hoping for a glimpse of gold.'

'Is that why you invaded our lands with no formal declaration and tried to steal the Lightstone from us? If not for the valor of King Yaravar at the Raaswash, who knows how many would have been killed?'

At this, Salmelu's small mouth set tightly with anger. Then he said, 'You speak of warriors being killed? As *your* people killed Elsu Maruth, who was a very great king.'

Although my father kept his face calm, his eyes flashed with fire as he said, 'Was he a greater king than Elkasar Elahad, whom you killed at the Diamond River twelve years ago?'

At the mention of my grandfather's name, I stared at Salmelu and the flames of vengeance began eating at me, too.

'Warriors die,' Salmelu said, shrugging off my father's grief with an air of unconcern. 'And warriors kill – as King Elkamesh killed my uncle, Lord Dorje. Duels are duels, and war is war.'

'War is war, as you say,' my father told Salmelu. 'And murder is murder, is it not?'

Salmelu's hand moved an inch closer to the hilt of his sword as his fingers began to twitch. Then he called out, 'Do you make an accusation, King Shamesh?'

'An accusation?' my father said. 'No, merely a statement of truth. There are some who say that my father's death was planned and call it murder. But you'll never hear me say this. War is war, and even kings are killed on the field of battle. No matter the intent, this can't be called murder. But the hunting of a king's son in his own woods – *that* is murder.'

For a long time, perhaps as many as twenty beats of my racing heart, my father sat staring at Salmelu. His eyes were like bright swords cutting away at Salmelu's outward hauteur to reveal the man within. And Salmelu stared at him: with defiance and a jealous hatred coloring his face. While this duel of the eyes took place before hundreds of men and women stunned into silence, I noticed Asaru exchange a brief look with Ravar. Then Asaru nodded toward a groom standing off to the side of the hall near the door that led to the kitchens. The groom bowed back and disappeared through the doorway. And Asaru stood up from the table, causing Salmelu to break eyes with my father and look at him instead.

'My lords and ladies,' Asaru called out to the room, 'it has come to my attention that the cooks have finally prepared a proper ending to the feast. If you'll abide with me a moment, they have a surprise for you.'

Now my father looked at Asaru with puzzlement furrowing his forehead. As did Lord Harsha, Count Dario, Lord Tomavar, and many others.

'But what does all this have to do with murder?' Salmelu demanded.

And Asaru replied, 'Only this: that all this talk of killing and murder must have made everyone hungry again. It wouldn't do to end a feast with everyone still hungry.'

Upon these curious words, the doors to the kitchen opened, and four grooms wheeled out one of the great serving carts usually reserved for the display of whole roasted boars or other large game. It seemed that one knight or another must have indeed speared a boar earlier that day in the woods, for a voluminous white cloth was draped over what appeared to be the largest of boars. Apparently it had taken all these many hours to finish cooking. The grooms wheeled the cart right out toward the front of the room, where they left it sitting just in front of the Ishkans' table.

'Is that *really* a boar?' I heard Maram ask one of the grooms. 'I haven't had a taste of a good boar in two years.'

Despite himself, he licked his lips in anticipation of this most succulent of meats. How anyone could still be hungry after all the food consumed earlier, I didn't know. But if any man could, Maram was certainly that man, and he eyed the bulging white cloth along with Master Tadeo and everyone else in the room.

Asaru came down from the dais and stepped over to the serving cart. He looked straight into Salmelu's troubled eyes. And then, with a flourish I hadn't known he possessed, he reached down and whisked the cloth away from the cart.

'Oh, my Lord!' Maram gasped out. 'Oh, Lord, Lord, Lord!'

All at once, many others gasped out with him in astonishment as they stared at the cart. For there, laid out on its bloodstained boards, was the body of the assassin that I had killed in the woods.

5

The man's face, I saw, was livid with the darkness of death. Although his eyes remained as I had closed them, no one had thought to change his dirty tunic, which was still moist with the blood that I had spilled.

'What is this?' Salmelu cried out, jumping to his feet. He rushed over to Asaru and stood facing him across the assassin's body. 'Who is this man? Are you saying that I murdered him?'

'No,' Asaru said, glancing up at me, 'no one will say that.'

'But who is he?'

'That we would all like to know,' Asaru said, looking first at my father and then out into the hall.

Salmelu flicked his hand toward the cart. 'But what did you mean by saying it wouldn't do to end a feast with everyone still hungry? This is no way to end a feast.'

'No, it isn't,' Asaru agreed. 'Not with all of us still hungry for the truth.'

I thought that my father had no knowledge of this ugly surprise that had been presented to his guests. It had all the markings of something that Asaru and Ravar had cooked up together, so to speak. But my father immediately saw their purpose. And so did I. With his bright eyes glistening, he looked out into the hall to see if anyone might give a sign that he recognized the assassin. I looked too, but with a sense deeper than that of sight. I thought I might detect the pangs of guilt or grief emanating from some knight who would prove to be the second assassin. But all I could feel was a great, spreading wave of revulsion that made me sick.

As all looked upon Asaru, he began telling of how two hooded men had tried to murder him in his father's own forest. Although he gave a full account of my killing the man upon the cart, it was obvious that he still believed the first assassin's arrow had been meant for him.

'If anyone present knows this man,' he said, pointing at the dead assassin, 'will he speak and tell us who he is?'

Of course, Asaru must have thought that no one would speak at all. So he was as surprised as everyone else when Count Dario suddenly rose and walked over to the cart.

'I know this man,' he announced, looking at the body. 'His name is Raldu. He joined our party in Ishka, just after we had crossed the Aru River.'

The other emissaries at the Alonian table, including two named Baron Telek and Lord Mingan, all looked at each other and nodded their heads in affirmation of what Count Dario had said.

'But who *is* he?' Asaru asked Count Dario. 'And how is it that emissaries of a great king came to share fellowship with a murderer?'

Count Dario stood pulling at his bristly red chin hairs; then he fingered the golden wand of the caduceus emblazoned on his blue tunic. He was a cool-headed man, I thought, and he evinced not the slightest sign that my brother's questions had insulted him.

'I do not know if this man has a name other than Raldu,' he said in a calm, measured voice. 'And so I cannot say who he truly is. *He* said that he was a knight of Galda who fled that land when it fell to the Lord of Lies. He said that he had been wandering among the kingdoms in hope of finding a way to fight him. When he learned the nature of our mission, he asked to join us. He seemed greatly excited at the prospect of the Lightstone being recovered. As we all are. I apologize that I let this excitement fan the flames of my own. My enthusiasm obviously overwhelmed my judgment. Perhaps I should have questioned him more closely.'

'Perhaps you should have,' Asaru said, touching his hair where the arrow had burned through it.

At this my father looked at him sternly. And then, to Count Dario, he said, 'It was not upon you to seek out the secrets of this Raldu's heart. He joined you as a free companion only, not as a servant, and so you can't be held responsible for his actions.'

'Thank you, King Shamesh,' Count Dario said, bowing.

My father bowed back to him, then continued, 'But we must ask you to search your memory deeply now. Did Raldu ever speak against myself or my house? Did he form any close associations with your other companions? Or with anyone while you were in Ishka? Did he ever say anything to indicate who his true lord might be?'

Count Dario moved back over to his table where he conferred with his countrymen for a while. Then he looked up at the King and said, 'No, none of us had cause to suspect him. On the journey through Ishka, he kept to himself and comported himself well at all times.'

So, I thought, if Count Dario spoke truly, Raldu had used the emissaries as cover to enter Mesh from Ishka. And then used the hunt as an opportunity to try to murder me.

'So, then,' my father said, as if echoing my thoughts, 'it's clear how Raldu found his way into Mesh. But what was he doing in Ishka? Is it possible that the Ishkans had no knowledge of this man's presence?'

My father turned to look at Salmelu then. And Salmelu looked back at him as his hand touched his sword and he snarled out, 'If you think to accuse us of hiring assassins to accomplish what good Ishkan steel has always done quite well, then perhaps we should add *that* to the list of grievances that only battle can address.'

My father's hand tightened into a fist, and for a moment it seemed that he might accuse the Ishkans of this very crime. And then Count Dario raised up his voice and said, 'Mesh and Ishka: the two greatest kingdoms of the Valari. And here you are ready make war against each other when the Lord of Lies is on the march again. Isn't there any way I could persuade you of what a tragedy this war will be?'

My father took a deep breath and relaxed his fingers. And then he spoke not just to Count Dario but to all those present in the Hall. 'War,' he said, 'has not yet been decided. But it is growing late, and we would like to hear from anyone who would speak for or against war with Ishka.'

As quickly as he could, Lord Harsha rose to his feet. He seemed in a combative mood, probably because he had lost his chance to chastise Maram. He rubbed the patch over his missing eye, then pointed at Raldu's body and said, 'We'll probably never know if the Ishkans hired this man or his friend. But it doesn't matter if they did. It's plain that what the Ishkans really want is our diamonds. Well, why don't we give them a bit of Meshian steel, instead?'

With that, he patted the sheath of his sword, and the cries of many of Mesh's finest knights suddenly rang out into the hall. As he sat back down, I noticed Salmelu smiling at him.

During the whole time of the feast, my grandmother, sitting six places from me near the center of our family's table, had been quiet. She was rather small for a Valari and growing old, but once she had been Elkamesh's beloved queen. I had never known a more patient or kinder woman. Although she was shrinking in her body as the years fell upon her, a secret light seemed to be gathering in her eyes and growing ever brighter. Everyone loved her for this deep beauty as she loved them. And so when Ayasha Elahad, the Queen Mother, arose to address the knights and ladies of Mesh, everyone fell silent to listen to her speak.

'It's been twelve years now since my king was killed in battle with the Ishkans,' she called out in a voice like aged wine. 'And many more since my first two sons met a similar fate. Now only King Shamesh remains for me – and my grandsons by him. Must I watch them be taken away as well over a handful of diamonds?'

That was all she said. But as she returned to her chair, she looked at me as if to tell me that it would break her heart if I died before she did.

Then Master Juwain arose and gazed out at the hundreds of warriors with his clear, gray eyes. 'There have been thirty-three wars,' he said, 'over the centuries between Ishka and Mesh. And what has either kingdom gained? Nothing.'

That was all he said, too. He sat back down next to Master Kelem, who sagely nodded his hoary old head.

'It's to be expected that Master Juwain would feel thusly,' Salmelu called out from where he still stood by the cart. 'The Brothers always side with the women in avoiding matters of honor, don't they?'

It is one of the tragedies of my people that the other Valari such as the Ishkans, do not esteem the Brotherhoods as do we of Mesh. They suspect them of secret alliances and purposes beyond the teaching of meditation or music – all true. But the Brothers, Maram notwithstanding, have their own honor. I hated Salmelu for implying that they – and noble women whom I loved – might be cowards.

I rose to my feet then. I took a drink of beer to moisten my dry throat. I knew that almost no one would want to hear what I had to say. But the kirax was beating like a hammer in my blood, and I still felt the coldness of Raldu's body in my own. And so I looked at Salmelu and said, 'My grandfather once told me that the first Valari were warriors of the spirit only. And that a true warrior would find a way to end war. It takes more courage to live life fully with an open heart than it does to march blindly into battle and die over a heap of dirt. And this is something women understand.'

Salmelu gave me barely enough time to return to my chair before firing his sneering words back at me: 'Perhaps young Valashu has been spending too much time with the Brothers and the women. And perhaps it's well that his grandfather is no longer alive to spread the foolishness of myths and old wives' tales.'

Again, as if I had drunk a cup full of kirax, a wave of hatred came flooding into me. My eyes hurt so badly that I could hardly bear to keep looking at Salmelu. But I couldn't tell if this poisonous emotion originated from myself or him. Certainly, I thought, he had hated *me* since the moment I had bested him at chess. How deep did this hate reach, I wondered? Could it be that this prince of Ishka was the man who had shot the arrow at me?

'You should be careful,' my father warned Salmelu, 'of how you speak of a man's ancestors.'

'Thank you, King Shamesh, for sharing your wisdom,' Salmelu said, bowing with exaggerated punctilio. 'And *you* should be careful of what decision you make here tonight. The lives of many warriors and women depend on this famous wisdom.'

As my father caught his breath and stared out at the great wooden beams that held up the roof of the hall, I wondered why the Ishkans had really come to our castle. Did they wish to provoke a war, here, this very night? Did they truly believe that they could defeat Mesh in battle? Well, perhaps they could. The Ishkans could field some twelve thousand warriors and knights to our ten, and we couldn't necessarily count on our greater valor to win the day as we had at the Diamond River. But I thought it more likely that Salmelu and his countrymen were bluffing: trying to cow us into ceding them the mountain by displaying their eagerness to fight. They couldn't really want war, could they? Who, I wondered, would ever want a war?

My father asked everyone to sit then, and so we did. He called for the council to continue, and various lords and ladies spoke for or against war according to their hearts. Lord Tomavar, a long-faced man with a slow, heavy manner about him, surprised everyone by arguing that the Ishkans should be allowed to keep their part of the mountain. He said that Mesh already had enough diamonds to supply the armorers for the next ten years and that it wouldn't hurt to give a few of them away. Other lords and knights – and many of the women – agreed with him. But there were many more, such as the fiery Lord Solaru of Mir, who did not.

Finally, after the candles had burned low in their stands and many hours had passed, my father held up his hand to call an end to the debate. He sighed deeply and said, 'Thank you all for speaking so openly, with reason as well as passion. But now it is upon me to decide what must be done.'

As everyone waited to hear what he would say and the room fell quiet, he took another deep breath and turned toward Salmelu. 'Do you have sons, Lord Salmelu?' he asked him.

'Yes, two,' he said, cocking his head as if he couldn't grasp the point of the question.

'Very well, then as a father you will understand why we are too

69

distraught to call for war at this time.' Here he paused to look first at Asaru and then at me. 'Two of *my* sons were nearly murdered today. And one of the assassins still walks free; perhaps he's among us in this room even now.'

At this, many troubled voices rumbled out into the hall as men and women cast nervous glances at their neighbors. And then Salmelu rebuked my father, saying, 'That's no decision at all!'

'It's a decision not to decide at this time,' my father told him. 'There's no need to hurry this war, if war there must be. The snows are not yet fully melted from the passes. And we must determine the extent of the diamond deposits before deciding if we will cede them or not. And an assassin remains to be caught.'

My father went on to say that the end of summer, when the roads were dry, would be soon enough for battle.

'We've come here to bring you King Hadaru's request,' Salmelu said, staring at my father, 'not to be put off.'

'And we've given you our decision,' my father told him.

'That you have,' Salmelu snapped out. 'And it's a *dangerous* decision, King Shamesh. You would do well to reflect upon just how dangerous it might prove to be.'

Truly, I thought, my father was taking a great chance. For thousands of years, the Valari had made war upon each other, but never towards the ends of conquest or the enslavement of the defeated. But if a king tried to avoid a formal war such as the Ishkans had proposed, then he ran a very real risk that a war of ravage, rapine and even annihilation might break out.

'We live in a world with danger at every turn,' my father told Salmelu. 'Who has the wisdom always to see which of many dangers is the greatest or the least?'

'So be it, then,' Salmelu snarled out, looking away from him.

'So be it,' my father said.

This pronouncement answered the first of the requests asked of him that night. But no one seemed to remember that a second remained to be made. For a long time, various lords and knights looked at their empty goblets while Salmelu stared at Lord Nadhru in the shame of having failed to wrest an immediate decision from my father. I could almost feel the hundreds of hearts of the men and women in the hall beating like so many war drums. And then Count Dario finally stood to address us.

'King Shamesh,' he called out, 'may I speak now?'

'Please do – it has grown very late.'

Count Dario touched the golden caduceus shining from his tunic, then cast his voice out into the hall. 'We *do* live in troubled times with dangers at every turn,' he said. 'Earlier today, two princes of Mesh went hunting for deer in a quiet wood only to find someone hunting them instead. And I have watched the noblest lords of Ishka and Mesh nearly come to blows over past grievances that no one can undo. Who has the wisdom to overcome this discord? Who has the power to heal old wounds and bring peace to the lands of Ea? *I* know of no such man now living, neither king nor Brother nor sage. But it is said that the Lightstone has this power. And that is why, with the Red Dragon uncaged once again, it must be found.'

He paused to take a deep breath and look around the room as my father nodded at him to continue.

'And it *will* be found,' he said. 'Before the snows of next winter come, men and women will behold the Cup of Heaven as in ancient times. This is the prophecy that the great scryer, Ayondela Kirriland, gave us before *she* was murdered. It is why King Kiritan has sent messengers into all the free lands.'

Although it was not Salmelu's place to speak, he looked Count Dario up and down with his dark eyes and snapped out, 'What are the words of this prophecy, then?'

Count Dario paused as if counting the beats of his heart. I thought that he couldn't have expected to encounter such rudeness among the Valari. And then, as all eyes turned his way and I held my breath, he told us, 'Her words are these: "The seven brothers and sisters of the earth with the seven stones will set forth into the darkness. The Lightstone will be found, the Maitreya will come forth, and a new age will begin."'

A new age, I thought as I gazed at the empty stand behind our table where once the Lightstone had shone. *An age without killing or war.*

'My king,' Count Dario continued, 'has asked for all knights wishing to fulfill the prophecy to gather in Tria on the seventh day of Soldru. There he will give his blessing to all who vow to make this quest.'

'Very well,' my father finally said, looking at him deeply. 'And a very noble quest this is.'

Count Dario, not knowing my father, took this as a sign of encouragement. He smiled at him and said, 'King Kiritan has asked that all kings of the free lands send knights to Tria. He would make this request of you, King Shamesh.'

My father nodded his head respectfully then looked across the hall at Lord Harsha, Lord Tomavar and his seneschal, Lansar Raasharu. He said, 'Very well, but before *this* decision is made, we would like to hear counsel. Lord Raasharu, what do you have to say?'

Lord Raasharu was a solid, cautious man renowned for his loyalty to

71

my family. He had long, iron-gray hair, which he brushed back from his plain face as he stood and said, 'Sire, how can we trust the prophecies of foreign scryers? The oracles of Alonia are known to be corrupt. Are we to risk the lives of knights on the words of this Ayondela Kirriland?'

As soon as he had sat back down, Lord Tomavar arose to take his place. In his slow, ponderous voice, he looked at my father and said, 'Risk the lives of our knights? Wouldn't it be more like throwing them away? Can we afford to do this at a time when the Ishkans are demanding our diamonds?'

Now Lord Tanu, a fierce, old warrior whose four diamonds flashed brilliantly from his ring, said simply, 'This quest is a fool's errand.'

His sentiment seemed to be that of most of the lords and knights in the hall. For perhaps another hour, my countrymen arose one by one to speak against King Kiritan's request. And nearly all this time, I sat staring at the empty granite stand behind my father's chair.

'Enough,' my father finally said, raising his hand. He turned to address Count Dario. 'We said earlier that hearing King Hadaru's request first might help us decide King Kiritan's request. And so it has. It seems that we of Mesh are all agreed on this, at least.'

He paused a moment and turned to point at the empty stand. 'Other kings have sent knights to seek the Lightstone – and few of these knights have ever returned to Mesh. The Lightstone is surely lost forever. And so even one knight would be too many to send on this hopeless quest.'

Count Dario listened as many lords and knights rapped their warrior's rings against the tables in affirmation of my father's decision. Then his face clouded with puzzlement as he half-shouted, 'But once your people fought the Lord of Lies himself for the Lightstone! And brought it back to your mountains! I don't understand you Valari!'

'It may be that we don't understand ourselves,' my father said gravely. 'But as Lord Tanu has said, we know a fool's errand when we hear of one.'

All present in the hall fell silent in respect of Count Dario's obvious disappointment. It was so quiet that I could almost hear the beating of my heart. The candles in their stands near the wall had now burned very low; this changed the angle of the rays of light cast against the great banner there so that the silver swan and the seven silver stars seemed to shimmer with a new radiance.

'It is *not* a fool's errand,' Count Dario said proudly, 'but the greatest undertaking of our time.'

'If my words offended you, please accept my apologies,' my father said.

'So, then, you do not believe Ayondela's prophecy?'

'Over the ages the scryers have made thousands of prophecies, but how many have ever been fulfilled?'

'So then, you will send no knights to Tria?'

'No, no knights will be sent,' my father said. 'However, no one who truly wants to go will be kept from going.'

Although I listened to my father speak, I did not really hear him. For on the wall behind our table, scarcely ten feet from my throbbing eyes, the largest of the banner's seven stars suddenly began gleaming brightly. It cast a stream of light straight toward the surface of the dusty stand. The silvery light touched the white granite, which seemed to glow with a soft, golden radiance. I remembered then the ancient prophecy from the *Epics* of the *Saganom Elu*: that the silver would lead to the gold.

I looked at my father as he called out to the many tables below ours: 'Is there anyone here who would make this quest?'

All at once, the many whispering voices grew quiet, and almost everyone's gaze pulled down toward the floor. Their lack of interest astonished me. Couldn't they see the silver star blazing like a great beacon from the center of the banner? What was wrong with them that they were blind to the miracle occurring before their eyes?

I turned back toward the stand then, and *my* astonishment made my breath stop and my heart catch in my throat. For there, on top of the stand, a golden cup was pouring its light out into the hall. It sat there as clear for all to see as the goblets on the tables before them.

The Lightstone will be found, I heard my heart whisper. *A new age will begin.*

Ravar, who must have seen me staring at the stand as if drunk with the fire of angels, suddenly began staring, too. But all he said was, 'What are you looking at, Val? What's the matter?'

'Don't you see it?' I whispered to him.

'See *what*?'

'The Lightstone,' I said. 'The golden cup, there, shining like a star.'

'You're drunk,' he whispered back to me. 'Either that or you're dreaming.'

Now Count Dario, who also appeared not to see the Lightstone where it shimmered from its ancient stand, suddenly called out to the knights and nobles in the room: 'Is there anyone here who will stand tonight and pledge himself to making this quest?'

While Lord Harsha scowled and traded embarrassed looks with Lord Tomavar, most of the knights present, both Ishkan and Meshian, kept staring at the cold floorstones.

'Lord Asaru,' Count Dario called out, turning toward my brother, 'You are the eldest of a long and noble line. Will you at least make the journey to Tria to hear what my king has to say?'

'No,' Asaru told him. 'It's enough for me to hear what *my* king has said: that this is no time for hopeless quests.'

Count Dario closed his eyes for a moment as if praying for patience. Then he looked straight at Karshur as he continued his strategy of singling out the sons of Shavashar Elahad.

'Lord Karshur,' he said, 'will you make this journey?'

Karshur, sitting between the Queen Mother and Jonathay, gathered in his great strength as he looked at Count Dario. And then, in a voice that sounded like an iron door closing, he said, 'No, the Lightstone is lost or destroyed, and not even the most adamant knight will ever find it.'

As Count Dario turned to query Yarashan, to the same result, I looked out toward the far wall at the most recent of my ancestors' portraits to have been hung there. The bright eyes of my grandfather, Elkamesh, stared back at me out of bold face bones and a mane of flowing white hair. The painter, I thought, had done well in capturing the essence of his character. I couldn't help being moved by this man's courage and devotion to truth. And above all, by his gift of compassion. The love that he had always held for me seemed still to live in dried pigments of black and white. If my grandfather were here in the flesh, I thought, he would understand my distress in seeing what no one else could see. If he sat beside me at my family's table, even as the loyal Jonathay and Ravar did, he would probably see it, too.

'Sar Mandru,' I heard Count Dario say to the last of my brothers, 'will you be in Tria on the seventh day of Soldru?'

'No,' Mandru said, gripping fiercely the sheath of his sword in his three fingers, 'my duty lies elsewhere.'

Now Count Dario paused to take a breath as he looked at me. All of my brothers had refused him, and I, too, felt the pangs of my loyalty to my father pressing at my heart.

'Valashu,' he finally asked, 'what does the last of King Shamesh's sons say?'

I opened my mouth to tell him that I had my duty as did my brothers, but no words came out. And then, as if seized by a will that I hadn't known I possessed, I pushed back my chair and rose to my feet. In less than a heartbeat, it seemed, I crossed the ten feet to where the Lightstone gleamed like a golden sun on its ancient stand. I reached out to grasp it with both hands. But my fingers closed upon air, and even as I blinked my eyes in disbelief, the Lightstone vanished into the near-darkness of the hall.

'Valashu?'

74

Count Dario, I saw, was looking at me as if I had fallen mad. Asaru had pushed back his chair, and had turned to look at me, too.

'Will you make the journey to Tria?' Count Dario said to me.

Along my spine, I suddenly felt the red worms of someone's hate gnawing at me as I had earlier. I longed to be free of my gift that left me open to such dreadful sensations. And so again I turned to stare at the stand that had held the Lightstone for so many thousands of years and for so few moments that night. But it did not reappear.

'Valashu Elahad,' Count Dario asked me formally, 'will you make this quest?'

'Yes,' I whispered to myself, 'I must.'

'What? What did you say?'

I took a deep breath and tried to fight back the fear churning in my belly. I touched the lightning-bolt scar on my forehead. And then, in a voice as loud and clear as I could manage, I called out to him and all the men and women in the hall: 'Yes, I will make the quest.'

Some say that the absence of sound is quiet and peace; but there is a silence that falls upon the world like thunder. For a moment, no one moved. Asaru, I noticed, was staring at me as if he couldn't believe what I had said, as were Ravar and Karshur and my other brothers. In truth, everyone in the hall was staring at me, my father the most intently of all.

'Why, Valashu?' he finally asked me.

I felt the deeper question burning inside him like a heated iron: *Why have you disobeyed me?*

And I told him, 'Because the Lightstone must be found, sir.'

My father's eyes were hard to look at then. But despite his anger, his love for me was no less real or deep than my grandfather's had been. And I loved him as I did the very sky and wanted very badly to please him. But there is always a greater duty, a higher love.

'My last born,' he suddenly called out to the nobles in the hall, 'has said that he will journey to Tria, and so he must go. It seems that the House of Elahad *will* be represented in this quest, after all, if only by the youngest and most impulsive of its sons.'

He paused to rub his eyes sadly, and then turned toward Salmelu and said, 'It would be fitting, would it not, if your house were to send a knight on this quest as well. And so we ask you, Lord Salmelu, will you journey to Tria with him?'

My father was a deep man, and very often he could be cunning. I thought that he wished to weaken the Ishkans – either that or to shame Salmelu in front of the greatest knights and nobles of our two kingdoms. But if Salmelu felt any disgrace in refusing to make the quest that the least of Shamesh's sons had promised to undertake, he gave no sign of it. Quite the contrary. He sat among his countrymen rubbing his sharp nose as if he didn't like the scent of my father's intentions. And then he looked from my father to me and said, 'No, I will not make this quest. My father has already spoken of his wishes. *I* would never leave my people without his permission at a time when war threatened.'

My ears burned as I looked into Salmelu's mocking eyes. It was one of the few times in my life that I was to see my father outmaneuvered by an opponent.

'However,' Salmelu went on, smiling at me, 'let it not be said that Ishka opposes this foolish quest. As our kingdom offers the shortest road to Tria, you have my promise of safe passage through it.'

'Thank you for your graciousness, Lord Salmelu,' I said to him, trying to keep the irony from my voice. 'But the quest is not foolish.'

'No? Is it not? Do you think *you* will ever recover what the greatest Valari knights have failed even to find?' He pointed toward the empty stand behind me. 'And even if by some miracle you *did* manage to gain the Lightstone, could you ever keep it? I think not, young Valashu.'

Even more than resenting Mesh's keeping the Lightstone in this castle for three millennia, the Ishkans reviled us for losing it. The story was still told in low voices over fires late at night: how many centuries ago, King Julumesh had brought the Lightstone from Silvassu to Tria to give into the hands of Godavanni Hastar, the Maitreya born at the end of the Age of Law. But Godavanni had never been able to wield the Lightstone for the good of Ea. For Morjin had broken free from Castle of Damoom, and he managed to slay Godavanni and steal the Cup of Heaven once again. King Julumesh and his men had been killed trying to guard it, and the Ishkans had blamed Mesh ever since.

'We will not speak of the keeping of that which is yet to be regained,' my father told Salmelu. 'It may be that the Lightstone will never be found. But we should at least honor those who attempt to find it.'

So saying he arose from his chair and walked toward me. He was a tall man, taller even than Asaru, and for all his years he stood as straight as a spruce tree.

'Although Valashu is the wildest of my sons, there is much to honor in him tonight,' he said. He pointed at Raldu's body, which still lay stretched out on the cart at the center of the hall. 'A few hours ago he fought and killed an enemy of Mesh – and this with only a knife against a mace. Possibly he saved my eldest son's life, and Brother Maram's as well. We believe that he should be recognized for his service to Mesh. Is there anyone here who would speak against this?'

My father had managed to save face by honoring my rebelliousness instead of chastising it, and it seemed that Salmelu hated him for that. But he sat quietly sulking in his chair all the same. Neither he nor Lord Nadhru nor any of the other Ishkans spoke against me. And, of course, none of my countrymen did either.

'Very well,' my father said. He reached inside the pocket of his tunic and removed a silver ring set with two large diamonds. They sparkled like the points of his crown and the five diamonds of his own ring. 'I won't have my son going to Tria as a warrior only. Val, come here, please.'

I stood up from my chair and went over to where he waited for me by the banner at the front of the hall. I knelt before him as he bade me. I noticed my mother watching proudly, but with great worry, too. Asaru's eyes were gleaming. Maram looked on with a huge smile lighting up his face; one would have thought that he congratulated himself for somehow bringing about this honor that no one could have anticipated. And then, before my family and all the men and women in the hall, my father pulled the warrior's ring from my finger and replaced it with the ring of a full knight. I sensed that he had kept this ring in his pocket for a long time, waiting for just such an occasion.

'In the name Valoreth,' he said, 'we give you this ring.'

My new ring felt cold and strange on my finger. But the heat of my pride was quickly warming it up.

My father then drew his sword from its sheath. It was the marvelous Valari kalama: a razor-sharp, double-edged sword that was light enough and well-enough balanced for a strong man to swing with one hand from horseback, and long and heavy enough to cut mail when wielded with two hands. Such swords had struck terror even into the Sarni tribes and had once defeated the Great Red Dragon. The sword, it is said, is a Valari knight's soul, and now my father brought this shimmering blade before me. With the point held upward as if to draw down the light of the stars, he pressed the flat of the blade between my eyes. The cold steel sent a thrill of joy straight through me. It made me want to polish my own inner sword and use it only to cut through the darkness that sometimes blinded me.

'May you always see the true enemy,' my father told me, repeating the ancient words of our people. 'May you always have the courage to fight it.'

He suddenly took the sword away from me and lifted it high over his head. 'Sar Valashu Elahad,' he said to me, 'go forth as a knight in the name of the Shining One and never forget from where you came.'

That was all there was to the ceremony of my being knighted. My father embraced me, and signaled to his guests that the feast had come to an end. Immediately Asaru and my brothers gathered close to congratulate me. Although I was glad to receive the honor which they had long since attained, I was dreadfully afraid of where my pledge to recover the Lightstone might take me.

'Val, congratulations!' Maram called out to me as he pressed through the circle of my family. He threw his arms around me and pounded my back with his huge hands. 'Let's go back to my room and drink to your knighthood!'

'No, let's not,' I told him. 'It's very late.'

In truth, it had been the longest day of my life. I had hunted a deer and been wounded with a poison that would always burn inside me. I had killed a man whose death had nearly killed me. And now, before my family and all my friends, I had promised to seek that which could never be found.

'Well,' Maram said, 'you'll at least come say goodbye to me before you set out on this impossible quest of yours, won't you?'

'Yes, of course,' I told him, smiling as I clasped his arm.

'Good, good,' he said. He belched up a bloom of beer and then covered his mouth as he yawned. 'Ah, I've got to find Behira and tell her the rest of the poem before I pass out and forget it. Would you by chance know where she might be quartered in this huge heap of stones of yours?'

'No,' I told him, committing my first lie as a knight. I pointed at Lord Harsha as he made his way with his daughter and several lords out of the hall. 'Perhaps you should ask Lord Harsha.'

'Ah, perhaps I *won't*, not just now,' Maram said as he stared at Lord Harsha's sheathed sword. It seemed that he had seen one kalama too many that night. 'Well, I'll see you in the morning.'

With that, he joined the stream of people making their way toward the door. Although I was as tired as I had ever been, I lingered a few more moments as I watched the Alonians and Ishkans – and everyone else – file from the hall. Once more I opened myself to see if I could detect the man who had fired the arrow at me. I couldn't. One last time I turned toward the white granite stand to see if the Lightstone would reappear, but it remained as empty as the air.

6

The next morning, the Ishkans departed our castle in a flurry of pounding hooves and muffled curses – so Asaru later told me. Apparently Salmelu wanted to bring King Hadaru the news of the war's postponement as quickly as possible. Likewise, the Alonians continued on their journey toward Waas and Kaash, where they would tell King Talanu and my cousins at his court of the great quest. Despite my intention to get an early start on the road to Tria, I slept almost until noon. My father had always upbraided me for liking my bed too well, and so I did. In truth, now that the time had come for me to leave the castle that I had never regarded as home, I was reluctant to do so.

It took me most of the day to make my preparations for the journey. I went from shop to shop among the courtyards as if moving in a dream. It seemed that there were a hundred things to do. Altaru's hooves needed reshoeing, as did those of our pack horse, Tanar. I had to visit the storerooms in the various cellars to gather rations for myself: cheeses and nuts, dried venison and apples and battle biscuits so hard they would break one's teeth if they weren't first dipped in a cupful of brandy or beer. These vital beverages I poured into twelve small oak casks which I carefully balanced on Tanar's back along with the waterskins. I worried that the weight would be too much for the brown gelding to carry, but Tanar was young and almost as heavily muscled as Altaru himself. He seemed to have no trouble bearing this load of consumables as well as my ground fur, cookware and other equipment that would make sleeping beneath the stars a delight rather than a misery.

He balked only when I strapped onto him my longbow and sheaves of arrows that I would use hunting in the forests between Silvassu and Tria. Once, at the Battle of Red Mountain, he had been struck in the flank by a stray arrow and had never forgotten it. I had to reassure him that we were embarking on a quest to regain a cup that would end such battles forever and *not* going out to war. But my appearance, unfortunately, belied any soothing words I could offer him. My father had insisted that I set forth as a knight of Mesh, and to honor him, I had gathered up the necessary accoutrements. By law, no knight could leave Mesh alone wearing our diamond armor; such displays would be likely to incite the envy and hatred of robbers who would murder for the gain of these priceless gems. So instead, I had donned a mail suit made of silver steel. Over its gleaming rings I had pulled a black surcoat bearing the swan and stars of Mesh. As well I bore a heavy charging lance, five lighter throwing lances, and, of course, the shining kalama that my father had given me on my thirteenth birthday. The massive war helm, with its narrow eye slits and silver wings projecting out from the sides, I would not put on until just before I was ready to leave the castle.

I spent at least two hours of the afternoon saying my farewells. I visited briefly with the master carpenter in his shop full of sawdust and riven wood. He was a thick, jowly man with an easy laugh and skillful hands that had made the frame of my grandfather's portrait. We talked about my grandfather for a while, the battles he had fought, the dreams he had dreamed. He wished me well and warned me to be careful of the Ishkans. This advice I also received from Lansar Raasharu, my father's seneschal. This sad-faced man, whom I had always loved as one of my family, told me that I should keep a tighter watch over my own lips than I did even over the enemy.

'They're a hot-headed bunch,' he said, 'who will fashion your own words into weapons and hurl them back at you toward disastrous ends.'

'Better that,' I said, 'than poison arrows fired in the woods.'

Lord Raasharu rubbed his rugged face and cocked his head, looking at me in surprise. He asked, 'Hasn't Lord Asaru spoken to you?'

'No, not since before the feast.'

'Well, you should have been told: it can't be Prince Salmelu who was your assassin. He and his friends crossed my path in the woods down by the Kurash at the time of your trouble.'

'And you're sure it was he?'

'As sure as that you're Valashu Elahad.'

'That is good news!' I said. I hadn't wanted to believe that Salmelu would have tried to murder me. 'The Ishkans may be Ishkans, but they're Valari first.'

'That's true,' Lord Raasharu said. 'But the Ishkans *are* still Ishkans, so you be careful once you cross the mountains, all right?'

And with that he clapped his hand across my shoulder hard enough to make the rings of mail jingle, and said goodbye.

It distressed me that I could find neither Maram nor Master Juwain to tell them how much I would miss them. According to Master Tadeo, who still remained in the Brothers' quarters, both Master Juwain and Maram had left the castle in great haste that morning while I had been sleeping. Apparently, there had been some sort of altercation with Lord Harsha, who had ridden off in a fury with Behira and their wagon before breakfast. But it seemed I had not been forgotten. Master Tadeo handed me a sealed letter that Maram had written; I tucked this square of white paper behind the belt girdling my surcoat, and vowed to read it later.

There remained only the farewells to be made with my family. Asaru insisted on meeting me by the east gate of the castle, as did my mother, my grandmother and my other brothers. In a courtyard full of barking dogs and children playing in the last of the day's sun, I stood by Altaru to take my leave of them. They each had presents for me, and a word or two of wisdom as well.

Mandru, the fiercest of my brothers, was the first to come forward. As usual, he carried his sword in the three remaining fingers of his left hand. It was rumored, I knew, that he slept holding this sword, and not his young wife, which might have explained his lack of children. For a moment, I thought that he intended to give me this most personal of possessions. And then I noticed that in his right hand, he held something else: his treasured sharpening stone made of pressed diamond dust. He gave this sparkling gray stone to me and said, 'Keep your sword sharp, Val. Never yield to our enemies.'

After he had embraced me, Ravar next approached to give me his favorite throwing lance. He reminded me always to set my boots in my stirrups before casting it, and then stepped aside to let Jonathay come nearer. With a faraway, dreamy look on his face, this most fatalistic of my brothers presented me with his chess set, the one with the rare ebony and ivory pieces that he loved playing with while on long campaigns. His calm, cheerful smile suggested to me that I play at the game of finding the Lightstone – and win.

Now it was Yarashan's turn to say goodbye. He strode up to me as if everyone in the castle was watching each of his lithe, powerful motions. He was even prouder than Asaru, I thought, but he lacked Asaru's kindness, innocence and essential goodness. He was a handsome, dashing man, and was considered the finest knight in Mesh – except for those who said this of Asaru. I thought that *he* considered he would make a better king than Asaru, although he was much too perceptive and loyal ever to say such a thing. He held in his hand a well-worn copy of the *Valkariad*, which was his favorite book of the *Saganom Elu*. He gave it to me and said, 'Remember the story of Kalkamesh, little brother.'

81

He, too, embraced me, then stepped aside as Karshur handed me his favorite hunting arrow. I had always envied this solid, simple man because he seemed never to have a doubt as to the right thing to do or the difference between evil and good.

Then I looked up to see Asaru standing between my mother and grandmother. As I listened to the distant sound of hammered iron coming from the blacksmith's shop, I watched him step over to me.

'Please take this,' he said to me. From around his neck, he pulled loose the thong binding the lucky bear claw that he always wore. He draped it over my head and told me, 'Never lose heart – you have a great heart, Val.'

Although he fell silent as he clapped me on the shoulder, the tears in his eyes said everything else there was to say.

I was sure that he thought I would be killed on some dark road in a strange kingdom far from home. My mother obviously thought this as well. Although she was a strong, brave woman, she too was weeping as she came forward to give me the traveling cloak which I knew she had been weaving as a birthday present. I guessed that she had stayed up all night finishing it; with its thick black wool trimmed out with fine silver embroidery and a magnificent silver brooch with which to fasten it, it was a work of love that would keep me warm on even the stormiest of nights.

'Come back,' was all she told me. 'Whether you find this cup or not, come home when it's time to come home.'

She kissed me then and fell sobbing against me. It took all of her will and dignity to pry herself loose and stand back so that my grandmother could give me the white, wool scarf that she had knitted for me. Ayasha Elahad, whom I had always called Nona, tied this simple garment around my neck. She stood in the darkening courtyard looking up at me with her bright eyes. Then she pointed at the night's first stars and told me, 'Your grandfather would have made this quest, you know. Never forget that he is watching you.'

I hugged her tiny body against the hardness of the mail that encircled mine. Even through this steel armor with its hundreds of interlocked rings, I could feel the beating of her heart. This frail woman, I thought, was the source of love in my family, and I would take this most precious of gifts with me wherever I went.

At last I stood away from her and looked at my family one by one. No one spoke; no one seemed to know any more words to say. I had hoped my father, too, would come to say goodbye, but it seemed that he was still too angry to bear the sight of me. And then, even as I turned to take Altaru's reins and mount him, I heard footsteps sounding hard against the packed earth. I looked out to see my father emerge from the gateway to the castle's adjoining middle courtyard. He was dressed in a black and silver tunic, and he bore on his arm a shield embossed with a silver swan and seven stars against a triangular expanse of glossy, black steel.

'Val,' he said as he walked up to me, 'it's good you haven't left yet.'

'No, not yet,' I said. 'But it's time. It seemed you wouldn't come.'

'It seemed that way to me, too. But farewells should be said.'

I stared at my father's sad, deep eyes and said, 'Thank you, sir. It can't be easy for you seeing me leave like this.'

'No, it's not. But you always went your own way.'

'Yes, sir.'

'And you always accepted your punishments when you did.'

'Yes,' I said, nodding my head. 'And sometimes that was hard; you were hard, sir.'

'But you never complained.'

'No – you taught me not to.'

'And you never apologized, either.'

'No, that's true.'

'Well,' he said, looking at my war lance and glistening armor, 'this time the hardships of your journey will be punishment enough.'

'Very likely they will.'

'And dangers,' he continued. 'There will be dangers aplenty on the road to Tria – and beyond.'

I nodded my head and smiled bravely to show him that I knew there would be. But inside, my belly was fluttering as before a battle.

'And so,' he said, 'it would please me if you would take this shield on your journey.'

He took another step closer to me, all the while keeping a watchful eye upon the snorting Altaru and his great hooves. Not wishing to arouse the ferocious stallion's protective instincts, he slowly held his shield out to me.

'But, sir,' I said, looking at this fine piece of workmanship, 'this is your war shield! If there's war with Ishka, you'll need it.'

'Please take it all the same,' he told me.

For a long moment, I gazed at the shield's swan and silver stars.

'Would you disobey in this, as well?'

'No, sir,' I said at last, taking the shield and thrusting my forearm through its leather straps. It was slightly heavier than my own shield, but somehow seemed to fit me better. 'Thank you – it's magnificent.'

He embraced me then, and kissed me, once, on my forehead. He looked at me strangely in a way that I had never seen him look at Karshur or Yarashan – or even Asaru. Then he told me, 'Always remember who you are.'

I bowed to him, then hoisted myself up onto Altaru's back. The great beast's entire body trembled with the excitement of setting out into the world.

I cleared my throat to say my final farewells, but just as I was about to speak, there came the sound of a horse galloping up the road beyond the open gate. A cloaked figure astride a big, panting sorrel came pounding into the courtyard. The rider wore a saber strapped to his thick black belt and bore a lance in his saddle's holster but seemed otherwise unarmed. His clothes, I saw, as his cloak pulled back, were of bright scarlet, and he wore a jeweled ring on each of the fingers of his two hands. I smiled because it was, of course, Maram.

'Val!' he called out to me as he reached forward to stroke and calm his sweating horse. 'I was afraid I'd have to intercept you on the road.'

I smiled again in appreciation of what must have been a hard ride down from the Brotherhood Sanctuary. My family all looked upon him approvingly for this act of seeming loyalty.

'Thank you for coming to say goodbye,' I told him.

'Say goodbye?' he called out. 'No, no – I've come to say that I'd like to accompany you on your journey. That is, at least as far as Tria, if you'll have me.'

This news surprised everyone, except perhaps my father, who gazed at Maram quietly. My mother gazed at him, too, with obvious gratitude that I wouldn't be setting out at night on a dangerous journey alone.

'Will I *have* you?' I said to him. I felt as if the weight of my unaccustomed armor had suddenly been lifted from my shoulders. 'Gladly. But what's happened, Maram?'

'Didn't you read my letter?'

I patted the square of paper still folded into my belt. 'No, my apologies, but there wasn't time.'

'Well,' he began, 'I couldn't just abandon my best friend to go out questing alone, now could I?'

'Is that all?'

Maram licked his lips as he glanced from my mother to Asaru, who was eyeing him discreetly. 'Well, no, it is not all,' he forced out. 'I suppose I should tell you the truth: Lord Harsha has threatened to cut off my, ah . . . head.'

As Maram went on to relate, Lord Harsha had discovered him talking with Behira early that morning and had again drawn his sword. He had chased Maram up and down the women's guest quarters, but his broken knee and Maram's greater agility, much quickened by his panic, enabled Maram to evade the threatened decapitation – or worse. After Lord Harsha's temper had cooled somewhat, he had told Maram to leave Mesh that day or face his sword when they next met. Maram had fled from the castle and returned to the Brotherhood Sanctuary to gather up his belongings. And then returned as quickly as he could to join me.

'It would be an honor to have you with me,' I told him. 'But what about your schooling?'

'I've only taken a leave of absence,' he said. 'I'm not quite ready to quit the Brotherhood altogether.'

And, it seemed, the Brotherhood wasn't ready to quit him. Even as Maram started in his saddle at the sound of more horses coming up to the castle, I looked down the road to see Master Juwain riding another sorrel and leading two pack horses behind him. He made his way through the gateway and came to a halt near Maram. He glanced at the weapons that Maram bore. Maram must have persuaded him that the lance and sword would be used only for their protection and not war. He shook his head sadly at having yet again to bend the Brotherhood's rules on Maram's behalf.

Master Juwain quickly explained that the news of the quest had created a great stir among the Brothers. For three long ages they had sought the secrets of the Lightstone. And now, if the prophecy proved true, it seemed that this cup of healing might finally be found. And so the Brothers had decided to send Master Juwain to Tria to determine the veracity of the prophecy. That he also might have other, and more secret, business in the City of Light remained unsaid.

'Then it isn't your intention to make this quest?' my father asked.

'Not at this time. I'll accompany Val only as far as Tria, if that's agreeable with him.'

'Nothing could please more, sir.' I smiled, unable to hide my delight. 'But it's my intention to take the road through Ishka, and that may not prove entirely safe.'

'Where can safety be found these days?' Master Juwain said, looking up at the great iron gate and the castle walls all around us. 'Lord Salmelu has promised you safe passage, and we'll have to hope for the best.'

'Very well, then,' I told him.

And with that, I turned to look at my brothers one last time. I nodded my head to my grandmother and my mother, who was quietly weeping again. Then I smiled grimly at my father and said, 'Farewell, sir.'

'Farewell, Valashu Elahad,' he said, speaking for the rest of my family. 'May you always walk in the light of the One.'

At last I put on the great helm, whose hard steel face plates immediately cut out the sight of my weeping mother. I wheeled Altaru about and nudged him forward with a gentle pressure of my heels. Then, with Master Juwain and Maram following, I rode out through the gate toward the long road that led down from the castle. And so my father finally had the satisfaction of seeing me set out as a Valari knight in all his glory.

It was a clear night with the first stars slicing open the blue-black vault of the heavens. To the west, Arakel's icy peak glowed blood-red in light of the sun lost somewhere beyond the world's edge. To the east, Mount Eluru was already sunk in darkness. The cool air sifted through the slits in my helm, carrying the scents of forest and earth and almost infinite possibilities. Soon, after perhaps half a mile of such joyous travel, I took off my helm, the better to feel the starlight on my face. I listened to the measured beat of Altaru's hooves against the hardpacked dirt as I looked out at the wonder of the world.

It seemed almost a foolish thing to begin such a long journey with night falling fast and deep all around us. But I knew that the moon would soon be up, and there would be light enough for riding along the well-made North Road that led toward Ishka. With the wind at my back and visions of golden cups blazing inside me, I thought that I might be able to ride perhaps until midnight. Certainly the seventh day of Soldru would come all too soon, and I wanted very badly to be in Tria with the knights of the free lands when King Kiritan called the great quest. Six hundred miles, as the raven flies, lay between Silvassu and Tria to the northwest. But I – we – would not be traveling as a bird flying free in the sky. There would be mountains to cross and rivers to ford, and the road toward that which the heart most desires is seldom straight.

And so we rode north through the gently rolling country of the Valley of the Swans. After an hour or so, the moon rose over the Culhadosh Range and silvered the fields and trees all about us. We rode in its soft light, which seem to fill all the valley like a marvelous shimmering liquid. The farmhouses we passed sent plumes of smoke curling up black against the luminous sky. And in the yards of each of those houses, I thought, no matter how tiring the day's work had been, warriors would be practicing at arms while their wives taught their children the meditative discipline so vital to all that was Valari. Only later would they take their evening meal, perhaps of cheese and apples and black barley bread. It came to me that I would miss these simple foods, grown out of Meshian soil, rich in tastes of the star-touched earth that recalled the deepest dreams of my people. I wondered if I were seeing my homeland for the last time even while strangely beholding it as if for the first time. It came to me as well that a Valari warrior, with sword and shield and a lifetime of discipline drilled into his soul, was much more than a dealer of death. For everything about me – the rocks and earth, the wind and trees and starlight – were just the things of life, and ultimately a warrior existed only to protect life and the land and people that he loved.

We made camp late that night in a fallow field by a small hill off the side of the road. The farmer who owned it, an old man named Yushur Kaldad, came out to greet us with a pot of stew that his wife had made. Although he hadn't been present at the feast, he had heard of my quest. After giving us permission to make a fire, he wished me well and walked back through the moonlight toward his little stone house.

'It's a lovely night,' I said to Maram as I tied Altaru to the wooden fence by the side of the field. There was thick grass growing all about the fence, which would make the horses happy. 'We don't really need a fire.'

Maram, working with Master Juwain, had already spread the sleeping furs across the husks of old barley that covered the cool ground. He moved off toward the rocks at the side of the road, and told me, 'I'm worried about bears.'

'But there aren't many bears in this part of the valley,' I told him.

'Not *many*?'

'In any case, the bears will leave us alone if we leave them alone.'

'Yes, and a fire will help encourage them to leave us alone.'

'Perhaps,' I told him. 'But perhaps it would only give them a better light to do their work in case they get really hungry.'

'Val!' Maram called out as he stood up with a large rock in either hand. 'I don't want to hear any more talk of hungry bears, all right?'

'All right,' I said, smiling. 'But please don't worry. If a bear comes close, the horses will give us warning.'

In the end, Maram had his way. In the space around which our sleeping furs were laid out, he dug a shallow pit and circled it with rocks. Then he moved off toward the hill where he found some dried twigs and branches among the deadwood beneath the trees and with great care he arrayed the tinder and kindling into a pyramid at the center of the pit. Then from his pocket he produced a flint and steel, and in only a few moments he coaxed the sparks from them into a cone of bright orange flames.

'You have a talent with fire,' Master Juwain told him. He dropped his gnarly body onto his sleeping fur and began ladling out the stew into three large bowls. Despite his years, he moved with both strength and suppleness, as if he had practiced his healing arts on himself. 'Perhaps you should study to be an alchemist.'

Maram's sensuous lips pulled back in a smile as he held his hands out toward the flames. His large eyes reflected the colors of the fire, and he said, 'It has always fascinated me. I think I made my first fire when I was four. When I was *fourteen*, I burned down my father's hunting lodge, for which he has never forgiven me.'

At this news, Master Juwain rubbed his lumpy face and told him, 'Perhaps you *shouldn't* be an alchemist.'

Maram shrugged off his comment with a good-natured smile. He clicked his fire-making stones together, and watched the sparks jump out of them.

'What is the magic in flint and steel?' he asked, speaking mostly to himself. 'Why don't flint and quartz, for instance, make such little lights? And what is the secret of the flames bound up in wood? How is it that logs will burn but not stone?'

Of course, I had no answers for him. I sat on my furs watching Master Juwain pulling at his jowls in deep thought. To Maram, I said, 'Perhaps if we find the Lightstone, you'll solve your mysteries.'

'Well, there's one mystery I'd like solved more than any other,' he confided. 'And that is this: How is it that when a man and a woman come together, they're like flint and steel throwing out sparks into the night?'

I smiled and looked straight at him. 'Isn't that one of the lines of the poem you recited to Behira?'

'Ah, Behira, Behira,' he said as he struck off another round of sparks. 'Perhaps I should never have gone to her room. But I had to know.'

'Did you . . . ?'

I started to ask him if he had stolen Behira's virtue, as Lord Harsha feared, but then decided that it was none of my business.

'No, no, I swear I didn't,' Maram said, understanding me perfectly well. 'I only wanted to tell her the rest of my poem and –'

'*Your* poem, Maram?' We both knew that he had stolen it from the *Book of Songs*, and so perhaps did Master Juwain.

'Ah, well,' Maram said, flushing, 'I never said outright that *I* had written it, only that the words came to me the first moment I saw her.'

'You parse words like a courtier,' I said to him.

'Sometimes one must to get at the truth.'

I looked at the stars twinkling in the sky and said, 'My grandfather taught me that unless one tries to get at the spirit of truth, it's no truth at all.'

'And we should honor him for that, for he was a great Valari king.' He smiled, and his thick beard glistened in the reddish firelight. 'But I'm not Valari, am I? No, I'm just a simple man, and it's as a *man* that I went to Behira's room. I had to know if she was the one.'

'What one, Maram?'

'The woman with whom I could make the ineffable flame. Ah, the fire that never goes out.' He turned toward the fire, his eyes gleaming. 'If ever I held the Lightstone in my hands, I'd use it to discover the place where love blazes eternally like the stars. *That's* the secret of the universe.'

For a while, no one spoke as we sat there eating our midnight meal beneath the stars. Yushur had brought us an excellent stew full of succulent lamb, new potatoes, carrots, onions and herbs; we consumed it down to the last drop of gravy, which we mopped up with the fresh bread that Master Juwain had brought down from the Sanctuary. To celebrate our first night together on the road, I had cracked open a cask of beer. Master Juwain had taken only the smallest sip of it, but of course Maram had drunk much more. After his first serving, as his rumbling voice built castles in the air, I rationed the precious black liquid into his cup. But as the time approached for sleeping, it became apparent that I hadn't measured out the beer carefully enough.

'I simply *must* see Tria before I die,' Maram told me in his rumbling voice. 'As for the Quest, though, I'm afraid that from there you'll be on your own, my friend. *I'm* no Valari knight, after all. Ah, but if I were, and I *did* gain the Lightstone, there are so many things I might do.'

'Such as?'

'Well, to begin with, I would return with it to Delu in glory. Then the nobles would have to make me king. Women would flock to me like lambs to sweet grass. I would establish a great harem as did the Delian kings of old. Then famous artists and warriors from all lands would gather in my court.'

I pushed the cork stopper into the half-empty cask as I looked at him and asked, 'But what about love?'

'Ah, yes, love,' he said. He belched then sighed as he rubbed his eyes. 'The always-elusive dream. As elusive as the Lightstone itself.'

In a voice full of self-pity, he declared that the Lightstone had certainly been destroyed, and that neither he nor anyone else was ever likely to find his heart's deepest desire.

Master Juwain had so far endured Maram's drinking spree in silence. But now he fixed him with his clear eyes and said, '*My* heart tells me that the prophecy will prove true. Starlight is elusive, too, but we do not doubt that it exists.'

'Ah, well, the prophecy,' Maram muttered. 'But who *are* these seven brothers and sisters? And what are these seven stones?'

'*That*, at least, should be obvious,' Master Juwain said. 'The stones must be the seven greater gelstei.'

He went on to say that although there were hundreds of types of gelstei, there were only seven of the great stones: the white, blue and green, the purple and black, the red firestones and the noble silver. Of course, there was the gold gelstei, but only one, known as *the* Gelstei, and that was the Lightstone itself.

'So many have sought the master stone,' he said.

'Sought it and died,' I said. 'No wonder my mother wept for me.'

I went on to tell him that I would most likely be killed far from home, perhaps brought down by a plunging rock in a mountain pass or felled by a robber's arrow in some dark woods.

'Do not speak so,' Master Juwain chastened me.

'But this whole business,' I said, 'seems such a narrow chance.'

'Perhaps it is, Val. But even a scryer can't see all chances. Not even Ashtoreth herself can.'

For a while we fell silent as the wind pushed through the valley and the fire crackled within its circles of stones. I thought of Morjin and his master, Angra Mainyu, one of the fallen Galadin who had once made war with Ashtoreth and the other angels and had been imprisoned on a world named Damoom; I thought of this and I shuddered.

To raise my spirits, Maram began singing the epic of Kalkamesh from the *Valkariad* of the *Saganom Elu*. Master Juwain kept time by drumming on one of the logs waiting to be burned. So I brought out my flute and took up the song's boldly defiant melody. I played to the wind and earth, and to the valor of this legendary being who had walked into the hell of Argattha to wrest the Lightstone from the Lord of Lies himself. It was a fine thing we did together, making music beneath the stars. My thoughts of death – the stillness of Raldu's body and the coldness of my own – seemed to vanish like the flames of the fire into the night.

We slept soundly after that on the soft soil of Yushur Kaldad's field. No bears came to disturb us. It was a splendid night, and I lay on top of my furs wrapped only in my new cloak for warmth. When the sun rose over Mount Eluru the next morning to the crowing of Yushur's cocks, I felt ready to ride to the end of the world.

And ride we did. After breaking camp, we set out through the richest farmland of the valley. It was a fine spring day with blue skies and abundant sunshine. The road along this part of our journey was as straight and well-paved as any in the Morning Mountains. Indeed, my father had always said that good roads make good kingdoms, and he had always gone to considerable pains to maintain his. Both Master Juwain and Maram could ride well, and Maram was tougher than he looked. And so we made excellent progress through the wind-rippled fields.

Around noon, after we had paused for a quick meal and the horses had filled up on some of the sweet green grass that grew along the curbs of the road, the country began to change. Toward the northern end of the Valley of the Swans, the terrain grew hillier and the soil more rocky. There were fewer farms and larger stands of trees between them. Here the road wound gently around and through these low hills; it began to rise at an easy grade toward the greater hills and mountains to the north. But still the traveling was easy. By the time the sun had crossed the sky and began dipping down toward the Central Range, we found ourselves at the edge of the forest that blankets the northernmost districts of Mesh. A few more miles would bring us to the town of Ki high in the mountains. And a few miles beyond it, we would cross the pass between Mount Raaskel and Mount Korukel, and go down into Ishka.

We made camp that night above a little stream running down from the mountains. The oak trees above us and the hill behind provided good cover against the wind. Master Juwain, although more knowledgeable than I in most things, allowed me to take the lead in choosing this site. As he admitted, he had little woodcraft or sense of terrain. He was very happy when I returned from the bushes along the stream with many handfuls of raspberries and some mushrooms that I had found. He sliced these last up and layered them with some cheese between slices of bread. Then he roasted the sandwiches over the fire that Maram had made. That night it was much cooler, and we were very glad for the fire as we edged close to it and ate this delicious meal. We listened to the hooing of the owls as they called to each other from the woods, and later, to the wolves howling high in the hills around us. After drinking some of the tea that Master Juwain brewed, we gathered our cloaks around us and fell soundly asleep.

The next morning dawned cloudy and cool. The sun was no more than a pale yellow disk behind sheets of white in the sky. Since I wanted to be well through the pass by nightfall and I was afraid a hard rain might delay us, I encouraged the groggy and lazy Maram to get ready as quickly as he could. The few miles to Ki passed quickly enough, although the road began to rise more steeply as the hills built toward the mountains. Ki itself was a small city of shops, smithies and neat little chalets with steep roofs to keep out the heavy mountain snows that fell all through winter.

One of the feeder streams of the Diamond River ran through the center of the town. Just beyond the bridge across these icy waters, where two large inns stood above the houses, the Kel Road from the east intersected the larger North Road. The Kel Road, as I knew from having traveled it, was one of the marvels of Mesh. It wound through the mountains around the entire perimeter of our kingdom connecting the kel keeps that guarded the passes. There were twenty-two of these high mountain fortresses spaced some twenty miles apart. I had spent a long, lonely winter at one of them watching for an invasion of the Mansurii tribe that never came.

Maram, citing the hard work of the morning (which in truth was mostly the horses' hard work), argued that we should stop for a few hours and bathe at one of these inns. He grumbled that the two previous nights' camps had afforded us neither the time nor the opportunity for such vital indulgence. It was almost a sacred ritual that a Valari would wash away the world's woes at the end of a day, and I wanted a hot bath as badly as he did. But I persuaded him that we should leave Ki behind us as swiftly as possible. Although it was late in the season, it could still snow, as I patiently explained to him. And so, after pausing at the inn only long enough to take a quick meal of fried eggs and porridge, we continued on our journey.

For seven miles between Ki and the kel keep situated near Raaskel and Korukel, the Kel Road ran contiguous with the North Road. Here, as the horses' hooves strove for purchase against the worn paving stones, the road rose very steeply. Thick walls of oak trees, mixed with elms and birch, pressed the road from either side, forming an archway of green leaves and branches high above it. But after only a few miles, the forest began changing and giving way to stands of aspen and spruce growing at the higher elevations. The mountains rose before us like steps leading to the unseen stars.

In many places, the road cut the sides of these fir-covered foothills like a long, curved scar against the swelling green. I knew that we were drawing close to the pass, although the lower peaks blocked the sight of it. As Maram complained, travel in the mountains was disorienting, and one could easily become lost. He had other fears as well. After I had recounted my conversation with Lansar Raasharu, he wondered aloud who the second assassin might be if he wasn't one of the Ishkans. Might this unknown man, he asked, stalk us along the road? And if he did, what were we doing venturing into Ishka where he might more easily finish what he had begun in the woods? With every step we took closer to this unfriendly kingdom, these unanswered questions seemed to hang in the air like the cold mist sifting down from the sky.

Around noon, just as we crested a low rise marked with a red standing stone, we had our first clear view of the pass. We stood resting the horses as we gazed out at the masses of Korukel and Raaskel that rose up like great guardian towers only a few miles to the north. The North Road curved closer to Raaskel, the smaller of these two mountains. But with its sheer granite faces and snowfields, I thought, it was forbidding enough. Korukel, whose twin peaks and great humped shoulders gave it the appearance of a two-headed ogre, seemed all too ready to pelt us with spears of ice or roll huge boulders down upon us. If not for the diamonds buried within its bowels, it hardly seemed like a mountain worth fighting for.

'Oh, my Lord, look!' Maram said, pointing up the road. 'The Telemesh Gate. I've never seen anything like it.'

Few people had. For there, across the barren valley just beyond the massive fortress of the kel keep, cutting the ground between the two mountains, was the great work of my ancestors and one of the wonders of Ea: it seemed that a great piece of mountain a fifth of a mile wide and a mile long had simply been sliced out of the earth as if by the hand of the Galadin themselves. In truth, as Maram seemed to know, King Telemesh had made this rectangular cut between the two mountains with a firestone that he had brought back from the War of the Stones. According to legend, he had stood upon this very hill with his red gelstei and had directed a stream of fire against the earth for most of six days. And when he had finished and the acres of ice, dirt and rock had simply boiled off into the sky, a great corridor between Mesh and Ishka had been opened. Indeed, until Telemesh had made his gate, this 'pass' between our two kingdoms had been considered unpassable, at least to armies marching along in their columns or travelers astride their weary horses.

'It's too bad the firestones have all perished,' Maram said wistfully. 'Else all the kingdoms of Ea might be so connected.'

'It's said that Morjin has a firestone,' I told him. 'It's said that he has rediscovered the secret of forging them.'

At this, Master Juwain looked at me sharply and shook his head. Many times he had warned Maram – and me – never to speak the Red Dragon's true name. And with the utterance of these two simple syllables, the wind off the icy peaks suddenly seemed to rise; either that, or I could feel it cutting me more closely. Again, as I had in the woods with Raldu and later in the castle, I shivered with an eerie sense that something was watching me. It was as if the stones themselves all about us had eyes. It consoled me not at all that my countrymen here in the north called Raaskel and Korukel the Watchers.

For a half a mile we walked our horses down to the kel keep at the center of the valley. Maram wondered why the makers of the fortress hadn't built it flush with the Gate, as of a wall of stone defending it.

I explained to him that it was better sited where it was: on top of a series of springs that could keep the garrison well-watered for years. It had never been the purpose of the keeps, I told him, to stop invading armies in the passes. They were intended only to delay the enemy as long as it took for the Meshian king to gather up an army of his own and destroy them in the open field.

We stopped at the keep to pay our respects to Lord Avijan, the garrison's commander. Lord Avijan, a serious man with a long, windburnt face, was Asaru's friend and not much older than I. He had been present at the feast, and he congratulated me on my knighthood. After seeing that we were well-fed with pork and potatoes brought up from Ki, he told me that Salmelu and the Ishkans had gone up into the pass early that morning.

'They were riding hard for Ishka,' Lord Avijan told me. 'As you had better do if you don't want to be caught in the pass at nightfall.'

After I had thanked him and he wished me well on my quest, we took his advice. We continued along the North Road where it snaked up the steeply rising slopes of the valley. About two miles from the keep, as we approached the Telemesh Gate, it grew suddenly colder. The air was thick with a moisture that wasn't quite rain nor mist nor snow. But there was still snow aplenty blanketing the ground. Here, in this bleak mountain tundra where trees wouldn't grow, the mosses and low shrubs in many places were still covered in snow. Against boulders as large as a house were gathered massive white drifts, a few of which blocked the road. If Lord Avijan hadn't sent out his warriors to cut a narrow corridor through them, the road would still have been impassable.

'It's cold,' Maram complained as his gelding drove his hooves against the road's wet stone. 'Perhaps we should return to the keep and wait for better weather.'

'No,' I said, laying my hand on Altaru's neck. Despite the cold, the hard work in the thin air had made him start sweating. 'Let's go on – it will be better on the other side of the pass.'

'Are you sure?'

I looked off through the gray air at the Telemesh Gate now only a hundred yards farther up the road. It was a dark cut through a wall of rock, an ice-glazed opening into the unknown.

'Yes, it will be better,' I reassured him, if not myself. 'Come on.'

I touched Altaru's flanks to urge him forward, but he nickered nervously and didn't move. As Master Juwain came up to join us, the big horse just stood there with his large nostrils opening and closing against the freezing wind.

'What is it, Val?' Master Juwain asked me.

I shrugged my shoulders as I scanned the boulders and snowfields all about us. The tundra seemed as barren as it was cold. Not even a marmot or a ptarmigan moved to break the bleakness of the pass.

'Do you think it could be a bear?' Maram asked, looking about, too. 'Maybe he smells a bear.'

'No, it's too early for bears to be up this high,' I told him.

In another month, the snow would be gone, and the slopes around us would teem with wildflowers and berries. But now there seemed little that was alive save for the orange and green patches of lichen that covered the cold stones.

Again, I nudged Altaru forward, and this time he whinnied and shook his head angrily at the opening to the Telemesh Gate. He began pawing at the road with his iron-shod hoof, and the harsh sound of it rang out into the mist-choked air.

'Altaru, Altaru,' I whispered to him, 'what's the matter?'

There was something, I thought, that he didn't like about this cut between the mountains. There was something I didn't like myself. I felt a sudden, deep wrongness entering my bones as from the ground beneath us. It was as if Telemesh, the great king, the grandfather of my grandfathers, in burning off the tissues of the mountain with his firestone, had wounded the land in a way that could never be healed. And now, out of this open wound of fused dirt and blackened rock, it seemed that the earth itself was still screaming in agony. What man or beast, I wondered, would ever be drawn to such a place? Well, perhaps the vultures who batten on the blood of the suffering and dying would feel at home here. And the great Beast who was called the Red Dragon – surely he would find a twisted pleasure in the world's pain.

He came for me then out of the dark mouth of the fire-scarred Gate. He was, even as Maram feared, a bear. And not merely a Meshian brown bear but one of the rare and very bad-tempered white bears of Ishka. I guessed that he must have wandered through the Gate into Mesh. And now he seemed to guard it, standing up on his stumpy hind legs to a height of ten feet as he sniffed the air and looked straight toward me.

'Oh, Lord!' Maram called out as he tried to steady his horse. 'Oh, Lord, oh, Lord!'

Now Altaru, seeing the bear at last, began snorting and stomping at the road. I tried to steady him as I said to Maram, 'Don't worry, the bear won't bother us if –'

'– if we don't bother him,' he finished. 'Well, I hope you're right, my friend.'

But it seemed that I couldn't leave the bear alone after all. The wind carried down from the mountain, and I smelled his rank scent which fairly reeked with an illness that I couldn't identify. I couldn't help staring at his small, questing eyes as my hand moved almost involuntarily to the hilt of my sword. And all the while, he kept sniffing at me with his wet black nose; I had the strange sense that even though he couldn't catch my scent, he could smell the kirax in my blood.

And then suddenly, without warning, he fell down onto all fours and charged us.

'Oh, Lord!' Maram cried out again. 'He's coming – run for your life!'

True to his instincts, he wheeled his horse about and began galloping down the road. I might have done the same if Altaru hadn't reared just then, throwing back his head and flashing his hooves in challenge at the bear. This move, which I should have anticipated, caught me off guard. For at that moment, as Altaru rose up with a mighty surge of bunching muscles, I was reaching toward my pack horse for my bow and arrows. I was badly unbalanced, and went flying out of my saddle. Tanar, my screaming pack horse, almost trampled me in his panic to get away from the charging bear. If I hadn't rolled behind Altaru, his wildly flailing hooves would surely have brained me.

'Val!' Master Juwain called to me, 'get up and draw your sword!'

It is astonishing how quickly a bear can cover a hundred yards, particularly when running downhill. I didn't have time to draw my sword. Even as Master Juwain tried to get control of his own bucking horse and the two pack horses tied behind him, the bear bounded down the snowy slope straight toward us. Tanar, caught between them and the growling bear, screamed in terror, all the while trying to get out of the way. And then the bear closed with him, and I thought for a moment that he might tear open his throat or break his back with a blow from one of his mighty paws. But it seemed that this stout horse was not intended to be the bear's prey. The bear only rammed him with his shoulder, knocking him aside in his fury to get at me.

'Val!' I heard Maram calling me as from far away. 'Run, now – oh, Lord, oh, Lord!'

The bear would certainly have fallen upon me then if not for Altaru's courage. As I struggled to stand and regain my breath, the great horse reared again and struck a glancing blow off the bear's head. His sharp hoof cut open the bear's eye, which filled with blood. The stunned bear screamed in outrage and swiped at Altaru with his long black claws. He grunted and brayed and shook his sloping white head at me. I smelled his musty white fur and felt the growls rumbling up from deep in his throat. His good eye fixed on mine like a hook; he opened his jaws to rip me open with his long white teeth.

'Val, I'm coming!' Maram cried out to the thunder of hooves against stone. 'I'm coming!'

The bear finally closed with me, locking his jaws onto my shoulder with a crushing force. He snarled and shook his head furiously and tried to pulp me with his deadly paws. And then Maram closed with him. Unbelievably, he had managed to wheel his horse about yet again and urge him forward in a desperate charge at the bear. He had his lance drawn and couched beneath his arm like a knight. But although trained in arms, he was no knight; the point of the lance caught the bear in the shoulder instead of the throat, and the shock of steel and metal pushing into hard flesh unseated Maram and propelled him from his horse. He hit the ground with a ugly slap and whooshing of breath. But for the moment, at least, he had succeeded in fighting the bear off of me.

'Val,' Maram croaked out from the blood-spattered road, 'help me!'

The bear snarled at Maram and moved to rend him with his claws in his determination to get at me. And in that moment, I finally slid my sword free. The long kalama flashed in the uneven light. I swung it with all my might at the bear's exposed neck. The kalama's razor edge, hardened in the forges of Godhra, bit through fur, muscle and bone. I gasped to feel the bear's bright lifeblood spraying out into the air as his great head went rolling down the road into a drift of snow. I fell to the road in the agony of death, and I hardly noticed the bear's body falling like an avalanche on top of Maram.

'Val – get this thing off me!' I heard Maram call out weakly from beneath the mound of fur.

But as always when I had killed an animal, it took me many moments to return to myself. I slowly stood up and rubbed my throbbing shoulder. If not for my armor and the padding beneath it, I thought, the bear would surely have torn off my arm. Master Juwain, having collected and hobbled the frightened horses, came over then and helped me pull Maram free from the bear. He stood there in the driving sleet checking us for wounds.

'Oh, my Lord, I'm killed!' Maram called out when he saw the blood drenching his tunic. But it proved only to be the bear's blood. In truth, he had suffered nothing worse than having the wind knocked out of him.

'I think you'll be all right,' Master Juwain said as he ran his gnarly hands over him.

'I will? But what about Val? The bear had half his body in his mouth!'

He turned to ask me how I was. I told him, 'It hurts. But it seems that nothing is broken.'

Maram looked at me with accusation in his still-frightened eyes. 'You told me that the bear would leave us alone. Well, he didn't, did he?'

'No,' I said, 'he didn't.'

Strange, I thought, that a bear should fall upon three men and six horses with such ferocious and single-minded purpose. I had never heard of a bear, not even a ravenous one, attacking so boldly.

Master Juwain stepped over to the side of the road and examined the bear's massive head. He looked at his glassy, dark eye and pulled open his jaws to gaze at his teeth.

'It's possible that he was maddened with rabies,' he said. 'But he doesn't have the look.'

'No, he doesn't,' I agreed, examining him as well.

'What made him attack us then?' Maram demanded.

Master Juwain's face fell gray as if he had eaten bad meat. He said, 'If the bear were a man, I would say his actions were those of a ghul.'

I stared at the bear, and it suddenly came to me that the illness I had sensed in him had been not of the body but the mind.

'A ghul!' Maram cried out. 'Are you saying that Mor . . . ah, that the Lord of Lies had seized his will? I've never heard of an animal ghul.'

No one had. With the wind working at the sweat beneath my armor, a deep shiver ran through me. I wondered if Morjin – or anyone except the Dark One himself, Angra Mainyu – could have gained that much power.

As if in answer to my question, Master Juwain sighed and said, 'It seems that his skill, if we can call it that, is growing.'

'Well,' Maram said, looking about nervously, 'if he can send one bear to kill Val, he can send another. Or a wolf, or a –'

'No, I think not,' Master Juwain interrupted. 'For a man or a woman to be made a ghul is a rare thing. There must be an opening, through despair or hate, into the darkness. And a certain sympathy of the minds. I would think that an animal ghul, if possible at all, would be even rarer.'

'But you don't really know, do you?' Maram pressed him.

'No, I don't,' Master Juwain said. He suddenly shivered, too, and pulled his cloak more tightly about him. 'But I *do* know that we should get down from this pass before it grows dark.'

'Yes, we should,' I agreed. With some handfuls of snow, I began cleaning the blood off me, and watched Maram do the same. After retying Tanar to Altaru, I mounted my black stallion and turned him up the road.

'You're not thinking of going *on?*' Maram asked me. 'Shouldn't we return to the keep?'

I pointed at the opening of the Gate. 'Tria lies that way.'

Maram looked down at the kel keep and the road that led back to the Valley of the Swans. He must have remembered that Lord Harsha was waiting for him there; it occurred to me that he had finally witnessed at first hand the kind of work that a kalama could accomplish, for he rubbed his curly beard worriedly and muttered, 'No, we can't go back, can we?'

He mounted his trembling sorrel, as did Master Juwain his. I smiled at Maram and bowed my head to him. 'Thank you for saving my life,' I told him.

'I *did* save your life, didn't I?' he said. He smiled back at me as if I had personally knighted him in front of a thousand nobles. 'Well, allow me to save it again. Who really wants to go to Tria, anyway? Perhaps it's time I returned to Delu. We could all go there. You'd be welcomed at my father's court and –'

'No,' I told him. 'Thank you for such a gracious offer, but my journey lies in another direction. Will you come with me?'

Maram sat on his horse as he looked back and forth between the headless bear and me. He blinked his eyes against the stinging sleet. He licked his lips, then finally said, 'Will I come with you? Haven't I said I would? Aren't you my best friend? Of *course* I'm coming with you!'

And with that he clasped my arm, and I clasped his. As if Altaru and I were of one will, we started moving up the road together. Maram and Master Juwain followed close behind me. I regretted leaving the bear unburied in a shallow pond of blood, but there was nothing else to do. Tomorrow, perhaps, one of Lord Avijan's patrols would find him and dispose of him. And so we rode our horses into the dark mouth of the Telemesh Gate and steeled ourselves to go down into Ishka.

7

Our passage through the Gate proved uneventful and quiet save for Maram's constant exclamations of delight. For, as he discovered, the walls of rock on both sides of us sparkled with diamonds. The fire of Telemesh's red gelstei, in melting this corridor through the mountain, had exposed many veins of these glittering white crystals. In honor of his great feat, the proud Telemesh had ordered that they never be cut, and they never had. I thought that the beauty of the diamonds somewhat made up for this long wound in the earth. But many visitors to Mesh – the Ishkans foremost among them – complained of such ostentatious displays of my kingdom's wealth. King Hadaru had often accused my father of mocking him thusly. But my father turned a stony face to his plaints; he would say only that he intended to respect Telemesh's law even as he would the Law of the One.

'But can't we take just *one* stone?' Maram asked when we were almost through the Gate. 'We could sell it for a fortune in Tria.'

Maram, I thought, didn't know what he was saying. Was anyone more despicable than a diamond seller? Yes – those who sold the bodies of men and women into slavery.

'Come,' he said. 'Who would ever know?'

'*We* would know, Maram,' I told him. I looked down at the corridor's smooth stone floor, which glittered with more than one diamond beneath patches of wind-blown grit and the occasional droppings of horses. 'Besides, it's said that any man who steals a stone will himself turn into stone – it's a very old prophecy.'

For many miles after that – after we debouched from the pass and began our descent into Ishka – Maram gazed at the rock formations by the side of the road as if they had once been thieves making their escape with illicit treasure in their hands. But as dusk approached, his desire for diamonds began to fade with the light. His talk turned to fires crackling in well-tended hearths and hot stew waiting to be ladled out for our evening meal. The sleet, which turned into a driving rain on the heavily wooded lower slopes of the mountain, convinced him that he didn't want to camp out that night.

It convinced me as well. When we reached the Ishkans' fortress that guarded their side of the pass, we stopped to ask if there were any inns nearby. The fortress's commander, Lord Shadru, told us that there were not; he offered his apologies that he couldn't allow a Meshian knight within the walls of his fortress. But then he directed us to the house of a woodcutter who lived only a mile farther down the road. He wished us well, and we continued plodding on through the icy rain.

A short time later, we turned onto a side road, as Shadru had directed us. And there, in the middle of a stand of trees dripping with water, we found a square chalet no different than ones that dot the mountains of Mesh. Its windows glowed orange with the light of a good fire burning within. The woodcutter, Ludar Narath, came out to greet us. After ascertaining who we were and why we had come to his door on such a stormy night, he offered us fire, bread and salt. He seemed determined that Ishkan hospitality should not suffer when compared to that of Mesh.

And so he invited us to share the spare bedroom that had once belonged to his eldest son, who had been killed in a war with Waas. Ludar's wife, Masha, served us a small feast. We sat by the fire eating fried trout and a soup made of barley, onions and mushrooms. There was bread and butter, cheese and walnuts, and a stout black beer that tasted little different than the best of Meshian brews. We sat at his huge table with his three daughters and his youngest son, who eyed me with great curiosity. I sensed that the boy wanted to come over to me, perhaps to pull at the rings of my mail or tell me a bad joke. But his forbearance overruled the natural friendliness bubbling up inside him. As it did with Ludar and the rest of his family. It didn't matter that I had spent my childhood in forests little different than theirs and had listened to the same after-dinner stories told before a warm fire; in the end, I was a knight of Mesh, and someday I might have to face Ludar in battle – and his remaining son as well.

Still, our hosts were as polite and proper as they could be. Masha saw to it that we had a good bath in the huge cedarwood tub that Ludar had made; while we soaked our battered bodies in the hot water that her son kept bringing us, Masha took away our blood-stained garments to clean them. She sent her daughters to lay out our sleeping furs on top of mattresses freshly stuffed with the cleanest of straw. And when we were finally ready for bed, she brought us cups of steaming ginger tea to warm our hearts before sleeping.

We spent a very comfortable night there in those wet woods on the wrong side of the mountains. With morning came the passing of the storm and the rising of the sun against a blue sky. We ate a quick meal of porridge and bacon as we listened to the sparrows chirping in the trees. Then we thanked Ludar and his family for the grace of their house; we saddled our horses and urged them down the path that led to the North Road.

That morning we rode through a misty countryside of high ridges and steep ravines. Although I had never passed this way before, the mountains beyond Raaskel and Korukel seemed strangely familiar to me. By early afternoon we had made our way through the highest part of them; stretching before us to the north, was a succession of green-shrouded hills that would eventually give way to the Tushur River valley. With every mile we put behind us, these hills grew lower and less steep. The road, while not as well-paved as any in Mesh, wound mostly downhill, and the horses found the going rather easy. By the time we drew up in a little clearing by a stream to make camp that night, we were all in good spirits.

The next day we awoke early to the birds singing their morning songs. We traveled hard through the rolling hill country which gradually opened out into the broad valley of the Tushur. There, the road curved east through the emerald farmland toward the golden glow of the sun – and toward Loviisa, where King Hadaru held his court. We debated making a cut across this curve and rejoining the road much to the north of the Ishkans' main city. It seemed wise to avoid the bellicose Salmelu and his friends, as Maram pointed out.

'What if Salmelu,' he asked me, '*hired* the assassin who shot at us in the woods?'

'No, he couldn't have,' I said. 'No Valari would ever dishonor himself so.'

'But what if the Red Dragon has gotten to him, too? What if he's been made a ghul?'

I looked off at the gleaming ribbon of the Tushur where it flowed through the valley below us. I wondered for the hundredth time why Morjin might be hunting me.

'Salmelu,' I said, 'is no ghul. If he hates me, it's of his own will and not the Red Dragon's.'

'If he hates you,' Maram said, 'shouldn't we avoid him altogether?'

I smiled grimly and shook my head. I told him, 'The world is full of hate, and there's no avoiding it. In front of his own countrymen, Salmelu has promised us safe passage, and he'll have to keep his word.'

After stopping for a quick meal, we decided that making a straight cut through the farms and forests of Ishka would only delay us and pose its own dangers: there would be the raging waters of the Tushur to cross and perhaps bears in the woods. In the end, it was the prospect of encountering another bear that persuaded Maram that we should ride on to Loviisa, and so we did.

We planned, however, to spend the night in one of Loviisa's inns; the following morning we would set out as early and with as little fanfare as possible. But others had made other plans for us. It seemed that our passage through Ishka had not gone unnoticed. As night approached and we rode past the farms near the outskirts of the city, a squadron of knights came thundering up the road to greet us. Their leader was Lord Nadhru, whom I recognized by the long scar on his jaw and his dark, volatile eyes. He bowed his head toward me and told me, 'So, Sar Valashu, we meet again. King Hadaru has sent me to request your presence in his hall tonight.'

At this news, I traded quick looks with both Maram and Master Juwain. There was no need to say anything; when a king 'requested' one's presence, there was nothing else to do except oblige him.

And so we followed Lord Nadhru and his knights through Loviisa, whose winding streets and coal-fired smithies reminded me of Godhra. He led us past a succession of square, stone houses up a steep hill at the north of the city. And there, on a heavily-wooded palisade overlooking the icy, blue Tushur, we found King Hadaru's palace all lit up as if in anticipation of guests. As Ludar Narath had told me, the King disdained living in his family's ancient castle in the hills nearby. And so instead he had built a palace fronted with flower gardens and fountains. The palace itself was an array of pagodas, exquisitely carved on its several levels out of curving sweeps of various kinds of wood. Indeed, it was famed throughout the Morning Mountains as the Wooden Palace. Ludar himself had cut dozens of rare shatterwood trees to provide the paneling of the main hall. Inside this beautiful building, if the stories proved true, we would find beams of good Anjo cherrywood and ebony columns that had come all the way from the southern forests of Galda. It was said that King Hadaru had paid for his magnificent palace with diamonds from the overworked Ishkan mines, but I did not want to believe such a slander.

We entrusted our horses to the grooms who met us at the entrance to the palace. Then Lord Nadhru led us down a long corridor to the hall where King Hadaru held his court. The four warriors guarding the entrance to this great room asked us to remove our boots before proceeding within, and so we did. They allowed me, of course, to keep

103

my sword sheathed by my side. One might better ask a Valari knight to surrender his soul before his sword.

The Ishkan nobles, Salmelu and Lord Issur foremost among them, stood waiting to welcome us near King Hadaru's throne. This was a single piece of white oak carved into the shape of a huge bear squatting on its hind legs. King Hadaru seemed almost lost against this massive sculpture, and he was no small man. He sat very straight in the bear's lap, back against the belly and chest, with the great white head projecting up and out above him. He himself seemed somewhat bearlike, with a large head covered by a mane of snowy white hair that showed ten red ribbons. He had a large, predatory nose like Salmelu's and eyes all gleaming and black like polished shatterwood. As we walked through the hall, with its massive oak beams arching high above us, his dark eyes never left us.

After Lord Nadhru had presented us, he took his place near Salmelu and Lord Issur, who stood near their father's throne. Other prominent knights attended the King as well: Lord Mestivan and Lord Solhtar, a proud-seeming man with a heavy black beard that was rare among the Valari. Two of the women present that night were Devora, the King's sister, and Irisha, a beautiful young woman who seemed about my age. Her hair was raven-black and her skin almost as fair as the oak of King Hadaru's throne. She was the daughter of Duke Barwan of Adar in Anjo, and it was said that King Hadaru had coerced him into giving her as his bride after his old queen had died. She stood in a bright green gown close to the King's throne, closer even than Salmelu. It was somewhat barbaric, I thought, that even a queen should be made to stand in the King's presence, but that was the way of things in Ishka.

'Sar Valashu Elahad,' the King said to me in a voice thickened with the bitterness of age. 'I would like to welcome you to my home.'

He nodded at Maram and Master Juwain, who stood on either side of me and continued, 'And you, Prince Maram Marshayk of Delu and Master Juwain of the Great White Brotherhood – you are welcomed, too.'

We thanked him for his hospitality, and then he favored me with a smile as brittle as the glass of the many windows of the hall. He told me, 'I hope you like your accommodations here better than those of that draughty old castle of yours.'

In truth, I already liked the palace of this sad, old king more than my father's castle, for it was a splendid thing. The vast roof of the hall, supported by great ebony columns, opened out in sweeping curves high above us like an indoor sky made of some sort of bluish wood. The panels of the walls were of the blackest shatterwood and red cherry, carved with battle scenes of Ishka's greatest victories. The darkness of these woods would have cast a gloom upon the hall if they hadn't been waxed and polished to a mirror-like finish. In their gleaming surfaces was reflected the light of the thousands of candles burning in their stands. As well, I saw thousands of leaping red flames in the deep gloss of the floor, which was of oak unadorned by any carpet. Its grainy whiteness was broken only by a circle some twenty feet across in front of the throne; no one stood upon this disk of red rosewood that must have been cut in Hesperu or Surrapam. I guessed that it symbolized the sun or perhaps one of the stars from which the Valari had come. I couldn't see a speck of dust upon it, nor on any other surface in the hall, which smelled of lemon oil and other exotic polishes.

'My cooks are preparing a meal, which we'll take in the dining room,' King Hadaru said to me. 'Now, I would like to know if there is anything you need?'

Maram, I noticed, was concentrating his attention on Irisha with a barely contained heat. I nudged him in the ribs with my elbow, and said to the King, 'We need only to travel as quickly as possible at first light.'

'Yes,' King Hadaru said, 'I've heard that you've pledged yourself to making this foolish quest.'

'That's true,' I said, feeling the eyes of everyone near the throne fall upon me.

'Well, the Lightstone will never be found. Your ancestor gave it to a stranger in Tria when he would have done better to bring it to Loviisa.'

His thin lips pulled together in distaste as if he had eaten a lemon. I could almost feel the resentment burning inside him. It occurred to me then that love frustrated turns to hate; hope defeated becomes the bitterness of despair.

'But what if the Lightstone *were* found?' I asked him.

'By you?'

'Yes – why not?'

'Then I have no doubt that you would bring it back to your castle and lock it away from the world.'

'No, that would never happen,' I told him. 'The Lightstone's radiance was meant to be shared by everyone. How else could we ever bring peace to the world?'

'Peace?' he snarled out. 'How can there ever be peace when there are those who would claim what is not theirs?'

At this, Salmelu traded sharp looks with Lord Nadhru, and I heard Lord Solhtar murmuring something about Korukel's diamonds. Lord

105

Mestivan, standing next to him in a bright blue tunic, nodded his head as he touched the red and white battle ribbons tied to his long black hair.

'Perhaps someday,' I said, 'all will know what is rightfully theirs.'

At this, King Hadaru let out a harsh laugh like the growl of a bear. And then he told me, 'You, Valashu Elahad, are a dreamer – like your grandfather.'

'Perhaps that's true,' I said. 'But all men have dreams. What is yours, King Hadaru?'

This question caught the King off guard, and his whole body tensed as if in anticipation of a blow. His eyes deepened with a faraway look; he seemed to be gazing through the beautiful woods of his palace out into the night-time sky. He suffered, I thought, from a stinginess of spirit in place of austerity, a brittle hardness instead of true strength. He strove for a zealous cleanliness when he should have longed for purity. If it came to war, he would fight out of pride of possessiveness rather than the protecting of that which he cherished most. And yet despite these turnings of the Valari virtues, I also sensed in him a secret desire that both he and the world could be different. He might fight against Waas or Mesh with all the cool ferocity for which he was famed, but his greatest battle would always be with himself.

'Of what do I dream?' he murmured as he pulled at the ribbons tied to his hair. His eyes seemed to grow brighter as they turned back toward me. 'I dream of diamonds,' he finally told me. 'I dream of the warriors of Ishka shining like ten thousand perfect, polished diamonds as they stand ready to fight for the riches they were born for.'

Now it was my turn to be caught off guard. My grandfather had always said that we were born to stand in the light of the One and feel its radiance growing ever brighter within ourselves, and I had always believed that he had told me the truth.

King Hadaru glanced at Lord Nadhru and asked, 'And of what do *you* dream, Lord Nadhru?'

Lord Nadhru fingered the hilt of his sword, and without hesitation, said, 'Justice, Sire.'

'And you, Lord Solhtar?' the King said to the man next to him.

Lord Solhtar fingered his thick beard for a moment before turning to look at the woman on his left. She had the thick bones and brown skin of a Galdan, and I wondered if she had come from that conquered kingdom. Lord Solhtar smiled at her in silent understanding, and then said, 'I dream that someday we Ishkans may help all peoples regain what is rightfully theirs.'

'Very good,' Lord Issur suddenly said. Although he was Salmelu's brother, he seemed to have little of his pugnaciousness and none of his arrogance. 'That is a worthy dream.'

King Hadaru must have caught a flash of concern from his young wife, for he suddenly looked at Irisha and said, 'Do you agree?'

I noticed Maram staring at Irisha intently as she brushed back her long hair and said, 'Of course it is worthy – worthy of our noblest efforts. But shouldn't we first look to the safeguarding of our own kingdom?'

This 'safeguarding,' I thought, might well mean the eventual incorporation of Anjo into Ishka. Although Irisha's father might owe allegiance to Anjo's King Danashu in Sauvo, Danashu was a king in name only. And so Adar, much to Duke Barwan's shame, had practically become a client state of Ishka. In truth, the only thing that kept Ishka from biting off pieces of Anjo one by one like a hungry bear was fear of Meshian steel.

For a while I listened as these proud nobles talked among themselves. They seemed little different, in their sentiments and concerns, from the lords and knights of Mesh. And yet the Ishkans *were* different from us in other ways. They wore colors in their clothing and battle ribbons in their hair in a time of peace, something that my dour countrymen would never do. And some of them, at least, had taken foreign-born wives. But worst of all, I thought, was their habit of frequently using the pronoun 'I' in their speech, which sounded vulgar and self-glorifying.

I remembered well my father telling me about the perils of using this deceptive word. And wasn't he right, after all? It is vain. It is a distracting mirror. It shrinks the soul and traps it inside a box of conceits, superficialities and illusions. It keeps us from looking out into the universe and sensing our greater being in the vastness of the infinite and the fiery exhalations of the stars. In Mesh, one used the word in forgetfulness or almost as a curse – or, rarely, in moments of great emotion as when a man might whisper to his wife in the privacy of their house, 'I love you.'

As it grew closer to the hour appointed for dinner, King Hadaru listened patiently to all that everyone had to say. Then finally, with a heaviness both in his body and spirit, he looked at Salmelu and asked, 'Of what do you dream, my son?'

Salmelu seemed to have been waiting for this moment. His eyes flared like a fire stoked with fresh coal as he looked at me and said, '*I* dream of war. Isn't that what a Valari is born for? To stand with his brothers on the battlefield and feel his heart beating as one with theirs, to see his enemies crumble and fall before him – is there anything better than this? How else can a warrior test himself? How else can he know if he is diamond inside or only glass that can be broken and ground beneath another man's boot, to blow away like dust in the wind?'

I took these words as a challenge. While King Hadaru watched me carefully, I held my knight's ring up so that it gleamed in the candlelight.

And then I said, 'All men are diamonds inside. And all life is a series of battles. It's how we face *this* war that determines whether we are cut and polished like the diamonds of our rings or broken like bad stones.'

At this, Master Juwain smiled at me approvingly, as did Lord Issur and many of the Ishkans. But Salmelu only stood there glowering at me. I could feel his malice toward me rising inside him like an angry snake.

'I myself saw your father give you that ring,' he said. 'But I can hardly believe what I see now: a Valari warrior who does everything that he can to avoid war.'

I took a deep breath to cool the heat rising through my belly. Then I told him, 'If it's war you want so badly, why not unite against the Red Dragon and fight *him*?'

'Because *I* do not fear him as you seem to. No Ishkan does.'

This, I thought, was not quite true. King Hadaru paled a little at the utterance of this evil name. It occurred to me then that he might not, after all, desire a war with Mesh that would weaken his kingdom at a dangerous time. Why wage war when he could gain his heart's desire through marriage or merely making threats?

'It's no shame to be afraid,' King Hadaru said. 'True courage is marching into battle in the face of fear.'

At this Salmelu traded quick looks with both Lord Nadhru and Lord Mestivan. I sensed that they were the leaders of the Ishkan faction that campaigned for war.

'Yes,' Salmelu said. 'Marching into *battle*, not merely banging on our shields and blowing our trumpets.'

'Whether or not there is a battle with Mesh,' the King reminded him, 'is still not decided. As I recall, the emissaries I sent to Silvassu failed to obtain a commitment for battle.'

At this, Salmelu's face flushed as if he had been burned by the sun. He stared at his father and said, 'If we failed, it was only because we weren't empowered to declare war immediately in the face of King Shamesh's evasions and postponements. If I were King –'

'Yes?' King Hadaru said in a voice like steel. 'What *would* you do if you were King?'

'I would march on Mesh immediately, snow or no snow in the passes.' He glared at me and continued, 'It's obvious that the Meshians have no real will toward war.'

'Then perhaps it is well that you're not King,' his father told him. 'And perhaps it's well that I haven't yet named an heir.'

At this, Irisha smiled at King Hadaru as she protectively cupped her hands to cover her belly. Salmelu glared at her with a hatefulness that I had thought he reserved only for me. He must have feared that Irisha would bear his father a new son who would simultaneously push him aside and consolidate the King's claims on Anjo.

King Hadaru turned to me and said, 'Please forgive my son. He is hotheaded and does not always consider the effects of his acts.'

Despite my dislike of Salmelu, I felt a rare moment of pity for him. Where my father ruled his sons out of love and respect, his father ruled him out of fear and shame.

'No offense is taken,' I told him. 'It's clear that Lord Salmelu acts out of what he believes to be Ishka's best interest.'

'You speak well, Sar Valashu,' the King said to me. 'If you weren't committed to making this impossible quest of yours, your father would do well to make *you* an emissary to one of the courts of the Nine Kingdoms.'

'Thank you, King Hadaru,' I said.

He sat back against the white wood of his throne, all the while regarding me deeply. And then he said, 'You have your father's eyes, you know. But you favor your mother. Elianora wi Solaru – now *there* is a beautiful woman.'

I sensed that King Hadaru was trying to win me with flattery, toward what end I couldn't see. But his attentions only embarrassed me. And they enraged Salmelu. He must have recalled that his father had once wooed my mother in vain, and had only married *his* mother as his second choice.

'Yes,' Salmelu choked out, ignoring his father's last comment. 'I agree that Sar Valashu should be made an emissary. Since it's clear that he's no warrior.'

Maram, standing impatiently next to me, made a rumbling sound in his throat as if he might challenge Salmelu's insult. But the sight of Salmelu's kalama sheathed at his side helped him keep his silence. As for me, I looked down at the two diamonds sparkling in my ring, and wondered if Salmelu was right, after all.

Then Salmelu continued, '*I* would say that Sar Valashu does favor his father, at least in his avoidance of battle.'

Why, I wondered, was Salmelu now insulting both my father and me in front of the entire Ishkan court? Was he trying to call me out? No, I thought, he couldn't challenge me to a duel since that would violate his pledge of a safe passage through Ishka.

'My father,' I said, breathing deeply, 'has fought many battles. No one has ever questioned his courage.'

'Do you think it's *his* courage I question?'

'What do you mean?'

Salmelu's eyes stabbed into mine like daggers as he said, 'It seems a noble thing, this pledge of yours to make your quest. But aren't you really just fleeing from war and the possibility of death in battle?'

I listened as several of the lords near Salmelu drew in quick breaths; I felt my own breath burning inside me as if I had inhaled fire. Was Salmelu trying to provoke me into calling *him* out? Well, I wouldn't be provoked. To fight him would be to die, most likely, and that would only aid him in inciting a war that might kill my friends and brothers. I was a diamond, I told myself, a perfect diamond which no words could touch.

And then despite my intentions, I found myself suddenly gripping the hilt of my sword as I said to him, 'Are you calling me a coward?'

If he called me a coward, to my face, then that *would* be a challenge to a duel that I would have to answer.

As my heart beat inside my chest so quickly and hard that I thought it might burst, I felt Master Juwain's hand grip my arm firmly as if to give me strength. And then Maram finally found his voice; he tried to make a joke of Salmelu's deadly insult, saying, 'Val, a coward? Ha, ha – is the sky yellow? Val is the bravest man I know.'

But his attempt to quiet our rising tempers had no effect on Salmelu. He just fixed me with his cold black eyes and said, 'Did you think I was calling you a coward? Then please excuse me – I was only raising the question.'

'Salmelu,' his father said to him sternly.

But Salmelu ignored him, too. 'All men,' he said, 'should question their own courage. Especially kings. Especially kings who allow their sons to run away when battle is threatened.'

'Salmelu!' King Hadaru half-shouted at him.

Now I gripped my sword so hard that my fingers hurt. To Salmelu, I said, 'Are you calling my father a coward, then?'

'Does a lion beget a lamb?'

These words were like drops of kirax in my eyes, burning me, blinding me. Salmelu's mocking face almost disappeared into the angry red sea closing in around me.

'Does an eagle,' he asked, 'hatch a rabbit from its eggs?'

The wily Salmelu was twisting his accusations into questions, and thus evading the responsibility for how I might respond. Why? Did he think I would simply impale myself on his sword?

'It's good,' he said, 'that your grandfather died before he saw what became of his line. Now there was a brave man. It takes true courage to sacrifice those whom we love. Who else would have let a hundred of his warriors die trying to protect him rather than simply defend his honor in a duel?'

As I choked on my wrath and stopped breathing, the whole world seemed to come crushing down upon my chest. I allowed this terrible lie to break me open so that I might know the truth of who Salmelu really was. And in that moment of bitterness and blood, his hate became my hate, and mine fed the fires of his, and almost without knowing what I was doing, I whipped my sword from its sheath and pointed it at him.

'Val,' Maram cried out in a horrified voice, 'put away your sword!'

But there was to be no putting away of swords that night; some things can never be undone. As Salmelu and his fellow Ishkans quickly drew their swords, I stared in silent resignation at this fence of gleaming steel. *I* had drawn on Salmelu, after all. Despite his taunts, I had done this of my own free will. And according to ancient law that all Valari held sacred, by this very act it had been I who had thus formally challenged him to a duel.

'Hold! Hold yourselves now, I say!' King Hadaru's outraged voice cut through the murmurs of anticipation rippling through the hall. Then he arose from his throne and took a step forward. To Salmelu, he said, 'I did not want this. I would not have you make this duel tonight – you needn't accept Sar Valashu's challenge.'

Salmelu's sword wavered not an inch as he pointed it toward me. He said, 'Nevertheless, I do accept it.'

The King stared at him for a long moment, and then sighed deeply. 'So be it, then,' he said. 'A challenge has been made and accepted. You will face Sar Valashu in the ring of honor when you are both ready.'

At this, Salmelu and the other lords slid their swords back into their sheaths, and I did the same. So, I thought, the time of my death has finally come. There was nothing more to say; there was nothing more to do – almost nothing.

Because Valari knights do not fight duels wearing armor, the King excused me for a few minutes so that I might remove my mail. With Maram and Master Juwain following close behind me, I repaired to an anteroom off the side of the hall. It was a small room, whose rosewood paneling had the look and smell of dried blood. I stood staring at yet another battle scene carved into wood as the heavy door banged shut and shook the entire room.

'Are you mad!' Maram shouted at me as he smacked his huge fist into the palm of his hand. 'Have you entirely taken leave of your senses? That man is the best swordsman in Ishka, and you drew on him!'

'It . . . couldn't be helped,' I said.

'Couldn't be helped?' he shouted. He seemed almost ready to smack his fist into me. 'Well, why don't you help it now? Why not just apologize to him and leave here as quickly as we can?'

At that moment, with my legs so weak that I could hardly stand, I wanted nothing more than to run away into the night. But I couldn't do that. A challenge had been made and accepted. There are some laws too sacred to break.

'Leave him alone now,' Master Juwain said as he came over to me. He helped me remove my surcoat, and then began working at the catches to my armor. 'If you would, Brother Maram, please go out to the horses and bring Val a fresh tunic.'

Maram muttered that he would be back in a few moments, and again the door opened and closed. With trembling hands, I began pulling off my armor. With my mail and underpadding removed, it was cold in that little room. Indeed, the entire palace was cold: out of fear of fire, the King allowed no flame hotter than that of a candle in any of its wooden rooms.

'Are you afraid?' Master Juwain asked as he laid his hand on my trembling shoulder.

'Yes,' I said, staring at the dreadful, red wall.

'Brother Maram is an excitable man,' he said. 'But he's right, you know. You could simply walk away from all this.'

'No, that's not possible,' I told him. 'The shame would be too great. My brothers would make war to expunge it. My father would.'

'I see,' Master Juwain said. He rubbed his neck, and then fell quiet.

'Master Juwain,' I said, looking at him, 'in ancient times, the Brothers would help a knight prepare for a duel. Will you help me now?'

Master Juwain began rubbing the back of his bald head as his gray eyes fell upon me. 'That was long ago, Val, before we forswore violence. If I helped you now, and you killed Salmelu, I would bear part of the blame for his death.'

'If you don't help me, and he kills me, you would bear part of the blame for mine.'

For as long as it took for my heart to beat twenty times, Master Juwain stared at me in silence. And then he bowed his head in acceptance of what had to be and said, 'All right.'

He instructed me to gaze at the stand of candles blazing in the corner of the room. I was to single out the flame of the highest candle and concentrate on its flickering yellow tip. Where did a candle's flame

112

come from when it was lit, he asked me? Where did it go when it went out?

He steadied my breathing then as he guided me into the ancient death meditation. Its purpose was to take me into a state of zanshin, a deep and timeless calm in the face of extreme danger. Its essence was in bringing me to the realization that I was much more than my body and that therefore I wouldn't fear its wounding or death.

'Breathe with me now,' Master Juwain told me. 'Concentrate on your awareness of the flame. Concentrate on your awareness, in itself.'

Was I afraid, he told me to ask myself? Who was asking the question? If it was *I* who asked, what was the 'I' who was aware of the one who asked? Wasn't there always a deeper I, a truer self – luminous, flawless, indestructible – that shone more brightly than any diamond and blazed as eternally as any star? What was this one radiant awareness that shone through all things?

For once in my life, my gift was truly a gift. As I opened myself to Master Juwain's low but powerful voice, his breathing became one with my breathing and his calm became my own. After a while, my hands stopped sweating and I found that I could stand without shaking. Although my heart still beat as quickly as a child's, the crushing pain I had felt earlier in my chest was gone.

And then suddenly, like thunder breaking through the sky, Maram came back into the room with my tunic, and it was time to go.

'Are you ready?' Master Juwain said as I pulled on this simple garment and buckled my sword around my waist.

'Yes,' I said, smiling at him. 'Thank you, sir.'

We returned to the main hall. King Hadaru and his court had gathered in a circle around the disc of rosewood at the center of the room. In Mesh, when a duel was to be fought, the knights and warriors formed the ring of honor at any convenient spot. But then, we did not fight duels nearly so often as did the bloodthirsty Ishkans.

As I made my way toward this red circle, the floor was so cold beneath my bare feet that it seemed I was walking on ice. Salmelu was waiting for me inside the ring of his countrymen. He had his sword drawn, and Lord Issur stood by his side. Although it took me only a few moments to join him there, with Maram acting as my second, it seemed like almost forever. Then we began the rituals that precede any duel. Salmelu handed his sword to Maram, who rubbed its long, gleaming blade with a white cloth soaked in brandy, and I gave Lord Issur mine. After this cleansing was finished and our swords returned, we closed our eyes for a few moments of meditation to cleanse our minds.

'Very good,' King Hadaru called out at last. 'Are the witnesses ready?'

I opened my eyes to see the ring of Ishkans nod their heads and affirm that they were indeed ready. Maram and Master Juwain now stood among them toward the east of the ring, and they both smiled at me grimly.

'Are the combatants ready?'

Salmelu, standing before me with his sword held in two hands and cocked by the side of his head, smiled confidently and called out, 'I'm ready, Sire. Sar Valashu was lucky at chess – let's see how long his luck holds here.'

The King waited for me to speak, then finally said, 'And you, Valashu Elahad?'

'Yes,' I told him. 'Let's get this over.'

'A challenge has been made and accepted,' King Hadaru said in a sad, heavy voice. 'You must now fight to defend your honor. In the name of the One and all of our ancestors who have stood on this earth before us, you may begin.'

For a few moments no one moved. So quiet was the ring of knights and nobles around us that it seemed no one even breathed. Some duels lasted no longer than this. A quick rush, a lightning stroke of steel flashing through the air, and as often as not, one of the combatants' heads would be sent rolling across the floor.

But Salmelu and I faced each other across a few feet of a blood-red circle of wood, taking our time. Asaru had once observed that a true duel between Valari knights resembled nothing so much as a catfight without the hideous screeching and yowling. As if our two bodies were connected by a terrible tension, we began circling each other with an excruciating slowness. After a few moments, we paused to stand utterly still. And then we were moving again, measuring distances, looking for any weakness or hesitation in the other's eyes. I felt sweat running down my sides and my heart beating like a hammer up through my head; I breathed deeply, trying to keep my muscles relaxed yet ready to explode into motion at the slightest impulse. I circled slowly around Salmelu with my sword held lightly in my hands, waiting, waiting, waiting . . .

And then there was no time. As if a signal had been given, we suddenly sprang at each other in a flurry of flashing swords. Steel rang against steel, and then we locked for a moment, pushing and straining with all our might against each other, trying to free our blades for a deadly cut. We grunted and gasped, and Salmelu's hot breath broke in quick bursts against my face. And then we leapt back from each other and whirled about before suddenly closing again. Steel met steel, once, twice, thrice, and then I aimed a blow downward that might have split him in two. But it missed, and his sword burned the air scarcely an inch above my head.

114

And then I heard Salmelu cry out as if in pain; I cried out myself to feel a sudden sharp agony cut through my leg almost down to the bone.

'Look!' Lord Mestivan called out in his high, nervous voice. 'He's cut! Salmelu has been cut!'

As Salmelu and I stood away from each other for a moment to look for another opening, I noticed a long, red gash splitting the blue silk of his trousers along his thigh. It seemed that my blow hadn't altogether missed him after all. The gash ran with fresh blood, but it didn't spurt, so most likely he wasn't fatally wounded. It was a miracle, I thought, that I had wounded him at all. Asaru had always said that I was very good with the sword if I didn't let myself become distracted, but I had never believed him.

And clearly the Ishkans suffered from the same disbelief. Gasps of astonishment broke from knights and lords in the ring around me. I heard Lord Nadhru call out, 'He's drawn first blood! The Elahad has!'

Standing across the circle from him, Maram let out a sudden, bellowing cheer. He might have hoped that Salmelu and I would put away our swords then, but the duel wouldn't end until one of us yielded.

Salmelu was determined that this would not be him. The steel I had put in his leg had sent a thrill of fear through him, and his whole body trembled with a panic to destroy me. I felt this dreadful emotion working at me like ice rubbed along my limbs, paralyzing my will to fight. I remembered my vow never to kill again, and I felt the strength bleed away from me. And in my moment of hesitation, Salmelu struck.

He sprang off his good leg straight at me, whirling his sword at my head, all the while snarling and spitting out his malice like a cat. Once again, his hate became my hate, and the madness of it was like a fire burning my eyes. As he cut at me, I barely managed to get my sword up to parry his. Again and again he swung his sword against mine, and the sound of steel against steel rang out into the hall like the beating of a blacksmith's hammer. Somehow I managed to lock swords with him to forestall this furious onslaught. In breaking free, however, he lunged straight toward my heart. It was only by the miracle of my gift that I felt the point pushing through my breast – and then pulled frantically aside a moment before it actually did so. But the point took me in my side beneath my arm. His sword drove clean through the knotted muscle there and out my back. I cried out for all to hear as he wrenched his sword free; I jumped backwards and held my sword in my good hand as I waited for him to come for me again.

'Second blood to Ishka!' someone near me called out. 'The third blood will tell!'

115

I stood gasping for breath as I watched Salmelu watching me. He took his time circling nearer to me; he moved as if in great pain, careful of his wounded leg. My left arm hung useless by my side; in my right hand, I gripped my long, heavy kalama, the bright blade that my father had given me. Experience should have told me that our respective wounds hampered each of us almost equally. But my fear told me something else. I was almost certain that Salmelu would soon find a way to cut through my feeble defenses. I felt myself almost ready to give up. But the combat, I reminded myself, wouldn't end until one of us yielded – yielded in death.

Again, Salmelu came at me. His little jaw worked up and down as if he were already chewing open my entrails. He now seemed supremely confident of cutting me open there – or in some other vital place. He had the strength and quickness of wielding his sword with two practiced arms, while my best advantage was in being able to dance about and leap out of his way. But the circle was small, and it seemed inevitable that he would soon catch me up near the edge of it. If I tried to break free from the ring of honor, angry Ishkan hands would push me back, into his sword. If I stood my ground, sword against sword, he would surely kill me. The seeming certainty of my approaching death unnerved me. Despite the fury of the battle, I began sweating and shivering. So badly did my body tremble that I could hardly hold my sword.

It was my gift, I believe, that saved me. It let me feel the intended devastation of his flashing sword and avoid it by a feather's edge, by a breath. And more, it opened me to much else. I sensed the deep calm of Master Juwain meditating at the edge of the circle, and my hate for Salmelu began dying away. I remembered my mother's love for me and her plea that I should someday return to Mesh; I remembered my father's last words to me: that I must always remember who I was. And who was I, really? I suddenly knew that I was not only Valashu Elahad who held a heavy sword in a tired hand, but the one who walked always beside me and would remain standing when I died: watching, waiting, whispering, shining. To this one who watched, the world and all things within it moved with an exquisite slowness: a scything sword no less than an Ishkan lord named Salmelu. I saw his kalama's steel flash at me then in a long, sweeping arc. There came an immense stillness and clarity. In that timeless moment, I leaned back to avoid the point, which ripped a ragged tear across my tunic. And then, quick as a lightning bolt, I slashed my sword in a counterstroke. As I had intended, it cut through the muscles of both of Salmelu's arms and across his chest. Blood leapt into the air, and his sword went flying out of his hands. It clanged against the floor even as Salmelu screamed out that I had killed him.

But, of course, I hadn't. The wound wasn't fatal, although it was terrible enough, and he would never hold a sword so easily again.

'Damn you, Elahad!' he snarled at me. He gazed down in disbelief at his bloody sword and the gashes it had torn in the wood of the floor. And then he looked at me in hatred as he waited for me to take his life away.

'Finish him!' King Hadaru commanded in a voice stricken with grief. 'What are you waiting for?'

As the blood flowed in streams from Salmelu's useless arms, his hateful eyes drilled into me. I felt his malice eating at *my* eyes like red, twisting worms. I wanted nothing more than to kill him so that I could keep this dreadful thing from devouring me or anyone else.

'Send him back to the stars!' Maram cried out.

The Brotherhoods teach that death is but a door that opens upon another world. The Valari believe that it is only a short journey not to be feared. I knew differently. Death was the end of everything and the beginning of the great nothingness. It was the dying of the light and a terrible cold. I looked at Salmelu almost ready to collapse in terror into the pool of his own blood, and I was even more afraid to kill him than I was to be killed.

'No,' I said to King Hadaru, 'I can't.'

'All duels are to the death,' he reminded me. 'If you stay your sword, you do my son a grave dishonor and bring no honor to yourself.'

I gripped my sword hard in my trembling hand. I watched as Salmelu's strength finally gave way and he collapsed to the floor. From the blood-soaked boards there, he stared up at me fearfully, all the while waiting, waiting, waiting . . .

'No, there will be no killing,' I finally said. 'No more killing.'

I walked over to Maram, who handed me a cloth to clean the blood from my sword. Then, with a loud ringing sound, I slid it back into its sheath.

'So be it,' King Hadaru said to me.

At that moment, the swords of Lord Issur and Lord Nadhru – and two dozen others – whipped out and pointed at me. By denying Salmelu his honorable death, I had shamed him even more seriously than he had me. And now his brother and friends meant to avenge my deadly insult.

'I challenge you!' Lord Issur shouted at me.

'I challenge you, too!' Lord Nadhru snarled out. 'If Lord Issur falls, then you will fight me!'

And so it went, various knights and lords around the ring of honor calling out their challenges to me.

'Hold!' King Hadaru commanded. He pointed his long finger at the blood still flowing from my side. 'Have you forgotten he's wounded?'

Valari codes forbade the issue of challenges to wounded warriors. And so Lord Nadhru and the others very angrily put away their swords.

'You have dishonored my house,' King Hadaru said, gazing at me. 'And so you are no longer welcome in it.'

He turned to look at Lord Nadhru, Lord Issur and other knights, and finally at his gravely wounded son. Then, in a trembling voice, he said, 'Valashu Elahad, you are no longer welcome in my kingdom. No one is to give you fire, bread or salt. My son has promised you safe passage through Ishka, and that you shall have. No knight or warrior shall harm you or delay your journey. But what happens after you cross our borders to another land is only justice and your fate.'

The sudden gleam in Lord Nadhru's eyes gave me to understand that he and his friends would pursue me into other kingdoms to exact vengeance – perhaps they would pursue me to the ends of the earth.

'So be it,' I said to King Hadaru.

Master Juwain stepped forward then and said, 'Your son is bleeding and should be tended immediately. I would like to offer my help and –'

'Do you think we don't have healers here?' King Hadaru snapped at him. 'Go with Sar Valashu and tend *his* wound. Go now before I forget the law of our land and make a challenge of my own!'

At this insult to his master, Maram shook his thick head like a bull. He cast a long look at Irisha standing across the circle from us. And then he called out, 'King Hadaru! Things shouldn't end this way! If I may speak, then I would hope to –'

'No, you may *not* speak, Maram Marshayk,' the King rudely told him. 'Men who covet other men's wives are not welcome in Ishka, either. Go with your friends unless you'd like a taste of Ishkan steel.'

Maram licked his lips as he looked at the kalama that King Hadaru wore. Then he turned to me and said, 'Come on, Val, we'd better go.'

There was nothing else do to. When a king ordered you to leave his kingdom, it was foolish to remain and argue.

And so I turned to lead the way back into the anteroom where I had left my armor. The Ishkan lords and ladies only reluctantly broke the ring of honor to allow me to pass from the circle. It was something of a miracle that no one drew his sword. But as we made our way through the long, cold hall, I felt dozens of pairs of eyes stabbing into me like so many kalamas. The pain of it was almost worse than that of the wound Salmelu had opened in my side.

8

The Ishkans let us alone while Master Juwain dressed my wound in that cold little room off the main hall. It was a strange coincidence, he remarked, that Salmelu had cut me so near the scratch that the arrow had made in my side. He told me that I was lucky that Salmelu's sword had cut the muscle lengthwise, along the grain. Such wounds usually healed of their own with no more treatment than being sown shut. That is, they healed if given the chance to heal, which I would not now have.

It hurt as Master Juwain punctured my flesh with a sharp, little needle and piece of thread. Working on my armor and surcoat hurt even more. Master Juwain fashioned a sling for my dangling arm, and then it was time to go.

We left King Hadaru's palace as we had entered it. Outside, at the bottom of the stairs beneath the front door, we found the grooms waiting for us with our horses. Lord Nadhru and Lord Issur – and an entire squadron of Ishkan knights mounted on their stamping horses – were waiting for us there, too.

'Oh, my Lord!' Maram called out when he saw them. 'It seems we have an escort.'

Master Juwain smiled grimly as he looked from the knights to me. Then he asked, 'Can you ride?'

'Yes,' I said. With a sharp gasp, I used my good arm to pull myself onto Altaru's back. The great beast's glossy coat was like black jade in the moonlight; he angrily shook his head at the Ishkan knights and their horses. 'Let's go,' I said.

We made our way slowly down the tree-lined road leading away from King Hadaru's palace. The sound of the horses' iron-shod hooves striking the paving stones seemed very loud against the stillness of the quiet grounds. It was now full night and falling cold. In the sky there were many stars. They rained their silver light upon the tinkling fountains and the rows of flowers that perfumed the air. Even though I vowed not to do so, I turned in my saddle to see this bright starlight glinting off the points of the Ishkans' lances and armor. Like me, they wore steel mail and not their diamond battle armor. They followed us at a distance of perhaps a hundred yards; as we turned onto the road leading to the bridge that crossed the Tushur, I was afraid that they intended to follow us all the way to Anjo.

'Shouldn't we return to Mesh?' Maram asked as rode his tired sorrel beside me. 'If we go on to Anjo, the Ishkans will kill us as soon as we cross the border.'

'If we return to Mesh,' I told him, 'they'll likely attack us as soon as we enter the Telemesh Gate.'

I went on to say that my death there, on Meshian soil, at the hands of the Ishkans, would make war between our two kingdoms almost certain.

'Perhaps *you* should return to Mesh,' I said to Maram. I looked at Master Juwain riding his sorrel to my right. 'And you, too, sir. It's not you that the Ishkans want.'

'No, it is not,' Master Juwain agreed. 'But if you journey without us, who will tend you if you fall to fever? And we can't just leave you alone to the Ishkans' lances, can we, Brother Maram?'

Maram, casting a glance back at Lord Nadhru and the other knights, let out a little moan of distress and said, 'Ah, no, I suppose we can't. But if we can't go back to Mesh, what are we to do?'

That, it seemed, was the question of the moment. Four points there are to the world, and one of these we could not follow. And as for the other three, each had its perils. To the west rose a wall of almost impassable mountains; beyond it were the warriors of the fierce Adirii tribe of the Sarni who patrolled the vast gray plains of the Wendrush. To the east, just beyond the Tushur, we would meet the King's Road which might take us into the kingdom of Taron. We could follow this road to Nar, where we would intersect the ancient Nar Road leading all the way to Tria. But the Taroners, while no friends of Ishka, were neither friendly with Mesh. In our war with Waas, Taron had sent knights to aid their ancient ally, and many of these my brothers had killed. Then too, the road to Nar led east, while if we were to make our quest, we must eventually turn around and journey northwest, toward Tria.

'It's only sixty miles to Anjo,' I said, looking across the dark landscape toward the bright north star. 'In that direction lies our best hope.'

'How so?' Master Juwain asked me. 'Brother Maram is right. With the Duke of Adar under King Hadaru's fist, the Ishkans will feel free to attack us as soon as we cross the Aru-Adar Bridge.'

'That's true,' I said. 'But there are other dukedoms in Anjo where the Ishkans might fear to ride. And other ways to cross into them.'

Without explaining too much, I told them that it was my intention to cross the border into Anjo much to the west of the bridge, where the waters of the Aru River did not flow so fiercely. Under the cover of night, we would simply ride into the mountains and lose the Ishkans somewhere in the thick, sloping forests.

'And *that* is your plan?' Maram said to me.

'Can you think of a better one?'

Maram waved his hand toward the lights of Loviisa glowing at the foot of the hill beneath us. 'King Hadaru's knights won't touch us so long as we remain in Ishka. Why not find an inn for the night and hope that morning will find his heart has softened?'

'His heart won't soften that soon,' I said. 'And besides, have you forgotten that he's denied us fire, bread and salt? So long as we remain in Ishka, we'll have only our supplies to eat, and after they're gone, we'll starve.'

Since Maram liked little in the world more than his evening meal, he rubbed his empty belly and agreed that we should leave Ishka as soon as possible. Neither he nor Master Juwain could think of a better course than the one I had suggested. And so we rode on into the night.

Loviisa, although not a large city, was spread out on both sides of the Tushur. We quickly found our way through its streets back to the North Road and the bridge that spanned the river. This great archway, with its stone pylons sunk down into the river's gurgling, black waters, was lit by torches along its rails. Lord Issur and his knights followed us across it. They kept a good hundred yards to our rear: not so close that they would have to suffer our presence, but not so far that we might lose them in the maze of streets winding through the northern half of the city.

Soon the buildings thinned out and gave way to the rolling farmland surrounding Loviisa. The moon shone upon fields of barley and wheat, whose new leaves glistened in the soft light. More than once, Maram cast a longing glance toward one of the little houses in the fields off the side of the road. We all listened to the lowing of cows and smelled the maddening aroma of roasting meat that wafted on the wind. We were very hungry, but all we had to eat was a few wheels of cheese and some battle biscuits pulled from the pack horses' bags. Maram complained that the iron-hard biscuits hurt his teeth; he bemoaned my duel with Salmelu, and then chided me, saying, 'Why couldn't you at least wait until *after* the feast before drawing on him?'

Eating the biscuits hurt my teeth, too. Everything about that nighttime flight from Ishka hurt. As always, Altaru sensed my condition and moved so as to ease the discomfiture of my wound. Even so, I could feel my outraged body throbbing with every beat of my heart. Around midnight, some clouds came up, and it rained. It grew suddenly colder. Maram pulled his cloak tightly around himself and then shook his fist at the sky as he growled out, 'I'm cold; I'm tired; I'm wet – and I'm still hungry. The merciless Ishkans can't expect us to ride all night, can they?'

It seemed they could. Soon after that, Master Juwain insisted that we stop to make camp for the night. But even as we were tethering our horses to the fence edging a farmer's fields, Lord Nadhru came thundering up the road on a huge war horse. I could barely make out his sharp features through the spattering of the rain. But his quick eyes found me easily enough. He stared straight at me and said, 'You've been denied any hospitality while in Ishka. Mount your horses, and don't try to stop again.'

'Are you mad?' Maram snapped at him. 'We've ridden since dawn, and our horses are exhausted, we are too, and –'

'Mount your horses,' Lord Nadhru commanded again, 'or we'll bind you with ropes and drag you from Ishka!'

Just then Lord Issur came riding up. He sat high on his horse while he regarded us through the rain. He was a spirited, graceful man, perhaps even kind in his own way, and I thought I might have liked him if we had met under different circumstances.

'Please mount your horses,' he told us. 'We've no liking to do as Lord Nadhru has said.'

Master Juwain stepped forward and looked up at these two towering knights on their horses. Although he was a small man, it seemed that he might be able to keep them at bay by the power of his voice alone.

'My friend is badly wounded and needs rest,' he said. 'If you have any compassion, you'll let us be.'

'Compassion?' Lord Issur cried out. 'We should all strive for such a noble estate, but does Sar Valashu? If he had any compassion at all, he would have slain my brother rather than condemning him to live in shame.'

'At least your brother is still alive,' Master Juwain said. 'And so long as he continues to draw breath, there's always hope that he'll find a way to undo his shame, is there not?'

'Perhaps,' Lord Issur said.

Master Juwain pointed at me and said, 'This journey might kill Valashu. *His* best hope lies in finding rest as soon as possible.'

'You don't understand,' Lord Issur said, shaking his head sadly. 'For him, there *is* no hope. He made his choice, and he must live by it –

and die by it. Now please mount your horses, or I'll have to let Lord Nadhru fetch his ropes.'

There was no arguing with him. Kind he might be, deep in his heart, but there was steel in him, too, and he seemed determined to execute King Hadaru's wishes no matter how bravely Master Juwain stood before him.

After he and Lord Salmelu had ridden back to the other knights, we prepared to set out again. Then Maram suddenly drew his sword and shook it at the dark road in their direction.

'How they speak to you!' he called out to me. 'Didn't they see what you did to Salmelu? *I've* never seen such sword work in my life! Tie us with ropes, they say! Why, if they even lay a hand on you, I'll –'

'Maram, please,' I broke in. 'Save your fight for our passage into Anjo. Now let's ride while we still can.'

The Sarni warriors, it is said, eat and sleep in the saddle, and let a little blood from a vein in their horses' necks for drink. Riding hard, they can cover a hundred miles in a day. We rode hard ourselves that night, although we did not cover nearly so many as a hundred miles. But we did well enough. As the rain pelted my cloak and the farmland gave way to rougher country, I struggled to remain awake. The pain in my side helped me. As for Maram, more than once he nodded off with a loud snoring, only to be jolted rudely awake when he felt himself slipping off his horse. Master Juwain, however, seemed to need little sleep. He admitted that his daily meditations had nearly overcome his need for such sweet oblivion. Beneath his vow of nonviolence and his kindly ways, he was a very tough man, as many of the Brothers are.

Sometime before morning, the rain stopped and the clouds pulled back from the night's last stars. Daybreak found us in a broad, green valley more than half the way to Anjo. To the east, a low range of mountains cut the golden-red disk of the rising sun. Its streaming rays fell upon us, not so warmly that it dried our garments, but not so weakly that we didn't all feel a little cheered. To the west, framed by the great snow-capped peaks of the Shoshan Range, the sunlight glinted off an expanse of blue water. I guessed that this must be Lake Osh, which was the largest and only real lake in Ishka. From the northern shore of its gleaming waters to the Ishkan border, if I remembered correctly, was a distance of only fifteen miles.

'Will I insult you,' Maram asked as he rode by my side, 'if I observe that this is a beautiful country? Almost as beautiful as Mesh.'

'Beauty can never be an insult,' I told him. I looked at him and tried to smile. 'Does it distress you that you might have remained to appreciate it if you hadn't ogled King Hadaru's wife?'

'Ogle, you say?' Maram's face flushed beet-red with resentment. 'But I wasn't ogling her!'

'What were you doing, then?'

'Ah, I was only *appreciating* her. You have to be grateful to a world that could bring such beauty into life.'

I smiled again and said, 'You sound as if you're in love with her.'

'Well, I am.'

'But you only just met her – you weren't even properly presented. How could you love her?'

'Does a fish need an introduction to love the water? Does a flower need more than a moment to love the sun?'

'But Irisha,' I said, 'is a woman.'

'Ah, yes, a woman indeed – just so. When you touch a woman's eyes with your own, you touch her soul. And then you know.'

'Do you think it's always so simple, then?'

'Of course it is – what could be simpler than love?'

What, indeed? Because I had no answer for him, I just rubbed my tired eyes and smiled.

Then Maram continued, 'How old do you think Irisha is – eighteen? Nineteen? King Hadaru has set himself to planting very old seed in some very fertile earth. I predict that nothing will grow from it. He won't live forever, either. And then someday I'll return for her.'

'But what about Behira?' I asked him. 'I thought you loved her.'

'Ah, sweet Behira. Well, I *do* love her – I think. But I'm sure I love Irisha even more.'

I wondered if Maram would ever return for either of these women – or even return at all. Even as the sparrows chirped in the fields around us and the sun began its climb into the sky, King Hadaru was still very much alive in his palace, and his knights were still pursuing us. A couple of hundred yards behind us, their brightly colored surcoats flapped in the early wind as they urged their horses forward.

We rode, too, as hard and steadily as we dared. More than once we stopped to feed and water the horses. The Ishkans made no complaint against these brief breaks. They might press us until we dropped from exhaustion, but being knights, they would have no wish to kill our horses. The morning deepened around us as the sun grew ever brighter. It heated up my armor, and I was grateful for the surcoat that covered most of its searing, steel rings. The warmth of the day made me drowsy, and I scarcely noticed the rocky slabs of the mountains to the east or the higher peaks that lay ahead of us. By noon, we had passed well beyond Yarwan, a pretty little town that reminded me of Lashku in Mesh. I guessed that the border to Anjo – and the Aru-Adar Bridge –

lay only ten or twelve miles farther up the road. And so I eased Altaru to a halt, and turned to talk with Maram and Master Juwain.

'It would be best,' I told them, 'if you go on from here without me.'

'What do you mean?' Maram asked.

I pointed up the road, which led north like a ribbon of gleaming stone.

'The Ishkans won't follow you across the bridge.'

'But where are you going?'

Now I pointed west to the hilly country that lay between Lake Osh and the mountains to the north.

'If what my father's minstrel once told me is true,' I said, 'there's a way through the mountains farther to the west. We'll part company for a few days and meet in Sauvo.'

In Sauvo, I explained, King Danashu would give us shelter, and there the Ishkans would not go.

Now Master Juwain nudged his horse over to me and touched his cool hand to my forehead. 'You're very hot, Val – you have a fever, and that might kill you before the Ishkans do. You need rest, and soon.'

'That might be,' I said. I closed my eyes for a moment as I tried to remember why I had set out on this endless journey. 'The world needs peace, too, but must go on all the same.'

'We won't leave you alone,' Master Juwain said.

'No, we won't,' Maram told me. Then, as he realized what he had committed himself to, doubt began to eat at his face, and he summoned up the bravado to bluster his way through it. 'We'll follow even through the gates of hell, my friend.'

'How did you know,' I said with a smile, 'where we were going?'

And with that, I turned Altaru toward the west and left the road. We began riding easily through the soft, green hills. The Ishkans, obviously alarmed at our new tack, tightened their ranks and followed us more closely. The soil beneath our horses' trampling hooves was too poor for crops, and so there were few farms about. Few trees grew, either, having been cut long ago for firewood or the Ishkans' wasteful building projects. I had hoped for more cover than this from Lord Issur's and Lord Nadhru's unrelenting vigilance. In truth, I had hoped for a thick forest into which we might dash wildly trying to make our escape.

There *were* forests in this part of Ishka, but only on the steep slopes of the mountains rising up to the north. I considered riding straight into them, but thought the better of it. I doubted if I or the horses, even Altaru, had any strength left for negotiating such rocky terrain. And even if we evaded Lord Issur and his knights, we would still have to make our way through one of the three passes along this part of the border. I was afraid that any of the garrisons guarding them might hold us up until Lord Issur tracked us down. The only unguarded pass – if it could be called that – still lay some miles ahead across these bare, undulating foothills. It took all my will to keep Altaru moving toward it, but I could think of nothing else to do.

And so I followed the sun, and Maram and Master Juwain followed me. It was the longest day of my life. My side felt as if Salmelu's sword was still stuck there, and every bone in my body, particularly those of my trembling legs, hurt. After some hours, the country around us seemed to dissolve into a sea of blazing green. I dozed in my saddle and I dreamed feverish dreams. More than once, I almost toppled off Altaru's back; but each time he moved with a knowing grace to check my fall. I marveled at the trust he had in me, leading him on toward a destination that none of us had ever seen. My trust in him – his surefootedness and his plain good sense – grew with every mile we put behind us; it seemed even more solid than the earth over which we rode.

Nightfall made our journey no easier. Indeed, if not for the full moon that rose over the hills about us, we wouldn't have been able to journey at all. I tried to set my gaze on a great, white-capped peak that swelled against the black sky straight ahead; there the lesser mountains to the north met the Shoshan Range like a great hinge of rock. But my eyes were dry as stones, and I could hardly keep them open. I was so tired that I couldn't even eat the pieces of bread that Master Juwain kept trying to urge into my mouth like a mother bird. It was all I could do to gulp down a few swallows of water. Soon, I knew, I would slip from Altaru's back no matter the great horse's agility and love for me. I would find oblivion in the sweet heather that blanketed the hills. And then Lord Nadhru would have to come for me with his ropes.

It was the Lightstone, I believe, that kept me going. I held the image of this golden cup close to my heart. From its deep hollows welled a cool, clear liquid that seemed to flow into me and give my body a new strength. It woke me up, at least enough so that my eyes didn't close in darkness.

It awakened me, too, to the sorry state of my friends, for they were nearly as tired as I was. And they were even more fearful of the unknown lands ahead. Their plight struck to my heart, and I vowed to do all that I could for them so long as any strength remained to me.

I rode side by side with them over the silver hills. And then, around midnight, just as we topped a hill crowned with many sharp rocks, I caught a moist, disturbing scent that jolted me wide awake. I stopped Altaru as I gazed at a depression in the generally rising terrain that seemed out of place. Patches of mist hung over it as of cotton balls floating in a great bowl. On the east side of it, the range of mountains along which we had been riding came to a sudden end. On the west side farther ahead of this dark scoop in the earth was the mountainous wall of the great Shoshan Range. Here, at last, was the hinge in the mountains that I had been seeking. And as I had hoped, the hinge was broken at its very joint, and the way into Anjo lay open before us.

'What is it?' Master Juwain said as he stared down across the moon-lit land.

Now a whiff of decay fell over me, and the air seemed suddenly colder. And then I said, 'It's a bog – and not a large one, either.'

I went on to tell both him and Maram what I knew about this unseemly break in the mountains. Indeed, it was more than unseemly, I said, it was an evil wound upon the land. For once, in the Age of Law, a mountain had stood upon this very spot. The Ishkans of old had named it Diamond Mountain in honor of the richest deposits of these gems ever to be found in the Morning Mountains. In their lust for wealth, they had used firestones to burn away layers of useless rock and uncover the veins of diamonds. Such wasteful mining, over hundreds of years, had burned away the entire mountain. It had left a poorly-drained depression that filled with silt and sand so that now, a whole age later, only a foul-smelling bog remained.

Maram, staring in horror at this miles-wide patch of ground, took me by the arm and said, 'You can't mean to ride down into that, can you? Not at night?'

If my father had taught me anything about war, it was that a king should never rely on mountains, rivers or forests – or even bogs – for protection. Such seemingly impenetrable natural barriers are often quite penetrable, sometimes much more readily than one might suspect. Often, hard work and a little daring sufficed for forcing one's way through them.

'Come on,' I said to Maram, 'it won't be so bad.'

'Oh no?' he said. 'Why do I suspect that it will be worse than bad?'

As we were debating the perils of bogs – Maram held that the quicksands in them could trap both man and horse and suck them down into a dreadful death – the Ishkans came riding up to us. Lord Issur and Lord Nadhru led eighteen grim-faced knights who seemed nearly as tired as we were. They sat shifting about uneasily in their saddles as the line of their horses stretched across the top of the hill.

'Sar Valashu!' Lord Issur called out to me. He pressed his horse a few paces closer to me and pointed down into the bog. 'As you can see, there is no way out of Ishka in this direction. Now you must return as you have come, and set out through one of the passes to the north.'

'No,' I said, looking down the line of his outstretched finger, 'we'll go this way.'

'Through the Black Bog?' he asked as his countrymen laughed uneasily. 'No, I think not.'

Maram wiped the sweat from his bulging forehead. 'The Black Bog, is it called? Excellent – now *there* is a name to inspire courage.'

'It will take more than courage,' Lord Nadhru put in, 'for you to cross it.'

'How so?' Maram asked.

'Because it is haunted,' Lord Nadhru said. 'There's something in there that devours men. No one who has ever gone into it has ever come out again.'

Now Master Juwain looked at me as I felt his belly suddenly tighten. But his steely will kept his fear from overcoming him; I smiled at him to honor his courage, and he smiled back.

To Lord Issur I said, 'Nevertheless, we will go into it.'

'No, you mustn't,' he said.

'Your father,' I told him, 'has said that we must leave Ishka. But surely the choice of our route out of it is ours to make.'

'Go back,' he urged me. There was a tightness in his own voice which I suspected he didn't like. 'It is death to go into this bog.'

'It is death for me to go into any of the passes if you follow so closely behind me.'

'There are worse things than death,' he said.

I stared down into the misty depression but said nothing.

'At least,' Lord Issur went on, nodding at Master Juwain and Maram, 'it will be your own death only. And you may die fighting with a sword in your hand.'

Just then, Altaru let out a whinny of impatience, and I patted his trembling neck to steady him. 'No, there's been enough fighting,' I said.

'Master Juwain?' Lord Issur called out. 'Prince Maram Marshayk – what will you do?'

In a voice as cool as the wind, Master Juwain affirmed that he would follow me into the bog. Maram looked at me for a long moment as our hearts beat together. And then, after taking a deep breath, he said that he would go with me, too. And then he muttered to the sky, 'Ah, the Black Bog indeed – why don't you just kill us here and save us the misery?'

For a moment it seemed that the Ishkans might do exactly that. The eighteen knights each gripped their lances more tightly as they looked at Lord Nadhru and Lord Issur and waited for their command.

'You must understand,' Lord Issur said to me, 'that it would be death as well for me to lead my men into the bog.'

128

'Perhaps,' I said.

'And that I will not do,' he told me.

I listened to the far-off howling of a wolf as I waited to see what he *would* do. Many miles before, I had foreseen that he might kill me on this very spot – and kill as well Master Juwain and Maram as witnesses to such a crime. But I had counted on him honoring Salmelu's promise that I wasn't to be harmed while on Ishkan soil. In the end, one is either a Valari or not.

'We won't follow where you're going,' he said. 'There's no need.'

At this, many of his knights sighed gratefully. But Lord Nadhru edged his horse closer to us and let his hand rest upon the hilt of his sword. To Lord Issur, he said, 'But what of the King's command that Sar Valashu and his friends leave Ishka?'

Again, Lord Issur pointed down into the bog. '*That* is no longer part of Ishka. It belongs to no kingdom on earth.'

He turned to me and said, 'Farewell, Valashu Elahad. You're a brave man, but a foolish one. We'll tell your countrymen, as we will our own, that you died in this accursed place.'

There was nothing to do then but go down into the bog. I said farewell to Lord Issur, then urged Altaru down the hill. Master Juwain and Maram, with the pack horses tied behind their sorrels, followed behind me. And so, for a few hundred yards, did the Ishkans. They watched us through the wavering moonlight to make sure that we did as we had said we would.

The slope of the hill gradually gave way to more even ground as we rode down into the depression. And the heather beneath our horses' hooves gave way to other vegetation: sedges and grasses and various kinds of moss. There was no clear line demarcating the bog from the land around it. But there came a point where the air grew suddenly colder and smelled even more pungently of decay. There Ataru suddenly planted his hooves in the moist ground and let out a great whinny. He shook his head at the mist-covered terrain before us, and would not go any farther.

'Come on, boy,' I said as I patted his neck. 'We have to do this.'

Master Juwain and Maram came up to us, and their horses pawed the ground uneasily, too.

'Come on,' I said again. 'It won't be so bad.'

I tried to clear my feverish head as Master Juwain had taught me. Some part of the calm I achieved must have passed into Altaru, for he turned his head to look back at me with his great, trusting eyes. And then he began moving slowly forward, into the bog.

The other horses followed him, and their hooves made moist

squishing sounds in the cold ground. It was strange, I thought, that although the ground over which we rode oozed with water, it seemed solid enough to look at. In few places were there actually patches of standing water. These almost black meres we avoided easily enough as we kept pressing forward. Our path through the bog, while not perfectly straight, was direct enough that I was sure we would soon be out of it.

I tried to keep us oriented toward the north so that we wouldn't lose direction in this trackless waste. After a while, I looked back to fix our position by the hill where we had left the Ishkans. Although it was hard to see very far, even in the bright moonlight, I thought I could make out their forms far off as they watched us from the top of the hill. And then a mist came up, covering us as it obliterated all sight of them. When it pulled back a few minutes later, the hill seemed barren of knights, or indeed, of any living thing. I couldn't even perceive the jagged rocks along the hill's crest. The hill itself seemed flatter and wider; it was as if the heavy air over the bog were like a spectacle maker's lens that distorted the world around us.

'Val,' Maram called out from behind me, 'I feel sick – it's like I'm falling.'

I, too, felt a strange, sinking sensation in the pit of my stomach. It was something like the time Asaru and I had jumped off the cliffs above Lake Silash into the dark, freezing waters. It seemed that the bog was pulling at us, pulling us down into the inconstant earth, even though at no point did its seeping water rise much above the horses' fetlocks.

'It will be all right,' I said as the mist slid along the ground and wrapped its gray-black tendrils around us. 'If we keep moving, it will be all right.'

And then, even as the mist opened slightly and I looked up at the sky, I knew that it would *not* be all right. For something about this accursed opening in the earth was distorting the sight of the very stars. The brightest of them – Solaru, Aras and Varshara – seemed strangely dulled and slightly out of place. I blinked my eyes and shook my head in disbelief. And the feeling of falling down into an endless dark hole grew only stronger.

'Maram,' I said. 'Master Juwain – there's something wrong here!'

I turned to tell them that we should stay close together. But when I peered through the swirling mist, I couldn't see either of them. And that was very strange because I had thought they were no more than ten yards behind me.

'Maram!' I called out. 'Master Juwain – where are you?'

I stopped Altaru and listened as carefully as I could. But the bog was quiet and deathly still. Not even a cricket chirped.

'Maram! Master Juwain!'

The shock of being suddenly alone was like a hammer striking me beneath my ribs. For many moments, I had trouble breathing the dank, stifling air. Had both Maram and Master Juwain, I wondered, plunged into a quicksand that had instantly sucked them down without a sound? Had they simply vanished from the earth?

I felt the sweat beading along my skin beneath my layers of armor and clothing. My whole body felt icy cold even as I shivered uncontrollably. For a moment, I covered my forehead and rubbed my fevered eyes. Was I mad, I wondered? Was I ill to my death and forever lost in this choking mist?

'Altaru,' I whispered as I stroked the coarse, long hair of his mane, 'where are they? Can you smell them?'

Altaru nickered nervously, then turned his head right and left. He pawed the sodden ground and waited for me to tell him what to do.

'Maram! Master Juwain!' I shouted. 'Why can't you hear me?'

There came a booming sound then as if the whole earth was shaking. It took me a while to realize that it was only the beating of my heart and not some gigantic drum. And then Maram called to me – but not from behind me as I had expected. A moment later, the mist parted again, and I could see him and Master Juwain riding their horses barely twenty yards ahead of me.

'Why did you leave me?' I called out as I rode up to them.

'Leave *you*?' Maram said. He leaned over on his horse and grasped my good arm with his as if to reassure himself that I was really there. 'It was you who left us.'

'Don't play games, Maram,' I said. 'How did you get ahead of me?'

'How did you get behind us?'

Because I had no strength to argue, I just sat astride Altaru looking at him in relief. I had never thought that the sight of his thick, brown beard and weepy eyes could please me so greatly.

Then Master Juwain came over to us and said, 'There *is* something wrong with this place. I've never heard of anything like it. Why don't we tie the horses together and stay closer to each other now?'

Both Maram and I agreed that this was an excellent idea. With some rope that we found in one of the horses' packs, we tied the sorrels close behind Altaru, and the pack horses behind them.

'Let's go,' I said, not wanting to spend another minute there. 'We must have come at least a couple of miles. It can't be much more than that to drier ground.'

131

Again, with me in the lead, we moved off toward what I thought was due north. In places, the mist was so thick that we couldn't see more than ten feet in any direction. The ground beneath us now was mostly of large, spongy mosses that made sucking sounds as the horses trampled over them. The air was cold and wet and smelled of dark scents that were strange to me. There were no animals to be seen or to be heard either. Even so, as we made our way across the drowned sedges and grasses and muck, I felt something following us. Although I thought that it couldn't be an animal – and certainly nothing like a wolf or a bear – I had an uneasy sensation that it could smell me from miles away even through the thickest of mists. And then I closed my eyes for a moment, and I was certain of nothing at all. For in my mind, I could see gray shapes on horseback riding hard in our pursuit. I was afraid that Lord Issur had changed his mind after all, and was coming to murder us.

I pressed Altaru more urgently then; the other horses, tied to my saddle with short lengths of rope, quickened their paces. We rode in near-silence for what seemed a long time. I couldn't guess how many miles we covered, for both time and distance in this terrible bog seemed to be different from that of the mountains and valleys in which I had spent my whole life. With every bit of sodden ground that we passed over, the sense that something or someone was following us grew stronger. I couldn't understand why we hadn't found the bog's northern edge and the safety of Anjo. And then, even as the mist thinned a little, Maram let out a cry of terror because he had found something else.

'Look!' he said as he pointed at the ground ahead of us. 'Oh, my – oh, my Lord!'

Now the moonlight seemed to wax stronger for a moment as it fell upon a form half-sunken into the mosses and muck. It was a man, I saw, or rather the remains of one. His bones, gleaming a dull white, were spread out along the ground. His eyeless skull seemed to stare straight at us, and his finger joints were wrapped around the hilt of a great, rusted sword. Almost the whole of his skeleton was encased in a suit of slowly rotting, diamond-studded armor. Its hundreds of stones, although smeared with mud, still had some fire to them. They caught my eye with their sparkle even as Maram and Master Juwain drew up beside me.

'Look!' Maram said again. He pointed to the nearby skeleton of a horse lying down among the mosses. 'How long do you think this knight has been here?'

I looked at the style of the armor, particularly at the aventail that hung down from the back of the knight's helmet, and I said, 'Perhaps a hundred years – perhaps more.'

'Why do you think he came here?'

'That's hard to say.'

'What do you think killed him, then?'

I studied the knight's armor, looking for any sign that it had been pierced or crushed. I shrugged my shoulders, then shook my head.

'Do you think he got lost?' Maram asked. 'Do you think he ran out of food and starved to death?'

There was a note of near-panic in his voice, and Master Juwain took hold of his arm and gently shook him. He said, 'There are some things it's better not to ask and better not to know. Now let's leave this place before we unnerve each other completely.'

Although Maram quickly agreed to that, he was already so unnerved that he didn't even suggest looting the knight of his armor, as I feared he might. We rode hard then for an hour or so. At those rare moments when I could see the sky, I tried to steer by the stars. But they kept shifting about in strange new patterns that didn't make sense to me. Master Juwain suggested trying to fix our position by the bright disk of the moon, and this I tried to do. But then, some miles from the spot where we had left the knight, I looked up to see half the moon missing as if some great beast had taken a bite out of it. I shook my head in disbelief, and sat there on top of Altaru blinking my eyes.

'Perhaps it's only an eclipse,' Master Juwain said to encourage me.

I looked at him and smiled as I shook my head. And then, as Maram let out a shriek of terror, I looked up at the sky again, and the moon was completely gone.

'Let's ride,' I said. 'Let's find a way out of here before we all lose our minds.'

And so yet again we set out in a direction that might have been north, south, east or west – or some entirely new direction that would take us nowhere forever. We rode hard for what seemed many hours. There was nothing to do but listen to the splashing that the horses made and breathe the chill air. Once, the stars returned to their familiar positions within their ancient constellations, and more than once, the full moon again burned a silvery circle through the black sky. We might have taken comfort from this bright disk, but then, as we were gazing up at it, a dark shape like that of a dragon or an impossibly huge bat flew straight across it. And then a moment later the moon vanished, and the mist closed around us like a wet, gray shroud.

'Val,' Maram said to me in a low voice, 'I'm afraid.'

'We all are,' I told him. 'But we have to keep going – there's nothing else to do.'

And then, seeing that my words had done little to cheer him, I nudged

Altaru closer to him and gripped his hand in mine. I said, 'It's all right –
I won't let anything happen to you.'

As we rode on in silence over the sucking mosses, I was very afraid
that the pain and fever of my wounded side would soon set me to
screaming. But even worse than this throbbing agony was the sensation
of something squirming in my head, clawing my eyes from inside. I
could still feel something or someone following us through the mist.
And something else – it felt like a vast, black, bloated spider – was
watching us and waiting for us even as it somehow called us toward
the darkest of places at the bog's very center. The more I tried to evade
this dreadful thing, the closer I seemed to be drawn to it – and Maram
and Master Juwain with me. It was only a matter of time, I thought,
until it seized me and tore me open to suck out my mind.

Before fear maddened me completely, I tried to use my mind to reason
our way out of the bog. Hadn't we been traveling through it for at least
twelve hours? Shouldn't we then have covered at least forty miles and
not merely the four or five miles of the bog's true width? Were we
moving in circles? Was the black, rippling mere to our right new to
us or one that we had left behind many miles ago? And if we kept the
mountains of the Shoshan Range always to our left – during those rare
moments when the mist lifted and we could see them – shouldn't we
have long since found our way into Anjo?

'Val, I'm so tired,' Maram said to me as our horses stepped through
a patch of sodden grasses. He waved his hand in front of his face as if
to dispel the mist nearly blinding us. 'Will this night never end?'

No, I suddenly thought, *the neverness of night has no end.*

'Where *are* we?' he asked. 'Why can't we find our way out of here?'

Master Juwain, riding beside him, touched his arm to steady him.
But he had no answer for him, and neither did I. I had no answers for
myself, and no hope, either. My command of direction, on which I had
always prided myself, seemed to have abandoned me utterly. I could
neither see nor sense my way out of this forsaken place. Perhaps there
was no way out, even as Lord Issur had said. Soon, we would all slip
off our horses and have to rest. We might awaken, once, twice, or even
twenty more times to continue our journey into the endless night. But in
the end, our food would run out and we would weaken beyond repair;
we would fall into the sleep from which there is no awakening, even
as the poor knight had. And then we would die in this desolate bog –
I was as certain of this as I was of the fever eating through my side into
my mind. Perhaps someday another knight would find *our* bones and
behold the fate that awaited him.

At last, I slumped forward in my saddle and threw my good arm around Altaru's neck to keep from myself plunging down into the wet earth. And then I whispered in his ear, 'We're lost, my friend, we're very lost. My apologies for bringing you here. Now go where you will, and bring yourself out, if you can.'

I closed my eyes then, and tried to hold on to his thickly muscled neck as the long column of it vibrated with a sudden nicker. He seemed to understand me, for he nickered again and surged forward with a new strength. Master Juwain's and Maram's sorrels, tied to him along with the pack horses, followed closely behind him. As I felt the rocking of Altaru's great body, my mind emptied and I drifted toward sleep. I was only dimly aware of him pausing before various meres and sniffing the air as he circled right or left and wound his way across the squishing mosses. My only thought was to keep hold of him and not let myself fall into the bog.

How long we traveled this way, I couldn't say. The heavy mist devoured both moon and stars. The darkness of the night seemed ever to deepen into a blackness as thick as ink. Although I knew that the fever must be working at me, my entire body felt as cold as death, and I couldn't stop shivering.

On and on we rode for many miles. I fell into a sleep in which I was strangely aware that I was sleeping. I dreamed that Altaru somehow found true north, and I felt the ground beginning to rise beneath us. And then this horse that I loved beyond all others let loose a tremendous whinny that shook me fully awake. The mist fell away from me. I opened my eyes to see both moon and stars and the jagged mountains of the Shoshan rising up to the west. Behind us – we all turned to look – the hazy bog steamed silver-gray in the soft light. But ahead us, a mile away on top of a steep hill, a castle stood limned against the glowing sky. Maram called out that we were saved, even as I let out a cry of joy. And then I finally let myself slip from Altaru's back, and I lay down against the hard, rocky, sweet, beautiful earth.

9

We were awakened from our sleep by the sound of trampling horses. With the sun dipping low toward the high mountains to the west, I guessed that we had slept all through the day and into the late afternoon. A mile behind us, the bog waited like a sea of dark green. In the clear daylight, it didn't seem nearly so threatening. Ahead us, however, up through the valley toward the castle on the hill, a small company of knights rode straight toward us across the rock-studded heather. There were five of them, and they seemed more worrisome. As I stood to greet them, I grasped the hilt of my sword because I didn't know their intentions.

'Who are these men?' Maram whispered to me as he stepped over to my side. 'Where in the world *are* we?'

The knights drew closer; I saw green falcons emblazoned on their shields and surcoats. I searched my memory for the lore that my father's heraldry master had taught me. Hadn't the Rezu clan, I wondered, taken the green falcon as its emblem?

'We must be in Rajak,' Master Juwain confirmed. Rajak, I recalled, was the westernmost duchy of Anjo. 'These must be Duke Rezu's men.'

The five knights rode straight up to us. As they drew nearer, I saw that only their leader wore the two diamonds of a full knight in his ring. He wore a suit of mail, even as I did, and his hand rested on the hilt of his sword. He had a sharp face and sharp eyes that flicked back and forth from our tired horses to our mud-spattered garments. He gazed for a long moment at my bandaged arm and even longer at the emblem that I wore.

'Who are you?' he called out in a rough but steady voice. 'From where have you come?'

'My name,' I said hoarsely, 'is Valashu Elahad.' Then I turned to present Master Juwain and Maram. 'We've come from Mesh.'

The knight presented himself as named Sar Naviru. Then he looked at me more closely and said, 'From Mesh, indeed – that I can see. But how did you come from there to here?'

I pointed at the bog behind us and said, 'We came through Ishka.'

'Through the bog? No, that's not possible – no one has ever come *out* of the Black Bog.'

Now his fist tightened around his sword, and he looked at us as if we had better give him a true accounting of our journeys.

'Nevertheless, we did,' I told him. 'We crossed it last night and –'

A sudden shiver of pain tore through my side, and I had to hold on to Maram for a moment to keep from falling. I stood there gasping for air. Then Master Juwain came over to me and held his hand against my burning forehead. He looked at Naviru and said, 'My friend has been wounded. Is there any way you can help us?'

Naviru pointed at me and said, 'If you are truly of Mesh and not demons, as has been said, you will be helped.'

Master Juwain pressed his hand to my side and then held it up for everyone to see. My bandage must have soaked through because his palm and fingers were covered with my blood.

'Does a demon,' Master Juwain asked, 'bleed?'

'I don't know,' Naviru said with a half-smile. 'I've never seen one. Now please come with us.'

It took most of Maram's considerable strength to boost me up onto Altaru's back and all of mine to keep me there during our short ride up to the castle. Master Juwain wanted to send Naviru's men for a litter, but I didn't want to greet Duke Rezu lying down. We rode across a long, open slope blazing a deep green with new spring grass. It looked like good country for grazing: off in the distance towards the bluish mountains to the east, a flock of sheep covered the side of a hill. Sar Naviru informed us that these low mountains to our right were those of the Aakash Range. On the other side of them, he said, was the duchy of Adar, from where we were fortunate not to have come.

The Rezu clan had built the Duke's castle against the backdrop of the much greater mountains of the Shoshan Range to the west. It was a small castle with only four towers and a single keep that also held the Duke's living quarters and hall. The walls, though not particularly high, were of a blue granite, and seemed in good repair. We rode into the castle across a moat on which floated many ducks and geese. I noted that the great chains that worked the drawbridge were free of rust and freshly greased. In the single courtyard, where some sheep milled about baahing nervously, three more knights wearing the green falcons of the Rezu clan stood waiting to greet us. The shortest of them – he was a sharp-faced man with sharp, quick eyes that reminded me of Sar Naviru's – wore a fresh black tunic and a kalama whose sheath was scarred with gouges. He greeted us warily and then presented himself as Duke Rezu of Rajak.

After Naviru had presented us and related our story, or as much as we had told him, the Duke looked straight at me for an uncomfortably long time. Then he said, 'Sar Valashu Elahad – I met your father at the tournament in Nar. You have his eyes, you know. And I hope you have his honesty as well: I can't believe that the son of Shavashar Elahad would tell *my* son anything other than the truth. Even so, it's hard to believe that you crossed the bog. It seems that you have stories for us. However, we won't ask you to tell them just now. You are wounded and need rest. That you shall have. And fire, salt and bread as well.'

And with that, he bowed to me, and took my hand in his to offer his hospitality. He summoned a groom to water, feed and comb down our horses. Then he instructed Naviru, who proved to be his third and youngest son, to take us to the guest quarters in the rooms above the great hall. This Naviru did without complaint. He seemed used to following his father's commands, and I sensed that they had fought in more than one battle together.

Naviru led us into the keep through an arched entrance surmounted with two carved falcons. Heavy wooden doors closed behind us, cutting off the sounds of the courtyard. The Duke's castle was like all castles: dark, dreary and cold. I shuddered at the prospect of being locked away in one again; I shuddered, too, because my entire body felt weak and cold. I was glad to lean against Maram's considerable bulk for support, but not glad at all to discover that the quarters to which we had been assigned lay on the keep's topmost floor. There were endless stairs to climb; with Maram's help, I somehow made my way up them. The far-off smell of baking bread encouraged me. And our rooms, when Naviru opened the door to them, gave me hope that the world was yet a fine place to live: along the west wall facing the Shoshan were many long windows letting in the late sunshine. There were two fireplaces lit with blazing logs, and our beds were stuffed with fresh straw and built off the floor on freshly waxed wooden platforms. Most wondrous of all was the large wooden tub in the bathing room that might be filled with hot water whenever we wanted a bath.

I spent all that night and most of the next three days in my very comfortable bed. Maram helped me wash away the muck of the bog, and Master Juwain fashioned a fresh dressing for my wound. He also made me a strong, bitter tea that tasted of turpentine and mold; he said it would fight my fever. After eating a little of the bread and chicken soup that Duke Rezu sent up for dinner, I slept long into the next morning. I awoke to find that my fever had broken, and I ate a much larger meal of bacon, fried eggs and porridge. And so it went for the next two days, the rhythm of my life settling in to successive rounds of eating and sleeping.

On the evening of the third day, Naviru returned to inquire if we would like join the Duke for dinner. He told us that the castle had guests whom the Duke wished us to meet. Although I wasn't particularly eager for company, I saw that Maram and Master Juwain had been confined much too long nursing me back to health. And so I quickly agreed to the Duke's summons. I put on my tunic, which Maram had sown and washed while I had been sleeping. And then we all went down to take our meal together.

The Duke's hall was not nearly so large as my father's. With its low, smoke-stained beams and a wooden floor lined with woven carpets, it seemed a rather cozy room for feasting. In it were crammed six smallish tables for Duke Rezu's warriors and knights, and a longer one that served his family and guests. That evening, only this longer table, made of planks of rough-cut hickory, was set with dishes.

The Duke stood waiting for us by his chair at the head of the table, while his wife took her place at the opposite end. Along the north side of the table gathered various members of the Rezu clan: Naviru and a nephew named Arashar; Chaitra, the Duke's recently widowed (and beautiful) niece, and his mother, Helenya, a small, dour woman whose eyes were as sharp as flints. Next to her stood an old minstrel named Yashku. Master Juwain, Maram and I took our places at the table's south side – I was glad that my sense of direction had returned to me – along with the Duke's two other guests. The first of these he presented as Thaman of Surrapam. I tried not to stare at this barbaric man with his mottled, pinkish skin and icy blue eyes. But how could I help looking at him again and again, especially at the bright red hair and beard that seemed to surround his head like a wreath of flames? Who had ever seen such hair on a human being? Well, of course I *could* help myself – hadn't my father taught me restraint? So instead of offending Thaman with the insolence of my gaze, I turned to regard the Duke's other guest instead.

This was a man with the strange and singular name of Kane. He wore loose, gray-green woolens without insignia or emblem that almost concealed the suit of mail beneath. I wondered from what land he had come. Although not as tall as most Valari, he had the brilliant black eyes and bold face bones of my people. But his accent sounded strange, as if he had been born in some kingdom far from the Morning Mountains, and he wore his snowy white hair cropped close to his head. I couldn't tell how old he was: the hair suggested an age of sixty while his sun-beaten features were those of a forty-year-old man. He moved, however, like a much younger warrior. In the highlands of Kaash, I had once seen one of the few snow tigers left in the world; Kane reminded me of that great beast in the power and grace of his muscular body, and most of all, in the fire I sensed blazing inside him. His dark eyes were hot, angry, wild and pained as if he were used to looking upon death, and I immediately mistrusted him.

'So, Valashu Elahad,' he said, drawing out the syllables of my name after the Duke had introduced us and we had all sat down. I felt his eyes cutting into the scar on my forehead. 'Of the Meshian Elahads – now there's a name that even *I* have heard.'

'Heard . . . where?' I asked, trying to ferret out his homeland.

But he only stared at me with his fathomless eyes as he scowled and the muscles above his tense jaws stood out like blocks of wood.

'So, you've journeyed from Mesh,' he continued. 'The Duke tells me you came through the bog.'

'Yes, we did,' I said, looking at Master Juwain and Maram.

Here the Duke's wife – a harsh-looking woman named Durva – fingered her graying hair and said, 'We've always counted on the bog being impassable. It's bad enough having to guard our border with Adar, to say nothing of the Kurmak raids. But if we have to worry about the Ishkans coming at us from the south, then we might as well just go into the bog ourselves and let the demons devour us.'

I shook my head as I smiled at her. Then I said, 'There aren't any demons in the bog.'

'No?' she asked. 'What *is* there in the bog?'

'Something worse,' I said.

While the Duke called for our goblets to be filled so that we could begin our rounds of toasting, I told of our passage through the bog. I had to explain, of course, why we had chosen to flee into it, and that led to an account of my duel with Salmelu and my reasons for leaving home. When I had finished my story, everyone sat looking at me quietly.

'Remarkable,' Duke Rezu said, staring at me down the ridge of his sharp nose. 'A sun that never rises, and a moon that vanishes like smoke! If I didn't have to worry about Duke Barwan, I'd be tempted to ride into the bog myself to witness these wonders.'

'Wonders?' Durva said. 'If those are wonders, then the Kurmak are angels sent to deliver us from our other enemies.'

The Duke took a sip of beer and then nodded at me. 'Perhaps your fever gave you visions of things that weren't there.'

'Master Juwain and Maram,' I said, 'didn't suffer from fevers, and they saw what I saw, too.'

At this, Maram took much more than a sip of beer, and nodded his head to affirm what I had said.

'Sleeplessness can cause one to view time strangely,' Duke Rezu said. He looked at his mother and smiled. 'Isn't that true?'

'It certainly is,' Helenya said crabbily. 'I haven't slept since Duke Barwan made an alliance with the Ishkans. I can tell you that a single night can well seem like a month.'

The Duke went around the table then, polling both family and guests as to what they thought of my story. Naviru, Chaitra and Arashar were inclined to believe me, while his mother and wife were more skeptical. Yashku, the old minstrel, however, seemed to doubt nothing of what I had said, even as Thaman shook his head and impatiently drummed his fingers against the table. As for Kane, his response surprised me. He took a long pull of his beer; then to Thaman, and the rest of us, he said, 'A man who has never seen a boat won't want to believe that mariners could cross the sea in one. So, there are many bad places in the world. And there are many things in Ea left from the War of Stones that we don't understand. This Black Bog is only one of them, eh?'

Duke Rezu agreed that this must be so, then complimented me on finding my way out of the bog. I took a sip of beer from my goblet as I shook my head. I admitted that it had been Altaru, and not I, who had led us to dry ground.

Kane's black eyes seemed to drink in my every word, and he said, 'The powers of animals run very deep. Few people anymore understand just how deep.'

It was a strange thing for him to say, and for a moment no one seemed to know how to respond. Naviru spoke of the nobility of his own horse, and Helenya told of a beloved dog that had once saved her from a robber's knife. Then Duke Rezu finally called for our meal to begin. His grooms brought out of the kitchen many platters of food: fried trout and rabbit stew, goose pie and nut bread and a big salad of spring greens. There were mashed potatoes, too, and three roasted legs of lamb. I found myself very hungry. I piled planks of trout and heaps of potatoes on my plate, and I watched as Maram, too, began to eat with a good appetite. After some moments of clanking dishes and beer being sloshed into our quickly emptied goblets, Maram nudged his elbow into my side. He nodded toward Kane, then whispered, 'I thought that *you* were the only one who could eat more than I.'

Not wanting to be too obvious, I glanced down the line of the table to see Kane working at his meal with a startling intensity. At the Duke's encouragement, he had taken a whole leg of lamb for himself. Using a dagger that he shook out of the sleeve of his tunic, he sliced off long strips of the rare meat with the skill of a butcher. His motions were so graceful and efficient that his hands and jaws – his whole body – seemed to flow almost languidly. He ate quite neatly, almost fastidiously. But as I watched his long, white teeth tear into the meat, I realized that he was devouring it with great speed. And with great relish, too: there was blood on his lips and fire in his eyes. In the time it took me to finish my first fillet of fish, he downed many gobbets of meat, all the while giving sound to murmurs of contentment from deep in his throat.

Duke Rezu seemed glad to provide Kane such toothsome joys, and he urged upon him other dishes and poured his beer with his own hand. From comments that he made and the silent trust of their eyes, I understood that Kane had done services for him in the past – what kinds of services I almost didn't want to know. As I watched Kane working with his dagger, I suspected that he could cut human flesh as easily as a lamb's.

'So, you wounded Lord Salmelu and left him alive,' he said to me as he looked up from his plate. He swallowed a huge hunk of lamb, almost without chewing, then smiled at me without humor. 'You should never leave enemies behind you, eh?'

I smiled, too, with no humor, and said, 'The world is full of enemies – we can't kill them all.'

At this, the bloodthirsty Durva shook her head and said, 'I wish you *had* killed Salmelu. And I wish your countrymen would kill the Ishkans, as many as possible. That would keep them from looking north, wouldn't it?'

'Perhaps,' I said. 'But there must be better ways to discourage the wandering of their eyes.'

Duke Rezu sighed at this and then pointed at the hall's empty tables. 'Even as we take this meal behind the safety of these walls, my eldest son, Ramashar, and my knights are riding the border of Adar. And we can only hope that the Kurmak clans won't mount an invasion this summer. Sad to say, we have enemies all around us. And so long as we do, the Ishkans will never be discouraged.'

'Enemies we have no lack of,' Durva agreed. Then she looked at her husband in silent accusation. 'And yet you chose this time to let our son go off on a hopeless quest.'

Duke Rezu took a gulp of beer as he regarded his outspoken wife. And then, to me and his other guests, he explained, 'Count Dario and the Alonians passed through Anjo before coming to Mesh. Ianar, my secondborn, has answered the call to the quest even as Sar Valashu and his friends have. He left for Tria ten days ago.'

This news encouraged me, and I felt a warmth inside as if I had drunk a glass of brandy. At least, I thought, I wouldn't be the only Valari knight in Tria.

The Duke looked at Thaman, who had hardly spoken ten words all night. Then he asked, 'And how is it in Surrapam? Have King Kiritan's emissaries reached your land, too?'

Thaman, dressed in stained woolens that had seen better days, used a napkin to wipe his hands. Then he ran his fingers through his thick red beard and said, 'Yes, they have. A ship arrived in Taylan late in Viradar. But few of my people have set out for Tria. This is not the time for us to be making such quests.'

'How so?' Duke Rezu asked him.

Thaman lifted back his head and drained the beer from his goblet. He grimaced as if he found the taste of the thick, black brew very bitter. Then he said, 'On the eighth of Viradar, at the Red Dragon's bidding, the armies of Hesperu marched against us. They've conquered our entire kingdom up to the line of the Maron River.'

At these words, everyone at the table grew still and looked at Thaman. These were the worst tidings to come to the Morning Mountains since the story of Galda's fall.

'So you see,' Thaman continued, 'we can spare few warriors to go off looking for golden cups that no longer exist.'

The Duke nodded his head and asked him, 'How is it then that your king can spare you?'

Thaman's small eyes blinked as if stung by particles of blowing snow. Then he drew his sword and laid it on the table alongside one of the half-eaten roasts. Its blade was shorter and thicker than that of a kalama, and notched in several places. He said, 'With this I've sent five Hesperuk warriors back to their ancestors. Do you question my courage?'

Thaman's sudden unsheathing of his sword caused Naviru and Arashar to grip the hilts of theirs. But Duke Rezu stayed their hands with a single look. He smiled coldly at Thaman and said, 'In the Morning Mountains, as Sar Valashu has found, we must be careful of unsheathing our swords. But you are new to our land, and must be forgiven for not knowing our ways. As for your courage, no, I do not question it – it is rather the opposite. You've made a journey across most of Ea that few would be willing or able to make. My only question is why your king would allow a brave man to make such a journey at a time when your sword must be badly needed.'

'It *is* needed,' Thaman admitted. 'I don't know how long we'll be able to hold. The Hesperuks fight like demons – it's believed that the Red Dragon's priests who lead their army have stolen their souls. They have done things I cannot speak of. My wife, my children . . .'

Thaman's voice suddenly died into the silence of the room. Although he kept his face as cold as stone and stared dry-eyed at the notched edge of his sword, I felt tears burning to break out from my own eyes at the great sorrow he held inside. An image of fish-scaled Hesperuk warriors ravaging the misty lands of far-off Surrapam came into my mind then. But I shook my head back and forth, trying not to let it take hold.

Duke Rezu refilled Thaman's goblet; bitterness or no, he drank the black beer almost in one gulp. Then he said, 'You speak of having enemies all around you. But for the peoples of Ea, there is only one true enemy, and his name is Morjin.'

At the sound of this name, I felt the arrow again bite into my side and the kirax burning in my blood. I turned to see Kane staring at Thaman with an even greater intensity than that with which he had attacked his meat.

'The Red Dragon's armies,' Thaman said, 'will soon control the entire south of Ea except for the Crescent Mountains and parts of the Red Desert.'

Now Kane's eyes, like black coals, began to burn with the heat of a hatred I couldn't comprehend.

'My king,' Thaman said, looking at Duke Rezu and then me, 'King Kaiman, has sent me to your land because it's said that the Valari are the greatest warriors in Ea. He hopes that you'll attack Sakai from the east before the Red Dragon swallows up what is left of Surrapam – and perhaps Eanna and Yarkona as well.'

I felt the sudden pressure of Maram's fat hand squeezing my leg beneath the table. Then he licked his lips as he winked at me. This was the very plan that he had proposed in Lord Harsha's field just before Raldu had almost murdered me.

Duke Rezu, who knew his history as well as anyone in Mesh, said to Thaman, 'Once we Valari fought our way across the Wendrush to attack the Red Dragon. He burned our warriors with firestones and crucified the survivors.'

At this, Thaman rapped his gold wedding ring against his sword. The thick steel blade rang out like a bell as he said, 'Someday, and sooner than you think, the Red Dragon will do worse than that to all your people.'

Duke Rezu shook his head sadly. 'This is not the time for the Valari to fight the Red Dragon together.'

'What would it take, then, to unite you?'

'I'm afraid,' the Duke said, 'that nothing less than an invasion of the tribes of the northern Sarni would unite Anjo. And to unite all the Valari kingdoms? Who can say? Only Aramesh was ever able to accomplish that, and we'll never see his like again.'

Despite myself, a thrill of pride swelled inside me. Aramesh was the great-grandfather of my grandfathers, and his blood still ran through my veins.

At that moment, I felt something like a dagger cutting into my forehead. I turned to see Kane staring at me, and his eyes were as hard and sharp as obsidian knives.

'It doesn't always take the united armies of the Valari to oppose Morjin,' he growled out. He nodded at Yashku and asked him, 'Do you know the Song of Kalkamesh and Telemesh?'

'Yes, I do,' Yashku said.

'So – sing it for us, then.'

It was unseemly for Kane to command Duke Rezu's minstrel, and so Yashku looked at the Duke to gain his assent. Duke Rezu slowly nodded his head and told him, 'We could use a song to hearten us tonight. But let's fill our goblets before you begin – if I remember correctly, it's a very long song.'

We began passing the big, brown jugs full of beer as I stared at the candles throwing up their bright flames. The Duke's grooms came out of the kitchen to remove the dishes, and the rattle of silverware and plates seemed very loud against the sudden quiet. Then Yashku, a wizened man with worn teeth, began pulling at his long, white hair and whispering to himself. His dark eyes danced with the candles' lights as he called to mind the key mnemonics that would help him remember the many verses of this epic poem.

The first part of it, which he sang out in a strong, mellow voice, told of the great crusade to liberate the Lightstone from Morjin at the end of the Age of Law. I listened to this history that I knew too well. Yashku sang of the alliance between Mesh, Ishka, Anjo and Kaash, and how these four kingdoms had sent armies across the Gray Prairies to join the Alonian army in assaulting Morjin's fortress of Argattha. He recounted the heroics and evil deeds of the Battle of Tarshid. There, against the Law of the One, King Dumakan of Alonia had used a red gelstei against Morjin's armies. But Morjin used the Lightstone to turn the firestones against the Alliance. Some of the firestones had exploded, destroying much of the Alonian army. Morjin had then turned his own firestones on the Valari armies, almost completely annihilating them. The survivors he had crucified along the road leading to Argattha. Then he and his priests had drunk the blood of their pierced hands in a great victory rite which heralded the coming of the Age of the Dragon. Yashku's words cut like swords into my heart:

A thousand men were bound in chains
Along the road where terror reigns,
And one by one were laid on wood
Where once Valari knights had stood.

In breaking of their flesh and bones,
Priests took up hammers hard as stones,
And iron spikes they drove through flesh,
And thus they killed the men of Mesh.

Their life poured out and reddened mud;
The Dragon's priests – they caught the blood
In clutching hands and golden bowls,
Then made a toast and drank their souls.

Here Yashku paused to take a sip of beer. Then he began singing about the courage of two men some eighty years after this terrible event. The first of these was Sartan Odinan, Morjin's infamous priest who had burnt the city of Suma to the ground with a firestone. But, in soul-searing remorse for this great crime, he had finally found his humanity and turned against Morjin. And so he made an alliance with a mysterious man named Kalkamesh – who was said to be the very same Kalkamesh who had fought beside Aramesh at the Battle of Sarburn thousands of years before. Vowing to regain the Lightstone by stealth where great armies had failed to take it by force, they had entered Argattha in secret. Sartan had led Kalkamesh through dark passageways that wound like worms through the underground city. After many perilous encounters, they had finally found the Lightstone locked away in one of Morjin's deepest dungeons at the very center of the city. Kalkamesh had managed to open the dungeon's iron door, but just as he was about to take the Lightstone in his hands, they were discovered.

What happened then in Argattha three millennia before, as told by Yashku, brought a gleam to everyone's eyes. While Kalkamesh had turned to fight Morjin's guards with a rare and terrible fury, Sartan had made his escape with the Lightstone. He had fled Argattha with the golden cup into the snowy wastes of Sakai where he and it had vanished from history.

'Very good,' Kane growled out as Yashku again paused to wet his throat. His eyes were as black and bottomless as I supposed the tunnels of Argattha to be. 'And now for Kalkamesh and Telemesh.'

The many verses of the poem, to this point, had been only a sort of preamble to the poet's true subject. This was the incredible valor of Kalkamesh and Telemesh. As we settled back in our chairs and sipped our beer, Yashku told of how Morjin had captured and tortured Kalkamesh. Believing that Kalkamesh must have known where Sartan intended to take the Lightstone, he had ordered Kalkamesh crucified to the mountain out of which was carved the city of Argattha. He had questioned him day and night, but Kalkamesh had only spat into his face. There, bolted naked to the side of the mountain, he endured every morning the rising of the blistering sun. And every morning as the sun's first rays touched Kalkamesh's writhing body, Morjin had arrived personally to cut open his belly with a stone knife and tear out his liver. He then used a green gelstei to aid this immortal man's already astonishing regenerative powers, and each night Kalkamesh's liver had grown back. It had been the beginning of the Long Torture that would last ten years.

But Morjin was never been able to break Kalkamesh. The story of his suffering and courage spread into every land of Ea. High in the Morning Mountains, the young Telashu Elahad, who would one day ascend the Swan Throne to become King Telemesh, heard of Kalkamesh's torment and vowed to end his misery. He had set out on his quest and crossed the Wendrush all alone. And then, on a night of lightning and storm, he had climbed Mount Skartaru in the dark to free Kalkamesh from his terrible fate. Yashku's words now rang out like silver bells deep in my soul:

> The lightning flashed, struck stone, burned white –
> The prince looked up into the light;
> Upon Skartaru nailed to stone
> He saw the warrior all alone.

> Through rain and hail he climbed the wall
> Still wet with bile, blood and gall.
> Where dread and dark devour light,
> He climbed alone into the night.

> And there beneath the blackened sky,
> He met the warrior eye to eye,
> The ancient warrior, hard as stone –
> He raised his sword and cut through bone.

> The lightning flashed, struck stone, burned red,
> And still the warrior wasn't dead.
> Where eagles perch and princes walk,
> He left his hands upon the rock.

147

And down and down they climbed as one
To beat the rising of the sun.
Through rain and ice and wind that wailed,
With strength and nerve that never failed.

They came into a healing place
Beneath Skartaru's bitter face.
And there, the One, the sacred spark,
Where love and light undo the dark.

The lightning flashed, struck stone, burned clear;
The prince beheld through rain and tear
The hands that held the golden bowl,
The warrior's hands again were whole.

'Very good,' Kane growled out after Yashku had finished reciting the poem. 'You sing well, minstrel. Very well indeed.'

Kane sat sipping his dark beer, which he had asked Duke Rezu's grooms to serve him hot like coffee. He was a hard man to read and an even harder one to look at. There was a heart-piercing poignancy beneath the brilliance of his black eyes, and he might have been considered too beautiful but for the harsh, vertical lines of a perpetual scowl that scarred his face. A scryer, it is said, with the aid of a crystal sphere can look into the future. There was something about him ageless and anguished as if he could look far into the past and recall all its hurts as his own. I wondered if he, like Thaman, had lost his family to the depredations of the Red Dragon. How else to explain the volcanic love and hate that threatened to erupt from him at every mention of Morjin's name?

'So,' he said, 'Kalkamesh and Telemesh – Sartan, too – defied Morjin. And shook the world, eh? I think it's shaking still.'

We all agreed that this was so, and we thanked Yashku for singing us the poem. Then Maram turned to Master Juwain and asked, 'What befell Kalkamesh after Argattha?'

'It's said that he perished in the War of the Stones.'

Thaman turned to Kane and regarded him coolly. 'And what of Sartan Odinan? He might have spirited away the Lightstone, but to where? The Song doesn't say.'

'No,' Kane agreed, 'it doesn't.'

'Surely, then, Sartan must have perished himself trying to make his escape. Surely the Lightstone must lie with his bones somewhere buried in the snows of Sakai or in the sands of the Red Desert.'

148

'No,' Kane said, shaking his large head. 'If Sartan was strong and cunning enough to enter Argattha, then surely he must have been resourceful enough make his escape unharmed.'

'Then why,' Thaman asked, 'do none of the epics tell of this?'

At this, Kane fell silent as he took a draw of his hot beer. And then Master Juwain interjected, 'But, of course, some of the epics do.'

We all turned to regard him with surprise. It was the first time on our journey from Silvassu that he had spoken of the Lightstone's fate.

'There is the Song of Madhar,' he said. 'And the Lay of Alanu. The first tells of how Sartan brought the Lightstone to the islands of the Elyssu and founded the Kingdom of Light early in the Age of the Dragon. The second tells that he hid the Lightstone in a castle high in the Crescent Mountains and studied its secrets. It's said that Sartan, too, gained immortality, and used the Lightstone to create an order of secret Masters who have journeyed across Ea for thousands of years opposing the Lord of Lies. And there are other legends, almost too many to mention.'

'Then why aren't these songs sung in Surrapam?' Thaman asked. He looked around the table at the curiosity on all our faces. 'Why aren't these legends told?'

Master Juwain rubbed the back of his bald head with his knotty hand. Despite his ugliness, he had a glowing presence that commanded respect. Maram, especially, regarded him proudly.

'Do you read ancient Ardik?' he asked Thaman. 'Do any of your countrymen?'

'No – we've no time for such indulgences anymore.'

'No,' Master Juwain agreed, 'it's been over three hundred years since your King Donatan closed the last of the Brotherhood schools in the west, hasn't it?'

Thaman took a gulp of beer and then grimaced in shame. He obviously didn't like it that Master Juwain knew so much about his country. I smiled proudly along with Maram because Master Juwain knew more about almost everything than anyone I had ever met.

'*I* read ancient Ardik,' Duke Rezu suddenly announced to everyone's surprise. 'And I've never heard of these legends, either.'

It was a victory for ignorance, I thought, that some of the Valari kingdoms had stopped sending their sons and daughters to the Brotherhood schools. But Anjo, at least, for all its troubles was not one of these.

'If you'd like,' Master Juwain told the Duke, 'later I'll show you a couple of books of the Lightstone legends that I've brought with me.'

'Yes, thank you,' Duke Rezu said, 'I'd like that very much.'

'Books, legends,' Thaman spat out. 'It's not words we need now but men with strong arms and sharp swords.'

Master Juwain's bushy eyebrows suddenly narrowed as he pointed his gnarly finger at my side. He said, 'Strong arms and swords we have in abundance here in the Morning Mountains. But without the knowledge of how to use them, they're worse than useless.'

'Use them against Morjin, then.'

'The Lord of Lies,' Master Juwain said, 'will never be defeated by the force of arms alone.'

'Then you think to defeat him by finding this golden cup that your legends tell of?'

'Does knowledge defeat ignorance? Does truth defeat a lie?'

'But not all the legends in your book can be true,' Thaman said.

'No,' Master Juwain agreed, 'but one of them might be. The trick is in discovering the right one.'

'But what if the Lightstone has been destroyed?'

'The Lightstone,' Master Juwain said, 'was wrought of gold gelstei by the Star People themselves. It can't be destroyed.'

'Well, then, what if it's lost forever?'

'But how can we know that?' Master Juwain asked. 'We can only say that it is lost forever if we stop seeking it and declare that it is forever lost.'

At this fencing of words, Thaman finally gave up and returned to his beer. He took a long drink of it and then asked, 'What do you think, Sar Kane?'

'Just Kane, please,' Kane said gruffly. 'I'm no knight.'

'Well,' Thaman asked him, 'will the Lightstone ever be found?'

Kane's eyes flashed just then, and I was reminded of lightning bolts lighting up the sky on a hot summer night. 'The Lightstone *must* be found,' he said. 'Or else the Red Dragon will never be defeated.'

'But defeated *how*?' Thaman asked, pressing him. 'Through knowledge or through the sword?'

'Knowledge is dangerous,' Kane said with a grim smile. 'Swords are, too. Who has the wisdom to use either, eh?'

'There's still wisdom in the world,' Master Juwain said stubbornly. 'There's still knowledge aplenty for those who open their minds to it.'

'*Dangerous*, I say,' Kane repeated, looking at Master Juwain. 'Long ago, Morjin opened *his* mind to the knowledge bestowed by the Lightstone, and he gained immortality, so it's said. So – who on Ea has benefited from this precious knowledge?'

As Duke Rezu's grooms arrived to bring out fresh pitchers of beer, Master Juwain sipped from the cup of tea that he had ordered. He regarded Kane with his large, gray eyes, obviously considering how to respond to his arguments.

'The Lord of Lies is the Lord of Lies,' he finally said. 'If he's truly the same tyrant who crucified Kalkamesh so long ago, then he makes a mockery of the immortality that is the province of the Elijin and Galadin.'

At this mention of the names of the angelic orders, Kane's eyes grew as empty as black space. I felt myself falling into them; it was like falling into a bottomless black pit.

'So,' Kane finally said, pinning Master Juwain with the daggers of his eyes, 'it's knowledge of the angels that you ultimately seek, isn't it?'

'Isn't that what the One created us to seek?'

'How would *I* know about that, damn it!' Kane growled out.

His vehemence startled all of us, and Master Juwain's voice softened as he said, 'Knowledge is power. The power to be more than animals or men of the sword. And the power to do great good in the world.'

'So you say,' Kane told him. 'Is that why you seek the Lightstone?'

Master Juwain forced a smile to his lips and looked at Kane with all the kindness he could muster. 'It's said that the Lightstone will bring infinite knowledge to him who drinks its golden light.'

'Is it really?' Kane said, showing his long white teeth in another grim smile. 'Isn't the true prophecy that the Lightstone will bring knowledge of the infinite?'

For a moment, I thought that the puzzled look on Master Juwain's face indicated that he had misremembered this particular bit of knowledge. Then, with a slow and measured motion, he removed a small copy of the *Saganom Elu* from the pocket of his robe and began thumbing through its dog-eared pages.

'Aha!' he finally said. From his other pocket, he had produced a magnifying glass, which he held over the pages of the opened book. 'The lines are here, in the seventy-seventh of the Trian Prophecies. And also, in the Visions, chapter five, verse forty-five. And if my memory serves, we'll find it written as well in the Book of Stars. Would you like to see?'

'No,' Kane told him. 'I try not to read such books.'

Kane might as well have told him that he tried not to smell the perfume of flowers or took no joy in the light of the sun. It was one of the few times I had ever seen Master Juwain moved to want to humble an opponent. He looked straight into Kane's unmoving eyes as he said, 'It would seem that you're wrong, wouldn't it?'

'So it seems,' Kane said. Although his words were agreeable enough, nothing in his tense, large-boned body suggested that he was yielding the point.

The Duke was used to battles, but not in his own hall. After lifting up his goblet and making a toast to the courage of Telemesh and Kalkamesh, he nodded at Kane. 'I think we're all agreed, at least, that we must oppose Morjin, however we can.'

'*That* I will agree to,' Kane said. 'I'll oppose Morjin even if it means seeking the Lightstone myself, and if I find it, letting the Brotherhoods take from it what knowledge they can.'

It was a noble thing for him to say, and his words warmed Master Juwain's heart. But not mine. I found that I could no more trust Kane than I could a tiger who purred softly one moment and then stared at me with hungry eyes the next.

'As it happens,' he told Master Juwain, 'I've business in Tria myself. If you'll let me, I'll accompany you there.'

Master Juwain sat sipping his tea as he slowly nodded his head. I sensed that he relished the opportunity to reopen his arguments with Kane, and he said, 'I would be honored. But the decision is not mine to make alone. What do you think, Brother Maram?'

Maram, who was busy making eyes with Chaitra, tore his gaze away from this lovely woman and looked at Master Juwain. He was more than a little drunk, and he said, 'Eh? What do *I* think? I think that even four is too few to face the dangers ahead that I don't even want to think about. The more the merrier!'

So saying, he turned back to Duke Rezu's widowed niece and flashed her a winning smile.

Master Juwain smiled too, in exasperation at the task of taming Maram. Then he said to me, 'What about you, Val?'

I turned toward Kane, who was staring at me with his unflinching gaze. It hurt to look at him too long, and so instead I glanced at the dagger that he still held in his large hands. And then I asked, 'What is your business in Tria?'

'My business is *my* business,' he growled at me. 'And *your* business, it would seem, is in reaching Tria without being killed. I'd think that you'd welcome the opportunity to increase your chances.'

Truly, I would, but did that mean welcoming this stranger to our company? I glanced at the sword sheathed at his side; it looked like a kalama. I thought that we might all welcome its sharp edges in fighting the unknown dangers that Maram was so afraid of. But a sword, as my grandfather used to say, can always cut two ways.

'We've come this far by ourselves,' I said to Kane. 'Perhaps it would be best if we continued on as we have.'

'So,' Kane said, 'if Morjin's men hunt you down in the forests of Alonia, you think to make it easy for them, eh?'

How, I wondered, had Kane sensed that Morjin might be pursuing me? Had Maram, in his drunken murmurings, blurted out clues that Kane had pieced together? Had the story of Raldu nearly murdering me somehow reached this little duchy of Rajak ahead of us?

'There's no reason,' I said, 'for the Lord of Lies to be hunting us.'

'You think not, eh? You're a prince of Mesh – King Shamesh's seventh son. Do you think Morjin needs any more reason than that to kill you?'

Kane spoke Morjin's name with so much hate that if words were steel, Morjin would now be dead. Watching Kane's neck tendons popping as he ground his teeth together, I couldn't doubt that he was Morjin's bitter enemy. But the enemy of my enemy, as my father liked to say, was not necessarily my friend.

'My apologies,' I said to him, 'but perhaps you can find other company.'

'Other company, you say? The outlaws who've taken over the wild lands beyond Anjo? The bears that infest the deeper woods?'

At the mention of Maram's least favorite beast, my love-stricken friend suddenly broke off his flirtation with Chaitra and said, 'Ah, Val, perhaps we *should* considering taking this Kane with us. To, ah, protect him from the bears.'

Kane's black eyes turned toward me to see what I would say. They were like enormous boulders used to crushing the will out of others.

'No,' I said, struggling to breathe. 'The bears will leave him alone if he leaves them alone. Surely he has enough woodcraft to avoid them.'

Both Master Juwain and Maram, while not agreeing with my decision, knew me well enough not to try to dissuade me. Master Juwain smiled at Kane and said, 'I'm sorry, but perhaps we can meet in Tria and continue our discussion about the prophecies.'

'So,' Kane snarled out. He ignored Master Juwain and continued to stare at me. 'You insist on making this journey alone, eh?'

'Yes,' I told him, trying not to look away from his blazing eyes.

'So be it, then,' he said with all the finality of a king pronouncing a sentence of death.

After that, Duke Rezu tried to return our conversation to the legends of the Lightstone. But the mood was broken. As it had grown very late, Yashku excused himself and went off to bed, followed in short order by Helenya, who complained of her aching joints and sleeplessness. Maram, of course, would have stayed there all night flirting with Chaitra if she hadn't suddenly winked at him and announced her need to go finish some undone knitting. As for me, the wound in my side pained me almost as much as the anguish of Kane's wounded soul puzzled me. Who was this man, I wondered, whose eyes looked as if they were

153

forged in some hellish furnace out of black iron fallen down from the stars? From where had he come? To where did he really intend to go? As we all pushed back our chairs and stood up from the table, I thought that I would never know the answers to these questions. For tomorrow, at first light, Master Juwain and Maram would join me in saddling our horses, and we would set out for Tria by ourselves.

10

As the sun brightened the bluish peaks of the Aakash Range to the east, we gathered in the castle's courtyard. It was a cool, clear day, and the sounds of roosters crowing and horses snorting filled the air. After I had greeted Altaru with a handful of warm bread that I had saved from breakfast, and Master Juwain and Maram had readied their sorrels, Duke Rezu came out into the courtyard to bid us farewell. Kane and Thaman accompanied him. I soon learned that Kane would be putting off his journey to Tria for at least another day – if indeed he really intended to travel in that direction. As for Thaman, our conversation over dinner had persuaded him that it would be useless to pursue his quest in either Ishka or Mesh at this time. And so later that morning he would continue on to Adar and then to the barony of Natesh before crossing the Culhadosh River and making his plea to the king of Taron.

'Farewell, Sar Valashu,' he said to me as I stood by Altaru. 'Forgive me if I spoke hastily last night. Sometimes I think the Red Dragon has poisoned my soul. But it may be that there is more than one way of fighting him. I wish you well on your quest.'

'And I wish you well on yours,' I said as we clasped hands.

Kane came up to me then, but not to touch hands in friendship. He stood with his arms folded across his chest, all the while eyeing the lines of Altaru's trembling body as well as my war lance couched in the holster at his side. Kane's dark gaze took in the hunting bow and arrows that my pack horse bore and then fell upon the kalama that I always kept close at hand. He nodded once, in seeming approval of these well-tested weapons, and then told me, 'I have no apologies for you, Valashu Elahad. Rain is gladly drunk by parched soil but runs off cold stone. If you've closed your heart to me, so be it. But please accept this last piece of advice in the spirit in which it's given: Beware the hill men west of the gap in the mountains. They're very fierce, and they don't like strangers.'

So saying, he nodded his head toward me, and I returned the gesture. Then Duke Rezu stepped over to my pack horse and patted his bulging saddlebags. He asked, 'Did my steward take care of your provisions? It's a long way to Tria from here.'

'Yes, thank you,' I told him. 'We've as much as we can carry.'

'Very well,' he said. He sighed as he pointed toward the castle's north tower. 'You'll find it easy riding from here into Daksh. You say that Duke Gorador is a friend of your father?'

'Yes,' I said. 'He gave him this horse.'

'Altaru, you call him, yes? Well, he's a magnificent animal – in all of Daksh, I doubt if you'll find another like him, and there are no horses like those the Dakshans ride, I'll give them that. As for Duke Gorador, I'm sure he'll welcome both you and your horse. But after you leave his castle, you should avoid the wild lands to the north. There are too many outlaws in those woods, I'm afraid. Instead, skirt around the Aakash Mountains and approach the Nar Road through the west of Jathay. Avoid Sauvo, if you can. There are plots against the King, and you won't want to be caught up in them. And stay well clear of Vishal – the Havosh River is its border. Baron Yashur has been pressing his claims against Count Atanu of Onkar, and they've been at war since last summer. But Yarvanu is safe. You should enter it from the southwest, through Jathay. My cousin, Count Rodru, has ruled Yarvanu for twenty-three years now, and he still keeps the bridge over the Santosh open.'

Having completed this little dissertation of the geography and politics of the broken kingdom of Anjo, Duke Rezu clasped my hand and wished me well. Then he watched me climb onto Altaru's back, which was no mean feat considering that I still had trouble using my left arm. But my right arm was strong enough, and I lifted it to wave goodbye. To Altaru, I whispered, 'All right, my friend – let's see if we can find this City of Light that everyone talks about.'

We rode down from the castle to the sound of the wind blowing across the heath. It was a high, fair country that the Duke called home, with mountains lining our way both on the east and west. There were only a few trees scattered across the green hills of Rajak's central valley, and our riding was easy, as the Duke had promised. Most of the land near his castle was given over to pasture for the many flocks of sheep basking in the early sun; their thick winter wool was as white and puffy as the clouds floating along the blue sky. But there were farms, too. Patches of emerald green, marked off by lines of stone walls or hedgerows, covered the earth before us like a vast quilt knit of barley and oats and other crops that the Duke's people grew. Here and there, a few fields lay fallow casting up colors of umber and gold.

156

Despite the pain in my side – which still cut into me like a knife whenever I moved my arm – it was good to be in the saddle again. It was good to smell grass and earth and the thick horse scent of Altaru's surging body. With neither the Ishkans nor any enemy we knew pursuing us, we set a slow pace toward Daksh and the lands that awaited us farther to the north.

Beautiful country or no, Maram could barely keep his eyes open to behold it. All that morning, he slumped in his saddle, yawning and sighing. Finally, after we had paused by a little stream to water our horses, Master Juwain took him to task for once again breaking his vows.

'I heard you get up last night,' Master Juwain told him. 'Did you have trouble sleeping?'

'Yes, yes, I did,' Maram said as he rode beside me. 'I wanted to take a walk around the walls and look at the stars.'

'I see,' Master Juwain said, riding beside him. '*Shooting* stars, they were, no doubt. The light of the heavenly bodies.'

'Ah, it's a wonderful world, isn't it?'

'Wonderful, yes,' Master Juwain admitted to him. 'But you should be careful of these midnight walks of yours. One night you might find yourself plunging off the parapets.'

Maram smiled at this, and so did I. Then he said, 'I've never been afraid of heights or of falling. To fall in love with a woman is the sweetest of deaths.'

'As you've fallen for Chaitra?'

'*Have* I fallen for Chaitra?' Maram asked as he pulled at his thick brown beard. 'Ah, well, I suppose I have.'

'But she's a widow,' Master Juwain said. 'And a newly made one at that. Didn't the Duke say that her husband had been killed last month in a skirmish with Adar?'

'Yes, sir, he did say that.'

'Don't you think it's cruel, then, to take walks in the starlight with a bereaved woman and then leave her alone the next day?'

'Cruel? Cruel, you say?' Maram was wide awake now, and he seemed genuinely aggrieved. 'The wind off Arakel in Viradar is cruel. Cats are cruel to mice, and bears – such as the one we fought at the Gate – live only to make me suffer. But a man's love for a woman, if it be true, can never be cruel.'

'No,' Master Juwain agreed, '*love* can't be.'

Maram rode on a few paces, all the while muttering that he was always misunderstood. And then he said, 'Please, sir, listen to me a moment. I would never think to dispute with you the declensions of the pronouns

157

in Ardik or the declinations of the constellations in Soldru. Or almost anything else. But about women – ah, women. Widows, especially. There's only one way to truly console a widow. The Brotherhood teaches us to honor our vows but that compassion is more sacred yet. Well, to make a woman sing where previously she has been weeping is the soul of compassion. When I close my eyes and smell the perfume that clings to my lips, I can hear Chaitra singing still.'

As I closed *my* eyes for a moment to listen to the chirping of the sparrows in the fields around us, I could almost hear Maram singing along with them. He seemed truly happy. And I had no doubt that Chaitra was doing the day's knitting with a song on her lips as well.

Maram's worldly ways obviously vexed Master Juwain. I thought that he might upbraid him in front of me or perhaps lay upon him some harsh punishment. But instead he gave up on instilling in Maram the Brotherhood's virtues – at least for the moment. He sighed as he turned to me and said, 'You young people these days do as you will, don't you?'

'Are you speaking of Kane?' I asked him.

'I'm afraid I am,' he said. 'Why did you refuse his company?'

I looked out at a nearby hill where a young shepherd stood guarding his sheep against marauding wolves; I thought a long time before giving him a truthful answer to his question.

'There's something about Kane,' I said. 'His face, his eyes – the way he moves the knife in his hands. He . . . burns. Raldu's accomplice put a bit of kirax in my blood, and *that* still burns like fire. But in Kane, there's more than a little bit of hell. He hates so utterly. It's as if he loves hating more than he could ever love a friend. How could anyone trust a man like that?'

Master Juwain rode next to me, thinking about what I had said. Then he sighed and rubbed the back of his head, which gleamed like a large brown nut in the bright sunlight. He said, 'You know that Kane has Duke Rezu's trust.'

'Yes, the Duke has need of men with quick swords,' I said. For a moment I listened to the thump of our horses' hooves against the stony soil. 'It's strange, isn't it, that this Kane showed up at the Duke's castle at the same time we escaped from the bog.'

'Perhaps it's just a coincidence,' Master Juwain said.

'You taught me not to believe in coincidence, sir,' I said to him.

'What do you believe about Kane, then?'

'He hates the Lord of Lies, that much seems certain,' I said. 'But *why* does he hate him so much?'

'I'm afraid it's only natural to hate that which is pure hate itself.'

158

'Perhaps,' I said. 'But what if it's more than that?'

'What, then?'

'There's something about Kane,' I said again. 'What if it was he who shot at me in the forest? And then somehow followed me into Anjo?'

'You think that it was *Kane* who tried to assassinate you?' Master Juwain asked. He seemed genuinely astonished. 'I thought we had established that it was the Lord of Lies who wished you dead. As you've observed, Kane hates him. Why should he then serve him?'

'That is what's puzzling me, sir. Perhaps the Lord of Lies has made a ghul of him. Or perhaps he has captured Kane's family and threatens them with death or worse.'

'Now *that* is a dark thought,' Master Juwain said. 'I'm afraid there's something dark about you, Valashu Elahad, to be thinking such thoughts on such a beautiful morning.'

I was afraid of the same thing, and I lifted up my face to let the bright sun drive away the coldness gnawing at my insides.

'Well,' Master Juwain continued, 'it's said that ghuls sometimes retain enough of their souls to hate their master. As for your other hypothesis, who knows? The Lord of Lies is certainly capable of doing as you said – and much worse.'

Master Juwain stopped to let his horse eat some grass. He began pulling at the folds of flesh beneath his chin. Then he said, 'But I don't think either hypothesis accounts for what I've seen of our mysterious Kane.'

'What do you think then, sir?'

He sat there on his horse on the middle of a gently rising hill, all the while regarding me with his large gray eyes. And then he asked, 'What do you know of the different Brotherhoods, Val?'

'Only what you taught me, sir.'

And that, I thought, was not very much. I knew that early in the Age of Law, in a time of rebirth known as the Great Awakening, the Brotherhood had finally come out from behind the Morning Mountains to open schools across all of Ea. The different schools took on different names according to the colors of the gelstei that were to become the soul of that brilliant civilization; each school specialized in pursuing knowledge that related to its particular stone, and eventually became its own Brotherhood. Thus the Blue Brotherhood concerned itself with communications of all sorts, especially languages and dreams, while the Red Brotherhood sought understanding of the secret fire that blazed inside rocks and earth and all things. And so on. While each of the seven new Brotherhoods eventually opened schools of their own across the whole continent, some were much stronger in certain lands: The

Silver Brotherhood predominated in far-off Surrapam while the Green Brotherhood came to its fullest flowering in the forest academies of Acadu. For two thousand years, the Brotherhoods had led civilization's rise into a golden age. And then, with the release of Morjin from his prison on the Isle of Damoom and his stealing of the Lightstone, had come the fall.

All during the Age of the Dragon, the various Brotherhoods had dwindled or were destroyed by Morjin's assassin-priests. The closing of the Silver Brotherhood's school in Surrapam that Master Juwain had lamented over dinner was among the last of these. Now, only the original Brotherhood remained to spread the light of truth throughout Ea. Although its Brothers had been the first to make vows to preserve the wisdom of the stars and raise up humanity to its birthright, they called themselves the Last Brotherhood.

'All of the Brotherhoods have been destroyed,' I said to Master Juwain. 'All except one.'

'Hmmm, have they indeed?' Master Juwain said. 'What do you know of the Black Brotherhood?'

'Only that they were once strongest in Sakai. And that when the Kallimun priests established their fortress in Argattha, they hunted down the Brothers and razed every one of their schools to the ground. The Black Brotherhood was completely destroyed early in the Age of the Dragon.'

Maram, taking an interest in our conversation, nudged his horse forward to hear better what we were saying.

Master Juwain turned about in his saddle, left and right, scanning the empty hills around us. And then, in a much-lowered voice, he said, 'No, the Black Brotherhood was never destroyed. The Kallimun only drove them out of Sakai into Alonia.'

He went on to tell us that the Black Brotherhood, seeking to understand the fire-negating properties of the black gelstei and the source of all darkness, had always been different from the other Brotherhoods. Early in the Age of Law, when the Brotherhoods had renounced war, the Black Brothers had rebelled against the new rule of non-violence. Believing that there would always be darkness in the world, they began taking up knives and other weapons to fight against it. And they fought quite fiercely, for thousands of years. As the other Brotherhoods – the Blue and the Red, the Gold and the Green – closed their schools all through the Age of the Dragon, the Black Brotherhood opened schools in secret in almost every land.

When Master Juwain had finished speaking, Maram sat very erect on his horse and said, 'I've never heard anyone speak of that.'

'We *don't* speak of it,' Master Juwain said. 'Certainly not to novices. And not usually to any Brother before he has attained his mastership.'

At this, Maram, who was no more likely to attain a mastership than I was to become a king, slowly nodded his head as if proud to be taken into Master Juwain's confidence. And then he said, 'I didn't know there were any black gelstei left in the world for *anyone* to study.'

'There may not be,' Master Juwain said. 'But the Black Brothers gave up the pursuit of such knowledge long ago.'

'They have? But what is their purpose, then?'

'Their purpose,' Master Juwain said, 'is to hunt the Kallimun priests who once hunted them. And ultimately, to slay the Red Dragon.'

Here he turned toward me and said, 'And that brings us back to Kane. I'm afraid that he might be of the Black Brotherhood. From what I've read about the Black Brothers, he has their look. Certainly he has their hate.'

I looked off at the soft green hills and the purplish Aakash Mountains just beyond them. The sun poured down its warmth upon the earth, and a sweet wind rippled the acres of grass. On such a lovely day, it seemed strange to speak of dark things such as the Black Brotherhood. Almost as strange as Kane himself.

'And so you asked Kane to ride with us,' I said to Master Juwain. 'Why, sir? Because you thought he might scare away any of the Red Dragon's men who might be hunting us? Or because you want to know more about the Black Brotherhood?'

Master Juwain laughed softly as he looked at me with his deep eyes. And then he said, 'I think you know me too well, Val. Kane was right about me, after all. I *do* seek knowledge, sometimes even in dark places. It's my curse.'

I looked up at the sun then as I thought about my own curse; I thought about the way that Kane's eyes had nearly sucked me down into the dark whirlpool of his soul. Would I, I wondered, ever find that which would heal me of my terrible gift of experiencing the sufferings of others?

'If Kane *is* of the Black Brotherhood,' I finally said to Master Juwain, 'why would he press to accompany us?'

But Master Juwain, who knew so much about so many things, only looked at me in silence as he slowly shook his head.

For the rest of the morning, as we journeyed north along the Aakash range, we talked about the Brotherhoods' role in the study and fabrication of the seven greater gelstei stones. The fine day opened into the long hours of the afternoon even as the valley through which we rode opened toward the plains of Anjo. The hills about us gradually lessened in elevation and began to flatten out. Maram wanted to pause on the top of one of these to eat our midday meal and take a nap. But despite the soreness of my side, I was eager to press on, and so we did. Late in the day, with the sun arching down toward the jagged Shoshan Mountains to the west, we crossed into Daksh. No river or border stones marked off this dukedom. We knew that we had entered Duke Gorador's domain only because a shepherd whom we passed told us that we had. He also told us that we would find the Duke's castle some five miles farther up the valley at the mouth of one of the canyons leading through the Aakash Mountains. And so we did. It was almost full night as we rode up to the castle's main gate and presented ourselves to the Duke.

Duke Gorador proved to be a heavy man with a long face like a horse and long lower lip, at which he pulled with his steely fingers as we told him our story. He seemed glad to hear that I had made enemies of Lord Salmelu and the Ishkans; apparently he regarded the enemy of his enemy as his friend, for he immediately offered us his hospitality, and ordered that we be feted. But before we sat down to take dinner with him, he insisted on looking at Altaru and taking his measure. He well remembered sending him to my father, and was astonished to see me astride him.

'I never thought anyone would ride this horse,' he said to me just inside his castle's gate. Unlike my father, he had the good sense to keep well away from him. 'Now come dine with me and tell me how you managed to win his friendship. It seems that we have many stories to tell tonight.'

That evening, over a meal of roasted lamb and mint jelly, we spoke of many things: of the warlords who terrorized the wild lands to the north of Daksh and the warriors of Duke Barwan who patrolled the passes of the mountains to the east. As it happened, Duke Gorador, too, had a son who had gone off to the great gathering in Tria. He gave us his blessings and told us to look for a Sar Avador, who would be riding a black gelding that might have been Altaru's cousin. Of Kane, whom he had met, he had nothing to say. For as he told us, his father had taught him that if he couldn't speak well of a man, he shouldn't speak at all. He did, however, have words of praise for Thaman and his cause. He surprised everyone by announcing that the Valari must someday unite under a single king. But it surprised no one that he thought this king should be of Anjo: perhaps even Lord Shurador, his eldest son.

We slept well that night to the music of the wolves howling in the hills. That is, Master Juwain and I slept well. Maram insisted on staying up until the dark hours writing a poem by candlelight. He intended to give Lord Shurador's wife his adoring words the next day since he couldn't manage to give her his love that night. But when the dawn broke its first light over the castle, both Master Juwain and I dissuaded him from this potentially disastrous act. We told him that if his verses were well-made and true, his passions would be preserved for all the ages. He could work on his poem as we journeyed north, and if he so desired, he could read it to the nobles and princes in Tria.

We said goodbye to the Duke near the gate where we had met him. Then we rode into the soft, swelling hills around his castle. The sky was as blue as cobalt glass; the soft wind smelled of dandelions and other wildflowers that grew on the grassy slopes. In the east, the sun burned with a golden fire.

It was a fine day for traveling, I thought, perhaps our finest yet. I determined that we should leave Daksh far behind us and cross well into Jathay before evening came. Perhaps some thirty miles of rolling country lay before us. We began our journey through it to the sound of Maram bellowing out the verses of his new poem. It was a measure of the safety that Duke Gorador provided his domain that we could ride without fear of Maram's noise provoking any enemy to attack us.

As the noon hour approached, the mountains to our east grew lower and lower like great granite steps leading down into the plains of Anjo. Their forested slopes gradually gave way to grassier terrain. At the border between Daksh and Jathay, they stopped altogether. Here, where one of the feeder streams of the Havosh led northeast toward Yarvanu and Vishal, we paused to eat a meal of lamb sandwiches and take our bearings.

'Ah, Val, listen to this,' Maram said between bites of his sandwich. 'Which line do you think is better? "Her eyes are pools of sacred fire?" Or, "Her eyes are fire feeding fire"?'

We sat on top of a hill above the west bank of the Havosh River. The day was still clear, and we could see many miles in any direction. To the east, just across the sparkling trickle of the river, the plains of Jathay glistened like a sea of green. Only some fifteen miles from us lay the city of Sauvo and the court intrigues that Duke Rezu had spoken of. To the northeast, along the line of the Havosh, were the fields of Vishal and Yarvanu, and some miles beyond their domains, the distant blue haze of the Alonian Sea. The Shoshan Range still rose like a vast wall of rock and ice to the west, but I knew that their jagged peaks gave way to a great gap some seventy-five miles to the northwest. Forty miles due north of our hill, the raging Santosh River flowed down from these mountains into the Alonian Sea. It formed the border between Alonia and Anjo's wild lands that both Duke Rezu and Duke Gorador had warned us against. From our vantage above them, they didn't seem so wild. Long stretches of swaying grass and shrubs were cut by stands

163

of trees in an irregular patchwork of vegetation. The ground undulated with soft swells of earth, as of the contours of a snake, but nowhere did it appear hilly or difficult to cross.

'Perhaps you don't like *either* line,' Maram said as I suddenly stood to gaze down at the thin, blue ribbon of the Havosh. 'How about, "Her eyes are windows to the stars"? Val, are you listening to me? What's wrong?'

I was barely listening to him. A sudden coldness struck into me as of something serpentine wrapping itself around my spine. It seemed to contract rhythmically, grinding my back-bones together even as it ate its way into my skull. Despite the dreadful chill I felt spreading through my limbs, I began to sweat. My belly tightened with a sickness that made me want to surrender up my lunch.

Now Master Juwain stood up, too, and laid his hand on my shoulder. He touched my head to see if my fever had returned. And then he asked, 'Are you ill, Val?'

'No,' I told him. 'It's not that.'

'What is it, then?'

I saw great concern on both my friends' faces. And I was concerned not to alarm either of them, especially Maram. But they had to know, so as gently as I could, I told them, 'Someone is following me.'

At this news, Maram leaped to his feet and began scanning the world in every direction. And so, more slowly, did Master Juwain. But the only moving things they detected were a few hawks in the sky and a rabbit startled out of the grass by Maram's darting back and forth across the top of the hill.

'We can't see anything,' Master Juwain said. 'Are you sure we're being followed?'

'Yes,' I said. 'At least, someone or something is seeking me and knows where I am. It's like they can scent out my blood.'

'Do you think it's Kane?' Maram asked. He turned south to peer more closely through the valley leading back to Duke Rezu's castle.

'It could be Kane,' I said. 'Or it could be someone waiting for us to ride into a trap.'

'Waiting *where*?' Maram asked. 'And who is it who's after you? The Ishkans? No, no – they wouldn't dare ride this far into Anjo. Would they? Do you think it's your assassin who has tracked you down?'

But I had no answers for him, nor for myself. All I could do was to smile bravely so that the flames of Maram's disquiet didn't spread into a raging panic.

Master Juwain, who had an intimation of my gift, nodded his head as if he trusted what I had told him. He asked, 'What should we do, Val?'

'We could try to set a trap of our own,' I said, touching the hilt of my sword.

'No, there's been enough of that already,' Master Juwain said. 'Besides, we have no idea how many might be pursuing us, do we?'

Maram nodded his head at the good sense of this, and said, 'Please, Val, let's leave this land as soon as we can.'

'All right,' I said. I pointed down at the Havosh River where it formed the border of Jathay and led toward Yarvanu and Vishal. 'If it *is* Kane who is after us, then he knows that Duke Rezu advised us to go in this direction. If it's someone else, then likely they'll be waiting for us along the Nar Road where it crosses through Yarvanu.'

'Of course they would,' Maram muttered. 'That's the only way over the Santosh into Alonia.'

'Perhaps not the only way,' I said.

'What do you mean?' Maram asked in alarm.

I pointed down into the wild lands that began at the base of our hill. I said, 'We could journey north, straight for the Santosh. And then into Alonia. If we keep northwest toward the Shoshan Range and then strike out north again, we should intercept the Nar Road in the Gap far from any of our pursuers.'

Maram looked at me as if I had suggested crossing the Alonian Sea on a log. Then he called out, 'But what of the wild lands we were warned against? The robbers and outlaws? Ah, perhaps the bears, too? And how will we cross the Santosh if there's no bridge? And if by some miracle we *do* cross it without drowning, how will we find our way through Alonia? I've heard there's nothing there but trackless forest.'

Some men are born to fear the familiar dangers that they see before their eyes; some take their greatest terror in the unknown. Maram was cursed with a sensibility that found threat everywhere in the world, from a boulder poised on the side of a hill to roll down upon him to his most wild imaginings. I knew that nothing I could say would assuage the dread rising like a flood inside him. Dangers lay before us in every direction. All we could do was to choose one way or another to go.

Even so, I grasped his hand in mine to reassure him. It was one of the times in my life that I wished my gift worked in reverse, so that some of my great hope for the future might pass into him. I fancied that some of it did.

We held council on top of that barren hill. All of us agreed that when facing an opponent, it was best to do the unexpected. And so in the end we decided on the course that I had suggested.

After packing up our food, we rode down into the wild lands with a new haste communicating into our horses. We moved at a bone-jolting

165

trot over fields overgrown with shrubs and weeds; but upon entering the various woods that lay upon our line of travel, we had to pick our way more slowly. The country through which we rode had once been rich farmland, some of the richest in the Morning Mountains. But now all that remained of civilization were the ruins of low stone walls or an occasional house, rotting or fallen in upon itself. We saw no other sign of human beings all that long afternoon. When evening came, we made camp in a copse of stout oaks. We risked no fire that night. We ate a cold meal of cheese and bread, and then agreed to take our sleep in turns so that one of us might always remain awake to listen for our pursuers. I took the first watch, followed by Maram. When it came time for me to rest, I fell asleep to the sound of wolves howling far out on the plain before us.

I was awakened just before dawn by a dreadful sensation that one of these wolves was licking my throat. I sprang up from the dark, damp earth with my sword in my hand; I believe I lunged at the gray shapes of these beasts lurking in the shadows of the trees. And then, as I came truly awake and my eyes cleared, I saw nothing more threatening than a few rotting logs among the towering oaks.

'Are you all right?' Master Juwain whispered. 'Was it a dream?'

'Yes, a dream,' I told him. 'But perhaps it's time we were off.'

We roused Maram then and quickly broke camp. Upon emerging from the woods, we rode straight toward the north star over a dark and silent land. But soon the sun reddened the sky in the east and drove away the darkness. With every yard of dew-dampened ground that we covered, it seemed that the world grew a little brighter. I took courage from this golden light. By the time full day came, I could no longer feel the serpent writhing along my spine.

Even so, I pressed Altaru to cross this forsaken country as quickly as we could. The ground fell gradually before us; in places, it grew damp and almost boggy – though nothing like the Black Bog that guarded the way into Rajak. The horses found their footing surely enough, and began to quicken their pace, urged on by clouds of biting, black flies. By noon we had covered nearly fifteen miles, and by late afternoon, another ten. And in all those miles, we saw nothing more threatening than a couple of foxes and the prints of a bear by the muddy bank of a stream.

And then, as we drew nearer the Santosh and entered a broad swathe of woods, we came upon a band of ragged-looking men whom Maram immediately took to be robbers. But they proved to be only outlaws exiled from Vishal for protesting the ruthless war that Baron Yashur was prosecuting against Onkar. With their matted hair and filthy tunics, they seemed scarcely Valari. But Valari they were, and they offered us no hindrance, only the roasted haunch of a deer that they had just killed. And more, when they heard that we were journeying to Tria, they offered to show us a way over the Santosh.

Meeting these 'wild' men that Maram had so feared was a great stroke of fortune. After we had eaten the gamy-tasting venison, they led us west along a track through the woods. A few miles of tramping along the black, hard-packed earth brought us close to the river. We heard this great surge of water through the trees before we could see it: the oaks and willows grew like a curtain right down to the bank. But then the track straightened and rose toward the causeway leading to an old bridge spanning the river. At the foot of this rickety structure, we paused to look down into the river's raging brown waters. There was no way, I knew, that we could have swum across them.

The outlaw Valari said goodbye to us there and wished us well on our quest. Crossing the bridge proved to be an exercise in faith. We all dismounted and led our horses across the bridge one by one, the better to distribute our weight across its rotten planks. Even so, Altaru's hoof broke through one of them with a sickening crunch, and it was all I could do to extricate it without my badly startled horse breaking his leg. But Altaru trusted me as much as I trusted him. After that, we picked our way across the rest of the bridge without incident. Master Juwain and Maram, with their lighter sorrels and the packhorses, encountered no problems.

As darkness was coming on, we camped there on moist, low ground near the bridge. Maram argued for a higher and drier campsite, but I convinced him that anyone pursuing us on horses would make a huge sound of hooves pounding against the drumlike boards of the bridge. This would alert us and allow us precious time either to flee or mount a defense.

And so we ate a joyless dinner in the damp next to the river. It was a cold, uncomfortable night. Sleep brought only torment. The season's first mosquitoes whined in my ear, bit, drew blood. After a time, I gave up slapping them and in exhaustion slipped down into the land of dreams. But there the whining grew only louder and swelled to a dreadful whimpering as of a prelude to a scream. Toward dawn I finally came screaming out of my sleep. Or so I thought. When my mind cleared, I realized that it was not I but Maram who was screaming: it turned out that a harmless garter snake had slithered across his sleeping fur and sent him hopping up from it on all fours like a badly frightened frog.

We were very glad to begin the day's journey. And very glad at last to have planted our feet on Alonian soil, if only the most southern and eastern part of it. It was a land that human beings had deserted many years ago. If any habitation had ever existed on this side of the river, the forest had long since swallowed it up. The oaks and elms through which we passed were more densely clustered than those of Mesh; there were many more maples, too, as well as hickories and moss-covered chestnuts. The undergrowth of bracken and ferns was a thick, green blanket almost smothering the forest floor. It would have been difficult to force our way through it if the forest had proved as trackless as Maram had feared. But the old road leading from the bridge – as on the other side of the river – turned into a track leading northwest through the trees. It seemed that no one except a few wandering animals had used it for a thousand years.

All that day we kept to this track, and to others we found deeper in the woods. As I had intended, we traveled on a fairly straight line toward the gap in the Shoshan Range through which the Nar road passed. Not far from the river, the ground began to rise before us and became drier. We saw no sign of man, and I began to hope that our cut across the wild lands of Anjo had either confused or lost whoever was hunting us. We slept that night at a higher elevation where we saw neither mosquitoes nor snakes.

Our next day's journey took us across several rills and streams flowing down from the mountains toward the Santosh. We had no trouble crossing them. Toward evening we encountered a bear feasting on newberries; we left him alone, and he left us alone. On our third day from the bridge, we entered the Gap in the Morning Mountains, where the land became hilly again. There I had intended to turn toward the Nar Road that cut through the Gap perhaps twenty miles to our north. But the folds of the hills and the only track we could find ran to the northwest. I decided that it wouldn't hurt to keep to these wild woods for another day or two before setting foot on the Nar Road.

In truth, I loved being so far from civilization. Here the trees lifted up their branches toward the sun and breathed their great, green breaths that sweetened the air. Here I felt at once all the wildness of an animal taking my strength from the earth and the silent worship of an angel walking proud and free beneath the stars. It would have been good to wander those woods for many more than a few days. But I had friends to lead out of them and promises to keep. And so on our fifth day in Old Alonia, I began seeking a track or a cut through the hills that would take us to the Nar Road.

'Where *are* we?' Maram grumbled to me as we made our way beneath the great crowns of the trees high above us. Through their leaves the sun shone like light through thousands of green, glass windows. 'Are you sure we're not lost?'

'Yes,' I told him for the hundredth time. 'As sure as the sun itself.'

'I hope you're right. You were sure we wouldn't get lost in the Bog, either.'

'This isn't the Black Bog,' I told him. As Altaru trod over earth nearly overgrown with ferns, I looked off at some lilies growing by the side of the track. 'We're only a few miles west of the Gap. We should find the Nar Road only a few miles north of here.'

'We *should* find it,' Maram agreed. 'But what if we don't?'

'And what if the sun doesn't rise tomorrow?' I countered. 'You can't worry about everything, you know.'

'Can't I? But it's you, with all your talk of men pursuing us, who has set me to worrying. You haven't, ah, sensed any sign of them?'

'Not for a few days.'

'Good, good. You've probably lost them in these dreadful woods. As you've probably lost us.'

'We're *not* lost,' I told him again.

'No? How do you know?'

An hour later, our track cut across a rocky shelf on the side of the hill. It was one of the few places we had found where trees didn't obstruct our view and we could look out at the land we were crossing. It was a rough, beautiful country we saw, with green-shrouded hills to the north and west. A soft mist, like long gray fingers, had settled down into the folds between them.

'I don't see the road,' Maram said as he stood staring out to the north. 'If it's only a few miles from here, shouldn't we see it?'

'Look,' I said, pointing at a strangely-formed hill near us. After rising at a gentle grade for a few hundred feet, it seemed to drop off abruptly as if cut with cliffs on its north face. At its top, it was barren of trees and all other vegetation except a few stunted grasses. 'If we climb it, we should be able to see the road from there.'

'All right,' Maram grumbled again. 'But I don't like the look of these hills. Didn't Kane warn of hill-men west of the Gap?'

Master Juwain came up and sat on his horse looking out at the misty hills. Then he said, 'I've been through this country before, when I traveled the Nar Road toward Mesh years ago. I met these hill-men that Kane spoke of. They waylaid our party and demanded that we pay a toll.'

'But this is the King's road!' I said, outraged at such robbery. In Mesh – as in all the Nine Kingdoms – the roads are free as the air men breathe. 'No one except King Kiritan has the right to charge tolls on any road through Alonia. And a wise king will never exercise that right.'

'I'm afraid we're far from Tria here,' Master Juwain said. 'The hill-men do as they please.'

'Well,' I said, 'perhaps we shouldn't cut toward the road just yet. Then we can't be charged for traveling upon it.'

This logic, however, did nothing to encourage Maram. He shook his head at Master Juwain and called out, 'But, sir, this is dreadful news! We don't have gold for tolls! Why didn't you tell me about these tolls?'

'I didn't want to worry you,' Master Juwain said. 'Now why don't we climb to the top of that hill and see what we can see?'

But Maram, hoping as always to put off potential disasters as long as he could, insisted on first eating a bit of lunch. And so we walked our horses down into the trees where we found a stream that seemed a good site for a rest. We ate a meal of walnuts, cheese and battle biscuits. I even let Maram have a little brandy to inspirit him. And then I led us down into a mist-filled vale giving out onto the barren hill to our north. After riding along a little stream for perhaps half a mile, the skin at the back of my neck began to tingle and burn. I had a sickening sense of being hunted, by whom or what I did not know.

And then, as suddenly as thunder breaking through a storm, the blare of battle horns split the air. TA-ROO, TA-ROO, TA-ROO – the same two notes sounded again and again as if someone was blowing a trumpet high on the hill before us. I tightened my grip around Altaru's reins and began urging him toward the hill; it was as if the horn – or something else – were calling me to battle.

'Wait, Val!' Maram called after me. 'What are you doing?'

'Going to see what's happening,' I said simply.

'I hate to know what's happening,' he said. He pointed behind us in the opposite direction. 'Shouldn't we flee, that way, while we still have the chance?'

I listened for a moment to the din shaking the woods, and then to a deeper sound inside me. I said, 'But what if the hill-men have trapped Sar Avador – or some other traveler – on the hill?'

'What if they trap *us* there? Come, please, while there's still time!'

'No,' I told him, 'I have to see.'

So saying, I pressed Altaru forward. Maram followed me reluctantly, and Master Juwain followed him trailing the pack horses. We rode along the dale and then through the woods leading up the side of the hill. As if someone had scoured the hill with fire, the trees suddenly ended in a line that curved around the hill's base. There we halted in their shelter to look out and see who was blowing the horn.

'Oh, my Lord!' Maram croaked out. 'Oh, my Lord!'

A hundred yards from us, ten men were advancing up the hill. They were squat and pale-skinned, nearly naked, with only the rudest covering of animal skins for clothing. They bore long oval shields, most of which had arrows sticking out of them. In their hands they clutched an irregular assortment of weapons: axes and maces and a few short, broad-bladed swords. Their leader – a thick-set and hairy man with daubs of red paint marking his face – paused once to blow a large, blood-spattered horn that looked as if it had been torn from the head of some animal. And then, pointing his sword up the hill, he began advancing again toward his quarry.

This was a single warrior who stood staring down at the men from the top of the hill. I immediately noted the long, blond hair that spilled from beneath the warrior's conical and pointed helmet; I couldn't help staring at the warrior's double-curved bow and the studded leather armor, for these were the accoutrements of the Sarni, which tribe I couldn't tell. A ring of dead men lay in the stunted grass fifty yards from the warrior farther down the hill. Arrows stuck out of them, too. In all of Ea, there were no archers like the Sarni and no bows that pulled so powerfully as theirs. But this warrior, I thought, would never pull a bow again because his quiver was empty and he had no more arrows to shoot. All he could do was to stand near his downed horse and wait for the hill-men to advance through the ring of their fallen countrymen and begin the butchery they so obviously intended.

'All right,' Maram murmured at me from behind his tree, 'you've seen what you came to see. Now let's get out of here!'

As quickly as I could, I nudged Altaru over to my pack horse where I untied the great helmet slung over his side. I untied as well the shield that my father had given me and thrust my arm through it. My side still hurt so badly that I could barely hold it. But I scarcely noticed this pain because I had worse wounds to bear.

'What are you doing?' Maram snapped at me. 'This isn't our business. That's a Sarni warrior, isn't it? A *Sarni*, Val!'

Master Juwain agreed with him that the course of action on which I was setting out perhaps wasn't the wisest. But since the Brotherhood teaches showing compassion to the unfortunates of the world, neither did he suggest that we should flee. He just stood there in the trees weighing different stratagems and wondering how the three of us – and one Sarni warrior – could possibly prevail against ten fierce and vengeful hill-men.

I slipped the winged helmet over my head then. I took up my lance and couched it beneath my good arm. How could I explain why I did this? I could hardly explain it to myself. After many miles of being hunted, I couldn't bear the sight of this warrior being hunted and bravely preparing to die. For Master Juwain, compassion was a noble principle to be honored wherever possible; for me it was a terrible pain piercing my heart. For some reason I didn't understand, I found myself opening to this doomed warrior. A proud Sarni he might be, but something inside him was calling for help, even as a child might call, and hoping that it might miraculously come.

'That man,' I told Maram, 'could have been Sar Avador. He could be my brother – he could be you.'

And with that, I touched my heels to Altaru's sides and rode out of the trees. I pressed him to a gallop; it was a measure of his immense strength that he quickly achieved this gait driving his hooves into the ground that sloped upward before us. I felt the great muscles of his rump bunching and pushing us into the air. He wheezed and snorted, and I felt his lust for battle. The hill-men had now drawn closer to the warrior, who stood waiting for them with nothing more than a saber and a little leather shield. His ten executioners, with their painted faces and bodies, advanced as a single mass, clumped foolishly close together. Their leader blew his bloody horn again and again to give them courage; they struck their weapons against their wooden shields as they screamed out obscenities and threatened fiendish tortures. This din must have drowned out the sound of Altaru pounding toward them, for they didn't see me until the last moment. But the warrior, looking downhill, did. He somehow guessed that I was charging toward the hill-men and not him; it must have mystified him why a Valari knight would ride to help him. But he left all such wonderings for a later moment. He let out a high-pitched whoop and charged the hill-men even as I lowered my lance and prepared to crash into them.

Just then, however, one of the hill-men turned toward me and let out a cry of dismay. This alerted the others, who froze wide-eyed in astonishment, not knowing what to do. I might easily have pushed the lance's point through the first man's neck. Altaru's snorting anger, and my own, drove me to do so; the nearness of death touched me with a terrible exhilaration. But then I remembered my vow never to kill anyone again. And so I raised the lance, and as we swept past the man, I used its steel-shod butt to strike him along the side of his head. He fell stunned to the side of the hill. One of his friends tried to unhorse me with a blow of his mace, but I caught it with my father's shield. Then the infuriated Altaru struck out with his hoof and broke through *his* shield and shoulder with a sickening crunch. He screamed in agony, even as I bit my lip in an effort not to scream, too.

Through the heat of the battle, I was somehow aware of the Sarni warrior closing with the hill-men's leader and opening his throat with a lightning slash of his saber. I immediately began coughing at the bubbling of blood I felt in my own throat. Then one of the hill-men swung his axe at my back, and only my Godhran-forged armor kept it from chopping through my spine. I whirled about in my saddle and struck him in the face with my shield. He stumbled to one knee, and I hesitated for an endless moment as I trembled to spear him with my lance.

And in that moment, the Sarni warrior cut through to him and ruthlessly finished him as well. A mail bevor fastened to the warrior's helm hid most of his face, but I could see his blue eyes flashing like diamonds even as his saber flashed out and struck off the man's head. His prowess of arms and rare fury – and, I supposed, my own wild charge – had badly dispirited the hill-men. When an arrow came whining suddenly out of the trees below us and buried itself in the ground near one of the hill-men to my right, he pointed downhill at Maram standing by a tree with my hunting bow. And then he cried out, 'They'll kill us all – run for your lives!'

In the panic that followed, the Sarni warrior managed to kill one more of the hill-men before his comrades turned their backs to us and fled down the hill toward the east, where a slight rise in the ground provided some cover against Maram's line of fire. I believe that the warrior might have pursued them to slay a few more if I hadn't slumped off my horse just then.

'No, please – no more killing,' I said as I held my hand palm outward and shook my head. I stood by Altaru, and grasped the pommel of his saddle to keep from falling.

'Who are you, Valari?' the warrior called to me.

I looked down the hill where the seven surviving men had disappeared into the woods. I looked at Maram and Master Juwain now making their way up the hill toward us. Except for the heavy breath steaming out of Altaru's huge nostrils, and my own labored breathing, the world had grown suddenly quiet.

'My name is Valashu Elahad,' I gasped out. I felt weak and disconnected from my body, as if my head had been cut off like the hill-man's and sent spinning into space. I pulled off my helm, then, the better to feel the wind against me. 'And who are you?'

The warrior hesitated a moment as I pressed my hand to my side. I felt the blood soaking through my armor. The battle had reopened the wound there, as well as the deeper wound that would never be healed.

'My name is Atara,' the warrior said, removing his helm as well. 'Atara Manslayer of the Kurmak. Thank you for saving my life.'

I gasped again, but not in pain. I stared at the long golden hair flowing down from Atara's head and the soft lines of Atara's golden face. It was now quite clear that Atara was a woman – the most beautiful woman I had ever seen. And though our enemies were either dead or dispersed, something inside her still called to me.

'Atara,' I said as if her name were an invocation to the angels who walked the stars, 'you're welcome.'

I suddenly knew that there was much more than a bond of blood between us. I looked into her eyes then, and it was like falling – not into the nothingness where she had sent the hill-men, but into the sacred fire of two brilliant, blue stars.

11

For what seemed forever, Atara held this magical connection of our eyes. Then, with what seemed a great effort of will, she looked away and smiled in embarrassment as if she had seen too much of me – or I of her.

She said, 'Please excuse me, there's work to be done.'

She walked back and forth across the hill, scanning the tree line for sign that the hill-men might attack again. She looked upon Maram and Master Juwain with scant curiosity, then quickly went about the blood-stained slope cutting her arrows out of the bodies of the fallen men. She used her saber with all the precision of Master Juwain probing a wound with a scalpel. And as she went from man to man, she counted out loud, beginning with the number five. At first, I thought her accounting had something to do with the number of arrows she had fired or recovered. But when she reached the body of the hill-men's leader, whom no arrow had struck, she quietly said, 'Fourteen.' And the headless body of the man she had beheaded was fifteen, whatever that might mean.

And then, as Maram and Master Juwain drew closer, I reflected upon Atara's strange second name: Manslayer. I remembered Ravar once telling of a group of women warriors of the Sarni called the Manslayer Society. It was said that a few rare women from each tribe practiced at arms and gave up marriage in order to join the fearsome Manslayers. Membership in their Society was almost always for life, for the only way that a Manslayer could be released from her vows was to slay a hundred of her enemies. Atara, in having slain four before she reached this dreadful hill, had already accounted for more men than many Valari knights. And in sending on twelve more, with arrow and sword, she had accomplished a great if terrible feat.

I stood watching her in awe as she cleaned the blood from her arrows and dropped them down into the quiver slung over her back. I thought that she couldn't be much older than I. She was a tall woman and big-boned, like most of her people. And she had their barbaric look. Her leather armor – all black and hardened and studded with steel – covered only her torso. A smoother and more supple pair of leather trousers provided protection for her legs. Her long, lithe arms were naked and burnt brown by the sun. Golden armlets encircled the upper parts of them. A golden torque, inlaid with lapis, encircled her neck. Her hair was like beaten gold, and the ends of it were wrapped with strings of tiny lapis beads. But it was her eyes that kept capturing my gaze; I had never hoped to see eyes like hers in all the world. Like sapphires her eyes were, like blue diamonds or the brightest of lapis. They sparkled with a rare spirit, and I thought they were more precious than any gem.

Just then, Maram and Master Juwain rode up to us, and Maram said, 'Oh, my Lord – it really *is* a woman!'

'A woman, yes,' I said to him. I was instantly jealous of the intense interest he showed in her. 'May I present Atara Manslayer of the Kurmak tribe? And this is Prince Maram Marshayk of Delu.'

I presented Master Juwain as well, and Atara greeted them politely before returning to the bloody work of retrieving her arrows. Both Master Juwain and Maram, as did I, wanted to know how a lone woman had come to be trapped on this hill. But Atara cut short their questions with an imperious shake of her head. She pointed to the top of the hill where her horse lay moaning, and she said, 'Excuse me, but I have one more thing to attend to.'

We followed her up the hill, but when we saw what she intended, we stood off a few yards to give her a bit of privacy. She walked straight up to her horse, a young steppe pony whose belly had been cut open. Much of his insides had spilled out of him and lay steaming on the grass. She sat down on the grass beside him; gently, she lifted his head onto her lap. She began stroking the side of it as she sang out a sad little song and looked into his large dark eye. She stroked his long neck, and then – even as I turned Altaru facing downhill – she drew the edge of her saber across his throat, almost more quickly than I could believe.

For a while Atara sat there on the reddening grass and stared up at the sky. Her struggle between pride of decorum and her grief touched me keenly. And then, at last, she buried her face in her horse's fur and began weeping softly. I blinked as I fought to keep from weeping as well.

After a while, she stood up and came over to us. Her hands and trousers were as bloody as a butcher's but she paid them no heed. She pointed at the bodies of the hill-men and said, 'They accosted me in the woods as I was climbing the hill. They demanded that I pay a toll for crossing their country. *Their* country, hmmph. I told them all this land belonged to King Kiritan, not them.'

'What else could you do?' Maram asked understandably. 'Who has gold for tolls?'

Here Atara moved back to her horse, where she freed a purse from his saddlebag. As she weighed it in her hand, it jangled with coins, and she said, 'It's not gold I lack – only a willingness to enrich robbers.'

'But they might have killed you!' Maram said.

'Better death than the dishonor of doing business with such men.'

Maram stared at her as if this principle were utterly alien to him.

'When the hill-men saw that I wouldn't pay them,' Atara continued, 'they became angry and raised weapons to me. They told me that they would take from me much more than a toll. One of them cut my pony with an axe to keep me from riding away. My *pony*! On the Wendrush, anyone who intentionally wounds a warrior's pony in battle is staked-out in the grass for the wolves.'

At this, Maram shook his head sadly and muttered, 'Well, better the wolves than the bears.'

It was a measure of Atara's wit – and grace – that she could laugh at this grim humor that she couldn't be expected to appreciate. But laugh she did, showing her straight white teeth as her face widened with a grim smile.

'But why were you even in the hill-men's country?' I asked her. I thought it more than strange that we should meet in the middle of this wilderness. 'And why were you climbing this hill?'

Atara pointed to the hill's ragged, rocky crest above us and said, 'I thought I might be able to see the Nar Road from here.'

We looked at each other in immediate understanding. I admitted that I needed to be in Tria on the seventh day of Soldru to answer King Kiritan's call to find the Lightstone. As did Atara. She told us of her journey then. She said that when word of the great quest had reached the Kurmak tribe, she had bade her people farewell and had ridden north along the western side of the Shoshan Mountains. Only by keeping close to these great peaks had she been able to bypass the Long Wall, which ran for four hundred miles across the prairies from the Shoshan to the Blue Mountains. Thus had Alonia protected its rich lands from the Sarni hordes for three long ages. But the Wall couldn't keep out one lone warrior determined to find a way around it. On Citadel Mountain, where the stones of the Wall flowed almost seamlessly into the blue granite of the Shoshan, Atara had discovered a track leading around it through the woods. Her nimble steppe pony had found footing on this rocky track where a larger horse such as Altaru would have broken his legs. And so Alonia, as in times past, had been invaded by the Sarni – if only a single warrior of the Manslayer Society.

'But the Sarni aren't at war with Alonia, are they?' I asked her. 'Why didn't you just pass the Wall through one of its gates?'

Atara looked at me strangely, and I felt her temper begin to rise. And then she said, 'No, there's no war, not yet. Other warriors, all men, have taken the more direct route along the Poru toward Tria. But the Alonians won't allow one such as I to pass through their gates.'

And so, she said, she had ridden north from the Wall into the hills west of the gap in the Shoshan Mountains. Even as we had ridden into them, from a different direction.

'I had hoped to cut the road by now,' she said. 'It can't be far.'

'You didn't see it from the top of the hill?' Maram asked worriedly.

'No, I didn't have time to look. But why don't we look now?'

Together, we walked the twenty yards to the hill's very top. As I had thought, the ground dropped off suddenly in a cliff as if a giant axe had chopped off the entire north part of the hill. From the exposed rocks along the line of this fault, we stood to look out. Forty or fifty miles away, the northern spur of the Shoshan Mountains was buried in the clouds. A cottony mist lay over the hill country leading up to them. We couldn't see much more of it than humps of green sticking out above the silvery swirls. But just below us, in a little valley, a blue-gray band of rock cut through the trees. It was wider than any road I had ever seen, and I knew that it must be the ancient Nar Road, which had been built from Tria to Nar before even the Age of Swords.

The question now arose as to what we should do. Maram, of course, favored the familiarity of good paving stones beneath his feet while I might have preferred to keep to the woods. I felt safer beneath the crowns of the great oaks than in proceeding along the line of an open road. But Master Juwain observed that if the hill-men were bent upon revenge, they could fall upon us anywhere in these hills that they chose. Therefore, he said, we might as well make our way down to the road. Atara agreed with him. And then she added that the hill-men were unlikely to attack us after losing so many men – especially since the arms of a Valari knight had now been added to the power of her great bow.

'But what about *my* bow?' Maram protested. He held up my hunting bow as if it belonged to him. 'It was *my* arrow, was it not, that finally frightened the men away?'

Atara looked down the hill to where Maram's arrow still stuck out of the grass. She said, 'Oh, you're right – what a magnificent shot! You probably managed to kill a mole or at least a few earthworms.'

I tried not to smile as Maram's face flushed beet red. And it was good that I didn't, for Atara had her doubts about me as well.

'I've heard that the Valari are great warriors,' she told me.

Yes, I thought, Telemesh and my grandfather were. My father is.

Atara pointed down at the body of the man I had spared. 'It must be hard to be a great warrior who is afraid to kill his enemies.'

Her eyes, which were as beautiful as diamonds, could be as cold and hard as these stones, too. They cut right through me and seemed to strip me naked.

'Yes,' I told her, 'it is hard.'

'Why did you ride to help me then?'

My gift, which sometimes let me see others' motivations so easily, often left me quite blind to my own. What could I say to her? That I had felt compassion for her plight? That even now I was afraid I might feel something more? Better then to say nothing, and so I stared off at the mist swirling over the hills.

'Well, you *did* help me, after all,' Atara finally said. 'You saved my life. And for that, I owe you a debt of blood.'

'No,' I said, looking at her, 'you owe me nothing.'

'Yes, I do. And I should ride with you until this debt is repaid.'

I blinked my eyes at the strangeness of this suggestion. A Sarni warrior ride with a Valari knight? Did wolves run with lions? How many times over the ages had the Sarni invaded the Morning Mountains – always to be beaten back? How many Valari had the Sarni sent on, and the Sarni slain of the Valari? Not even a warrior of the Manslayer Society, I thought, could count such numbers.

'No,' I said again, 'there is no debt.'

'Yes, of course there is. And I must repay it. Do you think I'd ride with you otherwise?'

Upon looking at the way she impatiently moved her hands as if to sweep away my obduracy, I sensed that she wouldn't. No, I thought, she would be much more likely to make her own way out of this wilderness – or even to fight me for the sheer joy of fighting.

'If the hill-men return,' she said, 'you'll need my bow and arrows.'

I touched my hand to my kalama and said, 'We Valari have always done well enough with our swords – even against the Sarni.'

Atara, who still held her saber in her long hands, glanced down at its curved blade and said, 'Yes, you've always had the superior weaponry.'

'You have your bows,' I said, pointing at hers, which she had left by her horse.

'We do,' she admitted. 'But the mountains have always proved bad ground for employing them to the best advantage. We've always had bad luck, as well.'

'That's true,' I said. 'At the Battle of the Song River, Elemesh's good generalship was your misfortune.'

We might have stood there arguing all day if Master Juwain hadn't observed that the sun wouldn't stop to listen and neither would the earth stand still to see who had prevailed. We should move on, and soon. Then he pointed out that Atara had no horse, and asked me if I truly intended to leave her alone in the woods.

'Are you sure you want to ride with us?' I asked her. Then I told her about Kane and the unknown men whom we suspected of hunting us since Anjo, and who might be hunting us still.

If I had thought to discourage her, however, I was disappointed. In answer to my question, she just stood there cleaning the blood from her sword and smiling as if I had proposed a game of chess on which she might gladly bet not only her bag of gold but her very life.

How, I wondered, could I ever trust such a woman? I looked at the bodies of the hill-men she had slain. Truly, she was the enemy of my enemies, but her people were also the enemy of mine. Was my enemy, then, so easily to become my friend?

'I pledge my life to the protection of yours,' she said simply. 'But I can't keep the hill-men away – or anyone else – if I don't ride with you.'

How could I *not* trust this courageous woman? I could almost feel her will to keep her word. I saw in her eyes a bright light and a basic goodness that touched me to the core. Even as I feared the fire building in my own eyes: if I let it, it might burn through me and consume me utterly. But if I ran away from this ineffable flame as I always had, then how would I be able protect *her* should evil men come for her again?

'Please,' I said, 'ride with us. We'll be glad of your company.'

I clasped hands with her then, and I felt the blood on her palm warm and wet against my own.

We spent most of the next hour readying ourselves for our journey. While Master Juwain redressed my wound, Maram shared out some of my hunting arrows with Atara. With her pony dead, we had to convert one of the pack horses to a mount. Atara reluctantly suggested riding my pack horse, Tanar. Although the big, bay gelding was quite strong, it had been a long time since he had borne a human being on his back. He was happy enough when I removed the bags of food and gear from him, but he shook his head and stamped his hoof when Atara buckled her saddle around him. Atara, however, had a gift for gentling horses. And for taking command of them. After convincing Tanar to accept the hard, iron bit in his mouth, she rode him about the hill for a while and announced that he would have to do until she could buy a better horse in Suma or Tria.

With one less horse available for carrying our supplies, I considered jettisoning the little casks of brandy and beer that Tanar had borne all the way from Silvassu. But this prospect horrified Maram. He protested that if necessary, he would dismount and carry the casks on his own back as far as Tria – or until he had managed to drain every dram from them, if that came first. Atara chided him, and all of us, for traveling so heavily burdened. A Sarni warrior, she said, could cross five hundred miles of the Wendrush with little more than a leather cloak and a bag full of dried antelope meat. But we were not Sarni. In the end, we redistributed our supplies as best we could over the backs and sides of our six horses.

We rode down from the hill then. After pausing by a stream so that Atara could clean herself, we found our way around the side of the hill into the valley we had seen from its top. A short distance through the trees brought us to a sudden break into bright sunlight where the Nar Road cut across the land. I marveled at the road's width: it was like a river of stone flowing through the forest. Grass grew in the many small cracks in it, and here and there, a tree grew out of larger breaks in its surface. But it was quite serviceable. Whole armies, I thought, could pass down this road. Whole armies had.

We traveled northeast along it for the rest of the day. We rode four abreast with the two remaining pack horses trailing behind us. If the hill-men were watching us from behind the walls of trees along the sides of the road, they didn't dare to show themselves. I thought that Atara was right, that they'd had enough of battle for one day. Even so, Atara and Maram kept their bows strung and close at hand as we all listened for breaking twigs or rustling leaves.

Master Juwain told us what he knew of the hill-men: he said they were descendants of a Kallimun army that had invaded Alonia early in the Age of the Dragon. The army's captain had been none other than Sartan Odinan, the very same Kallimun priest who had betrayed Morjin and then led Kalkamesh into Argattha to reclaim the Lightstone. After the rape and burning of Suma, Sartan's heart had softened and he had abandoned his bloodthirsty men. Morjin had then recalled the leaderless army to Sakai just as the conquest of Alonia seemed certain. But many of Sartan's men had remained to ravage the countryside. When King Maimun's soldiers began to hunt them down, they took refuge in the hills all about us, which their descendants had infested ever since.

'Sartan Odinan used a firestone to break the Long Wall,' Master Juwain said. 'Thus did his army force its way into Alonia. Even as the Sarni did in the Age of Swords.'

'No, the Sarni did *not* use a firestone to breach the Wall,' Atara said. 'The Sarni knew nothing of firestones then.'

As our horses clopped down the road and the slanting sun broke upon the canopies of the trees, Atara recounted the times of Tulumar Elek, who had united the Sarni tribes in the year 2,054 of the Age of Swords. According to Atara, Tulumar had been determined to conquer Alonia, then and still the greatest of Ea's kingdoms. And so Tulumar's armies had besieged the immense fortifications of the Long Wall for a year, without result. And then one day a mysterious man named Kadar the Wise had arrived in Tulumar's camp bearing casks of a red substance called *relb*. As Atara explained, *relb* was only a forerunner of the red gelstei, a first essay into the art of making these powerful stones. But it had power enough of its own: it concentrated the rays of the sun and set even stone on fire. Thus it was called the Stoneburner. Kadar the Wise persuaded Tulumar's Sarni warriors to spread the *relb* at night over a section of the Long Wall, and this they did, with great sacrifice. It looked much like paint or fresh blood, and the Alonians thought that the Sarni had gone mad.

But the next day, as the sun's rays at noon poured down upon the Long Wall, the *relb* burst into flame, melting stone to lava and killing thousands of the Wall's defenders. This great event had become known as the Breaking of the Long Wall. In the coming years, Tulumar would go on to conquer all of Alonia and Delu.

'Tulumar was a great warrior,' Atara said. 'One of the greatest of the Sarni. But Kadar the Wise tricked him.'

Master Juwain, rubbing his bald head as he rode along, looked at her in surprise. 'If your story is true – and I should say it's nowhere mentioned in the *Saganom Elu* or any of the histories of the Elekar dynasty – then it would seem that Tulumar owed much of his success to this Kadar the Wise.'

'No, Kadar tricked Tulumar,' Atara said again. 'For Kadar was really Morjin in disguise.'

'What!' Master Juwain called out. He rubbed his gnarly hands together as if in anticipation of a feast. I had never seen him so excited. 'The Red Dragon began his rise more than two hundred years after that!'

'No, it *was* Morjin,' Atara said. 'This is known. The stories have been told for two ages. Morjin tried to use Tulumar to conquer all of Ea. He tried to make a ghul of him, and in the end this killed him.'

'The *Saganom Elu* tells that Tulumar died of a fever after preparing an invasion of the Nine Kingdoms.'

'If he did, it was a fever born of poison and Morjin's lies.'

I thought about the poison burning in my own veins and what it

182

might eventually do to me. To distract myself from these dark thoughts, I said, 'Tulumar's son was Sagumar, I believe.'

'Yes,' Atara said. 'Morjin tried to enslave him, too.'

'And this was the same Sagumar, wasn't it, whom King Elemesh defeated at the Song River? If what you say is true, then King Elemesh defeated Morjin as well.'

'For a time,' Atara said bitterly, nodding her head. 'Morjin has always posed as the Sarni's greatest friend, but he is our greatest enemy. Even now, he is trying to win the tribes with promises of diamonds and gold. This is the key for him. If he wins the Sarni, he wins all of Ea.'

Although the sun was a bright yellow disk in the west, the world suddenly seemed cast into darkness. I asked Atara, 'Are the tribes listening to the Red Dragon then?'

'Some of them are. The Danladi and Marituk have practically pledged their swords to him. And half the clans of the Urtuk, it is said, favor an alliance with Sakai.'

At this news, I ground my teeth together. For the Urtuk commanded the steppe just to the west of the mountains of Mesh. 'And what about the Kurmak?' I asked her. 'Will your people ride with the Red Dragon?'

'Never!' Atara said. 'Sajagax himself would slay any warrior of the clans who even suggested following Morjin.'

She went on to tell us that this fierce, old chief of the Kurmak was her grandfather, and that he favored finding the Lightstone as a way of defeating Morjin. As did Atara.

As we made our way through the lovely afternoon, I thought about all that Atara had said. I thought about her as well. I liked her forceful and sportive temperament, and I liked her passion for justice even more. She had a wisdom I had never seen in a woman her age. And this was not simply a discerning knowledge of things unknown even to Master Juwain, but a keen sense for the ways of the world. Her eyes seemed to miss no detail of the forest we passed through, and her feel for terrain was even better than mine: more than once she was able to guess what streams we might find or how the road might turn beyond the wall of the hills before us. And that evening, as we halted by one of these streams, I discovered just how deep her understanding of animals ran. She told me that since I was wounded, I should rest and allow her to do much of the work of making camp. She insisted on unsaddling Altaru and brushing him down. When I insisted that my unruly horse might kill her if she drew too close to him, she simply walked up to his side and told him that they must be friends. Something in the dulcet tones of her voice must have worked a magic on Altaru, for he nickered softly and allowed her to breathe into his great nostrils. She stroked his neck for a long time then, and I could feel the beginning of love stirring in his great chest.

I was forced to admit that it was good that Atara had joined us; she was good company, and we all appreciated her enthusiasm and easy laughter. But she managed to vex us as well. Over the days of our journey, Master Juwain, Maram and I had grown used to each other and had established a certain rhythm in making camp. Atara changed all that. She was as meticulous in performing chores as she was precise in shooting her arrows. Water must be taken from a stream at its exact center so as to avoid collecting any unwanted sediment; the stones for the fire had to be set around the pit in a exact circle and the firewood neatly trimmed so as to fit the pit perfectly. She seemed tireless in making these devotions. For Atara, I thought, there was a right way and a wrong way of doing everything, and she attended each little action as if the fate of the world hung in the balance.

It must have been hard for her to demand so much of herself. I sensed in her a relentless war between what she wanted to do and what she knew she must do. At those rare moments when she relaxed and let down her guard, her wild joy of life came bubbling up out her like a fountain. She liked to laugh at even the most ridiculous of Maram's stories, and when she did, the peals rang out of her without restraint. That night, over a warm fire and a nip of brandy, she laughed and sang while I played my flute. I thought it was the finest music I had ever heard, and wished that we might have the chance again to make more.

The next day dawned bright and clear with the music of a million birds filling the forest. We traveled down the road through some of the most beautiful country I had ever seen. The hills were on fire with a deep and pure green, and glowed like huge emeralds; the sun was a golden crown melting over them. Wildflowers grew everywhere along the side of the road. With spring renewing the land, every tree was in leaf, and every leaf seemed to reflect the light of every other so that the whole forest shimmered with a perfect radiance.

Everything about the world that day touched me with astonishment at its perfection. It pleased me to see the squirrels scurrying after new shoots, and the sweetness of the buttercups and daisies filled my lungs with every breath. But I took my greatest joy from Atara for she seemed the greatest of the world's creations. As we passed down the road toward Tria, I found myself looking at her whenever I could. At times she rode ahead of me with Maram, and I listened to them talking spiritedly. When Atara laughed at one of Maram's rude jokes, my ears couldn't seem to get enough of the sound. My eyes drank in the sight of her long, browned arms and her flowing yellow hair, and were unquenchably thirsty for more. I marveled at even her hands for they were graceful and finely made, with long, tapering fingers – not at all the hands of a warrior. The image of her whole being seemed to burn itself into me: straight, proud, laughing, wise and allied with all the forces of life, a woman as a woman was born to be.

On the next day of our journey, we left the hills behind us, and the forest grew flatter. With nothing but wild land empty of human beings before us, we all began to relax a little. Around mid-morning, I found myself riding beside Maram while Atara and Master Juwain went on ahead us some thirty yards. Atara was telling Master Juwain of the Sarni's greatest stories and feats, which he was furiously scribbling down in his journal as he rode. I couldn't keep myself from admiring Atara's poise in the saddle, the way that the play of her hip and leg muscles seemed to guide Tanar effortlessly along. And Maram couldn't keep himself from noticing my absorption – and commenting upon it.

'You're in love, my friend,' he quietly said to me. 'At last, in love.'

His words caught me completely by surprise. The truth often does. It is astonishing how we can deny such things even when it is in our eyes and hearts. 'You think I'm in *love*?' I said stupidly. 'With Atara?'

'No, with your pack horse, whom you've been watching all morning.' He shook his head at my doltishness.

'But I thought it was you who loved her.'

'*I*? But what made you think that?'

'Well, she's a woman, isn't she?'

'Ah, a woman she is. And I'm a man. So what? A stallion smells a mare in heat, and it's inevitable that the inevitable will happen. But *love*, Val?'

'Well, she's a beautiful woman.'

'Beautiful, yes. So is a star. Can you touch one? Can you wrap your arms around such a cold fire and clasp it to your heart?'

'I don't know,' I said. 'If you can't, why should you think I can?'

'Because you're different from me,' he said simply. 'You were born to worship such impossible lights.'

He went on to say that the very feature I loved most about Atara unnerved him completely. 'The truth is, my friend, I can't bear looking at her damn eyes. Too blue, too bright – a woman's eyes should flow into mine like coffee, not dazzle me like diamonds.'

I looked down at the two diamonds of my knight's ring but couldn't find anything to say.

'She loves you, you know,' he suddenly told me.

'Did she say that?'

185

'Ah, no, not exactly. In fact, she denied it. But that's like denying the sun.'

'You see,' I said. 'She couldn't possibly love me. No one could love another so soon.'

'You think not? When you were born, did you need more than a moment to love the world?'

'That's different,' I said.

'No, my friend, it's not. Love *is*. Sometimes I think it's the only thing in the world that *really* is. And when a man and a woman meet, either they open themselves to this heavenly fire, or they do not.'

Again I looked at the stones of my ring shining in the bright morning light like two stars.

'Aren't you aware of the way Atara listens to you when you speak of even little things?' Maram asked. 'When you walk into a clearing, don't you see the way her eyes light up as if you were the sun?'

'No, no,' I murmured, 'it's not possible.'

'It *is* possible, damn it! She told me she was drawn to your kindness and that wild thing in your heart you always try to hide. She was really just saying that she loved you.'

'No, it's not possible,' I said again.

'Listen, my friend, and listen well!' Here Maram grasped my arm as if his fingers might convince me of what his words could not. 'You should tell her that you love her. Then ask her to marry you, before it's too late.'

'*You* say that?' I couldn't believe what I had heard. 'How many women have *you* asked to marry you, then?'

'Listen,' he said again. 'I may spend the rest of my life looking for the woman who was meant for me. But you, by rare good chance and the grace of the One – you've found the woman who was meant for you.'

We made camp that night off the side of the road in a little clearing where a great oak had fallen. A stream ran through the forest only fifty yards from our site; it was a place of good air and the clean scents of ferns and mosses. Maram and Master Juwain drifted off to sleep early while I insisted on staying awake to make the night's first watch. In truth, with all that Maram had said to me, I could hardly sleep. I was sitting on a flat rock by the fire and looking out at the stars when Atara came over and sat beside me.

'You should sleep, too,' I told her. 'The nights are growing shorter.'

Atara smiled as she shook her head at me. In her hands she held a couple of stones and a length of wood, which she intended to shape into a new arrow. 'I promised myself I'd finish this,' she said.

We spoke for a while of the Sarni's deadly war arrows which could pierce armor and their great bows made of layers of horn and sinew laminated to a wooden frame. Atara talked of life on the Wendrush and its harsh, unforgiving ways. She told me about the harsh, unforgiving Sajagax, the great war chief of the Kurmak. But of her father, she said little. I gathered only that he disapproved of her decision to enter the Manslayer Society.

'For a man to see his daughter take up arms,' I said, 'must come as a great shock.'

'Hmmph,' she said. 'A warrior who has seen many die in battle shouldn't complain about such shocks.'

'Are you speaking of me or your father?'

'I'm speaking of men,' she said. 'They claim they are brave and then almost faint at the sight of a woman with a bow in her hands or bleeding a little blood.'

'That's true,' I said, smiling. 'For me to see my mother or grandmother wounded would be almost unbearable.'

Atara's tone softened as she looked at me and said, 'You love them very much, don't you?'

'Yes, very much.'

'Then you must be glad,' she said, 'that you Valari forbid women to become warriors.'

'No, you don't understand,' I told her. 'We don't forbid women this. It's just the opposite: all our women are warriors.'

I went on to say that the first Valari were meant to be warriors of the spirit only. But in an imperfect world, we Valari men had had to learn the arts of war in order to preserve our purity of purpose, which we saw as being realized in women. It was only the Valari women, I said, who had the freedom to embody our highest aspirations. Where men were caught up with the mechanisms of death, the women might further the glories of life. It was upon women to approach all the things of life – growing food, healing, birthing, raising children – with a warrior's passion and devotion to flowingness, flawlessness and fearlessness.

'Women,' I said, 'are the source of life, are they not? And thus it is taught that they are a perfect manifestation of the One.'

And thus, I said, among the Valari, it was also taught that women might more easily find serenity and joy in the One. Women were seen as more easily mastering the meditative arts, and were very often the instructors of men. Of the three things a Valari warrior is taught – to tell the truth; to wield a sword; to abide in the One – his mother was responsible for the first and the last.

I stopped talking then, and listened to the stream flowing through the forest and the wind rustling the leaves of the trees. Atara was quiet for a few moments while she regarded me in the fire's soft light. And then she told me, 'I've never known a man like you.'

I watched as she drew the length of wood between the two grooved pieces of sandstone that she held in her hand, smoothing and straightening the new arrow. Then I said, 'Who has ever seen a women like you? In the Morning Mountains, the women shoot different kinds of arrows into men's hearts.'

She laughed at this in her spirited way, and then told me that healing, birthing, and raising children were indeed important and women were very good at them. But some women were also good at war, and this was a time when much killing needed to be done.

'A time comes to cut wheat and harvest it,' she said. 'Now it's time for the more bloody harvest of cutting men.'

She went on to say that for three long ages, men had ravaged the world, and now it was time for them to reap what they had sowed.

'No, there must be another way,' I told her. I drew my sword and watched the play of starlight on its long blade. 'This isn't the way the world was meant to be.'

'Perhaps not,' she said, staring at this length of steel. 'But it's the way the world *will* be until we make it differently.'

'And how will we do that?' I wondered.

She fell quiet for a long time as she sat looking at me. And then she said, 'Sometimes, late at night or when I look into the waters of a still pool, I can see it. *Almost* see it. There is a woman there. She has incredible courage but incredible grace, too. There hasn't been a true woman on Ea since the Age of the Mother. Maybe not even then. But this woman of the waters and wind – she has a terrible beauty like that of Ashtoreth herself. This is the beauty that the world was meant to bring into life. This is the beauty that every woman was born for. But that woman I will never be until men become what they were meant to be. And nothing will ever change men's hearts except the Lightstone itself.'

'Nothing?' I asked, dropping my eyes toward her arrow.

Here she laughed nicely for a moment and then admitted, 'I said before that I sought the Lightstone to unite all the Sarni. And that's true. And yet, I would like to see all men united. All men and all women.'

'That's a lovely thought,' I told her. 'And you're a lovely woman.'

'Please don't say that.'

'Why not?'

'Please don't say that the *way* that you say that.'

'My apologies,' I said, looking down as she slid the arrow between her sanding stones.

Then she put down both her arrow and her stones and waved her hands at the darkened trees all about us. 'It's strange,' she said, 'here we are in the middle of a wood that has almost no end, far from either the Wendrush or any city. And yet, whenever I come near you, I feel like I'm returning home.'

'It's that way for me, too,' I said.

'But it shouldn't be. It mustn't be. This isn't the time for anyone to be making homes together. Or anything else.'

'Such as children?'

'Children, yes.'

'Then you've no wish ever to be a mother?'

'Of course I have,' she said. 'Sometimes I think there's nothing I want more.' She looked straight at me and continued, 'But there are always choices, aren't there? And I was given the choice between making babies or killing my enemies.'

'So,' I said, 'if you kill enough bad men, the world will be a better place for babies?'

'Yes,' she said. 'That's why I joined the Society and made my vow.'

'Would you never consider breaking it then?'

'As Maram breaks his?'

'A hundred men,' I said, staring off at the shadows between the trees. Not even Asaru or Karshur, I thought, had slain so many. No Valari warrior I knew had.

'A vow is a vow,' she said sadly. 'I'm sorry, Val.'

I was sorry, too. I put away my sword then and took out my flute. The world about me was more peaceful than it had been since Mesh. The trees swayed gently beneath the starry sky while the wind blew cool and clean. On the other side of the fire, Maram snored happily and Master Juwain moved his lips in his sleep as if memorizing the lines from a book. And yet beneath this contentment was a sadness that seemed to touch all things, the ferns and the flowers no less than Atara and me. It was in recognition of the bittersweet taste of life that I began to play a song that my grandmother had taught me. The words formed up inside me like dried fruits stuck in my throat: *Wishes are wishing you would wish them.* What wish, I wondered, was waiting for me to give it life? Only that Atara and I might someday stand face to face, as man and woman, without the thunder of the war drums sounding in the distance.

And so I played, and each note was a step taking the music higher; my breath was the wind carrying this wish up into the sky. After a while, I played other songs even as Atara put away her arrow and looked at me. In her eyes danced the dark lights of the fire and much else. I couldn't help thinking of the words that Maram had called out some days before: *Her eyes are windows to the stars.* He had forgotten the lines of his new poem even more quickly than he had Duke Gorador's wife. But I hadn't. Neither had I forgotten the verse that he had recited the night of the feast in my father's hall:

> *Star of my soul, how you shimmer*
> *Beyond the deep blue sky*
> *Whirling and whirling – you and I whisperlessly*
> *Spinning sparks of joy into the night.*

Even as the crackling fire sent its own sparks spinning into the darkness, I was overwhelmed with a strange sense that Atara and I had once come from this nameless star. In truth, whenever she looked at me it seemed that we returned there. As we did now. For an age, it seemed, we sat there on our rock beneath the ancient constellations as the world turned and the stars whirled. Almost forever, I looked into her eyes. What was there? Only light. How, I wondered, even if she should miraculously fulfill her vow, could I ever hold it? Could I drink in the sea and all the oceans of stars?

Wordlessly, she reached out her hand and grasped mine. Her touch was like lightning splitting me open. All of her incredible sadness came flooding into me; but all of her wild joy of life came, too. In the warmth of her fingers against mine there was no assurance of passion or marriage, but only a promise that we would always be kind to each other and that we wouldn't fail each other. And that we would always remind each other where we had come from and who we were meant to be. It was the most sacred vow I had ever made, and I knew that both Atara and I would keep it.

It was good to be certain of at least one thing in a world where men tried to twist truth into lies. In the quiet of the night, we lost ourselves in each other's eyes and breathed as one.

And so for a few hours, I was happier than I had ever been. But when a door to a closed room is finally opened, not only does light stream in, that which was confined in the darkness is free to leap howling out. In my soaring hope, in my great gladness of Atara's company, I didn't dare see that my heart was wide open to the greatest of terrors.

12

Early the next morning my nightmares began again. I came screaming out of sleep convinced that the ground beneath my sleeping furs had opened up and I was plunging into a black and bottomless abyss. My cries of terror awoke myself and everyone else. Master Juwain came over to where I lay by the fire's glowing embers and rested his hand on my forehead.

'Your fever has returned,' he told me. 'I'll make you some tea.'

While he went off to fetch some water and prepare his bitter brew, Atara soaked a cloth in the cool water of the stream and returned to press it against my head. Her fingers – callused from years of pulling a bowstring – were incredibly gentle as she brushed back my sweat-soaked hair. She was quiet, her full lips pressed together with her concern.

'Do you think his wound is infected?' Maram said to Master Juwain. 'I thought it was getting better.'

'Let's see,' Master Juwain said as the water for the tea was heating. 'Let's get your mail off, Val.'

They helped strip me bare to the waist, and then Master Juwain removed my bandage to examine my wound. He probed it gently, and pronounced that it was healing again and looked clean enough. After bandaging my side and helping me dress, he sat by his pot of boiling water and looked at me in puzzlement.

'Do you think it's the kirax?' Maram asked.

'I don't think so,' Master Juwain said. 'But it's possible.'

'And what,' Atara asked, 'is kirax?'

Master Juwain turned to me as if wondering how much he should tell her. In answer, I nodded my head.

'It's a poison,' Master Juwain said. 'A terrible poison.'

He went on to recount how an assassin's arrow had wounded me in the woods outside Silvassu. He explained how the priests of the Kallimun sometimes used kirax to slay horribly at Morjin's bidding.

'Oh, but you make evil enemies, don't you?' Atara said to me.

'It would seem so,' I said. Then I smiled at Master Juwain, Maram and her. 'But also the best of friends.'

Atara returned my smile then asked, 'But why should Morjin wish you dead?'

That was one of the questions of my life I most wanted answered. Because I had nothing to say, I shrugged my shoulders and stared off at the glow of the dawn in the east.

'Well, if he does wish you dead and this man Kane is the one he has sent after you, I have a present for him.' So saying, Atara drew forth an arrow from her quiver and pointed it west, toward Argattha. 'Morjin's assassins aren't the only ones who can shoot arrows, you know.'

After that I drank my tea and ate a little breakfast. Although my fever faded with the coming of the day, a dull headache remained to torment me. Some big, dark clouds moved over the land from the north, and I could almost feel the pressure of them smothering the forest. Before we could even put away our cooking pots and break camp, it started to rain: a steady drumming of cold drops that drove down through the trees and beat against my head. Master Juwain pointed out that we would stay drier in the woods than on the open road; he suggested remaining there another day in order to recover our strength.

'No,' I said. 'We can rest when we get to Tria.'

Master Juwain, who could sometimes be cunning, shook his head at me and said, 'You're tired, Val. So are the horses.'

In the end, it was the condition of the horses that decided me. We had pressed them hard for many miles, and they hadn't had a good feed of grain since Duke Gorador's castle. Although they had found grass along our way, this wasn't enough to keep them fat and happy – especially Altaru, who needed some oats in his belly to keep his huge body driving forward. I realized that for a couple of days, he had been telling me that he was hungry, but I hadn't been listening. And so I consented to Master Juwain's suggestion. Against Maram's protests, I fed him and the other horses most of the oats that we had been reserving for our morning porridge. As I reminded Maram, we still had some cheese and nuts, and quite a few battle biscuits.

And so we remained there for the rest of the day. The rain seemed only to come down harder with each passing hour. We sat huddled beneath the meager shelter of the trees listening to its patter against the leaves. I was very grateful for the cloak that my mother had made for me; I kept it wrapped tightly about me, as I did the white, wool scarf my grandmother had knitted. To pass the time, I took out Jonathay's chess set. I played some games with Maram and then Atara. It surprised me

192

that she beat me every time, for I hadn't known the Sarni studied such civilized games. I might have blamed my poor play on my throbbing head, but I didn't want to diminish Atara's victory.

'Would you like to play me?' Atara asked Maram after I had lost my fourth game. 'You've been sitting out a while.'

'No, thank you,' Maram said. 'It's more fun watching Val lose.'

Atara began setting up the pieces for a new game as Maram shivered miserably beneath his red cloak and said, 'I'm cold, I'm weary, I'm wet. But at least this rain should keep the bears holed up. There hasn't been any sign of them – has there?'

'No,' I said to encourage him. 'The bears don't like rain.'

'And there's been no sign of Kane or anyone else – has anyone seen any sign?'

Both Master Juwain and Atara reassured him that, except for the rain, the woods had been as silent as they were wet. I wanted to reassure him as well. But I couldn't – nor could I comfort myself. For ever since I had awakened from my nightmare, I'd had a gnawing sensation in my belly that some beast was hunting for me, sniffing at the air and trying to catch my scent through the pouring rain. As the grayness of the afternoon deepened, this sensation grew stronger. And so I resolved to break camp and travel hard at first light no matter rain or fever or the tiredness of the horses.

That night I had worse nightmares. My fever returned, and Master Juwain's tea did little to cool it. But as I had promised myself, in the morning we set out on the road. It was grim work plodding over the drenched paving stones through the rain. The whole world narrowed to this tunnel of stone cutting east through the dark green woods and the even darker gray sky. Master Juwain said that in Alonia, it sometimes rained like this for days without end. Maram wondered aloud how it was that the sky could hold whole oceans among its cold currents of air. Atara said that on the Wendrush, it rained fiercely but rarely so steadily as this. Then, to cheer us, she began singing a song meant to charm the rain away.

Just before dusk, as we were making camp in the dripping woods, the rain finally broke. My fever didn't. It seemed to be centered in my head, searing all my senses, cooking my brain. I had no evil dreams that night only because I couldn't sleep. I lay awake on the cold, sodden earth tossing and turning and hoping that the sky might clear and the stars would come out. But the clouds remained thick and heavy long past midnight; through the long hours of darkness, the sky seemed lower than it should be. Morning's thin light showed a gray mist lying over the tops of the trees. It was a bad day for travel, I thought, but travel we must.

'You're still hot,' Master Juwain told me as he tested my head. 'And you're so pale, Val – I'm afraid you're growing weaker.'

In truth, I was so weak that I could hardly hold the mug of tea that Maram gave me or move my mouth to speak. But I had to warn them of my feeling of being followed because it was growing ever stronger.

'Someone is coming for us,' I said. 'Maybe Kane – maybe others.'

This news alarmed Maram almost as much as it surprised Atara. Her blonde eyebrows arched as she asked, 'But we've seen no sign of anyone since the hills. Why should you think someone is pursuing us?'

'Val has a sense about such things,' Master Juwain tried to explain.

Atara cast me a long, penetrating look and then nodded her head as if she understood. She seemed to see me as no one ever had before; she both believed me and believed *in* me, and I loved her for that.

'Someone is coming for us, you say,' Maram muttered as he stood by the fire scanning the woods. 'Why didn't you tell us, Val?'

I, too, stood staring off through the woods; I hadn't told them anything because I had doubted what I had sensed, even as I doubted it now. Only two days before, in my joy at finding Atara, I had opened myself to the whole world and had been stricken by the beauty of the sun and the sky, by the sweetness of the flowers and the trees and the wind. But what if my gift, quickened by the kirax in my blood, had also opened me to other things? What if I were picking up on every fox in the forest stalking the many rabbits and voles? What if I could somehow sense the killing instinct of every bear, racoon and weasel – as well as every fly-catching frog and worm-hunting bird and all the other creatures around us? Might I not have mistaken this flood of natural urges for a feeling that someone was hunting me?

And yet it was the sheer *unnaturalness* of what I now felt that filled me with dread. Something slimy and unclean seemed to want to fasten itself to the back of my neck and suck the fluids from my spine; something like a clot of worms gnawed continually at my belly. I was afraid that if I let them, they would eat their way up through my heart and head and bleed away my very life. And so, because I was afraid that this horrible thing might be coming for Atara and the others, too, I decided that it was long past time that I warned them of the danger.

'My apologies for not telling you sooner,' I said to Maram. 'But I had to be sure. There is a wrongness here.'

Maram, who remembered very well our near-death at the Telemesh Gate, drew in a quick breath and asked, 'Do you think it's another bear?'

'No, this is different. No beast could make me feel this way.'

'No beast except the Red Dragon,' he muttered.

'If it *is* men who are pursuing us,' Master Juwain said, 'then shouldn't we be on our way as soon as possible?'

'If it is men,' Atara said, slinging on her quiver, 'then as soon as they show themselves, my arrows will pursue *them*.'

She wondered if we shouldn't find a place of concealment by the side of the road and simply wait for whoever might be riding after us. But I couldn't countenance shooting at men from behind trees as my would-be assassin had shot at me. And I couldn't bear more killing in any case. Because our pursuers might still be untold miles away, it seemed the safest course to ride west as quickly as we could.

And ride we did. For most of the first hour of that day's journey, we moved along at a swift canter. Our horses' hooves struck the road in a three-beat rhythm of iron against stone, clop-clip-clop, again and again. When they grew tired, we slowed to a trot. At last we broke for a rest as Atara dismounted and pressed her ear to road to listen for the sound of other hooves.

'Do you hear anything?' Maram called to her from the side of the road. 'What do you hear?'

'Nothing except you,' Atara told him. 'Now please be quiet.'

But after a few moments, she stood up and slowly shook her head.

'Let's ride, then,' Maram said. 'I don't like the look of this wood.'

I smiled then because I thought it wasn't the trees or any growing thing that disturbed him. Some miles back, we had entered a hilly country again – but nothing so rugged or high as the tors along the gap of the Shoshan Range. Here the hills were low and rounded, and were covered in chestnut, yellow poplar, black ash and oak. In the broad valley through which we rode grew stands of beech, walnut, sycamore, elm and silver maple. Many of these giants of the forest were clothed in honeysuckle and wild grape. In truth, it was a lovely wood, sweet with fruits and singing birds, and I lamented that only man could bring any evil into it.

We rode through the rest of the day. Around noon, the sun boiled away the last of the mist, and the sky cleared to a hazy blue. It grew quite hot, and humid, too, with the earth's moisture flavoring the air like a fermy soup. I was hot from a fever that had now spread from my head into the rest of my body. Beneath my layers of surcoat, mail and underpadding, I began to sweat. For a long while, I suffered this torment as I had been taught. But then the worms in my belly seemed to ignite like writhing tendrils of flame; my skin felt like a tunic soaked in oil and set on fire. I wanted to pull off this wrapping of burning flesh, along with all my clothing and armor, and jump into the stream that ran by the roadside. Instead, I fixed my gaze on the white blister of the sun as it slowly made its way toward the west. I might have screamed at the agony of it all if I hadn't remembered that Valari warriors are not allowed to give voice to such pain.

We made camp that night in a grove of elms by a stream half a mile from the road. We risked no fire until it grew dark and the smoke from the damp wood we found would not be seen. Our meal that evening was as cold and cheerless as it was sparse: upon opening our food bags, we found that half our biscuits and all our cheese had grown a thick, green fur of mold. Although Master Juwain cut away as much of it as he could, neither Atara nor Maram had much appetite for what remained.

And I had none. Since I didn't have the strength to chew the leathery dried meat that Atara urged upon me, I sat back against a tree drinking some cool water. Although I insisted on staying awake to take the first watch – and perhaps the other watches as well – I almost immediately fell asleep. I never felt my friends' hands lifting me onto my bed of furs by the small fire.

I was vaguely aware that I was writhing and sweating there on the ground for most of the night. At times I must have dreamed. And then suddenly I found myself somehow awakening many miles away in a large room with rich furnishings. I stood by a magnificently canopied bed marveling at the gilded chests and wardrobes along the walls. There I saw three long mirrors, framed in ornate gold as well. The ceiling was like a chessboard, with squares of finely carved white wood alternating with the blackest ebony; an intricately woven carpet showing the shapes of many animals and men covered the floor. I couldn't find any window or door. I stood sweating in fear because I couldn't imagine how I had come to be there.

And then the mirror opposite me began rippling like still water into which someone had thrown a stone. A man stepped out of it. He was slightly above average height, slim and well-muscled, with skin as fair as snow. His short hair shone like spun gold, and the fine features of his face radiated an almost unearthly beauty. I gasped to behold his eyes, for they were all golden, too. He was elegantly dressed, in a golden tunic trimmed with black fur. Across the chest, the tunic was embroidered with an emblem that drew my eyes and held them fast: it was the coiled shape of a large and ferocious red dragon.

'You're standing on my head,' he told me in a strong, deep voice. 'Please get your muddy boots off it.'

I looked down to see that I was indeed standing on the eyes of a red dragon woven into the wool at the center of the carpet. I instantly found myself moving backward. No king I had ever known – neither

King Hadaru nor even my father – spoke with such command as did this beautiful man.

'Do you know who I am?' he asked me.

'Yes,' I said. I was sweating fiercely now; I wanted to close my eyes and scream, but I couldn't look away from him. 'You're the Red Dragon.'

'I have a name,' he said. 'You know what it is – please say it.'

'No,' I told him. 'I won't.'

'Say it now!'

'Morjin,' I said, despite my resolve. 'Your name is Morjin.'

'*Lord* Morjin, you should call me. And you are Valashu Elahad. Son of Shavashar Elahad, who is of the line of Elemesh, Aramesh and Telemesh. Do you know what these *men* did to me?'

'Yes – they defeated you.'

'Defeated? Do I look defeated?' Morjin positioned himself by one of his mirrors as he adjusted the folds of his tunic. He stood very straight, and his face took on a fierce and implacable countenance. It seemed that he was searching for fire and iron there and finding both in abundance. He looked into his own golden eyes for a long time. And then he turned to me and said, 'No, in the end, it was I who defeated them. They are dead and I am still alive.'

He took a few steps closer to me and said, 'But they did defy me. Even as you have, Valashu *Elahad*.'

'No,' I said, 'no, no.'

'No . . . *what?*'

'No, Lord Morjin.'

'You killed one of my knights, didn't you?'

'No, that's not true – are assassins knights?'

'You put your knife into him. You killed this man, and so you owe him a life. And since he was *my* man, you owe me your life.'

'No, that's a lie,' I said. 'You're the Lord of Lies.'

'Am I?'

'You're the Lord of Illusions, the Crucifier, the Great Beast.'

'I'm only a man, like you.'

'No – that's the worst lie of all! You're nothing like me.'

Morjin smiled, revealing small white teeth as lustrous as pearls. He asked me, 'Have you never lied, then?'

'No – my mother taught me not to lie. My father, too.'

'*That* is the first lie you've told me, Valashu. But not the last.'

'Yes, it is!' I said. I pressed my hand to my throbbing head. 'I mean, no, it isn't – I wasn't lying when I said it's wrong to lie.'

'Is it really?' he asked me. He took another step closer and said, 'It pleases me that you lie to me. Why not be truthful about what all men

197

do? You honor the truth, don't you? You're an *Elahad* aren't you? Then listen to this truth that I give to you freely: He who best knows the truth is most able to tell a falsehood. Therefore the man best at lying is the most true.'

'That's a lie!' I half-shouted. But my head hurt so bad I could hardly tell what was true and what was not. I tried to close my ears to the music that poured off Morjin's silver tongue. I tried to close my eyes and heart to him, but he just stood there smiling at me nicely as if he were my brother or best friend.

'Is *this* a lie then, Valashu? That there must be truth between us? That we already know the truth about each other, deep in our hearts?'

'No – you know nothing about me!'

'Don't I?'

Morjin pointed his long finger at my chest and said, 'I know that you're in love. Show her to me, please.'

I closed my eyes as I shook my head. In my mind there appeared a blazing image of Atara clasping hands with me, and I quickly shut it away in the stone-walled keep of my heart as I would the most precious of treasures.

'Thank you,' Morjin told me. 'I might have foreseen the irony of a Valari knight falling for a Sarni warrior. Do you congratulate yourself on the nobility of your making friends with your enemy?'

'No!'

'Well, she's a beautiful woman, in an animal kind of way. But then, you like riding horses, don't you?'

'Damn you!' I told him. I moved my hand to draw my sword, but I found that I wasn't wearing it.

'My apologies, that wasn't kind of me,' he said. 'And as you'll see, I'm really the kindest of men. 'But the truth is, this woman is as far beneath you as an earthworm.'

'I love her!'

'Do you? Or do you only love the benefits of loving her? When a man burns for a woman, all other hurts disappear, don't they? Tell me, Valashu, did you save her from my men out of love or so that you wouldn't have to suffer the agony of her violation and death?'

I made a fist to strike him then, but then he smiled as if to remind me of my vow not to harm others.

'You tell yourself that you honor truth, but sometimes it's too painful to face, isn't it? And so, like all men, you tell yourself lies.' Morjin's fine hands moved dramatically to emphasize his point; it seemed that such bright fires burned inside him that he couldn't stop moving. 'But please, do not chastise yourself. These little lies enable us to go on living.

And life is precious, is it not? The most precious gift of the One? And therefore a lie told in the service of the One is a noble thing.'

I stood there pressing my hands over my temples and ears. It felt like some beast was trying to break its way into my head.

'You've been told that I'm evil, but some part of you doubts this.' Morjin nodded his head at me, and I suddenly found myself nodding my head, too. 'It's a great suffering for you, isn't it, this doubt of yours? And most of all, I think, you doubt yourself.'

Again, I nodded my head.

'But wouldn't it be good to live without this doubt?' he asked me.

Yes, yes, I thought, *it would be very good*.

'How is evil known, then?' he asked. 'Is evil the light that shines from the One?'

'No, of course not – it's just the opposite,' I said. And then I quoted from the *Laws*: '"Darkness is the denial of the One; darkness is the illusion that all things are separate from the light of the One."'

'You understand,' he said kindly. 'Please don't separate yourself from the gifts I bring you, Valashu.'

I slowly shook my head, which throbbed with a deep agony at every beat of my heart.

'Please don't deny me.'

Now Morjin took the final step toward me and smiled. I was suddenly aware that he smelled of roses. I tried to move back, but found that I didn't want to. I told myself that I mustn't be afraid of him, that he had no power to harm me. Then he reached out his hand, which was long and beautiful with tapering fingers. He touched his forefinger to the scar on my forehead; the tip of it was warm, and I could almost feel it glowing with a deep radiance. He traced this finger slowly along the zig-zags of the scar, sinuously impressing it into me. He smiled warmly as he then cupped the whole of his hand around my head. Despite the delicacy of his fingers, I sensed that there was iron there and that he had the strength to crush my skull like an eggshell. But instead he only touched my temples with exquisite sensitivity and breathed deeply as if drawing my pain into him. And suddenly my headache was gone.

'There,' he said, stepping away from me. He waited a moment for me to speak, then told me, 'You're deciding if your Valari manners permit you to thank me, aren't you? Is it so hard to say the words, then?'

'To the Lord of Lies? To the Crucifier?'

'Men have called me that – they don't understand.'

'They understand what they see,' I said.

'And what do *you* see, young Valashu?'

Again he smiled, and the room lit up as with the rising of the sun.

For a moment, I couldn't help seeing him as an angel of light, as what I imagined the Elijin to be.

'They understand what you *do*,' I said. 'You've enslaved half of Ea and tortured everyone who has opposed you.'

'Enslaved? When your father accepts homage from a knight, is that enslavement? When he punishes a man for treason, is that torture?'

'My father,' I said, 'is a king.'

'And I am a king of kings,' he said. 'My realm is Sakai – and all the lands east, west, north and south. A long time ago, the land that you and your friends are traveling through belonged to me, and will once again.'

'By what right?'

'By the right of what is right,' he told me. 'Do you remember the words written in your book?'

He pointed at my hand, and I suddenly saw that I was holding Master Juwain's copy of the *Saganom Elu*. I hadn't been aware that I held it.

Morjin's face grew bright as he quoted from the *Commentaries*: '"The Lord called Morjin far excels the rest of mankind."'

'But you've left something out!' I accused him. 'Isn't the full passage: "The Lord Morjin far excels the rest of mankind *in doing evil*"?'

'Of course not,' he said. 'My enemies added those words after I had been imprisoned on Damoom and there was no one to gainsay their lies.'

I stood there watching the quick and elegant motions of his hands as he tried to convince me. I didn't know what to say.

'I'm more than seven thousand years old,' he told me. 'And I didn't come by my immortality by accident.'

'No – you gained immortality by stealing the Lightstone.'

'But how can a man steal what is his?'

'What do you mean? The Lightstone belongs to all of Ea.'

'It belongs to him who made it.'

I searched his face for the truth and his golden eyes seemed so bright and compelling that I didn't know what to think.

'The Lightstone,' I finally said, 'was brought here by Elahad and the Star People ages ago.'

At this, Morjin laughed softly. But there was no mockery in his voice, only irony and sadness. He said, 'You must know, Val – can I call you that? – you must know that is only a myth. *I* made the Lightstone myself late in the Age of Swords.'

'But all the histories say that you stole it, and that Aramesh won it back at the Battle of Sarburn!'

'The victors of that battle wrote the histories they wanted to write,' he said. 'And Aramesh *was* victorious – until death took him in its claws.'

Here I couldn't help staring at the claws of the dragon embroidered on his tunic.

'The Lightstone belongs to me,' he told me. 'And you must help me regain it.'

'No, I won't.'

'You *will*,' he told me. 'Scrying isn't the greatest of my talents, but I'll tell you this: someday you'll deliver it into my hands.'

'No, never.'

'You owe me your life,' he told me. 'A man who doesn't repay his debts is a thief, is he not?'

'No – there is no debt.'

'And *still* you deny me!' he thundered. Suddenly, he smacked his fist into his open hand. His face grew red and hard to look at. 'Just as you still shelter one who is worse than a thief.'

'What do you mean?'

'Who is that standing behind you?' he said, pointing his finger at me.

'What do you mean – there's no one behind me!'

But it seemed that there was. I turned to see a boy standing in the shadow that I cast upon the carpet. He was about six years old, with bold face bones, a shock of wild black hair and a scar shaped like a lighting bolt cut into his forehead.

'*There*,' Morjin said, stabbing at him with his long finger. 'Why are you trying to protect him?'

Morjin tried to step around me then to get at the boy. When I raised my arm to stop him, he touched my side with something sharp. I looked down to see that his finger had grown a long black claw tipped with a bluish substance that looked like kirax. My whole body began burning, and I suddenly couldn't move.

'Come here, Valashu,' Morjin said. Quick as a snapping turtle, he grabbed up the boy and stood shaking him near the wall. But the boy spat in his face and managed to bite off his clawlike finger. Morjin looked at the gaping wound in his hand and said to me, 'You'll have to help me now.'

'No, never!' I said again through my clenched teeth.

'Give me the arrow!' Morjin told me.

With one hand pinning the struggling boy against the wall, he reached out his other hand to me. I saw then that I really wasn't holding Master Juwain's book in my hand but an arrow fletched with raven feathers and tipped with a razor-sharp steel. It was the arrow that the unknown assassin had shot at me in the forest.

'Thank you,' Morjin said, taking it from me. He suddenly plunged it into the boy's side, and we both screamed at the burning pain of it. In moments, the kirax froze the boy's limbs so that he couldn't move.

'Do you have the hammer?' Morjin said to me. 'Do you have the nails?'

He turned from the boy, and took from me the three iron spikes that I held in my left hand and the heavy iron maul in my right. I saw then that I had been mistaken, that there really was a door giving out into the room: it was a thick slab of oak set into the wall just next to the boy. Morjin used the hammer to nail his hands and legs to it. I couldn't hear the ringing of iron against iron, so loud were the boy's screams.

'There,' he said when he had finished crucifying him. He smiled sadly at me and continued, 'And now you must give me what is mine.'

'No!' I cried out. 'Don't do this!'

'A king,' he said to me, 'must sometimes punish, even as your father punished you. And a warrior must sometimes slay in pursuit of a noble end even as you have slain.'

'But the boy! He's done nothing – he's innocent!'

'Innocent? He's committed a crime worse than treason or murder.'

'What is this crime?' I gasped.

'He coveted the Lightstone for himself,' he said simply. 'He couldn't bear the gift that the One bestowed upon him, and so when he heard his grandfather speak of the golden cup that heals all wounds, he dreamed of keeping it for himself.'

'No – that's not true!'

Morjin moved closer to the boy and let the blood streaming from his pierced hand run into his open mouth.

'No, don't,' I said.

'You must help me,' he said to me.

'No.'

'You must do me homage, Valashu Elahad, son of kings. You must surrender to me what is mine.'

The whole of my body below my neck couldn't move, but I could still shake my head.

'You must open your heart to me, Valashu. Only then will you find peace.'

His eyes now began to burn like two golden suns. Long black claws like those of a dragon grew from his hands in place of fingers.

'Don't hurt him!' I cried out. 'You can't hurt him!'

'Can't I?'

'No, you can't – this is only a dream.'

'Do you think so?' he asked. 'Then see if you can wake up.'

So saying, he turned to the terrified boy and made cooing sounds of pity as he tore him apart. When he was finished, he held the boy's still-beating heart in his claws so that I could see it.

You killed him! I wanted to scream. But the only sound that came from my ravaged throat was a burning sob.

'It's said that if you die in your dreams,' he told me, 'you die in life.'

He looked at the throbbing heart and said, 'But no, Val, I *haven't* killed him, not yet.'

And with that, he placed the heart back into the boy's chest and sealed the wound with a kiss from his golden lips. The boy opened his eyes then and stared at Morjin hatefully.

'Do you see?' he said to me with a heavy sigh. 'I can't *demand* that you open your heart to me. Such gifts must be truly given.'

I bit my lip then and tasted blood. The dark, salty liquid moistened my burning throat, and I cried out, 'That will never happen!'

'No?' he asked me angrily. 'Then you will truly die.'

Now his head grew out from his body, huge and elongated and red and covered with scales. His eyes were golden-red and glowed like coals. His forked tongue flicked out once as if tasting the fear in the air. Then he opened his jaws to let out a gout of fire that seared the boy from his head to his bloody feet. The boy screamed as his flesh began to char; Morjin screamed out his hatred in his fiery roar. And I screamed too as I pleaded with him to stop.

But he didn't stop. He let the fire pour out of his fearsome mouth as if venting ages of bitterness and hate. I felt my own skin beginning to blister; I knew that Morjin would soon renew it with the touch of his lips so that he could burn me again and again until I finally surrendered to him or died. I sensed that if I fought against this terrible burning, it would go on forever. And so I surrendered to it. I let its heat burn deep into my blood; I felt it burning the kirax *in* my blood. And suddenly I found myself able to move again. I swung my fist like a mace at the side of Morjin's head; it was like striking iron. But it stunned him long enough so that I could rush through the flames streaming from his mouth to the blackened, bloody door. The boy was now all black and twisted and screaming for me to help him. I somehow wrenched him free from the door with a great tearing of flesh and bones. And then, holding him close to me where I could feel as my own the wild beating of his heart and his screams, I opened the door.

I opened my eyes then to see Atara bending over me and pressing a cool, wet cloth against my head, which she held cradled in her lap. I was lying back against my sweat-soaked sleeping furs near the fire. I took me a moment to realize that I was screaming still. I closed my mouth then and bit my bloody lip against the burning in my body. Master Juwain, brewing up some more tea, held my hand in his, testing my pulse. Maram sat beside me pulling at his thick beard in concern.

'We couldn't wake you,' he told me. 'But *you* were screaming loud enough to wake the dead.'

I squeezed Atara's hand to thank her for her watching over me, and then I sat up. I found that I was still clutching my other hand against my heart, but the wounded boy I thought to find there was gone.

'Are you all right now?' Maram asked me.

I blinked my eyes against the burning there. I looked out at the trees, which were immense gray shapes in the faint light filtering through the forest. The crickets were chirping in the bushes, and a few birds were singing the day's first songs. It was that terrible time between death and morning when the whole world struggled to fight its way out of night.

I stood up, wincing against the flames that still scorched my skin. I took a step away from the fire.

'It's still night,' Atara said. 'Where are you going?'

'Down to the stream, to bathe,' I said. I wanted to wash away the charred skin from my hands and let the stream's rushing waters cool my burning body.

'You shouldn't go alone,' she told me. 'Here, let me get my bow –'

'No!' I said. 'It will be all right – I'll take my sword.'

So saying, I bent to grab up my kalama, which I always kept sheathed next to my bed when I was sleeping. And then I walked off by myself toward the stream.

It was eerie moving through the gray-lit woods. I imagined I saw dark gray shapes watching me through the trees. But when I looked more closely I saw that they were only bushes or shrubs: arrowwood and witch hazel and others whose names I couldn't quite remember. I plodded along the forest floor and crunched over twigs and old leaves. I smelled animal droppings and ferns and the sweaty remnants of my own fear.

And then suddenly I broke free from the trees and came upon the stream. It gurgled along its rocky course like a silver ribbon beneath the stars. I looked up at the glowing sky in deep gratitude that I could see these blazing points of light. In the east, the Swan constellation was just rising over the dark rim of the forest. Near it shone Valashu, the Morning Star – so bright that it was almost like a moon. I kept my eyes fixed upon this familiar star that gave me so much hope even as I bent to lave the stream's cool water over my head.

And then I felt a cold hand touch my shoulder. For a moment I was angry because I thought that Maram or Atara had followed me. But when I turned to tell them that I really did want to be alone, I saw that the man standing beside me was Morjin.

'Did you really think you could escape me?' he asked.

I stared at his golden hair and his great golden eyes, now touched with silver in the starlight. The claws were gone from his hands, and he was wearing a wool traveling cloak over his dragon-emblazoned tunic.

'How did you come here?' I gasped.

'Don't you know? I've been following you since Mesh.'

I gripped the hilt of my sword as I stared at him. Was this still a dream, I wondered? Was it an illusion that Morjin had cast like a painter covering a canvas with brightly-colored pigments? He *was* the Lord of Illusions, wasn't he? But no, I thought, this was no illusion. Both he and the fiery words that hissed from his mouth seemed much too real.

'I must congratulate you on finding your way out of my room,' he said. 'It surprises me that you did, though it pleases me even more.'

'It pleases you? Why?'

'Because it proves to me that you're capable of waking up.'

He gave me to understand that much of what had passed in my dream had been only a test and a spur to awaken my being. This seemed the greatest of the lies that he had told me, but I listened to it all the same.

'I told you that I was kind,' he said. 'But sometimes compassion must be cruel.'

'*You* speak of compassion?'

'I do speak of it because I know it better than any man.'

He told me that my gift for feeling others' sufferings and joys had a name, and that was *valarda*. This meant both the heart of the stars and the passion of the stars. Here he pointed up at the Morning Star and the bright Solaru and Altaru of the Swan constellation. All the Star People, he said, who still lived among these lights had this gift. As did Elahad and others of the Valari who had come to Ea long ago. But the gift had mostly been lost during the savagery of many thousands of years. Now only a few blessed souls such as myself knew the terrible beauty of *valarda*.

'I know it, too,' he told me. 'I have suffered from the *valarda* for a long time. But there is a way to make the suffering end.'

'How?' I asked.

He cupped his hands in front of his heart then, and they glowed with a soft golden radiance like that of a polished bowl. He said, 'Do you burn, Valashu? Does the kirax from my arrow still torment you?

205

Would you like to be cured of this poison and your deeper suffering as well?'

'How?' I asked again. Despite the coolness spraying up from the stream, my whole body raged with fever.

'I can relieve you of your gift,' Morjin told me. 'Or rather, the pain of it.'

Here he pointed at the kalama that I still held sheathed in my hand. 'You see, the *valarda* is like a double-edged sword. But so far, you've known it to cut only one way.'

He told me that a true Valari, which was his name for the Star People, could not only experience others' emotions but make them feel his own.

'Do you hate, Valashu? Do you sometimes clench your teeth against the fury inside you? I *know* that you do. But you can forge your fury into a weapon that will strike down your enemies. Shall I show you how to sharpen the steel of *this* sword?'

'No!' I cried out. 'That is wrong! It would be twisting the bright blade that the One himself forged. The *valarda* may be double-edged, as you say. But I must believe that it is sacred. And I would never pervert it by turning it inside-out to harm anyone. No more than I would use my kalama to kill anyone.'

'But you *will* kill again with that sword,' he said, pointing at my kalama. 'And with the *valarda*, as well. You see, Valashu, inflicting your own pain on others is the only way not to feel *their* pain – and your own.'

I closed my eyes for a moment as I looked inside for this terrible sword that Morjin had spoken of. I feared that I might find it. And this was the worst torment I had ever known.

'What you say, all that you say, is wrong,' I gasped out. 'It's evil.'

'Is it wrong to slay your enemies, then? Isn't it *they* who are evil for opposing your noblest dream?'

'You don't know my dream.'

'Don't I? Isn't it your dearest hope to end war? Listen to me, Valashu, listen as you've never listened before: there is nothing I desire more than an end to these wars.'

I listened to the rushing of the stream and the words from his golden lips. I was afraid that he might be telling me the truth. He went on to say that many of the kings and nobles of Ea loved war because it gave them the power of life and death over others. But they, he said, were of the darkness while dreamers such as he and I were of the light.

'It's death itself that's the great enemy,' he said. 'Our fear of it. And that is why we must regain the Lightstone. Only then can we bring men the gift of true life.'

'It is written in the *Laws*,' I said, 'that only the Elijin and the Galadin shall have such life.'

Morjin's eyes seemed to blaze out hatred into the dim gray light of the dawn. He told me, 'All the Galadin were once Elijin even as the Elijin were once men. But they have grown jealous of our kind. Now they would keep men such as you from making the same journey that they once did.'

'But I don't seek immortality,' I told him.

'That,' he said softly, 'is a lie.'

'All men die,' I said.

'Not *all* men,' he told me, smoothing the folds from his cloak.

'It's no failing to fear death,' I said. 'True courage is –'

'Lie to me if you will, Valashu, but do not lie to yourself.' He grasped my arm, and his delicate fingers pressed into me with a frightening strength. 'Death makes cowards of us all. You may think that true courage is acting rightly even though afraid. But *you* act not according to what is right but because you are afraid of your fear and wish to expunge it by facing it like a wild man.'

I didn't know what to say to this, so I bit my lip in silence.

'*True* courage,' he said, 'would be fearlessness. Isn't this what you Valari teach?'

'Yes,' I admitted, 'it is.'

He smiled as if he knew everything about the Valari. And then he spoke the words to a poem I knew too well:

> And down into the dark,
> No eyes, no lips, no spark.
> The dying of the light,
> The neverness of night.

'There is a way to keep the light burning,' he told me as he gently squeezed my shoulder. 'Let me show you the way.'

His eyes were like windows to other worlds from which men had journeyed long ago – and on which men who were more than men still lived. I felt his longing to return there. It was as real as the wind or the stream or the earth beneath my feet. I felt his immense loneliness in the bittersweet aching of my own. Something unbearably bright in him called to me as if from the wild, cold stars. I knew that I had the power to save him from a dread almost as dark as death even as I had saved Atara from the hill-men. And this knowledge burned me even more terribly than had his dragon fire or the kirax in my veins.

'Let me show you,' he said, forming his hands into a cup again. A fierce golden light poured out of them, almost blinding me.

'Servants I have many,' he told me. 'But friends I have none.'

I felt him breathing deeply as I drew in a quick, ragged breath.

'I will make you King of Mesh and all the Nine Kingdoms,' he told me. 'Kings I have as vassals, too, but a king of kings who comes to me with an open heart and a righteous sword – that would be a wondrous thing.'

I gazed at the light pouring from his hands, and for a moment I couldn't breathe.

'Help me find the Lightstone, Valashu, and you will live forever. And we will rule Ea together, and there will be no more war.'

Yes, yes, I wanted to say. *Yes, I will help you.*

There is a voice that whispers deep inside the soul. All of us have such a voice. Sometimes it is as clear as the ringing of a silver bell; sometimes it is faint and far-off like the fiery exhalations of the stars. But it always knows. And it always speaks the truth even when we don't want to hear it.

'No,' I said at last.

'*No?*'

'No, you lie,' I told him. 'You're the Lord of Lies.'

'I'm the Lord of Ea and you will help me!'

I gripped the hilt of the sword that my father had given me as I slowly shook my head.

'Damn you, Elahad! You damn yourself to death, then!'

'So be it,' I told him.

'So be it,' he told me. And then he said, 'I will tell you the true secret of the *valarda*: the only way you will ever expiate your fear of death is to make others die. As I will make *you* die, Elahad!'

The hate with which he said this was like lava pouring from a rent in the earth. I realized then that fear of death leads to hatred of life. Even as my fear of Morjin led me to hate him. I hated him with black bile and clenched teeth and red blood suddenly filling my eyes; I hated him as fire hates wood and darkness does light. Most of all, I hated him for lying to me and playing on my fears and making me sick to my soul with a deep and terrible hate.

It took only a moment for his dragon's head to grow out from his body and for his claws to emerge. But before his jaws could open, I whipped my kalama from its sheath. I plunged the point of it through the dragon embroidered on his tunic, deep into his heart. It was as if I had ripped out my own heart. The incredible pain of it caused me to scream like a wounded child even as my sword shattered into a thousand pieces; each piece lay burning with an orange-red light on the ground or hissed into the stream and sent up plumes of boiling water. I watched in horror as Morjin screamed, too, and his face fell away from the form of a dragon and became my own. Clots of twisting red worms began to eat out his eyes, *my* eyes, and his whole body burst into flames. In moments his face blackened into a rictus of agony. And then the flames consumed him utterly, and he vanished into the nothingness from which he had come.

For what seemed a long time, I stood there by the stream waiting for him to return. But all that remained of him was a terrible emptiness clutching at my heart. My fever left me; in the darkness of the dawn, I was suddenly very cold. Inside me beat the words to another stanza of Morjin's poem that I could never forget:

> *The stealing of the gold,*
> *The evil knife, the cold.*
> *The cold that freezes breath,*
> *The nothingness of death.*

13

A few moments later, Atara and Master Juwain, with Maram puffing close behind them, came running into the clearing by the stream. Atara held her strung bow in her hand, and Maram brandished his sword; Master Juwain had a copy of the *Saganom Elu* that he had been reading, but nothing more. The thought of him reciting passages or throwing his book at a man such as Morjin made me want to laugh wildly.

'What is it?' he asked me. 'We heard you cry out.'

Maram, who was more blunt, added, 'Ah, we heard you talking to yourself and shouting. Who were you shouting at, Val?'

'At Morjin,' I said. 'Or perhaps it was just an illusion – it's hard to say.'

I looked at the steel gleaming along the length of my sword, and I wondered how it had been remade.

'Morjin was *here*?' Atara asked. 'How could he be? Where did he go?'

I pointed toward the faint glow of the sun rising in the east. Then I pointed at the woods, north, west and south. Finally I flung my hand up toward the sky.

'Take Val back to camp,' Atara said to Master Juwain. She nodded at Maram, too, as if issuing a command. Then she started off toward the woods.

'Where are you going?' I asked her.

'To see,' she said simply.

'No, you mustn't!' I told her. I took a step toward her to stop her, but my body felt as if it had been drained of blood. I stumbled, and was only saved from falling by Maram, who wrapped his thick arm around me.

'Take him back to camp!' Atara said again. And then she moved off into the trees and was gone.

With my arms thrown across Maram's and Master Juwain's shoulders, they dragged me back to camp as if I were a drunkard. They sat me down by the fire, and Maram covered me with his cloak. While he rubbed the back of my neck and my cold hands, Master Juwain found a reddish herb in his wooden chest. He made me a tea that tasted like iron and bitter berries. It brought a little warmth back into my limbs. But the icy nothingness with which Morjin had touched my soul still remained.

'At least your fever is gone,' Maram told me.

'Yes,' I said, 'it's much better to die of the cold.'

'But you're not *dying*, Val! Are you? What did Morjin do to you?'

I tried to tell both Maram and Master Juwain something of my dream – and what had happened by the stream afterwards. But words failed me. It was impossible to describe a terror that had no bottom or end. And I found that I didn't want to.

After a while, with the hot tea trickling down my throat, my head began to clear and I came fully awake. Dawn began to brighten into morning as the sun's light touched the trees around us. I listened to the *shureet shuroo* of a scarlet tanager piping out his song from the branch of an oak; I gazed at the starlike white sepals of some goldthread growing in the shade of a birch tree. The world seemed marvelously and miraculously real, and my senses drank in every sight, sound and smell.

Just as I was steeling myself to strap on my sword and go look for Atara, she suddenly returned. She stepped out from behind the cover of the trees as silently as a doe. In the waxing light, her face was ashen. She came over and sat beside me by the fire.

'Well?' Maram asked her. 'What did you see?'

'Men,' Atara said. With a trembling hand, she reached for a mug of tea that Master Juwain handed her. 'Gray men.'

'What do you mean, *gray men*?' Maram said.

'There were nine of them,' Atara said. 'Or perhaps more. They were dressed all in gray; their horses were gray, too. Their faces were hideous: their flesh seemed as gray as slate.'

She paused to take a sip of tea as beads of sweat formed upon Maram's brow.

'It was hard to *see*,' Atara said. 'Perhaps their faces were only colored by the grayness of the dawn. But I don't think so. There was something about them that didn't seem human.'

Master Juwain knelt beside her and touched her shoulder. He told her, 'Please go on.'

'One of them looked at me,' she said. 'He had no eyes – no eyes like those of any man I've ever seen. They were all gray as if covered with cataracts. But he wasn't blind. The *way* that he looked at me. It was as if I was naked, like he could see everything about me.'

She took another sip of tea, then grasped my hand to keep her hand from shaking.

'I shouldn't have looked into his eyes,' she said. 'It was like looking into nothing. So empty, so cold – I felt the cold freezing my body. I felt his intention to do things to me. I . . . have no words for it. It was worse than the hill-men. Death I can face. Perhaps even torture, too. But this man – it was like he wanted to kill me forever and suck out my soul.'

We were all silent as we looked at her. And then Maram asked, 'What did you *do*?'

'I tried to draw on him,' she said. 'But it was as if my arms were frozen. It took all my will to pull my bow and sight on him. But it was too late – he rode off to join the others.'

'Oh, excellent!' Maram said, wiping his face. 'It seems that Val was right after all. Men *are* after us – gray men with no souls.'

As the sun rose higher, we sat by the fire debating who these men might be. Maram worried that the man who had faced down Atara might be Morjin himself – how else to explain the terrible dream and illusion I had suffered? Master Juwain held that they might be only in Morjin's employ; as he told us: 'The Lord of Lies has many servants, and none so terrible as those who have surrendered to him *their* souls.' I wondered if Kane might have hired them to murder me; I wondered if he was waiting for me farther along the road with a company of stone-faced assassins.

'But if they wanted to kill you,' Maram said, 'why didn't they just ride you down by the stream?'

I had no answer for him; neither could I say why the gray man and his companions hadn't charged Atara.

'Well, whoever they are,' Maram said, 'they know where *we* are. What are we going to do, Val?'

I thought for a moment and said, 'So long as we keep to the road, we'll be easy prey.'

'Ah, do you mind, my friend, if you don't refer to us as *prey*?'

'My apologies,' I said, smiling. 'But perhaps we should take to the forest again.'

I said that according to a map I had studied before leaving Mesh, the Nar Road curved north between the gap in the Shoshan Range and Suma, where the great forest ended and the more civilized reaches of Alonia began.

'We could cut through the forest straight for Suma,' I said. 'There will be hills to hide us and streams in which to lose our tracks.'

'You mean, rivers to drown us. Hills to hide *them*.' Maram thought a moment as he stroked his thick beard. Then he said, 'It worries me that the road should curve to the north. Why does it? Did the old Alonians built it so as to avoid something? What if the forest hides another Black Bog – or something worse?'

'Take heart, my friend,' I said, smiling again. 'Nothing could be worse than the Black Bog.'

On this point, Master Juwain, Maram and I were all agreed. After some further argument, we also agreed – as did Atara – that the cut through the forest offered our best hope.

Soon after that we broke camp and set out through the trees. We moved away from the road, bearing toward the west. I guessed that Suma must lie some thirty or forty miles to the northwest. If we journeyed too far in our new direction, we would pass by it much to the south. This prospect didn't discourage me, however, for we could always turn back north and cut the Nar Road when we were sure that we had eluded the men hunting us. In truth, I wanted to get as far away from the road as I could, and the deeper the woods through which we rode the better.

As the day warmed toward noon, the ground rose away from the stream. The trees grew less thickly, though they seemed taller, with the oaks predominating over the poplars and chestnuts. I could find no track through them. Still, the traveling wasn't difficult, for the undergrowth was mostly of lady fern and maidenhair, and the horses had no trouble finding footing. We rode in near-silence beneath the great, leafed archways of the trees. I took the lead followed by Master Juwain and the two remaining pack horses. Maram and Atara brought up the rear. All of us – except Master Juwain – rode with bows strung and swords close at hand.

We saw a few deer munching on leaves, and many squirrels, but no sign at all of the Stonefaces, as Maram named the gray men. I never doubted that they were somehow tracking us through the woods. With the sun high above the world, my fever came raging back, and my blood felt heavy as molten iron. It seemed that someone was aiming arrows of hate at me, for I could almost feel a succession of razor-sharp points driving into my forehead.

'I'm sorry I have no cure for what ails you,' Master Juwain said as he rode up beside me. He watched me rubbing my head, and looked at me with great concern.

'Perhaps there is no cure,' I told him. Then I said, 'The Red Dragon is so evil – how can anyone be this evil?'

'Only out of blindness,' Master Juwain said, 'so that he can't see the difference between evil or good. Or only out of the delusion that he is doing good when actually bringing about the opposite.'

The Red Dragon, he said, was certainly not evil by his own lights.

213

No one was. But I wasn't as sure of this. Something in Morjin's voice seemed to delight in darkness, and this still haunted me.

'He spoke to me,' I told Master Juwain. 'And I listened to him. Now his words won't leave my head.'

How, I asked myself, could I know what was the truth and what was a lie if I didn't listen?

To the rough walking gait of his horse, Master Juwain began thumbing rhythmically through the pages of the *Saganom Elu*. When he had found the passage he wanted, he cleared his throat and read from the *Healings*.

'I would advise you to meditate, if you can,' he told me. 'Do you remember the Second Light Meditation? It used to be your favorite.'

I nodded my head painfully because I remembered it well enough: I was to close my eyes and dwell on the dread brought on by the fall of night. And then, after gazing upon the blackness of the sky there as long as I could, I was to envision the Morning Star suddenly blazing as brightly as the sun. This fiery light I would then hold inside me as I would the promise that day would always follow night.

'It's hard,' I told him after some long moments of trying to practice this meditation. 'The Lord of Illusions has made light seem like darkness and darkness light.'

'The worst lie,' Master Juwain said, 'is that which misuses truth to make falseness. You'll have to look very hard for the truth now, Val.'

'You mean now that I've listened to Morjin's lies?'

'Please don't say his name,' he reminded me. 'And yes, I do mean that. You had to test your courage, didn't you? But you must never listen to him, not even in your dreams.'

'Are my dreams mine to make, then? Or are they his?'

'Your dreams are always *your* dreams,' he told me. 'But you must fight to keep them for yourself even more fiercely than you would to keep an enemy's sword from piercing your heart.'

'How, then?'

'By learning to be awake and aware in your dreams.'

'Is that possible?'

'Of course it is. Even in your dream, you weren't completely without will, were you?'

'No – or else the Red Dragon would have kept me in his room.'

Master Juwain nodded his head and smiled. 'You see, it's our will to life that quickens awareness. And our awareness that seeks our awakening. There are exercises in the dreamwork that you would have been taught if you hadn't left our school.'

'Can you teach me them now?'

214

'I can try, Val. But the art of dreaming at will takes a long time to learn.'

As we rode deeper into the woods, he explained some of the fundamentals of this ancient art. Every night while falling asleep, I was to resolve to remain aware of my dreams. And more, I was to create for myself an ally, a sort of dream self who would remain awake and watch over me while I slept.

'Do you remember the zanshin meditation I taught you before your duel with Lord Salmelu?'

'Yes – it's impossible to forget.'

'You may make use of that, then,' he said. 'The key is in the self looking at the self. You must continually ask yourself the question: Who am I? When you think you know, ask yourself: who is doing the knowing? This "who," this one who knows – this is your ally. It is he who remains always beside you, and is awake even as you sleep.'

He suggested that I practice an ancient exercise that could be found in the *Meditations*. I was to visualize in my throat a beautiful, soft lotus flower. The lotus should have light-pink petals which curled slightly inwards, and in the center there should be a luminous red-orange flame. He told me to visualize the top of the flame as long as possible, for the flame represented consciousness and the whole lotus was a symbol of awakening the consciousness of the self.

'Ultimately,' he explained, 'you'll learn to control and shape your own dreams even as they unfold.'

'Even if the Lord of Illusions is attacking me?'

'Especially then. Your dreams are sacred, Val; you must never let anyone steal your dreams.'

That night we made camp on a hill beneath the tall oaks. There was little enough cover to hide us – nothing more than some thickets of laurel and virburn – but at least we would have a more or less clear line of sight should the gray men try to charge at us up the hill. I fell asleep with Master Juwain's lotus blazing inside me. His exercises did me little good, however, for I had terrible dreams all night long. My cries kept the others awake. They were true allies, of flesh and blood, and they kept watch over me where Master Juwain's more ethereal ally did not.

Our next day's journey took us farther into the forest to the west. We covered only a few miles, though, because we spent most of the day attempting to elude our pursuers. We walked our horses for hours in shallow streams to leave no hoofprints; we walked them in circles around the tops of hills to confound anyone trying to read our tracks. We rode through blackberry thickets with sharp thorns. More than once,

215

we doubled back across our track. But if the sharp pain piercing my head was any sign, all such tactics failed.

'Whoever is following us,' Master Juwain said, 'is very likely reading more than the tracks that we leave in the mud.'

'Who *are* these Stonefaces, then?' Maram asked.

'Who knows?' Atara said. 'But if we can't escape them, then we should find a place to face them and kill them with arrows.'

'As you faced them by the stream?' Maram said to her. 'As you killed their leader with your arrow that you couldn't shoot?'

It was his revenge for her mocking his archery skills during the battle with the hill-men. Atara, whose freezing-up at the sight of the gray men still shamed her, looked off at the gray-green shapes of the sumac bushes hiding deeper in the woods. Then she said, 'I don't understand these Stonefaces. If they are many and we are few, why don't they just attack us and be done with it?'

'Have you never seen a bear-baiting?' Maram asked her. 'The hounds harry the bear and wear it down before it is killed.'

All that day, in the moist woods full of amanita and destroying angels and other poisonous mushrooms, I felt a mailed fist pounding at my head and trying to wear me down. I slept fitfully that night by a stream that gurgled like an opened throat. There the others – Atara and Maram – joined me in nightmare. Only Master Juwain seemed shielded against the terrible images that Morjin sent to rob us of sanity and sleep. But even he awoke the next morning with a fever and a fierce headache. As did Maram and Atara. Maram wondered if we had managed to drink some tainted water, perhaps from a stream poisoned by a dead animal who had eaten some of the overly abundant mushrooms. But Master Juwain doubted this possibility. He stood by his horse rubbing his bald head as he told him, 'This is no taint of rotten flesh or the poisoning of plants. No, Brother Maram, I'm afraid your hounds are getting bolder.'

To inspirit Maram, who groaned from fright as much as the fever in him, I said, 'If they are growing bolder, then so must we.'

'What do you intend to do?'

'Ride,' I told him. 'As fast and hard as we can. If the Stonefaces are wearing down our spirits, then at least we can try to wear down their bodies.'

'But, Val,' he said. 'They're wearing down our spirits *and* our bodies. Why should we help them?'

'Because,' I said, 'there's nothing else to do. Now let's get the horses ready.'

We rode all that morning across the gently rolling ground of the forest.

In places, where the trees grew less densely and the spaces between them were free of undergrowth, we pressed the horses to a fast canter, and twice, to a gallop. They wheezed and sweated at the effort of it, and so did we. It pained me to see the froth building up along Altaru's jaw. However, he made little complaint; he just charged on through the moss-hung trees hour after hour, driving at the earth with his great hooves. Maram's and Master Juwain's horses had a harder time of it. And Atara's horse was no mount at all. By the end of the afternoon, Tanar was near exhaustion, and it was only Atara's determination and skill that kept him moving.

'I'll have to whip him if you want any more work out of him today,' she said as we paused by a small river to water the horses. She stood by Tanar with a braided leather quirt in her hand. I had heard that the Sarni sometimes whipped their horses bloody, but Atara was obviously reluctant to follow this cruel custom.

'No, please don't,' I said. The horses' flanks were already scratched and bleeding from the blackberry brambles. I looked at Master Juwain, who stood leaning against his horse as if his shaking legs might buckle at any moment. Maram had already buckled. He lay by the riverbank holding a wet cloth against his head and moaning softly. I told him, 'We're all exhausted. We'll make camp and rest here.'

'Bless you, my friend. But, rest? I think I'm too tired to rest. My head feels as if your big, fat horse has been stepping on it all day. Please kill me now and save the Stonefaces the trouble.'

'We came far today,' I said. 'It may be that we lost them.'

But my dreams that night told me otherwise. And more than once, Atara's sharp cries startled me out of my sleep. I lay next to her by the little fire for hours listening to Maram's pitiful groaning and to the insects of the night: the katydids and the crickets in the bushes and the whining mosquitoes that came to suck our blood. I couldn't decide whether sleep or sleeplessness drained me more. If this was rest, I thought, we would do better to stumble about the forest and ride all night.

The next morning – I guessed it was the 28th of Ashte – dawned cloudy and cool. We all had trouble getting on our horses, even Master Juwain who had slept soundly enough when it hadn't been his watch. I remembered my father telling me that on long campaigns, even the doughtiest of warriors will weaken without good food and rest. We had had neither. The day before, we had eaten in the saddle: some moldy battle biscuits and walnuts that had gone rancid. I had been too exhausted to take dinner. Even Maram, when offered a bit of beer, complained that he had no head for it; he turned down as well the

217

leathery dried antelope that Atara offered him. He had no strength to chew it, he had said, and just wanted to sleep.

None of us had any strength that morning. We had been on the road for most of a month. The journey had worn the flesh off our bodies, and by his own ample standards even Maram was looking gaunt. We were dirty, our clothes torn by thorns and stained with mud. The hard riding of the previous day had reopened the wound in my side; beneath my armor, I felt the dampness of blood. Even so, I wanted to press Altaru to a canter. But the other horses had no heart for anything more than a quick walk. As the day dragged on, they gradually slowed their pace.

Sometime after noon – it was hard to measure the hour when we couldn't see the sun – I fell asleep in my saddle. A sudden splashing as Altaru stepped through a stream startled me awake. But after that I found myself frequently drifting off. Once, I swooned altogether and nearly fell to the ground. It was hard to keep Altaru to our course, which was now mostly to the northwest. At each of my lapses in consciousness, I found him turning toward the south as if he might find better browse or water in that direction.

'We're lost, aren't' we?' Maram asked as he looked around at the walls of trees on all sides. 'We're moving in circles.'

'No, not circles,' I reassured him. 'We're still on course.'

'Are you sure? Perhaps Master Juwain should take the lead for a while. He's the only one who can stay awake.'

But Master Juwain had little sense of direction, and even Atara seemed lost. With the sky hidden by the thick canopies of the trees and the even thicker gray clouds, we couldn't see the sun to read east or west. And no one except myself had enough woodcraft to read the moss on the elms or the lie of the flowers in the shadows of the birches. I knew well enough how to find our way; all I had to do was to keep from falling asleep.

As we moved off again, I resolved to let the pain in my side spur me to wakefulness. But very soon my eyes closed, for how long I couldn't say. When I finally opened them, I saw that Altaru had drifted again toward the south. I sensed in him a fierce desire to move in that direction; it was as if he could smell a mare deeper in the woods, and every muscle in his body trembled to find her. It was only by his instincts, I remembered, that we had escaped from the Black Bog. Perhaps his instincts might now help us escape the Stonefaces; certainly all my stratagems had failed in this. And so, without telling the others what was happening, I let Altaru go where he wished.

Thus we traveled quite a few miles due south. I sensed a gradual change in the air, and I thought that the trees here grew taller. Their great, green crowns towered over the forest floor perhaps as high as a hundred and twenty feet. From somewhere in their spreading branches and fluttering leaves, I heard the voice of an unfamiliar bird: his cry was something like the *raaark* of a raven, but was deeper and harsher and seemed to warn us away. Other things warned us away as well. I had a disquieting sense that I was crossing an invisible border into a forbidden realm. Whenever I tried to peer through the woods to see what might be drawing Altaru, however, it seemed that a will greater than my own caused me to become distracted and look away. It was as if the earth itself here was guarded by some sentinel whom I could not see. But strangely, I was never quite conscious that some being or entity might be watching these woods. At precisely those moments when I tried to bring these sensations into full awareness, I found myself touching my wounded side or gazing at the blood on my hand – or thinking of how I had fallen in love with Atara. It was as if my mind had slipped off the surface of a gleaming mirror to behold only myself.

I knew that the others, too, sensed something strange about these woods. I felt Atara's reluctance to go any farther and Maram's doubt pounding in him like a heartbeat that seemed to say: *Go back; go back; go back.* Even Master Juwain's great curiosity about the woods seemed blunted by his fear of them.

And then, after perhaps a couple of miles, the soft breeze grew suddenly cooler and cleaner. The sweet scent of the numinous seemed to hang in the air. I found that I could breathe more easily, and I gasped to behold the heights of the trees, for here the giant oaks grew very high above us, at least two hundred feet. The forest floor was mostly free of debris, being covered by carpet of golden leaves. But there were flowers, too: violets and goldthread and others that I had never seen before. One of these had many red, pointed petals that erupted from its center like flames. I called it a fireflower; but its fragrance filled me as if I had drunk from a sparkling stream. I felt my fever cooling and then leaving me altogether. My head pain vanished as well. All my senses seemed to grow keener and deeper. I could almost see the folds in the silvery bark of an oak three hundred yards away and hear the sap streaming through its mighty trunk.

How far we rode into these great trees I couldn't tell. In the abiding peace of the oaks, both distance and direction seemed to take on a new depth of dimension. Something about the earth itself here seemed to dissolve each moment into the next so that the whole forest opened onto a secret realm as timeless as the stars. I might have been walking these same woods a million years in the past – or a million years hence.

'What *is* this place?' Maram wondered as he stopped his horse to look up at the leaves fluttering high above us.

I climbed down from Altaru to give him a rest and stretch my legs. I reached down to touch a starflower growing out of a little plant. Its five white petals shone as if from a light within.

'My headache is gone,' Maram said. 'My fever, as well.'

Atara and Master Juwain admitted that they, too, had been miraculously restored. Along with Maram, they climbed off their horses and joined me on the forest floor. Then Master Juwain said, 'There are places of great power on the earth. Healing places – this must be one of them.'

'Why haven't I heard of these places?' Maram asked.

'Yes, indeed, why *haven't* you, Brother Maram? Do you not remember the *Book of Ages* where it tells of the vilds?'

'No, I'm sorry, I don't. Do *you* remember the passage, sir?'

Master Juwain nodded his head and then recited:

> There is a place tween earth and time,
> In some forgotten misty clime
> Of woods and brooks and vernal glades,
> Whose healing magic never fades.
>
> An island in the greenest sea,
> Abode of deeper greenery
> Where giant trees and emeralds grow,
> Where leaves and grass and flowers glow.
>
> And there no bitter bloom of spite
> To blight the forest's living light,
> No sword, no spear, no axe, no knife
> To tear the sweetest sprigs of life.
>
> The deeper life for which we yearn,
> Immortal flame that doesn't burn,
> The sacred sparks, ablaze, unseen –
> The children of the Galadin.
>
> Beneath the trees they gloze and gleam,
> And whirl and play and dance and dream
> Of wider woods beyond the sea
> Where they shall dwell eternally.

After he had finished, Maram rubbed his beard and said, 'I thought that was just a myth from the Lost Ages.'

'I hope not,' Master Juwain said.

'Well, wherever we are, it seems that we've finally lost the Stonefaces. Val, what do you think?'

I closed my eyes for a moment, trying to feel for the snake wrapping its coils around my spine. But my whole being seemed suddenly free from any wrongness. Even the burning of the kirax was cooled by the breeze blowing through the woods.

'We might have lost them,' I agreed. All around us grew fireflowers and starflowers and violets. In the trees, a flock of blue birds like none I had ever seen was trilling out the sweetest of songs. I had only ever dreamed a place that felt so alive as this. 'Perhaps they lost our scent.'

'Well, then,' Maram said, 'why don't we celebrate? Why don't we break out some of your father's fine brandy that we've been toting all the way from Mesh?'

We all agreed that this was a good idea; even Master Juwain consented to breaking his vows this one time. Atara, who might have chided him for going against his principles, seemed happy at the moment to honor the greater principle of celebrating life. After Maram had cracked the cask and filled our cups with some brandy, she eagerly held her nose over the smoky liquid as if drawing in its perfume. Master Juwain touched his tongue to it and grimaced; one might have thought he was touching fire. Then Maram raised his cup and called out, 'To our escape from the Stonefaces. Surely these woods won't abide any evil.'

Just as he was about to fasten his thick lips around the rim of his cup, a lilting voice called back to him from somewhere in the trees: 'Surely they won't, Hairface.'

A man suddenly stepped from behind a tree thirty yards away. He was short and slight, with curly brown hair, pale skin and leaf-green eyes. Except for a skirt woven of some silvery substance, he was naked. In his little hands he held a little bow and a flint-tipped arrow.

The unexpected sight of him so startled Maram that he spilled his brandy over his beard and chest. Then he managed to splutter, 'Who are you? We didn't know anyone lived here. We mean you no harm, little man.'

Quick as a wink, the man drew his arrow straight at Maram and piped out, 'Sad to say, we mean *you* harm, big man. So sad, too bad.'

And with that, even as Maram, Atara and I reached for our weapons, the little man let loose a high-pitched whistle that sounded like the trilling of the blue birds. Immediately, others of his kind appeared from behind trees in a great circle around us two hundred yards across. There were hundreds of them, and they each held a little bow fitted with an arrow.

'Oh, my Lord!' Maram cried out. 'Val, what shall we do?'

So, I thought, this was why the Stonefaces hadn't followed us here: we had ridden from one danger into a far greater one. I decided that the woodcraft of these little men must be very great for them to have stolen upon us unheard and unseen. But why, I wondered, hadn't I sensed them stalking me? Surely it was because in trying to close myself to the Stonefaces, I had also closed myself to them.

'Put down your weapons,' the man said as I drew my sword. 'Please, please don't move.'

At another of his whistles, the circle of little people began to close around us as both men and women approached us through the trees. It occurred to me that their strategy wasn't the best, for many of them stood in each other's line of fire should they loose their arrows at us and miss their marks. And then, after watching the graceful motions of their leader as he stalked me, it occurred to me that they wouldn't miss their marks. There was nothing to do except put down our weapons as he had said.

'Come, come,' he told me from in front of a tree where he had stopped ten yards away. The others had now closed their circle some twenty yards around us. 'Now stand away from your beasts, please – we don't want to pierce them.'

'Val!' Maram called to me. 'They mean to murder us – I really think they do!'

So did I think this. Or rather, I sensed that they intended to execute us for the crime of violating their woods. It was sad, I thought, that after facing seeming worse dangers together, we should have to die like cornered prey in this strange and beautiful wood.

'Come, come,' the man said again, 'stand away. It's sad to die, and bad to die like this – but it will be worse the longer we put it off.'

There was nothing to do, I thought, but die as he had said. For each of us, a time comes to say farewell to the earth and return to the stars. Now, at the sight of two hundred arrows pointing at our hearts, each of us faced his coming death in his own way. Master Juwain began chanting the words to the First Light Meditation. Maram covered his eyes with his forearm, as if blocking out the sight of the fierce little people might make them go away. He cried out that he was a prince of Delu and I a prince of Mesh. He promised them gold and diamonds if they would put down their bows; he told them, to no effect, that we were seekers of the Lightstone and that they would be cursed if they harmed us. Atara calmly reached back into her quiver for an arrow. She obviously intended to slay at least one more man and end her life in a joyous fight. I did not. It was bad enough that I should feel the great nothingness pulling me down into the dark; why, I wondered, should I inflict this terrible cold on men and women who sought only to protect their forest kingdom? And so, at last, I stood away from Altaru. I stood as tall and straight as I could. I lifted my hand from the hilt of my sword to brush back my hair, which my sweat had plastered to the side of my face. Then I looked at the man with the leaf-green eyes and waited.

For a moment – the longest of my life – the little man stood regarding me strangely. Then his drawn bow wavered; he relaxed the pull on his bowstring and pointed straight at my forehead. To the other men and women behind and all around him he said, 'Look, look – it's the mark!'

A murmur of astonishment rippled around the circle of little people. I noticed then that on each of their bows was burned a jagged mark like that of a lightning bolt.

'How did you come by the mark?' the man asked me.

'It was there from my birth,' I told him truthfully.

'Then you are blessed,' he said. 'And I am glad, so glad, for there will be no killing today.'

Maram let out a cry of thanksgiving while Atara still held her arrow nocked on her bowstring. The man asked her if she would consent to putting it away; otherwise, he said, his people would have to shoot *their* arrows into her arms and legs.

'Please, Atara,' I said to her.

Although obviously hating to disarm herself, Atara put her arrow back into her quiver and stowed her bow in the holster strapped to her horse.

'Too bad that we must bind you now,' the man said. 'But you understand the need for it, don't you? You big people are so quick with your weapons.'

So saying, he whistled again, and several women came forward with braided cords to bind our hands behind our backs. When they were finished, the man said, 'My name is Danali. We will take you to a place where you can rest.'

After presenting myself and each of the others in turn, I asked him, 'What *is* this place? And what is the name of your people?'

'This is the Forest,' he said simply. 'And we are the Lokilani.'

And with that he turned to lead us deeper into the woods.

14

We walked in line trailing our horses with the Lokilani swarming around us. With the abandon of children, they touched our garments and let out cries of surprise at Atara's leather trousers, and most of all, at the steel links of my armor. I gathered that none of them had seen such substances before. They were all dressed as was Danali, in simple skirts of what appeared to be silk. Many wore emerald or ruby pendants dangling from their delicate necks; a few of the women also sported earrings but were otherwise unadorned. None of them wore shoes upon their leathery feet.

Danali led us beneath the great trees, which seemed to grow still greater with every mile we moved into them. Here, in the deep woods, elms and maples mingled with the oaks. In places, however, we passed through groves of much lesser trees that were scarcely any taller than those of Mesh. They appeared all to be fruit trees: apple and cherry, pear and plum. Many were in full flower with little white petals covering them like mounds of snow; many were laden with red, ripe apples or dark red cherries. That they should bear fruit in Ashte seemed a miracle, and not the only one of those lovely woods. It amazed me to see deer in great numbers walking through the apple groves as if they had nothing to fear from the many Lokilani with their bows and arrows.

When Maram suggested that Danali should shoot a couple of them to make a feast for dinner, he looked at him in horror and said, '*Shoot* arrows into an animal? Would I shoot my own mother, Hairface? Am I wolf, am I weasel, am I a bear that I should hunt animals for food?'

'But what do you eat in these woods, then?' Maram asked as he shuffled along with his hands bound behind his back.

'We eat apples; we eat nuts – and much else. The trees give us everything we need.'

The Lokilani, as we found, wouldn't even eat the eggs taken from birds' nests or honey from the combs of the bees. Neither did they cultivate barley or wheat or any such vegetables as carrots, peas or beans. The only gardens they kept grew other glories from the earth: crystals such as clear quartz, amethyst and starstone as well as garnets, topaz, tourmaline and more precious gems. I marveled at these many-colored stones erupting from the forest floor like so many new shoots. They seemed always to be planted – if that was the right word – in colorful, concentric circles around trees like I had seen before only in my dreams. Though not very tall, these trees spread out like oaks, and their bark was silver like that of maples. But it was their leaves in all their splendor that made me gasp and wonder where they had come from; the leaves on these loveliest of trees shimmered like millions of golden shields and were etched with a webwork of deep green veins. Danali called them astors. I thought that the astors – and the bright gemstones growing around them – must be the greatest miracles of the Forest, but I was wrong.

By a circuitous route that seemed to follow no logic or path, Danali led us through the trees to the Lokilani's village. This, however, was no simple assemblage of buildings and dwellings. Indeed, there were no buildings such as castles, temples or towers; neither were there streets, for the only dwellings the Lokilani had were spread out over many acres, each house being built beneath its own tree.

Danali escorted us toward one of these strange-looking houses. Its frame was of many long poles set into the ground in a circle and leaning up against each other so as to form a high cone. The poles were woven with long strips of white bark like that of birch. Around it grew many flowers: dahlias and daisies, marigolds and chrysanthemums – and other kinds for which I had no name. Someone had adorned the doorway with garlands of white and gold blossoms whose petals formed little, nine-pointed stars. It was an inviting entrance to a space that was to be home, hospital and prison for the next two days.

Inside we found a circular expanse of earth covered with golden astor leaves. A small firepit had been dug into the ground at the house's center, but there was no furniture other than beds of fresh green leaves. Danali explained that this was a house of healing; here we would remain until our bodies and spirits were whole again.

After setting a guard around our house, Danali saw to our every need. He had food and drink brought to us; he had our clothes taken away to be mended and cleaned. That evening he led us under escort to a hot spring that bubbled up out of the ground near a grove of plum trees. Several of the Lokilani women climbed into the water with us and used handfuls of fragrant-smelling leaves to scrub us clean. One of them, a pretty woman named Iolana, immediately captured Maram's eye. She had long brown hair and the green eyes of all her people, but she was

225

almost as small as a child, standing no higher than the top of Maram's belly. The difference in their sizes, however, did not discourage him. When I remarked the incongruity of a moose taking up with a roe deer, he told me, 'Love will find a way, my friend. It always does. I'll be as gentle with her as a leaf settling onto a pond. Don't you find that there's something about these little people that inspires gentleness?'

I had to admit that, their bows and arrows notwithstanding, the Lokilani were the least warlike people I had ever met. They laughed easily and often, and they liked to sing to the accompaniment of each other's whistling or clapping of hands. They spoke with a light, lilting accent that was sometimes hard to understand, but they never spoke harshly or raised their voices, to one another or to us. Why they were so kind to us after nearly murdering us remained a mystery. Danali told us that all would be explained at a council to be held the next day, when we would be summoned to meet the Lokilani's queen. In the meantime, he said, we must rest and restore ourselves.

Toward this end, he later sent a beautiful woman named Pualani into our house. She had long, flowing chestnut hair and eyes as clear and green as the emerald she wore around her neck. They gleamed with concern as Master Juwain showed her the wound that Salmelu had cut into my side. With great gentleness, she pressed her warm fingers into my skin all around the wound, both in front and where his sword had emerged from my back. Then she had me drink a sweetish tea that she made and told me to lie back against my bed of leaves.

Almost immediately, I fell asleep. But strangely, all night long I was aware that I was sleeping, and also aware of Pualani pressing pungent-smelling leaves against my side. I thought I felt as well the coolness of her emerald touching me. My whole body seemed to burn with a cool, green light. When I awoke the next morning, I was amazed to discover that my wound had completely healed. Not even a scar remained to mark my flesh and remind me of my sword fight.

'It's a miracle!' Maram exclaimed when he saw what Pualani had done. In the soft light filtering through curving white walls, he ran his rough hand over my side. 'This wood is full of magic and miracles.'

'It would seem so,' Master Juwain said as he too examined me. 'It would seem that these people have much to teach us.'

As it happened, Master Juwain had much to teach them. When Pualani returned to check on me, she and Master Juwain began discussing herbs and various techniques of healing. She grew excited to discover that he knew of plants and potions of which she had never heard; then she invited him to walk among the trees so that she could show him the many medicinal mushrooms that grew in the Forest and nowhere else.

Later that day, after they had returned, Danali came to our house to escort us to a feast held in our honor. We all put on our best clothes: Maram found a fresh red tunic in the saddlebags of his pack horse while Master Juwain had only his newly cleaned green woolens. Atara, however, unpacked a yellow doeskin shirt embroidered with fine beadwork; it made a stark contrast with her dark leather trousers, but I liked it better than her studded armor. As for myself, I wore a simple black tunic emblazoned with the silver swan and seven stars of Mesh. Although I gladly left my mail suit in our house, I was more reluctant to abandon my sword. The Lokilani, however, wouldn't allow weapons at their meals. And so Maram left his sword behind, too, and Atara her bow and arrows, and together we stepped out from our flower-covered doorway and followed Danali through the woods to the place of the feast.

The whole Lokilani village had assembled nearby in a stand of great astor trees. There must have been nearly five hundred of them: men, women and children sitting on the leaf-covered ground and gathered around many long mats woven of long, green leaves. I saw at once that these mats served as tables, for they were heaped with bowls of food. Danali invited us to sit at a table beneath the boughs of a spreading astor, along with his wife and five children. And then, just as we were taking our places, Pualani walked into the glade. Her hair was crowned with a garland of blue flowers, and she wore a silvery robe that covered her from neck to ankle. Although we had supposed her to be quite young, she was accompanied by her grown daughter, who turned out to be none other than Iolana. With them walked her own husband, a slender but well-muscled man whom Danali introduced as Elan. He surprised us all by telling us that Pualani was the Lokilani's queen.

Pualani took the place of honor at the head of the table with Elan to her left. Master Juwain, Maram, Atara and I sat to one side of the table facing Danali and his family. Iolana knelt directly beside Maram, and they both seemed quite happy with this arrangement. She gazed at him much more openly than would any maid of Mesh.

Without fanfare, toasting or speeches, the meal began as Pualani reached out to pass a bowl of fruit to Elan. I saw that at the other tables surrounding us, the Lokilani were circulating similar hand-woven bowls. There was much food to heap on top of our plates, which were nothing more than single but very large leaves. As Danali had promised, all of our meal had come from trees or bushes in the Forest. Fruits predominated, and I had never seen so many served in one place: blackberries and raspberries, gooseberries, apples and plums. There were cherries, pears and strawberries, too, in great abundance, as well

227

as a greenish, apple-like thing that they called starfruit. And others. It was all quite ripe, and every piece I put into my mouth burst with fresh juices and sweetness. They made good use of the many seeds and nuts, which included not only familiar ones such as walnuts and hickories, but some very large brown nuts they called treemeats. Danali said that they were more sustaining than the flesh of animals; they tasted rich and earthy and seemed full of the Forest's strength. The Lokilani cooked them into a thick stew, even as they baked a bread of bearseed and spread it with various nut butters and jams. As well, we were passed bowls of green shoots that I had thought only a squirrel could eat, and at least four kinds of edible flowers. For drink, we had cups of cool water and elderberry wine. Although it seemed this last was too sweet to drink in quantity, Maram proved me wrong. He let the Lokilani refill his cup again and again even more times than he refilled his own plate.

'Ah, what a meal,' he said as he reached for a pitcher of maple syrup to drizzle over his bread. 'I've never eaten like this before.'

None of us had. The food was not only more delicious than any I had ever tasted, it was more alive. It seemed that the essence of the Forest was passing directly into our bodies as if breathed into our blood. By the time the feast ended, we all felt quite full but also light and animated, ready to dance or sing or tell stories according to the Lokilani's wont. As we discovered, our hosts and captors were quite fond of such after-dinner celebrations. But first, Pualani and the others had many questions for us, as we did for them.

'We should begin at the beginning,' Pualani told us in a voice as rich as the wine she poured us. Her deeply-set eyes caught up some of the color of the emerald necklace she wore, and I thought that she was not only beautiful but wise. 'We would all like to know how you found your way into our wood, and why.'

Since I – or rather Altaru – had led our way here, Master Juwain, Maram and Atara all looked at me to answer her.

'The "why" of it is easy enough to tell,' I said. 'We were fleeing our enemies, and our path took us here.'

I told her something of the Stonefaces who had been pursuing us for many miles through the wilds of Alonia. Of Kane I said nothing, nor did I relate my dream of Morjin.

'Well, Sar Valashu, that *is* a beginning,' Pualani said. 'But only the very beginning of the beginning, yes? You've told us the circumstances of your flight into the Forest but not *why* you've come to us. But perhaps you don't yet know. Too bad. And sad to say, neither do we.'

Maram, after taking yet another pull of his wine, looked at her and slurred out, 'Not everything has a purpose, my Lady.'

228

'But of course, all things do,' she told him. 'We just have to look for it.'

'You might as well look for the reason that birds sing or men drink wine.'

She smiled at him and said, 'Birds sing because they're glad to be alive, and men drink wine because they're not.'

'Perhaps that's true,' Maram said, squeezing his cup. 'But it tells us nothing of the *purpose* of my drinking this excellent wine of yours.'

'Perhaps the purpose is to teach you the value of sobriety.'

'Perhaps,' he muttered, licking the wine from his mustache.

Pualani turned toward me and said, 'Why don't we put aside the purpose of your coming here and try to understand just how you entered our woods.'

'Well, we walked into them,' I told her.

'Yes, of course – but *how* did you do this? No one just walks into the Forest.'

She explained that just as some peoples built walls of stone to protect their kingdoms, the Lokilani had constructed a different kind of barrier around their woods. She told us very little of how they did this. She hinted at the power of the great trees to keep strangers away and at a secret that the Lokilani shared with each other but not with us.

'Here the power of the earth is very great,' she said. 'It repels most people. Even many of the bears, wolves and higher beasts. A man walking in our direction would find that he doesn't want to walk this way. His path would take him in a great circle around the Forest or away from it.'

'Perhaps it would,' I said, remembering the sensations I had felt the day before. 'But if he came close enough, he would see the great trees.'

'Men come close to many things they never see,' Pualani said as she smiled mysteriously. 'Looking toward the Forest from the outside, most men would see *only* trees.'

'But what if they were looking *for* the Forest?'

'Men look for many things they never find,' she said. 'And who knows even to look? Even a Lokilani, upon leaving our woods, can forget what real trees are like and have a hard time finding his way back in.'

'Our coming must have been a wild chance, then.'

'No one comes here by chance, Sar Valashu. Few come at all.'

I pointed off toward a tree a hundred yards away where a young woman stood with a strung bow and arrow. I said, 'Your people don't hunt animals – what do they hunt, then?'

Pualani's face clouded for a moment as she exchanged dark looks with Elan and Danali. Then she said, 'For many years, the Earthkiller has sent his men to try to find our Forest. A few have come close, and these we've had to send back to the stars.'

'Who is this Earthkiller, then?'

'The Earthkiller is the Earthkiller,' she said simply. 'This is known from the ancient of days: he cuts trees to burn in his forges. He cuts wounds in the earth to steal its fire. By forge and fire he seeks the making of that which can never be made.'

Her words sounded familiar to me, as they must have to Master Juwain. I nodded at him as he pulled out his *Saganom Elu* and read from the *Book of Fire*:

> *He hates the flowers, soft and white,*
> *The grass, the forest's gentle breath,*
> *For all that lives and leaps with light*
> *Recalls the bitterness of death.*
>
> *With axe and pick and poison flame*
> *He wreaks his spite upon the land;*
> *His armies burn and hack and maim*
> *The ferns and flowers, soil and sand.*
>
> *And down through rocky vein and bore*
> *With evil eye and sorcery*
> *He plumbs the earth for golden ore*
> *In search of immortality.*
>
> *Thus wounding earth to steal her fire*
> *And feeding trees to forge and flame,*
> *He turns upon himself his ire*
> *And burns his soul with bitter blame.*
>
> *For golden cups that blaze too bright*
> *Make hateful, mortal men afraid,*
> *And that which makes the stellar light,*
> *In love, cannot itself be made.*

When he had finished, Pualani sighed deeply and said, 'It would seem that your people know of the Earthkiller, too.'

'We call him the Red Dragon,' Master Juwain said.

'You have named him well, then,' Pualani said. Then she pointed at his book and asked, 'But what is this animal skin encasing the white leaves crawling with bugs?'

We were all astonished that Pualani had never seen a book. Just as it astonished her and all the Lokilani when Master Juwain explained how the sounds of language could be represented by letters and read out loud.

'Your people bring marvels into our woods,' she said. 'And you bring great mysteries, too.'

She took a sip of wine and slowly swallowed it. Then she smiled at me and continued, 'When you approached the Forest, we thought the Earthkiller must have sent you. And so we sent Danali and the others to greet you. We couldn't have known that you would be wearing the mark of the Ellama.'

'What is this Ellama?' I asked her, touching the scar on my forehead.

'The Ellama is the Ellama,' she said. 'And the lightning bolt is sacred to him. And so it has been sacred to us for years beyond reckoning. This is the fire that connects the earth to the heavens, where the Ellama walks with the rest of his kind.'

'With the Star People?' I asked.

'Some think of them as people,' she said. 'But just as people such as you and I are also animals, we are something more. And so it is with them who are more than human, the Bright Ones, the Galad a'Din.'

'You mean, the *Galadin*?'

'You say words strangely. But yes, I mean they who walk among the stars. When Danali saw the mark on you, he wondered if it was perhaps the Ellama who really sent you to us.'

Maram suddenly dug his elbow into me as if to impel me to claim such exalted origins. Atara and Master Juwain both looked at me to see what I would say. Surely, I thought, the truth was a sacred thing. But life was more sacred still. If claiming to be the Galadin's emissary would keep the Lokilani from sending us back to them, shouldn't I then lie just this one time?

'We *are* emissaries,' I told Pualani. I watched her eyes deepen like cups that drank in my every word. If truth was a clear stream that replenished the soul, then wasn't a lie like poison? 'We're emissaries from Mesh and Delu, and from the Brotherhood and the Kurmak to the court of King Kiritan in Tria. He has called a quest to find the Lightstone, and we are journeying there to answer it and represent our peoples.'

While Danali poured more wine and the Lokilani at the other tables grew quiet, I told of how Count Dario had come to my father's castle on the first day of Ashte to announce the great quest. Something in Pualani's eyes made me want to relate as well the story of the assassin's arrow and all that had occurred since that dark afternoon. And so I told them of my duel with Salmelu and the Black Bog; I told them of Kane

231

and the Lord of Illusions and the stone-faced gray men who had nearly driven us mad.

When had I finished speaking, I took another long drink of wine and blamed it for loosening my tongue. But Pualani looked at me with the opposite of blame. She bowed her head and said, 'Thank you for opening your heart to us, Sar Valashu. Now at least it's clear how you entered our wood. You must be very wise to entrust your fate to your horse. And he must be blessed with much more than wisdom to be drawn by the Forest.'

She nodded toward a grove of apple trees nearby where the Lokilani had tethered our horses. Then she continued, 'If you hadn't been so forthcoming, we would have understood nothing about you. As it is, we can make sense of only a very little.'

She went on to say that the world of castles and quests and old books full of words were as unknown to the Lokilani as the stars must be to us. She had never heard of the Nine Kingdoms, nor even of Alonia, in whose great forests the Forest abided. In truth, she denied that any king could have a claim upon her woods or that it might be a part of any kingdom, unless that kingdom be the world itself. As she said, the Lokilani were the first people, the true people, and the Forest was the true world.

'Once, before the Earthkiller came and men cut down the great trees, there was only the Forest,' she told us. 'Here the Lokilani have lived since the beginning of time. And here we will remain until the stars die.'

Atara, who had been silent until now, caught Pualani's eye and said, 'It may be that King Kiritan has no true claim upon your realm. But he would think he had. Your woods lie very close to the more cultivated parts of Alonia. Aren't you afraid that the king's men will some day come to cut them down?'

'No, this we do not fear,' Pualani said. 'Your people build a world of stone cities and armies and swords. But this not *the* world. Very little in your world can touch the Forest now.'

'What about the Earthkiller?' I asked her.

Again, a dark look fell over Pualani's face; I was reminded of winter storm clouds smothering a bright blue sky.

'The Earthkiller has great power,' she admitted. 'And great allies, too. These Stonefaces of yours have tried to enter the Forest in our dreams even as they entered yours.'

'But they haven't tried to broach it, in their bodies?'

'No – they will never find their way into our woods. And if they do, they will never find their way out alive.'

'Still,' I said, 'it must be a great temptation for them to try. There are things here that the Lord of Lies would give a great deal to know:

how you grow trees to such great heights and grow gems from the very ground.'

'It is the earth that grows these things, not we. No more than a midwife grows the children she helps deliver.'

'Perhaps that's true,' I said. I touched my scar where the midwife's tongs had once cut me. 'But a midwife would be no more than a butcher without the skills taught her. It's this knowledge that the Lord of Illusions seeks.'

'You seem to know a great deal of what he would wish to know.'

Truly, I thought as I recalled my dream, I *did* know much more of Morjin's mind than I wanted to. I certainly knew enough to perceive that if he could, he would crush the secrets from the Lokilani as readily as he would grapes beneath his boots.

'There is one thing he seeks above all else,' I said. 'The same thing that we seek.'

'This is the Lightstone that you spoke of, yes? But what *is* this stone? Is it an emerald? A great ruby or a diamond?'

'No, it is a cup – a plain golden cup.'

Here, Master Juwain broke in to tell of the gelstei and of how these great crystals had been made through many long ages of Ea's history. And the greatest of all the gelstei, he said, was the gold, which most men believed had been created by the Star People and brought to earth at the beginning of the Lost Ages. But he admitted that many also thought that the Lightstone had been forged and cast into the shape of a cup in the Blue Mountains of Alonia sometime during the Age of Swords. Whatever the truth really was, the Lord of Lies sought not only the Lightstone itself but the secret of its making.

'He would certainly create a Lightstone of his own, if he could,' Master Juwain said. 'And so he would certainly steal from you any knowledge of growing and shaping crystals that might help him.'

Pualani sat very straight pulling on the emeralds of her necklace. She looked at Master Juwain for a long moment, and then at Atara, Maram and me. She asked us why we sought the Lightstone. We each answered as best we could. When we had finished speaking, she said, 'The gold gelstei brings light, as you say. And yet this lord of darkness seeks it above all other things. Why, we want to know, why, why?'

'Because,' Master Juwain said, 'the gold gives power over all the other gelstei except perhaps the silver. It gives immortality, too. And perhaps much else that we don't know of.'

'But it is light, you say, pure light bound into a cup of gold?'

'Even light can be used to read good or evil words in a book,' Master Juwain told her. 'Just as too much light can burn or blind.'

I sat thinking about this for a moment, and then I added, 'Even if this cup brought the Red Dragon no light at all, he would take joy in keeping others from it.'

'Oh, that is bad, very, very bad,' Pualani said. She bent forward to confer with Danali. After looking at Elan in silent understanding, she told us, 'There is great danger here for the Lokilani. A danger we never saw.'

'My apologies,' I said, 'for bringing such evil tidings.'

'No, no, you mustn't apologize,' Pualani said. 'And you've brought nothing evil into our woods, so we hope, so we pray. It may be that you're an emissary of the Ellama after all, even if you didn't know it.'

I looked down at the leaves on the ground because I didn't know what to say.

'The Ellama still watches over the Forest,' she told us. 'The Galad a'Din haven't forgotten the Lokilani, they would never forget.'

I smiled sadly at this because I supposed the Galadin had looked away from the ways and wars of Ea long ago.

'And we haven't forgotten them, we must never forget,' Pualani said to us. 'And so we celebrate this remembrance and their eternal presence among us. Will you help us celebrate, Sar Valashu Elahad?'

She looked straight at me then, and her eyes were twin emeralds, all green and blazing like life itself.

'Yes, of course,' I told her. 'Even as you've helped us.'

'And you, Prince Maram Marshayk – will you help us, too?'

Maram eyed his empty cup and the jug of wine that had found its way to the end of the table. He licked his lips and said, 'Help you *celebrate*? Does a bear eat honey if you hold it to his face? Does a horse have to be kicked to eat sweet grass?'

'Very good,' Pualani said, nodding at him. Then she smiled at Atara and asked, 'And what about you, Atara of the Manslayers? Will you celebrate the coming of the Galad a'Din?'

'I will,' Atara told her, nodding her head.

Pualani now turned to Master Juwain, and asked him this same question as if reciting the words to a ritual. And he replied, 'I would like very much to celebrate with you, but I'm afraid my vows don't permit me to drink wine.'

'Then you may keep your vows,' Pualani said, 'for it's not wine we drink in remembrance of the Shining Ones.'

At this news, Maram looked crestfallen, and he said, 'What *do* you drink, then?'

'Only fire,' Pualani said, smiling at him. 'But it might be more precise to say that we eat it.'

'Eat?' Maram said, groaning as he held his bulging belly. 'Eat *what*? I don't think I can eat another bite.'

'Does a bear eat honey when it's held to his face?' Pualani asked him with a coy smile.

'You have *honey*?' Maram asked her. 'I thought the Lokilani didn't eat honey.'

'We don't,' Pualani told him. 'But we have something much sweeter.'

So saying, she pulled off a silvery cloth from a bowl at the end of the table. Inside were piled many small golden fruits about the size of plums. She took one in her hand, and then passed the bowl to Elan, who did the same. The bowl quickly made its way around the table. I noticed that although Danali's three children all seemed quite interested in the bowl's gleaming contents, none of them touched the fruit. I gathered that just as a child in Mesh would never participate in our rituals of toasting and drinking beer, so the Lokilani children were forbidden to participate in what was to come.

'The fruit has probably fermented,' I said to Maram as I took one in my hand and squeezed its smooth, soft skin. 'You'll probably find all the wine inside that you wish.'

'Now *that* would be a miracle,' he said as he picked up one of the little fruits and regarded it doubtfully. He looked at Pualani and asked, 'What do you call this thing?'

'It's a timana,' she said. She pointed up at the golden-leafed tree above our table. 'You see, once every seven years, the astors bear the sacred fruit.'

Maram held the timana to his nose for a moment but said nothing.

'Long ago,' Pualani explained, 'the Shining Ones walked the Forest and planted the first astors. The trees were their gift to the Lokilani.'

She sat looking at the timana in her hand as I might look at the stars. Then she told us that the Galadin were angels and this was their flesh.

'We eat this fruit in remembrance of who the Shining Ones really are and who we were meant to be,' she explained. 'Please join us in our celebration today.'

Now the whole glade fell very quiet as the Lokilani at the other mats put down their cups of wine or water to watch us eat the timanas. I wondered why none of them had been given any fruit. I thought that it must be quite rare and used by only a few Lokilani at any one ritual.

Without any more words, Pualani bit into her timana, and all the men and women at our table did the same. As my teeth closed on the fruit, a waterfall of tastes exploded in my mouth. It was like honey and wine and sunlight all bound up into the most fragrant of juices. And

235

yet there was something bittersweet about the fruit as well. Beneath its succulent sugars was a flavor I had never experienced; it recalled mighty trees streaming with spring sap and the fire of a greenness that no longer existed on earth.

Even so, I found the fruit to be very good. Its savor was exquisite, and lingered on my tongue. Along with Pualani and Maram and everyone else, I took a second bite. The timana's flesh was reddish-orange and studded with a starlike array of tiny black seeds. It glistened in the waning light for an endless moment before I put the fruit in my mouth and ate the rest of it.

'We're so glad you've joined us,' Pualani said as the others finished theirs as well. 'Now you'll see what you'll see.'

'*What* will we see?' Maram asked, licking the juice from his teeth.

'Perhaps nothing,' Pualani said. 'But perhaps you'll see the Timpum.'

'The Timpum?' Maram asked in alarm. 'What's that?'

'The Timpum are the Timpum,' Pualani said softly. 'They are of the Galad a'Din.'

'I don't understand,' Maram said, rubbing his belly.

'The Galad a'Din,' Pualani said, 'are beings of pure fire. When they walked the earth in the ages before the Lost Ages, they left part of their being behind them. So, the fire, the beings that men do not usually see – the Timpum.'

'I don't think I *want* to understand,' Maram said.

'Few men do,' Pualani told him. Then she looked from him to Master Juwain and Atara, and last at me. She said, 'It's strange that you seek your golden cup in other lands when so much is to be found so much closer. Love, life, light – why not look for these things in the leaves of the trees and beneath the rocks and along the wind?'

Why not, indeed, I wondered as I looked up at the soft lights dancing along the trees' fluttering golden leaves?

'Am I to understand,' Maram said, breathing heavily, 'that this fruit you've fed us provides visions of these Timpum?'

'Yes,' Pualani said gravely, 'either that or death.'

We were all silent for as long as it took my heart to beat three times. Then Maram gasped out, 'What? What did you say?'

'You've eaten the flesh of the angels,' Pualani calmly explained. 'And so if it's meant to be, you'll see the angel fire. But not all can bear it. And so they die.'

At this news, Maram struggled to his feet, all the while puffing and groaning. He held his big belly as he cried out, 'Poison, poison! Oh, my Lord – I've been poisoned!'

He turned to bend and stick his fingers down his throat to purge himself of the dangerous fruit. Pualani stopped him with a few soft words. She told him that it was already too late, that he would have to live or die according to the grace of the Ellama.

'Why have you done this?' Maram shouted at her. His face was now almost as red as a plum. And so, I feared, were Master Juwain's, Atara's and mine. 'What have we done to deserve this?'

'Nothing that others haven't done,' Pualani told him. 'All the Lokilani, when we become women and men – we eat the sacred fruit. Many die, sad to say. But it must be so. Life without sight of the Timpum would not be worth living.'

'It would be to me!' Maram cried out. 'I'm not a Lokilani! Oh, my Lord – I don't want to die!'

'We're sorry this had to be, so sorry,' Pualani told us. She looked at Master Juwain, who sat frozen like a deer surrounded by wolves, and then she smiled at Atara and me. 'There are only two courses open to you. You may remain with the Lokilani and become as one of us. Or you must return to your world.'

My breath came hard and fast now as the woods about us seemed to take on the tones of the waning sunlight. It was a yellow like nothing I had ever seen, a waiting-yellow over the trees and through them. A watching-yellow that was very close and yet somehow faraway.

'Please forgive us, please do,' Pualani said. 'But if you *do* return to your world, we must be utterly certain of who you are. The Earthkiller's people could never bear the sight of the Timpum. And no one who has ever seen the Timpum could ever serve the Earthkiller.'

I noticed that the children at our table, and every table throughout the glade, were watching us with awe coloring their small, pale faces. It came to me that awe was nothing less than love and fear, and I felt both of these swelling inside me. Everyone was looking at us in fear for our lives, watching and waiting to see what we would see.

Suddenly, Maram threw his hands to the side of his face and let loose a wild, whoop of laughter. He fell to his knees, all the while shaking his head and laughing and crying out that he was being killed but didn't care.

'I see them! I see them!' he called to us. 'Oh, my Lord – they're everywhere!'

Master Juwain, who had been sitting as still as a statue, leapt to his feet and waved his hands about his bald head. 'Astonishing! Astonishing!' he shouted. 'It's not possible, it can't be possible. Val – do you see them?'

I did not see them. For at that moment, Atara let out a terrible cry and fell backward to the ground as if her spine had been cut with an axe. She screamed for a moment or two before her eyes closed. Then she grew quiet. The movement beneath her doeskin shirt was so slight that I couldn't tell if she was breathing. I fell over toward her and buried my face in this soft garment. Her whole body seemed as still as stone and colder than ice. I knew too well what it felt like for another to die; I would have died myself rather than feel this nothingness take away Atara. But the cold suddenly grew unbearable, and I knew with a dreadful certainty that she was leaving me. There was nothing but darkness inside her and all about me. I could see nothing because my eyes were tightly closed as I gripped the soft leather of her shirt and wept bitterly.

Then I, too, let out a terrible cry. My heart beat so hard I thought it would break open my chest. Everything poured out of me: my love for her, my tears, my whispers of hope that burned my lips like fire.

'Atara,' I said softly, 'don't go away.'

The pain inside me was worse than anything I had ever known. It cut me open like a sword, and I felt the blood streaming out of my heart and into hers. It took forever to die, I knew, while the moments of life were so precious and few.

And then, as if awakening from a dream, her whole body started. I looked down to see her eyes suddenly open. She smiled at me as her breath fell over my face. 'Thank you,' she said, 'for saving my life again.'

She struggled to sit up, and I held her against me with her head touching mine and my face pressing her shoulder. My breath came in shudders and quick gasps, and I was both weeping and laughing because I couldn't quite believe that she was still alive.

'Shhh,' she whispered to me, 'be quiet, be quiet now.'

As I sat there with my eyes closed, I became aware of a deep silence. But it was not a quietening of the world; now the songs of the sparrows came ringing through the trees, and I could almost hear the wildflowers growing in the earth all around me. It was more a silence within myself where the chatter of all my thoughts and fears suddenly died away. I could hear myself whispering to myself in a voice without sound; it seemed the earth itself was calling out a name that was mine but not mine alone.

'Oh, there are so many!' Atara said to me softly. 'Look, Val, look!'

I opened my eyes then, and I saw the Timpum. As Maram had said, they were everywhere. I sat up straight, blinking my eyes. Above the golden leaves of the forest floor, little luminous clouds floated about as if drawing their substance from the earth and returning to it soft showers of light. Among the wood anemone and ashflowers, swirls of fire burned in colors of red, orange and blue. They flitted from flower to flower like flaming butterflies drinking up nectar and touching each petal with their numinous heat. Little silver moons hovered near some cinnamon fern, and the ingathering of white sparks beneath the boughs of the astors reminded me of constellations of stars. From behind rocks came soft flashes like those of glowworms. The Timpum seemed to come in almost as many kinds as the birds and beasts of the Forest. They flickered and fluttered and danced and glittered, and no leaf or living thing in the glade appeared untouched by their presence.

'Astonishing! Astonishing!' Master Juwain called out again. 'I must learn their names and kinds!'

Some of the Timpum were tiny, no more than burning drops of light that hung in the air like mist. Some were as huge as the trees: the trunks of a few of the astors were ringed with golden halos that brightened and deepened as they spread out to encompass the great crowns of leaves.

Although they had forms, they had no faces. And yet we perceived them as having quite distinct faces – to be sure not of lips, noses, cheeks and eyes, but rather colored with various blendings of curiosity, playfulness, effervescence, compassion and other characteristics that one might expect to find on a human countenance. Most marvelous of all was that they seemed to be aware not only of the trees and the rocks, the ferns and the flowers, but of us.

'Look, Val!' Maram called to me. He stood above the table as he brushed the folds of his tunic. 'These little red ones keep at me like hummingbirds in a honeysuckle bush. Do you see them?'

'Yes – how not?' I told him.

All about him were Timpum of the whirling fire variety, and their flames touched him in tendrils of red, orange, yellow and violet. I turned to see a little silver moon shimmer in front of Atara for a moment as if drinking in the light of her bright blue eyes. And then I blinked, and it was gone.

'They seem to want something of me,' Maram said. 'I can almost hear them whispering, almost see it in my mind.'

The Timpum seemed to want something from all of us, though we couldn't quite say what that might be. I looked at Pualani to ask if it was that way for the Lokilani, too.

'The Timpum speak the language of the Galad a'Din,' she told us. 'And that is impossible for most to learn. Those that do take many years to understand only the smallest part of it. Even so, we *do* understand the Timpum sometimes. They warn us if outsiders are approaching our realm or of when we have hate in our hearts. On cloudy nights of no moon, they light up our woods.'

I looked off into the trees for a moment, and the great, shimmering spectacle before my eyes dazzled me. To Pualani I said, 'Do your people then see the world like this all the time?'

'Yes, this is how the Forest *is*.'

She told me that so long as we dwelled in the Forest, we would see the Timpum. If we some day chose to eat the sacred timanas again in remembrance of the Shining Ones, even as she and the others had eaten them, our vision of the Timpum would grow only brighter.

'If you decide to leave us,' she said, 'it will now be hard for you to bear the deadness of any other wood.'

Just then an especially bright Timpum – it was one of the ones like a swirl of flickering white stars – fell slowly down from the tree above me. It spun about in the space before my eyes as if studying the scar cut into my forehead. It seemed to touch me there with a quick silver light; I felt this as a deep surge of compassion that touched me to my core and brightened my whole being as if I had been struck with a lightning bolt. Then, after a moment, the flickering Timpum settled itself down on top of my head. Maram and the others saw it shimmering in my hair like a crown of stars, but I could not.

'How do I get it off me?' I asked as I brushed my hand through my hair and shook my head from side to side.

'Why would you want to?' Pualani asked me. 'Sometimes a Timpum will attach itself to one of us to try to tell us something.'

'What, then?'

'Only you will ever know,' she said as she gazed above my head. Then she told me, 'I think the "why" of your coming to our woods has finally been answered, however. You are here to listen, Sar Valashu Elahad. And to dance.'

And with that she smiled at me and rose from the table. This seemed a signal that Elan and Danali – and all the other Lokilani at the other tables – should rise, too. Along with Pualani, they came over to Atara, Master Juwain, Maram and me. They touched our faces and kissed our hands and congratulated us on eating the timanas and surviving to see the Timpum. Then Danali began singing a light, happy song while many of his people clapped their hands to keep time. Others began dancing. They joined hands in circles surrounding circles and spun about the forest floor as they added their voices to Danali's song. I found myself clasping hands with Atara and Maram, and turning with them. Although it was impossible to touch a Timpum, their substance being not of flesh but the fire of angels, there was a sense in which they danced with us and we with them. For they were everywhere among us, and they never stopped fluttering and sparkling and whirling about the golden-leafed trees.

Much later, after the sun had set and the Timpum's eyeless faces lit up the night, I took out my flute and joined the Lokilani in song. The Lokilani marveled at this slender piece of wood for they had never imagined music could be made this way. I taught a few of the children to play a simple song that my mother had once taught me. Atara sang with them, and Maram, too, before he took Iolana's hand and stole off into the trees. Even Master Juwain hummed a few notes in his rough old voice, though he was more interested in trying to ferret out and record the words of the Timpum's language.

I, too, wished to understand what they had to tell me. And so, even as Pualani had said, I stayed awake all night playing my flute and dancing and listening to the fiery voices that spoke along the wind.

15

O ur vision of the Timpum did not fade with the coming of the new day. If anything, in the fullness of the sunlight, their fiery forms seemed only brighter. It was impossible to look at them very long and imagine a life without them.

After a delicious breakfast of fruits and nutbread, Atara and I held council with Master Juwain and Maram. We stood by a stream not far from our house, inhaling the fragrance of cherry blossoms and marveling at the splendor of the woods.

'We must decide what to do,' I said to them. 'By my count, tomorrow will be the first of Soldru, and that gives us only seven more days to reach Tria.'

'Ah, but do we even *want* to go to Tria?' Maram asked as he stared at an astor sapling. 'That is the question.'

'There's very much to be learned here,' Master Juwain agreed. 'Very much more still to be seen.'

Atara smiled, and her eyes shone like diamonds. She said, 'That's true – and I would like to see it. But I've pledged myself to journey to Tria, and so I must go.'

'Perhaps we could stay here only a few more days,' Maram said. 'Or a few more months. Tria will still be there in Ioj or Valte.'

'But we would miss the calling of the quest,' Atara said.

'So what if we do? The Lightstone has been lost for three thousand years. Likely it will remain lost for three more months.'

'Unless, by chance,' I said, 'some knight finds it first.'

'By a miracle, that would be,' Maram said.

I pointed at the crown of lights that had floated from the top of my head and now hovered nearby over a blackberry bush. There, among the little ripe fruits, twinkled many Timpum that looked something like fireflies.

'Does it seem to you that the world lacks miracles?' I asked.

'No, perhaps it doesn't,' he admitted. His large eyes gleamed as if he were intoxicated – not with wine or even women but with pure fire.

'There's one miracle that I would like explained,' Master Juwain said to me. 'What happened last night between you and Atara?'

I looked at Atara a long moment before she answered him. 'After I ate the timana,' she said, 'I saw the Timpum almost immediately. It was like a flash of fire. It was so beautiful that I wanted to hold it forever – but can one hold the sun? I felt myself burning up like a leaf caught in the flames. And then I couldn't breathe, and I thought I was dying. Everything was so cold. It was like I had been buried alive in a crystal cave, so cold and hard, and everything growing darker. I *would* have died if Val hadn't come to take me back.'

'And how did he do that?' Master Juwain asked.

Again, Atara looked at me, and she said, 'I'm still not sure. Somehow I felt what he felt for me. All his love, his life – I felt it breaking open the cave like lightning and burning into me.'

Now Master Juwain and Maram looked at me, too, as the bluebirds sang and the Timpum glittered all about us. And Master Juwain said, 'That sounds like the *valarda*.'

Master Juwain's use of this word, utterly unexpected, fell out of the air like lightning and nearly broke *me* open. How did he know the name of my gift that Morjin had spoken to me? For many miles, I had wondered about this strange name, as I wondered about Master Juwain now. But he just smiled at me in his kindly but proud way, as if he knew almost everything there was to know.

It seemed that the time had finally come to explain about my gift, which they had already suspected lay behind my sensing of the Stonefaces and the other strangenesses of my life. And so I told them everything about it. I said that I had been born breathing in others' sufferings and their joys as well. I revealed my dream of Morjin and how he had prophesied that one day I would use my gift to make others feel my pain.

'It would appear,' Master Juwain said, looking from Atara to me, 'that you also have the power to make people feel much else.'

'Perhaps,' I said. 'But this is the first time this has happened. It's hard to know if it could ever happen again.'

'You say you are able to close yourself to others' emotions. Then surely it follows that you should be able to open them to yours.'

'Perhaps,' I said again. I didn't tell him that in order to do this, first I would have to open *myself* to the passions that blazed inside me, and that this was more terrifying than facing a naked sword.

243

'You should have come to us long ago,' Master Juwain told me. 'I'm sure we would have been able to help you.'

'Do you really think so?'

The Brotherhoods taught meditation and music, herbology and healing and many other things, but so far as I knew they knew nothing of this sense that both blessed and tormented me.

'Your gift is very rare, Val, but not unique. I read about it in a book years ago. I'm sure that there must be other books that could instruct you in its development and use.'

'Does one learn to play the flute from a book?' I asked him. I shook my head and smiled sadly. 'No, unless there is another who shares my affliction, there is only one thing that can help me.'

'You mean the Lightstone, don't you?'

'Yes, the Lightstone – it's said to be the cup of healing.'

If I could feel the fires that burned inside others and touch them with my own, then surely that meant there was a wound in my soul that allowed these sacred and very private flames to pass back and forth. This one time, perhaps, they had touched Atara and brought her back from the darkness. But what if the next time, through rage or hate, whatever was inside me flashed like real lightning and struck her dead?

Maram, who always understood so much without being told, came up to me and placed his hand above my heart. 'I think that this gift of yours must be like living with a hole in your chest. But Pualani healed you of the wound that Salmelu made. Perhaps she can heal this wound, too.'

Later that day, I went to Pualani's house to ask her about this. And there, inside a long door garlanded with white and purple flowers, she took my hand and told me, 'In the world, there are many sights that are hard to bear. Would you wish to be healed of the holes in your eyes so that you didn't have to see them?'

She went on to say that my wound, as I thought of it, was surely the gift of the Ellama. I must learn to use it, she said, as I would my eyes, my ears, my nose or any other part of me. If finding the Lightstone would help me in this, then I should seek it with all my heart.

That night in our house, I told Maram and Master Juwain that I must leave for Tria the next day.

'There will be knights from all the free kingdoms there,' I explained. 'Scryers and minstrels, too. One of them might tell of a crucial clue that would lead to the Lightstone.'

'I agree,' Atara said. 'In any case, King Kiritan will call all the questers to make vows together, and we should be there to receive his blessings.'

Master Juwain saw the sense of both these arguments, and agreed that we should all continue on to Tria together. Maram, when he saw that our minds were made up, reluctantly said that he would come with us as well.

'If you go without me,' he said, 'I'll never find either the strength or courage to leave these woods.'

'But what about Iolana?' I asked him. 'Don't you love her?'

'Ah, of course I do,' he said. 'I love the wine that the Lokilani serve, too. But there are many fine wines in the world, if you know what I mean.'

Maram's fickleness obviously vexed Atara, who said, 'I know little of wines. But there can't be another fruit on all of Ea like the timana.'

'And that is my point exactly,' Maram said. 'When I find the one wine that is to lesser vintages as the timana is to the more common fruits, I shall drink it and no other.'

The next morning I put on my cold armor and told Pualani that we would be leaving. After we had burdened the pack horses with a good load of fruit and freshly baked nutbread that the Lokilani provided us, we saddled Altaru and our other mounts. And then there, in the apple grove where they were tethered, the whole Lokilani village turned out to bid us farewell.

'It's sad to say goodbye,' Pualani told us. She stood beneath a blossom-laden bough with Elan, Danali and Iolana, who was weeping. Around them stood hundreds of men, women and children, and around all the Lokilani – everywhere in the grove – flickered the forms of the Timpum. 'And yet maybe some day you'll return to us as we all hope you will.'

From the pocket of her skirt, she removed a green jewel about the size of a child's finger. She pressed it into Master Juwain's gnarly old hand and said, 'You're a Master Healer of your Brotherhood. And emeralds are the stones of healing; they have power over all the growing things of the earth. If you should take wounds or illness, from the Earthkillers or any others, please use this emerald to heal yourselves.'

Master Juwain looked down at the gleaming emerald as if mystified. Then Pualani touched him lightly on his chest and said, 'There's no book that tells of this. To use it, you must open your heart. It has no resonance with the head.'

Master Juwain's bald head gleamed like a huge nut as he bowed and thanked her for her gift. Then she kissed him goodbye, and all the Lokilani, one by one, filed past us to touch our hands and kiss us as well.

'Farewell,' Pualani told us. 'May the light of the Ellama shine always upon you.'

Danali, with twenty or so of the Lokilani, had prepared an escort for us. As before, they each carried bows and arrows, but this time no one spoke of binding our hands. Because I thought it would be unseemly to mount our horses and sit so high above them when we already towered over them merely as we stood, we agreed to walk our horses through the Forest. Danali and the Lokilani led off while I followed holding Altaru's reins in my hand. Master Juwain and Maram came next, trailing both their sorrels and the pack horses. Atara walked next to Tanar in the rear.

It was a lovely morning, and the canopies of the astors shone above us like a dome of gold. The air smelled of fruits and flowers and the leaf-covered earth. Many birds were singing; their music seemed to pipe out in perfect time with the tinkling of the little stream that Danali followed. I thought that he was leading us west, but in the Forest I found my sense of direction dulled as if I had drunk too much wine.

We walked as quietly as we could in the silence of the great trees. No one spoke, not even to make little conversation or remark the beauty of some butterflies fluttering around a blackberry bush with their many-colored wings. An air of sadness hung over the woods, and we breathed its bittersweet fragrance with every step we took away from its center. The Timpum, so brilliant in their swirls of silver and scarlet, seemed less bright as we passed from the stands of astors into the giant oaks. There were fewer of them, too. We all knew that the Timpum could not live – if that was the right word – outside of the Forest. But to see them diminishing in splendor and numbers was a sorrowful thing.

Around noon, Danali left the stream and led us by secret paths through more thickly growing woods. Here the predominance of the oaks gave way to elms, maples and chestnuts, which, though still very tall, seemed stunted next to the giants of the deeper Forest. We walked along the winding paths for quite a few miles. The sun, crossing the sky somewhere above us, was invisible through the thick, green shrouds of leaves. I couldn't tell west from east or north from south.

After some hours, Danali finally broke his silence. He gave us to understand that the Forest could be almost as difficult to leave as it was to enter. Unless the Lokilani pointed themselves along certain, fixed paths out of it, they would find themselves wandering among the shimmering trees and being drawn back always toward its center.

'But it has been many years since any us has left the Forest,' he said. 'And many more since anyone, having left, found his way back in.'

Another couple of miles brought us to a place beyond which Danali and his people wouldn't go. Here, in a stand of oaks sprinkled with a few birch trees, we felt a barrier hanging over the Forest like an invisible curtain. There were only a few Timpum about, lingering among the oaks and shining weakly. It was hard to look beyond them into the dense green swaths of woods. For, only a few hundred yards from us, we could see nothing – only leaves and bark and ferns and other such things.

'We'll say goodbye here,' Danali said. He pointed down the narrow path cutting through the trees. 'Follow this, and do not look back. It will take you into your forest.'

The Lokilani embraced each of us in turn. After Danali had pressed his slender form against Maram's belly, he smiled at him and said, 'Take care, Hairface. I'm glad, so very glad, that we didn't have to kill you.'

And with that, the Lokilani stepped off into the trees to allow us to pass. I continued walking Altaru down the path, with Maram and the others following me. I listened as my horse's hooves struck deep into the soft loam of the forest floor. It was good to move without the pain in my side that had bothered me all the way from Ishka; but it was bad to have to leave friends behind, and as we made our way down the winding path, we tried not to look back at them.

After only a few hundred yards, the air lying over the woods grew heavier and moister. The leaves of the trees suddenly lost their luster as if some clouds had darkened the sky above them. Everything looked duller. The colors seemed to have drained from the woods and flattened out into various shades of gray. Even the birds had stopped singing.

The path ended suddenly about half a mile farther on. Despite Danali's warning, we turned to look back along it. We knew well enough that it should lead back into the Forest. But the scraggy scratch in the earth, crowded with bushes and vine-twisted trees, seemed to lead nowhere. In gazing through the thick greenery behind us, I felt repelled by a strong sensation pushing at my chest. It was as if I should proceed in any other direction but that one. And so I did. I walked Altaru through the woods toward what I thought to be the northwest. After a few hundred yards, the path vanished behind the walls of trees. A mile farther on, where the trees opened up a little and some dead elms lay down like slain giants, I would have been hard pressed to say exactly where the unseen Forest lay.

'We're lost, aren't we?' Maram said when we had paused to take our bearings. He turned this way and that toward the dark woods surrounding us, and the look on his face was that of a frightened beast. 'Oh, why did we ever leave the Forest? No more sweet wine for Maram. Not an astor to be seen here. Nor any Timpum.'

But this last proved to be not quite true. Even as Maram stood pulling nervously at his beard, a little light flashed in the air above us. It seemed to appear out of nowhere. Suddenly, framed against the leaves of some arrowwood, the little Timpum that had attached itself to me floated in the air and spun about in its swirls of silver sparks. We all saw it as clearly as we could the leaves on the trees.

'Look!' Maram said to me. 'How did it come here?'

Atara took a step closer to it, all the while fixing the little lights with her wide blue eyes. 'Oh, look at it!' she said. 'Look how it flickers!'

Maram, inspired by her words, took this opportunity to give a name to the Timpum. 'Well, then, little Flick,' he said to him, 'look around you and you won't see any of your kind. Sad to say, you're all alone in these dreary woods.'

Master Juwain pointed toward Flick, as I now couldn't help thinking of him. He said, 'Pualani was quite clear on this matter: the Timpum can't live outside of the Forest.'

'Nevertheless,' I said, looking at Flick, 'here he is, and here he lives.'

'Yes – but for how long?'

Master Juwain's question alarmed me, and I suddenly let go Altaru's reins to step forward toward the shimmering Timpum.

'Go back!' I said, waving my hands at Flick as if to shoo him away. 'Go back to your starflowers and astor trees!'

But Flick just floated in front of my eyes spinning out sparks at me.

'Maybe he's lost, as we are,' Maram said. 'Maybe he followed you here and can't find his way back.'

He proposed that we should return to the Forest in order to rescue Flick and spend at least one more night drinking wine and singing songs with the Lokilani.

'No, we must go on,' Atara said to him. 'If we did return to the Forest, even if we found our way back in, there's no certainty that Flick would follow us. And if he *did*, there's no reason why he wouldn't just follow us out again.'

Her argument made sense to everyone, even to Maram. But it saddened me. For I was sure that as soon as we struck off into these lesser woods that covered the earth before us, Flick would either die or slowly fade away.

'Do you think he might come with us a little farther?' Maram asked. 'Do you he might follow us toward Tria?'

'We'll see,' I said as I planted my boot in Altaru's stirrup and pulled myself up onto his back.

'But *where* is Tria? Val – do you know?'

'Yes,' I said, pointing off northwest into the woods. 'It's that way.'

'Are you sure?'

'Yes,' I said. I smiled with relief because my sense of direction had returned to me.

'But what about the Stonefaces?' he asked me. 'What if they find us here and follow us, too?'

I closed my eyes as I listened to the sounds of the woods and felt for anyone watching us. But other than a badger and a few deer, the only being that seemed aware of us was Flick.

'The Stonefaces must surely have lost us when we entered the Forest,' I told Maram. 'Now let's ride while we still have some day left.'

For a few hours more, we rode at a fast walk through the thick woods. No paths cut through the trees here, and in many places we had to force our way through dense undergrowth. But toward dusk, the trees opened again and the going was much easier. Our first concern was that we should keep to our course, bearing more north than west. And our second was this little array of lights that Maram had named Flick.

'Do you see?' he said when we had stopped by a stream to water the horses. He pointed at Flick, who hovered above the stream's bank like a bright bird watching for fish. 'He still follows us.'

'Yes,' I said. 'And he still shimmers, as before. This is hard to understand.'

'Well, we're still close to the Forest,' Master Juwain said. 'Perhaps he still takes his substance and strength from it.'

We decided to make camp there by the stream. It was our first night outside the Forest since our flight from the Stonefaces. As before, we took turns keeping watch. But no one came through the blackened trees to attack us. Nor did any dark dreams come to disturb our sleep. Even so, it was a hard night and a lonely one. Without the Lokilani's evening songs and the company of the Timpum, the hours passed slowly.

During my watch, I listened to the crickets chirping and the wind rustling the leaves of the trees above us. I counted the beats of my heart even as I looked for Flick in the dying flames of the fire or above me in the darkness, twinkling like a lone constellation of stars. I didn't know whether to resent or rejoice in his presence. For he was a very poignant reminder of a brighter place, where the great trees connected the earth to the sky and I had felt fully and truly alive.

During our next day's journey, we all suffered the sadness of leaving the Forest. As Pualani had warned us, the woods here seemed almost dead. And that was strange, because they were nearly the same woods through which I had walked as a child in Mesh and had loved. The maples still showed their three-pointed leaves, and the same gray squirrels ran up and down them clicking their claws against the silver-gray bark. The horned owls who hunted them were familiar to me, as were the robins singing their rising and falling song: *cheery-up, cheery-me*. Perhaps everything – the birds and the badgers, the thistles

249

and the flowers – were *too* familiar. Against my memory of the Forest's splendor, the trees here were ashen and stunted, and the animals all moved about in their same pointless patterns, dully and listlessly, as if drained of blood.

As we rode through the long day, we, too, began moving with a measured heaviness. It grew cloudy, and then rained for a while. The constant drumming of the large drops against our heads did little to lift our spirits. The whole world seemed wet and gray, and it smelled of the iron with which my armor had been made. The trees went on mile after mile, unbroken by any path and oppressive in their thick swaths of grayish-green that blocked out the sun.

Our camp that night was cheerless and cold. It rained so hard for a while that not even Maram could get a fire going. We all huddled beneath our cloaks, trying in our turns to sleep against our shivering. During my watch, I waited in vain for the sky to clear and the stars to come out. I looked for Flick, too. But in the dark, dripping woods, I couldn't find the faintest glint of light. By the time I fell off to sleep, I was sure that he was dead.

When dawn came, however, Atara espied him nestled down in my hair. It was the only brightness that any of us could find in that cool, gray morning. After a quick meal of some soggy nutbread and blackberries rimed with newly-grown mold, we set out into the rainy woods. The horses' hooves made rhythmic sucking sounds against the sodden forest floor. We listened for the more cheery piping of the bluebirds or even the whistles of the thrushes, but the trees were empty of any song.

The woods seemed endless, as if we might ride all that day and for ten thousand days all the way around the world and never see the end of them. We all knew in our heads that if our course were true, we must eventually cut the Nar Road. But our hearts told us that we were lost, moving in circles. We each began to worry that our food would run out or some disaster befall us long before we reached the road.

That afternoon the rain stopped, and the sun made a brief appearance. But it brought only a little thin light and no joy. As the day deepened toward dusk, even this glimmer began to weaken and fade. And so did our spirits weaken. Maram told us that he would have been better off letting Lord Harsha run him through with his sword, thus saving him from death by starvation in a trackless wilderness. Master Juwain sat astride his swaying horse staring at his book as if he couldn't decide which passage to read. Atara, whose courage never flagged, sang songs to cheer herself and us. But in the gloom of the woods, the notes she struck sounded hollow and false. I sensed her anger at herself for failing to uplift us: it was cold, hard and black as an iron arrowpoint. Compassion for other beings she might have in abundance, but for herself she spared no pity.

My despair was possibly the deepest for having the least excuse: I *knew* that we were moving in the right direction but allowed myself to doubt whether we would ever see the Nar Road or Tria. In my openness to my friends' forebodings, I allowed their doubts to become my own.

What is despair, really? It is a dark night of the soul and the remembrance of brighter things. It is a silent calling out to them. But the call comes from the darkest of places and is often heard by dark things instead.

That night as we camped beneath an old elm tree, we had dreams of dreadful things. Creatures of the dark came to devour us: we felt worms eating at our insides, bats biting us open and mosquitoes smothering us in thick black clouds and sucking out our blood. Gray shapes that looked like corpses torn from graves came to take our hands and pull us down into the ground. Even Master Juwain moaned in a tormented sleep, his meditations and allies having finally failed him. When morning came, all misty and gray, we spoke of our nightmares and discovered that they were very much the same.

'It's the Stonefaces, isn't it?' Maram said. 'They've found us again.'

'Yes,' I said, giving voice to what we all knew to be true. 'But have they found us in the flesh or only in our dreams?'

'You tell us, Val.'

I stood up from my bearskin and pulled my cloak around me. The woods in every direction seemed all the same. The oaks and elms were shagged with mosses, and a heavy mist lay over them – and over the dogwood and ferns and lesser vegetation as well. Everything smelled moist: of mushrooms and rotting wood. I had an unsettling sense that men were smelling *me* as from many miles away. I couldn't tell, however, how far they might be or whether they stalked the woods to the east or west, north or south. I knew only that they were hunting me and that their shapes were as gray as stone.

'We can't be far from the Nar Road,' I said. 'If we ride hard for it, we should reach it by dusk.'

'You're guessing, my friend, aren't you?'

In truth, I *was* guessing, but I thought it to be a good one. I was almost certain that the road couldn't lie much more than a day's journey to the north, or possibly two.

'What if the Stonefaces are waiting for us *on* the road?' Maram asked.

'No – they left the road to follow us through the forest. Probably they're as lost as you seem to think that we are.'

'*Probably*? Would you bet our lives on *probably*?'

'We can't wander these woods forever,' I said. 'Sooner or later, we'll have to return to the road.'

'We could return to the Forest, couldn't we?'

'Yes,' I said, 'if we could find it again. But likely the Stonefaces would find us first.'

Over the embers of the fire that had burned through the night, we held council as to what we should do. Atara said that all paths before us were perilous; since we couldn't see the safest, we should choose the one that led directly to Tria, which meant making straight for the Nar Road.

'In any case,' she said, 'none of us set out on this journey with the end of dying peacefully in our sleep. We should decide whether it's the Lightstone or safety that we seek.'

She pointed out that we must be nearing the civilized parts of Alonia; if we did reach the road, she said, likely we would find it patrolled by King Kiritan's men.

'We must have come as far west as Suma,' she said. 'The Stonefaces, whoever they are, would have to be very daring to ride openly against us there. It's said that King Kiritan hangs brigands and outlaws.'

Maram grumbled that, for a warrior of the Kurmak, she seemed to know a lot about Alonia. He doubted that King Kiritan kept his roads as safe as she said. But in the end, he agreed that we should strike for the road, and so he set to breaking camp with a resigned weariness.

We were all tired that morning as we rode through the woods. As well, we all had headaches, which grew worse with the constant pounding of the horses' hooves. Twice, I changed our course, to the east and due west through some elderberry thickets, to see if that might blunt the attack against us. But both times, my sense of someone hunting us did not diminish, and neither did our suffering. It was as if the sky, heavily laden with clouds, was slowly pressing at us and crushing our skulls against the earth.

By noon, however, the clouds burned away, and the sun came out. We all hoped to take a little cheer from its unexpected radiance. But the blazing orb drove arrows of fire into the forest, and it grew stifling hot. The sultry air choked us; gray vapors steamed up from the sodden earth. In the flatness of the land here, we could find no brook or stream, and so we had to content ourselves with the warm water in our canteens to slake our raging thirsts.

As we made our way north, the woods in many places broke upon abandoned fields on which grew highbush blackberry, sumac and other shrubs. Twice we found the remains of houses rotting among the meadow flowers. I took this as a sign that we were indeed approaching the civilized parts of Alonia that Atara had told of. We all hoped to find the Nar Road just a little farther on, after perhaps only a few more miles. And so we rode hard all that afternoon through forest and fields burning in the hot Soldru sun.

We came upon the road without warning just before dusk. As we were riding through a copse of mulberry, the trees suddenly gave out onto a broad band of stone. The road, as I could see, ran very straight here east and west through the flat forest. From the emptiness of this country, I guessed that Suma must lie to our east, which meant that we had bypassed this great city by quite a few miles. After some miles more – perhaps as few as eighty – we would find Tria down the road to the west.

'We're saved, then!' Maram cried out. He climbed down from his horse, and collapsed to his knees as he kissed the road's stones in relief.

'Shall we ride on until we find a village or town?'

I dismounted Altaru and stood beside him along the curb of the road. The day was dying quickly, and for the first night in many nights, we had a clear view of the sky. Already Valura, the evening star, shone in the blue-black dome to the west. In the east, the moon was rising: a full moon, as we could all see from its almost perfect circle of silver. The last time I had stood beneath a moon so bright had been in the Black Bog. I couldn't look upon it now without recalling that time of terror when I had feared that I was losing my mind.

Even as I now feared that men were attacking my mind. With the coming of night, the pain in all our heads grew suddenly worse. It seemed that the Stonefaces, whatever they were, took their greatest strength and boldness from the dark.

'If we ride,' I said, 'it would be very bad if the Stonefaces were waiting on the road to ambush us.'

I looked at Master Juwain slumped on his horse and at Atara forcing a smile to her worn-out face. We were all exhausted, I thought, and growing weaker by the hour. I doubted whether we could ride half the night to the next village.

'Wouldn't it be worse if they ambushed us here?' Maram asked.

'No,' I said, pointing behind us. 'We passed a meadow less than half a mile back. We could make camp there and fortify it against attack.'

'All right,' Maram said wearily. 'I'm too tired to argue.'

We mounted our horses again, and made our way back to the meadow. It was a broad, grassy expanse perhaps a hundred yards in diameter. Copses of mulberry and oak surrounded it. We hauled some deadfall from these woods to the center of the meadow where we built up around our camp a sort of circular fence. It took many trips back and forth to gather enough wood to construct such rudimentary fortifications. But when we were finished, we felt very glad to go inside it and lay out our bearskins.

It was full night by the time we finished our dinner. The moon had climbed above the meadow and silvered it with its cold light. Long, grayish grasses swayed in the gentle wind blowing in from the east. In the eerie sheen of the earth, the many rocks about us seemed as big as boulders. We had a clear line of sight fifty yards in any direction toward the rim of dark trees that surrounded us. Unless it grew very cloudy, no one could steal upon us unseen. And if anyone attacked us openly, we would kill them with arrows. Toward this end, Maram unpacked my arrows and bow and kept them close at hand. We checked our swords as well. Atara stood up against the breastwork of the fence as she practiced drawing her great, horn bow and aiming arrows over the top of it. She seemed satisfied that we had done all we could. After bidding us goodnight, she slipped down to the ground to sleep holding her bow as child might a blanket.

I took the first watch while the others slept fitfully. I knew they must be having evil dreams: Maram sweated and rolled about, while Master Juwain's small body twitched and started whenever he let out a low moan. Several times Atara murmured, 'No, no, no,' before falling into the ragged rhythms of her breathing.

When it came my turn to sleep, I couldn't bear the thought of closing my eyes. It was selfish of me, but I couldn't bring myself to wake up Master Juwain, either. And so I walked in a slow circle behind the fence looking out across the meadow. The horses, tethered outside the fence, were silently sleeping. So still did they stand that they looked like statues. As did the trees of the surrounding woods. In their dark shadows, I could see nothing. I listened for any telltale that men might be coming to attack us, but the only sounds were the crickets in the meadow and the distant howling of some wolves. Wherever these great, gray beasts stood, I thought, they must be looking upon the same moon as did I. I watched this pale disk climb the starry heavens inch by inch. I might have measured out the moments of its rise and fall by the painful beating of my heart, but the night seemed to deepen into a timelessness that had no end.

I let Maram sleep as well in place of standing his watch. And Atara, too. Despite the pain in my head, which drove through my eyes like nails, I was wide awake. The night was very warm, and I sweated beneath my armor. My legs shook with the effort of remaining standing. Even so, for many hours, I stared out across the meadow, listening and waiting. I walked around and around our camp trying to catch the sense of whoever might be hunting us.

Near dawn, without warning, Atara started out of her sleep and rose to stand by my side. When she saw the angle of the moon, she chided me for staying awake nearly all night. Then she sniffed the wind as might a tawny lioness and said, 'They're close, aren't they?'

'Yes,' I said, 'they are.'

'Then you should gotten some sleep to face them.'

'Sleep,' I said, shaking my head.

For a while we spoke of little things such as the direction of the wind and the grimness of the gray face of the moon. And then I looked at her and asked, 'Are you afraid to die?'

She thought about this for a long moment before saying, 'Death is like going to sleep. Should I be afraid of sleeping, then?'

I looked at Master Juwain as he lay against the ground moaning softly. I almost told Atara that death is cold, death is dark, death is an evil dream full of empty black nothing. But I kept myself from voicing such despair.

Even so, she seemed to sense my doubts. She smiled at me bravely and said, 'We take our being from the One. How can the One ever stop being? How can we?'

Because I had no answer for her, I looked up at the black spaces between the stars.

I felt her hand touch my face, and I turned to look at her as she asked me, 'Are you afraid?'

'Yes,' I told her. 'But most afraid for you.'

She smiled at me in the silent understanding that had flowed between us almost from our first moment together. Then her face fell serious as she said a strange thing: 'I can see them, you know.'

'See who, Atara?'

'The men,' she said. 'The gray men.'

'You mean, you saw them in your dreams?'

'Yes, that of course. But I can see them here, now.'

I looked at the gray trees standing in a circle all about us with their leafy arms raised toward the sky, but I saw no men standing with them.

Then Atara pointed out across the moonlit meadow and said, 'I can see them walking toward us with their knives.'

If the Stonefaces came to attack us, I thought, then surely they would stand behind the trees shooting arrows at us or charge us on horses with their swords drawn.

'Once, when I was a child,' she said, 'I saw a spider weaving a web in a corner of my father's house a month before she actually did. I can see the gray men the same way.'

I continued looking out around the meadow; other than the wind-rippled grasses, nothing moved. The moon seemed like a silver nail pinning still the sky. In between the soughs of Atara's breaths, I could almost feel each beat of her heart as it hung in the air like a boom of a great red drum.

And then Altaru came violently awake and let out a tremendous whinny, and I saw them, too. They suddenly appeared next to the trees as if the dark shadows had given them birth. Tall men they were, with hooded, grayish cloaks covering them from head to knee. As Atara had said, there were at least nine of them. Although we couldn't see their faces, they stood around the circle of trees watching us and waiting for something.

I quickly drew my sword.

Again, Altaru whinnied and stomped the earth as he pulled and rattled the fence. His noise shook Master Juwain and Maram awake.

'What is it?' Maram grumbled as he struggled to his feet rubbing his eyes. Then he looked across the meadow and cried out, 'Oh, no! Oh, my Lord – it's them!'

When pressed, Maram could move very quickly, big belly or no. It took only a moment for him to grab up his bow and join Atara and me by the fence.

'Don't shoot them!' Master Juwain pleaded as he stepped forward, too. By now, both Maram and Atara had arrows nocked to their bowstrings as they began to pull and sight on the gray men. 'We should try to talk to them first.'

Yes, we should, I thought. And so I called out, 'Who are you? What do you want of us?'

But their only answer was a silence that came with the sudden dying of the wind.

'Go away!' Maram called to them. 'Go away or we'll shoot you!'

But still the gray men didn't move, and the silence in the meadow grew only deeper.

'I'm going to give them a warning,' Maram said, squeezing his arrow between his fingers. 'I'm going to shoot this into a tree.'

Without waiting for me to say yea or nay, he quickly drew his bow. But his hands and arms suddenly started trembling; the arrow, when it came whining off his string, buried itself in the ground only forty feet from the fence.

'Hmmph – shooting at moles again,' Atara said. Then she too fired off a shot. But at the moment she released her arrow, her bow arm buckled as if broken at the elbow. Her arrow drove into the ground after covering even less distance than had Maram's.

Something moved then in the shadows of the trees. Twigs cracked, and even from fifty yards away, we could hear the rustling of leaves. A very tall man stepped forward into the moonlight. He was dressed as the others in gray trousers and a hooded cloak that covered his face. He had an air of command about him. When he turned his unseen face toward us and stood as if scenting us or staring intently into our souls, the others did too.

'Go away!' Maram cried again. 'Go away now, please!'

The gray men seemed not to hear him. Following their leader, they all drew forth long, gray knives and began walking across the meadow toward us, even as Atara had foreseen.

Atara and Maram fired more arrows at them, but they flew wild. The men advanced slowly as if taking care not to stumble over any branch or rock. Their gray-steel knives glinted dully in the moon's eerie light. When they had covered perhaps half the distance toward our camp, I caught a glimpse of their leader staring at me from beneath his cloak's gray hood. His face was long and flat, without expression and as gray as slate. There seemed to be something stuck to the middle of his forehead, where it was said one's third eye lies: it looked like a leech or some kind of flat, black stone.

'Go away,' I whispered. 'Go away, or one of us will have to die.'

Just then a swirl of little lights appeared as of stars dropping down from the heavens. It was Flick, spinning about furiously as he streaked back and forth in front of the gray men. It seemed that he was trying to warn them away or perhaps weaving a fence of light through which they couldn't pass. But the men took no notice of his presence. They walked slowly forward as if nothing stood between them and us.

In their disbelief at missing such easy marks, the urge to flee overcame Maram and Atara all at once. They began backing away from the gray men, all the while shooting arrows at the men as I joined them in edging up near the rear of the fence. Master Juwain pressed up close to us. And then the gray men's leader stood very still. The black stone on his forehead caught the moonlight, and gleamed darkly. At that moment, a crushing heaviness fell across my whole body. I dropped my sword, and my friends let go of their bows. My arms and legs were so weak that it seemed something had drained the blood from them. I wanted desperately to run, to will myself to move, but I could not. A terrible coldness spread quickly through me and froze me motionless like a fish caught in ice. I couldn't even open my mouth to scream.

And neither could my friends. But I sensed them screaming inside for the gray men to go away, and I knew that they could hear the screams of the horses, even as I could. The gray men's leader dispatched two of his confederates toward them. All of the horses were now whinnying and rearing and kicking the ground. Altaru aimed a mighty kick at the fence. It splintered the wood, and he pulled free from it, along with the two sorrels and Tanar, who immediately ran off into the woods. Altaru charged straight for the two men closest to the fence. But then they showed him their knives and something worse, and he suddenly changed course, galloping off into the woods, too. Although he was the bravest of beings, something about the gray men sent him into a panic.

The two men now closed on the remaining horses. They seemed bothered by their screaming and the beating of their hooves; it was as if the gray men sought silence in the outer world so that they could hear the voices of the inner. And so, moving with great care, they used their long knives to slash open the horses' throats.

No, I cried out in my voice of my mind, *no, no, no!*

The other gray men began pulling at the branches and logs of the fence, dismantling it and making an opening wide enough for all of them to pass. And still I stood with the others at the rear of the fence, watching them but unable to move.

And then the gray men's leader stepped forward and threw back his hood. The black stone on his forehead was a dark moon crushing us to the earth. The flesh of his face was gray as that of a dead fish. As Atara had told us, he had no eyes like any man I had ever seen. They were all of one hue and substance: a solid and translucent gray that covered them like dark glass. I couldn't guess how they let in any light; they let forth no light either, no hint of humanity or soul. They seemed utterly without pity, utterly empty, utterly cold. This cold struck straight into my heart like a lance of ice. It filled me with a wild fear. A steely voice spoke inside me then and told me that I couldn't move. I was nothing, it said to me; I was nothing more than an empty husk of flesh to be used as the gray men wished. I was one with the dead, and would take a long, long time in dying.

Evil, I knew then, was much more than darkness: it was a willful turning away from the light of the One. It was a poison that twists the soul, a madness, a terrible need to inflate one's self at the expense of others, as a tick swells on its victims' blood.

No – go back!

All the gray men now gathered around their leader at the opening to the fence. Their knives pointed toward us. Then they too threw back

258

their hoods. Although they wore no stones on their foreheads, their faces were as eyeless and stonelike as their leader's. They stood in the cold moonlight, watching us and waiting.

Oh, no! Oh, no! Oh, no!

I felt Atara's terror, and Master Juwain's and Maram's, thundering at me with the wild beating of their hearts. I couldn't close it out. Neither could I close my eyes as the gray men pierced me with theirs and began drinking from inside me that which was more precious than blood.

NO! NO! NO!

I wanted with all my soul to close my eyes and end this living nightmare from which I could not awaken. But then, even as I tried desperately to move my legs and run away, I looked across the meadow to see another cloaked figure break from the trees. This lone man, slightly shorter than the others, ran as silently as a wraith through the silvery grass. He had a sword drawn: it was longer than a knife, and longer than many swords, for it was a kalama. His powerful strides revealed the gleaming mail beneath his cloak. It took him only a few seconds to reach the wolf pack of men by the open fence. He crashed into them, sending two flying and slicing through the neck of a third. And then, even as the gray men finally realized they were under attack and turned toward him, he stabbed his sword straight through the back of their leader.

'Move!' he cried to us in voice like the roar of a tiger. 'Move now, I say!'

And then he drove into the men with his sword, whirling about powerfully yet gracefully, cutting at them with a rare and terrible fury.

With the death of the gray men's leader, I found myself suddenly free to move. A great surge of life welled up inside me and filled my hands with a new strength. Some of the gray men were running from the wild man at the opening of the fence; some were running at Atara and me. One of these aimed his knife at Atara's throat; without thinking, I picked up my sword and chopped off his arm in almost a single motion. Grayish-black blood sprayed into the air. It surprised me that he wore no armor and that the steel of my sword sliced through him so easily. The kalama is a fearsome weapon at any time, but most terrible to use against unprotected flesh. As I was forced to use it now. For in the rush of men coming at us with their gray, slashing knives, even as Maram and Atara drew their swords and laid about them in a wild death struggle, one of the men stole up behind her to stab her in the back. *His* back was to me, his knife poised to thrust home, and I was faced with a terrible choice: I could cut him down or let him kill her. It was no choice at all. And so, still reeling from the wound I had inflicted on the first man, I swung my sword at him. It sliced into his side and through his chest;

259

I felt its cold steel rip through his heart. Dark blood sprayed into my eyes; I could hardly see as he jumped in agony and turned to regard me for a moment in the strange silence of his hate. And then he died, and I almost died, too. I fell down to the blood-soaked earth screaming like a child as the darkness closed in and the battle raged all about me.

Later, when the last of the gray men had been killed and Maram and Atara stood panting with their bloody swords in their hands, the man who had run to our rescue let loose a howl of triumph. He stood in the moonlight holding his sword up to the stars. I felt his great joy at having slain so many of his enemies. Even through the death-agony covering my eyes like a dark, gray shroud, I watched him turn toward me. He threw back the hood of his cloak. His face blazed with a terrible beauty, his eyes all black and bright, and I gasped to see that it was Kane.

16

With Atara, Maram and Master Juwain still weak and trembling from what the gray men had done to us, Kane immediately took command. He ordered Master Juwain to tend to me while he walked around our camp counting the bodies of the slain. He numbered them at twelve, including the one that I had killed. Maram had managed to send two on to the other world, while Atara had added three more enemies toward her hundred. That meant Kane had accounted for six. As I lay with my head in Master Juwain's lap, I blinked my eyes in disbelief. I had never seen anyone fight with such quickness, skill and sheer ferocity.

After Kane had completed his tally, he knelt by the gray men's leader on the bloody earth. He used his sword to cut the black stone from his forehead. He studied this flat oval a long time before tightening his fist around it. Then he turned toward us and said, 'This is no place to remain, eh? The sun will be up soon. Let's get Val into the shade of the trees before it boils his brains.'

With Kane's help, my friends carried me into the trees. They found a nice dry spot beneath an old oak, and there they reestablished our camp. Atara laid out our sleeping skins while Maram got a fire going and Master Juwain went to work on making some tea. Kane brought over the packs from the dead horses. And then he went off into the woods to look for Altaru and the two sorrels. We heard his sharp whistles through the trees.

Sometime later he returned holding the reins of a big bay, which I took to be his horse. Altaru, Tanar and the sorrels followed them. I was as glad to see Altaru as he was me. He walked over to where I lay and bent his great head down to nuzzle me. Then Kane tethered him and the three other horses to a nearby tree.

'So, Valashu Elahad,' he said, looking down at me. 'I've wandered the wilds of Alonia looking for you. And now that I've found you, you're nearly dead.'

261

He spoke the truth. The coldness cutting through me was worse than that with which the gray men had touched me. I lay against the earth without the strength to rise. Having killed again, I wanted to die. But seeing the concern on Maram's face and the love on Atara's as they gathered around me, I wanted to live even more.

Maram laid his big hand on my head and said, 'Once before he recovered from something as bad as this.'

'Yes, after he killed Morjin's assassin,' Kane said. He seemed to know all about me – and much else besides. 'But that was before the Grays went to work on him.'

'Do you mean the Stonefaces?' Maram said. He pointed toward the meadow where the bodies of the gray men lay in the dawn's half-light.

'No – I mean the Grays,' Kane said. 'That is their name.'

'Who are they, then?'

'Servants of the Great Beast,' he growled out. 'They have the gift of speaking to themselves and others without using their tongues.'

Maram looked at Atara and Master Juwain as if they had never heard of such men before. Neither had I.

'They can see without using their eyes and smell the scent of others' minds,' Kane went on. 'That's how they tracked you all the way from Anjo.'

As the wind rose and the night began to fade, he told us that no one knew the Grays' true origins. 'It's said that the Great Beast bred them during the Age of Swords as one might breed horses. So, he looked for those with the gift of touching others' minds. Then he culled the weakest of them that the strongest might breed true.'

'But their faces, so gray,' Atara said, shuddering as she looked out into the field. 'Their eyes, too. No men on Ea have such eyes.'

'They don't, eh?' Kane said. Then he pointed up at the setting moon. 'It's also said that Morjin summoned the Grays from other worlds ages ago. From worlds even darker than this one.'

I stared out at the dim meadow as I lay looking at the Grays. Nothing could be darker, I thought, than the lightless world pulling me down into the cold earth.

'The Grays' favored method of killing,' Kane said, 'is to weaken their victims over many days. To drain them even as they drained you. Then, when they're too weak to move, they come for them with their knives.'

Master Juwain had finally finished preparing his tea, which he managed to make me drink with Maram's and Atara's help. Then, to Kane, he said, 'But we weren't so weak that we couldn't have fought them off. There was something else, wasn't there?'

262

Kane looked down at his fist for a while before opening it to reveal the black stone. He said, 'So, there *was* something else. The *baalstei*.'

'What's that?' Maram asked.

'The black gelstei,' Master Juwain said, staring at Kane's open hand. 'Can that truly be one of the great stones?'

Kane gazed at the stone, which seemed a crystal like the darkest obsidian. 'It *is* a gelstei,' he said. 'It's known that Morjin keeps at least three of the black stones.'

He told us that the black gelstei were very rare and very powerful. Originally created to control the terrible fire of the red gelstei, they had a much darker side. For the Grays and some of the priests of the Kallimun used them to dampen the life fires of their victims and weaken their wills. Thus they could be used to enslave others by mastering their very minds. Used ruthlessly, as by the Grays, they could blow out the ineffable flame, causing disease, degeneration and ultimately death.

'It may be,' Kane said, 'that at first the Grays were trying only to weaken Val.'

'For what reason?' Maram asked.

'Why, to make him into a ghul,' Kane said. He spoke of the darkest things as casually as Maram might the weather. 'Morjin would relish a slave such as Val, eh? But certainly after you fought off the Grays for so long and vanished into the Lokilani's wood, they intended to kill him – and all of you. They had no more time to do otherwise.'

He told us that the Grays had most likely attacked us physically in desperation before they were really ready. We had entered the parts of Alonia where it was dangerous for the Grays to ride openly. Certainly they would never seek to work their evil against us once we had reached Tria. For there the noise of thousands of minds would drown out the whispers of the Gray's poisonous voices. The Grays, he said, almost never sought their victims in large cities or during the day when people were awake.

'You seem to know a great deal about these Grays,' Maram said as he eyed Kane suspiciously.

'That I do,' Kane said, his black eyes burning. 'I know that your friend might very well die if we don't help him.'

His words seemed to blunt Maram's curiosity for the moment. I, too, had a hundred questions for Kane, but I was too weak to move my lips to ask them.

Master Juwain bent over me then, feeling my forehead and testing the pulses in my wrists and other places along my body. Then he said, 'I've given him a tisane of karch and bloodroot. Perhaps I should have added some angel leaf as well.'

'That's unlikely to do much good,' Kane muttered. 'It may warm him a little, but his real problem is the *valarda*, eh?'

Now Master Juwain and Maram – Atara, too – looked at Kane in surprise. No one had said anything to him of my gift.

'Val has had the life nearly sucked out of him,' Kane said. 'We must help him light the sacred fire again, eh?'

'Yes, but how?' Master Juwain asked. 'I'm afraid I've had no experience with this.'

'Neither have I,' Kane admitted. 'At least not for a long time. But just as Val has nearly died in touching the dead, he can be made well in feeling the fire of the living.'

So saying, he bade Master Juwain and Maram to remove my armor. As the sun rose over the meadow and the birds brightened the morning with their songs, they laid my body bare. I felt the sun's warm rays touching the skin of my chest. And then I felt my friends' hands there, too, as well as Kane's large, blunt hand. Together, the four of them made a circle of their hands over my heart. I heard Kane telling me that I must partake of the life they had to give me. This I tried to do. But I was too weak to open very far the door that I usually kept closed. Only the faintest of flames passed from them into me to warm my icy blood.

'It's not enough,' Kane said. 'He's still as cold as death.'

Just then, Flick appeared from behind the oak tree and streaked straight toward Master Juwain. He spun about just above the pocket of his robes. The swirls of his little form lit up as of a smiling face.

'Eh, what's this?' Kane said, looking at Flick. 'It's one of the Timpimpiri!'

'You can *see* him?' Maram said.

'As clearly as I can see your fat nose. But I never hoped to find one in woods such as these.'

Master Juwain, touched by Flick's numinous light, seemed suddenly to remember something. He reached into his pocket and pulled out the sparkling green jewel that Pualani had given him. He said, 'The queen of the Lokilani told me that this emerald was to be used for healing.'

Kane said nothing as he looked very closely at the emerald. His black eyes, like mirrors, fairly danced with the emerald's green fire.

'She said that I was to use my heart to touch the stone,' Master Juwain said.

'She did, eh? Well, use it then.'

Master Juwain held the emerald against his chest for many moments as if meditating. Then he opened his eyes and took out his copy of the *Saganom Elu*. His knotty fingers began dancing through the pages.

'I thought you were supposed to use your *heart*,' Maram said, pointing at the book. 'Won't all these words cloud your head?'

'Some of us,' Master Juwain said with a smile, 'must use our heads to reach our hearts. Now be quiet, Brother Maram, while I'm reading.'

Maram watched his eyes flicking back and forth across the page and said, 'Excuse me, sir, but if you wish the words to reach your heart, shouldn't you read them out loud? Didn't you teach me that the verses of the *Elu* were meant to be recited and *were* for hundreds of years before they were written down?'

'Oh, all right!' Master Juwain muttered. 'You've paid more attention to my lessons than I'd thought. This passage is from the *Songs*.'

He cleared his throat and began speaking in his most musical voice. He fairly sang out the words of *A Warrior's Heart*:

> A warrior's heart is like the sun,
>   She shines with golden light,
> Her golden sinews brightly spun
>   With angel-given might.

> A warrior's heart is like the sea,
>   Her love is very deep,
> She streams and swells with bravery
>   That makes the waters weep.

When he had finished, he again closed his eyes and held the emerald to his chest. He sat beside me as the sun rose and cast its rays into the woods. Atara sat beside me, too. She cupped her warm hand around mine. She remained silent, saying nothing with her lips. But her bright eyes said more than all the words in the *Saganom Elu*.

After most of an hour, Master Juwain opened his eyes and his hand. We were well-shaded by the leaves of the oak tree; even so, some fragment of sunlight fell upon the emerald and set it shimmering a brilliant green. Or perhaps I only imagined this: when I looked more closely, it seemed that the emerald shone with a deeper light. Master Juwain touched this beautiful stone to my chest then. He touched his hand there, and so did Atara, Maram and Kane, making a circle as before. Something warm and bright passed into me. It made me want to open myself to the touch of the whole world. I gasped suddenly, breathing in the sweetness of the air. I breathed in as well the essence of the oak trees streaming with hot spring sap and the very fire of the sun. For one blazing moment, I felt myself overflowing with the life of the forest – and with that of my three friends and the strange man named Kane.

'So,' Kane said to Master Juwain as he touched my face, 'this *emerald* of yours has great power, eh?'

As quickly as it had overcome me, the death-cold suddenly left me. Although I was still very weak, I managed to sit up and press my back against the oak tree.

'Thank you,' I told Master Juwain. Then I smiled at Maram, Kane and Atara. 'You saved my life.'

I pressed my hand to my side where Salmelu's sword had cut me. I remembered Pualani holding a green crystal there and my awakening the next day to find myself miraculously healed.

'I see,' Master Juwain finally said. He gazed at the green stone that he held in his hand. 'This can't be an ordinary emerald, can it?'

'No – you know it can't be,' Kane said. 'It's now proven: this is a *varistei*. A green gelstei.'

Master Juwain gripped the green stone as if he were afraid he might drop it and lose it among the leaves on the forest floor.

'I thought the green gelstei had all perished in the War of the Stones,' he said. 'This is a treasure beyond price. How did the Lokilani come by it?'

'That's a long story,' Kane said. 'Before I tell it, why don't we make a little breakfast so you can regain your strength.'

He stepped over to his horse's saddlebags, from which he removed a large round of bacon and a dozen chicken eggs. How he had found such fare in the middle of a wilderness I couldn't guess. He handed the supplies to Maram, who quickly set to work slicing strips of meat and frying it up in his pan. In little time, the delicious smell of sizzling bacon wafted out into the woods. It took only a little longer for Maram to fry up the eggs in the hot grease and serve us our meal.

'We should celebrate,' Maram said. 'It can't be every day that the Red Dragon's men are defeated and my best friend is saved. Why don't we have a little brandy?'

So saying, he broke out our last cask and filled our cups with the golden brandy. He made a toast to our freedom from the Grays' attacks. Then raised his cup and took a sip. I did too. I gasped as the fiery liquor burned sweetly down my throat. And Master Juwain gasped to see Kane throw back his head and guzzle his brandy like water before holding out his cup to be refilled by Maram. It was the strangest meal of my life, that breakfast of bacon, eggs and brandy in the woods beneath the rising sun.

'Excellent,' Kane said, licking his lips. 'Now I'll tell you what I know of the Lokii.'

'You mean, the Lokilani, don't you?' Maram said.

'No – that's not their true name,' Kane said. 'You see, the Lokii were one of the original tribes of Star People sent to Ea with the Lightstone ages ago.'

He went on to explain that there had been twelve of these tribes: the Danya, Weryin, Nisu, Kesari, Asadu, Ajani, Tuwari, Talasi, Sakuru, Helkiin and Lokii. And, of course, the Valari, headed by Elahad and entrusted with guarding the Lightstone. Each of the tribes had brought with them a single varistei meant to bring the new world to flower. For the green crystals had power over all living things and the fires of life itself. The Galadin and Elijin who had sent the twelve tribes to Ea had intended for them to create a paradise. But instead, Aryu of the Valari had risen up in envy to slay his brother, Elahad. He had stolen the Lightstone and broken the peace and hope of Ea.

'This much is known everywhere, if not always believed,' Kane said. 'But what is *not* known is that Aryu also stole the varistei from Elahad.'

He told us that Aryu, and many of the Valari who followed him, had set sail from Tria on three ships, fleeing into the Northern Sea. Near the Island of Nedu, a storm had driven two of the ships onto rocks, killing everyone aboard them save Aryu. But Aryu had been mortally wounded; at last, realizing his folly, he crawled ashore on a small island and hid the Lightstone in a cave. The Valari on the remaining ship, under his son, Jolonu, found Aryu's body but not the Lightstone. Jolonu then took the varistei from Aryu's dead hand and set sail for the most distant land he could find.

And so the renegade Valari came at last to the Island of Thalu in the uttermost west. There they used the green gelstei to slowly change their form to adapt to the cold mists of that harsh and rugged land. The followers of Aryu, or the Aryans, as they came to be called, became a tall, big-boned people, fair of face, with flaxen hair and blue eyes as bright as the sea.

Here Kane paused in his story to look at Atara. She sat on old leaves beneath the oak tree, and her bright, blue eyes were fixed on Kane's face. 'Have you never wondered at the origins of your people?' he asked her.

'No more than I have the origins of the antelope or the grass,' Atara told him. 'But it's said that the Sarni are the descendants of Sarngin Marshan.'

Prince Sarngin, she said, had fought with his brothers, Vashrad and Nawar, over the throne of Alonia late in the Age of the Mother. Vashrad had finally prevailed, killing Nawar. But he had spared Sarngin, whom he had loved. He had banished him and many of his followers, forbidding them ever to return to the lands of Alonia. And so Sarngin had come to the prairies of the Wendrush, where he and his followers had prospered and multiplied to become the ferocious Sarni.

'Sarngin and Vashrad were sons of Bohimir, eh?' Kane said.

'Yes,' Atara said. 'Bohimir the Great. He was Alonia's first king.'

'Ha, a king!' Kane said to her. 'He was an adventurer and a warlord. In three hundred ships, he sailed from Thalu with the Aryan sea rovers – descendants all of them of Aryu and Jolonu. That was in the year 2,177 of the Age of the Mother. The Dark Year, as it's now called. The Aryans entered the Dolphin Channel and sacked Tria. Bohimir crowned himself king. And *that* is the origin of your people.'

Kane paused to drink yet another cup of brandy. The potent liquor seemed to have little effect on him. While bees buzzed in the blossoms of a nearby dogwood and the day grew warmer, he sat looking back and forth between Atara and me.

'It's strange,' he muttered. 'Very, very strange.'

'What is?' I asked him.

He pointed at my hair and then held his hand toward my face as his black eyes burned into mine. 'It's said that all the Star People who came to Ea looked like you. Like the Valari. The Valari who settled the Morning Mountains were the only people to have had their varistei stolen. And so they were the only people of Ea to remain true to the Star People's original form.'

I looked down at the black hair spilling over my chest and at the ivory tones of my hands. I rubbed my long, hawk's nose and the prominent bones of my cheeks. Then I looked at Atara, whose coloring and cast of face couldn't have been more different.

'The Valari and the Aryans,' Kane said, 'were once of one tribe. Thus they're the closest of all peoples – and yet, ever since Aryu killed Elahad, they've always been the bitterest of enemies. The Sarni are ultimately the descendants of Aryu himself, and who has warred with the Valari more?'

Only the Valari, I thought, biting back a bitter smile.

'It's strange,' Kane said, bowing his head first at Atara and then at me, 'that you two should have made a peace between yourselves at a time when it's foretold the Lightstone will be found.'

In truth, it was more than strange; I couldn't remember hearing of any Valari ever making friends with a Sarni warrior. As the sun rose over the meadow where Atara and I had stood against our enemies together, I couldn't help wondering if the Age of the Dragon – and war itself – was finally coming to an end.

'Ah, this is all very interesting,' Maram said to Kane. 'But what does this have to do with the Lokii?'

'Just this,' Kane said. 'After Aryu stole the Lightstone and the Valari were broken into their two kindred, the remaining tribes scattered to every land of Ea. Each tribe carried its own varistei; they used the stones to adapt their forms to the various climes of Ea. The Lokii, being lovers of trees, disappeared into the Great Northern Forest. Over the ages, they came to look even as you've seen them.'

'Have *you* seen them, then?' Maram asked.

Kane ignored this question, regarding Maram as he might a fly that had a loud buzz but no bite. Then he told us more about the Lokii.

'Of all the tribes,' he said, 'they were the only one to fully understand the power of the green gelstei.'

The Lokii, he explained, became masters of growing great trees and things out of the earth, and of awakening the living earth fires called the telluric currents. After thousands of years, they learned how to grow more of the green gelstei crystals *from* the earth. They used these magic stones, as they thought of them, to deepen the power of their wood. So changed and concentrated did these telluric currents become that their wood separated from Ea in some strange way and became invisible to the rest of it. The Lokii called these pockets of deepened life fires 'vilds,' for they believed that there the earth was connected to the wild fires of the stars. Since the Lokii could not return to the stars, they hoped to awaken the earth itself so that all of Ea became as alive and magical as the other worlds that circled other suns.

'So, the vilds are invisible to almost all people except the Lokii,' Kane said. 'Even they have trouble finding their vild once they have left it. Which is why they never go far from their trees.'

'You say "vilds,"' Maram said. 'Are there more than one?'

Kane nodded his head and told us, 'During the Lost Ages, the Lokii tribe split into at least ten septs and bore varistei to other parts of Ea. There, they created vilds of their own. At least five of them remain.'

'Remain *where*?'

'Somewhere,' Kane said. 'They are somewhere.'

As he took another drink of brandy, Flick soared over to him and began spinning in front of his bright eyes. I could almost see the sparks passing back and forth between them. It was the longest I had ever seen Flick remain in one place.

'How is it,' Maram wondered, 'that Flick can live outside the vild?'

'*That* I would like to know, too,' Kane said.

'There can only be one answer,' Master Juwain said. 'If it's truly the telluric currents of the vilds that feed the Timpum, then here Flick must take his life from something else. And that can only be the Golden Band. Twenty years it's been since the earth entered its radiance. It must be the light of the Ieldra themselves that sustains him.'

'Perhaps,' Kane said. 'Perhaps we're coming into the time when the Galadin will walk the earth again.'

He knelt next to me by the tree, studying the scar on my forehead. Then he told me, 'This is why the Lokii spared your life. The mark of the lightning bolt – the Lokii believe that it's sacred to the archangel they call the Ellama. But others know this being as Valoreth. It's strange that you should bear his mark, eh?'

Maram, apparently not liking the look on Kane's face just then, turned to him and said, 'What's strange is that you should know so much that no one else knows.'

'It's a strange world,' Kane growled out.

'How did you know that the Red Dragon had sent assassins to kill Val?' Maram asked. 'And how did learn to fight as you do? Are you of the Black Brotherhood?'

As Maram tapped his empty cup against a stone, we all looked at Kane, who said, 'If I *were* of the Black Brotherhood, whatever you think that is, do you suppose I'd be permitted to tell you?'

Maram pointed at Flick, who now hovered over some flowers like a cloud of flashing butterflies. He said, 'If you can see the Timpum – ah, the Timpimpiri, as you called them – then you must have spent time in one of the vilds.'

'Must I have?'

Master Juwain sat holding his book and said, 'We of the Brotherhood spend our lives in search of knowledge. But even our Grandmaster would have much to learn from you.'

Kane smiled at this but said nothing.

'But how,' I asked him, 'did you find the vild and enter it?'

'Much the same as you did.'

He told us that he had spent much of his life crossing and recrossing Ea in search of knowledge – and something else.

'So, I seek the Lightstone,' he told us. 'Even as you do.'

'Toward what end?' I asked him.

'Toward the end of bringing about the end,' he growled out again. 'The end of Morjin and all his works.'

I remembered touching upon his bottomless hatred for Morjin at our first meeting in Duke Rezu's castle; I remembered the anguish in his eyes, and I shuddered.

'But what grievance do you have against him?' I asked.

'Does a man need a grievance against the Crucifier to oppose him?'

'Perhaps not,' I said. 'But to hate him as you do, yes.'

270

'Then let's just say he took from me that which was dearer than life itself.'

I remembered wondering if the Red Dragon had murdered his family, and I bowed my head in silence. Then I looked up and said, 'Your accent is strange – what is your homeland?'

'I have no home,' Kane said. 'No homeland that Morjin hasn't despoiled.'

'Who are your people, then?'

'I have no people whom Morjin hasn't killed or enslaved.'

'You almost look Valari.'

'I almost am. As with your people, I'm Morjin's enemy.'

As I sat staring into his dark, wild eyes, I couldn't help remembering the story of the Hundred Year March. After Aryu had killed Elahad and fled into the Northern Sea, Elahad's son, Arahad, had assembled a fleet of ten ships and set sail with the remaining Valari in pursuit. For ten years, they searched in vain from island to island and place to place. They faced many storms and adventures. Finally, having circumnavigated the whole of Ea, they had returned to Tria with only five remaining ships.

Arahad then decided – wrongly – that Aryu and the renegade Valari must have come to land and established themselves somewhere in the interior of the continent. And so again, Arahad and his followers set out in pursuit, this time on foot. Thus began the Hundred Year March. Arahad's Valari wandered almost every land of Ea looking for Aryu's descendants and the Lightstone. Finally, after Arahad's death, his son, Shavashar, led the remnants of the Valari tribe into the Morning Mountains, where they gave up their quest and remained. But it was said that some of the Valari lost heart long before this, and broke off from the rest of the tribe before they reached the Morning Mountains. In what land these lost Valari might have established themselves, not even the legends told. But I wondered if Kane might have been one of their descendants.

'You make a mystery of yourself,' I said to him.

'No more than the One has made a mystery of life,' he told me. 'So, it's not important who I am – only what I do.'

I turned toward the sunlit meadow to look upon the work that Kane had done. I still couldn't quite believe that he had killed the six Grays at close quarters without taking a scratch. I pointed at their bodies and said, 'Is *this* what you do, then?'

'As I told you at the Duke's castle, I oppose Morjin in any way I can.'

'Yes, by slaughtering his servants. How is it that you found them here? Were you following them – or us?'

Kane hesitated while he drew in a breath and looked at me deeply. Then he said, 'I've been looking for *you*, Valashu Elahad, for a year. When I heard that Morjin's assassins had found you first, I set out for Mesh as soon as I could.'

'But why should you have been looking for me at all? And how did you hear about the assassins?'

'My people in Mesh sent me the news by carrier pigeon,' he said.

'*Your* people?' I asked, now quite alarmed.

'So, there are brave men and women in every land who have joined to fight the Crucifier.'

'Are they of the Black Brotherhood, then?'

As he had with Maram, he ignored this question. And then he went on to say, 'When I heard that you had fought a duel with Prince Salmelu and were being pursued by the Ishkans along the North Road, I hurried through Anjo to Duke Rezu's castle to intercept you.'

'But how could you know that we'd come there? *We* certainly didn't know this until we escaped from the Black Bog.'

Now Kane's eyes began glowing as of coals heated in a furnace. He smiled savagely at me and said, 'So, I guessed. Duke Barwan eats from the Ishkans' hands like a dog, and so how much sense would it have made for you to cross the Aru-Adar Bridge into his domain? But where else could you cross into Anjo? Where could you hope to lose the Ishkans if not in the Bog? It was a good guess, eh?'

I nodded my head as Maram and Master Juwain looked at me in silent remembrance of the terrors of this nighttime passage. And then Kane continued, 'I knew that if you were who I thought you to be, you'd find your way out of the Bog – even as you found your way *into* the Lokii's vild.'

'But what *is* the Black Bog?' Maram asked, shuddering. 'It's like no place on earth I ever wanted to see.'

'That it's not,' Kane said. 'So, the Bog isn't wholly *of* the earth.'

He went on to tell us that there were certain power places in the earth – usually in the mountains – where the telluric currents gathered like great knots of fire. If they were disturbed, as the ancient Ishkans had done in leveling a whole mountain with firestones to create the Bog, then strange things could happen.

'Other worlds around other suns stream with their own telluric currents,' Kane said. 'The currents everywhere in the universe are interconnected. And so are the lands of the various worlds: in places such as the Bog, it's possible to pass from one world to another.'

'Do you mean to say that we were walking on other worlds like earth?' Maram asked.

'No, *not* like the earth, I hope,' Kane said. 'The Bog is known to connect Ea only with the Dark Worlds.'

I looked up at the sun pouring its light on the green leaves and the many-colored flowers of our woods; I didn't want to imagine what a Dark World might be. And neither, it seemed, did Maram or Atara. They looked utterly mystified by what Kane had said. But Master Juwain slowly nodded his head as he squeezed his black book in his little hands.

'The Dark Worlds are told of in the *Tragedies*,' he explained. 'They are worlds that have turned away from the Law of the One. "There the sun doesn't shine nor do men smile or birds sing." Shaitar was one such world. Damoom is another. Angra Mainyu is imprisoned there.'

Of course, even I had heard of Angra Mainyu, the Baaloch, the Dark Angel – the Lord of Darkness, himself. It was said that he had been the greatest of the Galadin before falling and making war against the One. But Valoreth and Ashtoreth, along with a great angelic host, had finally defeated him and bound him to the world of Damoom. That this world had somehow been darkened by his presence, however, I hadn't known.

'You should read the *Saganom Elu* more closely,' Master Juwain chided Maram and me. 'Then you might learn the true nature of darkness.'

I fought back a shudder as I smiled grimly; I didn't need a book to help me recall the hopelessness I had felt in the Black Bog.

To Kane, I said, 'If we passed from Ea to other worlds through the Bog, is it then possible for other peoples to pass from them to earth?'

'Not in any way that anyone could use,' Kane said, following my thoughts. 'There are no maps from the Bog to other such places. Openings to other worlds appear by chance and then vanish without warning like smoke. Anyone caught there quickly becomes maddened, exhausted, lost. The mind can't see its way out and wanders within itself even as *you* wandered with your bodies. But sometimes things escape from one world and find their way to another. Like the Grays: it's possible they originally came from one of the Dark Worlds. Perhaps even Damoom itself.'

My breakfast having put new strength in my limbs, I suddenly found myself standing up and stretching beneath the tree. It was good to feel the earth beneath my feet; it was good to be alive on a world such as Ea where the sun rose every day and the birds sang their sweet songs.

'The Grays,' I said to Kane, 'picked up our scent before we'd left Anjo.'

'Yes, I know,' Kane said. 'When Morjin's assassins failed to kill you, he must have decided to send his most powerful retainers against you.'

'You followed us from the Duke's castle, didn't you? Did you find the Grays following us, too?'

Kane slowly nodded his head, then stood up beside me. 'You were in great danger, though you couldn't have known the source. But *I* knew. So, I knew that they'd open you with their minds and then with their knives if I didn't follow them and kill them first.'

'If you truly wanted to help us,' I said, looking out into the meadow, 'you waited a long time.'

'That I did. There was no other way. It's impossible to steal upon the Grays and attack them unless their minds are completely occupied in immobilizing their victims.'

'So you used us as bait to spring your trap.'

'Would it have been better if I had walked into *their* trap and died with you?'

I nodded my head because what he had said made sense. Then I told him, 'We should thank you for taking such great risks to save our lives.'

'It's not your thanks I want,' he told me.

'What *is* it you want, then? You said you've spent a year looking for me – why?'

Now Master Juwain, Maram and Atara rose up and stood beside me facing Kane. We all waited to hear what he would say.

As the sun rose higher and the woods grew even warmer, Kane began pacing back and forth beneath the oak tree. His grim, bold face was set into a scowl; the large tendons along his neck popped out beneath his sun-burnt skin as his jaw muscles worked and he clamped his teeth together. Kane, I thought, was a man who fought terrible battles – the worst ones with himself. I felt in him a great doubt, and even more, a seething anger at himself for doubting at all. Finally, he turned toward me, and his eyes were pools of fire catching me up in their dark flames.

'So, I'll tell you of the prophecy of Ayondela Kirriland,' he said. The sounds issuing from his throat just then were more like an animal's growls than a human voice. 'Listen, listen well: "The seven brothers and sisters of the earth with the seven stones will set forth into the darkness. The Lightstone will be found, the Maitreya will come forth –"'

'"And a new age will begin,"' Maram said, interrupting him. 'Ah, we already *know* the words to the prophecy. King Kiritan's messenger delivered it in Mesh before we set out.'

'*Did* he?' Kane said, fixing his blazing eyes on Maram.

'Yes, we already know that the seven stones must be –'

'Be quiet!' Kane suddenly commanded him. 'Be quiet, now – you know nothing!'

Maram's mouth snapped shut like a turtle's. He looked at Kane in surprise, and not a little fear, as well.

'There's more to the prophecy than you'll have heard,' he told us. He turned to stare at me. 'These are the last lines of it: "A seventh son with the mark of Valoreth will slay the dragon. The old world will be destroyed and a new world created."'

As his voice died into the deepness of the woods, I stood there rubbing the scar on my forehead. I thought of Asaru, Karshur, Yarashan, Jonathay, Ravar and Mandru – my six brothers who were the sons of Shavashar Elahad. Then Maram turned toward me as if seeing me for the first time, and so did Atara and Master Juwain.

'If this is truly the whole prophecy,' I said to Kane, 'then why didn't King Kiritan's messenger deliver it?'

'Because he almost certainly didn't know it.'

He stared at my face as he told us of the tragedy of Ayondela Kirriland. It was well known, he said, that Ayondela was struck down by an assassin's knife just as she recited the first two lines of the prophecy. But what was not known was that the great oracle in Tria had been infiltrated by Morjin's priests who helped murder Ayondela. Just before she died, she whispered the second two lines of the prophecy to two of these Kallimun priests – Tulann Hastar and Seshu Jonku – who kept them secret from King Kiritan and almost everyone else.

'If the lines were kept secret, then how did you learn of them?' I asked.

'Tulann and Seshu informed Morjin, of course,' Kane said. His dark eyes gleamed with hate. 'And before Tulann died, he whispered the whole of the prophecy to *me*.'

I looked at the knife that Kane wore sheathed at his side; I didn't want to know how Kane had persuaded Tulann to reveal such secrets.

'Tulann was an assassin,' Kane said to me. 'And I'm an assassin of assassins. Some day I may kill the Great Beast himself – unless you do first.'

The scar above my eye was now burning as if a bolt of lightning had put its fire into me. I squeezed the hilt of my sword, hardly able to look at Kane.

'You bear the mark of Valoreth that Ayondela told of,' he said to me. 'And unless I've forgotten how to count, you're Shavashar Elahad's seventh son. *That's* why Morjin sent his assassins to kill you.'

Atara came up to me and put her hand on my shoulder. I felt within her a terrible excitement and her great fear for me as well. Master Juwain smiled happily as if he had just found a piece to a puzzle that he had thought lost. Maram bowed his head to me as a swell of pride flushed his face.

To Kane, I said, 'Why didn't you tell me all this at the Duke's castle?'

'Because you didn't trust me – why should I have trusted you?'

'Why should you trust me now?'

Kane's breath fairly steamed from his lips as he stared deep into my eyes. 'Why should I indeed, Valashu Elahad? Why, why? So, I trust your valor and the fire of your heart – and your sword. I trust the truth of your words. I trust that if you set out to seek the Lightstone, you won't turn back. Ha – I suppose I trust you because I *must*.'

So saying, he opened his hand to show me the black stone that he had torn from the Grays' leader's head. 'This, I believe, is one of the stones told of in Ayondela's prophecy.'

He nodded at Master Juwain and said, 'And I believe that the varistei that the Lokii queen gave you is another.'

Master Juwain took the green gelstei from his pocket and held the sparkling crystal up to the sun.

'The first two of the seven stones have been found,' Kane said. 'And here we stand, five of the seven brothers and sisters of the earth.'

'No, it's not possible,' I murmured. 'It can't be me that the prophecy told of. It can't be us.'

But even as I spoke these words, I knew that it was. I heard something calling me as from far away and yet very near. It was both terrible and beautiful to hear, and it whispered to me along the wind in a keening voice that I could not ignore. I felt it burning into my forehead and tingling along my spine and booming out like thunder with every beat of my heart.

'You can't choose your fate,' Kane said to me. 'You can decide only whether or not you'll try to hide from it.'

I stared into the centers of his black eyes; I sensed in him a whole sea of emotions: wrath, hope, hate, love – and passion for life in all its colors and shades of light and dark. There was a terrible darkness about him that I feared almost more than death itself.

He suddenly drew his sword which had sent on so many of the Grays. Its long blade gleamed in the sunlight filtering down through the trees. He said to me, 'You have the gift of the *valarda*. If you choose to, you can hear the truth in another's heart. Hear the truth of mine, then: I pledge this sword to your service so long as you seek the Lightstone. Your enemies will be my enemies. And I'll die before I see you killed.'

There was a darkness about Kane as black as space, and yet there was something incredibly bright about him, too. The same black eyes that had fallen upon his enemies with a hellish hate now shone like stars. It was this light that dazzled me; it was this bright being whom I looked upon with awe.

'Take me with you,' he said, 'and I'll fight by your side to the gates of Damoom itself.'

'All right,' I finally said, bowing my head. 'Come with us, then.'

And with that, I touched my hand to his sword. A moment later, he sheathed this fearsome weapon, and we grasped hands like brothers, smiling as we tested each other's strength.

It was rash for me to have spoken without the other's consent. But I knew that Master Juwain would welcome Kane's wisdom as would Maram the safety of his sword. As for Atara, she had nothing but respect for this matchless old warrior. She came up to him and clasped hands with him, too. And then she told him, 'If fate has brought us together, as it seems it has, then we should go forth as brothers and sisters. Truly we should. I'd be glad if you came with us – though let's hope we won't have to go quite so far as these Dark Worlds that you've told of.'

Master Juwain and Maram both welcomed Kane to our company, and we stood there in the shade of the oak tree smiling and taking each other's measure. Then Atara turned to Kane and said, 'There's one thing in your story that you glossed over.'

'Eh, what's that?'

Atara, who was as sharp as the point of one of her arrows, smiled at him and said, 'In your account of how Aryu stole the Lightstone, you claimed that he had hidden it in a cave before he died. If that's true, then how was it ever found?'

Kane let out a low, harsh laugh and said, 'That's a story that will certainly be told at the gathering in Tria. Can you wait until then?'

'Oh, if I really must,' she said.

I looked up at the sun and said, 'If we're to be at the gathering at all, we'd better saddle the horses and ride on. We've only two full days until King Kiritan calls the quest.'

And with that, we smiled at each other and turned to break camp.

17

A little later, when we were ready to set out, Kane sat atop his big brown horse and told us, 'We still must be careful. One of the Grays escaped us, and he may have gone to find reinforcements.'

This news dismayed all of us, Maram especially. 'Escaped?' he said to Kane. 'Are you sure?'

Kane nodded his head as he looked into the meadow. 'The Grays always hunt in companies of thirteen. I counted only twelve bodies. One of them must have run off into the woods in the heat of the battle.'

'Ah, this is very bad,' Maram said.

'No, it's not *that* bad,' Kane told him. 'The Gray won't be able to find any more of his kind – and almost certainly, no assassins of the Kallimun, either. At least not between here and Tria. But for the next few days, we should still keep our eyes open.'

And so we did. We quickly found our way through the woods back to the great road. I took the lead, keeping open much more than my eyes as I felt through the forested countryside for anyone who might be lying in wait for us. Atara, her bow at the ready, rode beside me, followed by Maram and Master Juwain. Kane insisted on taking the rear post. He was wise to the ways of ambuscade, he said, and he wouldn't let anyone steal upon us and attack us from behind.

After an hour of easy travel along the straight road, the forest gave out onto broad swaths of farmland, and we all relaxed a little. The ground here was flat, allowing a view across the fields for miles in any direction. It was a rich land of oats, barley and wheat – and cattle fattening in fallow fields next to little, wooden houses. I was surprised to find that we had fought our battle with the Grays so close to such intensely cultivated land. Later, when we had stopped for lunch and I remarked that I had never seen so many people packed so closely together outside of a city, Kane just laughed at me. He told me that the domains along the Nar Road were barren compared to the true centers of Alonian civilization, which lay along the Istas and Poru rivers.

'And as for true cities, you've never seen one,' he said. 'No one has until he's seen Tria.'

Since he had seen so much of the world and seemed to know so much about it, I asked him if he had learned the identity of the assassin who had shot at me that day in the woods outside my father's castle.

'No – it might've been anyone,' he told us. 'But most likely, a Kallimun priest or someone serving them. Master Juwain is right that they're the only ones to use the kirax.'

At the mention of this poison that would always drag its clawed fingers along my veins, I shuddered. 'It's strange, but it seemed that the Grays could smell the kirax in my blood. It seemed that the Red Dragon could – and still can.'

'So,' Kane said, 'the kirax is also known as the Great Opener – it opens one to death. But those it doesn't kill, it opens to worse things.'

I remembered my dream of Morjin, and ground my teeth together. I said, 'Could it be that the Red Dragon used it to torment me? To try to make me into a ghul?'

Kane favored me with one of his savage smiles. 'The kirax is designed to kill, quickly and horribly. The amount needed is tiny, eh? The amount *you* took inside is tinier still – it would be impossible to use it this way to make men into ghuls.'

I smiled in relief, which lasted no more than a moment as Kane told me, 'However, for you, who bears the gift of the *valarda*, it would seem that the kirax is especially dangerous. If Morjin tries to make a ghul of you, you'll have to fight very hard to stop him.'

'It's not easy to understand,' I said, 'why he doesn't just make ghuls of everyone and be done with it.'

'Ha!' Kane laughed out harshly. 'It's hard enough for him to make a ghul of *anyone*. And harder still to control him. It requires almost all his will, all his concentration. And *that*, we can thank the One, is why ghuls are very rare.'

As we resumed our journey, I tried not to think about Morjin or terrible poisons that might turn men into ghuls. It was a beautiful day of blue skies and sunshine, and it seemed almost a crime to dwell on dark things. As Master Juwain had warned me, the surest way to bring about that which we fear is to live in terror of it. And so I tried to open myself to other things: to the robins singing out their songs, *cheery-up, cheery-me*; to the farmers working hard in their fields; to the light that poured down from the sky and touched the whole earth with its golden radiance.

279

That night, in a town called Manarind, we found lodging at an inn, where we had a hot bath, a good meal and a sound sleep. We awoke the next morning feeling greatly refreshed and ready to push on toward Tria. The innkeeper, who looked something like a shorter Maram, patted his round belly and said to us, 'Leaving already, then? Well, I shouldn't be surprised – it's a good fifty miles to the city. You'll have to press hard to reach it by tomorrow.'

He went on to say that other companies of knights had stopped at his inn, but not for many days.

'You're the last,' he told us. 'I'm afraid you'll find all the respectable inns in Tria already full. No one wants to miss the King's celebration or the calling of the quest. I'd go myself, if I didn't have other duties.'

In the clear light of the morning, he looked at us more closely as he stroked his curly beard.

'Now where did you say you were from?' he asked us. He looked especially long at Atara. 'Two Valari knights and their friends. Well, for *my* friends, I can recommend an inn on the River Road not far from the Star Bridge. My brother-in-law owns it – he always keeps a room open for those I send on to him. For a small consideration, for my friends, of course, I could –'

'No, thank you,' Kane growled out. His eyes flashed, and for a moment, I thought he was ready to send this fat innkeeper on. 'We won't be staying in the city.'

This was news to all of us. Kane's insistence on secrecy disturbed me. It seemed that, at need, he could slide from truth into falsehood as easily as a fish changing currents in a stream.

'Well, then,' the innkeeper said, presenting Kane with the bill for our stay, 'I'll hope to see you on your return journey.'

Kane studied the bill for a moment as his face pulled into a scowl. Then he fixed his fierce eyes on the innkeeper and said, 'The oats you gave our horses we'll pay for, though not at the rate that you'd charge for serving men porridge. But the water they drank we won't pay for at all. This isn't the Red Desert – it rains every third day here, eh? Now fetch our horses, if you please.'

The innkeeper appeared inclined to argue with Kane. He started to say something about the great labor involved in drawing water from his well and hauling it to his stables. But the look on Kane's face silenced him, and he went off to do as Kane had told him.

The innkeeper's cupidity was my first experience of the Alonians' hunger for money but far from the last. (I didn't count the hill-men who had tried to rob Atara as Alonians.) As we rode out from the inn that morning, we passed the estates of great knights. In the fields surrounding their palatial houses, ragged-looking men and women worked with hoes beneath the hot sun. Kane called them peasants. They slept in hovels away from their masters' houses; Kane said that the knights permitted them to till their fields and let them keep a portion of the crops they cultivated. Such injustice infuriated me. Even the poorest Valari, I thought, lived on his own land in a stout, if small, stone house – and possessed as well a sword, suit of armor and the right to fight for his king when called to war.

'It's this way almost everywhere,' Kane told us. 'Ha, the lands ruled by Morjin are much worse. There he makes his people into slaves.'

'On the Wendrush,' Atara said, 'there are neither peasants nor slaves. Everyone is truly free.'

'That may be. Still, it's said that the Alonians are better off than most peoples and that Kiritan Narmada is a better king.'

Atara fell silent, and the clopping of the horses' hooves against the road seemed very loud. I felt in her a great disquiet, whether over the plight of the Alonians or something else, it was hard to say. I guessed that she felt ill at ease to be traveling through the lands of the Sarni's ancient enemy. And the closer we drew to Tria, the more apprehensive she became.

Around noon, we came to a village called Sarabrunan. There was little more there than a blacksmith's shop, a few houses and a mill above a swift stream grinding grain into flour. I wouldn't have thought of stopping there any longer than it took to water our horses and buy a few loaves of bread from the villagers. But then I chanced to look upon the hill to the north of the village: it was a low hump of earth topped with a unique rock formation that looked like an old woman's face. Its granite countenance froze me in my tracks and called me to remember.

'Sarabrunan,' I said softly. 'Sarburn – this is the place of the great battle.'

While Kane stared silently up at the Crone's Hill, as it was called, I found a villager who confirmed that indeed Morjin had met his defeat here. For a small fee, he offered to guide us around the battlefield.

'No, thank you,' I told him. 'We'll find our way ourselves.'

So saying, I turned Altaru toward the wheatfields to the north of the village. Maram protested that we had little enough time to reach Tria before the celebration the next night. But I wouldn't hear his arguments. I looked at him and said, 'This won't take long, but it must be seen.'

We followed the stream straight through the estate of some knight who had no doubt gone off to Tria. No one stopped us. After perhaps a mile of riding through the new wheat – and through fallow fields and occasional patches of woods – we came to a place where another stream joined the one flowing back toward the village. I pointed along these sparkling waters and said, 'This was once called the Sarburn. Here Aramesh led a charge against Morjin's center. He beat back his army across the stream. It's said that it turned red with the blood of the slain.'

We rode up this stream for a half mile and stopped. Five miles to the east, the Crone's Hill rose up overlooking the peaceful countryside. Other than a small knoll half a mile to our west – I remembered that it had once been called the Hill of the Dead – the land in every direction was level as the skin of a drum.

'The armies met in Valte, just after the harvest,' I said. 'The wheat had all been cut, and the chaff still lay in the fields when the battle began.'

I turned to ride toward the knoll, then. I found its slopes overgrown with thick woods where once meadows had been. While the others followed slowly behind me, I dismounted Altaru and walked him through the oak trees. Near one of them, I began rooting about in the bracken as I listened to a crow cawing out from somewhere ahead of me. I searched among old tree roots and the dense undergrowth for twenty yards before I found what I was looking for.

'Look,' I said to the others as I held up a long, flat stone for them to see. It was of white granite and covered with orange and brown splotches of lichen. Two long ages had weathered the stone so that the grooves cut into it were blurred and almost impossible to read.

'It looks like the writing might be ancient Ardik,' Master Juwain said as he traced his finger along one of the smooth letters. 'But I can't make out what it says.'

'It says this,' I told him. '"Here lies a Valari warrior."'

I handed the stone to him; it was the first time in my life I had ever given him a reading lesson.

'Ten thousand Valari fell that day,' I said. 'They were buried on this knoll. Aramesh ordered as many stones cut from a quarry near Tria and brought here to mark this place.'

At this, Maram and Kane began searching the woods for other death stones, and so did I. After half an hour, however, we had found only two more.

'Where are they all?' Maram asked. 'There should be thousands of them.'

'Likely the woods have swallowed them up,' Kane said. 'Likely the peasants have taken them to use as foundation stones to build their huts.'

'Have they no respect for the dead, then?' Maram asked.

'They were Valari dead,' I said, opening my hands toward the forest floor. 'And the army they fought was mostly Alonian.'

This was true. In ten terrible years toward the end of the Age of Swords, Morjin had conquered all of Alonia and pressed her peoples into his service. And in the end, he had led them to defeat and death here on this very ground upon which we stood. And so Aramesh had finally freed the Alonians from their enslavement – but at a great cost. Who could blame them for any bitterness or lack of gratitude they might feel toward the Valari?

For a long while, I stood with my eyes closed listening to the voices that spoke to me. Men might die, I thought, but their voices lingered on almost forever: in the rattling of the oak leaves, in the groaning of the swaying trees, in the whisper of the wind. The dead didn't demand vengeance. They made no complaint against death's everlasting cold. They asked only that their sons and grandsons of the farthermost generations not be cut down in the flush of life as they had.

All this time, Atara had remained as quiet as the stone that Master Juwain still held in his rough, old hands. She kept staring at it as if trying to decipher much more than its worn letters.

'You don't like to dwell in the past, do you?' I said to her.

She smiled sadly as she shook her head. She took my arm and pulled me deeper into the woods where we might have a bit of privacy.

'Surely you know that many Sarni warriors died in the battle, too,' she told me. 'But the past is the past. Can I change one moment of it? Truly, I can't. But the future! It's like a tapestry yet to be woven. And each moment of our lives, a thread. Each beautiful moment, everything we do. I have to believe that we can weave a different world than this. Truly, truly, we can.'

It was a strange thing for her to say, and I couldn't help thinking of the spider she had seen weaving its web in her father's house – and of the Grays walking toward us across the moonlit meadow before they actually had. I wondered, then, if she might be gifted with seeing visions of the future. But when I asked her about this, she just laughed in her easy, spirited way as her blue eyes sparkled.

'I'm no scryer,' she told me. 'Twice, only, I've seen these things. Surely it's just chance. Or perhaps for a couple of moments, Ashtoreth herself has given her sight directly into my eyes.'

It was neither the time nor the place to dispute what she said. I looked up at the sun, and led her back toward the others.

'It's growing late,' I told them. I bowed my head toward the stone that Maram held in his hand. 'There's nothing more here to see.'

'What should we do with this, then?' Maram asked.

I took the stone from him, and then used my knife to dig a trench in the leaf-covered ground. I planted the stone there; after a little more work with my knife, I set the other two stones back in the earth as well.

'Here lie ten thousand Valari warriors,' I said, looking about the knoll. 'Now come – there's nothing more we can do for them.'

After that we returned to the road as we had come. We rode in silence for a good few miles, west toward Tria, even as Aramesh had once ridden following his great victory.

That night we found another inn where we took our rest. We set out very early the next morning, and rode hard all that day. It was the seventh of Soldru – a day of clear skies and crisp air, perfect weather for riding. The miles passed quickly as a measure of the hours we spent cantering through the ever-more populated land. But measured by our anticipation of attending King Kiritan's birthday celebration, the time passed very slowly indeed.

Around noon, we entered a hilly country. I would have thought to find there fewer fields, but the Alonians had cut them out of the very land. Except on the steepest slopes, terraces of wheat and barley like green steps ran in contours around the hills. White stone walls supported each terrace and set one level off from another. It was a beautiful thing to see, and a hint of the Alonians' great skill at building things.

A few hours later, the proof of their genius was laid before us. The Nar Road cut between two of these hills; at the notch, where the road rose to its greatest elevation before winding down into lower and flatter lands, we had our first view of Tria. I could hardly believe what my eyes told me must be true. For there, to the northwest across some miles of gentle farmland, great white towers rose high above the highest wall I had ever seen. They sparkled as if covered with diamond dust, catching and scattering the brilliant sunlight, and cut like spears a quarter mile high into the blue dome of the sky. Other, lesser buildings – though still very great – formed a jagged line beneath them. Master Juwain told us that all these structures had been cast of living stone during the Age of Law, a marvelous substance of great beauty and strength. Although the secret of its making had long been lost, its splendor remained to remind men of the glories to which they might attain.

The City of Light, Tria was called. It stood before us in the late afternoon sun shimmering like a great jewel cut with thousands of facets.

It was sited at the mouth of the Poru River where it widened and flowed into the Bay of Belen. I saw these blue waters gleaming along the horizon beyond the city. It was my first glimpse of the Great Northern Sea. Jutting out of the bay were the dark shapes of many islands. The largest of these

– it looked almost like a skull made of black rock – was called Damoom. Master Juwain said that it had been named after the world where the Dark Angel, Angra Mainyu, was bound. For on this ominous-looking island, Aramesh had imprisoned Morjin after his defeat.

We rode down to the city, approaching it from the southeast. To our right was the Bay of Belen; to our left, the mighty Poru wound like a brown snake through the gentle, green countryside. We crossed fields and estates that led nearly up to the great walls themselves. Three thousand years ago, Master Juwain said, the city had overflowed for miles beyond the walls, encompassing the very ground over which we now rode. But, like Silvassu and other cities, it had diminished in size and greatness all during the Age of the Dragon. Only a few scattered houses, smithies and such remained outside the walls to hint of its former dimensions.

The Poru divided Tria into two unequal halves, west and east. East Tria, the older part of the city, was the smaller of the two – though still very much greater than any other city I had ever seen. The wall protecting it began at the banks of the bay and curved around it for a good four miles to the southwest, where it ended in a stout tower abutting the river. A mile to the west, across the river, the wall began again and ran almost straight for another four miles, before turning back toward the bay to form the defenses of the western part of the city. Nine gates, named after the nine Galadin who had defeated Angra Mainyu, were set into this great wall. The Nar Road led straight up to the Ashtoreth Gate, which opened upon the southern districts of East Tria. We rode past its iron doors unchallenged. And so we entered the City of Light late on the day that Count Dario had appointed as the date that his king would call the great quest.

'We'll still have to hurry if we're to be on time,' Kane said. 'We've the whole city still to cross.'

The King's Palace, he said, lay a good five miles across the river in West Tria. The Nar Road led almost straight towards it, and so we would keep to it for nearly the whole distance. It was hard to hurry, however, on such a crowded thoroughfare. With our cloaks pulled tightly around us to hide our faces, we rode in a line as quickly as we could, with Kane taking the lead. But carts drawn by tired horses and laden with wheat grain – and with barrels of beer, bolts of cloth and a hundred other things – blocked our way. Many hundreds of people crowded the street, too. Most were dressed poorly in homespun woolens, but there were also merchants wearing fine silks and not a few mercenaries clad in mail, even as Kane and I were. The din of horses whinnying, men shouting and iron-shod wheels rolling along the paving stones nearly deafened me. I had never heard such a noise other than on a battlefield. It came to me then that cities such as Tria, however beautiful, were dangerous places where men had to fight for a few feet of space or to keep themselves from being trampled – if not worse.

I should have kept my mind on forcing my way through the crowds and not allowing Altaru to strike out with his deadly hooves at anyone who drew too close. Instead, I stared at the many sights, even as Maram and the others did. Along the street were many stalls selling various viands: roasted breads, sausages, hams, apple pies and hot cakes sizzling in sesame oil. The smells of all these foods hung in the air and set our mouths watering. Maram eyed the stands of the beer sellers and almost stopped at a shop which advertised wines from Galda and Karabuk. I stared at a diamond seller, whose sparkling wares might have been looted from the dead Valari at the Sarburn and reset into brooches and rings. Other shops sold pottery from the Elyssu, Sunguru cotton as white as snow, glasswork handblown by the Delian masters of that art – almost anything made by the hand of man. And, in truth, the Trians sold many other things less substantial. Would-be scryers offered to read our futures for a few bronze coins while the astrologers did a brisk business casting horoscopes and drawing for their clients maps of the stars.

Everyone seemed eager to take our money. Hawkers shouted at us to enter shops selling fine jewelry; beautifully dressed – and beautiful – women came up to us and pulled insistently on our cloaks. Swarms of ragged children bravely darted in between our horses, holding out their hands as they stared at us with their big, sad eyes. Kane called them beggars. I had never seen such poor, gaunt-faced people before. Every few yards, it seemed, I reached into my purse to give one of them a silver coin. Kane cast a dark look at them, shooing them away as if they were flies. He told me that not even King Kiritan had enough money to feed all the poor of the world. But I couldn't help myself. I could feel the aching of their empty bellies. My coins couldn't feed everyone, but perhaps they would put bread into the mouths of these hungry people for a few days.

Atara, too, gave them coins: *gold* coins, of which she seemed to have many. She was a Sarni warrior, after all, and it was said that gold flows down to the Wendrush like the waters of the rivers to the sea. Kane chided her for attracting attention to us and wasting her money. He said that the Beggar King would likely rob the children of their new-found riches. Atara, however, met his hardened stare with an icy one of her own. She drew herself up straight in her saddle and told him, 'They're *children*. Have you no heart?'

Kane muttered something about the softness of women, and turned

286

to gaze upon a great tower near the city's wall. The Tur-Tisander, he said it was called. To distract us from the beggars, he told us more about Morjin's defeat. He said that following the Battle of Sarburn, Morjin had fled to the city and tried to hide behind its walls. But Aramesh had pursued him there; he had fought sword to sword with Morjin along the top of the great walls themselves. There, near the Tur-Tisander, between the Valoreth and Arwe Gates, Aramesh finally wounded and disabled Morjin, who laid down his sword and pleaded for his life. The kings and knights who had fought with Aramesh clamored for Morjin's death. But according to the Valari warrior codes, Aramesh was obliged to spare Morjin, although he hated to do so. Then, too, the scryer Katura Hastar had prophesied that 'the death of Morjin would be the death of Ea.' And so, after Morjin surrendered the Lightstone to Aramesh, he had Morjin bound in chains. He ordered an impregnable fortress built on a small island, which he renamed Damoom. There Morjin was to be imprisoned until 'all the earth grew green again and the people of all the lands returned to the stars.'

'Morjin should never have been freed,' Kane said, pointing north toward the dark island in the bay. 'But that's another story.'

He turned his horse and pressed on toward the river. We followed him through this crowded, old district. The Nar Road cut through it along a straight enough line, but most of the nearby streets curved and twisted like snakes. There were many small houses and tenements among the great towers, and many buildings where events of great moment had taken place. We passed the Old Sanctuary of the Maitriche Telu – or rather its ruins. I learned that in the year 2284 of the Age of Swords, six years before Morjin's downfall, he had tried to annihilate this Sisterhood of scryers and mind readers who opposed him. And so he had ordered their sanctuaries across Alonia torn down and the Sisters crucified. It was said that he had utterly destroyed their ancient order. But it was also said, by Kane and others, that the Sisters of Maitriche Telu still existed, dreaming their impossible dreams and plotting to remake the world from secret sanctuaries, perhaps even in Tria itself.

A couple of miles from the Astoreth Gate, the great boulevard led down to the river. Here the look of the city changed, giving way to many taverns, crumbling tenements and warehouses. There were shops making rope and sail, and others where hot pitch was poured into fat, wooden barrels. The air grew moist, and smelled of the faint, salt tang of the sea. We crossed a broad road just to the east of the river; along its muddy banks were many docks, at which great ships were anchored. I had never seen a real ship before, and the sight of them lined up along the quay – and pointed out into the river under full sail – made me think of storms whipping up raging seas and pirates venturing after treasure. Many of the men working on the ships even *looked* like pirates: there were sailors from Thalu with their sun-reddened skin and gold rings dangling from their ears. They wore bright bolts of cloth wrapped around their yellow hair and thick-bladed swords at their sides. Other sailors I took to be from the Elyssu, for their appearance was more like that of Master Juwain, except that most of them had a full head of hair. Master Juwain told me that when he had first come to Tria on a galley as a young man, he had had all his hair, too.

The Nar Road gave onto a great bridge named after an angel called Sarojin. With its huge stone pylons sunk down into the muddy waters of the Poru, I thought it the most magnificent such structure I had ever seen. But then, after we had progressed some hundred yards across it, the curve of the river allowed a view of a still greater bridge half a mile to the north. This was the famous Star Bridge. No pylons supported its immense mass. It seemed cast of a single piece of living stone that spanned the river in a great, sweeping, mile-long arch. All golden it was in the light of the setting sun, and Master Juwain called it by its more common name, which was the Golden Band. He said that the High King, Eluli Ashtoreth, had built it to remind his people of the Ieldra's sacred light that fell upon the earth at the end of every age.

'There's another light that *I'd* like to be reminded of,' Maram said as he looked at the bridge. 'Has anyone seen Flick since we entered the city?'

None of us had. We were all afraid that he had finally perished amidst the tumult of so many thousands of people and acres of stone – either that or simply evanesced into nothingness. But there was nothing we could do except to ride on and hope that he might soon reappear.

When we reached the Poru's west bank, just past the dockyards on that side of the river, we found a broad, tree-lined street leading straight up to a hill with a great tower and two palaces at the top. I supposed all this magnificence to be the residence of King Kiritan, but I was wrong. The tower, though not the city's largest, was *the* Tower of the Sun: the first such ever to be built in Tria or anywhere else. The southernmost palace was the abode of the ancient Marshan clan while the other one was named after the Hastars. After we passed from the shadow of a rectangular temple blocking our view, Kane directed my attention to a still greater hill a mile to the north of them. The palace rising from the top of it was larger than my father's entire castle. Built of living stone that gleamed like marble and with nine golden domes surmounting its various sections, it was the most impressive thing I had ever seen.

We made our way toward it along a broad street that cut the Nar

Road at an angle. In this district of the city, along a line of hills above the river, were the houses of the rich and powerful. They were mostly made of marble on three stories, and any one of them was greater than any lord's house in Mesh. Soon we came to a wall that surrounded the palace grounds. The guards at the gate blocked our way with spears until I told them that I was Sar Valashu Elahad of Mesh and that Count Dario had invited me and my friends to the King's celebration. As it was now growing dark, the guards' captain, a burly graybeard dressed in a fine new tunic, hesitated a moment as he studied my stained cloak and the long sword I wore beneath it. He stared even more dubiously at Kane, and cast Atara a long look as if deciding whether she was truly a Sarni warrior or only a serving girl whom we had dressed to play the part.

'You're an odd lot,' he said to us with the arrogance the Alonians hold for all other peoples. 'The oddest yet to pass this gate today. And, I hope, the last. You should have arrived an hour ago so that you might have been properly presented. Now you'll have to hurry if you're to be graced with the King's welcome.'

So saying, he waved us through the gate. Inside it we found a city within a city. The palace itself faced east overlooking the harbor and the Bay of Belen beyond. The grounds were laid out with many other great buildings and residences, a temple and two cemeteries, a guards' barracks, stables and a smithy. Between them a road lined with magnificent oak trees led up to the palace gates. We passed through great lawns of some of the lushest grass I had ever seen. There were gardens, fountains and long, still pools of water decked with white marble and reflecting the light of the rising moon.

Over them all loomed King Kiritan's palace, the most magnificent building I had ever seen. Grooms waited to take our horses. Kane didn't like it that I had so openly presented myself to the guards; he insisted that we now keep our cloaks pulled tightly around ourselves and make no mention of our names. He seemed more wary of the nobles waiting inside than he had been of the crowds of dangerous-looking men on the streets. As he put it, 'The Gray who escaped us must have known we'd come here. There'll be Kallimun priests among the knights here tonight – we can be sure of that. So let's watch each other's backs.'

With his dark cloak covering his face, he led the way up the steps to the colannaded portico. We passed between thick white pillars and through the doorway into the palace proper. There the guards waved us on, and we walked quietly through a magnificent hall. Its white walls shone like mirrors and the high ceiling was inlaid with squares of lapis and gold; it was so large that for a moment I wondered if we hadn't come too late after all and missed the entire gathering. But this proved to be only the entrance hall. Beyond it, through great wooden doors trimmed out in silver and bronze, was the King's great hall. The guards in front of the doors seemed put out that they should have to open them again for us. They did their duty, however, and we passed one by one into King Kiritan's immense throne room.

Three thousand people stood there beneath a great dome. From a distance, this dome had appeared golden; now, looking up at it past walls of a particularly bright living stone, I could see that it was as clear as glass. It let in the starlight, which fell like a shower of silver among the many people awaiting the King. Kane's dark eyes swept the room, which could easily have held three halls the size of my father's. In a low voice, he identified for us various princes from Eanna, Yarkona, Nedu, and the islands of the Elyssu. He pointed out the exiled knights of Galda, Hesperu, Uskudar, Sunguru and Karabuk. There were a dozen Sarni warriors, too, with their long blonde hair and drooping mustaches, and a few Valari from the kingdoms of Anjo, Taron, Waas, Lagash, Athar and Kaash. I was proud, of course, to stand for Mesh as Maram was for Delu. But most of those present that evening were Alonians: knights and nobles of the Five Families; barons from Alonia's every domain; and not a few adventurers and rogues. Not all of them would be making the quest, of course, but they wanted to be present at its calling. King Kiritan had invited his people to the greatest celebration in living memory, and the boldest and most powerful of them had taken advantage of his magnanimity.

We crowded into the very rear of the room, which was circular in shape. An aisle bisected it and was lined on both sides with guards in full armor and bearing both spears and brightly polished shields. Another aisle, also guarded, cut the room crosswise, thus dividing the crowd of people into four quadrants. Where the aisles gave out at the center of the room, under the apex of the star-washed dome, stood the King's throne. Mounted on a large pedestal, it was a massive construction, all covered in gold and encrusted with precious gems. Six great, deep steps led up to it. On each step, at either side, stood sculptures of various animals. Master Juwain explained to us that each pair symbolized the various spiritual and material forces that man must reconcile within himself.

To climb to his throne, the King had to pass first between a golden lion and a silver ox. These represented the sun and the moon, or the active and passive principles of life. On the next step awaited a lamb and a wolf, symbols of the pure heart and the devouring passions. A hawk and a sparrow framed the third step while on the fourth stood a goat and a great leopard, cast in bronze. The goat, I guessed, embodied the need for self-sacrifice, a calling that a king must never forget. The fifth step held both a falcon and a cock, reminders of obedience to the highest and the opposing gratification of lust. On the last step, across ten feet of a worn red carpet, there perched a golden eagle facing a peacock, cast of silver but completely covered in various gemstones so as to look like brightly-colored feathers. The eagle spoke of man's striving toward transcendence as Elijin and Galadin where the peacock represented the earthbound vanity and pride of the self. Set into the very top of the throne, beneath which the King would sit, was a golden dove, the great symbol of the peace to be attained at the end of this ascension. The final symbol, Master Juwain said, which wasn't really a symbol at all, was the starlight that fell upon the throne and called everyone to remember that shimmering place from which men had once come and to which they would someday return.

After we had stood pressed back against the wall for a bare few moments, the doors to our left opened, and heralds stationed there blew their trumpets to quiet us. Then the King, accompanied by a tall, handsome woman whom I took to be his wife, strode into the room. King Kiritan was himself a tall man; his golden crown, set with a large emerald on the front point, brought him up to about my height. Although his neatly trimmed beard was reddish-gray, his hair was all of silver and gold, and fell down to the shoulders of a magnificent, white ermine mantle. Beneath this he wore a blue velvet tunic showing the golden caduceus of the royal house. He wore a long sword at his side while in his hand he carried a very real caduceus of power and peace.

He made his way slowly down the aisle toward the throne. Although he walked with a slight limp, there was power yet in his stately gait and not a little pride. His face, cut with an unusual circular scar on his cheek, was as stern and unmoving as a stone; yet the glimpse I caught of his bright, blue eyes revealed a fierce devotion to lofty ideals and a strict moral order. He turned his head neither to the left nor right. His barons and the princes from the island kingdoms stood the nearest to the throne. There Count Dario and other nobles of the House Narmada waited as well for him to mount its six broad steps.

The King, however, paused before the first step while a herald came forward. The Alonians, as I would discover, loved their rituals, especially ancient ones. And the most ancient of all rituals in Tria was reminding the King of his duties and from where his power ultimately came. As the King's foot fell upon the first step, the herald called out to him, and to us, the first law for kings: 'You shall not multiply wives to yourself, nor shall you multiply lands, nor silver or gold.'

The next step brought the following injunction from the herald, who

291

would never think to speak to the king so boldly on any other occasion: 'You shall not suffer your people to live in hunger or want.'

Upon the third step, the herald told him: 'You shall not suffer any enemy to slay your people or make slaves of them.'

And so it went, step after step, until the king passed between the eagle and the peacock and drew up before his throne. Then, as the King lifted up his eyes toward the great dome, the herald cried out the final law: 'Know the One before whom you stand!'

Only then did King Kiritan sit upon his throne and prepare himself to act as judge and lord of his people.

'Welcome,' he called out to us in a strong, rich voice. He allowed himself a broad smile that hinted of warmth but failed to convey it. 'We welcome you with open heart and all the hospitality that we can command. As well, we thank you for gracing our house tonight, whether your journeys took you from only across the river or from as far away as the islands of the west or the southernmost steppes of the Wendrush.'

Here he paused to nod at a Sarni chieftain and at the gold-bearded giant standing next to him who proved to be Prince Aryaman of Thalu.

'Thirty years now,' King Kiritan said, 'we have sat upon this throne. And in all that time, there has never been an occasion like this. Truth to tell, Tria hasn't seen a gathering of such illustrious personages for an entire age. Now, it would be flattering to suppose that you've come here tonight to help us celebrate our birthday. That, however, would be more flattery than is good for any king to bear. Still, celebration *is* the essence of why we are here tonight. What is a birthday but the marking of a soul's coming into life? And what is this Quest that we've called you to answer but the coming of all of Ea into a new age and a new life?'

While the King went on about the great dangers and possibilities of the times in which we lived, I noticed Atara tensing her jaw muscles as she stood next to me watching him. I recalled that the Kurmak and Alonians had often been great enemies, and I sensed in her a great struggle to like or even trust this vain and arrogant king. Kane watched him closely, as well. We stood together with Maram and Master Juwain, pressed almost to the wall by a group of Alonian knights.

'Now, we must speak of this Quest,' King Kiritan told us. 'The Quest for the Cup of Heaven that has been lost for three thousand years.'

His square, handsome face fairly shone in the radiance falling down from the walls. There, set into curved recesses around the room, blazed at least fifty glowstones. These were regarded as only lesser gelstei – though to my mind, they were still marvelous enough. It was said that they drank in the light of the sun, held it, and gave it back at night. Master Juwain whispered to me that these same stones had illuminated this hall for more than three thousand years.

'Now, if you're all standing comfortably,' the King said, 'we'll tell you a story. Many of you already know parts of it; much of it is recorded in the *Saganom Elu* and other books. The whole of it, we suspect, is known to few. To these learned men and women, we beg your indulgence. After all, this is the King's birthday, and the finest gift we could receive would be all your attention and enthusiasm.'

So saying, he drew in a deep breath and favored us with another calculated smile. And then, as the stars poured down their light through the dome, as he sat on his immense and glittering throne beneath the golden dove of peace, he told us of the whole long and immensely bloody history of the Lightstone.

18

And so we listened and learned of how the golden cup had been made by the Elijin on another world and brought to Ea by the Star People at the beginning of the Lost Ages; and of how Aryu of the Valari tribe fell mad and killed his brother, Elahad, and stole the Lightstone only to lose it in death on an island near Nedu; of how the whole Valari tribe fell mad and set out on a futile mission to recover the Lightstone and avenge Elahad. And then King Kiritan told of the great First Quest, which had ultimately ended in success – though in bitter failure as well.

'This happened in the year 2259 of the Age of Swords,' King Kiritan told us. 'The story comes from a chronicle that should have been included in the *Saganom Elu*. But it *was* recorded in the *Damitan Elu*. We've had our scribe bring it over from the library to read it to you.'

He nodded at a pale, balding man standing near his throne. The man approached bearing a huge, leather-bound book in his hand. He opened it to a marked page, cleared his throat and began reading its account of the First Lightstone Quest.

That Quest, as well, had been foretold by an Alonian scryer and called by an Alonian king: Sartag Ars Hastar. Some of the names of the heroes who answered his summons were recorded in the *Damitan Elu*: Averin, Prince Garain, Iojin, Kalkin the Great, Bramu Rologar and Kalkamesh. And perhaps the greatest of the heroes, whose name was Morjin. For Morjin, before he fell into darkness, was renowned for his trueness of heart and was fair to look upon; he was said to be the finest swordsman of the age. According to the ancient account, he had led his six companions to the great library in Yarkona. There they had found an ancient map once drawn by Aryu's son, Jolonu, and passed down to his descendants for ages until it had finally found its way to the great library. The map showed the location of the island on which Aryu had died and hidden the Lightstone more than ten thousand years before.

After many adventures, the heroes had at last come to this little island near Nedu, where they found the Lightstone still sitting in a dark cave. The seven heroes then passed it from hand to hand as they beheld the intense radiance streaming out of the golden cup. Six of them it had filled with the splendor of the One. But the seventh, Morjin, was unable to bear its brilliant light. He fell mad, as had Aryu and the Valari; he began a long descent into the black caverns of envy and hate that open inside anyone who covets the infinite powers of creation itself. And so, on the voyage home to Tria, he secretly slew the great Kalkin and pushed him into the sea. One by one, he then murdered Iojin, Prince Garain, Averin and Bramu Rologar, for in touching the Lightstone they had gained immortality even as he had, and he was afraid that one of them would eventually kill *him* and claim the Lightstone for himself. Only Kalkamesh lived to avenge his companions. The *Damitan Elu* told that he had escaped by jumping into the shark-infested waters of the islands off the Elyssu. He had swum to safety, vowing to kill Morjin if it took him a thousand years and to reclaim the Lightstone for himself and all of Ea.

Here the scribe finished reading and closed his book. King Kiritan thanked him with a bow of his head. Then he resumed telling the Lightstone's history, giving a particularly detailed account of how Morjin had reappeared ten years later and had come to power in the Blue Mountains by usurping a duke named Patamon. From this base in the westernmost domain of Alonia, Morjin had founded the Kallimun; he had used the Lightstone to master the other gelstei, even as he used its beautiful light to master men. It took him only twelve years to conquer all of Alonia. And only eight more to crush the Sisters of the Maitriche Telu, conquer the Elyssu and most of Delu. And then he had nearly destroyed the Valari kingdoms as well. Only the fateful arrival of Kalkamesh at the Battle of Tulku Tor, he said, had turned the tide of Morjin's invasion and saved the Nine Kingdoms.

'Kalkamesh was a great hero,' King Kiritan said. 'Perhaps the greatest ever to arise from our land.'

As the crowds of Alonians rumbled their approval, I traded a quick look with Kane. His black eyes were blazing; so, I thought, were mine. I had been taught that Kalkamesh was Valari and of Mesh – hence his honored name. Kane must have thought this, too. He leaned his head close to me and whispered: 'Ha, Kalkamesh was no more Alonian than you or I!'

But King Kiritan seemed determined to claim this immortal man as his own, and so he continued his story: 'The scryer Rohana Lais had foretold that Morjin could be brought down only by a gelstei made of true silver, but no one in all of Ea knew how to fabricate such a stone. Except Kalkamesh. For in the years that Morjin spent on his illegitimate conquests, Kalkamesh had put the illumination gained by his touching the Lightstone to good use. We know that he was the first to forge the silver gelstei. And so he appeared at Tulku Tor wielding a sword made of pure silver gelstei. The Bright Sword, men called it. It was said to cut steel as steel does wood. Kalkamesh used it to cut a swath through Morjin's army. Thus he saved the battle for Aramesh. And two years later, at the Sarburn, he used this same sword to finally overthrow Morjin.'

King Kiritan paused to look out into the hall; I had a disquieting sense that he was singling out the few Valari present to bear his bitterness and opprobrium.

'After Morjin was taken,' he said, 'Kalkamesh had wanted to kill Morjin, as should have been done. Instead, Aramesh imprisoned him and took the Lightstone for himself. He took it back to the mountains of Mesh where it was selfishly kept in a tumbledown, little castle for all the Age of Law.'

Now the burn of my eyes spread to my ears. My father's castle, I thought, might not be especially large, but it had always been kept in excellent repair.

'For all the Age of Law!' King Kiritan's voice rang out again. 'For three thousand years, while men learned to forge all the gelstei except the gold and built a civilization worthy of the stars, the Valari kept the greatest of the gelstei from being used. By the time they finally saw their folly and returned the Lightstone to Tria, it was too late.'

The King's face fell cold and grave with judgment as he went on to tell of the tragedy of Godavanni Hastar. This great man, he said, had been born in Delu at a time when the whole Eaean civilization turned toward the dream of returning to the stars. Three hundred years before, the great Eluli Ashtoreth had united all of Ea – save the Nine Kingdoms – and had sat as High King on the very same throne before us. From Godavanni's birth, it was prophesied that he would someday become Ea's High King as well. He had the gift of healing and touching men's hearts, and many proclaimed him to be the Maitreya foretold for the end of the Age of Law. It was hoped that he would complete the task of healing the earth and lead the Return, as it was called. In the year 2939, Godavanni had become King of Delu. And two years later, upon the death of the High Queen, Morena Eriades (for in that time, there were ruling queens and well as kings), the Council of Twenty had elected Godavanni High King of Ea. And so Godavanni had come to Tria for his coronation and to sit on the Throne of the Golden Dove.

This event was the greatest of the great Age of Law. Kings and queens of Ea's many lands journeyed to Tria to honor Godavanni. One of these was Julumesh, who had befriended Godavanni and decided that the time had finally come for the Valari to surrender the Lightstone to one who could use it as the Elijin had intended. And so he brought the Lightstone from Silvassu to Tria to give into Godavanni's hands. As Godavanni took the Lightstone from him, a great light poured out of the cup and through him. He restored sight to old, blind King Durriken and touched many with a healing radiance. Everyone was touched with his compassion. But it was his compassion, and the deeper love from which it flowed, that proved to be his undoing – and Ea's, as well.

For this King of Kings known as Godavanni the Glorious wanted to show the people that a new age had begun. And so he ordered Morjin freed from the fortress on Damoom and brought to Tria. He believed that he had the power to heal Morjin, thus turning a once-great hero back toward the light, which would have been a great gift for all of Ea.

And perhaps Godavanni, through the Lightstone, *did* have this power. But there were other powers in the universe, too. Even as Godavanni opened himself completely and turned the radiance of the Lightstone toward Morjin, a window to the stars was opened. In an instant, Angra Mainyu, from his dark and distant world of Damoom, joined minds with Morjin. And with others in the hall, too. One of these – King Craydan of Surrapam – he caused to fall mad. And so King Craydan, who would ever after be known as Craydan the Ghul, sprang forward to give Morjin his sword. Morjin used it to stab Godavanni in the heart. He ripped the golden cup from Godavanni's hands. And then, with the help of his Kallimun priests who were hidden among the crowds in the hall, he made a daring escape, fleeing Tria and Alonia for the mountain fastness of Sakai.

This great catastrophe stunned the assembled royalty. After they recovered from the shock, everyone wanted to blame everyone else. As the light left Godavanni's eyes, the light seemed to go out of the whole Eaean civilization. In fit of fury, Julumesh killed King Craydan and then led his Valari guard on a mission to pursue Morjin. But an army of Kallimun priests intercepted them and slew them to the last man. The Delian nobles took Godavanni's body back to Delu to bury. The Council of Twenty Kings and Queens, now reduced by three, began arguing among themselves as to what should be done.

'In the coming years,' King Kiritan told us in a heavy voice, 'the Council could not agree on a High King or Queen. This was the Breaking of the Twenty Kingdoms. Then came the time of sorrows. The Delians blamed Alonia for letting their greatest king be killed. Everyone blamed Surrapam for the weakness of their king. The Zayak and Marituk tribes of the Sarni tried to invade the White Mountains to regain the Lightstone, but Morjin won them over with gold and promises of forging a great empire. King Yemon of Ishka accused the Meshians of carelessness in losing the Lightstone. And so the Valari fought among themselves, as is their wont, as they have always loved doing at the expense of all else. They fought kingdom against kingdom, even as Morjin's power grew and the kingdom of Sakai grew stronger. At last, King Dumakan Eriades called upon the Valari to end their futile wars and join him in a crusade against Sakai. He had with him great firestones. But Morjin used the Lightstone to turn the red gelstei against the King and his men. The stones exploded in a terrible fire; it melted steel, and the Alonian army was destroyed, the King and all of his men. Morjin crucified the Valari survivors along the road leading to Argattha. So began the War of the Stones and the Age of the Dragon, when all of Ea should have entered the Age of Light instead.'

King Kiritan paused to look around the room. His eyes settled on a Valari warrior bearing on his tunic the green falcons of the Rezu clan. I guessed that this must be Sar Ianar, Duke Rezu's son. King Kiritan regarded him scornfully. Great blame he had told of, and blame lived on in his icy blue eyes almost three thousand years after Godavanni's death.

As the King gripped his golden wand of rule and sat up even straighter upon his golden throne, he resumed his story. The part that he now told was more well known, for it had spread into all lands as the *Song of Kalkamesh and Telemesh* – the very same song that Duke Rezu's minstrel had sung for us in his castle. Now the King told of how Kalkamesh returned, and with the aid of one of Morjin's most trusted priests, the traitor Sartan Odinan, stole into the underground city of Argattha and stole the Lightstone; and of how Kalkamesh was captured and tortured while Sartan escaped with the Lightstone – only to lose it again or hide it somewhere unknown to history or to any man.

'Where the Lightstone now lies, no one knows,' King Kiritan said. 'But we *do* know that it will be found. You have all heard the prophecy of Ayondela Kirriland, but we will repeat it here for the words must not be forgotten: "The seven brothers and sisters of the earth with the seven stones will set forth into the darkness. The Lightstone will be found, the Maitreya will come forth, and a new age will begin."'

I waited for him to supply the missing lines of which Kane had told us, but of course he did not. Kane and I – and Atara, Maram and Master Juwain – all traded knowing looks as a great stir of excitement spread through the hall.

'Ayondela did not live to see this new age,' King Kiritan told us, 'for she was struck down by an assassin sent by Morjin, who would silence those who speak of hope. But he has no power to silence us now. We must now speak of *our* great hope: and that is the very dream of the Star People who came to Ea ages ago. It was their purpose to create a civilization that would give birth to men and women as they were born to be. Men who would transcend themselves, in body and spirit, and return to the stars as Elijin; immortal women shining like suns who would follow the Law of the One and go on to ever deeper life in the glorious forms of the Galadin themselves.

'But where are these men and women? Where is this great civilization? Where *is* the golden cup that will restore the lands of Ea to their promise and hope? We know that it was stolen from us by Aryu; and kept behind the Morning Mountains by selfish kings; and taken away by Morjin, only to become lost yet again. For all of an age, Morjin has sought it – only to be opposed and thwarted. By the Brotherhoods, by the Sisterhood of Scryers, by great kings, by brave people in all the free lands. But now Morjin has conquered Acadu and Uskudar; his priests rule Karabuk, Hesperu and Galda in his name. Surrapam may soon fall. If it is *he* who finds the Lightstone, all of Ea will surely fall. Then the seven brothers and sisters of the earth will go forth into the darkness and not return; the Maitreya will come forth only to be crucified; a new age will begin: the Age of Darkness that will last a thousand times three thousand years.'

King Kiritan, who was now breathing hard, paused to swallow painfully. I could almost feel his thirst and desire to call for a glass of water. But he would not be seen surrendering to his body's needs at such a moment. And so he pressed his thin, dry lips together as he sat tensely on his throne.

And then he cried out, 'And that is why it must be we who find the Lightstone first! One of us here in this hall tonight! Or seven, or seventy, or a thousand – who will join voices with me and vow to make this Quest?'

For a moment, no one in the hall moved. Then Count Dario, with his flaming red hair and burning eyes, put his hand to his sword as he cried out, 'I will seek the Lightstone!'

Behind him, two more Alonian knights touched hands to swords and shouted, 'I will!' as well. And then five knights from the Elyssu called out their promise, and all at once, like a fire shooting through dry wood, the fervor to regain this lost cup spread through the hall as hundreds of voices began crying out as one: 'I will! I will! I will!'

There was magic in that moment, and I found myself calling out the same pledge I had made in the hall of my father's castle. Atara and

299

Master Juwain joined me, and Maram, despite his doubts, added his booming voice to the clamor. Even Kane seemed swept away by the great passion of it all and growled out his assent.

After a while, when the multitude had quieted and the stones of the hall grew silent again, King Kiritan drew forth his sword and held it by the blade for all to see. He said to us, 'Swear this oath, then. By your swords, by your honor, by your lives – swear that you will seek the Lightstone and never rest until it is found. Swear that you will seek it by road, by water, by fire, by darkness, by the paths of the mind and the heart. Swear that your seeking will not end unless illness, wounds or death strike you down first. Swear that you will seek the Cup of Heaven for all of Ea and not yourselves.'

It was a harsh oath that King Kiritan called us to make, and more than one knight present bit his lip and shook his head. But many more called out that they would do what was asked of them. Atara, Kane and I did; Master Juwain, though no knight, did as well. I was afraid that Maram might balk at speaking such binding words. But he surprised me, and himself, by vowing to seek the Lightstone to his very death.

'Ah, Maram, my friend,' I heard him muttering to himself a moment later, 'what have you done?'

At first, I supposed that he had become drunk on the powerful wine of fellowship and had forgotten himself. And then I saw him staring at a pretty Alonian woman; she had hair like burnished bronze and full red lips and adoring eyes for all the knights who had vowed to make the quest. If Maram failed to catch her attention, I thought, there would be many other women in the coming years who would want to bless his bravery by giving him what gifts they could.

Now the time had come for King Kiritan to bless those who had made vows. These numbered perhaps a thousand of those present. King Kiritan called for them to move towards his throne. Even as my friends and I began pressing through the crush of people in the hall, King Kiritan stepped down from his throne. Then he called out to ten of his grooms, who walked down the southern aisle bearing a golden chest between each pair of them. They set the five chests at King Kiritan's feet near the first step of his throne. King Kiritan smiled as he bowed toward the handsome woman I had presumed to be his wife. And so she was. She had golden hair almost the color of Atara's and a haughty manner, and the King presented her as Queen Daryana Ars Narmada.

The Queen opened one of the chests and removed a large, gold medallion suspended from a golden chain. She held it high above her head for everyone to behold. The medallion was cast into the shape of a sunburst with flames shooting off of it. As I would soon see, a cup stood out in relief at its center. Seven rays, also in relief, streamed out of the cup towards the medallion's rim. There, around the rim, were written words in ancient Ardik that those making the quest should never forget: *Sura Longaram Tat-Tanuan Galardar.*

Queen Daryana gave this medallion to King Kiritan, who then draped it over the head of Count Dario, the first knight to have called out his pledge. After the King had given his blessing, Queen Daryana reached into the chest for another medallion, even as another knight stepped up to the King. This knight, too, received both medallion and blessing. And so it went, the Queen removing the medallions from the chest one by one as the King gave them with his own hands to the many questers lining up before him. As there were a thousand of us, however, this gift-giving took a long time. My friends and I were the last to enter the hall, and so we would be the last to receive our medallions.

While we stood waiting among the multitude in the hall, various knights announced their plans for finding the Lightstone. Many, of course, would journey to Ea's many oracles in hope of receiving prophecies that might direct them. Some would search the islands off Nedu, for they believed that perhaps the Lightstone that Morjin claimed at the end of the Age of Law was only one of the many False Gelstei and that the true and only Gelstei remained somewhere on the island where Aryu originally left it. Three knights from Delu were determined to journey into the Great Southern Forest of Acadu while others planned voyages across the sea. I heard knights vowing to seek the Lightstone in old sanctuaries or museums or in the ruins of ancient cities. A few decided to set forth alone, but many more were forming into bands of seven, for good luck and protection, but also because the prophecy spoke of 'the seven brothers and sisters of the earth with the seven stones.' These seven stones everyone presumed to be gelstei, but where the questers might find them, no one knew for most of the gelstei forged during the Age of Law had been destroyed or lost and those few that remained were jealously guarded like the treasures they were.

With Master Juwain pressed against my side, I thought of the varistei that Pualani had given him and of the black stone that Kane had cut from the Gray's forehead. Kane, standing just ahead of me, had surely secreted this stone on his person. I knew that he would guard it to the death from anyone who tried to take it from him. Of lesser treasures, he seemed to care nothing. He nodded toward King Kiritan and the chests of medallions and said, 'That's a pretty piece of gold that the King's handing out, and a thousand of them must have cost him dearly. But gold's only gold – it's the true gold that we're after. We've made our vows to find it. Now why don't we leave before something keeps us from our quest?'

'But we haven't received the King's blessing,' I whispered to him.

'If it's a blessing you want,' he grumbled, 'I'll give you mine.'

'Thank you,' I said. 'But you're not a king.'

At this, Kane ground his teeth together as he stared at me. Master Juwain said that we should certainly stay to receive King Kiritan's blessing while Maram, in his own mind, was likely already strutting before the ladies with his new golden medallion shining from his chest. As for Atara, she hadn't come all this way from the Wendrush and fought two battles to turn aside now. Each time Queen Daryana handed a medallion to the King, Atara's blue eyes flared like stars as a fierce desire ignited inside her.

The great nobles of Alonia were the first to receive their medallions that night. I heard them call out their names one by one. These included Belur Narmada, Julumar Hastar, Breyonan Eriades, Javan Kirriland and Hanitan Marshan. All were scions of the ancient Five Families, each of which had been founded in the Age of the Mother by the Aryan invaders who sailed with Bohimir Marshan. For three ages, the Alonian kings and queens had come from these clans. They built their palaces on Tria's seven hills, to which they had given their names. They also kept great estates on the lands surrounding the city. Many times the nobles had fought among themselves for the throne. They established dynasties, such as the renowned Marshanid dynasty, only to be overthrown and wait a hundred or five hundred more years to see their clan rise to preeminence again. Warriors their patriarchs had been, and warriors they remained. They wore well-used armor, and were fairer of hair and eyes than most of the Alonians I had seen in the streets.

Most recently, they and their fathers had made war upon the second group of nobles to stand before the King. These were the lords of Alonia's various domains. The greatest of them, Kane told me, were Baron Narcavage of Arngin and Baron Monteer of Iviendenhall. Two generations earlier, when Alonia had been reduced in power and size, the barons and dukes had ruled their possessions as independent lords. But King Sakandar the Fair, King Kiritan's grandfather, had begun the reconquest of Alonia's ancient realm. Before he died, he had forced the Duke of Raanan and the Count of Iviunn to do him homage and kneel to him. His son, King Hanikul, had continued the wars that he began. Only upon the ascension of *his* son, King Kiritan, however, had the reconquest been completed. King Kiritan had spent almost his entire reign riding at the head of his knights into one rebellious domain or another. Just two years before, the last of the lords had knelt before him and called him sire. And so Alonia had been restored to her ancient borders: from the Dolphin Channel in the north to the Long Wall in the south; and from the Blue Mountains in the west six hundred miles east all the way to the Alonian Sea. Many there were who had begun calling him King Kiritan the Great. It was said that although he hadn't sought this honorific for himself, neither did he discourage it.

It was also said – I heard these whispers and grumblings from various knights around me – that the King had more than one reason for calling the Quest. No one doubted that he loved Ea and wished to see her restored to her ancient splendor. No one doubted that he opposed Morjin with all his will and might. But neither did anyone doubt his need to check the power of his barons. And so he had called them to make vows: those who accepted his medallion would have to go forth upon the quest and leave their domains and intrigues behind them. Those who refused would shame themselves and mar their honor, thus diminishing their ability to mount any opposition to the King. As for King Kiritan himself, he would make *his* quest by seeking the Lightstone solely within Alonia's various domains. He would ride at the head of his knights into Tarlan or Aquantir as he always had, and so keep watch upon his realm. A cunning man was King Kiritan Ars Narmada, and a deep one, too.

After a long time, the last of the knights and nobles stepped away from the throne with their medallions shining brightly for all to see. Then it came time for my friends and me to stand before the King. As a great feast had been promised following this ceremony, everyone was now waiting for us to receive the King's blessing. Everyone grew quiet and watched as we approached the throne. Master Juwain was the first of us to throw back his cloak and call out his name: 'Master Juwain Zadoran,' he said, 'Greetings, King Kiritan.'

'Master Juwain Zadoran of what realm?' the King asked him as he studied his plain woolens doubtfully.

'Formerly of the Elyssu,' Master Juwain said. 'But for many years of that landless realm known as the Brotherhood.'

'Well, this *is* a surprise,' the King said with a smile. He turned to look at Queen Daryana and at Count Dario who stood nearby. 'A master of the Brotherhood will dare to undertake the Quest! We are honored.'

'The honor is mine, King Kiritan.'

'Well, it is growing late, and we still have many hungry bellies to feed,' the King said. He nodded at Queen Daryana, who reached into the fifth golden chest and removed a medallion. The King draped this over Master Juwain's bald head and told him: 'Master Juwain Zadoran, accept this with our blessing that you might be known and honored in all lands.'

Master Juwain bowed to the King and backed away as Maram now stepped up to him. With a great flourish, he loosened his cloak to reveal the red tunic and sword beneath. Then he called out: 'Prince Maram Marshayk of Delu.'

This announcement caused a great stir among the nobles in the room. At least forty knights present were from Delu's various dukedoms or baronies, and they looked at Maram with the shock of recognition brightening their faces.

'Now, this is an even greater surprise,' the King said. 'We were hoping that King Maralah might send one of his own to honor us this day. How is it that his son happens to be traveling with a master of the Brotherhood?'

'*That* is long story,' Maram said as he boldly stared at Queen Daryana. Although almost forty years old, she was still acclaimed for her beauty. 'Ah, perhaps I could tell it to you and your lovely queen later over a goblet of your finest wine.'

'Perhaps you could,' King Kiritan said, forcing a thin smile. 'We would like to hear it.'

And with that, he bestowed upon Maram his much-desired medallion and blessing.

Next Kane approached the King. With great reluctance, he uncloaked himself. And then, in a savage and almost disrespectful voice, he gave his name.

'Just "Kane"?' the King asked him as he gazed at him disapprovingly.

'So, just Kane,' Kane growled out. 'Kane of Erathe.'

The King seemed as curious to learn of his homeland as I was, and he asked, 'Erathe? We have never heard of that realm. Where does it lie?'

'Far away,' Kane said. 'It is very far away.'

'In what direction?'

But in answer, Kane only stared at him as his black eyes grew bright with the starlight pouring down through the dome.

'Who is your king, then?' King Kiritan asked him. 'Tell us the name of your lord.'

'No man is my lord,' Kane said. 'Nor do I call any man king.'

The King bit his lip in distaste and then said, 'You're not the first lordless knight to make vows tonight. But you *have* made vows, it seems. And so we will give you our blessing.'

As quickly as he could, the King took the medallion from Queen Daryana and dropped it over Kane's head. He looked away as Kane pressed his finger to the cup at the center of the medallion and stepped over to me.

'It's your turn,' he snarled out. 'Let's get this over and be done.'

It *was* my turn, and some three thousand knights, nobles and ladies were waiting for me to take it. But I sensed in Atara a great unease at so many people watching her. It would be hard to be the last to receive the King's blessing, I thought. And so I leaned my head back and asked if she wanted take my place.

'No, you go first,' she insisted. 'Please.'

'All right,' I said. Then I stepped up to King Kiritan, pulled back my cloak and told him my name: 'Sar Valashu Elahad of Mesh.'

For a moment, King Kiritan's face looked as if it had been slapped in front of the three thousand nobles quietly watching us. Then he recovered his composure; he nodded toward Count Dario as he said, 'We had heard that the son of King Shamesh would make this Quest. But it is a great distance between Silvassu and Tria. We had supposed you had lost your way in coming here.'

'No, King Kiritan,' I said as I glanced at Kane, 'we were delayed.'

'Well, then, we should rejoice that the Valari have sent a prince upon the Quest,' he said joylessly. 'We're honored that Shavashar Elahad sends us his *seventh* son.'

I winced as he said this, and so did Kane. I felt many eyes upon me. Who knew which pair of them had seen the words to the last two lines of Ayondela's prophecy?

'It is good,' King Kiritan continued, 'that a prince of Mesh will seek to put aright the great wrong done by his sires in ages past.'

Great pain the kirax in my blood still caused me, but it seemed slight against the burning I felt there now. King Kiritan knew nothing of my purpose in making the quest. And it was wrong for him to say that the kings of my line had done wrong. Even so, I did not gainsay him. I thought it more seemly to respect the decorum of the moment even if he did not.

'By my sword, by my honor, by my life,' I told him, 'I seek the Lightstone. For all of Ea and not myself.'

'Very good, then,' King Kiritan said looking at me closely. He held out his hand for a medallion, which he placed over my head. It seemed a great weight pressing against my chest. 'Sar Valashu Elahad, accept this with our blessing that you might be known and honored in all lands.'

I bowed and backed away, glad to done with him. Then Atara stepped forward. I was very glad that in only a few more moments, we would be free to leave the hall and set out on the next part of our journey.

'Look, it's the Princess!' I heard someone exclaim as Atara threw back her cloak.

I thought it a strange thing to say. The granddaughter of Sajagax she might be, but I had never heard the chiefs of the Sarni tribes called kings nor those of their lineage called princesses.

Atara, clad in her bloodstained trousers and black leather armor studded with steel, caused the assembled nobles to wag their fingers and begin talking furiously. Other Sarni warriors, similarly attired, had already stood before the King. But they had been men; it seemed that no one present had ever seen a woman warrior, much less one of the Manslayer Society.

She stepped straight up to the King and looked him boldly in the eyes. Then she said, 'Atara Manslayer of the Kurmak.'

The King's ruddy face paled with shock; his lips moved silently as he fought for words. Queen Daryana, too, stared at Atara as did Count Dario and all the other nobles near the throne.

'You,' the King said as he held his trembling hand out to Atara, 'have another name. Say it now so that we may hear it.'

Atara looked at me as if to beg my forgiveness. Then she smiled, drew in a breath and called out: 'Atara Ars Narmada – of Alonia *and* the Wendrush.'

I gasped in astonishment along with a thousand others. How it had come to be that this wild Sarni warrior was also a princess of the Narmada line, I couldn't understand. But that she was King Kiritan's daughter couldn't be denied. I saw it in the set of their square, stubborn faces and in the fire of their diamond-blue eyes; I felt it passing back and forth between them in fierce emotions that tasted both of love and hate.

'It's his daughter,' someone behind me whispered as if explaining Alonian court intrigues to an outsider. 'She's still alive.'

'*Is* she still our daughter?' King Kiritan asked, looking at Atara.

'Of course she is,' Queen Daryana said as she dropped the last medallion back into its chest. She hurried forward past the King and threw her arms around Atara. Not caring who was watching, she kissed her and stroked her long hair with delight. Tears were streaming from her eyes as she laughed out, 'Our brave, beautiful daughter – oh, you *are* still alive!'

King Kiritan stood very straight as he scowled at Atara. 'Six years it's been since you fled our kingdom for lands unknown. Six years! We had thought you dead.'

'I'm sorry, Father.'

'Remember where you are!'

'Excuse me . . . Sire.'

'That's better,' King Kiritan snapped. 'Are we to presume, then, that you've been living with the Kurmak all this time?'

'Yes, Sire.'

'You might have sent word to us that you were well.'

'Yes, I *might* have,' she said.

The King's eyes flicked up and down as he studied Atara's garments. Then he said, 'And now you return to us, on *this* night, in front of our guests, attired as . . . as what? A Sarni warrior? Is this how women dress on the Wendrush?'

Across the room I saw several Sarni warriors, with their drooping blonde mustaches and curious blue eyes, pressing closer.

'Some of them do,' Queen Daryana said. Standing next to her daughter, it was clear to see that they were of the same height and strong cast of body. They were both strong in other ways, too. The Queen seemed as unafraid of her husband as Atara had been of the hill-men. To King Kiritan she said, 'Did you not hear her name herself as a Manslayer?'

'No, we tried *not* to hear that name. What does it mean?'

'It means she is a warrior,' Queen Daryana said simply. Then a great bitterness came into her voice. 'You take little interest in my people beyond seeing that they remain outside your Long Wall.'

'*Your* people,' he reminded the Queen, 'are Alonians and have been for more than twenty years.'

In the heated words that followed, I pieced together the story of Atara's life – and some of the recent history of Alonia. It seemed that early in King Kiritan's reign, to protect his southern borders, he had felt compelled to cement an alliance with the ferocious Kurmak tribe. And so he had sent a great weight of gold to Sajagax in exchange for his daughter Daryana's hand in marriage. The Kurmak had made peace with Alonia, and more, had checked the power of the equally ferocious Marituk tribe who patrolled the Wendrush between the Blue Mountains and the Poru, from the Long Wall as far south as the Blood River. But there had been little peace between King Kiritan and his proud, fierce, headstrong queen. As she would tell anyone who would listen, she had been born free and would not be ruled by any man, not even Ea's greatest king. And so for every command or slight the King gave her, she gave him back words barbed like the points of the Sarni's arrows. It was said that King Kiritan had once dared to strike her face; to repay him, she had cut the scar marking his cheek with her strong, white teeth.

'The King,' she said to Atara, 'has told me that your grandfather and grandmother, and your mother's brothers and sisters and their children – all the warriors and women of the Kurmak – are not *my* people. If he cut out my heart, would he not see that my blood remains as red as theirs? But he is the King, and he has said what he has said. And this on a day when he has invited all the free peoples of Ea into our home to go forth on a great quest as one people. Is this worthy of the great man you love and revere as your Sire?'

It was also said that for many years, King Kiritan had given Daryana coldness in place of love. And so she had given him one daughter only and no sons.

I wondered why Daryana hadn't fled back to the Kurmak as Atara had done. In answer, almost as if she could hear my thoughts, she said, 'Of course some might say that since gold has been paid in dower to my father, that I now belong to him who paid it. A deal is a deal, and can't be broken, yes? But I hadn't heard that the Alonians had entered the business of buying and selling human beings.'

At this, the King flashed her a look of hate as he said, 'No, you're right – that is not our business. And you're also right to say that a deal cannot be broken. Especially one that was agreed upon freely, and as we remember, enthusiastically.'

Queen Daryana's eyes were full of sadness as she looked at Atara and said, 'Choices must always be made; seldom can they be unmade. I might have joined the Manslayers even as you have. But then I wouldn't have lived to bear such a beautiful daughter.'

Atara, who was blinking back tears, bowed her head to her mother and then looked down at the floor.

'Yes, a *daughter*,' the King said as if he had bit into a lemon. 'But how is a king to secure the continuance of his line and the peace of his lands without sons?'

Queen Daryana's eyes were like daggers of ice as she told him, 'It's said that the King doesn't lack sons.'

It was said – I learned this later from the Duke of Raanan – that King Kiritan had multiplied to himself many concubines, if not wives. And many of these had borne him bastard sons, whom he kept hidden in various estates among his domains.

Now the King's face grew as red as heated iron. His hand closed into a fist, and I was afraid he might strike Daryana. The Sarni warriors, I saw, were pulling at their mustaches and smiling at Daryana's defiance of him. Everyone was now watching King Kiritan, who must have felt the shame of their wondering how he could rule a kingdom if he couldn't even rule his own wife and daughter. But it seemed that he could at least rule his wrath. He looked down at his fist as if commanding it to relax and open. Then he turned to Atara and held this open hand toward her.

'It has been said,' he told her, 'that we know little of your grandfather's people. Especially this Society of Manslayers, as you call it. Would you please tell us more?'

This Atara did. Everyone in the hall pressed closer to hear stories of women warriors riding their ponies across the Wendrush and killing their enemies with arrows. By the time Atara told of being left naked in the middle of the steppe with nothing more than a knife to work her survival, and hinted at other fiercer and more secret initiations, the King's lips were white and pressed tightly together.

'A hundred of your enemies,' the King said, shaking his head. He looked at Count Dario and Baron Belur who stood near the throne. 'Few of even my finest knights have slain so many.'

'They haven't been trained by the Manslayers,' Atara said proudly.

The King ignored this slight against Alonian arms, and said, 'Then none of these women may marry until they've reached this number? Are there no exceptions?'

'No, Sire.'

'Not even for one who is also the daughter of the Alonian king?'

'I have made vows,' Atara told him.

'Do your vows then supersede your duty to your Lord?'

'And what duty is that?' Atara asked as she looked at Prince Jardan of the Elyssu. With his curled brown hair, he was a handsome man and a tall one – though the webwork of broken blood vessels on his red nose hinted of weakness and craving for strong drink. 'The duty to be sold in marriage to the highest bidder?'

It was well, I thought, that Atara had fled her home at the young age of sixteen. I saw that she vexed King Kiritan even more than did her mother. Again, his hand closed into a fist as he ground his teeth and his whole body trembled with rage. Because I couldn't allow him to strike her, I readied myself to rush forward and stand between them. But the King's guards saw my concern, and readied themselves to stop me. King Kiritan saw this, too.

'When did the sanctity of marriage come to be so little regarded?' he said to Atara. He cast me a dismissive look, then glowered at Maram and Kane. 'Is it right that you should forsake such a blessed union to take up with a ragtag band of adventurers?'

'Hmmph,' Atara said, 'you may call them that, but my friends are –'

'A bald, old man, a fat lecher, a mercenary and a knight of little name.'

Atara opened her mouth to parry his careless words. But warrior of the Manslayers though she might be, I could not allow her to fight my battles for me. I threw off my cloak then so that the King could see my surcoat and the silver swan and seven stars shining from it.

'My sires were kings, even as yours were, King Kiritan,' I said. 'And *their* sires were kings when the Narmadas were still warlords fighting the Hastars and Kirrilands for the throne.'

Now the hands of Count Dario and Baron Belur snapped toward the hilts of their swords. A dozen other knights grumbled their resentment of what I had said. It was one thing for the King's own wife and daughter to dispute with him, but quite another for an outland warrior to shame him with the truth.

'Sar Valashu Elahad,' the King huffed at me. 'It's said that your line is descended, father and son, from *the* Elahad. Well, it's also said that the Saryaks claim descent from Valoreth himself.'

'Many things are said, King Kiritan. And one of these is that a wise king will be able to tell what is true from what is false.'

'*We* tell you this then. *You* Valari are as prideful as you ever were.' His eyes flicked toward Atara, and he added, 'And as bold.'

'It's boldness that wins battles, is it not?'

'We haven't heard of any notable battles you've won of late,' he said. 'It would seem that you're too busy fighting among yourselves over diamonds.'

'That might be true,' I said bitterly. 'But once we fought for other things.'

'Yes, for a golden cup that does not belong to you.'

'At least the cup was won,' I said, recalling the white stones I had found on the Hill of the Dead the day before. 'At the Sarburn – you will have heard of that battle.'

'Indeed we have,' the King said. 'Eighty-nine Narmada knights fell there that day.'

'Ten *thousand* Valari are buried there!' I said. 'And their graves aren't even marked!'

'That is not right,' the King said with surprising softness. And then a note of bitterness crept back into his voice. 'But you can't blame my people for not wanting to honor outland warriors who invaded their land for plunder.'

'The Valari did not die for plunder,' I said.

'Nevertheless, Aramesh *did* take the Lightstone for his own. Just as he took for himself the crown of Alonia.'

At this, many grumbles of anger rolled through the room.

'He ruled, it is true, but for three years only until the Red Dragon's work was undone and he saw the kingship restored. It's nowhere recorded that he took the crown.'

'What right does any but an Alonian have to rule Alonia?'

'Some might say that if he hadn't ruled,' I said, looking around the hall and up at Kiritan's jewel-encrusted throne, 'there would have been nothing left for your sires to have ruled.'

'What was left of the Alonians' great sacrifice at the Sarburn,' King Kiritan asked, 'after Aramesh took the Lightstone back to Mesh and kept it behind his mountains?'

'He did *not* keep it for himself,' I said. 'He invited all to come and behold it. And in the end, Julumesh surrendered the cup to Godavanni, even as you have told of here tonight.'

'We have told of how the cup was lost. By Valari selfishness and pride.'

'The cup *was* lost,' I said. 'Which is why some of us have vowed to regain it.'

'We do not see many Valari here tonight,' the King said, looking out at the masses of people packed into the hall. 'And why is that?'

Because our hearts have been broken, I thought.

The King, answering his own question, said, 'Your land is long past its time of greatness. Now you Valari care for little more than your diamonds and your little wars. It's almost savage the way you glorify it: every man a warrior; your duels; meditating over your swords as if they were your souls. No, we're afraid that the Valari's day is done.'

Because I had nothing to say to this, I stared up through the dome at the stars. Then Atara touched my shoulder, and we looked at each other in a sudden, new understanding.

'Well, what's this, then?' the King said, glaring at us.

But neither Atara nor I answered him; we just stood there before three thousand people looking into each other's eyes.

'*You*,' the King said to Atara, 'will remain here now that you've returned.'

'But, Sire,' Atara said, turning toward him, 'I've made vows to seek the Lightstone. Would you have me break them?'

'You'll do your seeking in Alonia, then.'

Atara looked at me as she sadly shook her head. Then, to her father, she said, 'No, I'll go on the Quest with Val, if he'll have me.'

'If he'll *have* you!' the King thundered. 'Who is he to take you anywhere? To take you off to oblivion or death?'

'He has saved my life, Sire. Twice.'

'And who has given you life?' the King shouted. Quick as a cat, he turned to me and pointed his finger at my chest. 'Tell us the truth about what you want of our daughter!'

The first thing a Valari warrior is taught is always to tell the truth. And so I looked at King Kiritan and told him what my heart cried out, even though I had never said the words to anyone, not even myself: 'To marry Atara.'

For a moment, King Kiritan didn't move. It seemed that no one in the hall dared breathe. And then he shouted, 'Marry *our* daughter?'

'If she'll have me,' I said, smiling. 'And with your blessing.'

King Kiritan laughed at me then: a series of harsh, cutting sounds

311

that issued from his throat almost like the barking of a dog. Then his face purpled and he began raging at me: 'Who are *you* to marry her? An adventurer who hides himself in a dirty cloak? A seventh son who has no hope of ever becoming a king? And a king of what? A savage little kingdom no bigger than many of my barons' domains! You think to marry *our* daughter?'

In that moment, as King Kiritan's outraged voice thundered from the stone walls of his hall, I pitied him. For I saw that he resented having had to marry beneath himself, as he surely thought of his union with Daryana. And now he hoped to ennoble his line more deeply by marrying Atara to the crown prince of Eanna or possibly Prince Jardan of the Elyssu. Even Maram, I supposed, as a prince of the strategically important Delu, would have been considered a more suitable match than I if not for his lustful ways and friendship with me.

I saw another thing, too: that the King, unlike lesser men, was not at the mercy of his terrible rages. Rather, he summoned them from some deep well inside him like a conjuror, and more, wielded his wrath precisely as he might a sword to terrify anyone who stood against him. But I had lived with swords all my life. And I had one of my own.

'I love Atara,' I said to him. My eyes were now wide open, and much else as well. 'Will you bless our marriage, King Kiritan?'

In answer, he laughed at me again. And then, as his eyes filled with malice, in a mocking voice, he said, 'Yes, you may marry our daughter – when you've found the Lightstone and have delivered it here to this room!'

I was sure he expected me to cringe like a beaten dog or perhaps protest that the Cup of Heaven might be found only by the One's grace. Instead, I grasped the hilt of my sword and rashly told him, 'This I vow then.'

While he stared at me in disbelief, I took Atara's hand and kissed it. I told him, 'If you won't yet bless our marriage, then will you at least give Atara your blessing as you have everyone else so that we may set out on the Quest?'

'You dare too much, Valari!' he snapped at me. 'Should we then give her our own dagger so that she can stab us in the back?'

'Please, King Kiritan – give her your blessing.'

From somewhere to our side, a woman called out, 'Your blessing, King Kiritan!' Others picked up this cry so the hall rang with the sound of many voices, 'Give her your blessing!'

But the King was the King, and would not be so easily swayed. He stood before his jeweled throne, above the last chest of medallions, staring at both Atara and me as if we were rebellious barons who had dared enter his own hall to defy him.

How is it that we set out with so much love for our fathers, daughters or brothers, ready to make great sacrifices or even die for them – only to see this most sacred gift transmuted by an evil alchemy so that we caused them the greatest hurt and brought them its opposite instead?

As I stood there holding Atara's hand, I felt both her anguish and adoration for her father surging through her. It was strange, the sense I had that I could touch King Kiritan with either of these. In my dream, Morjin had told me that I would one day strike out at others with the black dagger of my hate; it hadn't occurred to me that I might also thrust the bright sword of another's love straight into their hearts.

'Don't look at me that way, Valari,' King Kiritan whispered to me. 'Damn your eyes – don't look at me!'

But I couldn't help looking at him. And he couldn't help turning toward Atara as a great tenderness softened his face. Few were close enough to see the tears welling in his eyes. And only Atara and Daryana – and I – could feel the great love pouring out of him.

'We were afraid you were dead,' he said to Atara.

'There have been many who tried to make me so,' Atara told him. 'But as you always said, Sire, we Narmadas are hard to kill.'

'Yes we are,' he said with a grateful smile. 'And by the grace of the One, as we set out on this Quest, may we continue to be.'

So saying, he nodded at Daryana, who reached into the chest to hand him a medallion. With a gentleness few would have suspected he possessed, he placed this over Atara's head and told her, 'Atara Ars Narmada, accept this with our blessing that you might be known and honored in all lands.'

To the cheers of almost everyone in the hall, he clasped her to him, kissed her fiercely on the forehead and stood there weeping softly. But it took him only a few moments to compose himself and put the steel back into his countenance. And the anger, too. He glared at me darkly as he called out to the knights and nobles around us: 'All who have wished have made their vows and have received our blessing. Now please join us outside that you might help us celebrate this great occasion and our birthday as well.'

And then, with a last, cutting glance at me, he turned and stormed from the hall.

313

19

For some time after that, I stood off to the side of the throne with Atara. Still stunned by what had just happened, all I could think to ask her was, 'Why didn't you tell me who you really were?'

'That's just it,' she said sadly. 'Atara Ars Narmada is who I *was*. But now I am Atara Manslayer.'

'Is that the only reason, then?'

'No – I was afraid that if you knew, you'd look at me differently. As I'm afraid you're looking at me now.'

'Please don't mistake my astonishment for anything else,' I told her. 'There's only one way I could ever see you. I *know* who you are.'

As my heart measured out the moments of my life in great, surging beats, I looked for that deep light in her eyes and found it. For a single, brilliant moment, we returned to our star. Then I smiled at her and said, 'It *is* astonishing what passed with your father. My apologies if what was said caused you embarrassment.'

'Please don't mistake *my* astonishment for anything else,' she said, returning my smile. 'But perhaps you should have asked me first if I would marry you.'

'Will you, Atara?'

'No, I won't,' she said sadly. 'I've made my vows, and I must keep them.'

'But if someday you fulfill them, then –'

'This is not the time for *anyone* to marry,' she said. 'Should I bear your children only to see them slain in the wars that must surely come?'

'But if the Lightstone were found and the Red Dragon defeated, war itself brought to an end, then –'

'Then it would be then,' she said, smiling at me. 'Then you may ask me about marriage – if that is still what you desire.'

She squeezed my hand, and turned toward Master Juwain, Maram and Kane, who were fighting the throngs streaming toward the doors.

They came up to us, their gold medallions showing beneath their cloaks.

'This is a kingly gift,' Maram said, cupping his hand beneath his medallion. 'I never thought to be given anything so magnificent.'

'And I never thought to hear you vow to seek the Lightstone,' Master Juwain told him. 'But you seem to have a fondness for making vows.'

'Ah, I do, don't I?' Maram said.

'I seem to remember you were to forsake wine, women and war.'

'Well, I suppose I'm not very good at forsaking, am I? And that's just the point, isn't it? I *won't* forsake this Quest.'

Maram's sudden earnestness made me smile. I clapped him on the shoulder and said, 'But why make vows at all? Didn't you set out only so far as to see Tria?'

'True, true,' he said. 'And I *have* seen Tria. And a great deal else.'

'We've vowed to seek the Lightstone until it is found,' I reminded him. 'We can't do very much of that seeking in taverns or boudoirs.'

'No, perhaps we can't, my friend. But maybe we'll find a few glasses of beer along our way.' Here he paused to eye a beautiful Alonian woman dressed in a blue satin gown. 'And perhaps great treasures as well.'

'We also vowed to go on seeking unless we're struck down first.'

'Ah, I *am* mad, aren't I?' he muttered as he shook his head and turned back toward me. 'But someone is bound to find this cup, and it might as well be us. Do you think I'd let you have all the fun yourself?'

With a brave smile, he clapped me on my shoulder. Then I nodded at Master Juwain and asked him, 'But what about you, sir? Didn't you come to Tria to verify the truth of the prophecy?'

'I did,' he said, 'but Kane has already verified it as much as these things can be. I'm afraid I must tell you, though, that my true business was always the finding of the Lightstone.'

We stood there wondering what to do next. All our plans and efforts had been directed toward bringing us to King Kiritan's palace by the seventh of Soldru; by the slimmest of chances (and more than one miracle), we had succeeded. But there were four points to the world, and five of us, and all directions beckoned with the gleam of gold upon the horizon.

'I'm too hungry to think about the Quest just now,' Maram said as he watched the last of the nobles leaving the hall. 'It's the King's birthday – why don't we help him celebrate it?'

'I think the King has seen enough of us for one night, eh?' Kane said. 'Others have seen us, too. So, we should find a quiet inn where we can sleep safely tonight.'

Kane's was the voice of prudence, and perhaps we should have heeded

315

it. But before leaving the palace, Master Juwain wanted to use the King's library, said to be one of the finest in the city. Atara wished to talk with her mother. As for me, now that I had already called attention to myself, I didn't want to have to slink away like a whipped dog.

'We've come this far through much worse,' I said. 'If King Kiritan has gone to so much trouble to honor us, then we should accept his hospitality.'

I led the way out of the north door of the hall. There we found a broad corridor giving out onto a vast lawn. The King's thousands of guests easily might have become lost upon it if not directed by a line of torches toward a long pool where many tables had been set with food. Against the backdrop of great, spraying fountains lit up with glowstones, these tables fairly groaned beneath the weight of mutton joints, beef roasts and whole roasted pigs. There were fowls and cheeses and breads, too, pastries and fruits, and many vegetables: buttered lentils with scallions, baked potatoes, asparagus drowning in a sauce made from lemons and eggs – and strange-looking roots called yams that were said to be grown in the Elyssu. This being Tria, the King's cooks had also set before us braised salmon, smoked herring and huge, insect-like shellfish called lobsters. I couldn't believe that human beings could eat such things, but the Trians seemed to relish and regard them as a delicacy. The nobles, I thought, were used to feasting on delicacies, and to drinking the finest wines, as well. These were set out in bottles on marble tables around the fountains. The best vintages, it was said, came from Galda before it had fallen and from the vineyards of Karabuk. Although the Alonians were forbidden to trade with this kingdom directly, cargoes of wine – and spices such as pepper, cloves and cinnamon – had somehow found their way into the holds of ships sailing up the coasts of Galda and Delu and then through the Dolphin Channel into Tria.

It was a clear, beautiful night, with a full moon and many stars. The city spread out in all directions below us. Little lights like those of fireflies flickered from the many houses and buildings. Some areas were dark, such as the Narmada Green, a two-mile long expanse of woods just to the west of the palace grounds. There the King rode to take his exercise and to hunt the few boar and deer that still remained there. To the south, the great Tower of the Sun stood like a silver needle between the Hastar and Marshan palaces, while to the north, arising from Narmada Hill and Eriades Hill, were the Tower of the Moon and the Tower of the Western Sun. East of the palace, on terraces cut into the lower slopes of the hill on which it was built, the Elu Gardens seemed almost suspended in space below us. In the bright light of the moon, I could still make out its many acres of lawns, flower beds and

316

well-tended trees. It formed a great barrier between the palace and the populous districts below it. A little farther to the east, the great, golden Star Bridge – now almost silver in the moonlight – spanned the Poru River and drew the eye out toward the harbor and the gleaming sea to the north.

Following Maram's lead, we all filled our plates with mounds of food, and found an empty table near some lilac bushes where we could take our meal in peace. But peace we could not have, for even as we finished eating and stood around the table drinking wine, various men and women began coming up to us and presenting themselves. The first of these I was very glad to see for he was a Valari knight whom I knew from my childhood: Sar Yarwan Solaru of Kaash, King Talanu's third son and my first cousin by my mother, who was sister to the King. Sar Yarwan, a striking man with a great, hawk's nose, clasped hands with me warmly, and then told me the names of the six other knights who accompanied him. These were Sar Manthanu of Athar, Sar Tadru of Lagash, Sar Danashu of Taron, Sar Laisu, also of Kaash, Sar Ianar of Rajak and Sar Avador of Daksh. These last two knights were the sons of Duke Rezu and Duke Gorador; I admitted to them that I had met their fathers on our passage through Anjo and that I had been told to look for them in Tria. Sar Ianar, who had his father's sharp features and sharpness of eye, looked at some Alonians milling about a nearby table and said, 'Sar Valashu Elahad, it's good to see another Valari here – so few of us made the journey.'

Sar Yarwan rested his hand on my shoulder and said, 'We all appreciate what you said to the King.'

'The truth is the truth and must be told,' I said.

'Nevertheless, it takes courage to tell it – especially when few wish to listen.' He bowed his head to me and continued, 'We didn't know you would be coming to Tria. It's too bad you arrived so late.'

Although he was my cousin, I didn't tell him about the Grays and that we'd had to fight for our lives to arrive at all.

'We would have asked you to join our company,' he said to me. His bright eyes seemed to be searching for something in mine. 'We would *still* ask you. There are seven of us, and that is good luck and accords with the prophecy. But we're all agreed that it would be even better luck to have you with us.'

'You honor me,' I said. Then I nodded at Kane, Maram, Atara and Master Juwain. 'But as you can see, we've already formed our own company.'

I presented my friends, who each bowed in turn to the Valari knights.

'Five is too few to make a company,' Sar Yarwan said. And then in that blunt, outspoken manner of too many of my people, he went on, 'Kane almost looks Valari, and he would be a welcome addition, too. And Atara Ars Narmada – Atara Manslayer. If any warriors are almost the equal of the Valari, it would be the Manslayers of the Sarni. But as for your other friends, well, we're a company of *knights*. Surely they could find other companions who shared their sensibilities and skills.'

Sar Yarwan's artless words seemed not to perturb Master Juwain in the slightest. But Maram stood there biting on his mustache and blushing. For once, he was speechless. And so I spoke for him instead, saying, 'Thank you, Sar Yarwan – we would certainly welcome your company, to say nothing of your swords. But we journeyed here together, and we'll journey from here together as well.'

'As you wish, Sar Valashu,' he said. He glanced at his companions again and nodded at me. '*We* wish all of you well, wherever your journeys take you. May you always walk in the light of the One.'

I said the same to him, and Atara did, too. Then she looked over towards one of the fountains and her face brightened. I turned to see Queen Daryana walking toward us accompanied by a large knight bearing the crest of two oaks and two eagles on his green tunic.

'Mother,' Atara said as she greeted the Queen, 'may I present Sar Valashu Elahad? I was hoping you might be able meet him in less difficult circumstances.'

I bowed to Queen Daryana, who smiled at me before glancing at the fountain where the King stood talking with two of his dukes. Then she said to me, 'It seems that all circumstances will be difficult so long as you remain in Tria.'

And with that, she motioned toward the knight standing next to her; with a wry smile, she said to me, 'This is Baron Narcavage of Arngin. The King has sent him with me to make sure that you don't attack me.'

I nodded my head slightly to this great Baron, who reluctantly returned the bow. He had a deep chest and great arms, and his large head was sunk down into a thick neck swollen with muscle or fat – it was hard to tell which on account of his thick, blond beard. His little blue eyes seemed the only small thing about him; they were almost lost beneath his overhanging forehead and bushy eyebrows. But they peered out at me with a sharp intelligence all the same. There was cunning and resentment there – and the wit to hide them as well.

'Sar Valashu Elahad,' he said to me, 'the King sends his regrets that he is too busy to further make your acquaintance. But he has also sent his finest wine to thank you for honoring him tonight.'

So saying, he showed everyone a large green bottle that he had held in

318

the crook of his arm. 'This comes from the Kinderry vineyards of Galda. May I pour you a glass?'

'Perhaps in a moment,' I said. 'We haven't finished making the presentations.'

I told the Queen the names of my friends, then presented Sar Yarwan and the Valari knights. She cast them, and me, a wary look. We were Valari, after all, and she was still the daughter of a Sarni chieftain.

As the moon rose higher over the cool lawns and bubbling fountains, we stood talking about the quest. Sar Yarwan announced his plan to journey to Skule in the wilds of northern Delu. He would search among the ruins of that once great city for any sign that Sartan Odinan might have brought the Lightstone there.

'Skule lies on the other side of the Straights of Storm,' Baron Narcavage said to him. 'If you'll be crossing them from Alonia, you'll have to pass through Arngin. Which you may do with my blessing.'

'Thank you, that would be the most direct route,' Sar Yarwan agreed.

'And the safest – to go back down the Nar Road and skirt along the Alonian Sea would take many months. You'd have to cross through most of Delu, which is now nothing more than a dozen savage provinces practically ruled by their warlords.'

'No, you're wrong about Delu,' a strong voice called out. Here Maram stepped forward and looked Baron Narcavage in the eye. 'Delu is certainly much more than you have said.'

'Forgive me, Prince Maram,' the Baron said, 'but I've journeyed through what is left of your father's kingdom while you've been off learning your dead languages at the Brotherhood's school.'

'Delu has its troubles,' Maram admitted. 'But it wasn't so long ago that Alonia had worse.'

To cool their rising tempers, I came between them and said, 'We live in a time of troubles.'

'We do indeed,' Baron Narcavage said, smiling at me. 'We've all heard that we can expect war between Ishka and Mesh.'

'That hasn't been decided yet,' I told him. 'We can still hope for peace.'

'How can there ever be peace in the Nine Kingdoms when each of your so-called kings insists on coveting his neighbors' lands?'

'What do mean, "so-called"?'

'Is the King of Anjo truly a king? Or Anjo a kingdom? And what of Mesh? My own domain is bigger than your entire realm.'

Now I felt my temper rising, too, and Maram gripped my arm to steady me. To Baron Narcavage, he said, 'That might be true, but at least his, ah, *sword* is longer than yours.'

319

Being well-pleased with his riposte, Maram grinned broadly and then winked at Queen Daryana.

Baron Narcavage shot him a dark look and then said, 'Yes, the famed Valari swords – used mostly to cut each other to pieces.'

I wondered at the Baron's purpose in belittling Maram's and my kingdoms. Perhaps it was pride in Alonian accomplishments; perhaps it was resentment. From talk I had heard in the hall, I gathered that the Baron's grandfather had fought fiercely with King Kiritan's grandfather to keep Arngin an independent domain. But in the end, he had knelt to King Sakandar even as Baron Narcavage kneeled to King Kiritan. It was said that Baron Narcavage was now the most trusted of the King's men and his greatest general. If so, then he must have harbored deep hurts that he chose to inflict on other people.

Queen Daryana seemed to like neither the Baron nor his usurping the conversation. To distract us all from squabbles almost as old as time – and to reclaim for herself the center of everyone's attention – she said, 'We live in a time of swords, and it's said that the Valari *do* have long ones. But this is a night of peace. Celebration and song. Who knows the *Song of the Swan*? Who will sing it with me?'

As I touched the silver swan embroidered on my tunic, she smiled at me, and I loved her for that. Her warmth and generosity of spirit moved me: this, after all, was Sajagax's daughter, who couldn't want me ever to marry Atara. But she chose to let our natural regard for each other shine forth even so.

Atara and I both drew close to her as we all started singing the song. It was mostly a sad song, telling of a king who falls in love with a great white swan. To gain her love in return, he builds a magnificent castle in which to keep her, and feeds her delicacies even as he dresses her in the finest silks. But the swan soon sickens and starts singing her death song. The grief-stricken king then goes among the people of his realm offering a great measure of gold to anyone who can tell him the answer to the riddle of how he may heal her without letting her go.

As we worked through the verses, Maram and the Valari knights joined us, and then other knights and their ladies came over and began singing, too. One of the women caught my eye: she had iron-gray hair and a pretty, pleasant face, and around her neck she wore the same gold medallion as did Atara and I. I remembered her earlier giving her name to King Kiritan as Liljana Ashvaran; she was one of the few Alonian woman to have vowed to make the quest. Although obviously no knight, she had an air of courage about her. She pressed in closer toward Queen Daryana, all the while singing with a measured assurance. When she thought I wasn't looking, she stole quick glances at me. Once, for a moment, we locked gazes, and I thought that her penetrating hazel eyes hid a great deal.

We stood there singing beneath the moon and stars for quite a while, for the song was a long one. When we reached the part of it where the king asks his people for advice, I took note of a new voice added to the chorus. Although in no way overpowering any other, it distinguished itself in subtle harmonies with its clarity and perfection of pitch. It came from a slender man whose black, curly hair gleamed in the light of the glowstones. He had the large brown eyes and the brown skin of a Galdan, those comeliest of people; his fine features seemed in perfect accord with the great beauty of his voice. His age was perhaps thirty or slightly more: the only lines I could make out on his face were the crow's-feet around his eyes – I guessed from smiling so much. He struck me as being spontaneous, witty, gifted, guileless and wild, and I liked him immediately.

I cocked my head, listening as we sang out the words to the king's terrible dilemma:

> *How do you capture a beautiful bird*
> *without killing its spirit?*

And then the answer came, from this man's perfectly formed lips and those of many others:

> *By letting it fly;*
> *By becoming the sky.*

The song ended happily with the king tearing down the walls of stone that he had built to imprison his beloved swan – and himself. For he realized that his true realm was not some little patch of earth, but of the heart and spirit, and was as vast as the sky itself.

The Queen took note of this man, too. When we had finished singing she called him over to her. He gave his name as Alphanderry of Galda. Although no noble, with his silk tunic trimmed in gold and elegance of carriage he managed to look more distinguished than any of the princes there. He was a minstrel, he said, exiled because his songs had offended Galda's new rulers. At the Queen's request, he lifted up his mandolet and sang one of these for us.

No bird, I thought, not even a swan, had a voice so beautiful as his. It spread out across the lawn and seemed to touch even the grasses with dewdrops of light. As we all grew quiet, it was much easier to appreciate its power and grace. His words were beautiful, too, and they told of the anguish of love and the eternal yearning for the Beloved. As with the *Song of the Swan*, its themes were bondage and the freedom that might be attained through the purest of love. Like the ringing of a perfect golden bell, his verses carried out in the night – so sweet and clear and full of longing that they were both a pain and a pleasure to hear.

And as he made his music, Flick suddenly appeared above him and whirled around and around like a tiny dancer raimented in pure light. Alphanderry, I thought, couldn't see him, nor could any of the nobles gathering around him. But I felt Maram's hand squeeze my shoulder as Atara flashed me a look of relief almost as sweet as Alphanderry's singing.

At the end of his song, he lowered his mandolet and smiled sadly. I, like everyone else, was filled with a sense that he had been singing just for me. We looked at each other for a moment, and he seemed to know how deeply his music had touched me. But there was no pride or vanity in him at this accomplishment, only a quiet joy that he had been gifted with the voice of the angels.

'That was lovely,' Queen Daryana said to him as she wiped the tears from her eyes. 'Galda's loss is Alonia's gain. And Ea's, as well.'

Alphanderry bowed to her, then gripped the gold medallion that King Kiritan had given him. Now his smile was happy and bright; like a butterfly among flowers, he seemed able to flit easily from one color of emotion to another.

'Thank you, Queen Daryana,' he told her. 'I haven't had the privilege of singing before such an appreciative audience for a long time.'

Baron Narcavage stepped forward and raised the wine bottle that he still held. He said, 'Allow us then to show our appreciation with some of this. I think you'll like the vintage – it's Galdan, from the King's special reserve. I was just about to pour Sar Valashu and the Queen a glass.'

So saying, he motioned to a groom, who brought over a tray of goblets. The Baron uncorked the wine, then poured the dark red liquid into eight of them. He handed the goblets one by one to me and my friends, and to Alphanderry and the Queen. The last one he took for himself. I thought it rude of him to ignore Sar Yarwan and the Valari knights – and everyone else who gathered around looking at us. Liljana Ashvaran seemed especially watchful of this little ceremony. She stood with her little nostrils sniffing the air as if any wine not offered to her must be sour.

'To the King,' the Baron called out. 'May his life be a long one. May we honor him in drinking his health as he has honored us in requesting our presence at his fiftieth birthday and the calling of the Quest.'

He nodded at the King, who was still talking with his dukes near the fountain while a dozen of his guards kept watch nearby. Kane, who stood a few yards from me scowling at his goblet, turned to scowl at the King instead. Then I gripped my goblet tightly in my hand as I looked down into the blood-red wine.

'It's not poison, Sar Valashu,' the Baron said to me. 'Do you think the King would poison you in front of his guests?'

I looked into the wine, which smelled of cinnamon and flowers and the strange spices of Galda. I could almost taste its fragrant sweetness.

'Do you think *I* would drink poison wine?' he said. Then he put the rim of the golden goblet to his thick lips and took a long drink. 'Come now, Sar Valashu, drink with me. All of you – drink!'

I sensed in him no intention to harm me, only a sudden exuberance and desire to win my good regard – most likely to atone for his previous unkindness. And that, I thought, was a noble thing indeed. Kane and my friends were watching to see what I would do. The Queen and Alphanderry, and Liljana Ashvaran – everyone was watching and waiting for me to take a drink of the King's wine.

Just as I was lifting the goblet to my lips, however, Liljana suddenly rushed toward me, crying out, 'No, it *is* poison – don't drink it!'

The certainty in her voice shocked me; I whirled around toward her to see if she might have fallen mad. Many things happened then almost in the same moment. Baron Narcavage, standing to the other side of me, looked toward King Kiritan and cried out, 'To me!' He drew a long dagger and lunged at my throat even as Liljana knocked the goblet from my hand. Alphanderry, who was nearer to me than any of my friends, suddenly jumped between me and the Baron. He grabbed at the Baron's knife arm with both hands and stood locked in a desperate struggle with him. If not for his inexplicable courage, the knife would surely have torn open my throat.

For that was surely the Baron's true intention. I saw it clearly now in the way his face fell into a fury of hate as he clubbed Alphanderry's head with his other hand, ripped free his knife and lunged at me again. Now, however, Liljana was close enough to grab his arm. She held onto it with all the tenacity of a hound, even as he cursed at her, beat at her with his other arm and knocked her about. Then I struck out with my fist straight into his bearded face. I felt my knuckles almost break against his thick jawbone. But he seemed invulnerable to pain and possessed of an insane strength. He shook his knife arm free and aimed another lunge toward my throat. He would have killed me if Kane hadn't come up then and run him through with his sword.

The Baron fell dead to the grass. Alphanderry stood dazed, shaking his bleeding head. From the trees planted across the palace grounds, the nightingales sang their songs.

Then I became aware of a great clamor toward the fountains. Spears clashed against shields; swords crossed with swords, and the sound of outraged steel rang out to a great chorus of curses and shouts. Knights and ladies were running away in great numbers, even as the King's guards fell upon one another. At first, I thought they had fallen mad. And then I saw the King slash his sword toward one of his dukes while five of his guards fought fiercely to protect him from the others. They were trying to kill the King, I realized. And other men – all with badges bearing the oaks and eagles of House Narcavage – were running toward us to kill the Queen.

Or so I thought, for it didn't occur to me that they might be coming to kill me. There were nearly thirty of these knights; they appeared out of the throngs of panicked people like vultures from the clouds. Their swords were drawn and gleaming in the moonlight. 'To me!' the Baron had called out, and now I understood to whom he had been calling. His men must have seen him fall, for their faces were masks of determination and hate as they came at us.

Queen Daryana cried out as she saw her husband fighting for his life and positioned herself near Alphanderry for the protection he offered, as did Liljana and Master Juwain. The rest of us stared at our attackers as we decided what to do.

We had no one to lead us, or rather too many: Sar Yarwan, Sar Ianar and the other five Valari knights – and Kane, Maram, Atara and myself. The leading of others into battle, my father once told me, is a strange thing. It depends not so much on rank or authority, but rather on the courage to see what must be done and the mysterious ability to communicate one's faith that victory is not only possible but inevitable. For only a moment, we stood there confused by the violence that Baron Narcavage had unleashed. And then I looked at the two diamonds shining like stars from my ring. A light flashed in my eyes, and in my heart, and I suddenly called out: 'Form a circle! Protect the Queen!'

For another moment, my command hung in the air. And then, as on the drill field, Sar Yarwan and the other Valari knights formed up into a circle around Queen Daryana. Savages the King had called us, and savages we were: savages whose swords were our souls, and we called kalamas.

We drew them now just in time to meet the attack of Baron Narcavage's men. Kane stood to my right, and Atara and Maram to my left – all of us facing outward. Sar Yarwan guarded the point of the circle directly across and in back of me. We were only eleven against some thirty knights. And yet when our swords were done flashing and stabbing and rending flesh, all of them lay dead or dying in the grass.

As I stood gasping for breath, I realized that the Baron's knights had not attacked us at random. A good number of them had come directly at me. And there, within a few yards of me and Kane's bloody sword, they sprawled in twisted heaps. I was almost certain that I had slain four of them myself. Their death agonies built inside me like great, cresting waves. But strangely, they never quite broke upon me and crushed me down into the icy dark. Perhaps it was because I remembered how Master Juwain and my friends had healed me after the battle with the Grays; perhaps I was able to open myself to the life fires blazing through Kane and Atara and everyone around me. Or perhaps I was only learning to keep closed the door to death and others' sufferings.

Even so, the great pain of it drove me to my knees and then caused me to collapse, moaning. Queen Daryana must have thought the Baron's men had run me through, for she suddenly called out, 'Over here! A man is wounded!'

For a moment, I couldn't imagine to whom she might be calling. Then, through the cold clouds of death touching my eyes, I saw a great number of the King's guards running toward us. I was afraid that they, too, were traitors come to kill the Queen; even if they weren't, I was afraid that Kane and the Valari knights would see them as such and begin the battle anew. But then the Queen cried out that my friends and I had saved her life. She called for everyone to put aside their swords, and this they did.

For what seemed an eternity, confusion reigned across the blood-spattered lawns of the palace grounds. Trumpets sounded while horses thundered across the grass some distance away. I heard women wailing and men screaming that the King had been killed. Then Queen Daryana took charge, calling out commands with a coolness that stilled the panic in the air. She deployed guards to see that the palace gates were closed to prevent any of the plotters from slipping away. Other guards she sent to hunt down any of the Baron's men who might be hiding around the palace. She ordered that the bodies of the slain be taken away and their blood washed with buckets of water into the earth. And she sent messengers to call up many new guards from the garrison that manned the city walls.

Word soon came that the King had only been wounded and borne away into the palace. He had called for Queen Daryana to come to his side.

'Your father isn't badly wounded,' Queen Daryana said to Atara. 'But it seems that your Valari knight might be. Please stay with him until I return.'

As Atara nodded her head, the Queen gathered up five guards and hurried off toward the palace.

Other guards drew up in a protective wall around us. King Kiritan's thousands of guests still milled about the fountains; despite their panic over Baron Narcavage's plot, they had nowhere to flee. But it seemed that most of the Baron's knights had died in attacking our circle. As for the traitorous guards, they had all been killed, too – or so it was hoped.

While the Valari knights gathered some yards away, Alphanderry and Liljana drew in closer above me. They watched Kane, Atara, Maram and Master Juwain kneel in a circle by my side. My friends removed my armor, as they had in the woods near the meadow where we had killed the Grays, and laid their hands upon me. So great was the power of their touch that I immediately felt a familiar fire warming me inside. Then Master Juwain drew out his green crystal and placed it over my chest. He and the others positioned their bodies to shield the sight of this healing from the guards and others looking on.

Very soon, I was able to stand up and move about again. In a low voice, Master Juwain marveled that he had hardly needed his green crystal to help revive me.

'Thank you, sir,' I said to him as I put on my armor again. I nodded to each of my friends. 'Thank you, all of you.'

I noticed Alphanderry looking at me curiously as if wondering why I had needed my friends' ministrations at all. He smiled at me in great relief, and my eyes asked him why he had risked his life for me as if he were my brother.

Because, his soft brown eyes answered me, *all men are brothers*.

Master Juwain's order, of course, taught this ideal of a higher love for all beings, even strangers. But Alphanderry's selfless act was the first time I had seen it embodied so unrestrainedly.

'Thank you,' I said to him. Then I turned to Liljana Ashvaran, whose courage had been no less than his. 'Thank you, too.'

Liljana bowed her head to me and smiled. Then she pointed at Master Juwain's pocket, where he had returned his green gelstei. In a voice pitched soft and low so that none of the guards or other onlookers might hear, she said, 'I think you have one of the stones told of in the prophecy.'

'What do you know of *that*?' Kane said sharply. He took a step closer to her; I was afraid he was about to draw his dagger and hold it to her throat. 'How did you know the wine was poisoned?'

Liljana folded her hands together as she stood there considering her answer. Her round face, I thought, was given to sternness as easily as kindness, and she seemed a thoughtful, unhurried and even relentless woman. She looked at Kane with her wise old eyes, and told him, 'I smelled it.'

'You *smelled* it?' he said. 'You must have the nose of a hound.'

'It was poisoned with wenrock,' she said. 'Its scent is almost like that of poppy. I've been trained to detect such things.'

'Trained by whom?'

'By my mother and grandmother,' she said. 'They were master tasters to King Kiritan's father and grandfather.'

'Then are you King Kiritan's taster?'

'Not any more,' she said. 'You see, I disobeyed him.'

As trumpets sounded and new guards took their places about the lawns, she told us a little of her past. Having studied very hard with her mother and grandmother, as a young woman she had entered King Kiritan's service in the very year he had ascended the throne. So devoted had she been to protecting him that she had forsaken marriage, as King Kiritan had demanded of her. But in the eighth year of her service, she had fallen in love with Count Kinnan Marshan and had married him against the King's wishes.

'He banished me from his court just before you were born,' Liljana said to Atara. 'He told me that love would cloud my senses and leave me unable to protect his family from his enemies. But I told him that love was like an elixir that *sharpened* all the senses. Unfortunately, he never believed me.'

And so Liljana had lived many unhappy years in the Count's house. Her three children had each died in infancy, while her husband had been called away almost constantly to fight in the King's many wars. One of these had ruined his leg while another had crippled his manhood. He had died soon after this, leaving Liljana a widow.

'When King Kiritan called the quest,' she said, 'I decided it was time for me to leave Tria and all its plots and poisons behind me.'

As she turned into the light of the moon, the medallion that she wore glowed with a soft golden light. And all the while, Kane's black eyes bored into her as if drilling for the truth.

'What *I* don't understand,' Maram said, stroking his beard, 'is why Baron Narcavage was willing to drink the wine if it was poisoned?'

'That should be clear enough,' Kane snapped. He nodded at Liljana and said, 'Tell him.'

Liljana nodded back at him, then explained, 'Certain men and women who use poisons such as wenrock take minute quantities of it over a period of years to build an invulnerability to it.'

'And who are these men and women?' Kane demanded.

327

'They're priests of the Kallimun,' Liljana said. 'The Kallimun uses such poisons.'

At the mention of this dreadful name, Alphanderry shuddered and said, 'Before Galda fell to the Kallimun, they poisoned many. And crucified many more. My friends. My brother.'

Kane seemed to forget himself for a moment, and laid his hand gently upon Alphanderry's head. 'So, the Baron was certainly Kallimun.'

'A priest, then?' I said. 'But when he served the wine, I was sure he wanted to celebrate with me.'

'The priests hide well, don't they? Especially beneath their own emotions. Celebrate, ha! He wanted to celebrate your death.'

As if troubled by his own tenderness, Kane suddenly snapped his hand away from Alphanderry's head and stared at me.

'And now,' I said to him, 'you celebrate his.'

'That I do,' Kane said savagely. He looked about the grass where only a short while before the bodies of Baron Narcavage and his men had lain. 'The Baron's plot must have been hastily planned – even so it nearly succeeded.'

'But were they plotting to kill the King and Queen or me?'

'Both,' he said. 'It's obvious that your death was to be the signal to attack them.'

He went on to say that all the Baron's men obviously belonged to the Kallimun, as did some of King Kiritan's guards.

'In Galda,' Alphanderry said, 'there were many such plots before the King was brought down.'

He rubbed the side of his head where Baron Narcavage had bludgeoned him with his fist. He looked at me and asked, 'But why would the priests want to kill you?'

Kane flashed me a warning glance then. Liljana, who was staring at my forehead, said softly, 'Because he has the mark.'

At this, Kane whirled upon her and demanded, 'What do you know of *that*?'

We were all waiting to hear what she would say, but she would not be hurried. She carefully drew in a breath, then said, 'Earlier, I overheard the Baron whispering to one of his knights that Val had the mark. I didn't know what he meant.'

'He meant that Val was marked out for death,' Kane said. 'Nothing more.'

But Liljana clearly did not believe him. Her eyes fell upon my face as if searching for the truth.

'You saved my life,' I said to her. 'Is there anything you would ask in return?'

My question seemed almost to offend her. 'Do you think I told you about the wine in hope of gain?'

'No, of course not,' I said. 'But in so doing, you've gained much, even so. My gratitude – my trust.'

She smiled, revealing her small, even teeth. She said, 'I've been looking for a company to join on the quest. It's not easy for a woman to take to the roads alone.'

Alphanderry smiled at me as well. 'I've been looking for companions myself. Would you consider adding two more to your company?'

'As you've seen tonight,' I said softly, looking first at Alphanderry and then at Liljana, 'there are those who would hunt me. If you joined us, you'd be hunted, too.'

Because I trusted them both – and because they needed to know – I told them how Morjin had sent assassins to kill me in Mesh; I told them of the Grays and of our battle in the woods; lastly, I gathered in all my faith and told them the full prophecy of Ayondela Kirriland.

'You *do* have the mark, then,' Liljana said, looking at me in wonder. 'I'd be sorry for you if I didn't feel so much hope. But hope or not, if what you say is true – and I'm sure it is – you need *more* companions to help you.'

Alphanderry, as well, looked happy, as if he were setting out on a great epic that he would one day sing about. All that he said to me was, 'Please, take me with you.'

And then Maram said, 'The prophecy told of the seven brothers and sisters of the earth. We've need of two more to make seven.'

'Yes – two more *warriors*,' Kane said.

'Warriors we already have,' I said, looking at Atara and Kane. 'Ours are not the only skills we might need on a long journey.'

'The seven brothers and *sisters*,' Master Juwain said. He smiled at Alphanderry and Liljana. 'It seems that this was meant to be.'

We all stood looking at each other. And then Atara whispered, 'Val – I can *see* them with us. On the road. In the forest by the sea.'

'Ah, I can see them, too,' Maram said, not quite understanding what she was talking about.

I turned to Kane and asked, 'Will you have them join us?'

'Is this what you truly want?'

'Yes,' I said, 'it is.'

Kane touched his sword and told me, 'I pledged this to your service in seeking the Lightstone. And that your enemies would be my enemies. Well, I suppose I should pledge that your friends will be mine as well.'

So saying, he held his hand out and laid it on top of mine. Then Atara covered his hand with hers, and so with Master Juwain and

Maram. Then Liljana carefully placed her hand on top of Maram's, while Alphanderry laughed happily as he slapped his hand down upon all of ours.

Soon after that, King Kiritan and Queen Daryana, accompanied by many guards, strode from the palace and rejoined the celebration. The guards from the garrison stood about with their shields and spears to provide a sense of enforced safety at odds with the gaiety that the King wished to encourage. After all, this was still the night of his fiftieth birthday and the calling of the quest, and he wasn't about to let a little poison and death spoil it for him.

The King and Queen walked straight toward us across the lawn. The glowstones around the fountains cast their pure white light upon them – and upon the faces of Belur Narmada, Julumar Hastar, Hanitan Marshan, Breyonan Eriades, and other great nobles of Tria who stood near us. Baron Maruth of Aquantir and Duke Malatam of Tarlan, waiting with other lords and their ladies, bowed their heads to the King. Even Sar Yarwan and Sar Ianar and the other Valari knights seemed glad to see that he was still alive.

The King drew up close to us; he stood stiffly and sternly, as if in great pain. I noticed that he seemed unable to use his right arm. His eyes fell upon me with a great heaviness as he said, 'Sar Valashu Elahad, we wish to thank you and your friends for saving the Queen's life. We had heard that the traitors wounded you.'

'They did,' I said, bowing my head. 'But it was nothing that Master Juwain couldn't take care of.'

The King smiled as if he didn't quite believe me. Then he turned to Liljana and said, 'It seems we should have kept you in our service after all. Perhaps you would have sniffed out the Baron's plot even as you did the poison in his wine.'

She returned his smile and told him, 'I'm sorry, Sire, but I had to follow my heart.'

'As you now follow Valashu Elahad and my daughter to lands unknown?'

The hard glint of his eyes told me that, gratitude or no, he would never relent in his pronouncement that I must bring the Lightstone into Tria if I ever hoped to marry Atara.

Liljana smiled at me, and then took this opportunity to speak on our behalf. She told the King that the power of love between a man and a woman was greater than the force that raised up mountains and must always be exalted. Then she said that the recovery of the Lightstone would be meaningless in the absence of this purest and most purifying of forces.

'Why else should we seek the Lightstone,' she said, 'if not to bring a little more love into the world?'

'Why, indeed?' King Kiritan said. Then he sighed and called out to us, 'Well, why don't we all drink to that, then?'

He nodded at a groom standing near the fountain. A few moments later, the water bubbling out of it gave way to a dark red liquid I mistook at first for blood. But it proved to be wine: a special vintage with which King Kiritan had filled this fountain and reserved for the ending of his celebration. The King, I saw, was a man who would insist on his child getting right back on a horse who had thrown her.

He motioned for us to follow him over to the fountain, and this we did. He took up a goblet and filled it with the rich red wine and invited us all to do the same. Considering the evening's earlier events, the King's guests were reluctant to drink it. And then Liljana sniffed the contents of her goblet and smiled, and many others did, too. Then the King raised his goblet and called out, 'To the finding of the Lightstone and to those who have pledged here tonight to seek it!'

I clinked goblets with my friends, and took a sip of the wine. The tang of the grapes touched my tongue, along with the fainter tastes of chocolate and oranges. We all stood about drinking and laughing with that nervous relief that comes after a narrow escape from death.

Then the King gave another signal, and the sky over the Elu Gardens filled with a booming like thunder. All at once, fireworks burst into the air like lightning splitting the night. Flowers of blue light opened outward in perfect spheres; millions of red and silver sparks spun through space and outshone the very stars. Flick, perhaps mistaking these lights for Timpum, spun with them. I saw him as a swirl of silver against the line of trees at the edge of the Gardens. Farther to the east, in the districts of the city running down to the river and beyond it, more fireworks were exploding: from the rooftops of buildings and above the various great squares and out above the dark islands at the mouth of the river. I was afraid they might set the nearby houses on fire, but Tria was a city of stone. And that night, it was a city of happy people, for the King had commanded that free bread and wine be distributed to them so that the whole populace might help him celebrate. The distant roar of their cheering spread out from the West Wall to the East Wall, and from the docks along the river to the Varkoth Gate, for now the sky above the whole of the city blazed like a fiery umbrella of light.

As I stood there with my friends, Maram admitted that he had never seen such a sight in all his life. None of us, I thought, had. It called us to hope that the Lightstone might someday be regained, even as we had vowed it would. Toward that end, we began discussing our dreams of finding it.

'When I set out from Mesh,' Maram said, looking out at the fireworks, 'all I wanted was to reach Tria safely. I never really thought about the Lightstone as existing somewhere, ah, you know, in a place where someone could actually go and find it. But now it's now. And now I suppose we *do* have to go looking for it. But who has any idea of where to look?'

At this, Alphanderry smiled at us and said, 'I know where.'

We all turned toward him as his large eyes lit up with a different kind of fireworks. He said, 'You see, I know where Sartan Odinan hid the Gelstei.'

And then, as three great, red flowers of fire burst in the air above us and my heart boomed like thunder, he smiled again as he told us where the Lightstone might be found.

20

Near Senta in the faraway reaches of the Crescent Mountains, there is a series of caverns whose walls are lined with colored crystals. Some are violet or emerald and hang like pendants from the caves' glittering ceilings; some shine like sapphires and arise in great blue pillars from the floors. All the crystals, whatever their shape or hue, vibrate like chimes in the wind. In truth, they sing.

For centuries, it is said, men and women from across Ea have come to the caverns to listen to these singing crystals and add their own voices to the music that pours out of them. For it is also said that the crystals will record any words that fall upon them so long as they are true and sung with the fire of one's soul.

Upon entering the caverns, all but the deaf hear a million voices trolling out the words of living languages and those long dead. The seven caverns resonate with ancient ballads, love songs, canticles, carols and the death songs of those who have come to say goodbye to the earth that bore them. Their walls, ashimmer with a radiance that also pours from the crystals, echo with plaints and whispers, with cries and prayers and exaltations. The great sound of it has been known to drive men mad. But others have found there a deep peace and an answer to the great mystery of life. For in the Singing Caves of Senta, people hear only what they are ready to hear. Even a deaf man, it is said, might hear the Galadin speaking to him, for the voices of the angels are not carried upon the wind alone and can sometimes be heard as a soundless music deep inside the heart.

All this Alphanderry told us on the lawn of King Kiritan's palace as we watched the fireworks. He told us as well of an Hesperan minstrel – his name was Venkatil – who had journeyed to Senta to learn the secrets of the caves. There, almost by chance, Venkatil had listened in wonder to the words of an old ballad that told of where Sartan Odinan had brought the Lightstone. Some months later, when he had heard that there would be a great quest to find it, he had set sail for Tria only to be shipwrecked in Terror Bay off Galda. .

'I met Venkatil in the forest west of Ar,' Alphanderry told us. 'He'd been set upon by robbers and mortally wounded. But before he died, he sang me the words to the ballad. They were in Old Ardik but their meaning was clear enough: "If you would know where the Gelstei was hidden, go to the Blue Mountains and seek in the Tower of the Sun."'

That particular Tower of the Sun, as Alphanderry told us, was also known by its more ancient name: the Tur-Solonu. Once the greatest of Ea's oracles, it had lain in ruins since Morjin had destroyed it in his first rise to power during the Age of Swords.

'Just so,' Kane muttered upon hearing what Alphanderry had to say. 'The Tur-Solonu *is* destroyed. There's nothing there but a heap of burnt stones. Why should we waste our time there?'

'Because,' Alphanderry said, 'the Singing Caves have never been known to tell anything but the truth.'

'So, it's gobbledegook they tell!' Kane said with inexplicable vehemence. 'I've been to the Caves, and I know. There may be truth somewhere in the babble you hear there, but who could ever know what it is?'

We debated the course of our journey long into the night. Kane and Maram both doubted the wisdom of exploring a dead oracle, and Master Juwain seemed inclined to agree with them. But Liljana pointed out that Sartan Odinan might indeed have brought the Lightstone to the Tur-Solonu, in order to hide it in a place that even Morjin might not think to search.

Such an accursed site, whose ruins were said to be haunted by the ghosts of the many scryers murdered there, would likewise be avoided by anyone making the quest. With knights journeying to every other oracle on Ea to find clues as to where the Lightstone was hidden, no one – especially not Morjin's priests or spies – would suspect our objective. And it was as good a place to start as any.

Atara, whose eyes took on the faraway glister of the stars, spoke the name of the Tur-Solonu in a strange voice. She looked to me for affirmation that we should journey there. But I hesitated a long time while I listened to the wind sweeping above the lawn's soft grasses.

'If we can't decide,' Maram said, 'perhaps we should take a vote.'

'No, there's to be none of that on this quest,' Kane said. 'We must agree, as one company, what we should do. And if we can't all agree, then one of our company must set our course.'

He proposed then that I lead us. It was I, he said, who had set out for Tria alone only to draw everyone else to me. It was I whom Morjin

334

sought and would first be killed if he found us. And it was I who bore the mark of Valoreth.

To my surprise, everyone agreed with him. At first I protested this decision, for it seemed to me that as elders, either Kane, Liljana or Master Juwain should more properly bear the burden of leadership. But something inside me whispered that perhaps Kane was right after all. I had a strange sense that if I did as he said, I would be completing a pattern woven of gold and silver threads and as ancient as the stars. And so I reluctantly bowed my head to my six friends and accepted their charge. And then we set the rules for our company.

These were simple and few. I was not to command as would a ship's captain or a lord. At all times, I was to ask the counsel of my friends in reaching any decision that must be made. And at any juncture in our journey, either along roads winding through dense forests or the even darker paths that lead down through the soul, any of us would be allowed to leave the company at any time. For freely we had come together as brothers and sisters, and freely we must all follow our hearts.

With my friends all looking at me to decide where we should go, I searched *my* heart for a long while. And then I drew in a breath and said, 'We'll journey to the Tur-Solonu, then. Liljana is right: it is as good a place to begin as any.'

We then agreed on our most important rule: that whoever first saw and laid hands upon the Lightstone, either at the Tur-Solonu or some other place, would be its guardian and decide what should be done with it.

We were among the last to leave the palace grounds that night. By the time we said goodbye to Sar Yarwan and the other Valari knights, and Atara bade her father and mother farewell, the sky in the east was brightening to a deep shade of blue. We might have remained as guests in one of the palace's many rooms, but Atara didn't want to sleep beneath her father's roof, and neither did any of the rest of us.

'Let's get away from here,' Kane whispered to me. He said that even inside the walled palace of a walled city protected by the armies of Tria's greatest king, I had nearly been killed. 'I know an inn down by the docks where we can stay and no one will ask our business.'

Maram, who knew something of cities, wrinkled his thick brows and asked, 'But is that safe?'

'Safe?' Kane said. 'Ha – no place on Ea is safe for us now.'

We retrieved our horses and made the short journey through Tria's deserted streets to the inn that Kane had suggested. It was called the Inn of the Seven Delights, and there we found large, clean rooms, hot baths and good food, if not the other delights promised by the inn's brightly painted sign. We stayed inside resting all that day and night. And then the following morning we began preparing for our journey to the Tur-Solonu.

There was much to do. Atara went off with Kane to the horse market just north of the Eluli Bridge, where she purchased a fine roan mare to replace the mount that she had lost fighting the hill-men. Inspired by the red hairs of the mare's flowing mane, she named her Fire. As well, she and Kane bargained for four more sturdy packhorses. These would bear the supplies we would need to reach the Blue Mountains.

Kane insisted that we travel lightly, and spoke against burdening the horses with tents or any unnecessary gear. But he also insisted that we pack as much weaponry as possible. Atara, of course, agreed with him. Arrows especially we might lose along the way, and so she went with him to an arrowmaker's shop, and they laid in a great store of long, feathered shafts. Kane said that Master Juwain, Liljana and Alphanderry should be able to defend themselves at close quarters, and toward that end, he went to the swordmaker's and selected three cutlasses that they might find easy to wield. Master Juwain, upon beholding his gleaming yard of steel, shook his head sadly and informed us that he would keep his vow to renounce war. Alphanderry said that he would rather sing than fight; but to please Kane, he strapped on his sword all the same. Liljana, too, seemed chagrined at Kane's gift. She stood holding her cutlass as she might a snake and then said a strange thing: 'Am I a pirate that I should begin carrying a pirate's sword? Well, perhaps we're *all* pirates, off to take the Lightstone by force. And this age, whatever men may call it, is still the Age of Swords.'

After that she went about Tria's streets with her cutlass concealed beneath a long, gray traveling cloak. It was she, with Maram's help, who took charge of laying in the food and drink for our journey. During the next two days they visited various shops near the river and gathered up dried apples, dried beef and dried salt cod as thin and hard as wooden planks. As well they bought casks of flour to be used to make hotcakes or to bake into bread. There were the inevitable battle biscuits wrapped in wax paper, and walnuts and almonds that had come from Karabuk. And much else. Since we would be traveling through a country of rivers and streams, there was no need for the horses to carry water. But Maram, from his own pocket, bought casks of other liquids to set upon their backs: brown beer from a little brewery near the docks and some good Galdan brandy. Such spirits, he said, would warm our hearts on cold nights, and I agreed with him. To my surprise, Kane and the others – even Master Juwain – did, too.

Our brief stay in the inn was marked by one ugly incident: on our second night there, Kane and I found Atara in the common room winning at dice, which proved to be one of the inn's seven delights. Her luck had been suspiciously good, and she had turned her few remaining coins into a considerable pile of gold. The men from whom she had won it – big, blond-haired sailors from Thalu who wore their cutlasses openly – didn't want to let her leave the table with so much of their money. They might have fought her over it but for a wild look that flashed in Kane's dark eyes, and, I supposed, in my own. As Kane put it, it was far better to warn men off before drawing bright steel from beneath our cloaks. Of course, we couldn't always hope for such men to back down before us and so keep ourselves concealed. Therefore, he said, we should leave Tria as soon as possible.

We completed our preparations on the evening of the tenth of Soldru. Although Kane thought it likely that we had evaded any Kallimun priests or others set to spy us out, we couldn't know this for certain.

'This inn may be watched even now,' he said as we gathered in the larger of our two rooms. 'So – it's certain that the Kallimun will have the gates watched. That will make it hard to leave the city, won't it?'

He proposed going down to the docks and renting a boat that might carry us out into the Bay of Belen; thus we might simply sail around Tria and her great walls. But Atara had another plan.

'The gates may be watched,' she said, 'but certainly not at night when they are shut.'

'If they are closed, how are we to pass through them?' Maram asked.

'That's simple: we'll open them,' she said. 'You see, I have the key.'

And with that, she drew forth her purse and hefted the clinking gold coins in her hand. Kane smiled at her, and so did I. None of us had really wanted to embark upon a strange boat anyway.

We waited until midnight and then assembled the horses on the empty street outside the inn's stable. The nearby shops – that of the sailmaker and the sawyer – were quiet and dark. I greeted Altaru by touching the white star at the middle of his forehead, then pulled myself onto his back. Atara, astride Fire, rode next to me while Master Juwain and Maram with their sorrels took up behind her. Behind them, they trailed the new packhorses, two by two, with Tanar behind them. Liljana and Alphanderry rode near the rear. Liljana's horse was a chestnut gelding a little past his prime; Alphanderry rode one of the magnificent Tervolan whites, which were famed for their fine heads and proud, arching necks. He called him by the strange name of Iolo. Kane, scanning the street left and right from atop his big bay, took up the point of greatest danger at the very rear.

And so we set out for the Tur-Solonu. In the stillness of the night, we made our way toward the city's walls, now gleaming eerily in the light of the moon. The clopping of our horses' hooves against the cobblestones seemed overloud; it reassured us that we heard no other such sounds, nor even the footfalls of furtive boots in the darkened alleys that we passed. In this poorer section of the city, few people were about: a band of drunken sailors returning to their ships; a street cleaner shoveling up horses' dung; and the beggars who slept beneath the bridges. None of them paid us much notice or followed us. We made our way north by narrow streets paralleling the much greater River Road. Here, the buildings around us seemed ten thousand years old – and perhaps some of them were. Just to the east of us, Atara told me, were the docks of the King's Fleet and the ancient fortresses that housed the sailors who manned his warships.

We passed onto a broad avenue and drew up before the Urwe Gate. The moon had dipped toward the west; it cast a rain of silver light upon the great iron gate set into the wall before us. We sat on our horses hoping that no spies were watching what we did. The street was lined with windowless houses, and the still air smelled of bread baking and the salty tang of the sea. One of King Kiritan's soldiers, arrayed in full armor, came out of the guardhouse next to the gate, sniffing at the air – and sniffing at us as if trying to suss out our identities. He demanded that we dismount, and this we did.

'The gate is closed!' he snapped at us. Then he drove the iron-shod butt of his spear against it as if to emphasize the law of the city. 'It won't be opened until morning.'

'The gates are meant to keep our enemies out,' Atara said to him. 'Not to keep Trians within.'

'And who are you to tell me what the gates are for?' the guard demanded.

Atara stepped forward and threw back the hood of her cloak. Then she said to him, 'I'm Atara Ars Narmada.'

Although it was hard to tell in the thin light, it seemed that the guard's face paled like the moon itself.

'Excuse me, Princess,' he said. He turned to peer at Kane and me, and the others. 'I'd heard that you'd taken up with strange companions.'

'Strange, hmmph,' she said. 'But you're right that they are my companions. We've vowed to make the Quest together. Will you let us pass?'

'At this hour? The King would have me flayed if I opened the gates before dawn, even for his own daughter.'

Atara pointed at the sally port set into the iron of the gate. This gate

within a gate – little wider than a horse and about thirty hands high –
was meant to allow the Trians to sally out to attack besieging soldiers.
At the guards' discretion, it could also be opened for travelers who might
arrive at the city after sunset.

'We would never think to ask you to open the main gate,' Atara said.
Then she pointed at the sally port. 'But if the King's knights can pass
this way, so can we.'

The guard stood staring at the sally port – and at us. He said, 'This is
most irregular. No one has ever made such a request of me.'

'How long have you stood guard here, then?' Atara asked.

'It's almost a year now,' he said. 'Ever since I was wounded in
Tarlan.'

'And before that – how long have you served the King?'

'Twenty-two years,' he said proudly.

'What is your name, then?'

'Lorand, they call me.'

'Well, Lorand – do you have a family?'

'Yes, Princess. Five boys and two girls. And my wife, Adalina.'

'You've taken wounds in the King's service,' Atara said, bowing her
head. 'My father is a great man, but he is not always able to reward his
men as they should be. It can't be easy feeding such a large family on
a soldier's pay.'

'No, Princess, it's not.'

'Please allow me, then, to reward your loyalty. The House of Narmada
won't forget it.'

So saying, Atara shook a dozen coins out of her purse and handed
them to Lorand one by one. The gold worked a magic almost as deep as
that of Master Juwain's gelstei: it turned the cranky, bleary-eyed guard
into an ally anxious to help us leave the city in the middle of the night.
He fairly leaped back into the guard house where he found an iron key
with which to open the sally port. A few moments later, he swung open
its creaking door, and the road to the Blue Mountains lay before us.

'Thank you,' Atara said. 'Truly, thank you.'

While Fire nickered impatiently, Atara touched Lorand's hand and
looked him straight in the eye. Then she said, 'You must have heard
what happened at the palace three nights ago. There may be more
assassins who would follow us, if they could.'

'But how could they, Princess?' Lorand said smiling at her. 'Since the
city's gates won't be opened until morning?'

'Well, there is always the sally port,' Atara said, smiling at him. Then
she handed him her purse, and closed his fingers around its heavy weight
of gold.

'No – I think opening it once tonight is enough,' Lorand said, returning her smile. Then he looked down at the purse in his hand and added, 'More than enough. Go quickly now, and don't you worry about assassins.'

And with that, he waved us to pass. We led the horses one by one through the narrow sally port and out onto the road leading away from the walls. The port clanged shut behind us. Then Kane turned to Atara and said, 'That was well done. I couldn't have bribed him better myself.'

In the intense moonlight, Atara's face suddenly fell sad. 'It's the same everywhere. Even on the Wendrush, men love gold too much.'

'So – gold's gold,' Kane said. 'And men are men.'

'Well, I just hope he *stays* bribed,' Maram said. 'The Kallimun priests must have gold, too.'

'Surely they do,' Atara said. 'But surely there's something that the guard must love more than gold.'

'Eh, what's that?' Kane asked. 'The King? The House Narmada?'

'No,' Atara said as her eyes gleamed. 'His honor.'

Liljana, who seemed able to scent out false intentions as she might poison, agreed with Atara that Lorand could be trusted. I decided not to worry. With the world opening out before us into the starry night, I felt wild and free as I hadn't for a long time. The wind off the unseen sea to the north carried the scent of limitless possibilities while the moon in the west called with its great, silvery face. I whistled to Altaru then, and we mounted our horses, forming up as before. And so, for the love of a different kind of gold, we rode toward the hills shining on the horizon.

It was a fine, clear night for travel; the moon was waning only three days past full and seemed as bright as a beacon. The road, though not quite so broad as the Nar Road, was a good one, with paving stones set at a contour to shed the rain and mile markers along our way. It led northwest, along the Bay of Belen where there were many fishing villages and little towns.

These were our first miles on the road together as a whole company and the first true night of the quest. For a long while, we spoke nothing of it. Even so, I felt my friends' excitement crackling like lightning along a rocky crag. The moon fell toward the earth as the white towers of Tria grew ever smaller behind us and we rode deeper into the beautiful night. Although each of us might have his own reasons for seeking the Lightstone, we moved as with one purpose, as if our individual dreams were only part of a greater dream. And *this* dream – as old as the earth and indestructible as the stars – like

340

a perfect jewel shone the more brightly with every facet with which it was cut.

About an hour before dawn, we stopped to take a little rest. We lay wrapped in our cloaks atop a grassy knoll overlooking the ocean. The sight of this great, shimmering water thrilled me and loosed inside me deep swells of hope. I fell asleep to the sound of waves crashing against rocks. I dreamed of the Lightstone: it sat on a pinnacle arising from the foamy surf. There, from this still point above the world, it poured out its radiance as from a deep and bottomless source. I wanted to open myself to this flowing light, to drink it in until I was full and vast as the ocean itself. I dreamed that I could hold whole oceans inside me, and more, perhaps even the sufferings and joys of those I loved.

When I awoke, the sun was a red disk glowing above the Poru valley behind us, and the sky was taking on the bright blue tones of morning. I sat on the grass looking out at the sea as I remembered my dream. It came to me that my reasons for wanting to find the Lightstone were changing, even as the days of Soldru grew ever brighter and hotter, and spring turned toward summer. It no longer seemed quite so important to gain renown or prove my courage to my father and brothers and the other knights of Mesh. And impressing King Kiritan and thus winning Atara's hand as my wife was certainly as vain as it was hopeless: even if he someday consented to our marriage, I thought it impossible that Atara would ever kill her hundred enemies and be released from her vows. There remained my deep desire to be healed of the *valarda* with which I had been born. To wish this only for myself now seemed a selfish and even ignoble thing. In truth, I questioned the very wish itself, for I was beginning to see that my gift might help my friends even as it tormented me.

Hadn't I, after Atara had eaten the timana and lay stricken in the Lokilani's wood, somehow called her back from death? And hadn't I called to King Kiritan's compassion and softened his heart toward her? What other possibilities might be lost if the *valarda* were simply expunged from me like a raging fever that gives visions of the angels along with convulsions?

Surely the Cup of Heaven held secrets unknown to any man. And surely the unbidden empathy that connected me to others held for me mysteries I might never understand.

For many years, I had thought of my gift as a door that might be opened or closed according to my will. Some terrible things, such as my killing Raldu in the woods, paralyzed my will and left me open to the greatest of pain. But only three nights before, I had slain Baron Narcavage's men and suffered something less than the icy touch of their deaths. Was I somehow learning to keep closed the door to my heart even as I struck cold steel into others'? Or was I only hardening, as tender flesh grows layers of callus to bear up beneath the world's outrages and thorns?

I didn't know. But my dream led me to hope that someday, in some mysterious way, the *valarda* might help me withstand the most violent of passions and emotional storms. I *did* know that whatever the cost, I must somehow keep myself open to my companions, for I had something vital to give them.

And I couldn't *not* give. They were as my brothers and sisters, and each of them was close to my heart in a different way. Each had weaknesses and even greater strengths that I was beginning to see ever more clearly. This was my gift, to see in others what they couldn't see in themselves. And in Kane and Atara, no less Maram and Master Juwain, was buried a finer steel than they ever knew.

Maram, my fat friend, lived in fear of the world and all that might come growling out of its dark shadows to harm him. But he also *lived*, passionately and with great joy, as few men dared to do, and I believed that someday his love of life would overcome his fright. Master Juwain might dwell too much in his books and his brain, but I knew that someday, and soon, he would find the door to his own heart and emerge from it as a healer without equal. Atara might be overzealous in striving to make the world and everything around her perfect. But in her, more than anyone I knew, blazed a deep love that was already perfect in itself and needed no refinement to touch others with its beauty. As for Kane, his hate pooled black and bitter as bile. But his rage at life was all the more terrible for concealing something sweet and warm and splendid as a golden apple shining in the sunlight. I prayed that someday he would remember himself and behold the noble being he was born to be.

Liljana and Alphanderry were harder for me to read, for I had known them only a few days. Already, however, on this very morning, Liljana's caring for others was obvious in the way she surprised us with a breakfast of bacon, eggs and some delicious crescent bread that she managed to coax out of a stone oven that she had painstakingly built while we had slept. She insisted on keeping our plates full while she waited to eat – and took nothing but joy at seeing our bodies and souls thus nourished. And Alphanderry, when we had finished our meal, picked up his mandolet and sang us a song with all his heart. He was incapable, I thought, of singing any other way. His music made our spirits soar and our feet eager to set out on the road before us.

I believed in my friends as I did the earth and the trees, the wind, the sky, the very sun. In their presence I felt more fully human, more alive. Often it seemed that I longed for their company as I did food and drink. Their smiles and kind words sustained me; the beating of their hearts reminded me of the power and purpose of my own. I loved the sound of Maram's deep voice, the smell of Atara's thick hair, even the wild gleam bound up in the darkness of Kane's black eyes. Their gift to me was greater than anything I could ever give to them. For it fed the fire of my *valarda*; it made me want to touch all things no matter the passion or pain, to burn away and be reborn like a great silver swan from the flames. In them I heard the whisper of my deepest self no less the calling of the stars.

We resumed our journey that morning with great good cheer. We rode without time pressing at us – and neither were we harried by wounds or men pursuing us with swords or knives. I was almost certain of this. The country through which we passed, with its little farms and fishing villages, was as peaceful as any I had ever seen. There was no smell of danger in the air, only the scent of the sea that blew over us in soft breezes and cooled the sun-drenched land.

We stopped to take our midday meal in a village called Railan. From a stand near the boats by the beach, we bought some fried fish and little slices of potatoes all crisp and golden and redolent with strangely spiced oils. I stood a long time staring out at the shining ocean and marveling at its size. And then Kane growled out that it was growing late and we should be on our way.

We left the coast road at Railan, from where it continued along the headland to the ancient town of Ondrar, built at the point of a peninsula sticking out into the ocean. Ondrar was famed for its museum housing many artifacts from the Age of Law; in setting out on the road toward this town, which lay northwest of Tria, we had hoped that anyone following us would suppose we would begin our quest there. But Kane was expert at maneuver and believed in always misdirecting the enemy. The Tur-Solonu, to the southwest, remained our objective. So, as we had decided the previous night, we turned toward it on a little dirt road leading out of Railan. It was scarred with potholes and wagon tracks, but so long as the weather held good, it would suit our purpose well.

'We're free,' Maram said to me that evening as we made camp on a farmer's field by a stream. 'Finally free. I'm sure no followed us from Tria. Ah, no one *is* following us, are they, Val?'

'No, they're not,' I said to reassure him. I looked at the farmland spread across the green hills around us and the occasional stands of trees along the streams. Then I smiled and said, 'It's likely that there aren't even any bears.'

The following morning we continued on into the fine spring sunshine.

Away from the coast, the air grew warmer, but never so hot that we suffered, not even Kane and I in our steel armor. All that day and the next our horses walked down the dry road. Fifty miles, at least, we covered with our steady plodding, and every mile was full of birds singing or bees buzzing in the flowers in the woods by the road. Along our way, the farms grew ever smaller and were separated by ever greater stands of trees.

Some time on the fourth day of our journey, we passed from Old Alonia into the barony of Iviunn. A woodcutter that we met along the road told us that we had crossed into Baron Muar's domains. He also told us that we would find few farms or towns thereabout. We had entered a forest, he said, that so far as he knew went on to the west for a good seventy miles.

'So,' Kane told us later, 'the forest goes on a *hundred* and seventy miles, all the way to the Tur-Solonu – and beyond, across the mountains into the Vardaloon. *That's* the greatest forest in all of Ea.'

The thought of such an unbroken expanse of trees awed me almost as much as had the sight of the ocean. I looked about us at the verdant swath of oaks and elms crowding the road – now reduced to a dirt track – and I said, 'So few people here.'

'Yes – that's what we wanted, isn't it?'

A long time ago, he said, this part of Alonia from Iviunn up into the domains of Narain and Jerolin, had been full of people. But the War of the Stones had laid waste the countryside, and the forest had reclaimed land once its own. There were still many people in Iviunn, but fifty miles to the south, along the Istas River.

'Ah, perhaps we should have traveled that way,' Maram said as he stared off into the darkening woods. 'There is a road that goes from Tria to Durgin, isn't there? A good road, it's said.'

'You're thinking of your bears again, aren't you?' Kane asked him.

'Well, what if I am?'

'So,' Kane said to him, 'you've seen bears and you've seen Morjin's men: Kallimun priests as well as the Grays. Which do you prefer?'

'Neither,' Maram said, shuddering. 'But we don't *know* that we'd find the Kallimun along the Durgin Road, do we?'

'We won't find them here,' Kane snapped at him. Then, as if remembering that Maram was now his sworn companion, his voice softened and he said, 'At least it's much less likely.'

We made camp under the cover of the trees that night. In this thick forest, among the oaks and elms, there were many that I had seen only rarely: black ash and locust, magnolia and holly. We laid out our sleeping furs near some thickets full of baneberry, with their tiny white flowers that looked like clumps of snow. The coming into our company of Kane, Alphanderry and Liljana had changed our daily routines – for the better, I thought. Atara had a talent for finding good clear water, and so set herself the task of filling our canteens and pots and bearing them back and forth from a nearby stream to our camp. I took charge of tending the horses: tethering and combing them down, and feeding them the oats that the packhorses carried. It gave me some moments to be alone with Altaru beneath the tree-shrouded stars. Maram, of course, gathered wood for his fires, while Kane worked furiously to fortify our camp, sometimes cutting brush or thornwood to place around it, sometimes hiding dry twigs among the bracken so that whoever stood watch might be warned of approaching enemies by hearing a sudden snap. Master Juwain took to helping Liljana prepare our meals. Although he had acquired some skill with the cookware since Mesh and could turn out a good plate of hotcakes, he had much to learn from Liljana, who immediately commandeered the food supply and practically turned him into her servant. But we were all grateful that she did. That night she conjured up a fish stew out of the ugly planks of salt cod and some roots, herbs, mushrooms and wild onions that she found in the forest. It was delicious. For dessert we had raspberries, accompanied by a little brandy. And then, while Master Juwain washed the dishes, Alphanderry played his mandolet and sang to us before we slept.

He really did little other work. To be sure, he might wander about the camp, joining me to brush the horses or helping Kane cut sharpened stakes to be driven into the earth – until Kane grew exasperated with his desultory axework and growled at him to be left alone. He flitted from one task to another, sometimes completing it, sometimes not, but always having a good time talking with whomever he chose to help. And we took great delight in his company, for he was always outgoing and cheerful, and always responsive to others' moods or remarks. If he saw it as his charge to keep our spirits uplifted, no one disputed that. In the end, despite whatever fine foods we found to put into our bellies, sharpened stakes or no, it would only be by strengthening our spirits that we would ever find the Lightstone.

That night, as we sat on top of our furs sipping our brandy, while Alphanderry's beautiful voice flowed out into the night, Flick appeared and spun about to the music. This lifted *my* spirits, and those of Master Juwain, Maram and Atara, for we hadn't seen much of him since we entered Tria. But since leaving the city, he had become ever more active and visible, and now the darkness between the trees filled with tiny, twinkling stars. I laughed to see him dancing among the flowers as he had in the Lokilani's wood. Even Kane smiled when Flick pulsed with little bursts of light to the rhythms of Alphanderry's song. He pointed off into the trees and said to me, 'Your little friend is back.'

Alphanderry, sitting toward the fire, suddenly put down his mandolet and turned to look into the woods. Then he looked around the fire at Atara, Maram, Master Juwain and me, and asked, 'What are you all staring at?'

Strangely, although Flick had been with us since the night of the fireworks, we hadn't yet remarked his presence. Does one make mention of the stars that come out every night? Sometimes, though, when the great Swan constellation and others are particularly bright, it is very hard not to look up in wonder. As it was now with Flick.

'It's one of the Timpimpiri,' Kane told Alphanderry. 'He's followed us through most of Alonia.'

Now Alphanderry blinked his eyes and stared hard toward the trees. Liljana did too. But neither of them saw anything other than shadows.

'You're having a joke with me, aren't you?' Alphanderry said as he smiled at Kane.

'A joke, is it?' Kane called out. 'Do I look like one to joke?'

'No, you don't,' Alphanderry admitted. 'And we'll have to change that before this journey is through.'

'You might as well try changing the face of the moon,' Maram put in.

Again, Alphanderry smiled as he studied the woods and suddenly said, 'Hoy, yes, I *do* see him now! He's got ears as long as a rabbit and a face as green as the leaves we can't see.'

'Ha – foolish minstrel,' Kane muttered as he took a sip of brandy. But his raising of his glass couldn't quite hide the smile that touched his lips.

'Here, Flick!' Alphanderry suddenly called to the trees. 'Why don't you come here and say hello?'

Alphanderry began whistling then, and this high-pitched sound was as sweet as any music that ever flowed from a panpipe. To our astonishment, and Kane's most of all, Flick came whirling out of the trees and took up position in front of Alphanderry's face.

'Oh, Flick,' Alphanderry said to the air in front of him, 'you're a fine little fellow, aren't you? But it's too bad we've eaten all of Liljana's good stew and have only bread to share with you.'

So saying, he found a crust of bread and held it out as he might to feed a squirrel.

'You really *can't* see him, can you?' Maram said to him.

'How could he,' Master Juwain asked, 'if he never ate the timana?'

'Of *course* I can see him,' Alphanderry said. 'He's a shy little one, isn't he? Come, Flick, this bread won't hurt you.'

To prove this, he ate most of it and left a large crumb between his lips. And then he held out his hand as if beckoning Flick to hop onto it and take the crumb from his mouth.

Once again, it astonished us when Flick moved onto the palm of his hand. The spiral swirls of his form flared with sparks and little purple flames.

'Ha!' Kane said, 'he must understand more than we thought. It would seem that there's more to the Timpimpiri than *anyone* thought.'

'Of course there is,' Alphanderry said, after swallowing the breadcrumb. 'They are magical beings, known to live in the deeper woods everywhere. If they've taken food from you, they must grant three wishes.'

'But Flick can't take food at all,' Maram said.

'Of course he can!' Alphanderry said. 'Of course he did! Didn't you *see* him?'

'Ah, I suppose I must have been looking away,' Maram said, grinning. 'What are your three wishes, then?'

'My first wish, of course, is that Flick grant all my future wishes.'

'That's cheating!' Atara called out.

'And my second wish,' he said, ignoring her, 'is that we accomplish the impossible and find the Lightstone.'

'That's better,' Atara said, smiling.

'And my third wish,' he continued, 'is that we accomplish the *truly* impossible and make our grim Kane laugh.'

Kane sat by the fire staring at Alphanderry with his hard eyes, and a stone statue couldn't have been more still.

'Now, then,' Alphanderry said, rising to his feet, 'the, ah, Timpimpiri are capable of many feats, magical and otherwise. Please watch closely, or you'll miss this.'

Alphanderry, it turned out, was skilled not only in music and singing but in the art of pantomime. He stood looking at his open hand and talking to Flick as if trying to persuade his invisible friend to entertain us. And all the while, his face took on different moods and expressions, and seemed as easily molded as a ball of Liljana's bread dough. The extreme mobility of his face, no less the sudden and comical deepening of his voice, made us all laugh a little – all of us except Kane.

'Now, Flick,' Alphanderry said in a voice all arrogant and stern like King Kiritan's, 'you've eaten our food and now must obey us. At my command, you'll jump into my other hand.'

Alphanderry now held his left hand out and away from his body. He looked down toward Flick in his right hand, and said, 'Are you ready?'

Just then his face underwent a sudden transfiguration and fell softer. His voice softened, too, becoming fully feminine, and when he spoke, its tone was unmistakably that of Queen Daryana. As if speaking to himself, this new voice called out, 'Is he a Timpimpiri or a slave? Why don't you set him free?'

Again, Alphanderry's face and voice took on the manner of King Kiritan. And he called out in response, 'Who rules here, you or I?'

Now he looked down at his hand and continued, 'When the King says jump, you jump.'

But before he, as King Kiritan, could get another word out, his face fell through yet another change. And speaking with Queen Daryana's voice, he said, 'The King has said you must jump, Flick. All right then, jump!'

All at once, Flick shot up off Alphanderry's hand and streaked up in a fiery arc to land on the other. And Alphanderry, who had yet again returned to his King Kiritan persona, pretended to watch this feat with outrage coloring his face. His eyes opened wide at his Queen's defiance and bounced like balls as they turned toward his other hand.

Now Kane's stony visage finally cracked. The faintest of smiles turned up his lips. Alphanderry's antics amused him much less, I thought, than did his utter blindness to Flick.

Alphanderry, still speaking as Queen Daryana, said, 'Quick, Flick – jump! Jump again, jump now!'

Each time he said this, Flick streaked from Alphanderry's one hand to the other, back and forth like a blazing rainbow. And with each jump, Alphanderry's face returned to the stern lines of King Kiritan as his eyes bounced up and down.

Maram and I – everyone except Kane – were now laughing heartily. Alphanderry's failure to move Kane must have distressed him, for he stopped his pantomime, looked at Kane, and in his own voice, he said, 'Hoy, man, what will it take to make you laugh?'

Kane didn't blink as he said, 'Make him spin on your nose.'

Alphanderry again became King Kiritan as he replied, '*That* would be beneath our dignity.'

And as Queen Daryana, he continued, 'Then perhaps I should make him spin on *my* nose. Flick, I want you to –'

'Enough!' Kane called out, holding up his hand. He stood up facing Alphanderry and pointed at Flick, who was spinning in the space just above Alphanderry's hand. 'The Timpimpiri *are* real. They dwell in the woods of the Lokilani.'

'And who are the Lokilani?' Alphanderry asked.

'They're the people of the woods,' Kane said. He held out his hand just below his chest as if measuring a man's height. 'The little people.'

'Oh – and I suppose they have long ears like a rabbit's and green faces,' Alphanderry said. He turned to wink at Maram and told him, 'You see, I *have* gotten him to joke.'

Kane pointed again at Flick and said, 'This is no joke. Although I can't understand it, the Timpimpiri seems to hear you and do as you bid.'

'Really? Then will he spin on my finger?' Alphanderry held up his finger as if pointing at the stars. 'I suppose he's spinning there now?'

No sooner had he spoken these words, then Flick flew up and turned about above his finger like a jeweled top.

Alphanderry abruptly took away his hand, and then bent to retrieve his personal kit from the foot of his furs. From it he removed a needle, which he held up to the light of the fire.

'And now,' he said, 'I suppose he's dancing upon this needle?'

And lo, in a flash, with perfect equipoise, Flick spun wildly about the point of the needle.

'Hoy, yes, and now, of course, he's spinning on my nose!'

To emphasize the foolishness of what he had said, his eyes suddenly crossed as if fixing on a fly on the tip of his nose. And there, unseen by him, Flick appeared doing his wild, incandescent dance.

This last proved too much for Kane. The crack in his obduracy suddenly widened into a bottomless chasm. His face broke into the widest smile I had ever seen as he let loose a great howl of laughter. He couldn't stop himself. He fell to his knees, laughing hard and deeply, tears in eyes, his belly heaving in and out as he sweated and gasped and his whole body shook. I thought the earth itself cracked open then, for the laughter that shook his soul was more like an earthquake than any human emotion. Out of him erupted blasts of smoke and fire, thunder and lightning – or so it seemed. He lay on the ground laughing for a long time as he held his belly, and we were all so awed by this sudden outburst that we didn't know what to do. In truth, there was nothing *to* do except laugh along with him, and this we did.

Finally, however, Kane grew quiet as he sat up breathing hard. Through his tears, his bright, black eyes seemed to shine with great happiness. I saw in him, for a moment, a great being: joyful, open, radiant and wise. He smiled at Alphanderry and said, 'Foolish minstrel – perhaps you *are* good for something.'

And then he regained much of his composure. The harsh, vertical lines returned to his face; flesh gave way before stone. He stared at Flick, who was now wavering in the air a few feet from Alphanderry.

Then came a time for explanations. While the fire burned down and the great constellations wheeled about the heavens, we took turns telling of our stay in the Lokilani's wood. Alphanderry came to see that we were not having a joke with him after all. I spoke to him of my first glorious vision of the many Timpum lighting up the forest, and he believed me; trust came easy to him. When Atara, with tears in her eyes, told of how she had almost died upon eating the timana, Alphanderry looked at me and said, 'You saved her life, then. With this gift that Kane calls the *valarda*. Is that why your Flick followed you out of the vild?'

Flick came over to me and hovered above my shoulder. I could almost feel the swirls of fire that made up his being. 'Who knows why he followed me?' I said.

'Perhaps for the same reason we all do,' Alphanderry said thoughtfully. 'Well, perhaps someday I'll be able to see him with you.'

All this time, Liljana had remained silent when she hadn't been laughing. Now, as it became clear that a great mystery had been set before her, she said simply, 'I'd like a taste of this timana, too.'

The following morning we made our way through a forest wide and thick enough to hide ten of the Lokilani's vilds. But we found neither another tribe of them nor their sacred fruit, and I thought that Liljana would have to wait a long time to be granted her wish. As we moved away from Old Alonia deeper into Iviunn, the gentle hills gave out onto a great forested plain. We made good progress along the track through the trees. Although it sometimes turned and narrowed as such tracks do, it mostly led straight toward the west. If we continued as we did, I calculated that we would reach the Blue Mountains in only seven more days.

And then the following day, great gray clouds moved in from the sea, and it began to rain. By late afternoon, our track had turned into a slip of mud. Although the deluge didn't slow us very much, it made the going miserable, for it was a cold, driving rain that soaked our cloaks and found its way into our undergarments. It didn't stop that day, nor even on the next or the one following that. By the fourth day of this weather, we were all a little on edge. We had all lost sleep, twisting and turning and shivering on the sodden earth.

'I'm cold, I'm tired, I'm wet,' Maram complained. 'But at least I'm not hungry – and we have Liljana to thank for that. Oh, my Lord, no one else could prepare such delicious meals in such foul weather!'

Liljana, riding her tired gelding who practically dragged his hooves through the squishing mud, beamed at his compliment. I noticed that just as she thrived on sacrificing herself and serving others, she relished their appreciation at least as much.

Her selflessness was an example to us all. She never minded being roused from even the deepest of sleeps and taking her turn standing watch. Twice, she even stayed awake in the exhausted Alphanderry's place to let him sleep; as she put it, some people needed more rest than others, and we had all observed that Alphanderry's talent for sleeping was almost as great as for making music and song.

As for myself, I often liked wandering about the camp when the hours grew darkest. On clear nights, I had a chance to be alone with the stars – or what I could see of them through the thick cover of the trees. And on rainy nights, I turned my marveling toward Flick. It almost seemed that he could sense my fervor to reach the Tur-Solonu, for with each passing day of the quest, his fiery form grew brighter as if to give me hope. The most bitter of rains passed right through him, dimming his light not even a little. In truth, he seemed to burn the brightest at precisely those moments when either rain or kirax or fear of the evils we faced damped my spirits and touched me with its cold.

On the fourth night of rain, I was awakened well before it was my turn to stand watch. I heard Kane shouting, and immediately grabbed for my sword. I sprang up from my wet furs, as did Atara and Liljana, followed more slowly by Maram and Master Juwain. We all rushed to the edge of our camp, where Kane had piled some brush. He stood glowering above Alphanderry, who sat in the drizzling rain looking bewildered. If not for the fire that Maram had made earlier – and the radiance pouring out of Flick – it was so dark that we wouldn't have been able to see them at all.

'He fell asleep!' Kane accused as he pointed at Alphanderry. His eyes were coals glowing like those of the fire. 'He couldn't even make it through an hour of his watch!'

'I don't know what happened,' Alphanderry said as he rose to his feet. He rubbed the sleep from his eyes, and then looked at Kane as he smiled sheepishly. 'It was so dark, and I was so tired, so I sat down, only for a moment. I just wanted to rest my eyes, and so I closed them and –'

'You fell asleep!' Kane thundered again. 'While you rested your damn eyes, we might have all been killed!'

His whole body tensed then, and I was afraid he might raise his arm to Alphanderry. So I clamped my hand around his elbow. He turned toward me and glared at me; again his body tensed with a wild power. I knew that if he chose to break free, I couldn't stop him. Could I hold a tiger? And yet, for a moment, I held him with my eyes, and that was enough.

'So, Val,' he said to me. 'So.'

As I let go of him, Liljana came up to Kane and poked her finger into his chest. Her pretty face had now grown as hard as Kane's. In her most domineering voice, she told him, 'Don't you speak to Alphanderry like that! We're all brothers and sisters here – or have you forgotten?'

Her admonishment so startled Kane that he took a step backward and then another as her finger again drove into his chest. Her zeal to defend Alphanderry completely overwhelmed Kane's considerable anger. I was reminded of something I had once seen near Lake Waskaw, when a wolverine, through the sheer force of ferocity, had driven off a much larger mountain lion trying to take one of her cubs.

'Brothers and sisters of the earth!' Liljana said again. 'If we fight with each other, how can we ever hope to find the Lightstone?'

Kane looked to me for rescue as he took yet another step backward. But for a few moments I said nothing while Liljana scolded him.

'All right, all right!' Kane said at last, smiling at her. 'I'll mind my mouth, if it bothers you so. But something must be done about what happened.'

He nodded toward Alphanderry, then looked at me. 'What befalls a Valari warrior caught sleeping on watch in the land of the enemy?'

Alphanderry ran his hand through his curly hair as he looked about the dark forest. 'But there are no enemies here!'

'You don't know that!' Kane snapped.

'Well, at least I don't *see* any enemies,' Alphanderry said, looking Kane straight in the eye.

I thought that the usual punishment meted out to overly sleepy warriors – being made to stay awake all night for three successive nights beneath the stinging points of his companions' kalamas – would do Alphanderry little good. He would likely wind up looking like a practice target – and then fall asleep in exhaustion during his next watch anyway. And yet something had to be done.

'It's not upon me to punish anyone,' I said. 'Even so, if everyone is agreeable, we might change the watches.'

I turned to Kane and said, 'You never have trouble staying awake, no matter the hour of your watch, do you?'

'Never,' he growled. 'I've had to learn how to stay awake.'

'Then perhaps you can teach this wakefulness to our friend. For the next few nights, why doesn't Alphanderry join you on your watch?'

Truly, it was my hope that, like a stick held to a furnace, Alphanderry might ignite with something of Kane's fire.

'Join me, eh?' Kane growled again. 'Punish *him*, I said, not me.'

With a bow of his head, Alphanderry accepted what passed for punishment. Then he smiled at Kane and said, 'I haven't had Flick's company to help keep me awake, but I'd welcome yours.'

The yearning in his voice as he spoke of Flick must have touched something deep in Kane, for he suddenly scowled and muttered, 'So, I suppose you *can't* see him, can you?'

352

Alphanderry shook his head sadly then said, 'I'm sorry I fell asleep – it won't happen again.'

The utter sincerity in his voice disarmed Kane. It seemed impossible for anyone to remain angry with Alphanderry very long, for he was as hard to pin down as quicksilver.

'All right, join me then,' Kane said. 'But if I catch you sleeping on *my* watch, I'll roast your feet in the fire!'

True to his word, Alphanderry kept wide awake during his watches after that. But his attention slipped from other chores that should have been simple: set him loose in the woods to find some raspberries, and he might wander about for hours before returning with a handful of pretty flowers instead. It was as if he couldn't hold on to *anything* in this world for very long. He was a dreamy man meant for the stars and for magical lands told of in songs.

It surprised us all that he and Kane became friends. None of us saw very much of what passed between them during Kane's nightly watches. But it seemed certain that Alphanderry was in awe of Kane's strength and immense vitality. He hinted that Kane was teaching him tricks to stay awake: walking, watching the stars, keeping the eyes moving, and composing music inside his head. As for Kane, he listened closely whenever Alphanderry sang his songs, especially those whose words were of a strange and beautiful language that we had never heard before. And it gladdened all our hearts to hear Kane laughing in Alphanderry's presence – more and more frequently, it seemed, with every day and night that passed.

On the morning following Alphanderry's failed watch, the rain finally stopped, and we had our first glimpse of the Blue Mountains. Through a break in the trees, we beheld their dark outline above the haze hanging over the world. They were old mountains, low to the earth with rounded peaks. But in that moment, I thought they were the most beautiful and magnificent mountains I had ever seen. The sight of them made me want to forget Alphanderry's flaws; it was he, after all, who had caused us to journey these many miles. Another two days' march, perhaps, would bring us to the ancient Tur-Solonu. And if the words that Alphanderry had heard in the Caves of Senta proved true, there, among the ancient ruins, we would find at last the golden cup that held so many of our hopes and dreams.

21

With the healing of the discord between Alphanderry and Kane, our company began working as a whole. Do the fingers of one's hand fight over which holes of a flute to cover when making music? No, and neither could we dispute with one another if we were to complete our quest. That we might be nearing the end of our journey, I didn't want to doubt. Already, since leaving my father's castle, we had been on the road some fifty days. And for most of them, I had been growing more and more homesick. The coming into our company of Alphanderry, with his quick smiles and playfulness, reminded me of my brother, Jonathay. My six companions, who every day were growing closer to my heart, reminded me of my six brothers left behind in Mesh. They would have been proud, I thought, to see us riding forth into the wilds of Alonia, united in our purpose like a company of knights.

As we drew closer to the mountains, the land through which we rode rose into a series of low hills running north and south. Kane told us that we had entered the ancient realm of Viljo; some seventy miles to the southwest, he said, Morjin had begun his rise to tyranny among the headwaters of the Istas River. There, in the year 2272 of the Age of Swords, he had founded the Order of the Kallimun. He had attracted six disciples to him, and then many more. Only ten years before this, he had made off with the Lightstone from the island where Aryu had hidden it; after that he used it in secret to attract converts at an astonishing rate. He persuaded many of Viljo's nobles to join him. But most took up arms against him – only to be defeated at the Battle of Bodil Fields. There, on that defiled ground, the Red Dragon had ordered the captured nobles slaughtered and had instituted the blood-drinking rites meant to lead to immortality.

'It's said that Morjin himself gained immortality from the Lightstone,' Kane told us. 'But he wouldn't suffer anyone else to behold it. So, he was afraid someone would steal it from *him*.'

And there had been those who almost did. A rebellion led by outcast knights had nearly succeeded in defeating him. For a time, Morjin had brought the Lightstone to the Tur-Solonu and had gone into hiding. But the scryers who dwelt at the oracle there had betrayed him; Morjin had barely escaped the Tur-Solonu fighting for his life. In revenge, four years later, when he had crushed the rebellion and captured the Tur-Solonu, he had ordered the scryers to be crucified and the Tower of the Sun destroyed.

'It's said that the scryers' blood poisoned the land about the Tur-Solonu, that nothing would ever grow there again,' Kane told us.

We had paused to eat a quick lunch on the side of a hill. From its grassy slopes, we had a good view of the mountains, now quite close to us in the west. Only a few miles away, one of the tributaries of the Istas ran down from them through the forest like a blue snake slithering through a sea of green. Just to the north was a spur of low peaks. If we followed the line of this spur, Kane said, we would find the ruins of the Tur-Solonu in the notch where it jutted out from the main body of the Blue Mountains.

'It can't be more than forty miles from here,' Kane said. 'If we ride steady, we should reach the ruins by sunset tomorrow.'

'Sunset!' Maram cried out as he drew a mug of beer from one of the casks. 'Just in time to greet the scryers' ghosts when they come out to haunt the ruins at night!'

We rode hard that day and the next into the notch in the mountains. Their wooded slopes rose to our right and left; in places bare rock shone in the sun to remind us of their bones, but they were mostly covered with trees and bushes all the way up their slopes. Like a huge funnel of granite and green, they directed us toward the notch's very apex, where the Tur-Solonu had been built late in the Age of the Mother, nearly a whole age before its destruction. I kept looking for the remnants of this tower through the canopies of the trees around us. All I saw, however, was a wild forest that might someday swallow up the very mountains themselves. If men and women had ever lived in this country, there was no sign of them, not even a fallen-in hut or gravestone to mark their lives and deaths.

And then, through a break in the trees, we saw it: the Tower rose up above the notch's floor like a great chess piece broken in half. Even in its destruction, it was still a mighty work, its remains standing at least a hundred and fifty feet high. The white stone facing us was cracked and scarred with streaks of black; in places, it seemed to have been melted and fused into great, glistening flows that hung down its curved sides like drips of wax. I wondered immediately if Morjin had used a firestone

355

to destroy it. But the first firestones, I thought, had been created only a thousand years later in the Age of Law.

'I'm afraid that is true,' Master Juwain said as we looked out at the ancient Tower of the Sun. 'Petram Vishalan forged the first of the red gelstei in Tria in the year 1319.'

'The first red gelstei that anyone *knew* about,' Kane muttered to us. 'Don't forget that it was Morjin, as Kadar the Wise, who spread the *relb* over the Long Wall and melted it for Tulumar's hordes to overrun Alonia long before that.'

'Are you saying that the Red Dragon forged a firestone and told no one of it?' Master Juwain asked.

'So – how else to explain what we see?' Kane said, pointing at the tower.

'Perhaps an earthquake,' Master Juwain said. 'Perhaps the eruption of a volcano would –'

'No – it's told that Morjin destroyed the Tur-Solonu.'

Master Juwain removed his leather-bound book from his cloak and patted it reassuringly. 'But it is not told in the *Saganom Elu*.'

'Books!' Kane snarled out with a sudden savagery. 'Books can tell whatever the damn fools who write them believe. Most books should be burned!'

Kane stood glaring at the book that Master Juwain held in his strong, old hand. The look of horror on Master Juwain's face suggested that he might as well have called for the burning of babies.

'If the Red Dragon forged firestones during the Age of Swords,' Master Juwain said, 'then why didn't he use them in his conquest of Alonia? And later, against Aramesh at the Battle of Sarburn?'

'I didn't say that he forged *firestones*,' Kane said. 'Perhaps he made only one – the one that destroyed this Tower.'

For a while, he stood arguing with Master Juwain in plain sight of the Tur-Solonu. The first red gelstei, he said, were known to be very dangerous to use: sometimes their fire turned against the one who wielded them, or the stones even exploded in their faces. Thus had Petram Vishalan died in 1320 – a fact that Kane gleefully pointed out *was* recorded in the *Saganom Elu*.

'Perhaps we'll never know what destroyed the Tower,' I said, looking at its jagged shape through the woods. 'But perhaps we should complete our journey and search there before it grows too late.'

And so we rode through the woods straight for the Tur-Solonu. The trees again obscured it from view, but soon we crested a little hill and there the trees gave way to barren ground. We came out onto a wedge-shaped desolation some three miles wide – but growing ever narrower toward the point of the notch where the spur met the main mountains. Walls of rock rose up on either side of us; the Tur-Solonu was now a great broken mass directly to the north at the middle of the notch. I wondered if the scorched-looking land about us was truly poisoned after all, for little grew there except a few yellowish grasses and some lichens among the many rocks. As we drew closer to the Tower, waves of heat seemed to emanate from the ground; Flick flared more brightly while Altaru suddenly whinnied, and I felt a strange tingling run up his trembling legs and into me. I had a sense that we were coming into a place of power and treading over earth that was both sacred and cursed.

The first ruins we came upon occupied an area about a half mile south of the tower. Much of the blasted stone there lay upon the ground in rectangular patterns or still stood as broken walls. We guessed it to be the remains of buildings, perhaps dormitories and dining halls and other such structures that the ancient scryers must have used. We dismounted, and began walking slowly among the mounds of rattling rock.

If the Lightstone lay buried beneath it, I thought, we might dig for a hundred years before uncovering it.

'But there is no reason that Sartan Odinan would have hidden it *here*,' Master Juwain said. He pointed straight toward the Tur-Solonu to the north, and then due east a quarter of a mile where stood the scorched columns of what must have been the scryers' temple. 'Surely he would have hidden it *there*. Or perhaps inside the Tower itself.'

Atara, standing with her hand shielding her eyes from the sun, pointed at another fallen-in structure a quarter mile due west of the Tower. It stood – if that was the right word – next to a swift stream running down from the mountains. 'What is *that*?' she asked.

'Probably the ruins of the baths,' Kane said. 'At least, that was my guess the first time I came here.'

'You never *did* tell us why you came here,' Atara said, fixing her bright eyes upon him.

'No, I didn't, did I?' Kane said. He gazed at the Tower, and it seemed he might retreat into one of his deep, scowling silences. And then he said, 'When I was younger, I wanted to see the wonders of the world. So, now I've seen them.'

Maram was now walking slowly among the shattered buildings; he paused from time to time as he looked back and forth toward the tower as if measuring angles and distances with his quick brown eyes. After a while, he said, 'Well, there's still much of the ruins *we* haven't seen. It's growing late – why don't we begin our search before it grows *too* late?'

'But where should we begin?' Master Juwain asked.

'Surely in the Temple,' Liljana said. Although her face remained calm and controlled as it usually was, I knew that she was tingling inside with a rare impatience.

'But what about the Tower?' Master Juwain asked. 'Shouldn't we climb it and see what is there?'

For a time, as the sun dropped quickly behind the mountains, the two of them argued as to where we should direct our efforts. Finally, I held up my hand and said, 'Such explorations will likely take longer than the hour of light we have left. Why don't we leave them until tomorrow?'

These were some of the hardest words I had ever spoken. If the others were trembling inside to find the Lightstone that very day, I was on fire.

'Why don't we walk around the Tower first,' I said, 'and see what we can see?'

The others reluctantly agreed to this, and so we began leading the horses in a wide spiral around the Tower. Soon we came to a circle of standing stones about four hundred yards from it. That is, some of the stones were still standing, while most were scorched and lying flat on the grass as if some impossibly strong wind had blown them over. Each stone was cut of granite, and twice the height of a tall man.

The entire area was also peppered with smaller stones, likewise melted, which we took to be the broken remains of the Tower. There were many of them, all of a white marble nowhere visible in the rock of the surrounding mountains.

'Look!' Maram said, pointing at the ground closer to the Tower. 'There are more stones over there.'

A hundred yards closer in toward the Tower, we found another circle of the larger stones half-buried in the grass. Only a few of these were still standing. They were covered with splotches of green and orange lichens that seemed to have been growing for thousands of years.

No sooner had we begun walking around these stones, than Maram descried yet a third circle of them fallen down closer still to the Tower. We moved from stone to stone around toward the east in the direction of the temple. Neither I nor any of the others was sure what we might be looking for among them if not the Lightstone itself. But their configuration was intriguing. Master Juwain believed they had been set to mark the precession of the constellations or some other astrological event. Liljana, however, questioned this. With one of her mysterious smiles that hid more than it revealed, she said, 'The *ancient* scryers, I think, cared more about the earth than they did the stars.'

Maram, who was in no mood for learned disputes, continued leading the way around the circle. Soon we found ourselves to the north of the

Tur-Solonu, directly along the line leading toward the apex of the notch. Without warning, Maram began walking toward the second circle as he studied the fallen stones and the scorch marks on the few standing ones with great care. When he reached the wide ring of stones, he stopped to point at a huge stone overturned and sunken into the ground. It lay by itself exactly at the midpoint between the second and third circles. It was thrice as long as any of the other stones and must have once stood nearly forty feet high.

'Look, there's something about this stone!' he said. Again, he stood measuring distances with his eyes. He was breathing hard now, and his face was flushed. Inside, he was all pulsing blood and pure, sweet fire. 'This is the place – I know it is!'

So saying, he hurried over to one of the packhorses and unslung the axe that it carried. With the axe in his hands and a wild gleam in his eyes, he rushed back to the end of the great stone and there fell upon it with a fury of motion most unlike him.

'Hold now! What are you doing?' Kane yelled at him. He rushed over and grabbed Maram from behind. 'You fat fool – that's good steel you're ruining!'

Maram managed one last swipe with the axe before Kane's grip tightened around him. By then it was too late: the axe's edge was already notched and splintered from chopping into cold, hard stone.

'Let me go!' Maram shouted, kicking at the ground like a maddened bull. 'Let me go, I said!'

And then the impossible happened: he broke free from Kane's mighty armlock. He raised the axe above his head, and I was afraid he might use it to brain the astonished Kane.

'It's here!' Maram shouted. 'A couple more good blows ought to free it!'

'*What* is here?' Kane growled at him.

'The gelstei,' Maram said. 'The firestone. Can't you see that when this stone was still standing, the Red Dragon must have mounted the red gelstei on top of it to burn down the Tower?'

Suddenly, we all *did* see this. Looking south toward the Tur-Solonu and all the other structures and stones in the notch, we could all see in our minds the blasts of fire that must have once erupted from this spot.

'Well, even if you're right,' Kane said to him, 'why should you think the firestone is still here?'

'How do I know my heart is here?' Maram said, thumping the flat of the axe against his chest. Then he pointed at the end of the stone, which was all bubbled and fused as if it had once been touched by

359

a great heat. 'It *is* here. Can't you see it must have melted itself into the stone?'

Again, he raised up the axe, and again Kane called to him, 'Hold, now! If you must have at it, don't ruin our axe beyond all repair.'

'What should I use then – my teeth?'

Kane strode over to the second packhorse, where he found a hammer and one of the iron stakes we used to picket the horses. He gave them to Maram and said, 'Here, use these.'

With his new tools, Maram set to work, panting heavily as he hammered the stake's iron point against the stone. Little gray chips flew into the air as iron rang against iron; dust exploded upward and powdered Maram all over. Twice, he missed his mark, and the hammer's edge bloodied his knuckles. But he made no complaint, hammering now with a rare purpose that I had seen in him only in his pursuit of women.

We all moved in close to see what this furious work might uncover. But it was growing dark, and Maram was bent close to the stone, using his large body for leverage. So that we wouldn't be blinded by the flying stone chips – as we were afraid Maram might be – we stepped back to give him more room to work and wait for him either to give up or announce that he had found the fabled firestone.

'Ha – look at him!' Kane said as he pointed at Maram. 'A starving man wouldn't work so hard digging up potatoes.'

All at once, with a last swing of the hammer and a great cry, Maram freed something from the rock. Then he held up a great crystal about a foot long and as red as blood. It was six-sided, like the cells of a honeycomb, and pointed at either end. It looked much like an overgrown ruby – but we all knew that it must be a firestone.

'So,' Kane said, staring at it. 'So.'

'It *is* one of the tuaoi stones,' Master Juwain said as he gazed at it in wonder. 'It would seem that the Lord of Lies really did make a red gelstei.'

Alphanderry, ducking as Maram carelessly swung the point of the crystal in his direction, laughed out, 'Hoy, don't point that at *me*!'

I stood beneath the night's first stars and watched as Flick appeared and described a fiery spiral along the length of the gelstei. With such a crystal, I thought, Morjin had once burned Valari warriors even as he had destroyed the Tur-Solonu.

'The seven brothers and sisters of the earth,' Liljana said quietly. 'The seven brothers and sisters with the seven stones will set forth into the darkness.'

The words of Ayondela Kirriland's prophecy hung in the falling darkness like the stars themselves. Seven gelstei Ayondela had spoken of, and now we had three: Master Juwain's varistei, Kane's black stone and a red crystal that might burn down even mountains.

'Prophecies,' Kane muttered. 'Who could ever know what hasn't yet happened? Why should we believe the words of this dead scryer?'

Despite his bitterness, the light in his eyes told me that he desperately wanted to believe them.

'Is this,' he asked, pointing at the firestone, 'the reason we've journeyed half the way across Ea to a dead oracle?'

His deep voice rolled out as if he were speaking his doubts to the wind. And it seemed that the wind answered him. A different voice, deeper in its purity if not tone, poured down the mountain slope to the west and floated across the field of stones: 'And who is it who has journeyed half the way across Ea to tell us that our oracle is dead?'

We all whirled about to see six white shapes appear in the darkness from behind the standing stones. Kane and I whipped free our swords even as Maram shouted, 'Ghosts! This place *is* haunted with ghosts!'

His eyes went wide, and he held out his crystal in front of him as he might a short sword.

Then the 'ghosts' began moving toward us. In the twilight, they seemed almost to float over the grass. Soon we saw that they were women, each with long hair of varying color; they each wore plain white robes that gleamed faintly: the robes, I saw, of scryers.

'Who are you?' their leader said again to Kane. She was a tall woman with dark hair and a long, sad face. 'What are your names?'

'Scryers,' Kane spat out. 'If you're scryers, you tell me, eh?'

Kane's rudeness appalled me, and I quickly stepped forward and said, 'My name is Valashu Elahad. And these are my companions.'

I presented each of my friends in turn. When I came to Kane, he practically cut me off and asked the scryer, 'So, what is *your* name, then?'

'I'm called Mithuna,' she said. She turned to the five women who accompanied her and said, 'And this is Ayanna, Jora, Twi, Tiras and Songlian.'

All of us, even Kane, bowed to the women one by one. And then Mithuna looked at Kane with her dark eyes and said, 'As you can see, the oracle of the Tur-Solonu is not dead.'

'Ha – I see a broken tower and scattered stones,' Kane said. 'And six women dressed up in white robes.'

'It's said that men and women see what they want to see,' Mithuna told him. 'Which is why they don't truly *see*.'

'Scryer talk,' Kane muttered. 'So it is with all the oracles now.'

361

'We speak as we speak,' Mithuna said. 'And you hear what you will hear.'

'Once,' Kane said, 'this oracle spoke the wisdom of the stars.'

'And you doubt that it still speaks this wisdom. So it is that the wind must blow; so the sun must rise and fall and the ages pass.'

She told us then what had happened in this very place in an age long past. After Morjin had destroyed the Tower of the Sun with the very crystal that Maram held in his hands, he had ordered the scryers who served the oracle to be crucified. But a few of them had eluded Morjin's murderous priests and had escaped into the surrounding mountains. There they had built a refuge in secret. And when Morjin and his men had finally abandoned the Tur-Solonu, the scryers had returned to the ruins to stand beneath the stars. The scryers grew old and died as all must do, but as the years passed, others had joined them. Thus had Mithuna's predecessors established a true and secret oracle in the ruins of the Tur-Solonu. And so, century after century, age after age, scryers from across Ea had come to this sacred site to seek their visions and listen for the voices of the Galadin on the stellar winds.

'But how would they know to come here?' I asked her.

'How did *you* know to come, Valashu Elahad?'

A savage look in Kane's eyes warned me to say nothing of our quest, and so for the moment I kept my silence.

'Surely,' she said, 'you came because you were called.'

I closed my eyes and listened to my heart beating strongly. Deeper, beneath my feet, the very earth seemed to beat like a great drum calling men to war.

'There *is* something about this place,' I said as I looked at her.

'Something, indeed,' she said. 'There is no other like it in all Ea.'

Here, she said, beneath the ground upon which we stood, the fires of the earth whirled in patterns that burned away time. Nowhere else in the world did the telluric currents well so deeply and connect the past to the future.

'This is why the standing stones were set into the ground,' she told us. 'This is why the Tur-Solonu was built, to draw up the fires from the earth.'

As Mithuna told of this, Master Juwain rubbed his bald head thoughtfully, then said, 'The Brotherhoods have suspected for a long time that there was a great earth chakra in the Blue Mountains. We should have sent someone to search it out long ago.'

'And now they have sent you,' Mithuna said. 'But I'm sorry to tell you that only scryers ever see visions here. Many are called but few are chosen.'

Here she smiled at Atara, and her eyes were like windows to other worlds. 'Thank you for making the journey. We can only hope that it is the One who has sent you to us.'

Atara looked at me, and I looked at her, and then to Mithuna she said, 'But I'm no scryer!'

'Aren't you?'

'No, I'm a warrior of the Manslayer Society! I'm Atara Ars Narmada, daughter of King –'

'It's all right,' Mithuna said, reaching out to grasp Atara's hand. 'Few know who they really are.'

A wild look flashed across Atara's face then. Her eyes fell upon me for reassurance as she said, 'I saw the spider spinning her web, and there were the gray men, too, but that must have all been chance. It *must* have been, mustn't it?'

I said nothing as I looked for the diamonds of her eyes in the failing light.

'And even if it wasn't chance,' she went on, 'I've *seen* so very little. That doesn't make me a scryer, does it?'

Maram, who was laughing softly to himself as he gripped his red crystal, said to her, 'Now I understand how you always win at dice.'

'But I'm just lucky!' Atara protested.

Mithuna stroked Atara's hand and told her, 'You *have* seen so very little of what there is to see. If you had been trained . . . . Oh, dear child, you've sacrificed much to forsake such training.'

Atara withdrew her hand and then looked at it as if trying to understand her fate from its many lines.

'It's *dangerous* to look into the future without being trained,' Mithuna said. 'Dangerous to look at all. And that is why you've come to us, so that we can help you.'

'No,' Atara said, 'I came here to look for the Lightstone. We all did.'

She touched the gold medallion that King Kiritan had given her; she spoke of the great quest upon which many knights had set out. Then she nodded toward Alphanderry and told Mithuna what his dead friend had heard in the Singing Caves.

'The Lightstone,' Mithuna said. She traded quick looks with Ayanna, who had white hair and a deeply lined face, and was the oldest of the scryers. 'Always the Lightstone.'

Here Kane smiled savagely and said, ''Ha – you didn't *see* that, eh?'

'No scryer has ever seen the Lightstone,' she said, staring back at him. 'At least, not in our visions.'

'But why not?' Atara asked her.

Now Mithuna favored the young and almond-eyed Songlian with one

363

of her faraway gazes before turning back to Atara. 'Because, dear child, all that is or ever will be flows out of a single point in time, and there the Lightstone always is. To look there is like looking at the sun.'

'Paradoxes, mysteries,' Kane spat out. 'You scryers make a mystery of everything.'

'No, it is not we who have made things so,' Mithuna reminded him.

In the light given off by Flick's twinkling form, Kane's face filled with both resentment and longing.

'The Singing Caves,' Alphanderry said to Mithuna, 'spoke these words: "If you would know where the Gelstei was hidden, go to the Blue Mountains and seek in the Tower of the Sun."'

'The Singing Caves always speak the truth,' Mithuna said. She pointed at Maram's red crystal and smiled. 'There is the gelstei.'

'Hoy, there it is,' Alphanderry agreed. 'But it is not *the* Gelstei.'

'It is difficult, isn't it, to know of which gelstei the Caves spoke?'

'But when one speaks of the Gelstei, what is always meant is the Lightstone.'

'Always?'

Kane, who was growing angrier by the moment, scowled as he looked about the starlit ruins and the dark mountains that towered above us.

'Are you saying that the Lightstone *wasn't* hidden here?' I asked.

'No,' Mithuna said, shaking her head, 'I wouldn't say that. Morjin hid it here long ago.'

'But it is not hidden here now?'

'No, I wouldn't say that either,' she said mysteriously. 'The Lightstone still *is* here. But if you truly want to recover it and hold it in your hands, you'll have to journey somewhere else.'

'So,' Kane muttered to the wind. 'Scryers.'

But I wasn't about to give up so easily. I said to Mithuna, 'So the Lightstone is here, somewhere, somehow – but it isn't here, as well?'

'Is the Tur-Solonu here?' she asked pointing at the broken tower above us. 'Are *you* here, Valashu Elahad? What would a scryer have said to this ten thousand years ago? What would she say ten thousand years hence?'

I took a deep breath as I asked, 'If the Lightstone is here, have you seen it, with your eyes?'

'No one sees the Lightstone with just the eyes,' Mithuna said. 'The eyes won't hold it anymore than hands will light.'

'But how do you know it isn't somewhere among these ruins, then?'

'Because,' she said, 'although I cannot see where it is, I can see where it is not.'

'But I thought you said it was everywhere.'

'That is true – it is everywhere and nowhere.'

I was beginning to see why Kane hated scryers. Was Mithuna, I wondered, willfully confounding us? Talking with her was like trying to eat the wind.

'We've come a very long way, Mistress Mithuna,' I told her. 'A great deal may depend on our finding the Lightstone. Would you mind if we searched the ruins for it?'

Mithuna's face fell sad; almost as if speaking to herself, she said, 'Should I mind the rising of tomorrow's sun? What should be shall be.'

She turned to Atara and said, 'It's growing late – will you sit with us tonight beneath the stars?'

Atara brushed back the hair from her eyes and stood up straight like the warrior she was. She said, 'Are you inviting my friends as well?'

'I'm sorry,' Mithuna said, 'but only scryers may see our refuge.'

'Do you mean, see with the eyes or . . . *see*?'

This made Mithuna smile, and she said, 'You see, you really *are* a scryer.'

She turned as if to make ready to leave, which prompted Maram to hold up his hand and say, 'No, don't go just yet! We've brandy and beer and Ea's finest minstrel to help us appreciate it. Won't you share this with us?'

He held the crystal carelessly so that it stuck straight out from his body. All his attention was turned on Mithuna, and I knew that he wanted to share much more with her than beer.

Mithuna looked at him a long time, then said, 'It was foretold that a man in red would find the firestone that destroyed the Tur-Solonu. I, myself, saw you in one of my visions.'

'You saw me, did you?' Maram said. His smile suggested that he had seen *her* in his dreams. 'And what did you see?'

'What do you mean? I saw you with the firestone.'

'And is that all?'

'Should there be more?' Mithuna asked as her eyes brightened.

'Oh, yes, indeed there should be,' Maram said as he gripped his crystal more tightly. 'Did you see my heart filling up with the fire of the sun? Did you see this fire pouring out of the gelstei?'

'I saw it melting the hardest rock,' she said with a smile.

'Did you? And did you, ah, see the earth shake, volcanoes erupting?'

'It is said that the firestones of old caused such cataclysms,' Mithuna admitted. 'They were very powerful.'

'Powerful, yes,' Maram said, holding his crystal pointing almost straight up. 'I suspect none of us knows just how powerful.'

'*That* is a dangerous thing,' Mithuna said, stretching her finger toward the firestone. 'We do know that.'

'Yes, but surely one can learn how to use it.'

'Perhaps some can. But can you?'

'Do you doubt me?' Maram said with a hurt look. 'Perhaps I should leave it where I found it?'

'No, surely it is yours to do with as you will.'

'Should I give it to you, then, Mistress Mithuna?'

'And what would I do with a firestone?'

'I wish I could, ah, give you *something*.'

Mithuna's face suddenly fell serious as if the whole weight of the world were pulling at it. In a sad voice, she said, 'Then give me your promise that you'll learn to use this stone wisely.'

'I *do* promise you that,' Maram said, glancing at the broken Tur-Solonu. Then his eyes covered her as he smiled. 'More wisely than did the Red Dragon.'

'Don't joke about such things,' she told him. Now she pointed fiercely at the firestone. 'You should know that a doom was laid upon this crystal: that it would bring Morjin's undoing. That is why he left it here.'

We all looked at the firestone more closely. And then Kane asked, 'And who laid this doom?'

'Her name was Rebekah Lorus,' Mithuna said. 'She was mistress of the murdered scryers.'

'Now *that* would be a strange justice,' Kane said, 'if the very gelstei that Morjin made unmade him.'

'But he didn't make it,' Mithuna said.

'What? Didn't make it, eh? Then who did?'

'A man named Kaspar Saranom. He was one of Morjin's priests.'

'And how do you know this?'

'Kaspar destroyed the Tur-Solonu at Morjin's command. The scryers who came before us have told of this for six thousand years.'

She went on to say that Morjin had never learned the art of making the red gelstei, for after nearly being killed creating the *relb*, he had grown deathly afraid of all such crystals. And so he had left their making to others. Kaspar Saranom had been the first on Ea to forge a firestone. That he had forged only one, Mithuna seemed certain.

'After the Tower was destroyed,' Mithuna said, 'Morjin wanted Kaspar to burn down every town from here to Tria. But Kaspar refused. For his defiance, Morjin had him crucified along with the scryers.'

Here Master Juwain came forward and said, 'This is news indeed. Then

366

Kaspar Saranom, not Petram, was the first to have made the red gelstei. His name will be remembered.'

'Ha,' Kane said, 'it's even greater news that Morjin didn't know the art of making the firestones. We can hope he never learned it.'

'Then this stone,' Master Juwain said, daring to touch Maram's crystal, 'would be the first firestone ever made.'

'So – and we can hope it's the last remaining on earth.'

We all looked at the firestone in a new light as Maram held it out and marveled at it.

'It's growing late,' Mithuna said again. 'Will you come with us, Atara?'

'No,' Atara said, 'I'll stay with my friends.'

'Then we'll return tomorrow,' Mithuna said. 'Good night.' And with that, she gathered her sister scryers around her, and they walked off into the deep shadows of the mountains.

'A beautiful woman,' Maram said to me after she was gone. 'How long do you think it's been since she did more than, ah, *look* at a man?'

'She's a scryer of an oracle,' I told him. 'Therefore she must have taken vows of celibacy.'

'Well, so have I.'

'Ha!' Kane said, stepping up to him. 'You might as well try to love this crystal as a scryer!'

Maram look down at the firestone in his hand and muttered, 'Ah, well, perhaps I will.'

We camped that night by the stream where the ancient scryers had built their baths. It was a long, dark night of dreams and brilliant stars. The wind blew unceasingly down from the mountains to the north. Altaru and the other horses were restless, more than once whinnying and pulling at their picket stakes. In the dark notch of the Tur-Solonu, the ruins gleamed faintly in the starlight like bleached and broken bones defying time.

Atara, lying on top of the inconstant earth with its whirling and numinous fires, sweated and turned in a sleep that wasn't quite sleep. Her murmurs and cries kept me awake most of the night. Nightmares I had suffered through with her before as she had with me. But this was something different. I felt something vast and bottomless as the sea pulling her down into its onstreaming currents. There, in the turbid darkness, Atara screamed silently in fascination and fear, and I wanted to scream, too.

We were all grateful the next day for the rising of the sun. When I asked Atara what she had seen in her sleep, she looked at me strangely as an uncharacteristic coldness came over her. Then she told me, 'If I had been blind from birth and asked you to describe the color of the sky to me, what would you say?'

I looked above the mountains, with their silvery rocks and emerald trees sparkling in the sun. There the sky was a blue dome growing bluer by the moment.

'I would say that it is the deepest of colors, the softest and the kindest, too. In the blue of morning, we find ourselves soaring with hope; in the blue of night, with infinite possibilities. In its opening out onto everything, we remember who we really are.'

'Perhaps you should have been a minstrel instead of a warrior,' she said with a wan smile. 'I'm sure I can't do as well.'

'Why don't you try?'

'All right, then,' she said. The sleeplessness that haunted her face convinced me that she had seen something much worse than ghosts. 'You spoke of remembrance, but who are we *really*? Infinite possibilities, yes, but only one can ever *be*. The one that shall be is the one that should be. But all of them *are*, always, and we are . . . so delicate. Like flowers, Val. Which is the one you will pick for me and tell me that you love me? And which is the one that can stand beneath the light of the sun?'

Already, I thought, she was beginning to talk like a scryer, and I didn't like it. To bring her back to the world of wind and grass and standing stones gleaming red beneath the rising sun, I suggested eating some of the delicious breakfast that Liljana was cooking, and this we did.

After that, we climbed the cracked stone steps of the Tur-Solonu to look for the Lightstone. It was cool and dark inside that broken tower, and except for the faint radiance streaming off Flick's spinning form, we wouldn't have been able to see very much. As it was, there was nothing much to see – nothing more interesting than a few cobwebs and the bones of some poor beast who had dragged itself inside the door to die there in peace. The Tower, much to our disappointment, held no rooms that might be explored, for it was only a series of steps winding up inside a tube of marble. The ancient scryers had used it only as means of standing closer to the stars. There was nowhere in its stark interior that Sartan Odinan could have hidden a golden cup.

'Perhaps there are secret recesses,' Maram said as he tapped the wall with the pommel of his sword. We were all gathered in the stairwell about seventy feet up inside the Tower. The outer wall curved dark and smooth around us, while the inner wall was like a pillar rising up as the Tower's core. 'Perhaps one of the stones is loose, and there Sartan hid the Lightstone.'

But try as we might, we could find no loose stone in the walls or steps of the well-made Tur-Solonu. We tested every one of them all the way to the top of the Tower, which was broken and open to the sun high above the mountains.

'It's not here,' I said, looking out over the standing stones below us. To the east, the ruins of the temple gleamed white in the harsh light. 'Sartan could not have hidden it here.'

Maram joined me upon the topmost unbroken step to stare out above the cracked and melted outer wall. He pointed at the temple's ruins below us and said, 'Perhaps there, then.'

'No, it won't be there,' I said. The taste of disappointment, I thought, was as bitter as the molds growing across the exposed stones. 'The words that Ventakil heard in the Caves told us to seek in the Tower of the Sun.'

'But shouldn't we at least go and see?' Maram asked.

'Of course we will,' I said. 'What else can we do?'

After breaking to eat a simple lunch of bread and cheese that Mithuna and the other scryers brought us, we spent the whole afternoon picking among the temple's ruins. If the Tower had suggested no possible places where a plain, golden cup could have been hidden, the scattered stones of the temple provided too many. Many sections of the walls had cracked and fallen down into great heaps of rubble; the Lightstone might have been buried in any one of them. During the centuries since Sartan had brought the Lightstone out of Argattha, wind had driven grit and soil into the cracks between the fallen stones, in some places, almost covering them altogether. And now grass grew in the soil, making a patchwork of green seams and turf among the many irregular-shaped mounds. Excavating any one of them could take many days, and there were many, many such mounds.

'Oh, my Lord, it's hopeless,' Maram said to me as we gathered near one of the temple's few standing pillars. The six scryers, with Mithuna at their center, stood off a few paces near a great slab of stone. 'What shall we do?'

Now Master Juwain and Liljana looked toward me with discouragement coloring their faces, while Alphanderry sat on a stone merrily munching on a handful of nuts. Kane stood staring at one of the mounds as if his eyes were firestones that might burn open the very ground. And Atara, next to me, was staring out into the nothingness of the deep blue sky.

'It's *not* hopeless,' I said to Maram. 'It can't be hopeless.'

Maram swept his hand out toward the remains of the temple and said, 'Shall we all take up shovels and start digging, then?'

'If all else fails, yes.'

'We'd dig for a hundred years.'

'Better that,' I said, 'than giving up.'

At the prospect of so much work, Maram groaned and Alphanderry ate another nut. Then Maram pointed his red crystal at one of the mounds and said, 'Perhaps I could melt the rock with this until the Lightstone was uncovered.'

'But wouldn't you melt it along with the rock?' Alphanderry asked.

'No,' Maram told him. 'It's said that nothing can harm the Lightstone in any way. It's said that even diamond won't scratch it.'

'But what if the sayings are wrong?'

Maram stared across the ruins of the temple as if realizing the folly of what he had suggested. And then Mithuna stepped forward and said to Atara, 'It would seem that your quest here has ended.'

Atara suddenly broke off staring at the sky. To Mithuna, she said, 'But how can it be since we haven't found what we came here to find?'

'Perhaps you have, Atara,' Mithuna said, smiling at her. 'Perhaps you should remain here with us.'

Atara looked at Mithuna for a long time, and I was afraid that she might accept her invitation. Our quest, at that moment, certainly seemed hopeless. Freely we had all joined together to seek the Lightstone, and freely any of us might leave the company – so we had agreed before setting out from Tria.

And then Atara turned toward me as her bright blue eyes filled with tears and a deeper thing. It was all warm and shimmering and more adamantine than diamond.

'No,' Atara finally said to Mithuna, 'I'll remain with my friends.'

'What should be shall be,' Mithuna said. 'In the end, we choose our futures.'

Atara looked over at the Tur-Solonu where it rose up a few hundred yards away. Her eyes grew dry and clear as diamonds and gleamed with a wild light. She pointed at it and said, 'Inside there is the future. I should have seen that all along.'

Without another word she began walking quickly toward the Tower, and we all followed her. It didn't take very long for us to wind our way among the standing stones and those lying down in the grass.

'You were right,' Atara said to Mithuna as we approached the Tower's door. 'The Lightstone *is* here.'

She stepped inside the door and so did I. And almost immediately I saw what I had missed before. On the Tower's inner wall, high up to the left, ran a jagged crack almost a foot wide. And wedged into it was a plain golden cup shining with a beautiful light.

'Atara!' I cried out. 'Atara, look!'

But the crack was high enough above the dusty floor that only a tall man could look into it. Or reach into it with arm and hand. This I now did, scraping the skin off my knuckles as I jammed my hand into the rock to feel for the cup. But even though I turned and twisted about and ran my whole arm up and down the crack, my fingers closed around nothing but cold marble and air.

'What are you doing?' Atara asked, coming over to my side. Kane, Maram and Liljana crowded inside the doorway. The others, along with the scryers, stared at me from outside to see if I had fallen mad.

A moment later, I withdrew my bleeding hand and stood back from the wall so that I could better see inside the crack. But the golden cup was gone.

'It was here!' I said. 'The Lightstone was here!'

Again, I thrust my arm into the crack, but it was as empty as the space between the stars.

'I don't understand!' I half-shouted, looking into the crack again.

Mithuna stepped inside the doorway then and touched my shoulder. She said, 'Scryers often see things that others do not.'

'But they don't see things that *are* not, do they?'

'That's true,' she said.

'Besides, I'm no scryer.'

'No, you're not,' she said. Her face drew out long and sad as she admitted, 'I don't understand this either.'

Atara took my bloody hand in hers as she used her other to touch the bottom of the crack. She said, 'The Lightstone isn't *here*, Val.'

'Where is it, then?'

She let go of my hand suddenly as she pointed toward the stairs and said, 'It's *there*.'

Without warning, she broke away from me and began climbing the stairs. In truth, she practically bounded up them three at a time. There was nothing to do except follow her.

And so we all raced up the winding stairs, Mithuna and Kane following me, while Maram puffed heavily behind him. Liljana, Alphanderry and Master Juwain were slower to begin their ascent, but climbed the more quickly to catch up. And the five scryers waited for us outside.

When Atara reached the broken opening that was now the top of the Tower, she paused on the highest step to gasp for air. I stood just below her, gasping too. For there, poised on the melted marble of the outer wall, was the Lightstone.

'Atara,' I said as before, 'look!'

I lunged forward to grasp it before it could disappear, but it suddenly winked into nothingness before my hands could close around it.

'Atara, please come down!' Mithuna suddenly called. She was standing with Kane and Maram just below me. In the narrow space of the stairwell, there was room for three people on any step, but no more. Now Master Juwain, Liljana and Alphanderry crowded in behind Maram and looked up at Atara.

'The Singing Caves *did* speak the truth,' Atara said. She carelessly rested her hand against the Tower's broken outer wall as she looked out at the mountains and sky.

'"If you would know where the Gelstei was hidden,"' Alphanderry reminded us, '"go to the Blue Mountains and seek in the Tower of the Sun."'

'If we would *know*,' Atara said. She stood with the wind whipping her hair about her face. 'If *I* would.'

She suddenly held her hands out toward the earth as she lifted back her head and gazed straight up into the sky. If her third eye was a door, she flung it wide open then. I felt her do this. And so, it seemed, did Mithuna.

'No, Atara – you don't know what you're doing!' Mithuna said.

But Atara was a warrior and as wild as the wind. She opened herself utterly to the invisible fires that streamed up through the Tur-Solonu. And then she let out a soft cry as her eyes rolled back into her head. She lost her balance and teetered at the edge of the Tower's wall. I moved quickly then to grab her back and clasp her to me; if I hadn't, she would have fallen to her death.

'Take her down from here!' Mithuna told me. 'Please!'

I lifted Atara in my arms and followed the others down through the Tower. Atara's eyes were now staring out at nothing, and she was breathing raggedly. I lost count of the Tower's steps, but there were many of them. By the time we reached the bottom, my arms were trembling with the weight of her body.

'Bring her over there!' Mithuna said, pointing at a standing stone in the direction of the temple. I and the others followed her a hundred yards over the swishing grass, where we sat Atara back against the huge stone.

'Atara!' Mithuna said, as she knelt beside her.

I knelt by her other side and tried to call her back to the world even as I had after she had eaten the timana. But the trance into which she had fallen, it seemed, was too deep.

Now Mithuna reached into the pocket of her robe and removed a clear, crystalline ball the size of a large apple. She pressed it into Atara's hands. The crystal, which sparkled like a diamond, caught the light of the sun and cast its brilliant colors into Atara's eyes.

'What's the matter with her?' Maram asked. He stood with Kane and the others peering above the half-circle that the scryers made around Atara. 'Will she be all right?'

'Quiet now!' Kane barked at him. 'Quiet, I say!'

At that moment, Flick appeared above Atara's head and spun about with a slowness that I took to be concern.

And then little by little, as all our breaths came and went like the whooshing of the wind, the light returned to Atara's eyes. She sat staring deep into the crystal.

'What *is* that?' Maram whispered to Master Juwain as he pointed at the crystal. 'A scryer's sphere?'

'A scryer's sphere indeed,' Master Juwain whispered back. 'Usually they're made of quartz – and more rarely, diamond.'

'That's no diamond, I think,' Liljana said as she pressed closer to look at the sphere. Something inside her seemed to be sniffing at it as she might a glass of wine.

Just then a shudder ran through Atara's body as her eyes blinked and she looked away from the crystal. She turned toward Mithuna and said, 'Thank you.'

She looked at me for a long moment and smiled before turning her gaze on Kane, Maram, Liljana, Alphanderry and Master Juwain.

'That's a *kristei*, isn't it?' Liljana said to Mithuna as she pointed at the crystal. 'A white gelstei.'

'It *is* a kristei,' Mithuna said. 'It was brought here long ago and has been passed down among us from hand to hand.'

The white gelstei, I remembered, were the stones of seeing. Through the clarity of such crystals, a scryer might apprehend things far away in space or time. It was said that during the Age of Law, each scryer had her own kristei. But now, only a very few did.

'Looking into the future,' Mithuna explained, 'is like gazing up into a tree that grows out toward the stars and has no end. The possibilities are infinite. And so it is easy to become lost in the branches of such visions. The kristei helps a scryer find the branch she is seeking. And find her way back to the earth.'

That was as clear an explanation of scrying as I was ever to hear from a scryer. Everyone looked at Atara then as I asked her, 'What did you see?'

'The Sea People,' she told me. 'Wherever I looked for the Lightstone, I saw them.'

'Do they have the Lightstone, then?'

'That's hard to say. I couldn't see that.'

'Do you think they might know where it is, then?'

'Perhaps,' she said. 'I only know that all the paths I could find led toward them.'

'Yes, but led *where*?'

Atara didn't know. The paths to the future, she said, were not like those that led through the lands of Ea. Although she'd had a clear vision of the Sea People, she couldn't tell us where we might find them.

'I'm afraid that no one knows anymore where the Sea People live,' Master Juwain said.

'*We* know,' Mithuna said. 'You'll find them at the Bay of Whales.'

We all looked at her as Maram let loose a long groan. The Bay of Whales lay at the edge of the Great Northern Ocean at least a hundred miles northwest across the great forest known as the Vardaloon.

'Are you *sure* they're there?' Maram asked Mithuna. 'Have you *seen* them?'

'Songlian has,' Mithuna said. She nodded at the shy young woman who smiled at us in affirmation of past visions. 'We've known about the Sea People for some time.'

Atara turned toward me and smiled, and I traded a knowing look with Kane. And Maram groaned again, louder this time, and said, 'Oh, no, my friends, please don't tell me that you're thinking of journeying to this Bay of Whales!'

We were thinking exactly that. It now seemed certain that we wouldn't find the Lightstone at the Tur-Solonu.

'But I'd hoped we would end our quest here!' Maram said. 'We can't just go tramping all over Ea!'

'Not *all* over Ea,' I said. 'Only a few more miles.'

We were all disappointed that we had gained nothing more in the Tower than a vision as to where the Lightstone might still be found. But none of us – not even Maram – was ready to break his vows and abandon the quest so soon. And so we held a quick council and decided to set out for the Bay of Whales the next day.

'I believe that would be your wisest course,' Mithuna told us.

Atara, who had now gained the strength to stand up, handed the crystal sphere back to her and said, 'Thank you for lending me this.'

Mithuna reached out her hands, and squeezed Atara's fingers the more tightly around the sphere. She said, 'But, dear child, this is our gift to you. If you really hope to find the Cup of Heaven, you'll need this more than I.'

The sunlight glazing off the crystal was so bright that it dazzled all of our eyes. For a moment, it seemed that Atara might disappear through its sparkling surface. And then she said, 'No, this is too much.'

'Please take it,' Mithuna insisted. 'It's time the kristei passed on.'

Atara continued staring at the stone. At last, she said, 'Thank you.'

This made Mithuna smile. She cast a long, sad look at the broken Tower and told us, 'It's said that when the Lightstone is found, the kristei will come into its true power, which is not merely to see the future but to create it. Then the Tur-Solonu will be raised up again. Then a new age will begin: the Age of Light we have all seen and yet feared could never come to be.'

With that, she leaned forward and kissed Atara upon the forehead. She told us that she and the other scryers would come to say goodbye to us the next morning, and then she walked off with them into the mountains.

For a while, as the sun dropped down toward their rounded peaks, we all stood staring at Atara's crystal sphere. There I saw the reflection of the ruined Tower. But there, too, in the shimmering substance of the white gelstei, in my deepest dreams, flickered the form of the Tower as it had once been and might be again: tall and straight and standing like an unbroken pillar beneath the brilliant stars.

22

The next morning we packed up the horses and gathered by the river. It was a cool day of big, puffy clouds that drifted slowly past the sun. As promised, Mithuna arrived with the other scryers to say goodbye. They brought cheeses and fresh bread to sustain us on our journey. Although we were grateful for their gift, we needed oats for the horses even more, and this they could not provide. Where we would be going, I thought, we would find no grain and precious little grass.

'The Vardaloon,' Maram said, shaking his head as he adjusted the saddle of his sorrel. 'I can't believe we're setting out to cross the Vardaloon.'

We might, of course, have retraced our path back through Iviunn and then proceeded north through Jerolin, hugging the mountains until we reached the sea. And there, we might have kept to the coast as we skirted along the edge of the great forest, all the way to the Bay of Whales. But Jerolin was said to be a Kallimun stronghold. And such a course would also be much longer, and might not even bring us to the end of our Quest. After the emptiness of the Tower, I feared dangers that fired up the spirit less than the discouragement of a journey that might seem to have no end.

'There *are* dangers in the great forest,' Mithuna whispered to me as I stroked Altaru's neck. 'There is something in there.'

'What is it, then?' I whispered back.

'I don't know,' Mithuna said, looking at Ayanna and the other scryers. 'We've never quite been able to see it – it's too dark.'

A shudder rippled through my belly then, and I told her, 'Please say nothing of this to my friends.'

But Maram needed no fell words from Mithuna to feed the flames of his already vivid imagination. He looked off toward the mountains to the west as he muttered, 'Ah, well, if any bears come for us, we've cold steel to give them. And if the forest grows too deep, we can always burn our way through the trees.'

Here he held up his firestone, which gleamed a dull red in the weak morning light.

Mithuna came over to him and pointed at the crystal. While the other scryers gathered around, and Kane and my friends looked on from where they stood by their horses, Mithuna's sad voice flowed out above the rushing of the river: 'You have a great fire in your heart, and now a great gelstei to hold it. But you must use it only in pursuit of the Lightstone – not for burning trees or against any living thing, if you can help it. This we have all seen.'

To our astonishment, Maram's most of all, she leaned forward and kissed him full upon the lips. Then she laughed out, 'I hope you won't mind leaving me with a little of this fire.'

After that, she pointed out a path along the river that led up into the woods surrounding the Tur-Solonu. 'If you follow this west, it will take you over the mountains into the Vardaloon.'

'And then?' Maram asked.

'And then we don't know,' Mithuna said. 'Farther than that, none of us has ever been. I'm afraid you'll have to find your own way through the forest.'

We went among Mithuna and her sister scryers, embracing them and making our final farewell. Then we mounted our horses and lined up in the same order as we had left Tria: I led forth and Kane rode warily at the rear. We left the scryers standing almost in the shadow of the Tur-Solonu as they watched us with cold, clear eyes that seemed as old as time.

For a few miles, we wound our way along the river through the rising woods. Then the path veered off to the right, where the trees grew thickest in an unbroken swath of gleaming leaves. It was a good path that Mithuna had shown us: wide enough for the horses to keep their footing, if a little overgrown. Its pitch was long and low, cutting as it did along the gentle slopes of one of the long, low Blue Mountains. High passes such as we had crossed from Mesh into Ishka we would not find here. Nor were there jagged escarpments ready to hurl down boulders upon us or biting cold. Our greatest obstacle, I thought, would be the forest itself, for it grew thickly all around us, the elms and chestnuts rising up through mats of oak fern and other bracken. Shrubs such as virburn and brambles made for low, green walls between the trees. If the path hadn't cut through this dense vegetation, we would have had to cut through it with our swords. Or burn through it with the firestone that Mithuna had said we must not use.

We traveled all that day through the peaceful mountains. It was quiet in the woods, with little more to listen to than the tapping of a woodpecker or the calls of the occasional thrush or tanager. And we were quiet as we picked our way along the path; our failure to gain the Lightstone drove all of us inside ourselves, there to ask our souls if we really had the courage to keep on seeking unless illness, wounds or death struck us down first. It was one thing, I thought, to make such a vow in the splendor of King Kiritan's hall, with thousands of shouting people, each of whom was convinced that he was the one destined to find the golden cup. And it was quite another to continue on through unknown lands after suffering great disappointment and the mud and cold of an already long journey.

And yet we all rode along toward the west in good spirits. We had cause for much faith. Atara's newly found gift and her vision of the Sea People gave us to hope that she might see our way through to the end of our quest. And we had not left the Tur-Solonu with empty hands. Maram had his firestone and Atara her kristei; with Kane's black stone and Master Juwain's healing crystal, that made four of the seven gelstei told of in Ayondela's prophecy. Was this nothing more than the rarest of chances? Or could it be that we *were* the ones destined to set forth into the darkness and win the Lightstone?

Of course, we all knew that it was not enough simply to have gained these four gelstei. Somehow we must learn how to use them. Toward that end, Master Juwain continued his own private quest of moving the dwelling of his soul from his head to his heart. Often, as we rode through the thick greenery, he would take out his green crystal and hold it up to the swaying leaves as if trying to capture their life-fire and hold it within himself. There, where his blood sang to the music of the birds and all living things, he would find a forest deeper and darker than a thousand Vardaloons. And with the aid of the gelstei he held in his hand, he must find his own way through it.

Atara had her own paths to negotiate. For her, scrying was a most difficult journey. Standing beneath the stars at night to unlock time's mysteries came unnaturally to her, for she was a creature of sun and wind and water rushing over open plains. Her temperament inclined her to want to look out upon all things with open eyes and go among the fields and flowers like a wild mare running free. And to leave all peoples or places she came across better for her passing. This was her will, to work her dreams upon the world. But now she had to call upon all her will to enter the otherworld of dreams of the future. And so, as she rode along behind me though the mountains, she brought forth her crystal sphere and fixed her bright eyes upon it. She turned inward into that dark place that she hated to go. And there brought what light she could.

As for Maram, he regarded his firestone as might a child who has been given a long-desired birthday present. Even while guiding his sorrel down the steepest segments of the path, he kept his crystal always at hand, now waving it about like a sword, now holding it tightly to his chest. He studied its dark, red interior with a diligence he had never applied to the *Saganom Elu* or the healing arts. He had a great passion to use this crystal, I thought, and I prayed that he had an equally great devotion to using it well.

Late that afternoon, as we made camp by a stream running through a pretty vale, he managed to coax the first fire from his stone. We all watched as he knelt over a pile of dry twigs and positioned the gelstei so that it caught what little light the sun drove through the forest's thick canopy. And it was good that the crystal drank in only a little light. For just as Maram's whole body trembled excitedly and he let loose a great gasp of wonder, the pointed end of the crystal erupted with a bolt of red flame. It shot like lightning into the firepit, instantly igniting and consuming the tinder, and turning it to black ash. The pit's stones cast the fire straight back into Maram's face so that it burned his cheeks and scorched his eyebrows. But he seemed not to mind this chastisement, or even to feel it. He jumped away from the pit and thrust his crystal toward the sky as he cried out, 'Yes! Oh, my Lord, yes – I've done it!'

After that, we all decided that Kane should stand over Maram whenever he practiced summoning the fires of the red gelstei, and this Kane did. The next morning, as Maram tried to burn holes in an old log just for the fun of it, Kane drew forth his black stone. His black eyes came alive to match the dark glister of his gelstei, but otherwise his whole being seemed to touch upon a place that utterly devoured light. The coldness that came over him chilled my heart and reminded me of things that I wished to forget. But it also seemed to cool the fires of Maram's crystal. In truth, Maram managed to call from it scarcely more than a candle's worth of flame – and this only after Kane had gathered his gelstei into his clenched fist. If Maram chafed at having to work with Kane and having his best efforts at firemaking dampened, Kane was wroth. When Maram complained that Kane had gone too far, Kane practically shoved the black gelstei in Maram's face and growled out, 'Do you think I *like* using this damn stone? Too far, you say, eh? What do you know about too far?'

His words remained a mystery to me until that night when we made our second camp in the mountains. Our two days of traveling had taken us almost all the way across this narrow range; just to the west, below us, gleamed the sea of green that was the Vardaloon. We found a shelf of earth on the side of a mountain overlooking it, and there we made our firepit and set out our furs. Around midnight, just after Alphanderry had finished his watch and gone to sleep, Kane and I stood together gazing at Flick's whirling form against the backdrop of the stars.

'Too far,' Kane said again in a low voice, 'always too far.'

'*What* is too far?' I asked, turning toward him.

He looked at me for a long few moments as his face softened and his eyes seemed to fill with starlight. Then he said, '*You* might understand. Of all men, you might.'

He smiled at me, and the warmth that poured out of him was a welcome tonic against the chill of the mountains. Then he opened his hand to show me the black gelstei and said, 'There is a place. One place, and one only, eh? All things gather there; there they shimmer, they whirl, they tremble like a child waiting to be born. From this place, all things burst forth into the world. Like roses, Val, like the sun rising in the morning. But the sun must set, eh? Roses soon die and return to the earth. The source of all things is also their negation. So, this is the power of the black gelstei. It touches upon this one place, this utter blackness. It *touches*: red gelstei or white, flowers or men's souls. And whatever fire burns there is sucked down into the blackness like a man's last gasp into a whirlpool.'

He paused to stare down at his stone, even as Flick spun faster and flared more brightly. I waited for him to go on, but he seemed caught in silence.

'To use this gelstei,' I said, 'you must touch upon this place, yes?'

'So, just so – I must,' Kane muttered, nodding his head. 'I cannot, but I must.'

'It is dangerous, yes?'

'Dangerous – ha! You don't know, you don't know!'

'Tell me, then.'

His voice fell strange and deep as he looked at Flick and said, 'This place I have told of – it's darker than any night you've ever seen. But it's something else, too. Out of it come the sun, the moon, the stars, even the fire of the Timpimpiri. The fire, Val, the light. There's no end to it. *This* is why the black stones are the most dangerous of the gelstei. Go too far, touch what may not be touched, and there's no end. Then instead of negation, its opposite. So, a light beyond light. If a black gelstei is used wrongly in controlling a firestone, then out of it might pour such a fire as hasn't been seen since the beginning of time.'

He looked over toward Maram where he slept by the fire holding his red crystal in his hand. Then he stared out at the blazing stars for a long time and said, 'No, Val, it's not the darkness I fear.'

We stood there on the side of the mountain talking of the gelstei as the sky turned and the night deepened. After a while, because he was

Kane, the man of stone who also held a deep and brilliant light, I told him of Mithuna's last words to me.

'There is something there,' I said as I looked off toward the dark hills of the Vardaloon. 'Some dark thing, Mithuna said.'

'So, stories are told of the Vardaloon,' Kane muttered.

'Tell me.'

'They're just stories.'

'Perhaps,' I said.

'You fear this thing, eh?'

I continued staring into the night for as long as it took for my heart to beat ten times, then said, 'Yes.'

'So,' he said. 'So it always is. It's fear that's the worst, eh? Well, let's at least slay this one enemy, if we can.'

Without other warning, he suddenly whipped his sword from its sheath. So quickly did he move that it seemed to burn the air. I heard its steel hissing scarcely inches in front of my face.

'What are you doing?' I asked him.

'Draw! Draw now, I say! It's time we had a little practice with these blades.'

'Here? Now? It must be nearly midnight.'

'So?'

'So it's too dark to see.'

'Of course it is – that's the point! Now draw before I lose my patience!'

'But we'll wake the others.'

'Let them wake, then, damn it! Now draw your sword!'

I looked over at our five friends sleeping soundly by the fire. There was little enough ground between them and the wall of thistles and branches we had cut to surround our camp. I looked back at Kane, and the change that had come over him chilled me. He stood glaring at me with his kalama held at the ready. The stars gave off just enough light that I could see it glinting behind his head.

'All right then,' I said, freeing my kalama from its sheath.

I should have been grateful that he deigned to fence with me. In all the battles I had fought, in all the duels I had ever watched, I had never seen his like with the sword. He knew things that even Asaru and my father's weapons master, Lansar Raasharu, did not. And it was his way to hold on to his secrets more tightly than a miser does gold. But now, it seemed, he was willing to share them with me.

'Ha!' he cried out. 'Ha, now, Valashu Elahad!'

His long steel blade leaped out of the dark like lightning from a blackened sky. I barely had a moment to raise up mine to parry it. The clash of steel against steel rang out across the side of the mountain. As I had feared, it brought Atara and the others flying out of their sleep. While Maram waved his crystal wildly in front of his face, Atara made a quick grab for her sword and might have charged toward us if Kane hadn't called out: 'It's only us, now go back to sleep! Or stay up and watch, if that's what you want!'

Again, his sword flashed out at me, and again I parried it – by inches, by the shrieking sound of it as much as sight. We stared at each other through the darkness as we each waited for the other to move.

And move Kane did, suddenly, explosively, attacking me in a fury of slashing steel. For several moments, we whirled about the dark ground, feinting and cutting at each other. Something dark came over him then – or came howling out of him like a tiger who hunts at night. It knew little of fellowship and nothing at all of the conventions of a friendly fencing match. I stood before Kane with drawn sword, and that was the only thing that mattered to him. In the madness of the moment, in the wildness of his black eyes that I could barely see, I had somehow become his enemy. And I wondered if he had become mine: had Morjin somehow suborned him? Had the Red Dragon's lies finally found their way to his heart? His sudden and utter viciousness terrified me, for I knew that he would destroy me, if he could.

'Ha!' he cried out gleefully. 'Ha – again!'

If not for my gift of sensing his movements – and the skills that my father had taught me – he might well have killed me then. He struck out with his sword straight toward me again and again, and I managed to dance out of his way or parry his ferocious blows only by the narrowest of distances.

'Again!' he called to me. 'Again!'

And again we circled each other, watching and waiting and exchanging slashes of our swords in a flurry of motion. We dueled thus for a very long time – so long that sweat soaked through my mail and the cool air that I gasped burned my lungs like fire. I lunged about the starlit earth looking for an opening that I couldn't find. At last, I retreated toward the fire where the others sat watching us. I held up my hand as I shook my head and leaned forward to catch my breath.

'Again!' Kane cried out. The fire cast its red light over his closely cropped white hair and harsh face.

'What are you doing?' Atara asked him. She was now clearly alarmed and gripped the hilt of her curved sword in her hand.

'Fight, Valashu!' Kane roared at me. 'Don't hide behind others! Now fight, damn it – fight, I say!'

I had no choice but to fight. If I hadn't raised my sword to parry his blow, he would have sent me on to the otherworld. Not even Atara could have moved quickly enough to stop him. The fury of his renewed attack caught me up like a whirlwind. His black eyes flashed in the fire's glow to the lightning strokes of his sword, and I felt my eyes flashing, too. I felt something else. His whole being burned with one purpose: to cut, to thrust, to tear and rend, to survive – no, to thrive, always and only to live deeply and completely, exultantly, destroying with joy anything that stood ready to destroy him. To *know* with utter certainty that he couldn't fail, that a light beyond light would always show him where his sword must strike and an infinite fire pooled always ready to fill his wild heart. His sword touched mine, and I suddenly felt this terrible will blazing inside me. I knew then that the light of it could always drive away any darkness that I feared. This was his first lesson to me, and the last.

'Good!' he cried out. 'Good!'

Zanshin's timeless calm in the face of extreme danger, I thought, was one thing; but this was quite another. I suddenly found the strength to spring forward and attack him with all the fury he had directed at me. The steel of my kalama caught up the starlight as I whirled the long blade at him. For a moment, it seemed that I might cut through his defenses. But he had more cunning and was better with the sword than I. He slipped beneath my blow and leaped forward with an unbelievable speed. And I suddenly found the point of his sword almost touching my throat.

'Good!' he cried out again. 'Very good, Valashu! That's enough for one night, eh?'

After that, he put away his sword and came forward to embrace me. Then I stood back looking at him.

'You would have killed me, wouldn't you?' I asked him.

'Would I have?' he said, almost to himself. Then his gaze hardened, and he growled, 'So – I *would* have, if you hadn't fought with all your heart. This quest of ours is no practice session, you know. We may only have one chance to gain the Lightstone, and we'd damn well better be ready to take it.'

I went to sleep thinking about what he had said to me – and taught me. I awoke the next morning strangely eager to cross blades with him again. But it was a day for travel into an unknown land. Kane promised another round of swordplay that evening if I were willing, and I had to content myself with that.

And so we went down into the Vardaloon. The path we had been following took us into a hilly country at the very edge of it. But soon the ground leveled out into a lowland of little streams and still ponds.

Although the forest was rather thick here, we had no trouble making our way through it. The elms and oaks were familiar friends; birds sang in their branches, while beneath them shrubs such as lowbush blueberries were heavy with fruit and promised a welcome addition to our meals.

And yet, there *was* something disquieting about these woods. The air was too warm and close, and too little light found its way through the unbroken cover of leaves. The squirrels who made their home here were rather sluggish in their motions and seemed too thin. A doe that crossed our path bounded out of the way too slowly; neither were her eyes as bright as they should have been. That there should have been a path at all in woods where no one had lived or gone for thousands of years disturbed us all. Perhaps, I thought, it was only an ancient game trail.

'Perhaps,' Maram said as we stopped to catch our breath, 'it is used by people.'

'I doubt that,' Kane said. 'I've never heard of people living in the Vardaloon.'

'They must,' Maram said as he slapped a mosquito that had landed on the side of his sweating neck. And then he waved his hand at another hovering near his ear. 'How else are these bloodsuckers fed?'

We resumed our journey, riding in order along the path as it wound its way west through the trees. We saw no people but there were plenty of mosquitoes, even in the full warmth of the day. They clung to the leaves of the bushes and took to the air in whining swarms as we brushed by them. They bedevilled our mounts as well, biting their ears and choking their nostrils. The dark woods soon filled with the sounds of slapping hands and horses snorting.

'I was wrong, Val,' Maram called from behind me. His big voice filled the spaces between the tall trees around us; it almost drowned out the whumph of Altaru's hooves and the whine of the mosquitoes biting us. 'People couldn't live here. And neither can we. Perhaps we should turn back.'

'Be quiet!' Kane called from behind him farther down the path. 'No one ever died from a few mosquitoes!'

'Then I'll be the first,' Maram complained. He sighed and said, 'Well, at least they can't get any worse.'

But that evening, as we made camp near some pretty poplars at least a hundred feet high, they got worse. With the bleeding away of the thin sunlight from the forest, the mosquitoes came out of the bushes like demons from hell. They sought us out in swarms of swarms, and now I began to fear that they might really kill us, draining us of blood or filling our noses and mouths so that we couldn't breathe. If not for an ointment made of yusage that Master Juwain found in his wooden chest, we might have been helpless before their onslaught. We lathered the reddish ointment over our faces, hands and necks, quickly exhausting Master Juwain's supply. While it didn't keep the mosquitoes from biting us and certainly didn't drive them off, it seemed that they attacked us in somewhat fewer numbers and with slightly less viciousness.

'I've never seen mosquitoes like these!' Maram said, waving his firestone and slapping at his face. 'They can't be natural!'

He sat with the rest of us between three smoky fires that he had built. We were all hunched over with our cloaks pulled tightly around our faces as we now choked on the thick streams of smoke that wafted this way and that. But it was better than being stung by the mosquitoes.

'They're just hungry,' Kane muttered to Maram. 'If you were that hungry, you'd carve up your own mother for dinner.'

At any other time, Maram might easily have found a riposte to Kane's jibe. But now it seemed to drive him into a sullenness and self-pity that he couldn't shake. Master Juwain tried to cheer him by reading an uplifting verse from the Book of Ages, but Maram waved his hand at his too-blithe words as if warding off yet another assault of mosquitoes. Liljana made him some mint tea sweetened with honey the way he liked it, but he said that the evening was too hot for tea. He even refused the cup of brandy that Atara brought him. And when Alphanderry brought out his mandolet and struck up a song, Maram complained that he couldn't hear the music against the whining of the mosquitoes' wings in his ears.

'We're all miserable,' I said as I came over and knelt by his side. 'Don't make it worse.'

'What shall I do, then?'

I walked off toward the stream and returned a few moments later with a large, round rock. I handed it to Maram and said, 'This is a beautiful thing, don't you think?'

'It's a rock, Val,' he said, looking at it dubiously.

'Yes,' I said, 'it is. But don't you think it has a beautiful shape?'

'Ah, I suppose so.'

'It lacks only one thing, though.'

'And what is that?'

'A hole.'

'A . . . hole?' He looked at me as if my head were full of holes.

'Yes, a hole,' I told him. 'Someday, when we return to Mesh with the Lightstone and tell the story of our journey, we'll show this as well. And everyone will marvel at the rocks of the Vardaloon that have holes in them.'

Maram's eyes shone with a sudden understanding as he hefted the rock in his hand and tapped it with his firestone.

'Make me a hole,' I said, smiling at him.

'All right,' he said, smiling back. 'For you, my friend, I'll make the most beautiful hole you've ever seen.'

And with that, he bent over it and went to work. There was just enough light left in the woods to bring his gelstei alive and summon forth a thin stream of flame. It melted out a little bit of rock before the light failed altogether, and with it the firestone. But Maram had the beginnings of a hole to show for his efforts, and this pleased him greatly. And it distracted him, for the moment, from the murderous mosquitoes.

When it grew dark, Kane and I further entertained him with another round of swordplay. Then it came time for sleep, which none of us managed very well. The merciless whining in our ears, I thought, was the song of the Vardaloon, and it kept us turning and slapping at the air far into the night.

We arose the next morning in very low spirits. All of our hands and faces were puffy from mosquito bites – all of us except Kane. He gazed out at the forest from behind his tough, unmarked face and explained, 'These little beasts drink blood for breakfast. Well, some blood is too bad even for them, eh?'

After we had saddled the horses, we held council and decided it was time we left the path. It was taking us ever farther into the Vardaloon toward the west, whereas we needed to cut off northwest to reach the Bay of Whales.

'The going will be rougher,' I said, looking off at the wall of green in that direction. 'But there may be higher ground that way, and so fewer mosquitoes.'

'Then let's go,' Maram called out as he waved his hand about his head. 'Nothing could be worse than these accursed mosquitoes.'

In our three days of travel from the Tur-Solonu, we must have come some fifty miles. That meant we had another fifty miles ahead of us before the Vardaloon gave out on the open country said to surround the Bay of Whales. If we found no swamps or large rivers to cross and rode hard, we might reach it in only two more days.

We rode as hard as we could. But the horses, drained of blood, moved off slowly, and we couldn't bring ourselves to drive them faster. As I had hoped, the ground rose away from the path, and it seemed that the swarms of mosquitoes grew thinner. The undergrowth, however, did not. We forced our way through some hobblebush and thickets of a dense shrub with pointed leaves. These scratched the horses' flanks and pulled at our legs. In a few places, we had to hack our way through with swords to keep the branches out of our faces.

Thus we endured the long morning. It was dark beneath the smothering cover of the trees – darker than in any woods I had ever been. The shroud of green above us almost completely blocked out the sun. In truth, we couldn't tell if the sun shone at all that day or whether clouds lay over the world, for the leaves were so thick we could see nothing of the sky.

'It's too damn dark here,' Maram said as we paused to take our lunch in a relatively clear space beneath an old oak tree. 'Not as dark as the Black Bog, but dark enough.'

He looked down at the red crystal he held in his much-bitten hand as if wondering how he might ever find enough light to fill it. Then he said, 'At least the mosquitoes aren't so bad here. I think the worst is . . .'

His voice suddenly died off as a look of horror came over his swollen face. His hand darted toward his other wrist, where his fingers closed like pincers, and he plucked something off him and cast it quickly to the ground. Then he jumped to his feet as he shuddered and began brushing wildly at his trousers and feeling with his panicked hands through his thick brown beard and hair.

'Ticks!' he cried out. 'I'm covered with ticks!'

We all were. The undergrowth here, it seemed, was infested with these loathsome insects. They were rather large ticks, flat and hard with tiny black heads. They clung to our garments and worked their way through their openings to find flesh to attach themselves. They crawled along our scalps beneath our hair.

We all jumped up then, and beat at our clothes to drive the ticks off us. Then we paired off to search through each other's hair. Atara carefully ran her fingers through my hair. She found at least seven ticks, which she pulled off me and threw back into the bushes. Then I parted her soft blond hair lock by lock and returned the favor. Master Juwain tended Liljana (for once I was envious of his bald head), while Alphanderry and Maram groomed each other like monkeys. Only Kane, the odd man out, seemed unconcerned with what might be hiding on his body. But he had great care for the horses. He went among them, laying his rough hands on their jumping hides, and combing through their hair as he began pulling off ticks by the tens and twenties.

'Let's ride,' he said when we had finished. 'Let's get out of here.'

I led the way through the woods, trying to keep a more or less straight line toward the northwest. But this way led through yet more undergrowth. We all looked down at the leaves of the bushes, hoping to espy any ticks there and pull our legs out of the way before they could cling to us. It was thus that our attention was turned in that direction. And so we did not see what hung from the branches above us until it was too late.

387

'What was *that*?' Maram shouted. He clapped his hand to his neck and sat bolt upright in his saddle. 'Val, did you throw something at me?'

'No,' I said, 'it must be –

'I can *feel* it,' Maram said, now pulling frantically at the collar of his shirt. 'Oh, my Lord, no, no – it can't be!'

But it was. Just then, as Maram looked up into the trees to see what had fallen on him, a dozen leeches dropped down upon his face and neck. They were black, wormy things at least four inches long – segmented, with bloated bodies thick in the middle but tapering off toward their sucking parts at either end. They fell upon the rest of us as well. They hung lengthwise from the branches above us in the hundreds and thousands like so many swaying seedpods. And as we passed beneath them they rained down upon us in streams of hungry, writhing flesh.

'I've got to get this off!' Maram shouted as he pulled at his shirt. 'I've got to get *them* off me!'

'No, not here!' I called back. Even as I felt something smooth and warm moving down my neck beneath my mail, I pulled my cloak around my head to cover myself from the leeches. 'Ride, Maram! Everyone ride until we're out of this!'

We pressed our horses then, but the undergrowth caught at their legs and kept them from moving very fast. They were weak, too, from being eaten by mosquitoes, as were we. We rode as hard as we could for a long while, perhaps an hour, and in all that time the leeches in the trees never stopped falling on us and trying to find their way inside our clothes. They drummed against my cloak and bounced off Altaru's sides – those that didn't fasten to his sweating black hide. After a while, I forgot to check the bushes for ticks. And I almost didn't notice the mosquitoes that still danced around my face.

'This is unbearable!' Maram called out from beside me. We had long since broken order, and now we rode as we could, strung out in a ragged line beneath the trees. 'I've *got* to get my clothes off! I can feel these bloodsuckers attached to me!'

We all could. I could feel the shuddering skin of my companions as my own. This was my gift and my glory – now my hell. Their horror of the leeches and their other sufferings only multiplied mine. Maram, especially, was fighting back panic, and everyone except Kane was near to despair.

'Atara,' I said as we stopped to catch our breaths, 'can you see our way out of this?'

She sat on her big roan mare, looking down into the crystal sphere that she held in her hands. For all of our journey from the mountains, she had struggled with her newly found skills of scrying. More than once, I thought, she had gazed with terror upon futures that she did not wish to see. But away from the time-annihilating fires of the Tur-Solonu, these visions seemed to come at their own calling, not hers. And so she looked up from her gelstei and smiled grimly. 'I see leeches everywhere. But I didn't need to be a scryer to see that.'

'Well, we've got to try to get them off us,' I said to her. I climbed down from Altaru and asked the others to dismount as well. 'Kane, Alphanderry, Master Juwain – please come here.'

While they approached me across the damp bracken, I whipped off my cloak and shook it out. Then, holding one corner of it above my head, I asked my three friends each to take a corner while Maram stood under it to disrobe.

'But, Val, your cloak!' Maram called out. 'You've nothing to cover yourself!'

'Hurry!' I told him. I stood with my eyes closed as a leech dropped down the back of my neck. 'Please hurry, Maram!'

I think that Maram had never moved so quickly to take off his clothes in all his life, not even at the invitation of Behira or other beauties. In a few moments, he stood bare to the waist, his big hairy belly and chest bare to the world. But my cloak, like a shield, protected him from the falling leeches. And so Liljana was able to join him beneath the makeshift canopy to cut away those that had already attached themselves along his sides and back. When she had finished, she rubbed one of Master Juwain's ointments into the half dozen wounds, which oozed copious amounts of blood. That was the strange thing about leech bites, the way they wouldn't easily stop bleeding.

'All right, Atara,' I said, 'you next.'

Maram dressed himself, taking care to pull his cloak so tightly around him that any leech would have to work very hard to force its way inside. Then Atara took his place as Liljana cut at her with her knife. I tried not look upon the splendor of her naked body. And so it went, each of us taking our turns one by one. Even Kane submitted to her ministrations. But he took no more care of the leeches fastened to him than he would twigs fallen into his hair. He dipped his finger into the blood dripping down his deep chest and said to me, 'So – it's as red as yours, eh?'

At last it came my turn. Atara helped me strip off my armor and its underpadding. While Maram held up my corner of my cloak, Liljana cut more than a dozen leeches from me. Then I quickly dressed, and when I had finished, my friends let my cloak fall around me so that I was well-covered against further assault.

Maram, looking around the forest at the many leeches that still hung from the trees, shook his head and said, 'This can't be natural.'

'Perhaps it's not,' Kane admitted.

'What do you mean?'

Kane's eyes swept the walls of green around us. 'There's a rumor that once Morjin went into the heart of the Vardaloon. To breed things. Leeches, so we've seen, and mosquitoes and ticks – anything that drinks blood as do his filthy priests. It's said he had a varistei, that he used it in essays of this filthy art.'

'Are you saying that it was he who made these things?' Maram asked.

'No, not *made*, as the One makes life,' Kane said. 'But made them to be especially numerous and vicious.'

'But why would he do that?'

'Why?' Kane grumbled. 'Because he's the Crucifier, that's why. He's the bloody Red Dragon. It's always been his way to torment living things until they find the darkest angels of their natures. And then to use them in his service.'

Kane's words disturbed us all, and as we set out again, we rode in silence thinking about them. After a while, Kane pulled his horse over toward me, and in a low voice, said, 'You lead well, Valashu Elahad. So, taking off your cloak – that was a noble gesture.'

A noble gesture – well, perhaps, I thought. But I wouldn't get very far on gestures alone or on merely putting up a good face. Soon, after a few more miles of this accursed forest, its creatures would slowly suck away my life and then my spirits would sink as low as Maram's.

That night, for me, was the worst of our journey since the Grays had attacked us. We made camp on the side of a low hill which I had thought might catch a bit of breeze to drive away the mosquitoes. But at dusk our whining friends came out in full force; there were many leeches here, and as I pulled off Altaru twenty ticks swollen as big as the end of my thumb, his sufferings touched me deeply. Another thing touched me, too. And that was a sense that something was once again hunting me. I thought it could smell my blood, which ran from the leech bites and stained my clothes. It was a dark thing that sought me through the forest, and it had the taste of Morjin.

23

For a long time I sat beneath the trees wondering what else the Red Dragon might have made. I said nothing of my speculations to my companions. They teetered on the brink of despair, and any news of yet another bloodthirsty creature pursuing us might push them over. To distract them from their torments – and me from mine – I called on Alphanderry to sing us a song.

'And what shall I play for you?' he said as we all sat between the five smoky fires that Maram had made.

'Something uplifting,' I said. 'Something that will take us far from here.'

He brought out his mandolet and tuned it with his puffy, bitten fingers. And then he began singing of the Cup of Heaven, of how the Galadin had forged it around a distant star long before it had come to Ea. At first, his words were Ardik, which we all knew fairly well. But soon he lapsed in that strange tongue that none of us understood. Its flowing vowels poured out of him like a sweet spring from the earth; its consonants filled the night like the ringing of silver bells. It seemed impossible to grasp with the mind alone, for it changed from moment to moment like the rushing of a moonlit river. It was musical in its very essence, as if it could never be spoken but only sung.

'That was lovely,' Atara said when he had finished.

We all agreed that it was – all of us except Kane, who sat staring at the fire as if he longed for its flames to burn him away.

'But what does it *mean?*' Maram asked. He watched as Flick did incandescent turns just above Alphanderry's head. 'Where did you learn this language?'

'But I'm still learning it, don't you see?'

'No, I don't,' Maram said, slapping at a mosquito.

Again, Alphanderry smiled, and he said, 'As I sing, if my heart is open, my tongue finds its way around new sounds. And I know the true ones by their taste. Because there is really only one sound and one taste. The more I sing, the sweeter the sounds and the closer I come to it. And that is why I seek the Lightstone.'

He went on to say that he believed the golden cup would help him recreate the original language and music of the angels, both Elijin and Galadin. Then would be revealed the true song of the universe and the secret of singing the stars and all of creation into light.

'Someday,' he said, 'I will find it, and then I will make real music.'

The music he made that night, I thought, was very fine as it was, for it poured from him like an elixir that gave both hope and strength. For a while, I paid no mind to the tightening of my belly that told me that something was coming for me through the forest. Instead, I looked off into the dark spaces between the trees. And there, sitting on top of a gnarly root or simply set down into the earth, I saw the Lightstone. It gleamed in many places even more brightly than it had in the Tur-Solonu. It gave me to remember why I had set out on the quest and why, at all costs, it must be found.

Moments of faith, when they fire the soul, seem as if they will last forever. And yet they do not. The morning brought a moist heat along with the mosquitoes, and we set out through the sweltering woods with a heaviness of limb and soul. Even the Vardaloon's many flowers – the snakeroot and ironweed, the baneberry and wild ginger – brought us no cheer. It was hard to stay wrapped in our rough wool cloaks; soon, I thought, we would have to choose between the leeches or heat stroke. I kept smelling the stifling air and looking for any sign that we might be drawing near the ocean. But I knew that we hadn't come as far as I had hoped. The Bay of Whales might still be two days away – or more. And two days, through these leech-infested woods that went on and on mile after mile, might as well be forever.

It was the seeming endlessness of the Vardaloon that oppressed me almost more than anything else. The whole world had become a vast tangle of trees, steaming bracken and bushes that tore at us and sheltered bloodsucking things. Although my mind knew very well that we must eventually come out upon the sea, the itch of my much-stung skin and the sweat burning along my leech bites told me otherwise. And even if we did survive this slow draining of our blood and somehow reached the Sea People, I couldn't guess how they might be able to help us, for they hadn't been known to speak to men and women for thousands of years. We might very well find the Bay of Whales a dead end from which we would have no retreat – unless we wanted to go back through the Vardaloon.

Around mid-afternoon, as the ground rose and the elms and maples began to give way before many more oaks, chestnuts and poplars, my sense of something hunting me rose as well. I knew that the dark thing that Mithuna had spoken of was coming closer. I tried to guess what it might be. Another bear that Morjin had made a ghul? A pack of maddened wolves trained to the taste of human blood? Or had Morjin somehow found us in this wild land and set another company of Grays upon us? I shuddered to think I might feel the helplessness of frozen limbs yet again as when I stood beneath the Grays' long knives and soulless eyes.

I nearly lost hope then. The sight of my companions slumped on their horses dispirited me even more. Maram's sullenness had deepened to an anger at the world – and me – for bringing him to such a dreadful place. Atara was haunted by what she saw in her scryer's sphere – and sickened by what awaited us in the trees. Her usually bright eyes seemed glazed with the certainty of our doom. Master Juwain couldn't find the strength even to open his book, while Alphanderry had lapsed into an unnerving silence. Liljana, stubborn and tough as she was, appeared determined to go on toward her inevitable death. I thought that she pitied herself and regretted even more that none of us would live to appreciate her sacrifice. Only Kane seemed untouched by this desolation – but, then, sometimes he hardly seemed human anyway. Hate was his shield against the evils of the Vardaloon, and he surrounded himself with it so that none of us dared even to look at him.

My friends' despair touched me deeply, and I wanted to make it go away. But first I had to make my own go away. No noble gesture would do.

'These damn trees,' Maram grumbled as he rode near me, 'there's no end to them! We'll never find our way out of here!'

I stared off into the gloom of the forest as I remembered that a light beyond light always shone within each of us to show the way. And so I said, 'Yes, we will.'

'No,' he said, 'it's impossible we'll ever come out of these woods.'

I felt this light now gathering in my eyes with all the inevitability of the rising sun. I had only to open myself to it, and it might touch Maram and remind him of his own. And so I said, 'It's impossible that we won't.'

For a moment, he sat very still in his saddle as he looked at me.

'Do you still have the stone?' I asked him.

He nodded his head as he reached into the pocket of his robe and removed the stone. His efforts with his gelstei had succeeded in burning a hole clean through it.

'Look through it, then,' I said, 'and tell me what you see.'

With a puzzled expression, he held the stone to his eye and said, 'Ah, I see trees and yet more trees. And leeches, and mosquitoes and other loathsome things.'

I held out my hand as I said, 'Give me the stone.'

He placed it in my hand, and then I looked through it at him and said, 'I see a glorious thing. I see a man in the likeness of the angels who burns so brightly even stone melts before him. Don't tell me that such a man can't find his way out of the woods.'

I smiled at him, and he at me, and suddenly his anger went away.

An hour later, as we rode higher into the hills, a new scourge descended upon us. Little black birds with red markings on their throats flew at us in angry flocks out of the trees. They drove their black beaks into the wounds on the horses' bodies to lap up their blood; they beat their wings and shrieked about our heads as they tried to get at the mosquito bites and leech cuts on our faces. Although they made no attack against any unmarked flesh, we bore enough wounds there that we were afraid they might pluck out our eyes. There seemed to be thousands of these bloodbirds, and they filled the air like a black cloud.

'Hoy, this is too much!' Alphanderry called out. He waved his hand in front of him as he tried to bury his head in his cloak. 'This is the end!'

The horses were all whinnying and stomping beneath the attacking birds. I managed to steady Altaru and urge him closer to Alphanderry and his bloody white horse. I waved my hand about violently, to no more effect than brushing frantic feathers. I looked at Maram, beginning to slip into despair again. I looked at Atara with her haunted eyes, and Liljana flinching beneath the birds' beaks. Their suffering made my eyes burn. And then I suddenly remembered that an infinite fire pooled always ready to fill my heart. It blazed there now, so hot and bright and full that it hurt, and I realized that it was nothing other than love. A wild and terrible love, perhaps, but love nonetheless. I whipped out my sword then, and a half-dozen birds fell in pieces to the ground. To Maram, I called out, 'Use your gelstei!'

The thousands of birds chittered and screamed as they darted and wheeled and kept diving at the horses and us. It was like being in the middle of a cloud of whirling feathers and stabbing beaks.

Maram gripped his red crystal in his hand as he called back to me, 'But Mithuna said that I shouldn't use it unless it was necessary!'

'It's necessary!' I said.

Maram struggled to position the gelstei so that it filled with light. Then something wild leaped inside him, and an orange flame shot from his stone and wrapped itself around twenty or thirty of the birds. They fell from the air like shrieking torches. I waited for another blast from the firestone to incinerate yet more of these pitiless creatures, but Maram shook his head as he shouted, 'That's all I can do for now!'

Kane, Atara and I were now laying about fiercely with our swords. But the birds had become wary of the flashing steel and mostly managed to avoid them. And then an inspiration came to me. I shielded my eyes as I called to Alphanderry, 'You found words to make the angels sing; now find those to drive away these demon birds!'

Alphanderry nodded his head as if he understood. Then he opened his mouth, and out of him poured the most bittersweet song I had ever heard. The notes of the music shifted and rose as he played with the harmonies; soon the sound of it grew so eerie and high-pitched that it hurt my ears. It seemed to unnerve the birds as well. As the song built louder and louder and filled all the forest with its terrible tones, the birds suddenly took wing as if moved by one mind, and vanished into the trees.

Alphanderry pressed his horse nearer to me, and his lips pulled back in a smile. 'I had never thought to do something like that,' he said.

Now the others gathered around us, and they were smiling, too.

'Do you think it will work against the mosquitoes?' Maram asked. 'And the leeches?'

'I don't know,' Alphanderry said.

I sat on Altaru wiping my sword as I looked about the woods. The oaks and poplars here were very tall, and there were fewer leeches among the vegetation than in other parts of the Vardaloon. The mosquitoes seemed less numerous as well. But whatever had been hunting us was now much closer. I felt its hunger like a gigantic leech wrapped around my spine.

'There is more here to worry about than vermin,' I said. Then I took a deep breath and told them of what I had sensed.

'But this is terrible!' Maram said. 'This is the worst news yet!'

We held council then and decided to go no farther that day. And so we gathered wood for the night's fires; we cut brush to fortify our camp. When we had finished it was growing late, with perhaps only an hour left until dark.

'What is it, Val?' Maram asked me. We all stood together near the rude fence we had made. 'Is it the Grays?'

I slowly shook my head as I looked for any movement about us. Next to me, Kane stared at the woods with hate-filled eyes. And then suddenly he walked over toward his horse and slid his bow out of its sling.

'What are you doing?' I asked him.

His jaws clamped together as he strung his bow and then slung on his quiver of arrows.

'Where are you going?' I asked.

He finally looked at me as his eyes took on the gleam of the black stone he held in his hand. And he growled out, 'I'm going hunting.'

He began moving toward the edge of the camp, and I rested my hand against his arm. I said, 'One alone in the woods will have no friends to stand with him.'

'That's true,' he said, looking at Atara as she, too, strung her bow. 'But one alone may go where others cannot.'

'Yes,' I said, 'all the way to the otherworld.'

'Ha – I'm setting out on no such journey!' he said. 'As with the Grays, I'll hunt whatever is hunting you.'

'Do you know what it is, then?'

'No – I only suspect.'

'You should have told me,' I said, staring at the shadows between the trees.

'And you should have told *me*,' he said, catching me up in the dark light of his eyes. 'You should have told me if it was this close.'

And with that, he carefully parted the brush surrounding our camp and stole off into the woods.

And so we waited. While Atara stood ready with an arrow nocked in her bowstring, Maram put aside his firestone in favor of his more reliable sword. Alphanderry and Liljana drew their cutlasses, and I my kalama, and we joined Master Juwain in gazing out through the curtains of green all around us.

'Surely it won't come for us here,' Maram said. 'Surely it will wait until tomorrow when we're lost in the forest. And then pick us off one by one.'

Maram, I knew, was exhausted – as we all were. In such ground, fear most easily takes seed.

'We survived the Grays,' I told him. 'We can survive this, too.'

And then I thought, no, not *survive*. But to thrive, yes, always and only to live with the wildness that makes eagles soar and wolves to sing. I clapped Maram on the shoulder then and traded smiles with him, and after that he spoke no more words of defeat.

Liljana, after doubtfully running her thumb across the edge of her sword, came over to inspect mine. She touched my kalama without my leave, and then she touched my arm as if testing its strength. She said, 'Listen, my dear, if there's to be a battle, shouldn't you eat something first? Perhaps I could make a little –'

'Liljana,' I said, 'your devotion is even more sustaining than your meals.'

I touched her face, which broke into a wide smile, and her fear of dying unheralded seemed to melt away.

Next to me, Master Juwain looked down at the varistei he held in his hand. His mind, I thought, like a sharpening wheel spinning out sparks, was turning around the same thoughts over and over.

'What is troubling you, sir?' I asked him.

He held up his green crystal and said, 'This is a stone of healing, as we've all seen. And yet I'm afraid it has no power over death.'

'No,' I said, 'its power is only in life.'

I smiled as I gripped his wiry forearm, and I felt his veins pressing against mine. His mind seemed to find a moment of peace even as his heart beat with a great surge of life.

Alphanderry, too, came closer as he stared out into the darkening woods. He said, 'A scryer once told me that I wouldn't die without finding the words to my song. Yet today, they seem as far away as the stars.'

'And what does that tell you?' I asked him.

'That scryers are usually wrong.'

This made Atara smile wryly, and I said to Alphanderry, 'Do you know what it tells me?'

'What, Val?'

'That this is not your day to die.'

Our eyes found each other then, and the light that came into his was almost as bright as the fire pouring out of Flick.

Atara stood staring out into the woods as if the whole world were a scryer's sphere. I stepped up to her and said, 'You've seen something, haven't you?'

'Yes,' she said, 'so many *people* here. In the forest, where the oaks grow along a stream. They were slaughtered. They *are* being slaughtered, or will be – oh, Val, I don't know, I don't know!'

I cupped my hand around her shoulder as she rubbed her bloodshot eyes. Death clung to her like a thousand leeches; it was written across her face like the letters of Master Juwain's book.

'I don't know what to do,' she said, 'because nothing can be done. It *can't* be, don't you see?'

I squeezed her shoulder and said to her, 'What is it the scryers always say? That in the end, we choose our futures, yes?'

I touched my forehead against hers and felt the lightning scar there pressing against her third eye. I felt her breath against my face and mine falling against hers like fire. When we pulled away from each other, her eyes were sparkling as if she had come alive again.

After that, we all stood watching the woods in silence. I was only dimly aware of the mosquitoes whining about and biting me; birds chirped and chittered from far off, but I was listening for other sounds. I gazed past the hanging leeches and the insect-eaten leaves, looking for something that was looking for me.

And then, out of the darkening woods, a terrible scream shook the trees. We all started at the anguish of it. I gripped my sword with sweating hands, as did Maram, Liljana and Alphanderry theirs, while Atara drew her bow and sighted her arrow in the direction from which it had come. A second scream ripped through the air, followed by another, and then came the sound of something large crashing through the bracken around our camp.

'What *is* it?' Maram whispered to me. 'Can you see –'

'Shhh!' I whispered back. 'Get ready!'

At that moment, a young woman broke from the cover of the trees running as fast as she could. Her long brown hair seemed torn, as was the homespun dress that barely covered her torn and bleeding body. She ran in a panic, now casting a quick look over her shoulder, now turning her head this way and that as if seeking an escape route through the woods. She stumbled past us barely fifty yards from our camp. But so great was her terror to flee whatever was pursuing her that she seemed not to see us.

'What shall we do?' Maram whispered to me.

'Wait,' I said, feeling my fingers curl around the hilt of my kalama. Next to me, Atara aimed her arrow at the trees behind the woman. 'Wait a few moments more.'

But Maram, who was now trembling with anger, had suffered through too many days of waiting. He suddenly waved his sword above his head and shouted, 'Over here! We're over here!'

At the sound of his huge voice, the woman stopped and turned toward us. The look of relief on her pretty face was that of a lost child who has found her mother. She ran straight for our camp, and we pulled aside the brush fence to let her in.

'Thank you,' she gasped from her bloody lips as we gathered around her. 'It . . . killed the others. It almost killed me.'

'*What* did?' I asked her.

But she was too spent and frightened to say much more. She stood near Maram trembling and weeping and gasping for air.

'Whatever it is,' Atara said, 'it likely won't show its face now.'

'No,' Alphanderry said, 'not until it grows dark.'

Maram, who was swelling with pity, opened his cloak to gather in the woman next to him. He wrapped it around her and asked, 'What is your name?'

'Melia,' the woman sobbed out. 'I'm Melia.'

Liljana sniffed at this bruised and beautiful woman as if jealous of Maram's gentleness toward her. And gentle Maram was, but I could also feel his desire rising like hot sap in a tree. It surprised me to feel as well a fierce desire for him burning through Melia's bleeding body.

'They're all dead,' Melia said, pointing out into the woods. 'All dead.'

I turned to peer through the trees. Behind me I heard Maram making strangled sounds as if his desire for Melia had caught in his throat.

'Ah,' he groaned, 'ah, ah, ahhh!'

I turned back to see Melia's face pressed into the curve of Maram's neck. Her hand was clutching there, too, as she pulled closer to him. It took me a moment to credit what my eyes knew to be true. Maram's eyes, I saw, were almost popping from his head as he struggled to scream. And all the while, Melia squeezed harder and harder as she fastened her teeth into him and bit open his neck.

'Ah,' Maram gasped through a burble of blood, 'ah, ah, ahhh!'

'Hold, there!' I shouted. 'What are you doing?'

I moved over to pull her away from the stricken Maram, but she raised an arm and knocked me to the ground with a shocking strength. As I was rising back up – and Liljana and Alphanderry moved toward them – Maram's cloak fell open to reveal Melia's changing shape. Now I couldn't credit what my eyes reported to me, for in only a moment Melia had transformed into a large, black, growling bear.

'Val,' Maram gasped as he struggled helplessly, 'ah, Val, Val!'

The bear – or whatever Melia really was – pushed its snout against Maram as it growled and bit and lapped his blood. Its black claws dug into his back, pulling him deep into this killing embrace. I swung my sword at it then. I expected to feel the kalama's razor edge bite through fur and flesh. Instead, it fell against the bear's hunched back as if striking stone. With a scream of tortured steel, it broke into two pieces. So broke the noble blade that my father had given me. I stared down at its jagged hilt-shard as if it were I who had been broken.

'Val, help us!' Liljana called to me.

I looked up to see her and Alphanderry ruin their blades against the bear as well. Atara shot an arrow point blank at the bear's back, but somehow, it glanced off its furry hide. Master Juwain finally found his heart and beat at the bear's head with his leather-bound book; but he might as well have beaten at a mountain. Suddenly the bear swiped out with one of its paws and knocked Master Juwain off his feet. Then, still gripping Maram with one arm, it struck out at Alphanderry and Liljana with the other, bloodying and stunning them. It didn't take long for it to rip apart the fence surrounding our camp. Now licking the blood that smeared its mouth, it carried Maram off into the woods.

'Val, they're getting away!' Atara shouted at me. She fired off another arrow, to no effect.

For only a moment, I hesitated. Then, gripping my broken sword, I sprang after them. I ran crashing and screaming like a wild man through the thick bracken. My feet pounded against the green-shrouded earth as my eyes fixed on the black, shaggy thing pulling Maram through the bushes with an unbelievable strength. It seemed impossible that I could hurt this unnatural creature in any way. Yet I suddenly knew with an utter certainty that I couldn't fail, that a light beyond light would show me where my sword must strike. And so as I closed with them and the bear-thing raised its paw to brain me, I ducked beneath it and stabbed out with all my strength. The splintered steel drove deep into the bear's armpit. It howled in a sudden rage as blood spurted and I wrenched my sword free. Then the bear's paw swiped out again, striking the side of my head and knocking me nearly senseless.

'Val!' Atara screamed from behind me. 'Oh, my lord, Val!'

I rose to one knee, breathing hard as I blinked and looked out upon an amazing sight. For the beast was shifting shapes and changing yet again – this time into what I took to be its true form. It had two arms and two legs, even as I did, and two hands, each ending in five thick fingers. It was entirely naked and hairless, and covered with a thick, black carapace more like the burnt iron of a meteor than skin. It couldn't have moved at all except for the joints in this stone-hard armor. Into one of these, I saw, between its mighty arm and blocky body, I had chanced to drive my sword. Although blood flowed from it freely, it seemed that it was not a fatal wound. It now dropped Maram onto the ground as it turned to regard me. It was a man, I thought, surely it must be a man. But only its eyes – large and lonely and full of malice – seemed human.

'Val!' Atara shouted. 'Get out of the way!'

This hideous man suddenly moved forward, growling and cursing at me. I saw from the blazing intelligence of his eyes that this time he didn't intend to present his more vulnerable parts to what was left of my sword. He would kill me, I knew, crushing me beneath his body as easily as he might a rabbit. I might have turned from him and fled back toward our camp. But then he would have had his way with Maram. And so instead, sensing the unbearable tension in Atara behind me, I suddenly dropped to the ground. I heard her bowstring twang as an arrow shrieked through the air above my head. It drove straight into the beast-man's eye. This stopped him dead in his tracks, though strangely he did not fall. And then another arrow, fired off with the blinding speed of which only Sarni warriors are capable, took him in his other eye.

'Father!' he cried out in a terrible voice that seemed to shake all the world. In this one sound were many deep emotions: astonishment, longing, relief and bitter hate. For only a moment, it seemed that a howl of grief answered him from far away. And then he died. He toppled backward to the ground like a tree and lay still among the ferns and flowers.

I was very weak, as if it had been my blood that he had drunk. Yet I managed to get up and go over to Maram. Atara and the others joined me there, too. Master Juwain found that the wounds to Maram's neck were not as grave as we had feared. It seemed that the beast-man had only pierced the vein there to take his meal. Maram, he said, had most likely fainted from the loss of blood.

'I hope that is the worst of it,' he said, looking through the woods at the body of the beast-man. 'Human bites are more poisonous than a snake's.'

He brought out his gelstei then and reached deep to find its healing fire. After a while, Maram opened his eyes, and we helped him sit up.

'Ah, Atara, you killed him!' Maram said as he looked into the woods. 'Good! Good! I guess that puts your count at twenty-two.'

The beast-man's last word troubled us, for he was so fell and hideous that we did not wish to see his father. And so when we heard something else crashing through the trees behind us, we jumped to our feet as we took up our weapons with trembling hands.

But it was only Kane. He came running at us through the bushes gripping his bow and arrows. He stopped before the body of the creature Atara had killed and stared down at it for a long moment. And then he growled out, 'I came upon his spoor a couple of miles from here. So, I was too late.'

Enough strength had returned to me that I was able to walk up to him and touch his shoulder. I asked, 'Do you know who this is?'

Kane slowly nodded his head. 'His name is Meliadus. He's Morjin's son.'

At this news, Atara shuddered, and so did I. Atara's gaze turned inward as if she were seeing some private vision that terrified her.

Master Juwain stepped up to Kane and cleared his throat. 'A son, you say? The Red Dragon had a son? But no one has ever told of that!'

'I myself thought it only a rumor until today,' Kane said, pointing at

Meliadus. 'He's an abomination. You can't begin to understand how great an abomination.'

He went on to tell us what was whispered about Morjin: that long ago, at the beginning of the Age of the Dragon, he had gone into the Vardaloon to breed a race of invincible warriors from his own flesh. Meliadus had been the first of this race – and the last. For Meliadus, upon growing to manhood and beholding the hideousness of his form, had conceived a terrible hate for his creator and had risen up against him. According to Kane, he had nearly killed Morjin, who had fled the Vardaloon and had left the vast forest to the vengeance of his mighty son.

'Once,' Kane said, waving his hand at the dark trees around us, 'the Vardaloon was a paradise. It's said that many people lived here. Meliadus must have been jealous of them. He must have hunted them down, man by man, tribe by tribe.'

Maram, sitting back against Liljana and Alphanderry, managed to cough out, 'But how is that possible? He can't have lived all that time!'

Master Juwain rubbed his bald head thoughtfully and told him, 'There's only one explanation: Morjin must have bestowed upon him his own immortality.'

'Immortality – ha!' Kane said. He moved over to Meliadus, and with the help of his knife, pried apart the fingers of his left hand. There he found a stone, which he brought over for us to see.

'What is it?' Maram asked.

The stone was a crystal, like in shape to Master Juwain's green gelstei. But its color was brown, and it was riven with many cracks so that it looked more like a withered leaf.

'It's a varistei,' Kane said. 'Possibly the same one that Morjin used to make his mosquitoes and leeches – and Meliadus.'

We all stared at this ugly crystal. And then Maram said, 'But that can't be a gelstei!'

'Can it not?' Kane said to him. 'You think the gelstei are immortal, but only the Lightstone truly is. The varistei especially are living crystals. And they can die, even as you see.'

'But what killed it?' Maram asked.

'He did,' Kane said, pointing again at Meliadus. 'He took the blood of men and women for hundreds of years, and that sustained him, in part. But he also took the life of this crystal.'

Master Juwain held out his hand to examine the brown crystal. Kane gave it to him, and Master Juwain asked, 'If this had no life left to give, what would Meliadus have done?'

'So, he would have continued sucking the blood out of deer and suchlike – and anyone who chanced to enter the Vardaloon,' Kane said. 'Then someday, and soon, he would have come out of it and crossed into other lands looking for another varistei.'

The thought of Meliadus ravaging the wilds of Alonia and finding the Forest of the Lokilani made my belly clutch up with dread. Unless the Lokilani were as keen shots as Atara, Meliadus might have slaughtered every last one of them.

I looked at Kane and asked, 'You said the Lord of Lies was Meliadus' father. But who was his mother, then?'

'That is not told,' Kane said. 'Likely Morjin got his son out of one of the tribeswomen who used to live here.'

The memory of the bleeding young woman whom Maram had taken beneath his cloak still burned in my mind. As did the growling bear. I told Kane about this, and we all looked at him as he said, 'Morjin must have bestowed upon Meliadus one thing at least. And that is his power of illusion. Or some small part of it, anyway. It would seem that Meliadus was able to shape only the image of how he appeared to you.'

Maram blushed in embarrassment at the way Meliadus had fooled him. But he was glad to be alive, and he said, 'Ah, I don't understand why Meliadus didn't just kill all of us once we had taken him inside our camp.'

'*That* should be obvious,' Kane snapped at him. 'Meliadus needed the blood of the living to go on living himself. After he had finished with you, he would have come back for the rest us one by one.'

I stood there breathing in the smell of blood that stained Maram's clothes and the dead leaves of the forest floor. I listened to the chirping of some birds, and wondered if they were the same ones that had tried to dip their beaks into us.

'If not for Atara's marksmanship,' Kane said, staring at the arrows that stuck out of Meliadus' eyes, 'he would have made meals of us all – all the way to the Bay of Whales.'

His words reminded us that we still had a journey to make and a quest to fulfill. The question now arose as to what we should do with Meliadus. Maram favored leaving him for the wolves. But as Master Juwain observed, they would only break their teeth against Meliadus' iron-hard hide.

'Why don't we bury him?' I said. 'Whatever else he was, he was a man first, and should be buried.'

We all agreed that it would be best to put him into earth and so at least return him to his mother. Liljana went to get the shovels then, and we dug at the tough, root-laced ground of the forest until we had a hole big enough to lay him in. We all stood for a moment looking at the feathered shafts embedded in what seemed the only human part of him. Arrows were dear to Atara, but these she did not retrieve. Then we covered him with dirt so that no one would ever have to see what a monster Morjin had made from a man.

Much later, as we gathered between the fires breathing in smoke, I sat holding the hilt-shard of what had once been my sword. It almost seemed that the ruin of this magnificent weapon had been too great a price to pay for my life. For a moment I felt as if it hadn't been a piece of steel that had broken against Meliadus but my very soul. And then I looked off into the woods towards his grave. There I saw the Lightstone shining out of the darkness and reminding me that the deepest fire that burned inside everyone was as inextinguishable as the light of the stars.

24

That night, I had my first dream of Morjin in nearly a month. He appeared to me with his unearthly beauty and golden, dragon's eyes; he told me that he had found me again and would never leave my side. A price, he said, must be paid for the slaying of his son. He would send other fell beings to hunt us down, and if they failed to take us, he would come for us himself.

I awoke drenched in sweat and beleaguered by a cloud of mosquitoes. Leeches still hung swaying from the surrounding trees. With Meliadus' death, the worst of the Vardaloon had perished, but we still remained in the thick of that horrible wood. And so, in the quiet of the cool, damp morning, we saddled our horses and determined to ride out of it as fast as we could.

We traveled all that day north and west toward the unseen ocean. We kept hoping to catch a glint of water through the wall of green before us. But the hills rose and fell like steps leading nowhere, and the forest covering them allowed only a rare few glimpses of the sky. Dusk found us fighting through some clumps of winged blackthorn and stands of yellow poplar. And so we were forced to spend yet another night in the company of our bloodsucking friends. That there seemed fewer of them in this part of the woods, I almost didn't notice. I lay awake most of the night, listening for worse things than mosquitoes.

In truth, I mourned the loss of my sword. Without it I felt naked and alone. How was I to defend my friends if a real bear should attack us or some servant of Morjin's surprise us in a fury of pounding hooves and well-tempered steel? My kalama was irreplaceable, I knew, for only the smiths of faraway Godhra made such wondrous swords. And even if I were willing to slide a lesser blade into my sheath, where would I find even a broadsword or longsword in the wild lands so many miles from any kingdom or civilized place?

'I'll give you my sword, if you wish,' Kane said to me the next morning as were preparing for yet another day of our journey. 'It's a kalama, too.'

'Thank you, but no,' I said to him. His concern astonished me. 'Your sword is your soul, and you can't just give it to anyone.'

'But you're not *anyone*, eh?'

I climbed on top of Altaru and touched the upraised lance holstered at his side. 'A knight has other weapons, yes?'

'Perhaps,' he said.

I looked down at the long blade buckled to his waist and said, 'Besides, we'll all ride more easily knowing that Ea's greatest swordsman still has his.'

Eight miles of hard travel that morning brought us to the crest of a line of hills. And there the Vardaloon suddenly ended. We felt this mostly as a cooling of the earth and a change in the air, for there were still many trees about us. But these were mostly white oak, magnolia and sycamore, and no leeches infested them. Neither did the wind stir with mosquitoes. Liljana, who had the keenest nose of us all, said that she could smell the faint, far-off scent of the sea. This good news caused us to make our way forward with renewed spirit. We were so excited that we didn't stop for lunch, and ate a cold meal of cheese and battle biscuits in our saddles.

Soon the hills began to grow smaller, and we came to a more open country. The woods were broken with fields and flats of hawthorn, elderleaf and highbush blueberry. And then, after another six or seven miles, we topped the last of the hills. And there, below us, windswept dunes were piled up east and west as far as the eye could see. Beyond them shone the blue waters of the Great Northern Ocean.

'Oh, my Lord – we did it!' Maram said as we rode down to the dunes. When we reached these castle-like mounds of sand, he practically fell from his horse and kissed the ground. 'We're saved!'

After whooping like a wild dog and throwing up handfuls of sand, he remounted, and we rode across the dunes toward the sea. Although we were all eager to stand before this great water, we had to make our way carefully along the dunes' shifting slopes. Master Juwain, who had been raised on the islands of the Elyssu, pointed out the various strange plants growing there and told me their names: the beach rose and the rounded shrubs of the beach plum; the matlike dusty miller, with its tiny yellow flowers and the blue-eyed grasses rippling in the wind.

After we had ridden down the last of the dunes, we came out upon a wide, sandy beach. There was much seaweed and many shells along the high-tide line. The air smelled of salt and carried the sound of the crashing surf. The sun was a great, golden chariot rolling down the clear blue sky toward the west. Because of the lateness of the hour, we decided to go no further that day. Of course, with the ocean only a hundred yards away, there was really nowhere else to go.

'Unless,' as Master Juwain observed, pointing out toward the sea, 'this isn't the Bay of Whales after all.'

'It *must* be,' Maram said, coming down off his horse.

Kane stood on the sand with his hand above his eyes, shielding them from the water's fierce glare. He seemed lost in memories as deep as the sea.

'What do you think?' I asked, coming up next to him.

Kane's hard hand swept out to the right and then the left. 'The coast here runs east and west. So it would be with the most inland part of the Bay of Whales.'

'And so it would be with the coast on either *side* of the Bay of Whales,' Master Juwain put in. He had studied his maps as well as any man, and was prepared to give us a geography lesson. 'If we came too far to the north, then the Bay of Whales will still lie to the west of us.'

'We didn't come too far north,' I assured him.

'And if we came too far west,' he said, looking at me, 'we will have overshot the Bay altogether. In that case, it would lie to the east.'

Kane's thick white hair rippled in the wind as he said, 'The Bay can't be more than sixty miles at its widest, eh? If this *is* the Bay and we ride west, the beach should begin curving toward the north soon enough.'

'But if it isn't,' Master Juwain said, 'we'll ride many miles to no good end. And then have to turn back.'

We stood there for several minutes debating what course to set the next day. Then Liljana came forward and laughed at us as if we were squabbling children.

'Of *course* this is the Bay,' she told us.

'But how do you know?' Maram asked, looking at her in surprise.

'Because,' she said, her nostrils quivering as she gazed out at the sea, 'I can smell the whales.'

We all smiled at this wild claim. But after remembering how she had saved me from Baron Narcavage's poisoned wine, I wasn't so sure.

'Why don't we make camp and decide tomorrow which way to turn,' I said. 'We'll think better if we're not so tired.'

Maram, I saw, was still exhausted from what Meliadus had done to him, and all of our faces were haggard and cut from our passage through the Vardaloon. I had seen warriors, after months of siege and starvation, who had looked better than we did.

And so we spread out our furs on the soft sand and helped Maram gather driftwood for a fire. Kane, foraging farther down the beach for logs or bushes with which to fortify our camp, came upon many blue crabs trapped in a tide pool between two belts of sand. He gathered up a hundred of these strange-looking beasts in his cloak and brought them back for Liljana to cook. Master Juwain dug up some clams from the hardpack near the ocean, and these he presented to Liljana as well. She added them to the stew that she was already cooking in her pot. Many of the crabs, however, she saved to be roasted on spits over the fire. It seemed to take hours for her to prepare this unusual meal. But when she had finished, all our mouths were watering. We sat around the fire cracking the crabs with stones and devouring the succulent meat. We mopped up the stew with some bread that Liljana made, and washed it all down with mugfuls of brown beer. In all my life, I had never had a finer feast.

The next morning, I awoke early to the harsh cries of seagulls fighting over the shells of the crabs. We spent a few hours in the shallows washing the blood from our clothing and bathing our wounded bodies. Master Juwain said that sea salt was good for mosquito bites and other hurts of the skin. The water was cold and rimed our clothing, but we all welcomed its healing touch.

After that, we gathered on the beach and looked out across the ocean for the Sea People. All we saw, however, were sparkling waters broken only by waves. Master Juwain brought out his varistei and pointed it at the rolling blue swells in the hope of sensing any kind of life. But all he found in the water were more crabs. Atara looked into her crystal sphere for a long time, but if she saw anything there resembling these mighty swimmers, she didn't say. Alphanderry took up his mandolet and sang to the sea in the sweetest of voices, but no one sang back.

'Ah, perhaps this *isn't* the Bay of Whales after all,' Maram said. 'Or perhaps the Sea People don't come here anymore.'

His words were as heavy as the sea itself. We stood staring out at the gleaming horizon as we thought about them. No one seemed to know what to do.

And then a strange look fell over Liljana's face. With great excitement, she began stripping off her still-moist tunic. When she had uncovered herself, she began walking quickly down toward the water. Modesty demanded that I look away from her, but I was afraid that her usual good sense had left her, for I felt in her an urge to swim far out into the surf. So I watched her dive into the breaking waves. She was a stocky woman, big-breasted with wide hips, and still quite strong for her years. She swam straight out to sea with measured strokes, and I marveled at her skill and power.

'Liljana, what are you doing?' Maram called to her. But the booming surf swept away his voice, and she seemed not to hear him. And so he turned to me and asked, 'Val – what is she doing?'

But I couldn't tell him. I could only watch as she swam farther out to sea.

'Ah, shouldn't you do something?' Maram asked me.

'What, then?'

'Swim after her!'

I watched Liljana pulling and kicking at the water, and I slowly shook my head. In truth, I was a poor swimmer. It took all my courage even to jump into a mountain lake.

'But she'll drown!' Maram said.

Atara came up and smiled at him. 'Drown, hmmph! She seems as likely to drown as a fish.'

'But the ocean is *dangerous*,' Maram said. 'Even for strong swimmers.'

'Then perhaps you should go after her.'

'I? I? Are you mad? I can't swim!'

'Neither can I,' Atara admitted.

And neither could any of us, I thought, swim as Liljana did. We all watched from the beach as she made her way far out past the line of the white-crested breakers.

And then Maram's puffy, mosquito-bitten face went as white as if another monster had drained him of blood. He pointed toward Liljana as two grayish fins suddenly cut the water near her, and he cried out, 'Sharks! Sharks! Oh, my Lord, she'll be eaten by sharks!'

In only a few more moments, as I drew in a deep breath and felt the hearts of my companions beating as quickly as mine, another ten or twelve fins appeared in a circle around Liljana. They were closing on her quickly, like a noose around a neck.

And then, without warning, a bluish shape leaped straight out of the water only a few yards from Liljana and fell back in with a terrific splash. Two more broached the surface and blew out their breaths in steamy blasts while others raised their heads out of the water and began talking in a high-pitched, squeaking language stranger even than the songs that Alphanderry sang for us. They had long, pointed snouts that seemed cast in perpetual smiles, and Master Juwain called them dolphins. He said that once they had been the most numerous, if the least powerful, of the Sea People.

For a long time, the dolphins swam near Liljana. They jumped out of the water, doing flips seemingly just for the fun of it. They nudged her with their noses and buoyed her up with their sleek, beautiful bodies. And all the while, they never stopped whistling and clicking and speaking to her. But what words of wisdom they imparted to her, none of us could tell.

After perhaps half an hour of such frolic, Liljana turned back toward the land. Two dolphins, one on either side of her, swam with her as far as the line of the breakers. They appeared to watch as she caught herself up in a gathering wave and let it carry her a good way toward the beach. As Liljana stood up suddenly in the shallows and streams of water dripped from her olive skin and dark brown hair, the dolphins gathered offshore as if holding a council of their own.

'How did you know the Sea People were here?' Maram asked Liljana after she dressed herself and rejoined us. 'Did you really smell them?'

'Yes, doubtful Prince,' she said, 'in a way, I did.'

She cast a quick look at the squeaking dolphins, and so did we.

'Did they speak to you?' I asked her.

'Yes, they did,' she said. Her hazel eyes fell sad and dreamy. Then she continued, 'But I'm afraid I didn't understand them.'

'So it's been for thousands of years,' Kane said. 'No one can speak to the Sea People anymore.'

Liljana looked out to where Flick spun like a silver wheel over the water in the direction of the dolphins. Then she said, 'They *want* to speak with us. I know they do.'

'Ha – why should the Sea People speak with us?' Kane asked. 'It's said that ever since the Age of Swords, men have hunted them like fishes.'

'We have much to tell each other,' Liljana said wistfully. 'I know we do.'

We stood on the beach for quite a while staring out at the immense barrier of water that separated us from the whales. Then Alphanderry suddenly stuck out his arm and said, 'Look, they're swimming away!'

Indeed, the whole dolphin tribe was now swimming slowly parallel to the shore toward the west. Liljana slowly nodded her head, watching them. And then she said, 'They want us to follow them.'

'But how do you know?' I asked her.

'I just know,' she told me.

'But where are they leading us, then?'

'Wherever they will,' she said, looking at me sternly. My doubt seemed to wound her, and she said, 'Have I asked *you*, young Prince, where you've been leading us all these long days?'

'But it's been clear that we've been heading toward the Bay of Whales.'

'And now we're here,' she said. She kept her voice calm and controlled, but I could feel a great excitement inside her. 'Will you help me discover what these people want from us?'

Her soft, searching eyes called to mind all the kindnesses she had done for me on our journey and suggested that I would be churlish to refuse her. Without waiting for me to answer, she began walking quickly down the beach, all the while keeping her gaze fixed upon the dolphins. It was left to me to gather up the others and break camp as quickly as we could.

We caught up with her about three miles down the beach. While Maram and Master Juwain took charge of the pack horses and Liljana's gelding, Alphanderry and I raced our horses with Kane's and Atara's along the water's edge. After the clutching vegetation of the Vardaloon, it was good to move over open country again. Altaru snorted and shook with a joyous power as I gave him his head. His hooves pounded against the wet, hardpacked sand leaving great holes in it. But although he was the strongest of the horses and faster than even Atara's very fast Fire, he could not quite keep up with Alphanderry as he sang to Iolo and urged his white Tervolan forward. What the dolphins made of us as we galloped clear past Liljana before wheeling about was impossible to say. For they just kept swimming a few hundred yards offshore as if they had all the time in the world to lead us toward some secret place.

'Perhaps they know where the Lightstone is,' Maram said as he and Master Juwain also caught up with Liljana. He handed Liljana the reins of her horse. 'Perhaps Sartan Odinan fled north from Argattha with the Gelstei and was stopped here by the ocean. Perhaps he died on this forsaken shore, and all knowledge of the Lightstone with him.'

What Maram had suggested seemed unlikely – but no more so than any other speculation as to the Lightstone's fate. We grew silent after that, each of us holding inside the image of this sacred golden cup. Our hopes fairly floated in the air like the puffy white clouds above the Bay. We were all a little excited, and we rode our horses at a bone-jarring trot as we tried to keep pace with the dolphins.

For hours, as the sun crossed the sky to the south, we made our way along the beach. The dunes gradually gave way to a headland of water-eaten limestone while the beach narrowed to a ribbon of rocky sand scarcely twenty yards wide. The horses hurt their hooves on this rough shingle. If we pressed them much harder, I thought, they would pull up lame. As it was, they were still weak from what the Vardaloon had taken from them and could not continue this way for long.

And then, just as I feared the beach would vanish to nothing between the headland to our left and the crashing surf, we came upon a cove cut into the stark, white cliffs. Great rocks broke from the shallows and the sand. There was little beach there, and most of it was covered with driftwood, pebbles and great heaps of shells. I did not think we could take the horses across it, not even if we dismounted and led them on foot. It seemed that we could follow the dolphins no further. And then I saw Liljana looking out to sea, and I looked, too. The dolphins had ceased their tireless swimming and were now gathered together in the rippling water. They whistled and clicked at us with great urgency. And all of their long, smiling faces were pointed straight toward the cove.

Liljana, of course, needed no further encouragement to dismount and begin searching along the beach. And neither did the rest of us. After we had tied the horses to a couple of great logs, we walked among the piles of shells, crunching them with our boots. Here and there, upon catching a glimpse of a pretty pebble or a golden shell, we would pause and drop to our knees as we dug at the beach. With every passing moment, as our breaths rushed in and out and the surf pounded wildly, it seemed more and more likely that Sartan Odinan had died here after all. Time and the relentless wash of the waves, we supposed, had buried his bones beneath layers of shells and sand. If we dug in the right place, we might find his remains – and the Lightstone.

All that long afternoon we searched there. Twice I thought I'd caught a glimpse of it. But we found no golden cup nor any other thing made by the hand of man – or the angels. We might have given up if the dolphins had swum away. And then at last, with the sun falling down toward the ocean like a flaming arrow, Liljana let out a little cry. She bent down and plucked something from the carpet of shells. She held it up in the slanting light for us all to see.

'What is it?' Maram asked, stepping over to her. 'It looks like glass.'

'Driftglass,' Master Juwain said, looking at it. 'I used to collect such things when I was a boy.'

The driftglass, if that it truly was, was deep blue in color and about the size of Liljana's thumb. It was old and chipped and scoured smooth by the sea.

'It looks like a whale,' Maram said. 'Don't you think?'

As Liljana turned it over and over in her tapering fingers, we saw that it was cast into a little figurine shaped like a whale. What it had been used for or how it had come here, no one could say.

And then Liljana suddenly made a fist around the glass and pressed it against the side of her head. Her eyes glazed as they stared out at the dolphins and then closed altogether.

'Liljana,' Master Juwain said to her, 'are you all right?'

But she didn't answer him. She just stood there utterly still facing the sea.

Strangely, the dolphins also fell silent. The only sounds about us were the cries of the seagulls along the cliffs and the ocean's long, dark roar. We were all concerned for Liljana, but we knew not to speak lest the spell be broken. And so we gathered around her, breathing in the smells of seaweed and the salty spray thrown up by the crash of the water against the rocks.

At last Liljana opened her eyes and smiled as she nodded her head. She looked down at the figurine gleaming dark blue in the palm of her hand. And then she said, 'This is no driftglass.'

Master Juwain bent his bald head down to get a better look at the figurine. He asked, 'May I see it?'

Liljana rather reluctantly gave it to him, and he turned it beneath his sparkling gray eyes.

'It's a gelstei,' Liljana said. 'Surely it is a gelstei.'

Master Juwain's bushy eyebrows pulled together as he looked at the figurine more closely.

'I spoke with the Sea People,' Liljana said. 'I could hear their words inside me.'

The blue gelstei, I recalled as I looked at the figurine, were the stones of truthsaying, languages and dreams. In certain gifted people, they also quickened the power of speaking mind to mind.

'I see, I see,' Master Juwain said, giving back the figurine. 'I believe it *is* a blue gelstei.'

We all crowded close to Liljana to get a better look at the stone. Kane's eyes shone with a deep light and for a moment seemed as blue as the sea.

'I didn't know you had the power of mindspeaking,' he said to Liljana as he looked at her strangely. 'It's very rare these days, eh?'

'I didn't know myself,' Liljana told him. 'I've never been good at much more than cooking and sniffing out poisons.'

She spoke with modesty, and there was little pride in her bearing. Yet something in her quiet composure gave me to suspect that finding the blue figurine and speaking with the dolphins had confirmed a secret sense she had of herself.

'Well,' Maram called out to her, 'what did the Sea People *say*, then? Did they tell of the Lightstone? Is it here?'

He looked farther down the beach at the shells piled up against a jutting black rock. He looked at the driftwood, at the cliffs, and his face was lit up with hope.

'No, they know nothing of the Lightstone,' Liljana said. 'They don't even understand what such a thing might be.'

'Ah, I hardly understand myself,' Maram said. 'But surely if they knew about your gelstei, they would have known about the Lightstone.'

413

'You're thinking like a man,' she said to him. 'But the Sea People don't think like we do.'

'Then they can't help us, can they?'

'Don't you give up so easily, my dear,' she scolded him. 'The Sea People are kind creatures, and they like puzzles as much as play. They've called others of their kind to come and talk with me.'

'Other dolphins?'

'I don't know,' she said. 'They called them the Old Ones.'

We looked out away from the land where the dolphins still swam in lazy circles around each other. Now the sun had disappeared into the ocean, and the blueness had left the water as if suddenly sucked away. Long, dark waves moved upon the darker deeps as the light slowly bled from the horizon. In the dusky sea, the dolphins waited, as did we. We stood on the windy beach looking out at the edge of the world where the evening's first stars blazed out of the immense, blue-black sky. They cast their silver rays upon the onstreaming waters and the great, gray shapes rising up from them. There, in the cold ocean, in that strange time that is neither day nor night, six immense whales suddenly broke the surface and blew their spray high into the air. Master Juwain, who knew about such things, named their kind as the *Mysticeti*. But I thought of them as Liljana did, and called them simply the Old Ones.

For a while, they spoke with one another in their long, mournful songs that were more like moans than music. Their great voices seemed to still the whole world. And then, as Liljana again pressed the blue gelstei against her head, they too fell silent. The stars filled the heavens and slowly turned above the shimmering sea.

This time, Liljana did not open her eyes. She stood nearly motionless on the shell-strewn beach. If not for the slow rise and fall of her breath, we would have thought that she had turned to stone.

'Master Juwain,' Maram said softly after some minutes had passed, 'what shall we do?'

'Do? What is there to do but wait?' Master Juwain said. Then he sighed and told him, 'I'm afraid the blestei are dangerous stones. I've always believed that the knowledge to use them has long been lost.'

But this was not good enough for Atara. She came up to Liljana and brushed the wind-whipped hair away from her face.

'We shouldn't just leave her like this,' she said, nodding at me. 'Horses can stand all night, but not a woman. Val, will you help me?'

I was afraid to touch Liljana just then, but together Atara and I, with Maram's help, managed to sit her down against a large rock facing the sea. Atara joined her there on the sand. She sat holding Liljana's free hand while Liljana continued holding the gelstei tightly to her head.

'Now we can wait,' Atara said. She looked out at the starlit sphere that was the world.

And wait we did. At first, none of us thought that Liljana would sit there entranced all night. We kept looking for some sign that she might open her eyes or the whales grow tired and swim away. But as a yellow half-moon rose in the east and the hours passed, we resigned ourselves to watching over Liljana for as long as it took. Maram got a fire out of some driftwood that he piled up nearby while Master Juwain managed to make us a meal of steamed clams and hotcakes. It was midnight by the time Alphanderry and Kane washed the dishes by the water's edge, and still Liljana did not move.

'I'm afraid for her,' Maram said to me as the fire burned lower. It cast its flickering light over Liljana's stricken face. 'You met minds with Morjin in your dreams, and it nearly drove you mad. What must it be like to speak this way with a whale?'

'Here, now,' Master Juwain said crabbily. He knelt in front of Liljana testing the pulse in her wrist. 'I've told you a hundred times not to name the Lord of Lies. And to name him in the same breath as the Old Ones – well, *that* is madness.'

He went on to say that the Sea People had never been known to make war or take their vengeance upon men, not even when men put their harpoons into them. Indeed the Sea People, through many long ages, had often rescued shipwrecked sailors from drowning, swimming up beneath them so that they could breathe and taking them toward land.

'That is true,' Kane said in a faraway voice. 'I've seen it myself.'

I thought about this as I sat on the cool sand and watched the great whales floating on the luminous surface of the sea. How was it, I wondered, that the Sea People had forsworn war where men had not? Had the Galadin sent them from the stars before even Elahad and Aryu and the stealing of the Lightstone? What would it be like to talk to such beings who obeyed the Law of the One so faithfully?

I waited there on the dark beach for Liljana to look at me and answer these questions. The wind blew across the water, from what source no one knew. The waves continued pounding against the shore like the beating of a vast and immortal heart. And the stars rose and fell into the blackness beyond the world and made me wonder if they were really distant suns or some kind of light-giving crystals created every night anew.

It was nearly dawn when Liljana opened her eyes and looked at us. As if saying goodbye, the whales sang their unfathomable songs and struck the water with their great tails. Then, along with the dolphins, they dove into the sea and swam away.

'Well,' Master Juwain said, as he knelt near Liljana, 'did you understand them? What did they tell you?'

But Atara, still sitting by Liljana, held up her hand protectively and said, 'Give her a moment, please.'

Liljana slowly stood up and walked back and forth along the water's edge. And then she turned and said, 'They told me many things.'

It was impossible for her to recount all that had passed between her and the Old Ones in their hours of conversation together. Nor, it seemed, did she wish to. She liked keeping secrets to herself almost as much as she delighted in bestowing upon others her cooking and her care. But she did admit that the Sea People were very doubtful of men.

'They said we were free,' she told us. 'They said that we were free but didn't know it. And not knowing this, that we weren't. They said we made chains – this is my word – out of our harpoons and ships and swords, and everything else. They said that wanting to master the world, we are made slaves of it. And so thinking ourselves cursed, we are. A cursed people bring death to themselves, and to the world. And worse, we bring forgetfulness of who we really are.'

She grew silent as the ocean sent its waves breaking against the shore. And then Master Juwain said, 'They must hate us very much.'

'No, my dear, it is just the opposite,' she said. 'Once, in the Age of the Mother, there was a great love between our kinds. They gave us their songs and we gave them ours. But at the end of the age, the Aryans came. Their wars destroyed all that. They hunted down all the sisters who could speak mind to mind to oppose them. Then they gathered up the blue gelstei and cast them into the sea.'

The Aryans, of course, had brought their swords to Tria – and the Age of Swords to all of Ea. They had prepared the way for the rise of Morjin, who hated the Sea People because he could find no way to make them serve him.

'It was the Red Dragon,' she said, 'who first began the hunting of the whales. The Old Ones told me that it had something to do with blood.'

'So,' Kane said in his grimmest voice, 'I've seen whale blood, too bad. It's darker than ours, redder and richer. To the Kallimun priests, it must be like gold.'

'To the Sea People,' Liljana said, 'our hunting of them is as much an abomination as if we hunted and ate our own kind. They think we've fallen mad.'

'Perhaps we have,' I said as I touched the hilt of my broken sword.

'So, it's a dark time,' Kane said. 'A dark age. But there will be others to come.'

Liljana scooped up a handful of wet sand and held it to the side of her face as if to ease a burning there. Then she said, 'The Old Ones spoke of that. They remember a time before we came to Ea. And they've told of a time when we will leave again, too.'

I stood a few yards from the crashing waves as I thought about this. I remembered what Master Juwain had once taught me about the beginning of the Age of Law. In those years, all of Ea had been sickened by the slaughter of the preceding age, and the peoples of all lands wanted only to return to their birthplace in the stars. But in the year 461, the great remembrancer, Sansu Medelin, had recalled the long-forgotten Elahad and his purpose in coming to earth. Sansu said that men and women must follow the Law of the One and create a new civilization before returning to their source. All who listened to him – they called themselves the Followers – fell out violently with the Returnists who wanted immediately to set out on ships and sail the cold seas of space. The War of the Two Stars, a great war lasting a hundred years, had been fought over these two different paths for humankind. Perhaps, I thought, in ages yet to come, other such wars would be fought as well.

'This *must* be the time,' Master Juwain said, giving voice to the old dream of the Brotherhoods – and many others besides. 'The earth has entered the Golden Band, this we know. Somewhere on Ea, the Maitreya has been born. It may be he who will lead the return to the stars.'

'Return?' Liljana said. 'What have we made here on earth? Ashes. The Red Dragon has burned all that was best of Ea to the ground. Should we return to the Star People bearing ashes in our hands?'

'What would you do, then, sow them into the soil and hope for gardens to grow?'

'From the ashes of its funeral pyre,' she said, 'the silver swan is reborn. There was a time when we built the Gardens of the Earth and the Temples of Life. And there will be a time when we will build them again.'

'But what of our leaving Ea that your Old Ones have told of?'

'We *will* leave someday, they say. They say we will leave either in glory or death. The Old Ones are waiting to see which it will be.'

She paused a moment, then said, 'They are waiting for us – waiting to welcome the Ardun to the higher orders.'

The Ardun, she explained, was her word for what the whales called the earth people. I turned toward the ocean to see if I could catch one last sight of them. But the waters were empty.

'Well, I'll choose glory, then,' Maram put in. 'It's what man was born for, isn't it?'

'And for what were women born?' Liljana asked. 'Being locked inside

417

their houses while men burn down their cities and spill each other's blood?'

At this Kane came forward and glared at Maram. Then he turned his gaze on Liljana and said, 'Whether the next age is one of darkness or light won't be decided just by men and women. All beings, I think, will play a part in what's to come. Maybe even the whales.'

Now he, too, looked out over the ocean. But aside from the ebbing of the tide, the only movement in that direction came from Flick as he darted and whirled among the sparkling waves.

I said to Liljana, 'Did you ask them about the Lightstone?'

Everyone, even Flick, moved a little closer to Liljana. And she said, 'Of course I did. I think it amuses them that we're seeking a *thing*, true gold or not, however powerful it might be.'

'And what do they seek, then?' I asked.

'Just life, my dear. The wisdom to live life as it should be.'

And that, I thought, as I looked at the golden cup that I saw gleaming from the rocks of the cliff, was a truly a great dream. But how, I wondered, could life be lived at all if a darkness that had no end fell upon the earth like a cold winter night?

'Do the Old Ones know where the Lightstone is?' I asked.

'They know where *something* is,' she said. 'They told me of a stone that gives much light.'

'Many stones give light,' Master Juwain said. 'Even the glowstones and the lesser gelstei.'

'This is no glowstone, I think,' she said. 'The Old Ones told of an island to the west where there is a great crystal. It's the most powerful gelstei they've ever sensed.'

'Yes, but is it *the* Gelstei?'

'I wish I knew,' she said to him.

Master Juwain held out a trembling finger to touch the figurine that Liljana was now staring at. Then he asked, 'Did the Old Ones tell what island this is?'

We all awaited the answer to this question as we held our breaths and looked at Liljana.

'Almost, they did,' she said. 'But their words are not our words. Understanding their names is like trying to grab hold of water.'

'I see,' Master Juwain said. 'But did they say *where* this island is, then?'

'It must be west of here – they said the evening sun sets upon it.'

'Very good, but how would anyone get to it? The whales must know.'

'Of course they do,' she said. 'But they don't steer by the stars, as we do. I think they . . . make pictures of the land and sea with sounds. With their words. When they speak to each other, they see these maps of the world. But I couldn't.'

'You couldn't see anything, then?'

'Only the shape of the island. It looked something like a seahorse.'

At this news, Master Juwain grew silent as his luminous eyes looked out toward the ocean.

Maram, still the student of the Brotherhood despite his failings, said, 'Nedu and Thalu lie to the west of here. And so do ten thousand other islands. Who would ever know if any of them were shaped like a seahorse?'

As it happened, Master Juwain did. The knowledge that he had gained from old books always astonished me. As did his memory.

'When I was a novice,' he told us, 'I read of a little island off Thalu where great flocks of swans gathered each spring. It was called the Island of the Swans, though it was said to be shaped like a seahorse.'

Now I, too, stared out at the ocean to the west. The sun was rising behind me; in the touch of its golden rays upon the world, I saw the Lightstone gleaming beyond the wild blue waters.

'We must go there, then,' I said.

I looked at Atara and Kane; I looked at Maram, Master Juwain, Alphanderry and Liljana. I couldn't hear the words of affirmation they spoke to themselves. But I didn't need a blue gelstei to know that their thoughts were mine.

'But, Val,' Master Juwain said to me, 'the account of this island that I read was *old*. There have been great wars since then. The firestones opened up the earth, you know. And the earth took back its own, in cataclysm and in fire. Many of the islands off Nedu and Thalu were blasted into rocks, utterly destroyed. Now the sea covers them.'

'The Old Ones told of this island,' I said. 'So it must still exist.'

A troubled look came over Liljana's face, and I asked her, 'What's wrong?'

'The Old Ones told of this island, yes,' she said. 'But I think they don't see time as we do. For them, what has been still is – and always will be.'

'They sound like scryers,' Maram said, smiling at Atara.

Atara smiled back at him. 'No, a scryer would say what will be always was. And never quite *is*.'

'And what does *this* scryer say?' I asked, smiling at her, too.

'Why, that we should search for this island. Of course we should.'

We decided to celebrate our passage of the Vardaloon and Liljana's great feat of speaking with the Sea People. We filled our cups with brandy, clinked them together, and drank to our resolve to find the Island of the Swans. As the fiery liquor warmed my throat and the sun warmed the world, I looked down at the silver swan shining from my surcoat. The Old Ones' revelation about the island, I sensed, was a great, good omen. For the swan was not only sacred to the Valari but a sign of bright things to come.

25

We traveled all that day toward the west. After retreating a few miles back down the beach, we found a path that led up along the headland overlooking the sea. This we followed for many more miles along the coast. It was rough terrain, broken by many cliffs and coves, and we found that we could best traverse it by keeping inland where the ground was somewhat level and covered with elderleaf and pepperbush and other such shrubs. We saw some seals on a rocky beach below us and many birds: cormorants and peregrine falcons and merlins splitting the air with their high-pitched cries. But the entire country seemed empty of people. Where we might find there fishermen or mariners with ships to take us over the ocean, none of us knew. Even so, we rode on in high spirits buoyed up by the bracing wind and our renewed hopes.

'It must be two hundred and fifty miles to Eanna's border,' Kane said as he cast his eyes west toward that old and distant kingdom. 'And again as much to Ivalo. There are galliots and whalers there, if I remember. And smaller ships. One of them would likely take us to this Island of the Swans.'

'Five hundred miles!' Maram complained. 'Well, we've come farther than that since Mesh. If we can cross the Vardaloon, we can cross this desolate country – and the sea.'

It was unlike him to be so cheerful, but the salty air and the brilliant waters below us seemed to work a magic upon him. He sat astride his sorrel humming to himself and quite pleased at having abundant sun with which to fill his firestone. More than once, along that windy and open track, he let loose a bolt of fire that incinerated a cluster of goldenrod or fused a patch of sand into glass. He might have aimed his crystal at the sea itself and tried to boil it away if Kane hadn't kept close to him with his black gelstei at the ready and his even blacker eyes watching him like an eagle.

421

Because we were all still tired, we didn't get very far that day. The horses were nearly spent, and none of us had the heart to push them – or ourselves. And so late in the afternoon, when the ground grew lower and we came upon a mead fairly rippling with long, green grass, we decided to make camp. We picketed the horses along the mead so that they could eat their fill, then spread out our furs on the beach just below it.

After piling up a good deal of driftwood for our fire and doing our other chores, we bathed in the ocean along with the anemones that floated in the shallows, and the sea lettuce and rockweed and other plants that Master Juwain named. We gathered up whelks and mussels, and sat around our fire pulling them out of their shells to make our evening meal. The gulls watched us closely even as we watched the sandpipers skipping along and making their *peetweet* cries. Out above the sea, the ospreys glided and swooped and grabbed up fish in their gray talons.

And then, like a cloud that had been building for most of a day, a casual comment cast a shadow on our bright mood.

'I wish we had some of those tomcods,' Liljana said, pointing at a wriggling length of silver that an osprey held. 'I know everyone would like a little fish for dinner.'

'Ah, but how did you *know* that?' Maram asked. 'None of us spoke of eating fish.'

He studied the blue figurine that she held in her hand, and then eyed her suspiciously.

'Well, you didn't have to. I saw the way you looked at them.'

'You did, did you? Ah, but did *you* by chance happen to look into *our* minds?'

Liljana's round, pleasant face reddened as if she had been slapped. 'No, Prince Maram Marshayk, I did not!'

It was strange, I thought, that although my friends rather welcomed my being able to sense their emotions, none of them wanted Liljana listening to their thoughts. And neither did I.

'Are you *sure* you couldn't hear what I was thinking?' Maram asked.

I stood up and walked around the fire past Kane before sitting down between Liljana and Maram. Then I told him, 'If Liljana says that she wasn't listening to your thoughts, you shouldn't doubt her.'

'Oh, shouldn't he?' Liljana said to me. 'And why shouldn't he, young Prince, since you doubt me yourself?'

'Did you hear me say anything about doubting you?' I asked.

'You didn't have to,' Liljana told me. 'Since your eyes say it all.'

Maram cracked opened a whelk with a sudden slap of a rock.

'Do you see, Val, she *can* hear your thoughts! It's that damn stone of hers.'

Liljana held up her blue gelstei and said, 'I don't need *this* for *that* when I have my eyes and nose.'

She turned toward me and said, 'What have I done to make you doubt me so? Do you think I haven't learned from bitter necessity to read the motives of powerful men, Valashu Elahad?' She squeezed the whale-shape figurine. 'Before I ever dreamed of finding this, I knew that your thoughts were turning in one direction.'

'And which direction is that?'

'From the hate in your voice, I would guess toward the Lord of Lies.'

I saw Kane, Atara and Master Juwain looking at me, and I said, 'Yes, this is true.'

'He's found you in your dreams again, hasn't he?' Liljana asked.

'In my dreams, yes.'

'And this makes you furious, doesn't it?'

'Yes,' I admitted, 'it does.'

'And you're afraid of this terrible fury of yours, aren't you? You think about ways of not being afraid, don't you?'

'That's true,' I said, staring out away from the beach.

'And so you think about the Lightstone – all the time.'

In truth, most of my waking hours – and many of my dreams – were spent in looking for the golden glow of the Lightstone inside myself. As I now looked for it above the streaming waters of the sea.

Liljana touched my hand and reassured me, 'I don't think I can go inside anyone's mind unless they let me. I don't think I could hear their thoughts unless they spoke them to me.'

'No, you don't have that power,' I said, looking at her. 'Not yet.'

I thought of the dream that Morjin had sent me. And then Kane, who was no mind-reader that I knew, pointed at Liljana's figurine and said, 'It's almost certain that Morjin has a blue gelstei, eh? He's always taken the deepest interest in the witches' stones.'

I noticed the puzzled looks on Atara's and Alphanderry's faces, and so I asked, 'Why do you call it that?'

But Kane clamped his jaws shut as he stared at the gelstei, and so Master Juwain answered for him: 'The blue gelstei are known to be both difficult and dangerous to use. You see, it's *very* dangerous to enter another's mind; few are born with the talent, and fewer still can do so without becoming lost or even maddened.'

He went on to recount something of the history of the blue gelstei, or blestei, as he called these crystals. He said that in the Age of the Mother, a physic made from the blue juice of the kirque plant had been found to aid the power of mindspeaking. But the kiriol, as it was called, was harsh on the body and shortened life. And so the alchemists of the Order of Brothers and Sisters of the Earth, inspired by the green gelstei, had tried to fabricate a blue crystal that would retain and magnify the mind-opening properties of the kiriol without its more deleterious effects.

'It took the alchemists a hundred years,' Master Juwain told us. Chule Ataru fabricated the first one – it was the first of the great gelstei made on Ea. He gave it to Rihana Hatar, who used it to speak with other Sisters in other lands – and the Sea People as well. That was the beginning of the great years of the Age of the Mother.'

Over the next century and a half, other such crystals had been made. Those who could use them – as with the scryers, these were mostly women – grew very powerful. But many were maddened by what they saw in others' minds, and men began to fear them. They covered their heads with their cloaks as they muttered protective charms and hurried past them. When the Aryans conquered most of Ea's free lands, they feared these mindspeaking Sisters, too, and called them witches. As many as they could find, they put to the sword. Their gelstei they buried or cast into the sea.

'In 2210 of that age,' Master Juwain said, 'a great conclave was held in Tria. Navsa Adami, foremost of the Brothers, favored arming any who would take up swords and using the blue gelstei to speak with others of like minds in other lands. He called for a rebellion that would cast off the Aryan yoke, almost in a night. But Janin Soli, and many of the Sisters, disagreed with him. She suggested opposing the Aryans by trying to grab hold of their minds and manipulating them from within.'

'*That* would be a horrible thing,' Maram said, shuddering again. 'But the witches never succeeded, did they, sir?'

'Don't you remember anything I've taught you?' Master Juwain said.

He told us then of how the Brothers and Sisters had argued violently as to how the blue gelstei should be used. In the end, Navsa Adami had fled from Alonia in great bitterness. He gathered up his followers and made his way to the Morning Mountains where he founded the first of the Brotherhood's schools.

'After that, King Vashrad began a great pogrom against what was left of the Order,' Master Juwain told us. 'He began killing *all* the Sisters, not just the mindspeakers, who were always quite few. It's said that he beheaded Janin Soli with his own sword.'

'But Janin had a daughter, didn't she?' Maram asked.

'Oh, you *do* remember your history, then?' Master Juwain said. 'Yes,

Janin Soli *did* have a daughter. But a daughter of the spirit, not the blood. Her name was Kalinda Marshan.'

Upon the destruction of the Order, he said, Kalinda had taken upon herself the ancient title of Materix, and had gathered the most advanced Sisters around her. They met in secret in the catacombs beneath the ruins of the Temple of Life in Tria. There Kalinda had vowed to avenge her beloved Janin's murder. There she and her other Sisters plotted the overthrow of the Aryan rule and the restoration of all the Temples of Life and Gardens of the Earth and all that was best of the Age of the Mother. And so was founded the very secret Maitriche Telu.

'So, the witches are still weaving their plots,' Kane said. 'Assassins, they are. Poisoners of minds. Makers of spells that capture men's souls.'

'But it's not known,' Master Juwain said, 'if the Maitriche Telu even still exists.'

'Ha, it exists!' Kane barked out. His black eyes flashed toward Liljana as he pointed at her gelstei. 'You should be very careful, Liljana. The Sisters must seek the blue gelstei since theirs have all likely been taken or lost. They'd give much gold for your little stone, eh?'

She nodded her head as if she agreed with him. Then she said, 'I suppose they would if there are any of these dread assassins and poisoners left. But *that's* not the kind of gold that I seek.'

'You shouldn't make jokes about the Maitriche Telu,' he growled at her. 'They'd kill you for that crystal, you know. If you're to keep it, you must keep it a secret, eh?'

Liljana smiled mysteriously and told us that she was good at keeping secrets; she promised that it would be safe with her. And then Master Juwain said, 'Yes, keep the blestei if you must, but please don't use it. Or else you'll risk falling mad like the ancient Sisters.'

Liljana opened her hand to show us her little blue crystal. Then she said, 'Do you think this came to me not to be used? What have I done that you think I would misuse it?'

'It's not you we doubt, Liljana,' Master Juwain said, 'but only the blue gelstei.'

'And what of the prophecy, then?'

We sat around the fire munching down roasted mussels as we spoke of Ayondela Kirriland's prophecy.

'"The seven Brothers and Sisters of the earth,"' Liljana reminded us, '"with the seven stones will set forth into the darkness."'

'Ah, well, if we *are* those seven,' Maram said, looking toward the south, 'at least we've already gone into the darkness. What could be darker than the Vardaloon?'

He brought out his red stone and gazed at it as if its fire might reassure him, while Kane turned his black gelstei around and around in his hard, thick fingers. Atara gripped her scryer's sphere even as Master Juwain studied his varistei and Liljana played with her bit of blue driftglass. And then Liljana said, 'If we are those seven, then we have two more gelstei to gain before the Lightstone can be found.'

'And if those two are of the greater gelstei,' Master Juwain said, 'they must be the purple and the silver.'

Everyone looked at me and Alphanderry then as if wondering which of us would gain which stone.

'The prophecy,' Alphanderry pointed out, 'said only that seven with the seven stones would set forth and that the Lightstone would be found. But we don't know that it will be found *after* the seven stones are gained.'

'If we find the Lightstone first,' Maram said, 'what would be the need of gaining the seven gelstei?'

'What would be the need of gaining them,' Liljana said, glancing at her figurine, 'if they are not to be used?'

I thought of how Morjin had used a varistei to make a monster named Meliadus and how the Grays had nearly stolen my soul with Kane's black stone. I said, '*All* the gelstei are dangerous, aren't they? Why should we single out Liljana's stone as being especially so?'

'But, Val,' Master Juwain said, 'consider this stone's origins. The blue gelstei captured some of the essence of the kiriol. And kiriol is made from an infusion of kirque juice, as is its more deadly cousin, kirax.'

The mere mention of this word intensified the pain of the poison that would always taint my blood. My thoughts turned again toward Morjin, and I feared yet again that the very act of thinking about him connected us heart to heart and mind to mind. As did the kirax.

I looked at Kane and asked, 'You said before that the Lord of Lies must have a blue gelstei – why do you think this?'

For a moment Kane stared into his black stone as if caught by a mirror. Then he looked up and told me, 'The Lord of *Illusions* has great powers, eh? What could be greater than the power to make others see what is not? But even he can't cast these illusions and nightmares all over Ea. For that he would surely need a blue gelstei.'

'He has seen my mind, then,' I said. 'He has seen me.'

Kane got up and stepped past the fire so that he could grab my arm and shake some courage into me. 'So, he's seen your mind, and that's too bad. But he hasn't seen your soul, I think. *That's* beyond any of the blue gelstei to reveal, even the most powerful.'

The strength of his hand reassured me a little. But his words disturbed

Maram, who said, 'But can he see Val, in his body? See where he is? If he can see him, then he can see us.'

'I don't think he can,' Liljana said. 'So long as Val keeps from speaking to his mind and revealing the details of what he sees about him, I would think that the Lord of Illusions would be able to do nothing more than sense his presence somewhere – but not know where.'

'This accords with what is known of the blue gelstei,' Master Juwain said. 'But we mustn't forget the poison that his man put into Val. I'm afraid that the kirax speaks for Val whether he wills it or not.'

'So, it speaks,' Kane said. 'But speaks *how*? Surely not to the mind. As we've seen by Val's most recent dream.'

'How so?' Master Juwain asked. 'Aren't dreams *of* the mind?'

'Ha, the mind!' Kane coughed out. 'I say that dreams are of the soul. But no matter. Val has been free from Morjin's dreams and illusions since we killed the Grays. Why this sudden dream, then?'

Master Juwain thought for a moment and then said, 'Meliadus.'

'Just so,' Kane said. 'When Meliadus died, the pain of it opened Val up. Morjin felt his son's death – and much else as well. It's the *valarda* that truly joins Val to Morjin. This is his greatest vulnerability, eh?'

As the fire sent up sparks into the darkening sky, we sat there speaking of the blue gelstei and the black, the purple and the silver and the gold – as well as the gifts of mindspeaking and the *valarda*. Finally, Kane held up his hand as if to ward off our most fearful speculations. And then he told us, 'No one knows everything about the Great Beast's powers. But this much we can take courage from: he can be fought. So, he casts illusions, but not all are maddened by them. He sends terrible dreams, but those there are who refuse to make them their own. He turns men and women into ghuls – but never the strongest, eh? In the end, I have to believe that each of us has the will to turn away from him.'

He went on to say that one's will must be tempered like the toughest of steels and sharpened so that it cut through all fear; it must be polished to a mirrorlike finish so as to cast back to Morjin all his illusions, nightmares and lies.

'Isn't this what I've always said?' Master Juwain asked, turning toward me. 'Have you been doing the exercises I taught you, Val?'

I remembered him telling me how I must create an ally who would watch over me in my sleep and guard me from evil dreams. I shook my head as I told him, 'After the Grays' deaths, there seemed no need.'

'I see,' Master Juwain said. 'Then perhaps it's time for some new lessons.'

'Yes, perhaps it is, sir.'

'And the dreams are the least of it,' he went on. 'While you're awake, you must try to turn your thoughts away from the Lord of Lies.'

I bowed my head in acknowledgement that this was so.

'And so must you, Liljana,' Master Juwain said, pointing at her blue crystal. 'Of all of us save Val, you must be the most careful.'

'Of *course* I will,' she told him. 'Have you known me to be otherwise?'

Master Juwain sighed as he rubbed the back of his head. 'Will you promise that if you *do* use your gelstei, you'll refrain from trying to see what is in the Red Dragon's mind?'

'Of *course* I will,' she said again. 'I think I know too well what is in such men's minds.'

Her offhand dismissal of Morjin as merely a man like any other alarmed me. As it did Atara. During our talk of the blue gelstei and mindspeaking, she had been mostly silent. But now she suddenly looked up from her clear crystal and said, 'Beware, Liljana – on the day you touch Morjin's mind, you'll smile no more, nor will you laugh again.'

And that, I thought, as we said good night to each other and settled down onto our sleeping furs, was a warning that we all should heed.

That night I was touched with dark dreams again, and I awakened long before sunrise to watch the clouds blowing in over the ocean and covering up the moon's feeble light. But then I meditated as Master Juwain had taught me; as I fell asleep again, I tried to remain aware of that part of me that never slept and remained always aware. It must have helped, for after that, I dreamed only of my family, whom I missed more than even the mountains of Mesh. My brothers – and my father, mother and grandmother, too – smiled at me from inside the castle of my soul and urged me to complete my quest and return home soon.

The clouds blew away with the rising of the sun, and we were given a fine, bright day for traveling. As we were saddling the horses, Master Juwain looked out at the ocean and said, 'Unless I've missed my count, today is the first of Marud. That's a good month for crossing the sea.'

'Hoy, it's the best of months,' Alphanderry said. 'But where are we to find a ship to cross it?'

That remained our most pressing problem, and we set out toward the west to solve it. We let the horses walk slowly along the beach for a couple of hours. Even though they had eaten their fill of grass during our camp, they were still sluggish in all their motions. They needed a good feed of oats, I knew, to fatten them up and renew their strength. But oats we had none, and neither in this country of sandy beaches and shrubs were we likely to find barley or rye or any other such grain. Altaru kept up his spirits even so. Twice, when I dismounted to walk beside him and give him a rest, he shook his head and kicked the sand as if offended that I doubted his ability to bear me. He was so great-hearted a beast, I thought, that he would have plunged into the sea in an effort to swim us across it. What he would make of a ship if ever we came upon one, I didn't know.

After perhaps ten miles, the shoreline curved toward the northwest, even as Kane and Master Juwain had decided it must if we had reached the Bay of Whales. Eanna, of course, lay almost due west of us, and we might have ridden straight toward it in that direction, thus cutting a good chunk of country – and many miles – from our journey. But to do so would have meant re-entering the Vardaloon. And as Maram put it, he'd rather ride around the coastline of all Ea than go back into that accursed forest again.

And so we hugged the coast as nearly as we could. But with its many coves, headlands and cliffs, we often found ourselves veering quite a few miles inland where the goldenrod, fleabane and other shrubs gave way to a forest of oaks and tall pines that fairly reeked of pitch. We were all very glad to find few mosquitoes there and no leeches or ticks. The bloodbirds that had tormented the horses so terribly seemed to be creatures of the deeper woods, and the fiercest flying things that we saw were some windcatchers who seemed happy to eat the mosquitoes rather than us.

The next day and the day after that found us still working our way to the northwest along the Bay of Whales. But on our fourth day since our talk about the blue gelstei, we came to a rocky prominence that pointed out toward the Northern Ocean. There the coast turned sharply toward the southwest. A hundred miles across these gray-green waters, Master Juwain said, the many small islands of the Nedu archipelago gave way to the those of the Elyssu. He told us that many ships sailed the sea between those islands and the bit of land upon which we stood. But that day we saw nothing but a few cormorants hovering over the sea.

'Something is worrying you, sir,' I said to Master Juwain as we gazed out at the ocean. The wind off the water whipped my hair about my head, as it did the horses' manes. But Master Juwain, bald as an egg, was spared this nuisance.

'Worrying me?' he said. 'Worrying, well, yes – I'm afraid there is.'

He turned to point along the coast to our left. 'Unless the old maps no longer show the world as it is, fifty miles from this cape, we'll come to a river. The Ardellan, it used to be called. It drains the whole of the Vardaloon and empties into the ocean. How are we to cross it?'

It might have vexed me that Master Juwain had waited until we had come so far to voice such doubts. But there was no help for it: he was a man who turned things over in his mind so thoroughly that he too often supposed what was obvious to him must be to others as well. As it happened, however, I had already discussed the crossing of the Ardellan with Kane.

'We'll build rafts,' I said, 'and float across it.'

'Rafts, is it?' Master Juwain said. 'And how are we to build such things?'

The failings of his knowledge made me smile. He could find a herb in a strange wood that would drive away some mysterious fever or tell of the making of the gelstei thousands of years ago. But the making of a simple raft seemed beyond him.

'We'll cut trees,' I told him, 'and tie them together.'

'Trees, is it? Yes, I see, I see.'

After making camp that night near a little stream that ran into the sea, we set out to the southwest along the coast early the next morning. The shoreline here grew straighter and gentler, and we found that we could keep to the beaches for many long stretches. Twenty-five miles we made that day at a slow walk, and our progress on the day following that was even more encouraging. By the late afternoon, we had our first signs that we were approaching the great river. We saw a flock of long-winged azulenes, and Master Juwain said that they were birds of fresh water, not salt. The horses, sniffing at the air, seemed to smell this water beyond the haze of trees and shoreline ahead of us. And so did Liljana.

'We're close,' she told us, pointing along the beach. Ahead of us some four miles, the coast seemed to take a turn to the south. 'That must be the mouth of the Ardellan.'

We rode straight toward it, now at a much quickened walk. The beach narrowed and then disappeared altogether, and we were forced to take to the forest that grew almost down to the sea. The trees here were the usual oaks and pines that found root in the sandy soil along this coast. They formed a thick wall blocking any view of the river that we must certainly be drawing nearer. I was glad for the tarry-smelling pines, for they grew straighter than the oaks and would be much easier to cut. Just as I was wondering how many it would take to build a raft large enough to bear up two or three of the horses, the woods gave out suddenly onto a line of fields. And just beyond these patches of green, I gasped to see a walled city built along the banks of the wide, blue river.

'I didn't know there were any cities in this part of the world,' Maram said, speaking for all of us. 'Who are these people?'

'Let's find out,' I said, nudging Altaru forward.

In truth, the city was more of a town, being much smaller than Tria – or even Silvassu. And the wall surrounding it was neither magnificent nor formidable: it was made of poles of wood planted down into the moist earth like a long line of rafts joined together. And most of it, we saw as we drew closer, was eaten with wormholes or rotten. The houses and all the buildings beyond it were made of the same rotting pine so that the whole city reeked of decay and the stench of tar and turpentine.

But the wall at least had a gate and a road leading up to it. We made our way down this dirt track past ragged peasants who ran from us as they cried out and covered their faces. They disappeared into their tiny wooden huts and shut the doors behind them.

'Ah, a friendly people,' Maram said as he rode next to me. 'Perhaps we shouldn't take advantage of their hospitality.'

'But they might be able to help us cross the river,' I told him. 'Besides, we should find out what has frightened them so.'

The peasants' cries had alerted the city's guards, who stood along a walkway behind the low walls looking down at us. They each had long blond hair and tangled blond beards. They wore tattered blue tunics emblazoned with crests showing an eagle clutching two crossed swords in its talons. Their iron helmets were pitted with rust, as were the poor, shortish swords they brandished at us.

'Who are you?' demanded one of these blue-eyed guards that I took to be their captain. 'From where do you come?'

We gave them our names and those of our lands; we told them that we needed help in crossing the Ardellan so that we could continue on our journey. After conferring with his fellows for a moment, the captain looked at us with his icy blue eyes and said, 'We know of Alonia and the Elyssu, but there are no kingdoms called Mesh and Delu that we have ever heard.'

'So, it's a big world,' Kane growled at him as he tossed a little stone against the gate. 'If you'll let us in, we'll tell you more about it.'

'The King will decide that,' the guard captain said. 'You'll wait here while he is summoned.'

As if to give more weight to his command, the other guards suddenly produced crossbows and aimed them at us. But the iron of their mechanisms seemed worn away, and I doubted if they would fire.

'What kind of king is it,' Maram whispered to me, 'who is summoned to greet us rather than we to him?'

For a while, as we sat on our horses and listened to the wind rattling across the potato fields surrounding the city, we awaited the answer to this question. And then we heard heavy steps behind the rickety old wall as of boots treading up wooden stairs. An old man suddenly showed his white-haired head and wispy white beard. I saw that he must have once been quite tall but was now stooped with age. He wore a faded purple mantle collared with white ermine that had seen better days. Upon his head was a silver crown that seemed to have been hastily polished in a vain effort to rub the tarnish away. The guard captain presented him as King Vakurun. The King looked down upon us with rheumy blue eyes that held no welcome but a great deal of fear.

'Tell us your names again,' he commanded us in a quavering voice. 'Speak up so that we can hear you.'

Again, we gave our names and waited for the gates to be opened.

'How do we know you are who you say?' he asked us.

'Who else could we be?' I replied.

King Vakurun traded a quick look with his captain, then pointed at the trees beyond the fields. 'Only evil things have ever come out of those woods.'

I smiled at Atara and Alphanderry, then called out, 'Do we look evil to you?'

'That which has slain my people,' he told us as he pointed his old finger at Atara, 'is said sometimes to appear as fair as this maiden.'

He went on to say that his realm had been attacked by a succession of enemies: great black bears deeper in the woods; an invincible knight mounted on a great white horse armored in diamonds; a tribe of warrior women; giant men with hideous faces and white fur; long, leechlike worms as big as whales – and other things.

Now it was my turn to trade looks with Kane and the others. Then I looked up at the King and said, 'It would seem that all these enemies were really one enemy. And he has been slain.'

We told of our passage through the Vardaloon and of Meliadus. We assured him that we had put this monster in the earth, from which he would never rise again. Then we told him about the quest and showed him the medallions that King Kiritan had given us.

'We have heard of King Kiritan,' King Vakurun said. The sunlight off the circles of gold we wore around our necks seemed to dazzle his eyes. 'And we have heard that he sent emissaries to all lands to call knights to Tria, though he never sent anyone to *our* realm.'

His hand swept out toward the fields around his rotting old town.

'And what realm is that?' I asked him.

'Why, Valdalon,' the King said. 'You're in Valdalon, didn't you know?'

He went on to say that he ruled all the lands from Eanna to the Blue Mountains and between the White Mountains and the sea.

'If you really did slay this Meliadus,' he told us, 'then we owe you a debt that must be repaid.'

I looked at the points of his crown and saw that the squares of amethyst there had fallen off two of them. I said, 'We ask only a safe passage through your kingdom and help crossing the river, if you can provide it.'

I admitted that we were on way to Ivalo, where we hoped to find a ship that would take us across the sea to the islands south of Thalu.

'If it's a ship you seek,' the King said, 'then perhaps we can help you cross much more than the river. There are two ships in our harbor, and one of them is due to sail for Ivalo this very day.'

This news sent a stir of excitement through us, especially Maram who had dreaded the hard work of chopping down trees to build a raft – to say nothing of riding hundreds of miles to Ivalo. After our various travails, we seemed to have been favored with a stroke of good fortune.

King Vakurun called for the gates to be opened then, and we rode into the city – if this assemblage of miserable houses and muddy streets could so be called. Forty of the King's men immediately surrounded us to act as an escort; none of these 'knights,' however, was mounted. It seemed that the King himself possessed the only horse in the city. He pulled himself on top of this sway-backed old gelding, then rode beside me as we made our way through the streets toward the river.

'We'll have to hurry if we wish to catch this ship,' he told us. 'It might be a long while before another sails for the west.'

With a sad look then, he recounted the story of his people. Many of these lined the streets to witness the unprecedented spectacle we must have provided them. All except the graybeards and crones had the same blond hair and blue eyes as our guards. All looked as if they might have been Atara's distant cousins – which indeed they proved to be.

The Valdalonians, King Vakurun said, were descendants of a great warrior named Tarnaran and his followers, who had set out from Thalu some three hundred years before. Tarnaran and his band of adventurers – these were not the King's words but only my understanding of them – claimed the great Bohimir as their ancestor. Dreaming as they did of regaining the glory of the ancient Aryans, they sought new lands to conquer. But Tarnaran was no Bohimir, and Thalu was long past its time of greatness. There was to be no sailing of the Thousand Ships or sack of Tria by bloodthirsty savages in this age. Five ships only Tarnaran gathered along the coast of the impoverished Thalu. He led them across the Northern Ocean and into the mouth of the Ardellan River. There they built their first city, and Tarnaran was crowned King of Valdalon.

But it was one thing to claim all the land from Eanna to the Blue Mountains, and quite another to subdue it. King Tarnaran had found it easy enough to cow the tribespeople along the coast into paying him a tribute of fish and furs; the tribes of the deeper forest proved more formidable. As did the forest itself. It took the Valdalonians a hundred years to establish towns farther inland along the Ardellan and its tributaries. Fighting the leeches and mosquitoes and thick walls of vegetation was bad enough. But as they tried to extend their power even further through their realm, they were assaulted and killed by the succession of enemies that King Vakurun had told of earlier.

'You can't begin to understand the terror this Meliadus caused my people,' King Vakurun told us. 'If it truly was this beast-man who slayed them.'

Meliadus, the King said, had slain much more than the Valdalonians. Over the second century of their rule, the tribes of the deeper woods began dying, followed by those of the coast. With no one left to pay them tribute, King Vakurun's people grew poorer. Then, one by one, their outposts in the forest came under assault. Dreadful tales were told: of a young warrior whose wife turned into a she-bear and devoured him; of children who had been stolen from their beds and later found drained of every ounce of blood. The third century of the Valdalonians' rule saw the gradual abandonment of towns along the Ardellan and the realm's other rivers. By the time of King Vakurun's father, King Vakurun said, his people had been reduced to eking out a living behind the walls of their original city.

'These have been bad times, the worst of times,' the King told us as we rode toward the river. 'But it's said that it's always darkest before the dawn. I pray that you'll find this Lightstone that you seek. As I do that my people will someday fill all of Valdalon from the White Mountains to the sea.'

His people, I thought, could barely fill the single city that remained to them. Many of the houses about us seemed abandoned or had even fallen in upon themselves. Aside from the few crops the Valdalonians pulled from the poor, sandy soil around their city and the hunting of the fur seals farther along the coast, they had little to sustain themselves. And so King Vakurun, early in his reign, had built a harbor in the hope of attracting the great ships that sailed the ocean to the south of the Elyssu and Nedu. From the pines that grew so abundantly nearby, his people had pressed forth pitch and turpentine with which to repair these ships. Thus they had been reduced from warriors to being caulkers and carpenters.

The two ships that he had told us about were still anchored at the harbor along the river's edge. Of course, to call four rickety docks sticking out into the river a harbor was something like calling a molehill a mountain. Still, I thought, the ships were impressive enough. One was a galliot being fitted with new oars while the other Master Juwain called a bilander. This stout, two-masted ship had pulled into the harbor to take on a cargo of furs and was bound for Ivalo.

We rode our horses right down onto the dock to which it was tied. Then King Vakurun called for the captain to come down the gangplank and meet us. The dozen sailors who had stopped their work to look at us made way for him. Captain Kharald, as the King presented him, was a burly man dressed like the men he commanded in a wool shirt, wide black belt and bright blue pantaloons. He had the flaming red hair of a Surrapamer and eyes as green as the sea. His face, burnt red from years of sun and wind, was creased with many lines like an old piece of leather. When he saw that the King intended us to take passage with him, it lit up with greed.

'Well, it's a clear hundred and fifty leagues from here to Ivalo,' he said, looking us over. 'And there are seven of you and eleven horses, two of them heavily laden.'

The captain, I thought, was a man who liked numbers and sums – and calculating profit to the thinnest piece of silver.

Atara started to draw forth the leather purse of coins that she had won at dice in Tria. But King Vakurun stayed her hand with an unexpectedly regal look. To Captain Kharald, he said, 'These people have done us a great service, and it is our wish that they should have passage to wherever they wish. You may take the cost of this from the price of the furs that we have agreed upon.'

I started to protest this largesse, but a look from Liljana silenced me. I saw what she saw: that a king, to be a king, needed opportunities to display his generosity. I saw another thing as well. King Vakurun, it seemed, was only too happy to rid his realm of seven strangers who might prove to be even more dangerous than Meliadus.

After that, we thanked the King and set about boarding the ship. As I had feared, there was some trouble getting the horses up the gangplank and then down into the stables in the ship's hold. Altaru, especially, did not want to be taken down into this dank, darkish place. Three of the sailors assured me that they had shipped horses before, and tried to take his reins from me. This was a mistake. Altaru kicked out at them, missing their heads by inches and almost splintering the topsides above the deck. Captain Kharald's green eyes blazed like a dragon's as he inspected the divots that Altaru's iron-shod hooves had left in the wood. He said nothing, but I could almost hear him tallying up the damage and subtracting it from the price of the furs he would pay to King Vakurun.

Finally, I took it upon myself to lead Altaru down the walkway into the hold. Atara and the others did the same with their horses. After making sure that their stables were clean and spread with fresh straw, we fed them oats from the ship's store and then went up to lay out our sleeping furs on the deck.

An hour later, with the ebbing of the tide and the night's first stars pointing our way west, the ship sailed out from the mouth of the Ardellan River into the Great Northern Ocean.

26

There was a full moon that night, and it rose over a world that was nothing but water in all directions. Long past the time that I should have been sleeping with my companions back near the stern, I stood alone at the bow gripping the railing there as I watched the ship splitting the waves of the moon-silvered sea. Sailing out of sight of the land terrified me. Merely looking out at the ocean threatened to drown me in its bright black vastness. To the south and west, east and north, I saw no bit of land upon which I could fix my gaze or hope of setting foot should a sudden storm take us under. My life, I realized, and those of my companions and everyone else aboard, was utterly tied to the fate of this rolling and pitching clump of wood that men had nailed together.

Captain Kharald had named his ship the *Snowy Owl*, and this gave me at least a little courage. Owls can see through the darkness, as could our red-bearded captain. He walked the deck for hours that first night of our voyage, now casting his eyes up at the wind-filled sails, now checking with the pilot who steered the ship to make sure that we held our course. This, I thought, he set by the stars. They were very bright that night. These millions of points of light streaked out of the black sky like diamond-tipped spears and almost outshone the moon itself. At no time in my life since I had climbed the mountains of my home had I felt so close to them.

I might have remained there all night gazing out into this unnerving splendor and smelling the salty spray of the sea. But then I heard steps behind me, and turned expecting to see Captain Kharald or one his crew of fifty sailors who worked the ship. Instead, a stranger stood limned in the moonlight. Or so I thought at first, for he wore neither the rough, wool shirt or pantaloons of Captain Kharald's men but rather a long traveling cloak with a deep hood that covered most of his face. And then he spoke, and I knew he was no stranger.

'Valashu Elahad,' he said, 'why are you trying to run from me?'

His voice was sweeter than Alphanderry's; when he threw back his hood, the moon's light fell across the most beautiful face I had ever seen. His hair gleamed like gold, and his eyes were like twin suns pouring a golden light into the darkness. Across the chest of his tunic, which was trimmed with black fur, there coiled a great, red dragon.

I tried not to look at him, but it seemed that my eyelids were pinned open as with nails. I tried not to listen to him, but his voice rose above the creaking of the ship's timbers and the howling wind: 'I know you murdered my son.'

I started to deny this, but then remembered that I mustn't speak to him at any cost.

Morjin then reached out his finely-made hand and touched the scabbard where my broken sword was sheathed. He said, 'I told you that you would slay with this sword again, and so you have.'

'No,' I whispered, 'it was he who –'

'MY SON!' Morjin suddenly roared at me. So great was this shout that I thought the force of it might crack the ship's masts. And so terrible was the anguish in Morjin's voice that I was afraid it might crack *me* apart.

'My son,' Morjin said in softer tones that slid into me like silken knives. 'My only son.'

I threw my hands up over my ears to shut out his words. Finally, I managed to close my eyes and blind myself to the immense suffering I saw on his face.

But then Morjin touched my hands with his hands; he touched my forehead, pressing his finger against the scar there. And I heard his voice pealing out like silver chimes inside my mind; I saw his eyes seeking me out and looking where no man should look.

'The last time we met,' he said, 'we agreed that you must die. But now that you have murdered Meliadus, you must die a thousand times. Shall I show you these deaths?'

Without waiting for me to answer, his hand lashed out, catching me full in the chest. The force of this blow was so great that it propelled me over the railing, and I fell through black space. And then I plunged into the even vaster blackness of the sea. I sank into the churning waves like a stone. I gasped for air, choked, breathed water. The salt burned my lungs even as the cold took me deeper and crushed the life from me.

And then the darkness of the sea gave way to a stinging glister, and I realized that I was not falling into its depths after all but rather caught in the cleft between two mountains as a blizzard raged all about me. Still I struggled to breathe as the liquid wind froze my limbs and needles of ice pierced my flesh. The pain of it grew

438

so great so that I was sure that cold steel knives were tearing into me.

And then I *was* being torn open – with the shouts of fierce, blue-skinned warriors who had somehow surrounded me and forced me up against a mountain wall. Their gleaming axes beat aside my father's shield and chopped through my armor into my belly. I opened my mouth to scream at the incredible agony of it all, but then another axe caught me in the face, and I had no mouth with which to utter any sound, not even the faintest whisper of how terrified I was of death.

And so it went. The Lord of Lies had promised me a thousand deaths. But as I stood there on the bow of the rolling ship with Morjin's hand touching my forehead, it seemed that I died a thousand times a thousand times.

'Do you see, Valashu?' he said to me. 'Do you see?'

For what seemed hours, as the moon dropped its chill radiance down upon us, I fought not to behold the terrible visions that Morjin gave me. But I didn't fight hard enough. Not even the fierce will to battle that I had learned from Kane was enough to drive them or him away.

Finally, Morjin took his hand away from me. He stood beneath millions of stars hanging like knives above our heads. And in the saddest of voices, he said to me, 'Now you have seen your fate. But know that there is one, and only one, who can change it. And only one way that I will be persuaded to let you live.'

So saying, he looked down at my hands, which I saw were grasping a plain golden cup. Before I could blink at my astonishment, he took this cup from me and held it so that I could look inside.

And there, in its shimmering depths that were deeper than the sea, I saw myself standing on top of the world's highest mountain before a great, golden throne. Morjin, sitting on top of this throne, came down off it and extended his hand toward me. Then he pointed east and west, north and south, at Delu and Surrapam, at Sunguru and Alonia and all the other kingdoms of the world. All these, he said, he would give me to rule. He would give me Atara as my queen, and I would reign for a thousand years as Ea's High King.

For a long time, I stared into the golden cup he held before me. I saw the Red Desert bloom with flowers and the Vardaloon changed into a paradise. I saw warriors in the thousands laying down their swords and peace brought to all lands.

When I finally looked up, I saw that Morjin had changed as well. If possible, he was even more beautiful than before. His golden eyes had softened with an immense compassion, and in place of his dragon-embroidered tunic, he seemed clothed in an unearthly radiance of many colors. Without him telling me so, I knew that he had been made from a man into one of the great Elijin themselves.

'For three ages,' he told me, 'in a hard and terrible world, I've had to do hard and terrible things. Many times I've slain men, even as you have, Valashu Elahad.'

The suffering I saw in his sad and beautiful eyes was real. It made *my* eyes burn and touched me more deeply than I could bear. Only the golden cup, which poured out a healing light like the coolest and sweetest of waters, kept me from falling down and weeping.

'But soon the Lightstone will be found,' he told me as he looked down into the cup. 'The old world will be destroyed and a new one created. And you and Atara – all your children and grandchildren – will live your lives in a world that knows only peace.'

Only Morjin knew how badly I wanted the things that he showed me. But it was all a lie. The most terrible of lies, I thought, is that which one desperately wants to be true.

'You're close, aren't you?' Morjin said to me.

I shut my eyes as I slowly shook my head back and forth.

'Yes, so very close now to finding it,' he said. 'Open your eyes to me that I might see where you are.'

I wanted with a terrible longing to open my eyes and see the world transformed into a place of beauty and light.

'Open your eyes, please – it's growing late and the morning will soon be upon us.'

I stood at the bow of the heaving ship, trying to listen to the wind instead of his golden voice. I knew that I couldn't fight him much longer.

'The stars, Valashu. Let me look at the same stars that you see.'

My hand closed about the hilt of my sword, but I remembered that it was broken. And so, at last, I opened my eyes to look upon the stars rising in the east. Master Juwain had once told me that darkness couldn't be defeated in battle but only by shining a bright enough light. And there, just above the dark line of the horizon, blazed a white star that was brighter than any other. I fixed my eyes upon this single shimmering light that was called Valashu, the Morning Star. As I opened myself to its radiance, it suddenly filled the sky like the sun. It consumed me utterly. And I vanished into it like a silver swan soaring into that sacred fire that has no beginning or end.

'Damn you, Elahad!' I heard Morjin's voice cursing me as from far away. But when I turned to look at him, he was gone.

I gripped the railing along the topsides as I gasped and gave thanks for my narrow escape. I breathed in the smell of the sea and the pungency of pitch that sealed the seams of the creaking ship. Although the night's constellations still hung in the sky like twinkling signposts, there was a red sheen in the east that heralded the rising of the sun.

When I returned to my companions where we had spread out our sleeping furs along the deck, I found that Kane was awake. He was always awake, it seemed. Or perhaps it was more true to say that he seldom slept.

'What is it?' he murmured to me as I sat down on my fur. 'You look like you've seen a ghost.'

'Worse,' I whispered back to him. 'Morjin.'

Many times, Master Juwain had warned me not to say this accursed name; now the mere utterance of it seemed to rouse him from his sleep. Of course, he liked to rise early anyway, and the ship's open deck was now glowing in the day's first light.

I told them both what had happened while I had stood alone by the railing. And Master Juwain said, 'You did well, Val. The Morning Star, you say? Hmmm, an interesting variation of the light meditations I've taught you.'

Kane's eyes were black pools darker than the night-time sea. They searched along the deck and behind the towering masts as if looking for Morjin. And then he said, 'It disturbs me how much he knows of his son's death. He's growing stronger, I think.'

Both he and Master Juwain agreed that I must continue my meditations. As well, I must practice the art of guarding the doorway to my dreams.

'And we must practice swords,' Kane told me. 'Not all our battles against Morjin, I think, will be with his damned illusions and lies.'

When I pointed out that I had no sword to cross against his, he said, 'So, why don't you make one, then? I'm sure Captain Kharald can spare a bit of wood.'

As it happened, Captain Kharald was only too glad to provide me with a piece of a broken old spar that one of his men fetched from the hold – for a price. He said that good oak was valuable, broken or not, and asked for a silver piece in payment. But silver we had none, only the gold coins in Atara's purse, any one of which would have bought a whole forest of oaks. And so we settled on shaving a coin's rim, and giving these gold splinters to Captain Kharald. Such debasement of royal coinage, of course, was a crime. Or would have been if the coin had been Alonian. But as it was stamped with the head of King Angand of Sunguru, who was Morjin's ally, no one on board seemed to mind.

I spent most of the morning whittling the hard oak spar. While the sails above me filled with a good following wind and the *Snowy Owl* fairly flew through the water, I shaved off long strips of wood with my dagger – the same blade that I had put into Raldu's heart. It wasn't the best tool for such work, but its Godhran steel cut well enough. By the time the fierce Marud sun was high above us and heating up the deck, I had a wooden sword as long as a kalama. Wood being lighter than steel, I had made it much thicker than the blade I was used to in order to preserve its heft. But its balance was good and it handled quite well – indeed so well that I held my own against Kane for most of our first round of swordplay. Although he finally cut through my defenses, it seemed that he was having to work ever harder to do so.

We sailed all that day and next night into the west beneath fair skies. A hundred miles we made from sunset to sunset, Captain Kharald told us. By the second morning of our voyage, we had reached a point just south of Orun off Nedu. There some clouds came up upon a rising wind as the sea grew rougher. The ship rocked and heaved to the swelling of ten-foot waves, and so did our bellies. A strange malady called sea-sickness stole upon us like a fever that comes from eating rotten meat. It grabbed hold of Maram and me the most tightly, while Atara, Alphanderry and Liljana were less troubled. Master Juwain, who had grown up around boats, said that he hardly felt sick at all. As for Kane, the ship might have rolled over on its side and cast us all into the ocean before he complained of any distress.

'Ah, oh, ohhhh!' Maram gasped. We knelt side by side and hung our heads over the ship's stern as we gave up our dinners to the sea. 'Oh, this is too much! This is the worst yet – I'll never get on a ship again.'

All about us, the wind howled like a stricken beast and the water churned a blackish-green. The ship's masts, trimmed back of much sail, groaned even more loudly than did Maram.

'I want to go back, Val,' Maram said as a wave slapped the side of the ship. 'I don't care if we ever find the Lightstone.'

Even though I knew we were close to laying our hands upon this long-sought cup, I pressed my fist into the pit of my belly and said, 'All right then – we'll go back.'

Maram looked at me through the spray that the ship cast up. 'Do you really mean that, my friend?'

'Yes, why not? We'll return to Mesh as soon as we can. We're sure to have a warm homecoming, even if we fail in our quest.'

'All your family would turn out to greet us, wouldn't they?'

'Of course they would,' I said. 'Lord Harsha, too.'

At the mention of this name, Maram moaned even louder and cried out, 'Oh, Lord Harsha – I'd almost forgotten about him!'

His belly heaved as he leaned even farther over the side of the ship

– so far in fact that I had to grasp hold of his belt for fear that he would fall into the sea. He might have been grateful that I had saved his life. But instead he groaned, 'Oh, just me let go and be done with it! Oh, I want to die, I want to die!'

It gave us little courage when Kane later told us that we would soon find our sea-legs, as with Captain Kharald and the others of his crew. After sipping some tea that Master Juwain brewed to ease our suffering, I cast my wretched, empty body down upon my furs and lay as still as I could upon the ship's rolling deck. I fell asleep and had dark dreams, dreams of death. Whether these nightmares came from Morjin or my own misery was hard to say. But it seemed that the ally Master Juwain had bade me summon to watch over my sleep was a poor guard that night.

By the next morning, however, the sea had quieted somewhat and so had my belly. I found myself able to stand and fix my gaze upon the wavering blueness of the horizon. One of Captain Kharald's men, another redbeard named Jonald, pointed out a hazy bit of land to the starboard and said that it was one of the Windy Isles. This was a long chain of rocky outcroppings that ran for more than three hundred miles between Nedu and the coast of Eanna to the south. We had made good speed, he said, coming some two hundred and fifty miles since setting sail from King Vakurun's little city. Another hundred and fifty should find us pulling in to the great harbor at Ivalo.

We took this opportunity to hold a brief council and decide the best course for reaching the Island of the Swans. Kane spoke for us all when he said, 'This Captain Kharald is a greedy man, but he knows his business. He has a good ship and good crew, I think. Why not let them take us to the island?'

Atara brought out her purse and hefted it so that the coins jingled. She said, 'Greedy, hmmph, I suppose he is. Well, we have gold for him then. But will it be enough?'

That question seemed settled an hour later when we took Captain Kharald aside and put our proposal to him. When he learned of where we truly hoped to journey, he looked aghast and said, 'The Island of the Swans, you say? Why would you want to go there? It's cursed.'

'Cursed how?' I asked him.

'No one knows for certain. But it's said there are dragons there. No one ever sails to that place.'

I told him that we must reach this island, and soon. I told him about the vows we had made in King Kiritan's palace and our hopes of regaining the Lightstone.

'The Lightstone, the Lightstone,' Captain Kharald sighed out. 'I've heard talk of little else in all the ports from Ivalo to the Elyssu. But surely your golden cup no longer exists. It must have been melted down into coinage or jewelry long ago.'

'Melted, ha!' Kane called out. 'Can the sun itself be melted? The Lightstone is no ordinary gold.'

'Perhaps it's not,' Captain Kharald said reasonably. 'But I've only ever known gold of one kind.'

Here he smiled significantly at Atara as if he could see beneath her cloak. Understanding only too well the meaning of this avaricious look, she brought out her purse and handed it to him.

'Aha, you *do* have gold, don't you?' he said. He took Atara's purse in one hand and weighed it carefully while he stroked his red beard with the other. Then he opened it, and his green eyes lit up like emeralds as he looked inside. 'Beautiful, beautiful – but where is the rest of it, then?'

Atara cast me a quick, sharp look, then said, 'That's all we have.'

'Well, if that's all you have, that's all you have,' he said as if consoling a poor widow who has to live on a meager inheritance. 'But the Island of the Swans lies more than three hundred miles from Ivalo. Across the Dragon Channel at that.'

'That's all the money we have,' Atara said again.

'I believe you,' he said. 'But gold's gold, and not all of it is pressed into coins.'

Here he pointed at the gold medallion that King Kiritan had slipped around Atara's neck. His eyes fixed on this brilliant sunburst and the golden cup standing out in relief at its center. Then he looked at Kane and Liljana and all the rest of us as well.

'Do you expect us to give you *these*?' she said, touching her medallion.

'My dear young woman, I expect nothing,' he said. 'But it is a very long way to this island you seek.'

Now Atara's fingers were twitching as if at any moment she might reach for her sword. I had never seen her so angry. 'The King gave us these with his blessing, that we might be known and honored in all lands.'

'A great man, is King Kiritan,' Captain Kharald said. 'And you are honored greatly. Who could bring more honor upon themselves than they who were willing to give the gold that all men desire for that finer metal of the Lightstone which so few have the courage to seek?'

His clever words shamed us, and we all looked at each other in silent understanding of what we would have to pay for our passage to the Island of the Swans.

'Very well,' I said, touching the words written around my medallion's rim. 'If that is what it takes.'

444

'Oh, I'm afraid it would take much more than that to cross the Dragon Channel,' he told us. 'That is a dangerous water. There are bad currents, many storms. And it's grown more dangerous of late, now that Hesperu has sent its ships to blockade Surrapam's ports.'

He spoke sadly about the war that had riven his homeland; he gave us to understand that he had lost a great fortune in fleeing his warehouses and ships to re-establish himself in Ivalo.

'So you see, this is a time for prudence,' he said. 'And prudence demands that great risks be undertaken only at the prospect of great gain.'

I nodded at the purse he still clutched in his hand. I said, 'The coins you may have. Our medallions as well. What more do you ask of us?'

'My good Prince,' he said, 'I ask nothing. At least nothing more than fair compensation for such dreadful risks.'

Now his gaze fell upon the ring that my father had given me. Its two diamonds sparkled brilliantly in the morning light.

'You want me to give you *this*?' I said, holding up my knight's ring. Would I give up my hand to gain the Lightstone? Would I give up my arm?

'Well,' he told me, 'diamonds *are* dearer than gold.'

Now it was my turn to be angry. I shook my ring at him as I said, 'Am I a diamond-seller, then?'

'Excuse me if I insulted you,' Captain Kharald said as he held out his hands. 'I don't like to argue.'

I took ten deep breaths as I tried to quiet the drumming of my heart. And then I said, 'All right, if it's diamonds you want, then you may have these two. But not the ring itself, do you understand?'

'Very well,' he said in a voice as cool as the sea. 'But *you* must understand that I could never risk my ship for even two such splendid diamonds as these.'

'How many would it take then?' I asked, clenching my teeth. If I had been wearing the diamond armor of a Valari warrior, I might have given him a whole fistful of diamonds – across the face.

'How many do you have?' he asked me.

'Only these two,' I said, nodding at my ring.

'Two only?' he said, shaking his head. 'And you a prince of Mesh?'

'In Mesh,' I told him, 'we set our diamonds into armor and such rings as you see. But we would never carry any outside our land.'

'Well, I've no liking to call any man a liar,' he said as he pulled on his red mustache. 'Neither do I like to haggle.'

I looked at Kane and the others, then told him, 'All that we have to give you for our passage, we have offered.'

Now Captain Kharald cocked his head as he looked at Atara's golden torque then turned to regard the rings that encircled each of Maram's fingers.

'You want *my* rings, too?' Maram said.

'Perhaps not,' Captain Kharald said, shaking his head again. 'Perhaps this journey of yours is just too dangerous. You must understand.'

At the coldness of his voice, Kane finally lost his patience. As quick as a flash, he whipped out his sword and held it reflecting the sun.

'So, I don't like to haggle either,' Kane said. 'We've offered you more than fair. Do *you* understand?'

'Do you draw your sword,' Captain Kharald said in an icy voice, 'against a ship's *captain*?'

Just then, Jonald and ten other of Captain Kharald's men came running toward us with their cutlasses drawn. All of them, however, had seen Kane's sword work, and they held back, forming a circle around us.

'No, not against *you*, Captain,' Kane said. 'I've no liking for mutiny, only exercise, eh?'

So saying, he slowly stretched his sword back behind him as if going through the first motion of the killing art that he had taught me.

'My men will never take you to the Island of the Swans without me,' Captain Kharald said. 'If you run me through, you gain nothing.'

'Nothing but satisfaction,' Kane growled at him.

'Kane!' I called out suddenly. I didn't like the look in his dark eyes just then.

Captain Kharald looked straight at Kane and said, 'You must do what you must. And I must do the same.'

Whatever Captain Kharald's failings, I thought, lack of courage wasn't one of them. I stepped forward then, and bade Kane put away his sword. I watched with relief as Captain Kharald's men sheathed theirs as well. To Captain Kharald, I said, 'You are certainly the captain of this ship – and the master of your own will as well. So long as the Red Dragon is kept at bay, you always will be.'

I went on to speak of the necessity of opposing Morjin so that he didn't make all men slaves. Recovering the Lightstone, I told him, was the key to everything. I tried to find clever words to persuade him. Without consciously wielding the sword of *valarda* that Morjin had told of, I opened my heart to him. But it seemed that it wasn't enough.

'There are other ships in Ivalo,' he informed us coldly. 'Perhaps one of them will take you where you wish to go.'

And with that he stormed off towards his cabin.

After his men had gone back to their duties, Maram said, 'Well, he's right that we'll find other ships and captains in Ivalo, isn't he?'

'So, we will,' Kane muttered. 'Pirates and war galleys and other merchantmen less principled than he.'

'Principled?' I said, looking at Kane.

'Just so,' he said. 'Captain Kharald has a keen sense of what he requires for our passage. He won't be swayed by any argument or threat.'

'Well,' Master Juwain observed, 'it's all very good to have principles, of course. But there are higher ones to live by.'

Maram nodded his head at this. 'Perhaps *we* weren't prepared to give everything, then. Perhaps we should have offered him one of our gelstei.'

Kane nodded toward the inner pocket of Maram's red tunic where he usually secreted his firestone. And then he said, 'Ha, I suppose *you're* willing to be the first to give up yours?'

Beneath the heat of Kane's blistering gaze, Maram flushed with shame as he slowly shook his head.

'I can't believe,' Liljana said, 'that we gained the gelstei only to use them to buy passage on a ship.'

We all agreed. But none of us could think of a way to persuade Captain Kharald to take us to the Island of the Swans.

'What are we to do then?' Maram asked.

And Kane said, 'So, we'll wait. Tomorrow we'll reach Ivalo. And there we'll have to find another ship.'

But this prospect discouraged us all, for we had come to have a strange trust in Captain Kharald and the *Snowy Owl*. That night, after dinner, we sat on her deck looking out on the stars in a deep melancholy. The cool, groaning wind off the lapping waves carried murmurs of lamentation from distant corners of the world. Even the waning moon seemed saddened to lose slivers of itself night after night.

Alphanderry, pulled by the great weight of this pale orb, took out his mandolet and began to sing. At first his words were of that impossible language it seemed no man could ever understand. There was a great pain in the sounds that poured from his throat but a great beauty, too. I had never heard him sing so well. Perhaps, I thought, his song had been made purer and clearer by listening to that of the whales. Even Flick seemed to apprehend this new quality of Alphanderry's music, for he hovered just above him and flared up like a cluster of shooting stars with every note.

Captain Kharald's men gathered around us then to listen to Alphanderry play his mandolet. I knew that they had never heard anything like it before. Then Captain Kharald came out of his cabin and stood staring at Alphanderry as if seeing him for the first time.

After Alphanderry had finally finished his song, he looked up and realized that he had an audience. 'Hoy,' he said, 'I'm getting closer, I think. Maybe someday, maybe someday.'

'What *was* that song?' Jonald asked in a rough voice. 'I couldn't understand a word of it.'

'I'm not sure I could either,' Alphanderry said, laughing along with Jonald and the other sailors.

'Well, do you know any songs we *can* understand?' Jonald asked.

'I don't know – what would you like to hear?'

It startled me when Captain Kharald suddenly stepped forward and said, 'What about *The Pilot King*? That's a good song for a night such as this.'

Alphanderry nodded his head agreeably and began tuning his mandolet. Then he smiled at Captain Kharald as he began to play:

> A king there was in Thaluvale,
>   His name was Koru-Ki,
> He built a silver ship to sail
>   The heavens' starry sea.

It was a sad song, full of wild longing and great deeds; it told of how King Koru-Ki, in the Age of Law, had sailed out from Thalu in search of the streaming lights of the Northern Passage, which was said to lead off the edge of the world up to the stars. It was a long song, too, and Alphanderry played for a long time. The moon was high in the sky by the time he finished.

'Thank you,' Captain Kharald told him politely. His men began drifting off, to their duties or beds. But he stood there a long while staring at Alphanderry strangely. 'Thank you, minstrel. If I had known you had such a voice, I wouldn't have let King Vakurun pay your passage.'

Then he, too, went off to bed and so did we.

We reached Ivalo late the next morning. We caught our first sight of it just as we rounded a hump of land along Eanna's northern coast. Like Varkall or Tria, it was a river city, built at the mouth of the Rune. But it had none of Tria's splendor and too much of Varkall's squalor. Too many of its houses and buildings were of wood and seemed jammed together in dirty, fetid districts that crowded the river. Unlike ancient Imatru a hundred miles farther up the Rune, it was a new city, scarcely a thousand years old. No great towers graced the muddy banks upon which it was sited. No gleaming bridges of living stone spanned the muddy Rune. Neither were there walls to catch the light of the midday sun. The Eannans, who were perhaps the greatest mariners in the world, liked to say that they were better protected with wooden walls, and these were their ships.

Many of them were docked in the harbor into which we sailed. We saw luggers and whalers, barks and bilanders – and, of course, the galliots and warships of the Eannan fleet. These were all lined up along the docks jutting out from the Rune's western bank. The eastern bank was given over to Ivalo's many warehouses and shipyards – and taverns and inns that served its sailors.

Here the *Snowy Owl* found berth along a wharf owned by one of Captain Kharald's friends. We tied up across the way from another bilander, commanded by a Surrapamer named Captain Toman. Both he and Captain Kharald were old friends. Like Captain Kharald, he was a thickset man with a shock of fiery hair – though his beard had gone gray. When he saw the *Snowy Owl* strike her sails, he came on board and greeted Jonald and others whom he knew. Then Captain Kharald showed him into his cabin so that they might drink a bit of brandy and speak of their homeland.

'Well,' I said to Kane, 'we'd better get the horses off and find ourselves another ship.'

We went down into the hold to attend to this task. Altaru and the other horses had fleshed out nicely during the voyage. They seemed only too happy to remain in their stalls and continue feasting on oats. If any of them had suffered from sea-sickness, they gave no sign.

Just as I was leading Altaru onto the deck, Captain Kharald came out of his cabin and walked over to me. He waited until my companions and their horses had joined me, and then astonished us all, saying, 'If it's still your wish to sail to the Island of the Swans, I'll take you there.'

'It *is* still our wish,' I said, speaking for my friends. 'But why this change of heart?'

Captain Kharald's face fell angry and sad. He said, 'I've had bad news from Surrapam. The Hesperuks have broken the line of the Maron and are laying waste the countryside. There is much hunger in my homeland. I've decided to take on a cargo of grain and sail for Artram as soon as we're loaded. I'm willing to put in to the Island of the Swans along the way.'

'So, you're willing, and we're all glad for that,' Kane said. 'But willing at what price?'

'The Princess' purse will be enough,' Captain Kharald told us. He pointed at Atara's medallion and then looked at my ring. 'These other things are dear to you, and you should keep them.'

I could not quite believe what I was hearing. I thanked Captain Kharald and smiled as Atara hurried to hand him her purse before he changed his mind again.

'Now I must excuse myself,' Captain Kharald said as he tucked the clinking coins into his pocket. 'There's much to do before we sail.'

He walked off toward the stern and left us there with our nickering horses and our confusion.

'I don't understand,' Maram said, watching the sailors and wharf hands swarm the deck in preparation for unloading and loading cargo.

And then Master Juwain explained: 'Their whole lives, men fight battles inside themselves. And sometimes, in a moment, the battle is suddenly won.'

After that, we took the horses down to the wharf and led them through Ivalo's noisome streets to give them some exercise. We spent the day wandering about the waterfront districts, trying to keep out of the way of the throngs of people who crowded by us. The Eannans, I saw, were a mixed people: many showed hair as red as Captain Kharald's while many more were fair-skinned blonds who must have traced their ancestry to the Aryans who had conquered this kingdom so long ago. There were women and men who had the brown hair and darker complexions of the Delians, even as did Maram, and more than a few bearing the lineaments of the Hesperuk race, with their mahogany skins and long, black curls. We tried to avoid them all. We kept our hoods close to our faces and kept to our business as well. For Eanna, as we had been told, was a land of assassins and spies, plots and usurpations. Here Morjin had great strength in the Kallimun priests who were said to have established themselves in secret citadels and even within the palace of old King Hanniban himself.

Late that afternoon, on a low hill about a mile from the shipyards, we found ourselves on a narrow lane called the Street of Swords. I visited the various smithies and shops there hoping to find a blade to replace the one I had broken. But the swords I saw were of poor quality, and I wouldn't consent to trade my medallion for any of them, even though I longed to fill up my scabbard with a length of good steel again. I resigned myself to practicing with the wooden sword I had whittled. It wouldn't do for battle, of course, but at least I could keep my skills sharp until I found something better.

We returned to the ship before dark, and there we waited for its bales of sealskins and barrels of whale oil to be unloaded and great canvas bags of wheat berries taken on. This took the wharf hands most of three days. When the holds were finally full again, Captain Kharald walked the decks inspecting the rigging and the balance of the ship. And then, on the tide, we sailed for Surrapam by way of the Island of the Swans.

The first hundred miles of our voyage were easy enough, with fair skies and good wind. On the following day, however, as we rounded the Cape of Storms at the very northwest corner of the continent, the seas grew much rougher. The skies darkened, too, though strangely there was no rain. With the great island of Thalu ahead of us somewhere to the west, we sailed south, into the Dragon Channel.

Here the wine-dark waters pitched the *Snowy Owl* up and down as if testing her timbers and the skills of those who sailed her. These, as I saw, were as great in their own way as any of my brothers' prowess with arms. Captain Kharald came alive with the rising of the wind and seas; often he stood near the bow grinning fiercely with his red hair blowing back behind him. At the sharp commands he barked out above the ocean's roar, Jonald and the other sailors turned the ship back and forth against the wind and made progress across the waves even so. The magic of this maneuver amazed me; Captain Kharald called it tacking. We spent most of the next three days tacking back and forth along a line leading mostly south toward Surrapam.

On our fifth day out from Ivalo, we came upon a sight that chagrined us all: this was the wreckage of a merchantman listing badly and dead in the water. As we drew closer to this stricken ship, however, we saw that it had not run aground on the numerous rocks and reefs off Thalu as Captain Kharald first supposed. Fire had taken her to her doom: the shreds of blackened sails still hanging from her spars and the charred wood there gave sign of this. There was also much sign of battle. Black arrows stuck from the masts like a porcupine's quills, and the hacked corpses of many sailors lay about the bloodstained deck. The terrible stench issuing from this death ship told us that none had survived this devastation. Captain Kharald wanted to board her to make sure this was so, but the rough seas about us prevented any such maneuver.

'Who do you think did this?' Maram asked him as everyone gathered along the *Snowy Owl's* port side to look at this ship.

'Pirates, likely,' Captain Kharald said. 'There are many pirate enclaves on Thalu.'

Maram shuddered at this and muttered that nothing could be worse than such lawless, marauding men. And then the sea turned the black ship slowly about, and what we saw told of something much worse. For there, nailed to the main mast, hung the burned and tormented body of a man.

451

'So, I've heard the Thalunes are without mercy,' Kane said. 'But I've never heard that they are crucifiers.'

'No, they're not,' Captain Kharald admitted. 'This is certainly the work of a Hesperuk warship. It's said the Hesperuks have taken to crucifying in the Red Dragon's name.'

'They'll crucify *us* if they catch us carrying wheat to Surrapam,' one of Captain Kharald's men said. 'Or feed us to the sharks.'

After that, Captain Kharald gave orders for an extra sailor to go aloft and stand watch on the crow's nest high on the foremast. We all cast nervous looks about the gray ocean as the wind drove the *Snowy Owl* ever further south and we left the death ship behind us.

But it is one thing to sail away from such sights on a fleet ship built of stout oak; it is quite another to leave them behind in one's soul. That night, terrible dreams nailed me to the deck of the ship. For what seemed hours, I tried to shield myself from Morjin's fell, whispered words that burned me like the breath of a dragon. It took all my will finally to fight myself awake. I sat up trembling and sweating and peering through the darkness for any sign of land. And wordlessly, whisperlessly, Atara came over to touch a dry cloth to my face.

'Here,' she said after a while, wiping my forehead, 'you were dreaming again.'

'Yes, dreaming,' I said.

The sea beneath us swelled and fell as the ship's wooden joints moaned like an old man. The wind off the cold water suddenly chilled me to the bone. It seemed that I could still smell the stench of the blackened ship we had passed.

'Of what were your dreams?' Atara asked me.

I looked at Maram snoring on top of his furs nearby and our other companions stretched out peacefully on the deck. And I said, 'Death. My dreams were of death.'

A terrible sadness fell over her then. She sat down facing me and wrapped her arms around my sweat-soaked back. She held me tightly against her warm body as she began weeping softly. And then, through her tears, she murmured, 'No, no, you can't die. You mustn't. You mustn't – don't you see?'

'See what, Atara?'

'That if you died, I'd want to die, too.'

For a long time she sat there kissing the tears from my own eyes as she stroked my hair. And then, to further comfort me, she said, 'Surely the Lightstone can take away any such dreams.'

'The Lightstone,' I said. 'Have you seen it, then?'

'No, I think Mithuna was right,' she told me. 'No scryer can ever behold it. But I know we're getting close to it, Val. We *must* be.'

I prayed that what she said must be true. As I held her against me, I looked over her shoulder, out into the darkness of the sea. And there, many miles to the south, beyond the black and rolling waves, I thought I saw a bit of golden light breaking through the clouds and drawing us on.

The next morning at sunrise, the lookout in the crow's nest called out that he had sighted the distant rocks of the Island of the Swans.

27

It was nearly noon by the time we had sailed close enough to the island to get a good look at it. This western part of the world was a realm of clouds and mists that lay low over the land and often obscured much of it. The rocks that the lookout had espied proved to be the highlands of four smaller islands just to the east of the Island of the Swans. The island itself, like a seahorse with its head pointed west and tail curling southeast, was a much greater prominence about fifty miles in length. Along its central spine, three conical mountains pushed their peaks toward the sky. From the centermost and tallest of these, it seemed that a great plume of smoke issued forth and fed the gray-black clouds above it. Captain Kharald's men feared that this must be dragon smoke; they called for the *Snowy Owl* to flee these accursed waters before the dragon descended upon us in a flurry of leathery wings and burned us with his fire.

'Dragons, hmmph,' Atara said as we all stood near the rail looking at the island. 'There hasn't been a dragon in Ea for two thousand years.'

'None but the Red Dragon,' Master Juwain agreed. 'And he has no power here.'

I clenched my teeth as I remembered the last night's dreams, but I said nothing.

'No men, I think, have power over the Island of the Swans,' Kane told us. 'It's said that men have never conquered it or made a kingdom here.'

If true, I thought that was very strange. The Island of the Swans lay scarcely sixty miles across the Dragon Channel from Surrapam, and even less distance from Thalu to the north. And while the Surrapamers had never been conquerors like the Thalunes, they weren't above grabbing bits of land to add to theirs like everyone else.

'If there are no dragons here,' Maram said, pointing at the smoking mountain, 'then what curse lies upon this land?'

454

None of us knew. Not even Captain Kharald could tell us why, for as long as anyone could remember, ships from Surrapam – as well as Eanna and Thalu – had avoided the Island of the Swans.

'Perhaps,' I heard one of his men grumble, 'it's because any ship that sails for this island never returns.'

His fear spread to his shipmates from tongue to nervous tongue, and even Jonald seemed reluctant to steer the *Snowy Owl* any closer to the island. Captain Kharald, his face set as sternly as the rocks toward which we sailed, walked among his crew and met them with his steely eyes to give them courage. If any decided that this was no voyage for them, he wanted to remind them of their duty before they began talking of mutiny.

We spent all that day sailing along the island's north shore looking for a place to land. But the forbidding walls of rock there warned us away; the currents were bad, too, and Captain Kharald kept a wary eye out for any reefs which might splinter his stout ship like kindling. We spent the night farther out at sea where we would be safe from running aground. And then the next morning, we rounded the island's westernmost point – the top of the seahorse's head – and made our way along its 'nose' for about five miles. When we reached its tip, we turned again, this time heading straight for the belly of the island, which bulged out to form a great deal of its southern shore. Here the waters grew calmer and the currents less swift. As we drew closer to this misty land arising out of the ocean, we saw beaches giving way to the green-shrouded heights beyond. Captain Kharald chose a likely looking expanse of sand, and steered the *Snowy Owl* toward it.

With one of his men sounding the water's depth with a length of a weighted and knotted rope, Captain Kharald finally ordered the *Snowy Owl* anchored about a quarter mile offshore. Along with Jonald and six other sailors, he joined us to the starboard and watched as Jonald directed the lowering of the skiff that would take us to the island.

'This far we've come against our better judgment,' Captain Kharald said to us. 'But I can't ask my men to accompany you onto the island.'

I stood armored in my mail, wearing my black and silver surcoat and my helmet with the silver swan wings projecting upward from the sides. I held the throwing lance that my brother Ravar had given me and my father's gleaming shield. Kane bore his long sword and Maram his shorter one; Atara had her saber and her deadly bow and arrows. Liljana and Alphanderry had strapped on their cutlasses, even though they had chipped them badly on Meliadus' rock-hard hide. And Master Juwain, of course, would carry no weapon. In his gnarly old hands, he clutched his copy of the *Saganom Elu* as if it contained whole armories within its leather-bound pages.

'Thank you for bringing us here,' I said to Captain Kharald. 'It will be enough if you'll wait until we return.'

From near the mast behind us, I heard one of his men mutter, 'If they *do* return.'

'Three days we'll wait, but no more,' Captain Kharald said. 'Then we'll have to sail for Artram. You must understand, my people are hungry.'

'Yes, they are,' I agreed. 'But hungry for more than bread.'

I stared off at the wall of green rising up beyond the beach. I was sure that somewhere on this lost island, we would finally behold the Lightstone that we had crossed the length of Ea to claim. And then we would find a way to end war and suffering, and people would never be hungry again.

We climbed down to the skiff on rope ladders hanging over the ship's side. It disquieted me that we would have to leave the horses behind, but there was no good way of getting them ashore. I sat in silence in the skiff with my companions as Jonald and the other sailors rowed the open boat toward the beach. The rhythmic sound of the oars dipping into the water seemed to measure out the remaining moments of our quest.

After Jonald and the others had put us ashore and set out to sea again, I stood with my friends on the beach's hard-packed sand. The island stretched out twenty-five miles to the west and as many to the east. We guessed that it must be at least ten miles wide at its widest part. In listening to the wind pour over this considerable length of land, I suddenly realized that I had no idea of where the Lightstone might be found.

And neither did any of my friends. Maram squinted against the squawking seagulls flying above us and said, 'Well, Val, what do we do now?'

I turned to Atara to ask her if she had seen anything in her crystal sphere. But in answer Atara only held out her hands helplessly and shook her head.

Four points there are to the world, and three of these were land while the fourth was ocean. I stood with my back to this gray water as I gazed at the smoking mountain to the north. When I looked in that direction, my heart beat more quickly. And so I began walking toward it.

The others followed close behind me across the beach. Soon its brownish sands gave out onto the wall of forest that had seemed so forbidding from the water. Up close, the tall trees and dense undergrowth proved nearly impenetrable. Search though we did for a few hundred yards up and down the beach, we could find no path cutting through them.

'Are you sure we should go this way?' Maram said, pointing into the forest. 'I don't like the look of it.'

'Come,' I said, taking a step forward. 'It won't be so bad.'

'That's what you said of the Vardaloon,' he moaned. Upon remembering our passage of that dark wood, he shuddered as he pulled the hood of his cloak up over his head. 'If I see a single leech, I'm turning back, all right?'

'All right,' I agreed. 'You can camp here on the beach and wait for us to return with the Lightstone.'

The thought of us gaining what he so deeply desired while he sat here on the sand sobered him. He suddenly found his courage, and muttered to me, 'All right, but you go first. If there are leeches here, maybe they'll drop first on *you*.'

But the forest turned out to hold none of these loathsome worms. Neither were we troubled by ticks, even though the undergrowth near the beach was very thick and brushed continually against us. As for mosquitoes, in all that thick band of woods, we saw only one. This, as it happened, landed right on Maram's fat nose. In his panic to swat it, he forgot the delicacy of this fleshy protuberance. His huge hand nearly flattened it out, causing him to shout in pain. Although the cunning little mosquito escaped this blow, he did manage to bloody himself. It was the funniest thing I had seen since Flick had spun about on Alphanderry's nose.

'Stop laughing at me!' Maram called out as he pressed his hand to his bleeding nose. 'Where's your compassion? Can't you see I'm *wounded*?'

This 'wound' Master Juwain tended with a few swipes of a cloth and a bit of a leaf tucked up into Maram's nostril. And then Kane came over and snapped at Maram, 'Save your valor for our real enemies. We don't know what we're going to find on this island.'

His rebuke reminded me that we knew almost nothing of the Island of the Swans. Dragons we surely need not fear, but what awaited us deeper in the forest, no one could say.

As we started off again, I used my shield to brush the ferns away from my face. I gripped my lance in my sword hand. But I saw nothing more threatening than a red fox darting out of our way and a few bumble bees. In truth, I immediately liked the feel of this ancient woodland. Its giant trees, towering far above the carpets of bracken along the forest floor, were hung with witch's hair and icicle moss as if arrayed in enchanted garments. Every living thing about us seemed soft and glowing with greenness; even the air smelled sweet and good.

I felt strangely at home here although there were many types of trees and plants that were strange to me. Master Juwain put names to a few of them: he pointed out the great cedars with their long strips of red bark and the yew trees and big-leaf maples. Others he had never seen either. But it turned out that Kane had. He showed us the sword ferns and the horsehair lichens, the lovely pink rhododendrons and the blue hemlocks shagged with old man's beard. Each name he spoke as if reciting that of an old friend. And each name Master Juwain dutifully recorded. I thought that it was part of his own private quest to remember the name of each and every thing in the world.

We made slow progress, for there were many new plants to identify, and the ground before us was thick with ferns and rose steeply. There were quite a few downed trees, too, which made the footing treacherous. Kane called some of these moss-covered trunks nurse logs. He said that in rotting apart into bits of crumbling wood, they served as nursery beds for other trees that took seed there. They were also homes to the red-backed voles and other animals we saw scurrying about the forest floor.

'I've never seen a wood so lush,' Maram said as he puffed along behind me. 'If the Lightstone *is* here, it could be *anywhere*. How are we to find it? I can't even find my own feet beneath me.'

Liljana came up to him then and reassured him that Sartan Odinan, if he had truly come here, wouldn't have just dropped the Lightstone down into a clump of moss. 'Don't you give up hope just yet, young prince. Perhaps we'll find a cave in one of the mountains we saw.'

These three peaks were now obscured by the wall of vegetation before us. But if we kept a straight line through the giant trees, after perhaps another five miles, we should come upon the slopes of the smoking mountain.

And so we fought our way up across the densely wooded ground that led toward it. It took us perhaps an hour to cover the first half mile. As there were few enough hours left in the day, and we had only three days until the *Snowy Owl* sailed again, it seemed that we would be able to explore only the tiniest corner of the island.

And then, after another half mile, the headland we were climbing came to a crest. The forest suddenly changed and thinned, and gave way to many more yews, maples and dogwoods. Through the gaps between them, we looked down into the most beautiful valley I had even seen.

'Oh, my lord!' Maram called out. 'There *are* people here!'

We saw signs of them everywhere. Between the crest on which we stood and the mountains some five miles away were many patches of green that could only be fields. Small stands of trees – they looked like cherry and plum – divided them from each other in darker green lines. Many pastures covered the long slope leading down to the valley's center. There a sparkling blue lake pooled at the base of the three mountains, which curved around its northern shore like a crescent moon. There, too, near the lake's southern shore, surrounded by what seemed to be many streets and colorfully painted houses, stood a great, square building whose white stone caught the sunlight streaming out of a break in the clouds. Liljana said that it reminded her of the ruins of the Temple of Life in Tria.

'We must go there then,' I said. Now my heart was beating very quickly.

'Whoever lives here,' Kane said, squinting as he looked about the valley, 'may not want us here at all. We should be careful, Val.'

I remembered how the Lokilani had stolen upon us and nearly killed us with arrows before rare chance had saved us.

'Careful we'll be, then,' I said. 'But when one walks into the lion's lair, there's only so much care that can be taken.'

And with that, I led off, walking warily through the woods. Atara kept pace with me just to my left; she held an arrow nocked in her bowstring as she looked off through the trees. Master Juwain came next, followed by Liljana and Alphanderry. Behind then, Maram trod carefully down the long slope, all the while fingering his firestone as he started at every squirrel or bird moving about in the branches above him. Kane, as usual, brought up the rear.

After about a half mile, the woods thinned even more and gave out onto a wide pasture on which only a few isolated trees grew. Here the grass was long and lush, and as green as grass could be. Many day's-eyes, with their sunlike yellow centers and long white petals, made a show of themselves, and thousands of dandelions brightened the grass as well. Bees buzzed from flower to flower in their slow but determined way, gathering up nectar peacefully. From somewhere ahead of us, across the lines of rolling and gradually descending ground, came the distant baahing of some sheep. If this was a lion's lair into which we were walking, I thought as I gripped my lance and shield, then surely we were the lions.

Another quarter mile brought us out onto a bowl-like pasture smelling of some sweet blue flowers and sheep droppings. We saw the flock ahead of us, fifty or sixty fat sheep spread out over the soft green grass, their white fleeces gleaming in the sun. We saw their shepherd, too. And he saw us. The look on his face as we suddenly appeared over a low rise above him was one of utter astonishment. But strangely, his bright, black eyes showed no sign of fear.

'*Di nisa palinaii,*' he said to us, holding out his hand as if in greeting. '*Di nisa, nisa – lililia waii?*'

The words he spoke made no sense to me. Nor did any of the others seem to understand him, not even Alphanderry, who held the seeds of all languages upon his fertile tongue.

'My name is Valashu Elahad,' I said, pressing my hand to my chest. 'What are you called, and who are your people?'

'*Kilima nisti,*' the man said, shaking his head. '*Kilima nastamii.*'

The shepherd, who was about my age, wore a long kirtle that seemed woven of the same white wool that covered his sheep. He was tall, almost my height, with ivory skin and a long, high nose that gave great dignity to his noble face – and a hint of fierceness, too. But there seemed nothing fierce about him. His manner was gentle, curious, welcoming. He wore no weapon on his braided and brightly colored cloth belt, and his hand held nothing more threatening than his shepherd's crook. This surprised me almost as much as did his appearance. For with his thick black hair and eyes like black jade, he might have been my brother.

'Oh, my lord!' Maram said as he came up beside me. 'He looks Valari!'

My friends, gathering around the shepherd, stared at him and remarked the resemblance as well. Master Juwain said, 'There's a mystery here: a lost island upon which stands a Valari warrior who seems no warrior at all. And who doesn't speak the language that all men do.'

If he was a mystery to us, we were an even greater one to him. He approached me as one might a wild animal; he slowly extended his hand and traced his finger along the swan and seven silver stars of my surcoat. He touched the steel links of my armor, too. Finally, he tapped his fingernail against my helmet as he slowly shook his head.

'*Di nisa, verlo,*' he murmured. '*Kananjii wa?*'

It seemed pointless, and a little rude, to continue talking with him from behind my helmet's curving steel plates. And so I took it off. The shepherd stood staring at me as if looking into a mirror for the first time.

'*Di nisa, nisa,* he said again, this time more doubtfully. '*Wansai paru di nisalu?*'

He turned to go among Maram and the others. He smiled at Liljana respectfully, then narrowed his eyebrows as he seemed to look for his reflection in the gleaming surface of Master Juwain's bald head. He put his finger to Alphanderry's dark curls then paused a moment as he looked at Kane. But he spent the longest time examining Atara. Everything about her seemed a marvel to him. He examined her leather armor and ran his finger along her bowstring; he touched her long blonde hair with all the reverence that Captain Kharald might have reserved for handling gold.

'*Di nisa athanu,*' he whispered. '*Athanasii, verlo.*'

'What language is this?' Maram asked, shaking his head. 'I can't understand anything of what he says.'

'I can *almost* understand,' Alphanderry said. 'Almost.'

'It sounds something like ancient Ardik,' Master Juwain told us. 'But, I'm afraid, no more than a pear is like an apple.'

Kane had now lost patience, perhaps with his own ignorance most of all. He nodded at Liljana and said, 'You spoke with the Sea People, eh? Can't you speak to this man?'

All this time Liljana had been clutching her little carved whale in her hand. Now she brought this figurine to her head. The blue gelstei, I suddenly recalled, were not only the stones of mindspeaking but also quickened the powers of truthsaying and apprehending languages and dreams.

'*Nomja?*' the shepherd said, looking at the figurine. '*Nomja, nisami?*'

A quick smile suddenly split Liljana's round face as if she were very pleased with herself. And then she opened her mouth and surprised us all by saying, '*Janomi . . . io di gelstei. Di blestei, di gelstei . . . falu.*'

After that, she began speaking the shepherd's language more rapidly. She paused only to allow him to return the discourse and ask her questions. And then, with a smile that lit up her whole being, she found her tongue again and managed to keep up a continual stream of conversation. The strange words poured out of her like a waterfall. The sheep baahed at each other and the sun dipped lower in the sky as she stood there talking with the shepherd.

After a while, she took the gelstei away from her head and told us, 'He says his name is Rhysu Araiu. And his people are called the Maii.'

'And this island?' Kane asked her. 'Does it have a name as well?'

'Of course it does,' Liljana said, smiling at him. 'The Maiians call it *Landaii Asawanu.*'

'And what does that mean, then?' Kane asked.

'It means,' she said, 'the Island of the Swans.'

Rhysu returned to his flock then, and we followed him across the pasture, which he had told Liljana he wanted us to do. Soon we came to rather large house, built of mostly of stone and wood that had been painted a bright yellow. Rhysu called out excitedly as we approached it. The door suddenly opened, and a tall woman with hair as straight and black as Rhysu's stepped out and greeted us. She had the high nose and exquisitely sculpted face bones of many Valari. Rhysu presented her as Piliri, and said she was his wife. Three more of his household soon joined us on the lawn: a young boy named Nilu and his older sister, Bria. Oldest of all, however, perhaps even older than Kane, was Piliri's grandmother, Yakira Araiu. Despite her years, despite an ailing hip and knee, which she painfully favored, she too was a tall woman; she stood proudly on the doorstep above her family as Rhysu presented us. That Rhysu so obviously deferred to her surprised me a little. And it surprised me even more to learn that she, not he, was the head of the Araiu family.

'Strange, isn't it,' Maram muttered, 'that he should take the name of his wife's grandmother? But then everything about this island is a little strange.'

Liljana bowed to Yakira, and stood talking with her for quite a while. And then she told us that the Maiians passed their family names from mother to daughter – and from mother to son.

'As it was in the ancient days,' she said.

She went on to say that here men did not rule their wives and daughters. No one, in truth, ruled anyone else: no king was there on the Island of the Swans, nor duke nor master nor lord. Their most prominent personage seemed to be a woman named Lady Nimaiu, who was also called the Lady of the Lake. Yakiru suggested that Piliri should present us to her.

'She says that she would take us down to the lake herself,' Liljana explained, 'but she can't walk so far anymore.'

It seemed that the Maii had no horses to ride nor even any oxen that might pull a cart. We might have managed to carry Yakiru the few miles down to the city by the lake, but this her dignity would not permit.

Here Yakiru spoke to Piliri for a few moments. Then Liljana translated her words: 'She said that Piliri must tell her everything that happens there.'

'Ah, I hope *nothing* happens,' Maram said. 'At least nothing more eventful than us finding that which we came to find.'

And with that, Piliri took her leave of her husband and family, and we set forth, with Piliri leading the way. Soon we came to a little road that led down the valley's center. It was paved with smooth stones cut so precisely that they showed only the narrowest of seams. Flowers of various kinds lined the sides of the road, which wound through the meadows and fields. With the soft sun providing just enough heat to warm us nicely and the many birds singing in the orchards to either side of us, it was one of the most pleasant walks I had ever made.

We stopped more than once to greet other shepherds and farmers curious as to the strange sight that we must have presented. After they had eyed my gleaming armor and studied my friends with amazement, more than one of them joined us. By the time we reached the edge of the city, we made a party perhaps thirty strong. And there, from the neat little houses painted yellow, red and blue, many more of the Maii stepped out to behold us. All of them had the look of my countrymen back in Mesh. Cries of, 'Nisa, Nisa!' sang out as Maiians emptied out of the shops and houses and lined the streets before us. As we passed, they closed in behind us and formed up into a procession of hundreds of excited men, women and children.

Piliri, walking now with great dignity, led the way straight toward the temple. From this massive structure, which appeared made of marble, bells began ringing and sent their silver peals out over the city. And now it seemed the whole of the city had been alerted to our coming, for thousands of people crowded the streets. In bright streams of kirtles and flowing garments dyed every color, they converged upon the temple from the south, west and east. There, in a tree-lined square beneath the temple's great, gleaming pillars, they gathered to greet us and witness what to them must have been an extraordinary event.

A tall woman, perhaps forty years of age, accompanied by six younger women, emerged from between the temple's two centermost pillars and slowly made her way down the steps toward us. She was as beautiful of face and form as my mother, and she wore a long white kirtle trimmed with green along the sleeves and hem. A filigree of tiny black pearls was sown into the kirtle's front while a fillet of much larger white ones had been set around her forehead and over her long, black hair. She stopped immediately in front of us. Then Piliri stepped forward, knelt and kissed the woman's hand. Upon straightening again, she said, 'Mi Lais Nimaiu-talanasii nisalu.'

She turned toward me and my companions and continued, 'Talanasii Sar Valashu Elahad. Eth Maramei Marshayk eth Liljana Ashvaran eth . . .'

And so it went until she had presented us all. Then she spoke to Liljana, who stepped closer with her blue gelstei to translate for her.

'Talanasii Lais Nimaiu,' Piliri said, presenting the tall woman to us. She spoke a few more words before nodding at Liljana.

Liljana pressed her little figurine to her head as she smiled at the tall woman. To us, she said, 'This is Lady Nimaiu. She is also called the Lady of the Lake.'

Lady Nimaiu, as Rhysu had, spent quite a few moments examining us. Atara's hair seemed to hold wonders for her as did Master Juwain's complete absence of it. But she reserved her greatest curiosity for me and my accoutrements. Her dark eyes took in the lineaments of my face, and then she rapped her fingernail against the steel of my helmet, which I held in the crook of my arm. With my leave, she touched this same elegant finger to the silver swan and stars embroidered on my surcoat. She gasped as if these shapes might be familiar to her. Her breathing quickened as she examined the hilt of my broken sword. She spent another few moments running her hand over the steel links of my mail and the swan and stars embossed on my father's shield. Finally, she wrapped her fingers lightly around my throwing lance before stepping back and regarding me warily.

With Liljana translating for us, she began conversing with me: 'You bring strange things to our land,' she said. 'Are suchlike common in yours?'

'Yes,' I admitted, 'most warriors, at least the knights, are accoutered thusly.'

Liljana hesitated a moment in her translation because she could find no words in Lady Nimaiu's language for knight or warrior. And so she simply spoke them as I did, leaving them untranslated.

'And what is *warrior*?' Lady Nimaiu asked me.

'A warrior,' I said, hesitating as well, 'is one who goes to war.'

'And what is *war*?'

Now the six women attending Lady Nimaiu pressed closer to hear my answer as did Piliri and many other of the Maii. I traded swift, incredulous looks with Master Juwain and Maram. And then I said, 'That might be hard to tell.'

I looked around at the gentle Maii, who stood regarding us with great curiosity but no fear. Could it be possible that they knew nothing of war? That the bloody history of the last ten thousand years had completely passed by their beautiful island?

As I stood there wondering what to say to Lady Nimaiu, she again touched the hilt of my sword. 'Is this an accouterment of *war*, then?'

'Yes,' I said, 'it is.'

'May I see it?'

I nodded my head as I drew what was left of my sword. Its broken hilt shard gleamed brightly in the light of the late afternoon sun.

'May I hold it, Sar Valashu?'

I did not want to let her hold my sword. Would I so readily give into her hands my soul? Nevertheless, upon remembering why we had come to her island, I fulfilled her request for the sake of a little good will.

'It's heavy,' she announced as her fingers closed around the hilt. 'Heavier than I would have thought.'

I did not explain that if the blade had been whole, it would have been heavier still. But Lady Nimaiu, whose bright eyes missed very little, seemed to understand this as she gazed at the ragged end of my sword where it had been broken.

'Of what metal is this made?' she asked me, tapping the blade.

'It's called steel, Lady Nimaiu.'

'What is this thing called, then?'

'It is a sword,' I said.

'And what is *sword* for?'

Before I could answer, she moved her finger from the flat of the blade and started to run it across its edge. 'Be careful!' I gasped. But it was too late: the kalama's razor-sharp steel sliced open her finger.

'Oh!' she exclaimed, instinctively clasping the wounded tip against her breast to stanch the bleeding. 'It's sharp – so very sharp!'

She gave me back my sword while one of the women close to her tended her cut finger. To the murmurs of grave disapproval spreading outward among the crowds around us, she explained that although the Maii used their bronze knives to shape wood and shear their sheep, none were so keen of edge that they cut flesh at the faintest touch.

'Oh, I see,' she said sadly as she held up her finger. The white wool of her kirtle was now stained with her blood. '*This* is what sword is for.'

I felt my own blood burning my ears with shame. I tried to explain a little about warfare then; I tried to tell her that all the peoples of Ea stood ready to protect their lands by going to war.

She spoke her amazement to Liljana, who continued to make her words understandable: 'But what do your lands need protecting *from*?' she asked me. 'Are the wolves that fierce where you live?'

Behind me Maram muttered, 'No, but the Ishkans are.'

Liljana either didn't hear this or chose to ignore it. And then I took upon myself the task of trying to explain how we Valari had to protect ourselves from our enemies – and each other.

I spoke for quite a while. But what I said made no sense to Lady Nimaiu – and, in truth, little to me. After I had finished my account of the world's woes, she stood there shaking her head as she said, 'How strange that brothers feel they must protect themselves from each other! What strange lands you have seen where men take up swords because they are afraid their neighbors will as well.'

'It . . . is not as simple as that,' I said.

'But why would men go to war?' Lady Nimaiu said. 'For pride and plunder, so you say. But do your men have no pride in anything other than their swords? Are your men thieves that they would take from each other what is not theirs?'

The Red Dragon is much worse than a thief, I thought. *And he would take from men their very souls.*

'It is not so simple as that,' I repeated. I wiped the sweat from my forehead and continued, 'What would your people do if two neighbors disputed the border of their lands and one of them made a sword to claim his part?'

While Liljana translated this, Lady Nimaiu looked at me thoughtfully. And then she said, 'We Maiians do not claim land as your people do. All of our island belongs to all of us. And so there is always enough for all.'

'As it was in the ancient days,' Liljana said quietly, pausing a moment in her translating duties.

I took a breath and asked Lady Nimaiu, 'But what if one of your men coveted one of his neighbor's sheep and tried to claim it as his own?'

'If his need was that great, then likely his neighbor would give it to him.'

'But what if he didn't?' I pressed her. 'What if he slew his neighbor, and then threatened others as well?'

What I had suggested plainly horrified Lady Nimaiu – and the other Maiians, too. Her face fell white, and her jaw trembled slightly as she gasped out, 'But none of us could ever do such a thing!'

'But what if someone *did*?'

'Then we would take his sword from him and break it, as yours is broken.'

'Swords are not so easy to take,' I told her. 'You would have to forge swords of your own to take such a man's sword.'

'No, we would never do that,' she said. 'We would simply surround him until he couldn't move.'

'But then many of your people would die.'

'Yes, they would,' she admitted. 'But such a price would have to be paid if one of us fell *shaida*.'

Now it was my turn to be puzzled as Liljana mouthed this Maiian word that had no simple translation into our tongue. After some further discussion between Lady Nimaiu and Liljana, I was given to understand that *shaida* meant something like the madness of one who willfully disregards the natural harmonies of life.

'But what would you do with such a *shaida* man once you had disarmed him?' I asked. 'Slay him with his own sword then?'

'Oh, no – we would never do that!'

'But if you didn't, he might just make another sword and more of your people would die.'

I started to tell her that once war between peoples had begun, it was very hard to stop. And then Lady Nimaiu said, 'But it could never come

to *war*, don't you see? Such a man would be given to the Lady, and all
would be restored.'

I stood there confused. I didn't know what she meant by 'given to the
Lady.' Wasn't *she* Lady Nimaiu, the Lady of the Lake? And what would
she do with such a murderous man?

After some rounds of Liljana passing our words back and forth to
each other, Lady Nimaiu smiled sadly and said to me, 'I am the Lady
of the Lake, as you've been told. But I am not *the* Lady, of course. It
is to Her that we would give your sword-making man.'

So saying, she pointed above the temple at the smoking mountain
across the lake. She said that anyone who fell *shaida* would be dropped
into its fiery cone.

'The Lady takes back everyone into herself,' she explained. 'But some
sooner than others.'

'Is this Lady the *mountain*, then?' I said, trying to understand.

My question seemed to amuse her, as it did many of the other Maii,
who gathered around laughing softly. And then Lady Nimaiu smiled
and told me, 'Oh, no, the mountain is only the Lady's mouth – and
only her mouth of fire at that. She has many others.'

She went on to explain that the wind was the Lady's breath and the
rain her tears; when the ground shook, she said, the Lady was laughing,
and when it quaked so violently that mountains moved, that was the
Lady's anger.

'The Maii,' she said, stretching out her wounded finger toward her
people, 'are the Lady's eyes and hands. And that is why none of us
would ever make a sword.'

I paused to look at the many men and women all around us. And
then I asked, 'And does this Lady have a name?'

'Of course she does,' Lady Nimaiu said. 'Her name is Ea.'

At the utterance of this single word common to both our languages,
the earth seemed to tremble slightly. Smoke continued pouring out of
the cone of the mountain above us, but whether this signaled the Lady
Ea's gladness at our arrival or displeasure, I couldn't tell.

We had a hundred questions for Lady Nimaiu and the Maiians, as
they had for us. They wanted to know everything about our peoples and
the lands from which we came. They were fascinated with Liljana's blue
figurine and her ability to shape the words of one language into that of
another. But they saved their greatest wonder toward the answering of
a single question.

'Why,' Lady Nimaiu said to me, 'have you come to our island?'

My first impulse was simply to blurt out that we had joined the great
quest to find the Lightstone. But Maram, fearing my artlessness, moved

up behind me and whispered in my ear, 'Be careful, Val. If the Lightstone *is* here, it's surely inside the temple. If we tell them that we're seeking what must be their greatest treasure, they'll likely give *us* to this bloodthirsty Lady of theirs.'

He advised telling Lady Nimaiu that we were on a mission to aid the besieged Surrapam and that we had stopped on the Island of the Swans to hunt for fresh meat to replace our dwindling stores. We should wait, he said, and contrive a way to enter the temple. Then we could determine if it really did house the Lightstone and devise a plan for its taking.

Maram was more cunning than I, yet not every situation called for this virtue. The Maiians, sensing something devious in Maram's quiet speech, which Liljana failed to translate, began murmuring among themselves and shifting about the square restlessly. I was reluctant to tell Maram's little lies and even more so to say anything that might get us pushed into a pool of fire. And so I looked at Lady Nimaiu and said, 'We're on a quest . . .'

A low groan from Maram behind me made me pause in my answer. And then I continued, 'We're on a quest to find truth, beauty and goodness. And the love of the One that is said to find its perfect manifestation somewhere in the world.'

My words, after Liljana had rendered them into the Maiians' tongue, seemed to please them. Although I had spoken only vaguely of the Lightstone's essence, what I had said was true enough.

Lady Nimaiu, who was now smiling, slowly nodded her head. And then she asked, 'But why should you think that you would find these things on our island, where none but the Maii have walked since the Lady stepped out of the starry night at the beginning of time?'

Liljana needed no prompting from me to answer this question. With more than a little pride flushing her intelligent face, she recounted the finding of her blue gelstei and her conversation with the Sea People.

Again, Lady Nimaiu nodded her head slowly. It seemed the most natural thing in the world to her that a woman should speak with whales.

'Thank you,' she said to Liljana. 'You have told us much about yourselves, though much more needs to be told. And perhaps tomorrow it shall be. Until then, we invite you to remain here as our guests.'

When a king extended such an invitation, it was really a command. But as Liljana had told us, the Maii had no kings, nor even queens. I sensed that Lady Nimaiu was giving us the freedom to go or remain as we pleased. And so we decided to remain.

After that, Lady Nimaiu dismissed the crowds of her people with a few kind words. We said goodbye to Piliri, who returned home to eat her evening meal with her family. Lady Nimaiu then took her leave of us, and went back into the temple with five of her attendants as she had come. The sixth attendant, a rather homely but voluptuous young woman named Lailaiu, was charged with the task of settling us in for the night.

She showed us to one of the out-buildings adjoining the west side of the temple but not really part of it. There we were given spacious rooms in the guest quarters. We were given food and drink as well: hot bread and white ewe's cheese, blackberries and plums and sweet salmon which the Maiians pulled from the rivers near the sea and smoked in juniper and honey. Our wine was rich, dark and red. After our feast, served by other temple attendants, Lailaiu returned to fill the sunken marble bath with hot water. She brought us herb-scented soaps and insisted on using them to lather up our worn flesh. All of us, even Kane, yielded to such an unexpected delight. Everything about the Maiians' dwellings and handiworks seemed designed to delight the senses. No corner of our rooms was unadorned, from the marble moldings carved with bold traceries to the tapestries and carpets that lined the walls and floors. Even the blankets that covered us that cool night, woven from the marvelously soft underhair of the Maiians' goats, were embroidered with brightly colored threads showing roses and violets, the two flowers most beloved of the Lady Ea.

'Ah, this is a fine place,' Maram said, after he had collapsed onto his bed with his seventh glass of wine. 'I've never seen a fairer land. So rich, so sweet.'

'Even Alonia isn't as rich as this island,' Liljana agreed. 'At least not outside the nobles' palaces.'

'Yes,' I said bitterly, 'the Maiians have time for creating such beauty since it seems they spend none of it waging war.'

'Who would have war when he could have beauty and love instead?' Maram wondered. 'And love, mark my words, is at hand here. Did you see the fire in Lailaiu's eyes as she sponged the soap from me?'

'Be careful,' Master Juwain warned as he settled onto his bed with his book in his hand. 'Fire burns.'

'Ah, no, no, not this,' Maram said thickly. 'It's the sweetest of flames; it's the radiance of the sun on beautiful summer day; it's the fire of a young, red, full-bodied wine in its finest and fruitiest blush; it's . . .'

He might have gone on in a like vein for quite a while. But then Kane, pacing the room like a caged tiger, scowled at him and said, 'Your Lailaiu looks a fruit that's never been picked. What do you think the Maiians do with men who take such from the vine before it's ripe? Likely they give them to the Lady. Now *there's* a fire you won't find so sweet.'

His words suddenly sobered Maram, who sat muttering into his wine. While Alphanderry took out his mandolet and Flick began spinning in anticipation of his music, Atara came over to Maram and laid her hand on his shoulder consolingly. And then she asked the question that puzzled all of us: 'Who *are* these people? They certainly *look* Valari.'

'They are certainly Valari,' Master Juwain said, looking up from his book. 'The question is, of which tribe? That of Aryu? Or that of Elahad?'

He went on to say that the Maiian's ancestors must be some of the Lost Valari: either the followers of Aryu after he had stolen the Lightstone or the companions of Arahad who had set out on the Hundred Year March to search for it.

'The Lost Valari, yes, that seems possible,' I said to Master Juwain. 'But how could they be of the tribe of Aryu?'

Here Kane stopped his pacing and came over to me. 'Do you remember what I told you after we killed the Grays? How Aryu had also stolen a varistei, which his people used to change their forms to suit Thalu's cold and mists? So, what if some of *his* tribe repented Aryu's crime? What if they fell out with their brethren before the varistei was used? If they fled Thalu to the south and came to land here, they would still look Valari, eh?'

'I'm afraid that seems the most likely explanation of the Maiians' origins,' Master Juwain agreed.

I sat on my bed staring at a tapestry showing a great oak tree in full leaf; I didn't quite want to admit that the Maiians were really Aryans who still retained the Valari form.

'But if what you say is true,' I said to Master Juwain, 'then how is it that the Aryans let the Maiians live here in peace so many thousands of years?'

'That we may never know,' Master Juwain said. 'Perhaps fortune favored them. Perhaps a curse was laid upon the Maiians and this island.'

'It would have to have been a mighty curse,' Liljana said, 'to have kept the Aryans from plundering it.'

We gathered around debating the mystery of the Maiians as the night deepened and their city fell quiet around us. And then Atara, who could often see things quite clearly with the natural keenness of her mind no less than with her second sight, twined her golden hair about her finger as she said, 'If Sartan Odinan sought a safe land in which to hide the Lightstone, he couldn't have found better than this lost island.'

That brought us back to the temple, which stood towering above us in the starlight only fifty yards to the east. We were all sure that the Lightstone must be waiting for us within its gleaming marble walls.

'We must find our way inside,' Maram said again. 'We must see if the cup is there.'

'And then what?' I asked him. I didn't like the greedy light that brightened his eyes just then.

'And then? Ah, I suppose we'll have to trade the Maiians something for it. Your shield, perhaps. Or your sword. They seemed interested in anything made of steel.'

I didn't believe that the Maiians would simply trade the Cup of Heaven for a broken sword, and I told Maram this.

'Hmmm, perhaps not,' he murmured as he pulled at his beard. 'But what if they don't *know* the cup's true value? After all these centuries, they *might* have lost the knowledge of what it is.'

'But what if they *do* know what it is?'

'Ah, well, I suppose we'll have to find a way to claim it, won't we?'

'Are we to plunder the temple, then? As the Aryans did Tria?'

Maram now sat up very straight, all signs of drunkenness gone from his reddened face. In its place was shame and other painful emotions.

'Ah, no, no – you misunderstand me, my friend! I'm only pointing out that there might be more than one way to gain the Lightstone.'

I drew my sword and sat staring at the ugly break in it. I said, 'Not this way, Maram.'

'But what if the Maiians don't see the need of our returning the Lightstone to the world? What if they take offense at us and declare us, ah, *shaida*? What if we *have* to fight for it?'

Atara, who now sat oiling her bow, suddenly plucked its braided string. It twanged out a note of discord utterly unlike the music that Alphanderry made with his mandolet.

'Fight, hmmph,' Atara said to Maram. 'And who is it that will lead in this fighting? You? Didn't you hear what the Lady Nimaiu said about her people throwing themselves on swords? And throwing anyone so mad as to draw them into their fire mountain?'

'It's one thing to speak of throwing oneself onto a sword,' Maram said. 'It's quite another to find the courage to do it. Why, Kane could fell a hundred of them before they knew what was happening. And you could shoot anyone who tried to pursue us. Surely we could cut our way through to the coast, if we had to.'

I suddenly stood up and slammed what was left of my sword back into its sheath. Then I moved over to Maram's bed. With a fury that astonished me, I grabbed the wine glass from Maram's hand and hurled it against the wall where it shattered into a thousand pieces.

'Tomorrow, we'll look through the temple,' I said. 'But tonight we'll sleep and put these careless words behind us.'

So saying, I stormed across the room and flung myself into my bed. My anger kept me from seeing that I would be wrong about both the assertions that I had just made.

28

As the chasm of disaffection between me and Maram seemed to widen with each passing hour, neither of us got much sleep that night – nor did any of the others. And the next morning, after a breakfast of fruit and cream which I hardly touched, we knocked at the great temple doors only to be turned away. The women who guarded them informed us that we could not pass within until we had been purified.

'And how does one become purified?' I asked her testily.

'Oh, by the Lady, of course,' she told us.

'But which Lady, then? Lady Nimaiu or Lady Ea?'

The guards – if that was the right word for them – giggled at this question as if it had been a child who asked it. Then the first of the women said, 'Only Lady Ea can purify, with her tears. But the Lady Nimaiu is her hands, and it is to her that you must go if you truly wish for purification.'

'We truly wish it,' I said, speaking through Liljana for all of us. 'May we see Lady Nimaiu that we may discuss this?'

As it happened, Lady Nimaiu would not see us that morning. She was busy attending to matters of great importance, the guard told us, and so we would have to wait.

'Ah, wait,' Maram muttered after the guards had closed the doors on us. 'How long can we wait? Two more days, and then the ship sails whether we're aboard her or not.'

'Then we'll wait two days, if we must,' I said. 'In the meantime, why don't we explore the island? The Lightstone might be anywhere.'

It was the Island of the Swans and the Maiians themselves that healed the wound opened by the shards of the glass I had broken. Maram and I went our own ways then, as did the others, each of us choosing a separate path through the city streets or among the fields and woods surrounding the lake. It surprised me that the Maiians allowed us to go about their land bearing our *shaida* weapons. But it was not their way to disallow anyone simple freedoms that even their children enjoyed. That they trusted us not to use our weapons touched me deeply. They had no fear of us, only a sweet and natural compassion for our urge to seek that which it seemed they already possessed. For the Maii were a contented people. They found their happiness neither in remembrance of the glories of ages past nor in dreams of future redemption, but rather in rock and leaf, wind and flower. The glint of the sun off the marble of their beautiful temple pleased them more than gold; the laughter of their children playing in pasture or field was to them a finer music than even Alphanderry could make. They were wholly wedded to the earth, and took great delight in that marriage.

I spent the morning wandering about the great gardens to the west of the temple. There, among the oak trees and cherry, where little streams ran through stone-lined channels into the lake, I found a few moments of peace. The gentle wind of that clime, in which summer seemed more like spring, cooled my anger. Many of the Maii worked unobtrusively around me, if efforts eagerly and joyfully undertaken could be called work. I understood that they counted it as a privilege to be chosen for the weeding, seed planting and building of the low stone walls that seemed perfectly to fit the well-tended earth. I watched them dirtying their hands in muck and manure, but they appeared to take no taint or displeasure from such substances. Indeed, the garden was so beautiful that it seemed impossible any ugliness could mar its perfection. It wasn't so much that it wouldn't abide evil; rather that which engendered evil – fear, wrath, hate – was out of place here and best left outside its flowering borders. With the birds piping out their songs of praise to the world, I found myself wanting to put aside my ill feeling for Maram (and for myself), much as I would remove a pair of muddy boots before entering a clean house or divest myself of my armor before sitting down to a family meal.

Although I didn't really expect to find the Lightstone set down into a bed of marigolds or filling with water in one of numerous stone fountains sculpted out of the earth, I kept an eye out for it all the same. But as the sun climbed toward its zenith and poured its honey-light over leaf and lake, I began to forget why I had come to the Maiians' island. For longings and lust, desires and dreams, also had a hard time taking root in that enchanted soil. For hours I sat drinking in the sight of the many flowers there: the redmaids and buttercups, the lilies and yarrow and roses. Their incredible fragrance devoured the day. The voluptuousness of the land in this lost valley was so full and sweet that it left little room for otherworldly hungers.

474

It was late afternoon when I came upon a stone bench perfectly sited for viewing two special trees growing atop a low rise near the garden's northern edge. To my astonishment, I saw that they were astors, with their silver bark and golden leaves. Though not so magnificent as those that grew in the Lokilani's wood, their long, lovely limbs spread out beneath the blue sky as if to embrace it and catch its light. The fire mountain, just beyond the quiet lake, perfectly framed their shimmering crowns. It came to me then that the transformation of the island into a paradise was not an altering of nature but rather its finest and fullest expression: for what could be more natural than the Maii, the Mother's eyes and hands, happily working their art upon the earth? I realized suddenly that I did not wish to leave them. It was as if I had journeyed across the whole length of Ea only to find my real home.

Just as the day's last light was fading from the astors' shield-like leaves, Maram came ambling down the path behind me and hailed me. He walked up to the bench and said, 'I heard you were here.'

I motioned for him to sit down beside me, then nodded toward the astors. 'Do you see them, Maram?'

'Yes, I see them,' he said. Then he sighed and continued, 'I'm sorry for what I said last night. I was a fool.'

'And I was worse than a fool,' I said. 'Will you forgive me?'

'Forgive *you*? Will you forgive *me*?'

We embraced then, and the chasm between us suddenly closed as if the earth had knitted itself whole again.

'Have you come across any sign of the Lightstone?' I asked him.

'The Lightstone? Ah, no, no, there's been nothing like that. But I *have* found love.'

He went on to tell me that he had spent most of the morning trying his wiles upon Lailaiu. But his efforts had seemed only to amuse her. Finally, she had held a finger to his clever lips and then offered herself to him as readily as a grover sharing some of the delicious red cherries that grew so abundantly in the many orchards of the valley.

'I was a fool to think of war when love was so close at hand,' he said. 'Why was I such a fool?'

'Perhaps because you wanted the Lightstone even more.'

'Ah, the Lightstone,' he said. 'Well, there's news as to that. Lady Nimaiu has agreed to our purification, whatever that may be. We're to meet by the lake tomorrow morning. After that, I suppose, we can enter the temple and see what is there.'

I returned with Maram to our rooms to join our friends in eating another delicious dinner. The mood at the table was one of quiet exaltation, as if the foods that passed our lips had been imbued with a rare, life-giving quality to be found here and nowhere else. Liljana waxed eloquent as she extolled the island's virtues and reminded us that during the Age of the Mother, nearly every part of Ea was like this. Alphanderry told of how he had spent the day teaching some of the Maiian children to play his mandolet. And they had taught him many things, not only their songs but the simplicity of their untutored voices, which had brought Alphanderry closer to the one Song that he truly wished to sing. Master Juwain, with Liljana acting as his interpreter, had gone about the city collecting stories of the Maiians' past toward the end of piecing together the puzzle of their origins. He had begun learning their language as well, and after another month, hoped to have it all written down. Atara told us that earlier she had walked halfway up the slopes of the fire mountain in order to get a better look at the island. Now, gazing out the window at the lake with dreamy eyes, she admitted that she never wanted to leave it.

Only Kane seemed untouched by the island's magic. After quaffing down the last of his wine, he paced about the room and paused only to growl out, 'So, it's a pretty paradise the Maiians have made for themselves. But if the Red Dragon ever sends a warship here, it will all be ashes.'

His grim words reminded us of why we had cajoled Captain Kharald into bringing us here. After that, we went to our beds in more somber spirits to get some rest and ready ourselves for the coming day.

The next morning before the sun had quite found its strength, we gathered by the lake's eastern shore. It was a fine, clear day with only a few clouds in the sky. Its almost perfect blueness was reflected in the calm, mirrorlike waters of the lake. Farther out upon it floated hundreds of swans, their folded wings snowy-white, their long, arched necks as lovely as the curve of the heavens themselves.

Maiians from all over the island had already arrived to witness whatever was to occur there that day. They wore plain white kirtles, and sat about the low shelves of lawn sculpted into the earth along the shore. I had a practiced eye, tutored in battle for taking in large numbers of men, and I counted at least five thousand of them. We stood on the lowest shelf of lawn with this multitude behind us and the lake almost directly in front of us. Only a series of white marble steps, following the contours of the lake's edge and actually leading down into it so that they were half-submerged, stood between us and the lapping waters of the lake itself.

Scarcely ten yards in the direction towards which these steps led, three pillars arose out of the lake's shallows. They seemed the remains of a much greater structure that must have once stood there. Liljana, after speaking in hushed tones to one of the temple attendants standing with us, told us that once the lake had been lower but over the ages had risen as it had filled with the Lady's tears. I understood then that we, too, were to be submerged in the water, and this I dreaded because it looked icy cold.

Soon Lady Nimaiu arrived with her six attendants following closely. The kirtle covering her long, graceful body was as white as the swans and embroidered with red roses. She stood with her back to the lake facing us and the thousands of her people behind us on the lawn. Her strong, clear voice carried out as she addressed us and told us that since we had freely requested to be purified, purification would be freely given.

For this occasion, we had all donned the flowing white kirtles of the Maii. They were spun of the same downy goat fur as our blankets, and were wonderfully soft. I had stripped myself of my armor, of course, as had Kane. But both of us still wore our swords: he because it was his will to do so, and I because I couldn't leave my soul aside even if it was broken.

What followed then was the simplest of ceremonies. Lady Nimaiu spoke of the sorrows which all must suffer, and which only the Mother's even greater sorrows could wash clean. For many ages, she said, since nearly the beginning of time, the Mother's tears had gathered into this lake that the Maii might taste the bitter pain of the world and rejoice in its splendor upon re-emerging from it.

'For this is why,' she told us, 'we were born in pain from the Mother's womb: we are that we might know joy.'

And with no further words, she led us down the steps in turns into the lake. One by one, she held us beneath its rippling surface. As I had feared, the water was very cold. In truth, it was bitter. But a short while later, as we stood yet again on the lawn above the steps, the sun warmed us and poured its golden radiance upon our soaked garments and dripping hair. Its light was incredibly sweet, and as we looked out into the long, green valley, we saw that the world was incredibly beautiful and good.

The Maii sitting on the grass all applauded our feat. In their front ranks, I noticed Piliri, Rhysu and their children smiling at us.

Then Lady Nimaiu came forward and addressed us, saying, 'Only in purification can there be truth, beauty and goodness. And the love from which they flow. Do you still seek these qualities, Sar Valashu Elahad?'

Although she directed this question to me, it was clear that she expected me to speak for all of us. The soft wind just then found its way through the wet kirtle plastered to my body; it seemed as cold and bracing as the lake itself.

'We do,' I said. I sensed that Lady Nimaiu was testing me, or rather calling me to embrace the truth which the lake's waters had set so clearly before me. And so I told her, 'We seek the gold gelstei that is called the Lightstone. We seek the Cup of Heaven that is said to hold these things inside it.'

At this, Maram began moaning; only the presence of Lailaiu as one of the temple attendants quieted him. Liljana was reluctant to translate my words, but I nodded at her to do so, and she did. And then I showed Lady Nimaiu my medallion and explained the meaning of the various symbols cast into it.

'It is good that you've given us the truth so freely,' Lady Nimaiu said, walking among the others of our company to examine their medallions as well. 'Allow me to return the favor: yesterday we consulted with the Sea People. They told us of your reason for coming here, that you seek this shining thing you call a *gelstei*.'

That the Maii seemed able to speak with the Sea People astonished me, as it did Liljana. She stared at Lady Nimaiu, her hazel eyes full of wonder and envy. She glanced at her figurine and muttered, 'As it was in the Age of the Mother – then they needed no blue gelstei to talk with the whales.'

Although she left this untranslated, Lady Nimaiu seemed to understand her all the same. She nodded at her and said, 'But the Sea People know nothing of a golden cup. Nor do we. There is none such on this island.'

I sensed that Lady Nimaiu was telling the truth, at least so far as she knew it. The disappointment I felt then was a palpable thing, as if an acid fruit had lodged in my throat. It didn't help that my friends' dashed hopes flooded into me as well.

'Perhaps the Lightstone was hidden here long ago,' I said, 'and the Maii have forgotten it.'

I couldn't help glance at the temple, so great was the bitterness burning inside me.

'I can tell you that you *won't* find it there,' she said. 'But now you are free to look, in the temple or anywhere else that you please.'

This news was small consolation, as little satisfying as a promise of delectable foods given a hungry man in place of a meal. I looked at Atara then, and saw that she, too, had almost abandoned her desire to search the temple. I looked at Maram, now lost in the depths of Lailaiu's eyes, and at Master Juwain, Liljana and Alphanderry. I saw Kane drop his gaze and scowl his frustration at the earth. We had journeyed too long and too far, I thought, and now it seemed that our quest must end here, on this lost island at the edge of the world.

'Now that you have tasted the Mother's tears,' Lady Nimaiu went on, 'you also are free to remain with us as long as you'd like. *We* would like this, that you live with the Maii forever.'

I had no power of mindspeaking, but I knew that my friends were all thinking of the vow we had made that our seeking the Lightstone would not end unless illness, wounds or death struck us down first. But couldn't the body, while not exactly stricken, grow exhausted of a succession of life-draining wounds? Couldn't the soul sicken? Couldn't hope die?

Lady Nimaiu glanced back at forth between Atara and me. Her face was as warm as the sun itself as she told us, 'You may make your homes here; you may marry, if that pleases you, either among us or each other. The Mother would smile upon your children and call them Maii.'

Atara looked at me, and the longing in her eyes hurt worse than any poison or sword that had been put into my flesh.

'Ah, I think I understand,' Maram murmured, still gazing at Lailaiu. 'I think perhaps the Aryans *did* come here to conquer. And the Maiians conquered them.'

For a while we stood there in silence, which spread to the crowds of Maii behind us. Now the sun, higher in the sky, was working to dry our garments. Out on the lake, the many swans there floated peacefully beneath its showers of light.

'Perhaps the golden cup *is* on this island, somewhere,' Alphanderry said. 'I wouldn't mind spending the rest of my life here searching for it.'

'Nor I,' Master Juwain said. His clear gray eyes were now full of the sky's puffy white clouds.

'Nor I,' Liljana admitted.

Kane, whom I expected to upbraid us for our faithlessness, lost his fathomless gaze in the blue waters of the lake.

'Atara,' I said, turning toward her, 'we have made vows. And you more than the rest of us.'

I expected this noble woman to affirm that vows must always be fulfilled. Instead she said, 'A vow is a sacred thing. But life is more sacred still. And I've never felt so alive as I do here.'

'Have you seen us remaining here, then?'

I was sure that she would confuse me with some sort of scryers' talk as to the different paths into the future tangling like the limbs of a thornbush. Instead, she surprised me, saying, 'Yes, I have. If we chose this, our lives would be long and happy, blessed with many children. The rest of Ea might go up in flames, but here there would be only peace.'

Only peace, I thought, looking out into the green pastures of the valley.

Wasn't peace what I truly wanted? Wasn't this really why I had set out to find the Lightstone in the first place?

I noticed Lady Nimaiu studying my face, but I feared that I wouldn't find the answers I sought in her soft, dark eyes which reminded me so much of my mother's. I didn't know where to look to find the wisdom that would decide my path. And then I chanced to see Flick glittering above the waters of the lake. His form was that of a whirling, white spiral of stars.

'Our children,' I said to Atara, 'would know peace here, yes?'

'Yes, they would,' she assured me.

'But what of *their* children? And their children's children? How long before the Dragon finds this island and destroys everything here?'

'A hundred years, perhaps,' Atara said. 'Perhaps a thousand, or perhaps never – I don't know.'

'And what of the rest of Ea?' I asked. 'What of the Wendrush and Alonia and Mesh?'

Atara had no answer for this; she just stared at me with her diamond-clear eyes that opened upon the future.

Then I heard inside myself the undying voice, whispering in fire. The same flame, I knew, burned inside Atara and my other friends.

'I can't remain here,' I told her.

Atara's eyes filled with a terrible sadness. Then she said, 'Nor I.'

'Nor I,' Liljana said, looking at Master Juwain.

'Nor I,' he said as well. 'I'm afraid the Lightstone *will* be found – if not by us or others who stood with us in Tria, then by the Red Dragon.'

And so it went, each of our company passing the ineffable flame back and forth as we remembered our purpose and reforged our wills to fulfill it. Even Maram broke off gazing at Lailaiu and said, 'I hate to leave this island, but it seems I must.'

I turned to Lady Nimaiu and said, 'Your offer that we may stay here is beyond mere graciousness. But we must continue our quest.'

'To find this gelstei that you call the Lightstone?'

'Yes, the Lightstone,' I said.

'But why would you risk your life for such a thing?'

I heard in her words a question beneath the obvious question, and I sensed that I was somehow being tested again. And so I asked myself for the thousandth time why this golden cup must be found. The answer, I was now certain, lay *not* in pleasing my father or brothers nor even winning Atara as my wife. As for my being healed of the *valarda* and the kirax that quickened my gift, what did the sufferings of a single man matter? If only I could find the strength, I would accept all the pain in the world and pass on the Lightstone to one more worthy if that meant

480

such as Meliadus would never be born and evil places like the Vardaloon would never blight the world again.

At last I looked at Lady Nimaiu and said, 'I would find the Lightstone to heal the lands of Ea and make them like yours. I'd fight all the demons of hell that this might be.'

After Liljana had translated this, a sad smile broke upon Lady Nimaiu's face. She bowed her head as if acknowledging the purity of my purpose and finding it distressful even so. And then, as the many people behind us on the lawn began murmuring quiet words of approval, she looked deep into my eyes for a long time.

'You are of the sword,' she finally said to me, glancing down at the hilt of my kalama. 'And so if you must fight, you should have a sword to fight with.'

She took my hand then and led me down the steps to the lake's edge. I had no idea what her intentions were; perhaps, I thought, she wanted to cleanse me of blood that I must someday spill in pursuit of this dream.

After taking many deep breaths, she suddenly let go my hand. And then she turned to walk down the steps into the water.

'What is she doing?' Maram cried out.

I, too, wondered this, as it seemed did everyone else. Many of the Maii stared at Lady Nimaiu as she took one final breath and disappeared into the lake. Their cries of concern told me that this was no part of any purification ceremony they knew.

My heart began beating quickly as if it were I who was holding my breath. I peered into the water and thought that I saw Lady Nimaiu swimming down toward a stone altar covered with silt and swaying with strands of lake moss. But then the mountains moved, casting a glow of fire into the sky and causing the earth to tremble. Gleaming ripples cut the lake's surface making it impossible to see very far into its icy depths.

'Quiwiri Lais Nimaiu?' a young man behind me half-shouted. Now he and many of his people were on their feet, pointing at the lake and murmuring, 'Quiwiri Lais Nimaiu?'

The pressure in my chest grew into a pain almost too great to bear. I couldn't move, so keen was the cold in my limbs that froze me to the shore gazing at the deep blue water.

And then, even as the swans suddenly cried out and leapt toward the sky with a great thunder of beating wings, a hand holding a sword broke the lake's surface. A moment later, Lady Nimaiu's face appeared as water streamed from her glistening black hair and she gasped for breath. Her feet found the marble steps, and she climbed them one by one, arising out of the lake while she held the sword high above her.

'The Sword of Flame,' I heard Alphanderry whisper behind me. 'The Sword of Light.'

Although I didn't dare believe that he might be right, I saw that the sword was bright enough to be called that and more. It was long and double-edged like the swords of the Valari; its blade shone more brilliantly than silver, and its edges were so keen they seemed to cut the very rays of the sun.

While all the Maii stood and the temple attendants stirred excitedly, while my friends looked on and Kane's eyes blazed like black coals, Lady Nimaiu approached to give me the sword. My hands closed around a hilt of black jade that was carved with swans and set with seven starlike diamonds; a much larger diamond, cut with many sparkling facets, formed its pommel stone. At the sword's first touch, fire leapt inside me. And something like a numinous flame ran along its silvery blade from the upswept guard to its incredibly sharp point, for it seemed suddenly to flare much brighter. I couldn't take my eyes from it or let it go. It was very heavy, as if truly wrought of silver or other noble metal, and yet strangely light, as if the sun itself were filling it with its radiance and drawing it toward the sky. I sliced the air with it a few times to get the feel for wielding it; its balance, I thought, was perfect. How such a marvelous weapon had come to be kept beneath the waters of the Maii's lake I couldn't imagine.

Now it came time for Lady Nimaiu to tell of this. Having shaken the water from her dripping kirtle and caught her breath, her hand swept out toward the sword as she recounted this story: Long ago in another age, she said, a Maiian fisherman named Elkaiu had cast out his net hoping to catch some of the silver salmon that swim off the coast of their island. But instead his net snagged on something heavy, and he hauled it in to find the silver sword gleaming among the folds of knotted rope. Elkaiu was amazed, not only because he had found an object for which he had no name, but because the sword bore no mark of rust or tarnish even though it had drifted for untold years along the currents of the salty sea. Elkaiu had brought the sword to his Lady, who had sensed that there was a great power in it. She sensed, too, that it had been cast into the sea to be cleansed, and so she had ordered it kept beneath the lake to continue its purification. The Lady had eventually grown old and died, of course, but she had passed on the knowledge of the sword to her successor. And so it had gone, generation after generation for many hundreds of years, the secret of the sword known only to the various Ladies of the Lake who preserved it. Over the centuries, Lady

Nimaiu said, there arose a legend that one day the sword's true owner would come to take it away.

'And that must be you, Sar Valashu,' she said as she pointed at my sheathed kalama whose hilt was also carved with swans and stars. 'And this *sword*, as you call it, must be the gelstei of which the Sea People told.'

Yes, I thought as I stared at the shimmering wonder of it, yes, it must be.

'The silver gelstei,' Master Juwain said, breathing deeply. 'So this is why we've come here.'

He went on to say that on all of Ea, throughout all the ages, he knew of no greater work of silver gelstei than this sword.

'If,' he said, 'this truly is the Sword of Light.'

For a moment, everyone fell silent as they looked at this long blade gleaming in the bright morning sunlight. Kane, who loved good steel almost more than life, seemed to gaze at it the longest and most deeply. And his eyes burned more brightly than anyone else's as he said, 'Alkaladur – so, Alkaladur.'

Here Alphanderry, standing by his side, rested his hand on his shoulder as he sang out:

> Alkaladur! Alkaladur!
> The Sword of Flame, the Sword of Light,
> Which men have named Awakener
> From ages dark and dream-dark night.

'What words are these?' Maram asked.

'So, they're from a much longer song telling of how Kalkamesh forged the Bright Sword,' Kane said. 'This was in the time after the First Quest when Morjin had nearly killed Kalkamesh and taken the Lightstone for himself.'

'Do you know the whole song?' Maram asked Alphanderry. 'Will you sing it?'

Alphanderry nodded his head, but then looked at Lady Nimaiu and her attendants who were combing out her tangled hair. It would have been rude for him to sing words that Liljana could have no hope of translating quickly and faithfully enough to be appreciated. But Lady Nimaiu, when apprised of this difficulty, asked Alphanderry to continue. She said that the spirit of the song would come through in his voice, and that was all that mattered. And so she stood smiling encouragingly at Alphanderry as all the Maii turned toward him and he began to sing:

When last the Dragon ruled the land,
The ancient warrior came to Mesh.
He sought for vengeance with his hand,
And vengeance bitter burned his flesh.

And yet a finer flame he held,
The sacred spark, aglow, unseen,
In hand and heart it brightly dwelled:
The fire of the Galadin.

He brought this flame into the realm
Of swans and stars and moonlit knolls
Where rivers ran through oak and elm
And diamond warriors called swords souls.

To Godhra thus the warrior came
Beside the ancient silver lake.
By might of mind, by forge and flame,
A sacred sword he vowed to make.

Alkaladur! Alkaladur!
The Sword of Flame, the Sword of Light,
Which men have named Awakener
From ages dark and dream-dark night.

No noble metal, gem or stone –
Its blade of finer substance wrought;
Of essence rare and form unknown,
The secret crystal ever sought.

Silustria, like silver steel,
Like silk, like diamond-frozen light,
Which angel fire has set its seal
And breath of angels polished bright.

Ten years it took to forge, ten years
To shape the crystal, make it whole;
The blade he quenched in blood and tears,
And in its length he left his soul.

A diamond for its pommel stone
Its swan-carved hilt was blackest jade

And set with seven gems that shone:
White diamonds in which starlight played.

Alkaladur! Alkaladur!
The Sword of Truth, the Silver Blade,
Which men have named the Vanquisher
Of bitter lies that men have made.

With Aramesh he rode to war
Upon the Sarburn's blood-drenched field;
He charged with knights tween wood and tor,
His bright avenging sword to wield.

He sought his foe with beating blood,
The Beast who stole the Stone of Light;
Through flashing steel and reddened mud
Pursued him all the day and night.

The silver sword, from starlight formed,
Sought that which formed the stellar light,
And in its presence flared and warmed
Until it blazed a brilliant white.

And there on Sarburn's battle ground,
Among the dying and the dead,
Where lords were killed and kings uncrowned,
The Dragon saw his doom and fled.

Alkaladur! Alkaladur!
The Sword of Sight, the Sword of Fate,
Which men have named the Harbinger
Of death to all who rule by hate.

In Tria thus the Dragon cowed,
Behind its star-flung walls of stone.
The ancient warrior, vengeance vowed,
Pursued him to his dragon throne.

But also came King Aramesh
At ending of the bitter strife,
And there despite his wounded flesh,
In ruth, he spared the Dragon's life.

The King then claimed the golden bowl,
Thus broke their star-blessed amity.
The warrior now with bitter soul:
He cast the sword into the sea.

And there it dwelled beneath the waves,
Through ages new and ages old.
But so it's told in ancient caves:
The silver gelstei seeks the gold.

Alkaladur! Alkaladur!
The ageless blade, immortal sword
Which men have named Deliverer –
To pure of heart will be restored.

Alphanderry fell silent as he stared at my sword; I stared at it, too, as did everyone else gathered around the lake.

Maram slowly nodded his head. Then he looked at Kane and said, 'If Kalkamesh *did* cast the sword into the sea in his anger at King Aramesh sparing Morjin, then it seems a rare chance that the sea carried it a thousand miles to this island only to be caught in this man Elkaiu's net.'

'Ha, chance,' Kane called out. 'There's much more at work here than mere chance.'

Now Alphanderry asked Liljana to tell the sword's story in the Maiian language, which she did. When she had finished, Lady Nimaiu gazed at the sword for a long while. 'Now I understand why it lay so long beneath the lake – and in the sea perhaps longer. Upon this sword, there must have been much blood.'

Perhaps once there had been, I thought. But now, as I held it up to the sun, the blade's silver surface reflected its light so perfectly that it seemed nothing could ever stain it or mar its beauty.

Master Juwain, whose mind turned over thoughts more times than the wind tossing about a leaf, nodded his bald head toward the sword and said, 'This must be the Awakener told of in the song. But we must be sure that it is before Val claims it as his own.'

'But, sir, how can we be any more sure than we are?' Maram asked.

'Well, there is the test to be made,' Master Juwain said. 'If it is truly of silustria and not some lesser gelstei or alloy, it will pass this test.'

'What test?' I asked him sharply.

'The silver gelstei is said to be very hard – harder than any stone save the Lightstone itself.'

486

He motioned for me to hold the sword with its blade flat to the earth so that he could get a better look at it. 'The sea carried it a thousand miles across its rocks and sands. Did they make many scratches? Do you see any mark upon it?'

I turned the sword over and over, trying to detect on its gleaming blade the faintest featherstroke of a line or scratch. But it was as unmarked as the surface of a still mountain lake.

'Hard is silustria – harder than adamant,' Master Juwain said as he looked at the two sparkling stones of my knight's ring. 'Why don't you use these diamonds to try to scratch this blade?'

Again I looked at the sword's wondrous finish. I no more wanted to scratch it than I did the lens of my eye.

'It must be tested, Val. It must be known.'

Yes, I thought, it must be. And so, making a fist, I touched the diamonds to the blade and drew them in a small arc across it near the hilt. The silver remained untouched. Now I singled out one of the stones and positioned it precisely; I found a point where three of its facets came together and pressed it as hard as I could against the silver, all the while trying to dig and drag the diamond down the entire length of the sword. But it slid off like light from a mirror and left not the slightest mark.

'Alkaladur,' Master Juwain said reverently. 'It *is* the Bright Sword.'

Now that our ceremony was completed, many of the Maii came down to congratulate us and get a better glimpse of this miraculous sword that had lain in their lake for so long unknown to them. Although they craned their necks to see it, none tried to touch it, nor would I have let them if they had.

'There are lines from the song I would like to understand better,' Maram said as he came up by my side. 'What does it mean that the silver gelstei seeks the gold?'

'Hmmph, that should be clear,' Atara said. 'Weren't you listening to what Alphanderry said?'

Her eyes fixed on the sword as she sang out:

> *The silver sword, from starlight formed,*
> *Sought that which formed the stellar light,*
> *And in its presence flared and warmed*
> *Until it blazed a brilliant white.*

'Yes, I see,' Master Juwain said, rubbing his shiny pate. 'The lines tell truly. Some believe that the Lightstone, far from merely coming from the stars, is the source of their light. It *is* known that the silver gelstei was first sought in an attempt to forge the gold. And so it has a deep resonance with it. It's said to love the Lightstone as a mirror does the sun. But whether it flares in its presence as the song has it, I do not know.'

'Why don't we put *that* to the test?' Kane growled out.

'An excellent idea,' Master Juwain said. 'But how? I believe that the Sea People also told truly: there *was* a great gelstei on this island. But not the Lightstone, it seems.'

I, too, believed what the great whales had said. But I turned to look at the temple even so.

'Why don't you point the sword toward it?' Kane said to me.

I did as he suggested, extending the sword's point directly toward the temple's pillars behind us to the south. But the silver blade, while marvelously full of light, seemed not to brighten even slightly.

'It's not there,' Maram muttered. 'I don't think it's there.'

We all fell silent then, and Liljana took this opportunity to explain our efforts to Lady Nimaiu and the Maiians. And then Master Juwain, still gazing at the sword as he scratched his head, told me, 'It might help if you meditated, Val. This, too, is said of the silustria.' He recited:

> To use the silver stone,
> The soul must dwell alone;
> The mind must be clear,
> Unclouded by fear.

As I stood there gazing at the reflection of my dark eyes in the sword's polished contours, I remembered what Master Juwain had once taught me about the silver gelstei: that it was the stone of the soul and therefore of the mind which arose out of it. At the moment, with thousands of people staring at me and this unlooked-for blade catching the bright morning sunlight, my mind was anything but clear.

'Why don't you try the seventh light meditation?' Master Juwain suggested.

And so I did. With the bees buzzing in the flower beds down by the lake to the west, I closed my eyes and envisioned a perfect diamond floating in the air. This diamond was just myself. Nothing could mar its incredibly hard substance – certainly not my fear of failing to gain the Lightstone. It was cut with thousands of facets, each one of which let in the sun's rays with perfect clarity, there to gather in its starlike heart with a brilliant fire that grew brighter and brighter and . . .

'Well, it seems there's nothing,' Master Juwain said, his voice coming as from far away. 'Nothing at all.'

I opened my eyes to find the blade unchanged.

'It seems the Lightstone really *isn't* on this island,' Maram said. And then he fell despondent and muttered, 'Ah, perhaps it's nowhere – perhaps your brothers were right that it's been destroyed.'

'No, it can't have been,' I said. 'I can almost feel it, Maram. I know it exists, somewhere on Ea.'

And with that, I held the image of the diamond inside myself again even as I held the sword out toward the Garden of Life to the west. But still its blade grew no brighter.

'Again, Val,' Kane encouraged me. 'Try a different direction.'

I slowly nodded my head. And then I lifted the sword toward the smoking mountain to the north, with as little result.

'Again, Val, again.'

Now I lightened my grip around the swan-carved hilt so that the seven diamonds set into the jade there wouldn't cut my hands so painfully. Then I pointed this sword that men had named Awakener toward that part of the world where the Morning Star arises in the east.

'It flares!' Kane called out suddenly. 'Do you see how it flares?'

It wasn't enough, I sensed, merely to clear my mind. And so I opened my heart to Alkaladur as I might to my brothers in a rare moment of trust. And the fire there suddenly blazed hotter, both purifying and reforging the secret sword that I had carried inside myself since my birth. I felt the two swords, the inner and outer, resonate like perfectly tuned crystals chiming out harmonies older than time. It was as if they each quickened each other's essence, aligning with each other, a fiery light passing back and forth, down the length of the sword, up and down the length of my spine and then out through my heart along the line of my arms held pointed out away from me and into Alkaladur.

'It flares!' Kane shouted. 'It flares!'

I opened my eyes to see the silver sword glowing faintly as from a light within. When my arms trembled and the sword's point wavered from slightly south of due east, so did its light.

'So, the Lightstone lies somewhere east of us,' Kane said. 'But it seems it's still far away.'

To the east of us, I thought, lay the Dragon Channel, Surrapam and the great Crescent Mountains. And farther: Eanna, Yarkona and the ancient library at Khaisham. And beyond that, the even greater White Mountains of Sakai and the plains of the Wendrush. And finally, the Morning Mountains of Mesh.

The Maiians, who had witnessed glories of the earth before but never one like this, gathered around gazing at my sword in wonder. After Liljana had explained to Lady Nimaiu about the silver gelstei, she nodded her head and smiled at me, saying, 'It would seem, Sar Valashu, that you won't leave our island with empty hands.'

'Yes, Lady Nimaiu,' I told her, 'and thanks to you.'

'But you still must leave, mustn't you?'

I looked at Atara and Kane and the others of our company, then turned back to her and said, 'Yes, we must.'

'But first, you'll share a meal with us, won't you?'

I glanced up at the sun, now high in the sky. The *Snowy Owl* would be sailing tomorrow on the morning tide.

'Yes,' I said, 'we'd be honored to dine with you.'

As the Maii began walking off toward the temple and the feast to be held there, she embraced me warmly. Then she touched her wounded finger to Alkaladur's blade and looked at me with her bright, black eyes.

It came time for me put away my new sword. But first I had to draw forth my old one. This I did, and I stared at the pieces of it with a great sadness in my heart. But there was also great joy there, too, and with Lady Nimaiu's permission, I flung the pieces of my broken kalama far out into the lake. They sank into its dark blue depths without a trace. Then I slid Alkaladur into the sheath. It fit perfectly. Tomorrow, I thought, as I rested my hand on its swan-carved hilt, we would journey east, toward the rising sun.

29

With a strong wind blowing at our backs, it took us only a day and a night of fast sailing to cross the Dragon Channel to Surrapam. There, the following morning, at Artram, the last of Surrapam's free ports and therefore crowded with ships coming and going through its bustling harbor, we said goodbye to Captain Kharald and the *Snowy Owl*. After the horses had been led onto the dock, he stood by us telling of the news that had just been brought to him.

'King Kaiman,' he said to us, 'is making a stand near Azam only forty miles from here. 'Its seems our wheat is needed very badly.'

I watched the lean, hungry-looking Surrapam dockmen unloading the bags of wheat from the *Snowy Owl*'s holds. From nearby smithies down Artram's busy streets came the sounds of hammered steel and the clamor of preparations for war.

'Your swords are needed badly, too,' he said to us. 'Would you be willing to raise them against the enemy that you say you oppose?'

I remembered Thaman's request to the Valari in Duke Rezu's castle; in the months since then, I thought, it had gone very badly for his people.

'Oppose the Hesperuk armies with *this*?' I asked him, showing him the wooden sword I had carved.

'Some,' he said grimly, looking around at the desperate Surrapamers, 'would fight him with their nails and teeth. But I think you have a better weapon than that piece of wood.'

The day before, when we had first returned to the ship, a chance gust of wind had whipped back my cloak, and Captain Kharald's quick eyes had fallen on Alkaladur's jeweled hilt. Since then, I had taken pains to keep it covered.

'You haven't told me what occurred on the island, and that's your business,' he said to me. 'But it's my business to help save the kingdom, if I can.'

Captain Kharald's new conscience had changed the direction of his efforts but not their vigor: I thought he would pursue his new business with all the cunning and force that he had applied toward making money.

'We failed to gain the Lightstone,' I said to him as Kane prowled about the horses, checking their loads. The others stood near me awaiting their turns to say goodbye as well. 'What more is there to tell?'

'Only *you* know that, Sar Valashu.'

Because I hoped it might give him courage, I finally confided in him the story of my receiving the Bright Sword. He looked at me with wonder lighting up his hard, blue eyes. 'Such a sword and a Valari knight to wield it would be worth a company of men. And with Kane and your friends behind you, a whole regiment.'

I smiled at this flattery, then told him, 'Even a hundred regiments arrayed against the Red Dragon wouldn't be enough to bring him down. But the finding of the Lightstone might be.'

'Then you intend to continue your quest?'

'Yes, we must.'

'But where will you go? It won't be long before the Hesperuk warships close the Channel.'

Kane, stroking the neck of Alphanderry's white Tervolan, shot me a warning look. Although our journey lay to the east, we hadn't yet decided its course.

'We'll go wherever we must,' I said to Captain Kharald.

'Well, go in the One's light then,' he told me. 'I wish you well, Valashu Elahad.'

I wished him well, too, and so did the others. And then, after clasping Captain Kharald's rough hand, we mounted our horses and rode north through Artram's narrow streets.

The choice of this direction was Kane's. Ever alert for enemies and Kallimun spies, he spared no effort in trying to throw potential pursuers off our scent. Artram was a rather small city of stout wooden houses and the inevitable shops of sailmakers, ropemakers and sawyers working up great spars to be used in fitting out the many ships docked in her port. There were many salteries, too, preserving the cargoes of cod and char that the fishing boats brought in from the sea. Most of these shops, however, were now empty, their stores having been requisitioned by King Kaiman's quartermasters. In truth, there seemed little food left in the city, and little hope for defeating Hesperu's ravaging armies, either.

Everywhere we went, we saw marks of woe upon the Surrapamers' gaunt faces. It pained me to see their children eyeing our well-fed horses and full saddlebags. Like Thaman and Captain Kharald, they were mostly red of hair, fair of skin and thick of body – or would have been in better times. Though nearly beaten, they carried themselves bravely and well. I resolved that if I ever returned to Mesh, I would speak out strongly for helping them, if only by taking the field against the Red Dragon.

Maram surprised us all by stopping to pull off his rings one by one and giving them to various beggars who crossed our path. After slipping his third ring into the hand of a one-legged old warrior, Kane chided him for such conspicuous largesse. And Maram chided *him*, saying, 'I can always get more rings, but he'll never get another leg. I regret that I have only ten fingers, with ten rings to give.'

The afternoon found us a few miles outside of the city, in a region of rich black earth and once-prosperous farms. But the King's quarter-masters had come here, too. Smokehouses that should have been stuffed with hanging hams were empty; barns that should have been full of dried barley and corn held only straw. Most of the grown men having been called to war, or already laid low by it, the fields of ripening wheat were tended by women, children and old men. They paused in their labor to watch us pass, obviously wondering that an armed company should ride unchallenged through their land. But there were few knights or men-at-arms left to stop and question us – or to offer us hospitality. I thought that the widows and worried wives who nodded to us would have been willing to share all they had, even if it was only a thin gruel. The Surrapamers were as generous of heart even as they were sometimes greedy, like Captain Kharald. But that day, we didn't put it to the test: we rode along in silence, exchanging nothing more than a few kind looks with those who watched us.

When we were sure that no one had followed us out of Artram, we turned east toward the mountains. Although the great Crescent Mountains were said to be very tall, we could not see even the tallest of their peaks, even though they lay only sixty miles away. Surrapam, it seemed, was a land of clouds and mists that obscured the sky – and sometimes even the tops of the trees pushing up into it. Master Juwain told us that here the sun shone only rarely. The Surrapamers' pale, pink skin drank up what little light there was; their thick bodies protected them from the sempiternal coolness clinging like moistened silk to its lush fields. But we were not so fortunate. That day, a thin drizzle sifted slowly down through the air. Although it was full summer, and the height of Marud at that, its chill made me draw my cloak tightly around me.

And yet, despite the gloom, it was a rich, beautiful land of evergreen forests and emerald fields glowing softly beneath the sky's gentle light. I could see why the Hesperuks might wish to conquer it. The farther we rode across its verdant folds, the more it seemed that we were journeying in the wrong direction. But three times that day I drew Alkaladur, and each time its faint radiance pointed us east. And east we must continue, I thought, even though great battles and the call to arms lay behind us.

We camped that night in a stand of spruce trees beside a swift-running stream. Its waters were clear and sweet, and full of trout, nine of which Alphanderry and Kane managed to catch for our dinner. Maram summoned forth a fire from some moist sticks, while Liljana set to with her pots and pans. It was the first time she had cooked a full meal for us since before Varkall.

We ate our fried fish and cornbread in the silence of those soft woods. We had cheese and blackberries for dessert, for these shiny little fruits grew abundantly in thickets along the roads we had ridden. By the time Master Juwain had brewed up a pot of Sunguran tea purchased in one of Artram's shops, we were ready to discuss the journey that still lay before us.

'Well, I had hoped the Lightstone might have come to Artram,' Maram said as he patted his well-filled belly. 'Though why I should have expected to find the Cup of Heaven in that sad little city not even the Ieldra know.'

I sat by the fire with my new sword unsheathed. Just to be sure that we had traveled in the right direction, I held it pointing toward Artram to the west. But the only light in its gleaming length came from the fire's flickering orange flames.

'No, I'm afraid it still lies east of us,' Master Juwain said. 'And I think it's more than a coincidence that Khaisham lies directly along the line which Val's sword has shown us.'

It was not the first time he had said this. Ever since the Island of the Swans, when it became clear that our journey might take us as far as Khaisham and the great library there, he had continually gazed off in its direction with a new excitement in his usually calm, gray eyes.

'I still don't see how the Lightstone could be there,' Maram said. 'The library has been searched a hundred times, hasn't it?'

'Yes, it has,' Master Juwain told him. 'But it's said to be vast, perhaps too vast ever to be searched fully. The number of books it holds is said to be thousands and thousands.'

Kane, sitting by Alphanderry who was tuning his mandolet, smiled gleefully and said, 'So, I've been to the Library once, many years ago. The number of its books is thousands *of* thousands. Many of them have never even been read.'

A new idea had suddenly come to Master Juwain, who sat rubbing his hands together as if in anticipation of a feast. 'Then perhaps one of them holds the Lightstone.'

'You mean, holds knowledge about it, don't you, sir?' Maram asked.

'No, I mean the Cup of Heaven itself. Perhaps one of the books has had its pages hollowed out to fit a small golden cup. And so escaped being discovered in any search.'

'Now *there's* a thought,' Maram said.

'It's as I've always told you,' Master Juwain said to him. 'When you open a book, you never know what you'll find there.'

We talked for quite a while about the library and the great treasures it guarded: not just the books, of course, but the numerous paintings, sculptures, works of jewelry, glittering masks studded with unknown gelstei and other artifacts, many of which dated from the Age of Law – and whose purpose neither the Librarians nor any one else had been able to fathom. For Master Juwain, a journey to the library was an opportunity of a lifetime. And the rest of us were eager to view this wonder, too. Even Atara, who had little patience for books, seemed excited at the prospect of beholding so many of them.

'I think there's no other choice then,' she said. 'We should go to this library, and see what we see.'

I looked at her as if to ask if she had *seen* us successfully completing our quest there, but she slowly shook her head.

'There's no other choice,' Master Juwain said. 'At least none better that I can think of.'

And so, despite Maram's objections that Khaisham lay five hundred miles away across unknown lands, we decided to journey there unless my sword pointed us elsewhere or we found the Lightstone first.

To firm up our resolve, we broke out the brandy and sat sipping it by the fire. This distillation of grapes ripened in the sun far away warmed us deep inside. Alphanderry began playing, and much to everyone's surprise, Kane joined him in song. His singing voice, which I had never heard, was much like the brandy itself: rich, dark, fiery and aged to a bittersweet perfection – and quite beautiful in its own way. He sang to the stars far above us which we could not see; he sang to the earth that gave us form and life and would someday take it away. When he had finished, I sat staring at my sword as if I might find my reflection there.

'What do you see, Val?' Master Juwain asked.

'That's hard to say,' I told him. 'It's all so strange. Here we are drinking this fine brandy – and it's as if the vintner who made it left the taste of his soul in it. In the air, there's the sound of battle, even though it's a quiet night. And the earth upon which we sit: can you feel her heart beating up through the ground? And not just *her* heart, but everyone's and everything's: the nightingale's and the wood vole's, and even that of the Lord Librarian in Khaisham half a world away. It beats and beats, and there's a song there – the same strange song that the stars sing. And truly, it's a cloudy night, but the stars are always there, in their spirals and sprays of light, like sea foam, like diamonds, like dreams in the mind of a child. And they never cease forming up and delighting: it's like Flick whirling in the Lokilani's wood. And it's all part of one pattern. And we could see the whole of it from any part if only we opened our eyes, if only we knew *how* to look. Strange, strange.'

Maram staggered over to me, and touched my head to see if I had a fever. He had never heard me speak like this before; neither had I.

'Ah, my friend, you're drunk,' he said, looking down at Alkaladur. 'Drunk on brandy or drunk on the fire of this sword – it's all the same.'

Master Juwain looked back and forth between the sword and me. 'No, I don't think he's quite drunk yet. I think he's just beginning to see.'

He went on to tell us that everyone had three eyes: the eye of the senses; the eye of reason; and the eye of the soul. This third eye did not develop so easily or naturally as the others. Meditation helped open it, and so did the attunement of certain gelstei.

'All the greater gelstei quicken the other sight,' he said, 'but the silver is especially the stone of the soul.'

The silustria, he said, had its most obvious effects on that part of the soul we called the mind. Like a highly polished lens, the silver crystal could reflect and magnify its powers: logic, deduction, calculation, awareness, insight and ordinary memory. In its reflective qualities, the silver gelstei might also be used as a shield against energies: vital, physical and particularly mental. Although not giving power *over* other minds, it could be used to quicken the working of another's mind, and was thus a great tool for teaching. A sword made of silustria, he thought, could cut through all things material as the mind cuts through ignorance and darkness, for it was far harder than diamond. In fact, in its fundamental composition, the silver was very much like the gold gelstei, and was one of the two noble stones.

'But its most sublime power is said to be this seeing of the soul that Val has told of. The way that all things are interconnected.'

Alphanderry, who seemed to have a song ready for any topic or occasion, sang an old one about the making of the heavens and earth. Its words, written down by some ancient minstrel long ago, told of how all of creation was woven of a single tapestry of superluminal jewels,

496

the light of each jewel reflected in every other. Although only the One could ever perceive each of the tapestry's shimmering emeralds, sapphires and diamonds, a man, through the power of the silver gelstei, might apprehend its unfolding pattern in all its unimaginable magnificence.

'"For we are the eyes through which the One beholds itself and knows itself divine,"' Alphanderry quoted.

And by 'we', he explained, he meant not only the men and women of Ea, but the Star People, the Elijin, and the great Galadin such as Arwe and Ashtoreth, whose eyes were said to be of purest silustria in place of flesh.

'What wonders would we behold,' he asked us, 'if only we had the eyes to see them?'

'Ah, well,' Maram said as he yawned and drank the last of his brandy, 'I'm afraid *my* eyes have seen enough of day for one day, if you know what I mean. While I don't expect anyone's sympathy, I must tell you that Lailaiu didn't allow me much sleep. But I'm off to bed to replenish my store of it. And to behold her in my dreams.'

He stood up, yawned again, rubbed his eyes and then patted Alphanderry's head. 'And *that*, my friend, is the only part of this wonderful tapestry of yours I care to see tonight.'

Because we were all quite as tired as he, we lay back against our furs and wrapped ourselves with our cloaks against the chill drizzle – everyone except Kane who had the first watch. I fell asleep to the sight of Flick fluttering about the fire like a blazing butterfly, even as I rested my hand on the hilt of my sword, which I kept at my side. Although I dreaded the dreams the Lord of Lies might send me, I slept well. That night, in my dreams, when I was trapped in a cave as black as death itself, I drew forth Alkaladur. The sword's fierce white light fell upon the dragon waiting in the darkness there, with its huge, folded wings and iron-black scales. Its radiance allowed me to see the dragon's only vulnerability: the knotted, red heart which throbbed like a bloody sun. And in seeing my seeing of his weakness, the dragon turned his great, golden eyes away from me in fear. And then, in a thunder of wings and great claws striking sparks against stone, he vanished down a tunnel leading into the bowels of the earth.

The next morning, after a breakfast of porridge and blackberries fortified with some walnuts that Liljana had held in reserve, we set out in good spirits. We rode across fallow fields and little dirt roads, neither seeking out the occasional farmhouses we came across or trying to avoid them. This part of Surrapam, it seemed, was not the most populated. Broad swaths of forest separated the much narrower strips of cultivated land and settlements from each other. Although the roads through the giant, moss-hung trees were good enough, if a little damp, I wondered what it would be like when we reached the mountains, where we might find no roads at all.

Maram, too, brooded about this. As we paused to make a mid-morning meal out of the clumps of blackberries growing along the roadside, he pointed ahead of us and said, 'How are we to take the horses across the mountains if there are no roads for them? The *Crescent Mountains*, Val?'

'Don't worry,' I told him, 'we'll find a way.'

Kane, whose face was so covered with berry juice that he looked as if he had torn apart a deer with his large teeth, grinned at him and said, 'If we find the mountains impassable, we can always go around them.'

He pointed out that this great mountain chain, which ran in a broad crescent from the southern reaches of the Red Desert up Ea's west coast through Hesperu and Surrapam, thinned and gave out altogether a hundred and fifty miles to the north of us in Eanna. We could always journey in that direction, he said, before rounding the farthermost point of the mountains and turning back south and east for Khaisham.

'But that would add another three hundred miles to our journey!' Maram groaned. 'Let's at least try crossing the mountains first.'

At this, Atara laughed and said, 'Your laziness is giving you courage.'

'It would give me more if you could *see* a road through the mountains. Can you?'

But in answer, Atara popped a fat blackberry into her mouth and slowly shook her head.

As we set out again, I wondered at the capriciousness of each of our gifts and the various gelstei that quickened them. Among us, we now had six; only Alphanderry lacked a stone, and so great were our hopes after my gaining Alkaladur that we were sure he would find a purple gelstei somewhere between Surrapam and Khaisham. Although Master Juwain brought forth his varistei with greater and greater frequency, he admitted that drawing upon its deepest healing properties might be the work of a lifetime. Kane, of course, kept his black stone mostly hidden and his doubts about using it secret as well. Liljana's blue figurine might indeed aid her in mindspeaking, but there were no dolphins or whales to be found in Ea's interior, and none among us with her talent. As she had promised to look away from the running streams of each of our thoughts unless invited to dip into them, she had little opportunity to gain any sort of mastery of her stone. As for Atara, she gazed into her scryer's sphere as often as I searched the sky for the sun. What she saw there, however, remained a mystery. I gathered that her visions were as uncertain as blizzards in spring, and blew through her with sometimes blinding fury.

Maram's talent proved to be the most fickle of any of ours – and the most neglected. Where he should have been growing more adept in using his firestone, he seemed almost to have forgotten that he possessed it. As he had said, his dreams were now of Lailaiu; at any one time, I thought, he was able to pour his passions into one vessel only. At the end of the day, after we had covered a good twenty-five miles through a gradually deepening drizzle, he tried to make a fire for us with his gelstei. But the red crystal brightened not even a little and remained dead in his hands.

'The wood is too wet,' he said as he knelt over a pile of it that he had made. 'There's too little light coming through these damn clouds.'

'Hmmph, you've gotten a fire out of your crystal before with as little light,' Atara chided him. 'I should think the test of it is at times such as these rather than in waiting for perfect conditions.'

'I didn't know I was being tested,' Maram fired back.

'Our whole journey is a test for all of us,' Atara told him. 'And all our lives may someday depend on your firestone.'

Her words cut deep into me and remained in my mind as I fell asleep that night. For I had a sword that I must learn to wield – and not by crossing blades with Kane every night during our fencing practice. Although Alkaladur might indeed be hard enough to slice through the hardest steel, it had more vital powers that I was only beginning to sense. It would take all my will, I thought, all my awareness and concentration of my lifefire to find myself in the silvery substance of the sword and it in me.

Morning brought with it a little sun, which lasted scarcely long enough for us to saddle the horses and break camp. It began to rain again, but much of its sting was taken away by the needles of the towering trees above us. Here were hemlocks and spruce two hundred feet high, and great King Firs perhaps even higher. They formed a vast shield of green protecting against wind and water, and sheltering the many squirrels, foxes and birds that lived here. I might have been content to ride through this lovely forest another month, for its smells of mosses and wildflowers pleased me greatly. Soon, however, the trees gave way to more farmland, cut with numerous streams running down from the mountains. In this more open country, the rain found us easy targets, and pelted us with icy drops that streaked down through the sky like silver arrows. It soaked our garments, making a misery of what should have been an easy ride. By late afternoon, with the ground rising steeply towards the mountains' foothills, we were all of us considering knocking on the door of some stout farmhouse and asking refuge for the night.

'But if we do that,' I said to my friends as we stopped to water the horses by a stream, 'these poor people will have to feed us, and they've nothing to spare.'

'Perhaps we could feed them,' Atara suggested. '*We've* plenty to spare.'

Liljana cast her a troubled look and said, 'If travelers came through the Wendrush offering food to their hosts, what would they think?'

'Ha,' Kane said, 'if travelers came through the Wendrush offering food to the *Kurmak*, they'd likely be put to the sword for the insult of it.'

Although Atara didn't respond to this remark about her people, her grim face suggested it might be true.

'I have an idea,' Maram said. 'It's time we began inquiring if anyone hereabouts knows of a road through the mountains. If anyone *happens* also to offer us shelter and also has enough food, we'll accept. Otherwise we'll ride on.'

It was a good plan, I thought, and the others agreed. We spent the next few hours riding from farmhouse to farmhouse, even as the rain grew stronger. But none of the Surrapamers knew of the road we sought. Most of them *did* offer us lodgings for the night, even though their sunken faces and bony bodies told us that this was an act of pride and politesse they could ill afford. It amazed me that they were willing to succor us at all, for we were strangers from distant lands of which few had heard; we were girt for war and riding across their fields at a time when many of their kinsmen had been taken by war – and many more might soon be. I thanked our stars that all their knights and warriors had ridden off, and so left these brave people little more than goodwill, and faith in *our* goodwill, with which to face us.

But as the day faded toward a gray, rainy evening, it seemed that I had given my thanks too soon. Just after we had knocked on the door of yet another farmhouse, a company of armed men came thundering down the road from the east and turned onto the farm's muddy lane. There were twenty of them, and they all wore rusted mail with no surcoat to cover it or identify their domains or houses. Shabby knights they seemed, and yet their lances appeared sharp enough and their swords ready at hand. Although they were quite as gaunt as the rest of their countrymen, they sat straight in their saddles and rode with good discipline.

'Who are you?' their leader called out to us as his large war horse kicked up clots of mud and came to a halt ten yards from us. He himself was a large man, with a thick gray beard and braided gray plaits hanging down from beneath his open-faced helmet. 'What are you doing in our land?'

The door of the house having been shut behind us, I stood by Altaru as he stomped about and eyed this man's horse ferociously. My companions had already mounted their horses; Atara was fingering her strung bow while Kane cast his black eyes on the men before us.

I gave the knight our names, and asked him his. He presented himself as Toman of Eastdale; he said that he and his men had been riding off to join King Kaiman at Azam.

'We'd heard there were strange knights about,' Toman said, studying my surcoat and other accouterments. 'We were afraid you might be Hesperuk spies.'

'Do we look like spies?' I said to him.

'No, you don't,' he admitted graciously. 'But not everyone is who they seem. The Hesperuks haven't won half our kingdom through force of arms alone.'

I pulled myself on top of Altaru and patted his neck to steady him. To Toman, I said, 'We're not Kallimun priests, if that's what you're thinking.'

'Perhaps not,' he said, 'but that is for the King to decide. I'm afraid you'll have to lay down your arms and come with us.'

At a nod from him, four of his knights rode up by his side with their lances held ready. Toman looked from Atara to Maram and then back at me. 'Please give me your sword, Sar Valashu.'

'I'll give you *mine*,' Kane growled as his eyes flashed and his hand moved quick as a snake's to draw his sword.

'Kane!' I said. With almost miraculous control, Kane caught himself in mid-motion and stared at me. 'Kane, don't draw on him!'

But all of Toman's knights had now drawn their swords. Unlike their armor, they showed no spot of rust.

'You must understand,' Toman said to me, 'that we can't allow you to go armed about our land – not with the Hesperuks knocking on our doors, too.'

'Very well,' I said, 'but we've no desire to go riding about Surrapam at all – only to find a way to leave it.'

I explained that we were journeying to the library at Khaisham; I told him that we had made vows to seek the Lightstone along with a thousand others in King Kiritan's hall in Tria.

'We've heard of this quest,' he said, pulling at his beard. 'But how do we know that you have truly set out upon it?'

I nudged Altaru forward, then drew forth the medallion that King Kiritan had given me. At the sight of this circle of gold, Toman's eyes held wonder but no greed. Then, at my bidding, my companions approached to show their medallions as well. Toman's knights, gathering around us, suddenly put away their swords at *his* bidding.

'We must honor the impulse behind this quest, even if we do not believe in it,' Toman said. 'If you truly oppose the Crucifier, you'd do better to come to battle with us.'

'That appears to be the thought of most of your countrymen,' I said. Then I told him of meeting Thaman at Duke Rezu's castle in Anjo, and his plea to the Valari.

'You know Thaman of Bear Lake?' one of Toman's men asked in surprise. He was scarcely eighteen years old, and proved to be Toman's grandson.

'It seems *you* do,' I said to him.

'He's my betrothed's cousin,' the man said, 'and a great warrior.'

Our acquaintance with Thaman finally decided Toman. He smiled grimly at us and said, 'Very well, you're free to go, then. But please leave our land before you frighten anyone else.'

'We'd leave it faster if we knew of a road through the mountains.'

Toman pointed off through the rain and dense greenery surrounding the farm and said, 'There *is* a road – it's about ten miles southeast of here. I would show it to you, but we've another hour before it's dark and must ride on. But my other grandson, Jaetan, will take you to it if you tell him of our meeting and my wishes.'

He proceeded to give us directions to his estate. Then he said, 'Well, we're off to the assembly at Iram. Are you sure you won't join us?'

'Thank you, no – we have our road, and it leads east.'

'Then farewell, Sar Valashu. Perhaps we'll meet in better times.'

And with that, he and his men turned their horses and rode off down the road to the west.

Toman's 'estate', when we found it an hour later, proved to be nothing more than a rather large, fortified house overlooking a barn and fields surrounded by a high fence of sharpened wooden poles. As he had promised, his family provided us shelter for the night. Toman's daughter and two grandsons were all that was left to him, his son having died in the battle of the Maron and two granddaughters taken by fever last winter. Toman's second grandson, Jaetan, was a freckle-faced redhead about thirteen years old – too young to ride off with his brother to war. And yet, I thought, I had gone to war at that age. It gladdened my heart, even as I filled with not a little pride, that even in the hour of their greatest need, the Surrapamers were not so war-loving as we Valari.

After we had laid our sleeping furs on the dry straw in the barn, Jaetan's mother, Kandra, insisted on calling us into the house for a meal, even as we had feared. But as they had nothing more than a few eggs, some blackberry jam and flour to be baked into bread, our dinner was a long time in coming. Kane solved the problem of our eating up Toman's family's reserves in the most spectacular manner: as he had with Meliadus, he grabbed up his bow and stole off into the darkening woods. A half hour later, he returned with a young buck slung across his broad shoulders. It was a great feat of hunting, Kandra exclaimed, especially so considering that the forest hereabouts had been nearly emptied of deer.

And so we had a feast that night and everyone was happy. Kandra kept the remains of the deer, which more than made up for the bread that she baked us. In the morning, we set out well fed, with Jaetan leading the way on a bony-looking old nag that was a little too big for him.

After a couple of hours of riding up a gradually ascending dirt road, we came to a notch between two hills where the road seemed to disappear into a great, green wall of vegetation. Jaetan pointed into it and told us, 'This is the old East Road. It's said to lead into Eanna. But no one really knows because no one goes that way any more.'

'Except us,' Maram muttered nervously.

Jaetan looked at him and told him, 'The road is good enough, I think. But you should be careful of the bears, Master Maram. It's said that there are still many bears in the mountains.'

'Oh, excellent,' Maram said, staring into the woods. 'Bears, is it now?'

We thanked Jaetan for his hospitality, and then he turned to Kane and asked, 'If you ever come back this way, will you teach me to hunt, sir?'

'That I will,' Kane promised as he reached out to rumple the boy's hair. 'That I will.'

With a few backward glances, Jaetan then rode back toward his grandfather's house and the warmth of the hearth that awaited him.

'Well,' Maram said, 'if the old maps are right, we've sixty miles of mountains to cross before we reach Eanna. I suppose we'd better start out before the bears catch our scent.'

But we saw no sign of bears all that day, nor the next nor even the one following that. The woods about us, though, were thick enough to have hidden a hundred of them. As the hills to either side of us rose and swelled into mountains, the giant trees of western Surrapam gave way to many more silver firs and nobles. These graceful evergreens, while not so tall as their lowland cousins, grew more densely. If not for the road, we would have been hard pressed to fight our way through them. This narrow muddy track had been cut along a snakelike course. And it turned like a snake, now curving south, now north, but always making its way roughly east as it gradually gained elevation. And with every thousand feet higher upon the green, humped earth on which we stood, it seemed that the rain poured down harder and the air fell colder.

Making camp in these misty mountains was very much a misery. The needles of the conifers, the bushes, the mosses and ferns about our soaked sleeping furs – everything the eye and hand fell upon was dripping wet. That Maram failed yet again with his fire dispirited us even more. When the day's first light fought its way through the almost solid grayness lying over the drenched earth each morning, we were glad to get moving again, if only because our exertions warmed our stiff bodies.

Three times the road failed us, vanishing into a mass of vegetation that seemed to swallow it completely. And three times Maram complained that we were lost and would never see the sun again, let alone Khaisham.

But each time, with an unerring sense, Atara struck off into the forest, leading us through the trees for a half mile or more until we found the road again. It was as if she could see much of the path that lay before us. It made me wonder if her powers of scrying were much greater than she let on.

On the fourth day of our mountain crossing, we had a stroke of luck. The rain stopped, the sky cleared, and the bright sun shone down upon us and warmed the world. The needles of the trees and the bushes' leaves, still wet with rain, shimmered as if covered with millions of drops of melting diamonds. Two thousand feet above us, the trees were frosted with snow. For the first time, we had a good view of the great peaks around us. Snow and ice covered these spurs of rock, which pushed up into the blue sky to the north and south of us. Our little road led between them; the ground that we still had to cross, as we could see, was not really a gap in the mountains, but only a stretch where they rose less high. Although we had covered a good thirty miles, as the raven flies, we still had heights to climb and as many more miles before us.

We broke then for our midday meal in a sparkling glade by a little lake. Maram, who still had his talent with flint and steel, struck up a fire, which Liljana used to roast a rock goat that Atara had managed to shoot. After some days of cold cheese and battle biscuits, we were all looking forward to this feast. While the meat was cooking, Maram discovered a downed tree-trunk, hollowed and swarming with bees.

'Ah, honeycomb,' he said to me as he pointed at the trunk and licked his lips. 'I can smell the honey in that hive.'

I watched from a safe distance as he built up another fire from wet

504

twigs to smoke the bees out of their home. It took quite some time, and many blows of the axe, but he finally pulled out a huge, sticky mass of waxen comb dripping with golden honey. That he suffered only a dozen stings from his robbery amazed me.

'You're brave enough when you want to be,' I said to him as he handed me a piece of comb. I licked a little honey from it. It was incredibly good, tasting of thousands of sun-drenched blossoms.

'Ah, I'd take a thousand stings for honey,' he said before cramming into his mouth a huge chunk of comb. 'In all the world, there's nothing sweeter except a woman.'

He rubbed some honey over the stings along his hands and face, and then we returned to the others to share this treasure.

We all gorged on the succulent goat meat and honey, Maram most of all. After he had finished stuffing his belly, he fell asleep on top of the dewed bracken near some thick bushes that Kane called pink spira. The rays of sun playing over his honey-smeared face showed a happy man.

We let him finish his nap while we broke our makeshift camp. After our waterbags had all been filled and the horses packed, we made ready to mount them and ride back to the road. And then, just as Liljana pointed out that it wouldn't do to leave Maram sleeping, we heard him murmuring behind us as if dreaming: 'Ah, Lailaiu, so soft, so sweet.'

I turned to go fetch him, but immediately stopped dead in my tracks. For what my eyes beheld then, my mind wouldn't quite believe: There, across the glade, in a break in the bushes above Maram and bending over him, crouched a large, black she-bear. She had her long, shiny snout pressed down into Maram's face as she licked his lips and beard with her long, pink tongue. She seemed rather content lapping up the smears of honey that the careless Maram had left clinging there. And all the while, Maram murmured in his half-sleep, 'Lailaiu, ah, Lailaiu.'

I might have fallen down laughing at my friend's very mistaken bliss. But bears, after all, were bears. I couldn't imagine how this one had stolen out of the bushes upon Maram without either Kane or the horses taking notice. As it was mid-summer, I feared that she had young cubs nearby.

Slowly and quietly, I reached out to tap on the elbow of Kane, who had his back to the bear as he tightened the cinch of his horse. When he turned to see what I was looking at, his black eyes lit up with many emotions at once: concern, hilarity, contempt, outrage and blood-lust. Quick as a wink, he drew forth his bow, strung it and fit an arrow to its string. This movement alerted the others as to Maram's peril – and the horses, too. Altaru, facing the wind, finally turned to see the bear;

he suddenly reared up as he let loose a tremendous whinny. Liljana's gelding and Master Juwain's sorrel, Iolo and Fire – all the horses added their voices to the great chorus of challenge and panic splitting the air. We had all we could do to keep hold of their reins and prevent them from running off. With Kane's bay stamping about and threatening to split his skull with a flying hoof, he couldn't get off a shot. And it was good that he didn't. For just as Maram finally awakened and looked up with wide eyes into the hairy face of his new lover, the bear started at the sudden noise and peered across the glade as if seeing us for the first time. She seemed more astonished than we were. It took her only a moment to gather her legs beneath her and bound off into the bushes.

'Oh, my Lord!' Maram called out upon realizing what had happened. He sprang up and raced to the lake's edge, where he knelt to wash his face. Then he said, 'Oh, my Lord – I was nearly eaten!'

Atara, keeping an eye out for the bear's return, walked up to him and poked a finger into his big belly. 'Hmmph, you're half a bear yourself. I've never seen anyone eat honey the way that you do. But the next time, perhaps you should be more careful how you eat it.'

That day we climbed to the greatest heights of our mountain crossing. This was a broad saddle between two great peaks, where lush meadows alternated with spire-like conifers. Thousands of wildflowers in colors from blazing pink to indigo brightened the sides of the road. Marmots and pikas grazed there, and looked at us as if they had never seen our kind before. But as they fed upon the grasses and seeds they found among the flowers, they kept a close watch for the eagles and ravens who hunted them. We watched them, too. Maram wondered if the Great Beast could seize the souls of these circling birds and turn them into ghuls as he had the bear at the beginning of our journey.

'Do you think he's watching us, Val?' Maram asked me. 'Do you think he can see us?'

I stopped to draw my sword and watch it glow along the line to the east. Its fire was of a faint white. In the journey from Swan Island, I had noticed that other things beside the Lightstone caused it to shine. In the glint of the stars, it radiance was more silver, while the stillness of my soul seemed to produce a clearer and brighter light.

'It's strange,' I said, 'but ever since Lady Nimaiu gave me this blade, the Lord of Lies seems unable to see me, even in my dreams.'

I looked up at a great, golden eagle gliding along the mountain wind, and I said, 'There's no evil in these creatures, Maram. If they're watching, it's only because *they're* afraid of us.'

My words seemed to reassure him, and we began our descent through the eastern half of the Crescent Range with good courage. For another three days, beneath the strong mountain sun, we rode on without incident. The road held true, taking us down the folded slopes and around the curve of lesser peaks. As we lost elevation and made our way east, the land grew drier, the forest more open. We crossed broad bands of white oak and ponderous pine, interspersed with balsamroot and phlox and other smaller plants. Many of the birds and animals who lived here were strange to me. There was a chipmunk with yellow stripes and a bluejay who ate acorns. We saw four more bears, smaller and of a grayish hue to their fur that lent them great dignity. They must have wondered why we hurried through their domain when the glories of the earth in midsummer ripened all around us.

And then, on the first day of Soal, with most of the great Crescent Range at our backs, we came out of a cleft in the foothills to see a vast plain opening to the east. It was like a sea of grass, yellow-green, and colored with deeper green lines where trees grew along the winding watercourses. Another hour's journey down some slopes of ponderous pine and rocky ridges would take us down into it.

'Eanna,' Kane said, pointing down into this lovely land. 'At least, this was once part of the ancient kingdom. But we're far from Imatru, and I doubt if King Hanniban holds any sway here.'

What peoples or lords we might find in the realm below us, he didn't know. But he admonished us to be wary, for out on the plain we would have no cover, either from men or the wolves and lions who hunted the antelope there.

'Wolves!' Maram exclaimed. 'Lions! – I think I'd rather keep company with the bears.'

But all that first day of our journey across Eanna, neither his fears nor Kane's took form to bring us harm. We left the road only a couple of miles from the mountains. It turned south, whether toward some lost city in this pretty country or toward nowhere, none of us could say. The Red Desert, Kane told us, lay not so very far in that direction, and its drifting vermilion sands and dunes had swallowed up more than one city over the millennia. We were lucky, he said, that Alkaladur seemed to point us along a path above this endless wasteland, for other than the fierce tribes of the Ravirii, no one could survive the desert's murderous sun for very long.

As it was, we felt a whiff of its heat even hundreds of miles north of the heart of it. But after the freezing rains of the mountains, we welcomed this sudden warming of the air, for it was dry like the breath of the stars and clean, and did not smother us. It did not last long, either, giving way soon after noon to gentle breezes that swept through the swaying grasses and touched our faces with the scents of strange new plants and flowers.

And at night, beneath the constellations that hung in the heavens like a brilliant, blazing tapestry, it fell quite cool – not so much that it chilled our bones, but rather that bracing crispness that sharpens all the senses and invites the marvel of the infinite.

We all slept quite well through that first dark out on the steppe – except during those hours when we were standing watch or simply gazing up at the stars from our beds on top of the long grass. The moon rose over the world like a gleaming half-shield; beneath it, from far out across the luminous earth, wolves howled and lions roared. I dreamed of these animals that night, and of eagles and falcons, and great silver swans that flew so high they caught the fire of the stars. When I awoke in the morning to a sky so blue that it seemed to go on forever, I felt this fire in me, warming my heart and calling me to journey forth toward the completion of our quest.

We rode hard all that day and the next, and the two following that. Although I worried we might press the horses too strenuously, they took great strength from the grass all around us, both in its sweet smell and in the bellyfuls they bit off and ate at midday and night. After many days of picking their way up and down steep mountain tracks studded with sharp rocks, they seemed glad for the feel of soft earth beneath their hooves. It was their pleasure to keep moving across the windy steppe, at a fast walk and sometimes at a canter or even a gallop. I felt my excitement flowing into Altaru and firing up his great heart, and his delight in running unbound across the wild and open steppe passing back into me. Sometimes he raced Iolo or Fire just for the sheer singing joy of it. And at such moments, I realized that our souls *were* free, and each of us knew this in the surging of our blood and our breaths upon the wind – and in the promises we made to ourselves.

It was hard for me, used to the more circumscribed horizons of mountainous or wooded country, to see just how far we traveled each day. But Atara had a better eye for distances here. She put the tally at a good fifty miles. So it was that we crossed almost the whole length of southern Eanna in very little time. And in all that wide land, dotted with cottonwood trees whose silver-green leaves were nearly as beautiful as astors', we saw almost no people.

'I should think *someone* would live here,' Liljana said on the fifth morning of our journey across the steppe. 'This is a fair land – it can't be the wolves that have scared them away. Nor even the lions.'

Later that day, toward noon, we came across some nomads who solved the mystery of Eanna's emptiness for us. The head of the thirty members of this band, who lived in tents woven from the hair of the shaggy cattle they tended, boldly presented himself as Jacarun the Elder.

He was a whitebeard whose bushy brows overhung his suspicious old eyes. But when he saw that we meant no harm and wanted only to cross his country, he was free with the milk and cheeses that his people got from their cattle – and with advice as well.

'We are the Telamun,' he explained to us as we broke from our journey to take a meal with his family. 'And once we were a great people.'

He told us that only a few generations before, the Telamun in their two great tribes had ruled this land. So great was their prowess at arms that the Kings in Imatru had feared to send their armies here. But then, after a blood-feud brought about by a careless insult, murder and an escalating sequence of revenge killings, the two tribes had gone to war against each other rather than with their common enemies. In the space of only twenty years, they had nearly wiped each other out.

'A few dozen families like ours, we're all that's left,' Jacarun said as he held up his drover's staff and swept it out across the plain. 'Now we've given up war – unless you count beating off wolves with sticks as war.'

He went on to say that their days as a free people were almost over, for others were now eyeing his family's ancient lands and even moving into them.

'King Hanniban has been having trouble with his barons, it's said, so hasn't yet been able to muster the few companies that it would take to conquer us,' he told us. 'But some of the Ravirii have come up from the Red Desert – they butchered a family not fifty miles from here. And the Yarkonans, well, in the long run, they're the real threat, of course. Count Ulanu of Aigul – they call him Ulanu the Handsome – has it in mind to conquer all of Yarkona in the Red Dragon's name and set himself up as King. If he ever does, he'll turn his gaze west and send his crucifiers here.'

He called for one of his daughters to bring us some roasted beef. And then, after fixing his weary old eyes on Kane and my other friends, he looked at me and asked, 'And where are you bound, Sar Valashu?'

'To Yarkona,' I said.

'Aha, I thought so! To the Library at Khaisham, yes?'

'How did you know?'

'Well, you're not the first pilgrims to cross our lands on their way to the Library, though you may be the last.' He sighed as he lifted his staff toward the sky. 'There was a time, and not so long ago, when many pilgrims came this way. We always charged them tribute for their safe passage, not much, only a little silver and sometimes a few grains of gold. But those days are past; soon it is *we* who will have to pay tribute for living here. In any case, no one goes to Yarkona anymore – it's an accursed land.'

He advised us that, if we insisted on completing our journey, we should avoid Aigul and Count Ulanu's demesne at all costs.

We ate our roasted beef then, and washed it down with some fermented milk that Jacarun called *laas*. After visiting with his family and admiring the fatness of their cattle – and restraining Maram from doing likewise with their women – we thanked Jacarun for his hospitality and set out again.

Soon the steppe, which had gradually been drying out as we drew further away from the Crescent Mountains, grew quite sere. The greens of its grasses gave way to yellow and umber and more somber tones. Many new shrubs found root here in the rockier soil: mostly bitterbroom and yusage, as Kane named these tough-looking plants. They gave shelter to lizards, thrashers, rock sparrows and other animals that I had never seen before. As the sun fell down the long arc of the sky behind us in its journey into night, it grew slightly warmer instead of cooler. We put quite a few miles behind us, though not so many as on the four preceding afternoons. The horses, perhaps sensing that they would find less water and food to the east, began moving more slowly as if to conserve their strength. And as we approached the land that Jacarun had warned us against, we turned our gazes inward to look for strength of our own.

And then, just before dusk, with the sun casting its longest rays over a glowing, reddened land, we came to a little trickle of water that Kane called the Parth. From its sandy banks, we looked out on the distant rocky outcroppings of Yarkona. There, I prayed, we would at last find the end of our journey and our hearts' deepest desire.

30

T he moon that night was just past full and tinged a glowing red. It
hung low in conjunction with a blazing twist of stars that some
called the Snake Constellation and others the Dragon.

'Blood Moon in the Dragon,' Master Juwain said. He sat sipping his
tea and looking up at the sky. 'I haven't seen suchlike in many years.'

He brought out his book then, and sat reading quietly by the firelight,
perhaps looking for some passage that would comfort him and turn his
attentions away from the stars. And then Liljana, who had gone off to
wash the dishes in a small stream that led back to the Parth, returned
holding some stones in her hand. They were black and shiny like Kane's
gelstei but had more the look of melted glass. Liljana called them Angels'
Tears; she said that wherever they were found, the earth would weep with
the sorrow of the heavens. Atara gazed at these three, droplike stones as
she might her much clearer crystal. Although her eyes darkened and I
felt a great heaviness descend upon her heart like a stormcloud, she,
too, sat quietly sipping her tea and saying nothing.

We slept uneasily that night, and Kane didn't sleep at all. He stood
for hours keeping watch, looking for lions in the shadows of the
moon-reddened rocks or enemies approaching across the darkling
plain. Alphanderry, who couldn't sleep either, brought out his mandolet
and sang to keep him company. And unseen by him, Flick spun only
desultorily to his music. He seemed to want to hide from the bloody
moon above us.

And so the hours of night passed, and the heavens turned slowly
about the rutilant earth. When morning came, we had a better look
at this harsher country into which we had ventured. Yarkona, Master
Juwain said, meant the 'Green Land,' but there was little of this hue
about it. Neither true steppe nor quite desert, the sparse grass here was
burnt brown by a much hotter sun. The yusage had been joined by
its even tougher cousins: ursage and spiny sage, whose spiked leaves

discouraged the brush voles and deer from browsing upon them. We saw a few of these cautious animals in the early light, framed by some blackish cliffs to the east. These sharp prominences had a charred looked about them, as if the sun had set fire to the very stone. But Kane said their color came from the basalt that formed them; the rocks, he told us, were the very bones of the earth, which the hot winds blowing up from the south had laid bare.

He also told us that we had made camp in Sagaram, a domain that some local lord had carved out of this once-great realm perhaps a century before. We looked to him for knowledge that might help us cross it. But as he admitted, he had come this way many years ago, in more peaceful times. Since then, he said, the boundaries of Yarkona's little baronies and possessions had no doubt shifted like a desert's sands, perhaps some of them having been blown away by war altogether.

'Aigul lies some sixty miles from here to the north and east,' he told us. 'Unless it has grown since then, and its counts have annexed lands to the south.'

These lands we set out to cross on that dry, windy morning. Sagaram proved to be little more than a thin strip of shrubs and sere grasses running seventy or so miles along the Parth. By early afternoon, we had made our way clear into the next domain, although no river or stone marked the border, and we didn't realize it at the time. It took some more miles of plodding across the hot, rising plain before we found anyone who could give us directions. This was a goatherd who lived in a little stone house by a well in sight of a rather striking rock formation to the east of us.

'You've come to Karkut,' he told us as he shared a little cheese and bread with us. He was a short man, neither young nor old, with a great flowing tunic pulled over his spare frame and tied at the waist with a bit of dirty rope. 'To the north of us lies Hansh and Aigul; to the south is the Nashthalan. That's mostly desert now, and you'll want to stay well to the north of it if you're to come to Khaisham safely.'

While his two young sons watered our horses, he advised us to make our way directly east along the hills above the Nashthalan; after crossing through Sarad, he said, we should turn north along the dip in the White Mountains and so come to Khaisham that way.

But even as we were sharing a cup of brandy with him and eating some dried figs, a knight wearing a green and white surcoat over his gleaming mail came riding down from the rock formation above us. He had the same browned skin and dark beard as the goatherd, but he rode with an air of confidence as if his lord commanded the lands hereabouts. He presented himself as Rinald, son of Omar the Quiet; he said that he was in the service of Lord Nicolaym, who had a castle hidden in the rocks above us.

'We saw you ride up to the well,' he told us, looking from me to my friends. 'We were afraid that you would pass this way unheralded.'

He came down from his horse and broke bread with us. He was only too happy to share some of our brandy, too, which was the nearly the last of the vintage we had carried from Tria.

'Lord Nicolaym,' he said to us, 'would like to offer his hospitality, for the night or as many nights as you wish.'

I thought of the golden cup that likely awaited us in Khaisham. An image sprang into my mind of time running out of it like the sands from an hourglass. If we came to Khaisham too late, I thought, we might find the Library emptied of the Lightstone, perhaps carried away by another.

'Sar Valashu?'

I looked up at the sun, still high in the cloudless sky. We had many hours left that day that we might travel, and I told Rinald this.

'Of course, you're free to ride on as you please,' Rinald said to us. 'Lord Nicolaym doesn't order the comings and goings of pilgrims or charge them tolls as some do. But you should be careful of where you go. Not everyone welcomes pilgrims these days.'

With an apology to the goatherd, he went on to dispute his advice that we should journey east through Sarad.

'Baron Jadur's knights are jealous of their borders there,' Rinald told us. 'Although they hate Count Ulanu, they've no love of Khaisham and the Librarians, either. It's said that for many years they've turned pilgrims away from their domain – those they haven't plundered or imprisoned.'

At this news, the goatherd took a drink of brandy and shrugged his shoulders. His business, he said, was keeping his goats fat and healthy, not in keeping apprised of the injustices of distant lords.

As for injustice, Rinald informed us sadly that there was too much of that in his own domain. 'Duke Rasham is a good enough man, but some of his lords have gone over to the Kallimun – we're not quite sure which ones. But there have been murders of those who speak for joining arms with Khaisham. We caught an assassin trying to murder Lord Nicolaym just last month. You should be careful in Karkut, I'm sorry to say, Sar Valashu. These are evil times.'

'It would seem that we must take care wherever we go in Yarkona,' I told him.

'That is true,' he said. 'But there are some domains you must avoid at all costs. Aigul, of course. And to the west of those crucifiers,

Brahamdur, whose baron and lords are practically Count Ulanu's slaves. And Sagaram – you were lucky to cross it unmolested, for they've been forced into an alliance with Aigul. To the north of us, between here and Aigul, Hansh has nearly lost its freedom as well. It's said that soon Count Ulanu will press Hansh levies into his army.'

Maram, of course, didn't like the news that he was hearing. He looked at me a long moment before asking Rinald, 'How are we to reach Khaisham, then?'

'The route through Madhvam would be the safest,' Rinald said, naming the domain just east of us. 'There's strength there for opposing Count Ulanu; their knights *would* join Khaisham in arms but for their bad blood with Sarad. That feud occupies all their attentions, I'm afraid. I haven't heard, though, that they have any quarrel with pilgrims.'

But Madhvam, as Maram learned, adjoined Aigul to its north, and that was too close for him. 'What if this Ulanu the Handsome attacks Madhvam while we're crossing it?'

'No, that's impossible,' Rinald said. 'We've just had word that Count Ulanu has marched against Sikar. The fortifications of that city are the strongest in all Yarkona. He'll be at least a month reducing them.'

Sikar, he said, lay a good sixty miles north of Madhvam up against the White Mountains, with the domain of Virad partially squeezed in between. He told us then what Duke Rasham and Lord Nicolaym supposed would be Count Ulanu's strategy for the conquest of Yarkona.

'Khaisham is the key to everything that Count Ulanu desires,' Rinald told us. 'Other than Aigul, it's the strongest domain in Yarkona, and Virad, Sikar and Inyam all look to the Librarians to lead the opposition against the Count. If Khaisham falls, the whole of the north will fall as well. Count Ulanu already has the west under his thumb. Hansh, too. The middle domains – Madhvam and Sarad, even Karkut – can't stand alone. And once Aigul has swallowed us all up, it will be nothing for the Count's army to take the Nashthalan.'

His words encouraged us to finish our brandy in quick swallows. And then Maram said, 'Ah, well, I should think that the Count's invasion of Sikar would lead all the free domains to join against him.'

'That is my lord's hope, too,' Rinald said. 'But I'm afraid that many lords think otherwise. They say that if Count Ulanu's conquest is inevitable, they should join *with* him rather than wind up nailed to crosses.'

'Nothing's inevitable,' Kane growled out, 'except such cowardly talk.'

'That is so,' Rinald said. 'Even Sikar's fall is uncertain. If only Khaisham's knights would ride to its aid . . .'

'Will they?' I asked.

'No one knows. The Librarians are brave enough, and none better at arms. But for a thousand years, they've used them only in defense of their books.'

'Then what about Virad? What about Inyam?' I asked, naming the domain north of Virad and between Sikar and Khaisham.

'I think they'll wait to see what Khaisham does,' Rinald says. 'If the Librarians stay behind their walls and Sikar falls, then likely they'll sue for peace.'

'You mean, surrender,' Kane snarled.

'Better that than crucifixion, many would say.'

Because Kane's flashing eyes were difficult to behold just then, I turned toward Maram, who was looking for reasons to abandon his courage.

'If the Red Dragon desires the conquest of Yarkona so badly,' he said, 'I don't see why he doesn't just send an army to reduce it. Sakai isn't so far from here, is it? What could stop him?'

'Niggardliness could,' Atara said perceptively. 'I think the Lord of Lies is very careful: he hoards his forces like a miser does gold.'

'Just so,' Rinald said. 'For him such a conquest would be an expensive campaign.'

'How so?' Maram asked.

'If I had a map, I would show you,' Rinald said. 'But there's no good route from Sakai to Yarkona. If a Sakayan army tried the Red Desert, the heat would kill them like flies if the Ravirii didn't first.'

'What about the direct route through the mountains?'

'That would be even more dangerous,' Rinald said. 'The White Mountains, at least the stretch of that range between Yarkona and Sakai, is the land of the Ymanir. *They* are much worse than the Ravirii.'

He went on to say that the Ymanir were also called the Frost Giants; they were savage men nearly eight feet tall and covered with white fur, who were known to kill all who entered their country and eat them.

'Frost Giants, is it now?' Maram exclaimed as he shuddered. 'Oh, too much, too much.'

I felt my own insides churning as I looked at the war-torn landscape to the east and tried to make out the great White Mountains beyond. In the haze of the burning distances, I saw a golden room whose great iron door was slowly closing like that of a vault. We had to enter the room safely and get out again before we were trapped inside.

'Val,' Maram said to me, 'I don't have a very good feeling about this land. Perhaps we should turn back before it's too late.'

I looked at him then, and the fire in my eyes told him that I wasn't about to come within inches of fulfilling the quest simply to turn back. This same fire blazed inside Kane and Atara, and in Liljana,

Alphanderry and Master Juwain. It smoldered, too, beneath the damp leaves of Maram's fear, even if he didn't know it.

'All right, all right, don't look at me like that,' Maram said to me. 'If we must go on, we must. But let's go soon, okay?'

And with that, we finished our little meal and thanked the goatherd for his hospitality. Then Rinald helped us finally decide our route: we would cut through Karkut and Madhvam toward the northeast along the line of the Nashbrum River. And then turn southeast through Virad's canyon lands, coming eventually to a little spur running down from the White Mountains that separated Virad and Inyam from Khaisham. There we would find a pass called the Kul Joram, and beyond that, Khaisham.

'I wish you well,' Rinald said to us as he mounted his horse. 'I'll remind Lord Nicolaym to keep a few rooms empty for your return.'

We watched him ride off toward the rocks above us and the castle that we couldn't see. And then we turned to mount our horses as well.

All that hot afternoon we rode along the line that Rinald had advised. We found the Nashbrum, a smallish river that ran down from the mountains and seemed to narrow and lose substance to the burning earth as it flowed toward the Nashthalan. Cottonwood trees grew along its course, and we kept their shimmering leaves in sight as we paralleled it almost all the way to Madhvam. We were lucky to come across none of the traitorous lords or knights who had gone over to the Kallimun. We made camp along the Nashbrum's sandy banks, keeping a careful watch.

But the night passed peacefully enough; only the howling of some wolves pointing their snouts toward the moon reminded us that we were not alone in this desolate country. When morning came, clear and blue and hinting of a sweltering heat later in the day, we set out early and rode quickly through what coolness we could find. It was good, I thought, that we kept close to the river; the sweating horses made free with its water and so did we. By the time the sun crested the sky, we decided to break for our midday meal beneath the shade of a great, gnarled cottonwood. No one was hungry enough to eat, but at least we had some cover from the blistering sun.

But soon enough, we had to set out again. Toward mid-afternoon, some big clouds formed up and let loose a quick burst of thunder and rain. It lasted only long enough to wet the ursage and dried grasses and the sharp rocks that tore at our horses' hooves. It was a measure of our desire to reach Khaisham that we still made a good distance that day. By the time the sun had left its fierceness behind it in the waves of heat radiating off the glowing land, we found ourselves in the domain

516

of Virad. To the north of us, and to the east, too, the knifelike peaks of the White Mountains caught the red fire of the setting sun.

'Well, that was a day,' Maram said. He wiped the sweat from his dripping brown curls and dismounted to look for some wood for the night's fire. 'I'm hot, I'm thirsty, I'm tired. And what's worse,' he said, pressing his nose to his armpit, 'I stink. This heat is much worse than the rain in the Crescent Mountains.'

'Hmmph,' Atara said to him, 'it's only worse because you're suffering from it *now*. Just wait until our return.'

'If we *do* return,' he muttered. He scratched at some beads of sweat in the thick beard along his neck as he looked about. 'Val, are you sure this is Virad?'

I pointed along the river where it abruptly turned north about five miles across the rocky ground ahead of us. I said, 'Rinald told us to look for that turning. There, we're to set our course to the southeast and so come to the pass after another forty miles.'

Directly to the east of us, I saw, was a large swelling of black rock impossible to cross on horses. And so, at the river's turning, we would ride up and around it.

'Well, then, we must have ridden nearly forty miles today.'

'Too far,' Kane said, coming over to us and studying the terrain around us. 'We pressed the horses too hard. Tomorrow we'll have to satisfy ourselves with half that distance.'

'I don't like the look of this country,' Maram said. 'I don't want to remain here any longer than we have to.'

'If we cripple the horses, we'll be here even longer,' Kane told him. 'Do you want to walk to Khaisham?'

That night, we fortified our camp with some of the logs and branches we found down by the river. The moon, when it rose over the black hills, was clearly waning though still nearly full. It set the wolves farther out on the plain to howling: a high-pitched, plaintive sound that had always unnerved Maram – and Liljana and Master Juwain, as well. To soothe them, Alphanderry plucked the strings of his mandolet and sang of ages past and brighter times to come when the Galadin and Elijin would walk the earth again. His clear voice rang out across the river, echoing from the ominous-looking rocks. It brought cheer to us all, though it also touched Kane with a deep dread I felt pulling at his insides like the teeth of something much worse than wolves.

'Too loud,' Kane muttered at Alphanderry. 'This isn't Alonia, eh? Nor even Surrapam.'

After that Alphanderry sang more quietly, and the golden tones pouring from his throat seemed to harmonize with the wolves' howls, softening them and rendering them less haunting. But then, above his beautiful voice and those of the wolves, from the north of us where the river turned into some low hills, came a distant keening sound that was terrible to hear.

'Shhh,' Maram said, tapping Alphanderry's knee, 'what was that?'

Alphanderry now put down his mandolet and listened with the rest of us. Again came the far-off keening, and then an answering sound, much closer, from the hills to the east. It was like the shrieking of a cat and the scream of a wounded horse and the cries of the damned all bound up into a single, piercing howl.

'That's no wolf!' Maram called out. 'What is it?'

Again came the howl, closer, and this time it had something of a crow's cawing and a bear's growl about it: OWRRRUULLL!

Kane jumped to his feet and drew his sword. It seemed to point of its own toward the terrible sound.

'Do you know what that is?' Maram asked him, also drawing his sword.

OWRRULLLLL!

Now all of us, except Master Juwain, took up weapons and stood staring at the moonlit rocks across the river.

'Ah, for the love of woman, Kane, please tell us if you know what we're facing!'

But Kane remained silent, staring off into the dark. The cry came again, but it seemed to be moving away from us. After a while, it faded and then vanished into the night.

'This is *too* too much,' Maram said. He turned toward Kane accusingly as if it was he who had called forth the hideous voices. 'Wolves don't howl like that.'

'No,' Kane muttered, 'but the Blues do.'

'The Blues!' Maram said. 'Who or what are the Blues?'

But it was Master Juwain who answered him. He knelt by the fire, reading from his book as he quoted from the *Visions*: '"Then came the blue men, the half-dead whose cries will wake the dead. They are the heralds of the Red Dragon, and the ghosts of battle follow them to war."'

He closed his book and said, 'I've always wondered what those lines meant.'

'They mean this,' Kane said. 'None of us will sleep tonight.'

He told us then what he knew of the Blues. He said that they were a short, immensely squat and powerful people, a race of warriors bred by Morjin during the Age of Swords. It was their gift – or curse – to have few nerves in their bodies and so to feel little pain. This gift was deepened by their eating the berries of the kirque plant, which enabled them to march into battle in a frenzy of unfeeling wrath toward their foes. The berries also stained their skin a pale shade of blue; most of their men accentuated this color by rubbing berry juice across their skin so that the whole of their bodies were blemished a deep blue the color of a bruise. Most of them, as well, displayed many scabs, open cuts and running sores across their arms and legs, for in their nearly nerveless immunity to pain, they were wont to wound themselves and take no notice of the injury. But others couldn't help noticing them: they went into battle naked wielding huge, terrible, steel axes. They howled like maddened wolves. They killed without pity or feeling as if their souls had died. Because of this, they were called the Soulless Ones or the Half-Dead.

'But if the Beast created these warriors during the Age of Swords for battle,' Master Juwain asked, thumping his book, 'why isn't more told of their feats in here?'

'There are other books,' Kane said, scanning the gleaming terrain about us. 'If we ever reach the Library, maybe you'll read them.'

As if realizing that he had spoken too harshly to a man he had come to respect, he softened his voice and said, 'As for their feats, they were almost too terrible to record. Great axes they wielded, remember, and they had even less care for others' flesh than they did their own.'

He went on to say that Morjin had employed the Blues in his initial conquest of Alonia. They had left almost no one alive to tell of their terror. They had also proved almost impossible to control. And so after one particularly vicious battle, Morjin – the Lord of Lies, the Treacherous One – had invited the entire host of Blues to a victory celebration. There, with his own hand, he had poured into their cups a poisoned wine.

'It's said that all the Blues perished in a single night,' Kane told us, looking toward the mountains to the north. 'But I think that some must have escaped to take refuge here. I've long heard it rumored that there was some terror hidden in the White Mountains – other than the Frost Giants, of course.'

In silence, we all looked at the great, snow-capped peaks glistering in the moonlight. And then Maram said, 'But we're still a good forty miles from the mountains. If it *is* the Blues we heard, what are they doing in the hills of Yarkona?'

'That I would like to know,' Kane told him. Then he clapped him on the arm and smiled his savage smile. 'But not *too* badly. And not tonight. Now why don't we at least try to sleep? Alphanderry and I will take the first watch. If the Blues come back to sing for us, we'll be sure to wake you.'

519

But the Half-Dead, if such they really were, did not return that night. Even so, none of us got much sleep. By the time morning came, we were all red-eyed and crabby, almost too tired to pull ourselves on top of our footsore horses. We prayed for a few clouds to soften the sun. Each hour, however, it waxed hotter and hotter so that it threatened to set all the sky on fire.

We rode through a land devoid of people. After we turned southeast at the bend in the river, we sought out the few scattered huts along the rock-humped plain to gather knowledge of the country through which we passed. But the huts were all empty, deserted it seemed in great haste. Perhaps, I thought, the cries of the Soulless Ones had driven their owners away. Perhaps they had fled for protection to a nearby castle of some local lord.

Late that morning, we saw some vultures circling in the sky ahead of us. As we rode closer, the air thickened with a terrible smell. Maram wanted to turn aside from whatever lay in that direction, but Kane was eager as always to see what must be seen. And so we pressed on until we crested a low rise. And there before us, growing out of the sage and grass like trees, were three wooden crosses from which hung the blackened bodies of three naked men. Vultures, perched on the arms of the crosses, bent their beaks downward, working at them. When Kane saw these death birds, his face darkened and his heart filled with wrath. He charged forward, waving his sword and growling like a wolf himself. At first, the vultures managed to ignore him. But such was his fury that when his sword leapt out to impale one of the vultures in the chest, the others sprang into the air and began circling warily about, waiting for the maddened Kane to leave them to their feast.

'How I hate these damn birds!' Kane raged as he dismounted to wipe his sword on the grass. 'They make a mockery of the One's noblest creation.'

We rode up to him, holding our cloaks over our noses against the awful smell. I forced myself to look up at these husks of once-proud men, which iron nails and the iron-hard beaks of the vultures had reduced so pitifully. To Kane, I said, 'You didn't tell us that the Blues learned the defilements of the Crucifier.'

'I never heard that they did,' he said, looking at the crosses. 'This may be the work of some lord who has gone over to the Kallimun.'

'What lord?' Liljana asked, nudging her horse closer to Kane. 'Rinald said that the lords of Virad looked to Khaisham for leadership.'

'So, it seems that some of them may look to Aigul.'

I dismounted Altaru and walked over to the center cross. I reached out and touched the foot of the man who had been nailed to it.

His flesh was soft, swollen and hot – as hot as the burning air itself.

'We should bury these men,' I said.

Kane stuck his sword down into the rock-hard earth. 'We *should* bury them, Val. But it would take us a day of digging, eh? Whoever put them here may come back and find us.'

Maram, whose hand was trembling as he held his cloak tightly covering his face, said, 'Come, please, let's go before it's too late!'

And then Kane, always a man of oppositions, snarled out, 'He's right, we should go. Let's leave these birds their meal. Even vultures must eat.'

And so, after a saying a prayer for the three men who had ended their lives in this desolate place, we mounted our horses and resumed our journey. But as we rode over the hot, tormented earth, Alphanderry wet his throat with a little blood from his cracked lips and gave us a song to hearten us. He made a hauntingly beautiful music in remembrance of the dead men, singing their souls up to the stars behind the deep blue sky. Despite the terrible thing we had just seen, his words were in praise of life:

> *Sing ye songs of glory,*
> *Sing ye songs of glory,*
> *That the light of the One*
> *Will shine upon the world.*

'Too loud,' Kane muttered as he scanned the low hills about us.

But Alphanderry, perhaps concentrating on an image of the Lightstone that lay somewhere before us, raised up his voice even louder. He sang strongly and bravely, with a reckless abandon, and his voice filled the countryside. Even the grasses, I thought, sere and stunted here, would want to weep at the sound of it.

'Too damn loud, I say!' Kane barked out, flashing an angry look at Alphanderry. 'Do you want to announce us to the whole world?'

Alphanderry, however, seemed drunk on the beauty of his own singing. He ignored Kane. After a while, strange and wonderful words began pouring from his lips in a torrent that seemed impossible to stop.

'Damn you, Alphanderry, come to your senses, will you?'

As Kane glowered at Alphanderry, he finally fell quiet. The look on his face was that of a scolded puppy. To Kane, he said, 'I'm sorry, but I was so close. So very close to finding the words of the angels.'

'If the crucifiers come upon us here,' Kane said, 'not even the angels will be able to help us.'

Even as he said this, Atara pointed at a far-off hill. I looked there and thought I saw a hazy figure vanish behind it.

'What is it?' Kane asked, squinting.

Atara, who had the best eyes of any of us, said, 'It was a man – he seemed dressed in blue.'

At this news, Maram sat swallowing against the fear in his throat as if he could so easily make it go away.

'I'm sorry,' Alphanderry said again. 'But maybe the blue man didn't see us.'

'Foolish minstrel,' Kane said softly. 'Let's ride now, and hope he didn't.'

And so we set out again, riding as swiftly as we dared for half an hour. And with each mile we covered, the air grew hotter so that it fairly roiled, and the stench of death stayed with us. We entered a country of rolling swells of earth like the waves of the sea; some were a hundred feet high and broken with rocky outcroppings. We kept a reasonably straight course, winding our way down their troughs. After a while, I felt a sick sensation along the back of my neck as if the vultures were watching me. I stopped and turned toward the left; I looked toward the top of the rise even as Atara did, too.

'What is it?' Maram said, reining up behind us. 'What do you see?'

We had been told to avoid Aigul, and so we had. But Aigul hadn't avoided us. Just as Maram swallowed another mouthful of air and belched in disquiet, a company of cavalry broke over the rise and thundered down the slope straight toward us. There were twenty-three of them, as I saw at a glance. Their mail and helms gleamed in the sun. And holstered and upraised from a horse near their leader was a long pole from which streamed their standard: a bright yellow banner showing the coils and fiery tongue of a great red dragon.

'Oh, my Lord!' Maram cried out. 'Oh, my Lord!'

Liljana, who had drawn her sword, looked about with her calm, penetrating eyes and said to me, 'Do we flee or fight, Val?'

'Perhaps neither,' I said, trying to keep my voice calm for Maram's sake – and my own. I turned, pointing toward the right, where a hummock stood like a grass-covered castle. 'Up there – we'll face them up there.'

'That's very right,' Master Juwain said reassuringly as he looked at the men bearing down on us. 'This is probably just some wayward lord and his retainers. If we flee, he'll think we're thieves or afraid of them.'

'Well, we are afraid of them!' Maram pointed out. He might have said more, but we had already turned to gallop up the hummock, and the shock of his horse's heaving muscles drove the wind from him.

It took us only a few moments to gain what little protection the hummock's height provided us. Its top was nearly flat, perhaps fifty yards across; we sat on our horses there as we watched the men approach. I didn't remark what we could now see quite plainly: that next to this great lord, who bore upon his yellow surcoat another red dragon, rode three naked men whose bodies seemed painted blue. Their little mountain ponies carried them up our hummock with greater agility than did the war horses of their more heavily armored companions. Each of the three men were short and immensely muscled, and they each brandished in their knotted fists an immense steel axe.

'I'm sorry,' Alphanderry said to Kane, who had his sword drawn as his black eyes stared down at the approaching company.

'It's not your sorrow that we need now, my young friend,' Kane said with a grim smile, 'but your strength. And your courage.'

The company drew up in a crescent on the slope below us. And then their leader, along with the standard-bearer and one of the blue men, rode forward a few paces. He was a quick-eyed man with a vulpine look to his hard face, which seemed all angles and planes, like pieces of chipped flint. Many would have called him handsome, a grace that he seemed to relish as he sat up straight on his horse in all his vanity and pride. His eyes were almost as dark as his well-trimmed beard; they fixed upon me like poisoned lances that pierced my heart with all the darkness of his.

'Who are you?' he called out to me in a raspy voice. 'Come down and identify yourselves!'

'Who are you,' I said to him, 'who rides upon us in surprise like robbers?'

'Robbers, is it?' he said. 'Be careful how you speak to the lord of this domain!'

I traded a quick look with Kane and then Atara, who held her strung bow down against her saddle. Rinald had told us that Virad's lord was Duke Vikram, an old man with scars along his white-bearded face. To this much younger man below us, I said, 'We had heard that the lord of this domain is Duke Vikram.'

'Not any more,' the man said with glee. 'Duke Vikram is dead. I'm the lord of Virad now. And of Sikar and Aigul. You may address me as Count Ulanu.'

It came to me, all in a moment, what the terrible stench in the air must be: the taint of many corpses rotting in the sun. Somewhere near here, I knew, a battle had recently been fought. And Count Ulanu claimed the lordship of Virad by right of conquest.

'You have my name, now give me yours,' the Count said to me.

'We're pilgrims,' I told him, 'only pilgrims bound for Khaisham.'

'Pilgrims with swords,' he said, looking at Kane, Maram and Liljana. Then he turned his gaze on me and studied my face for a long time. 'It's said that the Valari look like you.'

I slipped my hand beneath my cloak as I rested it on the hilt of my sword. I noticed Maram gripping his red crystal in his free hand even as Liljana held her blue stone to her head.

'What's that you've got in your hand?' Count Ulanu barked at her.

But Liljana didn't answer him; she just sat staring at him as if her eyes could drink up all the challenge in his and still hold more.

Count Ulanu bent his head to whisper something to one of the Blues, whose large, round head was shaved and stained darkly with the juice of the kirque berries, even as Kane had said. One of his ears was missing, and the skin about the hole there all scabbed over. Along his side, he showed an open wound, probably from a sword cut; in the dark red suck of it squirmed many white maggots eating away the decaying flesh there. As he pointed at Alphanderry and whispered back to Count Ulanu, I understood that this was the man who had sighted us earlier. Most likely, he had then gone to fetch the Count and his other men upon us.

'You picked an evil time for your pilgrimage,' the Count said, looking up at us. His raspy voice had now softened as if he were trying to lure a reluctant serving girl into his chambers. 'There has been unrest in Sikar and in Virad. Both Duke Amadam and Duke Vikram were forced to ask our help in putting down rebellions. This we did. We've recently fought a battle not far from here, at Tarmanam. Victory was ours, but sadly, Duke Vikram was killed. A few of the rebellious lords and their knights escaped us. They'll likely turn to outlawry now and fall upon pilgrims such as you. This country isn't safe. That is why we must ask you to lay down your arms and come with us for your own protection.'

I sat on top of Altaru sweating in the burning sun as I listened to him. I smelled the acridness of his own sweat and that of the knights about him. I knew that he was lying, even if I couldn't quite tell what the truth really was. I noticed Liljana suddenly close her eyes; it was strange how she seemed to be staring straight at him even so.

'You might ask us to lay down,' Kane told him, with surprising politeness, 'but we must respectfully decline your request.'

'I'm afraid we must to do more than ask,' Count Ulanu said, his voice rising with anger. 'Please lay down now and come with us.'

'No,' Kane told him. 'No, we can't do that.'

'When peace has been restored,' the Count went on, 'we'll provide you an escort to Khaisham so that you may complete your pilgrimage.'

'No, thank you,' Kane said icily.

'You have my word that you'll be treated honorably and well,'

Count Ulanu said, smiling sincerely. 'There's a tower for guests at Duke Vikram's castle – it overlooks the Ashbrum River. We'll be happy to set you up there.'

Now Liljana's nose pointed straight toward him as if she were sniffing out poison in a cup. She suddenly opened her eyes to stare at him as she said, 'He speaks the truth: there are many towers of wood now at the Duke's castle. He intends to set us on these crosses with the Duke's knights and his family.'

The sudden rage that enpurpled Count Ulanu's face just then was terrible to behold. He whipped out his saber and pointed it at Liljana as he shouted, 'Damn you, witch! Give me what's in your hand before I cut it off and take it from you!'

Liljana opened her hand to show him her blue gelstei. Then she smiled defiantly as she closed her hand about the stone and stuck her fist out toward him.

'Damn witch,' the Count muttered.

'There *was* a battle at Tarmanam,' she said to all who could hear. 'But there were no rebellious lords – only those faithful to Duke Vikram, who has been cruelly tortured to death.'

In her frightfully calm and measured way, she went on to tell us something of what she had seen in the Count's mind. She said that he and his army had marched into Sikar even as Rinald had told us. But there had been no siege of the mighty fortifications there. As soon as the Count's engineers had set up their catapults and battering rams, his army had been joined by a host of Blues. And then Kallimun priests within the city had assassinated the Duke of Sikar and his family; the Duke's cousin, Baron Mukal, bowing before the terror of these priests, had thrown open the city gates. Hostages had been taken and threatened with crucifixion. The Sikar army had then gone over to the Count, taking oaths of loyalty to him and his distant master. Thus Sikar had fallen in scarcely a day.

Count Ulanu had then gathered up both armies – and the companies of Blues. In a lightning strike, he had swept south, into Virad. Duke Vikram and his lords had had no time to watch events unfold in Sikar and to sue for peace on favorable terms; their only choice was to surrender unconditionally or to ride out to battle. With the Khaisham Librarians still preparing to send a force to Sikar, much too late, Duke Vikram chose to fight alone over bowing to Count Ulanu and the Red Dragon. But his forces had been slaughtered and many of the survivors crucified. And now his captured family awaited the same fate, imprisoned in his own castle.

'It was treachery that took Sikar,' Liljana said to us. 'And, listen, do you hear the lies in the Count's words? He promises us more treachery with every breath.'

As Count Ulanu stared at her, I was given to understand that he had been out riding with his personal guard in search of the best route to march his army through to Khaisham when one of his Blues had alerted him as to our presence.

On either side of the Count, two of his knights, clad in mail and armed with wicked-looking, curved swords, nudged their horses closer to him as if to steady him and show their support in the face of Liljana's barbs. It was to her that the Count now said, 'You know many things but not the one that really matters.'

'And what is that, dear Count?' Liljana asked.

'In the end, you'll beg to be allowed to bow before me and kiss my feet. How long has it been, *old witch*, since you've kissed a man?'

In answer, Liljana again held out her fist to him, this time with her middle finger extended.

The Count's face filled with hate, but he had the force of will to channel it into his derisive words: 'Why don't you try looking into my mind *now*?'

Then he, this priest of the Kallimun, turned upon her a gaze so venomous and full of malice that she gave a cry of pain. As something dark yet clear as a black crystal flared inside him, I felt the still-sheathed Alkaladur flare as well even through its jade hilt.

'What a gracious lord you are!' she said. She continued to stare at him despite her obvious anguish. 'I should imagine that all Yarkona has remarked your exemplary manners.'

I knew, of course, what she intended, and I approved her strategy: she was trying to use her blue gelstei and all the sharpness of her tongue to provoke the Count into an action against us. For surely there must be a battle between us; it would be best for us if we forced the Count and his men to fight it, here, upon this high ground, charging up this hill. This was our fate, perhaps written in the moon and stars, and I could see it approaching as clearly as could Atara. And yet it was also *my* fate that I must first speak for peace.

'Count Ulanu,' I said, 'you are now Lord of Sikar and Virad by conquest. But your domains were gained through treachery. No doubt the lords of Khaisham are preparing to take them back. Why don't you withdraw your men so that we may continue our journey? When we reach Khaisham, we'll speak to the Librarians concerning these matters. Perhaps a way can be found to restore peace to Yarkona without more war.'

It was a poor speech, I thought, and Count Ulanu had as much regard for it as I. His contemptuous eyes fell upon me as he said, 'If you *are* Valari, it seems you've lost your courage that you should suggest such cowardly schemes of running off to the enemy.'

For quite a few moments, he stared at the scar on my forehead. Then his eyes, which had caused Liljana nearly to weep, bored into mine. I felt something like black maggots trying to eat their way into my brain. My hand closed more tightly around Alkaladur's swan-carved hilt. I felt the fire of the silustria passing into me and gathering in *my* eyes. And suddenly Count Ulanu looked away from me.

'*Pilgrims*, are you?' he muttered. 'Seven of you, what's to be done with seven damn pilgrims?'

As the hot wind rippled the grasses about the hill, the Blue warrior with the shaved head impatiently turned to speak to the Count. His words came out in a series of guttural sounds like the grunts of a bear. He suddenly raised his axe, which caught the fierce rays of the sun. From his neck dangled a clear stone, which also gleamed in the bright light. It was a large, square-cut diamond like those that are affixed to leather breastpieces to make up the famed Valari battle armor. The other Blues sported identical gems. With the veins of my wrist touching my sword's diamond pommel, I saw in a flash how these Blues had acquired such stones: they had been ripped free from the armor of the crucified Valari after the battle of Tarshid an entire age ago. For three thousand years, Morjin had hoarded them against the day they might be needed. As now they were. For clearly, he had bought the service of the Blues' axes – and perhaps their forgetfulness of past treacheries – with these stolen diamonds.

'Urturuk here,' the Count said, nodding at the scabrous Blue, 'suggests that we *do* send you on to Khaisham. Or at least your heads.'

Like a perfect jewel forming up in my mind, I suddenly saw what Morjin's spending of this long-hoarded treasure portended: that he had finally committed to the open conquest of not only Yarkona but all of Ea.

'The Librarians,' the Count said, 'must be sent *some* sign that they've forfeited the right to receive more pilgrims.'

While the horses, ours and theirs, nickered nervously and pawed the earth, Count Ulanu stared up the grassy hill at us deciding what to do.

And then Liljana smiled at him and said, 'But haven't you already made your request to the Librarians?'

Again, the rage returned to Count Ulanu's face as he caught Liljana in his hateful eyes. And she stared right back at him, taking perhaps too much delight in her power to provoke him. Then she told us of the hidden thing that she had so painstakingly wrested from the Count's mind.

527

'After Tarmanam,' she said to him loudly so that all his men could hear, 'didn't you send your swiftest rider to Khaisham demanding a tribute of gold? And didn't the Librarians send *you* a book illumined with gilt letters? A book of *manners*?'

Her revelation of the Librarians' rebuke and the Count's secret shame proved too much for him. With his true motives for wanting to humble the Librarians exposed like a raw nerve, the Count's hand tightened on his horse's reins, pulling back its head until it screamed in pain. And then the Count himself suddenly pointed his sword at us and screamed to his men, 'Damned witch! Take her! Take them all! And be sure you take the Valari alive!'

This command pleased the three Blues greatly. They clanked their great axes together, and in harmony with the ringing steel, they let loose a long and savage howl: OWRRULLL!

Then the twenty knights kicked their spurs against their screaming horses' flanks, and the battle was joined.

31

The Count himself led the charge up the hill. He was daring enough to show brave, but cunning enough to know that his knights wouldn't let him ride right onto our swords unprotected and alone. As their horses wheezed and sweated and pounded up the steep slope, two of his knights spurred their mounts slightly ahead of him to act as living shields. And it was well for him that they did. For just then, behind me, a bowstring twanged and an arrow buried itself in the lead knight's chest. I heard Atara call out, 'Twenty-three!' A few moments later, another arrow sizzled through the roiling air, only to glance off the Count's shield. And then he and his men were upon us.

The first knight to crest the hill – a big, burly man with fear-maddened eyes – drove his horse straight toward me. But due to his uphill charge, he had little momentum and less balance in his saddle; with Altaru's hooves planted squarely in the earth, the point of my lance took him in the throat and drove clean through him. The force of his fall ripped the lance from my grasp. I heard him screaming, but then realized that he was going to his death in near silence, a wheeze of bloody breath escaping from his ruined throat and nothing more. The scream was all inside me. It built louder and louder until it seemed that the earth itself was shrieking in agony as it split asunder beneath me and pulled me down toward a black and bottomless chasm.

'Val!' Kane called out from somewhere nearby. 'Draw your sword!'

I heard *his* sword slice the air and cleave through the gorget surrounding a knight's neck. I was vaguely aware of Maram fumbling with his red crystal and trying to catch a few rays of sun with which to burn the advancing knights. Master Juwain, to my astonishment, scooped up the shield of the man I had unhorsed; he held it protecting Liljana from another knight's sword as she tried to urge her horse toward Count Ulanu. Behind me, to the right and left, Atara and Alphanderry worked furiously with their swords to beat back the attack of yet more knights who were trying to flank us along the rear of the hill and take us from behind.

With a trembling hand, I drew forth Alkaladur. The long blade gleamed in the light of the sun. The sight of the silver gelstei shining so brilliantly dismayed Count Ulanu and his men, even as it drove back the darkness engulfing me. My mind suddenly cleared and a fierce strength flowed up my hand into my arm, a strength that felt as bottomless as the sea. It was as if I were drawing Altaru's surging blood into me, and more, the very fires of the earth itself.

The Bright Sword flared white then, so brilliant and dazzling that the nearest knights cried out and threw their arms over their eyes. But other knights and the three Blues pressed toward me. Kane was near me, too, cutting and killing and cursing. Horses collided with each other, snorted and screamed. Altaru, steadying me and freely lending me his great strength, turned his wrath on any who tried to harm me. An unhorsed knight tried to hammer my back with his mace; Altaru kicked out, catching him in the chest and knocking him over. And then, even as Urturuk, the Blue with the missing ear, came for me with his huge axe, Altaru backed up to trample the fallen knight with his sharp hooves. He struck down with tremendous force, again and again until the knight's head was little more than white bones and broken brains beneath his crumpled helm.

'Val – on your right!'

I narrowly pulled back from Urturuk's ferocious axe blow that would have chopped through Altaru's neck. Altaru, now sensing the enemy's strategy of trying to kill him to get at me, furiously bit out at Urturuk, taking a good chunk of flesh from his shoulder. Urturuk seemed not to notice this ugly wound. He drove straight toward Altaru again, his mouth fairly frothing with wrath, this time trying to split open his skull.

At last I swung Alkaladur. It arced downward in a silvery flash, cutting through the axe's iron-hard haft and into Urturuk's bare chest, cleaving him nearly in two. The spray of blood from his opened chest nearly blinded me. I almost didn't see one of the Count's knights coming at me from the other side. But a sudden whinny and tensing of Altaru's body told me of his attack. I whirled about, swinging Alkaladur again. Its terrible, star-tempered edge cut through both shield and the mailed forearm behind it, and then bit into the steel rings covering the knight's belly. He cried out to see his arm fall away like a pruned tree limb, and plunged to the ground screaming out his death agony.

'Take him!' Count Ulanu screamed to his knights scarcely a dozen yards from me. 'Can't you take one damned Valari!'

Perhaps his men *could* have taken us but for Kane's fury and the suddenly unleashed terror of my sword. Then, too, they were disadvantaged by trying to cripple and capture us rather than kill. With knights now pressing us on all sides, I urged Altaru toward Count Ulanu. But Liljana, with Master Juwain still holding out the shield to protect her right side while Kane bulled his way forward on her left, had already reached him. She struck her sword straight out toward his sneering face. The point of it managed to slice off the tip of his nose even as one of his knight's horses knocked into hers. Blood streamed from this rather minor gash. But it was enough to unnerve Count Ulanu – and his men.

'The Count is wounded!' one of his captains cried out. 'Retreat! Protect the Count! Take him to safety!'

Although it hadn't been Count Ulanu who ordered this ignoble retreat, he made no move to gainsay his knight's command. He himself led the flight back down the hill. Two of his knights guarded his back as he turned his horse's tail to us – and paid with their lives. Kane's sword took one of them clean through the forehead while I pushed the point of mine straight through the other's armor into his heart. And suddenly the battle was over.

'Do we pursue?' Maram called out, reining in his horse at the top of the hill. He was either battle-drunk, I thought, or mad. 'I'll give them a taste of fire, I will!'

So saying, he drew out his gelstei and tried to loose a bolt of flame upon Count Ulanu and his retreating knights. But although the crystal warmed to a bright scarlet, it never came fully alive.

'Hold!' I called out. 'Hold now!'

Atara, who had her bow raised, fired off an arrow which split the mail of one of the retreating knights. He galloped away from us with a feathered shaft sticking out of his shoulder.

'Hold, please!'

With the three men I had killed lying rent and bleeding on the grass, I could barely keep from falling, too. Kane had dispatched two knights and the other two Blues. Atara had added two more men to her tally, while Maram, Alphanderry, Liljana and Master Juwain had done extraordinarily well in beating off the assault of armored knights without taking any wounds themselves. But now the agony of the slain took hold of my heart. A doorway showing only blackness opened to my left. The nothingness there beckoned me deeper toward death than I had ever been. To keep from being pulled inside, I held onto Alkaladur as tightly as I could. Its numinous fire opened another door through which streamed the light of the sun and stars. It warmed my icy limbs and brought me back to life.

'Val, are you wounded?' Master Juwain asked as he came up to me. Then he turned to take stock of the corpse-strewn hummock and called out to the rest of our company, 'Is anyone wounded?'

None of us were. I sat on top of the trembling Altaru, gaining strength each moment as I watched the last of Count Ulanu's men disappear over the same ridge from which they had come.

'What now, Val?' Liljana said to me as she wiped the Count's blood from the tip of her sword. '*Do* we pursue?'

'No, we've had enough of battle for one day,' I said. 'And we don't know how close the rest of the Count's army is.'

I looked up at the blazing sun and then out across Yarkona's rocky hills, calculating time and distances. To Liljana, to my other battle-sickened friends, I said, '*Now* we flee.'

They needed no further encouragement to put this hill of carnage behind us. We eased the horses down its slopes into the grassy trough through which we had been riding when the Count had surprised us. And then, wishing to cover ground quickly, we urged them to a fast canter toward the east. The pass into Khaisham called the Kul Joram, I guessed, lay a good twenty-five or thirty miles ahead of us. And beyond that, we would still need to ride another twenty miles to reach the Librarians' city.

We kept up a good pace for most of five miles, but then one of the pack horses threw a shoe, and we had to go more slowly as the sun-scorched turf gave way to ground planted with many more rocks. Here, too, there was a little ring-grass and sage pushing through the dirt, which the horses' hooves powdered and kicked up into the air. It was dry and hot, and the glazy blue sky held not the faintest breath of wind. The horses sweated even more profusely than did we. They kept driving onward through the murderous heat, snorting at the dust, making choking sounds in their throats and gasping until their nostrils and lips were white with froth. When we came across a little stream running down from the mountains, we had to stop to water them lest our dash across the burning plain kill them.

'I'm sorry,' I whispered to Altaru as he bent his shiny black neck down to the stream. 'Only a few more miles, old friend, only a few more.'

Alphanderry, gazing back in the direction from which we had come, spoke to all of us, saying, 'I'm sorry, but this is all my fault. If I hadn't opened my mouth to sing, we'd never have been discovered.'

I walked up to him and laid my hand on the damp, dark curls of his head. I told him, 'They might have found us in any case. And without your songs, we'd never have had the courage to come this far.'

'How far *have* we come?' Master Juwain said, looking eastward. 'How far to this Kul Joram?'

Liljana brushed back the hair sticking to her face as she caught my eye. 'There's something I must tell you, something else I saw in the Count's filthy mind. After Tarmanam, he sent a force to the Kul Joram to hold it for his army's advance into Khaisham.'

Maram, bending low by the stream to examine the hooves of his tiring sorrel, suddenly straightened up and said, 'Oh, no – this is terrible news! How are we to cross into Khaisham, then?'

'Don't you give up hope so easily,' Liljana chided him. 'There is another pass.'

'The Kul Moroth,' Kane spat out as he gazed into the wavering distances. 'It lies twenty miles north of the Kul Joram. It's an evil place, and much narrower, but it will have to do.'

Maram pulled at his beard as he fixed Liljana with a suspicious look. 'I thought you promised that you'd never look into another's mind without his permission? This was a sacred principle, you said.'

'Do you think I'd have let that treacherous Count nail you to a cross because of a *principle*?' Liljana said. 'Besides, I promised *you*, not him.'

Master Juwain came up to look into my eyes and said, 'It seems that you're growing ever more able to put up shields against others' agonies.'

'No, it's just the opposite,' I said, thinking of the three men I had slain. 'Each time a man goes over now, it carries me deeper into the death realm. But the *valarda*, even as it opens me to this void, also opens me to the world. To all its pain, yes, but to its life as well. The sword that Lady Nimaiu gave me only aids in this opening. When I wield it truly, it's as if the soul of the world pours into me.'

So saying, I drew Alkaladur and held it gleaming faintly toward the east.

'Then the sword lends you a certain protection against the vulnerabilities of your gift.'

'No, it is not so, sir. Someday when I kill, the death realm will grab hold of me so tightly that I'll never return.'

Because there was nothing for him to say to this, he stood looking at me quietly even as the others fell silent, too.

Then Atara, scanning the horizon behind us, drew in a quick breath as she pointed toward the west. 'They're coming,' she said. 'Don't you *see*?'

At first none of us did. But as we stared at the far-off hills until our eyes burned, we finally saw a plume of dust rising into the sky.

'How many are there?' Maram asked Atara.

'That's hard to say,' she told him.

But even as we stood there beneath the quick beatings of our hearts, the dust plume grew bigger.

'Too many, I think,' Kane said. 'Let's ride now. We'll have to leave the pack horses behind. They're practically lame and slowing us down.'

This imperious announcement sparked fierce protest from Maram and Liljana. Maram couldn't abide the thought of separating ourselves from most of our food and drink, while Liljana bitterly regretted having to forsake her beloved pots and pans.

'You have your shield,' she said to Kane, 'so why shouldn't I be allowed at least one pot for cooking a hot meal when we might most need one?'

'And what about the brandy?' Maram put in. 'There's little enough left, but we'll need it for our return from Khaisham.'

'Return?' Kane growled. 'We won't even reach Khaisham if we don't ride *now*. Now fetch your pot and your brandy, and let's be off.'

We made a quick redistribution of those vital stores that the pack horses carried, filling our mounts' saddlebags as full as we dared. Then we said goodbye to these faithful beasts that had carried our belongings so far. I prayed that they would wander over Yarkona's mounded plains until some kind farmer found them and put them to work.

With pursuit now certain, though still far away, we set out for the Kul Moroth. We rode hard, pressing the horses to a full gallop until it became clear that they couldn't hold such a pace. Altaru and Iolo were strong enough, and Fire, too, but Kane's big bay and Liljana's gelding had little wind left for such heroics. Master Juwain's sorrel seemed to have aged greatly since setting out from Mesh, while Maram's poor horse was in the worst shape of any of our mounts. His sore hoof, now bruised by hot stones, was getting worse with every furlong we covered. I worried that soon he would pull up ruined and lame. And Maram worried about this as well.

'Ah, perhaps you should just leave me behind,' he gasped as he urged his limping sorrel to keep up with us. For a moment, we slowed to a trot. 'I'll ride off in a different direction. Perhaps the Count's men will follow me, instead of you.'

It was a courageous offer, if a little insincere. I thought that he might hope that our pursuers would follow *us* instead of him.

'On the Wendrush,' Atara said from atop her great roan mare, 'that is how it must be. Where speed is life, a war party is only as fast as its slowest horse.'

Her words greatly alarmed Maram, who had no real intention of simply riding away from us. She saw his disquiet and said, 'But this is not the Wendrush and we are no war party.'

'Just so,' I said. 'Our *company* will reach Khaisham together or not at all. We have a lead; now let's keep it.'

But this proved impossible to do. As the ground grew even drier and rougher, Maram's sorrel slowed his pace even more. And the plume of dust behind us grew closer and thickened into a cloud.

'What are we to do?' Maram muttered. 'What are we to do?'

And Kane, bringing up the rear, answered him with one word, 'Ride.'

And ride we did. The rhythm of our horses' hooves beat against the ground like the pounding of a drum. It grew very hot. I squinted against the sun pouring down upon the rocks to the east of us. Its rays, I thought, were like fiery nails fixing us to the earth. Dust stung my eyes and found its way into my mouth. Here the soil tasted of salt and men's tears, if not those of the angels. Here, in this burning waste, it would be easy for horse and man to perish, sweated dry of all their water.

After some miles, my thoughts turned away from the men behind us and toward visions of water. I remembered the deep blue stillness of Lake Waskaw and the rivers of Mesh; I thought of the soft white clouds over Mount Vayu and its glittering snowfields melting into rills and brooks. I began to pray for rain.

But the sky remained clear, a hot and hellish blue-white that glared like fired iron. It consoled me not at all that Count Ulanu and his men must suffer this dreadful heat even as we did. I took courage, however, from the thought that if we endured it more bravely, we still might outdistance them.

But it was they who closed the distance between us. The cloud of dust following us grew ever larger and nearer.

'The Count,' Kane observed bitterly, looking back, 'can afford to leave his laggards behind.'

As the hours passed, we entered terrain in which a series of low ridges ran from north to south like dull knife-blades pushing up the earth. They roughly paralleled the much greater mountain spur still ahead of us where, if Kane's memory proved true, we would find the Kul Moroth. In most places, we had no choice but to ride up and over these sun-baked folds. This hot, heaving work tortured the horses. From the top of one of them, where we paused to rest our faithful and sweating friends, we had a better view of the men pursuing us.

'Oh, my Lord!' Maram groaned. 'There are so many!'

For now, beneath the roiling column of dust drawing closer to the west, we saw perhaps five hundred men on horses following the dragon

535

standard. I thought I caught a glimpse of another red dragon set against a yellow surcoat: surely that of Count Ulanu leading the pursuit. There were many knights behind him, both heavy cavalry and light, and even a few horse archers accoutered much as Atara. A whole company of Blues on their swift, nimble ponies galloped after us as well. It seemed that Count Ulanu had summoned the entire vanguard of his army to help him wreak his vengeance upon us.

During the next hour of our flight, clouds began moving in from the north and darkening the sky. They built to great heights with amazing quickness. Their black, billowing shapes blocked out much of the sun. It grew much cooler, a gift from the heavens for which we were all grateful.

Count Ulanu's men, though, drew as much relief from the approaching storm as did we. He sent some of his horse archers galloping forward in a wild dash finally to close with us. They fired off a few rounds of arrows, which fell to earth out of range.

'Hmmph, archers shouldn't waste arrows so,' Atara said. 'If they come any closer, I'll spare them a few of mine.'

They did come closer. As we began ascending yet another ridge, a feathered shaft struck the earth only a dozen yards behind Kane's heaving bay. Atara's great, recurved bow was strung and ready; I thought that she would wait until gaining the crest of the ridge before turning to shoot back at them.

The rapidly cooling air about us seemed charged with anticipation and death. The sky rumbled with great rolling waves of thunder. I felt an itch at the back of my neck as if something were pulling at my hair. And then a bolt of lightning flashed down from the clouds and burned the air. It struck the ridge above us, and sent a blue fire running along the rocks. Balls of hail fell down, too, pelting us and pinging off my helmet. Master Juwain and the others made a sort of canopy of their cloaks, holding them up to protect their heads. And still the lightning streaked down and set the very earth to humming.

It seemed pure folly to climb toward the ridgeline where the lightning was the fiercest. But behind us rode six archers firing off certain death from their bows. These steel-tipped bolts struck even closer than did the lightning. One of them glanced off my helmet like a piece of hail – only from a different direction and with much greater force. The sound of it dinging against the steel caused Atara to turn in her saddle and finally fire off a shot of her own. The arrow sank into the belly of the lead archer, who fell off his horse onto the hail-shrouded earth. But the others only charged after us with renewed determination.

I was the first to the ridge, followed in quick succession by Alphanderry,

Liljana, Master Juwain, Maram and Kane. Atara rode more slowly, the better to make her shots and fight her arrow duel. Another two found their marks, and she called out, 'Twenty-seven, twenty-eight!' Just as she reached the ridge-top, however, with the sky's bright fire sizzling the very rocks, the hail began to fall much harder. It streaked down from the sky at a slant like millions of silver bolts. Her arrows crashed into these hurtling balls of ice with sharp clacking sounds, sometimes shattering them into a spray of frozen chips and snow. The hail deflected the advancing archers' arrows, too. They fired off many rounds to no effect. But one of their arrows ripped through Atara's billowing cloak just before two more of hers raised her count to thirty. Then the remaining archer, sighting his last arrow with great care despite the rain and hail, fired off a desperate shot. Lightning flashed and thunder rent the sky, and somewhere beneath these terrifying events came the even more terrible twang of his bowstring. And then I gasped to see a couple feet of wood and feathers sticking out of Atara's chest.

'Ride!' she choked out as she kicked her horse forward. 'Keep riding!'

It wasn't fear that drove her on through the pain of such a grievous wound nor even will but regard for us and what must happen if her strength failed. I felt this in the way that she waved on Master Juwain every time he turned his worried gaze toward her; it was obvious in her brave smiles toward Kane and especially in the bittersweet protectiveness that filled her eyes whenever she looked at me. Of all the courageous acts I had witnessed on fields of battle, I thought that her jolting ride across the final miles of Virad was the most valorous.

Liljana, galloping by her side, suggested that we must stop to offer her a little water. But Atara waved her on, too, gasping out, 'Ride, ride now – they're too close.' There was blood on her lips as she said this.

Soon the thunder and rain stopped, and the dark clouds boiled above us as if threatening to break apart. The mountainous spur marking Khaisham's border came into view. It was a barren escarpment of reddish rock perhaps a thousand feet high. It stood like a wall before us. In many places along its length, it was cut with fissures starkly defining great rock forms that looked like pyramids and towers. From the miles of plain that still lay between us and it, it was hard to make out much detail. But I prayed that one of these dark openings into the upfolded earth would prove to be the pass named the Kul Moroth.

So began our wild dash toward whatever safety the domain of Khaisham might afford us. Count Ulanu and his men were close now, and thundering closer with each passing minute. We rode as fast as we could considering the lameness of Maram's horse and Atara's injury. I felt the jolts of pain that shot through her body with every strike of her horse's hooves; I felt her quickly weakening in her grip upon the reins as her vitality drained out of her. She was coughing up blood, I saw, not much but enough.

Kane pointed out a rent in the rocks ahead of us a little larger than the others. We rode straight toward it over the stony ground. Now, from behind us along the wind, came the high-pitched howling of the Blues; it chilled us more cruelly than had any rain or hail. It seemed to promise us a death beneath steel-bladed axes or even the gnashing teeth of enemies mad for revenge.

Death was everywhere about us. We felt it immediately as we found the opening to the Kul Moroth. As Kane had warned us, it seemed an evil place. Others, I knew, had died here in desperate battles before us. I could almost hear their cries of anguish echoing off the walls of rock rising up on either side of us. The pass was dark in its depths, and the sunlight had to fight its way down to its hard, scarred floor. And it was narrow indeed; ten horses would have had trouble riding through it side by side. We had trouble ourselves, for the ground was uneven and strewn with many rocks and boulders. Other boulders, and even greater sandstone pinnacles, seemed perched precariously along the pass's walls and top as if ready to roll down upon us at the slightest jolt. Long ago, perhaps, some great cataclysm had cracked open this rent in the earth; I prayed that it wouldn't close in upon us before we were free of it.

And that, it seemed as we drove the horses forward, we might never be. For just as we made a turning through this dark corridor and caught a glimpse of Khaisham's rough terrain a half mile ahead of us through the pass, Atara let loose a gasp of pain and slumped forward, throwing her arms around Fire's neck. She could go no farther. My first thought was that we would have to lash her to her horse if we were to ride the rest of the distance to the Librarians' city.

But this was not to be. I dismounted quickly, and Master Juwain and Liljana did, too. We reached Atara's side just as she slipped off her saddle and fell into our arms. We found a place where the fallen boulders provided some slight protection again Count Ulanu's advancing army, and there we laid her down, against the cold stone.

'There's no time for this!' Kane growled out as he gazed back through the pass. 'No time, I say!'

'Oh, my Lord!' Maram said, coming down from his horse and looking at Atara. 'Oh, my Lord!'

Now Alphanderry dismounted, too, and so did Kane. His dark eyes flashed toward Atara as he said, 'We've got to put her back on her horse.'

Master Juwain, after examining Atara for a moment, looked up at Kane and said, 'I'm afraid the arrow pierced her lights. I think it's cut an artery, too. We can't just lash her to her horse.'

'So, what *can* we do?'

'I've got to draw the arrow and staunch the bleeding somehow. If I don't, she'll die.'

'So, if you *do* she'll die anyway, I think.'

There was no time to argue. Atara was coughing up more blood now, and her face was very pale. Liljana used a clean white cloth to wipe the bright scarlet from her mouth.

'Val,' she whispered to me as the slightness of her breath moved over her blue lips. 'Leave me here and save yourself.'

'No,' I told her.

'Leave me – it's the Sarni way.'

'It's not *my* way,' I told her. 'It's not the way of the Valari.'

From the opening of the pass came the sound of many iron-shod hooves striking against stone and a terrible howling growing louder with each passing moment.

'Go now, damn you!'

'No, I won't leave you,' I told her.

I drew Alkaladur, then. The sight of its shimmering length cut straight through to my heart. I would kill a hundred of Count Ulanu's men, I vowed, before I let anyone come close to her. I knew I could.

OWRRULLL!

'Oh, my Lord!' Maram said taking out his red crystal. 'Oh, my Lord!'

As Master Juwain brought forth his wooden chest and opened it to search inside among the clacking steel instruments of its lower drawer, Alphanderry laid his hand upon Atara's head. He told her, 'I'm sorry, but this is my fault. My singing –'

'Your singing is all I wish to hear now,' Atara said, forcing a smile. 'Sing for me, now, will you? Please?'

Master Juwain found the two instruments that he was looking for: a razor-sharp knife and a long, spoonlike curve of steel with a little hole in the bowl near its end. Just then Alphanderry sang out:

> *Be ye songs of glory,*
> *Be ye songs of glory,*
> *That the light of the One*
> *Will shine upon the world.*

Maram, with tears in his eyes, stood above Atara as he tried to position his gelstei so that it caught what little light filtered down to the floor of the pass. He called out, to the rocks and the clouded sky above us, 'I'll burn them if they come close! Oh, my Lord, I will!'

The wild look in his eyes alarmed Kane. He drew out his black gelstei and stood looking between it and Maram's stone.

'Hold her!' Master Juwain said to me sharply as he looked down at Atara.

I put aside my sword, sat and pulled Atara onto my lap. My hands found their way between her arms and sides as I hung on to her tightly. Liljana bent to help hold her, too.

Master Juwain cut open her leather armor and the softer shirt beneath. He grasped the arrow and tugged on it, gently. Atara gasped in agony, but the arrow didn't move. Then Master Juwain nodded at me as if admonishing me not to let go of her. Sighing sadly, he used the knife to probe the opening that the arrow had made between her ribs and enlarge it, slightly. Now it took both Liljana and me to hold Atara still. Her body writhed with what little strength she had left. And still Master Juwain wasn't done tormenting her. He took out his spoon and fit its tip to the red hole in Atara's creamy white skin. Then he pushed his elongated spoon down along the arrow, slowly, feeling his way, deep into her. He twirled it about while Atara's eyes leapt toward mine; from deep in her throat came a succession of strangled cries. At last Master Juwain smiled with relief. I understood that the hole at the spoon's tip had snagged the tip of the arrow point; its curved flanges would now be wrapped around the point's barbs, thus shielding Atara's flesh from them so that they wouldn't catch as Master Juwain drew the arrow. This he now did. It came out with surprising smoothness and ease.

And so did a great deal of blood. It truth, it ran out of her like a bright red stream, flowing across her chest and wetting my hands with its warmth.

And all the while, Alphanderry knelt by her and sang:

Be ye songs of glory,
Be ye songs of glory,
That the light of the One
Will shine upon the world.

'Maram!' I heard Kane call out behind me. 'Watch what you're doing with that crystal!'

The quick clopping of many horses' hooves against stone came closer, as did the hideous howling, which filled the pass with an almost deafening sound: OWRRULLL!

Kane glanced down at Atara, who was fighting to breathe, much air now wheezing out of her chest along with a frothy red spray.

'So,' he said. 'So.'

Master Juwain touched her chest just above the place where the archer's arrow had ripped open her lungs. Everyone knew that such sucking wounds were mortal.

'She's bleeding to death!' I said to Master Juwain. 'We have to staunch it!'

He stared at her, almost frozen in his thoughts. He said, 'The wound is too grievous, too deep. I'm sorry, but I'm afraid there's no way.'

'Yes, there is,' I said. I reached my bloody hand into his pocket where he kept his green crystal. I took it out and gave it to him. 'Use this, please.'

'I'm afraid I don't know how.'

'Please, sir,' I said again to him. 'Use the gelstei.'

He sighed as he gripped his healing stone. He held it above Atara's wound. He closed his eyes as if looking inside himself for the spark with which to ignite it.

'I'm afraid there's nothing,' he said.

Maram, breaking off his fumblings with *his* crystal, said, 'Ah, perhaps you should read from your book. Or perhaps a period of meditation would –'

'There is no *time*,' Master Juwain said with uncharacteristic vehemence. 'Never enough time.'

OWRULLLLLLL!

Through my hand, I felt Atara's pulse weakening. I felt her life ready to blow out like a candle flame in an ice-cold wind. I didn't care then if Count Ulanu's men fell upon us and captured us. I wanted only for Atara to live another day, another minute, another moment. Where there was life, I thought, there was always hope and the possibility of escape.

'Please, sir,' I said to Master Juwain, 'keep trying.'

Again, Master Juwain closed his eyes even as his hard little hand closed tightly around the gelstei. But soon he opened them and shook his head.

'One more time,' I said to him. 'Please.'

'But there is no rhyme or reason to using this stone!' he said bitterly.

'No reason of the *mind*,' I said to him.

Atara began moving her lips as if she wanted to tell me something. But no words came out of them, only the faintest of whispers. The touch of her breath against my ear was so cold it burned like fire.

'What is it, Atara?' In her eyes was a look of faraway places and last things. I pressed my lips to her ear and whispered, 'What do you see?'

And she told me, 'I see you, Val, everywhere.'

In her clear blue eyes staring up at me, I saw my grandfather's eyes and the dying face of my mother's grandmother. I saw our children, Atara's and mine, who were worse than dead because we had never breathed our life into them.

A door to a deep, dark dungeon opened beneath Atara then. I was not the only one to look upon it. Atara, who could always see so much, and sometimes everything, turned and whispered, 'Alphanderry.'

Alphanderry stood up and smoothed the wrinkles out of his tunic, stained with sweat, rain and blood. He smiled as Atara said, 'Alphanderry, sing, it's time.'

Just as Count Ulanu and the knights of his hard-riding guard showed themselves down the pass's dark turnings, Alphanderry began walking toward them. I didn't know what he was doing.

'Oh, my Lord!' Maram said above me. 'Here they come!'

OWRRULLLL! sang the voices of the Blues riding behind Count Ulanu as they clanked their axes together.

And Alphanderry, with a much different voice, sang out, '*La valaha eshama halla, lais arda alhalla . . . .*'

His music had a new quality to it, both sadder and sweeter than anything I had ever heard before. I knew that he was close to finding the words that he had so long sought and opening the heavens with their sound.

'Valashu Elahad!' Count Ulanu called out as he rode with his captains and crucifiers inexorably toward us. 'Lay down your weapons and you will be spared!'

And then, as the Count reined in his horse and stopped dead in his tracks, Alphanderry began singing more strongly. The Count looked at him as if he were mad. So did his captains and the knights and Blues behind him. But then Alphanderry's song built ever larger and deeper, and began soaring outward like a flock of swans beating their wings up toward the sky. So wondrous was the music that poured out of him that it seemed the Count and his men couldn't move.

Something in it touched Master Juwain, too, as I could tell from the faraway look that haunted his eyes. He was staring into the past, I thought, and looking for an answer to Atara's approaching death in the fleeting images of memory or in the verses of the *Saganom Elu*. But he would never find it there.

'Look at her,' I said to Master Juwain. I took his free hand and brought it over Atara's and mine so that it covered both of them. 'Please look, sir.'

There was nothing more I could say to him, no more urgings or pleadings. I no longer felt resentment that he had failed to heal Atara, only an overwhelming gratitude that he had tried. And for Atara, I felt everything there was to feel. Her weakening pulse beneath my fingers touched mine with a deeper beating, vaster and infinitely finer. The sweet hurt of it reminded me how great and good it was to be alive. There seemed no end to it; it swelled my heart like the sun, breaking me open. And as I looked at Master Juwain eye to eye and heart to heart, he found himself in this luminous thing.

'I never knew, Val,' he whispered. 'Yes, I see, I see.'

And then Master Juwain, who turned back to Atara, *did* look and seemed suddenly to see her. He found the reason of his heart as his eyes grew moist with tears. He found his greatness, too. Then he smiled as if finally understanding something. He touched the wound in her chest. Then he held the varistei over it, the long axis of the stone exactly perpendicular to the opening that the arrow had made. He took a deep breath and then let it out to the sound of Atara's own anguished gasp.

I was waiting to see the gelstei glow with its soft, healing light. Even Kane, despite his despair, was looking at the stone as if hoping it would begin shining like a magical emerald. What happened next, I thought, amazed us all. A rare fire suddenly leaped in Master Juwain's eyes. And then viridian flames almost too bright to behold shot from both ends of the gelstei; they circled to meet each other beneath it before shooting like a stream of fire straight into Atara's wound. She cried out as if struck again with a burning arrow. But the green fire kept filling up the hole in her chest, and soon her eyes warmed with the intense life of it. A few moments later, the last of the fire swirled about the opening of the wound as if stitching it shut with its numinous light. As it crackled and then faded along her pale skin, we blinked our eyes, not daring to believe what we saw. For Atara was now breathing easily, and her flesh had been made whole.

'Oh, my Lord!' Maram sighed out from above us. 'Oh, my Lord!'

It seemed that neither Count Ulanu or his men witnessed this miracle, for Liljana's and Master Juwain's backs blocked their view of it. And before them unfolded a miracle of another sort. For now, at last, as Alphanderry stood in all his glory facing down the vanguard of an entire army, his tongue found the turnings of the language that he had sought all his life. Its sounds flowed out of him like golden drops of light. And words and music became as one, for now Alphanderry was singing the Song of the One. In its eternal harmonies and pure tones, it was impossible to lie, impossible to see the world other than as it was because every word was a thought's or a thing's true name.

And truth, I knew as I held Atara's hand and listened to Alphanderry sing, was really just beauty – a terrible beauty almost impossible to bear. Nothing like it had been heard on Ea since the Star People first came to earth ages ago. With every passing moment, Alphanderry's words became clearer, sweeter, brighter. They dissolved time as the sea does salt, and hatred, pride and bitterness. They called us to remember all that we had lost and might yet be regained; they reminded us who we really were. Tears filled my eyes, and I looked up astonished to see Kane weeping, too. The stony Blues had belted their axes for a moment so that they might cover their faces. Even Count Ulanu had fallen away from his disdain. His misting eyes gave sign that he was recalling his own original grace. It seemed that he might have a change of heart and renounce the Kallimun and Morjin, then and there with all the world witnessing his remaking.

In the magic of that moment in the Kul Moroth, all things seemed possible. Flick, near Alphanderry, was spinning wildly, beautifully, exultantly. The walls of stone around us echoed Alphanderry's words and seemed to sing them themselves. High above the world, the clouds parted and a shaft of light drove down through the pass to touch Alphanderry's head. I thought I saw a golden bowl floating above him and pouring out its radiance over him as from an infinite source.

And so Alphanderry sang with the angels. But he was, after all, only a man. One single line of the Galadin's song was all that he could call forth in its true form. After a while, his voice began to falter and fail him. He nearly wept at losing the ancient, heavenly connection. And then the spell was broken.

Count Ulanu, still sitting on his war horse in his battle armor, shook his head as if he couldn't quite believe what he had heard. It infuriated him to see what a dreadful sculpture he had made of himself from the sacred clay with which the One had provided him. His wrath now fell upon Alphanderry for showing him this. And for standing between him and the rest of us. A snarl of outrage returned to his face; he drew his sword as his knights pointed their lances at Alphanderry. The Blues, with unfeeling fingers, gripped their axes and readied themselves to advance upon him.

OWRRULLL! OWRRULLLLL!

At last, with the howls of the Blues drowning out the final echoes of Alphanderry's music, I grabbed up my sword and leaped to my feet. Kane gripped his gelstei as his wild black eyes fell upon Maram's red crystal.

544

'I'll burn them!' Maram called out. 'I will, I will!'

The clouds above the pass broke apart even more, and rays of light streamed down and touched Maram's firestone. It began glowing bright crimson.

Alphanderry, who had marched many yards down the pass away from us, turned and looked up toward his right. Something seemed to catch his eye. For a moment, he recaptured his joy and something of the Star People's lost language as he cried out: '*Ahura Alarama!*'

'What?' I shouted, gathering my strength to run to his side.

'I see him!'

'See *who*?'

'The one you call Flick.' He smiled like a child. 'Oh, Val . . . the colors!'

Just then, even as Count Ulanu spurred his horse forward, Maram's gelstei flared and burned his hands. He screamed, jerking the blazing crystal upwards. A great stream of fire poured out of it and blasted the boulders along the pass's walls. Kane was now working urgently with his black crystal to damp the fury of the firestone. But it drew its power from the very sun and fed the fires of the earth. The ground around us began shaking violently; I went down to one knee to keep from falling altogether. Stones rained down like hail, and one of them pinged off my helmet. Then came a deafening roar of great boulders bounding down the pass's walls. In only a few moments, the rockslide filled the defile to a height of twenty feet. A great mound stood between Alphanderry and the rest of the company, cutting off his escape. And keeping us from coming to his aid. We couldn't even see him.

But we could still hear him. As the dust choked us and settled slowly down, from beyond the heaped-up rubble I heard him singing what I knew would be his death song. For I knew that Count Ulanu, who spared no mercy for himself, would find none for him.

My hand gripped the hilt of my sword so fiercely that my fingers hurt; my arm hurt even as I felt Count Ulanu's arm pull back and his sword thrust downward. Alphanderry's terrible cry easily pierced the rocks between us. It pierced the whole world; it pierced my heart. My sword fell from my hand, even as I clasped my chest and fell myself. A door opened before me, and I followed Alphanderry through it.

I walked with him through the dark, vacant spaces up toward the stars.

32

The city of Khaisham was built on a strong site where the plains of Yarkona come up against the curve of the White Mountains. Directly to its east was Mount Redruth, an upfolding of great blocks of red sandstone that looked like pieces of a rusted iron breastplate. Mount Salmas, to the east and north, was more gentle in its rise toward the sky and slightly higher, too. Its peak pushed its way above the treeline like a bald, rounded pate. Out from the gorge between these two mountains rushed a river: the Tearam. Its swift flow was diverted into little channels along either side of it in order to water the fields to the north and west of the city. The city itself was built wholly to the south of the river. A wall following its curves formed the city's northern defenses. It rose up just above the Tearam's banks and ran east into the notch between the mountains. There it turned south along the steep slopes of Mount Redruth for a mile before turning yet again west through some excellent pasture. The wall's final turning took it back north toward the river. This stretch of mortared stone was the wall's longest and its most vulnerable – and therefore the most heavily defended. Great round towers surmounted it along its length at five hundred foot intervals. The south wall was likewise protected.

The men and women of Khaisham had good reason to feel safe in their little stone houses behind this wall, for it had never been breached or their city taken. The Lords of Khaisham, though, desired even more protection for the great Library and the treasures it held. And so, long ago they had built a second, inner wall around the Library itself.

This striking edifice occupied the heights at Khaisham's northeast corner, almost in the mouth of the gorge, and thus further protected by the Tearam and Mount Redruth. Unlike Khaisham's other buildings, which had been raised up out of the sandstone common in the mountains to the east, the Library had been constructed of white marble. No one remembered whence this fine stone had come. It lent the Library much of its grandeur. Its gleaming faces, which caught and reflected the harsh Yarkonan sun, showed themselves to approaching pilgrims even far out on the pasturage to the west of the city. The centermost section of the Library was a great, white cube; four others, forming its various wings, adjoined it to the west, south, east and north so that its shape was that of a cross. Smaller cubes erupted out of each of these four, making for wings to the wings. The overall effect was that of a great crystal, like a snowflake, with points radiating at perfect angles from a common center.

We came to Khaisham from the Kul Moroth almost directly to the west. I was never to remember very much of this twenty-mile journey for I was conscious during only parts of it. It was I, not Atara, whom my companions had to lash to his horse. At times, when my eyes opened slightly, I was aware of the rocky green pastures through which we rode and the shepherds tending their flocks there. More than once, I listened as Kane seemed to sigh out the name of Alphanderry with his every breath. I watched as his eyes misted like mirrors and he clamped shut his jaws so tightly that I feared his teeth would break and the splinters drive into his gums. At other times, however, the darkness closed in upon me, and I saw nothing. Nothing of this world, that is. For the bright constellations I had longed to apprehend since my childhood were now all too near. I could see how their swirling patterns found their likeness in those of the mountains far below them – and in Flick's fiery form, and in a man's dreams, indeed, in all things. In truth, from the moment of Alphanderry's death, I was like a man walking between two worlds and with my feet firmly planted in neither.

It was just as well, perhaps, that I couldn't touch upon my companions' grief. Can a cup hold an entire ocean? With the passing of Alphanderry from this world, it seemed that the spirit of the quest had left our company. It was as if a great blow had driven from each of us his very breath. I was dimly aware of Maram riding along on Alphanderry's horse and muttering that instead of burning the Kul Moroth's rocks, he should have directed his fire at Count Ulanu and his army. He voiced his doubt that we would ever leave Khaisham, now. The others were quieter though perhaps more disconsolate. Liljana seemed to have aged ten years in a moment, and her face was deeply creased with lines that all pointed toward death. Master Juwain was clearly appalled to have saved Atara only to lose Alphanderry so unexpectedly a few minutes later. He rode with his head bowed, not even caring to open his book and read a requiem or prayer. Atara, healed of her mortal wound, looked out upon the landscape of a terrible sadness it seemed that only she could see. And Kane, more than once, when he thought no

547

one was listening, murmured to himself, 'He's gone – my little friend is gone.'

As for me, the sheer evil of Morjin and all his works chilled my soul. It pervaded the world's waters and the air, even the rocks beneath the horses' hooves; it seemed as awesome as a mountain and unstoppable, like a rockslide, like the ocean in storm, like the fall of night. For the first time, I realized just how slim our chances of finding the Lightstone really were. If Alphanderry, so bright and pure of heart, could be slain by one of Morjin's men, any of us could. And if we could, we surely would, for Morjin was spending all his wealth and bending all his will toward defeating all who opposed him.

By the time we found our way past Khaisham's gates and into the Library, my desolation had only deepened as a cold worse than winter took hold of me and would not let go. Now the stars were all too near in the blackness that covered me; it seemed that I might never look upon the world again. For four days I lay as one dead in the Library's infirmary, lost in dark caverns that had no end.

My friends nearly despaired of me. Atara sat by my side day and night and would not let go my hand. Maram, sitting by my other side, wept even more than she did, while Kane stood like a statue keeping a vigil over me. Liljana made me hot soups which she somehow managed to make me swallow. As for Master Juwain, after he had failed to revive me with his teas or the magic of his green crystal, he called for many books to be brought to our room. It was his faith that one of them might tell of the Lightstone, which alone had the power to revive me now.

It was the Lightstone, I believe, no less the love of my friends, that brought me back to the world. Like a faint, golden glimmer, my hope of finding it never completely died. Even as Liljana's soups strengthened my body, this hope flared brighter within my soul. It filled me with a fire that gradually drove away the cold and awakened me. And so on the thirteenth day of Soal, and the one hundred and fifteenth of our quest, I opened my eyes to see the sunlight streaming through the room's south-facing windows.

'Val, you've come back!' Atara said. She bent to kiss my hand and then she pressed her lips to mine. 'I never thought . . .'

'I never thought I'd see you again either,' I told her.

Above me, Flick turned about slowly as if welcoming me back.

We spoke of Alphanderry for a long while. I needed to be sure that my memory of what happened in the Kul Moroth was real and true, and not just a bad dream. After Atara and my other friends attested to hearing Alphanderry's screams, I said, 'It's cruel that the most beloved of us should be the first to die.'

Maram, sitting to my left, suddenly grasped my hand and squeezed it almost hard enough to break my bones. Then he said, 'Ah, my friend, I must tell you something. Alphanderry, while dearer to all of us than I could ever say, was not the most beloved. You are. Because you're the most able to love.'

Because I didn't want him to see the anguish in my eyes just then, I closed them for a few moments. When I looked out at the room again, everything was a blur.

Master Juwain was there at the foot of my bed, reading a passage from the *Songs* of the *Saganom Elu*: '"After the darkest night, the brightest morning. After the gray of winter, the green of spring."'

Then he read a requiem from the *Book of Ages*, and we prayed for Alphanderry's spirit; I wept as I silently prayed for my own.

Food was then brought to us, and we made a feast in honor of Alphanderry's music which had sustained us in our darkest hours, in the pathless tangle of the Vardaloon and in the starkness of the Kul Moroth. I had no appetite for meat and bread, but I forced myself to eat these viands even so. I felt the strength of it in my belly even as the wonder of Alphanderry's last song would always fill my heart.

After breakfast, Kane brought me my sword. I drew forth Alkaladur and let its silver fire run down its length into my arm. Now that I was able to sit up and even stand, weakly, I held the blade pointing toward the Library's eastern wing. The silustria that formed its perfect symmetry seemed to gleam with a new brightness.

'It's here,' I said to my companions. 'The Lightstone must be here.'

'If it is,' Kane informed me gravely, 'we'd better go look for it as soon as you're able to walk. Much has happened these last few days while you've slept with the dead.'

So saying, he sent for the Lord Librarian that we might hold council and discuss Khaisham's peril – and our own.

While we waited in that sunny room, with its flowering plants along the windows and its rows of white-blanketed beds, Kane reassured me that the horses were well tended and that Altaru had taken no wound or injury in our flight across Khaisham from the pass. Maram admitted to having to leave his lame sorrel behind; it was his hope that some shepherd might find him and return him before we left Khaisham. If he took any joy from inheriting and riding Alphanderry's magnificent Iolo, he gave no sign.

Soon the door to the infirmary opened, and in walked a tall man wearing a suit of much-scarred mail over the limbs of his long body. His green surcoat showed an open book, all golden and touched with the sun's seven rays. His face showed worry, intelligence, command and pride. He had a large, jutting nose scarred across the middle and a long, serious face with a scar running down from his eye into his well-trimmed gray beard. His hands – long and large and well-formed – were stained with ink. His name was Vishalar Grayam, the Lord Librarian, and like his kindred, he was both a scholar and a warrior.

After we had been presented to each other, he shook my hand, testing me and looking at me for a long time. And then he said, 'It's good that you've come back to us, Sar Valashu. You've awakened none too soon.'

He went on to tell me what had happened since our passage of the Kul Moroth. Count Ulanu, he said, disbelieving that the mysterious rockslide might keep him from his quarry, had sent many of his men scrambling over it. They had all perished on Kane's and Maram's swords. Kane had then led the retreat from the pass, and Count Ulanu hadn't been able to pursue us. By the time he had raced his men south to the Kul Joram, our company had nearly reached Khaisham's gates.

Count Ulanu had then sent for his army, still encamped near Tarmanam in Virad. It had taken his men four days to march across to eastern Yarkona, pass through the Kul Joram and encamp outside of Khaisham. Now the forces of Aigul and Sikar, and the Blues, were preparing to besiege the city's outer walls.

'And if that isn't bad enough,' the Lord Librarian told us, 'we've just had grievous news. It seems that Inyam and Madhvam have made a separate peace with Aigul. And so we can't expect any help from that direction.'

And worse yet, he told us, was what he had heard about the domains of Brahamdur, Sagaram and Hansh.

'We've heard they've agreed to send contingents to aid Count Ulanu,' he said. 'They're being brought up as we speak.'

'Then it seems all of Yarkona has fallen,' Maram said gloomily.

'Not yet,' Lord Grayam told him. 'We still stand. And so does Sarad.'

'But will Sarad come to your aid?' I asked him. I tried to imagine the Ishkans marching out to aid Mesh if the combined tribes of the Sarni tried to invade us.

'No, I doubt if they will,' the Lord Librarian said. 'I expect that they, too, in the end, will do homage to Count Ulanu.'

'Then you stand alone,' Maram said, looking toward the window like a trapped beast.

'Alone, yes, perhaps,' the Lord Librarian said. He looked from Kane to Atara and then me. Lastly, he fixed Maram with a deep look as if trying to see beneath his surface fear and desperation.

'Then will you make peace with the Count yourselves?' Maram asked him.

'We would if we could,' the Lord Librarian said. 'But I'm afraid that while it takes two to make peace, it only takes one to make war.'

'But if you were to surrender and kneel to –'

'If we surrendered to Count Ulanu,' the Lord Librarian spat out, 'he would enslave those he didn't crucify. And as for our kneeling to him, we Librarians kneel to the Lord of Light and no one else.'

He went on to tell us that the Librarians of Khaisham were devoted to preserving the ancient wisdom, which had its ultimate source in the Light of the One. Theirs was the task of gathering, purchasing and collecting all books and other artifacts which might be of value to future generations. Much of their labor consisted of transcribing old, crumbling volumes and illuminating new manuscripts. They worked gold leaf into paper and vellum, and spent long hours in their calligraphy, penning black ink to white sheets with devout and practiced hands. Perhaps their noblest effort was the compilation of a great encyclopedia indexing all books and all knowledge – which was still unfinished, as Lord Grayam sadly admitted. But their foremost duty was to protect the treasures that the Library contained. And so they took vows never to allow anyone to desecrate the Library's books or to forsake guarding the Library, even unto their deaths. Toward this end, they trained with swords almost as diligently as with their pens.

'You've taken vows of your own,' he said, nodding toward my medallion. 'You're not the first to come here looking for the Lightstone, though none has done so for quite some time.'

He told us that once, many had made the pilgrimage to Khaisham, often paying princely sums for the right to use the Library. But now the ancient roads through Eanna and Surrapam were too dangerous, and few dared them.

'Master Juwain,' he said to me, 'has already explained that you've brought no money for us. Poor pilgrims you are, he tells me. That's as may be. But you have my welcome to use the library as you wish. Any who have fought Count Ulanu as you have are welcome here.'

From what he said then, it was clear that he regarded Master Juwain, Maram and Liljana as scholars, and esteemed Kane, Atara and me as warriors protecting them.

'We are fortunate to be joined by a company of such talents,' he said, searching in the softness of Maram's face for all that he tried to conceal there. 'I would hope that someday you might tell of what happened in the Kul Moroth. How very strange that the ground should shake just as you passed through it! And that rocks should have blocked Count

Ulanu's pursuit. And such rocks! The knights I sent there tell me that many of them were blackened and melted as if by lightning.'

Maram turned to look at me then. But neither of us – or our other companions – wished to speak of our gelstei.

'Well, then,' Lord Grayam said, 'you're good at keeping your own counsel, and I approve of that. But I must ask your trust in three things in order that you might have mine. First: If you find here anything of note or worth, you will bring it to me. Second: You will take great care not to harm any of the books, many of which are ancient and all too easy to harm. Third: You will remove nothing from the Library without my permission.'

I touched the medallion hanging from my neck and told him, 'When a knight takes refuge in a lord's castle, he doesn't dispute his rules. But you must know that we've come to claim the Lightstone and take it away to other lands.'

The Lord Librarian bristled at this. His bushy eyebrows pulled together as his hand found the hilt of his sword. 'Does a knight in *your* land then enter his lord's castle to claim his lord's most precious possession?'

'The Lightstone,' I told him, remembering my vows, 'is no one's possession. And we seek it not for ourselves but for all Ea.'

'A noble quest,' he sighed, relaxing his hand from his sword. 'But if you found the Cup of Heaven here, don't you think it should remain here where it can best be guarded?'

I managed to climb out of bed and walk over to the window. There, below me, I could see the many houses of Khaisham, with their square stone chimneys and brightly painted shutters. Beyond the city streets was Khaisham's outer wall, and beyond it, spread out over the green pastures to the south of the city, the thousands of tents of Count Ulanu's army.

'Forgive me, Lord Librarian,' I said, 'but you might find it difficult guarding even your own people's lives now.'

Lord Grayam's face fell sad and grave, and lines of worry furrowed his brow as he looked out the window with me.

'What you say is true,' he admitted. 'But it is also true that you won't find the Lightstone here. The Library has been searched through every nook and cranny for it for most of three thousand years. And so here we stand, arguing over nothing at a time when there's much else to do.'

'If we're arguing over nothing,' I said, 'then surely you won't mind if we begin our search?'

'So long as you abide by my rules.'

If we abided by his rules, as I pointed out to him, we would have to bring the Lightstone to him should we be so fortunate as to find it.

'That's true,' he said.

'Then it would seem that we're at an impasse.' I looked at Master Juwain and asked, 'Who has the wisdom to see our way through it?'

Master Juwain stepped forward, gripping his book, which Lord Grayam eyed admiringly. Master Juwain said, 'It may be that if we gain the Lightstone, we'll also gain the wisdom to know what should be done with it.'

'Very well then, let that be the way of it,' Lord Grayam said. 'I won't say yea or nay to your taking it from here until I've held it in my hands and you in yours. Do we understand each other?'

'Yes,' I said, speaking for the others, 'we do.'

'Excellent. Then I wish you well. Now please forgive me while I excuse myself. I've the city's defenses to look to.'

So saying, the Lord Librarian bowed to us and strode from the room.

I counted exactly three beats of my heart before Maram opened his mouth and said, 'Well, what are we waiting for?'

I drew my sword again and watched the light play about its gleaming contours.

'You must follow where your sword leads you,' Master Juwain told me, clapping me on the shoulder. Then he picked up a large book bound in red leather. 'But I'm afraid I must follow where *this* leads me.'

He told us that he was off to the Library's stacks to look for a book by a Master Malachi.

'But, sir,' Maram said to him, 'if we find the Lightstone in your absence –'

'Then I shall be very happy,' Master Juwain told him. 'Now why don't we meet by the statue of King Eluli in the great hall at midday, if we don't meet wandering around the other halls first? This place is vast, and it wouldn't do to lose each other in it.'

Liljana, too, admitted that she wished to make her own researches among the Library's millions of books. And so she followed Master Juwain out the door, each of them to go separate ways, and leaving Maram, Kane, Atara and me behind.

The infirmary, as I soon found, was a rather little room off a side wing connected by a large hall to an off-wing leading to the Library's immense south wing. Upon making passage into this cavernous space, I realized that it *would* be easy to become lost in the Library, not because there was anything mazelike about it, but simply because it was huge. In truth, the whole of this building had been laid out according to the four points of the world with a precise and sacred geometry. Everything about its construction, from the distances between the pillars holding up the roof to the great marble walls themselves, seemed to be that of cubes and squares. And of a special kind of rectangle, which, if the square part of it was removed, the remaining smaller rectangle retained the exact proportions of its parent. What these measures had to do with books puzzled me. Kane believed that the golden rectangle, as he called it, symbolized man himself: no matter what parts were taken away, a sacred spark in the image of the whole being always remained. And as with man, even more so with books. As any of the Librarians would attest, every part of a book, from its ridged spine to the last letter upon the last page, was sacred.

There were certainly many books. The south wing was divided into many sections, each filled with long islands of stacks of books reaching up nearly three hundred feet high toward the stone ceiling with its great, rectangular skylights. Each island was like a mighty tower of stone, wood, leather, paper and cloth; stairs at either end of an island led to the walkways circling them at their different levels. Thirty levels I counted to each island; it would take a long time, I thought, to climb to the top of one should a desired volume be shelved there. Passing from the heights of one island to another would have taken even longer but for the graceful stone bridges connecting them at various levels. The bridges, along with the islands stacked with their books, formed an immense and intricate latticework that seemed to interconnect the recordings of all possible knowledge.

As I walked with my friends down the long and seemingly endless aisles, I breathed in the scents of mildew and dust and old secrets. Many of the books, I saw, had been written in Ardik or ancient Ardik; quite a few told their tales in languages now long dead. By chance, it seemed, we passed by shelves of many large volumes of genealogies. Half a hundred of these were given over to the lineages of the Valari. Because my curiosity at that moment burned even brighter than my sword, I couldn't help opening one of them that traced the ancestry of Telemesh back son to father, generation to generation, to the great Aramesh. This gave evidence to the claim that the Meshian line of kings might truly extend back all the way to Elahad himself. My discovery filled me with pride. It renewed my determination to find the golden cup that the greatest of all my ancestors had brought to earth so long ago.

Alkaladur's faintly gleaming blade seemed to point us into an adjoining hall that was almost large enough to hold King Kiritan's entire palace. Here were collected all the Library's books pertaining to the Lightstone. There must have been a million of them. It seemed impossible that each of them had been searched for any mention of where Sartan Odinan might have hidden the golden cup after he had liberated it from the dungeons of Argattha. But a passing Librarian, hastily buckling on his sword as he hurried through the stacks to Lord Grayam's summons, assured us that they had. There were many Librarians, he told us, and there had been many generations of them since the Lightstone had become lost at the beginning of the Age of the Dragon long ago. That *his* generation might be the last of these devout scholar-warriors seemed not to enter his mind. And so he turned his faith from his pens to the steel of his sword; he excused himself and marched off toward his duty atop the city's walls.

Our search took us through this vast hall, with its even vaster silences and echoes of memory, into an eastern off-wing. And then into a side wing, where we found hall upon hall of nothing but paintings, mosaics and friezes depicting the Lightstone and scenes from its long past. And still my sword seemed to point us east. And so we passed into a much smaller, cubical chamber filled with vases from the Marshanid dynasty; these, too, showed the Lightstone in the hands of various kings and heroes out of history.

At last, however, we came to an alcove off a small room lined with painted shields. We determined that we had reached this wing's easternmost extension. We could go no farther in this direction. But I was sure that the Lightstone, wherever it was hidden, lay still to the east of us. Alkaladur gleamed like the moon when pointed toward the alcove's eastern window, and not at all when I swept it back toward the main body of the Library or any of the room's artifacts.

'So, we must try another wing,' Kane said to me. Maram and Atara, standing near him above an ancient Alonian ceremonial shield, nodded their heads in agreement. 'If your sword still shows true, then let's find our way to the east wing.'

Our search thus far had taken up the whole morning and part of the afternoon. Now we spent another hour crossing the Library's centermost section, also called the great hall. It dwarfed even the south wing, and was filled with so many towering islands of books and soaring bridges that I grew dizzy looking up at them. I was grateful when at last we passed into the east wing; in its cubical proportions, it was shaped identically to the others. One of its off-wings led us to a hall giving out on a side wing where the Librarians had put together an impressive collection of lesser gelstei. These were presented in locked cabinets of teak and glass. Atara gasped like a little girl to see so many glowstones, wish stones, angel eyes, warders, love stones and dragon bones gathered into one place. We might have lingered there a long time if Alkaladur hadn't pointed us down a long corridor leading to another side wing. The moment that we stepped into this chamber, with its many rare books of ancient poetry, my sword's blade warmed noticeably. And when we crossed into an adjoining room filled with vases, chalices, jewel-encrusted plates and the like, the silustria flared so that even Atara and Maram noticed its brightness.

'Is it truly *here*, Val?' Maram said to me. 'Can it be?'

I swept my sword from north to south, behind me and past the room's four corners. It grew its brightest whenever I pointed it east, toward a cracked marble stand on which were set two golden bowls, to the left and right, on its lowest shelves. Two more crystal bowls gleamed on top of the next higher ones, and at the stand's center on its highest square of marble sat a little cup that seemed to have been carved out of a single, immense pearl.

'Oh, my Lord!' Maram cried out. 'Oh, my Lord!'

Being unable to restrain himself – and wishing to be the first to lay his hands on the Lightstone and thus determine its fate according to our company's rules – he rushed forward as fast as his fat legs would carry him. I was afraid that in his excitement and greed, he would crash into this display. But he drew up short inches from it. He thrust out his hands and grasped the golden bowl to his right. Without even bothering to examine it, he lifted it high above his head, a wild light dancing in his eyes.

'Be careful with that!' Kane snapped at him. 'You don't want to drop it and dent it!'

'Dent the *gold* gelstei?' Maram said.

Atara, whose eyes were even sharper than her tongue, took a good look at the bowl in his hands and said, 'Hmmph! If that's the true gold, then a bull's nose ring is more precious than my mother's wedding band.'

Much puzzled, Maram lowered the bowl and turned it about in his hands. His brows narrowed suspiciously as he finally took notice of what was now so easy to see: the bowl was faintly tarnished and scarred in many places with fine scratches and wasn't made of gold at all. As Atara had hinted, it was only brass.

'But why display such a common thing?' Maram asked, embarrassed at his gullibility.

'Common, is it?' Kane said to him.

He walked closer to Maram and took the bowl from him. Then he picked up a much-worn wooden stick still lying on the shelf near where the bowl had been. With the bowl resting in the flat of one callused hand, he touched the stick to the rim of the bowl and drew it round

556

and round in slow circles. It set the bowl to pealing out a beautiful, pure tone like that of a bell.

'So, it's a singing bowl,' he said as he set it back on its stand. He nodded at the crystal bowls at the next highest level. 'So are those.'

'What about the one that looks like pearl?' Maram called out.

Not waiting for a answer, he picked up the pearly cup from the stand's highest level and tried to make music from it using the same stick as had Kane. After failing to draw forth so much as a squeak, he put it back in its place and scowled as if angry that it had disappointed him.

'It seems that this bowl,' he said, 'is for the beauty of the eye and not the ear.'

But I was not so sure. Just as I brought my sword closer to it and aligned its point directly toward its center, it began glowing very strongly. I thought that I could hear this pearly bowl singing faintly, with a soaring music that recalled Alphanderry's golden voice.

'There's something about this bowl,' I said. I took a step closer, and now Alkaladur began to hum in my hands.

Atara picked up the iridescent bowl and wrapped her long fingers around it. She said, 'It's heavy – much heavier than I would think a pearl of this size would be.'

'Have you ever *seen* a pearl so large?' Maram asked her. 'My Lord, it would take an oyster the size of a bear to make one so.'

Atara set this beautiful bowl back in its place. She stared at it with a penetrating sight that seemed to arise from a source much deeper than her sparkling blue eyes. And so did Kane.

'Can it be?' Maram said. Then he turned his head back and forth as if shaking sense into himself. 'No, of course it can't be. The Lightstone is of gold. This is pearl. Can the gold gelstei shimmer like pearl?'

'Perhaps,' Atara said, 'the Gelstei shimmers as one wishes it to.'

The silence that filled the chamber then was as deep as the sea.

'This must be it,' I said, staring into Alkaladur's bright silver and listening to the pearl bowl sing. 'But how can it be?'

My heart beat seven times in rhythm with Atara's, Maram's and Kane's. And then Atara, staring at the bowl as if transfixed by its splendor, whispered to me, 'Val, I can *see* it! It's *inside!*'

As we kept our eyes on the gleaming bowl, she told us that the pearl formed only its veneer; somehow, she said, the ancients had layered over this lustrous substance like enamel over lead.

'But it's no base metal that's inside,' she said. 'It's gold or something very like gold – I'm sure of it.'

'If it's gold, then it must be the true gold,' I said.

Kane's eyes were now black pools that drank in the bowl's light.

557

'So, we must break it open,' he told me. 'Strike it with your sword, Val.'

'But what about the Lord Librarian's second rule?' I asked.

Maram wiped the sweat from his flushed face. 'We weren't to harm any of the *books*, Lord Grayam said.'

'But surely the spirit of his rule was that we weren't to harm *anything* here.'

'Ah, surely,' Maram said, 'this is the time to abide by the *letter* of his rule?'

'Perhaps we should bring the cup to him and let him decide.'

Atara, who had a keener sense of right and wrong than I, nodded at the cup and told me, 'If you were Lord of Silvassu and your castle was about to fall by siege, would you want to be troubled by such a decision?'

'No, of course not.'

'Then shouldn't we abide by the highest rule?' she asked. And then she quoted from Master Juwain's book: '"Act with regard to others as you would have them act with regard to you."'

I was quiet while I gripped my sword, looking at the bowl.

'Strike, Val,' Kane told me. 'Strike, I say.'

And so I did. Without waiting for doubt to freeze my limbs, I swung Alkaladur in a flashing arc toward the bowl. Kane had taught me to wield my sword with an almost perfect precision; I aimed it so that its edge would cut the pearl to a depth of a tenth of an inch, but no more. The impossibly sharp silustria sliced right into the soft pearl. This thin veneer split away more easily than the shell of a boiled egg. Pieces of pearl fell with a tinkle onto the marble stand. And there upon it stood revealed a plain, golden bowl.

'Oh, my Lord! Oh, my Lord!'

Kane, ignoring the stricken look on Maram's face, picked it up. It took him only a moment to peel away the pieces of pearl that still clung to the inside of the bowl. Its gleaming surface was as perfect and unmarked as the silustria of my sword.

'It *is* the Lightstone!' Maram cried out.

A strangeness fell over Kane then. His face burned with wonder, doubt, joy, bitterness and awe. After a very long time, he handed the bowl to me. And the moment that my hands closed around it, I felt something like a sweet, liquid gold pouring into my soul.

'I wish Alphanderry was here to see this,' I said.

The coolness of the bowl's gold seemed to open my mind; I could hear inside myself each note of Alphanderry's last song.

As Atara next took the bowl, I saw Flick whirling above us as he had at the sound of Alphanderry's music. His exaltation was no less than my own. Then Maram's fat fingers closed around the bowl and he cried out again, louder now: 'The Lightstone! The Lightstone!'

We held quick council and decided that we must find Liljana and Master Juwain. But it was they who found us. At the sound of footsteps in the adjoining chamber with its poetry books, Maram quickly tucked the bowl into one of his tunic's pockets and very guiltily began sweeping the shards of pearl off the stand into his other pocket. When Liljana followed Master Juwain into the room, however, he breathed a sigh of relief and broke off hiding the signs of our desecration. He brought out the bowl and told them, 'I've found the Lightstone! Look! Look! Behold and rejoice!'

As Master Juwain's large gray eyes grew even larger, I again beheld this golden bowl and drank in its beauty. It was one of the happiest moments of my life.

'So *this* is what you've been shouting about,' Master Juwain said, staring at the bowl. 'We've been looking all over for you – did you know it's past midday?'

In this windowless room, time seemed lost in the hollows of the bowl that Maram held up triumphantly. In defense at missing our rendezvous by King Eluli's statue, he said again, 'I've found the Gelstei!'

'What do you mean, *you* found it?' Atara asked him.

'Well, I mean, ah, I was the first to pick it up. The first to see it.'

'*Were* you the first to see it?' Atara asked him.

She went on to say that Kane was the first to pick it up after I had cut away the pearl, and who could say who had first laid eyes upon it? Then she told him that it was ignoble to fight over who should receive credit for finding the Lightstone.

'I don't think that anyone has found the Lightstone,' Master Juwain said.

Maram looked at him in such disbelief that he nearly dropped the bowl. Atara and I clasped hands as if to reassure each other that Master Juwain had ruined his sight in reading his books all day. And Kane just stared at the bowl, his black eyes full of mystery and doubt.

Master Juwain took the bowl from Maram as Liljana stepped closer. He looked at us and said, 'Have you put it to the test?'

'It *is* the Gelstei, sir,' I said. 'What else could it be?'

'If it's the true gold,' he told me, 'nothing could harm it in any way. Nothing could scratch it – not even the silustria of your sword.'

'But Val has already struck his sword against it!' Maram said. 'And see, there is no mark!'

In truth, though, Alkaladur's edge had never quite touched the bowl. Because I had to know if it really was the Lightstone, I now brought out my sword again. And as Master Juwain held the bowl firmly in his hands, I drew the sword across the curve of the bowl. And there, cut into the gold, was the faintest of scratches.

'I don't understand!' I said. The sudden emptiness in the pit of my belly felt as if I had fallen off a cliff.

'I'm afraid you've found one of the False Gelstei,' he told me. 'Once upon a time, more than one such were made.'

He went on to say that in the Age of Law, during the hundred-year reign of Queen Atara Ashtoreth, the ancients had made quests of their own. And perhaps the greatest of these was to recapture in form the essence of the One. And so they had applied all their art toward fabricating the gold gelstei. After many attempts, the great alchemist, Ninlil Gurmani, had at last succeeded in making a silver gelstei with a golden sheen to it. Although it had none of the properties of the true gold, it was thought that the Lightstone might take its power from its shape rather than its substance alone. And so this gold-seeming silustria was cast into the form of bowls and cups, in the likeness of the Cup of Heaven itself. But to no avail.

'I'm afraid there is only one Lightstone,' Master Juwain told me.

'So,' Kane said, glowering at the little bowl that he held. 'So.'

'But look!' I said, pointing my sword at the bowl. 'Look how it brightens!'

The silver of my sword was indeed glowing strongly. But Master Juwain looked at it and slowly shook his head. And then he asked me, 'Don't you remember Alphanderry's poem?'

> *The silver sword, from starlight formed,*
> *Sought that which formed the stellar light,*
> *And in its presence flared and warmed*
> *Until it blazed a brilliant white.*

'It warms,' he said, 'it flares, but there's nothing of a blazing brilliance, is there?'

In looking at my sword's silvery sheen, I had to admit that there was not.

'This bowl is of silustria,' Master Juwain said. 'And a very special silustria at that. And so your sword finds a powerful resonance with it. It's what pointed you toward this room, away from where the Lightstone really lies.'

The hollowness inside me grew as large as a cave, and I felt sick to my soul. And then the meaning of Master Juwain's words and the gleam in his eyes struck home.

'What are you saying, sir?'

'I'm saying that I know where Sartan Odinan hid the Lightstone.' He set the bowl back on its stand and smiled at Liljana. 'We do.'

I finally noticed Liljana holding a cracked, leather-bound book in her hands. She gave it to him and said, 'It seems that Master Juwain is even more of a scholar than I had thought.'

Beaming at her compliment, Master Juwain proceeded to tell us about his researches in the Library that day – and during the days that I had lain unconscious in the infirmary.

'I began by trying to read everything the Librarians had collected about Sartan Odinan,' he said. 'While I was waiting for Val to return to us, I must have read thirty books.'

A chance remark in one of them, he told us, led him to think that Sartan might have had Brotherhood training before he had fallen into evil and joined the Kallimun priesthood. This training, Master Juwain believed, had gone very deep. And so he wondered if Sartan, in a time of great need, seeking to hide the Lightstone, might have sought refuge among those who had taught him as a child. It was an extraordinary intuition which was to prove true.

Master Juwain's next step was to look in the Librarian's Great Index for references to Sartan in any writings by any Brother. One of these was an account of a Master Todor, who had lived during the darkest period of the Age of the Dragon when the Sarni had once again broken the Long Wall and threatened Tria. The reference indicated that Master Todor had collected stories of all things that had to do with the Lightstone, particularly myths as to its fate.

It had taken Master Juwain half a day to locate Master Todor's great work in the Library's stacks. In it he found mention of a Master Malachi, whose superiors had disciplined him for taking an unseemly interest in Sartan, whom Master Malachi regarded as a tragic figure. Master Juwain, searching in an off-wing of the north wing, had found a few of Master Malachi's books, the titles of which had been indexed if not their contents. In *The Golden Renegade*, Master Juwain found a passage telling of a Master Aluino, who was said to have seen Sartan before Sartan died.

'And there I was afraid that this particular branch of my search had broken,' Master Juwain told us as he glanced at the False Gelstei. 'You see, I couldn't find *any* reference to Master Aluino in the Great Index. That's not surprising. There must be a million books that the Librarians have never gotten to – with more collected every year.'

561

'So what did you do?' Maram asked him.

'What did I do?' Master Juwain said. 'Think, Brother Maram. Sartan escaped Argattha with the Lightstone in the year 82 of this age – or so the histories tell. And so I knew the approximate years of Master Aluino's life. Do you see?'

'Ah, no, I'm sorry, I don't.'

'Well,' Master Juwain said, 'it occurred to me that Master Aluino must have kept a journal, as we Brothers are still encouraged to do.'

Here Maram looked down at the floor in embarrassment. It was clear that he had always found other ways to keep himself engaged during his free hours at night.

'And so,' Master Juwain continued, 'it also occurred to me that if Master Aluino *had* kept a journal, there was a chance that it might have found its way into the Library.'

'Aha,' Maram said, looking up and nodding his head.

'There is a hall off the west wing where old journals are stored and sorted by century,' Master Juwain said. 'I've spent most of the day looking for one by Master Aluino. Looking and reading.'

And with that, he proudly held up the fusty journal and opened it to a page that he had marked. He took great care, for the journal's paper was brittle and ancient.

'You see,' he said, 'this is written in Old West Ardik. Master Aluino had his residence at the Brotherhood's sanctuary of Navuu, in Surrapam. He was the Master Healer there.'

No, no, I thought, it can't be. Navuu lay five hundred miles from Khaisham, across the Red Desert in lands now held by the Hesperuks' marauding armies.

'Well,' Atara asked, 'what does the journal say?'

Master Juwain cleared his throat and said, 'This entry is from the 15th of Valte, in the year 82 of the Age of the Dragon.' Then he began reading to us, translating as he went:

Today a man seeking sanctuary was brought to me. A tall man with a filthy beard, dressed in rags. His feet were torn and bleeding. And his eyes: they were sad, desperate, wild. The eyes of a madman. His body had been badly burned from the sun, especially about the face and arms. But his hands were the worst. He had strange burns on the palms and fingers that wouldn't heal. Such burns, I thought, would drive anyone mad.

All my healings failed him; even the varistei had no virtue here, for I soon learned that his burns were not of the body alone but the soul. It is strange, isn't it, that when the soul decides to die, the body can never hold onto it.

I believe that he had come to our sanctuary to die. He claimed to have

*been taught at one of the Brotherhood schools in Alonia as a child; he said
many times that he was coming home. Babbled this, he did. There was
much about his speech that was incoherent. And much that was coherent
but not to be believed. For four days I listened to his rantings and fantasies,
and pieced together a story which he wanted me to believe – and which I
believe he believed.*

*He said his name was Sartan Odinan, the very same Kallimun priest who
had burned Suma to the ground with a firestone during the Red Dragon's
invasion of Alonia. Sartan the Renegade, who had repented of this terrible
crime and betrayed his master. It was believed that Sartan killed himself in
atonement, but this man told a different story as to his fate.*

Here Master Juwain looked up from the journal and said, 'Please
remember, this was written shortly after Kalkamesh had befriended
Sartan and they had entered Argattha to reclaim the Lightstone. That
tale certainly wasn't widely known at the time. The Red Dragon had
only just begun his torture of Kalkamesh.'

The stillness of Kane's eyes as they fell upon Master Juwain just then
made me recall the Song of Kalkamesh and Telemesh that Kane had
asked the minstrel Yashku to recite in Duke Rezu's hall. I couldn't
help thinking of the immortal Kalkamesh crucified to the rocky face
of Skartaru, and his rescue by a young prince who would become one
of Mesh's greatest kings.

'Let me resume this at the critical point,' Master Juwain said, tapping
the journal with his finger. 'You already know how Kalkamesh and
Sartan found the Lightstone in the locked dungeon.'

*And so he said that just as he and this mythical Kalkamesh opened the
dungeon doors, the Red Dragon's guards discovered them. While Kalkamesh
turned to fight them, he said, he grabbed the Cup of Heaven and fled back
through the Red Dragon's throne room whence they had come. For this
man, who claimed to have once been a High Priest of the Kallimun, had
again fallen and was now moved with a sudden lust to keep the Cup for
himself.*

*And now he reached the most incredible part of his story. He claimed that
upon touching the Cup of Heaven, it had flared a brilliant golden white
and burned his hands. And that it had then turned invisible. He said that
he had then set it down in the throne room, glad to be rid of it – this
hellishly beautiful thing, as he called it. After that, he had fled Argattha,
abandoning Kalkamesh to his fate. The story that he told me was that he
made his way into the Red Desert and across the Crescent Mountains and
so came here to our sanctuary.*

It is difficult to believe his story, or almost any part of it. The myth of an immortal man named Kalkamesh is just that; only the Elijin and Galadin have attained to the deathlessness of the One. Also, it would be impossible for anyone to enter Argattha as he told, for it is guarded by dragons. And nowhere is it recorded that the Cup of Heaven has the power to turn invisible.

And yet there are those strange burns on his hands to account for. I believe this *part of his story, if no other: that his lust for the Lightstone burned him, body and soul, and drove him mad. Perhaps he did somehow manage to cross the Red Desert. Perhaps he saw the image of the Lightstone in some blazing rock or heated iron and tried to hold onto it. If so, it has seared his soul far beyond my power to heal him.*

I am old now, and my heart has grown weak; my varistei has no power to keep me from the journey that all must make – and that I will certainly make soon, perhaps next month, perhaps tomorrow, following my doomed patient toward the stars. But I before I go, I wish to record here a warning to myself, which this poor, wretched man has unknowingly brought me: the very great danger of coveting that which no man was meant to possess. Soon enough I'll return to the One, and there will be light far beyond that which is held by any cup or stone.

Master Juwain finished reading and closed his book. The silence in that room of ancient artifacts was nearly total. Flick was spinning about slowly near the False Gelstei, and it seemed the whole world was spinning, too. Atara stared at the wall as if its smooth marble was as invisible as Master Aluino's patient had claimed the Lightstone to be. Kane's eyes blazed with frustration and hate, and I couldn't bear to look at him. I turned to see Maram nervously pulling at his beard and Liljana smiling ironically as if to hide a great fear.

And then, as from far away, through that little room's smells of dust and defeat, came a faint braying of horns and booming of war drums: Doom, Doom, Doom. I felt my heart beating out the same dread rhythm, again and again.

Maram was the first to break the quiet. He pointed at the journal in Master Juwain's hands and said, 'The story that madman told can't be *true* can it?'

Yes, I thought, as I listened to my heart and the pulsing of the world, it *is* true.

'Ah, no, no,' Maram muttered, 'this is too, too bad, to think that the Lightstone was left in Argattha.'

DOOM! DOOM! DOOM!

I looked at the False Gelstei sitting on its stand. I gripped the hilt of my sword as Maram said, 'Then the quest is over. There is no hope.'

I looked from him to Master Juwain and Liljana, and then at Atara and Kane. No hope could I see on any of their faces; there was nothing in their hearts except the beat of despair.

We stood there for a long time, waiting for what we knew not. Atara seemed lost within some secret terror. Even Master Juwain's pride at his discovery had given way to the meaning of it and a deepening gloom.

And then footfalls sounded in the adjoining chamber. A few moments later, a young Librarian about twelve years old came into the room and said, 'Sar Valashu, Lord Grayam bids you and your companions to take shelter in the keep. Or to join him on the walls, as is your wish.'

Then he told us that the attack of Count Ulanu's armies had begun.

33

We retreated through the Library's halls and chambers to the infirmary, where I retrieved my helmet and Atara her bow and arrows. There we said goodbye to Master Juwain and Liljana. Master Juwain would be helping the other healers who would tend the Librarians' inevitable battle wounds, and Liljana decided that she could best serve the city by assisting him. I tried not to look at the saws, clamps and other gleaming steel instruments that the healers set out as I embraced Master Juwain. He told me, and all of us, 'Please don't let me see that any of you have returned to this room until the battle is won.'

The young page who had found us earlier escorted Kane, Maram, Atara and me out of the Library and through the gates of the inner wall. He led the way through the narrow city streets, which were crowded with anxious people hurrying this way and that. Many were women clutching screaming babies, with yet more children in tow, on their way to take refuge in the Library's keep or grounds behind its inner wall. But quite a few were Librarians dressed as Kane and I were in mail, and bearing maces, crossbows and swords. Still more were Khaisham's potters, tanners, carpenters, papermakers, masons, smiths and other tradesmen. They were only poorly accoutered and armed, some bearing nothing more in the way of weaponry than a spear or a heavy shovel. At need, they would take their places along the walls with the Librarians – and us. But they would also keep the fighting men supplied with food, water, arrows and anything else necessary to withstanding a siege.

The flow of these hundreds of men, with their carts and braying donkeys, swept us down across the city to its west wall. This was Khaisham's longest and most vulnerable, and there atop a square mural tower near its center stood the Lord Librarian. He was resplendent in his polished mail and the green surcoat displaying the golden book over his heart. Other knights and archers were with him on the tower's ledge, behind the narrow stone merlons of the battlements that protected them from the enemy's arrows and missiles. We followed the page up a flight of steps until we stood at the top of the wall behind the slightly larger merlons there. And then we walked up another flight of steps, adjoining and turning around and up into the tower itself.

'I knew you would come,' the Lord Librarian said to us as we crowded onto the tower's ledge.

'Yes,' a nearby Librarian with a long, drooping mustache said, 'but will they stay?'

He turned to look down and out across the pasture in front of the wall, and there was a sight that would have sent even brave men fleeing. Three hundred yards from us, across the bright green grass that would soon be stained red, Count Ulanu had his armies drawn up in a long line facing the wall. Their steel-jacketed shields, spears and armor formed a wall of its own as thousands of his men stood shoulder to shoulder slowly advancing upon us. To our left, half a mile away where Khaisham's walls turned back toward Mount Redruth, I saw yet more lines of men marching across the pasture to the south of the city. And to the right, in the fields across the Tearam, stood companies of Count Ulanu's cavalry and other warriors. These men, blocked by the river's rushing waters, would make no assault upon the walls, but they would wait with their lances and swords held ready should any of Khaisham's citizens try to flee across it. Behind us to the east of the city, Lord Grayam said, between the east wall and Mount Redruth on ground too rough for siege towers or assaults, yet more of the enemy waited to cut off the escape of anyone trying to break out in that direction.

'We're surrounded,' Lord Grayam told us. He ran his finger along his scarred face as he watched the Count's army march toward us. 'So many – I had never thought he'd be able to muster so many.'

Out on the plain below us, I counted the standards of forty-four battalions. Ten bore the hawks and other insignia of Inyam and another five the black bears of Virad. There were masses of Blues, too, at least two thousand of them, huddled and naked and holding high their axes – and letting loose their bone-chilling howls.

OWRRULLL! OWRRULLLLLL!

'We should have sent for aid to Inyam,' Lord Grayam said. 'And we might have if we'd had more time. Too late, always too late.'

From out across the rolling pasture came the terrible sound of the enemy's war drums. It set the very stones of the walls to vibrating:

DOOM, DOOM, DOOM! DOOM, DOOM, DOOM!

'No, that wasn't it,' Lord Grayam said to a knight nearby whom I took to be one of his captains. 'I was too proud. I thought that we could stand alone. And now but for Sar Valashu and his companions, we do.'

Maram looked down at the advancing armies and took a gulp of air as if it were a potion that might fortify him. He seemed to be having second thoughts about joining the city's defense. Then he belched and said, 'Ah, Lord Grayam, as you observed before, I'm no warrior, only a student of the Brotherhoods and –'

'Yes, Prince Maram?'

Maram noticed that all the men at the top of the tower were looking at him. So were those along the wall below.

'– and I really shouldn't remain here, if I would only get in your way. If I were to join the others in the keep, then –'

'You mean, the women and the children?' Lord Grayam asked.

'Ah, yes, the . . . noncombatants. As I was saying, if I were to join them, then . . . .

Maram's voice trailed off; he noticed Kane had his black eyes fixed on him as did I my own.

Again he gulped air, belched and rolled his eyes toward the heavens as if asking why he was always having to do things that he didn't want to do. And then he continued, 'What I mean is, ah, although I'm certainly no swordmaster, I *do* have some skill, and I believe my blade would be wasted if I had to wait out this battle in the keep – unless of course *you*, sir, deem my inexpertise to be dangerous to the coordination of your defenses and would –'

'Good!' Lord Grayam suddenly called out, wasting no more time. 'I accept the service of your sword, at least for the duration of the siege.'

Maram shut his mouth then, having woven a web of words in which he had caught himself. He seemed quite disgusted.

'All of you,' Lord Grayam said, 'Sar Valashu, Kane, Princess Atara – we're honored that you would fight with us, of your own choice.'

In truth, I thought, listening to the booming of the drums, we had little choice. Our escape was cut off. And because the Librarians had succored us, especially me, in a time of great need, it would be ignoble of us to forsake them. And perhaps most importantly, Alphanderry's cruel murder needed to be avenged.

DOOM, DOOM, DOOM!

Maram, gulping again, drew his sword as he looked out one of the crenels of the battlements. He muttered, 'At least there's a good wall between us and them.'

But the wall, I thought, as I looked down at the Librarians lined up along it, might not provide as much safety as Maram hoped. It was neither very thick or high; the red sandstone its masons had built with was probably too soft to withstand very long a bombardment of good, granite boulders, if the Count's armies had the siegecraft to hurl them. The mural towers, being square instead of round, were also more vulnerable, and the wall had no machicolation: no projecting stone parapet at its top from which boiling oil or lime might be dropped down upon anyone assaulting it. Even now, in the last moments before the battle, the city's carpenters were hurriedly nailing into place hoardings over the lip of the wall to extend it outward toward the enemy. But these covered shelters were few and protected the walls only near the great towers at either side of the vulnerable gates. Since they were made of wood, fire arrows might ignite them. To forestall this calamity, the carpenters were also nailing wet hides over them.

'Sar Valashu,' Lord Grayam said to me as he placed his arm around the Librarian next to him, 'allow me present my son, Captain Donalam.'

Captain Donalam, a sturdy-looking man about Asaru's age, grasped my hand firmly and smiled as if to reassure me that Khaisham had never been conquered: if not because of her walls, then due to the valor of her scholar-warriors. Then he excused himself, and walked down the tower's stairs to the wall, where he would command the Librarians waiting for him there.

We, too, took our leave of the Lord Librarian. There was little room for us along the crowded ramparts in the tower. We walked down the stairs, thirty feet to the wall, and took our places behind the battlements. Maram bemoaned being that much closer to the enemy. And with every passing moment, as the drums beat out their relentless tattoo and the first arrows began hissing through the air, the enemy marched closer to us.

As they drew in upon the city in their lines of flashing steel, the nervousness in my belly felt as if I had swallowed whole mouthfuls of butterflies. I counted the standards of twenty-nine of Aigul's battalions. Among them fluttered the much larger standard of Count Ulanu's whole army: the yellow banner stained blood-red with its great, snarling dragon. Near it, on top of his big brown horse, was Count Ulanu himself. The knights of his vanguard rode with him. Soon enough, I thought, they would let the lines of their men advance forward past them to prosecute the very dangerous assault of the walls. But for the moment, Count Ulanu had the point of honor as the thousands of men on both sides of the wall turned their gazes upon him.

'Damn him!' Kane growled out beside me. 'Damn his eyes! Damn his soul!'

Everyone could see that we had hard work ahead of us. Four great siege towers, as high as the walls and with great iron hooks to latch

569

onto them, were being rolled slowly forward across the grass. They were shielded with planks of wood and wet hides; the moment they came up against the walls, many men would mount the stairs inside them and come pouring over the top. Three battering rams, each aimed at one of the west wall's gates, rolled toward us, too. But the most fearsome of the enemy's weapons were the catapults that had now ceased their advance and had begun heaving boulders at the city. One of these was a mangonel, which flung its missiles in a low arc against the wall itself. Even as I drew in a deep breath and grasped the hilt of my sword, a great boulder soared across the pasture and crashed into the wall a hundred yards to the south, shattering its battlements in a shower of stone.

Now it begins, I thought, with a terrible pulling inside me. *Again and always, it begins.*

As I did before any battle, I built up walls around me. These were as high as the stars and as hard as diamond; they were as thick as the mountains that keep peoples apart. My will was the stone that formed them, and my dread of what was to come was the mortar that cemented them in place. Already, the screams of men hit by flying rocks or pierced with arrows filled the air. But their agonies couldn't touch me.

'Oh, my Lord!' Maram cried out, hunched behind his stone merlon next to me. 'Oh, my Lord!'

Now the archers along the walls, working with crossbows or long-bows, firing from the arrow slits at the centers of the merlons, shot out great sheets of arrows at Count Ulanu's men. Warriors began falling, in their ones and tens, clutching their chests and bellies. And the enemy's archers returned our fire in great black clouds of whining bolts that arched high and fell almost straight down upon the walls in a clatter of steel points breaking upon stone and too often finding their marks in a throat or a hand or an eye.

'Oh, my Lord! Oh, my Lord!'

Most of the arrows, however, at this range were wasted. The battlements provided good cover from their trajectory. More worrisome were the shots fired off by the enemy's most skilled bowmen as their armies drew closer. Perhaps one in ten of these arrows, screaming through the air in straight lines, streaked right through the arrow slits. An archer standing only ten yards from me was killed by one of these. I tried not to look as he practically jumped back from the battlements, a feathered shaft sticking out of his opened mouth and look of vast surprise in his eyes.

There is no pain, I told myself. *Now there is only killing and death.*

We had skilled archers of our own, and none so fine as Atara. She stood beside me, firing off arrows at a rate that the nearby crossbowmen couldn't match. And few could match the range of her powerful, double-curved horn bow, and none her accuracy. Every one of her shots struck some man of Aigul or Virad or one of the naked Blues. Some deflected off a curve of armor or a shield; some found their mark in a shoulder or leg, and so did not kill. But as the moments of terror passed, with missiles shrieking out from and toward the walls, she slowly raised her count of the enemy she had slain.

'Thirty-two!' I heard her call out just after her bowstring had twanged yet again. And then, a few minutes later, 'Thirty-three!'

Kane, Maram and I might have taken our chances in this missile duel, but there were too few bows to be spared and even fewer arrows. In any case, the battle would not be decided by archers. When I dared to look out from the crenel beside me, I saw the many men behind the enemy's front lines bearing long ladders. I saw that the Count's armies, even as they tried to batter open the gates, would try to take the city by escalade. It was the most dangerous kind of assault, the most desperate. But then Count Ulanu must be desperate to invest Khaisham before I and the rest of our company found a way to escape.

I was certain that it was his rage to capture us that had led him to these tactics. I knew this, as I knew many things now since gaining my silver sword. And Kane seemed to know it, too. While Atara fired off her arrows and Maram cowered behind the battlements muttering prayers to the heavens, Kane looked at me and said, 'There can be no surrender for us, do you understand?'

'Yes,' I told him. And then, as a great rock crashed into the wall below us and set the stones to shaking, I said, 'They're going to try to scale the walls.'

'So, damn them,' he said. He looked down the long expanse of the wall and counted its defenders, who were all too few. He stood dangerously exposed, looking through the crenel as he counted the enemy. 'So, Count Ulanu has the men – if he has the will to waste them.'

'He has the will,' I said.

As his armies' lines drew closer, their drums boomed even louder now: DOOM, DOOM, DOOM!

Now a new terror fell upon us as the Aigul archers began shooting off flaming arrows, trying to set the hoardings above the gates, and the gates themselves, on fire. This tactic rankled Maram. He clearly regarded this fulminous substance as his prerogative. Astonishing both Kane and me, he suddenly stood straight up as he reached his hand into his pocket.

'Fire, is it?' he said, taking out his red crystal. 'I'll give them fire!'

Kane moved as if to grab Maram's arm, then checked himself. He looked at me, and our eyes told each other that if there was ever a time for using the red gelstei's flame against living flesh, this was it.

'Be careful!' Kane hissed at him. 'Remember what happened in the Kul Moroth.'

It was exactly this memory, I thought, which moved Maram to expose himself in the crenel. He knew, as did everyone, what would happen if we did not make a good defense here. And he suddenly saw that he had the power to harm the enemy grievously.

'I'll be careful,' Maram muttered, gripping his crystal. 'Careful to aim this at Count Ulanu's ugly face.'

As Maram positioned the crystal and the sun's rays fell upon it, a lancet of fire suddenly streaked out through the air. It fell upon one of Count Ulanu's knights and cut through the mail covering him. He fell screaming from his horse, trying to claw off the rings of molten steel burning into his chest.

'Ai, a firestone!' another knight called out fifty yards from the wall as he looked up at Maram. 'They have a firestone!'

This cry, picked up by others along the enemy's lines, practically halted the whole army's advance. Count Ulanu's warriors tried to cover themselves with their shields; they crouched behind their mantelets, those little rolling walls of wood that gave good protection against arrows if not fire. More than a few of them tried to duck down behind those warriors in front of them.

'Ai, a firestone! A firestone!' came their terrified cries.

The Librarians along the wall seemed only slightly less frightened by what they beheld in Maram's hand. They stared at him in amazement. Then Lord Grayam called down from the tower above us: 'It's a good thing you stood with us after all, Prince Maram. I wondered about the Kul Moroth. The angel fire you've been given to wield may yet win this battle!'

But I was not so sure of this. Firestones, as I had learned from my grandfather's stories, were notoriously difficult to wield in battle. And Maram's was an old stone with an uncertain hand upon it. It took a long time in drinking in the sun's rays before spitting them back out as fire. And despite Maram's boast, he had yet to learn to aim his crystal with anything like an archer's precision with bow and arrow. The next bolt of flame loosed from his stone shot out and burned through the grass dozens of yards from Count Ulanu or any of his men.

'Have pity on the poor moles!' Atara called to him, smiling as she reached for more arrows.

Count Ulanu, too, saw that the terror of Maram's crystal might be worse than its sear. With his captains, he rode along his lines, calling out encouragements and urging his men forward.

'To the walls!' his voice carried out over the corpse-strewn pasture. 'Be quick now, and we'll take them this very day!'

Archers on top of the walls fired their arrows at the Count; one of these whining shafts, shot by Atara, struck his shield and embedded itself there. But Count Ulanu seemed undeterred by this hail of death. Along with the knights of his guard, he bravely charged forward into it. Then his warriors from Aigul followed him, and a whole host of the screaming Blues ran toward us, too.

OWRRULLL! OWRRULLL!

'So,' Kane said. 'So.'

A tremendous blast from Maram's firestone burned a swath through one of Aigul's advancing companies. Twenty men fell like charred scarecrows. The men around them screamed and halted. But when no further fire issued forth, their captains got them moving again. They sprinted with their ladders straight toward the wall.

The enemy had more ladders than we did men. The moment these long wooden constructions touched the wall, the Librarians tried to push them away with forked poles. Many were the attackers that fell off, crying out as they thudded to the ground and perhaps breaking an arm or a leg. But many more fought their way up to the crenels. Here they were met with spear or mace or sword. The thousands of fierce, individual battles up and down the walls would determine whether the city was taken in this first assault.

Kane, working furiously at the crenel next to mine, stabbed out his sword six times, and six of the enemy's warriors flew out into space with mortal wounds reddening their bodies. Atara, to my right, stood firing arrows right into the faces of anyone who showed themselves at the top of their ladders. And Maram stood behind me, still trying to get a flame from his glowing crystal.

OWRRULLL!

One of the Blues came bounding up the ladder below my crenel with the dexterity of a great, squat ape. His face, stained a dark blue from the berries of the kirque plant, showed no emotion other than a rage to rip and rend. His blue eyes fixed on mine like fishhooks. Foam gathered about his mouth as he let loose a terrible cry. He ducked beneath the thrust of my sword and nearly caught me with his axe. But I backed away, and its steel edge scraped along the sandstone of the merlon, sending out sparks. My next thrust drove deep into his muscle-knotted arm, nearly severing it. He took as little notice of this spurting wound as I might a mosquito bite. With a dreadful quickness, he grabbed his axe with his other hand and swung it at me, all in one motion. Its edge bit almost through the mail covering my shoulder, shocking me and bruising the flesh beneath down to the bone. His next blow might have taken off my head if I hadn't swung my sword first, taking off his. Unbelievably, he stood headless at the mouth of the crenel for at least three heartbeats before toppling back from the wall.

There is no pain, I told myself. I stood blinking away the Blue's blood from my eyes and gasping for air. *There is no pain*.

Only my grip on Alkaladur kept me from falling off the rampart behind the battlements to the street below. My sword's shimmering silustria drew strength from the earth and sky, and I drew strength from it. Now other Blues showed themselves in the crenel in which I stood; my silver sword cut through their naked bodies as if through plums. Some of Count Ulanu's knights followed them up the ladder. I had only a little more difficulty in cutting through their mail and killing them one by one.

But many of the Librarians along the walls had less success than Kane and I. Many had fallen, hacked apart, bleeding and crying out their death agonies. Fifty yards down the wall to the left, a squadron of Blues had broken through their defenses. They were rampaging about the battlements, swinging their axes at anything that moved and howling hideously.

'How are we to kill them if they don't know themselves when they are already killed?' a Librarian near me cried.

From the tower high above the battlements, Lord Grayam's strong voice suddenly called down to us: 'Atara Ars Narmada! Our archers are fallen! Come up here now!'

Atara wasted no time in hurrying up the tower stairs in response to his summons. From this vantage high above the walls, she could shoot her arrows down at the Blues who now held an entire section of the wall.

Now, to the left and right, two of the great siege towers had nearly been brought up flush with the walls. And one of the battering rams already had. A hundred yards from us, Count Ulanu's warriors had positioned it in front of the centermost of the west wall's gates. It looked almost like a small chalet, with its steeply pointed triangular frame covered in a housing of wooden planks and wet hides. Inside it, hung on chains from the sturdy frame, was a great tree trunk whose head was black iron cast into the shape of a ram. The men inside the housing swung the log back and forth so that the ram's head struck the wooden gate, again and again, back and forth, threatening to shatter it into splinters.

DOOM! two, three, four, DOOM! two, three, four, DOOM! two, three . . .

'Oh, my Lord!' Maram said beside me. 'They're going to break in!'

574

He positioned his red crystal beneath the rays of the waning sun, but nothing happened.

'What's wrong with this stone!' he wailed out. And then, in a much softer voice, 'What's wrong with *me*?'

And still the great ram beat against the gates, DOOM! two, three, four, DOOM! two, three, four . . .

From the left came the yowling of the Blues, and from above us in the tower, the twang of Atara's bowstring as she fired arrows over our heads at them.

OWRRULLL! OWRRULLLL!

There is no pain, I told myself, hacking apart a young knight who had won through to the battlements. *There is only killing and death.*

'I'm out!' I heard Atara call down to someone in the street below the walls.

And then someone else cried out, 'More arrows! Send up more arrows!'

One of the city's tradesmen, climbing halfway up the wall's steps from the street below, heaved a sheaf of arrows up to me. I grabbed it by the binding cord, and ran up the tower steps to deliver them to Atara.

'Are you all right?' I said to her, looking her over for wounds.

'I'm fine, Val,' she said. Then she looked at my blood-spattered surcoat and mail and asked, 'Are *you* all right?'

'For now,' I said, cutting the cord around the sheaf of arrows.

As she fit one to her bowstring, Lord Grayam came over to me holding a long bow. He asked, 'Can you work one of these as you wield your sword?'

'No,' I said, 'but I *can* shoot.'

'Good – then aim your arrows at those Blues on the wall!'

For a moment, I turned to look at the battalions of Count Ulanu's men far below us crashing against the city's walls like steel waves. They stood bravely beneath the hail of our missiles, their shields held high, waiting to take their turns ascending ladders and die upon our swords – or deal out death themselves. A great many of them were massed beneath the section of wall that the Blues had taken. They were pouring up the numerous ladders there, trying to turn the stream of men that had topped the wall into a flood.

From the tower's vantage, Atara began shooting her arrows into the Blues with a deadly accuracy. I did, too. Where I had once pulled aside my bow to keep from wounding a deer, I now found myself firing feathered shafts into men's naked bellies and throats. Astonishingly, many of the Blues fought on even with half a dozen arrows sticking out of them. If it hadn't been for the valor of the Librarians on the wall, braving the Blues' ferocious axes as they counter-attacked them along the battlements from the north and south, that section of the wall might have been lost to the enemy's assault.

'Push them off!' Lord Grayam called down to his knights. 'Push them off and they'll lose heart!'

A hail of arrows aimed at the tower – at Lord Grayam and us – struck against its battlements, sending up chips of stone. And then a great boulder, hurled by the mangonel, nearly found its mark. It crashed into the wall just where it joined the tower, and broke a hole there. When the dust had settled and the tower stopped shaking, I looked down to see that the boulder had destroyed the stone stairway leading from the tower down to the walls.

DOOM! two, three, four, DOOM! two, three, four, DOOM! two, three . . .

And still the battering ram worked against the city's gates. I heard Maram gasp out a curse from thirty feet below me. Then I watched as he leaned out of a vacant crenel near Kane and held his crystal pointed toward the ram. A red fire that quickly built into swirling crimson flames leapt out from it. The flames fell upon the ram's housing like the breath of a dragon. In only moments, the wet hides nailed to the ram's frame steamed and began burning away as the wood beneath ignited in a great torment of fire. Screams split the air as the men inside it began burning, too.

'Ai! Ai! Ai!' they cried. 'Ai! Ai! Ai!'

More than one of Count Ulanu's men, upon witnessing this horror, turned to flee from the wall. Then ten more broke, and twenty, and soon whole companies from Aigul and Inyam were turning and running. Count Ulanu and his captains rode upon them, striking them with the flats of their swords and trying to turn back the tide of this uncalled retreat. But when men lose the courage to fight, there is little their leaders can do to make them.

'I'll give them fire!' Maram called out from the wall below the tower. 'I *will*!'

Just then his crystal flared a bright ruby red as a shaft of fire shot forth. It struck the siege tower, which had just been hooked onto the wall. Flames enveloped it, trapping fifty men inside its great height of crackling wood. I tried not to listen to their screams.

Suddenly the enemy's bugles along the burning pasture sounded a loud tattoo as Count Ulanu finally gave the order for a retreat. His men, who had mounted their ladders with so much bloodlust, now couldn't be kept from practically flying back down them. They left the company of Blues stranded on top of the wall. Although these nearly nerveless men fought valiantly, Atara's and my arrows picked them off one by one, and Lord Grayam's knights quickly finished them, closing in from north and south along the wall as they retook this blood-slicked section of it.

For the moment, the enemy's attack failed and the world seemed to stand still. All I could hear was the cries and pleading of the wounded, and the long, dark, terrible shrieking inside me. Then I took note of a tremendous clamor coming from the south of the city. A knight on top of a wounded horse came galloping through the streets from that direction. He stopped just beneath our tower and called up to Lord Grayam.

'My Lord!' he gasped, 'the Sun Gate is broken! Captain Nicolam is holding the entrance, but we are too few! He begs you to send more men!'

It took only a moment for Lord Grayam to call down to his son, Captain Donalam, to lead half a company of knights to this new crisis along the south wall. Kane, who had a sense for where the battle was to be the fiercest, looked up toward me and smiled savagely as he favored me with a quick nod of his head. Then he gripped his bloody sword and joined Captain Donalam's knights. They climbed down the wall to the street and began running behind the knight on his wounded horse. I would have gone with them, but the tower's steps were broken, and I had no good way down to them.

Doom, Doom, Doom, Doom . . .

Out on the pasture before the west wall, the enemy's war drums were booming again. Count Ulanu rode among his badly mauled battalions, screaming out orders and trying to reform his men. Surely, I thought, his heralds must have told him of the breaching of the Sun Gate. And so surely it wouldn't be long before he marched his thousands against the wall again.

'No, no,' Maram called out below me, seeming to read my thoughts, 'I'll burn him with starfire – I will!'

Flushed with the hubris of his recent triumphs, he stood leaning out between two of the battlements' arrow-scarred merlons. He pointed his gelstei toward Count Ulanu five hundred yards from us out on the pasture below. The slanting rays of the sun touched the fire-stone. It began to glow again, hellishly hot, it seemed to me. Ten thousand enemy warriors waited to see if its fire would fall upon them. Then Maram let out a painful cry as the sear of his stone burned his hand. He wailed as his fingers opened against his will, and he let go of it. It fell straight down in front of the wall like a shooting star.

'Oh, my Lord!' Maram cried. 'Oh, my Lord!'

'The firestone!' one of Lord Grayam's knights called out. 'He's dropped the firestone!'

Doom, doom, doom . . .

The bright crystal, now quickly cooling to a blood red, lay on the green grass of the pasture beneath the wall. A hundred of the Librarians had seen Maram drop it. And ten thousand of the enemy had.

'Maram Marshayk!' Lord Grayam called out next to me. He looked down from the tower at Maram almost alone beneath us. 'The gelstei! You've got to retrieve the gelstei!'

Maram peered over the crenel at the firestone where it lay among the bodies of fallen warriors thirty feet below him. He sadly shook his head and muttered, 'No, no – not I.'

Far out on the pasture, Count Ulanu had called up his archers who brought their bows to bear on our section of the wall.

'Maram!' I shouted, looking down at him. My eyes picked apart the broken masonry of the tower's stairway to see if there was any way I could climb down to him. There wasn't. 'Maram, you must not let them gain the firestone! Go now!'

'No!' Maram shouted back at me, 'I can't!'

'You can! You must!'

'No, no,' he said angrily. 'How could you ask this of me?'

Behind Count Ulanu, ten of his knights gathered in their horses' reins and turned their shining helms toward us.

'Maram!'

'No! No!'

Several Librarians near Maram chose that moment to haul themselves up over the battlements and climb down the outside of the wall on the ladders that Count Ulanu's men had left there. Arrows killed them. They fell down on top of the heaps of the dying and the dead.

'Maram!' I called out again.

'No, no! I won't go! Are you mad?'

He pulled back behind his merlon just as a rain of arrows clacked against the wall.

Atara, standing next to me on the tower's ledge, looked down at Maram and said, 'He'll never do it.'

'Yes,' I said to her, 'he will.'

Lord Grayam tapped me on the shoulder and pointed across the pasture where a company of cavalry had now gathered two hundred yards behind the archers to charge toward the wall. He started to call for five more of his Librarians, to Maram's left, to go down to the gelstei. But Atara stayed his command. With a strange light in her eyes, she said, 'No, it must be Maram, if it's anyone.'

'Maram!' I called again. 'The seven brothers and sisters of the earth with the seven –'

'Now we're only six and Alphanderry is dead! And I will be, too, if you ask me to go down there! How *can* you?'

How *could* I ask him this, I wondered? And then another thought, as clear and hard as a diamond: How could I not? I knew that the success of the quest depended on his regaining the firestone, as might the fate of Khaisham and much more. The whole world, I sensed, turned upon this moment.

'Maram!' I called out, but there was a silence below me.

It is a terrible thing to lead others in battle. Maram and my companions had elected me to lead us on our quest, and lead I must. But since there was no way I could go down to the firestone myself, I had to persuade him to do so. I wanted to give him all my courage then. But all I could do was to show him his own.

'Maram,' I said, though I did not speak with breath and lips. I drew Alkaladur and held it shining in the sun. Strangely, although I had killed many men with it, its silver blade was unstained, for the silustria was so smooth and hard that blood would not cling to it. Maram couldn't help seeing himself in its mirrored brightness. I opened my heart to him then and touched him with the *valarda*, this gift of the angels. My sword cut deep into him. And there, inside his own heart, he found a sword shimmering as bright as any kalama, if not so keenly honed.

'Damn you!' Maram called out to me. But his eyes told me just the opposite. And then, in a softer voice which I could barely hear, he muttered, 'All right, all right, I'll go!'

He turned to look out at what he must do, the muscles along his great body tensing as he gathered in all his strength. For a moment, I thought he was ready to go up and over the wall. And then he quickly pulled himself back behind the safety of the merlon. And still the drums along the enemy's lines beat almost as loud as my heart: Doom, doom, doom!

'I can't do this,' he said to himself. And then a moment later, 'Oh yes, you can, my friend.'

Again he faced the open crenel, and again he pulled back as he cried out, 'Am *I* mad?'

And still a third time he rushed to the crenel. He put his hands upon the chipped stone there, gathered in his breath, looked out . . . and heaved up his breakfast in a bitter spew. And then, to my pride and his own, he pulled himself up and turned facing the wall to let himself down the ladder there.

'Atara!' I cried, sheathing my sword and grabbing up my bow. 'Shoot now! Shoot as you've never shot before!'

Maram was climbing down the ladder with amazing speed as Count Ulanu's knights thundered across the pasture straight toward him. Atara's bow sang out, and so did mine – and those of the Librarians along the wall. Five knights fell from their horses with arrows sticking out of them. But the enemy's archers were now firing off arrows of their own. One of these struck Maram in his rump; he cried out in anger but kept climbing down the ladder. Then he suddenly let go of it and jumped the final five feet to the ground. He scooped up his crystal and leaped back toward the ladder.

Atara's bowstring twanged again, and another knight fell. I killed one, too – as did many of the archers along the wall. Thus the company of knights charging Maram melted beneath this hot rain of arrows. Only one of them managed to close the last twenty yards, slowing his horse as he neared the wall.

'Maram!' I called down to him. 'Behind you!'

Maram, about to be robbed of his treasure and perhaps his life, whipped out his sword even as he turned and ducked beneath the knight's lance. Then he lunged forward and stabbed his sword into the knight's thigh. In its quickness and ferocity, it was a move worthy of Kane.

Just then one of Atara's arrows burned down and took the knight through his throat. He clung desperately to his horse even as Maram turned to race back up the ladder.

'I'm saved!' he cried out. 'I'm saved!'

But he had spoken too soon. At that moment, an arrow whined through the air and buried itself in the other half of his fat rump. It seemed to push him even more quickly up the ladder. So it was, with feathered shafts sticking out of either of his hindquarters, he reached the top of the wall and heaved himself up over the crenel. Taking care to jump immediately behind one the merlons, he held up the firestone triumphantly.

'Behold!' he said to me. 'Behold and rejoice!'

Then he gazed lovingly at the crystal in his hand as he said, 'Ah, my beauty – did you *really* think I'd let anyone else have you?'

From the top of the tower, Lord Grayam called down to him, 'Thank you, Maram Marshayk!'

Other Librarians nearby by took up the cry: 'Maram Marshayk! Maram Marshayk!'

In a moment, their exultation spread up and down the wall so that knights and archers were now cheering out: 'Ma-ram! Ma-ram! Ma-ram! Ma-ram! . . .'

The sound of so many voices lifted up in praise carried out across the

580

pasture to where Count Ulanu sat on his horse. Hundreds of his men lay slaughtered beneath the wall, and only a few moments before, a whole company of his finest cavalry had perished. One of his siege towers and battering rams were now nothing but charred beams. And still Maram had his firestone. So when the enemy's bugles sounded again and Count Ulanu began pulling back his lines to make camp for the night, no one was surprised.

'Ma-ram! Ma-ram! Ma-ram! . . .'

A rope ladder was called for and cast up to the Lord Librarian – and to Atara and me. We climbed down it and embraced Maram, taking care with his wounds. The blood dripping down his legs caused him to turn and look back at the arrows embedded in him. And then he gasped in outrage and pain, 'Oh, my Lord, I'll never sit down again!'

'It's all right,' I said to him, 'I'll carry you, if I must.'

'*Will* you?'

I gripped his hand in mine with great joy as I watched him holding his red crystal in the other. I said, 'Thank you, Maram.'

In his soft brown eyes was a fire brighter than anything I had seen lighting up his gelstei. 'Thank *you*, my friend,' he told me.

Lord Grayam came forward and clasped his hand, too. 'You would do well, Prince Maram, to repair to the infirmary – with the other *warriors* wounded here today.'

Maram managed a painful but proud smile. 'We won, Lord Grayam.'

Lord Grayam stared down through the ruins of the wall at the bloody ground beneath us. He said, 'Yes, we won the day.'

But the Librarians, too, had lost many men, and the Sun Gate had been breached. Tomorrow, I thought, would be another day of battle and even more terrible.

34

S oon after that a messenger arrived to give Lord Grayam news that made his face blanch and set his hand to trembling: The enemy had been thrown back from the Sun Gate, but in its defense Captain Nicolam had been killed and Captain Donalam and several knights captured. The gate itself was ruined beyond repair; Kane and a hundred knights stood in a line behind it in case Count Ulanu should order a night assault of the city.

'They've taken my son,' Lord Grayam said. In his quavering voice, there was sadness, outrage and great fear. 'And if we try to hold as we did today, tomorrow they'll take the city.'

He issued orders then to abandon the outer wall – and with it, most of Khaisham. So many Librarians had fallen that day, he said, that there were just too few left to hold this extended perimeter. It was an agonizing decision to have to make, but a good one, or so I judged.

And so all the citizens of Khaisham not killed or captured by Count Ulanu's men retreated behind the city's inner wall. In its height and defenses, it was much like the outer wall; it surrounded the Library on all sides, its easternmost sections being almost flush with the outer wall where it turned along the contours of Mount Redruth. To the north, west and south of the inner wall, between its blocks of red sandstone and the houses of the city, an expanse of ground five hundred yards wide had been left barren of any buildings or structures. This provided a clear field of fire for Lord Grayam's archers, who quickly took up their stations behind the wall's battlements. It also kept any enemy from mounting an assault upon the wall from any convenient window or rooftop. That there had never been an assault of any kind upon the inner wall in all the thousands of years since the Library had been built cheered no one.

We took Maram to the infirmary to have his wounds tended. Atara and I half-carried him there, with his thick arms thrown across our shoulders. Master Juwain drew the arrows as he had with Atara. But

582

when he brought forth his green gelstei to heal him further, he had only a partial success. The varistei glowed with only with a dull light, as did Master Juwain himself. With the infirmary's beds filled with moaning warriors who had been hacked and maimed, it had been a very long day for him. Although he staunched the bleeding of Maram's wounds, they still required bandages. But at least Maram could still walk, if not sit very easily. It was more than most of the wounded could manage.

'Ah, thank you, sir, it's not so bad,' Maram said with surprising fortitude. He reached back his hand to pat himself where the arrows had pierced him. 'It's still very sore, but at least I won't be laid up here.'

I looked about this place of carnage and anguish that the infirmary had become. Its smells of medicinal teas and ointments assaulted my senses. I built up *my* inner walls even higher. Although I couldn't wait to get back to the open air of the battlements, it surprised me that Maram felt the same. Courage, once found, does not very quickly melt away.

We said goodbye to Master Juwain and Liljana and left them to a sleepless night of tending the wounded. Then we walked back through the Library. Almost everyone in Khaisham not dead or stationed along the walls had crowded into it. It was a vast place indeed, but it had been built to house millions of books, not thousands of people. It pained me to see aisle upon aisle of old men, women and children camped out there, trying to rest upon little straw mats that they had put down to cover the cold stone floor. It seemed that no yard of floor space in the Library's center hall or any of its wings was unoccupied. Even the walkways circling the great islands of books, at least at the lower levels, had been taken over by brave souls who didn't mind trying to sleep on a narrow bed of stone suspended thirty or fifty feet in space.

It was good to exit the Library through the great, arched doorways of its west wing and breathe fresh air again. We crossed a courtyard crammed with food carts, piles of planking, barrels of water, oil, nails and other things. Sheaves of arrows were stacked like wheat. And everywhere masons and carpenters hurried to and fro beneath the orange blaze of torches to prepare the inner walls for the next day's assault.

We took our places behind the battlements of the west wall. There we found one of Lord Grayam's knights speaking in low tones to Kane. It was very dark there, the only illumination being the fire of the torches in the courtyard below and the far-off glimmer of the stars. It wouldn't do to give the enemy's archers targets to shoot at if Count Ulanu should move them into range during the night.

'So,' Kane said, pointing out at the strip of dark, barren ground that separated the walls from the rest of the city. 'They'll at least try to move their siege engines in as close as they can before morning.'

I looked across the barren ground down toward the houses of the city. With no one left to light their hearths, they were strangely dark. Beyond them, in the thicker dark, farther to the west, I could just make out the lines of the outer wall. While we had been in the infirmary with Maram, Count Ulanu's engineers had breached its gates. The sounds of him bringing up his army lent a chill to the air. There came a squeaking of the axles of many carts and wagons, and iron-shod wheels rolling over the paving stones of the empty streets. Thousands of boots striking stone, jangling steel, whinnying horses, hateful shouts and the incessant howling of the Blues – this was the cacophony we had to endure those long hours after dusk in place of the nightingale's song or other music.

After a while, Lord Grayam walked down the battlements toward us and approached Kane. He told him, 'Thank you for your work at the gate. It's said that but for your sword, the enemy would have broken through.'

'So, my sword, yes,' Kane said, nodding his head. 'And those of a hundred others, Captain Donalam's foremost among them.'

In the dim torchlight, I thought I caught a gleam of water in Lord Grayam's eyes. 'I've been told that my son was stunned by an axe-blow and thus taken before he could regain his wits.'

Kane, who didn't like to lie, lied to Lord Grayam now. I sensed both untruth and a terrible sadness in him as his dark eyes filled with a rare compassion.

'I'm sure he never regained his wits,' he said. 'I'm sure he sleeps with the dead.'

'Let us hope so,' Lord Grayam said, swallowing against the lump in his throat. 'There's little enough hope left for us now.'

To cheer him, and myself, I finally told him of what we had found in the Library earlier that day. I brought forth the False Gelstei and pressed the little bowl into his hands. As the night deepened, Kane and Maram recounted the story of Master Juwain finding Master Aluino's journal. And then Atara, whose memory was like a glittering net that seemed to gather in all things, quoted from it almost word for word.

'Is it possible that Master Aluino told true?' Lord Grayam exclaimed. 'That the Lightstone is still in Argattha?'

He turned the False Gelstei about in his hands as if it might provide an answer to his question. And then he said to us, '*This* is why we fight. And this is why we must prevail tomorrow at any cost. Do you see what treasures we have here? How can we let them be lost?'

He thanked me for telling him of our find and delivering the cup to him, according to our promise. And then he told us, 'You're truly noble, all of you. With such virtue on our side, we might yet win this battle.'

Time is strange. That night near the ides of Soal, as measured by the sands of an hourglass, was rather short as summer nights are. But as measured by the sufferings of the soul, it seemed to drag on forever. Count Ulanu's men were determined that none of us should sleep. The half-moon rose to the Blues' relentless howls, which grew louder and more ferocious as the world turned past midnight. From the darkness beyond the wall came a clamor of axes being struck together and the pommels of swords banging against shields. Iron hammers beat against nails as terrible screams split the night.

We were closer to the Tearam here, and I listened for the river's cleansing sound beneath all this noise. Beyond it, to the north, Mount Salmas was humped in shadows as was Mount Redruth to the east. More than once I turned away from the wall facing this dark peak. In that direction lay Argattha and my home; from the east, in only a few hours or less, would come the rising of the sun and the hope of a new day.

But when the morning finally broke free from the gray of twilight and the forms of the dark earth began to sharpen, a terrible sight greeted all who stood behind the battlements. For there, set into the ground along the barren strip in front of the walls, were forty wooden crosses. The naked bodies of men and three women were nailed to them. The rising wind carried their moans and cries up to us.

'Oh, my Lord!' Maram said to me. 'Oh, too bad!'

Atara, pressing close to my side as she looked out the crenel before us, let loose a soft cry of her own, saying, 'Oh, no – look Val! It's Alphanderry!'

I stared along the line of her pointed finger, peering out into the dawn. My eyes were not as keen as hers; at first all I could make out was the torment of men writhing on their bloodstained wooden towers. And then as the light grew stronger, I saw that the middlemost of the crosses bore the body of our friend. Cords running across his brow bound his head to the cross so that it wouldn't fall forward and we could get a good look at his face. His eyes were open and gazed out at the sky as if he were still hoping to catch sight of the Morning Star before the sun rose and devoured the dreams of night in its fiery wrath.

'Is he *alive*?' Maram asked me.

For a moment, I closed my eyes, remembering. Then I looked at the remains of Alphanderry as I felt for the beating of his heart. 'No, he's dead. And five days dead at that.'

'Then why crucify him? He's beyond all pain now.'

'*He* is, but we're not, eh?' Kane said, clenching his fists in fury. If his fingernails had been claws, they would have torn open his palms. 'Count Ulanu desecrates the dead in order to kill the hope of the living.'

It was why he had crucified the others, too. These, however, were all still alive and all too keenly aware of the agonies that they suffered. It took at least two days to die upon the cross and sometimes much longer.

'Look!' one of the Librarians said, pointing at the cross next to Alphanderry's. 'It's Captain Donalam!'

Captain Donalam, hanging there helplessly, his anguished face caked with black blood, looked up toward the wall in silent supplication. I saw him meet eyes with his father. What passed between them was terrible to behold. I felt Lord Grayam's heart break open, and then there was nothing left inside him except defeat and a desire to die in his son's place.

'Look!' another Librarian said. 'There's Josam Sharod!'

And so it went, the knights on the wall calling out the names of their friends and companions – and of those few shepherds and farmers that Count Ulanu's men had captured outside the walls during his march upon the city.

A little while later, someone called out *our* names. We turned to see Liljana climbing the stairs to the wall, bearing a big pot of soup that she had made us for breakfast. She set it down and joined us in looking out at the crosses.

'Alphanderry!' she cried out as if he were her own child. 'Why did they do this to you?'

'So,' Kane growled, 'the Dragon's priests make every abomination, seek every opportunity to degrade the human spirit.'

Just then, four of Count Ulanu's knights rode out from behind the line of crosses. Atara fit an arrow to her bow to greet them, but she didn't fire it because one the knights bore a white flag. She listened, as we all did, when the knights stopped their horses beneath the walls and one of them called up to Lord Grayam requesting a parley.

'Count Ulanu would speak with you as to making a peace,' this proud-faced knight said.

'We spoke with him yesterday,' Lord Grayam called down. 'What has changed?'

In answer, the knight looked back at the crosses behind him and the broken outer wall of the city.

'Count Ulanu bids you to come down and listen to his terms.'

'Bids me, does he?' Lord Grayam snapped. Then, looking at his helpless son, his voice softened, and he said, 'All right then, *bid* Count Ulanu to come forward as you have, and we shall speak with him.'

'From behind your little wall?' the knight sneered. 'Why should the Count trust that you will honor the parley and not order your archers to fire at him?'

'Because,' Lord Grayam said, '*we* are to be trusted.'

The knight, seeing that he would gain no more concessions from Lord Grayam, nodded his head curtly. He signaled to his three companions; they turned to ride back through the crosses and return to their lines, which were drawn up across the barren ground with the city's houses just beyond them. After a few moments, Count Ulanu and five more knights rode back toward the wall, their dragon standard flapping in the early morning wind.

As soon as he had halted beneath the battlements, his eyes leaped out at us like fire arrows. He reserved the greatest part of his hate for Liljana. He stared at her with a pitilessness that promised no quarter. And she stared right back at him, at the wound her sword had gouged out of his face. What was left of his nose was a black, cauterized sore and looked as if the bitterest of acids had eaten it off.

'Hmmph,' Atara said, glancing at Liljana, 'I suppose he'll have to be called Ulanu the Not-So-Handsome now.'

For a few moments, Liljana and Count Ulanu locked eyes and contended with each other mind to mind. But Liljana had grown ever stronger and more attuned to her blue gelstei. It seemed that Count Ulanu couldn't bear her gaze, for he suddenly broke off looking at her. Then he spurred his horse forward a few paces and called out his terms to Lord Grayam: 'Surrender the Library to us and your people will be spared. Give us Sar Valashu Elahad and his companions and there will be no more crucifixions.'

'Supposing we believed you,' Lord Grayam said, 'what would befall my people upon surrender?'

'Only that they should do homage to me and swear to obey the wishes of Lord Morjin.'

'You'd make us slaves,' Lord Grayam said.

'The terms that you've been offered are the same we extended to Inyam. And they never crossed swords with us or murdered us with their cowardly fire.'

Here he looked up at Maram, who tried to hold his gaze but could not.

'You're very generous,' Lord Grayam called down sarcastically.

Count Ulanu pointed at the crosses and said, 'How many more of the children of your city are you prepared to see mounted thusly?'

587

'We cannot surrender the books to you,' Lord Grayam said. At this, many of the Librarians along the wall grimly nodded their heads.

'Books!' Count Ulanu spat out. Then he reached into the pocket of his cloak and pulled out a large book bound with leather as dark as the skin of a sun-baked corpse. He held it up and said, '*This* is the only book of any value. Either other books are in accord with what it tells, and so are superfluous, or else they mock its truth and so are abominations.'

I knew of this single volume of lies that he showed us: it was the *Darakul Elu*, the Black Book, which had been written by Morjin. It told of his dreams of uniting the world under the Dragon banner; it told of a new order in which men must serve the priests of the Kallimun, as they served Morjin – and that all must serve his lord, Angra Mainyu. It was the only book I knew that the Librarians refused to allow through the doors of the Library.

'We cannot surrender the books,' Lord Grayam said again, looking at Count Ulanu's book with loathing. 'We've vowed to give our lives to protect them.'

'Are books more precious to you than the lives of your people?'

Lord Grayam squared back his tired shoulders and spoke with all the dignity that he could command. It was then that I learned what hard men and women the Librarians truly were. His words stunned me and rang in my mind: 'The lives of men come and go like leaves budding on a tree in the spring and torn off in the fall. But knowledge is eternal – as the tree is sacred. We shall never surrender.'

'We shall see,' Count Ulanu snarled.

Lord Grayam pointed at the crosses and said, 'If you have any mercy, take these people down from there and bind their wounds.'

'Mercy, is it?' Count Ulanu shouted. 'If it's mercy you want, *that* you shall have. We'll leave their fate in your hands – or should I say, those of your archers?'

And with that, he smiled wickedly and turned his horse to gallop with his knights back toward his lines.

'Ah,' Maram said to me, 'I'm afraid to want to know what he meant by that.'

But the implication of his words soon became terribly clear. The Librarians along the wall began to call out to Lord Grayam to mount a sally outside the walls to rescue those who had been crucified. Lord Grayam listened for a few moments and then raised his hand to stay their voices. And then he said, 'Count Ulanu would like us to do just as you suggest. So that he could slaughter our knights while we attempted to rescue those for whom there can be no rescue other than death.'

'Then what are we to do?' a sad-faced knight named Jonatham asked. 'Watch them bake before our eyes beneath the sun?'

'We know what we must do,' Lord Grayam said. The bitterness in his voice hurt me worse than the poison that Morjin's man had put into my blood.

'No, no, please,' I said. 'Let's make a sally, while we can.'

A hundred knights called out to ride their war horses into the face of the enemy and free the crucified women and men. But again Lord Grayam held up his hand and said, 'You might kill many of the enemy, but there would be no time to pull our people down from their crosses. In the end, all of you would be killed or captured yourselves. And so we would lose what little hope of victory that remains to us.'

The Librarians, steeped in the wisdom of the books they guarded, bowed before this logic.

'Archers!' Lord Grayam called out. 'Take up your bows!'

I stood stunned in silence as I watched the archers along the walls fit arrows to their bowstrings and the crossbowmen set their bolts.

'Every abomination,' Kane said. 'Every degradation of the spirit.'

Atara, alone of the archers there, refused to lift her bow. Her brilliant blue eyes filled with tears and partially blinded her to sight of what must be.

'Ulanu the Merciful,' Liljana said bitterly. 'Ulanu the Cruel.'

'No, no,' I whispered, 'they mustn't do this!'

'No, Val, they must,' Kane said. 'What if it were *your* brothers crucified out there?'

Every perversion, I thought, listening to the moans of the dying. What could be more perverse than to twist a man's love for his son into the necessity of slaying him?

'Fire!'

And so it was done. The Khaisham archers fired their arrows into their countrymen and friends. Set upon their crosses only seventy yards from the walls, they were easy targets, as Count Ulanu had intended them to be.

'Damn him!' Kane snarled. 'Damn his eyes! Damn his soul!'

Lord Grayam slumped against the battlements as if he had fired burning arrows into his own heart. I listened for the cries of his son and the other crucified Librarians, but now there was only the moaning of the wind.

Kane stood staring at Alphanderry's body, whose arms were opened wide as if to ask the mercy of the heavens. After a while, his fury poured into me, as did his dark thoughts.

'We should at least ride out and recover the body of our friend,' I said. 'He shouldn't be left hanging for the vultures.'

'So,' Kane said, his eyes blazing into mine. 'So.'

I walked up to Lord Grayam and said, 'It *was* impossible to rescue your people, truly. But it may be that we could bring back our friend's body and a couple others for burial.'

'No, Sar Valashu,' Lord Grayam said, 'I couldn't allow that.'

'The enemy won't be expecting a sally now,' I said. 'We could ride like lightning and return before Count Ulanu could mount an attack.'

The knight named Jonatham called out to ride with us, and so did a dozen others. And then a hundred more along the wall turned toward Lord Grayam with a fire in their hearts and a steel in their voices that could not be gainsaid. And so Lord Grayam, not wanting their spirits to be broken like his own, finally agreed to our wild plan.

'All right,' he said to me. 'You and Kane may go and take ten others but no more. But go quickly before the enemy begins the day's assault.'

Already, Count Ulanu's war drums were booming out their terror as bugles blared out and called men to form up their battalions.

I pulled on my helmet, as did Kane his. Maram, due to his wounds, could not ride, and so would not be sallying forth with us. But Atara grabbed up some more arrows for her quiver, and the long, lean Jonatham came over to us, and we had two of our ten. He and Lord Grayam helped me in choosing the other eight knights for our sortie.

We climbed down from the wall and gathered in the courtyard below. Grooms brought up our horses from the stables. Lord Grayam had ordered his own family's armor fastened upon our horses. Altaru, who had taken me into battle against Waas, was used to the long, jointed criniere that protected the curve of his neck and the champfrein over his head and the other pieces of armor that protected him. And so was Kane's bay. But Fire was not; Atara chose to ride her fierce mare unencumbered, as the Sarni ride their steppe ponies into battle. Thus she could race her horse and turn her about with greater agility, the better to find her targets and fire off her arrows.

When we were all ready, we lined up behind the sally port set into the inner wall's main gate. Its iron-studded doors were thrown open, and we rode out, the twelve of us, across the rocky, barren ground. The cool morning wind found our faces and worked through the steel links of our armor. But it chilled us not at all because our hearts were now on fire. We galloped forward in a thunder of pounding hooves. It took only seconds to cover the ground between the wall and the line of crosses, but this was enough time for Count Ulanu's archers to begin firing at us and for him to order a whole company of cavalry to meet our unexpected charge.

590

An arrow pinged off my helmet and another struck my mail over my shoulder but failed to penetrate its tough steel. Another arrow deflected off the poitrel protecting Altaru's chest. But some of the knights behind me weren't so lucky. One of them, a powerful Librarian named Braham, cried out as a whining shaft suddenly transfixed his forearm. And one of the knight's horses on my left, a stout chestnut gelding, whinnied in pain as another buried itself in his hind leg beneath the croupiere. Even so, we reached the crosses in good order. We would have a few moments, but no more, before Count Ulanu's knights fell upon us.

I steadied Altaru beneath Alphanderry's cross. Even desecrated and left to hang uncovered in shame, he retained a beauty and nobility that defied death. Cords bound his arms to the beam while iron spikes, bent over against the palms like clamps, pierced either hand. Another spike had been driven through his feet. I saw immediately that had he been still alive, it would have been impossible to pull him down in the seconds that remained to us. But he was dead, and so, standing up in my stirrups, I drew my sword and touched it to the cords binding his head and arms; they parted like strands of grass. Then I swung Alkaladur three times, against Alphanderry's ankles and wrists. His body fell down toward me; Kane, who had brought his horse up close against mine, helped me catch it. We draped him across Altaru's back, between his steel-shod neck and my belly. His hands and feet we had to leave nailed to the cross.

Jonatham and Braham likewise managed to recover the body of Captain Donalam, even as a rain of arrows poured down upon us. Two more of Lord Grayam's Librarians cut down one of their companions as an arrow struck into his lifeless body and added insult to death. And then the arrow storm suddenly ceased. For Count Ulanu's knights rode upon us then, and his archers did not wish to kill them in trying to annihilate us.

Although we were outnumbered seven to one, we had that which overcame mere numbers. Atara, her blonde hair streaming back behind her in the wind, rode about wildly firing off death with every bend of her great bow. Jonatham charged the enemy knights once, twice, three times, and his lance became an instrument of vengeance, piercing throat or eye or heart with a lethal accuracy. Kane's sword flashed out with the fury of lightning and thunder, while I wielded the Bright Sword with all the terrible art he had taught me. I rode Altaru straight into the enemy knights where they gathered like a knot of shields and horses, and no matter the armor protecting them, their limbs and heads flew from their bodies like blood sausages encased in steel. The sun rising over Mount Redruth cast its rays upon Alkaladur, which blazed with a blinding light. The sight of it struck terror into even those knights who had yet to come near it. As if they were of one mind, like a flock of birds, they suddenly turned about toward their lines and put their horses to flight.

We managed to cut down five more crucified Librarians before the arrow storm began again. Behind the enemy's lines, Count Ulanu had finally gathered an entire battalion of cavalry to charge us. This force, which he must have intended to defeat any sortie, impelled us to regain the safety of the wall. We were all glad to pass back through the sally port bearing the bodies of friends and companions across our horses. Some of the Librarians, I saw, had taken arrows in payment of their valor. These went off to the infirmary to submit to the ministrations of Master Juwain and the other healers. The sortie had left Kane, Atara and me unwounded. We climbed down from our horses to the cheers of hundreds of Librarians along the walls.

Lord Grayam came down to meet us. He thanked Jonatham and Braham for rescuing his son's body, which had been laid upon a bier in the shadows beneath the wall. Lord Grayam knelt down and touched the bloody wound in his son's chest which Lord Grayam's archers had made. He kissed his son upon the eyes and lips, then stood up and said, 'There's little time for a proper burial, but it will be a while yet before the enemy begins their attack. Let's do for the slain what we can.'

He asked us if the Librarians could take care of Alphanderry's body, and we all agreed that this would be best. And so, forming a procession, Lord Grayam and twenty of his knights – along with Kane, Maram, Atara, Liljana and me – entered the Library through its great southern gate. There we were joined by Master Juwain and the families of the fallen knights. We made our way through long corridors turning right and left until we finally came to a monumental stairway leading down into the vast crypt beneath the Library. It took us a long time to descend these broad, shallow steps. We came down into a dim, musty space of many thick columns and arches holding up the floor of the Library above us. There we laid the dead in their tombs and covered them with slabs of stone. We prayed for their souls and wept. It would have been fitting, I thought, for us to give a favorite song into the silences of that cold, vast space, but this was not the Librarians' way. And so my companions and I sang our praises of Alphanderry inside our hearts.

A messenger came to tell Lord Grayam that the enemy was advancing and his presence was requested on the walls. Those of us who would fight with him there that day followed him to the battlements. Kane, Maram, Atara and I said goodbye to Master Juwain and Liljana, who returned to the infirmary to prepare for the terrible day that awaited us all.

We walked back through the Library as we had come. We crossed the courtyard along the southern wall until we came to the western wall where Lord Grayam had his post. He climbed up to the tower guarding the wall's gate, and Atara and Maram joined him there. Kane and I stood with the grim-faced knights beneath them along the wall where the fighting would be the fiercest.

As on the preceding day, the enemy's drums pounded out their promise of death, and Count Ulanu's steel-clad battalions marched in their gleaming lines toward the walls. The siege towers and battering rams rolled forward; the catapults hurled great stones crashing against the walls and the smooth marble of the Library itself. Arrows fell like rain, though not so many as before when the archers had more of them to shoot. The screams rang out as men began dying.

I was still safe behind the walls that I built for myself; Alkaladur, flashing brilliantly in the morning sun, gave me the strength to endure the deaths of those whom I would soon kill and those whom I had so recently sent on to the stars. Kane stood next to me with his sword held ready to drink the enemy's blood. He drew part of his strength from his hate. He stared down at the empty cross where Count Ulanu had put Alphanderry. I saw him scowling at the hands and feet that remained nailed to it. Lightning flashed in his eyes then. Thunder tore open his heart. A dark and terrible storm built inexorably inside him, awaiting only the advance of Count Ulanu and his men for its fury to be unleashed.

During the first assault, Count Ulanu sent a battalion of Blues against our part of the wall. Kane and I, no less Maram and Atara, had become familiar figures to the enemy. Many of them shrank back from facing us. But the bravest of them vied for the honor of slaying us, and none were so brave as the Blues. Atara killed them with her arrows and Maram with his fire, but it was not enough. Too many of them hurled themselves howling over the battlements to meet Kane's sword and mine with their murderous axes. Their rage seemed bottomless; they attacked us without fear. Alkaladur made a carnage of their frenzied, naked bodies, as did Kane's bloody blade. Even so, they came at us in twos and tens, and worked their way behind us. Twice I saved Kane from an axe splitting open his back, and three times he saved me. Thus our flashing swords forged deep bonds of brotherhood between us. For a few golden moments we fought back to back as if we were one: a single, black-eyed Valari warrior with four arms and two swords guarding both front and back.

593

The Blues could not overcome us. I killed many of them. And each time my sword opened up one of them, I myself was opened. Although they did not feel pain as did other men, their death agonies were strangely even more unbearable. For the very numbness of these half-dead men was itself a deeper and more terrible kind of suffering. The Soulless Ones, people called them, but I knew well enough they had souls, as all men do. It was just that the essence of what made them human seemed lost, damned in life to wander that gray and misty realm that lies between life and death. To feel no pain is to be robbed of joy as well. And so I found that I must not envy their invulnerability to that to which I was most vulnerable. I found, too, that I could not hate them. It was not the One but only Morjin who had originally called their kind into life.

At last Count Ulanu's buglers sounded the retreat, and the Blues and the rest of the enemy pulled back from the walls. Teams of pallbearers worked all up and down the battlements to dispose of the many enemy who had fallen there – and the bodies of the slain Librarians, too. Others came up to us with mops and buckets of water to clean the ramparts so that the remaining defenders wouldn't slip on all the blood spilled there or become disheartened at the sight of it. But it seemed that nothing could now lift the spirits of the Librarians. There were simply too many of the enemy and too few of them. Even the fire from Maram's crystal brought them little warmth of hope.

'It *is* difficult to use this in battle,' he said to me, holding up his gelstei and coming down from his tower to pay Kane and me a visit before the next assault. 'Difficult to aim. And the more fire I bring forth from it, the longer it takes to gather in the sun's rays for the next burst.'

'It's an old crystal,' Kane muttered. 'It's said that firestones of ages past were more powerful.'

I looked out to the left at the smoking ruins of the second siege tower that Maram had managed to set aflame. His firestone seemed fearsome enough. But fire was only fire, and the enemy was growing used to it. Death was only death, too, and what did it matter whether a warrior was killed by shooting flames or by boiling oil and red-hot sand poured down upon him from the hoardings above the gates?

Maram turned his red crystal about in his hands and said, 'I don't believe this will be enough to win the battle.'

'No, perhaps not,' Kane said. 'But it's kept us from losing it so far.'

'Do you *think* so?'

'I think that if any survive to sing of the deeds that were done here, your name will be mentioned first.'

Such praise, coming from Kane, surprised Maram and pleased him greatly. After a few moments of thought, however, he looked down at the lines of the enemy gathering at the edge of the barren ground, and he said, 'But there will be another assault, won't there? They have so many men.'

It was not yet noon when the day's second assault began. This time, Count Ulanu sent his finest knights against our part of the wall. They were almost harder to beat back than were the Blues, for they fought with greater skill, and their armor gave good protection against arrow and sword – all swords except Kane's kalama and Alkaladur.

There came a moment during the fiercest part of the attack when a dozen of these knights of Aigul fought their way over the battlements and won a bridgehead on the wall. Kane and I found ourselves separated, with the knights between us. They killed two Librarians standing near me, and a few more fighting near Kane. They had beards as black as Count Ulanu's and looked enough like him to have been his cousins; I thought they were some of the same knights that had pursued us into the Kul Moroth. They taunted Kane, telling him that soon they would capture him and have the pleasure of nailing him to a cross as they had Alphanderry.

It was the wrong thing to do. For Kane fell mad then. And so did I. Working along the wall toward the south, I wielded my sword with all the fury of the blazing Soal sun that poured down upon us. And Kane fought like a demon from hell, slashing and thrusting and rending his way north. Together, our flashing swords were like the teeth of a terrible beast closing upon our enemy. They died one by one, and then suddenly, the three knights still alive lost heart before our terrible onslaught. Two of them hurled themselves over the battlements, taking their chances with broken legs or backs in their plummet to the hard ground below. The remaining knight, seized with terror, threw down his sword. He knelt before Kane, placed his hands together over his chest and cried out, 'Quarter! I beg quarter of you!'

Kane raised his sword high to finish this hated enemy knight.

'Mercy, please!' the knight begged.

'So, I'll give you the same mercy your Count showed those he crucified!'

The madness suddenly left me. I called out, 'Kane! A warrior's code!'

'Damn the code!' he thundered. 'Damn him!'

'Kane!'

'Damn his eyes! Damn his soul!'

Kane's sword lifted higher as the knight looked at me, his dark eyes pleading like a trapped fawn's. There was a great pain inside him, the same bitter anguish I felt gnawing at my own heart. He burned for life; all of us do. In such circumstances, how could I allow it to be taken away from him?

I raised high my sword then so that its silustria caught the sun's rays and threw them back into Kane's eyes. For a moment he stood there dazzled by this golden light. His sword wavered. Then he looked at me, and I looked at him. There was a calling of our eyes, Valari eyes: black, brilliant and bottomless as the stellar deeps. There the stars shone, and there, too, Alphanderry's last song reverberated and sailed out toward infinity. I heard the haunting sound of it inside me, and in that moment, so did Kane. And in the opening of his heart, he began to remember who he really was and who he was meant to be. This was a bright, blessed being, joyful and compassionate – not a murderer of terrified men who had thrown down their weapons and asked for mercy. But he feared this shining one more than any other enemy. It was upon me to remind him that he was great enough of heart and soul that he need fear nothing in this world – nor that which dwelled beyond it.

'So,' he said, suddenly sheathing his sword as tears filled his eyes. He stepped past the kneeling knight and came up to me. He touched my sword, touched my hand, and then clamped his hand fiercely about my forearm. A bright, blazing thing, secret until now, passed between us. And he whispered, 'So, Val – so.'

He turned his back on the knight, not wanting to look at him. It seemed, as well, that he couldn't bear the sight of me just then. The Librarians came to take the knight away to that part of the Library where captives were being held. And all the while, Kane stared up at the sky as if looking for himself in the light that kept pouring from the bright, midday sun.

Three more times that long afternoon, Count Ulanu's armies made assaults upon the wall. And thrice we threw them back, each time with greater difficulty and desperation. Kane's newfound compassion did not keep him from fighting like an angel of death, nor did my own stay the terror of the sword Lady Nimaiu had given me. But all our efforts – and those of Maram, Atara and the Librarians – were not enough to defeat the much greater forces flung against us. Near the end of the third assault, with most of Count Ulanu's army in retreat from the walls, we suffered our greatest loss thus far. For one of the Blues, who had fought his way up to a section of wall where Lord Grayam stood with his sword trying to meet a sudden crisis, felled Lord Grayam with a blow of his axe. He himself was slain a moment later, but the deed was done. The Librarians set Lord Grayam down behind the wall's battlements. There he called for me and the rest of our company to come to him. While a messenger ran to summon Master Juwain and Liljana, I knelt with Kane, Atara and Maram by his side.

'I'm dying,' he gasped out as he leaned back against the bloodstained battlements.

I tried not to look at the bloody opening that the Blue had chopped through his mail into his belly. I knew it was a wound that not even Master Juwain could heal.

Jonatham and Braham called for a litter to carry the Lord Librarian to the infirmary. But he shook his head violently, telling them, 'There's no time! Never enough time! Now please leave me alone with Sar Valashu and his companions. I must speak with them before it's truly too late.'

This command displeased both Jonatham and Braham. But since they were unused to disobeying their lord, they did as he had asked, walking off down the wall and leaving us with him.

'The next attack will be the last,' he told us. 'They'll wait until the sun goes down so that Prince Maram can't use his firestone, and then . . . the end.'

'No,' I said, listening to the blood bubble from his belly. 'There's always hope.'

'Brave Valari,' he said, shaking his head.

In truth, unless a miracle befell us, the next assault *would* be the last. It was a matter of the numbers of Librarians still standing and the severity of their wounds; the promise of defeat was in the dullness of Librarians' eyes and in the exhaustion with which they held their notched and bloodstained weapons – no less the gaps the enemy's missiles had broken in the walls. A knowledge comes to men in battle when the battle is nearly lost. And now the enemy began reforming themselves in their companies and battalions in front of the houses of the glowing city; and now the Librarians peered out at this gathering doom as courageously as they could: without much fear but also without hope.

And then, from the tower to our left, one of the Librarians there pointed toward the west and shouted down, 'They're coming! I see the standards of Sarad! We're saved!'

It seemed that we had our miracle after all. I stood to look out the crenel, beyond Count Ulanu's armies and the houses of the city, beyond even the broken outer wall to the west. And there, perhaps a mile out on the pasture, cresting a hill and limned against the setting sun, was a great host of men marching toward Khaisham. The red sun glinted off their armor; their standards, in a direct line with this fiery orb, were hard to see. I told myself that I could make out the golden lions of Sarad against a flapping blue banner. But then one of the Librarians, from the tower to our right, peered through his looking glass and announced, 'No, the standards are black! And it is the golden dragons of Brahamdur!'

He then swept his glass from north to south and shouted, 'The armies of Sagaram and Hansh march with them! We are lost!'

A pall of doom descended upon all who stood there, worse than before. Count Ulanu had sent for reinforcements to complete his conquest, and with all the inevitability of death, they had come.

'Sar Valashu!' Lord Grayam called to me. 'Come closer – don't make me shout.'

I knelt beside him with my friends to hear what he had to say. Just then he smiled as he saw Liljana and Master Juwain mount the steps to the wall. He beckoned them closer, too, and they joined us.

'You must save yourselves, if you can,' he told us. 'You must flee the city while you can.'

I shook my head sadly; Khaisham was now surrounded by a ring of steel too thick for even Alkaladur to cut through.

'Listen to me!' Lord Grayam called out. 'This is not your battle; even so you have fought valiantly and have done all you can do.'

I looked from Atara to Kane, and then at Maram, who bit his lip as he tried desperately not to fall back into fear. Master Juwain and Liljana were so tired that they could hardly hold up their heads. They had seen enough of death during the past day to know that soon, like the coming of night, it would fall upon them as well.

'I should have bid you to leave Khaisham before this,' Lord Grayam told us, as if in apology. 'But I thought the battle could be won. With your swords, with the firestone that I suspected Prince Maram possessed . . . .'

His voice trailed off as a spasm of agony ripped through his body and contorted his face. And then he gasped, 'But now you must go.'

'Go *where*?' Maram muttered.

'Into the White Mountains,' he said. 'To Argattha.'

The name of this dreadful city was as welcome to our ears as the thunder of Count Ulanu's war drums booming out beyond the walls.

'You must,' he told us, 'try to recover the Lightstone.'

'But, sir,' I said, 'even if we could break out, to simply forsake those who have stood by us in battle –'

'Faithful Valari,' he said, cutting me off. His eyes stared up and through me, up at the twilight sky. 'Listen to me. The Red Dragon is too strong. The finding of the Lightstone is the only hope for Ea. I see this now. I see . . . so many things. If you forsake your quest, you truly *do* forsake those who have fought with you here. For why have we fought? For the books? Yes, yes, of course, but what do books hold inside them? A dream. Don't let the dream die. Go to Argattha. For my sake, for the sake of my son and all who have fallen here, go. Will you promise me this, Sar Valashu?'

Because a dying man had made a request of me with almost his last breath – and because I thought there was no way we could ever escape the city – I took his hand in mine and told him, 'Yes, you have my promise.'

'Good.' With all the strength that he could manage, he reached inside the pocket of his cloak and pulled out the False Gelstei that we had found in the Library the day before. He gave the gold-colored cup to me and told me, 'Take this. Don't let it fall into the enemy's hands.'

I took the cup from him and put it in my pocket. Then he closed his eyes against another spasm of pain and cried out, 'Jonatham! Braham! Captain Varkam!'

Jonatham and Braham, accompanied by a grim, gray-haired knight named Varkam, came running along the wall. They joined us, kneeling at Lord Grayam's feet.

'Jonatham, Braham,' Lord Grayam said. 'What I must tell you now, you mustn't dispute. There is no time. Everyone has noted your valor in rescuing my son's body. Now I must call upon a deeper courage.'

'What is it, Lord Librarian?' Jonatham asked, laying his hand on Lord Grayam's feet.

'You are to leave the city tonight. You will –'

'Leave the city? But how? No, no, I couldn't –'

'Don't argue with me!' Lord Grayam interrupted him. He coughed, once, very hard, and more blood flowed out of him. 'You and Braham will go into the Library. With horses, at least two of them. Take the Great Index. We can't rescue the books, but at least we should have a record of them so that copies might someday be found and saved. Then go with Sar Valashu and his companions into the hills. From there, they will go . . . where they must go. And you will go to Sarad. For a time: soon Count Ulanu will fall against it and take it as well. He'll take all of Yarkona. And so you must flee to some corner of Ea where the Dragon hasn't yet come. I don't know where. Flee, my knights, and gather books to you that you might start a new Library.'

He placed his hands over his belly and moaned bitterly as he shuddered. Then he sighed, 'Too late – much too late.'

Beyond the wall, the beating of the drums thundered louder.

Lord Grayam drew in a deep breath and said, 'Captain Varkam! You will hold the walls as long as you can. Do you understand?'

'Yes, Lord Librarian,' he said.

'All of you, I must tell you how sorry I am that I misjudged, that there just wasn't enough time, and that I, in my pride, didn't see –'

'Ah, Lord Grayam?' Maram said, interrupting him. He alone, of all of us, felt compelled to put need before decorum. 'You spoke of fleeing into the hills. But how are we to leave the city?'

Lord Grayam closed his eyes then, and I felt him slipping off into the great emptiness. But then he suddenly looked at me and said, 'Long ago, my predecessors built an escape tunnel from the Library to the slopes of Mount Redruth. Only the Lord Librarians have kept this secret. Only the *Lord* Librarian has the key.'

Here he weakly tapped his chest. We loosened the gorget covering his throat and pulled back his mail. There, fixed to a chain around his neck, was a large steel key.

'Take it,' he said, pressing it into my hand. After I had lifted the chain over his head, he continued, 'In the crypt, there is a door. It's plastered over, but . . . .'

Another spasm ripped through him. His whole body shivered and convulsed, and his eyes leaped out like a siege tower's hooks and fastened onto the great wall surrounding the city of night. So Lord Grayam died. Like many men, he went over to the other side before he was really ready, before he thought it was his time to die.

'Oh, too bad, too bad!' Maram said, touching his throat. Then he looked at Atara as his thoughts turned away from Lord Grayam to the problem at hand. 'We'll never find the door now. Can *you* help us?'

Atara shook her head even as Master Juwain closed Lord Grayam's onstaring eyes.

Doom, doom, doom, doom . . .

'Well, Lord Grayam said to go into the crypt, so I suppose we should go,' Maram said.

'Yes, but *which* crypt?' Jonatham asked. 'There is the one where we buried your friends. And one beneath each of the Library's wings.'

Now the sun had set, and the sentinels cried out that the armies of Brahamdur, Sagaram and Hansh were approaching the city's outer wall.

It would have been hopeless, of course, to search each of the crypts, tapping along their subterranean walls for the sound of a hidden door. And so Liljana, seized with inspiration, took out her blue gelstei and laid her hand on Lord Grayam's head. Her touch lasted only a few moments. But that was enough for her to reach into that land of ice and utter cold – enough, as her grip closed upon the last gleam of Lord Grayam's mind, to freeze her soul. Her eyes suddenly rolled back in her head, showing nothing but white, and I was afraid that she would join Lord Grayam in eternity. Then she shuddered violently as she ripped her hand away and looked at me.

'Oh, Val – I never knew!' she whispered to me.

'Brave woman,' I said, taking her cold hand in mine. I smiled and said softly, 'Foolish woman.'

Maram licked his lips as the drums kept up their relentless tattoo. He looked at Liljana and asked, 'Could you *see* anything?'

'I saw where the door is,' Liljana suddenly breathed out. 'It's in the main crypt. I can find it, I think.'

I stood up then, and so did my companions. To Captain Varkam, who was looking at us strangely, I said, 'It seems that there may be a way out for us, after all. And yet –'

'Go!' he said to me with great urgency. 'This was the Lord Librarian's last command, and it must be obeyed.'

He motioned for Lord Grayam's body to be placed on a bier. And then he told me, 'Farewell, Sar Valashu. May you walk always in the light of the One.'

Then he quickly clasped my hand and turned to look to the Library's last defense.

We sent for our horses and took them into the Library. The men and women of Khaisham looked at us incredulously as we led them clopping their iron-shod hooves down the long halls. The word soon spread that we had found a means of escaping this vast building – and the city itself. At first, many clamored to go with us. But when it became known that we were going into the mountains to the east, their panic to flee the city gave way to even greater fears. For that was the land of the man-eating Frost Giants from which none had ever returned.

'What will happen to them?' Maram asked as we began our descent down the broad steps leading to the crypt. Although no one had wanted to go with us, we all felt guilty at leaving them behind.

'Likely they'll be enslaved,' Kane said. 'So, likely they'll live longer than we will.'

We met Jonatham and Braham in the gloom of the crypt. They had four horses between them, each of whose saddlebags was packed with their portion of the eighty-four huge volumes of the Great Index. It made a heavy load for the horses, but not nearly so great as the burden that they themselves must bear.

Liljana located a place on the crypt's eastern wall, where the light of the torches through the arches showed most brightly. We brought forth the sledgehammers the Librarians had given us and broke through the veneer of plaster hiding the door. This was a huge slab of steel, untouched by rust and still gleaming dully despite the march of the centuries since it had been hung there. With the help of a little oil in its lock, the Lord Librarian's key opened it. Before us was a tunnel wide enough to drive a cart through – and dark enough to send shudders of doubt through all our hearts.

Our passage through it was like a nightmare. Once the door had closed behind us – this cold piece of steel that would take Count Ulanu's men half the night to break from its jamb – it seemed that the earth itself had devoured us. The torches we carried sent an oily smoke into the stale air and choked us; the red sandstone through which the tunnel had been carved seemed stained with the blood of all who had died along the Library's walls. The horses hated going down into that dank, foul-smelling place. Twice, Altaru whinnied and balked, setting his hooves against the stone like a mule which no threat will move. I had to whisper to him that we were going to a better place and would soon breathe fresh air again. Only his love for me, I thought, impelled him to move on and lead the other horses forward.

We walked down and down for a long time. The tunnel twisted like a worm in the earth, right and left. In its dark hollows sounded the echoes of our footfalls and the deeper murmurs of our despair. I thought I could feel the souls of all those who had been placed in the crypt, Alphanderry most of all, wandering about in this endless tunnel, forever lost. It was only Lord Grayam's dying wish, like a beckoning hand, that led me on.

At last the tunnel began to rise. After what seemed hours but must have been much less time, we came to another door, like the first. It opened onto a much larger space that had once been the shaft of a mine. Now, as we could tell from the strong animal scent clinging to the rocks here, it had been taken over as the lair of a bear. The sudden knowledge that we were so close to one of Maram's furry friends set him to singing nervously, so that any bear here would be warned of our passage and perhaps flee instead of attacking us. But it seemed that whatever beast lived in this ancient mine was not at home. We passed unmolested out of the mine's opening, which was overgrown with bushes and trees.

And so at last we stood on the slope of Mount Redruth beneath the night's first stars. In the air was a sharp coolness as well as a howling coming from the city below us. We could see all of Khaisham quite clearly in the starlight and in the sheen of the bright half moon. The Library, rising like a vast salt crystal from Khaisham's highest hill, was ringed by thousands of little lights that must have been torches. Many of these flickered from atop the inner wall; from this sign I knew that it had fallen. The Librarians, no doubt, were making their final defense from behind the Library's immense wooden doors. I wondered how much longer they would stand before Count Ulanu's fire arrows and battering rams.

'You should go now,' I said to Jonatham. He stood with Braham by their horses, looking down at his conquered city. I pointed along the curve of the mountain, south toward Sarad. 'It won't be long before our escape is discovered. Count Ulanu will surely send pursuit.'

'If he does, then they will be slain,' Jonatham said with a black certainty. 'As we will, all of us. We've entered the Frost Giants' country here, and they'll likely find us before Count Ulanu's men do.'

'They may,' I said. 'But there is always hope.'

'No, not always,' Jonatham said, taking my hand in his. 'But it gladdens my heart that you say that. I shall miss you, Sar Valashu.'

'Farewell, Jonatham,' I told him. 'May you walk in the light of the One.'

Then I clasped Braham's hand, as did my friends, one by one, quickly making their farewells. We watched as they led their horses across the trackless slope of the mountain until they vanished behind its contours into the dark.

I stood on the rocky, slanting earth with my hand on Altaru's neck, trying to ease his strained nerves for the journey that we still must make. Maram stood by Iolo near me, as did Atara and Liljana with their horses, and Master Juwain and Kane.

'Oh, what are we to do!' Maram said, gazing down at the city.

'There's only one thing *to* do,' I said.

Maram looked at me with horror filling up his face. 'But, Val, you can't really be thinking that –'

'I gave my promise to Lord Grayam,' I told him.

'But surely that's not a promise you can think to keep!'

Could I keep this promise, I wondered? I, too, stared down at Khaisham. The thousands of torches had now closed in around the Library like a ring of fire.

'My promise,' I said to Maram and the others, 'was given from me to Lord Grayam. It doesn't bind any of you.'

'But surely it doesn't bind *you*, either,' Master Juwain told me. 'You can't promise to do the impossible.'

Atara was quiet for a few moments as she looked off at Khaisham – and far beyond. And then she spoke with the clear, cool logic that was one of her gifts. 'If we don't go east, then what direction should we choose?'

As she pointed out, we could not return west through Yarkona as we had come. To the south lay Sarad, which would soon fall as Khaisham had, and beyond that, the deathly hot Red Desert. And north, across the White Mountains, infested in those parts with the tribes of the Blues, we would come to the thickest part of the Vardaloon, which might hold monsters even worse than Meliadus.

'Then we must go east,' I said. 'To Argattha, to find the Lightstone.'

'But we don't know that it's even there!' Maram said. 'What if Master Aluino's journal was a hoax? What if *he* was mad, as he thought of the man claiming to be Sartan Odinan?'

I stared at the blazing torches as I relived Lord Grayam's urging that I should enter Argattha. I tried to imagine an invisible cup guarded by dragons and hidden in the darkest of places – the last place on earth that I would ever wish to go. Then I drew Alkaladur and pointed it toward the east. Its blade flared with a silvery light, the brightest I had yet seen.

'It's there,' I said, knowing that it must be. 'It's still there.'

Master Juwain came forward and set his hand on my arm. He said, 'Val, there is a great danger here. Danger for us, if we covet the Lightstone as Sartan did and fall maddened by it. Perhaps it would be best to leave the Lightstone wherever it was that he set it down. It might never be found.'

'No,' I said, 'it *will* be found – by someone. And soon. This is the time, sir. You said so yourself.'

Master Juwain fell silent as he stared up at the stars. There, it was told, the Ieldra poured forth their essence upon the earth in the ethereal radiance of the Golden Band.

'The seven brothers and sisters of the earth,' I said, citing Ayondela's prophecy, 'with the seven stones will set forth into the darkness and –'

'And that's just it!' Maram broke in. 'With Alphanderry gone, we're only six. And we've only six gelstei. How are we to find the seventh in the wastes that lie between here and Argattha?'

I pressed my hand over my heart. I said, 'You're wrong, Maram. Alphanderry is still with us, here, in each of us. And as to the seventh gelstei, who knows what we'll find in the mountains?'

'You have a strange way of interpreting prophecies, my friend.'

I smiled grimly and told him, 'Of this part of the prophecy, we both must agree: that if we go into Argattha, we'll surely be setting forth into the very heart of darkness.'

The quiet desperation that fell upon Maram told me that he agreed with every fear-quivered fiber of his being.

Of all my friends, only Kane seemed pleased by the prospects of this desperate venture. The wind off his dark face and rippling white hair carried the scents of hate and madness. A wild look came into his eyes, and he said, 'Once Kalkamesh entered Argattha, and so might we.'

'But that's madness!' Maram said. 'Surely you can see that!'

'Ha – I see that the plan's seeming madness is its very strength. Morjin will continue to seek the Lightstone in every other land but Sakai. He'll seek us there, too, eh? He'd never dream we'd be witless enough to try to enter Argattha.'

'*Are* we that witless?' Maram asked.

Liljana patted his hand consolingly and said, 'It *would* be foolish to attempt the impossible. But is it truly that?'

We all looked at Atara, who stared out at Khaisham as from the vantage of the world's highest mountain. And then, in a soft voice that struck terror into me, she said, 'No, not impossible – but almost.'

From high up on the Library's south wing came a flicker of light, as of a flame brightening a window. I thought of all the Librarians who had died in its defense and the thousands of men, women and children taking refuge inside. I thought of my father and mother, of my brothers and all my countrymen in far-off Mesh – and of the Lokilani and Lady Nimaiu and even the greedy but sometimes noble Captain Kharald. And, of course, of Alphanderry. I knew then that even if there was only one chance in ten thousand of rescuing the Lightstone out of Argattha, it must be taken. My heart beat out its thundering affirmation of this dreadful decision. There comes a time when a life not willingly risked for the love of others is no longer worth living.

'I will go to Argattha,' I said. 'Who will come with me?'

Now more flames appeared in the other windows of the south wing, and then in those of the other wings, as well. When it became clear that Count Ulanu's men had fired the Library, Maram called out, 'The books! Everyone trapped inside! How can he do this? How, Val, how?'

He fell against me, weeping and clutching at the rings of my mail to keep from falling down in despair. I forced myself to stand like a wall, or else I would have fallen, too – and never to arise again.

'Oh no!' Liljana said, looking down at the burning Library, 'it can't be!'

Her arms found their way around Atara, who was now sobbing bitterly and silently as she pressed her face against Liljana's chest.

'I should never have used my firestone,' Maram gasped out. 'All the burning led only to this. I swear I'll never turn fire against men again.'

Master Juwain had both hands held against the sides of his head as he stared down at the horror before us. He seemed unable to move, unable to speak.

'So,' Kane said, with death leaping like dark lights in his eyes.

As the fire found the millions of books that the Librarians had collected over the centuries, a great column of flame shot high into the air. It seemed to carry the cries of the damned and the dying up toward the heavens. I smelled the sweet-bitter boil of death in the sudden burning that swept through me like an ocean of bubbling kirax. Fire ravished me. It blazed like starlight in my heart and hands and eyes.

'So,' Kane said as I turned to look at him, 'I will go with you to Argattha.'

I bowed my head to him, once, fiercely, as our hands locked together. Then I looked at Master Juwain, who said, 'I will go, too.'

'So will I,' Liljana said, gazing at me in awe of what we must do.

'And I,' Atara said softly. Her eyes found mine; in their depths was a blazing certainty that she would not leave my side.

Maram finally pulled away from me and forced himself to stop sobbing. I saw the flames from the Library reflected in the water of his dark eyes – and something else.

'And I,' he said, 'would *want* to go with you, too, if only I –'

He suddenly stopped speaking as he drew in a long breath. For a long few moments, he stood looking at me. He blinked at the bitter smoke as if remembering a promise that he had made to himself. He pulled himself up straight, shook out his brown curls, and stood for a moment like a king.

'I *will* go with you,' he told me with steel in his voice. 'I'd follow you into hell itself, Val, which is certainly where we are going.'

I clasped his hand in mine to seal this troth as our hearts beat as one.

After that, we all turned to behold the destruction of the Library. There was no desire to utter another word, no need to speak the prayers that would burn forever in our hearts. The fire, fed by many books and bodies, raged high into the sky and seemed to fill all the world, and that was hell enough.

35

And so, that very night, we went up into the mountains. We turned our horses east and picked our way across the rocky slopes of Mount Redruth. We had no track to follow, only the gleam of my sword and the glimmer of the stars. These points of white and blue grew more vivid as we left Khaisham's glowing sky behind us and climbed higher. Bright Solaru of the Swan Constellation gave me hope, as did the brilliant swath of stars called the Sparkling Stairs. They reminded me that there were better places in the One's creation where men did not kill each other with steel and flame.

As the night deepened, it grew cooler, and I surrounded myself in my cloak, which my mother had made of lamb's wool and embroidered with silver. It gave good warmth, as did those of my companions. But not enough to please Kane. His eyes cut through the dark ahead of us, peering out at the ghostly white shapes of the greater mountains rising up to the east. And he said, 'We'll need thicker clothing than this before long.'

'But it's still summer,' Maram said, walking his horse near him.

'In the deeper mountains, it's already fall,' Kane said, pointing ahead of us. 'And in the high mountains, winter. Always winter.'

His words quickened the chill in the air. They brought us back to the dangers all about us. These were numerous and deadly. Pursuit by Count Ulanu's men was the least of them. Although we listened for the sound of his warriors hurrying after us, it would be morning at the earliest before there would be enough light for them to follow our tracks. More worrisome, at the moment, was losing our way in the dark and plunging off an unexpected cliff. Or having one of the horses break a leg on the jagged rocks of the uncertain terrain, and thus being forced make a mercy killing. Certainly there were bears about, as Maram imagined seeing behind every tree. And we all looked for the shapes of the dreaded Frost Giants lying in wait for us, perhaps just behind the next ridge, or the one behind that.

All that night, however, we saw no sign of these fearsome creatures. Nor did we catch sight of the twinkling form of Flick. This dispirited all of us, not as much as had Alphanderry's death, but enough. Maram supposed that Flick had the good sense not to enter a land guarded by bears and man-eating giants. I wondered if the evil of what had happened in Khaisham had simply driven him away. I was almost ready to say a requiem for him when he suddenly reappeared just before dawn. As the Morning Star showed brightly in the east, he winked into a fiery incandescence that reminded me of the sparks thrown up by the library's burning. I took this as his own manner of saying a requiem – or at least a remembrance of all those who had died that night in the hellish flames.

'Flick, my little friend!' Maram cried out when he saw him spinning through the grayness of the twilight. 'You've come back to us!'

'Maybe he's been with us all along, and we just couldn't see him,' Atara said.

Liljana, leaning against her horse, said, 'It's strange, isn't it, that Alphanderry *did* see him just before he died? How can that be?'

We looked at each other in puzzlement and wonder; the world was full of mysteries.

'Ah, I'm tired,' Maram yawned. 'Too tired to think about such things now. I think I'd better lie down before I fall down.'

We were all exhausted. We were at the end of our second sleepless night; none of us, except perhaps Kane, could pass another day without at least a few hours of rest. As for myself, my body hurt from a dozen bruises gained in battle. My shoulder, into which the Blue had swung his axe, was the worst of these torments. With the coolness of the night and the muscles' inevitable stiffening, it ached so badly that Master Juwain had to rig a sling to take up the weight of my arm. And yet it was nothing against the aching I felt in my heart whenever I thought of Alphanderry hanging from his cross and all the Librarians who had died before my eyes. From such ghastly visions, I and all my friends longed for surcease.

And so we found a level place in a hollow between two ridges and set out our sleeping furs for a quick nap. Kane insisted on remaining awake to keep watch over us, and none of us argued with him. I fell off into a sleep troubled with images of fire and terrible screams. And it wasn't Morjin who sent these dreams to me, only the demons of war that had fought their way deep into my mind.

We awoke beneath a bright sun to vistas of icy mountains rising up before us. While Liljana went to work on our breakfast, we held a quick council and decided that we had eluded whatever pursuit that Count Ulanu had sent after us – if indeed he had sent anyone at all. Kane thought it possible that the Library had been fired before our escape route through the crypt had been discovered, and Atara agreed. Perhaps, she said, the Library had collapsed into a smoking ruin, forever sealing off access to the escape tunnel and the steel door that guarded it.

'Likely Count Ulanu thinks we're dead,' Atara told us. 'Likely he'll spend many days searching through the ruins for our bodies – and for our gelstei.'

'Well, this is a stroke of luck, then!' Maram said. 'Perhaps luck is turning our way.'

Atara said nothing as she stared out at the great mountains before us. We all knew that we would need much more than luck to cross them.

The smell of bubbling porridge wafted into the air. Liljana stood by her little cauldron stirring the oats with a long wooden spoon. Her face told me that she was still unhappy at having had to jettison her cookware on our flight across Yarkona. She was unhappy, too, that there hadn't been time to gather the necessary supplies for our journey.

'We've enough food for most of a month, if we stretch it,' she told us as we gathered around the little fire to eat. 'How far is it to Argattha?'

'If the old maps are right, two hundred and fifty miles, as the raven flies,' Master Juwain said. Then his face furrowed as he rubbed his bald head. No one knew very much about Sakai, not even the mapmakers.

'Well, then,' Maram said, 'we need make only eight or nine miles per day.'

'So,' Kane said, 'we won't be traveling as the raven flies. And in the mountains, we'll be lucky to make even that.'

While Liljana brewed up the last of our coffee and its sweet, thick aroma steamed out into the air, we sat discussing our route into Sakai. It was unnerving to know so little about the land that we proposed to cross. According to Master Juwain, Sakai was a vast, high plateau entirely ringed by mountains. The White Mountains, he said, rose up like an immense wall from the lake country of Eanna in the northwest and ran for a thousand miles toward the southeast to make up Ea's spine. Somewhere to the east of us, it divided into two great ranges: The Yorgos in the south, and in the north, the Nagarshath, where it was said were the highest mountains on earth. The realm of Sakai lay between them. Master Juwain thought that various spurs of these ranges ran north and south across the plateau, but he wasn't sure.

'At least we know that Skartaru lies along the very northern edge of the Nagarshath,' he said. 'It's known that the Black Mountain looks out over the Wendrush.'

'Then we should follow the line of the Nagarshath until we come to it,' I said. I looked at my sword, whose radiance was almost lost in the greater blaze of the sun. It pointed us east and slightly south – straight along the course I imagined the Nagarshath to run.

'We should follow it,' Kane agreed, 'but follow how? We can't make our way through the range itself. Its mountains are said to be impassable. That leaves a journey across the plateau, keeping the mountains to our left. But there, we'll certainly find Morjin's people – or be found by them.'

'But what other choice do we have?' Liljana asked.

'None that I can see,' Kane said.

We all looked at Atara, who shook her head and told us, 'None that I can see, either.'

We were silent as we scanned the mountains about us. Maram stared off behind us, still looking for pursuit, while I gazed ahead at the great, white peaks rising up like impossibly high merlons directly ahead of us.

'How far is it,' I asked Master Juwain, 'until we come to where the two ranges part and the plateau begins?'

'I'm not really sure,' he said. 'Sixty miles. Perhaps seventy.'

I felt my belly tighten. Seventy miles of such mountains as these seemed like seventy thousand. Trying to show a courage that I didn't feel, I pointed my sword east into their heart. Then I said, 'We'll just have to cut straight across them.'

'Ha, straight is it?' Kane laughed out, clapping me on my good shoulder. 'So you say – and you a man of the mountains.'

I laughed with him. Then Maram pointed out that the only thing straight about the journey ahead of us was that we were going straight into hell.

That day we had some of the hardest work of our journey. Without any map or track to follow, we had to make our way across the rocky ridges with little more than intuition to guide us. Twice, my sighting of a possible pass through the rising ground before us proved a dead-end, and we had to turn back to find another route. It was exhausting to lead the horses up toward the snowline along a slope strewn with boulders and scree; it was even more dispiriting to retreat down these same uncertain steps to seek out another path. Although there was beauty all about us in the gleam of the great mountains and in the sky pilots and other wildflowers that brightened their sides, by the time we made camp that evening, we were all too tired to appreciate it. The thin air cut our throats, and Master Juwain complained of the same dull headache I felt building at the back of my neck. It grew quite cold – and this faint frost of the falling night was only a promise of the ice and bitterness that still lay before us.

Thus for three days we fought our way east. Mostly, the weather held fair, with the air so thin and dry that it seemed it could never hold the slightest particle of moisture. But then, late on the third afternoon, dark clouds appeared as if from nowhere, and we had a few fierce hours of freezing rain. It cut our eyes with lancets of sleet and stung our lips; it coated the rocks with a glaze of ice, making the footing for both man and beast treacherous. As we could find no shelter from this torment, we sat huddled beneath our cloaks waiting for it to end. And end it did as the clouds finally opened to reveal the frigidity of night. As we could neither retreat nor go forward with any degree of safety, we were forced to spend the night high up on the saddle between two great mountains. There Maram knelt with his flint and steel, trying to get a fire out of the wood that the horses had toted up into this barrenness.

'I'm cold; I'm wet; I'm tired,' Maram complained as he struck off another round of sparks into his tinder. His hands shook as he shivered and said, 'Ah, no, the truth is, I'm *very* cold.'

While Atara and Kane gathered snow to melt and Liljana waited to cook our dinner, I walked over to Maram and placed my hand on the back of his neck to rub the knotted muscles there. Some of the fire that kept me going must have passed into him, for he sighed and said, 'Ah, that's good, that's very good – thank you, Val.'

A tiny flame leaped up from the tinder and spread to the little twigs that Maram had gathered around it. He watched it grow until he had quite a good blaze going.

'Ah,' he said, relaxing beneath the sudden heat, 'you took more blows in the battle than I. And so it is *I* who should rub *your* neck.'

The pain at the back of my neck felt as if a mace had broken through the bones there to open up my brain. But I said, 'You took two arrows saving us, Maram. It was a great thing that you did.'

'It was, wasn't it?' he said. He gingerly touched his hindquarters where the arrows had pierced him. 'Still, fair is fair, and I owe you a massage, all right?'

'All right,' I said, smiling at him. He smiled as well, proud to have freely taken on such a little debt.

An hour later we gathered around the fire and ate some boiled salt pork and battle biscuits. Master Juwain made us tea and poured it into our mugs, which we rolled between our hands to draw in its warmth. It was a time for song, but none of us felt like singing. And so

I drew forth my flute and played a melody that my mother had taught me. It was nothing like the music that Alphanderry had made for us, but there was love and hope in it even so.

'Ah, that's *very* very good,' Maram said as he held his cloak before the fire to dry it. 'Look, Flick is dancing to your song!'

Limned against the starry eastern sky, Flick was spinning about in long, glittering spirals. His fiery pirouettes *did* seem something like dancing. We all took courage from his presence. Master Juwain pointed at him and said, 'I'm beginning to think that *he* might be the seventh told of in Ayondela's prophecy.'

It was a strange thought with which to lie against the cold ground and fall off to sleep that night. It made me recall with great clarity Alphanderry's death and the despair that had gripped my heart afterwards. And through this dark doorway, Morjin came for me. In my dreams, he sent a werewolf who looked like Alphanderry sniffing through the shadows for the scent of my blood. This demon howled in a rage to show me yet another of my deaths; then it sang sweetly that I should join him in the land from which there is no return. It tried to kill me with the terror of what awaited me. But that night, I had allies watching over me and guarding my soul.

Flick, I somehow knew, spun above my sleeping form like a swirl of stars warding off evil. My mother's love, felt in the deep currents of the earth beneath me, enveloped me like a warm and impenetrable cloak. Inside me shone the sword of valor that my father had given me, and outside, on the ground with my hand resting on the hilt, was the sword called Alkaladur. It quickened the fires of my being so that I was able to strike out and drive the demon away. It cut through the black smoke of the nightmare realm into the clear air through which shone the world's bright stars. And so I was able to awaken beneath the mountains, covered in sweat and shaking but otherwise unharmed.

I opened my eyes to see Atara sitting by my side and holding my hand. It was just past midnight and her turn to take the watch. On the other side of the fire, with their furs spread on top of the snow, Maram, Liljana and Master Juwain were sleeping. Kane, who lay breathing lightly with his eyes closed, was probably sleeping too, but with him it was harder to tell.

'Your dreams are growing darker, aren't they?' Atara said softly.

'Not ... darker,' I said, struggling for breath. I sat up facing her and looked for her eyes through the thickness of the night. 'But they're worse – the Lord of Lies tries to twist the love of a friend into hate.'

She squeezed my hand in hers while she held her scryer's sphere in her other. I gathered that she had been gazing into this clear crystal when I had cried out in my sleep.

'He *sees* you, doesn't he?' she asked.

'In a way,' I said. 'But it is more as if he can smell the taint of the kirax in me. Whatever Count Ulanu has communicated to him as to our deaths, he knows that I'm still alive.'

'He is still seeking you, then?'

'Yes, seeking – but not quite finding. Not as he would like.'

'He *mustn't* find you,' she said with a quiet urgency in her voice.

'Time is on his side,' I told her. 'It is said that the Lord of Lies never sleeps.'

'Do not speak so. You mustn't say such things.'

Of course, she was right. To anticipate one's own defeat is to bring it about with utter certainty.

There was a new fear in her voice when she spoke of Morjin and a new tenderness in her fingers as she stroked my hand. I pointed at the sphere of gelstei she clutched against her breast, and I asked, 'Have *you* seen him then? In your crystal?'

'I've seen many things,' she said evasively.

I waited for her to say more but she fell into a deep silence.

'Tell me, Atara,' I whispered.

She shook her head and whispered back, 'You're not like Master Juwain. You don't need to know everything about everything.'

'No, not everything,' I agreed.

Maram, snoring loudly on the other side of the fire, rolled over in his sleep as Liljana shifted about against the cold and pulled her cloak more tightly about her neck. I sensed that Atara was afraid of waking them. So it didn't surprise me when she stood up, took my hand and walked with me a few dozen yards across the snowy ground into the darkness surrounding our camp.

'It's so hard for me to tell you, don't you see?' she said softly.

'Is it that bad then? Is it any worse than what I've seen?'

I told her about the thousands of deaths I had died in my dreams. This touched something raw inside her. I felt her seize up as if I had stuck my finger into an open wound.

'What is it?' I asked her.

Her whole body shook as if suddenly stricken with the night's deep cold.

'Please tell me,' I said, holding her against me.

'No, I can't, I shouldn't – I shouldn't have to,' she whispered.

And then she was kissing my hands and eyes, touching the scar on my forehead, kissing that, holding me tightly – and then she collapsed to her knees as she threw her arms around my legs and buried her face against my thighs as she sobbed.

I called to her as I stroked her hair, 'Atara, Atara.'

A little later, with the night's wind cooling her grief, she managed to stand again and look at me. And she told me, 'Almost every time I see Morjin, I see you. I see your death.'

The wind off the icy peaks around us suddenly chilled me to the bone. I smiled grimly at her and asked, 'You said *almost* every time?'

'Almost, yes,' she said. 'There are other branchings, you see, so few other branchings of your life.'

'Please tell me, then.'

She took a deep breath and said, 'I've seen you kneeling to Morjin – and living.'

'*That* will never be.'

'I've seen you turning away from Argattha, too. And going far away from him. With me, Val. Hiding.'

'That can't ever be,' I said softly.

'I know,' she whispered through her tears. 'But I *want* it to be.'

I held her tightly as her heart beat against mine. I whispered in her ear, 'There must be a way. I have to believe that there's always a way.'

'But what if there isn't?'

The star's light reflected from the snow was just enough for me to behold the terror in her eyes. And I said, 'If you've seen my death in Argattha, you should tell me. So that I might fight against it and make my own fate.'

'You don't understand,' she said, shaking her head.

She went on to tell me something of her gift with which she had been touched. She tried to describe how a scryer's vision was like ascending the branches of an infinite tree. Each moment of time, she said, was like a magical seed quivering with possibilities. Just as a woman lay waiting to blossom inside a child, the whole tree of life was inside the seed. Every leaf, twig or flower that could ever be was there. A scryer opened it with her warmth and will, with her passion for truth and her tears. To move from the present to the future, as a scryer does, was to find an eternal golden stem breaking out of the seed and dividing into two or ten branches, and each one of these dividing again and again, ten into ten thousand, ten thousand into trillions upon trillions of branches shimmering always just beyond her reach. The tree grew ever higher toward the sun, branching out into infinite possibilities. And the higher the scryer climbed, the brighter became this sun until it grew impossibly bright, as if all the light in the universe were pulling her toward a single, golden moment at the end of time that could never quite be.

'It sounds glorious,' I said to her.

'You *still* don't understand,' she said sadly. 'Morjin, and his lord, Angra Mainyu – they are poisoning this tree. Darkening even the sun. The higher I climb, the more withered branches and dead leaves.'

The wind in my face seemed to carry the stench of the burning Library in its sharp gusts. For the thousandth time, I wondered how many people had died in this terrible conflagration.

'But there must be a branch that is whole,' I said to her. 'Leaves that even he cannot touch.'

'There might be,' she agreed. 'I wish I had the courage to look.'

'What do you mean?'

She put her crystal in her pocket and grasped my hands. She said, 'I'm afraid, Val.'

'You, afraid?'

She nodded her head. The starlight seemed to catch in her hair. Then she told me that the tree of life grew out of a strange, dark land inside her.

'There be dragons there,' she said, looking at me sharply.

My heart ached with a sudden, fierce desire to slay this particular dragon.

'A scryer,' she said, 'a true scryer must never turn back from ascending the tree. But the heights bring her too close to the sun. To the light. After a while, it burns and blinds – blinds her to the things of the world. *Her* world grows ever brighter. And so she lives more for her visions than for other people. And living thus, she dies a little and grows ugly in her soul. Old, ugly, shriveled. And that is why people grow to hate her.'

I pressed her hand against my wrist so that she could feel the beating of my heart there. I said, 'Do you think I could ever hate you?'

'I'd want to die if you did,' she said.

In the dark I found her eyes as I took a deep breath. I said, 'There must be a way.'

There must be a way that she could stand beneath this brilliant, inner sun and return in all her beauty bearing its light in her hands.

'Atara,' I whispered.

I knew that for me, too, there was a way that the *valarda* could not only open others' hearts to me, but mine to them.

'Atara,' I said again.

What is it to love a woman? It is just love, as all love is: warm and soft as the down of a quilt yet hard and flawless like a diamond whose sheen can never be dimmed. It is sweeter than honey, more quenching of thirst than the coolest mountain stream. But it is also a song of praise and exaltation of all the wild joy of life. It makes a man want to fight to the death protecting his beloved just so this one bit of brightness and beauty, like a perfect rose, will remain among the living when he has gone on. Through the hands and eyes it sings, calling and calling – calling her to open up the bright petals of her soul and be a glory to the earth.

I touched the tears gathering at the corner of Atara's eye and then wiped away my own. I looked at her a long time as she looked at me. She grasped my hand and pressed it against her wet cheek. At last she smiled and said, 'Thank you.'

Then she took the white gelstei out of her pocket. She held it so that its polished curves caught the faint light raining down from the sky. Inside it were stars, an infinitude of stars. For a moment, her eyes were full of them as they seemed to grow almost as big as her crystal sphere. And then she disappeared into it as if plunging through an icy lake into a deeper world.

I waited there on the cold snow for her to return to me; I waited a long time. The constellations wheeled slowly about the heavens. The wind fell down from the sky with a keening that cut right through me. It sent icy shivers along my veins and set my heart to beating like a great red drum.

'Atara,' I whispered, but she didn't hear me.

Somewhere behind me, Maram snored and one of the horses nickered softly. These sounds of the earth seemed a million miles away.

'Atara,' I said again, 'please come back.'

And at last she did. With a great effort, she ripped her eyes from her crystal to stare at me. There was death all over her beautiful face, now tightening with a sudden, deep anguish. Something worse than death haunted her eyes and set her whole body to trembling. She shook so badly that her fingers opened and the gelstei fell down into the snow.

'Oh, Val!' she sobbed out.

Then she fell weeping against me and I had to hold her up to keep her from collapsing altogether. I was afraid that I would have to carry her back to our camp. But she was Atara Ars Narmada of the Manslayer Society, after all, and it wasn't in her to allow herself such weakness for very long. After a few moments, she gathered up her dignity and stood away from me. She dried her tears with the edge of her cloak. Then she bent to retrieve her scryer's sphere from the snow.

I waited for her to tell me what she had beheld inside it. But all she said was, 'Do you see? Do you see?'

I saw only that she had been stricken by some terrible vision and was afraid that she was now mutilated in her soul. Whatever this affliction was, I wanted to share it with her.

'Tell me what you saw, then.'

'No . . . I never will.'

'But you must.'

'No, I must *not*.'

'Please, tell me.'

She stared out at the snow-white contours of the mountains around us. Then she looked at me and said, 'It's so hard to make you understand. To make you *see*. Just talking about this one thing can change . . . everything. There are so many paths, so many futures. But only one that can ever *be*. We can choose which one. In the end, we always choose. *I* can, Val. That's what makes this seeing so hard. I blink my eyes just one time, and the world isn't the same. Master Juwain once said that if he had a lever long enough and a place to stand, he could move the world. Well, I've been given this gift, this incredible lever of mine. Shouldn't I want to use it to preserve what is most precious to me and save your life? And yet, how *should* I use it if in saving you, you are lost? And the world along with you?'

She had told me almost too much; more than this I did not wish to hear. And so I gave voice to what my soul whispered to be true: 'There must be a way.'

'A way,' she said, her voice dying into the bitterness of the wind.

If there *was* a way she would never tell it to me for fear of what might befall. And yet, I knew that she had found some gleam of hope in the dragon-blackened tree inside her. Her eyes screamed this to me; her pounding heart could not deny it. But it was a terrible hope that was tearing her apart.

'Do you see?' she asked me. 'Do you see why scryers are stoned and driven off to live in the ruins of ancient towers?'

'That is not what I see, Atara.'

She stood before me with a new awareness of life: prouder, deeper, fiercer, more tender, more passionate and devoted to truth – and this was a beauty of a wholly different order. This was her grace, to transform the terrible into a splendor that shone forth from deep inside her. And she, who could see so much, could not see this. And so I showed it to her. With my eyes and with my heart, which was like a mirror wrought of the purest silustria, I showed her this beautiful woman.

'Valashu,' she said to me.

What is it to love a woman? It is this: that if she hurts, you hurt even more to see her in pain. It is your heart stripped of protective tissues and utterly exposed: soft, raw, impossibly tender; if a feather brushed against it, it would be the greatest of agonies. And yet also the greatest of joys, for this, too, is love: that through its fiery alchemy, what was once two miraculously becomes one.

We gazed at each other through the darkness, locking eyes as we called to each other – calling and calling. My heart, fed with fire, swelled like the sun. Suddenly it broke open in a blaze of light. It broke her open, too. She called to me, and we closed the distance between ourselves like two warriors rushing to battle. She flew into my arms, and I into hers. Our mouths met in a fury to breathe in and taste each other's souls; in our haste and artlessness, we bruised our lips with our teeth, bit, drew blood. We were like wild animals, clawing and pulling at each other, and yet like angels, too. In the heat of her body was a fierce desire that I tear her open to reveal the beautiful woman she really was. And that I should join her in that secret place inside her. She called me to fill her with light, with love, with burning raindrops of life. Only then could she feel all of the One's glory pouring itself out through her, as well. Only then could we both drive back death.

Valashu.

I felt her hand against my chest, pressing the cold rings of my armor against my heart. She suddenly pulled her lips away from mine. She fought herself away from me, and stood back a few paces, trembling and sweating and gasping for breath.

'No!' she suddenly sobbed out. 'This can't be!'

I teetered on top of the snow, sweating and trembling, too, stunned to find myself suddenly standing alone. There was a terrible pressure inside me that made me want to scream.

'Don't you see?' she said to me as her hands covered her belly. Her eyes, fixed on the emptiness of the night, suddenly found mine. 'Our son, our beautiful son – I can't *see* him!'

I didn't know what she meant; I didn't *want* to know what she meant.

'I'm sorry,' she said, taking my hands in hers. 'But this can't be, not yet. Maybe not ever.'

The wind, falling down from the sky, chilled my inflamed body. The stars in the blackness above me told me that I must be patient.

'I know that there is hope,' I said to her. 'I know that there is a way.'

She drew herself up to her full height and gazed at me as from far away. Then she asked me, 'And how do you know this?'

'Because,' I said, 'I love you.'

It was a foolish thing to say. What did love have to do with overcoming the world's evil and making things come out all right? My wild words were sheer foolishness, and we both knew this. But it made her weep all the same.

'If there *is* a way,' she said, pressing her hand against the side of her face, 'you'll have to find it. I'm sorry, Val.'

She leaned forward then and kissed me, once, on my lips with great tenderness. And then she turned to walk back toward our camp, leaving me alone beneath the stars.

I didn't sleep the rest of the night – and not because the Lord of Lies sent evil dreams to torment me. The remembrance of the terrible hope that I had seen in Atara's eyes was torment enough. So was the taste of her lips that seemed to linger on mine.

In the morning we made our way down from the saddle between the two mountains into a long, narrow valley. It was a lovely place and heavily wooded, with blue spruce and feather fir and other trees. A sparkling river ran down its center. Its undulating forests hid many birds and animals: bear, marten, elk and deer. Although we were deep in the White Mountains and it was rather cool, the air held none of the bitterness of the high terrain we had just crossed. And so we decided to make camp by the river and rest that day. The horses' hooves needed tending and so did our sorely worked bodies. Despite our worry about the Frost Giants, Atara went off by herself to hunt, hoping to take a little venison to replace our dwindling stores. Although we needed the meat badly enough, I knew that she mostly just wanted to be alone.

I was not the only one to notice this new inwardness that had come over her. Later that afternoon, as I sat with Maram and Liljana on the rocks by the river washing our clothes, Maram said to me, 'How she looks at you now! How she looks at herself! What happened between you two last night?'

'That is hard to say,' I told him.

'Well, whatever it is, she's a new woman. Ah, the power of love! As soon as this quest of ours is over, my friend, I'd advise you to marry her.'

And with that he stood up, gathered up his wet clothes and pointed at some dry, high ground above us where he had built up a good fire. 'Well, I'm going to take a nap. Please keep an eye out for the Frost Giants. And bears. I don't want to be eaten in my sleep.'

After he had ambled off, I looked at Liljana and said, 'Here we are in the middle of the wildest country on earth and he thinks of marriage.'

Liljana's big breasts swayed beneath her tunic as she beat our soiled garments upon the rocks. She looked up from her work and smiled at me, saying, 'I think you do, too.'

'No,' I said, looking toward the forest to the south where Atara had disappeared, 'this is no time to think of that.'

'With a woman like Atara, how could you think otherwise?'

'No,' I said, 'she's a scryer, and scryers never marry. And she's a warrior who must –'

'She's a *woman*,' Liljana said to me as she wrung out one of Master Juwain's small tunics. 'Don't you ever forget that, my dear.'

Then she sighed and lowered her voice as if confiding in me a great secret. 'A woman,' she said, 'plays many roles: princess, weaver, mother, warrior, wife. But what she really wishes for, deep in her heart, is to be someone's beloved.'

She looked at me kindly and smiled. Then she, too, gathered up her clothes and left me sitting by the river.

Later that night, over a fine feast of roasted venison, we all sat around the fire discussing the long journey that still lay ahead of us. None of us had forgotten what had happened in the Kul Moroth or in Khaisham. But the meat we devoured filled us with a new life. And something in the gleam of Atara's eyes communicated to us a new hope, as terrible as it might be.

'It's strange,' Maram said, 'that we've come this far and seen no sign of these Frost Giants. Perhaps they don't really exist.'

'Ha!' Kane laughed out, wiping the meat's bloody juices from his chin. 'You might as well hope that bears don't exist.'

'I'd rather meet a bear here than a Frost Giant,' Maram admitted. 'One of the Librarians told me that they use men's skin for their water bags and make a pudding from our blood. And that they grind our bones to make their bread.'

'Perhaps they do – so what? Do you think *they're* not made of flesh and blood? Do you think steel won't cut them or arrows kill them?'

While Kane and Maram sat debating the terrors of these mysterious creatures, Master Juwain suddenly looked up from the book he was reading. 'If they *do* exist, then perhaps they make their dwellings only in the higher mountains. Why else would they be called Frost Giants?'

Here he pointed toward the white peaks of the great massif rising up to the east of the valley.

'Well, then,' Maram said, looking about nervously, 'we should keep to the valleys, shouldn't we?'

But, of course, we couldn't do that. The cast of the mountains here was mostly from north to south, with the ridgelines of the peaks and the valleys between them running in those directions. To journey east, as we did, was to have to cut across these great folds in the earth wherever we might find a pass or an unexpected break. And that made a hard journey a nearly impossible one.

The next morning we gathered over a breakfast of venison and porridge to study the lay of this long valley in which we had camped.

We could see no end to it either to the north or south. We had to turn one way or the other, however, for just to the east rose a great, jagged wall of peaks that not even a rock goat could have crossed.

'I say we should turn south,' Maram said, looking off into the white haze in that direction. 'That way, it grows warmer, not colder.'

We all looked at Atara, but her eyes held no eagerness to set out in any direction. She said nothing, staring off toward the sky.

'Perhaps we should go north,' Master Juwain said. 'We wouldn't want to stray too far from the line of the Nagarshath when we come out onto Sakai's plateau.'

'If we go too far north,' Kane said, 'we'll find the country of the Blues.'

'Better they than the Frost Giants,' Maram said.

'I thought you wanted to go south, eh?'

'*I* don't want to go anywhere,' Maram said. 'Not anywhere but home. Why is it that *we* have to go to Argattha to find the Lightstone?'

'Because,' I said, 'it must be done, and it is upon us to do it.'

I drew my sword, pointing it east and slightly south as I watched it glow in the cool, clear air. Then I said, 'We'll go south.'

And so we did. We packed the horses and rode along the river through the sweet-smelling forest. The trees here were not so high or thick that we couldn't catch glimpses of the great range to the east of us. We rode all that day for twenty miles across gradually ascending ground until we came to a little lake at the bottom of a bowl with mountains all around us. And there, just to the south of these blue waters, was the break in the mountain wall that I had been hoping for. It was only a quarter mile wide and narrowed quickly as its rocky slopes rose toward ridgelines to either side of it. But it seemed like a pass, or at least an opening onto other valleys beyond it.

As it was too late to begin our ascent, we made camp by the lake and settled in early for a night of good rest. We ate more venison, sweetened with some pine nuts that Liljana shook out of their cones. We watched the beavers that made their mounded homes on the lake and the geese that swam there, too.

We set out very early, almost at first light. The climb toward the pass was a steep one, with our route following a little stream that wound down from the heights, here cutting through a ravine, there spilling in clear cascades over granite escarpments. We walked the horses higher and higher, leading them by their halters and taking care that they had good footing on the rocky terrain. By late morning, we had climbed beyond the treeline. There the slope leveled out a little but there was no end of it in sight. To our right was a vast wall of mountain, sharp as the blade of a knife. To our left, a huge pyramid of ice and granite – one of the highest that I had ever seen – turned its stark, uncaring face toward us. These great, jagged peaks seemed to bite the sky itself and tear open the entrails of heaven.

Early that afternoon, we reached the snowline, and there it grew much colder. Clouds came up and blocked out the sun. The wind rose, too, and drove little particles of ice against the horses' flanks – and into our faces. It was so frigid that it set us to gasping and nearly stole our breath away. We gathered our cloaks around us, and all of us wished for the warmer clothing of which Kane had spoken a few nights before.

'I'm tired and I'm cold,' Maram grumbled as he led Iolo through the snow behind me. Atara and Fire followed him, and then Master Juwain and Liljana with their horses, and finally Kane and his bay. 'I can't see our way out of this miserable pass – can you?'

I listened to the sound of my boots breaking through the crusts of snow, and the horses' hooves crunching ice against rock. I peered off through the clouds of spindrift whipping through the pass. It seemed to give out onto lower ground only a half mile ahead of us.

'It can't be much farther,' I said, turning back to look at Maram.

'It better not be,' he said, as he flicked the ice from his mustache. 'My feet are getting numb. And so are my fingers.'

But when we had covered this slight distance, made much longer and nearly unbearable by the thin and bitter air, we found that our way turned along the back side of the sharp ridgeline on our right. And there another long, white slope lay before us. It led up between two crests to an even higher part of the pass.

'It's too high!' Maram called out when he saw this. 'We'll have to turn back!'

Atara came up to us then, and so did the others. We all stood staring up at this distant doorway through the mountains. Liljana, who could calculate distances as readily as the nuances of people's faces, rubbed her wind-reddened hands together and said, 'We can be through it by midafternoon.'

'Perhaps,' Master Juwain said. 'But what will we find on the other side?'

He turned to Atara in hope that she might answer this question. But her eyes flashed, and I knew that she was growing weary of everyone always looking to her to read the terrain of the future. And so she smiled at him and said, 'Likely we'll find the other side of the mountain.'

'But what if we can't easily get down from there?' Maram said. 'Or what if this is really no pass at all? I don't want to spend a night this high up.'

'So, we've wood for a fire,' Kane said. 'And if the worst befalls us, we can always burrow into the snow like rabbits. I think we'll survive the night.'

'One night, maybe,' Maram said.

I took his cold hand in mine and blew on his fingertips to warm them. Then I said, 'We have to take some chances. Or else we'll wander here, and that's the worst chance of all. Now why don't we go on while we still have the strength?'

I led forth, and Altaru and I broke track through the snow for the others. It was very hard work, even worse for the horses, I thought, than for us. Faggots of wood were slung across their backs, weighing them down heavily. I watched the breath steam from Altaru's nostrils as he leaned his neck forward and drove his great hooves into the snow. But he made no complaint, nor did any of the other horses. I marveled at their trust in us, marching onward at our behest into a snowy waste that seemed to have no end.

A short while later it began to snow. It was not a heavy storm, nor did it feel as if it would be a long one. But the wind caught up the downy flakes and drove them like tiny spears against us. It was hard to see, with bits of ice nearly blinding our eyes. The snow burned my nose and found its way down my neck. It piled up beneath my boots, making the work of walking upward much harder.

And so we continued our ascent for at least an hour. We all suffered from the cold in near silence, except Maram, who made deep growling sounds in his throat as if this noise might simply drive the storm away. And then the snow lightened, a little, even as we drew near the pass. But we gained no relief, for the wind suddenly rose and grew more bitter. A cloud of snow whirled about us and tore at our flesh. I began shivering and so did the others. My face burned with the sting of the snow, and my nose felt numb and stiff. My fingers were stiff, too. I could hardly feel them, hardly keep my grip on the ice-encrusted leather of Altaru's halter. I bent forward, into the wind, driving my numbed feet into the snow mounding into drifts all around us. I could hardly see; my eyes were nearly frozen shut, and I kept blinking against the biting snow, blinking and blinking as I tried to peer through this blinding white wall ahead to make out the shrouded rock forms at the lip of the pass.

It was there, perhaps a hundred yards from our much-desired objective, that many great white shapes rose up out of the storm as if from nowhere. At first it seemed that the swirls of snow had formed themselves up into ghostly beings that haunted such high places; in truth, the snowdrifts themselves seemed to come alive with a will of their own. And then, with the whinnying and stamping of the horses, I saw huge, white-furred beasts descending from the walls of rock around us. And closing in from behind us, too. There were at least twenty of them, and they came for us out of the storm in utter silence, with murderous intent.

'The Frost Giants!' Maram cried out. 'Run for your lives!'

But with this new enemy encircling us, there was nowhere to run, nor did any of us have the strength for flight. The Frost Giants, if such they really were, were advancing upon us with a shocking speed. Their footing through the snow seemed sure and stolid. And they were not beasts at all, I saw, but only huge men nearly eight feet tall. Although they were entirely unclothed, their shaggy white hair was so long and thick that it covered them like gowns of fur. Their furry faces were savage, with ice-blue eyes peering out from beneath browridges as thick as slabs of granite. There was a keen intelligence in these cold orbs, and death as well. In their hands, they each gripped huge clubs: five-foot lengths of oak shod with spiked iron. A blow from one of these would break a horse's back or crumple even plate armor. What it would do to flesh and bones was too terrible to contemplate.

'Circle!' I cried out. 'Circle the horses!'

I cried out as well, to the Frost Giants, that we were not their enemies, that we wished only to cross their land in peace. But either they didn't understand what I said or didn't care.

'Oh, my Lord!' Maram shouted. 'Oh, my Lord!'

We tried to make a wall of the horses; their deadly, kicking hooves, especially Altaru's, might deter even these terrible men. From behind them, we might take up our bows and defend ourselves with a hail of arrows. But the horses were whinnying and stamping, pulling frantically at their halters and would not cooperate. And in any case, there was no time. The Frost Giants were nearly upon us, raising up their great clubs behind their heads as easily as I might have held a chicken leg.

'Val! Val!' Maram cried out. 'Val – my fingers are frozen!'

Mine almost were. I tried to bring forth my bow and string it, but my fingers were too numb for such work. So were Atara's. I saw her behind me attempting to fit an arrow to her bowstring; but she was shivering so badly and her hands were so stiff that she couldn't quite nock it. Kane didn't even bother to try his bow. He drew his sword from its sheath, and a moment later, so did I.

I waited in the blinding snow for the Frost Giants to complete their charge. Then, I was certain, we would fight our last battle before finding one of the numerous deaths that Atara had seen two nights before in her cold, crystal sphere.

36

It is strange that compassion can be a force powerful enough almost to stop the turning of the world. Maram, standing by my side, his frozen fingers fumbling in his pocket, finally managed to draw forth his red crystal. He held it clamped between his hands, pointing it at the Frost Giants. His terrified voice wheezed in my ear, 'Val – should I burn them?'

And then, as he remembered his vow never again to turn fire against men, his hands shook and he couldn't quite use it. His hesitation saved our lives.

'Hrold!' one of the Frost Giants suddenly called out. 'Hrold now!'

The white-furred men halted twenty feet from us in a ring around us. Their spiked clubs wavered in the air.

The Frost Giant who had spoken, a vastly thick man with a broken nose and eyes the color of a frozen waterfall, pointed at Maram's crystal and said, 'It is a firestone.'

The man next to him in the circle peered through the snow at us and said, 'Are you sure, Ymiru?'

Ymiru slowly nodded his head. Then his large blue eyes squinted as they fixed on the sword that I held ready at my side. With the moment of my death at hand, Alkaladur began shimmering with a soft, silver light.

'And that is *sarastria*,' he said. His huge, deep voice rumbled out into the pass like thunder. 'It must be *sarastria*.'

Sarastria, I thought. Silustria. The Frost Giants spoke familiar words with a strange turning of the tongue, but I could still understand what they said.

'Little man,' Ymiru said, pointing his club at me, 'how came you to find *sarastria*?'

It astonished me that this savage-seeming Frost Giant should know anything at all about the silver gelstei – or the firestones. I looked at him and said, 'It was acquired on a journey.'

'What kind of journey?'

I traded quick looks with Kane and Atara; I was reluctant to tell these strange men of our quest.

'Come!' Ymiru roared out, raising up his club. 'Speak now! And speak truthfully or else you and your friends will soon find death.'

I had a strange sense that I could trust this giant man – to do exactly as he said. And so I opened my cloak to show him the gold medallion that King Kiritan had placed there. I told him of the great gathering in Tria and of our vows to seek the Lightstone.

'You speak of the Galastei, yes?' Ymiru said. His eyes lit up with a sudden fire, and so did those of his companions. 'You speak of the golden cup made by the Galadin and brought down from stars? It is a marvelous substance, this gold galastei, this Stone of Light. Inside it is the secret of making all other galastei – and the secret of *making* itself.'

He went on to say that the Lightstone was the very radiance of the One made manifest – and therefore that which moved the very stars and earth and all that occurred upon it.

'But for one entire elu, the Lightstone has been lost,' Ymiru said, losing himself in his thoughts. 'And so all hope for Ea has been lost, too.'

He paused to take a deep breath and then let it out in a cloud of steam. Then, returning to the matter at hand, he continued, 'And now, you say, you hope it will be found. You've made vows to find it. But find it *where*? Surely not in land of the Ymanir!'

'No, not in your land,' Kane said from behind me. 'We seek only to cross it as quickly as we can.'

'So you say. But cross it towards the east? *That* is land of Asakai.'

At the mention of this name, the Ymaniris' hands tightened around their clubs. Their savage faces grew even more savage and pulled into masks of hate.

I didn't want to tell Ymiru that we proposed to cross Sakai and enter Argattha to seek the Lightstone. I doubted that he would believe me; even more, I feared that he would.

'Perhaps they're really *of* Asakai,' a young-looking man near Ymiru said. 'Perhaps they're spies returning home.'

'No, Havru,' Ymiru said. 'They come from Yrakona, I am sure. They're not Morjin's kind.'

The giant young man named Havru, whose chin pointed like a spur of rock, shook his club at us and growled out, 'It's said that Morjin's kind have the power to seem like other kind. Shouldn't we kill them to be certain?'

Across the circle, a man with a reddish tint to his fur bellowed, 'Yes, kill them! Take the galastei, and let's be done!'

Others picked up his cry as they began thumping their clubs into the snow and calling out, 'Kill them! Kill them!'

'Hrold! Hrold now!' Ymiru shouted back at them, raising up his club.

Altaru, standing to the left of me, trembled as he shook his head at the falling snow and beat his hoof downward. Any of the Ymanir attacking me, I thought, would find themselves assaulted with the four terrible clubs attached to the ends of his legs.

'Hrold, Askir!' Ymiru said again to the man with the reddish fur.

But then, across the circle from him, a one-eyed giant let loose a tremendous cry and shook his club at us. He shouted, 'If they be Morjin's men, I'll break their bones to dust!'

This so alarmed Maram that he cringed and called out to me, 'Val! It's as I said! They mean to kill us and eat us! They really do!'

The Ymanir may have been savages, but they were still men, with the same range of feelings as had other men. Ymiru turned his face toward Maram, and I could feel in him the same quick rush of emotions that surged through many of the Ymanir: astonishment, insult, horror. Then their mood shifted yet again as Ymiru's pale lips pulled back in a sad, savage smile. He pointed his club at Maram and called out to his companions: 'You may have any of the others you want. But the fat one is mine!'

'Val!'

Ymiru's smile had now been taken up by the young Havru, who said, 'But, sir, that is unfair of you. Our rations have been thin, and I'm very hungry. I could get at least ten meals from him.'

'Ten?' a sardonic man named Lodur half-shouted. 'He's fat enough for twenty, I should think.'

'Let's roast him over coals!' another man said.

'No, let's make a soup of him!'

'All right,' Havru laughed out wickedly, 'but let's save his bones for our bread.'

All at once, the twenty Ymanir fell into a long and thunderous laughter. But there was no malice in their huge voices, only a vast amusement. They were only having a joke with Maram, and with us.

'Savages!' Maram shouted at them when he realized this. His face reddened as he wiped the sweat from it. 'It's cruel sport you make.'

'Cruel?' Ymiru coughed out. 'Was it any crueler than your suggestion that we are eaters of men?'

Maram didn't know what to say to this. He looked from Ymiru to me and then back at Ymiru as he stammered out, 'Well, I had heard that . . . ah, that is to say, the Yarkonans believe that you are killers of men and –'

'Hrold your tongue!' Ymiru said, cutting him off. 'We're certainly killers of men: any who serve the Great Beast. And any who would enter our land without our leave.'

He suddenly motioned to Askir and two other men, who walked around the outside of the circle of the Ymanir and came over to him. While we stood shivering in the driving wind, they gathered in close with each other and conferred in low, rumbling tones.

After a while, Ymiru looked at Maram and said, 'You are certainly not of Asakai. No man of Morjin's would hrold a firestone against us and fail to use it. We thank you, little fat man, for your forbearance. We wouldn't have wanted to wind up roasted on *your* dinner plate.'

'Ah, well,' Maram said, 'thank you for your forbearance in letting us pass through –'

'Hrold your noise!' Ymiru commanded him. His furry hand suddenly tightened around his club. 'We have forborne nothing. You have set foot upon Elivagar and cast your eyes upon this sacred land. So by our law, you must be put to death.'

Maram's hand shook as he tried to position his gelstei so as to catch what little light filtered through the snow-gray clouds. And then I laid my hand on his shoulder to steady him. I waited on the cold, windy slope, looking up at Ymiru and the grim-faced Ymanir. And so did Kane, Liljana and my other companions.

'However, these are strange times, and you are a strange people,' he went on in his slow, sad way. 'You seek that which we seek, too. Our law is our law. But there is a higher law that speaks of things beyond the commonplace. Our elders are the keepers of it. It is to them that we will take you, if you are agreeable. The Urdahir shall decide your fate.'

I looked from Maram to Atara, then at Liljana and Master Juwain. Their nearly frozen faces told me that anything was better than standing here in this killing wind. But Kane was not so eager to offer up his surrender, nor was I. And so I turned to Ymiru and asked him, 'And what if this is not agreeable to us?'

'Then,' Ymiru said, raising high his club, 'the best that we can give you is a good burial. You have my promise we won't let the bears eat you.'

I saw that it would be hopeless to fight the Ymanir or to try to escape. And it seemed that our fate, in the hands of these giants, was sweeping us along, moving us step by step closer to Argattha. And so, speaking for the others, I told Ymiru that we would accompany them to the council of their elders.

'Thank you,' Ymiru said. 'I wouldn't have wanted your blood on my *borkor.*'

Here he patted his club as he looked at me. Then he asked our names, which we gave, and he told us theirs.

'Very good, Sar Valashu Elahad,' he said. 'Now if you'll just throw down your weapons, we'll blindfold you and take you to a place that only the Ymanir know.'

I could hardly feel my hands' grip around the hilt of Alkaladur, but I was sure it suddenly tightened. I couldn't let anyone touch my sword. And neither did my friends want to surrender their weapons.

'Come, Sar Valashu!'

'No,' I told him. 'My apologies, but we can't do as you ask.'

All at once, twenty thick borkors raised up like trees ready to crush us to the earth.

'Hrold!' Ymiru cried out yet again. He looked at me and asked, 'How can you think to walk armed into our land?'

'How can you think to blind us?' I countered.

For a long ten beats of my heart, Ymiru stared at me as we took each other's measure. I didn't have to tell him that at least a few of his people would die if they tried to kill us. And he didn't have to tell me that these deaths, ours included, would serve only our common enemy.

'Very well,' he said to me at last. 'You may keep your weapons. But while in Elivagar, you must keep your bows unstrung and your swords sheathed. Do you agree to this?'

'Yes,' I said, looking at my friends, 'we do.'

'But, Ymiru!' Askir suddenly shouted, 'what if they –'

'Sar Valashu,' Ymiru said, cutting him off, 'if you break your word, which I have accepted in good faith, the Elders will put *me* to death. And then you and your companions.'

There was a keenness to this huge man's gaze that cut right to my heart. Somehow, without being told, he knew that the possibility of my causing his death in this manner would bind my hands more surely that the tightest cords.

'But about the blindfolding,' he continued, 'there can be no argument. No one except the Ymanir can see the way toward the place we are taking you.'

In the end, we agreed on this compromise. It was strange and disturbing to watch as they found a roll of red cloth in the pack that Havru bore and cut it up to fashion six blindfolds. Despite the hugeness of their hands, they worked quickly in the cold with an amazing dexterity. Ymiru appointed Havru to tie the blindfolds over our eyes, and this he did. He moved from Kane to Atara and Liljana, and then tied broad, red strips around Master Juwain's and Maram's heads and finally mine. As this great, furry being towered over me, I had to stand fast and steady Altaru, or else my ferocious horse would have kicked out in terror and wrath. I held my breath as the blindfold's soft fabric pulled tight over my eyes. With the world plunged into darkness, I suddenly noticed Havru's smell, which was of woodsmoke and wool and cold wind off a frozen lake.

Wise Ymiru also appointed Havru and four others to be our guides. He himself took my hand in his and began leading me up toward the pass. There was a comforting warmth and great strength in the press of his flesh against mine. I heard Maram sigh out behind me, and I could almost feel his fingers thawing in Havru's encompassing grip. Although none of us liked walking blind through the snow, the Ymanir had a friendship with this bitter substance that communicated to us through the sure, gentle pulling of hand against hand. It was remarkable, I thought, that we were led over ice and rocks, and none of us stumbled or tripped. In this way, from guide to guided, a seemingly unbreakable trust was born.

As Maram had feared, the rise toward which we climbed proved not to be the end of the pass. Ymiru, walking in front of me and leading me upward, was loath to say much about the mountains here. But he did tell us that our path would take us over a still higher rise, before descending into the difficult terrain beyond. From what he said, it was clear that we would have to spend the night at a very high elevation. But we would not have to spend it in the open. For the Ymanir, he told us, had built a hut that they used for sleeping less than a mile from where we stood.

In truth, this 'hut' turned out to be more like a fortress, as we found when we reached it a little later. Although Ymiru bade us keep our blindfolds on, the moment that we walked through the doorway of this unseen structure, I had a sense of a cold, vast, open space where the echoes of our snow-encrusted boots fell off of thick walls of stone. We were all shivering by the time the Ymanir closed the doors behind us and led us to what I took to be a sleeping area where thick wool mats were laid out in front a fire. As someone heaved on a few fresh logs, flames leaped out at us to thaw our frozen bodies. We were very glad for the heat, and gladder still for the bowls of steaming soup that our hosts ladled out into huge bowls and pressed into our hands. Their hospitality, I thought, was flawless. They gave their beds up to us, and took our boots away to be dried in front of the fire. They even served us a mulled cider that had almost as much flavor and punch as the finest Meshian beer.

'Ah, this isn't so bad,' Maram said, sipping his cider on the bed next to mine. 'In fact, it's really quite good.'

It was strange not being able to see the food that we ate or the drink that passed our lips. But soon it came time for lying back in our beds, and the darkness of our blindfolds gave way to that of sleep. We rested well that night. In the morning, the Ymanir served us porridge mixed with goat's milk, dried berries and nuts before we set out again.

As I could tell from the warmth of the sun on my face, we had a clear day for traveling. Half the Ymanir remained near their hut to guard the pass. One man Ymiru sent on ahead to alert the Elders of our coming. And then he and the remaining Ymanir led us even higher into the mountains.

We walked rather slowly for a couple of hours up a steep slope. And then, at the crest of the pass, where the wind blew so fiercely that it nearly ripped the blindfolds from our faces, we began a long descent through what seemed a chute of rock. We walked for a couple more hours, breaking only for a quick lunch. We offered the Ymanir some of the salted pork that we had tucked away in the horses' packs, but this food horrified them. Havru called us Eaters of Beasts; the loathing in his voice suggested that we might as well have been cannibals. Askir explained that although the Ymanir might borrow milk and wool from their goats, they would never think to take their meat. Their gentleness toward animals was only the first of the surprises that awaited us that day.

Our afternoon's journey took us down below the snowline, where Ymiru led us onto what felt like a broad dirt track. Here there were many more rocks to negotiate, which made the going much more difficult. The track turned sharply north and climbed steeply before veering eastward and downward again. I was as sure of these directions as I was of the beating of my heart. I didn't need the thin heat of the falling sun to tell me which way we walked. But I failed to mention this to Ymiru. He seemed content to lead me by the hand, whistling a sad song as he walked on a couple of paces ahead of me.

By early afternoon, the track turned yet again, this time toward the south. It rose in a series of snakelike switchbacks up what seemed to be the slopes of a good-sized mountain. Soon the smells of spruce and dirt gave way to ice as we again crossed onto a snowfield. Frozen crusts crunched beneath our feet. With my left hand in Ymiru's and my right hand pulling on Altaru's halter, I led my horse through some rather thick drifts of snow. We climbed ever higher. Maram, walking to the rear of me, puffed and wheezed in the thin, bitter air. I felt his fear that we would climb too high and fall to cold or sudden stroke of breathlessness. The burning in my lungs told me that I had never been so high in the mountains in all my life; my nearly frozen cheeks and the pulsing of my eyes against the blindfold told me that Maram's fears might soon become my own.

And then, without warning, we crested yet another pass. The wind shifted and blew strange scents against my face. I heard one of the Ymanir sigh out with anticipation as if he would soon be rejoined with his wife and family. Something very deep stirred in Ymiru, too. He led us down through the snow for perhaps a quarter of a mile to a more level ground where the wind didn't cut so keenly. And there, with the crest of the pass at our backs, he finally let go of my hand.

'Sar Valashu,' he said to me, 'we have come to the place that I have told of. None except the Ymanir have ever looked upon it. And none ever must. And so I ask you, whatever fate befalls you, that you keep this sight to yourself. Do you agree to this?'

With the blindfold still tight around my eyes, I didn't know what I was agreeing to. But I was eager to have it removed, so I said, 'Yes, we are agreed.'

Ymiru's voice carried out behind me as he called out, 'Prince Maram Marshayk, do you agree to this?'

And so it went, one by one, Ymiru formally calling each of us to pledge his silence, and each of us giving what he had asked. Then I felt his fingers at the back of my head working against the blindfold's knot. In a few moments, he had it off. The sun, even at this late hour, pierced my eyelids with such a dazzling white light that I could not open them. I stood toward the south with my hand to my forehead, trying to block out some of its intense radiance.

And then, as my eyes slowly adjusted to this new level of illumination, I fought them open, blinking against the stab of the tears there, blinking and blinking at the blinding haze of indistinct forms that was all I could perceive at first. And then my vision suddenly cleared. The features of the world came into sharp focus. And I, along with Atara, Maram and my other friends, drew in a sudden gasp of air almost with one breath. For there, spread out beneath the blue dome of the sky, was the most astonishing sight I had ever beheld.

'Oh, my Lord!' Maram murmured quietly from behind me.

Far below us, a broad valley opened out between great walls of white-capped mountains. And in its center, built on either side of an ice-blue river, rose a city more marvelous than I had ever dreamed. It filled most of the valley. Although not as large as Tria, it had a splendor that even the Trians might have envied. Many great towers and spires, made of glittering sweeps of living stone, seemed to grow out of the valley's very rock. Some of these were half a mile high and nearly vanished into the sky. Their building stones were of carnelian and violet, azure and aquamarine and a thousand other soft, shifting hues. The city's broad avenues and streets were laid out with precision from east to west and north to south as if to mark the four points of the world. The late afternoon sun poured down these thoroughfares like rivers of gold. The various palaces and temples caught up its light. But the magnificence of the buildings, I thought, was not in their number nor even their size. Rather, it was their perfect proportions and sparkle that caught the eye and stirred the soul. The houses along even the side streets seemed to cast their colors at each other and reflect those of their neighbors. Their lovely lines and arrangement bespoke an almost seamless blending with the earth – and with each other. It was as if the whole city was a choir of sight, intoning deep and startling harmonies, giving the song of its beauty to the wind and the sky, to the moon and the sun and the stars.

Above the city, on the slope of a mountain to the east, huge and fantastic sculptures gleamed. A few of these were diamond-like figures a mile high; near them, immense but delicate-looking crystals opened beneath the sun like glittering flowers. It seemed like something that only the Galadin themselves could have created. Ymiru saw me staring at it, and told me that the Ymanir called this great work the Garden of the Gods.

As striking as were these marvels, they paled beneath the greatest glory of this place. This was a mountain to the west that overlooked the whole valley. Ymiru said it was the highest mountain in the world. Standing above the lesser peaks to either side, it rose straight into the sky in a great upward thrust of stone and ice. It had an almost perfect symmetry, like that of a pyramid. Although its pointed summit and upper reaches were crowned in pure, white snow, the main body of it appeared to be made of amethyst, emerald, sapphire and jewels of every color. I could not imagine how it had come to be.

'That is Alumit,' Ymiru said as he watched me and my friends staring at it. 'We call it the Mountain of the Morning Star.'

This name, as he spoke it in his deep voice that rumbled like thunder, stunned me into silence.

'And your city?' Maram asked, standing next to his horse behind us. 'What do you call it?'

'Its name is Alundil,' Ymiru told us. 'This means the "City of the Stars" in the old language.'

As the wind whipped swirls of snow about our legs, I stared down at this fantastic place for quite a while. It was strange, I thought, that all the legends and old wives' tales had told of the Ymanir as only savage and man-eating Frost Giants. And with their fearsome borkors and harsh laws, savage they might truly have been. But they had built the most beautiful creation on earth. And no one, it seemed, except my companions and I, and the Ymanir themselves, had ever beheld it.

Kane, gazing down into the valley as if its splendor had swept him away to another world, suddenly looked at Ymiru and said, 'All these years, walking among the other cities of the world, and other mountains – even without wearing a blindfold, I might as well have been.'

'I've never imagined seeing such a thing,' Maram added, blinking his eyes. He looked up at Ymiru and asked, 'Did your people make this? How could they have?'

How, indeed, I wondered, staring down at the great sculptures of the Garden of the Gods? How could naked giants with spiked clubs have built a greater glory than had even the ancient architects of Tria during the great golden Age of Law? How could anyone?

'Yes, we did – that is who we Ymanir are,' Ymiru said proudly. 'We are workers of living stone; we are mountain shapers and gardeners of the earth.'

He went on to say that the Ymanir's greatest delight was in making things out of things. They especially loved coaxing out of the earth the secret and beautiful forms hidden there. Ymiru told us that his people were devoted to discovering how to forge substances of all kinds, and none more so than the gelstei crystals.

'But the secret of their making has been lost to us for most of an age,' he said sadly. 'At least the making of the greater galastei.'

'In other lands,' Master Juwain told him, 'it has been forgotten how to forge even the lesser gelstei.'

'So much has been lost,' Ymiru said bitterly. 'And that is why the Urdahir, some of them, seek the secret of the ultimate making.'

'And what is that?' Maram asked, staring at the jeweled mountain called Alumit.

'Why, the making of the golden crystal of the Galastei itself,' Ymiru said. 'That is why we, too, seek the cup you call the Lightstone. We believe that only the Lightstone itself will ever reveal the secret of how it was created.'

With this secret, he told us, the Ymanir could not only reforge the great gelstei crystals of old and a new Lightstone, but the very world itself.

That was a strange thought to take with us on our descent to the city. We followed a well-marked track that cut through the pass's snowfields and wound down through the treeline of the mountain beneath us. It was nearly dark before we came out of the mouth of a narrow canyon onto Alundil's heights. Immediately upon setting foot in this enchanting city, with its graceful houses and stands of silver shih trees,

I had a strange sense of simultaneously walking my horse down a quiet street and standing a thousand miles high. The sweep of the great spires seemed to draw my soul up toward the stars. In this marvelous place, I was still very much of the earth and on it, never more so – and yet I felt myself suddenly opened like a living crystal that is transparent to other worlds and other realms. Lovely was my home in the Morning Mountains, and magical were the woods of the Lokilani. But in no other place on Ea had I felt myself to be so great and noble a being as I did here.

We proceeded through the streets and onto one of the city's broad avenues, all of which were deserted. Likewise, no fire or light brightened the windows of the houses and buildings that we passed. Maram, somewhat vexed at this strangeness, asked Ymiru if his people had once been more numerous. Had they, he asked, abandoned this part of the city for other districts?

'Yes, once the Ymanir were a much greater people,' he told us. His voice was heavy with a bitter sadness. 'Once, we claimed nearly all of the mountains as our home. But when the Great Beast took the Black Mountain, he sent a plague to kill the Ymanir. The survivors were too few to hrold. He drove us off, into the westernmost part of our realm – into Elivagar. He and his Red Priests did dreadful things to our hrome. And thus sacred Sakai became Asakai, the accursed land.'

He went on to tell us that, even before Morjin's rise, there had never been enough of his people to fill a city so large as Alundil. And as large as it was, it would grow only larger, for the Ymanir continued to add to it stone by stone and tower by tower as they had for thousands of years.

'I don't understand,' Maram said, blowing out his breath into the cold, darkening air. 'If Alundil is already too big for your people, why build it bigger?'

'Because,' Ymiru said, 'Alundil is not for us.'

The clopping of the horses' hooves against the stone of the street suddenly seemed too loud. Ymiru, Havru and Askir – and the other Ymanir – suddenly stood as straight and proud as any of the sculptures in the Garden of the Gods.

The look on Maram's face suggested that he was now totally mystified, as were the rest of us. And so Ymiru explained, 'Long ago, our scryers looked toward the stars and beheld cities on other worlds. It is our greatest hope to recreate on earth these visions that they saw.'

'But why?' Maram asked.

'Because someday the Star People will come again,' Ymiru said. 'They will come to earth and find prepared for them a new hrome.'

It was upon hearing this sad history and sad dreams of the future that

Ymiru and the others took us to meet with their Elders. As Ymiru had said, Alundil was not for the Ymanir, and so his people had built their own town in the foothills east of the valley. This consisted mostly of great, long, stone houses arrayed on winding streets. The Ymanir had applied only a little of their art in raising up these constructions. None were of the marvelous living stone that formed the buildings of the dark city below. Rather, they were made of blocks of granite, cut with great precision and fitted together in sweeping arches that enclosed large spaces. The Ymanir, we soon found, liked open spaces and built their houses accordingly.

They had built their great hall this way, too. We approached this castle-like building along a rising road, lined with many Ymanir who had left their houses to witness the unprecedented arrival of strangers in their valley. Hundreds of these tall, white-furred people stood as straight and silent as the spruce trees that also lined the road. I caught a scent of the deep feelings that rumbled through them: anger, fear, curiosity, hope. There was a great sadness about them, and yet a fierce pride as well.

We tethered our horses to some trees outside the great hall. Inside it, we all understood, the Ymanir called the Urdahir were waiting to decide our fate.

37

Ymiru, Havru and Askir escorted us inside the hall where their Elders had gathered – along with many more of the Ymanir, too. A good two hundred of them were lined up by mats woven of the wonderfully soft goat hair that we had encountered the night before in Ymiru's mountain hut. They faced nine aged men and women who stood near similar mats on a stone dais at the front of the room. We were shown to the place of honor – or inquisition – just below this dais. We joined Ymiru on the floor there as everyone in the room sat down together in the fashion of his people: our legs folded back beneath us, sitting back on our heels with our spines straight and our eyes slightly lowered as we waited for the Elders to address us.

This they wasted no time in doing. After asking Ymiru our names, the centermost and eldest of the Urdahir introduced himself as Hrothmar. Then he presented the four women to his left: Audhumla, Yvanu, Ulla and Halda. The men, to his right, were: Burri, Hramjir, Hramdal and Yramu. They all turned slightly toward Hrothmar, allowing him to speak on their behalf.

'By now,' he said, his gruff old voice carrying out into the hall, 'everyone in Elivagar knows of Ymiru's extraordinary audacity in breaking our law by bringing these six strangers here. And everyone *thinks* he knows certain facts concerning this matter: that the little fat man known as Maram Marshayk bears with him a red galastei, while Sar Valashu Elahad bears a sword of *sarastria*. And that these same two and their companions seek *the* Galastei. We are met here to determine if these facts are true – and to uncover others. And to discuss them. All may help us in this truthsaying. And all may speak in their turn.'

Hrothmar paused a moment to catch his breath. With his much-weathered and wrinkled skin about his sad old eyes, few of the Ymanir in the hall had more years than he. And none had greater height or stature, not even the giant guards who stood around the walls of the hall bearing their great borkors at their sides.

'And first to speak,' he wheezed out, 'shall be Burri. He'll speak for the law of the Ymanir.'

The man sitting next to him, who had an angry look to his long, lean face, stroked the silver-white fur of his beard as he looked down at us. Then he said, 'The law, in this matter, is simple. It says that any Ymanir who discovers strangers entering our land without the Urdahir's permission shall immediately put them to death. This should have been done. It was not. And therefore, also according to the law, Ymiru and all the guard of the South Pass, should be put to death.'

Ymiru, listening quietly near me, seemed suddenly to sit up very straight. I hadn't realized the terrible risk that he had taken merely in sparing our lives.

Burri stared at Ymiru with his cold, blue eyes and said, 'Have you no respect for the law that you break it the first chance that you get?'

His gaze turned on Atara, Kane and me as he added, 'And you, strangers – you drew weapons to oppose Ymiru's execution of the law. And thus are yourselves in violation of it. It would have been easier if you had allowed Ymiru to do his duty. Why didn't you?'

It surprised me when Liljana stood up and answered for us. She brushed back her gray hair and looked up at the Urdahir, her round face filling with a steely obstinacy. To Burri, she sad, 'Do you mean that we should have allowed Ymiru to kill us out of hand?'

'Yes, little woman, I do mean that,' he told her in a voice that fell like a club. 'Thus you would have spared yourselves the false hope of your continued existence.'

Liljana smiled at his thinly veiled threat; her coolness beneath Burri's savage gaze lent me the forbearance to keep my hand away from my sword. Then Liljana nodded at him and said, 'If we had acquiesced in our own murders, by our law, we would become murderers, too.'

'Do you carry your own law with you, then, into others' lands?'

'We carry it in our hearts,' Liljana said, pressing her hand between her breasts. 'There, too, we carry something greater than the law. And that is life. Is the law made to serve life, or life to serve the law?'

'The law of the Ymanir,' Burri told her, 'is made to serve the Ymanir. And so each of us must serve it.'

'And this is for the good of your people, yes?'

'It is for my people's *life*,' he growled at her.

Liljana stared out into the immense room, with its stone walls covered with marvelous golden hangings and sweeping arches high overhead. Built into recesses of the columns that supported this great vault were glowstones giving off a soft, white light. The walls themselves, at intervals of ten feet, were set with blocks of hot slate, which radiated a steady heat. And these lesser gelstei were not the only ones visible in the room that night. Many of the Ymanir wore warders about their necks; more than a few sported dragon bones, and at least one old woman rolled a music marble between her long, furry hands. Not even in Tria had I seen so many surviving works of the ancient alchemists. From what Ymiru had said, I thought that these gelstei might not be so ancient. For the Ymanir had surely preserved the art of forging them. They had as much pride in this, I sensed, as they did sadness in being slaughtered by the Red Dragon and driven into this lost corner of their ancient realm. They were a strange people and a great one; I could not blame them for savagely enforcing laws that preserved what little they had left.

Liljana's round face fell soft and kind as she gathered in all her compassion and looked back up at Burri. She said, 'The lowest law is the law of survival, and even the beasts know this. But a human being knows much more: that she may not live at the sacrifice of her people.'

'Just so,' Burri growled again.

'And so each of us must obey the law of her people.'

'Just so, just so.'

'And a people,' Liljana went on, smiling at him, 'may not live at the sacrifice of their world. And so any people's law must always give way before the higher law.'

Burri, not liking to be swayed by Liljana's relentless calm, suddenly lost his temper and thundered down at her: 'And how do you know of the Ymanir's higher law?'

'I know,' she said, 'because the higher law is the same for all peoples. It is just the Law of the One.'

Burri suddenly stood up to his full height of eight feet. His hands opened and closed as if they longed to grip a borkor. He turned toward the other elders and said, 'We all knew that Ymiru would invoke the higher law. And so he has, through this little woman. But what could possibly persuade us of the need? The fact that two of the strangers bear greater galastei? That they are seekers of *the* Galastei? The Red Dragon's priests are seekers of the same and have come to us with firestones in their hands – to burn us. And so no one has ever objected to us sending them to their fate.'

Liljana waited for him to finish speaking and said simply, 'We are not the Red Dragon's priests.'

'But how do we *know* this?' Burri said, looking out at the hundreds of

Ymanir in the hall. 'The Red Dragon has set clever traps for us before. And who among us be more clever than he? No, no, we Ymanir are clever with our hands, but not in this way. And so we've made our law. And so we should use it.'

'Before hearing what we have to say?' Liljana asked him.

'We've all heard the cleverness of your words, little woman,' Burri said to her. 'Must we hear more?'

He turned to look at Hramjir, a gnarled old man with only one arm. He spoke to him, and to the other Elders, saying, 'Hrothmar has told us that all should be allowed to speak. But I say this be folly. Let us not wonder if the strangers speak lies. Such doubt be a poison to the heart. Let us execute the law, now, before it be too late.'

With a glance at the guards along the walls and by the door, he called for the Elders to decide our fate then and there. And this, also by the Ymanir's law, they were forced to do. And so they gathered in a circle and put their heads together as they conferred in their long, low, rumbling voices. And then they took their places again on their mats, and Hrothmar stared down at us as he waited for silence in the room.

'Burri has spoke for the Ymanir's law,' he told us. 'And Ulla and Hramjir would see this law immediately executed. But most of us would not. Therefore, we'll call on others to speak for other concerns. Audhumla will speak for the Law of the One.'

Now Audhumla, an old and rather small woman, for the Ymanir – she couldn't have been an inch over seven feet – smoothed back the silky white fur of her face. Then in a raspy voice she said, 'The essence of this law be simple: that throughout the stars the One must unfold in the glory of creation. The Ymanir's part in this be also simple: We are to prepare the way for the Elijin's and Galadin's coming to earth. This be why we *be*. Only then will Ea be restored to her place in the creation of the true civilization, which has been lost for six long ages.'

She paused to take a breath and continued, 'If the strangers' lives are to be spared in consideration of the higher law, if our lives are to be put at risk in sparing theirs, it must be shown that they also have a place in our purpose. Or have an equally great purpose of their own.'

Here a young man behind us – I gathered he was a friend of Ymiru's – stood up and said, 'But it has already been told that the strangers seek the Galastei. What could be a greater purpose than that?'

'If it be true,' Audhumla said to him. 'If it be true.'

'If it be true,' Hrothmar added, 'that would still not be enough. The strangers would still have to show that they had a chance to find it.'

He turned his penetrating gaze upon me and asked, 'Sar Valashu – will you now speak for your people?'

Maram, sitting next to me, nudged me in the ribs to stand up. Atara, Master Juwain and Liljana each looked at me and smiled encouragingly. Kane's black eyes buried themselves in mine. I felt him urging me to speak, and speak well. I felt also that if the Ymanir guards should ever come at us with their borkors, he would not honor my promise to keep our swords sheathed in the Ymanir's land.

'Yes,' I said, standing before the Elders. 'I will speak for us.'

And so I did. While the glowstones shone on sempiternally through the night, I told the Ymanir a tale such as they had never heard before. I began it six long ages past, when Aryu had killed Elahad and had stolen the Lightstone. Its history, much of it unknown to the Ymanir, I then recounted, much as King Kiritan had when he had gathered the thousands of knights in his hall and called the great quest. My part in this, and my friends', I explained with as much candor as I could. I told of the black arrow and the kirax that had poisoned my blood; I even told them of Ayondela Kirriland's prophecy and pointed out the scar that had saved us from the Lokilani's arrows. The hundreds of men and women in the room fell into a deep silence as I went on with the story of our long journey that had taken us across most of Ea to the Library at Khaisham. What we had found there, however, I did not tell. It would be very dangerous, I thought, to announce the Lightstone's hiding place to so many people.

'Your story,' Burri said, shaking his head when I had finished, 'be too fantastic to be true.'

'It be too fantastic *not* to be true,' Yvanu countered. She was the youngest of the Urdahir and a beautiful woman, whose long white fur about her head and neck had been twisted into long braids.

All the Elders were now staring at me, as was everyone else in the room. Still shaking his head, Burri said to me, 'How will we ever know if you speak the truth?'

'You'll know,' I said softly. 'If you listen, you'll know.'

But Burri, like many people, did not wish to listen to his own heart. He pointed his clublike finger at me and demanded, 'But where are the proofs of your story? Let us see the proofs.'

I met eyes with each of my friends then, and they brought forth their gelstei. The sudden sight of Maram's firestone and Atara's crystal sphere, no less Liljana's little blue whale, Master Juwain's varistei and Kane's black stone, stunned everyone in the room. Nowhere on Ea are any people so in awe of the gelstei as are the Ymanir.

'And where be the *sarastria*, then?' Burri asked.

Ymiru gave me permission to draw my sword, and this I did. As I swept it toward the east, its silver length gleamed with a deep light.

'Do you see?' Ymiru said, standing to face Burri. 'Their story must be true.'

All at once, a hundred giant men and women called out that a miracle had befallen the Ymanir, and that our lives should be spared. But this wasn't good enough for Burri.

'We must know if these stones truly be the greater galastei,' he said, pointing down at what we held in our hands. 'They must be put to the test.'

But it was hard to test Maram's red crystal with no sun to fire it. And hard, too, to test the powers of my friends' other gelstei. And so Burri had to satisfy himself with Hrothmar's suggestion: that a diamond be brought forth to see if Alkaladur's blade could mark it. Ulla, the oldest of the Urdahir, sacrificed the perfection of her wedding ring for this test. She held out her hand to me and bade me come forward with my sword. She watched utterly spellbound as I set its edge and cut the diamond.

'It *is* the silver,' she exclaimed, holding up her ring for all to see. Then her old eyes fixed on my sword. 'The silver will lead to the gold.'

At first I thought she knew the words of the song that Alphanderry had sung after I had gained Alkaladur. And then many of the Ymanir in the room began murmuring their ancient belief that the secrets of the silver gelstei would lead to the *making* of the gold.

'This be a very great thing that you've been given,' Hrothmar said to me, staring at my sword. 'Who would ever have thought that a stranger would bring the silver galastei into our land?'

The gleam in Burri's eyes as they fell upon my sword told me that he didn't want it ever to *leave* his land.

'The silver galastei,' he muttered, 'what do these strangers know of it? What do they truly know of *any* of the galastei?'

'We know this,' I told him, sheathing my sword. 'We know that the silver has sometimes led to covetousness of the gold.'

So saying, I reached into the pocket of my tunic and drew forth the False Gelstei that we had found in the Library. I moved across the dais and set it into Burri's outstretched hand.

'The Galastei! It is the Galastei!' many voices cried out at once.

But Burri, who had a more practiced eye, held the goldish cup beneath the glowstones' light. As I explained what it was, he nodded his long head in acceptance of the truth.

'In ages past,' he said, looking at the cup in amazement, 'it's said that the Ymanir made many such cups. Perhaps even this very one.'

'If that is so,' I said, 'then perhaps it would be fitting that you keep it, for your people.'

642

Burri's icy blue eyes froze into mine. He said, 'You can't buy our mercy.'

I felt my spine stiffen with pride; I felt my father in me as words that he would have spoken formed themselves upon my lips: 'In my land, when a gift is given, we usually just say "thank you." And it is not your mercy that we seek – only justice.'

But I knew that such a speech would not convince Burri that I truly wanted to help his people. My rebuke wounded him. His fingers closed angrily about the cup, and it nearly disappeared in his huge hand.

'There be much of the strangers' story for which we can never have proofs,' he called out. 'His claim of descent from this Elahad. This twinkling Timpum being that only the strangers can see. This golden-voiced minstrel –'

'*We* saw Khaisham burn,' a stout man said as he stood to address the room. 'My brother and I were returning from the South Reach, and we saw the fire.'

'Do not interrupt me again!' Burri thundered at him. He turned to stare down at the other elders. 'Do you see how the strangers have already put us off our manners? Should they also put us off doing justice?'

'We shall do justice,' Hrothmar assured him. 'After we know the truth.'

'But we can never know the truth here!'

Just then, Audhumla brought forth a bluish stone about the size of an eagle's egg. It looked something like lapis, and she rolled it between her thin, graceful hands. And then she said, 'You're wrong, Burri. We shall soon know the truth of the strangers' story.'

After asking Burri and me to sit back down, she announced to the Elders, and to the assembled Ymanir in the hall, that she held a truth stone in her hands.

'But that can't be!' Burri said. 'We haven't made a truth stone for a thousand years.'

'No, we haven't,' Audhumla said. 'This be a family heirloom.'

In the discussion that followed, I learned that the truth stones were a kind of lesser gelstei related to Liljana's blue gelstei. Although they did not allow sight into another's mind, they were able to record certain impressions from it, such as falseness or truth.

Burri looked at Audhumla doubtfully, and with ill-concealed loathing. 'There hasn't been a truthsayer among us for a thousand years.'

'None except the women of my family.'

'If that be true,' Burri said, 'then why haven't they made themselves known?'

'So that the hateful can cast scorn upon them?'

Liljana's eyes, I noticed, filled with tears as she said this.

'Scorn would be the least that a truthsayer would deserve,' Burri said, 'if she failed to use her gift for her people.'

'And how should she use it if, for a thousand years, no stranger has come among us to be tested?'

The Elders again gathered in a circle to discuss this unexpected turn. Then they took their places on their mats, and Hrothmar's voice carried out into the room: 'We believe the truth of what Audhumla has told us, if nothing else. And so we've agreed to allow Sar Valashu to be tested this way, if he be willing.'

With two hundred Ymanir suddenly looking at me, and my six friends as well, I saw that I had little choice. And so I said, 'Then test me, if you will.'

Audhumla bade me to come forward again and kneel before her on the dais. She held her blue stone out to me, cupped in her hands. I placed my hand upon it. It was warm from the heat of Audhumla's body, and felt more porous that the crystal of the greater gelstei. It seemed to drink in my sweat and the pulsing of the blood that beat through my hand. I remembered that such gelstei were also called touchstones because they seemed to touch all of one's flesh straight through to the heart.

I looked straight into Audhumla's eyes and said, 'All that I have told tonight is true.'

I took my hand away and watched Audhumla's much larger hands close upon the stone. Her eyes closed as she stroked it; she was like a mother gathering in her child's emotions from the touch of a tear-stained cheek.

At last she looked at me and said, 'All that you have told *is* true. But you have not told *all* that is true.'

The two hundred Ymanir in the hall waited for her to say more. But she had no more to say. Hrothmar, however, did. This wise old man needed no gelstei, lesser or greater, to discern the part of my story that I had left incomplete.

'Sar Valashu,' he said to me, 'you have told that you and your companions have sought the Lightstone across the length of Ea. But you have not told why you entered our land to seek it.'

No, I thought, I hadn't. But I saw that I finally must. And so I took a deep breath and told them about Master Aluino's journal. Then I admitted that my friends and I had vowed to journey into Sakai and enter the underground city of Argattha.

For a long time, no one in the hall spoke. No one even moved. I felt the great hearts of the hundreds of Ymanir beating out a great thunder of astonishment.

At last, Hrothmar found his voice and spoke for all his people, even Burri. He said to me, 'Even the bravest of the Ymanir seldom go any more into Asakai, where once we went so freely. Either you and your companions are mad or you are possessed of a great courage. And I do not believe you are mad.'

A roar of voices cascaded through the room like a suddenly unleashed flood. Hrothmar let his people speak for quite a while. Then he held up his hand for silence.

'The strangers have brought us the greatest chance that we Ymanir have ever had,' he said in his grave, deep voice. 'And the greatest peril, too. How are we to decide their fate – and our own?'

He paused to rub his tired eyes. Then he said, 'Let us not try to make this decision tonight. Let us reflect and sleep and dream. And let us all gather before first light in the great square, that we might call upon the wisdom of the Galadin to help us.'

He dismissed the assemblage and stood, as did everyone else. Then the men who had guarded the hall escorted us to Ymiru's house at the edge of the town, where we had been offered quarters. Compared with the other Ymanir houses on the wooded slopes nearby, it was a small affair of stacked stone and rough-hewn beams – but quite large enough to accommodate us.

Ymiru proved an excellent host. He laid out extra sleeping mats by the fire that he lit in the hearth. There, too, he set out a block of cheese that it might soften so we could dip crusts of bread into it for our evening meal. He drew baths for us and later poured our tea into small blue cups with his huge hand. He seemed glad for our company and bemused that his fate seemed to have tied itself up with ours.

'When I awoke yesterday, it was a morning like any other,' he told us as he joined us by the fire. 'And now here I sit with six little people, talking about the Lightstone.'

He went on to say that the next morning would come soon enough and that we should get a good night's rest to prepare us for what was to come.

'I don't think I'll sleep at all,' Maram said, as he cast his eyes around the room to catch sight of a bottle of brandy or beer. 'That Burri gave us a bad enough time today.'

Ymiru's eyes fell sad, and he surprised us, saying, 'Burri be a good man. But he has many fears.'

He explained that once, years ago, he and Burri, along with others in the hall, had lived in the same village in the East Reach near

Sakai. And then one day, Morjin had sent a battalion to annihilate it.

'We were too few to hrold,' he told us. He took a sip of the bitter tea in his cup. 'I lost my wife and sons in the attack; Burri lost much more. The Beast's men murdered his daughters and grandchildren, his mother and brothers, too. And the Ymanir lost part of Elivagar. Burri has vowed that we won't lose any more.'

After that he fell into a deep silence from which he could not be roused. He brought out a song stone, a little sphere of swirling hues; he sat listening to the voice of his dead wife long after Maram – and Atara, Liljana and Master Juwain – had gone to sleep.

It was cold the next morning when we gathered at the appointed hour in Alundil's great square. The city's empty towers and buildings were even darker than the sky, which was hung with many stars. Ten thousand men, women and children crowded shoulder to shoulder facing a great spire just to the west of the square. At the head of them were Hrothmar and Burri and the others of Urdahir. We stood with Ymiru near them, ringed by thirty Ymanir gripping borkors in their massive hands. The sharp wind falling down from the icy mountains all around us seemed not to touch them. But it pierced us nearly to the bone. I stood between Atara and Master Juwain, shivering as they did, waiting with them and our other companions, for what we didn't know.

'Why are we meeting *here*?' Maram asked for the tenth time.

And for the tenth time, Ymiru answered him, saying, 'You will see, little man, you will see.'

Now many of the Ymanir behind us had turned to look out above the spire to the east of the square. There, above the Garden of the Gods, above the icy eastern mountains, the sky was beginning to lighten with the rising of the sun. There, too, the Morning Star shone, brightest of all the heavens' lights. It cast its radiance upon us, touching Alundil's houses and spires, illuminating the faces of all who gazed upon it. Through the clear air and straight across the valley streaked this silver light, where it fell upon the shimmering face of Alumit. It was still too dark to make out the colors of this great mountain that seemed to overlook the whole of the world. I wondered yet again how it had come to be. Ymiru had told us that his ancestors had raised up the sculptures of the Garden of the Gods; but it seemed that the building of an entire mountain had been beyond even the ancient Ymanir. Ymiru believed that once, long ago, the Galadin had come to earth to work this miracle. As he believed that someday they would come again.

As the wind quickened and our breaths steamed out into the air, the eastern sky grew even brighter. The rising of the sun stole the stars' light one by one until only the Morning Star remained shining. Then it, too, disappeared into the blue-white glister at the edge of the world. We waited for the sun to crest the mountains behind us. Ahead of us, to the west of the square above the spire, Alumit's great, white peak caught the sun's first rays before the valley below it did. Its pointed crown of ice and snow began glowing a deep red. Soon this fire fell down the slopes of the mountain and drew forth its colors. Again I marveled at the crystals from which it was wrought, the sparkling blues that seemed to pour forth from sapphire, the reds of ruby and a deep, vivid, emerald green.

At last the sun broke over the flaming ridgeline to the east. The air warmed, slightly, as the morning grew brighter. And still we waited, facing this great Mountain of the Morning Star. And then, to the thunder of ten thousand hearts and the rising of the wind, the colors of the mountain began to change. Slowly its jewel-like hues deepened and grew even more splendid. They seemed to flow into each other, red into yellow, orange into green, miraculously transforming into a single color like nothing I had ever dreamed. It was *not* a blending or a tessellation of colors, but one solid color – though perhaps not so solid at all, for in staring at it, I seemed to fall into it and become aware of infinite depths. How could this be, I wondered? How could there exist in the world an entirely new color of the spectrum that no one ever saw? It was as different from red or green as those colors are from violet or blue. And yet I could only describe it to myself in terms of the more common colors, for that was the only way I could make sense of such an amazing thing: it had all the fire of red, the brightness and expansiveness of yellow, the deep peace of the purest cobalt blue.

'How is this possible?' I heard Maram whisper behind me. 'Oh, my Lord, how can this be?'

I shook my head as I stared at the great mountain, now wholly shimmering with a single hue, at once like living gold and cosmic scarlet, like the secret blue inside blue that people do not usually see.

'What is it?' Maram gasped, directing his words at Ymiru. 'Tell me before I fall mad.'

'It be glorre,' Ymiru said to him. 'It be the color of the angels.'

Glorre, I thought, glorre – it was so beautiful that I wanted to drink this color into my deepest self; it was almost too real to be real. And yet it *was* real, the truest and loveliest thing I had ever beheld. I melted into it; I felt it washing through my entire being, carrying into every part of me the clear, sweet, numinous taste of the One that is just the essence of all things.

'But yesterday,' Maram gasped out, 'the mountain didn't appear so!'

'No, it did not,' Ymiru agreed. 'It takes on this color only once each day, in the light of the Morning Star – with the rising of the sun.'

Atara stared at Alumit as intensely as she ever had her scryer's sphere. Behind her, Master Juwain asked Ymiru, 'Has it always taken on this color?'

'No, only for the last twenty years,' Ymiru said. 'Ever since the earth entered the Golden Band.'

'I see,' Master Juwain said, rubbing his bald head. 'Yes, I see.'

Liljana looked upon the mountain in awed silence while Kane stood stricken beside her. His fathomless eyes were fixed on the glorre of the mountain. He didn't move; he seemed not even to breathe. If one of the Ymanir had fallen on him with a club just then, I did not think that he would have drawn his sword to defend himself.

'The mountain speaks to those who listen,' Ymiru said softly. 'As we must listen now.'

The silence that descended upon the square was a strange and beautiful thing. We stood with ten thousand Ymanir looking up at the sacred Alumit to the west, and not a single child fidgeted or called for his mother to take him home. I tried to listen with the same concentration as did they. As I my eyes drank in this mountain of a numinous hue seen only in the stars, I became aware of voices singing as from far away. Far but almost impossibly near: every building in the city seemed suddenly to vibrate with these sweet sounds, which I felt resonating inside me. It was like the ringing of bells and gentle laughter carried along the wind. The music reminded me of that which Alphanderry had sung in the Kul Moroth. I tried to understand the words that formed up in my mind, breaking like the crest of a wave always just beyond my reach. And yet I knew that I could always keep them within me, in my heart and hands, if only I had the courage to hold onto them.

Others, however, were more practiced or gifted at such apprehension. Liljana stood with her gelstei pressed to her forehead over her third eye. The little blue whale seemed to have deepened to the color of glorre. Liljana's eyes, wide open, flicked about with the little movements of one who is deep in dream.

'What does she see?' Maram whispered to me.

'You might better ask yourself,' Ymiru told him, 'what she *hears*.'

We soon had our answer. As the sun rose still higher in the sky, Liljana's hand fell down to her side. She smiled at Master Juwain in her peacable way, and then turned to Atara and me. She said, 'They're waiting for us, you know. On many, many worlds, the Star People are waiting for us to complete the quest.'

The nine Elders of the Urdahir, led by Hrothmar, turned our way.

The guards around us pulled aside to allow him room to step forward.

'They *are* waiting,' he told us. 'As are the Elijin and Galadin themselves. We feared that it would be so.'

He sighed as he pulled at the white fur of his chin and looked at me. 'Sar Valashu, we believe that you and your friends *must* try to enter Argattha and recover the Lightstone. If you agree, we'd like to help you.'

Audhumla and Yvanu, standing just behind him, smiled as he said this; Hramjir and Hramdal nodded their massive heads, while even Burri seemed to have been moved by the wonder of what he had just heard.

Maram muttered something about the madness of forcing Argattha's gates, and Hrothmar, not quite understanding him, nodded his head gravely, saying 'Then you may remain here as our guests for as long as you live – or until the Star People return.'

I couldn't help smiling at Maram's consternation. To Hrothmar I said, 'We would welcome whatever help you have to give us.'

'Very good,' his huge voice rumbled out. He looked from Atara to Liljana, and then at Kane, Maram, Master Juwain and me. 'The prophecy you told us spoke of the seven brothers and sisters with the seven stones of the greater galastei. And seven you were until you lost the minstrel in Yrakona. Therefore, you need one more to complete your company. And so we must ask that we send one of our people with you to Argattha.'

I knew from the set of his hard, blue eyes that there could be no disputing this demand. I looked toward the edge of the square at the guards, with their fearsome borkors. Either we accepted one of these giants into our company, I thought, or we must remain here forever.

'Who would you send with us then?' I asked him.

He turned to Ymiru and said, 'I have seen in you a desire to make this journey. It would be fitting, wouldn't it, that after breaking the lower law, you should fulfill the higher?'

'Yes,' Ymiru said, 'it would.'

'Will you show the little people the way through Asakai?'

'Yes, I will.'

Hrothmar looked at me. 'Well, Sar Valashu – will you take Ymiru into your company?'

I met eyes with Ymiru and smiled at him. 'Gladly,' I said. Then I reached out to grasp Ymiru's huge hand with mine.

Now, as the sun rose still higher and the glorre of Alumit began to break apart into its usual, brilliant colors, the thousands of people in the square all turned their attention on Ymiru and the nine Elders – and us.

'But we've still only six gelstei,' Maram pointed out. 'How can Ymiru come with us without a gelstei?'

Hrothmar's sudden grin seemed bigger than the sky. I noticed then that he was holding a small, jeweled box in his hand. He gripped this tightly next to his furry hip. Then he lifted it up and said to us, 'You have found six of the galastei on your journey; now we would like to give you the seventh.'

And with that, he opened the box. He pulled out a large, square-cut stone, clear and bright and purple as wine.

'This be a lilastei,' he said, handing it to Ymiru. 'It be the last one remaining to our people. Take it with our blessing. For with you goes the hope of our people.'

Ymiru held the gelstei up to the sun. Its bright rays passed through it and fell upon the ground. The stone there seemed to soften in the deep violet light.

'Thank you,' Ymiru said.

Maram came forward then and took Ymiru's free hand. 'This is a lucky day for us. With you by our side, we'll be more like seventeen than seven.'

Atara was the next to welcome Ymiru into our company, followed by Liljana and Master Juwain. And then Kane stepped up to him. He clasped hands with Ymiru, fiercely, like a tiger testing the strength of a bear. He said nothing to him. But the fire of fellowship in his bright eyes said more than words ever could.

Hrothmar swept his hand toward the seven of us and said, 'Your courage in undertaking this journey cannot be questioned. But we must ask you to find an even greater courage within yourselves: that should fate fall against you, you will seek death before revealing to the Beast the secrets of Alundil.'

Ymiru agreed to this grim demand with a bow of his head. As did Master Juwain, Liljana and I. Atara smiled with a chilling acceptance of what must be. And Maram, his face flushed with fear, looked at Hrothmar and said, 'Set your mind at ease. I'll gladly seek death before torture.'

Hrothmar turned to Kane and asked, 'And you, keeper of the black stone?'

Kane looked toward the east in the direction that we soon must travel. In his black eyes was death and defiance. He said, 'No torture of Morjin's will ever make me speak.'

So great was the will that steeled his being that Hrothmar did not question him further.

'Very good,' Hrothmar said, to him and to us. Then he embraced us one by one and gave us his blessing.

Hramjir, with his one arm, did likewise as well as he could, followed by Audhumla, Yvanu and the other Urdahir. Burri was the last to approach us. After wrapping me up in a mound of living fur, he took out the cup that I had given him. He looked down at me and said, 'Thank you for your gift, Sar Valashu. We have lost our last lilastei only to gain one of the greatest of the silver galastei.'

Then he turned to Ymiru and told him, 'I was wrong about the little people. And about you.'

He embraced Ymiru with an unexpected tenderness. Then shocked us all, saying, 'I'm sorry, my son.'

From the mist that gathered in Burri's blue eyes, and Ymiru's, I knew that even the hardest ice could melt and be broken.

To direct my attention elsewhere, Burri suddenly pointed above the square toward Alumit. There, limned against the last patch of glorre to light up the mountain, Flick danced ecstatically through the air, whirling and diving, describing incendiary arcs. His being blazed with silver, scarlet and gold – and now, too, with glorre. I must have been blind, I thought, never to have beheld this dazzling color within him. As others were now beholding it as well. At least a hundred of the Ymanir nearby had their long fingers aimed at him, and their large eyes seemed suddenly larger with wonder. And Burri, perhaps, held the most wonder of all.

'I think you did tell one lie, Sar Valashu,' he said to me. 'You told that the Timpum twinkled. But these lights – they be a glorious thing.'

Glorious indeed, I thought, watching Flick spin beneath the shining mountain that the Galadin had made. As Burri and the other Elders began wishing us well on our journey, it gave me hope to enter another mountain whose faces were as hard as iron and whose color was as black as death.

38

It took us four days to set out from Alundil. Much of this was spent in gathering supplies for our journey: rations such as cheeses and dried fruit, pine nuts and potatoes and the Ymanir version of the inevitable battle biscuits. To Maram's delight, Ymiru laid in a few small casks of a fermented goat's milk called *kalvaas*. I thought it a foul, rancid-smelling brew, but Maram announced that drinking it gave him visions of the angels or beautiful women – to him, it seemed, the same thing.

'Now take these Ymanir women,' he said to me one night after we had worked very hard to reshoe the horses. 'Now it's true, they are, ah, rather large. But they have a certain comeliness of form and face, don't you think? And, oh my Lord, they would keep a man warm at night.'

As it happened, the Ymanir women were working very hard to keep us *all* warm on our journey. It took Hrothmar's daughters – along with Audhumla, Yvanu, Ulla and others – most of four days to make for us long coats that covered us from head to ankle. They were wonderfully soft and thick, woven from the long fur that the Ymanir women had sheared from their own bodies. Their whiteness, like that of snow, would help hide us against the frozen slopes of the mountains to the east.

The Ymanir men were equally clever at the making of things. They filled Atara's empty quivers with arrows, a few of which were tipped with diamond points for piercing the hardest plate armor. One of their smiths presented Liljana with a new set of cookware, forged from a very light but very strong goldish metal that he called *galte*. Burri himself, on this last night of our stay in Alundil, brought Ymiru a map that one of their ancestors had fashioned some generations before. He kept this gift wrapped in brown paper and string, and admonished Ymiru not to reveal its secrets to us until we were well away from the city.

'For the time, this be for your eyes only,' he said to Ymiru. 'And for your hands only – only the fathers and sons of our line have ever touched this.'

The mystery that he made of the map aroused our curiosity. There was much, as well, that we wished to know about Ymiru and his family. After Burri had gone, we asked Ymiru why he hadn't told us outright that he was his father. And Ymiru, staring at the paper-covered package in his hands, fell into a deep, brooding silence. And then he said, 'I thought I did.'

In truth, he had told us only that he had lost his children to the Red Dragon, and Burri his grandchildren – and this was his way of making known to us certain truths that tormented him. Clever he might be in shaping things with his huge hands, but he was not very good at bringing forth memories and sadnesses from the gloom inside him.

We did learn, however, one of the reasons that the Urdahir had chosen him to show us the way toward Argattha: when he was younger, it seemed, he had led raids into Sakai in a fierce effort to beat back the encroachments of the Red Dragon's armies. Although he and the other Ymanir had killed many with their borkors, in the end they were too few, and much of the East Reach had been lost.

'The Dragon grows ever stronger while we weaken,' he told us. 'Burri and Hrothmar, all of the Urdahir, know that we can hrold Elivagar for another generation, perhaps two – but not forever. And so they were willing to take the dreadful chance of sending me with you to Argattha.'

Evil omens, he said, were everywhere: in the stars, in the fall of Yarkona, in the rumor of a fire-breathing dragon that Morjin held ready to unleash upon those who opposed them. Even the new color of Alumit, he admitted, was not wholly a good thing, for in the wisdom that the Elders gleaned from the Star People there was not only hope but the murmurings of doom.

'Elivagar might be the last place on Ea to fall,' he said to us. 'But fall it finally will. And so the Star People will never come.'

'No, don't speak so,' I told him. 'There's always hope.'

'Hrope,' he said bitterly. 'I have had none since the Beast took my children from me. And now –'

I gripped his massive forearm, wondering if he could feel the incredible strength there that I did.

'And now, tomorrow,' he said, 'the seven of us will leave for Argattha. Be there really any hrope in this quest? I suppose we must at least *act* as if there be.'

Ymiru's sudden melancholy, which fell upon him like an ice-fog, seemed to evaporate the following morning when the Elders and many of the Ymanir again gathered in the great square to wish us farewell. He had girded himself for our journey, strapping onto his back a huge pack and taking into his hand the great borkor that had felled many of his enemies. As well, he had taken on the task of leading the thirty Ymanir guards who would escort us from Alundil; now he was all business and bluff good cheer, checking the guards' loads, calling out commands in his thundering voice. He moved about with an almost frenetic activity, with the air of a captain who is certain of victory. His new mood, that sunny morning, was that of his people. They swarmed around us, cheering and calling out encouragements. When it came time for us to set out, they formed up on either side of us like living mountains of fur. Down one of Alundil's broad avenues, as through a valley, we passed between them as they cast sprigs of laurel at us and sang out their prayers.

We left Alundil by way of a great road leading through the valley to the south of the city. Here, along the banks of the blue Ostrand, were many fields planted with barley, rye, potatoes and other hardy crops. I rode on top of Altaru, leading the line of my friends on their mounts. And the Ymanir led us. With Ymiru at their head, our guard marched along with huge strides, matching the pace of our horses. For a moment, I wished that these thirty giants might accompany us all the way to Argattha where they might simply batter down its gates with their huge clubs.

Some miles outside of the city, where the farms gave way to forests and wilder country, we turned onto a side road leading east toward what seemed a break in the mountains. As Altaru carried me forward, I searched the undulations of the sharp white peaks very carefully, measuring angles and distances with my eye, trying to see with my mind's eye how the terrain into which we were journeying would unfold. And then it came time for me to look no more. Ymiru halted our company and asked us to dismount. He brought out the same blindfolds that had covered our eyes on our passage into Alundil. Now we must wear them again, so that if by ill fate we *were* captured, we might tell of Alundil's existence but not the way into it.

Thus we walked blind as bats for the rest of the day. As on our approach to Alundil we each had one of the Ymanir to guide us. I had worried that the presence and the smoky smell of so many men who stood almost as high as great white bears might spook the horses. But men are men, not beasts, and the horses knew this well enough. They accepted the Ymanir as they might any people. But the Ymanir did not easily accept them. They were unused to horses, and the idea of riding an animal disturbed them deeply. As Ymiru put it, 'The hrorse was made with four legs to flee from lions and wolves, not to bear a man's weight when his two legs have grown 'too tired.' It was, I thought, a strange and compassionate way to look at the world.

I worried that the horses would have a hard time crossing the mountains ahead of us. There might be places there, on steep slopes of scree or sheer rock, where two legs – and two hands – would be much better than four. But if Ymiru shared my concern, he showed no sign of it. Neither did he discuss the route that he intended to take out of Elivagar and into Sakai. I wondered if he might be reluctant to tell of this in front his countrymen, who didn't really need to know it. I wondered, too, if he simply wished to spare us the imagining of its terrors.

It was disquieting and uncomfortable walking along with a piece of cloth wrapped around my eyes. It would be terrible, I thought, to be truly blind. And yet, with the negation of this most vital of the senses, I became more aware of my others. The road led up a winding way through a forest into the mountains. I felt this steep gradient through the angle of my feet as I felt the air growing colder and colder with every yard higher we climbed. The wind on my face carried scents of spruce, feather fir and new flowers that I had never smelled before. I listened to the sweet *cheer-lee churr* of what sounded like a bluebird and to the bellows and whistles of the elk from deeper in the woods. And then my senses drove deeper, and I dwelled on the pull of Ymiru's hand against mine and the rushing of the breath from his lips. My heart told me that he was hiding something in his great, booming heart, keeping from us some dark secret that he didn't want us to know.

We made camp that night by a little river, where it pooled just beneath a waterfall. It seemed a lovely place, with the smell of spray off the rocks and some nearby yarrow perfuming the air. All of us, I knew, longed to take off our blindfolds and look upon it. But this Ymiru would not permit. Neither would he let us gather wood for a fire or cook our meal. He assigned his countrymen these chores and others. He left only the care of the horses to us. Even a blind man, I thought, as I patted Altaru's neck, could comb down a horse or hold a bag of oats to his eager lips.

The next day we set out early and spent most of the morning climbing over a snow-steeped pass. There were turnings and twistings to our route – and risings and fallings, too. But mostly risings: we climbed beneath a bright sun into cold air that grew thinner and thinner as the mountain beneath us thrust itself up into the sky. We plowed through snowdrifts up to our thighs; in places, we slipped upon ice-glazed rocks. But Ymiru's guidance, and that of the Ymanir who had my other companions' hands, proved steady and true. That night we found shelter in yet another of the stone huts that the Ymanir had built through the high country of their land.

On our third day out from Alundil, we wound our way down into a deep valley before climbing a jagged ridgeline that led to yet another pass. We crested this cleft between two mountains late in the afternoon. After making our way down through the snow past a field of scree, Ymiru found a shelf on the mountain's east slope where he called for a halt and a rest. He also called for our blindfolds to be removed. As on our approach to Alundil, the sudden touch of the sun dazzled our eyes. It was quite a few moments before our sight returned to us. When I again managed to make out the world's forms, I saw that that a high valley lay below us. All around us were the sculpted white peaks of mountains as far as the eye could see.

We said goodbye to our escort, there on that cold mountain. Maram, who had come to appreciate the comfort of these thirty giants, did not want to see them leave. Two of them especially, Lodur and a young man named Asklin, he had befriended on our journey through Elivagar. After clasping hands with them and watching them march off with the others, he sighed and said, 'I don't understand why they can't accompany us to Argattha. They would be a great strength.'

Ymiru stood with his furry feet splayed out upon the snow. He nodded at the line of his retreating countrymen and said, 'Their numbers might prove a weakness rather than a strength. Above all else, on our way through Sakai, we must avoid being detected. If we are, it won't matter if we are thirty times thirty.'

'Besides,' Atara reminded him, 'the prophecy spoke of the seven brothers and sisters of the earth – not *their* thirty brothers as well.'

With the hour fallen so late, we hastened our descent down the mountain. Even so, we were forced to make camp fairly high up, barely within the shelter of the trees that blanketed the mountain's lower slopes. But at least there was no snow beneath the swaying spruces, and we found some level ground where we laid out our sleeping furs. When the wind rose later that night and it grew cold, we had a good, crackling fire to warm us – as well as the thick coats that Hrothmar's daughters had made for us.

'Ah, this isn't so bad,' Maram whispered to me, drawing his white coat around himself. He fingered its collar and added, 'It's as though the best part of the world is keeping me warm. Such softness – I wonder if the Ymanir women are so soft. Now *that* is something I would like to live to discover.'

He must have thought that Ymiru, lying on the bare ground between Kane and Liljana with only his own fur to cover him, was asleep. But it seemed that he was only deep in thought. And his hearing, as Maram discovered to his embarrassment, was very keen. He turned about, facing the fire – and Maram. And then he laughed and said, 'And just what would you do with one of our women, little man?'

'Little?' Maram said. 'Ah, I confess that there aren't any yet who have found me so.'

'No? Are you considering the size of your mouth? Or perhaps you speak of your head, which seems swollen with unattainable dreams?'

'Ah, well, my head,' Maram muttered. He shot me a quick, knowing look as if giving thanks that Lord Harsha hadn't cut it off. 'Let's just say I'm speaking of the size of my, ah, soul.'

'Your *soul*, is it?' Ymiru said. 'Now *that* be a great and glorious thing, I'm sure. Even a little man can have a great soul.'

'Just so, just so.'

'It must be your plan, then, to find a willing woman and fill her with this magnificent, questing soul of yours?'

'Ah, you *do* understand.'

'I do indeed,' Ymiru said, letting loose a laugh that shook the side of the mountain. 'Now that would be something *I* would like to live to see.'

We all laughed with Ymiru and Maram, and felt the better for it. Since Alphanderry's death, we'd had little enough opportunity for laughter and even less inclination. In truth, making jokes again around a campfire made us miss his mirthful ways terribly and seemed almost to mock his memory. But it would have been worse, I thought, if we had kept to our mournful mood forever. Alphanderry, of all people, would not have wanted it so. He would have wished upon us music and song, dancing and friendship and laughter. I knew that the only way we could ever really honor his death was to live our lives more deeply and take his spirit into us.

The coming of Ymiru into our company made this easier in some ways and more difficult in others. He had a wit to match Alphanderry's and a song in his heart – but the melodies that sounded there were less often light and sweet than complex, dark and deep. His quiet glooms and occasional enthusiasms reminded us that he could never simply replace Alphanderry as the seventh of our company. He was his own person, as brooding and mysterious as Alphanderry was cheerful and open. Although we already appreciated his thoughtfulness and courage, no less his steadiness and strength, he would have to find his way toward us, and we toward him.

At least, I thought, we would have many miles in our coming together toward our common cause. From Alundil to Argattha, Burri had told us, was a distance of a good two hundred and fifty miles. Perhaps thirty of these we had already covered. How long would the remaining miles take us to cross? A month? Already, it was near the end of Soal, and Ioj was nearly upon us. If Valte, with its snows, found us still in the mountains, it might be very bad for us indeed.

After breakfast the following morning we crossed a high valley peopled with only a few dozen Ymanir families. One of these served us a big lunch of vegetable and barley soup, cream cheese sandwiches and applesauce. They shared a little kalvaas with us, too, before wishing us well on our journey.

That afternoon we crossed over a rather low ridgeline into a wild country broken with many tors. We snaked our way around these rocky prominences, working our way through mostly barren furrows toward the east. The air grew cold as we gradually gained elevation. The horses, driving their newly shod hooves against the icy rocks and patches of snow, moved steadily forward, bearing the six of us on their backs as Ymiru walked a few paces ahead of them. Of all of horses, I thought, only Altaru knew how much I worried over the finding of grass for them in the even more forbidding land into which we were headed.

We made camp well before sunset by a stream that flowed out from between two good-sized hills. The faces of these rocky heaps were jacketed with slabs of sandstone, growing out of the earth at a steep angle like huge flatirons. After the work of gathering water, making a fire and preparing dinner had been done – and after we had eaten the thick cheese and potato soup that Liljana made – Ymiru sat by the fire playing with some chips of sandstone that he had found. Then, from a pouch on the great black belt that he wore, he took out the gelstei Hrothmar had given him. He held the flat, purple crystal over the sandstone chips in various positions, turning it this way and that. His ice-blue eyes were afire with the intensity of his concentration.

'Ah, may I ask what you're doing?' Maram said as he held a mug of kalvaas in his hand and sat nearby looking on.

When Ymiru didn't answer him, Atara came close and said, 'That should be obvious.'

'Well, it's not obvious to me.'

Now Liljana moved closer, and so did Kane. And Atara said, 'You might say he's trying to make a silk purse out of a sow's ear.'

Ymiru's faint, curving smile suggested that he had heard Atara's words as from far away.

'*Trying*?' Maram said. 'But he's a Frost Giant! Don't they all know how to use these stones?'

He then began a long speech – made much longer by the quantity of kalvaas that he drank – about the wonders of Alundil. After he went on and on extolling the great, crystalline sculptures of the Garden of the Gods, which could only have been formed through the power of the purple gelstei, Ymiru had finally had enough. He held up his great hand for silence. Then he said to Maram, 'The Garden of the Gods was made long ago, with knowledge that has been lost to us. And with much greater galastei than this one.'

As he looked at the gleaming stone in his hand, Master Juwain came over and said, 'It's told that the purple crystals sing with the deeper vibrations of the earth. And thus, in many ways, they are the hardest to use.'

'And who tells this?' Ymiru asked him.

'My Brotherhood's alchemists.'

'Have they worked with many of the lilastei, then?'

Master Juwain shook his head. 'Not for three thousand years. The purple stones have been lost to us, too. The alchemists' knowledge comes from books.'

'So does mine,' Ymiru said, fingering his crystal. 'And from the teachings of the elders. Many of my people are instructed in the ways of the lilastei, should the Ymanir ever find the secret of making more of them.'

And with that, he bent over to direct his attention to the task at hand, trying to unlock the secrets of his violet-colored crystal.

After a while, Liljana and Atara went to work on cleaning the pots and dishes while Maram slipped off into a drunken doze. I stood up to cover the horses with the white blankets that the Ymanir women had woven for them. Kane stood because he hated sitting; he walked about the perimeter of our camp, staring off into the darkness to look for enemies that he was unlikely to find within the safety of the Ymanir's land.

And then, just as I was feeding Altaru a chunk of carrot that I had saved from my soup, I heard Master Juwain cry out with delight: 'Do you see? He's done it after all! Val, Kane, Liljana – come here and look!'

As Maram awoke with a loud, breaking snore, we all gathered around Ymiru. I looked down at the ground beneath his purple gelstei. Where only a few moments before a pile of sandstone chips had been, now three long, clear, quartz crystals grew out of a fused mass of stone.

'What is it?' Maram asked. He struggled to sit up as he peered at Ymiru's work through his bleary eyes. 'What *is* this – sleight of hand?'

He looked at Ymiru suspiciously, as he might a street magician who has been given a bauble to play with. I did not think that he would ever be willing to lend Ymiru a gold coin for fear that Ymiru would return to him only a lump of lead.

'There's your silk purse,' Atara said, pointed at the newly-formed quartz crystals. 'It's good work – they're lovely, Ymiru.'

'So small,' he said, holding the crystals up to the light of the fire. 'And stived with flaws. But it be a beginning.'

Master Juwain had his own crystal in his hand as he looked at Ymiru approvingly. He couldn't have helped noticing, I thought, that just as Ymiru's knowledge and will had brought out the power of the purple stone, the stone had also brought out *his* power and exalted him.

'It *is* a beginning,' Master Juwain said, to Ymiru and to all of us. 'Or, I should say, a completion. Now, for perhaps the first time since the Age of Law, seven of the greater gelstei have been brought together.'

He explained that the seven greater gelstei were each emanations of the gold gelstei and held something of its virtue. Used together, they were much more powerful than all of the stones used separately. They were like the fingers of a hand gripping the cup of fate that is also called the Lightstone.

'And as with the gelstei, so with us,' he said, looking at Ymiru. 'For we are only emanations of the One. Each of us – all have some seeds of the great gifts. It's the gelstei's purpose to quicken these gifts.'

Maram let loose a loud belch and said, 'You seem happy, sir.'

'I *am* happy, Brother Maram. Do you see? It's as I've always said – there is only one pattern to everything, a single tapestry. And we are its threads.'

Maram, still trying to wake up, rubbed his eyes and said, 'Ah, I don't quite understand.'

'One pattern,' Master Juwain said to him again. 'And the Lightstone holds the secret of its making. Its *making*. And I've sought just the opposite. All my life, looking for the knowledge to cut through and understand, the way to unravel the tapestry – all my life. And now, when perhaps there is not much left of it, I see that I was misguided.'

He turned to look at Liljana and Atara, and then at Kane and me. He said, 'We've been seeking to quicken our gifts and use the gelstei in order to find the Lightstone. But perhaps we should seek the Lightstone in order quicken our gifts.'

He went on to tell us that our work with the gelstei had great merit, as did our lives, even if we failed in our quest.

'Alphanderry said it best,' he reminded us. 'Do you remember his words?'

We are the songs that sing the world into life, I thought. And then I said them aloud for all to hear.

I sat staring up at the stars, wondering if Alphanderry's music had ever found its way toward these eternal lights. And then Kane's gruff voice brought me back to earth.

'Our lives are our lives, and we shouldn't give them up too easily,' he said to Master Juwain. 'So, I'll sing better when we hold the Lightstone in our hands.'

I fell off to sleep that night holding the hilt of Alkaladur in my hand. I prayed for the thousandth time that I might never again use this sword to take others' lives in defense of mine, but only to find my way through to the Lightstone.

The next day we had our first sight of Sakai. After a breakfast of fried eggs and toasted rye bread, we set out and soon pushed our way between the two hills where we had encamped. A line of low mountains lay ahead of us. We found a pass cutting through this chain, and worked our way over it. And when we crossed over to the other side, we found that we had come to the end of the Ymanir's country.

By chance, it seemed, Ymiru had led us to the exact spot on earth that we had first sought. For here was the great hinge in the White Mountains. To our right, toward the south, the line of mountains that we had just crossed quickly gained elevation as they built toward a wall of white peaks running off into the distance. These were the mountains of the Yorgos Range, and most of Elivagar was spread across their ridges and valleys. To our left, toward the south and east, rose the rocky masses of the Nagarshath. It chilled me merely to look up the unbroken chain of these vast upthrustings of the earth, with their jagged, white, ice-frozen crests. There was no way, I thought, that either man or beast could survive in such great heights. Surely our only hope, as we had discussed, was to pass through Sakai by way of the broad plateau opening out between the two mountain ranges straight ahead of us.

'So that is Sakai,' Maram said as we stood by the horses on the side of the mountain. The wind was out of the west, at our backs, and threatened to push us down its slopes. 'Well, I don't like the look of it.'

Neither did I. The land below was windswept and sere, its brown grasses and patches of bare earth already showing occasional shags of snow. It went on and on toward the gray haze of the horizon. I thought I could make out, off in the distance, outcroppings of dark rock marking the face of this forbidding plateau. It did not seem a place where people would live. And yet I knew that when we went down into it, we would likely find nomads herding their flocks – or the Red Dragon's cavalry riding the borders of his dreadful realm.

'So,' Kane said as the wind whipped up his snowy hair. 'So.'

Atara stood near me, staring down into Sakai as if she had seen it before in her crystal sphere.

Maram looked at Ymiru doubtfully. 'You said that you've led raids down into *that*?'

'No, not here,' Ymiru said. 'Our battles with the Beast's armies were almost a hundred miles to the south.'

'But you still propose to lead us across it?'

'No,' Ymiru said, 'I don't.'

We all looked at him in surprise, even as did Maram, who said, 'But you were to lead us through Sakai. Has seeing it changed your mind?'

'I *will* lead you through Sakai,' Ymiru said. His hard blue eyes looked to the left as he pointed at the mountains of the Nagarshath. 'That, too, be Sakai.'

Although the wind was burning Maram's face bright red, for a moment the color drained from his cheeks. 'But there's no way through those mountains!'

'No, there be a way,' Ymiru said. The coldness of his eyes made me want to shiver. 'An ancient way – we call it the Wailing Way.'

He told us that long ago his ancestors had built a system of roads, tunnels and bridges through the Nagarshath in order to help them fight their wars against Morjin. There, along the icy peaks of these high mountains, the wind wailed almost continually. And there, too, the mothers of the Ymanir had wailed for many hundreds of years to see so many of their sons and daughters slain.

'It took the Beast a long, long time to drive us from the Nagarshath,' Ymiru told us. 'But the mountains were too vast, and we were too few to defend them. So in the end we had to retreat to Elivagar.'

'But surely, then,' Maram said, 'the Red Dragon's men now guard this Wailing Way of yours.'

'No, they would have no reason to – none of my people has been that way for a thousand years.'

'You haven't either?'

'No, I haven't.'

'Then how do you know it still exists?'

'It *must* still exist,' Ymiru said. 'You've seen how my people build things.'

'But what if the Red Dragon has destroyed it?'

'It is my hrope that he has not,' Ymiru said. 'You see, it was a *secret* way, and it may be that his men never found it.'

We all stood wondering if Ymiru could find his way through these terrible mountains and so lead us to Argattha through Sakai's back door. In answer, he took off his pack and removed the paper-wrapped package

662

that Burri had given him. It took him only a moment to open it and take out his father's map.

'What *is* that?' Maram said, crowding close to look at it.

Ymiru held in his hands what seemed a pair of lacquered boards, square in shape and inlaid with various dark woods. With great care, Ymiru suddenly pulled away the top board, which was set neatly against the bottom board's rune-carved frame so as to protect its interior surface. This was a smaller square within a square, wrought of a reddish-brown substance that looked much like clay. Indeed, Ymiru called it living clay, and said that his great-grandfather had crafted it nearly ninety years before.

'This be one thing my people haven't lost,' Ymiru said. 'Almost every Ymanir family has such a map.'

Maram suddenly reached out his finger to run it over the clay's smooth, unbroken surface. And then Ymiru's great voice suddenly bellowed out and froze him motionless: 'Don't touch that! The living clay must never be touched, or else you'll ruin the map!'

Maram jerked back his hand as if from a heated iron. He said, 'I don't understand how you can call this a map.'

'Watch, little man,' Ymiru said to him. 'If I be steady of hand and clear of mind, you'll see something you've never seen.'

As Ymiru oriented his father's map toward the mountains of the Nagarshath, we all gathered in as close as we could. We watched as Ymiru closed his eyes and slowly shifted the position of his furry feet about the bare ground. He seemed to draw strength from it and something else. Almost as slowly as the turning of the earth, he rotated the clay-laden board, apparently seeking to position it along lines that only he could apprehend.

And then without warning, the map's living clay began moving about as if being molded by invisible hands. In places, fissures and furrows marked its rippling surface even as bits of clay formed themselves into ridges and crests, and thrust upward in long, jagged lines that looked like miniature mountain ranges. It took very little time for this transformation to occur. But when it was completed, as I saw to my amazement, Ymiru held in his hands an exact replica of the mountains that lay before us.

'This be a map of the nearer mountains of the Nagarshath,' Ymiru said, opening his eyes. He pointed down with his chin. 'Do you see the valley behind the front range?'

Of course, we could all make out the deep groove in the clay behind the map's front mountains. But when I looked out at the world, through the cold air that hung heavy beneath the blue sky, all I could see was a vast, white wall of rocky peaks edging Sakai's umber plateau. If a valley lay beyond these very real mountains, the map could see it but I couldn't.

'If the map is true,' Master Juwain said, pointing his finger at the gleaming clay, 'then it seems the valley runs for many miles.'

'The map be true,' Ymiru said, looking down at it proudly. 'And the valley be nearly eighty miles long. It will take us a third of the way to Argattha.'

'But what is the magic of this map?' Maram asked him. 'I've never *heard* of such magic.'

Ymiru's eyes warmed as he looked out upon Sakai. And then to Maram, he said, 'The world be a great and glorious place. And through it, along its valleys and rivers and within its hills, pulses the currents of the earth – much as your blood pulses through your big nose and follows its contours. The living clay resonates with these currents. And so it hrolds within its form the forms of the earth.'

Master Juwain's clear gray eyes fixed on the map. And then he said, 'But not *all* the earth, it seems.'

'No, there be a limit to what the map can model,' Ymiru said. 'If it be oriented with the greatest skill, it will show the terrain ahead to a distance of a hundred miles but no more.'

'Then,' I said, pointing at the edge of the map, 'there is no way for us to know what lies beyond this valley.'

'No, not until we've covered some further distance,' Ymiru said, 'But it be my hrope that we'll find other valleys paralleling this one. The line of Nagarshath runs toward Argattha, and so must its valleys.'

'And this Wailing Way of yours?' Kane asked him. 'Does it follow the Nagarshath's valleys, too?'

'It be said that it does.'

'Do you think you can find it?'

Ymiru looked down at the map as he nodded his head. 'That be my hrope.'

With his marvelous map revealing a possible way through the mountains, it seemed that we might not have to brave Sakai's plateau after all. But I was reluctant to commit to this new course. At least on the plateau below us, there would be abundant grass for the horses.

'There be grass in the mountains' valleys, I think,' Ymiru said. 'At least the lower valleys.'

As he pointed out, the horses' packs were still full of the oats that we had gathered for our journey. 'And if the worst befalls and the horses starve, you can always eat them and continue the journey afoot.'

Just then Altaru nickered nervously, and I looked at Ymiru as if he had suggested eating my own brother. Ymiru, who had watched in horror as we savored the taste of our salted pork, could not quite understand the different kind of love that we held for our horses.

'Come, Val,' Kane said to me. 'There are risks in whatever path we take.'

After a quick council, it was decided that the greater risk was in riding straight across Sakai's plateau with barely a rock for cover. And so, as Ymiru turned his attention away from his map and its surface molded itself back into a flat sheet of clay, we steeled ourselves to cross over the Nagarshath's great mountains and approach Argattha along the Wailing Way.

39

nd so we went into Sakai. It was the work of the rest of the day to fight our way over the nearest pass in this towering front range. We had a bad time of it. Atara slipped on an ice-glazed rock and nearly broke her leg. The horses suffered grievously in the thin air, panting and sweating until their fur froze in the cold. We put blankets over them to ease their shivering, but it didn't seem to help very much. When the wind rose to a screaming howl as we crested the pass, whipping up flurries of snow, it seemed that our great, white coats didn't help us much, either.

'I'm cold, I'm tired,' Maram complained as he drove himself into the wind and pulled at Iolo's reins. To either side of us were towers of rock and clouds of snow; beneath the powder at our feet was a mat of old snow made hard as ice by a season of melting and refreezing. 'In fact, I'm *very* cold,' Maram called out into the bitter air. 'I'm so cold that I'm . . . frozen! Oh, my Lord, my fingers are frozen! I can't feel them!'

I hastened to his side and helped him pull off the mittens that Audhumla had knitted him. The tips of his fingers were hard and white. I placed them between my hands and blew on them to warm them. Then Master Juwain came over to take a look.

'I was afraid of this,' Master Juwain said, gently pressing his knotty fingers against Maram's.

Dread cut through Maram like a shark's fin breaking cold waters. He said, 'Is there anything you can do? Never to touch a woman again, never to feel –'

'I *think*,' Master Juwain said, 'we can save the arm.'

He winked as he said this, and his obvious care and confidence reassured Maram somewhat. He told me to keep working on Maram's fingers until I had completely thawed them; he told Maram to keep his hands in his pockets close to his body until we made camp that night and he could heal Maram's savaged flesh with his varistei.

'All right,' Maram said. 'But if this is Sakai, I've had enough of it already.'

So had I. So, I thought, had all of us – except perhaps Ymiru, who consented to take Iolo's reins and lead the descent down into the valley that his map had showed. Here, in this windy groove in the earth tens of miles long, we found a few stunted dead trees that provided us wood for a fire. There was a little grass for the horses, too, and water that ran down its center in a little brown stream. The valley seemed too high to shelter much life beyond some marmots and a few rock goats. Blessedly, we seemed the only people to have set foot here for a thousand years.

Our camp that night was a cold one. Master Juwain, his green crystal in hand, accomplished the minor miracle of fully restoring Maram to himself. Maram vowed to exercise more caution on the long journey that still lay ahead of us. I knew that he would. No man, I thought, had a greater fondness for his various appendages.

For the next four days we worked our way down the valley. I didn't like it that we had so little cover here. But there seemed no one to see us, except the occasional vultures circling on the mountain thermals high above us. We made good time and good distance. The horses held steady and so did we. By the afternoon of our fifth day in Sakai, with the valley abruptly coming to an end in a great massif that blocked our way, we were all gathering our strength for yet another foray into the grim, mountain heights.

Ymiru's map showed a pass off to our right, hidden by a great buttress of the massif ahead of us. We climbed up the rocky slope at the valley's very end, praying that the map proved true. And so it did. After an hour of hard, panting work, we came upon a break in the massif, the highest pass yet that we had tried to cross. Master Juwain took his first look at this huge saddle of snow and ice, and thought it was *too* high to cross. And so, for a moment, did I. And then, at the very center of the pass, I noticed what seemed a cleft cut straight through it. It looked much like the Telemesh Gate that we had passed through from Mesh into Ishka.

'So,' Kane said to Ymiru, looking at him strangely, 'your people once used firestones against the earth.'

As Ymiru stared up at the pass, I sensed some deep, dark thing devouring his insides. There was great doubt in him, and great sadness, too.

'Yes, we used firestones,' he said, pointing upward. 'Thus we made the Wailing Way.'

Liljana shifted about uneasily, as if trying to gain respite from the fierce wind pounding against the shawl she had wrapped around her head. I felt within her the same dread that crept up my legs into my spine: that here it wasn't just the wind that wailed but the very earth itself.

If ever there had been a road leading up to the pass, snow and the relentless work of the seasons had long since obliterated it. But the cleft through the pass itself remained much as the Ymanir's firestones had burned it long ago. And on the other side, below some of the deepest snowfields we had plowed through yet, we found an ancient track leading down from the heights.

We followed this band of packed earth and stone for many miles, all that afternoon and for the next ten days. It wound its way toward the southeast through the furrows between great ice-capped prominences. In places, where it led across a mountain's slope, it was cunningly cut so as to be hidden behind rock and ridgeline from the vantage of the valleys farther below. In other places it disappeared altogether, and there Ymiru had to trust his instinct, following the logic of the land around pinnacles, across basins, until he found the track again. It was a high road, this Wailing Way that the Ymanir had built. In most of the valleys through which it ran, we could find only a little grass for the horses; a few were altogether barren and seemed nothing more than chutes of rocky earth.

This starkness of Sakai appalled us all. But it was nothing, I thought, against the much deeper ugliness that had been worked into the land by the hand of man. The occasional tunnels – through icy ridges too high to cross – seemed like holes cut through the flesh of the earth into her very bones. And worse, by far, were the open pits scooped out the high meadows or basins, sometimes out of the sides of the mountains themselves. They were like sores in the earth, like festering wounds that hadn't healed after even thousands of years. Something in their making, perhaps the piles of slag torn up from the ground, seemed to have poisoned the earth currents that Ymiru had spoken of, for near them nothing would grow. I was given to understand that other parts of Sakai were much more devastated and blighted than this.

'This *must* be the work of the Beast,' Ymiru explained to us, pointing at a circular pock in the valley far below us. 'It be told that his men have dug such pits all across Sakai.'

'But why?' Maram asked him. 'Are there diamonds here? Gold?'

I had my sword drawn and pointing east to see if the Lightstone still lay in that direction. In the reflected sunlight off its silvery surface, a sudden thought flashed through my mind.

'The Red Dragon *does* seek gold,' I said. 'The true gold, from which he hopes to forge another Lightstone.'

Ymiru looked at me strangely, with a deep sadness. 'So it be, so it be.'

This mark of the Beast disturbed me, and all of us, for if Morjin's men had once come here, they might come again. I felt his presence all around me, in the jagged knifeblades of the ridgelines, in the pinnacles' icy spears, and most of all, in the bitter wind. As promised, it swept across the Nagarshath as through a dragon's teeth and wailed without relief. It bit at my bones; it carried in its icy gusts whispers of torment and death. As we drew closer to Morjin and the seat of his power on earth, it seemed that he was seeking me even as I sought the Lightstone, calling me as always to surrender up my will and dreams and kneel before him.

I doubted that he could perceive my actual physical presence in these terrible mountains he claimed as his own. But the kirax still poisoned my blood and connected us in ways that chilled me with a growing dread. I knew that he could sense my soul. The howling wind told me this, as did the silent screaming of my lungs. In the icy wastes through which we passed for many days, he sent illusions to confuse and break me. In many of these, I saw myself chained to the face of some rock and being tortured with fire and steel; in others, the frozen ground beneath me suddenly gave way, and I found myself plunging into a black and bottomless abyss.

But the hardest illusion for me to bear was the one in which I had regained the Lightstone and used it to restore the tormented lands of Ea. The imagined *pleasure* of simply touching this golden cup nearly overwhelmed me. It seduced me into covetousness and pride, and made me want to possess the Lightstone for myself alone and never suffer another even to behold it. So great was the greed for the golden light that Morjin aroused in me that I made for myself illusions of my own. In the dazzling whiteness of Sakai's snows, in the glare and glister of the sun off glacier ice, I began seeing the Lightstone everywhere: on rocky ledges, dropped down into frozen drifts or even floating in the air. It was there, in the nearly blinding fastness of the White Mountains, that I began the fiercest battle yet for my sanity and my very soul.

I drew great strength to join it from my friends, of course, particularly Atara. But they each had battles of their own. And in the end, one must journey far out into the icy wastes of despair to face one's demons alone. I *did* have a mighty weapon with which to fight. Alkaladur's silustria, like a perfect mirror, threw Morjin's deceits back at him and shielded me from his hideous golden eyes and the worst of his hate. And more, as I attuned to it, it helped me cut through all illusion to see the world as it really is. My whole being began opening to the numinous and the true: in the stark, snowy landscapes of the White Mountains and in the shimmering stars above them, but also within myself. For there shone the bright sword of my soul. I saw that it was indeed possible to polish it more brilliantly than even the silustria itself. And with every bit of rust that I rubbed from it, as I cleansed myself of pride and fear, I felt this sword gleaming brighter and brighter and pointing me on toward my fate.

One night, just past the ides of Ioj, we made camp at the foot of a glacier. Maram got a fire going out of the last of our wood, and there Ymiru sat with a huge chunk of ice between his legs as he chiseled it with his knife. He worked with a quick, fierce concentration. It was as if he were trying to bring forth the image of some perfect thing that he longed to create. He would not tell us what this was. He did not speak to us, for he had fallen deep into one of his glooms. He even refused the tea that Master Juwain made him. He was, I thought, a man who held onto the dark side of his feelings, afraid that if the demons of his melancholy were driven from him, the angels of his ecstasies would be, too.

'What is it you're carving there?' Maram asked, sidling closer. 'It almost looks like Val's mother.'

It looked like, I thought, the great carving of the Galadin Queen I had seen passing through the Ashtoreth Gate on our entrance to Tria.

But Ymiru didn't answer him. He just set his sculpture down into the snow and then took up a flaming brand from the fire. He held it so that it melted the ice of the sculpture's surface. Then he brought out his purple gelstei, positioning it in front of the sculpture's face.

'What are you doing?' Maram asked him.

None of us knew. But we were all curious, so we gathered around to watch.

And then, as the starlight flickered off the blade of my drawn sword, a sudden thought came to me. I said, 'He's trying to turn his carving to stone.'

'Turn ice to stone?' Maram said. 'Impossible!'

Ymiru suddenly looked up from his work, staring at me in amazement. 'How did you know that?' he asked me.

How *did* I know, I wondered? I looked down at the star-sparkled length of my sword. Its silver gelstei gave me to know many things from the slightest hint.

'It be impossible to turn ice to stone, truly,' Ymiru said. 'But to turn *water* to stone – this be one of the powers of the lilastei.'

'But how?' Maram asked.

Ymiru ran his finger over the sculpture's dripping surface. 'When water falls cold, it wants to turn to ice. This be its natural crystallization. But there be another, too, and that is the clear stone called *shatar*. The purple galastei makes water want to freeze into this stone. And stone it truly be: shatar be as hard as quartz and never thaws.'

As he moved to put away his violet stone, Maram said, 'What are you doing? Aren't you going to show us this shatar of yours?'

'No,' Ymiru said, 'I can't *make* the lilastei make the water want to freeze this way. I haven't the power.'

'Perhaps not yet.'

Ymiru said nothing as he stared at his sculpture's wet face, now freezing in the wind like that of a spurned lover.

'But what else can the lilastei do?' Maram asked. 'You've told us so little about them, or your people.'

The silence into which Ymiru now fell seemed greater than the expanse of all the mountains of the Nagarshath. He looked east, along the line toward which my gleaming sword pointed.

'The lilastei,' I said, gasping at the images that flooded into my mind, 'can mold rock, as the firestones can burn it. That was how the Ymanir made Argattha.'

As Kane's eyes went wide with wonder, everyone looked at me in astonishment. And Ymiru thundered at me, 'Who told you that?'

I felt Alkaladur's bright blade almost humming in the starlight. I said, 'Is it true, Ymiru?'

Ymiru suddenly slumped back, his great chest deflating like a bellows emptied of air. And then he sighed out, 'Yes, it be true.'

'But how?' Maram asked. 'How can it be?'

Ymiru rubbed his broken nose for a few moments and sighed again. 'How? How, you ask? You see, there was a time when we Ymanir thought that Morjin was our friend.'

The story he now told us was a sad one. Long, long ago, he said, during Morjin's first rise at the end of the Age of the Swords, he had gone to Sakai to win the Ymanir to his cause. At this time his evil deeds were mostly unknown. Morjin was fair of form and graceful with his words; he flattered the ancient Ymanir and brought them gifts: of diamonds and gold, but greatest of all, the purple gelstei.

'It was the Beast himself,' Ymiru said, 'who gave us the first lilastei and taught us to use them. It was he who suggested that we seek beneath Skartaru for the true gold that we might use it to forge a new Lightstone.'

Toward this end, Morjin had called his Red Priests into Sakai to teach the Ymanir and aid in the excavations beneath Skartaru that would come to be the city called Argattha. They remained as counselors when Morjin went off to conquer Alonia and eventually be defeated at the Sarburn. It was they who poisoned the ancient Ymaniris' minds and seduced them into believing terrible lies: that Morjin only wished to unite Ea under one banner to bring peace to its torn lands; that his fall had been brought by treachery and the evil of his enemies. And so, when Morjin had been imprisoned on Damoom for all the Age of Law, Ymiru's ancestors had worked hard and long to prepare Argattha for Morjin's return.

'We built a city fit for kings,' Ymiru said. 'Argattha was a great and glorious place, as we may yet live to see.'

Maram, sipping a mug of kalvaas as he listened to Ymiru speak, said, 'I don't care what we see there – I just want to live to come back out.'

'Tell us,' Kane said, watching Ymiru with his dark eyes, 'what happened when the Lord of Lies *did* return.'

'That be easy to tell,' Ymiru said sadly. 'Easy, but the hardest of tales: in the time that followed Morjin's second coming to Argattha, we discovered that the Lord of Light, as he called himself, was really the Lord of Lies. He had taken back the Lightstone then, but he kept us digging beneath Skartaru all the same. He used it to try to bend us to his will and tried to make us slaves. But no one will rule the Ymanir – not even other Ymanir. And so began our war with the Beast that has lasted until this day.'

After he had finished speaking, Atara sat listening to the wind as she stared into her white crystal. Master Juwain gripped his old book and looked at Liljana, who had taken out her blue whale. Kane, crouching near Ymiru like a tiger ready to spring, growled, 'Damn his golden eyes.'

Maram was nearly drunk, but he had a clear enough wit to appreciate that as far as we were concerned, Ymiru's story might not be wholly tragic. 'If your people made Argattha,' he said, 'did they keep any maps of its streets?'

'No,' Ymiru said, 'all such perished in the wars.'

'Ah, too bad, too bad,' Maram said. 'I had hoped, for a moment, that there might be a way into the city other than through one of its gates.'

For a hundred miles, at least, we had discussed the problem of entering Argattha and finding our way to Morjin's throne room. I had thought that our knowledge of the city was scarcely more than anyone's: that Argattha had been built up through the black mountain on seven levels, with Morjin's palace and throne room at the highest. And that five gates, named in mockery of Tria's, opened upon its streets. Each gate, it was said, was guarded by ferocious dogs and a company of Morjin's men. And perhaps, as Kane suggested, by the mind-reading Grays as well.

'There *be* another way into Argattha,' Ymiru said. 'A dark way, an ancient way.'

We all looked at him, waiting for him to say more.

672

'When Morjin came to Argattha with the Lightstone,' he explained, 'he feared that his enemies would assault the mountain and trap him inside. And so my people built escape tunnels for him. Secret tunnels, and the knowledge of all of them has been lost to us – except one.'

'Do you know where this tunnel is?' Maram asked.

'No, I don't know,' Ymiru said, to Maram's bitter disappointment. 'But I know where it might be found.'

Maram's face immediately brightened again as Ymiru brought out his map and oriented it toward the east. For quite a few days now, we had used it to set our course on the greatest of the mountains to show through the clay along the map's eastern edge. This was Skartaru, whose shape was famous across Ea: as seen from the east, from across the Wendrush, its twin peaks thrust like the points of pyramids high into the sky. And now, as Ymiru told us of a secret way into this dread mountain, we studied the model of it in the map that he held in his huge, furry hands.

'I can't see *anything* here,' Maram said, peering at the living clay in the fire's flickering light.

'No, the scale be much too small,' Ymiru said. 'The map shows only the mountain's greater features.'

'Then how do you hope to find this tunnel of yours?'

'Because there be a verse,' Ymiru said. 'Words that have survived where paper or clay have not.'

'What is it, then?'

Ymiru cleared his throat, and then recited for us six ancient lines:

> Beneath the Diamond's icy walls,
> Where brightest sunlight never falls;
> Beside the Ogre's knobby knee:
> The cave that leads to liberty.
> The rock there marked with iron ore
> Which points the way to Morjin's door.

We sat there listening to the wind shriek across the high mountains around us. It seemed to carry the whisperings of the frozen rocks and echoes ten thousand years old.

'So,' Kane said, pointing his finger at Ymiru's map, 'this Diamond that the verse tells of must be Skartaru's north face.'

The black mountain's north face, I saw, was indeed shaped like a standing diamond three miles high, with great buttresses to either side seeming to hold it up.

'That is confirmed by the verse's next line,' Master Juwain said.

'But what about the Ogre?' Liljana asked, looking at the map's dark clay. 'I don't see any such formations beneath the north face.'

'No, the scale be too small,' Ymiru said. 'And so we can deduce that this Ogre rock formation will be rather small, in relation to the rest of the mountain. We won't be able to find the cave until we actually stand beneath it.'

'We won't find *anything*,' Kane said, 'if the verse doesn't tell true.'

'I believe that it be true,' Ymiru said.

Maram took another swig of his kalvaas, then asked him, 'This matter of the verse, ah, your people making escape tunnels, making Argattha itself – why didn't you tell us all this before now?'

'I didn't want to arouse false hrope.'

I sat beneath the stars of the bright Owl constellation, which I could see reflected in the silver of my sword. Then I looked up and said, 'Isn't there another reason, Ymiru?'

Ymiru looked straight at me then, but seemed not to see me. His great heart was booming like a drum.

'The ancient Ymanir,' I said to him, 'sought the true gold beneath Skartaru, but they also sought something else, didn't they?'

'Yes,' he finally said, as everyone stared at him. 'You see, beneath the White Mountains, the earth currents are very strong – the strongest on all of Ea. And they touch the currents of other worlds.'

Kane's black eyes seemed to flare up in the firelight and fall upon Ymiru like hot coals. I remembered him telling us how the telluric currents of all worlds were interconnected.

'My ancestors believed,' Ymiru said, 'that if they could open the currents beneath Skartaru, they might open doors to other worlds. The worlds of the Galadin. They built Argattha to welcome them to Ea.'

'And who,' I asked Ymiru, 'suggested to the ancient Ymanir that such doors might be opened?'

'Morjin did.'

If my sword had shattered into a thousand pieces just then, I would have been able to see the whole of it from a single glittering shard. I found Ymiru's eyes in the dark and said to him, 'Seeking the true gold was never Morjin's real purpose either, was it?'

'No,' Ymiru whispered. As the wind cut at us with icy knives, we waited for him to say more. Then he looked down at his map and told us, 'Morjin wanted to open a door to the Dark World where the Baaloch, Angra Mainyu, is imprisoned. And he came close, we believe, so very close.'

I could hardly bear Kane's presence just then, so deep and dark was the well of hate that opened inside him.

He knows, I thought. *Somehow, he knows.*

'And what, do you believe,' Kane growled at Ymiru, 'kept Morjin from opening this door?'

'Kalkamesh did,' Ymiru said. 'And Sartan Odinan. When they took the Lightstone out of the dungeon where it was kept, they took away Morjin's greatest chance of freeing the Baaloch.'

'How so?' Master Juwain asked.

'Because the Lightstone,' Ymiru said, 'is attuned to the galastei and all things of power, but especially to the telluric currents. With it, Morjin almost certainly would have been able to see exactly where in the earth beneath Skartaru he must send his slaves to dig.'

All this time, even as Atara stared silently into her crystal, Liljana had been nearly as quiet. But now she fingered her blue gelstei and turned to Ymiru, saying, 'When I stood beneath Alumit and its colors changed, I thought I heard the voices of the Galadin. Speaking to me, speaking to everyone. There was a warning about Angra Mainyu, I think. A warning told of in a great prophecy.'

Now Atara finally looked up from her gleaming sphere at Ymiru as she waited for him to speak.

'Yes, there be a great, great prophecy,' Ymiru said. 'An old prophecy – ages old. The Elders know of this. They have heard the Galadin speak of it.'

He went on to tell us what the grandfathers and grandmothers of the Urdahir had gleaned from the otherworldly voices that poured out of Alumit's singular color. He said that ages ago, when the Star People discovered Ea, their greatest scryer, Midori Hastar, had prophesied two paths for this sparkling new world: either it would give birth to the Cosmic Maitreya who would lead all worlds everywhere to a glorious destiny, or else it would descend into the darkest of worlds and bring forth a dark angel who would free the Baaloch, thus loosing upon the entire universe a great evil and possibly destroying it.

'The Galadin,' Ymiru told us, 'took a terrible chance in sending the Lightstone to Ea. And the dice they shook six ages ago are tumbling still.'

I felt my heart beating in rhythm with Ymiru's and with the deeper pulsing of the earth. My sword gleamed in my hand as the distant stars called to me. I saw in their shimmering lights a grand design that had long awaited completion. Some great event, I sensed, had been coming for untold years, set into motion ages of ages ago with the force of whole worlds tumbling through space. I knew then that I, and my friends, *must* face Morjin in Argattha. For that, too, was one of the virtues of the silver gelstei, that it let me see the way that my fate

675

was aligned with the much greater fate of the world and the whole universe itself.

'You should have told us,' Atara said to Ymiru. 'You should have told us before this.'

'I'm sorry,' Ymiru said, 'I *should* have. But I didn't want to crush your hrope.'

Maram was now drunk on the potent kalvaas – but not quite drunk enough to suit him. He took another swallow of it, belched and sighed out, 'Ah, to think we've come this far for nothing.'

'What do you mean, little man?'

'Well, surely in light of what you've told us, the risk of entering Argattha is too great. Surely you can see that. If we *should* find the Lightstone, and Morjin finds us, then . . . . ah, I don't like to think about *then*.'

'*I* can't see that,' Atara said, squeezing her white gelstei in her hand. 'We've known for many miles that we were taking a great risk.'

Master Juwain nodded his lumpy head, agreeing with her. To Maram, and all of us, he said, 'The Galadin, in their wisdom, sent the Lightstone to Ea, hoping for the best. So we should hope, too.'

'So we should,' Liljana added. 'It's not upon us to weigh this risk down to the last grain. Only to take it.'

Maram took yet another pull of his drink. He looked at me and asked, 'Does that mean we *are* still going to Argattha?'

'Ha!' Kane said, clapping him on the back, 'it means just that.'

'Does it, Val?' Maram asked me.

'Yes,' I said, 'it does.'

With the exception of Ymiru, who insisted on staying awake to take the first watch, we all retired to our furs. But I, at least, could not sleep. Great things had been told that night. Far beneath Skartaru's pointed summit, in the bowels of the earth, Morjin labored long and deep to free the Dark Lord from his prison on the world of Damoom. And now we must labor to find the door into Argattha. What we would find on the other side, I thought, not even the Galadin themselves could know.

40

We were all quiet when we set out the next morning. Our breath steamed out into the bitter air, and our boots crunched against the cold, squeaking snow. It was enough, I thought, to avoid tripping and tumbling down some steep slope, enough merely to keep placing one foot ahead of the other and continue plowing through Sakai's frozen wastes. But I couldn't help thinking of Angra Mainyu, this great, fallen Galadin whose dreadful face could darken whole worlds. I knew that somehow, through Morjin, he, too, sensed my defiance and trembled to crush me in his wrath.

And so for two days we worked our way closer to Argattha. Our approach led us through a wild, broken country where we lost the thread of our road. Finally, following Ymiru's map and the lines of the land, we came to a great gorge running for forty miles to either side of us, north and south. It was hundreds of feet wide and very deep: standing at the lip of it, we looked down and saw a little river winding its way past layers of rock far below. Ymiru had hoped to find a bridge here, but it seemed that the only way across the gorge was to fly.

'Is there no way down it?' Atara asked, looking over the edge. I think she knew there wasn't. A very agile man, perhaps, might be able to climb down such a forbidding wall, but no horse ever could.

Liljana looked up and down the gorge, at the mountains framing it, and then at the map which Ymiru held out before him. She said, 'It would be hard work to walk around this. I should think it would add a hundred miles to our journey.'

'That's too far,' Master Juwain said. 'The horses would starve.'

As we stood with the horses on the narrow shelf of land above the gorge, I felt Altaru's belly rumbling with hunger – as I did my own. We had run out of oats for the horses and had little enough food for ourselves.

'Perhaps the bridge you seek is farther up the gorge,' Liljana said to

Ymiru. Then she turned to look at the rent earth toward the right and said, 'Or perhaps that way.'

'I had thought the bridge would be right here,' Ymiru said despondently.

He walked away from us, along the ragged lip of the gorge, looking down at the rocks below for any sign of a fallen bridge. Then he sat down on a rock and bent his head low as he stared down at the ground in silence.

'So,' Kane said, 'seeking for non-existent bridges up and down this gorge would be as futile as trying to walk around it.'

'Then we *will* have to turn back,' Maram said.

'Turn back?' Kane said to him. 'To what?'

After a while, I gave Altaru's reins to Atara, and went over to Ymiru where he sat fifty yards away, now staring down into the gorge as if he were contemplating throwing himself into it.

'I was *sure* the bridge would be here,' he said, not even bothering to look up at me. 'Now I've put us in a hrorrible spot.'

'You can't blame yourself,' I said, sitting down beside him. 'And you can't give up hope, either.'

'But, Val, what are we to do?' he asked as he pointed at the gorge. 'Walk across this on air? You might as well put your hropes into old wives' legends.'

Something sparked in me as he said this. And so I asked him, 'What legends are these?'

He finally looked up at me and said, 'There are stories told that the ancients built invisible bridges. But no one believes them.'

'Perhaps you *should* believe them,' I said, gazing at the sun-filled spaces of the gorge. 'What else is there to do?'

'Nothing,' he said. 'There be nothing *to* do.'

'Are you sure?'

He smiled at me sadly and said, 'That be what I love about you, Val – you never give up hrope.'

'That's because there always *is* hope.'

'In you, perhaps, but not in me.'

Inside him, I sensed, was a whole, dark, turbid ocean of self-doubt and despair. But there, too, was the sacred spark: the ineffable flame that could never be quenched so long as life was in life. And in Ymiru this flame burned much brighter than it did in other men. How was it that he, who could feel so much, couldn't feel this?

'Ymiru,' I said, grasping his huge hand. It was much warmer than mine, and yet as my heart opened to him, I felt a knife-like heat passing from me into him. 'You've led us this far. Now take us the rest of the way toward Argattha, or else the work of your father and all your grandfathers will have been in vain.'

His ice-blue eyes suddenly lit up as he squeezed my hand almost hard enough to break it. He looked across the gorge and said, 'But Val, even if there *were* such a bridge here, how would I ever find it?'

'Your people are builders,' I said to him. 'If you were to build a bridge across this ditch, where would you put it?'

A fire seemed to flare up inside him then. He gathered up a great handful of stones and leapt to his feet. His hard eyes darted this way and that, measuring distances, assessing the lay of the great, columnar buttresses of rock along the length of the gorge. He began walking along it with great strides and great vigor. Here and there, he paused a moment to hurl a stone far out into the gorge and watch it plunge through the air down towards the river below.

'What did you say to him?' Master Juwain asked as Ymiru came up to the place where he and the others waited with the horses. 'What is he doing?'

Ymiru cast another stone arcing out into space, and Maram said, 'No doubt he's calculating how long it will take us to fall to the bottom if we're foolish enough to try to climb down this wall. Ah, we're not *that* foolish, are we, Val?'

At that moment, one of Ymiru's stones made a *tinking* sound and seemed to bounce up into the air before continuing its fall into the gorge. As Maram watched dumbfounded – along with Kane and the others – Ymiru threw another stone slightly to the right and achieved the same effect. Then he flung all the remaining stones in his hand out into space, and many of them bounced and skittered along what could only be the unseen span of one of the bridges told of in the Ymanir's old wives' tales.

'I suppose I'll have to pay more attention to old wives,' Maram said after Ymiru had explained things to him. 'Invisible bridges indeed! I suppose it's made of frozen air?'

Ymiru, looking out at the gorge with a happy smile, said, 'Our Elders have long sought the making of a crystal they called *glisse*. It be as invisible *as* air. This bridge, I'm sure, be made of it.'

It seemed a miracle that the gorge should be spanned by a crystalline substance that no one could see. All that remained was for us to cross over it.

'Perhaps,' Master Juwain suggested to Maram, 'you should lead the way.'

'I? I? Are you mad, sir?'

'But didn't you tell us, after your little escapade at Duke Rezu's castle, that you're unafraid of heights?'

'Ah, well, I was speaking of the heights of *love*, not this.'

Ymiru stepped forward and laid his hand on Maram's shoulder. He said, 'Don't worry, little man. I think you're going to *love* walking on air.'

As we made ready to cross the gorge, we found that the horses would not step very close to the edge of it; surely, I knew, they would balk at setting their hooves down on seemingly empty space. And so in the end, we had to blindfold them. We found some strips of cloth and bound them over their eyes.

'You'd do better to blindfold *me*,' Maram muttered as he fixed the cloth around Iolo. 'We're not really going to step out onto this *glisse*, are we, Val?'

'We are,' I said, 'unless you first discover a way to fly.'

Ymiru, who was the only one of us freed from the burden of leading a horse, borrowed Kane's bow so that he could feel the way ahead of him. He stepped to the very edge of the gorge. Slowly, he brought the tip of the bow down through the air until it touched the invisible bridge. And then, as we all held our breaths, he stepped out into space onto it.

'It be true!' he shouted. 'The old tales be true!'

In all my life, I had seen nothing stranger than this great, furry man seeming to stand on nothing but air. And now it was our turn to join him there.

And so, as Ymiru led forth, tapping the bow ahead of him like a blind man, we followed him one by one out onto the invisible bridge. With Maram and Iolo right behind him, we kept as straight a line as we could. Our lives depended on this discipline and exactitude. Ymiru discovered that the bridge wasn't very wide: little more than the width of a couple of horses. And it had no rails that we could grasp onto or keep us from slipping over its edge. It was, quite simply, just a huge span of some flawlessly clear crystal that had stood here for perhaps a thousand years.

For the first half of our crossing, we walked up a gradually curving slope. The horses' hooves clopped against the unseen glisse as they might any stone. We tried not to look down at what our boots were touching, for beneath the bridge, straight down hundreds of feet, were many rocks and boulders that had fallen into the gorge and piled up along the river's banks. It was all too easy to imagine our broken bodies dashed upon them. The wind – the icy, merciless wind of the Wailing Way – howled through the gorge and cut at us like some great battle-axe, threatening to drive us over the edge. It set the bridge swaying through space with a sickening motion that recalled the pitching and rolling of Captain Kharald's ship.

'Oh,' Maram gasped ahead of me as he clutched his belly with his free hand, 'this is too much!'

'Steady!' I called out to him from behind Master Juwain and Liljana. 'We're almost across.'

In truth, we were just cresting the highest part of the bridge, with the river directly below us.

'Oh,' Maram groaned, 'perhaps I *shouldn't* have drunk that kalvaas before trying this.'

My anger as he said this was an almost palpable thing. It seemed to reach out from me unbidden, like an invisible hand, and slap him across the face. 'But you'll wreck your balance!' I called to him.

'I only had a nip,' he called back. 'Besides, I thought I needed courage more than coordination.'

It seemed, as I watched him stepping daintily behind Ymiru, that he had coordination enough to complete the crossing. He moved quite carefully, with a keen awareness of what lay beneath him. And then, as he grabbed at his churning belly yet again and the wind hit the bridge with a tremendous gust at the same moment, his foot slipped on the glisse as against ice. He lost his balance – as the rest of us nearly did, too. He grabbed at Iolo's reins to steady himself, but just then Alphanderry's spirited horse stamped and whinnied and shook his head. This was enough to further throw Maram off his center. With a great cry and terror in his eyes, with his arms and legs flailing like windmills, he began his plunge into space.

He surely would have died if Ymiru hadn't moved very quickly to grab him. I watched in disbelief as Ymiru's great hand shot out and locked onto Maram's hand. For a moment, he held him dangling and kicking in mid-air. Maram, despite what Ymiru liked to call him, was no little man. He must have weighed in at a good eighteen stone. And yet Ymiru hauled him back onto the bridge as easily as he might a sack of potatoes.

'Oh, my Lord!' Maram gasped, falling against Ymiru and grabbing on to him. 'Oh, my Lord – thank you, thank you!'

Almost as quickly, Ymiru had moved to grasp Iolo's reins with his other hand and steady him. Now he pressed these leather straps into Maram's hand and told him, 'Here, take your hrorse.'

Maram did as he was bade, and he stroked Iolo's trembling side as if to calm him – and himself. And then he gathered up the best of his courage, turned to Ymiru and said, 'Thank you, big man. But I'm afraid we both missed a great chance.'

'And what be that?'

'To see if I could really fly.'

We completed the rest of the crossing without further incident. When we reached the far side of the gorge, Maram let loose a great shout of triumph and insisted on drinking a little kalvaas to celebrate. My nerves were so frayed that I agreed to this indulgence. Maram smiled, glad to be forgiven his foolishness, and passed me his cup. The disgusting brew was just as greasy and rancid as it always was. But at that moment, with our feet firmly planted on ground that we could see, it tasted almost like nectar.

That was the last great obstacle we faced along the Wailing Way. Five days later, after traversing a good part of the Nagarshath to the south of the headwaters of the Blood River, we came out around the curve of a mountain through some foothills to behold the great, golden grasslands of the Wendrush. To the east of us, as far as the eye could see, was a rolling plain opening out beneath a cloudless blue sky. There antelope gathered in great herds and lions hunted them. There, too, the tribes of the Sarni rode freely over the wind-rippled grass, hunting the antelope – and each other. Many times before, facing west from the kel keeps of Mesh's mountains, I had lost myself in the vast sweeps of this country. And now I wondered what it would be like to ride across it, five hundred miles, toward Vashkel and Urkel and the other mountains I knew so well.

'That way be your hrome,' Ymiru said as we gathered on the side of a great hill. Then he turned and pointed to the south of us, where the easternmost mountains of the Nagarshath edged the grasslands. 'And that be Skartaru.'

The sight of this grim, black mountain struck an icy dread deep into my bones. If Alumit had been made by the Galadin, Skartaru might have been carved by the Baaloch himself. It was a great mound of basalt, cut with sharp ridges and points like the blades of knives. Snow and glaciers froze its upper slopes; sheer walls of forbidding rock formed its lower ones. I marveled at Ymiru's feat of navigation, for he had brought us out on the side of a mountain just to the north and east of it. From this vantage, we had a good look at two of its faces. The famed east face was shaped like an almost perfect triangle, save that near its higher reaches, a notch seemed to have been cut from it between its two great peaks. Far beneath the higher and nearer of these – a great pointed horn of black rock three miles high – a road led out of one of Argattha's gates and sliced across the Wendrush. Along this road, I thought, the ancient Valari had been crucified after the Battle of Tarshid. And a thousand feet above the gate, on the east face's sun-baked

682

rock, Morjin had crucified the great Kalkamesh for taking the Lightstone from him.

I stared at this glowing black sheet, and almost unbidden, the ancient words formed upon my lips:

> *The lightning flashed, struck stone, burned white –*
> *The prince looked up into the light;*
> *Upon Skartaru nailed to stone*
> *He saw the warrior all alone.*

'It doesn't seem possible,' I whispered to the wind.

'What doesn't?' Maram asked me. 'That Kalkamesh could have survived such torture?'

'Yes, that,' I said. 'And that Telemesh could have climbed that wall at night and brought Kalkamesh down.'

I was not the only one struck with the marvel of this great feat. Liljana and Atara stared at the mountain's east face, while Ymiru pointed his furry finger at it and Master Juwain shook his head. And as for Kane, his black eyes were so full of fire that they might have melted the mountain itself. Sometimes I could sense the swell of the passions and hates that streamed inside him. But now there was only a burning, bottomless abyss.

'Skartaru,' he growled. 'The Black Mountain.'

He tore his eyes from its east face and pointed at the darker north one. 'There's the Diamond,' he said.

A few miles from where we stood, across some grassy buttes where the plains came up against the mountains, we had a good view of the long-sought Skartaru's north face. As shown by Ymiru's map, this was a towering diamond of black rock, at least three miles high, framed on either side by enormous, humped buttresses. We looked between them for the rock formation told of as the Ogre. But either we were too far away or lacked the proper angle for viewing, because we couldn't discern it.

'It be there, I'm sure of it,' Ymiru said. 'But we've got to get closer.'

So began the final leg of our journey toward Argattha. We might simply have ridden straight across the mounded grasslands toward the valley that cut beneath Skartaru's north face. But such exposure, so near to the enemy's secret city, would have been a great foolishness. As it was, standing here on the side of a mountain above the lands of the Zayak tribe of the Sarni – and in clear sight of Argattha – we were taking a great risk. And so we decided on the longer, and relatively safer, route toward our objective. This would keep us close to the mountains, hugging their curve toward the south and through their foothills. It would take us over wooded slopes and around rocky ridges, past the mouths of two small canyons giving out onto the Wendrush's plain. And so it would take us much longer. But now that we had come so near to our fate, whatever that might be, none of us felt much hurry to meet it.

We spent the rest of the day walking through the foothills. Here, so close to Argattha, every flight of a bird and every sound was a call to grip our weapons more tightly. Atara, who had the best eyes of any of us, kept a tense vigil, watching the ridgelines above us, peering far out on the plains of the Wendrush. Kane brought up the rear of our company, and he seemed able to sense danger through every pore of his skin. And yet despite Skartaru's looming presence and the dread that crushed down upon us like immense, black boulders from its heights, our luck held good. We reached a little canyon to the north of the mountain without sighting anyone. Here, in this grassy hollow where only a single ridge blocked the way toward Skartaru's north face, we came to the moment that I had been dreading almost more than entering the mountain. For here we decided that we must set the horses free.

'Ah, perhaps *one* of us should remain with them,' Maram said, looking about the canyon.

Actually, it was more of a great bowl scooped out of the side of the mountain to the west, with ridges framing it to the north and south. A few trees ran around the curve of these ridges, but in between was a half mile of good grass.

'Hmmph,' Atara said to Maram, 'has coming so close to Argattha made you forget the prophecy?'

'I know, I know,' he said, 'the seven of us must go forth . . . to where we must go. But what will happen to the horses? And what will happen to *us* should our quest prove a success and we return to find the horses gone?'

He suggested that we should perhaps hobble the horses or even picket them so that they remained in the valley.

'No, there are wolves and lions about,' I said, looking down into the plain. 'If we tie the horses, they'd be unable to run or defend themselves. And if we don't return . . .'

Maram watched my face for sign of despair, and then asked, 'But what are we to do?'

I moved quickly to ungird Altaru's saddle and remove his harness. When he was free of these encumbrances and naked as an animal should be, I faced him stroking his neck and looking into his eyes. In these large, brown orbs was something deep and ancient that brought a

684

mist to mine. I stood there breathing my love for him into his nostrils, while he gave voice to the covenant of friendship that had always been between us.

'Stay with the other horses,' I told him as he nickered softly. 'Don't let them leave this valley – do you understand?'

He nickered again, this time louder, and I was seized with a strange, soaring sense that somehow he *did* understand.

It took Atara and the others only a few moments to loose their horses, too. We hid the saddles and tack in some bushes beneath the nearby trees. After taking up our weapons and some supplies, we turned to leave the horses grazing on the canyon's brown grass.

We might have done well to wait for night and approach Skartaru under the cover of darkness. But we needed to find the Ogre and the cave leading into Argattha, and for this we needed light. And so in the day's last hours, we crossed the ridge to the south and then made our way across the narrow canyon cutting beneath the mountain's north face. We found what cover we could among the trees and stony outcroppings there. Now Skartaru loomed so high and huge above us that it blocked the sun and most of the sky. Its black rock seemed the whole of the world; looking at this stark and terrible face, I could almost feel Kalkamesh's blood running down its jags and cracks, even as the cries of those still trapped inside the underground city sounded from inside it.

We walked almost straight up a rocky slope toward the base of the Diamond. We expected to be caught at any moment. But except for a few birds and deer keeping a watch for lions, the valley seemed empty of anyone except us.

'Look!' Ymiru said in a low voice that broke into the quiet air like thunder. He pointed at a great hump of rock five hundred feet high swelling out the Diamond's dark wall. 'Does that look like an Ogre to anyone?'

'Almost,' Liljana said. 'But it's hard to tell from this angle.'

We changed the course of our hike slightly toward the west. After a couple of hundred yards, we came to the very bottom of the Diamond's lower point, in a hollow pressed between the north face's two immense buttresses. And there, jutting out of this dread face, the hump of rock did indeed look like an ogre kneeling down on one knee.

We rushed up to this knob-like prominence, looking for the cave told of in Ymiru's verse. But no cave, to either side of it, could we find. The black rock of the Diamond was scarred with many cracks, but otherwise unmarked. Even though we spread out along the wall searching more carefully, we found no sign of any cave.

'But it must be here!' Ymiru said, pounding the cold rock with his great fist.

Maram, breathing deeply against the day's exertions, leaned back against what must have been the Ogre's knee and sighed, 'Well, who's ready to try one of Argattha's gates?'

Liljana fixed her eyes upon the mountain's rock; suddenly she spoke to both of them, saying, 'Don't you give up so soon. Don't you remember the verse's last two lines?'

Even as she said this, Atara, standing back from the wall, descried a vein of red running through the black rock. Now we all stood back as she pointed at it. It was surely iron ore, I thought, and it ran in jagged bands that pointed like an arrow straight toward the base of the wall just to the right of the Ogre's knee.

'But there be no cave there!' Ymiru said. 'There be nothing but rock.'

'Only rock,' Kane muttered. Then he stepped back toward the wall and began moving his hands over it. 'And smooth rock at that, eh? Ymiru, come here and look at this! Tell me if you've ever seen a mountain's rock so smooth.'

Ymiru joined him there, as did the rest of us. And then Ymiru said, 'It looks like the rock that the ancients cut through the passes of the Wailing Way.'

'So, cut with firestones,' Kane said. 'Melted out of the mountains – as this mountain has been melted down over the cave.'

He told us them that Morjin, perhaps after making other escape tunnels from Argattha, must have sealed off this one.

'But why?' Maram asked. 'Just to confound us, no doubt.'

'Who knows why?' Kane said, rapping his knuckles against the wall. 'Maybe too many knew about this. But I'd wager our lives we'll find the cave behind this rock.'

We all looked at each other in the grim certainty that we *were* wagering our lives here. And then Ymiru, after first casting quick glances up and down the valley, began tapping his borkor at various points along the wall. When he reached the place beneath the bands of iron ore, the reverberations from the rock sounded slightly hollow.

'There be *something* behind here,' he said.

Now he raised his iron-shod club straight back and struck the wall a tremendous blow. The rock rang as if hammered by a god. Chips of black basalt sprayed out into the air. But if Ymiru had hoped to break through to the hidden cave, he failed.

Thrice more he wielded his club, before turning to Kane and saying, 'The rock be too thick. And I haven't the right tools to mine into it.'

'No, you don't,' Kane said. Then he looked at Maram. 'But he does.'

Maram drew forth his firestone and stood looking up at the sky. He said, 'There's not much light here, and I've never burned rock like this, but . . . .'

He pointed his red crystal at the wall and told us, 'Stand back now!'

We did as he bade us. A moment later, a thin tendril of flame flickered out from his crystal and licked the wall. But it scarcely heated up the rock there.

'It's too dark here,' Maram muttered. 'There's too little light.'

'So,' Kane told him, 'I think it's not only light that fires your stone.'

Maram nodded his head and closed his eyes as he searched inside himself. And then, as his gelstei began glowing bright red, he looked straight at the wall, concentrating on the exact spot that he wished to open. At that moment, a great bolt of lightning shot from his crystal and burned into the rock, which vaporized in a tremendous blast. Fire flew back into Maram's face, scorching it lobster-red and singing his beard and eyebrows. Lava ran down from the wall in thick, glowing streams. Maram had to be careful that it didn't engulf his feet and melt away his flesh into a hellishly hot soup.

'Be careful with that stone or you'll kill us all!' Kane shouted at him. He looked at the shallow hole that Maram had melted in the rock. 'Here, I'd better help you.'

He took out his black gelstei and held it facing Maram's firestone. Then he nodded at him and said, 'All right.'

For the next half hour, he and Maram worked together to open the way into the mountain. At times, when the red crystal flared too brightly and great sheets of flame fell out against the rock, Kane used his black gelstei to damp the fury of the firestone. At other times he had to desist altogether, for all Maram's efforts sufficed only in coaxing from his stone a dull red glow. Little by little, however, Maram melted away layers of rock and cut deeper into the face of Skartaru.

All this time, Atara and I had been keeping watch. Now she nudged me gently and pointed down the valley out toward the plain. 'Val, look!' she said.

I squinted and strained my eyes to see some twenty men on horses riding straight toward the canyon.

'Do you think they saw us?' Liljana asked Atara, looking toward the riders, too.

'They saw *something*,' Atara said. 'Probably the flashes of the firestone.'

Ymiru approached the hole that Maram had made in the wall, and rammed his club against the still-glowing rock there. But he failed to break through. He said, 'It still be too thick.'

'Get down!' I said to him, waving my hand toward the ground. The men were approaching the mouth of the canyon. 'Get down, Ymiru – they mustn't see you!'

I pointed at a nearby rock formation to our left and told him to hide behind it. Then I nodded at some trees to our right, and told Liljana, Master Juwain and Atara to wait there.

'So, Val,' Kane said looking down the canyon. 'So.'

'Oh, my Lord!' Maram said, hurrying down from the scorched wall over to where I stood. 'Val – shouldn't we flee?'

'No, they might already have seen us,' I said. 'They would catch us wherever we ran. Or give the alarm.'

'But what are we to do, then?'

I smiled at him and said, 'Bluff it out.'

And so, there beneath Skartaru's dark face, with the Ogre's grim, black eyes staring down at us, we waited as the twenty riders drew closer. Maram, who was clever enough at need, busied himself gathering wood as if for a fire. Kane sat back against a rock and began whittling a long pole with his knife. And I gathered some round stones and set them in a circle as for a firepit.

Soon we saw that the riders were wearing the livery of Morjin: their surcoats showed blazing red dragons against a bright yellow field. They had sabers girded at their sides and bore long lances pointing at us. At a very quick pace, they urged their snorting mounts up the rocky slope straight toward the place where we sat.

'Who are you?' their leader called out to us. He was a thickset man with long yellow hair that spilled out from beneath his iron helm. His drooping mustaches couldn't hide the scars cut into his long, truculent face. 'Stand up and identify yourselves!'

After grabbing up a stone in either hand, I did as he bade us, and so did Maram and Kane. We gave the scowling captain names and stories that we had made up on the spot. He glowered at us as if he didn't like our look and said, 'Three more vagabonds come to sell their swords to the highest bidder. Well, you've come to the right place – show us your passes!'

'Passes?' Maram asked him.

'Of course – you're in Sakai now. How did you come this far without being given a pass?'

Now he gripped his lance more tightly as he looked at us suspiciously. He told us that no one was permitted to move about Sakai without the proper scroll signed by an officer of the border guard – or without one of the seals of the kingdom which the Red Priests bestowed upon the especially privileged.

So saying, he touched the heavy gold disk that hung on a chain from his neck. It was hard to tell across a distance of twenty feet, but it seemed embossed with a coiled, fire-breathing dragon.

'Oh, *that*,' Maram said with a nonchalance that I knew he didn't feel. 'We didn't know you called them passes.'

And with that he opened his cloak to show the captain the gift that King Kiritan had given him. I did the same, and so did Kane.

Our medallions, cast with the Cup of Heaven at their centers, gleamed in day's last light. For a moment, I thought that this mistrustful captain might let us go. And then, as he spurred his horse forward, he called out, 'Let me see those!'

We waited for him and three of his men to come closer, and then Kane growled out, 'I'll let you see *this*!'

And with that, he cast the pole that he had been whittling straight through the captain's eye, killing him instantly. I hurled the two stones in my hands at two of the knights bearing down on us, and managed to strike one of them full in his face, knocking him off his horse. And then, at the call of one of the captain's lieutenants, the remaining knights whipped up their horses and thundered down upon us, and the battle began.

The knights clearly intended to make quick work of us. And so they might have if their lieutenant, a young man with a dark, vulpine look that reminded me of Count Ulanu, hadn't pointed his sword at us and said, 'Take them alive! Lord Morjin will want to question them!'

But it was not so easy for anyone to take Kane this way – or to kill him. With a lightning-quick motion he reached back the hand holding his knife and whipped it forward. The knife spun through space, and its sharp point tore straight into the lieutenant's mouth, which he hadn't had time to close. At the same moment, from the right, an arrow hissed out from behind a tree as Atara found her mark and killed another of Morjin's men. Three more arrows followed in a quick, sizzling succession before the knights even realized that a hidden archer was firing upon them. They had counted on their greater numbers and the great advantage in height that their charging horses gave them to strike terror into us.

And then, from the left, with a great, thundering war-cry that shook even me to my bones, Ymiru arose from behind his rock. His face contorted with a ferocious look as he raised his huge club above his head.

'The Yamanish!' one of the knights cried. 'The Yamanish are upon us!'

Ymiru stood as high as the knights upon their horses; with four quick, savage blows, he knocked four of them off them. None got up.

And then the remaining nine knights, who had given up all thought of maiming and capturing us, fell upon Kane, Maram and me. They tried to kill us with their lances, swords and maces. And we tried to kill them. Kane drew his sword; I drew Alkaladur and cut one of the knights off his mount. Ymiru swung his club against the side of a knight's neck, and struck his head clean off. Blood sprayed the air as more arrows hissed out. Horses flailed their hooves against the earth, reared and screamed. I heard Maram call out the name of his father as he met a flashing saber with his sword and then managed a clean thrust through the belly of one of the knights – just in time to keep him from skewering me with his lance. And Kane, as always, fought like an angel of death in the thickest part of the battle, growling as horses knocked against him, grabbing their bits and tearing them from their mouths, parrying the blows of the knights, cutting and thrusting and snarling out his hate.

And then, miraculously, it was over. The agony of the men I had killed came flooding into me as I stared at the bodies of the nineteen dead knights and fought to keep myself from falling down and joining them.

'Look!' Ymiru called out. 'One of them is getting away!'

Indeed, one of the knights, in the heat of the battle, had turned his horse around and was now galloping straight toward the mouth of the canyon.

Atara came out from behind her tree then to get a better angle upon him. She pulled back the string of her great bow, sighting one of her diamond-tipped arrows on the red dragon of the surcoat covering the knight's back. It was a long shot that she trembled to make – made even longer with every second that she hesitated loosing her arrow.

'Shoot, damn it!' Kane shouted. 'Shoot now, I say, or all is lost!'

Atara finally let fly the arrow. It split the air in an invisible whining and drove straight through the knight's surcoat and armor, burying itself in his back. He remained in his saddle for only a few strides of his bounding horse before plunging off to crash against the rocky ground.

During the next few minutes, Kane went about the mountain's slope with his sword making sure that none of Morjin's men remained alive. And then Master Juwain noticed that some of the blood dripping from his white hair was not the enemy's but his own. It seemed that one of the knights had sliced off his ear.

'Oh, my Lord!' Maram said.

None of us had ever seen Kane wounded. But as always, he made no complaint, not even when Maram set a brand afire and Master Juwain used it to cauterize the bloody hole at the side of his head.

'So, that was close,' he said as Master Juwain fixed a bandage over what remained of his ear. 'The closest yet, eh?'

All the rest of us were untouched. But I was still shaking from the deaths I had meted out, and Maram stood staring at his bloody sword, not quite daring to believe that he had used it to kill two armored knights.

'You did well, Maram,' Kane said to him. 'Very well. Now let's get back to work before anyone else comes, eh?'

Maram cleaned his sword and sheathed it. He took out his red crystal. But he was not quite ready to use it. He walked off a way, up a slight rise, and stood staring down at the carnage that we had made.

After a while, after the shooting pains were gone from my chest and I could breathe again, I went over to him and said, 'You did do well, you know. You saved my life.'

'I *did*, didn't I?' he said as he smiled brightly. And then the horror returned to his face as his eyes fell upon the bodies of the slain. 'Kane was right, I think. That *was* the closest yet.'

He turned to look at the dark hole that he had burned in Skartaru's dark north face. Then he said, 'And yet I think that perhaps worse awaits us inside there.'

'Perhaps,' I said.

'Perhaps it's the end of the road, for all of us.'

'Don't worry,' I said to him, grasping his hand. 'I won't let you die.'

'Ah, death,' he said, smiling sadly. 'I must die someday. It seems strange, but I know it's true.'

I squeezed his hand harder, trying not to think of the lines of the poem that had haunted me ever since I had killed Raldu in the forest beneath my father's castle.

'And when I *do* die, Val,' he said, 'if I could choose, I'd rather have it come fighting beside you.'

'Maram, listen to me, you mustn't speak –'

'No, I *must* speak of this, now, because I might not have another chance,' he told me. Then he looked straight into my eyes. 'Ever since we set out from Mesh, you've shown me a realm I never dreamed. I . . . I was born the prince of a great kingdom. But it's you who have made me noble.'

He clasped me to him then and hugged me as hard as he could. And then, as he dried his eyes and I did mine, he took a step back and said, 'Now let's finish this nasty business and get out of here, if we can.'

There was a man whom Maram wished to be. This man now gathered up all of his bravura and stood up straight and tall. Then he gripped his red crystal and marched up to Skartaru's darkening face without hesitation.

As before, with Kane's help, he used his firestone to melt the mountain's black rock. He stood there, by the base of the Ogre's knee, for most of an hour, working flame against the wall. And at last, in the failing light, he broke through to the hidden cave spoken of in the ancient verse. He stepped aside from this black, glowing gash in the earth. And then he smiled proudly to show us that the door to Argattha had been opened.

41

We spent some time in gathering up the knights' horses and divesting them of their saddles and tack, which we piled up inside the cave. We dragged the dead knights inside, as well; it wouldn't do for the vultures or other animals to find them and so alert another patrol as to what had happened here. After driving off the horses – we hoped they would gallop off into the Wendrush and lose themselves on its endless grasslands – we made our final preparations for entering Argattha. Ymiru unpacked some torches, which he had anticipated needing as far back as Alundil. He also brought out and donned his disguise for making his way through the city. This was a great, black, cowled robe that covered him from head to foot. A veil, built into the cowl, hid his face, while he had a huge pair of boots and black gloves to pull on over his furry feet and hands. Thus did the very tall Saryaks of Uskudar dress. Of course, the Saryaks were not *quite* so tall as the Ymanir, and not nearly so thick. And their black skins were smooth, like jet. And so Ymiru's disguise would not bear close scrutiny. But this, we hoped, he was unlikely to endure since we had found a way of bypassing Argattha's gates.

'And if we *are* stopped,' Kane said, holding up one of the knights' medallions, 'these should win our way through.'

At his bidding, we each put on a medallion and hid away our own.

'I *hate* wearing such,' Liljana said, tapping her finger against her new medallion's gold dragon.

We all did. And we hated even more the idea of stripping the dead of their armor and surcoats and dressing as Morjin's knights, which Maram suggested. 'Thus we might simply walk into the Dragon's throne room,' he said.

'No,' Kane told him, shaking his head, 'thus we might be stopped by Morjin's other knights, wondering why strangers are wearing the livery of their friends. Or asking us the name of our company. The risk here, I deem, is greater than the gain.'

We all agreed that it was so. And so we would go forth into the city, dressed in our mail and tattered tunics, looking for all the world like vagabonds come to sell our swords, as the knights' captain had suggested.

Our final preparations having been completed, Ymiru heaved a few great boulders over the cut into the mountain that Maram had made so that any passersby might not notice it. And then, standing inside the cave with the bodies of the men we had slain, we lit the torches. Their acrid, oily smoke filled the black cavity around us. Their flickering yellow flames gave enough light to show the cave's curving roof and black walls – and the tunnel at its far end: black and rectangular and opening like a gate into hell.

Holding a torch in one hand and my father's shield in the other, I led the way into it. Ymiru, whose people had once bored this channel through hard rock, was little help here. He had told us all that he knew about this secret passage: that it wound its way beneath Argattha's first level, long since abandoned by Morjin and the city's other denizens. Ymiru thought that the tunnel might give out in the old throne room or onto stairs leading to it. It must give out *somewhere* on the first level, he said. And from there, we could make our way up to the second level where people lived, and so up to the higher levels until we came to Morjin's new throne room on the seventh and highest level of the city.

In the dark tunnel, it was cold and close. Although it had been cut high enough for Ymiru to walk without stooping – barely – it was so narrow that we had to walk in single file. I moved forward slowly, not knowing what my torch would show in the curving, black passage ahead of me. Its walls, of greasy-looking basalt, seemed to press upon me from either side and crush the breath from my chest. The air was stale and smelled bad, having pocketed here for perhaps a thousand years. In its cloying moistness were the scents of decay, suffering and death.

Ymiru paced along just behind me, awkward in his new boots. Maram kept close to him, followed by Master Juwain, Liljana, Atara and finally Kane. Their dread of this dark place was like a scent of its own that I could no more avoid than the torches' oily smoke. I smelled Maram's nervous sweat and the rancidness of the kalvaas in his mustache and beard. Atara was fighting hard to keep her spirit from being crushed away in the chilling gloom. And I sensed some dark thing eating at Kane's insides that dwelled even deeper than his hate.

We marched on for perhaps an eighth of a mile, stepping over broken boulders and the occasional crack through the tunnel's floor. The rock here, I thought, seemed to hold shrieks and screams ages old. Moisture clung to the tunnel's walls as if blood had been sweated and tortured from them. The slick floor ran with a trickle of water and other liquids that must have seeped down from the levels of the city above us. In places it pooled inches deep: a foul-smelling effluvia of metallic sludges, rotting garbage and human waste. As Ymiru slogged along, he admitted that he was very glad for his boots – as were we all.

We came to a place where the tunnel divided. Each fork, the right and the left, looked equally ominous. I turned to Ymiru and asked, 'Do both these lead to the old throne room?'

'I don't know,' he told me, shaking his head. He patted the pack on his back, where he had stowed his father's map. 'I wish the living clay showed earth forms so small as these.'

I called for Atara to come up, and he pressed himself flat against the tunnel's wall to allow her room to squeeze by. She stood next to me at the fork in the tunnel, looking right and looking left.

'Which way, Atara?' I asked her. 'Can you see our way through?'

She brought out her scryer's crystal and held it before her. And then without hesitation, she said, 'Right.'

As we resumed our journey through the dark, I wondered if she had simply chosen this direction at random to reassure us. Soon we came to a sudden rent through the tunnel's rock. It split the ceiling and the walls, and ran through the floor deep into the earth. I almost tripped into this black chasm. Maram suggested sounding its depths with a dropped stone, but quickly thought the better of such recklessness. As the chasm was some yards across, I needed a running jump to clear it, as did Ymiru and Maram. And Master Juwain needed more than this. When it came his turn to make the leap, he fell a little short, and only Maram, grabbing onto Master Juwain's arm, kept him from falling back into the blackness.

'Thank you,' Master Juwain told him, his cheeks puffing from exertion. With Maram, he stood at the chasm's edge, not daring to look back at it.

'You're welcome, sir,' Maram said. 'Don't worry – I wouldn't let you die.'

His smile told me that he was very proud to have saved Master Juwain's life, as Ymiru had saved his.

When the others had each crossed the chasm and we stood safely on the other side, we set out again. We walked as quietly as we could though the stifling darkness. We came to other branchings in the tunnel and other cracks through it. One of these was so wide that it had been spanned by a narrow stone bridge. This arch seemed so worn and old that I feared it might crumble at the first footfall. And yet it bore me up and then Ymiru's considerably greater weight. After Maram had crossed over it, too, he stood holding his hand out as if to feel the air.

'It's warm,' he said. 'Ah, it's almost hot.'

I crowded back close to him, letting this upwelling of hot air blow across my face. In its searing jets, I thought I heard the sound of beating iron, cracking whips and men crying out in pain.

'What lies beneath here?' I asked Ymiru.

'Only the mines, I think.'

'And how many levels are there to these?'

'To the mines there be no levels,' he said. He told us that the mines beneath Argattha had been tunneled like the twistings of a man's bowels, leading far down into the earth.

'But how far, then?'

'I don't know, Val,' he said. 'There be seven levels to the city, and each of them five hundred feet thick. It be said that the mines ran twice as deep as all the levels were high, together. And that was more than two thousand years ago.'

How far, I wondered? *How far had Morjin come toward finding the dark currents in the earth that he sought and freeing the Lord of Death known as Angra Mainyu?*

'Come, Val,' Ymiru said as we stood at the edge of this pit. He rested his gloved hand on my shoulder. 'Do not look down – look up. We've still far to go.'

I nodded my head, and then waited for the others to cross the bridge, too. And then I led off again, thrusting the blazing torch ahead of me as I pushed forward deeper into Argattha.

After a while, the foul smell began to work at me and burn like a poison in my blood; the distant drip of water beat at my head like a relentless hammer. In places, air shafts broke through the tunnel's floor or ceiling. But these brought no relief against the oppressive darkness, only more bad smells, muffled cries and the slow slip of muck and mire working its way down into the earth. Although my torch gave little enough light, it was enough to warn away the rats that jumped out of the darkness in their panic to flee from us. Some of these were nearly as big as cats; their glowing red eyes were like hot coals as they scurried along with their claws scraping against rock – and more than once across my boots. The rapaciousness of these trapped, maddened creatures made me shudder. I wondered what they had here for food, but I did not really want to know.

The tunnel wound mostly toward the south, across more chasms, into the middle of the mountain. After about a mile, we came to another forking where the tunnel curved off toward the right and the left as if cut along the lines of a perfect circle. I was reluctant to go forward in either direction. Even Atara, when she came forward, seemed unable to decide which way to go.

'I don't know,' she said to me at last, shaking her head. 'You choose.'

'Very well, then,' I said. 'We'll go right.'

And so we did. But after a hundred yards, we came to another node and another choice of directions. Again, I led toward the right and we moved off, circling that way.

And so it went, the nodes coming one after another, the tunnel turning sharply west and then north, and then curving back south again. Thrice we came to dead ends and had to retrace our steps. We circled east for a way before the tunnel bent yet again, taking us back toward the north, the opposite of the way that we needed to go. Soon it became apparent that we had entered a labyrinth – and that we were lost within it.

'This is too much,' Maram said as we gathered in the space of one of the nodes. A hungry rat, bolder than many, lunged at him, trying to bite a chunk out of his leg. He kicked it squealing away from him and muttered, 'Ah, this is like hell.'

Liljana, who was having a hard time breathing in the fetid air, turned to Ymiru and said, 'You didn't tell us we'd find a labyrinth here.'

'I didn't know,' Ymiru said. 'Morjin must have had it built to confound assassins or anyone pursuing him out of the city.'

'Well, it's certainly confounding *us*,' she said. 'How are we to find our way through it?'

But he didn't have an answer for her, nor did I or anyone else. Finally, Kane, who had tired of standing still, shook his torch at the corridor off to the left and said, 'Let's walk then, eh? What else is there to do?'

And so we walked, as he had said. For a long time we wandered through the labyrinth's curves, which ate through the bare rock like dark, twisting worms. After a while we grew very tired. Liljana's torch, its oil all burned, was the first to sputter out. We used the sooty end of it to mark the wall where we stood, in the hope of orienting ourselves should we come upon this part of the labyrinth again. But the black char seemed lost against the blackness of the rock here. Soon, I thought, all of our torches would die, and then we wouldn't be able to see any marks upon the walls – or even the walls themselves.

'It's cold down here,' Maram grumbled. 'My feet are wet and sore. And I'm tired. And I'm hungry, too.'

We were all hungry, and so we paused to sit down on a dry patch of the cold stone floor and eat a quick meal. We shared some hard cheese and battle biscuits with each other, trying to ignore the pervasive stench in the air as we swallowed these rough foods. We tried to swallow back our belly-churning fear, too, which was growing with the darkness as our torches flickered out one by one.

After a while, after we stood yet again and resumed our wanderings, only two torches remained afire. I took one of these to lead the way while Kane, in the rear, took the other. Ymiru, Maram, Master Juwain, Liljana and Atara walked in the darkness between these two sickly yellow lights.

At last we came to a large, circular chamber at what I guessed to be the labyrinth's very center. There our last torch died, and much of our hope with it as we huddled together in the utter blackness.

'Ah, this is the end,' Maram muttered, 'surely the end.'

Master Juwain, whose tenacity seemed to grow with the severity of our plight, said to him, 'Surely this is *not* the end. Surely we've come to the center of this maze, and that must be counted as progress.'

'I think not, sir,' Maram said. 'Didn't you notice that there was only one way into this chamber? And so only one way out. Now we'll just have to go back and get lost all over again.'

His logic drove Master Juwain to silence. For a moment, we all stood there in the dark listening to the sound of our breathing and the scurrying of the rats around us. One of these tried to bite Maram again, and he shook it off with a desperate curse and shuddering frenzy.

'The rats seem to like you,' Atara said to him. 'Maybe they smell all that disgusting kalvaas you've spilled on yourself.'

'Ah, these accursed rats,' Maram said, shuddering more violently. 'I think they're worse than anything we found in the Vardaloon.'

He paused to do a breathing exercise that Master Juwain had taught him. Then he gave up and said, 'And this accursed place is worse than the Black Bog.'

Now it was my turn to shudder; I stood there in the black bowels of the earth wondering how we would ever escape from its endless twistings, especially if we could not see our way out of them. I was afraid that if we didn't escape from this city of dreadful night soon, I would begin to hate myself for leading us into it, and more, hate the whole world for calling such dark creatures as Morjin into life.

And then, at last, I drew my sword. It glowed with a soft, silver light. It was not enough to fill the chamber and illumine its dark walls, but it brightened our spirits all the same.

When I pointed my sword upward, its sheen deepened, slightly. It was strange to think that the Lightstone might be so close, somewhere above us through half a mile of rock in Morjin's throne room. Morjin, I thought, was near there, too. I could almost feel our hearts beating with the same poisoned blood and sense his mind seeking mine. This connection that he had made between us with a bit of kirax suddenly darkened my soul. For a single moment, I allowed my dread of him to take hold of me. As if I had drunk the foul waters running through the cold rock here, my belly filled with doubt. It quickly worked at me and split me open. And through this dark crack in my being, beasts and demons came for me. At first I was so shocked by this sudden attack that I didn't realize that it was an illusion. Black, birdlike things with razor talons and the faces of those I had slain fell at me out of the air. I cut at them with my sword, and its touch caused them to burst into flame and scream so pitifully that I thought I was screaming myself. And then a huge shape lunged through the chamber's doorway. It had great, golden eyes, scales as red as rust and hooked claws that sought to tear me open. Through its slashing white teeth, it breathed fire at me, as the dragons of old were said to do. I swung my sword against its writhing neck, and watched in horror as its bright blade shattered into a hundred glittering shards. And then the fire caught me up in its incredible heat and began burning through my mail, melting the steel into a glowing lava that ate into my heart, burning and burning and . . .

'Val!' someone called to me.

A sudden shimmering radiance poured out into the chamber. It was Flick, I saw, spinning about in swirls of silver and iridescent blue. Once again, he had returned to us. And beneath his reassuring form, Master Juwain stood in front of me with his varistei pointing at my chest. It flared a deep and bright green. I felt its healing touch, like cool waters, quench the evil fire inside me. And then my mind cleared as I slowly shook my head.

Kane, his sword drawn, stood next to him looking at me intently. I remembered that in my madness, I had swung my sword at him – and at my other friends. Only Kane's great skill in parrying my wild slashes, it seemed, had saved them from being hacked in half.

'Val, what happened?' Master Juwain asked me.

'That . . . is hard to say, sir,' I told him. I looked at Alkaladur's bright blade. 'When my sword first flared, there was a moment of hope. And I saw it leading us to the Lightstone. But there the Red Dragon waited, too – always watching and waiting. And my hope turned into despair.'

Master Juwain nodded his head gravely and said, 'There is a great danger for you here – and for all of us. Danger beyond death or even capture and torment. This turning that you have told of: it seems that the Lord of Lies has a great talent for poisoning even the strongest of trees and twisting good into evil.'

He went on to ask me if I had been practicing the exercises he had taught me, particularly the light meditations.

'Yes, sir, all the time,' I told him. 'And my sword has helped me. The silustria has. It has shielded me all through the Nagarshath. And so I began to think that the battle against the Dragon's lies had been won.'

'*That* battle can never be won,' Master Juwain told me. 'And it is lost most surely the moment we *think* that it is won.'

Kane tapped his sword against mine, and its steel rang throughout the semi-lit chamber. 'So, even the best of shields is useless if it's lowered, eh?'

I nodded my head that this was so. 'Thank you for reminding me.'

'As you've reminded us,' he said, smiling fiercely. 'From the first, you've had more fire in you for finding the Lightstone than any of us, and we wouldn't have come this far without it.'

His deep eyes searched in mine for faith, and Master Juwain, Atara and the others looked at me in this way, too. They looked to me to find a way out of this seemingly endless labyrinth and see our way toward the Lightstone.

And suddenly I knew that there *was* a way out. In my connection to the dark corridors of Morjin's mind, I became aware of a twisted logic that ordered its turnings. It was the logic of his life and all the works of his hand, this labyrinth among them. For hours upon hours, I had wandered through part of it. Its curved passages and nodes were recorded inside me as if my blood were a liquid, living clay. And now, as I gazed at the bright, silver crystal of my sword and my mind opened, in a flash of light, I saw the whole of the labyrinth from this chamber at its very center.

'Come,' I said, leading forth toward the doorway. 'We've only a little farther to go.'

We lined up as before, with Ymiru just behind me. He shuffled along the winding corridors, keeping his eyes fixed on my glowing sword. Of all my companions save Liljana, he was the only one unable to see Flick and thus was blinded to this strange being's dancing lights. But the others perceived him well enough, and marveled that he had now fallen into a steady, flaming spiral just above my head. His presence gave them to move with more confidence through the turnings of the labyrinth.

At last, after circling east and north and then abruptly reversing our direction through a black tube of rock, we came to a break in the curving wall that opened upon a new passage. As this led straight toward the south, I knew that we had finally found our way out of the labyrinth's south end.

'Are you sure this way be south?' Ymiru asked me. 'I admit I've been turned around for quite a while.'

'Val has a sense of direction,' Maram said from behind him. 'He never gets turned around.'

Not *never*, I thought, remembering the disappearing moon of the Black Bog. But now, it seemed, I had led us true. For after a hundred yards, the tunnel suddenly gave out onto a set of stairs.

'Saved!' Maram cried out. 'These must be the stairs to the first level!'

'Quiet now!' Kane hissed back at him. 'We don't know what we'll find there!'

The stairs wound up through the rock, spiraling left, like those in my father's castle. Ymiru had said that the distance between the levels of Argattha was five hundred feet. But Morjin had built his escape tunnel just beneath the first level, it seemed, and so we did not have to climb nearly so far. After a few minutes, the stairs gave out onto a short corridor that led through an open doorway into a huge hall.

I was the first to step into it, and I saw at once that it was dimly lit by the few ancient glowstones still set into its steeply rising walls. Great columns of rock, many now broken into the cracked wheels of basalt that littered the hall's hard floor, supported the curving ceiling three hundred feet above us. The sheer vastness of this place, carved from the heart of the mountain, struck me with awe. There was terror there, too – and not only mine. For just as Ymiru and the others joined me a few feet beyond the doorway, I saw that we were not alone. At the south end of the hall, off to the left, a small, ragged figure was struggling mightily against the chain and shackle locked around his ankle.

'Look!' Atara said to me. 'It's a child.'

I started straight for him, but Kane suddenly laid his hand on my shoulder and said, 'Be careful – this might be a trap!'

The child, if that he really was, saw us almost immediately. And now he lunged against his chain as his eyes leaped with terror.

'It's all right,' I whispered, 'we won't hurt you!'

Again, I started across the rubble-strewn floor, fighting the child's scent of fear and the overpowering foulness of the air. This stank of cinnamon and sweat, of burning pitch and heated rock and evil as old as the mountain itself.

'Who are you?' I said to him, crossing the distance between us cautiously. 'Who chained you here?'

I saw that he was indeed a child, a boy, about nine years old. Greasy rags barely covered his skinny body. His hair was black and hung about his dirty face in tangles. He had the dark skin and almond eyes of the Sung – and yet he clearly belonged to Morjin. For upon his forehead was tattooed the sign of his slavery: a red dragon coiled as if burned deep into his flesh.

'Look!' Kane said to me as he came running up to my side. He pointed at the far end of the room toward the north. There, between two great pillars, stood a pyramid of skulls perhaps twenty feet high. Their curving bones and empty eye hollows gleamed a ghastly yellow in the glowstones' dim light.

'Oh, I don't like this place!' Maram said. 'Let's get out of here.'

He looked toward a great, open portal along the west wall opposite the stairs by which we had entered the hall. The doors of both of these openings, I saw, had long since been torn off their hinges. What use, I wondered, did Morjin now make of this foul chamber? A dungeon for the torture and execution of his enemies? But how could a child be anyone's enemy, even Morjin's?

'What is your name?' I said to the terrified boy, laying my hand on his head. 'Where is your mother? Your father?'

He jumped at my touch. He knocked my hand away and looked frantically toward the portal, where once a great iron gate had been.

'He's coming!' he said to me in a sweet voice made bitter by bondage. 'He's coming!'

'*Who* is coming?' I asked him.

I looked down at the boy's bare leg. So hard had he lunged against the shackle there that its iron had torn him bloody. There were bite marks about the ankle, as well. I did not want to admit what I knew to be true: that this poor boy, like a trapped animal, had tried to gnaw off his own leg.

'Who is it?' I asked him again.

He looked at me as if trying to decide who *I* might be. And then, with a deep courage pushing away some of his fear, he said, 'It's the Dragon.'

'Morjin, here?' Kane snarled, shaking his sword at the air.

The boy pulled to the limit of the chain attached to a bolt in the floor. He fell to his knee and crunched down upon some bones there. All about him, I saw, were piles of rat skulls and their skeletons. His torn tunic was stained with the guts and gore of rats, which it seemed he had eaten.

'It's the Dragon,' the boy said again. 'Can't you *hear* him?'

The vast hall rumbled with distant sounds of the other parts of the city. Water trickled and iron beat against stone; the stone itself seemed to beat like a great, black heart with rhythms as old as time.

702

'Listen, Rat Boy,' Maram said, coming up close to him. 'You've been here too long and must be hearing things that aren't –'

'No, it's the Dragon! We've got to get out of here!'

Now he stretched out his thin hand as if beckoning toward the rat leavings littered across the floor. And there, among these gnawed white bones, just beyond his reach, lay a black, iron key.

'Every abomination,' Kane muttered as I bent to pick up the key. 'Every degradation of the spirit.'

I turned to see if the key would indeed fit the locked shackle. And as I bent low, Atara stroked the boy's trembling head and asked him, 'Was it the Dragon who locked you here?'

'No, it was Morjin. Lord Morjin.'

'And you think he's coming back here?'

'No! I told you – it's the Dragon who's coming!'

Now Liljana and Master Juwain both drew out their gelstei. Liljana was fingering her blue whale, clearly contemplating entering the boy's mind to see where it had cracked. And Master Juwain wanted only to heal him of his delusions and terror.

I pushed the key through the hole in the lock. It slipped in with a loud click. The boy's heart was now beating even more rapidly than my own: *doom, doom, doom*.

'Quick!' the boy said to me, 'we've got to run!'

Now the smells of cinnamon and burning pitch suddenly grew overpowering as a blast of hot air blew into the room. From the dark corridor beyond the hall's open portal came a loud, rhythmic, thumping sound: *Doom, Doom, Doom*.

'Quick, Val!' Maram called to me. 'Back to the stairs! Something *is* coming.'

I turned the key, screeching metal against metal, right and then left. I jiggled it in the lock as the boy pulled with all his might against the chain. The sweaty cinnamon smell grew much stronger. And now the thunder of shaken stone filled the hall: DOOM! DOOM! DOOM!

The shackle's lock suddenly snapped open just as Atara sighted an arrow on the opening of the portal. And then there, in that dark, huge rectangular space, a great shape appeared. It stood fifteen feet high and was perhaps thrice that long. Scales, red like rusted iron, covered the whole length of its long, sinuous body nearly down to the knotted tip of its tail. At the end of its great hind legs, claws as sharp as steel cut grooves into the rock of the floor. Its leathery wings were folded back along its sides like a cat's ears before a battle. Its great, golden eyes fixed on the boy with a malign intelligence. As I pulled the shackle from his leg, they fixed on me.

'Oh, Lord!' Maram said, fumbling for his firestone. 'Oh, my Lord!'

It was, as the boy had tried to tell us, a dragon – and a female at that. And she was clearly angry that we had just robbed her of her feast.

'Liljana! Master Juwain!' I shouted. 'Take the boy back to the stairs!'

Liljana grabbed the boy's hand and started running toward the stairs with Master Juwain close behind him. And then, just as the dragon sprang forward, Atara loosed her arrow at one of the dragon's eyes. But the dragon turned her head just in time so that the arrow glanced off her scales along her great jaws.

These now opened to show sharp white teeth as long as knives. I sensed that the dragon longed to charge Atara and bite her in two. And so I stepped forward, pointing my sword at the dragon as I raised up my shield. It was good for me that I still had my father's shield.

'Val, the fire!' Maram called to me. I thought, for a moment, that he must be speaking of his gelstei. 'The fire, beware!'

Suddenly, as the dragon seemed to quiver and cough, all at once, a great breath of flame shot from her mouth. It fell in an orange stream against my shield, burning the silver swan embossed there as black as the curving black steel around it. Some of the flame spilled over my shield's rim and scorched my face. I rushed forward then to strike the dragon dead before she could draw breath and summon her fire again.

As did Ymiru and Kane. Kane closed in toward the dragon's side and thrust his sword at the dragon's belly. It struck sparks against the scales there, and glanced off her, as did the second arrow that Atara fired at the dragon's eyes. Ymiru had greater success swinging his borkor at the dragon's still-open mouth. With tremendous force, it cracked into the jaw, breaking off two huge teeth and shaking the dragon to her bones. But then the dragon used her great, knotty head like a club of her own, swinging it sideways into Ymiru's chest, cracking ribs and knocking him off his feet. Her tail suddenly lashed out at Kane; if he hadn't been quick to duck beneath its terrible sweep, the mace-like spikes at the tip would have taken off his head.

The dragon having been distracted, I worked in close to her huge, heaving body. I thrust my sword straight at her chest. But Alkaladur's gleaming silustria, which had split open even plate armor, failed to pierce the dragon deeply. It drove between two of the thick scales to a distance of perhaps an inch. It was enough only to wound the dragon – as a bloodbird might peck at me.

'Val, she's too strong!' Atara called to me. 'Back to the stairs!'

Maram wasted no time in heeding her call to retreat. Gripping his gelstei, which had failed to produce the slightest spark, he turned to run back toward the narrow opening to the east. While Kane helped Ymiru regain his feet, I stood before them, covering them with my shield. The dragon, dripping blood from her battered mouth, regarded Ymiru with wariness and hate. Then she suddenly opened her jaws again to burn us.

This time I saw that her breath was not really of fire. Rather, as she coughed and heaved, she spit straight at us a stream of a reddish and jellylike substance. Upon touching the air, it burst into flame. It clung to my shield with all the stickiness of honey. It burned into the steel there, etching it as might a blazing acid.

'Retreat, Val!' Kane shouted at me.

He and Ymiru, following Atara, had already started toward the stairs. I backed away from the dragon as quickly as I could. Once more, the dragon aimed a fiery blast at us. I caught it again on my shield, and then turned to run back toward the stairs before the dragon could summon up more of this evil, red liquid. I reached the doorway and bounded down the stairs just as another stream of fire poured through. Some drops of the jelly stuck to my mail and burned into my back. But at least my friends and I were safe. There was no way the dragon could force her huge body through the narrow doorway.

But there was no way either that we could go forward. It seemed that we were trapped in the deeps of Argattha.

42

'That was close!' Maram gasped as we gathered in the winding stairwell just below the corridor leading to the dragon's hall. When I peeked over the top stair into the corridor, I could see the dragon's golden eyes looking back at me through the doorway. 'Are you all right, Val?'

I was not quite all right. The dragon's fire had burned holes clean through my armor. This I now removed so that Master Juwain could tend the seared flesh along my back.

'A dragon!' Maram marveled, not quite daring to look into the corridor. 'I never really believed the old stories.'

He and Atara stood just beneath me on the steps. And beneath them were Kane and Ymiru, and then Liljana, who had her arms wrapped around the boy that we had found.

As Master Juwain held his crystal above my back, I looked down the stairs at the boy and asked him, 'Do you have a name?'

This time he answered me, looking me straight in the eyes as he said, 'I'm called Daj.'

'Just "Daj"?' I asked him.

His eyes burned with old hurts as if he didn't want to tell me anything more about his name. And so I asked him what land he hailed from. But this, too, it seemed, touched upon terrible memories.

'Well, Daj, please tell us how you came to be chained up there.'

'Lord Morjin put me there,' he said.

'But why?'

'Because I wouldn't do what he wanted me to.'

'And what was that?'

But Daj didn't want to answer this question either. A deep loathing fell over him as his little body began to shudder.

'Are you a slave?' Atara asked him, looking at his tattooed forehead.

706

'Yes,' he said, pressing back into Liljana's bosom. 'That is, I was. But I escaped.'

The story he now told us was a terrible one. A couple of years before, after watching his family slaughtered by Morjin's men and being enslaved in some distant land that he wouldn't name, he had been brought in chains to Argattha. And there – in the city above us – Morjin had taken this handsome boy as his body servant. For a slave, it had been a relatively easy life, tending to Morjin's needs in the luxury of the private rooms of his palace. But Daj had hated it. Somehow he had found a way to displease his master. And so Morjin had consigned him to the mines far below Argattha's first level. There, in tunnels so narrow that only young boys slight of body could squeeze through, Daj was given a pick and told to hack away at the veins of goldish ore running through the earth. His life became one of bleeding hands and gashed knees, of whips and curses and the terror of despair. He had slept with the corpses of the many other boys who had died around him; some of the other starved boys, he said, had been forced to eat from these bodies. And somehow, the brave and clever Daj had contrived a way to escape from this living hell.

'I found a way from the mines up to the first level,' he told us, pointing up toward the top of the stairs. 'That's where the dragon is kept. And so no one usually goes there.'

For some months, he told us, he had survived by wandering the first level's abandoned streets and alleys; he had captured rats for food and ripped them apart with his hands and teeth. When the dragon drew near, he hid beyond the doorways of ancient apartments or in crumbling store rooms or even in cracks in the earth. But finally, his dread of the dragon – and his hunger – had grown too great. And so he had tried to steal up into the second level of the city.

'They captured me there,' he said. Then he pointed at his forehead. 'The mark gave me away – that's why all the slaves are tattooed. Lord Morjin himself came to see me taken back down to the first level and chained in the great hall. He gave me to the dragon. Just like he's given all the others.'

I thought of the pyramid of skulls in the hall above us and shuddered.

Maram, moved to great pity by Daj's story, began weeping uncontrollably. But he seemed to realize that his tears might only inflame the boy's grief. So instead he forced out a brave laughter as if trying to inspirit him. He said, 'Oh, you poor lad – how old are you?'

'Older than you.'

Maram looked at him as if he had fallen mad. 'How can you say that?'

'You laugh and cry like a little boy, but I haven't laughed for years, and I don't cry anymore. So you tell me, who is older?'

None of us knew what to say to this. So I turned to Daj and asked him, 'How long were you chained there, then?'

'I don't know – a long time.'

'But why did the dragon take so long in coming?'

'She *did* come, all the time,' he said. 'She brought me rats to eat. I think she wanted to fatten me up before she ate *me*.'

After Master Juwain had finished with his crystal, he rubbed an ointment into my cooked skin, and then I put my armor back on with much wincing and pain. And then I looked down the dim stairwell at Daj and asked him, 'How is it that the Lord of Lies and his men could have chained you without the dragon adding their skulls to his stack? Have they enslaved it, too?'

'In a way,' Daj told me. 'Lord Morjin said not all his chains are iron.'

'Of what be this particular chain made?' Ymiru asked him.

Daj looked up at Ymiru in obvious wonder at his great height; it seemed that he was trying to peer beneath Ymiru's cowled robe and get a better look at him.

'I heard Lord Morjin tell a priest something about the dragon,' Daj explained. 'He said that long ago, he brought the dragons here from somewhere else.'

'From where?' Kane asked him sharply.

'I don't know – somewhere.'

'You said *dragons*. How many were there?'

'Two of them, I think. A dragon king and his queen. But Lord Morjin poisoned the king; he took the eggs from the queen. A dragon queen lays only a single clutch of eggs, you know.'

He paused to let Liljana pick a few lice from his head before continuing. But I had already guessed what he would say.

'Lord Morjin keeps the eggs in his chambers,' he told us. 'They won't hatch if they're kept cold. And that's why the dragon won't touch Lord Morjin. Because if she does, she knows the eggs will be destroyed.'

Morjin, I suddenly knew, was keeping the dragon bound for his final war of conquest of the world.

Master Juwain rubbed his head as he smiled at Daj. He said, 'I see, I see. But you said that Morjin took the eggs long ago. They can't still be viable?'

'What does that mean?'

'Still alive and capable of hatching.'

'Oh, well, dragons live forever – like Lord Morjin,' he said. 'And so do their eggs.'

It was strange to think that the terrible, fire-spewing creature above us could so love her eggs that she was held in thrall by fear of their being destroyed. And what Daj told us next was stranger still.

'The dragon is making a pyramid of the skulls of all the men she's killed,' he said. 'Because of Lord Morjin, she hates all men. But she hates Lord Morjin most of all. She's saving the very top place on the pyramid for his skull.'

We all fell quiet for a moment as we listened to the dragon thundering about the chamber above us. And then Master Juwain asked Daj, 'But how could you possibly know that?'

'Because I heard the dragon say this.'

'The dragon talks to you?'

'Not with words, not like you do,' Daj said. He pressed his finger into his ratty hair above his ear. 'But I heard her inside here.'

'Are you a mindspeaker then?'

'What's that?'

Master Juwain looked at Liljana, who continued stroking Daj's hair as she tried to explain something about her powers that her blue gelstei quickened and magnified.

'I don't know anything about that,' Daj said. 'The only one I ever heard speak that way was the dragon.'

'So it is with dragons,' Kane suddenly growled out. 'It's said that they have this power.'

I looked at him in amazement and asked, 'But what do you know about dragons?'

'Very little, I think. It's said that they're stronger in their minds than men and darker in their hearts.'

'But where did you hear that?' Master Juwain asked him. 'It's known that the ancient accounts of this matter were fabricated.'

Kane pointed up the steps and said to him, 'Was this beast fabricated then? She came from *somewhere*, as the boy said.'

'But where?' I asked.

Kane's eyes were hot pools as he looked me. 'It's said that dragons live on the world of Charoth and nowhere else.'

'But Charoth is a dark world, isn't it?'

'That it is,' Kane said. 'Morjin must have opened a gateway to it. So, he must be very close to opening a gate to Damoom and freeing the Dark One himself.'

I risked another peek above the top of the stairs. It seemed more important than ever that we get past the dragon and complete our quest.

'What do you see, Val?' Maram called to me.

The dragon, it seemed, had given up staring through the doorway into the corridor above the stairs. But I sensed that she was still waiting for us in the hall. And so, as lightly as I could, I stole along the corridor until I came to the doorway. I looked out of it to see the dragon coiled around her skull pyramid as if guarding a treasure. Her golden eyes were lit up and staring at the doorway; I thought that she was daring us to make a dash across the hall for the great portal that opened upon the abandoned streets of Argattha's first level.

'She's guarding the portal,' I said when I returned to the others. I looked down into the stairwell at Daj. 'Is there any other way out of the hall?'

'Only these stairs,' he told us.

'What will we find beyond the portal?'

'Well, there's a big passage to a street, and then a lot of streets, like a maze almost – they lead mostly east toward the old gates in the city. They're all closed now, so the dragon can't escape.'

'But you said that there *is* a way up to the second level?'

'Yes, that's right – there are some stairs about a mile from here. But they're too narrow for the dragon to use.'

'Could you find these stairs again?'

'I think so,' he said.

Maram looked at me in horror of what he knew I was planning. He said, 'You're not thinking of just running for these stairs, are you?'

'Not *just* running,' I said.

'But shouldn't we wait for the dragon to leave? Or, ah, to go away?'

Upon questioning Daj further, we determined that the dragon never slept. And as for waiting, it seemed, the dragon could wait much longer than we. We had very little food, less water and no time.

'The dragon,' Liljana unexpectedly announced, 'is waiting for something. I think the Red Priests are due to bring another here. What will they think when they find the boy gone and his shackles unlocked?'

'But how do you know that?' Kane asked her.

'I *know*,' she said, tapping her blue stone against her head, 'because the dragon is in my mind.'

'So,' Kane murmured as rubbed his bandaged ear.

Liljana's face suddenly contorted as she shook her head violently back and forth. And she gasped out, 'She's trying . . . to make a ghul of me!'

Kane waited for her to regain control of herself and then snarled out, 'So, perhaps *you* should try to go into her mind. And make a ghul of her.'

This suggested an elaboration on the desperate plan that I was considering: We would all rush out into the hall. And then, while Liljana used her blue gelstei to engage the dragon's mind, Atara would shoot arrows into her eyes. This would allow me to steal in close and try once more to cut through the dragon's iron hide.

Master Juwain, his green crystal in hand, looked at me and said, 'I shouldn't be telling you how to kill *anything*, not even a dragon. But the place in the chest that you stabbed – that's not where her heart is, I'm sure. If my stone tells true, you'll find it beating three feet farther down, just where the scales darken, closer to the curve of her belly.'

Ymiru had his purple gelstei in hand as he listened to Master Juwain tell us this, and he slowly nodded his great head.

But Maram remained horrified by what we were about to do. He shot me a quick look and said, 'But what of the dragon's fire? Are you so eager to be burnt again?'

'What of your own fire?' I countered, looking at Maram's red crystal.

'Ah, what of it? There's no sun in this accursed city to light it.'

'But didn't you once tell me that you thought the firestone might be able to hold the sun's light and not just focus it?'

'Ah, perhaps, one bolt of flame, no more – if only I could find it.'

'Find it, then,' I said, smiling at him.

Kane, standing below me on the stairs, caught my glance and said, 'This red jelly that bursts into flame – it's very much like the *relb*, eh?'

I remembered the story of Morjin, posing as Kadar the Wise, painting the Long Wall with relb and watching as the rising sun set it aflame and melted a breach in the stone for Tulumar's armies to ravage Alonia.

'And the relb,' Kane went on, gripping his black stone, 'was a forerunner of the firestones, was it not?'

'That it was,' I said, smiling at him as well. The brightness of his black eyes gave me hope that we really might win the coming battle.

Atara, holding her gelstei in her hands, looked up from her stone as her haunted eyes found mine. Her face was white as she said, 'I see one terrible chance, Val.'

I smiled at her, too, although it tore my heart open to do so. And I said, 'Then one chance will have to be enough.'

I turned to take council with the others. And there, in the dim, curving confines of the stairwell, smelling of sweat and fear and the burning reek of relb, we decided that if we weren't to abandon the quest, we would have to fight the dragon.

'But what about the boy?' Maram asked, looking at Daj. 'We can't take him with us, can we?'

Of course we couldn't. But we couldn't *not* take him, either. I might lead him back through the labyrinth to the cave we had opened into the mountain. But what then? Should he simply wait there for our return? And what if we *didn't* return? Then he would have to flee into the valley beyond Skartaru, where he would simply be captured all over again – either that or wander about Sakai facing starvation and death.

In the end, it was Daj who decided the question for us. Despite his words to Maram earlier, he was still only a boy. He gripped onto Liljana's tunic, pressing himself into her soft body. Then he said, 'Don't leave me here!'

Either we left him here, I thought, or we must abandon the quest to take him back to our homelands. Or else we must take him with us to the upper levels of Argattha.

'Please,' he pleaded, 'let me go with you!'

I sensed that his fear of Morjin and reentering the inhabited parts of the city was less than his dread of being left alone. There was terrible risk for him, it seemed, no matter what path we chose.

Unless, I thought, *we do flee back to Mesh*.

But this, I knew, we couldn't do, not even to save this poor child. How many more children, I wondered, would Morjin enslave and murder if he weren't defeated? And how would anyone ever accomplish this miracle so long as the Lightstone remained in Argattha?

'His fate is tied to ours now,' Atara said to me softly. 'The moment you turned the key in the lock, it was so.'

'Have you *seen* this?' I asked her.

'Yes, Val,' she said, squeezing her crystal sphere, 'I have.'

'All right,' I said, bowing my head to Daj, 'you can come with us, then. But you must be brave, as we know you can be. Very, very brave.'

And with that, I turned to lead the way into the corridor. Very quietly, we walked in file through it to the doorway of the hall. As I had feared, the dragon remained coiled around her skulls, watching us – watching us break into a run as we made for the portal across the hall. She sprang up from the skulls with a frightening speed. She bounded straight toward us, clearly intending to cut us off. Her great hind claws tore at the floor as she thundered closer. So quick were her bunching, explosive motions that I knew we had no hope of outrunning her.

Her first fire fell upon my shield just as Ymiru broke from our formation to grab up a great slab of fallen rock. He used this as a shield of his own, holding the immense weight in front of him in order to work in close to the dragon. The dragon turned her fire upon him. The flaming relb blasted against the slab and began burning the stone into lava. And then Atara pulled back the string of her bow and loosed an arrow at the dragon's eye.

As before, however, she sensed her intention just as the bowstring twanged. She turned her head at the last instant, and the arrow skittered off her iron scales. I knew that she was ready to leap at us, to rend us with her great teeth and claws, to stomp us into a bloody pulp. But just then Liljana, holding her blue whale against her head, managed to engage the dragon's mind. I felt the light of her golden eyes burning into Liljana as she froze in her tracks.

And in that moment, I dashed forward. So did Ymiru, who cast down his rock shield. I ran straight in beneath the dragon's long, twisting neck, where her huge chest gave way to her belly. I saw the place on the curve of her heaving body where the scales darkened, even as Master Juwain had said. And there I thrust my sword. This time it penetrated to a distance of perhaps two inches. The dragon roared out her pain and wrath, and kicked her claws into my shield, sending me flying. I hit the floor backward; the force of the fall bruised my back and knocked the breath from me. I lay there gasping for air, watching in puzzlement and horror as Ymiru worked in still closer to the dragon with his gelstei in hand.

'Ymiru – what are you doing?' Kane called to him.

As Atara fired off another arrow, to no effect, Ymiru brought his flaring purple crystal up to the place on the dragon's belly where I had stabbed her. The scale there seemed to darken to a pitted, reddish black. And then Liljana, still staring at the dragon, cried out in pain. I could almost feel her connection with the dragon's mind break like snapped wood. The dragon, finally and completely unbound, quickly turned about in a snarling, spitting rage and bit out at Ymiru. Her jaws closed about Ymiru's arm, and she tore it clean off, swallowing it whole. A fount of blood sprayed the air. Ymiru cried out as he gripped his gelstei in his remaining hand and tried to move backward, away from the dragon. But the dragon was too quick and Ymiru was in too much pain. Again the dragon's jaws opened. I was sure that she was about to rend Ymiru into meat or burn him. And then Atara shot off still another arrow.

This time it drove straight into the dragon's mouth. But not quite straight enough: the shaft stuck out from between two of the dragon's teeth like a long, feathered toothpick. The dragon, turning her attention from the quickly retreating Ymiru, shook her head furiously in futile effort to dislodge it. Blood as red as Ymiru's leaked from her wounded gums. And she gazed hatefully at Atara as she opened her jaws again to spit fire at her.

713

'Atara!' I cried as I sprang to my feet. 'Atara!'

I raced across the few feet separating us just in time to take the full blast of the dragon's fury upon my shield. It was a great gout of flaming relb that the dragon spewed at me. It melted huge holes in the steel of the shield and burned straight through to the leather straps covering my forearm. I had to take it off and cast it from me lest I lose an arm as had Ymiru. Once again – and for the last time – my father's shield had saved my life.

But now there was nothing except air between me and the dragon. She glared at me with her ancient glowing eyes in her promise to burn me. I had hoped that Kane might keep me from this fate. All this time, he had stood with his black gelstei in hand trying in vain to steal the dragon's fire. And so, to my astonishment, it was Maram who saved me – and Daj. Quick as a bounding rat, the agile boy broke from behind Liljana and dashed across the room. He scooped up a large stone and hurled it at the pyramid of skulls, knocking a couple of them from the top. This drew the dragon's attention and all her wrath toward him. And in that moment, Maram moved.

He suddenly stood away from the others and pointed his firestone at the dragon. A tremendous blast of flame, like a lightning bolt, leaped out from the crystal even as Maram let out a great cry of agony. I saw the firestone crack in his seared hands. And the flame drove straight into the dragon's neck, wounding her terribly. She let out a great roar of anguish. In a few quick bounds, she sprang toward the part of the room where Daj had been chained. There she backed into the corner, roaring and stinking of burnt blood, dropping her huge head low to the floor as she shook and glowered and waited for me.

'Val, no!' Atara said, laying her hand upon my shoulder as I started forward. 'She'll burn you!'

I shook off her hand, wondering how I could get at the dragon's belly, now pressed down against the hall's hard floor. The dragon, I sensed, was shocked and very weak.

'I've seen you dead here!' she said to me.

She grasped my hand and pulled at it even as Kane bellowed out, 'Run, damn it! All of you run for the portal!'

At the opposite end of the room, Daj heaved a last stone into the stack of skulls, shattering one of them. And then he bolted for the portal. So did Atara, Kane, Maram and I. Liljana and Master Juwain, who had just finished wrapping a cord around Ymiru's severed arm, followed quickly after us.

We raced through it and out into a corridor leading to a dimly lit street. This great tunnel – fifty feet wide and thirty feet high – opened

714

through the black rock ahead of us. Once, perhaps, there had been stalls here selling food and water, silks and jewels. But now it was empty save for a few broken rocks, dead rats and heaps of steaming dragon dung. We made our way east past the rotted-out doorways of ancient rooms and apartments. Smaller streets, every sixty yards or so, gave out onto what I took to be one of this level's great boulevards. Just after the place where it bent sharply toward the north, Daj led us to the left onto one of these side streets. We hurried as quickly as we could, but Ymiru could not run very fast missing one arm and clutching his great war club in his remaining hand.

'Here,' Master Juwain said, calling for a halt. He gathered us up close to a dark doorway in the side of the street. 'Ymiru, please let me see your arm.'

Master Juwain pulled aside Ymiru's robe to look at his wounded arm, bitten off at the elbow. The cord tied above it had stopped the spurting, but a good deal of blood still leaked from the raw, red stump. Master Juwain brought out his emerald crystal then. He summoned from it a bright green fire that cauterized the wound without burning and set the exposed and ragged flesh to healing. The sweet flame filled Ymiru like an elixir and took away his pain and shock. This gave Maram hope that someday he might be whole again.

'The arm *will* grow back, won't it?' Maram asked.

'No, I'm afraid not,' Master Juwain said. 'The varistei hasn't that power.'

As Kane rubbed the bandage over his missing ear, Ymiru looked at him sadly as if to find confirmation of his gloomy view of the world. But he had no pity for himself. He looked down as Master Juwain bandaged the stump and arranged the torn robe over it. Then he said, 'The dragon took my arm from me, but at least he didn't take this.'

He opened his other hand to show us his purple gelstei. 'And if the dragon comes for us again, this might prove her death.'

'*Will* the dragon follow us?' Maram asked.

Daj, who was growing more impatient by the moment, pulled at my hand as he said, 'The dragon is very strong. She'll come soon – let's go!'

Liljana looked at me as she nodded her head. 'She'll come,' she said with certainty.

I knew she would. And so I turned to Daj and said, 'Take us out of here, then.'

Daj led forth just ahead of me; Maram puffed and panted behind me followed by Liljana, Kane, Master Juwain and Ymiru. Atara insisted on bringing up the rear. If the dragon caught us here on the open streets, she said, she still might be able to turn and stop her with a few well-placed arrows.

And so we made our way through dark tunnels of rock that twisted through the earth. We passed by scoops in the mountain's basalt where once people had burrowed like moles. Daj led us through a snarl of streets almost as complex as the labyrinth. I had hoped that if the dragon *did* pursue us, we might lose her in this maze. But the dragon, I sensed, could track us by the scent of our sweat no less than of our minds. And since she had been imprisoned here untold years, perhaps no one or nothing knew the streets of Argattha's first level so well.

It was just as we had turned onto a narrow street that we heard a deep drumming of the dragon's footfalls behind us: *Doom, doom, doom*. Daj took a quick look behind him and then called out, 'Run! Faster now! The stairs are close!'

We ran as fast as we could. My boots slapped against dark, dirty stone as Maram wheezed along behind me. Farther back, Master Juwain was working very hard to keep up, while Ymiru's breath broke upon the fetid air in great gasps. His strength amazed me. He seemed to have shaken off the shock of his terrible wound. As had the dragon.

She was drawing closer now, gaining upon us with a frightening speed. Her great body, no doubt filling most of the narrow tunnel, seemed to push the air ahead of her. Her thick cinnamon scent carried to us and stirred up a thrill of fear. And the sound of her clawed feet echoed down the twisting tube of rock: *Doom, doom, doom*!

'Quick!' Daj shouted to us as his feet flew across the rock. 'We're almost there!'

He led us onto a long, winding street that seemed not to intersect any others or have any outlet. If we were caught here, I thought, it *would* be the end. And then, to the drumming of the dragon's feet and the growing stink of relb, as I had begun to fear that Daj had forgotten the way toward the stairs, he ran down the street's final turning and through a portal into an immense open space. This, it seemed, had once been a great hall or perhaps an open square where people had gathered – in Argattha there was really no difference. Long ago, it seemed, the mountain had moved, opening a huge rent through the rock here. A chasm thirty feet wide ran almost straight through the center of this cavernous square. It would have blocked our way if not for the narrow stone bridge that led across it.

'Come on!' Daj shouted to us as he made for the bridge.

On the other side of it was a huge shelf of rock about as large as the dragon's hall. And at the far end of the chamber, two hundred yards away, loomed a large portal.

716

'Val!' Maram shouted, 'she's coming!'

Even as he said this, the chamber shook with a terrible sound: DOOM, DOOM, DOOM.

'Run!' I called.

Daj was the first across the crumbling old bridge, followed by me, Maram and Liljana. But just as Kane set foot upon it, Atara's bowstring cracked, and I turned to see the dragon thunder into the chamber. She drove her great, scaled body bounding toward us as she hissed and growled. Her golden eyes were as full of hate as her throat was of the poisonous relb. There was no time, I saw, for anyone else after Kane to cross the bridge. And so I turned and pointed at a crack that ran deep into the chamber's side wall. To Master Juwain, I shouted, 'Hide!'

Master Juwain, trapped on the rock shelf on the other side of the chasm, jumped toward the crack and fairly pulled Atara into it. Ymiru followed them a moment later. I was afraid that the dragon, striking sparks with her great claws, might thrust her head into the crack and burn them with her fire. But the dragon's eyes were fixed upon Maram, who was running behind Daj toward the portal. It was he who had wounded the dragon with his fire. And so it would be he, I sensed, whom the dragon would burn first before rending him with her terrible teeth.

DOOM! DOOM! DOOM!

But there was no way that he, or any of us, could now escape the dragon by running. With great, heaving bounds, she leapt toward us. Her wings beat out just as her huge hind feet struck down upon the center of the bridge. There was a loud cracking of stone and a flurry of driven air. The dragon descended upon the other side of the chasm just as the bridge swayed and shuddered and broke into great pieces in its plummet into the earth's dark and fathomless deeps.

'Val!' Atara called to me from the other side of the chasm. She had stepped out of the crack and had her hands up to her mouth. 'Don't attack yet! If you move, you die!'

Behind me, Daj and Maram were still running for the portal. But Kane stood on the huge rock shelf by my right side and Liljana on my left. My sword was drawn, and I had determined that I must charge the dragon to give them time to flee.

The dragon, in her fury of driving feet and beating wings, thundered closer. Liljana waited calmly next to me, staring into her great eyes. Kane had his black stone in hand as his black eyes fixed upon the dragon's snarling face.

'Val!' Atara called again. 'Wait until she rises! There will be a moment – you will *see* the moment!'

Now the dragon, closing quickly upon me from some yards away, opened her jaws. I wondered if I could endure the burning of her fire long enough to put my sword into her before I died.

Doom, doom, doom. I felt my heart beating out the moments of my life: *doom, doom, doom.*

The dragon's throat suddenly contracted and tightened even as mine did. And I heard Kane growling at my side, 'So . . . so.'

The relb spurted at me in a great red jet of jelly. But just then, Kane finally found his way into the depths of his black crystal. The gelstei damped the fires of the relb and kept it from igniting. It splattered upon me like gore hacked out of an enemy's body. It was warm, wet and sticky, but it burned no worse than blood.

The dragon, catching sight of this miracle with her intelligent eyes, dug her claws into the rock as she reared back and rose up above me. Her long neck drew back like a snake's so that she could strike out at me with her jaws and teeth.

'Val!' Ymiru's huge voice rang out. He stood next to Atara on the other side of the chasm, pointing his purple crystal at the dragon. 'Can you see the scale?'

I saw the scale, the one just above the dragon's belly that was now darker than all the others. Ymiru had given his arm so that he could work the magic of his gelstei against this stone-hard scale and soften it.

Doom, doom, doom.

The dragon's eyes stared down at me like searing suns. Her spicy, overpowering stench sickened me as she watched and waited like a giant cobra. I knew that she would never allow me to get close to her exposed belly.

'ANGRABODA!'

With all the power of her stout body, Liljana suddenly shouted out this name that she had wrested from the dragon's mind. It was the dragon's true name, the breath of her soul, and for a moment it chilled her soul and froze her motionless. And in that moment I struck.

I rushed in forward, Alkaladur held high. Its bright blade flared with a silver light. It warded off the last, desperate, paralyzing poison of the dragon's mind. And then I thrust it straight through the softened scale, deep into her heart. And a terrible fire, like blood bursting into flames, leapt along the length of my sword, into *my* blood – straight into my heart. If Atara hadn't cried out for me to move, I would have fallen beneath the dragon even as she fell to the chamber's floor with a tremendous roar of anguish and a crash that shook the mountain's stone.

It took me a long time to return from the dark world to which the dragon's death had sent me. Only my sword's shining silustria, quickened by Flick's twinkling lights, called me back to life. When I opened my eyes again, I found myself lying on the cold stone floor of a cavern deep in the earth. The dragon lay dead ten feet away from me. And Liljana, Kane, Maram and Daj all knelt above me rubbing my cold limbs.

'Come on,' Daj said, pulling at my hand. He pointed at the portal at the far end of the chamber. 'We're almost at the stairs.'

I sat up slowly, gripping the diamond-studded hilt of my sword. Strength flowed into me even as the dragon's heart emptied the last of her blood into the great pool of crimson gathering upon the floor. I wanted to weep because I had killed a great, if malignant, being. But instead I stood up and walked over to the lip of the chasm.

'Val – are you all right?' Atara called to me.

She stood with Ymiru and Master Juwain on the other side, thirty feet away. It might as well have been thirty miles. There was nothing left of the stone bridge that had spanned it only a few minutes before.

'Daj,' I said, looking at the boy, 'how can they get over to us?'

'I don't know,' he said, 'that was the only way.'

He pointed behind us at the portal and added, 'That corridor leads right to the stairs to the second level. There's nowhere else we can go.'

'No other streets join the corridor?'

'No.'

'But are there any other stairs on this level that lead up to the next?'

As it happened, there was another set of stairs, back through the first level two miles beyond the dragon's hall. Daj told Master Juwain, Ymiru and Atara how to reach them.

'Then where,' I asked Daj, 'can we meet on the second level?'

'I don't know,' Daj said. 'I don't know that level at all.'

'But you know the seventh level, don't you?'

'As well as I know this one.'

'Is there a place we can meet there?' I asked.

'Yes, there's a fountain near Lord Morjin's palace. It's called the Red Fountain. Everyone knows where it is.'

We held quick council then, shouting back and forth across the chasm. We decided that it would be foolish to try to wander about the city's second level hoping to run into each other somewhere in its twisting streets. And so we resolved to find the fountain that Daj had told of and meet there before stealing into Morjin's throne room.

'But we've never been separated before,' Maram said, looking back at Master Juwain. 'I don't like this at all.'

None of us did. But if we were to complete our quest, we had no choice. And so we stood facing our friends across a dark crack in the earth and said goodbye to them.

'If something should happen and we don't reach the fountain, don't wait for us,' I called to Atara. 'Find your own way into the throne room. Find the cup and take it out of this place, if you can.'

'All right,' she called back. 'And you, too.'

With a last look that cut deep into me, she turned to lead Master Juwain and Ymiru out of the chamber the way that they had come. And then, with Daj pulling at my hand, we turned the other way toward the portal and the dark corridor that pointed toward the stairs to Argattha's upper levels.

43

The opening to the stairway proved quite narrow. There was no way, I saw, that the dragon could ever have forced her body into it. Daj informed us that there was a much larger passage from the first level to the second: a great road that wound up through the layers of rock and into the next level, where an enormous iron gate, kept closed, blocked the dragon from escaping into the inhabited parts of Argattha.

It was into these parts, with great wariness, that we finally made our way. As in ascending a castle's high tower, we climbed five hundred feet up the winding stairs. In this turning tube of rock, it was cold and dark, with only my sword and Flick's lights providing any illumination. Few ever used this stairway, Daj told us. The Red Priests, torches in hand, might bear a struggling offering for the dragon down the stairs, but no one else would ever think of daring its domain. Likewise, none looked for anyone to emerge from the stairway into the second level. We found that the stairs gave out into a deserted corridor leading to a quiet street in the western district of the city. No one was about the street as we debouched onto it. The doors of the apartments along this tunnel of rock were closed. I wondered if it was night; in the twistings of the labyrinth and our fight with the dragon, we had utterly lost the thread of time.

'It *is* night,' Kane said to us as we made our toward the noise of a larger street ahead of us. 'In this accursed city, always night.'

Daj was little help to us here. Some days ago, he said, he had made his way up the stairs, even as we just had, only to be captured very near this district.

'Lord Morjin's spies,' he said, 'saw the mark and captured me.'

To cover this foul mark inked into his forehead, Master Juwain had rigged a length of cloth around his head. It looked, Kane told us, something like the flowing kaftafs worn by the tribesmen of the Red Desert.

I worried how well Daj's disguise would hold up. I worried about Ymiru, as well. It was bad enough that he had to go forth dressed as a Saryak. Would his missing arm, I wondered, attract even more attention his way?

In this matter, at least, we had little to fear. Soon we reached a street where many people were about. And many of them, I saw, were veterans of Morjin's conquests. Quite a few of those not dressed in his livery, mostly the invalided and old, showed signs of service in faraway lands: they had scars upon their faces and arms – that is, if their arms and other limbs hadn't long since been hacked off. Other people – blacksmiths, potters, masons, carpenters, bakers, and especially the tattooed slaves – bore the marks of Morjin's displeasure. The Red Dragon, as Daj told us, had settled upon mutilation as punishment for even minor offenses. As we made our way through the crowds behind rolling carts laden with iron ore, hay, water barrels and other supplies, we saw men and women with branded faces, notched ears and gouged-out eyes. Thieves who hadn't been given to the dragon lacked hands with which to cut others' purses. In no other city had I seen so many carved-up, burnt, tortured, unfortunate people. Ymiru, I thought, would attract no attention on account of his severed arm.

It reassured me as well that we passed several Saryaks hurrying past us. These very tall men were dressed as Ymiru in black robes whose cowls covered their faces. They were girded with maces and curved swords; they served Morjin freely, for pay, as did other mercenaries whose appearance and dress led me to believe that their homelands were Sunguru and Uskudar – and even Surrapam, Delu and Alonia. Many Sarni warriors, accoutered in leather armor as Atara, rode their steppe ponies boldly through the streets. Kane identified their tribes as Zayak, Marituk and western Urtuk, all of whom were said to have made alliances with Sakai. As well, we passed a band of Blues with their battleaxes and companies of marching levies from Hesperu, Karabuk and Galda, which Morjin's Red Priests had conquered outright in his name. It seemed that Morjin was gathering a great host under his banner and sheltering them here in this dark, impregnable city. If any of Argattha's residents looked our way, I hoped they would think that we were just a few more warriors come to sell our swords.

Daj explained to us that the various levels of the city were mostly devoted to differing activities. Thus on the seventh level were to be found Morjin's palace and throne room, many of Argattha's temples, and other chambers given over to matters of ceremony and state. There lived the Red Priests and nobles, while the higher artisans such as painters and sculptors had shops on the sixth level, with weavers, clothmakers and dyers on the fifth, and so on down to the second level, the city's largest, where Morjin's armies were quartered in dim, cramped barracks and the blacksmiths and armorers labored over their forges preparing for war.

We saw signs of the coming cataclysm all around us. Carts stacked with yew and horn, bound for the bowmakers' shops, rolled past us. Other carts laden with sheaves of arrows moved the other way. Slaughterhouses laying in pork for long campaigns shook with the squeals of pigs having their throats cut; their blood flowed out into the streets' gutters, there to be drunk by the scurrying rats or the clouds of flies that plagued Argattha.

From smithies came the constant hammering of steel as men beat mauls against white-hot metal and made spearheads, swords, maces, arrowheads, helmets, shields and suits of mail. From the many forges billowed a thick smoke that choked the streets. Although numerous air shafts opened like chimneys upon the ironworks and dank corridors, they were too few to carry away the fumes and stinks of the city. The foul mixture of smoke, rotting blood and fear was the smell of Argattha, and I worried that it would cling not just to my clothes and hair but to my soul.

And how much worse, I thought, was the assault of this dreadful place on those who were forced or had chosen to dwell here. Mercenaries scurried like rats themselves through the dirty streets. Mole-like merchants spent their years in little shops no better than pits and in scooped-out apartments that were worse. To the crack of whips, slaves dug new passages out of solid rock, and in long lines bore boulders and other debris out of Argattha's tunnels. They reminded me of ants more than men. Men and women, I thought, were not made to live so. We were noble beings who had come from far away to make a better world than this. We should have roses and starlight and hopes swelling like the Poru in flood. We should have great, soaring cities like Alundil and forests like the Lokilani's magical wood. A true king, my father once told me, turned all his thoughts and actions toward fulfilling the dreams of his people. In the end, he became *their* servant. But Morjin had bent the will of his subjects toward serving his dark design. They were a twisted people, bearing marks of woe upon their bodies and stunted in their souls.

I thought that if I couldn't soon lay my hands upon the Lightstone and escape from this city, the sufferings of these thousands of tortured men, women and children would drive me mad. And escape, it seemed, was near. After stopping a broken, old women to ask directions, we found our way onto one of this level's boulevards. This great bore through the mountain's basalt, lit with oil lamps and lined with shops, ran almost straight from the Gashur Gate in the east face of Skartaru to the Vodya

Gate in the west. It intersected another similar boulevard connecting the Lokir Gate and the Zun Gate, long since closed. Gashur, Lokir, Vodya and Zun – four of the great Galadin who had joined Angra Mainyu's rebellion against the angelic hosts and had been imprisoned with him on the world of Damoom. Their names were reminders of why we had come to Argattha – and why we *couldn't* just flee out of the city's gates.

And so we turned northeast toward the Zun Gate, as the old woman had advised us. The city's great central stairs, she had said, opened onto the boulevard only a quarter mile farther along. We passed bakeries, taverns and mess halls carved out of solid rock. The smells of hot bread, beer and roasted chicken mingled with the reek of sewage and the dung that the gong farmers hauled out of the city in wicker baskets. Although it had been a long time since our last meal and we were fairly starving, we couldn't quite bring ourselves to stop and eat. But we must, as Maram pointed out, find something to drink. Atara had been carrying our water, and we had not the slightest drop to wet our parched throats.

'I'm thirsty,' Maram complained as we made our way against the jostling crowds in the street. He walked beside me, with Daj behind him and Kane and Liljana following protectively. 'I don't like to think that I'd drink the water in this filthy place, but I suppose I must.'

Although time was pressing us like a great boulder set rolling down a mountain, we decided to duck into a waterseller's shop and buy a few glasses of this precious liquid. But after we had drunk our fill of the greasy-seeming water, which tasted faintly of iron and blood, we found that we couldn't leave.

'Look,' Daj said to me, pointing out of the shop's doorway. I followed the line of his finger toward some men who were sitting around a table outside of the tavern next door. 'I know that man – he's one of Lord Morjin's spies.'

The man he had indicated, tall and blond like the Thalunes and dressed in a plain tunic and mail like many mercenaries, had his chair positioned facing the doorway to the waterseller's shop. His cruel blue eyes swept the street, no doubt looking for a way that he could transmute his betrayal of others into gold. It would be impossible, I knew, for us to walk past him without him seeing us.

'What should we do?' Maram whispered to me.

'Wait,' I whispered back.

And so wait we did. We ordered more glasses of water and sat drinking them around a table at the rear of the shop. There was a chess set there, too, and Kane and I set up the pieces and began a game in the most desultory of ways. Maram chided me for losing my knight in a vain effort to forestall an attack upon my queen. But I had no mind for a game at such a time, when my heart beat out like thunder at every round of laughter or curses that sounded from the tavern next door.

It took most of an hour for the spy and his friends to finish their ale and leave. We waited another quarter of an hour before daring to leave ourselves; the spy, we feared, might be skulking somewhere on the street nearby. Maram thanked the stars that we didn't see him anywhere in the crowds that streamed past us as we hurried along. But that didn't mean anything, as Kane pointed out. It was the essence of spying, he said, to seek out others without being seen.

But luck, I thought, had finally turned our way. We reached the central stairs without further incident. These great steps, a hundred feet wide, opened onto the boulevard exactly as the old woman had said. Streams of people poured down them on the left, while many others puffed laboriously up them on the right. We waited a few moments at the foot of them, hoping we might catch sight of Atara, Ymiru and Master Juwain in the throngs about us. But if they had kept to our plan, they had no doubt reached this spot before us and had gone on ahead.

And so with a final glance at the street, we began our climb up to Argattha's seventh level. With five levels to ascend and five hundred feet per level, we had to work our way up a distance of almost a half mile, straight up through the heart of the mountain. It took us a long time to make this climb. The stairs drove up toward the east until giving way to a great landing, before turning back west on their rise again. And so it went, with many, many turnings as the seemingly endless stairs took us through the black rock past the openings to the third, fourth, fifth and sixth levels. At last, with Maram fairly wheezing and dripping sweat from his thick, brown beard, we came out onto one of the boulevards of the seventh level.

'Ah, here it is,' Maram said, puffing as we stepped out onto the huge street. 'Well, it doesn't look like much.'

Indeed, the street looked like every other tunnel in this unnatural city, save that it was even larger: it was a great, square-cut channel through black rock that was lit with foul-smelling oil lamps and pitted with doorways that were the openings to dank living spaces and shops. Although we were close to Morjin's throne room, as Daj told us, no vistas of magnificent domed buildings or soaring arches were to be seen, for Morjin's 'palace' was just another series of rat holes in a mountain gnawed with thousands of such dark places.

'The palace is that way,' he said, pointing almost due south at a wall of stone.

To the west of the palace, he said, was the great Gardens: a huge hall where flowering plants were bathed in the light of the thousands of glowstones on the walls. To the east of the palace was a passage that only Morjin was permitted to use. This led past a series of private stairs to the lower levels, a mile and a half straight toward an opening cut onto Skartaru's east face. Daj called it Morjin's Porch, and there the Red Dragon liked to sit each morning to watch the rising of the sun. There, too, long ago, on the naked rock face, he had nailed the immortal Kalkamesh and tortured him for ten long years.

'I'd like to see this porch of his,' Maram said, looking about the dim street. 'I'd give anything to feel real light on my face again.'

'Don't be a fool!' Kane snapped at him. 'You won't be seeing it anytime soon unless Morjin puts *you* there.'

'He may put all of us there,' Maram said bravely. 'And it may be that someday the poets will sing of us and what we tried to do here. Do you think so, Val?'

'Perhaps,' I said to him. 'But it would please me more if Alphanderry were here to sing of the stars.'

The boulevard led us a quarter mile toward the east, where it intersected another running from north to south – directly toward the throne room of Morjin's Palace. In the great square where these two streets came together had been built a fountain. Men and women sat around it in the spray of a great plume of water, red as rust, as if it had been forced through ancient iron pipes.

We sat there by this crimson pool, too, waiting for our friends. We watched carts full of silks and wine barrels roll past; one cart, stacked with glowstones that reminded me of the skulls in the dragon's hall, was clearly being taken outside of Argattha so that these gelstei could be refilled with the light of the sun. Hundreds of people from the boulevards poured in streams of living flesh around the fountain. Many of these wore red robes embroidered with golden dragons: the vestments of the Red Priests of the Kallimun. These men – and they were almost all men – strode along with an air of rectitude and dominion, as if all things and peoples about them were their province. More than one of them cast us suspicious looks. And we were, I thought, a suspicious company: three men dressed like mercenaries, a noble-looking woman and a ragtag child. It was very good, I thought, that only we could see Flick.

After a while, it became clear that there were few mercenaries on this level of the city – but many captains and lords of Morjin's armies. One of these, dressed in an ice-blue tunic with a broadsword buckled at the waist, swaggered up to us and demanded that we identify ourselves. Only the medallions that we had lifted off the dead knights kept us from being taken and bound in chains.

'That was close,' Maram said, after the captain had stalked off. We had hinted that we were spies, and that Morjin would be very displeased if the captain interfered with our mission. 'Too, too close.'

Liljana sat with her arms thrown protectively around Daj as might his mother. But there was something fierce and unyielding in her watchful gaze, as if she would reluctantly sacrifice him or any of us – or herself – in order to gain the Lightstone.

'We can't wait here much longer,' she whispered against the fountain's splatter.

I looked up and down the boulevards, praying that I might catch sight of Atara and the others.

'With our delay at the waterseller's, likely they're already come,' Kane said. 'And likely they've already gone on to the throne room.'

He pointed down the boulevard toward the south. According to Daj, it gave out onto Morjin's Palace little more than a quarter mile from the fountain.

'Perhaps we should wait just a few minutes longer,' I said. I looked for Atara's flowing blond mane among the mostly darker-haired women who seemed to populate Argattha.

'We agreed not to wait,' Kane reminded me. 'Likely they're trying to find their way into the throne room even as we waste our time here. And likely they'll need our help with the guards.'

Here Liljana fingered her blue figurine while Kane rested his hand on the haft of his dagger.

It seemed a desperate business to try to fool or force our way into the throne room past Morjin's guards. Although fortune often favored such boldness, I was reluctant to attempt this frontal assault even so. And then Daj surprised me, and all of us, saying, 'There's another way into the throne room.'

He told us that three great gates, on the throne room's east, west and north sides, opened upon the streets of the city and were always guarded. But a door inside the throne room, on its west wall, opened upon an unguarded passage that led directly through the palace to Morjin's private quarters.

'Oh, excellent,' Maram said to Daj. 'And I suppose you know a way to get inside the Red Dragon's rooms without just knocking at his door?'

'I *do*,' Daj said, and our surprise turned to amazement. 'There's a secret passage *from* Lord Morjin's rooms into the city.'

He went on to tell us that Morjin often used this passage to leave his palace unnoticed; he would go about the city in disguise, Daj said, acting as his own most trusted spy to ferret out any plots or slanders made against him.

'But why didn't you tell us this?' I asked him.

'Because I was afraid,' he said, looking at Kane grip his dagger.

'Afraid of what?'

'Afraid that you've come to kill Lord Morjin.'

He went on to say that an ancient curse had been laid upon anyone who would dare to try to slay the Red Dragon. And so he had been afraid, he said, to lead us through his private chambers.

'But why are you telling us this now, then?' I asked him.

'Because I don't care anymore,' he said. His dark, youthful eyes suddenly filled with hate, like Kane's 'About the curse, I mean. I hope you *do* kill him. I'll never sleep well again until he's dead.'

The hurt inside him cut me like a heated knife. And I said to him, 'But we haven't come here to kill anyone. We're not assassins, Daj.'

As Kane's eyes flared like coals, I went on to tell him that we meant to enter Morjin's throne room in order to recover something that had once been stolen from the king's palace in Tria.

'What is it then, treasure?' he asked. 'There's plenty of that in the throne room.'

'Yes, treasure,' I said. And then, to myself, I whispered: *The greatest treasure in the world*.

We decided that Daj should take us through the district outside Morjin's Palace to the secret passage that led into it. But first we must reconnoiter the streets around the gates to the throne room, in the hope that we might find Atara and the others seeking a way inside. Then we might rejoin them and tell of our new plan for gaining entrance.

When we reached the street facing the throne room's north gate, however, we found many people milling about the food stalls and fortune tellers there, but none of them were our friends. The gate itself – great iron doors twenty feet high and as wide – was guarded by four of Morjin's men. We might simply have rushed upon them and murdered them; it would then be easy to push open the doors and storm our way into the throne room and begin our search for the Lightstone. But even if we completed our quest within a few minutes, the alarm would have been given, and we would have to try to fight our way back out against perhaps a hundred hastily summoned guards.

'Does this street ever grow quiet?' I asked Daj. I looked at the silksellers hawking their wares from their carts and other merchants displaying golden bangles, silver brooches and jeweled rings.

'At night it does,' he said.

Maram pulled at his beard and muttered, 'But how can you tell when it's night in this accursed place?'

'Well, the criers come to call out the curfew.'

'So,' Kane said, 'if our friends have discovered that, then perhaps they're waiting for night to clear the streets.'

'Perhaps,' I said, as I watched a nearby vendor roasting a baby pig over a little fire. The spit and hiss of its dripping fat sent a greasy, black smoke out onto the noisy street.

'Perhaps we *should* wait here, after all,' Maram said. 'If we're to steal through the Red Dragon's rooms, it would be better to do so at night when he's sleeping.'

'But he *doesn't* sleep,' Daj said. 'He stays up all night reading his books. Or playing chess with himself. Or . . . other things.'

'And during the day?' I asked, looking for some ray of light driving down the airshafts that opened upon the street.

'During the day,' Daj said, 'he could be anywhere in the city.'

I pulled my cloak more tightly about myself as he said this. I felt the eyes of many people about the street watching us.

'Anywhere except the throne room,' Liljana said.

'Yes, that's right,' Daj said, nodding toward the iron gate. 'The doors are almost always open when Lord Morjin is holding court.'

'*Almost* always?' Liljana asked him.

Daj nodded his head. 'Yes, sometimes he holds . . . private audiences.'

I felt my heart beating like a hammer and sweat running beneath the padding of my armor. I said, 'All right, the throne room is likely empty, as we stand here talking. And our friends, if they haven't been taken, are likely waiting somewhere for night to fight their way into it.'

'And if they *have* been taken?' Maram asked.

I tried not to look at the heated iron running through the sizzling pig or listen to the scream building inside me. I said, 'Then all the more reason that we should hasten to find this secret passage that Daj has told of. And if our friends are safe, we'll no doubt find them outside one of the gates tonight, after we've completed our quest.'

Everyone agreed that it would be best if we attempted the secret passage now, before we were discovered or our courage failed. And so Daj led the way into the district to the northwest of the palace. Here the streets were narrow and twisted like tunnels that would have confused an ant. Nobles, mostly, lived here between the shops of the bakers, vintners and others who served their needs. The stares of these people as we quickly passed by disquieted all of us. But we moved along without any trouble until we came to another square, much smaller than that of the Red Fountain.

Here, on a great wooden cross caked with layers of old blood, a nearly naked man had been crucified for all to see. A crowd had gathered to watch his death throes, and for a moment we joined them. I couldn't take my eyes off the man's head, which was slumped down against his chest as if he were watching his heart's last flame about to be blown out.

Almost against my will, I found my hand sliding beneath my cloak and gripping the hilt of my sword. And then Kane's steely fingers gripped *my* arm as he shook his head and told me, 'You can't save everyone, Val.'

'But what was his crime?' I whispered to him.

No one around us seemed to know. One old woman, likely the wife of some great lord, gathered in her silks and told her attendant that she believed the condemned man had somehow insulted Morjin.

'Come, now,' Kane said, pulling at my arm. 'Let's take our revenge on Morjin by stealing from him what he covets most.'

I nodded my head, and we pushed our way out of the crowd. Daj led us onto a dim street that turned toward the north, in the direction of the great stairs. But then it turned again, west and south. We walked on a little way. Then Daj pointed at an open doorway next to a butchery where many fly-blown chickens and lambs were hung. It was an unusual doorway, the rock on either side of it being carved with standing dragons that framed it like pillars. It gave into a little chamber that was one of Argattha's many sanctuaries. Inside, as we found, was little more than a single glowstone hanging from the low ceiling. This one light, Daj said, symbolized the Light of the One. The meaning of our passage through the pillars was clear: that the way toward the One was through the way of the Dragon.

'People are supposed to come here and meditate,' Daj told us. We stood at the center of the deserted chamber, staring at a tapestry of various Elijin and Galadin on the far wall. 'But no one ever comes.'

'Why not?' Maram asked him.

'Because it's said that Lord Morjin seeks his sacrifices from the most faithful and finds them in the sanctuaries.'

Such tales, I thought, were an excellent way of keeping the sanctuaries empty – so that Morjin could reserve them for his private use.

With Maram standing watch in the doorway, we moved over to the tapestry, and Liljana held it away from the wall. Behind it was a door, barely perceptible as such: a crack ran horizontally through the black rock just above the level of our heads, while two others cut lengthwise framing a large basalt slab. If pushed against, I thought, it would revolve and open onto the secret passage.

I pushed against it now, but it was like pushing against a solid wall, and the door didn't move. And Daj said to me, 'You have to know the password.'

'I presume you know what this is?' Kane said to him.

'Yes, there's a door like this at the other end of the passage – in Lord Morjin's rooms. One time, I hid there and watched him use it. And then followed him here.'

'Brave boy,' I said, nodding my head in acknowledgement of his feat.

'Yes, you're a brave little spy,' Kane said, grinning savagely. 'Well, let's see if Morjin has kept the password. What is it?'

'*Memoriar-damoom*,' Daj said softly. 'I don't know what it means.'

'It means,' Kane said, translating the ancient Ardik, '"Remember Damoom."'

He stood directly facing the door and spoke the word clearly, louder this time. And from within the door came a clicking sound as of a lock being slid open.

As Maram hurried across the room to view this marvel, Kane's grin grew larger, and he said, 'In the Age of Law, many locks were made thusly. Song stones, keyed to a word or a voice, turn at the touch of the right sound and set the locking mechanism in motion.'

Now he set his hand against the edge of the door and leaned his weight into it. The part that he pushed against swung inward smoothly while the left edge of the slab revolved out into the room. Beyond the opening lay a dark tunnel.

'So,' he said.

He started straight into the tunnel, followed by Daj and me. But when it came Maram's turn to step forward, he hesitated and said, 'Ah, I don't like the look of this at all.'

'Come,' I said, turning back toward him. 'Where's your courage?'

'Ah, where indeed, my friend? I'm afraid that almost all of *that* coin has been spent.'

'There's always more,' I said to him.

'For you, perhaps, but not for me. After all, I'm no Valari.'

'What do you mean?'

'Well, I mean that for you Valari, courage is a birthright. You breathe it in as easily as others do air.'

'No, you're wrong, Maram,' I told him, shaking my head. My belly churned as if I had swallowed a nest of writhing snakes. 'Courage never gets to be a habit. Each time . . . it gets harder to find. As it is now for me.'

'For you?'

'Yes,' I said, glancing at Kane and Liljana. And then I looked straight at Maram. 'Without you by my side, I don't know how I'd ever be able to do this.'

'Do you really mean that?'

I clasped his hand in mine and smiled at him. 'Will you come with me this last mile?'

He hesitated another long moment before slowly nodding his head. And then he sighed out, 'All right, then, I'll come. But this has to be the *last* time.'

Then he, too, stepped into the tunnel, followed by Liljana, who had so arrayed the tapestry that it fell back over the door as we pushed it shut. Darkness swallowed us; for a moment we stood nearly blind beneath the black shroud of night. Then I drew my sword. Daj stared at the glowing blade in wonder, but seemed too afraid to ask by what miracle it gave light. All that he said was: 'The last time I was here, all I had was a candle. But this is better.'

He started off down the tunnel, with me, Maram, Liljana and Kane close behind. The dark tube of rock seemed empty even of rats. We walked quietly, but the scrape of our boots echoed off the bare rocks. After a while we came to a place where another tunnel joined ours. Daj told us that he thought it led to another sanctuary somewhere on the seventh level. Or perhaps, he said, it gave out onto the passage that led to Morjin's Porch on Skartaru's east face. Along that way was to be found Morjin's Stairs, which led down to Argattha's lower levels and the secret escape tunnels there that Morjin still kept open.

'Do you know these tunnels?' I asked him.

'Well, I know *about* them,' Daj said. 'But I was never able to find out where they were.'

We walked on for another two hundred yards and came across two more of these adjoining tunnels. And then, after turning left, toward the east, our tunnel ended abruptly in what seemed a wall of solid rock.

'He's sealed it off!' Maram whispered when he saw this. 'We're trapped!'

I smiled as I brought my sword up close to the wall to reveal the cracks running through it, outlining a door – the door that must open onto Morjin's private chambers. I pressed my ear to the cold rock and listened for any sounds from the room beyond it.

'What do you hear?' Maram whispered, pressing close.

'Only your breath in my ear. Now be quiet.'

I continued listening for a murmur of voices, the slap of boots against stone, silverware clacking against a plate – for anything at all. But the rock was as quiet as a skull. The only sound I heard was the drumming of my heart up through my ear.

'All right,' I said, turning back to look at Liljana and Kane. 'Is everyone ready?'

Both of them had their swords drawn, as did Maram and I. I gripped Alkaladur's hilt more tightly as I faced the door and said, 'Memoriar Damoom!'

There came a clicking from within the rock of the door. I placed my hand on the edge of it; it felt wet as from dripping water, but I realized that it was only my sweat. Slowly, I pushed against the door. It opened directly into a cloth that I discovered to be another tapestry. I squeezed out from behind its clinging folds and stepped into a well-lit room.

'This is it,' Daj said, joining me there. 'Lord's Morjin's room.'

I knew that it was. All at once, a sickly-sweet odor as of incense mixed with decay made my stomach churn. As the others moved out from behind the tapestry and then pushed the door shut, I looked out at a large, richly furnished room. Intricate tapestries, like the one hiding the door behind us, completely covered the room's four walls so that not a square inch of bare rock remained exposed to remind Morjin that he had chosen to live inside a mountain. We stood with our backs to the room's west wall. To our left, along the north wall, was a heavy bronze door cast with roses and other flowers – the door to the rest of Morjin's palace. Straight ahead stood another door, like in size, but it showed a great, spreading tree beneath a bronze sun. Daj said that it opened upon the passage that led to the throne room.

Before starting toward this door, I quickly took in the room's other features. Above the great bed along the south wall was hung a blue-black canopy embroidered with thousands of tiny diamonds. These were set in the patterns of the constellations' stars. On either side of the bed were gilded chests and wardrobes; three long mirrors, framed in ornate gold, were set into the east, north and west walls. The ceiling was a chessboard of white and black wood squares, while the floor was covered with a single carpet woven with the shapes of knights on horses, winged lions and ferocious beasts. As before, when Morjin had brought me to this room through the doorway of nightmare and illusion, I looked down to see that I was standing on the head of a fire-breathing dragon.

'Look, Val!' Maram whispered to me as he nudged my side. 'That's a touchstone, isn't it!'

I turned to see him pointing at a massive desk on which many books lay open. There, too, set out as if Morjin had been studying them, were warders, wish stones, dragon bones and other lesser gelstei. I saw three precious music marbles as well as a sleep stone, with its many swirling colors that looked something like a fire agate. Maram took a step straight toward the desk, perhaps intending to touch or take one of these treasures. But I grabbed his elbow and said, 'We don't have time for this.'

Kane, moving quickly, swept up a few bloodstones glowing with a dreadful red light and pocketed them. Then he pointed his sword at a large stand next to the desk. He snarled out, 'So, we have time for *this*, then.'

I saw that the stand, which looked something like a brazier, held six large eggs thrice the size of an eagle's. Before I could stop him, Kane crossed the room and thrust his sword straight through one of the eggs, breaking open the leathery shell. Five more times he thrust out, and when he was done, the steel of his sword dripped with a thick, blood-orange yolk. Thus did he destroy the eggs of Angraboda, one of the dragons that Morjin had summoned here from Damoom.

'But there were *seven* eggs!' Daj whispered as he crossed the room to where Kane stood snarling down at the broken, oozing mass of shells.

'Seven, eh? Are you sure?'

Daj nodded his head, looking about the room, as did Kane. He stalked across it to wipe his sword contemptuously on the silk coverings of Morjin's bed.

'Kane, there's no time!' I said, making for the door with the great tree. 'We've got to go!'

'You go,' he said, casting his eyes about the room. 'This is a rare chance.'

'To destroy an egg?'

'Yes, that,' he said, stabbing his sword into one of the bed's feather pillows. 'And to destroy Morjin.'

Now he looked at the door on the north wall that led to the rest of the palace; he gazed fiercely at the tapestry covering the door by which we had entered the room. And then he said, 'So, I'll wait here for him. And when he comes, I'll send him back to the stars.'

Liljana, who had a cooler head than mine, went over to him and touched his sword arm. 'You might wait days then. And what are *we* to do while you wait to make this murder?'

'Complete your quest.'

'But what if we need your help?'

'You won't,' he snapped. Then his savage gaze fell upon her. 'I know that you want him dead almost as badly as I do.'

'Perhaps,' Liljana said, looking away from him. 'But not as badly as I want to find what we came here to find.'

I, too, found it hard to bear the fire in Kane's blazing eyes just then. But I stared straight at him and said a single word: 'Please.'

There was a moment when I thought he would turn inward to that

734

burning ocean of hate that pulled him ever downward into the hell of his own being. But once, near a little clearing littered with the bodies of the gray men that we had slain, he had pledged his sword to my service so long as I sought the Lightstone. The deep, knowing touch of our eyes told me that he remembered this promise. And that he would keep it.

'All right,' he said, pointing his sword toward the east door that led to Morjin's throne room. 'Let's finish this damn quest of yours then!'

I stepped over and twisted the knob of the door, which was unlocked and pulled open like any other. Behind it was a hallway, draped with flowing silks, that ran straight east. I led the way into it, and then Kane shut the door behind us.

We marched forward for a distance of a few hundred yards. No other doors or passages gave out onto this new tunnel. On either side of us and above us, Daj said, were the rooms of Morjin's palace that could only be reached from his room through its north door. Many people, I sensed, were all about us through thin walls of rock. As we hurried along, my breath came more quickly in bursts that seemed to burn my nostrils and mouth. And yet the air was cold, as was the rock beneath the thin, silk wall coverings. The door at the opposite end of the hallway was cold, too. We came upon it in a rush of driving feet and beating hearts. Like the door to Morjin's room, it was cast of bronze and unlocked.

With a last look back at Kane and the others, I pushed it open. And then I stepped out into Morjin's throne room.

'Oh, my Lord!' Maram whispered in my ear. 'Oh, my Lord!'

We stood along the west wall of one of the largest enclosed spaces I had ever beheld. The vast chamber, carved out of solid rock, must have been three hundred feet high and nearly as long and wide. Immense pillars rose up from the floor like giant stone trees and fluted out to support the dark ceiling high above. Everything about this cold, vaulted hall seemed dark, with its acres of bare, black basalt. Yet Morjin and the hall's makers had applied all their art toward filling it with light. In the walls and ceiling were set many hundreds of glowstones, throwing out their soft, silky sheen. The pillars were jacketed in gold leaf, which reflected this radiance out into the hall. Various statues, encrusted with rubies, sapphires and other gems, added to the glitter. And yet, it was not quite enough to reach into the farthest corners and drive away the shadows. In the midst of all this ancient and hideous splendor hung an air of dread that seemed to ooze from the exposed rock along the ceiling, floor and walls; here echoed the memory of torments as old as the ages and the future cries of hopelessness and doom.

For a moment, I pressed back against the bronze door to still my dizziness and orient myself. I noted the three closed gates, along the east, north and west walls. Opposite the door to Morjin's rooms where we gathered, at the center of the hall and toward its southern end, stood a great throne. It had been built, it seemed, in imitation or mockery of the king's throne in Tria. Six broad steps led up to it, and each step was framed at either end by the sculptures of Gashur and Zun and other Galadin who had become as monsters. The greatest of these was the coiled, red dragon monument to Angra Mainyu into which the throne itself was set. When Morjin took his place on this seat of power, his head would be framed just below the huge dragon's head, which looked out into the room with golden eyes carved out of two huge amber stones.

Leaving the door behind us open should we have to beat a hasty retreat, we moved out into the great hall as we began what I hoped would be the final moments of the quest. But even as Alkaladur's blade shone with a new light, my hope faded. For in truth, the silustria blazed too brightly. It whatever direction I pointed it – north, east, south and west – I could detect not the slightest change in its luminosity. I knew from this frightful radiance that the Lightstone must be very close – so close that my silver sword could lead us no farther. But how we were otherwise to find it in so vast a space, I didn't know.

For there were a thousand places where Sartan Odinan might have set down a little golden cup. Behind the throne, and in other parts of the room, there were altars, cabinets and pedestals that might have been the Lightstone's resting place. And cold braziers, lamp stands, benches, shelves and even the plinths of the great stone pillars holding up the ceiling. Along the huge walls themselves – carved with dragons, demons and a huge bas-relief of the Baaloch and the dark angels imprisoned with him on Damoom – there were recesses and rocky projections, any one of which might have hidden the Lightstone.

'Well?' Maram said to me as we walked out into the room.

'It's here,' I said. 'But it's so close, my sword can't tell us where.'

'Then how are we to find it?' He stopped by the line of pillars running down the hall to the right of the throne. He bent to feel along a pillar's massive, square-cut plinth, tapping his hands along the stone like a blind man. 'My Lord – we can't just hope we'll stumble across it!'

We worked our way straight across the hall, passing between the throne and an evil-looking, circular area with several great standing stones arising from the floor. We came to the line of pillars running down the hall to the left of the throne. And there, suddenly, Flick appeared. His small, scintillating form, now throwing out sparks of silver and gold, shot straight up into the air like fireworks. He whirled about ecstatically, then dived down like a firebird and began weaving his way in and out of the mighty pillars in streaks of violet flame.

'Do you think he knows where it is?' Maram asked. 'Do you think he is trying to tell us?'

Flick looped in and out of the pillars and then spun directly over the circular area with its standing stones, which looked to be used for rituals. Flick, I thought, certainly knew where the Lightstone was. And more, it seemed he was drinking in its presence through every sparkling bit of his being and growing ever brighter. But I sensed that he couldn't simply tell us where it had been hidden. For whatever Flick really was, it couldn't have occurred to him that for my friends and me, the Lightstone remained invisible.

It was the greatest torment of Argattha to stand so close to the Lightstone, almost to *feel* its numinous presence charging the air as before a storm, but not be able to see it.

Daj, watching us look across the room as Flick streaked about, must have thought we had fallen mad. He could not make out the Timpum's fiery shape. And so he was the first of us to behold another sight.

'Val – over there!' he suddenly cried as he pulled on my arm. He pointed across the ritual area at the gate on the west side of the hall. 'They're coming!'

And even as my eyes fell upon the gate's iron doors, they flew open, swinging inward. Many guards, dressed in mail and yellow livery stained with angry, red dragons, charged into the hall. Many of them bore swords and halberds in their hands; some had long, thrusting spears. Their captains arrayed them in four lines, two on either side of the doorway. Almost without thinking, I took a quick count of their numbers: there were about twenty-five of them in each line.

'So,' Kane muttered. Just then the door to Morjin's private chamber by which we had entered the hall slammed shut. 'Four of us against a hundred – so.'

Without any more prompting, Maram ran over to the gate on the east wall behind the pillars where we gathered. He pounded against it, but it was locked.

'Trapped!' he cried out. 'Now we're truly trapped!'

So we were. As Maram quickly rejoined us and we stood with our backs to the pillars, there came a flurry of motion from outside the open gate to the throne room. And then a man dressed in a golden tunic, trimmed with black fur and emblazoned with a ferocious, red dragon, strode through the doorway. He was almost tall and bore himself with an unshakeable air of command. His close-cropped hair shone like gold while the beauty of his form and face seemed almost too perfect. His eyes appeared golden, too. For he was, of course, Morjin the Fair – the Lord of Lies and the Great Beast who had so often come for me with his claws and illusions in the worst of my nightmares.

'Ah, my friend,' Maram said to me as we pressed back against the pillars, preparing for a last stand. 'This is the end – finally, the end.'

Morjin took another step forward, before pausing to beckon with his hand to his guards. He stared across the room straight at me – and at Kane, Maram, Liljana and Daj. There was utter triumph in his hideously beautiful eyes. And then, without a word, his face fell into a mask of hate as he and his guards began marching toward us.

44

Morjin left half of his men to guard the open gate while he deployed the fifty others around the ritual area facing us. I had supposed that he and his guards would simply charge us when they drew close enough. But it seemed that he had other plans.

'Back toward the wall!' Maram hissed at me.

I was reluctant to retreat from the line of the pillars to the wall, for there we would be trapped with no room to maneuver. And Morjin seemed loath to force this retreat. He stood at the center of the circular area staring at us across some seventy feet of the bare stone floor, and his guards stood there, too.

'No, hold here,' I said to Maram. 'Let's see what he's waiting for.'

A moment later, six red-robed men walked through the gate, down the line of the guards posted there and crossed the room to join Morjin. They were of various ages, heights and colorings, but they all had the long, lean, hungry look of wolves.

'The Red Priests!' Kane snarled out. 'Damn their eyes!'

Even as he said this, I felt a sharp stab of despair at the base of my skull, and men that I dreaded even more than these drinkers of blood entered the room. There were thirteen of them, all wearing hooded gray cloaks over their gray garments. Their faces were as gray as rotting flesh, while their eyes – what little we could see of them – were like cold gray marbles empty of life. There was nothing inside them, I thought, except a ravenous desire to drink *our* lives and our very souls.

'Oh, no!' Maram muttered as he stood trembling beside me. 'The Stonefaces!'

Liljana held one hand protectively over Daj's heart, while she gripped her gelstei in the other. She watched the thirteen Grays take their place inside the circle with Morjin. She said, 'It is they. I'm almost certain it was they who gave us away.'

Hearing this, Maram whispered, 'Then perhaps our friends are still safe. Perhaps they'll find a way to –'

'Hold your noise!' Kane snapped at him. 'And guard your thoughts!'

The leader of the Grays, a tall man with a pitiless contempt stamped into his stony face, turned his cold gaze upon me. A terrible fear suddenly pinned me back against the pillar as if a dozen lances of ice had pierced my body.

And then Liljana brought her little figurine up to her head, engaging his mind, fighting him and his dreadful company for all our sakes, and the lances suddenly snapped as I felt a new life returning to my chilled limbs.

'Liljana,' I said, looking at her. 'Can you hold them?'

Liljana stood valiantly facing the Grays. Her wise, willful eyes fought off their soul-sucking stares. Sweat poured down her deeply creased face. And she gasped out, 'I think I can . . . for a while.'

Mighty was the power of the blue gelstei, I thought, and mighty was the mind of Liljana Ashvaran. A surge of hope shot through me then. But not for us: I could only pray that Atara and the others would discover that we had been taken and that Liljana's valor would give them time to flee Argattha.

And then, as if Morjin could read *my* mind, he turned toward the still-open gate. His gloat of victory disfigured his fine face. My heart almost broke to see two guards dragging Atara into the throne room in chains. Another likewise led Master Juwain toward the ritual area. And then five men, each pulling at long chains like leads on a mad dog, strained to jerk the furiously struggling Ymiru into the room. Five more men followed him with chains pulled tight around the shackles binding his huge wrist, neck and waist. His black Saryak's robe had been stripped from him. Blood stained his fur where the shackles cut into him. It took all the strength of these ten large men to control him and move him toward the circle where Morjin stood with his priests, guards and the terrible Grays.

Seeing the guards manhandle Atara, I lifted up Alkaladur and took a step forward. Its blade radiated my hate. And then Morjin, his eyes fixed fearfully on my bright sword, finally spoke to me. His words rang out like steel into the hall: 'If you come any closer, Valashu Elahad, she will be killed.'

The Red Priests swarming over Atara, I saw, had jeweled knives fastened onto their belts. And the Grays, of course, had their knives drawn: gray-steel daggers as sharp as death. The guards deployed around the circle pointed their swords, halberds and spears at Kane and me.

'Chain her!' Morjin commanded his guards. He turned his golden eyes upon Master Juwain and the raging Ymiru. 'Chain them, too!'

Guards came forward with hammers then, and beat at our friends' chains with a dreadful clang of metal against metal. They bound them to the iron rings sunk into the standing stones. With the cruel chains pulling their arms straight out from their sides, they could barely move.

My fear for Atara – and for Master Juwain, Ymiru and all of us – almost chained *me* back against the pillar. I could only gaze helplessly into Atara's clear blue eyes as I held my sword at my side and waited for Morjin to speak.

The Lord of Lies seemed steeped in thought as he paced around the circle. He had ordered Ymiru's club and Atara's bow and arrows, like the key to Daj's shackles, placed on the floor just beyond their reach. There too lay Master Juwain's varistei, Ymiru's purple gelstei and Atara's crystal sphere. Now Morjin came over and held his hands above the gelstei as if to draw up their power. He glanced at Ymiru's great, iron-shod club and nudged it with his boot. He bent to slip a feathered arrow from Atara's quiver; he stood staring at the sharp, steel point. Then, as if remembering other times when he had held court here, he looked down at the dark etchings in the floor. I suddenly took keen note of what I had so far scarcely perceived: that the stonework of the ritual area was carved with a great, coiled dragon. The dragon's head formed the very center of the circle, and its mouth was open as if to swallow the blood that must run through the grooves in the dark, sticky stone.

'All right then,' he called out as the doors closed, 'we may begin.'

His voice, as I remembered from my nightmares, was clear and strong like the ringing of a silver bell. But now that we had finally met in the flesh, here in the fastness of his hall, he seemed to have abandoned all desire to charm or persuade me. His smiles were chill and full of malice, as little alluring as the stare of a snake. His manner was brusque and cruel as if he had come to mete out justice with an iron hand.

'Stay where you are, Valari!' he suddenly commanded me. 'I would speak with you but I don't wish to shout!'

He summoned twenty of his guards and his Red Priests to walk slowly toward us where we stood by the line of pillars. They drew up forty feet away with ten guards on either side of him. I knew that he wanted something from me.

'So,' Kane muttered, 'so.'

I could feel Kane's large body tensing to spring forward like a tiger's even as I trembled to hold back my own. His black eyes flashed fire at Morjin as he calculated numbers and distances. He held himself in check only because it was obvious that Morjin could retreat under cover to the circle before we could get at him.

Morjin turned to nod at the fiercest-looking of his priests, a man with the black skin of Uskudar and the dark, hungry eyes of the damned. He spoke to this priest, and to his other men, saying, 'Well, Lord Salmalik, it's as I've foretold. The enemy has sent assassins to murder me.'

He pointed a long, elegant finger back toward the circle at Ymiru and said, 'It's obvious that the Ymanish led them here. No doubt out of vengeance, bearing his people's false claim. Do you see what comes of the bitterness of believing ancient lies?'

'It be *you* who lies!' Ymiru roared out as he lunged against his chains. 'Argattha be *our* hrome!'

Morjin nodded at a guard, who slammed the butt end of his spear into Ymiru's face, smashing his teeth and bloodying his lips. He shook his dazed head slowly back and forth as Morjin continued to address him:

'Your people were paid good gold for the work they did here,' he said. 'And they did good work, it's true, but there is much we've improved upon.'

Ymiru stared down at the dragon carved into the floor, then cast his eyes upon the dragon throne. Finally he turned to look at the Red Dragon himself as he said, 'You've taken a hroly place and made it into something hrorrible!'

Again Morjin nodded at his guard. This time the man thrust the point of his spear into Ymiru's side, tearing open a bloody hole in his fur.

'Thus to assassins,' Morjin called out.

His golden eyes now fell upon Master Juwain. 'For ages, the Brotherhoods have opposed us. And now the Great White Brotherhood sends one of its Masters – a Master Healer, no less – to slay rather than mend body and soul together.'

Master Juwain stared fearlessly at Morjin and opened his mouth as if to gainsay this lie. But, mindful of the guard's bloody spear, he decided that there was little point in disputing Morjin.

'If he touches him,' Maram said, looking at Master Juwain, 'I'll . . .'

His voice suddenly died as he looked down at the red crystal in his hand. The cracked firestone was now useless and couldn't summon forth even a wooden match's worth of flame.

Now Morjin pointed the arrow that he still held at Atara. He called out, 'Princess Atara Ars Narmada, daughter of the usurper of the realm that still belongs to us! The Manslayer who must have seen me dead beneath her assassin's arrows! Well, scryer, what future do you see now?'

I, too, wondered what Atara saw; she stared at the figures of the fallen Galadin carved into the walls, and her eyes were full of horror.

I recalled the last part of Ayondela Kirriland's prophecy, that the dragon would be slain. Well, the dragon named Angraboda *had* been slain, but Morjin must have feared that the prophecy really spoke of him. Could it be, I wondered, that he truly thought we were assassins? Was it possible that he didn't know our real reason for entering Argattha?

He mustn't know then, I thought. *At all costs, he mustn't know.*

Morjin turned away from Atara toward us where we took shelter beneath the pillars. He pointed at Daj, and spoke with great bitterness: 'Well, young Dajarian, I've been merciful, but this time for you, it's the cross.'

Daj pulled back behind Liljana, who was still fighting off the Grays. He began trembling as he cast his eyes about the room like a trapped fawn.

'And Prince Maram Marshayk,' Morjin said, looking at my best friend. 'Why *you* have joined this conspiracy is a mystery to me.'

'Ah, it's a mystery to me as well,' Maram muttered. He, too, trembled to flee, but he held his ground bravely even so.

'And Liljana Ashvaran,' Morjin said, watching her stare down the leader of the Grays. 'At least your motives are more obvious, witch.'

He added his dreadful stare to that of the Grays, trying to beat open her mind. And I shouted, 'Leave her alone! She's just a poor widow!'

Morjin suddenly smiled at me and said, 'Is that what you've thought? She's the Materix of the Maitriche Telu. The ruling witch herself.'

Liljana's eyes were fixed on the Grays, but some flicker of pride fired up inside her then, and I knew that Morjin had told true.

'Well, witch, did you keep this a secret from your companions?'

Kane, I thought from the look on his face, *might* have known Liljana's true rank. And so might have Atara. But this news clearly amazed Maram, Master Juwain and Ymiru – as it did me.

Morjin nodded at the priest named Salmalik and said, '*Maitriche Telu*, do you see? Poisoners and assassins, all of them. If not for men such as you, they would have murdered their way to the rule of Ea long ago.'

At being singled out for praise, Lord Salmalik swelled with pride. But Morjin hadn't saved his accolades for him alone. He walked among his priests and guards, here smiling at an old priest as if giving thanks for long service, there placing his hand on a young man's arm to show his gratitude for his risking his life on Morjin's behalf. The Lord of Lies, I saw, was a great seducer who made a show of his preeminence and played to his people's desires with all the skill of a magician.

At a nod from Morjin, the leader of the Grays suddenly looked away from Liljana. And she turned to me and said, 'I *am* the Materix of the Maitriche Telu. Perhaps I should have told you – I'm sorry, Val.'

Liljana, I thought, had given me a dozen clues that this was so. Why hadn't I seen this?

'And we have killed,' she went on, 'but only when we've had to.'

My amazement only deepened. The Maitriche Telu, it was said, had secret sanctuaries and chapter houses in almost every land. If Morjin was more powerful than any king, even King Kiritan, then Liljana was the most powerful woman in Ea.

'But Morjin lies,' she told me, 'when he says that we desire rule. We seek only to restore Ea to the ancient ways.'

'You might want to be careful whom you call a liar, old witch,' Morjin snapped at her. He pointed at another iron ring on the side of the standing stone to which Atara was bound. 'It's an evil tongue you have, and I might decide to tear it out.'

Liljana pointed her figurine at the Grays and said, 'Of course you speak of such things – that's the only way you have to silence me.'

Morjin turned back toward the Grays' leader. Something seemed to pass back and forth unspoken between them. And then, as if explaining this exchange to his Red Priests and guards, Morjin said to him, 'Soon enough you shall have the witch's blue gelstei. And the black stone that was stolen from your brother.'

Now Morjin whirled about facing Kane. Their eyes locked together like red-hot iron rings hammered into a chain. Emotions as fiery and deep as a volcano's molten rock blasted out into the room. It was impossible for me to tell whose hate was vaster, Morjin's or Kane's.

'*You*,' Morjin said to him. 'You dare to come here again.'

'So, I do dare.'

'What is it you call yourself now – "Kane"?'

'What is it you call *yourself* now – King of Kings? Ha!'

Morjin stood before his priests and snapped at Kane, 'I should have torn out *your* tongue long ago!'

'Do you think it wouldn't have grown back in the mouths of ten thousand others to tell the truth of who you really are?'

'Be careful of what you say!'

'So, I'm free to speak as I will.'

'For the moment.' Morjin's face flushed with rage, and he pointed at the iron rings sticking out the side of Ymiru's stone. He said, 'When you're chained there, who will set you free?'

'Ask that,' Kane said, pointing his sword at Morjin, 'after you've put me there.'

Morjin stared so hard at Kane that his eyes seemed to redden from burst blood vessels. And he demanded, 'Give me the stone!'

Kane held up the black gelstei that he had cut from the Gray's forehead in Alonia on the night of the full moon. And then he snarled out, 'Take it from me!'

My old suspicions of Kane came flooding back into me. I wondered for the thousandth time at his grievance against Morjin. It seemed they had known each other long ago in another place.

Morjin saw me looking at Kane, and he turned his spite upon me. He said, 'You've taken a madman into your company, Valari.'

'Do not speak so,' I told him, 'of my friends.'

'Kane, your friend?' Morjin sneered. He pointed at Alkaladur, which I held gleaming by my side. 'He's no more your friend than that is your sword.'

I knew from the pounding of his heart that he feared this bright blade as he did death. It seemed that he could hardly bear to look at it.

'Alkaladur,' he said softly. 'How did you find it?'

'It was given to me,' I told him.

I sensed that the sword's shimmering presence made him recall dark moments in dark ages long past, as well as visions yet to come. I knew, as he did, that it had been foretold that the sword would bring his death.

'Surrender the sword to me, Valari!' he suddenly shouted. 'Surrender it, now!'

This sudden command, breaking from his throat like a clap of thunder, shocked every nerve in my body. His golden eyes dazzled me; the tremendous power of his will beat at my bones, almost breaking *my* will to keep hold of my sword.

'Surrender and save yourself!' he told me. 'And save your friends.'

What need, I wondered, had Morjin of his Grays when he had his own mind and malice to poison others? As his eyes found mine, the hatred that poured out of him smothered me like burning pitch. The Red Dragon, in the flesh, was far worse than in any of my illusions or dreams. Only my resolve to oppose him – magnified by the shielding powers of my sword – kept me from falling down and groveling at his feet.

'Do you see how strong the Valari are?' Morjin said, turning to the leader of the Grays. Then he looked at Salmalik and his other Red Priests. 'And so the savages send one of their strongest to murder me.'

I stared at him down the length of the shining sword that I pointed at him. I *did* badly want to murder him. How could I deny this?

'Conspirators, thieves and murderers,' he said. 'They defiled my chambers. And they would have trapped and tortured me there, if they could have.'

This, of course, was a lie. But how could I deny it without giving away our purpose?

Lord Salmalik caught Morjin's eye and said, 'Torture, Sire?'

Morjin nodded his head and spoke to all gathered in the room: 'These seven, save the Ymanish, all journeyed to Tria to the lure of Kiritan's illicit summons. They've made quest for the Lightstone across half of Ea. I'm certain that they've gathered clues as to where it was hidden.'

He doesn't know! I thought. *He truly doesn't know that the Lightstone lies somewhere in this room*!

'And these clues,' he continued, 'led them here. To me. They must have thought that *I* possess the key clue to their stealing of what is rightfully mine. And so they came to torture this knowledge from me.'

I held myself very still, staring at him. And he said to me, 'Do you deny this, Valari?'

No, I thought, I couldn't. But neither could I affirm such a lie. And so held myself cloaked in silence.

'Do you see how proud the Valari is?' Morjin said to Salmalik. 'Proud and vain – it is the curse of his kind. Telemesh. Aramesh. Elemesh. Murderers, all. How many have been slaughtered in wars because of them? Because they, who are savages at heart, put their glory above others? Descendants of Elahad they claim to be! Elahad, whom the Valari claim brought the Lightstone to Ea. Elahad, the murderer of his own –'

'Elahad *did* bring the Lightstone to Ea!' I shouted. 'The Valari were its guardians!'

'Be quiet while I'm speaking!' Morjin roared at me. He turned to look back at the ritual area and touch eyes with his guards, who stood in rapt attention. 'Do you see how the Valari twists this false claim of guardianship into an excuse to break into my home and torture me? From such a people, are any outrages impossible?'

'You lie!' I said to him.

Morjin paused to stare at me as he gathered in his breath. He was working himself up into a frenzy of spite. And now his all hate fell upon me like an infected wound bursting with pus.

'Look at the Valari standing there!' he said to his priests. 'So tall in his arrogance! The long sword. The black eyes – who has ever seen such eyes outside nightmares where demons haunt the dark? Many have said that the Valari have made a pact with demons. But I say they are demons themselves – fiends from hell. They are a plague upon the world; they are a stab in the back of the body of humanity; they are a corruption of

746

all that is good and true. It's in their blood, like poison. The taint goes back to the beginning of time. But it will have an ending, in time, an antidote of fire and steel. Haven't I foretold that if war comes, this last war we've all been dreading, that the Valari race will disappear from the face of the earth? That race of warlords and savages has on its conscience the dead of every great conflict in Ea's history. Would it be too much to ask that they be given new homes in the Red Desert or on trees that shall grow out of the ground in entire forests to accommodate them?'

Once before, I thought, after the battle of Tarshid, Morjin had put a thousand Valari warriors on such 'trees.' And now he proposed the slaughter of the whole Valari people. Or did he?

'It's not entirely disadvantageous,' he went on, 'that rumor attributes to us the plan for carrying out this fate. Terror can be a salutary thing.'

How, I wondered, could Morjin speak with such passion and conviction when he must have known the enormity of his deceit? In looking at my sword's shining silustria, a terrible thought came to me. People believe what they see others believing most strongly. Long ago, Morjin had perfected those expressions, gestures and intonations of voice designed to convince his followers that he believed his own lies. And after hundreds of years, this greatest of deceits had worked an evil alchemy upon Morjin: it had overcome him and his sense of the real so that he truly *did* believe his lies. This communicated to his audiences like lightning. And thus shocked into frenzies of false faith, his listeners returned his passion to him and further strengthened his own belief.

His own lies had possessed him, I thought. And so he had made of himself a ghul.

For a moment, I was moved to pity him. But the gleam in his golden eyes told me that he would use any such emotions against me. As he now used his gift of *valarda* to further enchant and enslave his people.

Again he pointed at me as he thundered: 'The arrogance of the Valari! Who else could steal the Lightstone and keep it behind their mountains for most of an age? Is there a greater crime than this in all of history?'

I felt Morjin's hate beating at me like a hammer, directly from his heart to mine – as it beat at his guards and Grays and everyone else gathered in the hall.

Morjin stepped over to one of his priests, a young man whose handsome face was marred with patches of scar as if it had been burned by heated iron. I thought that he might possibly be the least cruel of the Red Priests. Morjin said to him, 'Lord Uilliam, if such criminals came into your care, what would you recommend be done with them?'

Morjin's eyes touched Lord Uilliam's; his tongue seemed to shoot invisible streams of relb at Lord Uilliam so that the young man's tongue caught up the flames of malice, and he said, 'Purify them with fire!'

Morjin breathed out the fire of his approval and set the young man's blood burning with a raging desire to punish his enemies.

'Oh, oh!' I heard Maram moan next to me. He stood by the great, black pillar, looking at Atara and the bloody Ymiru as he squeezed his ruined crystal.

Morjin next addressed an older priest whose long, narrow face and great beak of a nose gave him the appearance of a vulture. 'Lord Yadom, if such criminals were persuaded to tell of clues that helped you recover the Lightstone, what would you do with it?'

'I would bring it to you, Sire.'

'But what if I had been abducted for torture and imprisoned?'

Lord Yadom clearly understood that Morjin was testing him. And so he said, 'Then I would wait for your release.'

'What if you waited thirty years?'

'The Kallimun waited a hundred times as long for your release from Damoom.'

'Yes, but then you didn't have the Lightstone. Wouldn't you use it to free your own king?'

'I would *want* to, Sire,' Yadom said with apparent sincerity. 'But the Lightstone is not to be used this way.'

Morjin stared at him and then called out into the hall: 'Wise Yadom! Is anyone wiser than the first of my priests?'

Even as he said this, his golden eyes seemed to swell like suns. And Yadom swelled with overweening pride, like a flower too full of nectar. Morjin's faith in Yadom that he beamed forth was so pleasurable that it made my whole body shudder.

And so it went as he paced about the room, here pausing to question one of his guards, there nodding at one of the Grays or his priests. He played to his people: with cunning words that fell easily off his silver tongue, with long, soulful looks, with veiled threats and promises and deceits. One man he flattered; another he frightened; too many his malice opened like a black knife and set loose their animal ferocity. I hated how Morjin perverted the gift we both had been given: he played men like instruments, plucking at their heartstrings as if he were a twisted minstrel making the most evil of music.

Morjin nodded across the hall at one of his guards, who brought a brazier heaped with hot coals into the ritual circle. He set it down in front of Atara, Ymiru and Master Juwain, and then thrust a pincers and three long, pointed irons into the coals to heat them.

'The Lightstone *will* soon be recovered,' Morjin shouted. 'Haven't

I foretold that this is the time when it will again be seen in this hall? And what should be done with this cup when it returns to its rightful place?'

One of his guards, an old soldier with a grim face and a strange hunger in his eyes, knew the right answer to this question. And he called out, 'Pour from it eternal life!'

Now every pair of eyes in the hall fixed on Morjin. His men looked at him with an almost electric anticipation.

'Eternal life!' Morjin suddenly cried out. '*This* is the gift that the Lightstone may bestow upon men and its true purpose. But is it a gift for everyone? Can a beast appreciate a flute or a book placed into its paws? No, and so it is that only those chosen to receive the true gold of the Lightstone will ever know immortality.'

As Kane stared at Morjin defiantly, I suddenly understood that the powerful seek power for its own sake because it gives them the illusion that they have power over death.

But fear of death, I thought, *leads to hate of life*.

With these few words, whispered inside my mind, I knew that I had condemned myself should the door that *I* most feared be flung open before me. For Morjin, with all his vainglory and hate, was like a mirror reflecting back at me a shape that I did not want to see.

'And who are these chosen?' Morjin continued. He nodded sternly at Lord Uilliam and Lord Yadom. 'They are the priests who have served the Kallimun so faithfully; they are my guards and soldiers who have given their lives for a greater purpose, and so it is only fitting that they shall have greater life themselves.'

Morjin, the sorcerer who had lived thousands of years, stood before his men as the living embodiment that what he promised was possible.

'And who,' he quietly asked, 'shall be the one to pour the nectar of immortality from the golden cup? Only the Maitreya. But who *is* this man? That will be determined only when the Lightstone is placed in his hands.'

So saying, he reached his hands out to the hundred and twenty men who had followed him into the room. In their many eyes was a terrible lust for the Lightstone and all that Morjin had vowed to give them. And then a remarkable thing occurred. As if light itself were pouring out of his hands, he used the *valarda* to touch all who gazed upon him with bliss.

'So,' Kane muttered next to me. There came a rumbling sound of hate from deep inside his throat. 'So.'

All people have a love and longing for the One, for that is our source, at once father and mother and breath of the infinite in which we take our being. And Morjin had tried to fool people into turning this love onto him. In his smile was the false promise of all joy and happiness, but in the end he would bring the world only sorrow and death.

Now he turned to me and said, 'You've taken a vow to seek the Lightstone. And now you can fulfill it by helping us to recover it. You must help us, Valari.'

I gripped my sword more tightly as I fought off the waves of bliss that he beamed at me. It was strange to think that he wanted my hate and fear less than he did my love.

'Surrender your sword,' he again commanded me. 'Surrender yourself.'

'No,' I said, my heart beating fast like a bird's.

'You must surrender, Valari.'

He stood before me with his fingers outstretched as if waiting for me to place my sword in his hands. His eyes called to me. I knew that he required the surrender of my will and all my adoration so that he might counterfeit a sense of the One within himself.

'Is it death you want?' he asked me. His eyes now seemed as golden as the Lightstone itself. 'Or life?'

I took a few deep breaths to slow the racing of my heart. And then I said, 'It's not upon you to give me either.'

'Is it not? That we shall see.'

I lifted my sword back behind my head in readiness should Morjin send his guards against us. And I told him, 'I'll never surrender to you!'

My contempt for Morjin was in my eyes for all to behold. Even if I hadn't possessed the gift of *valarda*, not a man in the hall would have been spared feeling my defiance.

'Damn you, Valari!' he suddenly thundered at me. His face contorted into a mask of ugliness as rage took hold of him. If he couldn't have love, he was ready to embrace hate. 'Never surrender, you say? That, too, we shall see.'

He shook Atara's arrow at me, and then pointed its head back at the circle directly at Master Juwain. He shouted, 'What is it *you* know about the Lightstone?'

'What?' Master Juwain said as if he didn't quite understand the question.

'Didn't you hear me?' Morjin roared out. Upon beckoning Lord Uilliam to follow him, he turned and strode back into the circle. He plucked one of the irons from the brazier and handed it to Lord

Uilliam. 'Master Juwain's ear is stopped with wax – clean it out.'

As Lord Uilliam gazed at the iron's glowing red point, Morjin commanded the guards still posted near the door to join the others around the circle. They took their places there, and Lord Uilliam looked over at Master Juwain, sweating and biting his lip as he pulled at the chains that bound him to the standing stone.

'Put it in his ear!' Morjin commanded.

Lord Uilliam still hesitated, and he said, 'But he's just an old man!'

'Do it!' Morjin hissed.

'I can't, Sire.'

Morjin grabbed the iron from Lord Uilliam's trembling hand and pointed it at Master Juwain. He said, 'He is old, but *is* he a man?'

I didn't know what he meant; I didn't want to know. Beside me, Maram now had his sword drawn, as did Liljana and Kane. I was ready to charge forward in an effort to cut our way through to Master Juwain – and to Ymiru and Atara. But we were only four against a hundred.

'Be strong,' Kane said to me. 'You must be strong now, eh?'

Morjin now turned to Lord Uilliam; it seemed for a moment that he might put the iron in *him* for failing to do his bidding. But he surprised me. He drew up closer to the young man, and laid his arm about his shoulder as he bent his head to whisper in his ear. From seventy feet away, I could not hear what he said to him. But I had a keen sense that he was trying to persuade his priest that Master Juwain was not really a man at all but some kind of beast.

'It's hard, I know,' Morjin called out so that everyone could hear him. Compassion seemed to pour from him like rain.

'Sire?' Lord Uilliam said as Morjin gave him back the iron. He looked at Master Juwain.

I looked at him, too. His face, tight with fear, seemed even uglier than it usually did. It was all twisted and knotted with lumps, bristly like a boar's and scarcely human.

'Do as I've commanded you!' Morjin said to Lord Uilliam.

And then his eyes fell upon Lord Uilliam, and he breathed the terrible fire of his wrath into him. Lord Uilliam suddenly stiffened as if he could feel the heat of the iron up through his hand and all throughout his body. He turned to step closer to Master Juwain. As one of the guards slammed Master Juwain's head back against the standing stone and held it clamped there, Lord Uilliam pushed the burning point of the iron into the opening of Master Juwain's ear. There came a hissing and the stench of burnt flesh.

Lord Uilliam snarled and gnashed his teeth together; he kept pushing the iron deeper, twisting it, reaming it around in circles as his hate poured out of him.

'Master Juwain!' Maram called out, and he burst into tears.

The pain burning through my head was so great that I could barely keep standing. But the sheer valor with which Master Juwain faced his torture sent a thrill of strength shooting through me. Not once did he cry out for mercy. His whole body quivered with the shock of what the priest was doing to him. Although his face contorted with agony, I saw that it was really beautiful after all – beautiful with a luminous will that overmatched Morjin's and kept him from surrendering his soul to him.

'Master Juwain!' Maram cried out again. 'Master Juwain!'

True men, I thought looking at Maram, didn't need the gift of *valarda* to suffer another's pain.

At last, the iron's point quenched in Master Juwain's blood, Lord Uilliam stood away from him. His face was white; he held the iron in his trembling hand. He could barely stand himself. Morjin stepped closer to him, and wrapped his arm around his back to help hold him up.

'Well done, my priest,' Morjin told him. He touched his finger to the iron's bloody point; then he touched his finger to his tongue. 'Have I not said many times that the priests of the Kallimun must do the hard things and so sacrifice themselves for the sake of Ea?'

After Lord Uilliam could stand on his own again, Morjin shook his fist at Master Juwain and shouted, 'Is this what you wanted? That you, a master healer, should cause such sickness in my priest's soul?'

But I did not think that Master Juwain could hear him, even with his remaining good ear. His head had fallen down against his chest, and the weight of his body pulled against the chains binding him.

'Where is the Lightstone?' Morjin screamed at him. He stepped over and slapped Master Juwain's face. 'What have you learned about it?'

Master Juwain finally opened his eyes and lifted up his head. His gray eyes blazed with defiance. And he told Morjin, 'Only that you'll never have from it what you wish.'

Again Morjin slapped Master Juwain's face, which snapped his head back against the great stone. He looked at the greatly enlarged red hole in Master Juwain's ear. And he said to him, 'I would be doing you a favor to order your death. But until I know where the Lightstone is, I'm not permitted to extend such mercies.'

He motioned for his six priests to gather around him. He stood talking to them in hushed tones as the thirteen silent Grays waited nearby and the hundred guards circled the ritual area with the steel of their swords and spears. It was a mortar of torture and blood-crime that bound this evil brotherhood together. It was well for them, I thought, that they hid their secrets inside the windowless vaults of a black mountain.

'Val,' Maram whispered to me as he stared at the standing stones. He was sweating even more profusely than Master Juwain. 'Stab your sword into my heart – I don't think I have the courage to fall on mine.'

'Be strong!' Kane called to him. 'Strong as stone now, I say!'

Maram closed his eyes then. It was said that the Brotherhoods taught meditations that could forever still the beating of one's heart. But it seemed that Maram had been too busy with other pursuits to learn them.

'I can't,' he finally said, looking at me. 'I can't will myself to die.'

'Will *them* to die!' Kane growled out, pointing his sword at Morjin and his priests.

Now Morjin stepped over to Atara and looked at her, and a new terror struck into me. Atara looked back at him boldly, her eyes as clear as diamonds. There was a terrible fear in their bright blue depths, but something else as well. It seemed that she was seeing the future and trying to surrender herself to what must be. This was *her* will, as a warrior and a woman, to fulfill her purpose in being born on such a savage world as Ea.

'Don't you ever look at me like that!' Morjin suddenly raged at her. He slapped her face with his left hand, turning her head, and then backhanded her, turning her head again. But she summoned up all her courage and held her head up proudly as she continued to stare at him. I sensed that she was seeing something in him that no one else could see.

'Damn you!' he snarled out, slapping her again and bloodying her mouth. Then he whirled about to face me. 'And damn *you*, Valari!'

He paused to catch his breath. Then he called out, 'Lay down your sword!'

I turned to catch Kane's stare and said, 'Let's charge them now and make an end to this.'

Kane eyed the hundred guards waiting around the circle, and he said, 'It would be our death.'

'There's no help for that now.'

'No – there may yet be a chance.'

'What, then?'

Kane's dark eyes picked over the walls of the room, the great throne, the pillars and the bolted iron doors. Then he said, 'I wish I knew.'

Morjin, hating to be ignored, waved Atara's arrow at me and shouted again: 'Lay down your sword and I will spare your woman!'

'No!' Atara cried out to me. 'You must never surrender!'

'Do it!' Morjin hissed at me. 'Now!'

'No!' Atara said again. 'The sword is his death – can't you see how he fears it?'

Morjin tore his gaze from my flashing sword to stare at Atara. And then he screamed at her, 'And what do you fear, scryer? Not death, I think. And scarcely pain. Something worse. What is it you see when you look at *my* eyes now? Look as long as you can, scryer – look deep.'

Atara looked at him in utter loathing and contempt, and then spat the blood from her broken lip straight into his eyes.

'Damn you!' he shouted. He wiped his sleeve across his face and blinked furiously. He shook the arrow at her and cried out, 'Is this one of the arrows you shot into my son's eyes?'

I stood almost unable to breathe watching the rage flow into Morjin's face as I remembered the deadly accuracy of Atara's arrows in the darkness of the Vardaloon.

'Meliadus,' Atara said clearly for all to hear, 'was a monster.'

'HE WAS MY SON!'

Morjin screamed this so loudly that the rock of the archways three hundred feet above the circle rang with his anguish and wrath. He suddenly reached out with his left hand and grabbed Atara's long hair. He slammed her head back against the standing stone and held it there. And then, with blinding speed, he stabbed the arrow's barbed point into her left eye. It took only a moment for him to rip it free and plunge the bloody steel straight through the center of her right eye.

I surged forward then to kill as many priests and guards as I could in my rage to get at Morjin. But Kane suddenly grabbed me from behind and wrapped his iron arm around my throat. Maram grabbed my right arm; Liljana held fast to my left. From somewhere behind me, I heard Daj screaming and cursing and gasping out his fear of Morjin, all at once.

Morjin didn't even pause to glance at me. He cast down the bloody arrow. And then, like a bird of prey, like a rabid cat, like the demon he truly was, he fell upon Atara with all his fury and hate. He spat and hissed as he drove his clawlike fingers into her face. He stood fastened to her, shaking and snarling and gouging, pulling ferociously, tearing at her – driving his fingers beneath her brows and tearing out her eyes. He suddenly jumped back and held the bloody orbs up for all to see. Then he crossed over to the brazier and cast these lumps of flesh into the burning coals.

For a long time, it seemed, my world went dark, and I could not see for the terrible burning that blinded my own eyes. A high, hideous scream broke upon the hall. At first I thought it was Atara giving voice to what Morjin had done to her; then I realized that the sound had been torn from deep inside me. When I could finally see again, it was not by virtue of the glowstones' dim light but only the hate that filled my heart and head and utterly possessed me. I looked over at the circle to see Atara shaking and sobbing as she wept blood instead of tears from her reddened eye hollows. Morjin stood holding a cup to her cheek, catching the blood that flowed out of them. More blood – a whole ocean of it, it seemed – flowed off Atara's chin in streams. It fell to the floor and ran through the dark grooves cut into the stone there; it disappeared into the dragon's open mouth like water gurgling down a hole.

Kane's arm was an iron collar bound around my throat; his body behind me was a pillar of stone that I could not break or pull down. And his breath in my ear was the red-hot flame of vengeance: 'Damn Morjin and all his kind!'

Now Morjin stood back from Atara and gazed at her ruined face. He took a drink from the cup that he held in his bloody hands. Then he passed it to Lord Yadom, who likewise drank from it before passing it on to another priest.

With great effort, Atara pulled back her head and oriented it facing Morjin, as if she could smell or sense his presence. Her heart beat with her contempt for him. And then an incredible thing happened. I perceived Morjin as she had, just before her blinding. The mask of illusion was suddenly ripped away from him, and he stood revealed as he truly was: no longer beautiful in face and form, but rather terrible and ghastly to behold. His eyes were not golden at all. They were a sickly red, with pigments of ocher and iron settled into the irises, while the whites were bloodshot as if he was never able to sleep. His pale, mottled skin was likewise disfigured with a webwork of broken blood vessels. There were pouches under his eyes, and much of his limp, grayish hair had fallen out. In the skin that drooped from his neck and in his predatory countenance was a ravenous hunger for vitality and lost love.

I knew that I would never be able to see him otherwise again. As his tongue darted out like a snake's and he licked the blood from his lips, I saw something else: that he had blinded Atara not because of Meliadus but because she had seen through the veil of his most precious illusion and had shown him in the mirror of her eyes what an evil being he truly was.

He knows! I suddenly realized. *All this time, he has known!*

Somewhere, beneath the lies and trickeries that he crafted for himself and others, lived a man who knew very well the wrong of what he did – and chose to do it anyway. And why? Because people were less than animals to him.

What is hate? It is a black abyss full of fire hotter than a dragon's breath. It is a poison that burns a thousand times as painfully as kirax. It is a black and bitter bile that gathers at the center of one's being, seething to a boil. It is a stabbing pain in the heart, a pressure in the head, a gathering in of all the world's anguish and an overwhelming desire to make another suffer as you have. It is lightning. But not the thunderbolt of illumination, but rather its opposite which maims and burns and blinds. And its name is *valarda*.

MORJIN!

As he had once promised I would, I struck out at him with the gift that the angels had bestowed upon me. Something very like a thunderbolt of pure, black hate shot out from my heart along the line of my sword and struck his heart. It staggered him. He gasped as he stared at me in astonishment. He dropped to one knee, gasping and clutching at his chest, even as Kane held me from behind and kept me from collapsing in the sudden agony of what I had done to him.

'Oh, Valari!' Morjin gasped as he struggled to breathe.

I, myself, had stopped breathing. For few moments, I think, my heart stopped beating, too, and I nearly died. And then, as Morjin regained his strength, I felt hate pouring into my limbs again and firing up my being.

'Oh, Valari!' Morjin said again as he stood up and gazed at me. On his pale, fell face was a look of utter triumph. '*That* is the last time you'll catch me off-guard. You're stronger than I would have believed, but there's much you have to learn. Shall I show you how it's done?'

So saying, he whirled upon Atara and fixed her with his terrible red eyes. A storm of hate gathered inside him. His heart beat in rhythm with mine.

'No!' I cried.

'Then throw down your sword!'

'No!' I cried again.

'What befalls your woman now,' he said, pointing at her, 'is upon you.'

'No, that's not true!'

'You'll see her die, but not until *you've* died a thousand times.' And with that, he stepped over to the brazier and removed the glowing pincers.

'Damn you!' I screamed at him.

'Damn *you*, Valari, for making me do this!' He looked at the pincers' red-hot iron and shouted, 'I'll tear out her vile tongue and roast it on the coals! I'll send lepers to ravish her! I'll give her to the rats and let you watch as they eat what's left of her face!'

The thirteen Grays, with their cold eyes and long knives, stood in the circle of death with Morjin waiting to see what he would do. The six priests of the Kallimun looked pitilessly at Atara as they must have many other victims. The hundred guards ringing the circle waited with their swords and spears and axlike halberds. The whole world, it seemed, waited for me to speak or move.

'You must not surrender!' Atara suddenly called to me. She stood tall and brave and eyeless in eternity.

'In a moment, I'll tear out your tongue,' Morjin promised her. 'But first you *will* call for the Elahad to surrender.'

He took a step closer to her as I gripped my sword more tightly. Once before, in the land of nightmare, he had told me that the *valarda* was a double-edged sword. He, himself, could now only cut and kill with his. But it haunted him that I might still be able to open myself to others' joys and sufferings. Hating me for the grace that he had long ago lost, he fell into a sickening fury. I sensed that he wanted to test my compassion for Atara. It was his will to torture her terribly and for a long time. Because he hated her, yes, but more because he wanted to break me utterly. He wanted me perverted, crushed in spirit, enslaved. He wanted me to kneel before him in the sight of all the men gathered in the hall almost as much as he wanted the Lightstone itself.

'Atara,' I whispered.

What is hate? It is a wall ten thousand feet high surrounding the castle of despair. Since the moment that Morjin had blinded Atara, I had built this wall higher and higher so that I would not have to know what she really suffered. But now she had turned toward me, and in looking at the blood pooling in her eye hollows and dripping down her cheeks, her face emptied of all hope of that which she most deeply desired, this wall of stone suddenly split asunder as if the earth beneath it had cracked open. And I cried out in the greatest anguish I had ever known, for the love that bound Atara and me together was the greatest I had ever known.

'Hold!' I shouted to Morjin. 'Take me instead of Atara!'

The world, I knew, was a place of infinite suffering, infinite pain. In the end I was the weakest of our company. I could bear Atara's torture much less than she herself.

'Throw down, then!' Morjin called to me, turning away from Atara.

I shook myself free from Kane, who stared at me, waiting to see what I would do. And I shouted at Morjin, 'First free Atara!'

I looked at Master Juwain bound to his stone and at Ymiru pulling with his only whole arm against his chain. 'Free my friends, too! Let them leave Argattha!'

'No,' Morjin said to me. 'First throw down and step forward into our circle, and then I shall do as you ask.'

He stared at me, smiling triumphantly.

'Val, don't do it!' Liljana said to me, pulling on my arm. 'He lies!'

'So, his promise is worth rat dung,' Kane growled out.

I called out to Morjin, 'What surety do we have that you will keep your word?'

'I am King of Ea, and what more surety can there be?' he said. 'It is *we* who need surety, Valari. How is it to be believed that a proud Valari knight will go willingly to his death with no sword in his hand?'

I knew that he didn't believe that I would give my life in Atara's place, especially if it meant first untold days of hideous torture. And yet, he willed and wanted with every fiber of his being that I should make this surrender. His red eyes filled with a raging bloodlust that was terrible to behold.

How can I do what I must do? I asked myself.

Kane had said that there still might be a chance for us, and now I saw that there was. But not for me. I might buy my friends' lives with mine. Morjin had given his word before his priests and men, and there was a chance that he might keep it.

'Val!' Atara called to me.

What is love? It is the warm, healing breath of life that melts the bitterest ice. It is the hot pain of joy in one's heart impossible to quench. It is the fire of the stars that burns clean the soul. It is a simple thing – the simplest thing in the world.

'Atara,' I whispered as I looked at her. Her bloody, mutilated face, I thought, was the most beautiful thing I had ever seen.

I stood there facing the circle where Atara and my friends were bound, and my hands sweated to feel the diamonds in Alkaladur's hilt for the last time. There was a sickness in my belly; my chest ached with a crushing pain. Death waited there for me. My old enemy was cold and black and terrifying; it was a terrible emptiness that had no end. It didn't matter. In looking at Atara look toward me, so full of love, so full of light, I suddenly wanted to die for her. I burned with a fierce desire to accept any torment and annihilation in order to keep her living in the land of light.

'Well, Valari?' Morjin called out to me.

I glanced at him and nodded my head. Even if there was only one chance in ten thousand that he would spare Atara and my friends, I had to take it.

And then, even as I bent to lay Alkaladur down upon the dark stone of this vast, dark hall, at the darkest moment of my life, the Bright

Sword began shining with an intense radiance that I also felt inside myself. At that moment, the world was strangely full of light. For I, and I alone, suddenly saw the Lightstone everywhere: on top of pedestals and gleaming golden in the recesses of the rocky walls; on the altar near the throne and on tables and even shimmering amidst the red-hot coals in the brazier into which Morjin had cast his offering of flesh. The whole of the throne room blazed with a brilliant golden light. It blinded me to the Lightstone's true presence as surely as my flaws of fear and faithlessness had always blinded me to myself.

'Valari!' Morjin called to me.

And then Alkaladur flared silver-white, more brightly than it ever had before. In the mirror of the polished and perfect silustria of my sword, I saw who I really was: Valashu Elahad, son of Shavashar Elahad, who was the direct descendent of Telemesh and Aramesh and all the kings of Mesh going back to the grandsons of Elahad himself. In me still burned the soul of the Valari – we who long ago had brought the Lightstone to earth. The Valari, I suddenly remembered, were once guardians of the Lightstone, and would someday be again.

'Damn you, Valari, throw down now or I'll take your woman's tongue!'

But what or who were we to guard the Lightstone *for*? Not for glory or the ending of pain. Not for invulnerability or immortality or power. Not for the victory of the Maitriche Telu or the vengeance of Kane. Nor for great kings such as Kiritan who would give their daughters to triumphant warriors, nor even for wise queens such as the Lady of the Lake. And certainly not for false Maitreyas such as Morjin who would use it to work great evil instead of good.

The Lightstone is for one and one only, I thought. *The true Maitreya told of in the great prophecy, the Lightbringer who will arise from Ea to defeat the Lord of Darkness and lead all the worlds into a new age.*

To gain this cup and guard it so that I could place it in the Maitreya's hands was my purpose; it was my deepest desire and fate.

What is love? It is the radiance of the One; it is the blazing of the Morning Star in the eastern sky that calls men to wake up.

All my life, it seemed, I had worked to polish and sharpen the sword of my soul, rubbing away the rust and honing the steel finer and finer to put on it an exceedingly keen edge. And now, through a love beyond love, with the hand of the One bestowing this final grace, the polishing was at last completed and nothing of myself remained. And yet, paradoxically, everything. And so the true sword was revealed. It cut with an infinitely fine edge and was impossibly bright.

I suddenly stood straight and gripped Alkaladur more tightly. And with the deeper sword that the One had placed in my heart, I finally slew the great dragon whose names are Vanity and Pride. The evil of my hate left me. And then both swords, the one that I held in my hand and the other inside me, blazed like suns. The light was so intense that it completely outshone the illusions all around me and made the thousands of Lightstones that I saw simply disappear. And in this luminous state, my eyes finally opened and drank in the sight of *the* Lightstone.

As the songs had told, it was just a plain golden cup that would easily fit into the palm of my hand. And as Sartan Odinan had told, it still remained in the vast, dark hall where he had set it down thousands of years before. Even as Morjin and his priests shielded their eyes against the sheen of my sword, I looked to the south of the ritual circle at the great throne. And there, on top of the eye of the coiled red dragon that framed the throne, the Lightstone waited all golden and glorious as it always had.

'Valari!' Morjin called to me.

I somehow knew that if I could only hold the Lightstone in my hands, everything would come out all right. And so I broke from our shelter by the pillars and sprinted for the throne at the same moment that Morjin's voice filled the hall.

'Guards!' he called out. 'He's trying to run away!'

The hundred men of his Dragon Guard, no less his Red Priests and the murderous Grays, waited for him to order an attack. But Morjin, confused at my seeming cowardice, all the while realizing that there was something here that he didn't quite see, hesitated a heartbeat too long.

And in that moment, Flick suddenly appeared. From out of the hall's dark depths he streaked like a bolt of lightning straight toward the ritual circle. As I ran, I looked back over my shoulder to see Flick fall upon Morjin's face in swirls of white and violet sparks. Morjin, his eyes wide with astonishment, dropped the iron pincers to the floor and used his hands to try to beat Flick's fiery form away from his head. And he gasped out, 'Damn you, Valari! What is this trick of yours?'

It took me only a few seconds to reach the steps to the throne. I bounded up them, taking but little notice of the statues of the fallen Galadin that stared silently at me from their sides. I stood on the hard stone before the seat of the throne itself. I rested my sword there. And then I reached out and grasped the Lightstone in my hands.

Upon its touch, at once cool as grass and warm as Atara's cheek, Morjin's cries and the dark glitter of the hall faded away as in the passing of a dream. A deeper world blazed forth. Everything seemed touched with a single color, and that was glorre. The cup overflowed with shimmering cascades of light that fell over my hands and arms and every part of me. I felt its incredible sweetness through my skin and brightening my blood. Suddenly the cup began ringing with a single, pure note like a great golden bell. Then the gold gelstei of which the Lightstone was wrought turned transparent, and there was an astonishing clarity. Inside it were swirling constellations of stars – all the stars in the universe. Their light was impossibly deep; it was more brilliant and beautiful than anything I had ever beheld. I dissolved like salt into this infinite clear sea of radiance. And at last I knew the indestructible joy and bottomless peace of diving deep into the shimmering waters of the One.

When I returned to the throne room a single moment and ten thousand years later, I knew why the Lightstone's touch had killed Sartan Odinan. For the gold gelstei, far from healing my hurts, quickened my gift of *valarda* almost infinitely. Inside the cup was all of creation, and so long as I held it, I was open to all of its joy and pain.

Infinite pain, I whispered. And then, as I felt within myself the polishing of the true substance of which I was wrought, there came a greater realization: *But infinite capacity to bear it.*

And so I finally understood words that I had read once in the *Saganom Elu*: 'To drink in the world's suffering, you must become the ocean; to bear the burning of the fire, you must become the flame.'

I grasped the Lightstone, and all fear left me. And I smiled to see that I was holding only a small golden cup in my hand.

The others saw it, too. But only for a moment. As the face of everyone in the hall turned toward me, the gold of the Lightstone fell clear as a diamond crystal and began radiating light like the sun. Brighter and brighter grew this light until it poured out like the starfire of ten thousand suns. It dazzled the very soul, and for a few moments, blinded every pair of eyes in the hall save my own.

Morjin was especially stricken by this terrible and beautiful light. He stood at the center of the black circle on top of the dragon's open mouth, gasping in terror because he was suddenly more blind than Atara. And then, finally, with a sickening jolt, he realized why my friends and I had really entered Argattha. He saw that the brilliance of my sword had come not from my hate but from a deeper resonance that he had long been denied. And so he opened his mouth and let loose a terrible cry that filled all the hall:

VALARIII!

His raw, outraged voice shook the stones of the pillars to the sides of the throne even as he shook his head about and howled like a mad dog. His hatred was a terrible thing. It blasted out into the hall like the fire of a furnace from hell. He hated me, and all of us, with a black, bitter fury for keeping this secret from him. And even more, he hated his own blindness that had lasted thirty centuries and lasted still.

'Guards!' he screamed. 'Kill the Valari! Take the Lightstone!'

I saw that the Lightstone's radiance was now beginning to fade and would soon return to a simple golden sheen. After taking a last look at it, I tucked the little cup down beneath my mail shirt over my heart. And then, lifting up my bright, long sword, I hurried down the steps of the throne and rushed forward to do battle to defend it.

45

To be cast into darkness is the cruelest of fates. Morjin's sudden blindness struck terror into him. He waved his hand in front of his face and screamed out, 'Guards! To me! To me!'

Like writhing, sightless insects, his guards stumbled about and managed to swarm around Morjin and protect him with their frantically waving spears. More than one of these steel-tipped shafts pierced a hand or eye of a neighboring guard, and their screams fell out into the hall as well. I sensed that I had only moments before they regained their vision. And so I sprinted from the throne straight across the hall toward the circle where Atara, Ymiru and Master Juwain were bound.

Three guards, no doubt hearing the pounding of my boots against the floor, stabbed out their spears blindly to stop me. I parried their clumsy thrusts and cut them down. And then I pushed my way through other guards until I came to the standing stone holding up Atara. I swung Alkaladur twice, with great precision; its incredibly sharp silustria cut clean through her chains in a shriek of snapping iron. I wrapped my arm around her back as I led her over to Master Juwain's and Ymiru's stones and likewise freed them.

Four more guards tried to hinder me – or perhaps they were only fleeing *into* me in their blindness. I reddened my sword in the warm, wet sheaths of their bodies. I led Atara over to the part of the circle where our weapons and gelstei had been heaped. And then the still-blind Master Juwain and Ymiru.

It took only a moment for me to grab up Ymiru's great war club and press it into his remaining hand. He suddenly regained his vision even as his huge fingers closed around the haft.

'*Now* there be blood!' he roared out as his eyes leaped with light. He stood glaring at the nearby guards as I tucked his violet crystal into the pouch on his belt. 'Now they'll know what real hrorror be!'

As Master Juwain espied his green gelstei lying on the bloodstained floor, Ymiru raised up his club and began laying about Morjin's guards with a terrifying ferocity. Flesh and bones broke like eggshells with a sickening crunch as gouts of flesh sprayed out into the air. Four more men fell like bludgeoned chickens. The gargoyles carved into the walls and pillars of the hall – to say nothing of the statues of the fallen Galadin – smiled their hideous smiles to behold a bloody horror that would make even stone itself quail.

And all the while, Morjin kept screaming out, 'Guards! To me! To me!'

'Master Juwain!' I said as he held his crystal in front of Atara's face to stop the bleeding there. 'Stay close!'

Blood still trickled from his ruined ear, and he nodded his head.

'Atara!' I said, putting her sword into her hand. 'Stay by me!'

I worried that she would be too weak to stand; I didn't quite see how I could protect both her and the Lightstone in the battle that was building around us. And then she astonished me by moving precisely to gather up her bow and arrows as if she could sense how they lay on the floor. She strapped on her quiver and then turned her eyeless head toward me, saying, 'No, Val – stay with the others. I've men to slay.'

She smiled grimly and broke away from me; she took off at a run, dodging or stabbing guards who tried to block her way. When she had fought clear of the circle, she began running straight for Morjin's throne.

How is it possible! I wondered. *How is it possible that the sightless can see?*

I had no time to ponder this mystery. Even as Atara bounded up the throne's steps, leaped upon the seat of the throne and climbed up the face of the dragon to stand on top of its head, the sight began returning to our enemies, one by one. A few were so bold as to attack Ymiru or me, and these quickly died. But soon the entire host of Morjin's guard would be able to see us and direct their spears and halberds in a coordinated assault. And then they would surely cut us down.

'To me!' a strong voice called out like the roar of a lion. 'Val, to me!'

Across the circle, at its edge in the direction of the pillars and the hall's eastern gate, Kane had also regained the use of his eyes. He had wasted no time or pity in butchering Morjin's men; at least seven of them lay dead beneath his dripping sword. His efforts, however, weren't directed against these spear carriers and halberd wielders. It seemed that he was trying to slash his way toward Morjin, who stood near the center of the ritual area ringed by several circles of still-dazzled guards.

'Val, kill the Grays first, if you can!' Kane shouted.

Between Morjin and Kane gathered the thirteen Grays. These dreadful men might have paralyzed any and all of us but for the wrath of Liljana, who fought by Kane's side along with Maram. She held her blue gelstei up before her. I could almost feel it resonating with the Lightstone close to my heart and gaining great power. It seemed to pour forth an ethereal radiance like that of a hot blue star. So fierce was Liljana's attack upon the Grays' minds that they grabbed their heads and howled in helplessness. And Kane howled out as well, 'To me!' And then, with Maram fighting frantically by his side and covering him, he finally broke through the ring of guards around the Grays and began matching their long knives with his much longer sword. It took him only a few moments to slaughter all of them.

As the last of them fell, Liljana joined Kane in fixing her eyes on Morjin. And the Great Beast suddenly bellowed out, 'Get out of my mind, witch!'

I could almost feel the blast of pure mental fire that Morjin directed at Liljana. For a moment she stood utterly stricken. It was as if she stood writhing in the midst of all the flames of hell. And then she turned on him a terrible fire of her own.

Now many more of Morjin's guards were able to see, and they closed ranks to protect their lord. Kane, Maram and Liljana were forced to retreat back a few dozen yards toward the throne. Ymiru and I, with Master Juwain behind us, fought our way around the edge of the circle and joined them a hundred feet from the throne and about as far from the line of pillars to the east. It was an exposed position with the bare, black stone of the floor all around us. Behind us rose the dragon throne, upon which Atara now stood holding her great, curved bow. Ahead of us was the mass of guards shielding Morjin inside the circle. For us, I saw, further retreat would be futile; soon Morjin's men would drive us back to the corner of the room. And so I called for us to form up into a five-pointed star: I stood facing Morjin, with Kane on my right and Ymiru on my left. Maram and Liljana stood farther back, with Master Juwain in the star's center.

At that moment, Atara loosed the first of her arrows. It burned through the air and struck through the face of a tall guard standing in front of Morjin. Atara cried out, 'Sixty-one!' Then, in quick succession, three more arrows sang out and found their marks in the guards surrounding Morjin. She would have slain the great Red Dragon himself if Morjin and his priests hadn't ducked down beneath their shields of living flesh.

'Atara!' I cried out. 'Kill the captains first!'

I didn't understand how Atara's arrows found these four steel-clad men. It took her only six more shots to send them on to the stars. As death rained down all about Morjin and he cowered at the center of the circle, his naked fear beat out into the room.

He was perhaps the last person in the hall to regain his sight. As he finally did, and one of his priests pointed out where Atara stood on top of his throne with her great bow like an angel of death, he shouted, 'Kill her!'

'Kane!' I called out. None of Morjin's captains remained standing to lead the charge against Atara. In only moments, Morjin would see his strategy for victory: he would deploy perhaps twenty of his remaining seventy guards to charge the throne and slay Atara. Then, freed from the murderous flight of her arrows, he would be able to order the rest of his guards against us. They would soon flank us in a well-coordinated assault and annihilate us.

'Everyone,' I called again, 'attack!'

I led forth into the clot of men gathered around Morjin and his priests. Four guards stabbed their spears toward me. I swung Alkaladur and cut through the shafts of all the spears in a single stroke; on the backstroke, I took off the head of one of these guards and cut clean through another's arm deep into his chest. Kane, at my right, quickly butchered two more as Ymiru's club fell straight down and crushed a halberd-bearing guard to a bloody pulp.

A few guards, on their own initiative, had tried to circle around us. Liljana stabbed one of these through the neck while Maram worked his sword against the sword and spear of two others. I sensed a great strength flowing into him. He cut and parried and thrust, all the while grunting like a bear. Although his gelstei was cracked, the presence of the Lightstone seemed to cause some of its fire to ignite his heart and limbs. He suddenly snarled as he drove his sword clean through the opposing swordsman's chest. And then whipping it free, he turned to parry a spear thrust and bury his sword in its owner's eye.

We had slain many but many more stood before us. The stone eyes of Angra Mainyu looking out upon the battle might have recorded that we were still badly outnumbered. But I knew that the numbers favored us. For we were more than six warriors against sixty. Kane fought beside me with the strength and fury of ten men, and all that he had taught me came out in the speed and precision of my sword, which flashed and cut as if I wielded ten swords in my hands. My father was there beside me as well, and his weapons master, Lansar Rashaaru, and Asaru, Karshur, Yarashan and all my brothers. My mother fought with me like a lioness, calling out encouragements and warnings, protecting me, urging me to live at all costs and return home to her. In truth, the entire host of the Valari was in the hall that day, the Ishkans with the Meshians, the

Waashians and the warriors of Kaash, and it was as if we slashed ten thousand bright steel kalamas into the soul of our ancient enemy.

Panic, in battle, is a terrible thing. The victors strike it into the vanquished in the furious clash of steel against steel, in the lionlike roar of their hearts and in the blaze of their eyes. It spreads among the doomed like a disease: here a guard cries out in dismay while another sprays his neighbor in a fountain of blood; there a halberd wavers in the air and a spearman pulls back behind the imagined safety of others around him while many others begin falling back as well and even a few break and run. Panic also communicates from commander to commanded like wildfire through dry grass. When a king, on the field of battle, loses heart, he has no hope of victory.

Even as Ymiru's club crumpled steel and my sword cut through the guards' armor as if it were cloth, as Atara's arrows sizzled through the air and struck down guards and priests like lightning falling from the heavens, Morjin was seized with a great fear of death. I felt it come quivering alive within his chest and then spread out in waves through the men bunched around him. In truth, they now fought like maddened beasts rather than men. They bunched and screamed and swarmed about Morjin. And his voice rose above the clamor of the spears and clashing steel: 'Retreat! Retreat to the gate!'

A commander who cannot view all of his forces arrayed against the enemy will find battle to be a vast, boiling cloud of unknowing. For a warrior caught in the thick of flashing swords and blood, battle is a tunnel of fire. I, who held the Bright Sword in my hands, suddenly saw the ferocious fight through Morjin's throne room as from the vantage of an eagle high above and as a fiercely struggling knight swinging sword against sword – all at once. And I saw this with an astonishing clarity. In front of me, the mass of men moved a few yards toward the southwest, and I knew that Morjin intended to flee through the door leading to his private chambers rather than through the room's west gate. Already one of his priests had broken from the circle to run and open this door. Although the tightly pressed guards prevented my view of his flight, I heard his boots pounding against the floor even as Atara's bowstring sang out its twanging tune of death. And so I 'saw' him clutch his chest against the arrow sticking out of it and fall to the floor. Likewise I became aware of Liljana behind me slipping her sword through a guard's defenses and thrusting its steel point through the mail covering his belly. His scream was as strangled and deep as the knot of his suddenly pierced intestines. Nearby, Maram matched sword against sword with a master warrior. The clanging of steel reverberated with rhythms in my blood as Maram fought with a fury and skill I hadn't known he possessed. In truth, in that moment with his brilliant sword and his heart of fire, he fought like a Valari knight. He suddenly killed his man with a quick thrust and then turned to cross swords with another.

In this most desperate of battles, we even had help from two unexpected sources. At the center of the star whose five points were Kane, Liljana, Maram, Ymiru and I, Master Juwain stood with his green gelstei blazing and pouring new life into our tired limbs and souls. And as we inched slowing toward the door leading to Morjin's rooms, Daj suddenly darted out from behind a pillar and grabbed up a cast-off spear. He went forth mercilessly finishing off the wounded and dying where they lay sprawled and groaning on the floor. One guard, outraged at his temerity, closed and swung his halberd at his head. Daj dropped low, beneath the blow even as he thrust up with the spear. It drove straight into the guard's groin. In the wrath of his awful scream, the guard's backstroke would have split open Daj's brains if Ymiru hadn't come up and brained *him* with his terrible club.

'Val!' Kane called out to my right. His sword flashed and a hand flew though the air nearby. 'Don't let Morjin escape!'

I was closer to him than was Kane. Now, through the mass of men in front of me, I caught glimpses of Morjin's golden tunic. He still crouched low, taking cover behind his frantically battling guards. But as Atara fired off the last of her arrows and her mighty bow fell silent, he stood up straight and drew his sword. His eyes found mine across ten yards of the blood-slick floorstone. His hatred poured out of them and something more: he tried to murder me with a sudden blast of the *valarda*. The shining silustria of my sword, however, shielded me from this deadly assault – as it did my companions. And as I raised Alkaladur high above my head, he looked upon it and saw his death.

I fought with a rare fury to kill him then. But this came not from a desire for vengeance. The only way for me to guard the Lightstone was to slay my enemies, not in fear, anger or hate, but only in knowledge, prowess and necessity, even out of love – a vast and terrible love beyond love that would destroy such diseased beings as Morjin so that new and greater life could be. He was a poisonous serpent who must be slain if I was to protect others. And more, he was a cracked vessel who could not hold light but only darkness. He had lived ages too long, and it was long past time that the One made a new cup out of this particular clay.

It was the destroying wrath of the One itself that fell upon me and blazed forth through the lightning strokes of my sword. I swung Alkaladur and struck off a guard's head; I lunged and drove its point through the mail covering a guard's chest, clean through his body and into the chest of the guard pressed up close behind him. In wrenching its blade free, I killed two more. A few moments later, another guard tried to parry a quick blow. My sword cut the steel of his – and then cut straight down through his shoulder, cleaving his body in two. The terror of my sword caused the guards behind him to panic. But they were bunched around Morjin too close simply to flee.

At last, I understood the Valari ideal of fearlessness, flawlessness and flowingness, not just with my head, but in the exquisite pressure of the black jade of my sword's hilt against my hands, and in the surging of my heart and deep in my soul.

Fearlessness: I was at one with the death that I dealt out, and so with the wild joy of life that poured into me. If I saw that a guard's spear thrust might be taken square upon my armor, I didn't flinch from it, but rather trusted to the strength of its steel rings forged by the master armorers of Mesh. Thus I was free to thrust and cut myself, like a whirlwind whipping a silver blade among my foes, lunging and parrying and killing – all the time dancing the wild and delicate dance of death.

Flawlessness: In the grace bestowed upon me, nothing could pierce the perfect diamond clarity of my awareness and will to fulfill my fate. All of my soul was in my sword, and my sword was in me, and so I cut my way through steel and flesh straight toward Morjin.

Flowingness: This desperate fight of guards screaming and hacking and spinning about had a logic and pattern that was not mine to control. But as in a storm at sea, there was a still point around which all the winds of violence whirled, and this quiet place was inside of me. And so I became one with the pattern of the battle, moving among men like water, always flowing down the red channels of death toward the great Red Dragon whose name was Morjin.

As Kane and my other friends battled beside me and guarded my back, I fought my way closer to him. Now only two tall guards, aiming spears at me, stood between us. I looked past them and locked eyes with him; he waited to slash his sword into me. His snarl of rage promised endless torments, but he no longer had the power of illusion to make me feel them, nor would he ever again. His hideousness stunned me. Now that we were so near each other, I knew that he didn't really smell of roses as his illusions suggested. Rather, he gave off the sick reek of fear, fouler than a bloody flux, putrid as death. It hit like the blow of a war hammer deep into my belly. My bones ached with the urge to destroy this twisted being. From the circle of the carved stone beneath us came the gurgle of the blood of many dead men being sucked down the drain of the dragon's mouth; it sounded out like a roaring from deep inside the mountain itself.

'Morjin!' I cried out even as I cut my way through these last two guards.

And his cry joined mine in echoing from the cold stone of the hall, 'Valari!'

We crossed swords then, and my greater fury bore him back into the guards massed about him. The sharp edge of a halberd slammed into the mail covering my side, but I scarcely felt it. A spear thrust at my face, and I pulled back my head to let it slip harmlessly past a couple of inches from my eyes. I raised back my sword.

'Val!' From on top of the throne, Atara's strong, clear voice rang out like a bell through the hall. 'You mustn't kill him!'

I suddenly remembered the prophecy that the death of Morjin would be the death of Ea.

'Val.'

It was said by some that Morjin was the finest swordsman on Ea. And perhaps he was. But now his hatred of me and the rigidness of his lust to take my head betrayed him. I felt his murderous intentions deep in my throat, and ducked beneath the vicious slash of his sword at the last moment. And then, rising quickly, I saw my chance. I thrust my sword over the shoulder of a quickly closing guard into Morjin's neck. It was a terrible wound, a mortal wound – but it failed to kill him.

'His fate is yours,' Atara called to me. 'If you kill him, you kill yourself!'

'I don't care!' I cried out.

I knew what she said was true. I stood in the land of death with all the men I had slain. If I now killed Morjin, this great immortal being with whom I was connected by the poison in my blood and the dark weave of fate, I would never leave it. Already, with the muscles and veins of Morjin's neck ripped open into a bloody hole, I could barely stand, barely see. Again, I raised back my sword.

'Val, if you kill yourself, you kill me!'

Atara's warning seemed to crack the stone of the mountain and stop the earth itself from turning. I suddenly knew something else: that Atara's blinding had shocked her to a wholly new level of scrying. Thus, even though eyeless, she had been able to 'see' to fire her arrows into Morjin's guards. I sensed that she was seeing things both far and near in space and time. And now she fired a different kind of arrow into me. Even as I hesitated and Morjin's guards closed in and came between us, she called out that she loved me more than life. If I died, she told me, she would die, too.

Her words tore open my heart. How much more must this beautiful, tortured woman be made to lose? I looked through the ring of guards to see Morjin choking on his blood and gasping for breath. His eyes closed even as his guards tried desperately to bear him back away from me.

'Atara,' I whispered.

My sword lowered as I cast a terrible look at the nearby guards to warn them away from me. I knew that I couldn't kill Morjin. It was the strangest and bitterest turning of fate that out of compassion for the one I most loved, I must spare Morjin's life.

'Damn it, Val!' Kane thundered from my right. 'You're letting him get away!'

He started after the mass of guards, many fewer in number now, who were bearing Morjin's gravely wounded body toward the southwest corner of the room. There, one of his guards had finally managed to open the door to his chambers. I suddenly grabbed Kane's arm and looked into his furious black eyes. I'd had enough of killing for one day.

'Damn you!' Kane said again. 'If you can't kill him, I will!'

He wrenched his arm free from my grip to pursue Morjin. He ran across the hall, savagely cutting down the few guards who tried to stop him. I ran after him. By the time I reached his side, however, the guards and remaining priests had succeeded in dragging Morjin through the open doorway. A dozen guards stood in front it, waiting their turn to enter the passageway beyond. Kane fell upon them, all the while stabbing and slashing and howling out his frustration that Morjin was escaping him.

'Let him go!' I shouted. 'It would be your death to follow him!'

Not even Kane, I thought, could fight his way through such a narrow passageway held by so many men.

'I don't care!' Kane roared. 'Morjin must die!'

Perhaps Morjin *would* die of his dreadful wound, but it was too late to inflict any other. In order to save Kane's life, I came up behind him and wrapped my arm like an iron band across his chest. He surged against me like an enraged tiger. By the time he again broke free, the last of the guards fled into the passageway, and the door slammed shut in our faces.

MORJINNN!

Kane screamed out his great enemy's name as he leaped forward to pound the pommel of his sword against the heavy, locked door. Then he whirled about facing me. There was blood in his eyes and dripping from his sword.

'What's wrong with you!' he shouted at me, pointing at the door. 'We might have killed them all!'

From across the hall to the east, from on top of the throne, Atara's clear voice called out, 'No – if we had pursued them there, they would have killed all of us.'

'So *you* say, scryer,' Kane snarled out.

I looked over at the throne to behold Atara. But she, who had seen clearly enough to shoot her arrows across the dim hall into our enemy's throats or eyes, seemed now to be suddenly and completely blind. She fumbled and groped about with her hands as she tried to climb down from the throne. I ran across the hall to help her. Kane ran after me. And then a few moments later, Maram, Liljana and the others joined us there as well, and we gathered beneath the steps to the throne.

'We're trapped!' Maram cried as he turned about to look at the room's locked gates. 'We kill a hundred men, and we're still trapped!'

I stood with my arm around Atara's back, helping her stand. She had spent nearly the last of her strength. Her bloody, beautiful head rested heavily on my shoulder.

'So, not quite a hundred,' Kane said. He stood looking toward the standing stones and the carnage that we had wrought. Across the blood-soaked ritual circle, the hacked and torn bodies of our enemies lay everywhere. 'And not quite enough – never enough death for them.'

But it was more than enough death for me. As I gazed at those whom I had slain, only my grip on Alkaladur's diamond-set hilt kept me from falling down and joining them.

'I'm sorry,' Atara said to Kane. She managed to lift up her head and orient her face toward him. 'But I saw . . . that is, I *knew* that Val needed to remain alive. You, too, Kane, and myself – all of us. We all must live to guard the Lightstone for the Maitreya.'

Upon these words I removed the Lightstone from beneath my armor. It seemed more than a lifetime ago that I had put it there. And it seemed almost a dream that I had finally found it after all. Only the warm hardness of the little golden cup in my hand reassured me that it was real.

'So,' Kane muttered. His black eyes were bright as moons as they drank in the cup's golden sheen. His thirst for its light, I thought, was nearly infinite. 'So.'

He broke his gaze and turned toward Atara. He said, 'Morjin and others have killed every Maitreya born on Ea. Killing *him* was the best hope we had of putting this cup in the next Maitreya's hands.'

'Hrope,' Ymiru said bitterly. He leaned over his bloody war club as he turned his attention from the wonder of the Lightstone to the room's great bronze gates. 'How long will it be before more guards are summoned? Or before the Red Priests call up the whrole army from the first level?'

Maram, tearing his eyes from the Lightstone, looked at me and asked, 'Is there no way out of here, then?'

'There *is* a way out,' Liljana said, staring at the Lightstone. She wiped her sword on a tunic torn from one of the dead and sheathed it. 'A secret passage leading from the throne room – I saw this in Morjin's mind.'

'Where is it, then?' Maram shouted at her.

'I saw *that* it is,' she told him, 'but not *where* it is.'

I looked at Daj, who was standing slightly behind Liljana. He still held his killing spear in his little hands. 'Do you know where this passage is?' I asked him.

'No, Lord Morjin never spoke of it,' he said. Then his courage finally failed him, and he began trembling and said, 'I want to go home!'

As Liljana put her arm around him and pulled him closer, she said to Atara, 'Have *you* seen the door to this passage, my dear?'

'No, I . . . can see nothing now,' Atara murmured, shaking her head.

Maram ran over to the wall near the door to Morjin's chambers and began searching it for the telltale cracks that might demarcate a secret door. But the throne room's acres of walls were everywhere cracked and carved with fissures and swirls that formed the shapes of dragons and other beasts, and so it seemed that Maram had set himself a hopeless task. Master Juwain moved up in front of Atara with his varistei held over the crown of her head. A brilliant green light poured out of it as of a rain shower that has taken on the color of new spring leaves. It gave her new life. But it failed to restore her vision.

Liljana laid her hand on Atara's shoulder as she addressed Master Juwain, saying, 'If Atara can't find her way to visions of the otherworld, then perhaps you can restore her sight of this one.'

'I?' Master Juwain said. 'How?'

'By growing new eyes for her.'

Master Juwain looked at his crystal as he sadly shook his head. He told her, 'As I've said before, I'm afraid my gelstei hasn't that power.'

'Not by itself, perhaps. But the Lightstone must have that power.'

She turned straight toward Kane and recited the lines from the *Song of Kalkamesh and Telemesh*:

> *The lightning flashed, struck stone, burned clear;*
> *The prince beheld through rain and tear*
> *The hands that held the golden bowl,*
> *The warrior's hands again were whole.*

'Kalkamesh,' she told him, 'had touched the Lightstone before his torture – before Telemesh freed him by cutting him away from his crucified hands. But he grew *new* hands, didn't he?'

'So,' Kane said as his eyes darkened. 'So the old songs say.'

'Kalkamesh,' she said again, 'gained this power thusly, didn't he?'

'How should *I* know?' Kane muttered, shaking his head.

'*Didn't* he?'

'No,' Kane snarled, 'you're wrong – you know nothing.'

'I know what I see.'

So saying, Liljana pointed at the side of Kane's head. There, during the ferocity of the battle, the bandage that Master Juwain had fixed after the earlier battle with the knights beneath Skartaru's north face had come loose. I stared through the dim light near the throne, and gasped at what I saw. For beneath Kane's white hair, where the knight's sword had sheared off his ear, a small, pink, new ear the size of a child's was growing from his head.

'Kalkamesh,' Liljana said, staring at him. 'You are he.'

'No,' Kane murmured, shaking his head. 'No.'

'Morjin spoke to you as if you'd known him long ago. As you spoke to him.'

'No, no,' Kane said.

'And the *way* you looked at him! Your hate. Who could ever hate him so much?'

Kane looked at Atara and then me but said nothing.

'And the way you fight!' Liljana continued. 'Who could ever fight as Kalkamesh did?'

Kane bowed his head to me and said, 'Valashu Elahad can.'

I returned his bow, then asked him, '*Are* you really Kalkamesh?'

'No,' he said as he stared at the Lightstone. 'That is not my name.'

'Then what *is* your name? Your true name? It's not Kane, is it?'

'No, that is not my name either.'

I waited for him to say more as my heart pounded like the distant hammering that I could hear from beyond the throne room's doors. A battle a thousand times fiercer than the one we had just fought raged inside him.

'My name,' he whispered, 'is Kalkin.'

He drew himself up as straight as a king and pointed his sword at the door to Morjin's chambers. And a single, terrible cry broke from his throat like thunder and shook the hall:

'KALKIN!

'Do you hear that, Morjin! My name is Kalkin, and I've come to return you to the stars!'

It hurt my ears to hear him shout this name; it hurt my heart. As the hall fell silent again, we all looked at him in amazement. And then Master Juwain, who had a better memory than any of us, turned to him and said, 'The *Damitan Elu* speaks of Kalkin. He was one of the heroes of the first Lightstone quest.'

I suddenly remembered King Kiritan telling of this in his great hall: of how Morjin had led heroes on the first quest, only to fall mad upon beholding the Lightstone and slaying Kalkin and all the others – all except the immortal Kalkamesh.

As Master Juwain began recounting this ancient tale, Kane shook his sword at him and cut him off. He said, 'I've warned you that many of these ancient histories do not tell true. Morjin never led that quest. And he did *not* kill Kalkin, as you can see.'

'I don't *know* what I see,' Master Juwain said, looking at him strangely. 'If you're not Kalkamesh, then whatever happened to him?'

'*I* happened to him!' Kane said. 'Do you understand? After the first quest, Kalkin *became* Kalkamesh. And an age later, after the Sarburn, when Kalkamesh cast Alkaladur into the sea, *he* became Kane, do you understand?'

As I looked down at my sword, my amazement deepened. And then I squeezed the Lightstone more tightly in my hand as I asked him, 'But if you are really Kalkin, *didn't* the touch of this cup bestow upon you immortality?'

Kane, or the man that I had known by that name, began pacing about like a caged tiger as he cast quick, ferocious glances at the doors of the hall. He suddenly stopped and snarled out, 'Listen, damn you, and listen well – we haven't much time.'

He stared down at the blackish blood pooled on the floor as if looking far into the past. Then he looked up and said, 'Once there was a band of brothers, a sacred band.'

He nodded at Master Juwain and went on, 'We were *not* of any of your Brotherhoods; ours was much older. So, much older, much more glorious, I, you – you can't understand . . .'

From beyond the hall's western gate came a pounding as of many boots against stone. We all pressed closer to Kane to hear what he had to tell us.

'I will say their names, for they should be heard at least once in every age,' Kane said. 'There were twelve of us: Sarojin, Averin, Manjin, Balakin and Durrikin. And Iojin, Mayin, Baladin, Nurijin and Garain.'

'That's only ten,' Maram pointed out.

'The eleventh was myself,' Kane said. He pointed at the door to Morjin's chambers. 'And you know the name of the twelfth.'

Now many voices shouted from beyond the hall's eastern doors. I knew that we should be searching for the secret passage that Liljana had spoken of. But the gleam of my sword, in whose silver I saw reflected the Lightstone, gave me to understand that it was somehow more important to listen to Kane.

'We came to Tria early in the Age of Swords,' Kane told us. 'So, it was a savage time, even worse than this. Manjin was killed in a Sarni raid. Mayin was murdered on the Gray Prairies looking for clues as to where Aryu had taken the Lightstone. Nurijin, Durrikin, Baladin, and Sarojin, Balakin, too, and then even Iojin, sweet, beloved Iojin – all killed. All except Garain and Averin, who set out with Morjin and Kalkin on a ship captained by Bramu Rologar to seek the Lightstone.'

Kane paused to stare at the cup that I held, and then continued, 'And find it we did. The Lightstone was *made* to be found. But on the voyage back to Tria, Morjin enlisted the aid of Captain Rologar and his men to kill Averin and Garain. So, and Kalkin, too. But Kalkin was harder to kill, eh? So, *he* killed Captain Rologar and four of his men and damned himself, do you understand? He killed, in violence to his soul, killed *men*, before Morjin stabbed him in the back and cast him into the sea.'

Now, beyond the hall's northern door, came a clamor as of shields banging together. I knew that I, or all of us, should begin cutting arrows out of the dead in the event that Atara miraculously regained her second sight.

Instead, I nodded at Kane and asked him, 'But how did Kalkin live to tell such a tale?'

'The dolphins saved him. They were friends with men, once upon a time.'

'But that still doesn't explain Kalkin's immortality,' I pointed out.

Master Juwain, ever the student of history, caught Kane's eyes and said, 'You've recounted that Kalkin and his band of brothers came to Tria early in the Age of Swords. But the first quest took place *late* in that age, didn't it?'

'So,' Kane said, his eyes flashing, 'so.'

'Hundreds of years later,' Master Juwain said. 'But if Kalkin and Morjin, and the others as well, lived all that time, then they *didn't* gain their immortality by touching –'

'The Lightstone has no such power!' Kane suddenly shouted, cutting him off. 'Haven't I made that clear?'

'Then how,' Master Juwain asked, 'did Kalkin become immortal?'

'The way that men do,' Kane told him. 'By becoming more than men.'

It was as if a cold wind had fallen down from the nighttime sky and found the flesh along the back of my neck. A shiver, like a lightning bolt made of ice, ran up and down my spine. I stood staring at Kane, waiting for him to say more.

'It was the Galadin who sent us here to recover the Lightstone,' he told us. 'For them, who were immortal and could not be killed, Ea was deemed too perilous. For us, who were merely immortal, this world proved to be perilous enough, eh?'

How was it possible, I wondered? How was it possible that this man who stood before us – grim, angry, pained and still dripping with the blood of those whom he had slain – could be one of the blessed Elijin?

'Five men Kalkin put to the sword, eh? But *we* were forbidden to kill men. And so in breaking with the Law of the One, Kalkin broke with the One, perhaps forever.'

Kane stared at the cup in my hand, and there was an immense and endless blackness inside him waiting to be filled with light. How long he had been waiting, I thought! For he, who had once held the Lightstone and had beheld its perfect radiance even as I had, had been cast into a lightless void and had endured a dark night of the soul that had lasted nearly seven thousand years.

Maram, suddenly understanding this, gazed at Kane in awe. 'No wonder you fought so hard to bring us here to recover the Lightstone.'

'Ha!' Kane called out. 'I never thought we *would* find the Lightstone here. I never believed the account of Master Aluino's journal. *I* knew Sartan Odinan, and I never thought it possible that his greed would have permitted him simply to drop the Lightstone down on top of Morjin's damn throne.'

Maram looked at him nervously and said, 'If that's true, then you must have wanted –'

'Revenge!' Kane cried out. He raised up his bloody sword and swept it about the hall. 'I came here to put this into Morjin's treacherous heart! Does anyone deserve death more? What's one more murder against all those I have slain?'

'Perhaps,' I said, remembering Atara's warning, 'one too many.'

'*You* say that?' he growled at me, looking at my sword. 'How many have *you* slain with that today?'

'Too many,' I said as I looked about the hall. Then I held Alkaladur out toward him and said, 'If you are really Kalkamesh, then you forged this sword. And so it is yours.'

'No, it's yours now. You're better at killing with it than I ever was.'

'But if you were to take it back, the silver gelstei might –'

'It's not your damn bloody sword I want!' he thundered at me. There was a strange, faraway look in his eyes – and the faint fire of madness, too. 'It's not the *silver* gelstei that I want.'

Now the red flames in his eyes built hotter as he stared at the Lightstone. His voice filled with anger and a choking desire as he pointed at the cup and called out, 'So, Morjin has escaped me, eh? But it seems that fate has put the Lightstone in my hands.'

'In *Val's* hands,' Maram said, stepping forward. 'That was the rule we made in Tria, that whoever found the Lightstone would have final say as to what would be done with it.'

'So,' Kane said, taking a step closer to me. His knuckles were white around the hilt of his sword. 'So.'

'You pledged your sword to Val's service!' Maram reminded him.

'So I did,' Kane said. 'I pledged it only so long as he sought the Lightstone. Well, the Lightstone has been found, and so he seeks it no longer.'

I didn't know if Kane had fallen so far that he would kill me to claim the Lightstone; I didn't know if I could kill him, even in its defense. I doubted that I *could* kill him. Despite his words of praise as to my prowess with the Bright Sword that he had forged, he was an angel of death who gripped in his hands a killing sword of his own.

'Kalkin,' I said to him.

'Don't call me that!'

'No matter how many you kill, even Morjin, even Angra Mainyu himself, it will never bring back the light.'

'Damn you!'

We met eyes suddenly, and the anguish that I saw in him cut open my heart. I knew then that I could never kill this brave blessed man whom I loved.

Without a further glance at my sword, I quickly sheathed it. I looked deep into Kane's black eyes, so like my own. As the Valari were sons and daughters of the Star People, so were the Elijin – in transcendence and immortality. Kane, I thought, was Valari in his soul, and something more.

I held the Lightstone out to him then. I said, 'Take it. If you will promise to guard and keep it for the Maitreya, then I would have the Lightstone go with you.'

Kane stepped forward and reached out to grasp the Lightstone with his left hand. My hand, suddenly freed from this slight weight, suddenly felt a thousand times heavier.

'So,' he whispered, 'so.'

He stood looking back and forth between the cup in his left hand and the sword in his right. He blinked his eyes in rhythm with the beating of my heart. His belly tightened into a hard knot, and his hands, first the left and then the right, began to tremble.

'Kalkin,' I said.

With a great effort, he broke off gazing at the Lightstone and looked at me. His grim mouth could make no words, but his heart spoke to me all the same. In the quiet deep thunder of the blood that we shared, in the touching of each other's unfathomable suffering and pain, his soul cried out that I had offered him something more precious than a small, golden cup, and that was friendship and trust.

What is it to love a man? This above all: that you want with all the polished silver of your being to show him the glory of his own.

Now Kane's jaws clamped shut as if he were trying to bite back the worst of pains. I felt him swallowing against a hard knot in his throat that would not be dislodged. A great pressure built in his chest and burned up through his eyes. He took a long, deep look at the Lightstone.

'Valashu,' he gasped.

He suddenly cast his sword clanging down upon the bare rock floor. I felt tears burning in my eyes a moment before his filled as well. And then, at last, the storm broke. He lifted the Lightstone up high and threw back his head. His mouth opened wide as he let loose a terrible sound: 'KALKIN!' No torture of Morjin's could have torn such a cry of agony and despair from a man. He fell down to his knees before me, weeping for himself and the world. In his wracking sobs was all his grief at losing Alphanderry to death – and much, much else that he had held inside for years beyond counting. His breath burst out so violently that the stone of the hall seemed to shake and the very heavens open up even through miles of rock and ice. For a moment his tears, and my own, flowed so freely that they seemed almost to wash away the blood spilled here this terrible day.

I rested my hand on top of his thick, white hair as he reached his hand behind my leg and pressed his forehead against the hard rings of steel covering my knee. The tremors ripping through his powerful body took a long time to subside. At last, when he had grown quiet again, as I listened to Atara's pained breaths breaking out into the air behind me and to Maram weeping like a child, he looked up at me. He pulled away from me, slightly, and pressed the Lightstone back into my hand.

'*You* take it,' he said to me. 'Guard it for the Maitreya. So, guard it with your life – that is your fate.'

I gave the cup to Maram to hold, and his large hand closed around it.

'Some wounds,' Kane said, 'only he can heal.'

I reached out to grasp Kane's hard hand in mine as I helped him to his feet. Then he let go of me and pulled himself up tall and straight. The tears in his eyes were gone. I looked deep into their bright, black depths; as had been the Lightstone, they were full of stars.

'Valashu,' he said, smiling at me.

For millennia he had waged the bitterest of wars against himself, but angels cannot so easily be killed. A broken man had knelt before me, but here rose up another. The lines of his face seemed to lose their hardness and rigidity. Years fell from him, untold years, and I saw him as he must have been in his youth when he had walked with the One. His skin gleamed all golden like the sun, and his white hair had taken on the silver tones of silustria; a crown of light surrounded his head and fell about his shoulders like a lion's mane set on fire. He seemed raimented all in glorre, while his whole being was transparent to the hopes and dreams of a deeper world. A man he truly was, like the first man to walk the earth and perhaps the last.

And yet he was also something more, for here he stood all noble, wise, beautiful and radiant, blazing like a star, as one of the great Elijin.

But only for a moment. He moved over to Atara and laid his hand on her face to turn her toward him. Then, with infinite gentleness, he touched his thumbs into the hollows of her eyes. And the angel fire passed into her and out of him.

'Val!' Atara cried out. 'I know where the passageway is!'

Once, speaking of Morjin, Kane had asked what could be greater than the power to make others see what is not. And here, in this beautiful woman restored for a moment to her vision, the only answer: the power to help them see what really is.

Maram gave the Lightstone to Ymiru, who stood holding it in his single hand a few moments before turning it over to Liljana. Then Maram, looking at Kane in awe, said, 'Lord Kalkin, you are –'

'Don't say that name again!' Kane told him. Much of the light had now gone out of him; with its passing, Kane had returned to us – but never quite the same Kane again. 'So, you'll call me as you have, do you understand?'

'All right, then,' Maram said.

Kane smiled grimly as he bent to pick up his sword.

Liljana, after gazing into the Lightstone as long as she dared, gave the cup to Master Juwain, who held it only a moment before placing it in Atara's hands. While Daj stood close to Liljana, looking on in awe, Flick suddenly appeared and looped around the cup as if spinning out strands of a silvery cocoon of light.

'So, the second quest ends,' Kane said, casting one last look at the Lightstone. As a great noise of pounding boots and shaking steel sounded from outside the hall, his eyes flashed around the throne room's three gates. 'And it will be the end of us if we don't find our way out of here soon. It sounds as if they're bringing up the whole damn army!'

'Come,' Atara said softly, taking my hand.

She gave the Lightstone back to me, and I returned it to its resting place beneath my armor. Then she led us over to the wall behind the throne. There, set into the fearsome face of a carving of Angra Mainyu, she found the hidden door. It took only a few moments to open it.

'Come,' she said again, this time taking Daj's hand. 'Let's go home.'

Then she turned into the tunnel beyond the open door and bravely led the way into the bright, black darkness.

46

The passageway took us straight toward the southeast for a distance of a few hundred yards. It gave onto a much larger corridor running east and west. Just at the juncture, however, we found our way blocked by lines of iron bars running from the ceiling down into the floor. An iron door, like one leading from a jail cell, was set into the middle of the bars.

'Locked!' Maram cried out as he rushed forward to try it. 'Then we're still trapped in this forsaken place!'

None of us knew how long it would be before Morjin's men burst into the throne room behind us and found their way to this secret passage.

'Hrold your noise!' Ymiru said softly, stepping up to the bars.

Then he brought forth his purple gelstei and worked its magic upon them. Its violet light transformed the crystal within the iron into a softer substance – soft enough so that Ymiru's great strength, with Maram, Kane and me helping, sufficed to bend them. Daj danced through this opening, and as for the rest of us, only Ymiru had much trouble squeezing through.

'There!' he huffed out after leaving shreds of white fur upon the rough iron bars. 'We're *not* trapped! I'll never allow myself to be trapped and taken again.'

'But how *did* Morjin take you?' Maram asked him.

'It was bad chance,' he said. 'After Val killed the dragon, we made it back past the old throne room and up to the seventh level without much trouble. Then we ran into that company of Grays.'

The Grays, as he explained, had scented out the secrets of their minds, and had used *their* frightful minds to freeze them with fear until Morjin's guards – and Morjin himself – could be summoned to bind them in chains.

'It was hrorrible,' Ymiru said, nodding at Atara and Master Juwain. 'We fought them as hard as we could, with the light meditations, but how

782

long can one hrold against such creatures? And then Morjin suggested taking us into the throne room; he said that the torture of our bodies might help the Grays break into our minds.'

'Are you sure they *didn't*?' Kane asked him.

'I think not,' Master Juwain said, stepping up to Ymiru. 'When Morjin discovered that you and Val had broken into the throne room, he was very keen to have the Grays turn their minds toward you.'

'So, then it's possible that the enemy doesn't know how we entered Argattha?'

'It's likely,' Master Juwain said. 'I heard Morjin give orders to double the guard at the city's gates. He berated the captain of his guards for allowing a giant such as Ymiru to pass through unchallenged.'

'Then they will likely look for us at these gates,' Maram said. 'If we can find our way back as we came, we may yet have time to make our escape.'

'A little time, perhaps,' Kane said. 'But we must hurry.'

And so hurry we did, out onto the larger corridor, which was lit with numerous glowstones set at intervals into the black, basalt walls. To the west, as Kane told us, the corridor led back toward Morjin's palace. And to the east, this bore through solid rock would take us straight through the mountain to the window carved into its side known as Morjin's Porch.

'But how did you know that?' Daj asked him. 'If this is the way toward Morjin's Porch, only Lord Morjin is ever allowed to use it.'

'Not *ever*, lad,' Kane said grimly as he stared down the corridor. 'Once, a long time ago, one named Kalkamesh was taken this way and crucified to the face of the mountain.'

Daj, who apparently hadn't heard this story, stared at Kane in awe.

'If I remember aright,' Kane said, 'it also leads to Morjin's Stairs.'

As Daj had told us, Morjin's Stairs would take us down to Argattha's lower levels, perhaps as far down as the abandoned first level – though not even Daj or Ymiru could say where it might give out.

'Can you see where?' Kane asked Atara.

Atara, who could 'see' well enough to keep from stumbling along this dim corridor, shook her head and told us, 'It's too far.'

'Let's find out, then,' Kane said.

We had no trouble in finding Morjin's Stairs about a quarter mile to our left. They spiraled deep into the dark mountain, turning around and around, and down and down for hundreds of feet. After a while, we came to a landing giving out onto a tunnel, which we supposed led to the secret tunnel system and sanctuaries on the sixth level. It was quiet in that direction. This gave us good hope as we turned the other way and resumed our journey down the endlessly winding stairs. Thus we passed openings to the fifth, fourth, third and second levels. There, as we had prayed, the stairs didn't end; they led us another five hundred feet down to the first level of Argattha.

'What is this?' Maram said, pointing ahead of us. The stairs let us out onto a very short corridor that seemed to end abruptly in a wall. 'Another trap?'

'Ha, another secret door, most likely!' Kane said, clapping him on the shoulder. Then he stepped forward and called out, '*Memoriar Damoom!*'

Remember Damoom, I thought as Kane pushed open the carefully concealed door. I looked back at Atara and the one-armed Ymiru, and I knew that all of us, live though we might another thousand years, would always remember Argattha.

By great, good fortune, we discovered that the door opened upon Morjin's old throne room. We stepped out into the great hall where we had fought our first battle with the dragon. Here, with its great, cracked columns of basalt and the pyramid of skulls, the floor was still caked with the blood from Ymiru's severed arm. And across from the great portal leading out to the first level, the doorway to the stairs by which we had first entered the hall still stood open.

It was strange and disquieting to cross this vast open space where once had thundered a dragon. We were glad to gain the shelter of the stairwell. And glad, too, to climb down a little way to the corridor leading back toward the labyrinth. Daj, who had explored many of the tunnels of Argattha's first level, had never dared to enter this dark, twisting place. As I held high Alkaladur, now blazing brilliantly in the Lightstone's presence, he and the others followed closely behind me around and through its turnings. At last we came out of it as we had entered it. And so we stepped into the close, foul-smelling, rat-infested tunnel system leading to the cave hidden behind Skartaru's north face.

We found the cave as we had left it: piled with the bodies of the knights we had slain, as well as the saddles of their driven-off horses and other accouterments. Here, despite our fear of pursuit, despite the awful fetor of the rotting bodies, we had to pause to search through the knights' gear. We took away as many saddlebags of food as we could carry, and the smallest saddle that we could find. Atara was very happy to lay her hands on a full quiver of arrows; although they were not so well-made as those that the Sarni carefully shaped and fletched, she said that they would likely fly straight enough if only she could aim them at our enemies.

When we were finally ready, we rolled aside the great rocks with which we had sealed the cave. We stepped outside into a brilliant night. In all my life, the air that I breathed had never smelled so clean and sweet – even though that air was still of Sakai. A cold wind blew down from the Nagarshath through the valley to the north of the mountain. It set all of us except Ymiru to shivering; even so we were glad for the scent of ice and pines that it carried along in its frigid gusts.

'What time is it?' Maram asked softly as he gazed at the shadowed rockscape of the valley.

I looked up at the sky; to the east of us, above the dark, rolling plains of the Wendrush, the Morning Star stood like a beacon among the bright constellations. 'It's nearly dawn,' I told him.

'What *day* is it?'

None of us seemed to know. In the lightless hell of Argattha, we might have journeyed and fought for two days – or two years.

'I would guess it's the 24th,' Master Juwain said. 'Or perhaps the 25th.'

'The 25th of Ioj?' Maram asked.

Kane came up to him and rumpled his curly hair. 'Ioj it still is, my friend. We've still time to make it home before the snows come.'

We started walking down through the valley then. First light found us working our way across the ridge that hid the little canyon to the north of Skartaru. With nerves laid bare by what we had endured, we listened and looked for any sign of pursuit. But the slowly brightening foothills rang with the cries of wolves and bluebirds rather than the hoofbeats of Morjin's cavalry. We knew that it would be only a matter of time before he or one of his priests sent out riders to patrol the approaches to Skartaru. How much time we had, however, not even Atara could say.

And so we came down into the grassy bowl where we had left the horses; there my heart cried out with what it took to be the greatest stroke of fortune of all our journey. For there, in the center of the bowl, his black coat burning in the light of the rising sun, Altaru stood sniffing the air as for enemies. Atara's roan mare, Fire, was feeding on the lush grass nearby him, while twelve other horses – all of them mares as well – took their breakfast with her. I was sure that these were the mounts of the knights in the cave. Altaru had obviously gathered a harem about him. But he seemed to have driven off the magnificent Iolo, for what stallion will endure another sniffing about his new brides? When Maram discovered this, he wanted to weep bitter tears that he would have to find another horse to carry him homeward. Kane, Liljana and Master Juwain had better luck: their geldings stood off about a quarter mile from the herd as if awaiting our return.

We walked down into the bowl, where I whistled for Altaru. His ears pricked up, and he let loose a great whinny in return; it was like the music of the earth carried along with the day's first wind. I waited to see if he would come to me. It seemed a shame to take him from his newly-found freedom, to say nothing of his harem. But he and I had a covenant between us. So long as we had breath in our lungs and blood in our veins, we were fated to face, and fight, our enemies together.

At last he came trotting over to greet me. He nuzzled my face; I breathed into his nostrils and told him that a dragon had been killed – although the Great Red Dragon remained alive. We still had very far to ride together, I said, if he was willing to bear my weight. In answer, he nickered softly and licked my ear. His great heart beat like a war drum. He pawed the ground impatiently as I brought forth the saddle that I had hidden with the others and put it on his back.

The others saddled their horses, too. Maram chose out of the herd a big mare to ride; the smallest we gave to Daj, who had surprised us all by declaring that he *could* ride.

'My father,' he told us, 'was a knight.'

'In what land, lad?' Kane asked him.

Finally Daj consented to naming his homeland. He looked at Kane in the deepest of trust and said, 'Hesperu. My father, all the knights of the north – there was a rebellion, you see. But we were defeated. Killed and enslaved.'

'Hesperu is very far away,' Kane told him. 'I'm afraid there's no way we can take you home.'

'I know,' he said. And then a moment later, he admitted, 'I have no home.'

He said no more as he buckled around his horse the small saddle that we had taken from Morjin's men. It was still too big for him. But he rode well enough, I thought, patting his mare on the neck and being gentle with her flanks, which were scarred from the spurs of its previous owner.

Most of the day, however, we spent in walking, rather than riding, along the foothills of the White Mountains. The sun was high in the sky by the time we reached the canyon by which we had come down out of the Nagarshath. There we said goodbye to Ymiru. He would be traveling west, while we must journey east.

'But it's too dangerous for you to cross the mountains alone!' Maram said to him. He looked at the remains of his arm and shook his head. 'And surely you're still too weak from what the dragon did to you.'

Ymiru bowed his huge head to Master Juwain, and then said, 'I've had the help of Ea's greatest healer – I feel as strong as a *bear*.'

At the mention of Maram's least favorite animal, he cast his eyes about the tree-shrouded hills to look for one of the great, white bears that were said to haunt the Nagarshath. Then he studied Ymiru. Master Juwain had healed his pierced side, and his green gelstei seemed to have restored him to his great vitality.

'Still,' Maram said, 'those mountains, two hundred and fifty miles of them, and you alone. And with winter coming on, it's a journey that –'

'Only I can make,' Ymiru said, clapping him on the arm. 'Don't worry, little man, I shall be all right. But I must go hrome.'

He went on to say that he must tell his people the great news that the Lightstone had been found. Such a miracle, he said, surely heralded the return of the Star People, and so Alundil must be prepared for this great event.

'And the Ymanir must prepare for war,' he said. 'The Great Beast told me that my people would be the next to feel his wrath.'

Liljana came forward and laid her hand on his white fur. 'I saw this in his mind. His hatred of your land, and the desire to destroy it.'

'He has the strength, I think,' Ymiru admitted. His sad smile made me recall the hosts of men and the preparations for war that we had seen in Argattha. 'But we can still fight a while longer.'

'You won't fight alone,' I promised him.

Ymiru's face brightened as he asked me, 'Will the Valari take up the sword against him, then?'

'We'll have to,' I assured him. 'With what we've seen on this journey, what other choice will we have?'

He smiled again as he put down his club; then we clasped hands like brothers.

'I shall miss you, Valashu Elahad,' he said to me.

'And I, you,' I told him.

Liljana brought up one of the mares, which she and Master Juwain had heaped with most of the saddlebags of food. Ymiru would need every last biscuit of it on his long journey.

'Farewell,' she told him. 'May you walk in the light of the One.'

The others, too, said their goodbyes. And then, one last time, I took out the Lightstone and placed it in Ymiru's hand. Its radiance spilled over him like the gold of the sun.

'Someday,' he told me, 'I'll have to journey to Mesh to learn this cup's secrets.'

'You'll always be welcome,' I said to him.

'Or perhaps someday,' he said, handing the Lightstone back to me, 'you'll bring this to Alundil.'

'Perhaps I will,' I said.

Gone from his fearsome face was any hint of gloom; I saw there instead only bright, shining hope. He bowed his head to me, and then turned to tie the mare's reins around his mutilated arm. And he called out, 'A hrorse! Who would ever have thought that a Ymanir would make company of a hrorse!'

And then, leading his horse with one hand, his great war club in the other, he turned to the west and began his long, lonely walk up into the great white mountains of the Nagarshath.

After he had disappeared around the curve of the canyon, we made our final preparations for our journey. Since we had sixteen horses among the seven of us, we had remounts to tie behind us. And Master Juwain had a bandage to tie around Atara. Because she could not bear us to endure the sight of her missing eyes, she begged Master Juwain to cover them. In his wooden chest, he found a bolt of clean white cloth, which he pulled over her eye hollows and temples. I thought it looked less like a bandage than a blindfold.

At last we were ready to leave Sakai. And so we mounted our horses and turned them toward the east. Just below the foothills, the golden plains of the Wendrush gleamed in the sunlight as far as the eye could see. We rode straight down into them; there was nothing else to do. Now, as we found ourselves in the middle of a sea of grass or crested a rise, we would be visible from miles away: clear targets for Morjin's cavalry or any of the Sarni who might decide to divest us of our horses, our lives or more precious treasure.

In truth, on all of Ea there is no other place more perilous to travelers than the Wendrush. Here, between the Morning Mountains and the White, prides of lions hunted antelope and the great, shaggy sagosk; sometimes a darkness fell upon their fierce, red hearts, and then they hunted men. Of all the Sarni tribes, in their plundering for sport or gold, perhaps only the Kurmak or Niuriu tempered their ferocity with mercy – and even they had no love of strangers. The worst of the tribes, it was said, was the Zayak, whose country we now had to cross. Somehow, Morjin had made allies of them – if it was possible to enlist the aid of warriors so proudly independent that they were said to demand tribute even of Morjin's men should they wish to ride across their lands.

For all that first day of our flight from Argattha, we saw no sign of Sarni or of pursuit from Sakai. We rode as fast as we dared, over the swaying grasses of the soft, black earth. The sky was an immense blue dome resting upon the fundament of the far-off horizon; all about us was grass made golden by autumn's last heat. When night came, still we didn't pause in our rush across the plains. With the rising of the wind, we rode long past the twilight hour into the falling darkness.

The stars came out like a million candles lighting the black ocean of the heavens. They called us ever onward; their splendor lifted up our spirits and reminded us how good it was to be free.

The next day, however, as we looked back toward the Black Mountain still looming over the plain, we found ourselves pursued by riders. They crested a knoll behind us; there were twenty of them, bearing neither the shining mail nor lances of Morjin's knights but rather the leather armor and great curved bows of the Sarni.

'So,' Kane said to Atara, 'it's your people.'

He turned his horse about and made ready for one last battle. We all knew that it was hopeless to try to outdistance the Zayaks' lithe steppe ponies with our larger mounts – especially with so great and stolid a war horse as Altaru.

'Please don't call them my people,' Atara said to Kane. 'Anyone sent by Morjin is as much my enemy as yours.'

As we soon discovered, these twenty warriors with their blue-painted faces and wildly streaming yellow hair *had* been sent by Morjin – or rather by the captains of his cavalry that his priests had sent after us. They charged straight at us, firing arrows as they rode. And we charged them. Two of the warriors underestimated Altaru's speed over short distances; these died quickly beneath my long lance, which had the weight of Altaru's driving body behind it. A third warrior got in the way of Kane's falling sword, and so surrendered his spirit to the sky. A fourth cried out, 'Give us the treasure that you stole from Lord Morjin!' even as Maram ducked beneath an arrow that he loosed and managed to race forward and duel with him to his death.

Still, the battle would have gone badly for us if Atara hadn't countered the Zayaks' arrows with a murderous stream of her own. She shot off five of them with astonishing accuracy before most of the enemy came close enough to use their bows. And five warriors fell from their ponies with feathered shafts sticking out of their chests. It was the finest archery I had ever seen – and the Zayaks must have thought that, too. The sight of the blinded Atara, whipping her red horse about and firing off death with every crack of her bowstring, utterly unnerved these bold but superstitious warriors. Their leader, a fierce man with a huge, drooping, yellow mustache, cast her an awe-stricken look and cried out: 'Imakla! The Manslayer is *imakla*!'

And with that, he pointed his pony toward the rolling land to the north and led the survivors of his company in a wild, galloping retreat over the plains.

We did not escape this brief but deadly encounter unscathed. An arrow killed Liljana's horse beneath her; she barely managed to avoid being

789

crushed in its fall, and had to choose out another from our remounts. One of the Zayaks' arrows had buried itself in Altaru's flank. It was a bad wound, and Master Juwain drew it only with difficulty. If not for the radiance of the green gelstei, now blazing like emerald fire in its nearness to the Lightstone, it might have been many days before Altaru would have been able to walk without limping. Likewise Master Juwain helped heal Kane of the wound caused by an arrow that had pierced his mail and transfixed his shoulder.

After we had made ready to set out again, I turned to Atara and asked, 'What does *imakla* mean?'

She seemed reluctant to answer me. But finally, she turned her blindfolded head toward me and said, 'The *imakil* are the immortal dead warriors of ages past, heroes who have done some great deed. Some warriors are said to ride with them and draw upon their strength. They are *imakla*, and may not be touched.'

And with that, this brave woman who rode with the dead, pointed her horse toward the rising sun and led us through the Zayaks' country. As we trotted along, Maram offered his opinion that we had surely outdistanced Morjin's cavalry, for why else would they have sent the Zayaks after us?

'They spoke of the cup,' he said to her. 'Do you think they know it's the Lightstone?'

'Hmmph!' Atara said to him. 'If they knew that, they'd have called down the entire Zayak host upon us. And then Morjin would have lost all hope of regaining it.'

We discovered the next day that the Zayaks almost certainly knew nothing of the treasure that we bore through their land. About seventy miles out onto the plain, we ran into a much larger band of warriors. At the sight of Atara leading us toward them, they turned their horses and fled from us. It seemed that word of a blind, *imakla* warrior of the Manslayers had spread ahead of us like fire through dry grass.

Still, we took no assurance from this seeming miracle. We resolved to leave the Zayaks' county as quickly as we could. Our straightest path across the Wendrush would have taken us across most of their land, which was bordered by the White Mountains in the west, by the Blood River in the north, and by the Jade in the south. It was toward this river that we now turned. We didn't mind adding a few extra miles to our journey. In any case, soon we must cross the Astu River, and it would be much easier first to cross the Jade and then the Astu to the south of where the Jade emptied into it.

And so the following day, with the fording of the cold waters that flowed down from the White Mountains, we passed into the country

790

of the Danladi tribe. Their warriors, too, seemed to have been warned of Atara, for they let us ride through their lands unmolested. They were no friends of Morjin; but neither did they extend amity to a warrior of the Kurmak – and most especially not to Maram or Kane or any of the rest of us. It didn't matter. The weather held fine, with warm days of abundant sunshine and cold, clear nights. Thus we had no need of shelter, for we made our beds on the soft prairie grass and covered ourselves in our cloaks. When our food ran out, Atara shot an antelope, which gave us the sweetest of meats. Maram washed this feast down with the last of the kalvaas that we had brought from Alundil. Then he turned his eyes eastward in anticipation of some good, thick Meshian beer.

It took us most of three days to cover the hundred and twenty miles between the Jade and the Astu. This great river, here, to the south of where the Jade and the Blood flowed into it, was not nearly so wide as it grew on its course toward the Poru – which eventually wound its way across the plains and forests of Alonia, all the way to Tria. Still, it was wide enough. We had to swim the horses across it. By the time we reached the other side, Maram vowed that he would never swim a river again.

'At least not until we cross the Poru,' Atara reminded him.

'Oh, the Poru!' Maram cried out. 'I'd forgotten the Poru!'

But this queen of all rivers still lay a hundred and fifty miles to the east. The country to the west of it, here at this latitude, was that of the Niuriu tribe – who were friendly with the Kurmak. When an outrider of one of their clans trotted our way and discovered that Atara was the granddaughter of the great Sajagax, he offered us shelter, meat and fire. We spent that night in the great felt tent of his war chief. As with the other Sarni whom we encountered, Atara remained untouchable: any warrior approaching her to offer food or drink was careful to avert his eyes and *very* careful not to lay his hands on her or even brush against her garments. This restraint, however, did not in any way diminish the Niuriu's hospitality. As we discovered, the Sarni's enmity toward strangers was overmatched only by the generosity they showed to their friends. The chieftain's warriors and wives brought forth platters heaped with roasted antelope, sagosk steaks and coneys grilled over sweetgrass fire. As well, we had rounds of hot, yellow bread dripping with butter and honey and bowls of mare's milk. To Maram's delight, the chieftain himself, who was named Vishakan, brought forth a bottle of brandy and poured it into our cups with his own hand. And before we fell off to a contented sleep, he presented each of us with a braided leather quirt, with handles trimmed out in beaten silver.

On the next day – it proved to be the first of Valte – we made fifty miles over the flat, short-grass steppe. And on the two days following that, we did as well, riding past the great herds of sagosk long past sunset. Although the air grew slightly cooler here in the middle of the Wendrush, the sky deepened to an even more beautiful blue, and the red-orange paintbush and the golden leaves of the cottonwood trees along the watercourses made a great show of color. It would have been the finest leg of our journey homeward if Atara hadn't thrice lost her way for a few hours before regaining her sense of the terrain.

On the morning of the fourth of Valte, we came to the mighty Poru River. Atara assured Maram that the waters were not nearly so deep as in the spring or summer, when they raged brown down from the mountains. Even so, Maram dreaded this immersion. His unease must have communicated to his horse, because they floated downstream much too far, and so came out upon the Poru's eastern bank a hundred yards from the rest of us. This precipitated the only real crisis of this part of our journey. A great, black-maned lion, lying in wait by the grasses along the river, decided to chase Maram and his horse across the steppe. He almost certainly would have sunk his claws into the flanks of Maram's mare and dragged them down if Atara hadn't killed him with a single arrow shot into his heart.

'Ah,' Maram said to Atara as we all gathered around the dead lion, 'I suppose I should thank you for saving my life.'

'I suppose you should,' Atara said to him with a broad smile. 'But I think we're all long past saying thanks for saving each other's lives.'

Atara's feat of shooting down a charging lion was heralded not only by us. As it happened, two warriors of the Manslayer Society, with long hair even yellower than Atara's and wearing leather armor decorated much the same as hers, were out hunting along the Poru that morning. They immediately thundered our way to greet one of their bloodsisters. It didn't matter that Atara was of the Kurmak while they counted themselves as Urtuk – and eastern Urtuk at that. And they only honored Atara, as *imakla*, for gracing their country with her presence. When they studied the dead lion, killed so cleanly, they insisted that Atara return to their camp and share wine with them. They produced knives and quickly skinned the lion. It was their intention to dress the fur and make for Atara a lion-skin cloak so that all might appreciate her prowess.

They were reluctant, however, for the rest of us to accompany them. Liljana they might have taken into their confidence, but they looked at Kane, Maram, Master Juwain, Daj and me with the challenge that they reserved for all males. They fired their arrows of suspicion especially at me, for I was a knight of Mesh and therefore the Urtuks' ancient enemy.

It cooled their bellicosity not at all that I assured them that our peoples were not at war and that I was only returning homeward. Only Atara's claim that we were great warriors who had killed many of Morjin's men softened these two warriors. Atara also insisted that we remain together, and more, that the Manslayers of the Urtuk provide us escort as far as the Morning Mountains. So great had Atara's reputation now grown – to say nothing of her will – that the two Manslayers took a long look at the blindfold wrapped around her face and agreed to her demand.

Later that day, when we returned with them to their camp, their other sisters met in counsel and decided to honor their decision. They made only a single demand of their own: that Atara remain with them and teach three of the younger sisters her skill with the bow while the older sisters were preparing her lion skin.

And so there, along a stream sheltered by great cottonwoods, we waited for five long days. I felt the passing of time most keenly; an overwhelming sense that I must return home as soon as possible beat like a drum though my blood. Still, I was glad to make friends with these fierce women. At night, we sat around the fire sharing food with them and stories. It amazed them – and us – when one night Flick appeared and entertained them with his dance of silver sparks. We offered them no explanations as to this little miracle. We, ourselves, could only believe that the Lightstone's power had somehow quickened Flick's being and brought forth his colors for all to see.

At last, when the sisters had finished tanning the lion's skin and sewing into it a lining of purest, Galdan satin, they brought it to Atara to put on. With the black fur of the lion's mane framing her blond hair and her white blindfold circling her striking face, she did indeed look like one of the *imakil* heroes of past ages come to life.

The next morning, we set out to cross the Urtuks' country. Twelve of the Manslayers, acting as escort, rode out before us. After cutting across a little triangle of the steppe for thirty miles, we came to the Diamond River and followed it east. This band of clear water, flowing down from the Morning Mountains, reminded me how close I was to my home. I prayed that I would reach it without further incident. I needn't have worried. Although a company of fifty Urtuk warriors rode north from their winter camp father down along the Poru to witness the strange sight of the Manslayers leading seven outlanders toward Mesh, they did not challenge us or offer battle. Indeed, they offered us cheers in the form of their terrible war cries, for they had heard that we had entered Sakai and had slain many of the Red Dragon's men.

A hundred miles, as the raven flies, it is from the confluence of the Poru and Diamond Rivers to Mesh, and we rode nearly as straight. It took us only a day to cover half this distance. By the morning of the eleventh, when we awoke to a few puffy white clouds floating along the sky, the mountains of Mesh were a purplish haze along the horizon. As we urged the horses toward them during that long, long, day, the mountains grew ever greater and more distinct. By noon, I was able to make out the lines of Mount Tarkel's soaring white summit. Although I had never seen it from this vantage, there was only one mountain that stood just south of the Diamond River and overlooking the golden grasses of the Wendrush.

That evening we made camp scarcely three miles from the foothills beneath its western face. The pounding of my heart demanded that we ride up into Mesh even through the falling darkness; but my head told me that it would be foolhardy to brave the wild, rocky approaches to Tarkel at night. And more, such a course would be ungracious and sad beyond thinking because Maram, Master Juwain and I would have little time to say goodbye to the rest of our friends.

It was only during the five hundred miles of our flight from Argattha that I had gradually come to accept the rightness of the breaking of our company, though I hadn't yet made peace with this difficult decision. After we had thanked the Manslayers for their kindness and they had ridden off back toward their camp, the seven of us gathered around the fire that Maram had made for a last council.

It was a cold, clear night of many stars and a moon just past full. Flick spun about against the backdrop of the sky, and his swirling form seemed to match the twinkling lights of the constellations. The wind carried down the scents of my homeland and set my heart to beating more quickly. Before us was a little fire of burning sagosk bricks that smelled surprisingly sweet.

We spoke of many things; for a while, we told stories of Alphanderry, whose voice we now listened for in the wind and in the music of the stars. We had decided that Kane should inherit his mandolet, which was all we had left of him – except that we had our memories and a song in our hearts, and that was everything. Kane sat plucking at the mandolet's strings and singing to us. When he wished, he, too, had a fine, clear voice, as strong and beautiful as an eagle soaring across the sky. I thought that he was trying to recapture the words of Alphanderry's last song; I knew that someday he would.

'That's a music that should be heard in Mesh,' I said to him. 'Are you sure you won't reconsider your plans?'

Kane put down his mandolet and looked at me; I wondered if he would waver in his decision.

'It would be an honor if you could meet my father,' I said to him. Then I laid my hand on top of the diamond pommel of the sword that he had forged in Godhra so long ago. 'And my brothers, certainly my mother and grandmother. All my countrymen. Your name is still remembered in Mesh.'

'*That* name you have promised not to speak, eh?' He bowed his head to me in trust that I would keep this promise. And then he said, 'No, I'm sorry but I must return to Tria – I've business there.'

Master Juwain, holding his gnarled hands out to the fire, looked up at him and asked, 'The business of the Black Brotherhood?'

In all our miles together, Kane had said very little about this secret brotherhood of men whom we supposed he led. And he told us only a little more now, saying, 'The Great Beast must be opposed with any weapons we can find.'

'Even assassination?' Master Juwain said to him. 'Even poison, terror, deceit?'

Kane looked far off into the star-spangled heavens. Somewhere, unseen, golden bands of light streamed out from their center, touching many of the universe's earths.

'No, perhaps not those things,' Kane finally said. He looked over at me and stared at Alkaladur. 'Perhaps it's time we found other means of fighting.'

'I've said before,' Master Juwain told him, 'that evil cannot be defeated with the sword.'

'No, perhaps not,' Kane admitted. 'But evil people can.'

He cast me a long, sad look, and my hand tightened around Alkaladur's hilt. I feared that fate would once more call me to draw it before the world was rid of such as Morjin. And yet I knew that Master Juwain was right, that even the greatest of swords could never put an end to war.

'There are still battles to be fought,' I said. I drew forth the Lightstone and sat gazing at it. 'Different *kinds* of battles.'

As I remembered why I had fought so hard for this little cup and why the Galadin had sent it to Ea, it suddenly began pouring out an intense, golden radiance. For a moment, I held in my hands a little sun whose light could perhaps been seen from the mountains to the east of us, if any were looking.

'There *will* be battles, and soon,' Kane assured us. He nodded his head at the Lightstone and added, 'Now that we've taken *this* from the Beast, he'll bend all his will toward getting it back.'

'Then you believe he'll recover from his wound?' Maram asked.

'Yes, his kind cannot be killed so easily,' Kane said. 'A sword through the heart, or the severing of the head – that's almost the only way to kill one of the Elijin.'

He went on to say that Morjin would now be forced to accelerate his plans for his conquest.

'So, he's always looked to Alonia and to the Nine Kingdoms, Delu too, for he knows that if they fall, all of Ea falls, too.' He nodded at Atara, Liljana and me. 'But with the Sarni divided and much of the Wendrush held against him, to say nothing of the Long Wall, he can't attack your lands directly, eh? So, first he'll surround you – that's been his strategy all along.'

'Do you think he'll invade Delu from Galda?' Maram asked nervously.

'Not yet, he hasn't the strength,' Kane said. 'No, he'll move first against Eanna.'

'But if Surrapam holds,' Maram said, 'then he'll have to –'

'Surrapam *won't* hold,' Kane said. 'We all saw that.'

'Perhaps not,' I said. 'But the Hesperuks can't consolidate their conquest of Surrapam *and* attack Eanna.'

Kane nodded his head savagely and said, 'Not by themselves. That's why Morjin needs a backdoor into Eanna. And now he has that, with Yarkona.'

The Lightstone's radiance had now faded, and I gave the cup to Maram to hold. I sat staring at the fire. In its flames I saw the conflagration of the great Library; I saw the hateful eyes of Count Ulanu, as well.

'Count Ulanu,' I said to Kane, 'still isn't strong enough to attack Eanna.'

'He will be soon,' Kane said. 'Morjin will reinforce him.'

'Through Elivagar?'

'Just so – that's the key to his conquest, eh? Once the Ymanir's land is taken, he'll have a road through the mountains to march his armies into Yarkona and so into Eanna. And when Eanna falls, so will Thalu and the whole northwest.' Kane paused to catch his breath, and continued, 'And then nothing will stop Morjin from assembling a fleet and sailing his armies past Nedu and through the Dolphin Channel to attack Alonia.'

I watched the fire's flames gather in the Lightstone's bowl; in Maram there now gathered a different kind of fire.

'Then we must,' he said, 'stop Morjin first.'

Again, I gripped my sword as a great bitterness ate at my belly. And I said, 'Perhaps I *should* have killed him.'

Kane reached over and laid his hand on my shoulder. And then he said a strange thing, 'You did what you did out of compassion, and there's nothing to be sorry for in that. Would that we all had such compassion.'

Atara, who was now holding the Lightstone, faced me from next to Maram and said, 'Not even a scryer can see all ends, you know. If you had died in Argattha, *we* might never have escaped. And so one of Morjin's Red Priests might be holding this even now.'

It was one of those moments when the Lightstone's gold seemed to reveal a clear light within its depths – as did Atara. She nodded at me and asked, '*Will* the Valari come to the Ymanir's aid and fight Morjin?'

'Yes,' I told her. 'If we don't fight each other.'

Maram looked at Kane and then said, 'I couldn't bear it if the Beast ever saw Alundil. He would destroy it, I think. Is there no way that the Star People *might* return and send help?'

We all understood that Kane was forbidden to speak of other worlds around other stars, even as he forbade himself to speak of his past. And so he surprised us, saying, 'They *did* send help, once. But they'll never come again so long as Morjin is free to work his evil. You tell of the glory of Alundil. It's nothing against that of the cities of the Star People and the Elijin. And the Galadin, so, the Galadin. What if Morjin or another were to place the Lightstone in the Dark One's hands? So, they'll not risk the destruction of worlds and a splendor that you cannot imagine.'

Liljana, who had been passed the Lightstone, nodded at Kane and said, 'And that is why we must first and always look to *this* world. And that is why I must return to Tria. The Sisterhood must prepare for what is to come.'

She said as little about the Maitriche Telu as Kane did his Black Brotherhood. But it gladdened my heart when she looked at Master Juwain and said, 'Perhaps the time has come when our two orders can make our purposes known to each other.'

She gave the Lightstone to him, and his ugly face brightened with the most beautiful of smiles. 'The time *has* come, I see. I would like nothing more than for us to call each other Sister and Brother.'

As Daj next took the Lightstone, his eyes wide with the wonder of it, Liljana clasped Master Juwain's hand.

Now Master Juwain took out his varistei and sat gazing at it. Seized with inspiration, he held it in front of Daj's forehead. The Lightstone seemed to pour its radiance into the green stone. Then a green light leaped from the crystal, and its rays seared into the tattoo of the red dragon disfiguring Daj. After a few moments, the crystal grew quiet. And we all stared at Daj through the fire's flames to see that the tattoo was gone.

'Is it really?' Daj said, handing the Lightstone to Kane. He scurfed his fingers across his forehead as if feeling for the hated tattoo. 'I want to see! Val, will you show me, in your sword?'

I drew Alkaladur so that he could behold himself in its gleaming silver. But the sword, in the Lightstone's presence, suddenly flared so brightly that for a moment *none* of us could see. After it had returned to only a mirror-like brilliance, Daj sat looking at himself in wonder.

'It *is* gone,' he said. 'Now they won't stare at me in Tria.'

We had decided that he would go with Kane and Liljana to Tria, where Liljana would look after him. Atara would accompany them along the mountains facing the Wendrush; she must pay her respects to Sajagax and the Kurmak, she said, before continuing on with Kane and the others to Tria to conclude her business with her father.

'King Kiritan,' she said, 'must be told that the Lightstone has been found and the Quest fulfilled. And I must tell him.'

'*That* I would like to see,' Kane said, gazing at the cup that he held. His eyes, like the black stone he kept hidden away, seemed to touch upon the fiery light of creation itself. 'Almost as much as I'd like to see his face when Val shows him *this*.'

He passed the Lightstone on to me and asked, 'Are you sure you won't reconsider *your* plans?'

I squeezed the cup between my hands and said, 'The Lightstone must first be brought to the Valari. We are its guardians, and we can't guard it if I alone of my people take it into Tria.'

'But, Val,' Maram reminded me, 'King Kiritan is expecting its finder to bring it to him. Our vows –'

'We vowed to seek the Lightstone for all of Ea and not for ourselves,' I said. 'For *Ea*, Maram – not for King Kiritan.'

'But what about *your* vow, then?'

Now the gold of the Lightstone suddenly felt as cold as ice in my hands. I remembered too well standing in King Kiritan's hall before thousands of knights and nobles, and promising King Kiritan that I would bring the Lightstone to him and so claim Atara as my bride.

I looked over at Atara sitting rigidly as a statue, and I said, 'That vow is not mine to fulfill. Not mine alone.'

After that, our talk turned toward the remembrance of all that we suffered together, the glories as well as the sorrows. Kane recounted the story of Flick spinning on Alphanderry's nose; this made Daj break open with an easy, boyish laughter that was a delight to hear. We had thought that he would never laugh again. His sudden joy made us weep, especially Liljana, who seemed to have lost her own laughter, even as Atara had warned on the beach of the Bay of Whales. For she had looked too deep into Morjin's mind and seen there an evil so great that her own joy of life seemed forever dimmed. Even the Lightstone's gleaming presence was not enough to restore her peaceable temperament and her lovely smiles.

At last it came time to begin the long and painful rounds of making our goodbyes. Master Juwain sat telling Daj of the Great White Brotherhood and gave him his copy of the *Saganom Elu*; Daj promised to read it and someday make the journey to Mesh. I gave Kane the sharpening stone of pressed diamond dust that my brother, Mandru, had once given me. Alkaladur's edge never needed sharpening, but the kalama that Kane bore would. In return, he gave me one of the bloodstones that he had taken from Morjin's chambers, and instructed me in its use. Much past midnight, with the moon dropping lower in the sky, I spoke with Liljana about a few of the things she had seen in Morjin's mind.

Still later, I walked with Atara through the swishing grass at the edge of our camp. Twice she almost stumbled as the long grasses snared her feet. It was one of those times when she was truly blind. I offered her my arm, but she wouldn't take it.

'I must learn to get on by myself,' she told me.

'No one was meant to get on alone,' I said to her. 'If this quest has taught me anything, it's that.'

'Still, you can't walk for me. You can't see for me.'

'No,' I said, touching the mail over my chest where I had returned the Lightstone. 'But now that this has been found, I can marry you.'

'I still have *my* vow,' she reminded me.

I stopped to look off across the steppe, west, toward Argattha. I asked her, 'How many men have you slain, then? Sixty? Seventy?'

'Would you have me slay more?'

I listened to the beating of my heart, then said, 'Your vow isn't what keeps you from wanting to make vows with me.'

'No,' she said softly, touching the cloth around her face. 'I can't marry you like *this*.'

'But your sight will return,' I said, speaking of her powers of scrying, which seemed to be growing ever stronger. 'In Argattha, when Kane touched –'

'Kane will go his way, and I will go mine,' she told me. 'And Kane is still Kane, don't you see?'

I looked back toward the fire where Kane stood like a lonely sentinel surveying the steppe in all directions. Despite our nearness to Mesh, he hadn't ceased his eternal watch for enemies.

'Sometimes now,' she said to me, 'Kane walks with the One. But too often, he still walks with himself. He hasn't the power to make me *see*. In Argattha, for a moment, he helped me find *my* way back to the One. But I . . . can't always remain there. And so then I'm utterly blind.'

'I don't care,' I told her.

'But I *do* care,' she said to me. 'Someday, if I bear your son, as I have wished a thousand times and *will*, if only I could, my son . . . when I hold him to me and give him my milk, when I look down at him, if I can't see him, if I can't see him *seeing* me, then it would break my heart.'

I stood beneath the blazing stars that she could not perceive. In their brilliance, the patterns of life and death were stitched by the silver needle of fate. And fate, I thought, was forged in our hearts, whether with the fire of hate or love, it was our will to decide.

'I understand,' I told her. How could I love this woman if I didn't guard her heart as I would my own heart, as I would the Lightstone itself?

'I know it's vain of me,' she said, 'I know it's selfish, but I –'

'I understand,' I said again.

I moved to stroke her hair, gleaming like silver-gold in the starlight. But she shook her head and pulled back from me. And she murmured, 'No, no – I'm *imakla* now, haven't you heard? I'm *imakla*, and may not be touched.'

'I don't care, Atara.'

I knew that she couldn't bear for me to touch her – and even more, that she couldn't bear *not* being touched. And so one last time, I kissed her. My lips burned with a pain worse than when the dragon had seared me with her fire.

After that, I sat with her on the cold grass holding hands as we waited for the sun to brighten the sky over the mountains to the east. When it came time to say goodbye, she squeezed my hand and said, 'I wish you well, Valashu Elahad.'

For a moment, my eyes burned and blurred, and I was almost as blind as she. Then I told her, 'May you always walk in the light of the One.'

She got up to saddle her horse with the others while I sat staring at the last of the night's stars. After a while Maram came over to me. He somehow knew what had occurred between us, and I loved him for that.

'Take courage, old friend, there may yet be hope,' he told me. 'If you've taught me anything, it's that.'

I slipped the Lightstone out from beneath my armor and held it before me. Its hollows suddenly filled with the first rays of the sun rising over Tarkel's slopes, and I knew what he said was true.

'Thank you, Maram,' I said as he grabbed my hand and pulled me to my feet. I pointed east at Tarkel. 'Now why don't we go get some of that beer I've promised you for at least the last thousand miles?'

The smile brightening his face reminded me that no matter how fiercely I might miss Atara and the rest of our company, others whom I loved were waiting for me beneath the shining mountains of my home.

47

About a mile from our camp, Atara found a ford over the Diamond River and led Liljana, Daj and Kane across it. Thus they entered the lands of the Adiri tribe, who were presently allied with the Kurmak. As she rode north on her red horse draped in her black-maned lion's skin, I had no fear for her – only a great doubt if I would ever see her again.

In the quiet of the morning, I rode with Maram and Master Juwain east along the river. There were no boundary stones to mark the exact place where Altaru first set his hoof upon Meshian soil. But when the steppe gave way to the low foothills fronting the Shoshan Range of the Morning Mountains, I knew that we would find no Sarni farming the rocky ground or tending flocks of sheep on the pastures, but only Valari warriors who followed the standard of King Shamesh.

A fortress, built beneath Tarkel's lower slopes, stood looking down upon the Diamond River and the valley through which it cut. It was a great square construction, with thick granite walls – one of the twenty-two kel keeps that ringed my father's kingdom. Politeness demanded that we make our way up to it and pay our respects to its commander. And the knights and warriors who manned its walls would have demanded this too if we had tried to ride past it. In truth, there was no way that three unknown men could simply ride out of the Wendrush into Mesh along the river without being seen and stopped.

And so we were met at the north gate by fifty warriors in mail and the keep's commander, a long-faced, jowly man whose long hair had gone almost completely gray. He presented himself as Lord Manthanu of Pushku. He had summoned forth the entire garrison to witness the strange sight of three men, who obviously were not Sarni, coming unscathed out of the Sarni's lands.

'And who,' Lord Manthanu called out as we stopped just inside the gate, 'are you?'

His men were lined up on either side of the road leading from the gate, their hands gripping their kalamas should they need to draw them. I did not recognize any of them. It seemed that the keep was garrisoned with warriors from the lands along the Sawash River, a part of Mesh I had visited only once ten years before.

'My name,' I said, throwing back my cloak to reveal the swan and stars of my much-worn surcoat, 'is Valashu Elahad.'

Like a lightning flash, Lord Manthanu whipped out his kalama and pointed it at me. And nearly as quickly, his fifty warriors drew their swords, too.

'Impossible!' Lord Manthanu called out. 'Sar Valashu was killed last spring in Ishka, in the Black Bog. We had reports of it.'

'*That* is news to me,' I said with a smile. 'It would seem that the Ishkans reported wrongly. My name is as I've said. And my friends are Prince Maram Marshayk of Delu and Master Juwain of the Brotherhood.'

After much discussion we convinced them of who we really were. It turned out that one of the keep's stonemasons making repairs to its battlements had once done work for the Brothers at their sanctuary near Silvassu. Upon being summoned, he greeted Master Juwain warmly, for Master Juwain had once healed him of a catarrh of the eyes that had nearly blinded him.

'Sar Valashu, my apologies,' Lord Manthanu said. He sheathed his sword and clasped my hand. 'But the Ishkans *did* send word that you had perished in the Bog. How did you escape it?'

Maram took this opportunity to say, 'That might be a story best told over a glass of beer.'

'It might,' Lord Manthanu admitted, 'but this is no time for drinkfests.'

'How so?' Maram asked.

'Haven't you heard? But of course not – you've been off on that foolish quest. Did you ever make it as far as Tria?'

'Yes,' I said, smiling again, 'we did. But please tell us these tidings that have all your men drawing swords on their countrymen.'

Lord Manthanu paused only a moment before saying, 'We received word only yesterday that the Ishkans are marching on Mesh. We're to meet in battle on the fields between the Upper Raaswash and the Lower.'

So, I thought, it had finally come to this. Autumn having reached its fullness, and the year's barley safely grown and harvested, the Ishkans had succeeded in calling out the battle that they had long sought.

'Has a date been appointed?' I asked.

'Yes, the sixteenth.'

'And today is the twelfth, is that right?'

Lord Manthanu's eyes widened as he asked, 'Where have you been that you are in doubt of the date?'

'We have been,' I told him, 'in a dark place, the darkest of places.'

It seemed that while all the Sarni tribes from Galda to the Long Wall knew of our adventure in Argattha, word of this had not yet penetrated beyond the wall of the Morning Mountains. I decided that this was no time to tell of our journey – and certainly not to show the golden cup that we had brought out of the bowels of Skartaru.

I bowed my head then and said, 'Lord Manthanu, as you can see, we haven't much time. Will you supply us with food and drink that we might ride on as soon as possible?'

Maram was now quite alarmed by what he heard in my voice. He looked at me and said, 'But Val, you can't be thinking of riding to this battle?'

I was thinking exactly that, and he knew it. I told him, 'The King has called all free knights and warriors to the Raaswash. And the King himself gave me this ring.'

I made a fist to show Maram my knight's ring with its two sparkling diamonds. The fifty warriors lined up by the gate looked on approvingly. And so did Lord Manthanu.

'It's our duty to remain here and miss the greatest battle in years, and more's the pity,' he said. 'But, Sar Valashu, it seems that fortune has favored you. You've arrived home just in time seek honor and show brave.'

So I had, I thought. But I feared that fate had brought me back to Mesh so that I must witness the death or wounding of my brothers beneath the Ishkans' swords.

Maram, who hadn't yet reconciled himself to another battle, looked at me and said, 'It's a good hundred miles from here to the Raaswash – and mountain miles at that. How can we hope to cover this distance in only four days?'

'By riding fast,' I told him. 'Very fast.'

'Oh, oh,' he said, rubbing his hindquarters. Despite Master Juwain's ministrations, he still complained of hurts taken from the two arrows shot into him in the battle for Khaisham. 'My poor body!'

While five of Lord Manthanu's men went to take charge of filling our saddlebags with oats, salt pork and other supplies, I turned to Maram and said, 'This isn't your battle. No one will think worse of you if you remain here and rest or go straight on to the Brotherhood's sanctuary with Master Juwain.'

'No, I suppose they wouldn't,' he said. 'But *I* would think worse of myself. Do you think I've ridden by your side across half of Ea to leave you to the Ishkans at the last moment?'

We clasped hands then, and he gripped mine so hard that his fingers squeezed like a vise against my knight's ring.

'I'm afraid I won't be leaving either,' Master Juwain said. He rubbed the back of his bald head and sighed. 'If a battle must be fought, if it really *is*, then there will be much healing to be done.'

After Lord Manthanu had seen to our provisioning, we thanked him and bade him farewell. Then we rode forth out of the gate and found our way to the Kel Road leading along the border of Ishka. As always, my father's men had kept it in good repair. We urged the horses to a greater effort and so cantered at a fast pace toward the northeast corner of my father's kingdom.

All that day the weather held fair, and we made good time. It was one of the most beautiful seasons of the year with the foliage of the trees just past the most brilliant colors. The maples lining the road waved their bright red leaves in the sun while on the higher slopes, the yellows of the aspens were a yellow blaze against the deep blue sky. We passed by pastures whitened with flocks of sheep and by fields golden with the chaff of freshly cut barley. That night we took shelter in the house of a woman named Fayora. She fed us mutton and black barley bread, and asked us to look for her husband, Sar Laisu, if we should see him on the field of the Raaswash.

The next day – the thirteenth of Valte – found us struggling across and around some of the Shoshan's highest peaks. We pounded across a bridge spanning one of the tributaries of the Diamond, then came to two more kel keeps before crossing over this icy blue river's headwaters where they wound down from the south toward Ishka. We had hoped to make it as far as Mount Raaskel by evening; but for the horses' sake, to say nothing of Maram's poor hindquarters, we felt compelled to spend the night at the kel keep only a few miles from the bridge.

'You'll have some hard travel tomorrow,' Master Tadru the keep's commander told us. 'From here to the North Road, the way is very steep.'

And so it was. In the hard frost of the next morning, before the sun had risen, the horses' breath steamed out into the air as they drove forward up the Kel Road. Here, its ice-slicked stones turned away from Mount Raaskel, rising up like a white horn to the north of us. The road led south for a few miles, before turning back north and east again. We passed up a hot meal offered us at the keep where the Kel Road intersected the North Road. On our journey into Ishka, we had stopped here to greet the keep's commander, Lord Avijan. But the keep's new commander, Master Sivar, informed us that we would be hard-pressed to join Lord Avijan in time for the meeting with the Ishkans two days hence.

'The battle is to begin in the morning,' he admonished us, 'and it won't wait upon one late knight, even if he is King Shamesh's son.'

We paused at the keep only long enough to give the horses oats and water – and to gaze up the North Road where it led through the Telemesh Gate into Ishka. There, on the snowfield between Raaskel and Korukel, with its twin peaks and ogre-like humps, the white bear sent by Morjin had attacked us and nearly put an end to our quest at its very beginning. It gave us grim satisfaction to know that the Lord of Illusions would not be making ghuls of animals or men for quite some time to come.

That afternoon we passed through Ki; as on our journey into Ishka, we found that we didn't have time for a hot bath at one of its inns, nor for the beer that I had promised Maram. We left its little chalets and shops quickly behind us. Only one kel keep graced the long stretch of road between Ki and the Raaswash, and I wanted to reach it before nightfall.

We found this cold, spare fortress to be nearly emptied of supplies, which had been sent off in wagons toward the battlefield to the east. Our rest there that night was brief and troubled. For the first time since Argattha, I had bad dreams, none of which had been sent by Morjin. I was only too happy to arise in the darkness before dawn and saddle Altaru for another long day's ride.

It was a good thirty miles from the keep to the Lower Raaswash, and then perhaps another seven to the appointed battlefield. I didn't know how we would be able to cover this distance in a single day. It was a cold morning with wisps of clouds high in the sky and a shifting of the wind that presaged a storm. Although the forest beyond the keep's battlements smelled sweetly of woodsmoke and dry leaves, there hung in the crisp autumn air a certain bitterness: both our remembrance of what we had lost on our long journey and a presentiment of what the following day's battle might still take from us.

I didn't need spurs or the silver-handled quirt that the Niuriu's chieftain, Vishakan, had given me to hurry Altaru onward. As always, he sensed my urgency to cover ground quickly, and he led the other horses in moving down the road with all the speed their driving hooves could purchase against the worn paving stones. My fierce warhorse smelled battle ahead of us – and not a battle where he must hide behind walls while the Blues and other warriors came howling over battlements, but a great gathering of warriors in long, shining lines and companies of cavalry thundering over grass toward each other. He was a fearless animal, I thought, and I envied him his trust that the future would somehow take care of itself and come out all right.

It grew colder all that day as we rode along; by early afternoon, the sky was growing heavy with clouds. The first snowflakes of the season's first snow began falling a few hours later. Maram, pulling his cloak around himself, offered his opinion that the hand of fate had fallen against us, and now we had no hope of reaching the battlefield by the morrow.

'Perhaps they'll call the battle off,' he said as our horses clopped along the road. 'It's no fun fighting through snow.'

I looked at him past the fluffy white crystals sifting slowly down from the sky. I said to him, 'They won't call off the battle, Maram. And so we must ride, even faster, if we can.'

'Ride through the snow, then?'

'Yes,' I said. 'And we'll ride through the night, if we have to.'

Although we had suffered much worse cold in the Nagarshath, we had been hoping by this day for the warmth of our home fires and our journey's end. If the storm had proved a heavy one, it might have gone badly for us. As it was, however, it snowed for only a couple of hours. And a couple of hours after that, the clouds began breaking up. By dusk, with the air growing dark and icy, the sky was beginning to fill with stars.

'It seems,' I said to Maram, 'that fate may yet offer us a chance.'

'Yes, to throw ourselves onto the Ishkan's spears,' he muttered. He wiped the frost from his mustache, then said to me, 'Do you remember that day in Lord Harsha's fields? He said that the next time the Ishkans and Meshians lined up for battle, you'd be there at the front of your army.'

Master Juwain, making a rare joke, looked at Maram from on top of his tired horse and said, 'I didn't know Mesh produced such scryers. Perhaps we should have taken him with us on our journey as well.'

This suggestion produced nothing but groans from Maram. He turned toward me and said, 'Lord Harsha is too old to go off to war, isn't he? Now there's a man I don't want to meet decked out for battle.'

'We're likely to meet only the dead on the battlefield' I said to him, 'if we don't hurry.'

That evening we ate our supper in our saddles: a cold meal of cheese, dried cherries and battle biscuits that nearly broke our teeth. We rode far into the cold night. The many stars and the bright half-moon opened up the black sky and gave enough light so that we could follow the whitened road as it wound like a strand of shimmering silver along the mountains toward the east. It would have been safest for us to cleave to the Kel Road and take it all the way to the keep by the gorge of the Lower Raaswash.

There the road from Mir, by which my father's army had marched, came up from the south and followed the river for seven miles as it flowed northeast toward the Upper Raaswash. But for us, coming from the west, this was not the quickest way toward the battlefield. I knew of another road that led straight from the Kel Road down to the Upper Raaswash.

'Are you asking us to cut through the mountains on a snowy night?' Maram asked incredulously when I told him of my plan. 'Have you lost your wits?'

'Is this wise?' Master Juwain asked as we stopped the horses for a quick rest. 'Your shortcut will save only a few miles.'

I looked up at the stars where the Swan constellation was practically flying across the sky. I said, 'It may save an hour of our journey – and the difference between life and death.'

'Very well,' he said, steeling himself for the last leg of a hard ride.

'Ah, I think I've lost *my* wits,' Maram said, 'following you this far.'

'Come on,' I said, smiling at him. 'We've dared much worse than this.'

The path that gave upon the Kel Road, when we finally found it, proved to be not nearly as bad as Maram had feared. True, it was unpaved and quite steep, leading up and over the side of a small mountain. But there were few rocks to turn the horses' hooves, and the path was quite clear. It took us through a swath of evergreens dusted in white and gleaming in the moonlight. Soon enough the road began its descent through some elms and oaks mostly bare of leaves; by the time the sky ahead of us began growing lighter, the quiet woods through which we rode were covered with only a couple of inches of snow.

I guessed that the confluence of the two Raaswash rivers lay only four or five miles from here. We rode quickly over ground that gradually fell off toward the northeast, our direction of travel. As we lost elevation, the trees around us showed many more leaves. The rising sun was just beginning to melt the snow from them. The woods around us rang with the patter of falling water, like rain. And from ahead of us came a deeper, more troubling sound: the booming of war drums shaking the air and calling men to battle.

At last we crested a small hill, and through a break in the trees we saw the armies of Ishka and Mesh spread out below us. The clear morning sun cast a great glimmer upon ranks of shields, spears and polished steel helms. The Upper Raaswash was to our left; the Ishkan lines – perhaps twelve thousand men – were drawn up about five hundred yards to the south of it. They ran along the river, from the base of our hill to the Lower Raaswash, which joined the Upper about a mile farther on to the east. There King Hadaru had anchored his left flank, which were all warriors on foot, against these bright waters. He himself had gathered the knights of his cavalry to him on his right flank at the base of our hill. I sensed that Salmelu, Lord Issur and Lord Nadhru were there, sitting on top of their snorting and stamping mounts as they awaited the command to charge. I counted nearly seven hundred knights around them, all looking toward the standard of the white bear that fluttered near King Hadaru.

Facing them across the snow-covered ground were the lines of the ten thousand warriors and knights of Mesh. A mile away, by the Lower Raaswash, two hundred Meshian knights on horse were massed to the right of the foot warriors. I knew that Asaru would be there leading them, and perhaps Karshur and one or two of my other brothers as well. Although my father always made good use of terrain, he didn't believe in relying upon rivers, hills or suchlike for protecting his flanks. It gave men, he always said, a false sense of security and weakened their will to fight. And my father's will toward fighting, I knew, was very strong. Having tried to avoid this battle with all his wiles and good sense, now that he had finally taken the field against the Ishkans, I pitied any knight or warrior who dared to cross swords with him.

He sat on top of a great chestnut stallion with five hundred knights on their horses at the base of our hill, off toward our right. I couldn't make out his countenance from this distance, but his flapping standard of the swan and stars was clear enough as was the white swan plume that graced his helm. I made out the blazons of the Lords Tomavar, Tanu and Avijan nearby him, and of course, the gold field and blue rose of his seneschal, Lord Lansar Raasharu. Much to Maram's chagrin, Lord Harsha had taken a post just to their right. It seemed that he was not too old for war, after all.

Maram, Master Juwain and I had only a few moments to drink in this splendid and terrible sight before a signal was given and the trumpeters up and down the Meshian lines sounded the attack. Now the drummers ahead of the lines beat out a quicker cadence in a great booming thunder as ten thousand men began marching forward. Their long, black hair, tied with brightly colored battle ribbons won in other contests, flowed out from beneath their helms and streamed out behind them. Around their ankles they wore silver bells which sounded the jangling rhythm of their carefully measured steps. This high-pitched ringing had been known to unnerve whole armies and put them to flight before a single arrow was fired or spear clashed against shield. But our enemy that day were Ishkans, and they sported silver bells of their own, as did all the Valari in battle. And every man on the field, Ishkan or Meshian, warrior or king, was dressed in a suit of the marvelous Valari battle armor: supple black leather encrusted with white diamonds across the chest and back, covering the neck, and gleaming along the arms and legs down to the diamond-studded boots.

The brilliance of so many thousands of men, each sparkling with a covering of thousands of diamonds, dazzled the eye. Who had ever seen so many diamonds displayed in one place? The wealth of the Morning Mountains was spread out on the snowy field below us – and not just her gemstones. For it was men, I thought, and the women who would grieve for them, who were the true treasure of this land. Warriors such as Asaru, pure of heart and noble-souled, born of the fertilest and finest soil – these were the only diamonds that had true worth. And they mustn't, I knew, be squandered.

'Come on!' I said to Maram and Master Juwain. I urged Altaru forward down the hill. 'It's nearly too late.'

Already, on the battlefield ahead of us through the trees, the archers behind the opposing lines were loosing their arrows. The whine of these hundreds of shafts shivered the air; their points clacked off armor in a cacophony of steel striking stone. Soon enough, some of these arrows would drive through the chinks between the diamonds and find their way into flesh.

I rode hard for the edge of the woods and the quickly narrowing gap between the two advancing armies. Maram, clinging to his bounding horse, somehow managed to catch up to me. He pointed through the trees off to the right, towards my father's standard and his cavalry. And he gasped out, 'Your lines are that way! What are you trying to do?'

'Stop a battle,' I said.

And with that I drew forth the Lightstone and charged out onto the field. I held it high above my head. The sun filled the cup with its radiance, and it gave back this splendor a thousandfold. A sudden blaze poured out of it, drenching the warriors of both armies in a brilliant golden sheen. More than twenty thousand pairs of eyes turned my way. With Maram to my right, and Master Juwain to my left, we rode straight past the lines of men to either side of us as down a road. Thus did Lord Harsha's prediction come true as we found ourselves in the middle of the battlefield in front of both advancing armies.

'Hold!' I cried out to the warriors around me as Altaru galloped through the snow. 'Hold now!'

An arrow, shot from behind the Ishkans' ranks, whistled past my ear. Then I heard one of the Ishkans shout, 'It's the Elahad – back from the dead!'

Many men were now giving voice to their amazement. I recognized Lord Harsha's gruff old voice booming out above others of the knights grouped around my father, 'They've returned! The questers have returned! The Lightstone has been found!'

Suddenly the trumpets stopped blowing and the drums fell silent. The captains calling out the cadences up and down the lines gave the order for a halt. The silver bells bound around the warriors' legs ceased their eerie jingling as the twenty thousand men along the Ishkan and Meshian lines drew up waiting to see what their kings would next command.

I stopped Altaru at the middle of the field. Master Juwain and Maram joined me there. The Lightstone was now like the sun itself in my hand. It was a call for a truce, the like of which hadn't been seen among the Valari for three thousand years.

My father, along with Lansar Raasharu, Lord Tomavar, Lord Harsha and several other lords and master knights, was the first to ride toward us beneath a fluttering white flag. A few moments later, King Hadaru gathered up his most trusted lords and called for one of his squires to hold up a white flag as well. Then he, too, led his men slowly toward us. It was not quite the thundering charge that either the Meshian knights or the Ishkans had anticipated.

'Stop the battle, you said!' Maram muttered at me, holding his hand to his chest. 'Stop my heart, I say!'

My father had signaled for Asaru to join the parlay; now he broke from the ranks to the east down by the river and urged his dark brown stallion across the field. It took him only a few minutes to canter across the half mile that separated us. As he drew closer and the Lightstone's radiance showed the long, hawk's nose and the noble face that I had nearly given up hope of seeing again, *my* heart soared and tears filled my eyes.

Then my father, who had drawn up with his lords in a half circle around Master Juwain, Maram and me, called out my name, and his voice touched my soul, 'Sar Valashu, my son – you *have* returned to us. And not with empty hands.'

He sat straight and grave in his sparkling armor as he regarded the Lightstone with marvel and me even more so. We were like new men to each other. His black eyes, so like Kane's in their brilliance, found mine, and embraced my entire being with gladness and love. In his fierce gaze burned a certainty that he had not lived his life in vain.

As King Hadaru and the Ishkans formed up on the other side of me facing him, my father studied my torn cloak and nearly ragged surcoat. Then he asked me, 'Where is the shield that I gave you when you set out on your journey?'

'Gone, Sire,' I told him. 'Consumed in dragon fire.'

At this, even the greatest lords of both Ishka and Mesh gasped out their amazement as if they were still unbloodied boys. They all pressed closer. No one seemed to know if what I had said should be taken literally.

'Dragon fire, is it?' King Hadaru said. He sat all bearlike and irritable on top of his huge horse as he looked at me skeptically. His great beak of a nose pointed straight at me as if threatening to pry out the truth. 'And where did you fight this dragon?'

'In Argattha,' I said.

This name, dreadful and ancient, loosed in the lords another round of gasps and cries. All their eyes now lifted up and fixed on the golden cup still pouring forth its light from above my hand.

'It was in Argattha,' Maram said, 'that we found the Lightstone.'

Prince Salmelu, nudging his horse closer to his father, held his hand covering his eyes as he shook his head. The scar running down the side of his face to his weak chin burned a goldish-red. Then he tore his gaze from the Lightstone. His cold, dark eyes fell upon me in challenge. He looked at me with a great hate that had only grown in poisonousness during the months since I had wounded him in our duel.

'Is it your claim, then,' he said to me in a bitter voice, 'that *this* is the Lightstone?'

'There's no claim to me made,' I told him. 'It is, as you can see, the cup that our ancestors brought to earth.'

He pressed his horse a few paces forward as if to get a better look at the cup that I held. His ugly, furtive eyes showed but little of its light.

'And you claim to have entered the forbidden city and brought forth this cup?' Salmelu asked me.

'In fulfillment of our quest, yes,' I said to him.

'What proofs can you give us, then?' he called out to me. 'Why should we believe the word of a man who has dishonored himself in fighting duels that he didn't have the courage to finish?'

Despite my resolve to keep a cool head, I suddenly found myself gripping Alkaladur's hilt. And Salmelu, moving slightly more slowly due to the wounds I had cut into his arms and chest, curled his fingers around his kalama.

'Val,' Master Juwain reminded me with an urgent whisper, 'if you truly wish to stop this battle, this is no place for pride.'

'Perhaps not pride,' I told him, 'but certainly honor.'

Then I fought to turn away from the ever-beckoning and burning black pool of hatred that would consume me if I let it, my father's clear voice rang out: 'Sar Valashu, on this day no knight on all of Ea has more honor than you.'

His words washed through me like a thrill of cold water. I suddenly let go of my sword.

But my father's praise only inflamed Salmelu and deepened his spite. And so, before two kings and the assembled lords of Ishka and Mesh, with the thousands of warriors of two armies waiting in their lines and looking on, he sneered at me, saying, 'And still you lack the courage to test whether the swordstroke that cut me so dishonorably was skill or only evil luck!'

I took a deep breath and said, 'We haven't journeyed to the end of Ea and returned here today to make more tests – only to tell of what we've seen.'

I informed the assembled lords then of the battle for Surrapam and the conquest of Yarkona by Count Ulanu and his dreadful Blues. I spoke of the armed might that Morjin was assembling behind the rocky shield of Skartaru. And then I called for a peace between Ishka and Mesh. I said that the Valari must now join together and renounce our petty squabbles, duels and formal combats. For someday Morjin would recover from the wound that I had dealt him. And someday we would have to fight a war without rules or mercy, a terrible war to determine the fate of the world – and perhaps much else.

'A great scryer named Atara Ars Narmada has told that we can die bravely as Ishkans and Meshians,' I called out. 'Or live as Valari.'

Salmelu nudged his horse a step closer as he pointed at the Lightstone. He said, 'And *still* Sar Valashu will say anything to avoid battle. How should we believe anything of what he has told us? How do we know that this is really the cup of our ancestors and not just one of the False Lightstones told of in the ancient chronicles? Or even some glowstone gilded over to fool us?'

Truly, a poisonous serpent was Salmelu. And the time had come to pull his fangs.

'Those who serve the Lord of Lies,' I said to him, 'will hear lies in the truth that others tell.'

As Salmelu froze in a hateful stare, all the Ishkan lords except King Hadaru grabbed at the hilts of their swords. He sat beneath the white flag held by his squire, looking at Salmelu and the others as if to remind them that we had gathered here in sacred truce. Then he turned toward me. In a deathly calm voice, he asked, 'Do you accuse my son of treachery?'

'Treachery, yes, and more,' I said. I looked straight into Salmelu's black, boiling eyes. 'It was he who shot the poison arrow at me in the woods. He is an assassin, sent by the Red Dragon to –'

I had expected that Salmelu might not be able to bear the shame of his iniquity. And so I was prepared for him to whip free his sword and deliver an underhanded cut at me. But at the last moment, even as he screamed and spurred his horse straight at me, I was seized with a sudden premonition that if I drew forth Alkaladur to defend myself, I would touch off the very battle that I had come here to prevent.

'Damn you, Elahad!' he screamed at me again.

He aimed his kalama in a silvery flash at my hand holding the Lightstone; its razor-sharp edge easily would have cleaved off my arm. But I suddenly gripped the cup tightly and turned it into the plane of his swordstroke. The gold of the gelstei – of *the* Gelstei – met cold steel in a shiver of shrieking metal. His sword shattered into pieces, and he stared down in disbelief at the hilt-shard sticking out from his spasming fist.

'Hold!' King Hadaru called out, spurring his horse forward. He motioned to Lord Issur, Lord Nadhru and Lord Mestivan. 'Hold him, now! Let it not be said that we Ishkans are trucebreakers!'

As the Ishkan lords and knights swarmed around Salmelu, grabbing at him and the reins of his horse, King Hadaru himself wrested the broken sword from his son's hand. He spat on it and cast it to the ground. Then he raised back his gauntleted hand and struck Salmelu across the face. And he raged at him, 'Trucebreaker! You have dishonored yourself in the sight of both friend and foe!'

My father, sitting on his horse between Asaru and Lord Harsha, stared at the livid welt raised up on the side of Salmelu's face. He had little liking for this man, but even less desire to see a king savage his own son.

'And you!' King Hadaru said, whirling about on top of his horse to point at me. 'You bring no honor to yourself if you cast careless words at one whom you have already wounded! He who provokes the breaking of a truce may be called a trucebreaker himself!'

'None of my words has been careless, King Hadaru,' I said. 'Your son has called for war with Mesh at the command of the Red Dragon. He was to weaken your realm and my father's. His reward, after the Red Dragon had sent his armies to conquer us, was to have been the overlordship of both Mesh and Ishka – and eventually all of the Nine Kingdoms.'

'No, no,' King Hadaru said, his red face falling white with a cold, deadly wrath, 'that is not possible!'

Although I pitied him, and his pain was like a great, hard knot in my chest, I looked at him and said, 'Your son is one of the Kallimun.'

Now a terrible silence descended upon all those assembled beneath the flapping white flags and spread out like death across the battlefield. For a moment, no one dared to move.

'Who has ever heard a Valari knight speak such evil of another?' King Hadaru said, staring at me. 'How could you possibly know such a thing?'

'Because,' I said, 'one of my companions saw this in Morjin's mind.'

'Proof!' Salmelu suddenly screamed out. 'He has no proofs!'

King Hadaru pointed at him and commanded, 'Hold him!'

Lord Issur and Lord Nadhru, who had their horses pressed up close to Salmelu's, gripped his arms while Lord Mestivan dismounted and pulled him off his horse. Then three other Ishkan lords dismounted as well, and helped Lord Mestivan subdue the furiously struggling Salmelu.

'There *are* proofs,' I said to King Hadaru. I gave the Lightstone to Maram to hold, then climbed down from Altaru and stepped over to Salmelu. 'Watch closely.'

I pulled out the bloodstone that Kane had given me. Its dreadful red light fell upon Salmelu's face. And there, at the center of Salmelu's forehead, was revealed a tattoo of a coiled, red dragon.

'It's the mark of the Kallimun,' I said. 'The Red Priests affix it to their own with an invisible ink. The bloodstones bring it out into view. Thus do the Red Priests know each other.'

'It's a trick!' Salmelu cried out, shaking his head back and forth. 'An evil trick of this gelstei!'

'Salmelu's murder of me,' I said, ignoring him, 'was to have been his final initiation into Morjin's priesthood.'

The Ishkan lords murmured among themselves and cast Salmelu looks of loathing. Lansar Raasharu pressed his horse forward as he stared at him. Then he turned toward me and said, 'But Sar Valashu, this cannot be! I've already told that I saw Prince Salmelu in the woods by Lake Waskaw on the afternoon you say he shot at you.'

Lord Raasharu *had* told this to Asaru and me, if no other, and it was courageous of him to declaim before two kings what he supposed was the truth – even if it aided Salmelu.

'You did *not* see Prince Salmelu there as you thought,' I told him. 'When he failed at my murder, the Lord of Lies sent an illusion to the most trusted man in Mesh so that suspicion wouldn't fall upon his priest.'

'What you say disquiets me greatly,' Lord Raasharu said. 'To think that the Lord of Lies could make me see what is not.'

'It has disquieted me, as well,' I told him.

'Illusion!' Salmelu cried out again. His squinting at the bloodstone crinkled the red dragon tattooed into his forehead. 'What you see is surely an illusion cast by this evil stone!'

I put away the bloodstone then, and watched as the red mark disappeared.

'Do you see?' Salmelu said. 'It's gone, isn't it?'

I drew my sword an inch from its sheath. I touched my thumb to its blade, drawing blood. Then I pressed my thumb to the middle of Salmelu's forehead. The ink seared into his flesh grabbed at my blood and held some part of it. When I pulled back, the dragon tattoo now stood out red as blood for all to see.

'A trick!' he called. 'Another trick!'

He managed to wrench free his arm, and he clawed his hand furiously at his forehead in a vain attempt to rub away the mark that would remain there to his death.

'Is this a trick?' I asked him.

As the Ishkan lords regained their hold on him, I placed my hand on the dagger at his belt and drew it. I showed it to King Hadaru. Its blade was coated with a dark blue substance that could only be kirax.

'During the battle,' I said to him, 'if you weren't struck down, he was to have touched you with this.'

King Hadaru's eyes locked on Salmelu in disbelief. 'Why?' he asked him softly.

Salmelu, now seeing that his lies would no longer be believed, tried hate and terror instead.

'Because you're a blind old fool who can't see what must be done!' He tried to twist free from the men holding him, but could not. 'All the Valari – fools! Can't you see that Morjin *will* rule Ea? If we oppose him, he'll annihilate us. But if we serve him, he'll make us kings and lords over other men!'

King Hadaru climbed down from his horse. He drew out his sword and stepped in front of me. Then he raised it up above Salmelu's neck. In his wrathful eyes was horror and hate of his son – and a terrible love as well.

'Hold!' my father called out from on top of his horse. 'King Hadaru, hold! None of us would see a man slay his own son.'

'If not I, then who else?' King Hadaru said. 'My son has earned this death – no man more so.'

'So he has,' my father agreed. 'But let there be no blood spilled here today.'

His eyes met mine in a twinkle of light, and then he glanced down at my hand. 'No more blood, that is.'

King Hadaru's sword wavered above Salmelu's neck. I knew that he did not want to kill him. And my father knew this as well.

'May a king ask another king for mercy?'

'Very well,' King Hadaru said.

As quickly as he had drawn his sword, he sheathed it. Although it was he who should have thanked my father, his manner suggested that he had granted him a great boon.

'Let me go, then!' Salmelu screamed out.

'Yes, let him go,' King Hadaru commanded his men.

As Lord Mestivan and the others set Salmelu free, King Hadaru took the tainted dagger from me, then bent and thrust it through the snow into the ground beneath. He walked over to Salmelu's horse. He grabbed up the shield slung there and cast it to the ground as well. His war lance and three throwing lances followed in quick succession. Then, as Salmelu's cold eyes met the even colder stare of his father, King Hadaru commanded that Salmelu's helmet, armor, and ring be stripped from him. This was done. He stood almost naked in his underpadding before the lords of Mesh and Ishka waiting to hear his father pronounce his judgment.

'This is not yet Ishkan soil,' King Hadaru said, 'and so not even the King of Ishka can banish you from it. But you *are* so banished from Ishka, forever. No one in my realm is to give you fire, bread or salt.'

'And in my realm as well, Prince Salmelu,' my father said, 'you are denied fire, bread and salt.'

As twenty thousand men watched the badly shaking Salmelu, he climbed on top of his horse. Again he rubbed at the red dragon marking his forehead. And then, kicking his heels into his horse, he screamed out, 'Damn you, Valari!'

And with that he thundered off across the battlefield cursing and screaming. When he reached the Lower Raaswash, he drove his horse in a savage gallop through its swift waters. From the Raaswash to the Culhadosh was a distance of ten miles. And on the other side of that river was the kingdom of Waas.

After Salmelu had disappeared into the woods beyond the Raaswash, I turned to address his father and my own.

'King Hadaru,' I said. Then I looked at my father, 'Sire, in all the Morning Mountains, no other kings have so great renown. But a war between Ishka and Mesh will only diminish both realms. It will only please the Lord of Lies – he who has schemed and sent out assassins so that this war might take place. Will you do the bidding of a false king?'

'The King of Ishka,' King Hadaru said, touching the white bear of his purple surcoat, 'does his own bidding and no other.'

With his bushy white hair whipping about in the wind, I could see that he was still wroth over what had occurred with Salmelu. He scowled at my father and said, 'The Lord of Lies' schemes notwithstanding, there are still grievances between our kingdoms. There is still the matter of Korukel and its diamonds.'

I took back the Lightstone from Maram and stood holding it. Then I looked at my father and said, 'Sire, let the Ishkans have the diamonds. They'll need many diamonds to make armor to face the Dragon in the wars that are to come. All the Valari will.'

My father, Shavashar Elahad, known throughout the Morning Mountains as King Shamesh, was not a vindictive or grasping man. For a long time, it seemed, he had been looking for a good reason to cede the Ishkans their half of Mount Korukel. Only the stubbornness and ferocity of his lords such as Lord Tanu and Lord Harsha had kept him from this course. But now, in light of all that had occurred here this day, their hearts softened, and the greatest lords of Mesh nodded their heads to my father in assent of what I had suggested.

'Very well,' he said to King Hadaru. He dismounted and walked over to him. 'You shall have your diamonds.'

At this grace, Asaru and others struck their lances against their shields that my father's wisdom had finally prevailed.

King Hadaru inclined his head very slightly in acceptance of his offer. And then, most ungraciously, he said, 'It is perhaps easy to surrender one treasure when a greater one has so unexpectedly been gained.'

And with that, he turned toward me to stare at the Lightstone.

I held the golden cup higher for all to see. Once before, on this same ground, Mesh and Ishka had fought over its possession, and the Ishkan king, Elsu Maruth, had been killed. As I looked upon the thousands of warriors who had taken the field here this day, I prayed that we would not fight over it again.

'King Hadaru,' I said, 'the Lightstone is to be kept by all the Valari. We are its guardians.'

And with that, much to his astonishment, I stepped forward and placed it in his hands.

While Ishkan lords and Meshians came down from their horses and pressed closer, he gazed at the cup in wonder. His grim, old eyes were wide like a child's. Something coiled tightly inside him seemed suddenly to let go. Then he raised his head up and stood straight and tall, looking like one of the Valari kings of old. And in a clear voice he called out, 'Ishka will not make war with Mesh.'

He surprised even himself, I thought, in surrendering the Lightstone to my father. As his hands closed upon it, a golden radiance fell upon him. And in his noble countenance was revealed the lineaments of Telemesh, Aramesh and even Elahad himself.

'And Mesh,' my father told the assembled lords and knights, 'will not make war with Ishka.'

Holding the cup in one hand, he stepped forward and clasped King Hadaru's hand with his other.

817

As squires were sent off to report this news to the captains of the two armies, my father looked at the Lightstone and asked me, 'How were you led to find it?'

'This led me,' I said. And with that I drew Alkaladur and held it shining brilliantly before the Lightstone.

'There are stories to be told here,' my father said. His awe at the ancient silver sword was no less than that of the other lords staring at it. 'Great stories, it seems.'

As he passed the cup to Lord Issur, I began giving an account of our quest. I told of our nightmare journey through the Black Bog and the even greater nightmare of being pursued by the fearsome Grays. I told of meeting Kane and Atara, Liljana and Alphanderry. His death in the Kul Moroth was still a raw wound inside me; it opened in my father and in King Hadaru the anguish of sacrifice, for in their long lives they had witnessed many feats of heroism, and none had touched them quite like this. Both of them were surprised – as were Asaru and Lord Harsha – when they heard of how Maram had almost singlehandedly saved the day at the siege of Khaisham. They nodded their heads when I declared that a great Maitreya had been born somewhere on Ea, and that the Lightstone must be guarded for him. They smiled to hear of Master Juwain's brilliant solving of the final clue that had led us into Argattha. And of the gaining of the seven gelstei and Atara's blinding that sometimes helped her truly to see, they listened with amazement.

Now it was Asaru's turn to hold the Lightstone; he gazed at the cup as if he couldn't quite believe it was real. Then he turned to me with a great smile and said, 'You've done well, little brother.'

'They've all done well,' my father said. 'It's too bad their other companions aren't here to see this.'

He suddenly turned his head and called out, 'Ringbearer! Send squires to summon the ringbearer! And Sar Valashu's brothers, too.'

At that moment Flick appeared and settled his sparkling form down into the bowl of the Lightstone like a bird into his nest. Asaru blinked his eyes, not quite daring to credit what they beheld. A dozen lords and knights shook their heads in awe.

'It seems,' Asaru said, 'that you've yet many more stories to tell.'

While he gave the Lightstone to Lord Nadhru, a thunder of hooves announced the arrival of my father's ringbearer and my other brothers. As they reined in and dismounted, I ran forward to greet them.

'Karshur!' I cried out throwing my arms around his solid body. 'Ravar! Yarashan!'

Quick-witted Ravar cast a glance at the Lightstone as if he thought that I had proved quite clever in finding it, after all. Yarashan, of course, was

818

envious of my feat; but his pride in being my brother was greater still. He embraced me warmly and kissed my forehead, as did the fierce and valorous Mandru. Jonathay, when he saw Lord Tomavar holding the Lightstone, let loose a great laugh of triumph as sweet and clear as a mountain stream.

With King Hadaru holding up his hand for silence, my father approached Master Juwain and said, 'Without your guidance, Sar Valashu might never have found the road that led him to seek the Lightstone. And without your courage and insight, none of you would have found your way to Argattha. Therefore it is my wish that the treasure that would have been wasted upon this battle be spent in raising up a new building for your sanctuary. There you shall gather gelstei to you that their secrets might be revealed. There, from time to time, the Lightstone shall be brought. And it shall be as it was in another and better age.'

Master Juwain bowed his head and said, 'Thank you, King Shamesh.'

My father next turned to Maram and said, 'Prince Maram Marshayk! Your courage at Khaisham and in Argattha was extraordinary; your prowess with the sword was the equal of great warriors; your faithfulness on this quest was as adamantine as diamond and worthy of a Valari.'

Then he smiled and said, 'Ringbearer!'

A young knight named Jushur stepped up to my father holding a broad, flat, wooden case. He opened it to reveal four rows of silver rings pressed into a lining of black velvet. The rings in the first row were set with a single diamond, while those in the second row showed two, and so on. It was my father's pride and pleasure, as king, to reward heroism by promoting knights and master warriors on the field of battle.

After studying Maram's fat fingers, he chose out the largest ring from the second row. Its two diamonds sparkled in the strengthening sun. My father grasped Maram's hand and slipped the ring onto his finger. It was the ring of a Valari knight, even as the one that I wore.

'For your service to my son,' he said, clasping Maram's hand. 'For your service to Mesh and all of Ea.'

As the lords of Mesh and Ishka crowded around Maram to stare at his knight's ring, Maram flushed with pride and thanked my father. For a hundred years, none but Valari warriors had been bestowed with such an honor.

Now my father turned to me and pulled off my knight's ring. He selected another from the case's fourth row. Then he placed this silver band with its four bright diamonds on my finger; he kissed my forehead and said, 'Lord Valashu, Knight of the Swan, Guardian of the Lightstone.'

The golden cup, I saw, was now being held by one of the Ishkans whom I did not know. Others were whispering that they had never heard of a Valari knight being made directly into a lord.

Master Juwain came over to Maram to get a better look at his new ring. He said to him, 'I'm afraid that now you're a Valari in spirit.'

'Ah, I'm afraid I am, sir.' The diamonds of his ring dazzled his eyes. 'Ah, I'm afraid that I must formally renounce my vows to the Brotherhood.'

At this, Master Juwain smiled and bowed his head in acceptance. He said, 'I think you renounced them many miles ago.'

As the two kings sent squires to call for their armies to come closer and view the Lightstone, Lord Harsha limped over to us. On his bluff, old face was the brightest of smiles. His single eye fell upon me, and he said, 'Lord Valashu – you can't know how glad it makes me to say that.'

Maram, I saw, had pulled back behind the cover of Karshur's thick body. He looked away from Lord Harsha like a child at school who is afraid that his master might call upon him.

'And Sar Maram!' Lord Harsha said, finding him easily enough. 'We're all glad to see you.'

'You are?' Maram asked. 'I had thought you might be distressed, ah, about things that had distressed you.'

Lord Harsha looked at the two diamonds of Maram's ring and said, 'It might have been so. But my poor daughter has talked of little else but you since you went away. And *that* distresses me.'

'Behira,' Maram said as if struggling to remember her name, 'is a lovely woman.'

'Yes, the loveliest. And she will be delighted to see that you've been knighted. What honor could we bestow upon you to equal that which you've brought to us?'

'Ah, perhaps some of your excellent beer, sir.'

'That you shall have, Sar Maram. And much else as well. The month of Ashte is a lovely time for a wedding, don't you think?'

'Sir?'

'Yes, a lovely time.' Lord Harsha stepped forward favoring his crippled leg. He embraced Maram and said, 'My son!'

'Ah, Lord Harsha, I –'

'There is only one thing in the world that could distress me on such a fine day as this,' Lord Harsha added. He smiled at Maram as he rested his hand on his kalama. 'And that would be to see my daughter further distressed. Do you understand?'

Maram *did* understand, and he looked at me as if pleading that I might come to his rescue. But this one time, I was powerless to help him.

'Ashte,' I said to him, as Lord Harsha walked off, 'is half a year away. Much might happen between now and then.'

'Yes,' Maram said optimistically, 'I might come to love Behira, mightn't I?'

'You might,' I told him. 'Isn't it love that you really sought?'

Now, as the Lightstone was passed back and forth between knights arriving at our encampment on the middle of the field, as my father stood conferring with King Hadaru, and Maram showed Yarashan the rock with the hole that he had burned with his red gelstei in the Vardaloon, Asaru took my hand. Our lord's rings clicked together, and he said, 'My apologies for doubting that the Lightstone might be found. Our grandfather would have been proud of you.'

'Thank you, Asaru,' I told him.

'But you had me worried,' he said. 'When the news came from Ishka, about the Bog, we all gave up hope.'

I looked deep into the essential innocence gathering in his dark eyes, and I said, 'All except you.'

We clasped hands so tightly that my fingers hurt. And he said, 'You've changed, Valashu.'

All at once, as if ice were breaking beneath me, I felt myself plunging into unbearably cold waters. There pooled all the pain of Atara's blinding, of Kane's darkened soul, of Alphanderry's death.

'Valashu,' my brother said.

I blinked my eyes to see him suddenly weeping as all the anguish inside me flowed into him. I knew then that the gift of *valarda* that my grandfather had bestowed upon me had not left Asaru untouched. It lay waiting to be awakened in all Valari, perhaps in all men.

Now the twelve thousand warriors of Ishka and the ten thousand of Mesh had finally closed and met all about us in the middle of the field. At the commands of the warlords and captains, they laid their spears and shields down upon the snow. Its white crystals, like millions of diamonds, shimmered with blues and golds and reds. Soon the morning sun would melt the ground's cold covering, even as the Lightstone melted six thousand years of hatred, envy and suspicion. I turned to watch the warriors of King Hadaru and King Shamesh passing the cup from hand to hand, along the ranks, up one file and then down another. The Valari drank in its radiance through their bright eyes and through their hands. It blazed like the sun through their beings. In each of them, as in Asaru, I saw a golden cup pouring out its light from inside their hearts. It melted them open, melted the very diamond armor encasing them. And in this miracle that seemed almost an illusion but was as real as the water in my eyes, as real as my love for Asaru and for my brothers, for my father and King Hadaru and all the Ishkans, it melted even me.

'Look,' Asaru said, pointing up at the sky, 'there's a good sign.'

I followed the line of his finger to see a great flock of swans winging their way south as they flew over the Upper Raaswash into Mesh. As my heart opened to this glorious sight, and to the hearts of the twenty thousand jubilant Valari all around me, I knew that the *valarda* was truly the greatest of gifts. For the joy of my brothers in arms and fellow guardians came flooding into me, and I felt myself soaring through the sky as well.

'Tonight,' Asaru said, still looking at the swans, 'they'll sleep at home. As we will soon enough, since there will be no war. What will you do, Valashu, now that you've found the Lightstone?'

What *would* I do, I wondered?

I turned to watch the swans disappear over the mountains to the south. In that direction lay the Valley of the Swans and the three great peaks above my father's castle. My mother and grandmother would be waiting for me there – even as my grandfather waited in another place. Atara was waiting in darkness for our son to be born and behold the beauty of the world. Where the stars burned cold and clean and bright, there the Elijin and Galadin waited for the Shining One to come forth. All people everywhere, and all things, always waiting.

And I must wait a little longer, too. The Quest had been fulfilled but one task remained: I must show my grandfather the golden cup that he knew would one day be found. And so, soon, on a clear winter night, I would climb Mount Telshar or Arakel and stand upon the summit with the Lightstone in my hand. I would breathe the cold breath of all those who had come before me; I would dream my fiery dreams and speak my promise to the stars: that darkness would be defeated, that men and women would soar the heavens with wings of light, that someday the Lightstone would be returned to that bright, blazing place from which it came.

APPENDICES

HERALDRY

THE NINE KINGDOMS

The shield and surcoat arms of the warriors of the Nine Kingdoms differ from those of the other lands in two respects. First, they tend to be simpler, with a single, bold charge emblazoned on a field of a single color. Second, every fighting man, from the simple warrior up through the ranks of knight, master and lord to the king himself, is entitled to bear the arms of his line.

There is no mark or insignia of service to any lord save the king. Loyalty to one's ruling king is displayed on shield borders as a field matching the color of the king's field, and a repeating motif of the king's charge. Thus, for instance, every fighting man of Ishka, from warrior to lord, will display a red shield border with white bears surrounding whatever arms have been passed down to him. With the exception of the lords of Anjo, only the kings and the royal families of the Nine Kingdoms bear unbordered shields and surcoats.

In Anjo, although a king in name still rules in Jathay, the lords of the other regions have broken away from his rule to assert their own sovereignty. Thus, for instance, Baron Yashur of Vishal bears a shield of simple green emblazoned with a white crescent moon without bordure as if were already a king or aspiring to be one.

Once there was a time when all Valari kings bore the seven stars of the Swan Constellation on their shields as a reminder of the Elijin and Galadin to whom they owed allegiance. But by the time of the Second Lightstone Quest, only the House of Elahad has as part of its emblem the seven silver stars.

In the heraldry of the Nine Kingdoms, white and silver are used interchangeably as are silver and gold. Marks of cadence – those smaller charges that distinguish individual members of a line, house or family – are usually placed at the point of the shield.

Mesh

House of Elahad – a black field; a silver-white swan with spread wings gazes upon the seven silver-white stars of the Swan constellation
Lord Harsha – a blue field; gold lion rampant filling nearly all of it
Lord Tomavar – white field; black tower
Lord Tanu – white field; black, double-headed eagle
Lord Raasharu – gold field; blue rose
Lord Navaru – blue field; gold sunburst
Lord Juluval – gold field; three red roses
Lord Durrivar – red field; white bull
Lord Arshan – white field; three blue stars

Ishka

King Hadaru Aradar – red field; great white bear
Lord Mestivan – gold field; black dragon
Lord Nadhru – green field; three white swords, points touching upwards
Lord Solhtar – red field; gold sunburst

Athar

King Mohan – gold field; blue horse

Lagash

King Kurshan – blue field; white Tree of Life

Waas

King Sandarkan – black field; two crossed silver swords

Taron

King Waray – red field; white winged horse

Kaash

King Talanu Solaru – blue field; white snow tiger

Anjo

King Danashu – blue field; gold dragon
Duke Gorador Shurvar of Daksh – white field; red heart
Duke Rezu of Rajak – white field; green falcon
Duke Barwan of Adar – blue field; white candle
Baron Yashur of Vishal – green field; white crescent moon
Count Rodru Narvu of Yarvanu – white field; two green lions rampant

Count Atanu Tuval of Onkar – white field; red maple leaf
Baron Yuval of Natesh – black field; golden flute

FREE KINGDOMS

As in the Nine Kingdoms, the bordure pattern is that of the field and charge of the ruling king. But in the Free Kingdoms, only nobles and knights are permitted to display arms on their shields and surcoats. Common soldiers wear two badges: the first, usually on their right arm, displaying the emblems of their kings, and the second, worn on their left arm, displaying those of whatever baron, duke or knight to whom they have sworn allegiance.

In the houses of Free Kingdoms, excepting the ancient Five Families of Tria from whom Alonia has drawn most of her kings, the heraldry tends toward more complicated and geometric patterns than in the Nine Kingdoms.

Alonia
House of Narmada – blue field; gold caduceus
House of Eriades – Field divided per bend; blue upper, white lower; white star on blue, blue star on white
House of Kirriland – White field; black raven
House of Hastar – Black field; two gold lions rampant
House of Marshan – white field; red star inside black circle
Baron Narcavage of Arngin – white field; red bend; black oak lower; black eagle upper
Baron Maruth of Aquantir – green field; gold cross; two gold arrows on each quadrant
Duke Ashvar of Raanan – gold field; repeating pattern of black swords
Baron Monteer of Iviendenhall – white and black checkered shield
Count Muar of Iviunn – black field; white cross of Ashtoreth
Duke Malatam of Tarlan – white field; black saltire; repeating red roses on white quadrants

Eanna
King Hanniban Dujar – gold field; red cross; blue lions rampant on each gold quadrant

Surrapan
King Kaiman – red field; white saltire; blue star at center

Thalu

King Aryaman – Black and white gyronny; white swords on four black sectors

Delu

King Santoval Marshayk – green field; two gold lions rampant facing each other

The Elyssu

King Theodor Jardan – blue field; repeating breaching silver dolphins

Nedu

King Tal – blue field; gold cross; gold eagle volant on each blue quadrant

THE DRAGON KINGDOMS

With one exception, in these lands, only Morjin himself bears his own arms: a great, red dragon on a gold field. Kings who have sworn fealty to him – King Orunjan, King Arsu – have been forced to surrender their ancient arms and display a somewhat smaller red dragon on their shields and surcoats. Kallimun priests who have been appointed to kingship or who have conquered realms in Morjin's name – King Mansul, King Yarkul, Count Ulanu – also display this emblem but are proud to do so.

Nobles serving these kings bear slightly smaller dragons, and the knights serving them bear yet smaller ones. Common soldiers wear a yellow livery displaying a repeating pattern of very small red dragons.

King Angand of Sunguru, as an ally of Morjin, bears his family's arms as does any free king.

The kings of Hesperu and Uskudar have been allowed to retain their family crests as a mark of their kingship, though they have surrendered their arms.

Sunguru

King Angand – blue field; white heart with wings

Uskudar

King Orunjan – gold field; 3/4 red dragon

Karabuk
King Mansul – gold field; $3/4$ red dragon

Hesperu
King Arsu – gold field; $3/4$ red dragon

Galda
King Yarkul – gold field; $3/4$ red dragon

Yarkona
Count Ulanu – gold field; $1/2$ red dragon

THE GELSTEI

THE GOLD

The history of the gold gelstei, called the Lightstone, is shrouded in mystery. Most people believe the legend of Elahad: that this Valari king of the Star People made the Lightstone and brought it to earth. Some of the Brotherhoods, however, teach that the Elijin or the Galadin made the Lightstone. Some teach that the mythical Ieldra, who are like gods, made the Lightstone millions of years earlier. A few hold that the Lightstone may be a transcendental, increate object from before the beginning of time, and as such, much as the One or the universe itself, has always existed and always will. Also, there are people who believe that this golden cup, the greatest of the gelstei, was made in Ea during the great Age of Law.

The Lightstone is the image of solar light, the sun, and hence of divine intelligence. It is made into the shape of a plain golden cup because 'it holds the whole universe inside'. Upon being activated by a powerful enough being, the gold begins to turn clear like a crystal and to radiate light like the sun. As it connects with the infinite power of the universe, the One, it radiates light like that of ten thousand suns. Ultimately, its light is pure, clear and infinite – the light of pure consciousness. The light inside light, the light inside all things that *is* all things. The Lightstone quickens consciousness in itself, the power of consciousness to enfold itself and form up as matter and thus evolve into infinite possibilities. It enables certain human beings to channel and magnify this power. Its power is infinitely greater than that of the red gelstei, the firestones. Indeed, the Lightstone gives power over the other gelstei, the green, purple, blue and white, the black and perhaps the silver – and potentially over all matter, energy, space and time. The final secret of the Lightstone is that, as the very consciousness and substance of the universe itself, it is found within each human being, interwoven and interfused with each separate soul. To quote from the *Saganom Elu*, it is 'the perfect jewel within the lotus found inside the human heart'.

The Lightstone has many specific powers, and each person finds in it a reflection of himself. Those seeking healing are healed. In some, it recalls their true nature and origins as Star People; others, in their lust for immortality, find only the hell of endless life. Some – such as Morjin or Angra Mainyu – it blinds with its terrible and beautiful light. Its potential to be misused by such maddened beings is vast: ultimately it has the power to blow up the sun and destroy the stars, perhaps the whole universe itself.

Used properly, the Lightstone can quicken the evolution of all beings. In its light, Star People may transcend to their higher angelic natures while angels evolve into archangels. And the Galadin themselves, in the act of creation only, may use the Lightstone to create whole new universes.

The Lightstone is activated at once by individual consciousness, the collective unconscious and the energies of the stars. It also becomes somewhat active at certain key times, such as when the Seven Sisters are rising in the sky. Its most transcendental powers manifest when it is in the presence of an enlightened being and/or when the earth enters the Golden Band.

It is not known if there are many Lightstones throughout the universe, or only one that somehow appears at the same time in different places. One of the greatest mysteries of the Lightstone is that on Ea, only a human man, woman or child can use it for its best and highest purpose: to bring the sacred light to others and awaken each being to his angelic nature. Neither the Elijin nor the Galadin, the archangels, possess this special resonance. And only a very few of the Star People do.

These rare beings are the Maitreyas who come forth every few millennia or so to share their enlightenment with the world. They have cast off all illusion and apprehend the One in all things and all things as manifestations of the One. Thus they are the deadly enemies of Morjin and the Dark Angel, and other Lords of the Lie.

THE GREATER GELSTEI

THE SILVER

The silver gelstei is made of a marvelous substance called silustria. The crystal resembles pure silver, but is brighter, reflecting even more light. Depending on how forged, the silver gelstei can be much harder than diamond.

The silver gelstei is the stone of reflection, and thus of the soul, for the soul is that part of man that reflects the light of the universe. The silver reflects and magnifies the powers of the soul, including, in its lower emanations, those of mind: logic, deduction, calculation, awareness, ordinary memory, judgment and insight. It can confer upon those who wield it holistic vision: the ability to see whole patterns and reach astonishing conclusions from only a few details or clues. Its higher emanations allow one to see how the individual soul must align itself with the universal soul to achieve the unfolding of fate.

In its reflective qualities, the silver gelstei may be used as a shield against various energies: vital, mental, or physical. In other ages, it has been shaped into arms and armor, such as swords, mail shirts and actual shields. Although not giving power *over* another, in body or in mind, the silver can be used to quicken the working of another's mind, and is thus a great pedagogical tool leading to knowledge and laying bare truth. A sword made of silver gelstei can cut through all things physical as the mind cuts through ignorance and darkness.

In its fundamental composition, the silver is very much like the gold gelstei, and is one of the two noble stones.

THE WHITE

These stones are called the white, but in appearance are usually clear, like diamonds. During the Age of Law, many of them were cast into the form of crystal balls to be used by scryers, and are thus often called 'scryers' spheres'.

These are the stones of far-seeing: of perceiving events distant in either space or time. They are sometimes used by remembrancers to uncover the secrets of the past. The kristei, as they are called, have helped the master healers of the Brotherhoods read the auras of the sick that they might be brought back to strength and health.

THE BLUE

The blue gelstei, or blestei, have been fabricated on Ea at least as far back as the Age of the Mother. These crystals range in color from a deep cobalt to a bright, lapis blue. They have been cast into many forms: amulets, cups, figurines, rings and others.

The blue gelstei quicken and deepen all kinds of knowing and communication. They are an aid to mindspeakers and truthsayers, and confer a greater sensitivity to music, poetry, painting, languages and dreams.

THE GREEN

Other than the Lightstone itself, these are the oldest of the gelstei. Many books of the *Saganom Elu* tell of how the Star People brought twelve of the green stones with them to Ea. The varistei look like beautiful emeralds; they are usually cast – or grown – in the shape of baguettes or astragals, and range in size from that of a pin or bead to great jewels nearly a foot in length.

The green gelstei resonate with the vital fires of plants and animals, and of the earth. They are the stones of healing and can be used to quicken and strengthen life and lengthen its span. As the purple gelstei can be used to mold crystals and other inanimate substances into new shapes, the green gelstei have powers over the forms of living things. In the Lost Ages, it was said that masters of the varistei used them to create new races of man (and sometimes monsters) but this art is thought to be long since lost.

These crystals confer great vitality on those who use them in harmony with nature; they can open the body's chakras and awaken the kundalini fire so the whole body and soul vibrate at a higher level of being.

THE RED

The red gelstei – also called tuaoi stones or firestones – are blood-red crystals like rubies in appearance and color. They are often cast into baguettes at least a foot in length, though during the Age of Law much larger ones were made. The greatest ever fabricated was the hundred-foot Eluli's Spire, mounted on top of the Tower of the Sun. It was said to cast its fiery light up into the heavens as a beacon calling out to the Star People to return to earth.

The firestones quicken, channel and control the physical energies. They draw upon the sun's rays, as well as the earth's magnetic and telluric currents, to generate beams of light, lightning, heat or fire. They are thought to be the most dangerous of the gelstei; it is said that a great pyramid of red gelstei unleashed a terrible lightning that split asunder the world of Iviunn and destroyed its star.

THE BLACK

The black gelstei, or baalstei, are black crystals like obsidian. Many are cast into the shape of eyes, either flattened or rounded like large marbles. They devour light and are the stones of negation.

Many believe them to be evil stones, but they were created for a great good purpose: to control the awesome lightning of the firestones. Theirs is the power to damp the fires of material things, both living and living crystals such as the gelstei. Used properly, they can negate the working of all the other kinds of gelstei except the silver and the gold, over which they have no power.

Their power over living things *is* most often put to evil purpose. The Kallimun priests and other servants of Morjin such as the Grays have wielded them as weapons to attack people physically, mentally and spiritually, literally sucking away their vital energies and will. Thus the black stones can be used to cause disease, degeneration and death.

It is believed that that baalstei might be potentially more dangerous than even the firestones. For in the *Beginnings* is told of an utterly black place that is at once the negation of all things and paradoxically also their source. Out of this place may come the fire and light of the

834

universe itself. It is said that the Baaloch, Angra Mainyu, before he was imprisoned on the world of Damoom, used a great black gelstei to destroy whole suns in his war of rebellion against the Galadin and the rule of the Ieldra.

THE PURPLE

The lilastei are the stones of shaping and making. They are a bright violet in hue, and are cast into crystals of a great variety of shapes and sizes. Their power is unlocking the light locked up in matter so that matter might be changed, molded and transformed. Thus the lilastei are sometimes called the alchemists' stones, according to the alchemists' age-old dream of transmuting baser matter into true gold, and casting true gold into a new Lightstone.

The purple gelstei's greatest effects are on crystals of all sorts: but mostly those in metal and rocks. It can unlock the crystals in these substances so that they might be more easily worked. Or they can be used to grow crystals of great size and beauty; they are the stone shapers and stone growers spoken of in legend. It is said that Kalkamesh used a lilastei in forging the silustria of the Bright Sword, Alkaladur.

Some believe the potential power of the purple gelstei to be very great and perhaps very perilous. Lilastei have been known to 'freeze' water into an alternate crystal called shatar, which is clear and as hard as quartz. Some fear that these gelstei might be used thus to crystallize the water in the sea and so destroy all life on earth. The stone masters of old, who probed the mysteries of the lilastei too deeply, are said to have accidentally turned themselves *into* stone, but most believe this to be only a cautionary tale out of legend.

THE SEVEN OPENERS

If man's purpose is seen as in progressing to the orders of the Star People, Elijin and Galadin, then the seven stones known as the openers might fairly be called greater gelstei. Indeed, there are those of the Great White Brotherhood and the Green Brotherhood who revered them in this way. For, with much study and work, the openers each activate one of the body's chakras: the energy centers known as wheels of light. As the chakras are opened, from the base of the spine to the crown of the head, so is opened a pathway for the fires of life to reconnect to the heavens in a great burst of lightning called the angel's fire. Only then can a man or a woman undertake the advanced work necessary for advancement to the higher orders.

The openers are each small, clear stones the color of their respective chakras. They are easily mistaken for gemstones.

THE FIRST (also called bloodstones)

These are a clear, deep red in color, like rubies. The first stones open the chakra of the physical body and activate the vital energies.

THE SECOND (also called passion stones or old gold)

These gelstei are gold-orange in color and are sometimes mistaken for amber. The second stones open the chakra of the emotional body and activate the currents of sensation and feeling.

THE THIRD (also called sun stones)

The third stones are clear and bright yellow, like citrine; they open the third chakra of the mental body and activate the mind.

THE FOURTH (also called dream stones or heart stones)

These beautiful stones – clear and pure green in color like emeralds – open the heart chakra. Thus they open one's second feeling, a truer and deeper sense than the emotions of the second chakra. The fourth stones work upon the astral body and activate the dreamer.

THE FIFTH (also called soul stones)

Bright blue in color like sapphires, the fifth stones open the chakra of the etheric body and activate the intuitive knower, or the soul.

THE SIXTH (also called angel eyes)

The sixth stones are bright purple like amethyst. They open the chakra of the celestial body located just above and between the eyes. Thus their more common name: theirs is the power of activating one's second sight. Indeed, these gelstei activate the seer in the realm of light, and open one to the powers of scrying, visualization and deep insight.

THE SEVENTH (also called clear crowns or true diamonds)

One of the rarest of the gelstei, the seventh stones are clear and bright as diamonds. Indeed, some say they are nothing more than perfect diamonds, without flaw or taint of color. These stones open the chakra of the ketheric body and free the spirit for reunion with the One.

THE LESSER GELSTEI

During the Age of Law, hundreds of kinds of gelstei were made for purposes ranging from the commonplace to the sublime. Few of these have survived the passage of the centuries. Some of those that have are:

GLOWSTONES
Also called glowglobes, these stones are cast into solid, round shapes resembling opals of various sizes – some quite huge. They give a soft and beautiful light. Those of lesser quality must be frequently refired beneath the sun, while those of the highest quality drink in even the faintest candlelight, hold it and give back in a steady illumination.

SLEEP STONES
A gelstei of many shifting and swirling colors, the sleep stones have a calming effect on the human nervous system. They look something like agates.

WARDERS
Usually blood-red in color and opaque, like carnelians, these stones deflect or 'ward-off' psychic energies directed at a person. This includes thoughts, emotions, curses – and even the debilitating energy drain of the black gelstei. One who wears a warder can be rendered invisible to scryers and opaque to mindspeakers.

LOVE STONES
Often called true amber and sometimes mistaken for the second stones of the openers, these gelstei partake of some of their properties. They are specific to arousing feelings of infatuation and love; sometimes love stones are ground into a powder and made into potions to achieve the same end. They are soft stones and look much like amber.

WISH STONES
These little stones – they look something like white pearls – help the wearer remember his dreams and visions of the future; they activate the will to manifest these visualizations.

DRAGON BONES
Of a translucent, old ivory in color, the dragon bones strengthen the life fires and quicken one's courage – and all too often one's wrath.

HOT SLATE

A dark, gray, opaque stone of considerable size – hot slate is usually cast into yard-long bricks – this gelstei is related in powers and purpose, if not form, to the glowstones. It absorbs heat directly from the air and radiates it back over a period of hours or days.

MUSIC MARBLES

Often called song stones, these gelstei of variegated, swirling hues record and play music, both of the human voice and all instruments. They are very rare.

TOUCH STONES

These are related to the song stones and have a similar appearance. However, they record and play emotions and tactile sensations instead of music. A man or a woman, upon touching one of these gelstei, will leave a trace of emotions that a sensitive can read from contact with the stone.

THOUGHT STONES

This is the third stone in this family and is almost indistinguishable from the others. It absorbs and holds one's thoughts as a cotton garment might retain the smell of perfume or sweat. The ability to read back these thoughts from touching this gelstei is not nearly so rare as that of mindspeaking itself.

BOOKS OF THE SAGANOM ELU

Beginnings
Sources
Chronicles
Journeys
Book of Stones
Book of Water
Book of Wind
Book of Fire
Tragedies
Book of Remembrance
Sarojin
Baladin
Averin
Souls
Songs
Meditations

Mendelin
Ananke
Commentaries
Book of Stars
Book of Ages
Peoples
Healings
Laws
Battles
Progressions
Book of Dreams
Idylls
Visions
Valkariad
Trian Prophecies
The Eschaton

THE AGES OF EA

The Lost Ages (18,000 – 12,000 years ago)
The Age of the Mother (12,000 – 9,000 years ago)
The Age of the Sword (9,000 – 6000 years ago)
The Age of Law (6,000 – 3,000 years ago)
The Age of the Dragon (3,000 years ago to the present)

THE MONTHS OF THE YEAR

Yaradar	Marud
Viradar	Soal
Triolet	Ioj
Gliss	Valte
Ashte	Ashvar
Soldru	Segadar